EXTRAORDINARY PRAISE FOR
NELSON DeMILLE'S *CATHEDRAL*

"From the beginning...until the final chapters when you find yourself frantically turning pages, it's truly impossible to lay aside *CATHEDRAL*."
—***Dallas Times Herald***

"TOO TRUE TO LIFE FOR COMFORT...ENTERTAINS...The writing is crisp, terse, and highly realistic."
—***New York Daily News***

"THOROUGHLY CREDIBLE AND ABSOLUTELY ABSORBING...Motivation, characterization, and plotting are all exceptional...Will keep readers engrossed till the final page."
—**United Press International**

"CHILLINGLY BELIEVABLE, PEOPLED WITH RECOGNIZABLE CHARACTERS...*CATHEDRAL* ENTERTAINS WITH THE UNIMAGINABLE."
—***Publishers Weekly***

"FAST-PACED, BREATHTAKING."
—***Chattanooga Times***

"THE MOST FRIGHTENING THING ABOUT THIS STORY IS THAT IT AT NO TIME SEEMS IMPLAUSIBLE."
—***Newark Star-Ledger***

Cathedral

Novels by Nelson DeMille

By the Rivers of Babylon
Cathedral
The Talbot Odyssey
Word of Honor
The Charm School
The Gold Coast
The General's Daughter
Spencerville
Plum Island
The Lion's Game
Up Country
Night Fall
The Gate House
The Lion

WITH THOMAS BLOCK
Mayday

Nelson DeMille

Cathedral

GRAND CENTRAL
PUBLISHING

New York Boston

Copyright © 1981 by Nelson DeMille
Introduction copyright © 2011 by Nelson DeMille

All rights reserved. Except as permitted under the U.S. Copyright Act of 1976, no part of this publication may be reproduced, distributed, or transmitted in any form or by any means, or stored in a database or retrieval system, without the prior written permission of the publisher.

Lyrics from "Danny Boy" by F. E. Watherley: © 1918 by Boosey & Co.; Renewed 1945. Reprinted by permission of Boosey & Hawkes, Inc.

Lines from "The Men Behind the Wire" from SONGS OF STRUGGLE AND PROTEST edited by John Donnell, published by Gilbert Dalton Limited, Co., Dublin, Ireland.

This Hachette Book Group edition is published by arrangement with the author.

Grand Central Publishing
Hachette Book Group
237 Park Avenue
New York, NY 10017

www.HachetteBookGroup.com

Printed in the United States of America

Originally published in hardcover by Hachette Book Group.

First Trade Edition: June 2011

10 9 8 7 6 5 4 3 2 1

Grand Central Publishing is a division of Hachette Book Group, Inc. The Grand Central Publishing name and logo is a trademark of Hachette Book Group, Inc.

The publisher is not responsible for websites (or their content) that are not owned by the publisher.

LCCN: 80029126

ISBN: 978-1-4555-0163-2 (pbk.)

For Lauren, my PhD,
and Alex,
my Master of Fine Arts

Acknowledgments

I wish to thank the following people for their editorial help, dedication, and above all, patience: Bernard and Darlene Geis, Joseph Elder, David Kleinman, Mary Crowley, Eleanor Hurka, and Rose Ann Ferrick. And very special thanks to Judith Shafran, to whom this book would have been dedicated had she not been an editor and therefore a natural enemy of authors, albeit a noble and forthright one.

For their expertise and technical assistance I'd like to thank Detective Jack Lanigan, NYPD, Retired; and Michael Moriarty, Carm Tintle, and Jim Miller, Seanachies.

The following organizations have provided information for this book: The New York Police Department Public Information Office; The St. Patrick's Parade Committee; The 69th Infantry, NYARNG; Amnesty International; the Irish Consulate; the British Consulate; and the Irish Tourist Board.

There were other individuals and organizations who gave of their time and knowledge, providing colorful threads of the narrative tapestry presented here, and to them—too numerous to mention—I express my sincere appreciation.

And finally, I want to thank The Little People, who refrained, as much as could be hoped, from mischief.

Introduction

Cathedral was first published in 1981, and when I sat down to write this book, the Irish Troubles were front page news with bombings and murders in Belfast and London, and all over England and Northern Ireland. The Irish Republican Army prisoners in British jails were on hunger strikes, and each side was engaged in ever-worsening acts of violence against the other. I was actually in London on a day when an IRA bomb went off. I'd been standing on the steps of my hotel when the ground shook. I hadn't heard anything, but the doorman said, almost nonchalantly, "IRA bomb," which indeed it turned out to be. That, more than anything I'd seen on the TV news over the years, made this conflict real and frightening.

My first instinct as I contemplated writing this book was *not* to write it; it was a touchy and inflammatory subject at the time. Passions were running high in the Irish-American community, especially in New York where I live, and it seemed that half the cars in the metropolitan area had bumper stickers saying, "England out of Ireland." Additionally, there were a good number of Irish citizens in New York who were here "on business," meaning, they were raising money for the IRA, and also giving press interviews. A few of these men and women frequented the same Irish pubs that I did in those days, and when the word went out that I was writing a novel about the Irish Troubles—something I probably should not have mentioned, except that I needed some information—I was given not only information, but also unsolicited advice, some of which could be construed as a warning to be easy on the boys who were fighting to reunite Ireland. So, as I said, I thought about finding a safer subject. But in the end, I decided to press on and see if I, as a novelist, could find some middle ground, or at least some truth and understanding of both sides of this age-old conflict.

When *Cathedral* was published, it got a lot of attention. Most reviewers loved the book and thought it accurately reflected the ongoing conflict without taking sides or being a propaganda tool for either cause. A few reviewers and columnists, however—mostly in Irish-American publications—had a less positive view of *Cathedral*. Some of them suggested that I, an American with no Irish ancestry, should not be writing about something I could not possibly understand. My belief, however, is that the truth is the truth, and that you don't need to be emotionally or genetically involved to be a good reporter or a good writer. Just the opposite. In fact, as most of my Irish friends agree, one of the best novels ever written about the Irish struggle was written by an American Jew: *Trinity* by Leon Uris, published in 1976, about a year before I began writing *Cathedral*. *Trinity* was, in fact, what got me interested in the subject.

In the weeks after publication, I received a number of letters, mostly unsigned, that could be construed as veiled threats. Some of these letter writers thought I had not presented the Irish Catholic cause in a good light, and some thought I was taking the English or Protestant side. Also, during my cross-country publicity tour, I sometimes found myself on radio shows speaking to angry callers and on TV shows with other guests who'd apparently been invited to argue with me. Also, there were some unfriendly people at my book signings. Again, passions were running high then, though now it's hard to go back in time and memory to understand how divisive this conflict was. But to understand how a work of fiction about the Irish Troubles could inflame such passions, think about a similarly controversial novel today about Islam; *The Satanic Verses* comes to mind.

Ironically, as I said, I had gone out of my way to present both sides, but that only served to annoy each side.

When I returned to New York, which was then, along with Boston, the center of IRA sympathy in America, I decided to meet the beast, so to speak. So I gathered a group of Irish-American friends and two or three Irish nationals (who may have had IRA connections) and went pub hopping, or as we used to say, we did a pub crawl.

I'd asked the publisher to drop off or send multiple copies of *Cathedral* to a few dozen pubs right after publication, and some of these copies were prominently displayed on the bar shelves, and I autographed them. Many of the bartenders, wait staff, and patrons I ran into that night had read the book and were happy to discuss it. The pub reviews were generally favorable, though a few people said I treated the IRA unfairly, while others thought I had glamorized it. I was reminded of an old adage that says one man's terrorist is another man's freedom fighter.

One Irish pub, Ryan McFadden's on the corner of Second Avenue and 42nd Street, was the favorite watering hole of a number of British journalists who had offices across the street in the Daily News building. I had become friendly with a number of them, and I invited them to meet me at McFadden's one night. They also had been sent copies of *Cathedral*, and we discussed the book. Most of them felt that I had not glamorized the Irish Republican Army, and most of them thought I'd been fair in regard to the British position on the issues of Northern Ireland. A few, however, had the opposite opinion. My opinion, for what it's worth, is that I'd done a good job of pleasing or annoying everyone.

In a related story, when Prince Charles and Lady Diana were married on July 29, 1981—two months after *Cathedral* was published—the British journalists who frequented Ryan McFadden's asked if they could have a party in the pub to celebrate the marriage. The owners agreed and the scheduled party made the news: British royal wedding celebration in Irish pub. The party started at 4 a.m. to coincide with live television coverage coming from London, where it was 10 a.m. By dawn, the bar was full of revelers of all ancestry and religious beliefs, myself included. The two owners of the bar, both Irish-Americans, received no fewer than three telephoned IRA bomb threats during the party, which they announced, though no one left the premises. The quite logical belief was that these threats were hoaxes, and that the Irish Republican Army would not blow up an Irish pub in New York City and kill a lot of Americans just to blow up a dozen British journalists. The British journalists believed that, too, and we all watched the royal couple on TV and had beer and bangers for breakfast.

The point of this story is that the Irish conflict, while brutal, had a few rules, one of which was that the Troubles were not going to spill over into America. Our current war on terrorism has no such rules, obviously. *Cathedral*, however, is about just such a scenario: the Irish war spills over into America—specifically, New York City—and does so in a very dramatic way.

Without giving away the plot, a splinter group of the Irish Republican Army plans to seize St. Patrick's Cathedral on New York's Fifth Avenue. And they decide to do it on St. Patrick's Day during the Fifth Avenue parade when over a million marchers, spectators, and partiers are crammed into midtown Manhattan. All the ingredients for chaos are in place—the media are covering the parade, the Cardinal and church dignitaries are on the steps of the cathedral, the reviewing stands on Fifth Avenue are filled with politicians and VIPs, the police are over-stretched, and the citizens are...well, not feeling any pain. The only people who have any clear idea of what is happening are the people who are about to seize the cathedral and take hostages.

Where do I get ideas like this? Well, it had been my privilege for many years to be included as a guest on the steps of St. Patrick's Cathedral during the annual parade, along with church dignitaries, city officials, police brass, and other worthy citizens. Maybe they should not have invited an action/adventure writer with an overactive imagination to be among those upstanding citizens.

In 1977, while I was putting the finishing touches on *By the Rivers of Babylon*, I took time out to go to the parade on March 17. It was a cold but clear day, and as I stood on the steps of St. Pat's and watched the tens of thousands of people parading up Fifth Avenue, I had a thought. A police captain I knew was standing next to me, and I said to him, "What if the IRA seized the cathedral now and took the Cardinal hostage?"

He didn't like that "what if" and replied, "Bite your tongue, son." Then he said, "Impossible."

Nothing is impossible—especially in fiction. I needed an idea for my next book and I'd just found it.

The next day, I began my research. First, I wrote to the Rec-tor of St. Pat's, whom I knew, and without bothering him with the plot, I asked him if he'd help me with my research on a book about the cathedral, especially the physical layout. He referred me to a man named Knight Sturgis, the consulting architect of St. Patrick's, now deceased.

Mr. Sturgis took the time to give me several tours of the usu-ally inaccessible parts of the cathedral, including the bell tower,

the attic, crypt, and underground passages. He also provided
me with detailed blueprints of the cathedral, some of which
are reproduced in this book. Mr. Sturgis did not know exactly
what my book was going to be about, and that was just as well.
He did, however, see from a book reviewer an advance reading
copy of *Cathedral*, in which I cited Mr. Sturgis's assistance in the
Acknowledgments. He asked me to delete his name from the
final copy, which I did, so you won't see him listed in the Acknowledgments here or in earlier editions, though through an
oversight he is listed in the original book club edition. Similarly, St. Patricks' rector, whose name I won't mention, though
he's also deceased, asked me to expunge his name from the cred-
its. After *Cathedral* was published, I became persona non grata
on the steps of St. Patrick's during the parade—but I was still
welcome the other 364 days of the year, especially for Saturday
Confession.

Also after *Cathedral* was published, there was some debate in
the media about irresponsible authors giving ideas to potential
terrorists. My position was and remains that "what if" fiction
is a cautionary tale, a wake-up call to citizens and to the people
who are entrusted with our security. Prior to *Cathedral* being
published, there were no contingency plans in place if something like I describe in this book actually happened in real life.
As a result of the Munich Olympics tragedy, New York City
had just formed a Hostage Negotiation Unit headed by Captain Frank Bolz, whom I knew, and there was a relatively small
NYPD SWAT team in place. But other than that, there was no
clear plan of action in the event of a takeover of a public building or a historic landmark. One of the things that resulted, I've
been told, from the publication of *Cathedral* was that the NYPD
began acquiring blueprints of places like St. Patrick's, Grand
Central Station, the Empire State Building, the U.N. Headquar-

ters, foreign consulates, and other buildings that could be at risk for a takeover or attack by terrorist groups.

Anti-terrorism in those days was in its infancy, and writers of fiction and nonfiction were often far in advance of the security apparatus in terms of terrorist scenarios that could be played out in America. That has changed, of course, but the people who wish to do us harm only have to be half a step ahead of us to succeed. Books like this, then, can help, not hurt, the cause of national security. *Cathedral* didn't give the IRA any ideas; it gave the police some ideas.

We're much more sophisticated now than we were in the early 1980s, and we've seen things happen that not even a novelist with a good imagination could have conceived. But back then, we believed if we didn't write about it, or think about it, it wouldn't happen, (i.e., "bite your tongue"). We all wish that were true, but we know it's not.

I'm not suggesting that this book was published as a public service. It was controversial and I took some flak for it. But with the passage of time, most of the public, the media, and the people entrusted with our security view books like this as a reflection of reality, or as I said, a warning to be prepared.

The Irish Republican Army never did come to America to cause us harm—only to raise money and buy guns and explosives— but it goes without saying that America is now in the crosshairs of many other groups who have and will cause us harm.

Upon publication, *Cathedral* was an instant bestseller and a Main Selection of the Literary Guild. It's been translated into over twenty foreign languages and is still in print around the world. *Cathedral* is very cinematic, and it had the most movie interest of any of my novels, but if you think you've missed the movie, you haven't; it's never been made. In the end, most moviemakers thought it was too controversial or too inflammatory, which is similar to how Hollywood feels today about Islamic terrorist themes.

Cathedral was my second hardcover novel, following *By the Rivers of Babylon*, and because of its success, I felt I had overcome what is called in the business Second Book Syndrome, which is the inevitably bad and self-conscious book that follows an author's bestselling debut. I credit this success in part to the subject matter, i.e., it was the right book at the right time, as was *By the Rivers of Babylon*.

When I recently re-read *Cathedral*, I was concerned that I might find it almost quaint and unsophisticated by today's standards of terrorist novels, and terrorist reality. The reader, too, might find something that seems to belong in another era. But the book and the story have stood up very well to the passage of time, and it has remained one of my bestselling novels for over thirty years. The book's characters on both sides—inside and outside the cathedral—are as engaging and complex as when I first created them. The passion is alive on the pages, and the double-crossing and deceit are all too familiar. Maybe some of what was high-tech then is not so high-tech now, but this story is more about the human mind and our capacity for good and evil, and our justifications and motivations for both.

When you read this story, keep in mind that it is about a conflict that we as Americans had trouble understanding, partly because we were not a target of that conflict for a change. We, or most of us, feel an affinity for the Irish and the English, and it made us unhappy that they were killing each other. This is what I try to capture in this story— the media's and the public's ambivalence as the Irish Republican Army perpetrates this attack on American soil, in a holy place that is also holy to the perpetrators. The issues were complex and the hate was not always comprehensible, not even to those directly involved. And maybe for that reason this conflict has apparently come to an end. In the final analysis, it was senseless and the modern world overtook the ancient hatreds.

But now, let's return to the early 1980s at the height of the Troubles. It is St. Patrick's Day in New York City, and on this day everyone is Irish and everyone is having a grand time. Until the first shot is fired.

Nelson DeMille
New York, 2011

Author's Note

Regarding places, people, and events: The author has learned that in any book dealing with the Irish, literary license and other liberties should not only be tolerated but expected.

St. Patrick's Cathedral in New York has been described with care and accuracy. However, as in any work of fiction, especially in one set in the future, dramatic liberties have been exercised in some instances.

The New York police officers represented in this novel are not based on real people. The fictional hostage negotiator, Captain Bert Schroeder, is not meant to represent the present New York Police Department Hostage Negotiator, Frank Bolz. The only similarity shared is the title of Hostage Negotiator. Captain Bolz is an exceptionally competent officer whom the author has had the pleasure of meeting on three occasions, and Captain Bolz's worldwide reputation as innovator of the New York Plan of hostage negotiating is well deserved. To the people of the city of New York, and especially to the people whose lives he's been instrumental in saving, he is a true hero in every sense of the word.

The Catholic clergy represented in this work are not based on actual persons. The Irish revolutionaries in this novel are based to some extent on a composite of real people, as are the politicians, intelligence people, and diplomats, though no individual character is meant to represent an actual man or woman.

The purpose of this work was not to write a roman à clef or to represent in any way, favorably or unfavorably, persons living or dead.

The story takes place not in the present or the past but in the future; the nature of the story, however, compels the author to use descriptive job titles and other factual designations that exist at this writing. Beyond these designations there is no identification meant or intended with the public figures who presently hold those descriptive job titles.

Historical characters and references are for the most part factual except where there is an obvious blend of fact and fiction woven into the story line.

St. Patrick's
Cathedral
First Floor Plan

Key:

Altars–A
Archbishop's
Sacristy–Ar
Archbishop's
Throne–T
Bookstore–B
Bride's Room–BR
Bronze Plate–BP
Chimney–C
Clergy Pews–CP
Confessional–Co
Elevators–E
Organ
Keyboard–Or
Spiral
Staircases–S

◀ N

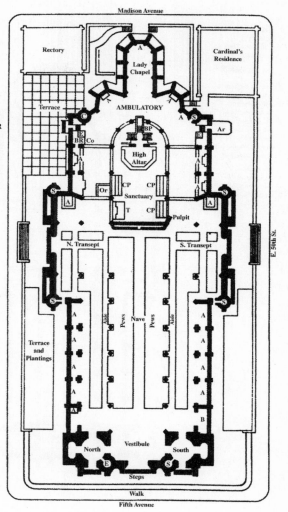

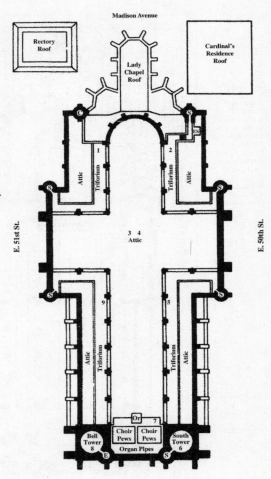

**St. Patrick's
Cathedral
Triforium Plan
and Attics**

Key (clockwise):

Eamon Farrell–1
Frank Gallagher–2
Jean Kearney–3
Arthur Nulty–4
George Sullivan–5
Rory Devane–6
Jack Leary–7
Donald Mullins–8
Abby Boland–9

Chimney–C
Elevator–E
Elevator Shaft–ES
Organ Keyboard–Or
Spiral Staircases–S

← N

Madison Avenue

Rectory Roof

Cardinal's Residence Roof

Lady Chapel Roof

Attic

Triforium

1

2

Triforium

Attic

E. 51st St.

3 4
Attic

E. 50th St.

9

5

Attic

Triforium

Triforium

Attic

Or   7

Bell Tower 8

Choir Pews

Choir Pews

South Tower 6

Organ Pipes

Fifth Avenue

BOOK I

Northern Ireland

Now that I've learned a great deal about Northern Ireland, there are things I can say about it: that it's an unhealthy and morbid place, where people learn to die from the time that they're children; where we've never been able to forget our history and our culture—which are only other forms of violence; where it's so easy to deride things and people; where people are capable of much love, affection, human warmth and generosity. But, my God! How much we know how to hate!

Every two or three hours, we resurrect the part, dust it off and throw it in someone's face.

Betty Williams,
Northern Irish peace
activist and winner of
the Nobel Peace Prize

CHAPTER 1

T he tea has got cold." Sheila Malone set down her cup and waited for the two young men who sat opposite her, clad in khaki underwear, to do the same.

The younger man, Private Harding, cleared his throat. "We'd like to put on our uniforms."

Sheila Malone shook her head. "No need for that."

The other man, Sergeant Shelby, put down his cup. "Let's get done with it." His voice was steady, but his hand shook and the color had drained from under his eyes. He made no move to rise.

Sheila Malone said abruptly, "Why don't we take a walk?"

The sergeant stood. The other man, Harding, looked down at the table, staring at the scattered remains of the bridge game they'd all passed the morning with. He shook his head. "No."

Sergeant Shelby took the younger man's arm and tried to grip it, but there was no strength in his hand. "Come on, now. We could use some air."

Sheila Malone nodded to two men by the fire. They rose and came up behind the British soldiers. One of them, Liam Coogan, said roughly, "Let's go. We've not got all day."

Shelby looked at the men behind him. "Give the lad a second or two," he said, pulling at Harding's arm. "Stand up," he ordered. "That's the hardest part."

The young private rose slowly, then began to sink back into his chair, his body trembling.

Coogan grasped him under the arms and propelled him toward the door. The other man, George Sullivan, opened the door and pushed him out.

Everyone knew that speed was important now, that it had to be done quickly, before anyone's courage failed. The sod was wet and cold under the prisoners' feet, and a January wind shook water off the rowan trees. They passed the outdoor privy they had walked to every morning and every evening for two weeks and kept walking toward the ravine near the cottage.

Sheila Malone reached under her sweater and drew a small revolver from her waistband. During the weeks she had spent with these men she had grown to like them, and out of common decency someone else should have been sent to do it. Bloody insensitive bastards.

The two soldiers were at the edge of the ravine now, walking down into it.

Coogan poked her roughly. "Now, damn you! Now!"

She looked back toward the prisoners. "Stop!"

The two men halted with their backs to their executioners. Sheila Malone hesitated, then raised the pistol with both hands. She knew she would hit only their backs from that range, but she couldn't bring herself to move closer for a head shot. She took a deep breath and fired, shifted her aim, and fired again.

Shelby and Harding lurched forward and hit the ground before the echo of the two reports died away. They thrashed on the ground, moaning.

Coogan cursed. "Goddamn it!" He ran into the ravine, pointed his pistol at the back of Shelby's head, and fired. He looked at Harding, who was lying on his side. Frothy blood trickled from his mouth and his chest heaved. Coogan bent over, placed the pistol between Harding's wideopen eyes, and fired again. He put his revolver in his pocket and looked up at the edge of the ravine. "Bloody stupid woman. Give a woman a job to do and..."

Sheila Malone pointed her revolver down at him. Coogan stepped backward and tripped over Shelby's body. He lay between the two corpses with his hands still held high. "No! Please. I didn't mean anything by it. Don't shoot!"

Sheila lowered the pistol. "If you ever touch me again, or say anything to me again... I'll blow your fucking head off!"

Sullivan approached her cautiously. "It's all right now. Come on, Sheila. We've got to get away from here."

"He can find his own bloody way back. I'll not ride with him."

Sullivan turned and looked down at Coogan. "Head out through the wood, Liam. You'll pick up a bus on the highway. See you in Belfast."

Sheila Malone and George Sullivan walked quickly to the car waiting off the lane and climbed in behind the driver, Rory Devane, and the courier, Tommy Fitzgerald.

"Let's go," said Sullivan.

"Where's Liam?" asked Devane nervously.

"Move out," said Sheila.

The car pulled into the lane and headed south toward Belfast.

Sheila drew from her pocket the two letters the soldiers had given her to mail to their families. If she were stopped at a roadblock and the Royal Ulster Constabulary found the letters... She opened the window and threw her pistol out, then let the letters sail into the wind.

Sheila Malone jumped out of her bed. She could hear motors in the street and the sounds of boots against the cobbles. Residents of the block were shouting from windows, and trash-can lids were being beaten to sound the alarm. As she began pulling her slacks on under her nightdress her bedroom door crashed open, and two soldiers rushed in without a word. A shaft of light from the hall made her cover her eyes. The red-bereted paratroopers pushed her against the wall and ripped the slacks from around her legs. One of them raised her nightdress over her head, and then ran his hands over her body, searching for a weapon. She spun and swung her fists at him. "Get your filthy hands..."

One of the soldiers punched her in the stomach, and she doubled over and lay on the floor, her nightdress gathered up around her breasts.

The second soldier bent down, grabbed her long hair, and dragged her to her feet. He spoke for the first time. "Sheila Malone, all I'm required to tell you is that you are being arrested under the Special Powers Act. If you make one fucking sound when we take you out to the trucks, we'll beat you to a pulp."

The two soldiers pushed her into the hall, down the stairs, and into the street, which was filled with shouting people. Everything passed in a blur as she was half-carried to the intersection where the trucks were parked. Voices called insults at the British soldiers and the Royal Ulster Constabulary who were assisting them. A boy's voice shouted, "Fuck the Queen." Women and children were crying, and dogs were barking. She saw a young priest trying to calm a group of people. An unconscious man, his head bloodied, was dragged past her. The soldiers picked her up and threw her into the back of a small truck filled with a dozen other prisoners. An RUC guard stood at the front of the truck, fondling a large truncheon. "Lie down, bitch, and shut your mouth."

She lay down by the tailgate and listened to her own breathing in the totally silent truck. After a few minutes the gates of the truck closed and it pulled away.

The guard shouted above the noise of the convoy. "The Pope is a fucking queer."

Sheila Malone lay against the tailgate, trying to calm herself. In the dark truck some men slept or were unconscious; a few were weeping. The guard kept up an anti-Catholic tirade until the truck stopped and the tailgate swung open, revealing a large, floodlit enclosure surrounded by barbed wire and machine-gun towers. Long Kesh, known to the Catholics of Northern Ireland as Dachau.

A soldier shouted into the truck, "Clear out! Quick! Move it!"

A few men scrambled over and around Sheila, and she heard the sounds of blows, shouts, and cries as the men left the truck. A voice cried out, "Take it easy, I'm an old man." A young boy clad in pajamas crawled over her and tumbled to the ground. The RUC guard was kicking everyone toward the tailgate now, like a trash man sweeping the floor of his truck clean at the dump. Someone pulled her out by her legs, and she fell on the soft, wet earth. She tried to stand but was knocked down.

"Crawl! Crawl, you bastards!"

She picked up her head and saw two lines of paratrooper boots. She crawled as quickly as she could between the gauntlet as blows fell on her back and buttocks. A few of the men made obscene remarks as she passed by on her hands and knees, but the blows were light and the obscenities were shouted by boyish, embarrassed voices, which somehow made it all the more obscene.

At the end of the gauntlet two soldiers picked her up and pushed her into a long Nissen hut. An officer with a swagger stick pointed to an open door, and the soldiers pushed her onto the floor of a small room and shut the door as they left. She looked up from where she lay in the center of the tiny cubicle.

A matron stood behind a camp table. "Strip. Come on, you little tramp. Stand up and take them off."

Within minutes she was stripped and searched and was wearing a gray prison dress and prison underwear. She could hear blows being struck outside the small cubicle and cries and shouts as the harvest of the sweep was processed— transformed from sleeping civilians into gray, terrified internees.

Sheila Malone had no doubt that a good number of them were guilty of some kind of anti-British or antigovernment activity. A few were actually IRA. A smaller number might even be arsonists or bombers...or murderers like herself. There was a fifty-fifty chance of getting out of internment within ninety days if you didn't crack and confess to something. But if they had something on you—something as serious as murder...Before she could gather her thoughts and begin to formulate what she was going to say, someone placed a hood over her head and she was pushed through a door that closed behind her.

A voice shouted directly in her ear, and she jumped. "I said, spell your name, bitch!"

She tried to spell it but found to her surprise that she could not. Someone laughed.

Another voice shouted, "Stupid cunt!"

A third voice screamed in her other ear. "So, you shot two of our boys, did you?"

There it was. They knew. She felt her legs begin to shake.

"Answer me, you little murdering cunt!"

"N-n-no."

"*What*? Don't lie to us, you cowardly, murdering bitch. Like to shoot men in the back, do you? Now it's your turn!"

She felt something poke her in the back of the head and

heard the sound of a pistol cocking. The hammer fell home and made a loud, metallic thud. She jumped and someone laughed again. "Next time it won't be empty, bitch."

She felt sweat gather on her brow and soak the black hood.

"All right. Pull up your dress. That's right. All the way!"

She pulled her skirt up and stood motionless as someone pulled her pants down to her ankles.

After an hour of pain, insults, humiliation, and leering laughter, the three interrogators seemed to get bored. She was certain now that they were just fishing, and she could almost picture being released at dawn.

"Fix yourself up."

She let her aching arms fall and bent over to pull up her pants. Before she straightened up she heard the three men leave the room as two other people entered. The hood was pulled from her head, and the bright lights half-blinded her. The man who had taken the hood moved to the side and sat in a chair just out of range of her vision. She focused her eyes straight ahead.

A young British army officer, a major, sat in a chair behind a small camp desk in the center of the windowless room. "Sit down, Miss Malone."

She walked stiffly toward a stool in front of the desk and sat slowly. Her buttocks hurt so much that she would almost rather have remained standing. She choked down a sob and steadied her breathing.

"Yes, you can have a bed as soon as we finish this." The major smiled. "My name is Martin. Bartholomew Martin."

"Yes...I've heard of you."

"Really? Good things, I trust."

She leaned forward and looked into his eyes. "Listen, Major Martin, I was beaten and sexually abused."

He shuffled some papers. "We'll discuss all of that as soon as we finish with this." He picked out one sheet of paper. "Here it is. A search of your room has uncovered a pistol and a satchel of gelignite. Enough to blow up the whole block." He looked at her. "That's a dreadful thing to keep in your aunt's house. I'm afraid she may be in trouble now as well."

"There was no gun or explosives in my room, and you know it."

He drummed his fingers impatiently on the desk. "Whether they were there or not is hardly the point, Miss Malone. The point is that my report *says* a gun and explosives were found, and in Ulster there is not a great deal of difference between the charges and the realities. In fact, they are the same. Do you follow me?"

She didn't answer.

"All right," said the major. "That's not important. What is important," he continued as he stared into her eyes, "are the murders of Sergeant Thomas Shelby and Private Alan Harding."

She stared back at his eyes and displayed no emotion, but her stomach heaved. They had her, and she was fairly certain she knew how they had gotten her.

"I believe you know a Liam Coogan, Miss Malone. An associate of yours. He's turned Queen's evidence." An odd half smile passed over his face. "I'm afraid we've got you now."

"If you know so goddamned much, why did your men—"

"Oh, they're not my men. They're paratroop lads. Served with Harding and Shelby. Brought them here for the occasion. I'm in Intelligence, of course." Major Martin's voice changed, became more intimate. "You're damned lucky they didn't kill you."

Sheila Malone considered her situation. Even under normal British law she would probably be convicted on Coogan's testimony. Then why had she been arrested under the Special Powers

Act? Why had they bothered to plant a gun and explosives in her room? Major Martin was after something else.

Martin stared at her, then cleared his throat. "Unfortunately, there is no capital punishment for murder in our enlightened kingdom. However, we're going to try something new. We're going to try to get an indictment for treason—I think we can safely say that the Provisional Irish Republican Army, of which you are a member, has committed treason toward the Crown."

He looked down at an open book in front of him. "'Acts that constitute treason. Paragraph 811—Levies war against the Sovereign in her realm....' I think you fill that bill nicely." He pulled the book closer and read, "'Paragraph 812—The essence of the offense of treason lies in the violation of the allegiance owed to the Sovereign....' And Paragraph 813 is my favorite. It says simply"—he looked at her without reading from the book—"'The punishment for treason is death by hanging.'" He stressed the last words and looked for a reaction, but there was none. "It was Mr. Churchill, commenting on the Irish uprising of 1916, who said, 'The grass grows green on the battlefield, but never on the scaffold.' It's time we started hanging Irish traitors again. You first. And beside you on the scaffold will be your sister, Maureen."

She sat up. "My sister? Why...?"

"Coogan says *she* was there as well. You, your sister, and her lover, Brian Flynn."

"That's a bloody lie."

"Why would a man turn Queen's evidence and then lie about who committed the murders?"

"Because *he* shot those soldiers—"

"There were two calibers of bullets. We can try two people for murder—any two. So why don't you let me work out who did what to whom?"

"You don't care who killed those soldiers. It's Flynn you want to hang."

"*Someone* must hang." But Major Martin had no intention of hanging any of them and making more Irish martyrs. He wanted to get Flynn into Long Kesh, where he could wring out every piece of information that he possessed about the Provisional IRA. Then he would cut Brian Flynn's throat with a piece of glass and call it suicide.

He said, "Let's assume that you escape the hangman's noose. Assume also that we pick up your sister, which is not unlikely. Consider if you will, Miss Malone, sharing a cell with your sister for the rest of your natural lives. How old are you? Not twenty yet? The months, the years pass slowly. *Slowly.* Young girls wasting their lives...and for what? A philosophy? The rest of the world will go on living and loving, free to come and go. And you...well, the real hell of it is that Maureen, at least, is innocent of murder. You are the reason she'd be there—because you wouldn't name her lover. And Flynn will have found another woman, of course. And Coogan, yes, Coogan will have gone to London or America to live and—"

"Shut up! For God's sake, shut up!" She buried her face in her hands and tried to think before he started again.

"Now there *is* a way out." He looked down at his papers, then looked up again. "There always is, isn't there? What you must do is dictate a confession naming Brian Flynn as an officer in the Provisional IRA—which he is—and naming him as the murderer of Sergeant Shelby and Private Harding. You will be charged as an accessory after the fact and be free within...let's say, seven years."

"And my sister?"

"We'll put out a warrant for her arrest only as an accessory. She should leave Ulster and never return. We will not look for her and will not press any country for extradition. But this arrangement is operative only if we find Brian Flynn." He leaned forward. "Where is Brian Flynn?"

"How the hell should I know?"

Martin leaned back in his chair. "Well, we must charge you with something within ninety days of internment. That's the law, you understand. If we don't find Flynn by the ninetieth day, we will charge you with double homicide—perhaps treason as well. So, if you can remember anything that will lead us to him, please don't hesitate to tell us." He paused. "Will you think about where Flynn might be?"

She didn't answer.

"Actually, if you really don't know, then you're useless to me...unless...You see, your sister will try to free you, and with her will be Flynn...so perhaps—"

"You won't use me for bait, you bastard."

"No? Well, we'll have to see about that, won't we?"

"May I have a bed?"

"Certainly. You may stand now."

She stood. "No more Gestapo tactics?"

"I'm sorry, I don't understand." He rose from his chair. "The matron will escort you to a cell. Good night."

She turned and opened the door. A hood came down over her head, but before it did she saw not the matron but two young Royal Ulster Constabulary men and three grinning paratroopers.

CHAPTER 2

Brian Flynn looked up at Queen's Bridge, shrouded in March mist and darkness. The Lagan River fog rolled down the partially lit street and hung between the red-brick buildings of Bank Road. The curfew was in effect, and there was no traffic.

Maureen Malone looked at him. His handsome, dark features always seemed sinister at night. She pulled back the sleeve of her trench coat and looked at her watch. "It's after four. Where the hell are—"

"Quiet! Listen."

She heard the rhythmic footsteps coming out of Oxford Street. In the mist a squad of Royal Ulster Constabulary appeared and turned toward them, and they crouched behind a stack of oil drums.

They waited in silence, their breathing coming irregularly in long plumes of fog. The patrol passed, and a few seconds later they heard the whining of a truck changing gears and saw the headlights in the mist. A Belfast Gas Works truck pulled up to the curbstone near them, and they jumped in the open side door. The driver, Rory Devane, moved the truck slowly north toward the bridge. The man in the passenger seat, Tommy Fitzgerald, turned. "Road block on Cromac Street."

Maureen Malone sat on the floor. "Is everything set?"

Devane spoke as he steered slowly toward the bridge. "Yes. Sheila left Long Kesh in an RUC van a half hour ago. They took the A23 and were seen passing through Castlereagh not ten minutes ago. They'll be coming over the Queen's Bridge about now."

Flynn lit a cigarette. "Escort?"

"No," said Devane. "Just a driver and guard in the cab and two guards in the back, according to our sources."

"Other prisoners?"

"Maybe as many as ten. All going to Crumlin Road Jail, except for two women going up to Armagh." He paused. "Where do you want to hit them?"

Flynn looked out the rear window of the truck. A pair of headlights appeared on the bridge. "Collins's men are set up on Waring Street. That's the way they'll have to go to Crumlin Road." He wiped the fog from the window and stared. "Here's the RUC van." Devane cut off the engine and shut the lights.

The black, unmarked RUC van rolled off the bridge and headed into Ann Street. Devane waited, then restarted his truck and followed at a distance with his lights off. Flynn said to Devane, "Circle round to High Street."

No one spoke as the truck moved through the quiet streets. They approached Waring Street, and Tommy Fitzgerald reached under his seat and pulled out two weapons, an old American Thompson submachine gun and a modern Armalite automatic rifle. "The tommy gun is for you, Brian, and the light gun for my lady." He passed a short cardboard tube to Flynn. "And this... if, God forbid, we run into a Saracen." Flynn took the tube and stuck it under his trench coat.

They swung off Royal Avenue into Waring Street from the west at the same time the RUC van entered from the east at Victoria Street. The two vehicles approached each other slowly. A black sedan fell in behind the RUC van, and Fitzgerald pointed. "That'll be Collins and his boys."

Flynn saw that the RUC van was moving more slowly now, the driver realizing that he was being boxed in and looking for a way out.

"Now!" shouted Flynn. Devane swung the truck so that it blocked the road, and the RUC van screeched to a stop. The black sedan following the van came to a halt, and Collins with three of his men jumped out and ran toward the rear of the van with submachine guns.

Flynn and Maureen were out of the truck and moving toward the trapped van twenty-five yards up the road. The RUC guard and driver dropped below the windshield, and Flynn pointed his rifle. "Come out with your hands raised!" But the men didn't come out, and Flynn knew he couldn't shoot at the unarmored van filled with prisoners. He yelled to Collins, "I've got them covered! Go on!"

Collins stepped up to the van and struck the rear doors with his rifle butt. "Guards! You're surrounded! Open the doors and you won't be harmed!"

Maureen knelt in the road, her rifle across her knees. She felt her heart beating heavily in her chest. The idea of freeing her sister had become an obsession over the months and had, she realized, clouded her judgment. Suddenly all the things that were wrong with this operation crystallized in her mind—the van riding very low as though it were weighted, the lack of an escort, the predictable route. "Run! Collins—"

She saw Collins's surprised face under the glare of a streetlamp as the doors swung out from the RUC van.

Collins stood paralyzed in front of the open doors and stared at the British paratrooper berets over the top of a sandbag wall. The two barrels of the machine guns blazed in his face.

Flynn watched as his four men were cut down. One machine gun continued to pour bullets into the bodies while the other shifted its fire and riddled the sedan with incendiary rounds, hitting the gas tank and blowing it up. The street echoed with the explosion and the chattering sound of the machine guns, and the night was illuminated by the fire of the burning sedan.

Maureen grabbed Flynn's arm and pulled him toward their truck as pistol shots rang out from the doorway where the guard and driver had disappeared. She fired a full magazine into the doorway and the shooting stopped. The streets were alive with the sounds of whistles, shouting, and running men, and they could hear motor vehicles closing in.

Flynn turned and saw that the truck's windshield was shot out and the tires were flat. Fitzgerald and Devane were running up the street. Fitzgerald's body jerked, and he slid across the cobblestones. Devane kept running and disappeared into a bombed-out building.

Behind him Flynn could hear soldiers jumping from the RUC van and racing toward them. He pulled Maureen's arm, and they started to run as a light rain began to fall.

Donegall Street entered Waring Street from the north, and they turned into it, bullets kicking up chips of cobble behind them. Maureen slipped on the wet stone and fell, her rifle clattering on the pavement and skidding away in the darkness. Flynn lifted her, and they ran into a long alleyway, coming out into Hill Street.

A British Saracen armored car rolled into the street, its six huge rubber wheels skidding as it turned. The Saracen's spotlight came on and found them. The armored car turned and came directly at them, its loudspeaker blaring into the rainy night. "HALT! HANDS ON YOUR HEADS!"

Behind him Flynn could hear the paratroopers coming into

the long alley. He pulled the cardboard tube from his trench coat and knelt. He broke the seal and extended the telescoped tubes of the American-made M-72 antitank weapon, raised the plastic sights, and aimed at the approaching Saracen.

The Saracen's two machine guns blazed, pulverizing the brick walls around him, and he felt shards of brick bite into his chest. He put his finger on the percussion ignition switch and tried to steady his aim as he wondered if the thing would work. A disposable cardboard rocket launcher. Like a disposable diaper. Who but the Americans could make a throwaway bazooka? *Steady, Brian. Steady.*

The Saracen fired again, and he heard Maureen give a short yell behind him and felt her roll against his legs. "Bastards!" He squeezed the switch, and the 66mm HEAT rocket roared out of the tube and streaked down the dark, foggy street.

The turret of the Saracen erupted into orange flame, and the vehicle swerved wildly, smashing into a bombed-out travel agency. The surviving crew stumbled out holding their heads from the pain of the deafening rocket hit, and Flynn could see their clothes smoking. He turned and looked down at Maureen. She was moving, and he put his arm under her head. "Are you hit badly?"

She opened her eyes and began to sit up in his arms. "I don't know. Breast."

"Can you run?"

She nodded, and he helped her up. In the streets around them they could hear whistles, motors, shouts, tramping feet, and dogs. Flynn carefully wiped his fingerprints from the Thompson submachine gun and threw it into the alley.

They headed north toward the Catholic ghetto around New Lodge Road. As they entered the residential area they kept to the familiar maze of back alleys and yards between the row houses. They could hear a column of men double-timing on the street, rifle butts knocking on doors, windows opening, angry exchanges, babies wailing. The sounds of Belfast.

Maureen leaned against a brick garden wall. The running had made the blood flow faster through her wound, and she put her hand under her sweater. "Oh."

"Bad?"

"I don't know." She drew her hand away and looked at the blood, then said, "We were set up."

"Happens all the time," he said.

"Who?"

"Coogan, maybe. Could have been anyone, really." He was fairly certain he knew who it was. "I'm sorry about Sheila."

She shook her head. "I should have known they would use her as bait to get us.... You don't think *she*..." She put her face in her hands. "We lost some good people tonight."

He peered over the garden wall, then helped her over, and they ran through a block of adjoining yards. They entered a Protestant neighborhood, noticing the better built and maintained homes. Flynn knew this neighborhood from his youth, and he remembered the schoolboy pranks—breaking windows and running like hell—like now—through these alleys and yards. He remembered the smells of decent food, the clotheslines of white gleaming linen, the rose gardens, and the lawn furniture.

They headed west and approached the Catholic enclave of the Ardoyne. Ulster Defense League civilian patrols blocked the roads leading into the Arodyne, and the Royal Ulster Constabulary and British soldiers were making house searches. Flynn crouched behind a row of trash bins and pulled Maureen down beside him. "We've gotten everyone out of their beds tonight."

Maureen Malone glanced at him and saw the half smile on his face. "You enjoy this."

"So do they. Breaks the monotony. They'll swap brave tales at the Orange lodges and in the barracks. Men love the hunt."

She flexed her arm. A stiffness and dull pain were spreading outward from her breast into her side and shoulder. "I don't think we have much chance of getting out of Belfast."

"All the hunters are here in the forest. The hunters' village is therefore deserted."

"Which means?"

"Into the heart of the Protestant neighborhood. The Shankill Road is not far."

They turned, headed south, and within five minutes they entered Shankill Road. They walked up the deserted road casually and stopped on a corner. It was not as foggy here, and the streetlights were working. Flynn couldn't see any blood on Maureen's black trench coat, but the wound had drained the color from her face. His own wound had stopped bleeding, and the dried blood stuck to his chest and sweater. "We'll take the next outbound bus that comes by, sleep in a barn, and head for Derry in the morning."

"All we need is an outbound bus, not to mention an appearance of respectability." She leaned back against the bus-stop sign. "When do we get our discharge, Brian?"

He looked at her in the dim light. "Don't forget the IRA motto," he said softly. "Once in, never out. Do you understand?"

She didn't answer.

A Red Bus appeared from the east. Flynn pulled Maureen close to him and supported her as they mounted the steps. "Clady," said Flynn, and he smiled at the driver as he paid the fare. "The lady's had rather too much to drink, I'm afraid."

The driver, a heavy-set man with a face that looked more Scottish than Irish, nodded uncaringly. "Do you have your curfew card?"

Flynn glanced down the length of the bus. Less than a dozen people, mostly workers in essential services, and they looked mostly Protestant—as far as he could tell—like the driver. Perhaps everyone looked like Prods tonight. No sign of police, though. "Yes. Here it is." He held his wallet up close to the driver's face.

The driver glanced at it and moved the door lever closed, then put the bus in gear.

Flynn helped Maureen toward the rear of the bus, and a few of the passengers gave them looks ranging from disapproval to curiosity. In London or Dublin they would be dismissed for what they claimed to be—drunks. In Belfast people's minds worked in different directions. He knew they would have to get off the bus soon. They sat in the back seat.

The bus rolled up Shankill Road, through the Protestant working-class neighborhood, then headed northwest into the mixed neighborhoods around Oldpark. Flynn turned to Maureen and spoke softly. "Feeling better?"

"Oh, quite. Let's do it again."

"Ah, Maureen..."

An old woman sitting alone in front of them turned around. "How's the lady? How are you, dear? Feelin' better, then?"

Maureen looked at her without answering. The citizens of Belfast were capable of anything from murder and treachery to Christian kindness.

The old woman showed a toothless smile and spoke quietly. "Between Squire's Hill and McIlwhan's Hill is a wee valley called the Flush. There's an abbey there— you know it—Whitehorn Abbey. The priest, Father Donnelly, will give you lodgings for the night."

Flynn fixed the woman with a cold stare. "What makes you think we need a place to stay? We're headed home."

The bus stopped, and the old woman stood without another word and trundled off to the front of the bus and stepped off.

The bus started again. Flynn was very uneasy now. "Next stop. Are you up to it?"

"I'm not up to one more second on this bus." She paused thoughtfully. "The old woman...?"

Flynn shook his head.

"I think we can trust her."

"I don't trust anyone."

"What kind of country do we live in?"

He laughed derisively. "What a bloody stupid thing to say, Maureen. *We* are the ones who helped make it like it is."

She lowered her head. "You're right, of course...as usual."

"You must accept what you are. I accept it. I'm well adjusted."

She nodded. With that strange logic of his he had turned the world upside down. Brian was normal. She was not. "I'm going to Whitehorn Abbey."

He shrugged. "Better than a barn, I suppose. You'll be needing bandaging...but if the good rector there turns us in..."

She didn't answer and turned away from him.

He put his arm around her shoulders. "I *do* love you, you know."

She looked down and nodded.

The bus stopped again about a half-mile up the road, and Flynn and Maureen moved toward the door.

"This isn't Clady," said the driver.

"That's all right," answered Flynn. They stepped off the bus and into the road. Flynn took Maureen's arm. "That bastard will report us at the next stop." They crossed the road and headed north up a country lane lined with rowan trees. Flynn looked at his watch, then at the eastern sky. "Almost dawn. We have to be there before the farmers start running about—they're almost all Prods up here."

"I know that." Maureen breathed deeply as they walked in the light rain. The filthy air and ugliness of Belfast were far behind, and she felt better. Belfast—a blot of ash on the green loveliness of County Antrim, a blot of ash on the soul of Ireland. Sometimes she wished that the city would sink back into the bog it grew out of.

They passed hedgerows, well-tended fields, and pastures dotted with cattle and bales of fodder. An exhilarating sodden scent filled the air, and the first birds of morning began to sing.

"I'm not going back to Belfast."

He put his arm around her and touched her face with his hand. She was becoming feverish. "I understand. See how you feel in a week or two."

"I'm going to live in the south. A village."

"Good. And what will you do there? Tend pigs? Or do you have independent means, Maureen? Will you buy a country estate?"

"Do you remember the cottage overlooking the sea? You said we'd go there some day to live our lives in peace."

"Someday maybe we will."

"I'll go to Dublin, then. Find a job."

"Yes. Good jobs in Dublin. After a year they'll give you the tables by the window where the American tourists sit. Or the sewing machine by the window where you can get a bit of air and sun. That's the secret. By the window."

After a while she said, "Perhaps Killeen..."

"No. You can never go back to your own village. It's never the same, you know. Better to go to any other pig village."

"Let's go to America."

"No!" The loudness of his own voice surprised him.

"No. I won't do what they all did." He thought of his family and friends, so many of them gone to America, Canada, or Australia. He had lost them as surely as he had lost his mother and father when he buried them. Everyone in Ireland, north and south, lost family, friends, neighbors, even husbands and wives and lovers, through emigration. Like some great plague sweeping the land, taking the firstborn, the brightest, and the most adventurous, leaving the old, the sick, the timid, the self-satisfied rich, the desperately poor. "This is my country. I won't leave here to become a laborer in America."

She nodded. Better to be a king of the dunghills of Belfast and Londonderry. "I may go alone."

"You probably should."

They walked quietly, their arms around each other's waists, both realizing that they had lost something more than a little blood this night.

CHAPTER 3

The lane led into a small, treeless valley between two hills. In the distance they saw the abbey. The moonlight lit the white stone and gave it a spectral appearance in the ground mist.

They approached the abbey cautiously and stood under a newly budded sycamore tree. A small oblong cemetery, hedged with short green plants, spread out beside the abbey wall. Flynn pushed through the hedge and led Maureen into the cemetery.

The churchyard was unkempt, and vines grew up the gravestones. Whitehorn plants—which gave the abbey its name and which were omens of good luck or bad luck, depending on which superstition you believed—clogged the narrow path. A small side gate in a high stone wall led into the abbey's cloister. Flynn pushed it open and looked around the quiet court. "Sit on this bench. I'll find the brothers' dormitory."

She sat without answering and let her head fall to her chest. When she opened her eyes again, Flynn was standing over her with a priest.

"Maureen, this is Father Donnelly."

She focused on the elderly priest, a frail-looking man with a pale face. "Hello, Father."

He took her hand and with his other hand held her forearm in that way they had of claiming instant intimacy. He was the pastor; she was now one of his flock. Presto. Everyone's role had been carved in stone two millennia ago.

"Follow me," he said. "Hold my arm."

The three of them walked across the cloister and entered the arched door of a polygon-shaped building. Maureen recognized the traditional configuration of the chapter house, the meeting place of the monks. For a moment she thought she was going to face an assemblage, but she saw by the light of a table lamp that the room was empty.

Father Donnelly stopped abruptly and turned. "We have an infirmary, but I'm afraid I'll have to put you in the hole until the police and soldiers have come round looking for you."

Flynn didn't answer.

"You can trust me."

Flynn didn't trust anyone, but if he was betrayed, at least the War Council wouldn't think him too foolish for having trusted a priest. "Where's this hole, then? We don't have much time, I think."

The priest led them down a corridor, then opened the door at the end of the passage. Gray dawn came through stained glass, emitting a light that was more sensed than seen. A single votive candle burned in a red jar, and Flynn could see he was in the abbey's small church.

The priest lit a candle on a wall sconce and took it down. "Follow me up the altar. Be careful."

Flynn helped Maureen up to the raised altar sanctuary and watched the priest fumble with some keys and then disappear behind the reredos wall in back of the altar.

Flynn glanced around the church but neither saw nor heard anything in the shadows to signal danger. He noticed that the oppressive smell of incense and tallow was missing, and the church smelled like the outside air. The priest had told him that the abbey was deserted. Father Donnelly was apparently not the abbot but served in something like a caretaker capacity, though he didn't seem the type of priest that a bishop would exile to such a place, thought Flynn. Nor did he seem the type to hide members of the provisional IRA just to get a thrill out of it.

The priest reappeared holding his candle in the darkness. "Come this way." He led them to a half-open door made of scrolled wrought iron in the rear of the altar. "This is the place we use." He looked at the two fugitives to see why they weren't moving toward it. "The crypt," he added as if to explain.

"I know what it is. Everyone knows there's a crypt beneath an altar's sanctuary."

"Yes," said Father Donnelly. "First place they always look. Come along."

Flynn peered down the stone steps. A candle in an amber glass, apparently always kept burning, illuminated a wall and floor of white limestone. "Why is it I've not heard of this abbey as a place of safety before tonight?"

The priest spoke softly, evenly. "You had no need of it before tonight."

Typical priests' talk, thought Flynn. He turned to Maureen. She looked down the stairway, then at the priest. Her instincts, too, rebelled against entering the crypt. Yet her conditioned response was to do what the priest urged. She stepped toward the stairway and descended. Flynn glanced at the priest, then stepped through the doorway.

Father Donnelly led them along the limestone wall past the tombs of the former abbots of Whitehorn Abbey. He stopped and opened the bronze door of one of the tombs, marked *Fr. Seamus Cahill,* held up his candle, and entered the tomb. A wooden casket lay on a stone plinth in the middle of the chamber.

Father Donnelly passed the candle to Flynn and raised the

lid of the casket. Inside was a body wrapped in heavy winding sheets, the linen covered with fuzz of green mold. "Sticks and straw," he said. He reached into the casket and released a concealed catch, and the coffin bottom swung downward with the bogus mummy still affixed to it. "Yes, yes. Melodramatic for our age, but when it was conceived, it was necessary and quite common. Go on. Climb in. There's a staircase. See it? Follow the passageway at the bottom until you enter a chamber. Use your candle to light the way. There are more candles in the chamber."

Flynn mounted the plinth and swung his legs over the side. His feet found the top step, and he stood in the casket. A dank, almost putrid smell rose out of the dark hole. He stared at Father Donnelly questioningly.

"It's the entranceway to hell, my boy. Don't fear. You'll find friends down there."

Flynn tried to smile at the joke, but an involuntary shudder ran up his spine. "I suppose we should be thanking you."

"I suppose you should. But just hurry on now. I want to be in the refectory having breakfast when they arrive."

Flynn took a few steps down as Father Donnelly helped Maureen up the plinth and over the side of the casket onto the first step. Flynn held her arm with one hand and held the candle high with the other. She avoided the wrapped figure as she descended.

Father Donnelly pulled the casket floor up, then shut the lid and left the tomb, closing the bronze door behind him.

Flynn held the candle out and followed the narrow, shoulder-width passageway for a distance of about fifty feet, grasping Maureen's hand behind him. He entered an open area and followed the wall to his right. He found candles in sconces spaced irregularly around the unhewn and unmortared stone walls and lit them, completing the circuit around the room. The air in the chamber was chilly, and he saw his own breath. He looked around slowly at the half-lit room. "Odd sort of place."

Maureen wrapped herself in a gray blanket she had found and sat on a footstool. "What did you expect, Brian—a game room?"

"Ah, I see you're feeling better."

"I'm feeling terrible."

He walked around the perimeter of the six-sided room. On one wall was a large Celtic cross, and under the cross was a small chest on a wooden stand. Flynn placed his hand on the dusty lid but didn't open it. He turned back to Maureen. "You trust him?"

"He's a priest."

"Priests are no different from other men."

"Of course they are."

"We'll see." He now felt the fatigue that he had fought off for so long, and he sank down to the damp floor. He sat against the wall next to the chest, facing the stairway. "If we awake in Long Kesh..."

"My fault. All right? Go to sleep."

Flynn drifted off into fitful periods of sleep, opening his eyes once to see Maureen, wrapped in the blanket, lying on the floor beside him. He awoke again when he heard the casket bottom swing down and strike the wall of the passageway. He jumped up and stood at the entrance to the passage. In a shaft of light from the crypt he could see the coffin floor hanging, its grotesque mockery of a dead man stuck to it like a lizard on a wall.

The torso of a man appeared: black shoes, black trousers, the Roman collar, then the face of Father Donnelly. He held a tea tray high above his head as he made his way. "They were here and they're gone."

Flynn moved down the passageway and took the tray that the priest passed to him. Father Donnelly closed the coffin, and they walked into the chamber, Flynn placing the tray on a small wooden table.

Father Donnelly looked around the chamber the way a host examines a guest room. He stared at Maureen's sleeping figure, then turned to Flynn. "So, you blew up a sixer, did you? Rather daring, I'd say."

Flynn didn't answer.

"Well, anyway, they traced you as far as the McGloughlin farm up the lane. Good, loyal Ulstermen, the McGloughlins. Solid Presbyterians. Family came over from Scotland with Cromwell's army. Another three hundred years and they'll think this is their country. How's the lady?"

Flynn knelt beside her. "Sleeping." He touched her forehead. "Feverish."

"There's some penicillin tablets and an army aid kit along with the tea and bacon." He took a small bottle from his pocket. "And some Dunphy's, if you've the need of it."

Flynn took the bottle. "Rarely have I needed it more." He uncorked it and took a long drink.

Father Donnelly found two footstools, pulled them to the table, and sat. "Let her sleep. I'll take tea with you."

Flynn sat and watched the priest go through the fussy motions of a man who took food and drink seriously. "Who was here?" asked Flynn.

"The Brits and the RUCs. As usual the RUCs wanted to tear the place apart, but a British army officer restrained them. A Major Martin. Know him, do you? Yes, he's quite infamous. Anyway, they all played their roles wonderfully."

"I'm glad everyone had a good time. I'm only sorry I had to waken everyone so early."

"You know, lad, it's as if the participants in this war secretly appreciate each other. The excitement is not entirely unwelcome."

Flynn looked at the priest. Here was one man, at least, who didn't lie about it. "Can we get out of here?" he asked as he sipped the hot tea.

"You'll have to wait until they clear out of the hedgerows. Binoculars, you understand. Two days at least. Leave at night, of course."

"Doesn't everyone travel at night?"

The priest laughed. "Ah, Mister..."

"Cocharan."

"Whatever. When will this all stop?"

"When the British leave and the northern six counties are reunited with the southern twenty-six."

The priest put down his teacup. "Not true, my boy. The real desire of the IRA, the most secret dark desire of the Catholics, no matter what we all say about living in peace after the reunification, is to deport all the Protestants back to England, Scotland, and Wales. Send the McGloughlins back to a country they haven't seen in three hundred years."

"That's bloody rubbish."

The priest shrugged. "I don't care personally, you understand. I only want you to examine your own heart."

Flynn leaned across the table. "Why are you in this? The Catholic clergy has never supported any Irish rebellion against the British. So why are you risking internment?"

Father Donnelly stared down into his cup, then looked up at Flynn. "I don't involve myself with any of the things that mean so much to you. I don't care what your policy is or even what Church policy is. My only role here is to provide sanctuary. A haven in a country gone mad."

"To anyone? A murderer like me? Protestants? British troops?"

"Anyone who asks." He stood. "In this abbey was once an order of fifty monks. Now, only me." He paused and looked down at Flynn. "This abbey has a limited future, Mr. Cocharan, but a very rich past."

"Like you and me, Father. But I hope not like our country."

The priest seemed not to hear him and went on. "This chamber was once the storage cellar of an ancient Celtic Bruidean house. You know the term?"

"Yes, I think so."

"The House of the Hostages, it was called. A six-sided structure where six roads met. Coincidentally—or maybe not so—chapter houses are traditionally polygons, and the chapter house we passed through is built on these foundations." He gestured above. "Here in the Bruidean a traveler or a fugitive could shelter from the cold, dark road, protected by tradition and the king's law. The early Celts were not complete barbarians, after all." He looked at Flynn. "So you see, you've come to the right place."

"And you've taken it upon yourself to combine a bit of paganism with Christian charity."

The priest smiled. "Irish Catholicism has always been a blend of paganism and Christianity. The early Christians after Patrick specifically built their churches on Druid holy spots such as this. I suspect early Christians burnt this Bruidean down, then constructed a crude church on its foundations. You can still see the charred foundation stones. Then the Vikings destroyed the original monastery, and the next one was destroyed by the English army when Cromwell passed through. This is the last abbey to be built here. The Protestant plantations took all the good land in Ireland, but the Catholics held on to most of the good church sites."

"What more could you want?"

The priest regarded Flynn for a long time, then spoke softly. "You'd better wake the lady before the tea gets cold."

Flynn rose and crossed the floor to where Maureen was lying, knelt beside her, and shook her. "Tea."

She opened her eyes.

He said, "Hold on to me." He stood her up and helped her to his stool. "How are you feeling?"

She looked around the candlelit room. "Better."

Flynn poured the tea, and Father Donnelly extracted a pill from a vial. "Take this."

She swallowed the pill and took some tea. "Did the British come?"

The priest felt her forehead. "Came and went. In a few days you'll be on your way."

She looked at him, He was so accepting of them, what they were and what they had done. She felt disreputable. Whenever her life was revealed to people not in the movement, she felt not proud but ashamed, and that was not the way it was supposed to be. "Can you help us?"

"I am, dear. Drink your tea."

"No, I mean can you help us...get out of this?"

The priest nodded. "I see. Yes, I can help you if you want. It's rather easy, you know."

Flynn seemed impatient. "Father, save souls on your own time. I need some sleep. Thank you for everything."

"You're quite welcome."

"Could you do one more favor for us? I'll give you a number to call. Tell the person who answers where we are. Tell them that Brian and Maureen need help. Let me know what they say."

"I'll use a phone in the village in case this one is tapped."

Flynn smiled appreciatively. "If I've seemed a bit abrupt—"

"Don't let it trouble you." He repeated the number Flynn gave him, turned, and disappeared into the narrow passageway.

Flynn took the bottle of Dunphy's from the table and poured some in Maureen's teacup. She shook her head impatiently. "Not with the penicillin, Brian."

He looked at her. "We're not getting along, are we?"

"I'm afraid not."

He nodded. "Well, let's have a look at the nick, then."

She stood slowly, pulled her wet sweater over her head, and dropped it on the stool. Flynn saw that she was in pain as she unhooked her bloodied bra, but he didn't offer to help. He took a candle from the table and examined the wound, a wide gash running along the outside of her right breast and passing under her armpit. An inch to the left and she would have been dead. "Just a graze, really."

"I know."

"The important thing is that you won't need a doctor." The wound was bleeding again from the movement of her undressing, and he could see that it had bled and coagulated several times already. "It's going to hurt a bit." He dressed the wound while she stood with her arm raised. "Lie down and wrap yourself in the blanket."

She lay down and stared at him in the flickering light. She was cold, wet, and feverish. Her whole side ached, and the food had made her nauseous, though she was very thirsty. "We live like animals, licking our wounds, cut off from humanity...from..."

"God? But don't settle for this second-class Popish nonsense, Maureen. Join the Church of England—then you'll have your God, your respectability, and you can sit over tea with the Ladies' Auxiliary and complain about the IRA's latest outrage."

She closed her eyes, and tears ran down her cheeks.

When he saw that she was sleeping, he took the cup of Dunphy's and drained it, then began walking around the cellar. He examined the walls again and saw the scorch marks. How many times had this place been put to the torch? What made this location holy to both the Druids and the Christians? What spirit lived here in the heart of the earth? He carried a candle to the wooden chest and studied it. After some time he reached out and lifted the lid.

Inside he saw fragments of limestone that bore ancient Celtic inscriptions and a few unidentifiable pieces of metal, bronze, rusted iron. He pushed some of the objects aside, revealing a huge oval ring crusted with verdigris. He slipped it on his ring finger. It was large, but it stayed on his finger well enough. He clenched his fist and studied the ring. It bore a crest, and through the tarnish he could make out Celtic writing around a crudely molded bearded face.

He rubbed his fingers over the ring and wiped away some of the encrustation. The crude face stared back at him like a child's rendering of a particularly fearsome man. He felt dizzy and sensed his legs buckling under him. He was aware of hitting the floor. Then he blacked out.

CHAPTER 4

Brian Flynn woke to find a face staring down at him.

"It's noon," said Father Donnelly. "I've brought you some lunch."

Flynn focused on the ruddy face of the old man. He saw that the priest was staring at the ring on his finger. He got to his feet and looked around. Maureen was sitting at the table wearing a new pullover and eating from a steaming bowl. The priest had been there for some time, and that annoyed him. He walked over and sat opposite her. "Feeling better?"

"Much."

Father Donnelly pulled up a stool. "Would you mind if I joined you?"

"It's your food and your table," said Flynn.

The priest smiled. "One never gets used to dining alone."

Flynn took a spoon. "Why don't they send you a...monk or something?" He took a spoonful of stew.

"There's a lay brother who does the caretaking, but he's on leave." He leaned forward. "I see you've found the treasure of Whitehorn Abbey."

Flynn continued to eat as he spoke. "Sorry. Couldn't resist the temptation."

"That's all right."

Maureen looked up. "What are we talking about, please?"

Flynn slipped off the ring, passed it to her, and motioned toward the opened chest.

She examined the ring, then passed it to Father Donnelly. "It's an extraordinary ring."

Father Donnelly toyed with the ring. "Extraordinarily large, in any case."

Flynn poured a bottle of Guinness into a glass. "Where did it come from?"

The priest shook his head. "The last abbot said it was always here with the other things in that box. It may have been excavated here during one of the rebuildings. Perhaps under this floor."

Flynn stared at the ring in the priest's hand. "Pre-Christian?"

"Yes. Pagan. If you want a romantic story, it is said that it was a warrior king's ring. More specifically, Fenian. It's certainly a man's ring, and no average man at that."

Flynn nodded. "Why not MacCumail's ring? Or Dermot's?"

"Why not, indeed? Who would dare wear a ring larger than this?"

Flynn smiled. "You've a pagan streak in you, Father. Didn't Saint Patrick consign the departed Fenians to hell? What was their crime, then, that they must spend eternity in hell?"

"No crime. Just born at the wrong time." He smiled. "Like many of us."

"Right." Flynn liked a priest who could laugh at his dogma.

The priest leaned across the table. "When Oisin, son of Finn MacCumail, returned from the Land of Perpetual Youth, he found Ireland Christian. The brave warrior was confused, sad. Oisin rejected the ordered Christian society and longed with nostalgia for the untamed lustiness of old Erin. If he or his father, Finn MacCumail, came into Ulster today, they would be overjoyed at this Christian warfare. And they would certainly recognize the new pagans among us."

"Meaning me?"

Maureen poured tea into three mugs. "He's talking to you, Brian, isn't he?"

Father Donnelly rose. "I'll take my tea in the refectory."

Maureen Malone rose, too. "Don't leave."

"I really must." His demeanor had changed from paternal to businesslike. He looked at Flynn. "Your friends want you to stay here for two more days. They'll contact me and let me know the plan. Any reply?"

Flynn shook his head. "No."

Maureen looked at Flynn, then at Father Donnelly. "I have a reply. Tell them I want safe passage to Dublin, a hundred pounds, and a work visa for the south."

The priest nodded. He turned to go, hesitated, and came back. He placed the ring on the small table. "Mister..."

"Cocharan."

"Yes. Take this ring."

"Why?"

"Because you want it and I don't."

"It's a valuable relic."

"So are you."

"I won't ask you what you mean by that." He stood and looked hard at the priest, then took the ring from the table and placed it on his finger. Several new thoughts were forming in his mind, but he had no one to share them with. "Thank you." He looked at the ring. "Any curse attached to it that I should know about?"

The priest replied, "You should assume there is."

He looked at the two people standing before him. "I can't approve of the way you live your lives, but I find it painful to see a love dying. Any love, anywhere in this unloving country." He turned and made his way out of the cellar.

Flynn knew that Maureen had been talking to the priest while he'd been sleeping. He was having difficulty dealing with all that had happened in so short a time. Belfast, the old lady and the abbey, a priest who used pagan legends to make Christian statements, Maureen's aloofness. He was clearly not in control. He stood motionless for a time, then turned toward her. "I'd like you to reconsider about Dublin."

She looked down and shook her head.

"I'm asking you to stay . . . not only because I . . . What I mean is . . ."

"I know what you mean. Once in, never out. I'm not afraid of them."

"You should be. I can't protect you—"

"I'm not asking you to." She looked at him. "We're both better off."

"You're probably right. You understand these things better than I."

She knew that tone of voice. Remote. Sarcastic. The air in the cellar felt dense, oppressive. Church or not, the place made her uneasy. She thought about the coffin through which they had entered this hole, and that had been a little like dying. When she came out again she wanted to leave behind every memory of the place, every thought of the war. She looked at the ring on his hand. "Leave the damned thing here."

"I'm not only taking the ring, Maureen, I'm taking the name as well."

"What name?"

"I need a new code name . . . Finn MacCumail."

She almost laughed. "In any other country they'd treat you for megalomania. In Northern Ireland they'll find you quite normal, Brian."

"But I am normal."

"Not bloody likely."

He looked at her in the dim candlelight. He thought he had never seen anyone so lovely, and he realized that he hadn't thought of her in that way for a long time. Now she was flushed with the expectation of new beginnings, not to mention the flush of fever that reddened her cheeks and caused her eyes to burn bright. "You may well be right."

"About your being a lunatic?"

"Well, that too." He smiled at the small shared joke. "But I meant about you going off to Dublin."

"I'm sorry."

"Don't be. I'm only sorry I can't go with you."

"Perhaps, Brian, some day you'll get tired of this."

"Not bloody likely."

"No."

"Well, I'll miss you."

"I hope so," she said.

He stayed silent for a moment, then said, "I still don't know if we can trust him."

"He's a saint, for God's sake, Brian. Take him for what he appears to be."

"He appears different to me. Something odd about him. Anyway, we're not home free yet."

"I know."

"If anything happens and I don't have time to make a proper parting...well..."

"You've had time enough over the years to say what you felt. Time wasn't the problem. Tea?"

"Yes, please."

They sat silently, drinking their tea.

Flynn put down his cup. "Your sister..."

She shook her head. "Sheila is beyond our help."

"Maybe not."

"I don't want to see anyone else killed...."

"There are other ways...." He lapsed into silence, then said, "The keys to the jails of Ulster are in America."

A month later, when spring was firmly planted in the countryside and three weeks after Maureen Malone left for Dublin, Brian Flynn hired a car and went out to the abbey to thank Father Donnelly and to ask him about possible help in the future.

He found all the gates to the abbey locked, and no one answered any of the pull bells. A farmer riding by on a cart told him that the abbey was looked after by villagers employed by the diocese. And that no one had lived there for many years.

BOOK II

New York

English, Scotchmen, Jews, do well in Ireland—Irishmen, never; even the patriot has to leave Ireland to get a hearing.

George Moore,
Ave (Overture)

CHAPTER 5

B rian Flynn, dressed in the black clothing and white collar of a Roman Catholic priest, stood in the dim morning light near the south transept entrance to St. Patrick's Cathedral. He carried a small parcel wrapped in white paper decorated with green shamrocks. A few older women and two men stood at the base of the steps near him, huddled against the cold.

One of the two large transept doors swung open, and the head of a sexton appeared and nodded. The small crowd mounted the steps and passed through the side vestibule, then entered the Cathedral. Brian Flynn followed.

Inside the Cathedral, Flynn kneeled at the communion rail. The raised marble area, the altar sanctuary, was decked with fields of green carnations, and he studied the festive decorations. It had been four years since he had left Whitehorn Abbey; four years since he had seen her. Today he would see her again, for the last time.

He rose and turned toward the front of the Cathedral, slipping his right hand into his black overcoat pocket to feel the cold steel of the automatic pistol.

Father Timothy Murphy left his room in the rectory and made his way to the underground passage between the rectory and the

Cathedral. At the end of a corridor he came to a large paneled door and opened it, then stepped into a dark room and turned on a wall switch. Soft lights glowed in the marble-vaulted sacristy.

He walked to the priests' chapel in the rear of the sacristy and knelt, directing his prayers to St. Patrick, whose feast day it was, and asking as he did every year for peace in Northern Ireland, his native land. He asked also for good weather for the parade and a peaceful and relatively sober day in his adopted city.

He rose, crossed the sacristy, mounted a short flight of marble stairs, and unlocked a pair of brass gates. He rolled the gates back on their tracks into the marble archway, then continued up the steps.

On the first landing he stopped and peered through a barred door into the crypt that contained the remains of the past archbishops of New York. A soft yellow light burned somewhere in the heart of the crypt.

The staircase split in two directions on the landing, and he took the flight to the left. He came around the altar and walked toward the high pulpit. He mounted the curving stone steps and stood beneath the bronze canopy high above the pews.

The Cathedral spread out before him, covering an entire city block. The lighter spots of the towering stained-glass windows—the flesh tones of faces and hands—picked up the early morning light, changing the focus of the scenes from the Scriptures depicted on them in a way that their artisans never intended. Disembodied heads and limbs stared out of the cobalt blues and fiery reds, looking more damned than saved.

Father Murphy turned away from the windows and peered down at the worshipers. A dozen people were widely scattered over the length and breadth of this massive-columned house, none of them with any companion but God. He lifted his eyes toward the great choir loft over the front portals. The large pipe organ rose up like a miniature cathedral, its thousands of brass pipes soaring like spires against the diffused light of the massive rose window above them.

From his pocket Father Murphy drew his typed sermon and laid it over the open pages of the lectionary, then adjusted the microphone upward. He checked his watch. Six-forty. Twenty minutes until Mass.

Satisfied with these small details, he looked up again and noticed a tall priest standing beside the altar of St. Brigid. He didn't recognize the man, but St. Patrick's would be filled with visiting priests on this day; in fact, the priest appeared to be sightseeing, taking in the wide expanses of the Cathedral. A country bumpkin, thought Murphy, just as he himself had been years before. Yet there was something self-assured about the man's bearing. He seemed to be not awed but critical, as though he were considering buying the place but was unhappy with some of the appointments.

Father Murphy came down from the pulpit. He studied the bouquets of green-dyed carnations, then snapped one off and stuck it in the lapel of his coat as he descended the steps of the altar sanctuary and walked down the center aisle. In the large vestibule under the bell tower he came within a dozen feet of the tall priest, that area of space within which greeting had to be made. He paused, then smiled, "Good morning, Father."

The tall priest stared. "Morning."

Father Murphy considered extending his hand, but the other priest had his right hand deep in his overcoat pocket and held a gift-wrapped box under his other arm. Murphy passed by the priest and crossed the cold stone vestibule to the front door. He drew the floor bolt, then pushed the door open and stepped out to the front steps of the Cathedral. His clear blue eyes drifted across Fifth Avenue and upward to the top of the International Building in Rockefeller Center. A glint of sunlight reflected from the bronze work of the building. It was going to be a sunny day for the Irish, a great day for the Irish.

He looked to his right. Approaching from the north was a vehicle with flashing yellow lights. Hissing noises emanated from it as it drew opposite the Cathedral. Murphy saw the stream of Kelly-green paint coming from the rear of the machine, drawing a line down the middle of Fifth Avenue and covering the white traffic line.

His eyes focused on the huge bronze statue of Atlas—facing him from across the street in front of the International Building—holding up the world in a classic pose, heroic but pagan. He had never liked that statue—it mocked his church. Rockefeller Center itself mocked his church, its gray masonry buildings a colossal monument to the ego of one man, soaring above the marble spires of the Cathedral.

He stared at the naked physique of the god opposite him and was reminded of the tall priest in the Cathedral.

Brian Flynn moved to an arched oak door in a wall of the vestibule below the bell tower, opened it, and stepped into a small elevator. He pushed the only button on the panel, and the elevator rose. Flynn stepped out into the choir practice room, walked through it into the choir loft, and stood at the parapet rail.

Flynn looked beyond the sea of wooden pews toward the raised altar, its bronze work bathed in soft illumination and its marble gleaming from unseen light sources. White statuary reflected the ambient lighting and seemed—as it was supposed to seem—ethereal and animated. The statue of St. Patrick opposite the pulpit appeared to be looking up at him. Behind the carnation-decked altar was the rounded apse that held the Lady Chapel, the tall, slender, stained-glass windows alight with the rising sun. The fifteen altars that stood on the periphery of the Cathedral were aglow with votive candles.

If the intention was to awe, to mystify, to diminish man in the face of God, then this Gothic structure accomplished its purpose very well. What masters of suspense and mystery these Catholics were, Flynn thought, what incredible manipulators of physical reality and, hence, inner reality. Bread and wine into flesh and blood, indeed. Yet inside this Cathedral the years of childhood programming had their effect, and his thinking was involved with too many forgotten emotions. Outside the Church was a world that didn't diminish him or play tricks with his mind and eyes. He gave the Cathedral a last look, then made his way to a small door off the choir loft and opened it.

A rush of cold air hit him, and he shivered as he stepped into the bell tower. When his eyes had adjusted to the darkness he moved forward and found a spiral staircase with handrails in the center of the tower and began to climb, steadying himself with one hand and holding the parcel with the other.

The tower was dark, but translucent glass let in a grayish light. Flynn could see his breath as he climbed. The stairs gave way to ladders, and the ladders became shakier at each succeeding landing. He wondered if anyone ever came up here; he couldn't imagine why they would. He stopped to catch his breath on a landing below what he believed to be the first bell room.

He saw some movement to his right and drew his pistol. He walked in a crouch toward the movement, but it was only the straps of the bells hanging down the wall in a sinister fashion, swaying in the drafts as they passed through a hole in the landing.

He looked around. The place was eerie. The diffused light added to the effect, and the sounds of the surrounding city were changed into odd noises that seemed to come from the tower itself. The draft was eerie also because he couldn't quite tell from which direction it came. It seemed to come from some hidden respiratory organ belonging to the Cathedral itself—in a way, the secret breath of St. Patrick's—or St. Patrick himself. Yet he felt somehow that this breath was not sanctified and that there was an evil about the place, He had felt that in Whitehorn Abbey, and afterward realized that what the faithful took to be the presence of the Holy Spirit was something quite different for the faithless.

He tried to light a cigarette, but the matches would not stay lit. The brief light illuminated the small, polygon-shaped chamber of the tower, and again his thoughts were drawn back to the subbasement of Whitehorn's chapter house. He rubbed his hand over the large ring that he still wore. He thought of Maureen and pictured her as he had last seen her in that basement: frightened, sick, saddened at their parting. He wondered what her first words to him would be after these four years.

He looked at his watch. In ten minutes the bells would ring the Angelus, and if he were near them he would be deafened. He mounted the ladder and ascended. He had an impulse to shout a blasphemy up into the dark tower to rouse those spirits in their aerie, to tell them that Finn MacCumail was approaching and to make way.

The ladder reached into the first bell room, which held three of the Cathedral's nineteen cast-bronze bells hanging from a crossbeam. Flynn checked his watch again. Eight minutes to seven. Setting a flashlight on a crossbeam, he worked swiftly to unwrap the package, exposing a black metal box. He found the electrical wire that led to the utility work light fixed on the beam and cut the wire, connecting each end to terminals in the metal box. He set an electrical timer on the box to 5:00 P.M., then pulled the chain of the utility light. The bell room was partially illuminated, revealing the accumulated dust and cobwebs of a century, and the timer began ticking loudly in the still room.

He touched one of the bronze bells and felt its coldness, thinking that today might be the last day New York would hear it.

CHAPTER 6

Maureen Malone stood naked in front of the full-length door mirror, cold water clinging to her face and shoulders and glistening in the harsh bathroom light. Her hand moved to her right breast, and she felt the cold, jagged flesh along the side of it. She stared at the purple gash. God, the damage a tiny bullet could do. She had once considered plastic surgery, but the wound went down into her soul where no surgeon's hands could reach it.

She took a hotel bath towel, wrapped herself in it, and stepped into the bedroom. She walked slowly across the thick carpet, parted the heavy drapery, and looked out into the city from the forty-second floor of the Waldorf's north tower.

She tried to focus on the lights a few at a time. Strings of highway and bridge lamps cut across the waterways and flatlands around the island, and the island itself was jammed with incredibly huge buildings. She scanned the buildings closest to her and saw the Cathedral laid out in the shape of a cross, bathed in a cold blue light. The apse faced her, and the entrance was on a wide avenue. Its twin spires rose gracefully amid the rectangular hulks around it, and she could see traffic moving on many of the city's streets, an incredible thing at that hour, she thought.

The lights of the city blurred in her eyes, and her mind wandered back to the dinner in the Empire Room downstairs where she had been a speaker. What had she told those ladies and gentlemen of Amnesty International? That she was there for the living and dead of Ireland. *What was her mission?* they asked. To convince the British to release the men and women interned in Northern Ireland under the Special Powers Act. After that, and only after that, would her former comrades-in-arms talk peace.

The newspapers had said that her appearance on the steps of St. Patrick's Cathedral on the saint's feast day, with Sir Harold Baxter, the British Consul General in New York, would be a historical precedent. Never had a Cardinal allowed anyone remotely political to stand with him on the steps on this day. The political types mounted the steps, she was told, saluted the Prince of the Church and his entourage, then rejoined the parade and marched to the reviewing stands fourteen blocks farther north. But Maureen Malone, ex-IRA terrorist, had been invited. Hadn't Jesus forgiven Mary Magdalene? the Cardinal had asked her. Wasn't this what Christ's message was all about? She didn't know if she liked the comparison with that famous whore, but the Cardinal had seemed so sincere.

Sir Harold Baxter, she knew, was as uncomfortable with the arrangement as she was, but he could not have accepted without the approval of his Foreign Office, so that at least was a breakthrough. Peace initiatives, unlike war initiatives, always had such small, meek, tentative beginnings.

She felt a sudden chill by the window and shivered. Her eyes went back to the blue-lit Cathedral. She tried to envision how the day would end but couldn't, and this frightened her. Another chill, a different kind, ran down her spine. *Once in, never out.*

Somehow she knew Brian Flynn was close, and she knew he would not let her get away with this.

* * *

Terri O'Neal woke to the sound of early morning traffic coming through the second-story window. She sat up slowly in the bed. A streetlight outside the window partially illuminated the room. The man next to her—Dan, yes, Dan—turned his head and stared at her. She could see that his eyes were clear, unclouded by either drink or sleep. She suspected that he had been awake for some time, and this made her uneasy, but she didn't know why. "Maybe I should get going. Work today."

He sat up and held her arm. "No work today. You're going to the parade. Remember?"

His voice, a light brogue, was not husky with sleep. He *had* been awake—and how did he know she wasn't going to work today? She never told her pickups anything more than they had to know—in case it didn't go well. "Are *you* going to work today?"

"I am at work." He laughed as he took a cigarette from the night table.

She forced a smile, swung her legs out of bed, and stood. She felt his eyes taking in her figure as she walked to the big bay window and knelt in the window bench facing the street. She looked out. A lovely street. Sixty-something—off Fifth, a street of brownstone and granite town houses.

She looked westward. A big police van was parked on the corner of Fifth, and across the street from it was a television truck. On the far side of the Avenue were the reviewing stands that had been assembled in front of the park.

She looked directly below her. A long line of police scooters were angle-parked on the street. Dozens of helmeted police officers were milling about, blowing into their hands or drinking coffee. Their proximity made her feel better.

She turned and sat facing the bed. She noticed that he had

put on his jeans, but he was still sitting on the bed. She became apprehensive again, and her voice came out low and tremulous. "Who—who are you?"

He got off the bed and walked to her. "I'm your lover of last evening, Mrs. O'Neal." He stood directly in front of her, and she had to crane her neck to look up into his face.

Terri O'Neal was frightened. This man did not act, look, or talk like a crazy—yet he was going to do something to her that she was not going to like. She was sure of that. She pulled free of his stare and turned her eyes slightly toward the side panel of the bay window. A loud scream would do it. She hoped to God it would do it.

Dan Morgan didn't follow her eyes, but he knew what was out there. "Not a peep, lass. Not a peep..."

Reluctantly she swung her head back toward him and found herself staring into a big, black silencer at the end of a bigger black pistol. Her mouth went dry.

"...or I'll put a bullet through your pretty, dimpled kneecap."

It was several seconds before she could form a thought or a word, then she said softly, "What do you want?"

"Just your company for a while."

"Company?" Her brain wasn't taking in any of this.

"You're kidnapped, darlin'. Kidnapped."

CHAPTER 7

Detective Lieutenant Patrick Burke sat huddled against the cold dawn on the top riser of the reviewing stands and looked down into the Avenue. The freshly painted green line glistened in the thin sunlight, and policemen stepped carefully over it as they crossed the street.

A bomb squad ambled through the risers picking up paper bags and bottles, none of them containing anything more lethal than the dregs of cheap wine. A bum lay covered with newspaper on the riser below him, undisturbed by the indulgent cops.

Burke looked east into Sixty-fourth Street. Police motor scooters lined the street, and a WPIX television van had taken up position on the north corner. A police mobile headquarters van was parked on the south corner, and two policemen were connecting the van's cables to an access opening at the base of a streetlamp.

Burke lit a cigarette. In twenty years of intelligence work this scene had not changed nearly so much as everything else in his life had. He thought that even the bum might be the same.

Burke glanced at his watch—five minutes to kill. He watched the uniformed patrolmen queue up to a PBA canteen truck for coffee. Someone at the back of the line was fortifying the cups of coffee with a dark liquid poured from a Coke bottle, like a priest, thought Burke, sprinkling holy water on the passing troops. It would be a long, hard day for the uniformed cops. Over a million people, Irish and otherwise, would crowd the sidewalks of Fifth Avenue and the bars and restaurants of midtown Manhattan. Surprisingly, for all the sound and fury of the day there had never been a serious political incident in over two centuries of St. Patrick's days in New York. But Burke felt every year that it would happen, that it must happen eventually.

The presence of the Malone woman in New York disturbed him. He had interviewed her briefly in the Empire Room of the Waldorf the previous evening. She seemed likable enough, pretty, too, and undaunted by his suggestion that someone might decide to murder her. She had probably become accustomed to threats on her life, he thought.

The Irish were Burke's specialty, and the Irish, he believed, were potentially the most dangerous group of all. But if they struck, would they pick *this* day? This day *belonged* to the Irish. The parade was their trooping of the colors, their showing of the green, necessary in those days when they were regarded as America's first unwanted foreigners. He remembered a joke his grandfather used to tell, popular at the turn of the century: What is St. Patrick's Day? It's the day the Protestants and Jews look out the windows of their town houses on Fifth Avenue to watch their employees march by.

What had begun as America's first civil rights demonstration was now a reminder to the city—to the nation—that the Irish still existed as a force. This was the day that the Irish got to fuck up New York City, the day they turned Manhattan on its ear.

Burke stood, stretched his big frame, then bounded down the rows of benches and jumped onto the sidewalk. He walked behind the stands until he came to an opening in the low stone wall that bordered Central Park, where he descended a flight of stone steps. In front of him rose the huge, castlelike Arsenal—actually a park administration building—flying, along with the American flag, the green, white, and orange tricolor of the Republic of Ireland. He circled around it to his right and came to a closed set of towering wrought-iron gates. Without much enthusiasm he climbed to the top of the gates, then dropped down into the zoo.

The zoo was deserted and much darker than the Avenue. Ornate lamps cast a weak light over the paths and brick buildings. He proceeded slowly down the straight lane, staying in the shadows. As he walked he unholstered his service revolver and slipped it into his coat pocket, more as a precaution against muggers than professional assassins.

The shadows of bare sycamores lay over the lane, and the smell of damp straw and animals hung oppressively in the cold, misty air. To his left seals were barking in their pool, and birds, captive and free, chirped and squawked in a blend of familiar and exotic sounds.

Burke passed the brick arches that supported the Delacorte clock and peered into the shadows of the colonnade, but no one was there. He checked his watch against the clock. Ferguson was late or dead. He leaned against one of the clock arches and lit another cigarette. Around him he saw, to the east, south, and west, towering skyscrapers silhouetted against the dawn, crowded close to the black treelines like sheer cliffs around a rain forest basin.

He heard the sound of soft footsteps behind him and turned, peering around the arch into the path that led to the Children's Zoo deeper into the park.

Jack Ferguson passed through a concrete tunnel and stepped into a pool of light, then stopped. "Burke?"

"Over here." Burke watched Ferguson approach. The man

walked with a slight limp, his oversized vintage trench coat flapping with every step he took.

Ferguson offered his hand and smiled, showing a set of yellowed teeth. "Good to see you, Patrick."

Burke took his hand. "How's your wife, Jack?"

"Poorly. Poorly, I'm afraid."

"Sorry to hear that. You're looking a bit pale yourself."

Ferguson touched his face. "Am I? I should get out more."

"Take a walk in the park—when the sun's up. Why are we meeting here, Jack?"

"Oh God, the town's full of Micks today, isn't it? I mean we could be seen anywhere by anybody."

"I suppose." Old revolutionaries, thought Burke, would wither and die without their paranoia and conspiracies. Burke pulled a small thermal flask from his coat. "Tea and Irish?"

"Bless you." Ferguson took it and drank, then handed it back as he looked around into the shadows. "Are you alone?"

"Me, you, and the monkeys." Burke took a drink and regarded Ferguson over the rim of the flask. Jack Ferguson was a genuine 1930s City College Marxist whose life had been spent in periods of either fomenting or waiting for the revolution of the working classes. The historical tides that had swept the rest of the world since the war had left Jack Ferguson untouched and unimpressed. In addition he was a pacifist, a gentle man, though these seemingly disparate ideals never appeared to cause him any inner conflict. Burke held out the flask. "Another rip?"

"No, not just yet."

Burke screwed the cap back on the Thermos as he studied Ferguson, who was nervously looking around him. Ferguson was a ranking officer in the Official Irish Republican Army, or whatever was left of it in New York, and he was as burnt out and moribund as the rest of that group of geriatrics. "What's coming down today, Jack?"

Ferguson took Burke's arm and looked up into his face. "The Fenians ride again, my boy."

"Really? Where'd they get the horses?"

"No joke, Patrick. A renegade group made up mostly from the Provos in Ulster. They call themselves the Fenians."

Burke nodded. He had heard of them. "They're here? In New York?"

"Afraid so."

"For what purpose?"

"I couldn't say, exactly. But they're up to mischief."

"Are your sources reliable?"

"Very."

"Are these people into violence?"

"In the vernacular of the day, yes, they're into violence. Into it up to their asses. They're murderers, arsonists, and bombers. The cream of the Provisional IRA. Between them they've leveled most of downtown Belfast, and they're responsible for hundreds of deaths. A bad lot."

"Sounds like it, doesn't it? What do they do on weekends?"

Ferguson lit a cigarette with unsteady hands. "Let's sit awhile."

Burke followed him toward a bench facing the ape house. As he walked he watched the man in front of him. If ever there was a man more anachronistic, more quixotic than Jack Ferguson, he had never met him. Yet Ferguson had somehow survived in that netherworld of leftist politics and had even survived a murder attempt—or an assassination attempt, as Ferguson would have corrected him. And he was unusually reliable in these matters. The Marxist-oriented Officials distrusted the breakaway Provisionals and vice versa. Each side still had people in the opposite camp, and they were the best sources of information about each other. The only common bond they shared was a deep hate for the English and a policy of hands-off-America. Burke sat next to Ferguson. "The IRA has not committed acts of violence in America since the Second World War," Burke recited the conventional wisdom, "and I don't think they're ready to now."

"That's true of the Officials, certainly, and even the Provisionals, but not of these Fenians."

Burke said nothing for a long time, then asked, "How many?"

Ferguson chain-lit a cigarette. "At least twenty, maybe more."

"Armed?"

"Not when they left Belfast, of course, but there are people here who would help them."

"Target?"

"Who knows? No end of targets today. Hundreds of politicians in the reviewing stands, in the parade. People on the steps of the Cathedral. Then, of course, there's the British Consulate, British Airways, the Irish Tourist Board, the Ulster Trade Delegation, the—"

"All right. I've got a list too." Burke watched a gorilla with red, burning eyes peering at them through the bars of the ape house. The animal seemed interested in them, turning its head whenever they spoke. "Who are the leaders of these Fenians?"

"A man who calls himself Finn MacCumail."

"What's his real name?"

"I may know this afternoon. MacCumail's lieutenant is John Hickey, code name Dermot."

"Hickey's dead."

"No, he's living right here in New Jersey. He must be close to eighty by now."

Burke had never met Hickey, but Hickey's career in the IRA

was so long and so blood-splattered that he was mentioned in history books. "Anything else?"

"No, that's it for now."

"Where can we meet later?"

"Call me at home every hour starting at noon. If you don't reach me, meet me back here on the terrace of the restaurant at four thirty... unless, of course, whatever is to happen has already happened. In that case I'll be out of town for a while."

Burke nodded. "What can I do for you?"

Ferguson acted both surprised and indifferent, the way he always did at this point. "Do? Oh, well... let's see.... How's the special fund these days?"

"I can get a few hundred."

"Fine. Things are a bit tight with us."

Burke didn't know if he was referring to himself and his wife or his organization. Probably both. "I'll try for more."

"As you wish. The money isn't so important. What is important is that you avoid bloodshed, and that the department knows we're helping you. And that no one else knows it."

"That's the way we've always done it."

Ferguson stood and put out his hand. "Good-bye, Patrick. *Erin go bragh.*"

Burke stood and took Ferguson's hand. "Do what you can, Jack, but be careful."

Burke watched Ferguson limp away down the path and disappear under the clock. He felt very chilled and took a drink from his flask. *The Fenians ride again.* He had an idea that this St. Patrick's Day would be the most memorable of all.

CHAPTER 8

Maureen Malone put down her teacup and let her eyes wander around the hotel breakfast room.

"Would you like anything else?" Margaret Singer, Secretary of Amnesty International, smiled at her from across the table.

"No, thank you—" She almost added ma'am but caught herself. Three years as a revolutionary didn't transform a lifetime of inbred deference.

Next to Margaret Singer sat Malcolm Hull, also of Amnesty. And across the round table sat a man introduced only as Peter who had his back to the wall and faced the main entrance to the dining room. He neither ate nor smiled but drank black coffee. Maureen knew the type.

The fifth person at the table was recently arrived and quite unexpected: Sir Harold Baxter, British Consul General. He had come, he said frankly, to break the ice so there would be no awkwardness when they met on the steps of the Cathedral. The British, reflected Maureen, were so civilized, polite, and practical. It made one sick, really.

Sir Harold poured a cup of coffee and smiled at her. "Will you be staying on awhile?"

She forced herself to look into his clear gray eyes. He looked no more than forty, but his hair was graying at the temples.

He was undeniably good-looking. "I think I'll go on to Belfast tonight."

His smile never faded. "Not a good idea, actually. London or even Dublin would be better."

She smiled back at his words. Translation: After today they'll surely murder you in Belfast. She didn't think he cared personally if the IRA murdered her, but his government must have decided she was useful. Her voice was cool. "When the Famine killed a million and a half Irish, it also scattered as many throughout the English-speaking world, and among these Irish are always a few IRA types. If I'm to die by their bullets, I'd rather it be in Belfast than anywhere else."

No one said anything for a few seconds, then Sir Harold spoke. "Certainly you overestimate the strength of these people outside of Ulster. Even in the south, the Dublin government has outlawed them—"

"The Dublin government, Sir Harold, are a bunch of British lackeys." There. She had really broken the ice now. "The only hope for the Catholics of the six counties— or Ulster, as you call it—has become the Irish Republican Army—not London or Dublin or Washington. Northern Ireland needs an alternative to the IRA, so Northern Ireland is where I must be."

Harold Baxter's eyes grew weary. He was sick to death of this problem but felt it his duty to respond. "And you are the alternative?"

"I'm searching for an alternative to the killing of innocent civilians."

Harold Baxter put on his best icy stare. "But not British soldiers? Tell me, why would Ulster Catholics wish to unite with a nation governed by British lackeys?"

Her response was quick, as his had been. They both knew their catechism. "I think a people would rather be governed by their own incompetent politicians than by foreign incompetents."

Baxter sat back and pressed his palms together. "Please don't forget the two-thirds of the Ulster population who are Protestant and who consider Dublin, not London, to be a foreign capital."

Maureen Malone's face grew red. "That bunch of Bible-toting bigots does not recognize any allegiance except money. They'd throw you over in a second if they thought they could handle the Catholics themselves. Every time they sing 'God Save the Queen' in their silly Orange Lodges, they wink at each other. They think the English are decadent and the Irish Catholics are lazy drunks. They are certain *they* are the chosen people. And they've guiled you into thinking they're your loyal subjects." She realized that she had raised her voice and took a deep breath, then fixed Baxter with a cold stare to match his own. "English blood and the Crown's money keep Belfast's industry humming—don't you feel like fools, Sir Harold?"

Harold Baxter placed his napkin on the table. "Her Majesty's government would no more abandon one million subjects—loyal or disloyal—in Ulster than they would abandon Cornwall or Surrey, madam." He stood. "If this makes us fools, so be it. Excuse me." He turned and headed toward the door.

Maureen stared after him, then turned toward her host and hostess. "I'm sorry. I shouldn't have picked an argument with him."

Margaret Singer smiled. "That's all right. But I'd advise you not to argue politics with the other side. If we tell the Russians what bullies they are and then try to get a Soviet Jew released from the camps, we don't have much luck, you know."

Hull nodded in assent. "You won't agree, but I can assure you that the British are among the fairest people in this troubled world. If you want to get them to end internment, you'll have to appeal to that sense of fairness. You broke with the IRA to travel this path."

Margaret Singer added, "We all must deal with our devils—and we do." She paused. "They hold the keys to the camps."

Maureen took the gentle rebuke without answering. The good people of the world were infinitely more difficult to deal with than the bad. "Thank you for breakfast. Excuse me." She stood.

A bellhop came toward the table. "Miss Malone?"

She nodded slowly.

"For you, miss." He held up a small bouquet of green carnations. "I'll put them in a nice vase in your room, ma'am. There's a card I can give you now, if you wish."

She stared at the small buff envelope, then took it. It was blank. She looked questioningly at Singer and Hull. They shook their heads. She broke the seal on the envelope.

Maureen's mind went back to London five years earlier. She and Sheila had been hiding in a safe house in an Irish neighborhood in the East End. Their mission had been secret, and only the Provisional IRA War Council knew of their whereabouts.

A florist had come to the door one morning and delivered a bouquet of English lavender and foxglove, and the Irishwoman who owned the house had gone up to their room and thrown the flowers on their bed. "Secret mission," she had said, and had spit on the floor. "What a bloody bunch of fools you all are."

She and Sheila had read the accompanying card: *Welcome to London. Her Majesty's government hope you enjoy your visit and trust you will avail yourself of the pleasures of our island and the hospitality of the English people.* Right out of a government travel brochure. Except that it wasn't signed by the Tourist Board but by Military Intelligence.

She had never been so humiliated and frightened in her life.

She and Sheila had run out of the house with only the clothes on their backs, and spent days in the parks and the London Underground. They hadn't dared to go to any other contacts for fear they were being followed for that purpose. Eventually, after the worst fortnight she had ever passed in her life, they had made it to Dublin.

She pulled the card half out of its envelope to read the words. *Welcome to New York. We hope your stay will be pleasant and that you will take advantage of the pleasures of the island and the hospitality of the people.*

She didn't have to pull the rest of the card out to see the signature, but she did anyway, and read the name of Finn MacCumail.

Maureen closed the door of her room and bolted it. The flowers were already on the dresser. She pulled them from the vase and took them into the bathroom. She tore and ripped them and flushed them down the toilet. In the mirror she could see the reflection of the bedroom and the partly opened door to the adjoining sitting room. She spun around. The closet door was also ajar, and she hadn't left either of those doors open. She took several deep breaths to make sure her voice was steady. "Brian?"

She heard a movement in the sitting room. Her knees were beginning to feel shaky, and she pressed them together. "Damn you, Flynn!"

The connecting door to the sitting room swung open. "Ma'am?" The maid looked across the room at her.

Maureen took another long breath. "Is anyone else here?"

"No, ma'am."

"Has anyone been here?"

"Only the boy with the flowers, ma'am."

"Please leave."

"Yes, ma'am." The maid pushed her cart into the hall. Maureen followed her and bolted the door, then sat in the armchair and stared at the Paisley wallpaper.

She was surprised by her calmness. She almost wished he would roll out from under the bed and smile at her with that strange smile that was not a smile at all. She conjured up an image of him standing in front of her. He would say, "It's been a damned long time, Maureen." He always said that after they had been separated. Or "Where are my flowers, lass? Did you put them in a special place?"

"Yes, very special," she said aloud. "I flushed them down the goddamned john."

She sat there for several minutes carrying on her imaginary conversation with him. She realized how much she missed him and how she wanted to hear his voice again. She was both excited and frightened by the knowledge that he was close and that he would find her.

The phone next to her rang. She let it ring for a long time before she picked it up.

"Maureen? Is everything all right?" It was Margaret Singer, "Shall I come up and get you? We're expected at the Irish Pavilion—"

"I'll be right down." She hung up and rose slowly from the chair. The Irish Pavilion for a reception, then the steps of St. Patrick's, the parade, and the reviewing stands at the end of the day. Then the Irish Cultural Society Benefit Dinner for Ireland's Children. Then Kennedy Airport. What a lot of merrymaking in the name of helping soothe the ravages of war. Only in America. The Americans would turn the Apocalypse into a dinner dance.

She walked across the sitting room and into the bedroom. On the floor she saw a single green carnation, and she knelt to pick it up.

CHAPTER 9

Patrick Burke looked out of the telephone booth into the dim interior of the Blarney Stone on Third Avenue. Cardboard shamrocks were pasted on the bar mirror, and a plastic leprechaun hat hung from the ceiling. Burke dialed a direct number in Police Plaza. "Langley?"

Inspector Philip Langley, head of the New York Police Department's Intelligence Division, sipped his coffee. "I got your report on Ferguson." Langley looked down from his thirteenth-story window toward the Brooklyn Bridge. The sea fog was burning off. "It's like this, Pat. We're getting some pieces to a puzzle here, and the picture that's taking shape doesn't look good. The FBI has received information from IRA informers that a renegade group from Ireland has been poking around the New York and Boston IRA—testing the waters to see if they can have a free hand in something that they're planning in this country."

Burke wiped his neck with a handkerchief. "In the words of the old cavalry scout, I see many hoofprints going in and none coming out."

Langley said, "Of course, nothing points directly to New York on Saint Patrick's Day—"

"There is a law that says that if you imagine the worst possible thing happening at the worst possible moment, it will usually happen, and Saint Patrick's Day is a nightmare under the best of circumstances. It's Mardi Gras, Bastille Day, Carnivale, all in one. So if I were the head of a renegade Irish group and I wanted to make a big splash in America, I would do it in New York City on March seventeenth."

"I hear you. How do you want to approach this?"

"I'll start by digging up my contacts. Barhop. Listen to the barroom patriots talk. Buy drinks. Buy people."

"Be careful."

Burke hung up, then walked over to the bar.

"What'll you be having?"

"Cutty." Burke placed a twenty-dollar bill on the bar. He recognized the bartender, a giant of a man named Mike. Burke took his drink and left the change on the bar. "Buy you one?"

"It's a little early yet." The bartender waited. He knew a man who wanted something.

Burke slipped into a light brogue. "I'm looking for friends."

"Go to church."

"I won't be finding them there. The brothers Flannnagan. Eddie and Bob. Also John Hickey."

"You're a friend?"

"Meet them every March seventeenth."

"Then you should know that John Hickey is dead—may his soul rest in peace. The Flannagans are gone back to the old country. A year it's been. Drink up now and move along. You'll not be finding any friends here."

"Is this the bar where they throw a drunk through the window every Saint Patrick's Day?"

"It will be if you don't move along." He stared at Burke.

A medium-built man in an expensive topcoat suddenly emerged from a booth and stood beside Burke. The man spoke softly, in a British accent. "Could I have a word with you?"

Burke stared at the man, who inclined his head toward the door. Both men walked out of the bar. The man led Burke across the street, stopping on the far corner. "My name is Major Bartholomew Martin of British Military Intelligence." Martin produced his diplomatic passport and military I.D. card.

Burke hardly glanced at them. "Means nothing."

Martin motioned to a skyscraper in the center of the block. "Then perhaps we'd better go in there."

Burke knew the building without looking at it. He saw two big Tactical Policemen standing a few yards from the entrance with their hands behind their backs. Martin walked past the policemen and held open the door. Burke entered the big marble lobby and picked out four Special Services men standing at strategic locations. Martin moved swiftly to the rear of the lobby, behind a stone façade that camouflaged the building's elevators. The elevator doors opened, and both men moved inside. Burke reached out and pushed floor nine.

Martin smiled. "Thank you."

Burke looked at the man standing in a classical elevator pose, feet separated, hands behind his back, head tilted upward, engrossed in the progression of illuminated numbers. Despite his rank there was nothing military about Bartholomew Martin, thought Burke. If anything he looked like an actor who was trying to get into character for a difficult role. He hadn't mastered control of the mouth, however, which was hard and unyielding, despite the smile. A glimpse of the real man, perhaps.

The elevator stopped, and Burke followed the major into the corridor. Martin nodded to a man who stood to the left, dressed in a blue blazer with polished brass buttons.

On the wall of the corridor, opposite Burke, was the royal coat of arms and a highly polished bronze plaque that read: BRITISH INFORMATION SERVICES. There was no sign to indicate that this was where the spies usually hung out, but as far as Burke knew, nobody's consulate or embassy information office made that too clear.

Burke followed Martin through a door into a large room. A blond receptionist, dressed in a blue tweed suit that matched the Concorde poster above her desk, stood as they approached and said in a crisp British accent, "Good morning, Major."

Martin led Burke through a door just beyond the desk, through a microfilm reading room, and into a small sitting room furnished in a more traditional style than the rest of the place. The only detail that suggested a government office was a large travel poster that showed a black and white cow standing in a sunny meadow, captioned: "Find peace and tranquility in an English village."

Martin drew the door shut, locked it, and hung his topcoat on a clothes tree. "Have a seat, Lieutenant."

Burke left his coat on, walked to the sideboard and took the stopper out of a decanter, smelled it, then poured a drink. He looked around the well-furnished room. The last time he'd been in the consulate was a week before last St. Patrick's Day. A Colonel Hayes that time. Burke leaned back against the sideboard. "Well, what can you do for me?"

Major Martin smiled. "A great deal, I think."

"Good."

"I've already given Inspector Langley a report on a group of Irish terrorists called the Fenians, led by a Finn MacCumail. You've seen the report?"

"I've been apprised of the details."

"Fine. Then you know something may happen here today." Major Martin leaned forward. "I'm working closely with the FBI and CIA, but I'd like to work more closely with your people—pool our information. The FBI and CIA tell us things they don't tell you, but I'd keep you informed of their progress as well as ours. I've already helped your military intelligence branches set up files on the IRA, and I've briefed your State Department intelligence service on the problem."

"You've been busy."

"Yes. You see, I'm a sort of clearinghouse in this affair. British Intelligence knows more about the Irish revolutionaries than anyone, of course, and now you seem to need that information, and we have a chance to do you a good turn."

"What's the price?"

Major Martin played with a lighter on the coffee table. "Yes, price. Well, better information from you in future on the transatlantic IRA types in New York. Gunrunning. Fund raising. IRA people here on R and R. That sort of thing."

"Sounds fair."

"It *is* fair."

"So what do you want of me particularly?"

Major Martin looked at Burke. "Just wanted to tell you directly about all of this. To meet you." Martin stood. "Look here, if you want to get a bit of information to me directly, call here and ask for Mr. James. Someone will take the message and pass it on to me. And I'll leave messages for you here as well. Perhaps a little something you can give to Langley as your own. You'll make a few points that way. Makes everyone look good."

Burke moved toward the door, then turned. "They're probably going after the Malone woman. Maybe even after the consul general."

Major Martin shook his head. "I don't think so. Sir Harold has no involvement whatsoever in Irish affairs. And the Malone woman—I knew her sister, Sheila, in Belfast, incidentally. She's in jail. An IRA martyr. They should only know—but that's another story. Where was I?—Maureen Malone. She's quite the other thing to the IRA. A Provisional IRA tribunal has condemned her to death in absentia, you know. She's on borrowed time now. But they won't shoot her down in the street. They'll grab her someday in Ireland, north or south, have a trial with her present this time, kneecap her, then a day or so later shoot her in the head and leave her on a street in Belfast. And the Fenians, whoever they are, won't do anything that would preempt the Provos' death sentence. And don't forget, Malone and Sir Harold will be on the steps of Saint Patrick's most of the day, and the Irish respect the sanctuary of the church no matter what their religious or political beliefs. No, I wouldn't worry about those two. Look for a more obvious target. British property. The Ulster Trade Delegation. The Irish always perform in a predictable manner."

"Really? Maybe that's why my wife left me."

"Oh, you're Irish, of course...sorry...."

Burke unbolted the door and walked out of the room.

Major Martin threw back his head and laughed softly, then went to the sideboard and made himself a martini. He evaluated his conversation with Burke and decided that Burke was more clever than he had been led to believe. Not that it would do him any good this late in the game.

BOOK III

The Parade

Saint Patrick's Day in New York is the most fantastic affair, and in past years on Fifth Avenue, from Forty-fourth Street to Ninety-sixth Street, the white traffic lines were re-painted green for the occasion. All the would-be Irish, has-been Irish and never-been Irish, seem to appear true-blue Irish overnight. Everyone is in on the act, but it is a very jolly occasion and I have never experienced anything like it anywhere else in the world.

Brendan Behan,
Brendan Behan's New York

CHAPTER 10

In the middle of Fifth Avenue, at Forty-fourth Street, Pat and Mike, the two Irish wolfhounds that were the mascots of the Fighting 69th Infantry Regiment, strained at their leashes. Colonel Dennis Logan, Commander of the 69th, tapped his Irish blackthorn swagger stick impatiently against his leg. He glanced at the sky and sniffed the air, then turned to Major Matthew Cole. "What's the weather for this afternoon, Major?"

Major Cole, like all good adjutants, had the answer to everything. "Cold front moving through later, sir. Snow or freezing rain by nightfall."

Logan nodded and thrust his prominent jaw out in a gesture of defiance, as though he were going to say, "Damn the weather—full speed ahead."

The young major struck a similar pose, although his jaw was not so grand. "Parade'll be finished before then, I suspect, Colonel." He glanced at Logan to see if he was listening. The colonel's marvelously angular face had served him well at staff meetings, but the rocklike quality of that visage was softened by misty green eyes like a woman's. Too bad.

Logan looked at his watch, then at the big iron stanchion clock in front of the Morgan Guaranty Trust Building on Fifth Avenue. The clock was three minutes fast, but they would go when that clock struck noon. Logan would never forget the newspaper picture that showed his unit at parade rest and the clock at three minutes after. The caption had read: THE IRISH START LATE. Never again.

The regiment's staff, back from their inspection of the unit, was assembled in front of the color guard. The national and regimental colors snapped in a five-mile-an-hour wind that came down the Avenue from the north, and the multicolored battle streamers, some going back to the Civil War and the Indian wars, fluttered nicely. Logan turned to Major Cole. "What's your feel?"

The major searched his mind for a response, but the question threw him. "Feel...sir?"

"Feel, man. *Feel.*" He accentuated the words.

"Fine. Fine."

Logan looked at the battle ribbons on the major's chest. A splash of purple stood out like the wound it represented. "In 'Nam, did you ever get a feeling that everything was not fine?"

The major nodded thoughtfully.

Logan waited for a response that would reinforce his own feelings of unease, but Cole was too young to have fully developed that other sense to the extent that he could identify what he felt in the jungle and recognize it in the canyons of Manhattan Island. "Keep a sharp eye out today. This is not a parade—it's an operation. Don't let your head slide up your ass."

"Yes, sir."

Logan looked at his regiment. They stood at parade rest, their polished helmets with the regimental crest reflecting the overhead sunlight. Slung across their shoulders were M-16 rifles.

The crowd at Forty-fourth Street, swelled by office workers on their lunch hour, was jostling for a better view. People had climbed atop the WALK–DON'T WALK signs, the mailboxes, and the cement pots that held the newly budded trees along the Avenue.

In the intersection around Colonel Logan newsmen mixed with politicians and parade officials. The parade chairman, old Judge Driscoll, was patting everyone on the back as he had done for over forty years. The formation marshals, resplendent in black morning coats, straightened their tricolor sashes and top hats. The Governor was shaking every hand that looked as if it could pull a voting lever, and Mayor Kline was wearing the silliest green derby that Logan had ever seen.

Logan looked up Fifth Avenue. The broad thoroughfare was clear of traffic and people, an odd sight reminiscent of a B-grade science-fiction movie. The pavement stretched unobstructed to the horizon, and Colonel Logan was more impressed with this sight than anything else he had seen that day. He couldn't see the Cathedral, recessed between Fiftieth and Fifty-first Streets, but he could see the police barriers around it and the guests on the lower steps.

A stillness began to descend on the crossroads as the hands of the clock moved another notch toward the twelve. The army band accompanying the 69th ceased their tuning of instruments, and the bagpipes of the Emerald Society on the side street stopped practicing. The dignitaries, whom the 69th Regiment was charged with escorting to the reviewing stands, began to fall into their designated places as Judge Driscoll looked on approvingly.

Logan felt his heart beat faster as he waited out the final minutes. He was aware of, but did not see, the mass of humanity huddled around him, the hundreds of thousands of spectators along the parade route to his front, the police, the reviewing stands in the park, the cameras and the newspeople. It was to be a day of dedication and celebration, sentimentality and even sorrow. In New York this day had been crowned by the parade, which had gone on uninterrupted by war, depression, or civil strife since 1762. It was, in fact, a mainstay of Irish culture in the New World, and it was not about to change, even if every last man, woman, and child in old Ireland did away with themselves and the British to boot. Logan turned to Major Cole. "Are we ready, Major?"

"The Fighting Irish are always ready, Colonel."

Logan nodded. The Irish were always ready for anything, he thought, and prepared for nothing.

Father Murphy looked around him as a thousand guests crowded the steps of the Cathedral. He edged over and stood on the long green carpet that had been unrolled from the main portal between the brass handrail and down into the street. In front of him, between the handrails, stood the Cardinal and the Monsignor, shoulder to shoulder. Flanking them were the British consul, Baxter, next to the Cardinal, and the Malone woman next to the Monsignor. Murphy smiled. The arrangement wasn't strictly protocol, but they couldn't get at each other's throats so easily now.

Standing in loose formation around the Cardinal's group were priests, nuns, and church benefactors. Murphy noticed at least two men who were probably undercover police. He looked up over the heads of the people in front of him toward the crowd across the Avenue. Boys and girls had climbed to the top of the pedestal of the Atlas and were passing bottles back and forth. His eyes were drawn to a familiar face: Standing in front of the pedestal, with his hands resting on a police barricade, was Patrick Burke. The man towered above the crowd around him and seemed strangely unaffected by the animated throng pressing against him on the sidewalk. Murphy realized that Burke's presence reassured him, though he didn't know why he felt he needed that assurance.

The Cardinal turned his head toward Harold Baxter and spoke in a voice that had that neutral tone of diplomacy so like his own. "Will you be staying with us for the entire day, Mr. Baxter?"

Baxter was no longer used to being called mister, but he didn't think the Cardinal meant anything by it. He turned his head to meet the Cardinal's eyes. "If I may, Your Eminence."

"We would be delighted."

"Thank you." He continued to look at the Cardinal, who had now turned away. The man was old, but his eyes were bright. Baxter cleared his throat. "Excuse me, Your Eminence, but I was thinking that perhaps I should stand away from the center of things a bit."

The Cardinal waved to well-wishers in the crowd as he spoke. "Mr. Baxter, you *are* the center of things today. You and Miss Malone. This little display of ours has captured the imagination of political commentators. It is, as they say, newsworthy. Everyone loves these precedents, this breaking with the past." He turned and smiled at Baxter, a wide Irish smile. "If you move an inch, they will be pulling their hair in Belfast, Dublin, London, and Washington." He turned back to the crowds and continued moving his arm in a blending of cheery waving and holy blessing.

"Yes, of course. I wasn't taking into account the political aspect—only the security aspect. I wouldn't want to be the cause of anyone being injured or—"

"God is watching over us, Mr. Baxter, and Commissioner Dwyer assures me that the Police Department is doing the same."

"That's reassuring on both counts. You've spoken to him recently? The Police Commissioner, I mean."

The Cardinal turned and fixed Baxter with a smile that showed he understood the little joke but did not find it amusing.

Baxter stared back for a moment, then turned away. It was going to be a long day.

Patrick Burke regarded the steps. He noticed his friend Father Murphy near the Cardinal. It must be a strange life for a man, he reflected. The celibacy. The paternal and maternal concern of monsignors and mother superiors. Like being an eternal boy. His mother had wanted that for him. A priest in the family was the ultimate status for those old Irish, but he had become a cop instead, which was almost as good in the old neighborhoods, and no one was disappointed, least of all himself.

He saw that the Monsignor was smiling and talking with the ex-IRA woman. Burke focused on her. She looked pretty, even from this distance. Angelic, almost. Her blond hair moved nicely in the breeze, and she kept brushing wisps of hair from her face.

Burke thought that if he were Harold Baxter or Maureen Malone he would not be on those steps at all, and certainly not together. And if he were the Cardinal, he would have invited them for yesterday, when they could have shared the steps with indifferent pigeons, bag ladies, and winos. He didn't know whose idea it had been to wave this red flag in the face of the Irish rebels, but if it was supposed to bring peace, someone had badly miscalculated.

He looked up and down the Avenue. Workers and high school kids, all playing hooky to get in on the big bash, mingled with street vendors, who were making out very well. Some young girls had painted green shamrocks and harps on their faces and wore *Kiss Me, I'm Irish* buttons, and they were being taken up on it by young men, most of whom wore plastic leprechaun bowlers. The older crowd settled for green carnations and *Erin Go Bragh* buttons.

Maureen Malone had never seen so many people. All along the Avenue, American and Irish flags hung from staffs jutting out of the gray masonry buildings. A group in front of the British Empire Building was hoisting a huge green banner, and Maureen read the familiar words: ENGLAND GET OUT OF IRELAND. Margaret Singer had told her that this was the only political slogan she would see, the only one sanctioned by the Grand Marshal, who had also specified that the banners be nearly made with white lettering on green background. The police had permission to seize any other banner. She hoped Baxter saw it; she didn't see how he could miss it. She turned to Monsignor Downes. "All these people are certainly not Irish."

Monsignor Downes smiled. "We have a saying in New York. 'On Saint Patrick's Day, everyone is Irish!' "

She looked around again, as though she still didn't believe what she was seeing. Little Ireland, poor and underpopulated, with its humble patron saint, almost unknown in the rest of the Christian world, causing all this fuss. It gave her goose bumps, and she felt a choking in her throat. Ireland's best exports, it was said bitterly, were her sons and daughters. But there was nothing to be bitter about, she realized. They had kept the faith, although in an Americanized version.

Suddenly she heard a great noise coming from the crowd and turned her head toward the commotion. A group of men and women, about fifteen of them, had unfurled a green banner reading: VICTIMS OF BRITISH INTERNMENT AND TORTURE. She recognized a friend of her sister's.

A police mounted unit galloped south down the Avenue, Plexiglas helmet-visors down, long batons raised above their heads. From the north side of the Cathedral on Fifty-first Street, scooter police roared past the mobile headquarters truck and onto Fifth Avenue.

A man with a bullhorn shouted, "LONG KESH! ARMAGH PRISON! CRUMLIN ROAD JAIL! CONCENTRATION CAMPS, BAXTER, YOU BASTARD! MAUREEN MALONE—TRAITOR!"

She turned and looked at Harold Baxter across the empty space left by the Cardinal and Monsignor who had been moved up the steps by the security police. He remained in a rigid position of attention, staring straight ahead. She knew there were news cameras trained on him to record his every movement, every betrayal of emotion, whether anger or fear. But they were wasting their time. The man was British.

She realized that cameras were on her as well, and she turned away from him and looked down into the street. The banner was down now, and half the demonstrators were in the hands of the police, but the other half had broken through the police barricades and were coming toward the steps, where a line of mounted police waited almost nonchalantly.

Maureen shook her head. The history of her people: forever attempting the insurmountable and, in the end, finding it indeed insurmountable.

Maureen watched, transfixed, as one of the last standing men cocked his arm and threw something toward the steps. Her heart skipped a beat as she saw it sailing through the air. It seemed to hang for a second before drifting downward slowly; the sunlight sparkled from it, making it difficult to identify. "Oh God." She began to drop to the ground but caught a glimpse of Baxter out of the corner of her eye. He hadn't moved a muscle and, whether it was a bomb or a carnation heading his way, he acted as if he could not care less. Reluctantly she straightened up. She heard a bottle crash on the granite steps directly behind her and waited for the sound of exploding petrol or nitro, but there was only a choked-off exclamation from the crowd, then a stillness around her. Green paint from the shattered bottle flecked the clothing of the people standing closest to where it hit. Her legs began to shake in relief, and her mouth became dry.

Sir Harold Baxter turned his head and looked at her. "Is this traditional?"

She could not control her voice sufficiently to speak, and she stared at him.

Baxter moved beside her. Their shoulders touched. Her reaction was to move away, but she didn't. He turned his head slightly. "Will you stand next to me for the rest of this thing?"

She moved her eyes toward him. Camera shutters clicked around them. She spoke softly. "I believe there's an assassin out there who intends to kill me today."

He didn't appear to react to this information. "Well, there are probably several out there who intend to kill me.... I promise I won't throw myself in front of you if you promise the same."

She let herself smile. "I think we can agree on that."

Burke stood firm as the crowd pushed and shoved around him. He looked at his watch. The episode had taken just two minutes. For a moment he had thought this was it, but within fifteen seconds he knew these were not the Fenians.

The security police on the steps had acted quickly but not really decisively in front of the partisan crowd. If that bottle had been a bomb, there would have been more than green paint to mop up. Burke took a long drink from his flask. He knew the whole day was a security problem of such magnitude that it had ceased to be a problem.

Burke considered the little he knew of the Fenians. They were veterans, said Ferguson, survivors, not suicidal fanatics. Whatever their mission they most probably intended to get away afterward, and that, thought Burke, would make their mission more difficult and make his job just a little easier. He hoped.

Colonel Dennis Logan was calming Pat and Mike, who had been aroused by shouts from the crowd.

Logan straightened up and looked at the stanchion clock. One minute past noon. "Oh, shit!" He turned to his adjutant, Major Cole. "Start this fucking parade."

"Yes, sir!" The adjutant turned to Barry Dugan, the police officer who for twenty-five years had blown the green whistle to begin the parade. "Officer Dugan! Do it!"

Dugan put the whistle to his lips, filled his lungs, and let out the longest, loudest whistle in all his quarter century of doing it.

Colonel Logan placed himself in front of the formation and raised his arm. Logan looked up the six blocks and saw the mass of newsmen and blue uniforms milling around a paddy wagon. They'd take their time if left to their own devices. He remembered his regiment's motto: Clear the way! He lowered his arm and turned his head over his right shoulder. "Foo-waard—MARCH!" The regiment stepped off.

The army band struck up the "Garryowen," and the two hundred and twenty-third St. Patrick's Day Parade began.

CHAPTER 11

Patrick Burke walked across the Avenue to the curb in front of the Cathedral and stood by the barricades. The 69th Regiment came abreast of the Cathedral, and Colonel Logan called the regiment to a halt.

The barriers behind Burke were parted where the green carpet came into the street, and a group of men in morning dress left the parade line and approached the Cathedral.

Burke remembered that the Cardinal had mentioned, casually, to the newspapers the day before that his favorite song was "Danny Boy," and the army bandleader apparently had taken this as a command and ordered the band to play the sweet, lilting air. Some of the people on the steps and many in the crowd around the Cathedral broke into spontaneous song. It was difficult for an Irishman, thought Burke, not to respond to that music, especially if he had had a few already.

> "O Danny Boy, the pipes, the pipes are calling
> From glen to glen, and down the mountain side,
> The summer's gone, and all the roses falling,
> 'Tis you, 'tis you, must go and I must bide."

Burke watched the entourage of dignitaries as they mounted the steps: the marshals, Mayor Kline, Governor Doyle, senators, congressmen, all the secular power in the city and state, and many from the national level. They all passed through the space in those barriers, walked across the narrow carpet, and presented themselves to the Cardinal, then left quickly, as protocol demanded. The faithful knelt and kissed the green-jeweled ring; others bowed or shook hands.

"But come ye back when summer's in the meadow,
Or when the valley's hushed and white with snow,
For I'll be here in sunshine or in shadow,
O Danny Boy, O Danny Boy, I love you so."

Maureen felt the excitement, the heightening of perceptions that led to fear, to apprehension. Everyone was smiling and bowing, kissing the Cardinal's ring, shaking her hand, the Monsignor's hand, Baxter's hand. Hands and wide smiles. The Americans had super teeth. Not a bad one in the lot.

She noticed a few steely-eyed men near her who wore the same expression of suppressed anxiety that she knew was on her face. Down by the space in the barriers she recognized Lieutenant Burke from the Waldorf. He was eyeing everyone who approached, as though they were all ax murderers instead of important citizens, and she felt a little comforted.

Around her the crowd was still singing, trying to remember the words and humming where they couldn't, as the flutes and horns of the army band played.

"But when ye leave, and all the flowers are dying,
And I am dead, as dead I may well be,
Then will ye come and find the place where I am lying,
And kneel and say an Ave there for me?"

Maureen shook her head. What a typically morbid Irish song. She tried to turn her thoughts to other things, but the intrusive words of the ballad reminded her of her own life—her own tragic love. Danny Boy was Brian, as Danny Boy was every Irish girl's lover. She could not escape its message and meaning for her as an Irishwoman; she found her eyes had gone misty, and there was a lump in her throat.

> "And I shall hear tho soft ye tread above me,
> And tho my grave will warmer, sweeter be,
> And you shall bend and tell me that you love me,
> And I shall sleep in peace until you come to me."

Burke watched the 69th move out. When the last unit was clear of the Cathedral, he breathed easier. The potential targets were no longer clustered around the Cathedral, they were scattered again—on the steps, moving around the regiment in small groups, some riding now in limousines up Park Avenue to the reviewing stands, some on their way home or to the airports.

At the end of the 69th Regiment Burke saw the regimental veterans in civilian clothes marching in a unit. Behind them was the Police Emerald Society Pipes and Drums, kilts swirling and their bagpipes wailing as their drums beat out a warlike cadence. At the head of the unit their longtime commander, Finbar Devine, raised his huge mace and ordered the pipers to play "Danny Boy" as they passed the Cathedral. Burke smiled. One hundred and ninety-six marching bands would play "Danny Boy" for the Cardinal today, such was the combined power of the press and the Cardinal's casual remark. Before the day was out His Eminence would wish he had never heard the song and pray to God that he would never hear it again as long as he lived.

Burke joined the last rank of the old veterans at the end of

the 69th Regiment. The next likely point of trouble was the reviewing stands at Sixty-fourth Street, where the targets would
again be bunched up like irresistibly plump fruit, and on St. Patrick's Day the fastest way to get uptown was to be in the parade.

Central Park was covered with people on hillocks and stone outcroppings, and several people were sitting in trees.

Colonel Logan knew that thousands of marchers had fallen
in behind him now. He could feel the electricity that was passing
through his regiment into the crowd around him and down the
line of marchers, until the last units—the old IRA vets— had
caught the tempo and the spirit. Cold and tired in the fading
light, the old soldiers would hold their heads high as they passed
the spectators, who by this time were jaded, weary, and drunk.

Logan watched the politicians as they left the march and
headed toward the reviewing stands to take their seats. He gave
the customary order of "eyes left" as they passed the stands and
saluted, breathing more easily now that his escort mission had
been accomplished.

Patrick Burke left the parade formation at Sixty-fourth Street,
made his way through the crowd, and entered the rear door of
the police mobile headquarters van. A television set was tuned
to the WPIX news program that was covering the parade. Lights
flashed on the consoles, and three radios, each tuned to a different command channel, crackled in the semidarkness. A few men
occupied with paperwork or electronics sat on small stools.

Burke recognized Sergeant George Byrd from the Bureau of
Special Services. "Big Byrd."

Byrd looked up from a radio and smiled. "Patrick Burke, the
scourge of Irish revolutionaries, defender of the faith."

"Eat it, George." He lit a cigarette.

"I read the report you filed this morning. Who are the Finnigans? What do they want?"

Burke sat on a small jump seat. "Fenians."

"Fenians. Finnigans. Micks. Who are they?"

"The Fenians were a group of Irish warriors and poets. About 200 A.D. There was also an Irish anti-British guerrilla army in the nineteenth century who called themselves Fenians—"

Byrd laughed. "That's kind of old intelligence, Burke. Must have been held up in Police Plaza."

"Filed with your promotion papers, no doubt."

Byrd grunted and leaned back against the wall. "And who's Finn Mac— something?"

"Head of the original Fenians. Been dead seventeen hundred years now."

"A code name?"

"I hope so. Wouldn't want to meet the real one."

Byrd listened to the radios. The command posts up and down the Avenue were reporting: The post at the Presbyterian church at Fifty-fourth Street reported all quiet. The post on the twentieth floor of the General Motors Building reported all quiet. The mobile headquarters at the Cathedral reported all quiet. Byrd picked up the radiophone and hesitated, then spoke softly. "Mobile at Sixty-fourth. All quiet at the reviewing stands. Out." He replaced the phone and looked at Burke. "Too quiet?"

"Don't start that shit." Burke picked up a telephone and dialed. "Jack?"

Jack Ferguson glanced at the closed bedroom door where his wife slept fitfully, then spoke in a low voice. "Patrick"—he looked at a wall clock in the kitchen—"it's twelve-thirty. You're supposed to call me on the hour."

"I was in the parade. What do you have?"

Ferguson looked at some notes scribbled on a pad near the telephone. "It's hard to find anyone today."

"I know, Jack. That's why today is the day."

"Exactly. But I did learn that the man called MacCumail has recruited some of the more wild-eyed members of the Boston Provisional IRA."

"Interesting. Any line on weapons? Explosives?"

"No," answered Ferguson, "but you can buy anything you want in this country, from pistols to tanks."

"Anything else?"

"A partial description of the man called MacCumail—tall, lean, dark—"

"That could be my mother."

"He wears a distinctive ring. Always has it."

"Not very smart."

"No. He may believe it's a charm of some sort. The Irish are a superstitious lot. The ring is oversized, probably an antique or a family heirloom. Also, I did find out something interesting about this MacCumail. It's only hearsay...but apparently he was captured once and possibly compromised by British Intelligence."

"Hold on." Burke tried to arrange his thoughts. It occurred to him, not for the first time, that there was more than one game in town today. Where there was an Irish conspiracy, there was sure to be an English conspiracy. After eight hundred years of almost continuous strife, it was as though the two adversaries were inseparably bonded in a bizarre embrace destined to last eternally. If the Irish war was coming to America, then the English would be here to fight it. It was Major Bartholomew Martin's presence in New York, more than anything Ferguson said, that signaled an approaching battle. And Major Martin knew more than he was telling. Burke spoke into the mouthpiece. "Do you have anything else?"

"No...I'm going to have to do some legwork now. I'll leave messages with Langley at Police Plaza if anything turns up. I'll meet you at the zoo at four-thirty if nothing has happened by then."

"Time is short, Jack," Burke said.

"I'll do what I can to avoid violence. But you must try to go easy on the lads if you find them. They're brothers."

"Yeah...brothers...." Burke hung up and turned to Byrd. "That was one of my informers. A funny little guy who's caught between his own basic decency and his wild politics."

Burke left the van and stood in the crowd at the corner of Sixty-fourth Street. He looked at the reviewing stands across Fifth Avenue, thick with people. If there was going to be trouble, it would probably happen at the reviewing stands. The other possible objectives that Major Martin suggested—the banks, the consulates, the airline offices, symbols of the London, Dublin, or Belfast governments—were small potatoes compared to the reviewing stands crowded with American, British, Irish, and other foreign VIPs.

The Cathedral, Burke understood, was also a big potato. But no Irish group would attack the Cathedral. Even Ferguson's Official IRA—mostly nonviolent Marxists and atheists—wouldn't consider it. The Provisionals were violent but mostly Catholic. Who but the Irish could have peaceful Reds and bomb-throwing Catholics?

Burke rubbed his tired eyes. Yes, if there was an action today, it had to be the reviewing stands.

Terri O'Neal was lying on the bed. The television set was tuned to the parade. Dan Morgan sat on the window seat and looked down Sixty-fourth Street. He noticed a tall man in civilian clothes step down from the police van, and he watched him as

he lit a cigarette and stared into the street, scanning the buildings. Eventually the police, the FBI, maybe even the CIA and
British Intelligence, would start to get onto them. That was
expected. The Irish had a tradition called Inform and Betray.
Without that weakness in the national character they would
have been rid of the English centuries ago. But this time was going to be different. MacCumail was a man you didn't want to
betray. The Fenians were a group more closely knit than an ancient clan, bound by one great sorrow and one great hate.

The telephone rang. Morgan walked into the living room,
closed the door behind him, then picked up the receiver. "Yes?"
He listened to the voice of Finn MacCumail, then hung up
and pushed open the door. He stared at Terri O'Neal. It wasn't
easy to kill a woman, yet MacCumail wasn't asking him to do
something he himself wouldn't do. Maureen Malone and Terri
O'Neal. They had nothing in common except their ancestry and
the fact that both of them had only a fifty-fifty chance of seeing
another dawn.

CHAPTER 12

Patrick Burke walked down Third Avenue, stopping at Irish pubs along the way. The sidewalks were crowded with revelers engaged in the traditional barhopping. Paper shamrocks and harps were plastered against the windows of most shops and restaurants. There was an old saying that St. Patrick's Day was the day the Irish marched up Fifth Avenue and staggered down Third, and Burke noticed that ladies and gentlemen were be beginning to wobble a bit. There was a great deal of handshaking, a tradition of sorts, as though everyone were congratulating each other on being Irish or on being sober enough to find his hand.

Burke approached P. J. Clarke's at Fifty-fifth Street, an old nineteenth-century brick relic, spared by the wrecker's ball but left encapsulated in the towering hulk around it—the Marine Midland Bank Building, which resembled a black Sony calculator with too many buttons.

Burke walked in through the frosted glass doors, made his way to the crowded bar, and ordered a beer. He looked around for familiar faces, an informant, an old friend, someone who owed him, but there was no one. Too many familiar faces missing this afternoon.

He made his way back into the street and breathed the cold north wind until his head cleared. He continued to walk, stopping at a half-remembered bar, an Irish-owned shop, or wherever a group of people huddled and spoke on the sidewalk. His thoughts raced rapidly and, unconsciously, he picked up his pace to keep abreast of the moving streams of people.

This day had begun strangely, and every incident, every conversation, added to his sense of unreality. He took a cigarette from his pocket, lit it, and headed south again.

Burke stared up at the gilt lettering on the window of J. P. Donleavy's, a small, inconspicuous pub on Forty-seventh Street. Donleavy's was another haunt of the quasi-IRA men and barroom patriots. Occasionally there would be a real IRA man there from the other side, and you could tell who he was because he rarely stood at the bar but usually sat alone in a booth. They were always pale, the result of Ireland's perpetual mist or as a result of some time in internment. New York and Boston were their sanctuaries, places of Irish culture, Irish pubs, Irish people without gelignite.

Burke walked in and pushed his way between two men who were talking to each other at the bar. He slipped into his light brogue for the occasion. "Buy you a drink, gentlemen. A round here, barkeeper!" He turned to the man on his left, a young laborer. The man looked annoyed. Burke smiled. "I'm to meet some friends in P.J.'s, but I can't remember if they said P. J. Clarke's, P. J. O'Hara's, P. J. Moriarty's, P. J. O'Rourke's or here. Bloody stupid of me—or of them." The beer came and Burke paid for it. "Would you know Kevin Michaels or Jim Malloy or Liam Connelly? Have you seen them today?"

The man to Burke's right spoke. "That's an interesting list of names. If you're looking for them, you can be sure they'll find *you*."

Burke looked into the man's eyes. "That's what I'm counting on."

The man stared back but said nothing.

Burke smelled the sour beer on the man's breath, on his clothes. "I'm looking, too, for John Hickey."

Neither man spoke.

Burke took a long drink and put his glass down. "Thank you, gentlemen. I'm off to the Green Derby. Good day." He turned and walked down the length of the bar. An angled mirror reflected the two men huddled with the bartender, looking at him as he left.

He repeated his story, or one like it, in every bar that he thought might be promising. He switched from whiskey to stout to hot coffee and had a sandwich at a pub, which made him feel better. He crossed and recrossed Third Avenue, making his way southward. In every bar he left a forwarding address, and at every street corner he stopped and waited for the sound of shoes against the cold concrete to hesitate, to stop behind him. He was trolling, using himself as bait, but no one was rising to it today.

Burke picked up his pace. Time was running out. He looked at his watch; it was past four, and he had to be at the zoo at four-thirty. He stopped at a phone booth. "Langley? I need five hundred for Ferguson."

"Later. You didn't call for that."

Burke lit a cigarette. "What do you know about a Major Bartholomew Martin?"

There was a long silence on the phone, then Langley said, "Oh, you mean the British Intelligence guy. Don't worry about him."

"Why not?"

"Because I said so." Langley paused. "It's very complicated...CIA..."

"Tell me about it someday. Anything else I should know?"

"The FBI has finally decided to talk to us," Langley said. "They've uncovered an arms buy in New Jersey. A dozen M-16 ri-

fles, a few sniper rifles, pistols, and plastic explosives. Also, a half
dozen of those disposable rocket launchers. U.S. Army issue."

"Any other particulars?"

"Only that the buyers had Irish accents, and they didn't arrange for shipping to Ireland the way they usually do."

"Sounds ominous."

"I'll say—what are they *waiting* for?"

Burke shook his head. "I don't know. The parade has less
than an hour to run. The weapons should be a clue to the type
of operation."

"Martin thinks they're going to knock over a British bank
down in the Wall Street area. The Police Commissioner has di-
verted detectives and patrolmen down there," said Langley.

"Why should they come all the way here to knock over a British bank? They want something...something they can only get
here."

"Maybe." Langley paused. "We're really not getting any
closer, are we?"

"Too many targets. Too much beach to guard. The attackers
always have the initiative."

"I'll remember that line when I stand in front of the Commissioner."

Burke looked at his watch. "I have to meet Ferguson. He's
my last play." He hung up, stepped into Third Avenue, and
hailed a cab.

Burke passed through the open gate beside the armory. The zoo
looked less sinister in the light of day. Children with parents or
governesses walked on the paths, holding candy or balloons, or
some other object that was appropriate to their mission and the
setting.

The Delacorte clock showed four thirty. Brass monkeys in

the clock tower suddenly came to life, circled the bell with hammers raised, and struck it. As the mast gong sounded a recording played "MacNamara's Band."

Burke found Ferguson in the Terrace Restaurant at a small table, his face buried in *The New York Times*. Two containers of tea steamed on the table. Burke pulled up a chair opposite him and took a container.

Ferguson lowered the newspaper. "Well, the word on the street is that there is to be a robbery of a major British bank in the Wall Street area."

"Who told you that?"

Ferguson didn't answer.

Burke looked over the zoo, scanning the men on the benches, then turned back to Ferguson and fixed him with a sharp look.

Ferguson said nothing. "Major Martin," Burke said, "is what is known as an agent provocateur. What his game is, I don't know yet. But I think he knows more than he's telling any of us." Burke ground out his cigarette. "All right, forget what Martin told you. Tell me what *you* think. Time is—"

Ferguson turned up the collar of his trench coat against the rising wind. "I know all about time. It's very relative, you know. When they're kneecapping you in that new way with an electric drill instead of a bullet, then time moves very slowly. If you're trying to discover something by dusk, it goes quickly. If you were ten minutes early instead of late, you might have had the time to do something."

"About what?"

Ferguson leaned across the table. "I just came from the Cathedral. John Hickey, who hasn't been inside a church since he robbed Saint Patrick's in Dublin, was sleeping in the first pew. The old man wears a beard now, but I'd know him anywhere."

"Go on."

"The four o'clock Mass is ending soon, and there'll be thousands of people coming out of the Cathedral. Quitting time for most citizens is also at five."

"Right. It's called rush hour—"

"The counties and the IRA vets are marching now. Both groups are composed of people in civilian dress, and there are people who don't know each other in each unit. Anyone could be infiltrated among them."

"I'm listening, but hurry it up."

"I have to give you my thoughts so you can deduce—"

"Go on."

"All right. The police are tired. Some units are going off duty, the crowd is restless, drunk."

"I hear you."

"Events are moving inexorably toward their end. The gathering storm is about to break."

"No poetry, please."

"Finn MacCumail is Brian Flynn. Before Maureen Malone's desertion from the IRA, she and Brian Flynn were lovers."

Burke stood. "He's going after her."

"It's the kind of insane thing a man who calls himself Finn MacCumail, Chief of the Fenians, would do."

"At the Cathedral?"

"What better place? The Irish have a love of spectacle, grand gestures. Whether they win or not is unimportant. Ireland will always remember her martyrs and heroes for their style, not their success or lack of it. So, who will soon forget the resurrected Finn MacCumail and his Fenians when they kidnap or kill his faithless lover at Saint Patrick's Cathedral in New York on Saint Patrick's Day? No, it won't be soon forgotten."

Burke's mind raced. "I didn't believe they'd hit the Cathedral...but it fits the facts—"

"To hell with the facts. It fits their characters. It fits with history, with destiny, with—"

"Fuck history." Burke ran toward the terrace steps. "Fuck
destiny, Jack." He tore down the path toward Fifth Avenue.

Ferguson called out after him. "Too late! Too late!"

Terri O'Neal watched the IRA veterans pass on the television
screen. The scene shifted from Sixty-fourth Street to a view from
the roof of Rockefeller Center. The County Tyrone unit passed
in front of the Cathedral, and the camera zoomed in. She sat
up and leaned closer to the television set. Her father's face suddenly filled the screen, and the announcer, who had recognized
him, made a passing comment. She put her hand over her face
as the enormity of what was going to happen—to her, to him,
to everyone—at last dawned on her. "Oh, no.... Dad! Don't let
them get away with this...."

Dan Morgan looked at her. "Even if he could hear you,
there's not a thing he can do now."

The telephone rang, and Morgan answered it. He listened.
"Yes, as ready as I'll ever be." He hung up, then looked at his
watch and began counting off sixty seconds as he walked into
the bedroom.

Terri O'Neal looked up from the television and watched
him. "Is this it?"

He glanced at the parade passing by on the screen, then at
her. "Yes. And God help us if we've misjudged...."

"God help you, anyway."

Morgan went into the bedroom, opened the side panel of the
bay window, and waved a green shamrock flag.

CHAPTER 13

B rendan O'Connor stood with the crowd on Fifth Avenue. He looked up and saw the shamrock flag waving from the window on Sixty-fourth Street. He took a deep breath and moved behind the reviewing stands where pedestrian traffic was allowed to pass under the scrutiny of patrolmen. He lit a cigarette and watched the smoke blow southward, over his shoulder.

O'Connor reached his right hand into the pocket of his overcoat, slid the elastic off the handle of a grenade that had the pin removed, and held the handle down with his thumb. As he moved through the closely pressed crowd he pushed the grenade through a slit in his pocket and let it fall to the sidewalk. He felt the detonator handle hit his ankle as it flew off. He repeated the procedure with a grenade in his left pocket, pushing quickly through the tight crowd as it fell.

Both seven-second fuses popped in sequence. The first grenade, a CS gas canister, hissed quietly. The second grenade, a smoke signaling device, billowed huge green clouds that floated south into the stands. Brendan O'Connor kept walking. Behind him he could hear the sounds of surprise as the CS gas rose to face level, followed by the sounds of fear and panic as the smoke and choking gas swept over the crowd on the sidewalk and up to the reviewing stands. O'Connor released four more canisters through his pockets, then walked through an opening in the stone wall and disappeared into the park.

Patrick Burke vaulted the low stone wall of Central Park and barreled into the crowd on the sidewalk near the reviewing stands. Billowing green smoke rolled over the stands toward him, and even before it reached him his eyes began to tear. "Shit." He put a handkerchief to his face and ran into the Avenue, but panic had seized the marchers, and Burke was caught in the middle of the confusion. The banner of the unit had fallen to the pavement, and Burke glimpsed it under the feet of the running men—BELFAST IRISH REPUBLICAN ARMY VETERANS. As he fought his way across the Avenue, Burke could see that their ranks were laced with agitators and professional shriekers, as he called them. *Well planned,* he thought. *Well executed.*

James Sweeney put his back to the streetlight pole at Sixty-fourth Street and held his ground against the press of people around him. His hands reached through the pockets of his long trench coat and grabbed a long-handled bolt cutter hanging from his belt. He let the skirts of his coat fall over the cable connections from the mobile headquarters van as he clipped the telephone lines and then the electric power lines at the base of the pole.

Sweeney took three steps into the shoving crowd and let the bolt cutter slide into the storm drain at the curb. He allowed himself to be carried along with the flow of the moving mass of marchers and spectators up Sixty-fourth Street, away from the Avenue and the choking gas.

* * *

Inside the mobile headquarters van the telephone operators heard an odd noise, and the four telephones went dead. All the lights in the van went out a second later. One of the operators looked up at George Byrd silhouetted against a small side window. "Phones out!"

Byrd pressed his face to the small window and looked down at the base of the streetlight. "Oh Christ! Sons of bitches." He turned back and grabbed at a radio as the van driver started the engine and switched to internal power. Byrd transmitted: "All stations! Mobile at Sixty-fourth. Power line cut. We're operating radios on generator. Telephone lines cut. Situation unclear—"

Burke burst through the door and grabbed the radiophone from Byrd's hand. "Mobile at Fifty-first—do you read?"

The second mobile van beside the Cathedral answered. "Roger. All quiet here. Mounted and scooter units headed your way—"

"No! Listen—"

As the nineteen bronze bells in the north spire of St. Patrick's Cathedral chimed five o'clock, the timer on the box resting on the crossbeam above the bells completed the electrical circuit. The box, a broad-band transmitter, began sending out static over the entire spectrum of the radio band. From its transmitting point, high above the street, the transmitter jammed all two-way radios in the midtown area.

A high, piercing sound filled Burke's earphone. "Mobile at Fifty-first—do you read? Action will take place at *Cathedral....*" The sound grew louder and settled into a pattern of continuous high-pitched static. "Mobile at Fifty-first..." He let the radio-phone fall from his hand and turned to Byrd. "Jammed."

"I hear it—shit!" Byrd grabbed at the radio and switched to

alternate command channels, but they were all filled with static. "Bastards!"

Burke grabbed his arm. "Listen, get some men to the public telephones. Call Police Plaza and the rectory. Have them try to get a message to the police around the Cathedral. The mobile van there may still have telephone communication."

"I doubt it."

"Tell them—"

"I know, I know. I heard you." Byrd sent four men out of the van. He looked out the side window at the crowd streaming by and watched his men pushing through it. He turned around to speak to Burke, but he was gone.

On the steps of the Cathedral, Maureen watched the plain-clothesman standing in front of her trying to get his hand radio to work. Several policemen were running around, passing on messages and receiving orders, and she could tell by their manner that there was some confusion among them. Police were moving in and out of the van on the corner to her right. She noticed the spectators on the sidewalks; they seemed to have received some message that those on the steps had not. There was a murmur running through the crowd, and heads craned north, up the Avenue, as though the message had come from that direction as in a child's game of Pass-It-On. She looked north but could see nothing unusual except the unsettled crowd. Then she noticed that the pace of the marchers had slowed. She turned to Harold Baxter and said quietly, "Something is wrong."

The bells struck the last of the five chimes, then began their traditional five o'clock hymns with "Autumn."

Baxter nodded. "Keep alert."

The County Cork unit passed slowly in front of the Cathedral, and behind them the County Mayo unit marked time as

the parade became inexplicably stalled. Parade marshals and formation marshals spoke to policemen. Maureen noticed that the
Cardinal looked annoyed but not visibly concerned about the
rising swell of commotion around him.

Office workers and store clerks began streaming out of the
lobbies of Rockefeller Center, the Olympic Tower, and the surrounding skyscrapers onto the already crowded sidewalks. They
jostled to get away from the area, or to get a better view of the
parade.

Suddenly there was a loud cry from the crowd. Maureen
turned to her left. From the front doors of Saks Fifth Avenue
burst a dozen men dressed in black suits and derbies. They wore
white gloves and bright orange sashes across their chests, and
most of them carried walking sticks. They pushed aside a police barricade and unfurled a long banner that read: GOD SAVE
THE QUEEN. ULSTER WILL BE BRITISH FOREVER.

Maureen's pulse quickened, and her mind flashed back to Ulster, to the long summer marching season when the Orangemen
paraded through the cities and villages, proclaiming their loyalty
to God and Queen and their hate of their Catholic neighbors.

The crowd began to howl and hiss. An old IRA veteran fortified with spirits crashed through the police barrier and ran into
the street, racing at the Orangemen, screaming as he ran, "Fucking bloody murdering bastards! I'll kill you!"

A half dozen of the Orangemen hoisted bullhorns and broke
into song:

> "A rope, a rope, to hang the Pope!
> A pennyworth o' cheese to choke him!
> A pint o' lamp oil to wrench it down,
> And a big hot fire to roast him!"

Several of the enraged crowd broke from the sidewalks and ran into the street, spurred on by a few men who seemed to have materialized suddenly as their leaders. This vanguard was soon joined by streams of men, women, and teen-agers as the barriers began falling up and down the Avenue.

The few mounted police who had not headed to the reviewing stands formed a protective phalanx around the Orangemen, and a paddy wagon escorted by patrol cars began moving up Fiftieth Street to rescue the Orangemen from the crowd that had suddenly turned into a mob. The police swung clubs to keep the surging mob away from the still singing Orangemen. All the techniques of crowd control, learned in the Police Academy and learned on the streets, were employed in an effort to save the dozen Orangemen from being lynched, and the Orangemen themselves seemed finally to recognize their perilous position as hundreds of people ran out of control. They laid down their bullhorns and banner and joined the police in fighting their way to the safety of the approaching paddy wagon.

Patrick Burke ran south on Fifth Avenue, weaving in and out of the spectators and marchers who filled the street. He drew up in front of a parked patrol car, out of breath, and held up his badge. "Can you call mobile at the Cathedral?"

The patrolman shook his head and pointed to the static-filled radio.

"Take me to the Cathedral. Quick!" He grabbed the rear-door handle.

The uniformed sergeant sitting beside the driver called out. "No way! We can't move through this mob. If we hit someone, they'll tear us apart."

"Shit." Burke slammed the door and recrossed the Avenue. He vaulted the wall into Central Park and ran south along a path paralleling the Avenue. He came out of the park at Grand Army Plaza and began moving south through the increasingly disorderly mob. He know it could take him half an hour to move the remaining nine blocks to the Cathedral, and he knew that the parallel avenues were probably not much better, even if he could get to them through a side street. He was not going to make it.

Suddenly a black horse appeared in front of him. A young policewoman, with blond hair tucked under her helmet, was sitting impassively atop the horse. He pushed alongside the woman and showed his badge. "Burke, Intelligence Division. I have to get to the Cathedral. Can you push this nag through this mob with me on the back?"

She regarded Burke, taking in his disheveled appearance. "This is not a nag, Lieutenant, but if you're in so much of a hurry, jump on." She reached down. Burke took her hand, put his foot in the stirrup, and swung heavily onto the rear of the horse.

The policewoman spurred the horse forward. "Giddyap! Come on, Commissioner!"

"I'm only a lieutenant."

The policewoman glanced over her shoulder as the horse began to move forward. "That's the horse's name—Commissioner."

"Oh. What's your...?"

"Police Officer Foster...Betty."

"Nice. Good names. Let's move it."

The trained police horse and the rider were in their element, darting, weaving, cutting into every brief opening, and scattering knots of people in their path without seriously injuring anyone.

Burke held tightly to the woman's waist. He looked up and

saw that they were approaching the intersection at Fifty-seventh Street. He shouted into her ear, "You dance good, Betty. Come here often?"

The policewoman turned her head and looked at him. "This run had damned well better be important, Lieutenant."

"It's the most important horse ride since Paul Revere's."

Major Bartholomew Martin stood at the window of a small room on the tenth floor of the British Empire Building in Rockefeller Center. He watched the riot that swirled around the Cathedral, then turned to the man standing beside him. "Well, Kruger, it appears that the Fenians have arrived."

The other man, an American, said, "Yes, for better or for worse." He paused, then asked, "Did you know this was going to happen?"

"Not exactly. Brian Flynn does not confide in me. I gave him some ideas, some options. His only prohibition was not to attack British property or personnel—like blowing up this building, for instance. But you never quite know with these people." Major Martin stared off into space for a few seconds, then spoke in a faraway voice. "You know, Kruger, when I finally caught up with the bastard in Belfast last winter, he was a beaten man—physically as well as mentally. All he wanted was for me to kill him quickly. And I wanted very much to accommodate him, I assure you, but then I thought better of it. I turned him around, as we say, then pointed him at America and set him loose. A dangerous business, I know, like grabbing that tiger by the tail. But it's paid off, I think."

Kruger stared at him for a long time, then said, "I hope we've calculated American public reaction correctly."

Martin smiled as he took some brandy from a flask. "If the American public was ambivalent about the Irish problem yesterday, they are not so ambivalent today." He looked at Kruger. "I'm sure this will help your service a bit."

Kruger replied, "And if it doesn't help, then you owe us a favor. In fact, I wanted to speak to you about something we have planned in Hong Kong."

"Ah, intrigue. Yes, yes, I want to hear all about it. But later. Enjoy the parade." He opened the window, and the sound of crashing windows, police sirens, and thousands of people filled the small room. "*Erin go bragh,* as they say."

CHAPTER 14

Maureen Malone felt someone tap her on the shoulder. She turned to see a man holding a badge in front of her face. "Bureau of Special Services, Miss Malone. Some of the crowd is turning their attention up here. We have to get you into the Cathedral. Mr. Baxter, you too. Please follow us."

Baxter looked down at the crowd in the street and at the police line, arms locked, at the curb. "I think we're perfectly safe here for now."

The man answered, "Sir, you have to get out of here for the safety of the other people on the steps—please—"

"Yes, yes, I see. All right. Miss Malone, he's quite right."

Maureen and Baxter turned and mounted the steps. Maureen saw the red vestments of the Cardinal as he moved through the crowded steps in front of them, flanked by two men.

Other BSS men on the steps had moved around the Monsignor and the other priests and church people, eyeing the crowd closely. Two BSS men noticed that the Cardinal, Malone, and Baxter were being led away by unknown men and began to follow, pushing their way toward the portals. Two priests on the top step fell in behind them, and the two BSS men felt the press of something hard on their backs. "Freeze," said one of the priests softly, "or we'll blow your spines open."

The police in the mobile headquarters van beside the Cathedral had lost radio communication as static filled the frequencies, but they were still reporting by telephone. Without warning an ambulance coming down Fifty-first Street swerved and sideswiped the headquarters van. The van shot forward, and the lines connecting it to the streetlamp snapped. The ambulance drivers abandoned their vehicle and disappeared quickly into the crowded lobby of the Olympic Tower.

Maureen Malone, Harold Baxter, and the Cardinal walked abreast down the main aisle of the crowded Cathedral. Two men walked behind them, and two men set the pace in front. Maureen could see that the priest in the pulpit was Father Murphy, and another priest was kneeling at the communion rail. As she moved closer to the kneeling priest she was aware that there was something familiar about him.

The Cardinal turned and looked back up the aisle, then asked his escort, "Where is Monsignor Downes? Why aren't the others with us?"

One of the men answered, "They'll be along. Please keep moving, Your Eminence."

Father Murphy tried to continue the Mass, but he was distracted again by the shouts and sirens outside. He looked out over the two thousand worshipers in the pews and in the aisles, and his eye caught a movement of brilliant red in the main aisle. He stared at the disturbing sight of the Cardinal walking toward the altar, flanked by Malone and Baxter and escorted by security men. The thought that something was happening outside to mar this great day upset him. He forgot where he was in the Mass and said abruptly, "The Mass is ended. Go in peace." He added hurriedly, "No. Wait. Stay until we know what is happening. Stay in your seats, please."

Father Murphy turned and saw the priest who had been kneeling at the communion rail now standing on the top step of the pulpit. He recognized the tall priest with the deep green eyes and was, oddly, not surprised to see him again. He cleared his throat. "Yes?"

Brian Flynn slipped a pistol from under his black coat and kept it near his side. "Stand back."

Murphy took a deep breath. "Who the hell are you?"

"I'm the new archbishop." Flynn pushed Murphy into the rear of the pulpit and took the microphone. He watched the Cardinal approaching the altar, then began to address the worshipers who were still standing in the pews. "Ladies and gentlemen," he began in a carefully measured cadence, "may I have your attention...."

Maureen Malone stopped abruptly in the open area a few feet from the altar rail. She stared up at the pulpit, transfixed by the tall, dark figure standing there in the dim light. The man behind her nudged her forward. She turned slowly. "Who are you?"

The man revealed a pistol stuck in his waistband. "Not the police, I assure you." The New York accent had disappeared, replaced by a light brogue. "Keep walking. You, too, Baxter, Your Eminence."

One of the men in front opened the gate in the marble altar railing and turned. "Come in, won't you?"

Patrick Burke, seated uneasily on the horse, looked over the heads of the crowd. Two blocks beyond he could see mass confusion, worse than that which swirled around him. The shop windows of Cartier and Gucci were broken, as were most of the other windows along the Avenue. Uniformed police stood in front of the displays of many of the shops, but there was no apparent looting, only that strange mixture of fighting and reveling that the Irish affectionately called a donnybrook. Burke could see the Cathedral now, and it was obvious that whatever had sparked this turmoil had begun there.

The crowd immediately around him was made up of marching units that were staying together, passing bottles, and singing. A brass band was playing "East Side, West Side," backed by an enthusiastic chorus. The policewoman spurred the horse on.

Midway down the block before the Cathedral the crowd became tighter, and the horse was straining to sidestep through. Bodies crushed against the riders' legs, then fell away as the horse made another lunge. "Keep pushing! Keep going!" called Burke.

The policewoman shouted, "God, they're packed so tight...." She pulled back on the reins, and the horse reared up. The crowd scattered, and she drove into the opening, then repeated the maneuver.

Burke felt his stomach heave and caught his breath. "Nice! Nice! Good work!"

"How far do I have to get?"

"When Commissioner is kneeling at the communion rail, I'll tell you!"

Brian Flynn waited until the Cardinal and the others were safely inside the railing of the high altar, then said into the microphone, "Ladies and gentlemen, there is a small fire in the basement. Please stay calm. Leave quickly through the doors, including the front doors."

A cry went up from the congregation, and a few men interspersed throughout the Cathedral shouted, "Fire! Fire! Run!"

The pews emptied rapidly, and the aisles streamed with people pushing toward the exits. Racks of votive candles went down, spilling and cracking on the floor. The bookshop near the south spire emptied, and the first wave of people filled the vestibules and surged through the three sets of front doors, pouring out onto the steps.

The spectators on the steps suddenly found themselves pushed by a sea of people coming through the portals, and were swept down across the sidewalk, into the police barricades, through the line of policemen, and into the riot on Fifth Avenue.

Monsignor Downes tried to fight against the tide and get into the Cathedral, but found himself in the street squeezed between a heavy woman and a burly police officer.

The two bogus priests who had been pressing guns into the backs of the Bureau of Special Services men blended into the moving throng and disappeared. The two BSS men turned and tried to remount the steps but were carried down into the Avenue by the crowd.

Police scooters toppled, and patrol cars were covered with people trying to escape the crush of the crowd. Marching units broke ranks and became engulfed in the mob. Police tried to set up perimeters to keep the area of the disturbance contained, but without radio communication their actions were uncoordinated and ineffective.

Television news crews filmed the scene until they were overwhelmed by the surging mob.

Inspector Philip Langley peered down from the New York Police Department command helicopter into the darkening canyons below. He turned to Deputy Police Commissioner Rourke and shouted above the beat of the rotor blades. "I think the Saint Patrick's Day Parade is over."

The Deputy Commissioner eyed him for a long second, then looked down at the incredible scene. Rush hour traffic was stalled for miles, and a sea of people completely covered the streets and sidewalks as far south as Thirty-fourth Street and as far north as Seventy-second Street. Close to a million people were in the small midtown area at this hour, and not one of them was going to get home in time for dinner. "Lot of unhappy citizens down there, Philip."

Langley lit a cigarette. "I'll hand in my resignation tonight."

The Deputy Commissioner looked up at him. "I hope there's somebody around to accept it." He looked back at the streets. "Almost every ranking officer in the New York Police Department is down there somewhere, cut off from communication, cut off from their command." He turned to Langley. "This is the worst yet."

Langley shook his head. "I think the worst is yet to come."

In the intersection at Fiftieth Street, Burke could see the bright orange sashes of men being led into a paddy wagon. Burke remembered the Irish saying: "If you want an audience, start a fight." These Orangemen had wanted an audience, and he knew why; he knew, too, that they were not Orangemen at all but Boston Provos recruited to cause a diversion—dumb Micks with more courage than brains.

The policewoman turned to him as she urged the horse on. "Who are those people with orange sashes?"

"It's a long story. Go on. Almost there—"

Brian Flynn came down from the pulpit and faced Maureen Malone. "It's been a damned long time, Maureen."

She looked at him and replied in an even voice, "Not long enough."

He smiled. "Did you get my flowers?"

"I flushed them."

"You have one in your lapel."

Her face reddened. "So you've come to America after all, Brian."

"Yes. But as you can see, on my terms." He looked out over the Cathedral. The last of the worshipers were jamming the center vestibule, trying to squeeze through the great bronze doors. Two Fenians, Arthur Nulty dressed as a priest and Frank Gallagher dressed as a parade marshal, stood behind them and urged them on through the doors, onto the packed steps, but the crowd began to back up into the vestibule. All the other doors had been swung closed and bolted. Flynn looked at his watch. This was taking longer than he expected. He turned to Maureen. "Yes, on my terms. Do you see what I've *done*? Within half an hour all of America will see and hear this. We'll provide some good Irish theater for them. Better than the Abbey ever did."

Maureen saw in his eyes a familiar look of triumph, but mixed with that look was one of fear that she had never seen before. Like a little boy, she thought, who had stolen something from a shop and knows he might have to answer for his transgression very shortly. "You won't get away with this, you know."

He smiled, and the fear left his eyes. "Yes, I will."

Two of the Fenians who had posed as police walked around the altar and descended the stairs that led down to the sacristy. From the open archway on the left-hand wall of the sacristy, they heard footsteps approaching in the corridor that led from the rectory. Excited voices came from a similar opening on the opposite wall that led to the Cardinal's residence. All at once priests and uniformed policemen burst into the sacristy from both doors.

The two Fenians drew the sliding gates out of the wall until they met with a loud metallic ring, and the people in the sacristy looked up the stairs. A uniformed sergeant called out, "Hey! Open those gates!" He advanced toward the stairs.

The Fenians tied a chain through the scrolled brasswork and produced a padlock.

The sergeant drew his pistol. Another policeman came up behind him and did the same.

The Fenians seemed to pay no attention to the officers and snapped the heavy lock on the ends of the wrapped chain. One of them looked up, smiled, and gave a brief salute. "Sorry, lads, you'll have to go round." Both Fenians disappeared up the stairs. One of them, Pedar Fitzgerald, sat near the crypt door where he could see the gate. The other, Eamon Farrell, came around the altar and nodded to Flynn.

Flynn turned to Baxter for the first time. "Sir Harold Baxter?"

"That's correct."

He stared at Baxter. "Yes, I'd enjoy killing you."

Baxter replied without inflection, "Your kind would enjoy killing anyone."

Flynn turned away and looked at the Cardinal. "Your Eminence." He bowed his head, and it wasn't clear if he was mocking or sincere. "My name is Finn MacCumail, Chief of the new Fenian Army. This church is now mine. This is my Bruidean. You know the term? My place of sanctuary."

The Cardinal seemed not to hear him. He asked abruptly, "Is this Cathedral on fire?"

"That depends to a large extent on what happens in the next few minutes."

The Cardinal stared at him, and neither man flinched. The Cardinal finally spoke. "Get out of here. Get out while you can."

"I can't, and I don't want to." He looked up at the choir loft over the main doors where Jack Leary, dressed as a colonial soldier, stood with a rifle. Flynn's eyes dropped to the main doors nearly a block away. People still jammed the vestibule, and noise and light passed in through the open doors. He turned to Father Murphy, who stood next to him. "Father, you may leave. Hurry down the aisle before the doors close."

Murphy strode deliberately to a spot beside the Cardinal. "We are both leaving."

"No. No, on second thought, we may find a use for you later." Flynn turned to Maureen again and moved closer to her. He spoke softly. "You knew, didn't you? Even before you got the flowers?"

"I knew."

"Good. We still know each other, don't we? We've spoken over the years and across the miles, haven't we, Maureen?"

She nodded.

A young woman dressed as a nun appeared at the altar rail holding a large pistol. In the front pew a bearded old man, apparently sleeping on the bench, rose, stretched, and came up behind her. Everyone watched as the two people ascended the steps of the altar sanctuary.

The old man nodded to the hostages and spoke in a clear, vibrant voice. "Your Eminence, Father Murphy, Miss Malone, Sir Harold. I am John Hickey, fancifully code-named Dermot, in keeping with the pagan motif suggested by our leader, Finn MacCumail." He made an exaggerated bow to Flynn. "I am a poet, scholar, soldier, and patriot, much like the original Fenians. You may have heard of me." He looked around and saw the signs of recognition in the eyes of the four hostages. "No, not dead, as you can plainly see. But dead before the sun rises again, I'll wager. Dead in the ruins of this smoldering Cathedral.

A magnificent funeral pyre it'll be, befitting a man of my rank. Oh, don't look so glum, Cardinal, there's a way out—if we all keep our senses about us." He turned to the young woman beside him. "May I present our Grania—or, as she prefers her real name, Megan Fitzgerald."

Megan Fitzgerald said nothing but looked into the face of each hostage. Her eyes came to rest on Maureen Malone, and she looked her up and down.

Maureen stared back at the young woman. She knew there would be a woman. There always was with Flynn. Flynn was that type of man who needed a woman watching in order to stiffen his courage, the way other men needed a drink. Maureen looked into the face of Megan Fitzgerald: high cheekboned, freckled, with a mouth that seemed set in a perpetual sneer, and eyes that should have been lovely but were something quite different. Too young, and not likely to get much older in the company of Brian Flynn. Maureen saw herself ten years before.

Megan Fitzgerald stepped up to her, the big pistol swinging nonchalantly from her left hand, and put her mouth close to Maureen's ear. "You understand that I'm looking for an excuse to kill you."

"I hope I find the courage to do something to give you one. Then we'll see how *your* courage stands up."

Megan Fitzgerald's body tensed visibly. After a few seconds she stepped back and looked around the altar, sweeping each person standing there with a cold stare and meeting Flynn's look of disapproval. She turned, walked down from the altar, and then strode down the main aisle toward the center doors.

Flynn watched her, then looked past her into the vestibule. The doors were still open. He hadn't counted on the crowd being so large. If they couldn't get the doors closed and bolted soon, the police would force their way in and there would be a fire fight. As he watched, Megan passed into the vestibule and raised her pistol. He saw the smoke flash from the upturned muzzle of her gun, then heard the report roll through the massive church and echo in and out of the vaults and side altars. A scream went up from the crowd in the vestibule, and their backs receded as they found a new strength and a more immediate reason to push through the crowd blocking the steps.

Flynn watched Megan bring the gun down into a horizontal position and aim it at the opening. Nulty and Gallagher maneuvered around, and each took up a position behind the doors, pushing them against the last of the fleeing worshipers.

Megan dropped to one knee and steadied her aim with both hands.

Patrick Burke shouted to the policewoman, "Up the steps! Up to the front door!"

Betty Foster spurred the horse up the steps where they curved around to Fifty-first Street, and moved diagonally through the crowd toward the center doors.

Burke saw the last of the worshipers flee through the doors, and the horse broke into the open space between them and the portals. The policewoman reined the horse around and kicked its flanks. "Come on, Commissioner! Up! Up!"

Burke drew his service revolver and shouted, "Draw your piece! Through the doors!"

Betty Foster held the reins with her left hand and drew her revolver.

A few yards from the portals the big bronze ceremonial doors—sixteen feet across, nearly two stories high, and weighing ten thousand pounds apiece— began closing. Burke knew they were pushed by unseen persons standing behind them. The dimly lit vestibule came into sight, and he saw a nun kneeling there. Behind her, the vast, deserted Cathedral stretched back a hundred yards, through a forest of stone columns, to the raised altar sanctuary where Burke could see people standing. A figure in bright red stood out against the white marble.

The doors were half closed now, and the horse's head was a yard from the opening. Burke know they were going to make it. And then...what?

Suddenly the image of the kneeling nun filled his brain, and his eyes focused on her again. From her extended arm Burke saw a flash of light, then heard a loud, echoing sound followed by a sharp crack.

The horse's front legs buckled, and the animal pitched forward. Burke was aware of Betty Foster flying into the air, then felt himself falling forward. His face struck the granite step a foot from the doors. He crawled toward the small opening, but the bronze doors came together and shut in his face. He heard, above all the noise around him, the sound of the floor bolts sliding home.

Burke rolled onto his back and sat up. He turned to the policewoman, who was lying on the steps, blood running from her forehead. As he watched, she sat up slowly.

Burke stood and offered her his hand, but she got to her feet without his aid and looked down at her mount. A small wound on Commissioner's chest ran with blood; frothy blood trickled from the horse's open mouth and steamed in a puddle as it collected on the cold stone. The horse tried to stand but fell clumsily back onto its side. Betty Foster fired into his head. After putting her hand to the horse's nostrils to make certain he was dead, she holstered her revolver. She looked up at Burke, then back at her horse. Walking slowly down the steps, she disappeared into the staring crowd.

Burke looked out into the Avenue. Rotating beacons from

the police cars cast swirling red and white light on the chaotic scene and across the façades of the surrounding buildings. Occasionally, above the general bedlam, Burke could hear a window smash, a whistle blow, a scream ring out.

He turned around and stared at the Cathedral. Taped to one of the bronze ceremonial doors, over the face of St. Elizabeth Seton, was a piece of cardboard with handlettering on it. He stepped closer to read it in the fading light.

THIS CATHEDRAL IS UNDER THE CONTROL OF THE IRISH
FENIAN ARMY

It was signed, FINN MACCUMAIL.

BOOK IV

The Cathedral: Siege

Friendship, joy and peace! If the outside world only realized the wonders of this Cathedral, there would never be a vacant pew.

—Parishioner

CHAPTER 15

Patrick Burke stood at the front doors of St. Patrick's Cathedral, his hands in his pockets and a cigarette in his mouth. Lightly falling sleet melted on the flanks of the dead horse and ran in rivulets onto the icy stone steps.

The crowds in the surrounding streets were not completely under control, but the police had rerouted the remainder of the marching units west to Sixth Avenue. Burke could hear drums and bagpipes above the roar of the mob. The two hundred and twenty-third St. Patrick's Day Parade would go on until the last marcher arrived at Eighty-fourth Street, even if it meant marching through Central Park to get there.

Automobile horns were blaring incessantly, and police whistles and sirens cut through the windy March dusk. *What a fucking mess.* Burke wondered if anyone out there knew that the Cathedral was under the control of gunmen. He looked at his watch—not yet five thirty. The six o'clock news would begin early and not end until this ended.

Burke turned and examined the bronze ceremonial doors, then put his shoulder to one of them and pushed. The door moved slightly, then sprang back, closing. From behind the doors Burke heard a shrill alarm. "Smart sons of bitches." It wasn't going to be easy to get the Cathedral away from Finn

MacCumail. He heard a muffled voice call out from behind the door. "Get away! We're putting mines on the doors!"

Burke moved back and stared up at the massive doors, noticing them for the first time in twenty years. On a righthand panel a bronze relief of St. Patrick stared down at him, a crooked staff in one hand, a serpent in the other. To the saint's right was a Celtic harp, to his left the mythical phoenix, appropriated from the pagans, rising to renewed life from its own ashes. Burke turned slowly and started walking down the steps. "Okay, Finn or Flynn, or whatever you call yourself—you may have gotten in standing tall, but you won't be leaving that way."

Brian Flynn stood at the railing of the choir loft and looked out over the vast Cathedral spread out over an area larger than a football field. Seventy towering stained-glass windows glowed with the outside lights of the city like dripping jewels, and dozens of hanging chandeliers cast a soft luminescence over the dark wooden pews. Rows of gray granite pillars reached up to the vaulted ceiling like the upraised arms of the faithful supporting the house of God. Flynn turned to John Hickey. "It would take some doing to level this place."

"Leave it to me, Brian."

Flynn said, "The first priority of the police is that mob out there. We've bought some time to set up our defense." Flynn raised a pair of field glasses and looked at Maureen. Even at this distance he saw that her face was red, and her jaw was set in a hard line. He focused on Megan who had assembled three men and two women and was making an inspection of the perimeter walls. She had taken off the nun's wimple, revealing long red hair that fell to her shoulders. She walked quickly, now peeling off her nun's habit and throwing the black and white garments carelessly onto the floor until she was clad in only jeans and a T-shirt, which had a big red apple on it and the words *I Love New York*. She stopped by the north transept doors and looked up at the southeast triforium as she called out, "Gallagher!"

Frank Gallagher, dressed in the morning coat and striped pants of a parade marshal, leaned over the balcony parapet and pointed his sniper rifle at her, taking aim through the scope. He shouted back, "Check!"

Megan moved on.

Flynn unrolled a set of blueprints and rested them on the rail of the choir loft. He tapped the plans of the Cathedral with his open hand and said, as though the realization had just come to him, "We took it."

Hickey nodded and stroked his wispy beard. "Aye, but can we keep it? Can we hold it with a dozen people against twenty thousand policemen?"

Flynn turned to Jack Leary standing near the organ keyboard beside him. "Can we hold it, Jack?"

Leary nodded slowly. "Twenty thousand, or twenty, they can only come in a few at a time." He patted his modified M-14 rifle with attached scope. "Anyone who survives the mines on the doors will be dead before he gets three paces."

Flynn looked closely at Leary in the subdued light. Leary looked comical in his colonial marching uniform and with his green-painted rifle. But there was nothing funny about his eyes or his expressionless voice.

Flynn looked back over the Cathedral and glanced at the blueprints. This building was shaped like a cross. The long stem of the cross was the nave, holding the main pews and five aisles; the cross-arms were the transepts, containing more pews and an exit from the end of each arm. Two arcaded triforia, long, dark galleries supported by columns, overhung the nave, running as far as the transepts. Two shorter triforia began at the far side of

the transepts and overlooked the altar. This was the basic layout
of the structure to be defended.

Flynn looked at the top of the blueprints. They showed the
five-story rectory nestled in the northeast quadrant of the cross
outside the Cathedral. The rectory was connected to the Cathedral by basement areas under the terraces, which did not appear
on the blueprints. In the southeast quadrant was the Cardinal's
residence, also separated by terraces and gardens and connected
underground. These uncharted connections, Flynn understood,
were a weak point in the defense. "I wish we could have held the
two outside buildings."

Hickey smiled. "Next time."

Flynn smiled in return. The old man had remained an
enigma, swinging precipitantly between clownishness and deci-
siveness. Flynn looked back at the blueprints. The top of the
cross was the rounded area called the apse. In the apse was the
Lady Chapel, a quiet, serene area of long, narrow stained-glass
windows. Flynn pointed to the blueprint. "The Lady Chapel
has no outside connections, and I've decided not to post a man
there—can't spare anyone."

Hickey leaned over the blueprints. "I'll examine it for hidden
passages. Church architecture wouldn't be church architecture,
Brian, without hollow walls and secret doors. Places for the
Holy Ghost to run about—places where priests can pop up on
you unawares and scare the hell out of you by whispering your
name."

"Have you heard of Whitehorn Abbey outside of Belfast?"

"I spent a night there once. Did you get a scare there, lad?"
Hickey laughed.

Flynn looked out over the Cathedral again, concentrating on
the raised area of black and white marble called the altar sanctuary. In the middle of the sanctuary sat the altar, raised still higher

on a broad marble plinth. The cold marble and bronze of the area was softened by fields of fresh green carnations, symbolizing, Flynn imagined, the green sod of Ireland, which would not have looked or smelled as nice on the altar.

On both sides of the sanctuary were rows of wooden pews reserved for clergy. In the pews to the right sat Maureen, Baxter, and Father Murphy, all looking very still from this distance. Flynn placed his field glasses to his eyes and focused on Maureen again. She didn't appear at all frightened, and he liked that. He noticed that her lips were moving as she stared straight ahead. Praying? No, not Maureen. Baxter's lips were moving also. And Father Murphy's. "They're plotting dark things against us, John."

"Good," said Hickey. "Maybe they'll keep us entertained."

Flynn swung the field glasses to the left. Facing the hostages across the checkered marble floor sat the Cardinal on his elevated throne of red velvet, absolutely motionless. "No sanctuary in the sanctuary," commented Flynn under his breath.

Leary heard him and called out, "A sanctuary of sorts. If they leave that area, I'll kill them."

Flynn leaned farther over the rail. Directly behind the altar were the sacristy stairs, not visible from the loft, where Pedar Fitzgerald, Megan's brother, sat on the landing holding a submachine gun. Fitzgerald was a good man, a man who knew that those chained gates had to be protected at any cost. He had his sister's courage without her savagery. "We still don't know if there's a way they can enter the crypt from an underground route and come up behind Pedar."

Hickey glanced again at the blueprints. "We'll get the crypt keys and the keys to this whole place later and have a proper look around the real estate. We need time, Brian. Time to tighten our defense. Damn these blueprints, they're not very detailed. And damn this church. It's like a marble sieve with more holes in it than the story of the Resurrection."

"I hope the police don't get hold of the architect."

"You should have kidnapped him last night along with Terri O'Neal," Hickey said.

"Too obvious. That would have put Intelligence onto something."

"Then you should have killed him and made it look like an accident."

Flynn shook his head. "One has to draw a line somewhere. Don't you think so?"

"You're a lousy revolutionary. It's a wonder you've come as far as you have."

"I've come farther than most. I'm here."

CHAPTER 16

Major Bartholomew Martin put down his field glasses and let out a long breath. "Well, they've done it. No apparent casualties...except that fine horse." He closed the window against the cold wind and sleet. "Burke almost got himself killed, however."

Kruger shrugged. It never paid to examine these things too closely.

Major Martin put on his topcoat. "Sir Harold was a good sort. Played a good game of bridge. Anyway, you see, Flynn went back on his word. Now they'll want to kill poor Harry as soon as things don't go their way."

Kruger glanced out the window. "I think you planned on Baxter getting kidnapped."

Major Martin moved toward the door. "I planned *nothing*, Kruger. I only provided the opportunity and the wherewithal. Most of this is as much a surprise to me as it is to you and the police." Martin looked at his watch. "My consulate will be looking for me, and your people will be looking for you. Remember, Kruger, the first requirement of a successful liar is a good memory. Don't forget what you're not supposed to know, and please remember the things you *are* supposed to know." He pulled on his gloves as he left.

* * *

Megan Fitzgerald motioned to the three men and two women with her and moved quickly toward the front of the Cathedral. The five of them followed her, burdened with suitcases, slung rifles, and rocket tubes. They entered the vestibule of the north tower, rode up the small elevator, and stepped off into the choir practice room in the tower. Megan moved into the choir loft.

Jack Leary was standing at the end of the loft, some distance from Flynn and Hickey, establishing his fields of fire. Megan said curtly, "Leary, you understand your orders?"

The sniper turned and stared at her.

Megan stared back into his pale, watery eyes. Soft eyes, she thought, but she knew how they hardened as the rifle traveled up to his shoulder. Eyes that saw things not in fluid motion but in a series of still pictures, like a camera lens. She had watched him in practice many times. Perfect eye-hand coordination—"muscle memory" he had called it on the one occasion he had spoken to her. Muscle memory— a step below instinct, as though the brain wasn't even involved in the process— optic nerves and motor nerves, bypassing the brain, controlled by some primitive bundle of fibers found only in the lower forms of life. The others stayed away from Leary, but Megan was fascinated by him. "Answer me, Leary. Do you know your orders, man?"

He nodded almost imperceptibly as his eyes took in the young woman standing in front of him.

Megan walked along the rail and came up beside Flynn and Hickey. She placed the field phone on the railing and looked at the outside telephone on the organ. "Call the police."

Flynn didn't look up from the blueprints. "They'll call us."

Hickey said to her, "I'd advise you not to upset Mr. Leary.

He seems incapable of witty bantering, and he'd probably shoot you if he couldn't think of anything to say."

Megan looked back at Leary, then said to Hickey, "We understand each other."

Hickey smiled. "Yes, I've noticed a silent communication between you—but what other type could there be with a man who has a vocabulary of fourteen words, eight of which have to do with rifles?"

Megan turned and walked back to the entrance of the choir practice room where the others were waiting, and she led them up a spiral iron staircase. At a level above the choir practice room she found a door and kicked it open, motioning to Abby Boland. "Come with me," she said.

The long triforium stretched out along the north side of the Cathedral, an unlit gallery of dusty stone and air-conditioning ducts. A flagpole of about twenty feet in length jutted out from the parapet over the nave, flying the white and yellow Papal flag.

Megan turned to Abby Boland, who was dressed in the short skirt and blue blouse of a twirler from Mother Cabrini High School, a place neither of them had heard of until a week before. "This is your post," said Megan. "Remember, the rocket is to use if you see a Saracen—or whatever they call them here—coming through your assigned door. The sniper rifle is for close-in defense, if they come through the tower door there—and for blowing your own brains out if you've a mind to. Any questions? No?" She looked the girl up and down. "You should have thought to bring some clothes with you. It'll be cold up here tonight." Megan returned to the tower.

Abby Boland unslung her rifles and put them down beside the rocket. She slipped off her tight-fitting shoes, unbuttoned her constricting blouse, and sighted through the scope of the sniper rifle, then lowered it and looked around. It occurred to her that rather than freeing her husband, Jonathan, she might very well end up in jail herself, on this side of the Atlantic, too long a distance to intertwine their fingers through the mesh wire of Long Kesh. She might also end up dead, of course, which might be better for both of them.

Megan Fitzgerald continued up the stairs of the bell tower and turned into a side passage. She found a pull chain and lit a small bulb revealing a section of the huge attic. Wooden cat-walks ran over the plaster lathing of the vaulted ceiling below and stretched back into the darkness. The four people with her walked quickly over the catwalks, turning on lights in the cold, musty attic.

Megan could see the ten dormered hatches overhead that led to the slate roof above. On the floor, at intervals, were small winches that lowered the chandeliers to the floors below for maintenance. She turned and moved to the big arched window at the front peak of the attic. Stone tracery on the outside of the Cathedral partially blocked the view, and grime covered the small panes in front of her. She wiped a section with her hand and stared down into Fifth Avenue. The block in front of the Cathedral was nearly deserted, but the police had not yet cleared the crowds out of the intersections on either side. Falling sleet was visible against the streetlights, and ice covered the streets and sidewalks and collected on the shoulders of Atlas.

Megan looked up at the International Building in Rocke-feller Center directly across from her. The two side wings of the building were lower than the attic, and she could see people moving through the ice, people sitting huddled on the big concrete tubs that held bare plants and trees. The uniformed police had no rifles, and she knew that the Cathedral was not yet surrounded by the SWAT teams euphemistically called the

Emergency Services Division in New York. She saw no soldiers, either, and remembered that Americans rarely called on them.

She turned back to the attic. The four people had opened the suitcases and deposited piles of votive candles at intervals along the catwalks. Megan called out to Jean Kearney and Arthur Nulty. "Find the fire axes, chop wood from the catwalks, and build pyres around the candles. Cut the fire hoses up here and string the wire for the field telephone. Be quick about it. Mullins and Devane, grab an ax and come with me."

Megan Fitzgerald retraced her steps out of the attic, followed by the two men who had posed as BSS Security, Donald Mullins and Rory Devane. She continued her climb up to the bell tower. Mullins carried a roll of communication wire, which he played out behind him. Devane carried the weapons and axes.

Arthur Nulty offered Jean Kearney a cigarette. He looked over her Kelly-green Aer Lingus stewardess uniform. "You look very sexy, lass. Would it be a sacrilege to do it up here, do you think?"

"We'll not have time for that."

"Time is all we've got up here. God, but it's cold. We'll need some warming and there's no spirits allowed, so that leaves..."

"We'll see. Jesus, Arthur, if your wife—what happens to us if we get her out of Armagh?"

Arthur Nulty let go of her arm and looked away. "Well...now...let's take things one a time." He picked up an ax and swung it, shattering a wooden railing, then ripped the railing from its post and threw it atop a pile of votive candles. "Whole place is wood up here. Never thought I'd be burning a church. If Father Flannery could see me now." He took another swing with the ax. "Jesus, I hope it doesn't come to that. They'll give in before they see this Cathedral burned. In twenty-four hours your brothers will be in Dublin. Your old dad will be pleased, Jean. He thought he'd never see the boys again." He threw a post on the woodpile. "She called them pyres, Megan did. Doesn't she know that pyres refer only to places to burn corpses?"

CHAPTER 17

Patrick Burke posted patrolmen at each of the Cathedral's portals with the warning that the doors were mined, then came back to the front of the Cathedral and approached a parked patrol car. "Any commo yet?"

The patrolman shook his head. "No, sir. What's going on in there?"

"There are armed gunmen inside, so keep pushing the crowd back. Tell the officer in charge to begin a cordon operation."

"Yes, sir." The patrol car moved away through the nearly deserted Avenue.

Burke remounted the steps and saw Police Officer Betty Foster kneeling in the ice beside her horse.

She looked up at him. "You still here?" She looked back at the horse. "I have to get the saddle." She unhooked the girth. "What the hell's going on in there?" She tugged at the saddle. "You almost got me killed."

He helped her pull at the saddle, but it wouldn't come loose. "Leave this here."

"I can't. It's police property."

"There's police property strewn up and down Fifth Avenue." He let go of the saddle and looked at the bell tower. "There'll be people in these towers soon, if they're not there already. Get this later when they recover the horse."

She straightened up. "Poor Commissioner. Both of them."

"What do you mean?"

"Police Commissioner Dwyer died of a heart attack—at the reviewing stands."

"Jesus Christ." Burke heard a noise from the bell tower overhead and pulled Betty Foster under the alcove of the front door. "Somebody's up there."

"Are you staying here?"

"Until things get straightened out."

She looked at him and said, "Are you brave, Lieutenant Burke?"

"No. Just stupid."

"That's what I thought." She laughed. "God, I thought I was going to pass out when I saw that nun—I guess it wasn't a nun—"

"Not likely."

"That woman, pointing a gun at us."

"You did fine."

"Did I? I guess I did." She paused and looked around. "I'm going to be on duty for a long time. I have to go back to Varick Street and get remounted."

"Remounted?" A bizarre sexual image flashed through his mind. "Oh. Right. Keep close to the wall. I don't know if those people up in the tower are looking for blue targets, but it's better to assume they are."

She hesitated. "See you later." She moved out of the alcove, keeping close to the wall. She called back, "I didn't just come back for the saddle. I wanted to see if you were all right."

Burke watched her round the corner of the tower. This morning neither he nor Betty Foster would have given each other a second glance. Now, however, they had things going for them—riots, gunpowder, horses—great stimulants, powerful aphrodisiacs. He looked at his watch. This lull would not last much longer.

Megan Fitzgerald climbed into the bell room and stood catching her breath as she looked around the cold room, peering into the weak light cast by the single bulb. She saw Flynn's radio jamming device on a crossbeam from which hung three huge bells, each with a turning wheel and a pull strap. Gusts of cold March wind blew in from the eight sets of copper louvers in the octagon-shaped tower room. The sound of police bullhorns and sirens was carried up into the eighteen-story-high room.

Megan grabbed a steel-cut fire ax from Rory Devane, turned suddenly, and swung it at one of the sets of louvers, ripping them open and letting in the lights of the city. Mullins set to work on the other seven louvers, cutting them out of their stone casements as Devane knelt on the floor and connected a field telephone.

Megan turned to Mullins, who had moved to the window overlooking Fifth Avenue. "Remember, Mullins, report *anything* unusual. Keep a sharp eye for helicopters. No shooting without orders."

Mullins looked out at Rockefeller Center. People were pressed to the windows opposite him, and, on the roofs below, people were pointing up at the ripped louvers. A police spotlight in the street came on, and its white beam circled and came to rest on the opening where Mullins stood. He moved back and blinked his eyes. "I'd like to put that spot out."

Megan nodded. "Might as well set them straight now."

Mullins leaned out of the opening and squinted into his sniper scope. He saw figures moving around at the periphery of the spotlight. He took a long breath, steadied his aim, then squeezed the trigger. The sound of the rifle exploded in the bell room, and Mullins saw the red tracer round streak down into the intersection. The spotlight suddenly lost its beam, fading from white to red to black. A hollow popping sound drifted into the bell room, followed by sounds of shouting. Mullins stepped back behind the stonework and blew his nose into a handkerchief. "Cold up here."

Devane sat on the floor and cranked the field phone. "Attic, this is bell tower. Can you hear me?"

The voice of Jean Kearney came back clearly. "Hear you, bell tower. What was that noise?"

Devane answered. "Mullins put out a spot. No problem."

"Roger. Stand by for commo check with choir loft. Choir loft, can you hear bell tower and attic?"

John Hickey's voice came over the line. "Hear you both. Commo established. Who the hell authorized you to shoot at a spotlight?"

Megan grabbed the field phone from Devane. "I did."

Hickey's voice had an edge of sarcasm and annoyance. "Ah, Megan, that was a rhetorical question, lass. I knew the answer to that. Watch yourself today."

Megan dropped the field phone on the floor and looked down at Devane. "Go on down and string the wire from the choir loft to the south tower, then knock out the louvers and take your post there."

Devane picked up a roll of communication wire and the fire ax and climbed down out of the bell room.

Megan moved from opening to opening. The walls of the Cathedral were bathed in blue luminescence from the Cathedral's floodlights in the gardens. To the north the massive fifty-one-story Olympic Tower reflected the Cathedral from its glass sides. To the east the Waldorf-Astoria's windows were lit against the black sky, and to the south the Cathedral's twin tower rose up, partially blocking the view of Saks Fifth Avenue. Police stood on the Saks roof, milling around, flapping their arms against the cold. In all the surrounding streets the crowd was being forced back block by block, and the deserted area around the Cathedral grew in size.

Megan looked back at Mullins, who was blowing into his hands. His young face was red with cold, and tinges of blue showed on his lips. She moved to the ladder in the middle of the floor. "Keep alert."

He watched Megan disappear down the ladder and suddenly felt lonely. "Bitch." She was not much older than he, but her movements, her voice, were those of an older woman. She had lost her youth in everything but her face and body.

Mullins looked around his solitary observation post, then peered back into Fifth Avenue. He unfastened a rolled flag around his waist and tied the corners to the louvers, then let it unfurl over the side of the tower. A wind made it snap against the gray marble, and the Cathedral's floodlights illuminated it nicely.

From the street and the rooftops an exclamation rose from the reporters and civilians still in the area. A few people cheered, and a few applauded. There were a few jeers as well.

Mullins listened to the mixed reaction, then pulled his head back into the tower and wiped the cold sleet from his face. He wondered with a sense of awe how he came to be standing in the bell tower of St. Patrick's Cathedral with a rifle. Then he remembered his older sister, Peg, widowed with three children, pacing the prison yard of Armagh. He remembered the night her husband, Barry Collins, was killed trying to take a prison van that was supposed to contain Maureen Malone's sister, Sheila. He re-

membered his mother looking after Peg's three children for days
at a time while Peg went off with hard-looking men in dark coats.
Mullins remembered the night he went into the streets of Belfast
to find Brian Flynn and his Fenians, and how his mother wept
and cursed after him. But most of all he remembered the bombs
and gunfire that had rocked and split the Belfast nights ever since
he was a child. Thinking back, he didn't see how he could have
traveled any road that didn't lead here, or someplace like it.

Patrick Burke looked up. A green flag, emblazoned with the gold
Irish harp, hung from the ripped louvers, and Burke could make
out a man with a rifle standing in the opening. Burke turned
and watched the police in the intersection wheeling away the
smashed spotlight. The crowd was becoming more cooperative,
concluding that anyone who could put out a spotlight at two
hundred yards could put them out just as easily. Burke moved
into the alcove of the tower door and spoke to the policeman
he had posted there. "We'll just stand here awhile. That guy up
there is still manufacturing adrenaline."

"I know the feeling."

Burke looked out over the steps. The green carpet was white
with sleet now, and green carnations, plastic leprechaun hats,
and paper pompoms littered the steps, sidewalks, and street. In
the intersection of Fiftieth Street a huge Lambeg drum left by
the Orangemen lay on its side. Black bowlers and bright orange
sashes moved slowly southward in the wind. From the buildings
of Rockefeller Center news cameramen were cautiously getting
it all on film. Burke pictured it as it would appear on television.
Zoom-in shots of the debris, a bowler tumbling end over end
across the icy street. The voice-over, deep, resonant—"Today the
ancient war between the English and the Irish came to Fifth Avenue...." The Irish always gave you good theater.

* * *

Brian Flynn leaned out over the parapet rail of the choir loft and pointed to a small sacristy off the ambulatory as he said to Hickey, "Since we can't see the outside door of the bishop's sacristy or the elevator door, the police could theoretically beat the alarms and mines. Then we'd have policemen massed in that small sacristy."

Leary, who seemed to be able to hear things at great distances, called out from the far end of the choir loft. "And if they stick their heads into the ambulatory, I'll blow—"

Hickey shouted back, "Thank you, Mr. Leary. We know you will." He said softly to Flynn, "God Almighty, where'd you get that monster? I'll be afraid to scratch my ass down there."

Flynn answered quietly, "Yes, he has good eyes and ears."

"An American, isn't he?"

"Irish-American. Marine sniper in Vietnam."

"Does he know why he's here? Does he even know where the hell he *is*?"

"He's in a perch overlooking a free-fire zone. That's all he knows and all he cares about. He's being paid handsomely for his services. He's the only one of us besides you and me who has no relatives in British jails. I don't want a man up here with emotional ties to us. He'll kill according to standing orders, he'll kill any one of us I tell him to kill, and if we're attacked and overcome, he'll kill any of us who survives, if he's still able. He's the Angel of Death, the Grim Reaper, and the court of last resort." "Does everyone know all of this?"

"No."

Hickey smiled, a half-toothless grin. "I underestimated you, Brian."

"Yes. You've been doing that. Let's go on with this. The Arch-bishop's sacristy— a problem, but only one of many—"

"I wish you'd brought more people."

Flynn spoke impatiently. "I have a great deal of help on the outside, but how many people do you think I could find to come in here to die?"

A distant look came over the old man's face. "There were plenty of good men and women in Dublin on Easter Monday, 1916. More than the besieged buildings could hold." Hickey's eyes took in the quiet Cathedral below. "No lack of volunteers then. And faith! What faith we all had. In the early days of the First War, sometime before the Easter Rising, my brother was in the British Army. Lot of Irish lads were then. Still are. You've heard of the Angels of Mons? No? Well, my brother Bob was with the British Expeditionary Force in France, and they were about to be annihilated by an overwhelming German force. Then, at a place called Mons, a host of heavenly angels appeared and stood between them and the Germans. Understandably the Germans fell back in confusion. It was in all the papers at the time. And people *believed* it, Brian. They believed the British Army was so blessed by God that He sent His angels to inter-vene on their behalf against their enemy."

Flynn looked at him. "Sounds like a mass hallucination of desperate men. When we start seeing angels here, we'll know we've had it, and—" He broke off abruptly and looked at Hickey closely in the dim light. For a brief second he imagined he was back in Whitehorn Abbey, listening to the stories of the old priest.

"What is it, lad?"

"Nothing. I suppose one shouldn't doubt the intervention of the supernatural. I'll tell you about it tomorrow."

Hickey laughed. "If you can tell it tomorrow, I'll believe it."

Flynn forced a smile in return. "I may be telling it to you in another place."

"Then I'll surely believe it."

Megan Fitzgerald came up behind George Sullivan setting the last of the mines on the south transept door. "Finished?"

Sullivan turned abruptly. "Jesus, don't do that, Megan, when I'm working with explosives."

She looked at Sullivan, dressed splendidly in the kilts of a bagpiper of the New York Police Emerald Society. "Grab your gear and follow me. Bring your bagpipes." She led him to a small door at the corner of the transept, and they walked up a spiral stone staircase, coming out onto the long south triforium. A flagpole with a huge American flag hanging from it pointed across the nave toward the Papal flag on the opposite triforium. Megan looked to the left, at the choir loft below, and watched Flynn and Hickey poring over their blueprints like two generals on the eve of battle. She found it odd that such different men seemed to be getting on well. She hadn't liked the idea of bringing John Hickey in at the last moment. But the others felt they needed the old hero to legitimize themselves, a bona fide link with 1916, as though Hickey's presence could make them something other than the outcasts they all were.

She saw no need to draw on the past. The world had taken form for her in 1973 when she had seen her first bomb casualties in downtown Belfast on the way home from school, and had taken meaning and purpose when her older brother Tommy had been wounded and captured trying to free Sheila Malone. The distant past didn't exist, any more than the near future did. Her own personal memories were all the history she was concerned with.

She watched Flynn pointing and gesturing. He seemed not

much different from the old man beside him. Yet he had been different once. To Tommy Fitzgerald, Brian Flynn was everything a man should be, and she had grown up seeing Brian Flynn, the legend in the making, through her older brother's eyes. Then came Brian's arrest and his release, suspicious at best. Then the break with the IRA, the forming of the new Fenian Army, his recruiting of her and her younger brother Pedar, and, finally, her inevitable involvement with him. She had not been disappointed in him as a lover, but as a revolutionary he had flaws. He would hesitate before destroying the Cathedral, but she would see to it that this decision was out of his hands.

Sullivan called out from the far end of the triforium, "The view is marvelous. How's the food?"

Megan turned to him. "If you've no qualms about feasting on blood, it's good and ample."

Sullivan sighted through his rifle. "Don't be a beast, Megan." He raised the rifle and focused the scope on Abby Boland, noticing her open blouse. She saw him and waved. He waved back. "So near, yet so far."

"Give it a rest, George," said Megan impatiently. "You'll not be using it for much but peeing for yet a while." She looked at him closely. George Sullivan was not easily intimidated by her. He had that combination of smugness and devil-may-care personality that came with handling high explosives, a special gift of the gods, he had called it. Maybe. "Are you certain Hickey knows how to rig the bombs?"

Sullivan picked up his bagpipe and began blowing into it. He looked up. "Oh, yes. He's very good. World War Two techniques, but that's all right, and he's got the nerve for it."

"I'm interested in his skill, not his nerve. I'm to be his assistant."

"Good for you. Best to be close by if it goes wrong. Never

feel a thing. It'll be us poor bastards up here who'll be slowly crushed by falling stone. Picture it, Megan. Like Samson and Delilah, the temple falling about our heads, tons of stone quivering, falling.... Someone should have brought a movie camera."

"Next time. All right, George, the north transept is your sector of fire if they break in. But if they use armor through that door, Boland will lean over the north triforium and launch a rocket directly down at it. Your responsibility for armor is the south transept door below you. She'll cover you and you'll cover her with rifle fire."

"What if one of us is dead?"

"Then the other two, Gallagher and Farrell, will divide up the sector of the dead party."

"What if we're all dead?"

"Then it doesn't matter, does it, George? Besides, there's always Leary. Leary is immortal, you know."

"I've heard." He put the blowpipe to his mouth.

"Can you play 'Come Back to Erin'?"

He nodded as he puffed.

"Then play it for us, George."

He took a long breath and said, "To use an expression, Megan, you've not paid the piper, and you'll not call the tune. I'll play 'The Minstrel Boy' and you'll damn well like it. Go on, now, and leave me alone."

Megan looked at him, turned abruptly, and entered the small door that led down to the spiral stairs.

Sullivan finished inflating the bagpipe, bounced a few notes off the wall behind him, made the necessary tuning, then turned, bellied up to the stone parapet, and began to play. The haunting melody carried into every corner of the Cathedral and echoed off the stone. Acoustically bad for an organ or choir, Sullivan thought, but for a bagpipe it was lovely, sounding like the old Celtic warpipes echoing through the rocky glens of Antrim. The pipes were designed to echo from stone, he thought, and now that he heard his pipes in here, he would recommend their use in place of organs in Ireland. He had never sounded better.

He saw Abby Boland leaning across the parapet, looking at him, and he played to her, then turned east and played to his wife in Armagh prison, then turned to the wall behind him and played softly for himself.

CHAPTER 18

Brian Flynn listened to Sullivan for a few seconds. "The lad's not bad."

Hickey found his briar pipe and began filling it. "Reminds me of those Scottish and Irish regiments in the First War. Used to go into battle with pipes skirling. Jerry's machine guns ripped them up. Never missed a note, though—good morale-builder." He looked down at the blueprints. "I'm beginning to think whoever designed this place designed Tut's tomb."

"Same mentality. Tricks with stone. Fellow named Renwick in this case. There's a likeness of him on one of those stained-glass windows. Over there. Looks shifty."

"Even God looks shifty in stained glass, Brian."

Flynn consulted the blueprints. "Look, there are six large supporting piers— they're towers, actually. They all have doors either on the inside or outside of the Cathedral, and they all have spiral staircases that go into the triforia.... All except this one, which passes through Farrell's triforium. It has no doors, either on the blueprints or in actuality."

"How did he get up there?"

"From the next tower which has an outside door." Flynn looked up at Eamon Farrell. "I told him to look for the way into this tower, but he hasn't found it."

"Aye, and probably never will. Maybe that's where they burn heretics. Or hide the gold."

"Well, you may joke about it, but it bothers me. Not even a church architect wastes time and money building a tower from basement to roof without putting it to some use. I'm certain there's a staircase in there, and entrances as well. We'll have to find out where."

"We may find out quite unexpectedly," said Hickey.

"That we may."

"Later," said Hickey, "perhaps I'll call on Renwick's ghost for help."

"I'd settle for the present architect. Stillway." Flynn tapped his finger on the blueprints. "I think there are more hollow spaces here than even Renwick knew. Passages made by masons and workmen—not unusual in a cathedral of this size and style."

"Anyway, you've done a superb job, Brian. It will take the police some time to formulate an attack."

"Unless *they* get hold of Stillway and his set of blueprints before our people on the outside find him." He turned and looked at the telephone mounted on the organ. "What's taking the police so long to call?"

Hickey picked up the telephone. "It's working." He came back to the rail. "They're still confused. You've disrupted their chain of command. They'll be more angry with you for that than for this."

"Aye. It's like a huge machine that has malfunctioned. But when they get it going again, they'll start to grind away at us. And there's no way to shut it down again once it starts."

Eamon Farrell, a middle-aged man and the oldest of the Fenians, except for Hickey, looked down from the six-story-high northeast triforium, watching Flynn and Hickey as they came out of the bell-tower lobby. Flynn wore the black suit of a priest, Hickey an old tweed jacket. They looked for all the world like a priest and an architect talking over renovations. Farrell shifted his gaze to the four hostages sitting in the sanctuary, waiting for some indication as to their fate. He felt sorry for them. But he also felt sorry for his only son, Eamon, Jr., in Long Kesh. The boy was in the second week of a hunger strike and wouldn't last much longer.

Farrell slipped his police tunic off and hung it over the parapet, then turned and walked back to the wooden kneewall behind him. In the wall was a small door, and he opened it, knelt, and shone his flashlight at the plaster lathing of the ceiling of the bride's room below him. He walked carefully in a crouch onto a rafter, and played the light around the dark recess, moving farther out onto the wooden beam. There was a fairly large space around him, a sort of lower attic below the main attic, formed by the downward pitch of the triforium roof before it met the outside wall of stone buttresses.

He stepped to the beam on his right and raised his light to the corner where the two walls came together. In the corner was part of a rounded tower made of brick and mortar. He made his way toward it and knelt precariously on a beam over the plaster. He reached out and ran his hand over a very small black iron door, almost the color of the dusty brick.

Eamon Farrell unhooked the rusty latch and pulled the door open. A familiar smell came out of the dark opening, and he reached his hand in and touched the inside of the brick, then brought his hand away and looked at it. Soot.

Farrell directed the light through the door and saw that the round hollow space was at least six feet across. He angled the light down but could see nothing. Carefully he eased his head and shoulders through the door and looked up. He sensed rather than saw the lights of the towering city above him. A cold down-draft confirmed that the hollow tower was a chimney.

Something caught his eye, and he pointed the light at it. A rung set into the brick. He played the light up and down the chimney and saw a series of iron rungs that ran up the chimney to the top. He withdrew from the opening and closed the thick steel door, then latched it firmly shut. He remained crouched on the beam for a long time, then came out of the small attic and moved to the parapet, calling down to Flynn.

Flynn quickly moved under the triforium. "Did you find something, Eamon?"

Farrell hesitated, then made a decision. "I see the tower as it comes through behind the triforium. There's no doorway."

Flynn looked impatient. "Throw me the rope ladder, and I'll have a look."

"No. No, don't bother. I'll keep looking."

Flynn considered, then said, "That tower has a function—find out what it is."

Farrell nodded. "I will." But he had already found it, and found an escape route for himself, a way to get out of this mess alive if the coming negotiations failed.

Frank Gallagher looked out from the southeast triforium. Everyone seemed to be in place. Directly across from him was Farrell. Sullivan, he noticed, was making eyes at Boland across the nave. Jean Kearney and Arthur Nulty were in the attic building bonfires and discussing, no doubt, the possibility of getting in a quick one before they died. Megan's brother, Pedar, was on the crypt landing watching the sacristy gates. He was young, not eighteen, but steady as a rock. *For thou art Peter, and upon this Rock,* thought Gallagher, who was devoutly Catholic, *upon this Rock, I will build my church; and the gates of hell shall not prevail against it.* The Thompson submachine gun helped, too.

Devane and Mullins had the nicest views, Gallagher thought, but it was probably cold up there. Megan, Hickey, and Flynn floated around like nervous hosts and hostess before a party, checking on the seating and ambience.

Frank Gallagher removed the silk parade marshal's sash and dropped it on the floor. He sighted his rifle at the choir loft, and Leary came into focus. He quickly put the rifle down. You didn't point a rifle at Leary. You didn't do anything to, with, or for Leary. You just avoided Leary like you avoided dark alleys and contagion wards.

Gallagher looked down at the hostages. His orders were simple. *If they leave the sanctuary, unescorted, shoot them.* He stared at the Cardinal. Somehow Frank Gallagher had to square this thing he was doing, square it with the Cardinal or his own priest later—later, when it was over, and people saw what a fine thing they had done.

CHAPTER 19

Maureen watched Flynn as he moved about the Cathedral. He moved with a sense of purpose and animation that she recognized, and she knew he was feeling very alive and very good about himself. She watched the Cardinal sitting directly across from her. She envied him for what she knew was his absolute confidence in his position, his unerring belief that he was a blameless victim, a potential martyr. But for herself, and perhaps for Baxter, there was some guilt, and some misgivings, about their roles. And those feelings could work to undermine their ability to resist the pressures that the coming hours or days would bring.

She glanced quickly around at the triforia and choir loft. *Well done, Brian, but you're short of troops.* She tried to remember the faces of the people she had seen close in, and was fairly certain that she didn't know any of them except Gallagher and Devane. Megan and Pedar Fitzgerald she knew of through their brother, Tommy. What had become of all the people she once called sisters and brothers? The camps or the grave. These were their relatives, recruited in that endless cycle of blood vengeance that characterized the Irish war. With that kind of perpetual vendetta she couldn't see how it would end until they were all dead.

She spoke to Baxter. "If we run quickly to the south transept doors, we could be in the vestibule, hidden from the snipers, before they reacted. I can disarm almost any mine in a few seconds. We'd be through the outer door and into the street before anyone reached the vestibule."

Baxter looked at her. "What in the world are you talking about?"

"I'm talking about getting out of here alive."

"Look up there. Five snipers. And how can we run off and leave the Cardinal and Father Murphy?"

"They can come with us."

"Are you mad? I won't hear of it."

"I'll do what I damned well please."

He saw her body tense and reached out and held her arm. "No, you don't. Listen here, we have a chance to be released if—"

"No chance at all. From what I picked up of their conversation, they are going to demand the release of prisoners in internment. Do you think your government will agree to *that*?"

"I'm...I'm sure something will be worked out..."

"Bloody stupid diplomat. I know these people better than you do, and I know your government's position on Irish terrorists. No negotiation. End of discussion."

"...but we have to wait for the right moment. We need a plan."

She tried to pull her arm away, but he held it tightly. She said, "I wish I had a shilling for every prisoner who stood in front of a firing squad because he waited for the right moment to make a break. The right moment, according to your own soldier's manual, is as soon after capture as possible. Before the enemy settles down, before they get their bearings. We've already waited too long. Let go of me."

"No. Let me think of something—something less suicidal."

"Listen to me, Baxter—we're not physically bound in any

way yet. We must act now. You and I are as good as dead. The Cardinal and the priest may be spared. We won't be."

Baxter took a long breath, then said, "Well...it may be that I'm as good as dead...but don't you know this fellow, Flynn? Weren't you in the IRA together...?"

"We were lovers. That's another reason I won't stay here at his mercy for one more second."

"I see. Well, if you want to commit suicide, that's one thing. But don't tell me you're trying to escape. And don't expect me to get myself killed with you."

"You'll wish later you'd taken a quick bullet."

He spoke evenly. "If an opportunity presents itself, I *will* try to escape." He paused. "If not, then when the time comes I'll die with some dignity, I hope."

"I hope so, too. You can let go of my arm now. I'll wait. But if we're bound or thrown into the crypt or something like that—then, as you're thrashing about with two shattered kneecaps, you can think about how we could have run. That's how they do it, you know. They kneecap you hours before they shoot you in the heart."

Baxter drew a deep breath. "I suppose I lack a sufficiently vivid imagination to be frightened enough to try anything...But you're supplying me with the necessary picture." He took his hand away from hers and sat watching her out of the corner of his eyes, but she seemed content to sit there. "Steady."

"Oh, take your bloody British steady and shove it."

Baxter remembered her bravery on the steps and realized that part of that, consciously or unconsciously, was for him, or more accurately, what he represented. He realized also that her survival was to some extent in his hands. As for himself, he felt indignant over his present position but felt no loss of dignity. The distinction was not a small one and would determine how each of them would react to their captivity, and if they were to die, how they would die. He said, "Whenever you're ready... I'm with you."

Pedar Fitzgerald looked up the right-hand stairs as his sister came down toward him. He stood and cradled the Thompson submachine gun under his arm. "How's it going, Megan?"

"Everything's set but the bombs." She looked down the stairs through the gate into the empty sacristy. "Any movement?"

"No. Things are quiet." He forced a smile. "Maybe they don't know we're here."

She smiled back. "Oh, they know. They know, Pedar." She drew her pistol and descended the stairs, then examined the lock and chain on the gates. She listened, trying to hear a sound from the four side corridors that led into the sacristy. Something moved, someone coughed quietly. She turned and said to her brother in a loud voice, "When you shoot, boys, shoot between the bars. Don't damage the lock and chain. Those Thompsons can get away from you."

Pedar smiled. "We've handled them enough times."

She winked at him and climbed back up the stairs, sticking the pistol in the waistband of her jeans. She moved close to him and touched his cheek lightly. "We're putting all we've got on this, Pedar. Tommy is in for life. We could be dead or in an American prison for life. Mum is near dead for worry. None of us will see each other again if this goes badly."

Pedar Fitzgerald felt tears forming in his eyes but fought them back. He found his voice and said, "We've all put everything on Brian, Megan. Do you... do you trust him...? Can he do it, then?"

Megan Fitzgerald looked into her brother's eyes. "If he can't and we see he can't, then... you and I, Pedar... we'll take over.

The family comes first." She turned and climbed up to the sanctuary, came around the altar, and looked at Maureen sitting in the pew. Their eyes met and neither looked away.

Flynn watched from the ambulatory, then called out, "Megan. Come take a walk with us."

Megan Fitzgerald turned away from Maureen and joined Flynn and Hickey as they began walking up the center aisle. "There are people in the sacristy corridors," she said.

Flynn nodded as he walked. "They won't do anything until they've established who we are and what we want. We've a little time yet."

When they reached the front door, Flynn ran his hands over the cold bronze ceremonial doors. "Magnificent. I'd like to take one with me." He examined the mines, then turned back and motioned around the Cathedral. "We've set up a perfect and very deadly cross fire from five long, concealed perches protected by stone parapets. As long as we hold the high spots we can dominate the Cathedral. But if we lose the high ground and the fight takes place on the floor, it will be very difficult."

Hickey relit his pipe. "As long as there's no fighting in the bookstore."

Megan looked at him. "I hope you keep your sense of humor when the bullets start ripping through the smoke around your face."

He blew smoke toward her. "Lass, I've been shot at more times than you've had your period."

Flynn interrupted. "If you were a police commander, John, what would you do?"

Hickey thought a moment, then said, "I'd do what the British Army did in downtown Dublin in 1916. I'd call in the artillery and level the fucking place. Then I'd offer surrender terms."

"But this is not Dublin, 1916," said Flynn. "I think the people out there have to act with great restraint."

"You may call it restraint, I'd call it cunning. They'll eventually have to attack when they see we won't be talked out. But they'll do it without the big guns. More tactics, less gunpowder—gas, helicopters, concussion grenades that don't damage property. There's a lot available to them today." He looked around. "But we may be able to hold on."

Megan said, "We *will* hold on."

Flynn added, "We have gas masks, incidentally."

"Do you, now? You're a very thorough man, Brian. The old IRA was always going off half-cocked to try to grab the British lion's balls. And the lion loved it— loved feasting on IRA." He looked up at the triforia, then down at the deserted main floor. "Too bad, though, you couldn't find more men—"

Flynn interrupted. "They're a good lot. Each of them is worth twenty of the old-type ruffians."

"Are they, then? Even the women?"

Megan stiffened and started to speak.

Flynn interjected, "Nothing wrong with women, you old bastard. I've learned that over the years. They're steady. Loyal."

Hickey glanced at the sanctuary where Maureen sat, then made an exaggerated pretense of looking away quickly. "I suppose many of them are." He sat at the edge of a pew and yawned. "Tiring business. Megan, lass, I hope you didn't think I included you when I spoke about women."

"Oh, go to hell." She turned and walked away.

Flynn let out a long breath of annoyance. "Why are you provoking her?"

Hickey watched her walk toward the altar. "Cold, cold. Must be like fucking a wooden icebox."

"Look, John—"

The telephone on the chancel organ beside the altar rang loudly, and everyone turned toward it.

CHAPTER 20

Brian Flynn put his hand on the ringing phone and looked at Hickey. "I was beginning to believe no one cared—one hears such stories about New York indifference."

Hickey laughed. "I can't think of a worse nightmare for an Irish revolutionary than to be ignored. Answer it, and if it's someone wanting to sell aluminum siding for the rectory, I suggest we just go home."

Flynn drew a deep breath and picked up the receiver. "MacCumail here."

There was a short silence, then a man's voice said, "Who?"

"This is Finn MacCumail, Chief of the Fenians. Who is this?"

The voice hesitated for a moment, then the man said, "This is Police Sergeant Tezik. Tactical Patrol Unit. I'm calling from the rectory. What the hell is going on in there?"

"Not much of anything at the moment."

"Why are the doors locked?"

"Because there are mines attached to each one. It's for your own protection, actually."

"Why...?"

"Listen, Sergeant Tezik, and listen very closely. We have four hostages in here— Father Timothy Murphy, Maureen Malone, Sir Harold Baxter, and the Cardinal himself. If the police try to

force their way in, the mines will explode, and if they keep coming, the hostages will be shot and the Cathedral will be set afire.
Do you understand?"

"Jesus Christ..."

"Get this message to your superiors quickly, and get a ranking man on the phone. Be quick about it, Sergeant Tezik."

"Yeah...all right.... Listen, everything's pretty screwed up
here, so just take it easy. As soon as we get things sorted out,
we'll have a police official on the phone with you. Okay?"

"Make it quick. And no nonsense or there will be a great
number of dead people you'll have to answer for. No helicopters
in the area. No armored vehicles on the streets. I have men in
the towers with rockets and rifles. I've got a gun pointed at the
Cardinal's head right now."

"Okay—take it easy. Don't—"

Flynn hung up and turned to Hickey and Megan, who had
joined them. "A TPU sergeant—spiritual kin to the RUCs and
the Gestapo. I didn't like the tone of his voice."

Hickey nodded. "It's their height. Gives them a sense of superiority." He smiled. "Easier targets, though."

Flynn looked at the doors. "We caused a bit *too* much confusion. I hope they reestablish some chain of command before the
hotheaded types start acting. The next few minutes are going to
be critical."

Megan turned to Hickey and spoke quickly. "Do you want
Sullivan to help you place the bombs?"

"Megan, love, I want *you* to help me. Run along and get what
we need." He waited until Megan left, then turned to Flynn.
"We have to make a decision now about the hostages—a decision about who kills which one."

Flynn looked at the Cardinal sitting straight on his throne,
looking every inch a Prince of the Church. He knew it wasn't

vanity or affectation he was observing but a product of two thousand years of history, ceremony, and training. The Cardinal would be not only a difficult hostage but a difficult man to make a corpse of. He said to Hickey, "It would be a hard man who could put a bullet into him."

Hickey's eyes, which normally twinkled with an old man's mischief, turned narrow and malevolent. "Well, I'll do him, if"—Hickey inclined his head toward Maureen— "if you'll do her."

Flynn glanced at Maureen sitting in the clergy pews between Baxter and Father Murphy. He hesitated, then said, "Yes, all right. Go on and plant the bombs."

Hickey ignored him. "As for Baxter, anyone will kill him. You tell Megan to do the priest. The little bitch should draw her first blood the hard way—not with Maureen."

Flynn looked at Hickey closely. It was becoming apparent that Hickey was obsessed with taking as many people with him as possible. "Yes," he said, "that seems the way to handle it." He looked out over the vast expanse around him and said, more to himself than to Hickey, "God, how did we get in this place, and how can we get out?"

Hickey took Flynn's arm and pressed it tightly. "Funny, that's almost exactly what Padraic Pearse said when his men seized the General Post Office in Dublin, Easter Monday. I remember it very clearly. The answer then, as it is now, is that you got in with luck and blarney, but you'll not get out alive...." He released Flynn's arm and slapped him on the back. "Cheer up, lad, we'll take a good number of them with us, like we did in 1916. Burn this place down while we're about it. Blow it up, too, if we get those bombs in place."

Flynn stared at Hickey. He might have to kill Hickey before Hickey got them all killed.

* * *

Megan Fitzgerald mounted the sanctuary, carrying two suitcases. She walked rapidly to the right side of the high altar, and placed them beside a bronze plate set into the marble floor, then lifted the plate. John Hickey came up beside her and picked up the suitcases. "Go on."

Megan descended a shaky metal ladder, found a light chain, and pulled it. Hickey climbed down and handed the suitcases to Megan, who placed them gently on the floor. They examined the unevenly excavated crawl space. Building rubble, pipes, and ducts nearly filled the space around them, and it was difficult to move or to see clearly. Megan called out, "Here's the outer wall of the crypt."

Hickey called back, "Yes, and here's the wall of the staircase that continues down into the sacristy. Come along." Hickey turned on a flashlight and probed the area to his front as he moved, dragging one of the suitcases behind him.

They followed a parallel course to the descending staircase wall, hunching lower as they progressed. The dirt floor turned to Manhattan bedrock, and Hickey called out, "I see it up ahead." He crawled to a protruding mound from which rose the footing of a massive column. "Here it is. Come closer." He played the light around the dark spaces. "See? Here's where they cut through the old foundation and footing to let the sacristy stairs pass through. If we dug down farther, we'd find the sacristy's subbasement. It's somewhat like the layout of a modern split-level home."

Megan was skeptical. "Damned confusing sort of place. The fire in the attic is much surer."

"Don't be getting cold feet, now, Megan. I'll not blow you up."

"I'm only concerned with placing them properly."

"Of course." Hickey ran his hand over the column. "Now the story is that when they blasted the new stairs through the foundation in 1904 they weakened these flanking columns. In architectural terms, they're under stress. The old boy whose father worked on the blasting told me that the Irish laborers believed only God Almighty kept the whole place from collapsing when they set the dynamite. But God Almighty doesn't live here anymore, so when we plant this plastic and it blows, nothing will hold up the roof."

"And if it does hold up, will you be a believer then?"

"No. I'll think we didn't place the explosives properly." Hickey opened the suitcase and pulled out twenty white bricks wrapped in cellophane. He tore the cellophane from the white, putty-like substance and molded a brick into the place where the bedrock met the hewn and mortared stone of the column footing. Megan joined him, and they sculpted the bricks around the footing. He handed her the flashlight. "Hold this steady."

Hickey implanted four detonators, connected by wires to a battery pack, into the plastic. He picked up an alarm clock and looked at his watch. "It's four minutes after six now. The clock doesn't know A.M. from P.M., so the most time I can give it is eleven hours and fifty-nine minutes." He began turning the clock's alarm dial slowly counter-clockwise, talking as he did. "So I'll set the alarm for five minutes after six— no, I mean three minutes after six." He laughed as he kept turning the dial. "I remember once, a lad in Galway who didn't understand that. At midnight he set the timer to go off at one minute after twelve, in what he thought would be the afternoon. British officer's club, I think it was. Yes, lunchtime, he thought. Anyway, at one minute past midnight...he was standing before his Maker, who must have wondered how he became so unmade." He laughed again as he joined the clock wire to the batteries.

"At least don't get us killed until we've set the one on the other side."

"Good point. Did I do that right? Well, I hope so." He pulled the clock switch, and the loud ticking filled the damp space. He looked at her. "And don't forget, my sharp little lass, only you and I know exactly where these are planted, which gives us some advantages and a bit of power with your friend, Mr. Flynn. Only you and I can decide if we want to give an extension of the deadline to meet our demands." He laughed as he pushed the clock into the explosives and molded the plastic around it. "But if the police have killed us before then, well, at three minutes after six—which incidentally happens to be the exact time of sunrise—they'll get a message from us, directly from hell." He took some earth from the floor and pressed it into the white plastic. "There. That looks innocent, doesn't it? Give me a hand here." He spoke as he continued to camouflage the plastic explosives. "You're young. You don't want it to end so soon, I know, but you must have some sort of death wish to get mixed up in this. Nobody dropped you in through the roof. You people planned this for over a year. Wish I'd had a year to think about it. I'd be home now where I belong."

He picked up the flashlight and turned it onto her face. Her bright green eyes glowed back at him. "I hope you had a good look at this morning's sunrise, lass, because the chances are you'll not see another one."

Patrick Burke moved carefully from under the portal of the bronze ceremonial doors and looked up at the north tower. The Cathedral's floodlights cast a blue-white brilliance over the recently cleaned stonework and onto the fluttering harp flag of green and gold, reminding Burke irreverently of a Disney World castle. Burke looked over the south tower. The louvers were torn open, and a man was looking down at him through a rifle scope. Burke turned his back on the sniper and saw a tall uniformed patrolman of the Tactical Patrol Unit hurrying toward him through the sleet.

The young patrolman hesitated, then said, "Are you a sergeant or better?"

"Can't you tell?"

"I . . ."

"Lieutenant, Intelligence."

The patrolman began speaking rapidly. "Christ, Lieutenant, my sergeant, Tezik, is in the rectory. He's got a platoon of TPU ready to move. He wants to hit the doors with trucks—I don't think we should do anything until we get orders—"

Burke moved quickly across the steps and followed the north wall of the Cathedral through the gardens and terraces until he came to the rear of the rectory. He entered a door that led to a large vestibule. Scattered throughout the halls and offices and sitting on the stairs were about thirty men of the Tactical Patrol Unit, an elite reaction force, looking fresh, young, big, and eager. Burke turned to the patrolman who had followed him. "Where's Tezik?"

"In the Rector's office." He leaned toward Burke and said quietly, "He's a little . . . high-strung. You know?"

Burke left the patrolman in the vestibule and moved quickly up the stairs between the sitting TPU men. On the next landing he opened a door marked RECTOR.

Monsignor Downes sat at his desk in the center of the large, old-fashioned office, still wearing his topcoat and smoking a cigarette. Burke stood in the doorway. "Monsignor, where's the police sergeant?"

Monsignor Downes looked up blankly. "Who are you?"

"Burke. Police. Where is—?"

Monsignor Downes spoke distractedly. "Oh, yes. I know you. Friend of Father Murphy...saw you last night at the Waldorf...Maureen Malone...you were—"

"Yes, sir. Where is Sergeant Tezik?"

A deep voice called out from behind a set of double doors to Burke's right. "I'm in here!"

Burke moved through the doors into a larger inner office with a fireplace and bookshelves. Sergeant Tezik sat at an over-sized desk in the rear room. "Burke. ID. Get your men out of the rectory and on the street where they belong. Help with crowd control."

Sergeant Tezik stood slowly, revealing a frame six-and-a-half feet tall, weighing, Burke guessed, about two seventy-five. Tezik said, "Who died and left you in charge?"

Burke closed the door behind him. "Actually, Commissioner Dwyer *is* dead. Heart attack."

"I heard. That don't make *you* the PC."

"No, but I'll do for now." Burke moved farther into the room. "Don't try to take advantage of this mess, Tezik. Don't play macho man with other people's lives. You know the saying, Tezik: When a citizen is in trouble he calls a cop; when a cop is in trouble he calls Emergency Service."

"I'm using what they call personal initiative, Lieutenant. I figure that before those bastards get themselves dug in—"

"Who have you called? Where are your orders coming from?"

"They're coming from my brains."

"That's too bad."

Tezik continued, unperturbed, "I can't get an open line no place."

"Did you try Police Plaza?"

"I *told* you, I can't get through. This is a revolution, for

Christ's sake. You know?" He hesitated, then added, "Only the interphone in the Cathedral complex is working.... I spoke to somebody..."

Burke moved to the desk. "Who did you speak to?"

"Some guy—Finn?—something. Name's on the Cathedral doors."

"What did he say?"

"Nothing." He thought a moment. "Said he had four hostages."

"Who?"

"The Cardinal—"

"Shit!"

"Yeah. And they got a priest, too—Murphy. And some broad whose name I don't remember—that peace woman, I think. Name was in the papers. And some English royalty guy, Baker."

"Jesus Christ. What else did he say, Tezik? Think."

Tezik seemed to be thinking. "Let me see.... He said he'd kill them—they always say that. Right? And burn the Cathedral—how do you burn a Cathedral—?"

"With matches."

"Not possible. Stone don't burn. Anyway, the doors are supposed to be rigged with explosives, but, shit, I have thirty-five TPU in the rectory, ready to go. I got a dozen more standing in the halls that lead to the sacristy. I got four-wheel-drive equipment from the Sanitation Department, with my men driving, ready to hit the doors, and—"

"Forget it."

"Like hell. Look, the longer you wait, the deeper the other guy digs in. That's a fact."

"Where did you learn that fact?"

"In the Marines. 'Nam."

"Sure. Listen, Tezik, this is midtown Manhattan, not Fuck

Luck Province. A great cathedral full of art treasures has been seized, Tezik. And *hostages,* Tezik. The dinks never held hostages, did they? Police policy is containment, not cavalry charges. Right?"

"This is different. The command structure's broken down. One time, near Quangtri, I was on patrol—"

"Who cares?"

Tezik stiffened. "Let me see your shield."

Burke held out his badge case, then put it away. "Look, Tezik, these people who've taken the Cathedral do not present a clear or immediate danger to anyone outside the Cathedral—"

"They shot out a spotlight. They hung a flag from the steeple. They could be Reds, Burke—revolutionaries.... Fenians...what the hell *are* Fenians?"

"Listen to me—leave this to Emergency Services and the Hostage Negotiator. Okay?"

"I'm going in now, Burke. Now, before they start shooting into the city—before they start shooting the hostages...or burning the Cathedral—"

"It's stone."

"Back off, Lieutenant. I'm the man on the spot, and I have to do what I have to do."

Burke unbuttoned his topcoat and hooked his thumbs into his belt. "No way."

Neither man spoke for several seconds, then Tezik said, "I'm walking to that door."

Burke said, "Try it."

The office was very still except for the ticking of a mantel clock.

They both sidestepped clear of the desk, then faced off, each man knowing that he had unwittingly backed the other against a wall, and neither knowing what to do about it.

CHAPTER 21

Father Murphy addressed Maureen and Baxter sitting beside him on the pew. "I'm going to speak to His Eminence. Will you come with me?"

Maureen shook her head.

Baxter said, "I'll be along shortly."

Father Murphy crossed the marble floor, knelt at the throne and kissed the episcopal ring, then rose and began speaking to the Cardinal in a low voice. Maureen watched them, then said to Baxter, "I can't stay here another moment."

He studied her closely. Her eyes were darting around wildly, and he saw that her body was shaking again.

He put his hand on her arm. "You really must get a grip on yourself."

"Oh, go to hell! How could you understand? For me this is like sitting in a room full of nightmares come to life."

"Let me see if I can get you a drink. Perhaps they have tranquilizers—"

"No! Listen, I'm not afraid of..."

"Talk about it if it will help."

Maureen tried to steady her shaking legs. "It's lots of things.... It's *him*. Flynn. He can...he has a power...no, not a power...a way of making you do things, and afterward you

wished you hadn't done them, and you feel awful. Do you understand?"

"I think—"

"And...these people...They're my people, you see, yet
they're not. Not anymore. I don't know how to react to them....
It's like a family meeting, and I've been called in because I've
done something terrible. They're not saying anything, just
watching me...." She shook her head. *Once in, never out.* She
was beginning to understand what that really meant, and it had
nothing to do with them but with oneself. She looked at Baxter.
"Even if they don't kill us...There are worse things...."

Baxter pressed her arm. "Yes...I think I understand—"

"I'm not explaining myself very well."

She knew of that total suppression of ego that made hostages
zombies, willing participants in the drama. And afterward the
mixed feelings, confusion, guilt. She remembered what one psychologist had said, *Once you're a hostage, you're a hostage for the
rest of your life.* She shook her head. No. She wouldn't let that
happen to her. No. "No!"

Baxter squeezed her hand. "Look here, we may have to die,
but I promise you, I won't let them abuse you...us. There'll be
no mock trial, no public recanting, no..." He found it difficult
to say what he knew her fears were. "No sadistic games, no psychological torture..."

She studied his face closely. He had more insight into these
things than she would have thought of a prim career diplomat.

He cleared his throat and said, "You're a very proud woman....
It's easier for me, actually. I hate them, and anything they do to me
just diminishes *them*—not *me*. It would help if you established the
proper relationship between yourself and them."

She shook her head. "Yes. I feel like a traitor, and I'm a patriot. I feel guilty, and I'm the victim. How can that be?"

"When we know the answers to that, we'll know how to deal with people like Brian Flynn."

She forced a smile. "I'm sorry I bothered you with all of this." Baxter started to interrupt, but she went on. "I thought you had a right to know, before I—"

Baxter grabbed at her arm, but she vaulted into the pew behind her, then jumped into the last row and grabbed at the two wooden columns of the carved screen, swinging her legs up to the balustrade before jumping down to the ambulatory six feet below.

Frank Gallagher leaned over the edge of the triforium. He pointed his rifle straight down at the top of her head, but the rifle was shaking so badly he didn't fire.

Eamon Farrell sighted across the sanctuary at her back but shifted his aim to her left and squeezed off a single round, which exploded into the stillness of the Cathedral.

George Sullivan and Abby Boland in the long triforium at the front of the Cathedral looked quickly at the source of the shot, then down at the aim of Farrell's rifle, but neither moved.

Leary had read the signs before Maureen even made her first move. As she came out of the pew he leaned farther over the parapet of the choir loft and followed her through his rifle scope. As she swung up to the balustrade he fired.

Maureen heard the sharp crack of Farrell's fire ring out behind her, then almost simultaneously heard the report roll down from the choir loft. Farrell's shot passed to her left. Leary's shot passed so close over her head she felt it touch her hair, and the wooden column near her left ear splintered in her face. Suddenly a pair of strong hands grabbed her shoulders and yanked her backward into the pew behind her. She looked up into the face of Harold Baxter. "Let go of me! Let go!"

Baxter was agitated and kept repeating, "Don't move! For God's sake, don't move!"

A sound of running footsteps came to the sanctuary, and Maureen saw Megan leaning into the pew, pointing a pistol at her face. Megan spoke softly. "Thank you." She cocked the pistol.

Baxter found himself sprawled over Maureen's body. "No! For God's sake, don't."

Megan screamed. "Move, you stupid bastard! Move!" She struck Baxter on the back of the head with her pistol, then pushed the muzzle into Maureen's throat.

The Cardinal was halfway across the sanctuary, shouting, "Stop that! Let them alone!" Father Murphy moved quickly behind Megan and grabbed her forearms. He picked her up high into the air, spun around, and dropped her on the floor. Megan slid on the polished marble, then shot up quickly into a kneeling position, and pointed the gun at the priest.

Brian Flynn's voice came clearly from the communion rail. "No!"

Megan pivoted around and stared at him, her pistol still leveled in front of her.

Flynn jumped over the gate and mounted the steps. "Go into the choir loft and stay there!"

Megan knelt on the floor, the pistol shaking in her hand. Everyone stood around her, motionless.

John Hickey quickly mounted the sanctuary steps. "Come with me, Megan." He walked to her, bent over at the waist, and took her arms in his hands. "Come on, then. That's it." He pulled her to her feet, and pushed her gunhand down to her side. He led her down the steps into the center aisle.

Flynn walked to the side of the pews and looked down. "Baxter, that was very gallant—very knightly. Stupid, too."

Harold Baxter picked himself up, then pulled Maureen up beside him.

Flynn looked at Maureen. "You won't get off that easy. And you almost got Sir Harry killed, too."

She didn't answer.

Baxter pressed a handkerchief to Maureen's cheek, where she had been hit by the wooden splinters.

Flynn's arm shot out and knocked Baxter's hand away. He went on calmly, "And don't think Mr. Leary is a bad shot. Had you gotten to the door he would have blown both your ankles away." Flynn turned. "And that goes as well for His Eminence and the good Father. And if by some miracle someone does get out of here, someone else dies for it." He looked at each of them. "Or should I just bind you all together? I'd rather not have to do that." He fixed each of the silent hostages with a cold stare. "Do not leave this sanctuary. Do we all understand the rules? Good. Everyone sit down." Flynn walked behind the altar and descended the steps to the crypt door landing. He spoke quietly to Pedar Fitzgerald. "Any movement down there?"

Fitzgerald answered softly. "Lot of commotion in the corridors, but it's quiet now. Is anyone hurt? Is my sister all right?"

"No one is hurt. Don't leave this post, no matter what you hear up there."

"I know. Look out for Megan, will you?"

"We're all watching out for Megan, Pedar."

A TPU man burst into the Monsignor's suite and ran to the inner office, out of breath. "Sergeant!"

Tezik and Burke both looked up.

The patrolman said excitedly, "The men in the corridors heard two shots fired—"

Tezik looked at Burke. "That's it. We're going in." Tezik moved quickly past Burke toward the door. Burke grabbed his shoulders and threw him back against the fireplace.

Tezik recovered his balance and shouted to the patrolman, "Arrest this man!"

The patrolman hesitated, then drew his service revolver.

The telephone rang.

Burke reached for it, but Tezik snatched the phone away and picked up the receiver. "Sergeant Tezik, NYPD."

Flynn sat at the chancel organ bench and said, "This is Finn MacCumail."

Tezik's voice was excited. "What happened in there? What's all that shooting?"

Flynn lit a cigarette. "Two shots hardly constitute 'all that shooting,' Sergeant. You ought to spend your next holiday in Belfast. Mothers fire two shots into the nursery just to wake the children."

"What—"

"No one is hurt," interrupted Flynn. "An automatic rifle discharged by accident." He said abruptly, "We're getting impatient, Sergeant."

"Just stay calm."

"The deadline for the demands I'm going to make is sunrise, and sunrise won't come any later because you're fucking around to find your chiefs." He hung up and drew on his cigarette. He thought about Maureen. He ought to tie her up for her own good, and for the good of them all, but perhaps he owed it to her to leave her options open and let her arrive at her own destiny without his interference. Sometime before sunrise they would be free of each other, or if not free, then together again, one way or the other.

CHAPTER 22

Sergeant Tezik replaced the receiver and glanced at Burke. "An automatic rifle went off by accident—that's what he said.... I don't know." Tezik seemed to have calmed down somewhat. "What do you think?"

Burke let out a long breath, then moved to the window overlooking the Cathedral and pulled back the drapes. "Take a look out there."

Sergeant Tezik looked at the floodlit Cathedral.

"Have you ever seen the inside of that place, Tezik?"

He nodded. "Holy Name Society communions. Couple of ... funerals."

"Yeah. Well, remember the triforia—the balconies? The choir loft? The acre or so of pews? It's a deathtrap in there, Sergeant, a fucking shooting gallery, and the TPU will be ducks." Burke let the drape fall and faced Tezik. "My intelligence sources say that those people have automatic weapons and sniper rifles. Maybe rockets. What do you have, Tezik? Six-shooters? Go back to your post. Tell your men to stand fast."

Tezik walked to a sideboard, poured a glass of brandy, drank it, then stared off at a point in space for a full minute. He looked at Burke and said, "Okay, I'm no hero." He forced a smile.

"Thought it might be a piece of cake. Couple of medals. Mayor's commendation... media stuff. You know?"

"Yeah, I've been to a lot of funerals like that."

The other TPU man holstered his revolver and left as Tezik moved sullenly toward the door.

"And no funny stuff, Sergeant."

Tezik walked into the outer office, then called back. "They want to speak to a high-ranking police official. Hope you can find one."

Burke moved to the desk and dialed a special number to his office in Police Plaza. After a long delay the phone rang and a woman answered. "Jackson."

"Louise, Burke here."

Duty Sergeant Louise Jackson, a middle-aged black woman, sounded tired. "Lieutenant! Where are you?"

"In the rectory of Saint Patrick's Cathedral. Put Langley on."

"The Inspector's in a helicopter with Deputy PC Rourke. They're trying to establish a command structure, but we lost radio contact with them when they got close to the Cathedral. Jamming device there. Every telephone line in the city is overloaded except these special ones, and they're not so good either. Everything's pretty crazy here."

"It's a little messy here, too. Listen, you call the Hostage Negotiator's office upstairs. Have them get hold of Bert Schroeder, quick. We have a hostage situation here."

"Damn it. That's what we thought. The BSS guarding the VIPs on the steps just called in. They lost some people in the shuffle, but they were a little vague about who and how."

"I'll tell you who and how in a second. Okay, call the Emergency Service office— Captain Bellini, if he's available. Explain that the Cathedral is held by gunmen and tell them to assemble siege equipment, snipers, and whatever other personnel and equipment is necessary, in the Cardinal's residence. Got that?"

"This one's going to be a bitch."

"For sure. Okay, I have a situation report and a message from the gunmen, Louise. I'll give it to you, and you call the Commissioner's office. They'll call everyone on the Situation A list. Ready to copy?"

"Shoot."

"At approximately 5:20 P.M. Saint Patrick's Cathedral was seized by an unknown number of gunmen—" Burke finished his report. "I'm designating the rectory as the command post. Get Ma Bell on the horn and have them put extra phone lines into the rectory according to existing emergency procedures. Got that?"

"Yes.... Pat, are you authorized—?"

Burke felt the sweat collecting around his collar and loosened it. "Louise, don't ask those kinds of questions. We've got to wing this one. Okay?"

"Okay."

"Do your best to contact those people. Stay cool."

"I'm cool. But you ought to see the people here. Everybody thinks it's some kind of *insurrection* or something. Albany and Washington called the PC's office— couldn't get a straight answer from City Hall or Gracie Mansion—PC's office called here. Want to know if it's an insurrection—or a race riot. Can you tell if it's an insurrection? Just for the record."

"Tell Albany and Washington that nobody in New York cares enough to start an insurrection. As far as I can make out, the Fenians provoked a disturbance to cover their seizing of the Cathedral. It got out of hand—a lot of happy citizens cutting loose. Do you have any reports from our people in the field?"

"Not a one. You're the first."

"One more thing. Get John Hickey's file sent here as soon as possible. And see what we have on a Northern Irishman named Brian Flynn." He hung up.

Burke walked into the outer office. "Monsignor?"

Monsignor Downes put down his telephone. "I can't get through to *anyone*. I have to speak to the Vicar General. I have to call the Apostolic Delegate in Washington. What's happening? What is going on here?"

Burke looked into Downes's ashen face, moved to the coffee table, and picked up a bottle of wine and a glass.

"Have some of this. The phones will be clear later. Couple of million people are trying to call home at the same time, that's all. We're going to have to use this rectory as a command post."

Monsignor Downes ignored the wine. "Command post?"

"Please clear the rectory and evacuate all the office personnel and priests. Leave a switchboard operator on until I can get a police operator here." Burke looked at his watch and considered a moment, then said, "How do I get into the corridor that connects with the sacristy?"

Monsignor Downes gave him a set of involved and disjointed instructions.

The door swung open and a tall man in a black topcoat burst in. He held up his badge case. "Lieutenant Young. Bureau of Special Services." He looked at the Monsignor, then at Burke, and said, "Who are you?"

"Burke. ID."

The man went directly to the coffee table and poured a glass of wine. "Christ— excuse me, Father—damn it, we've accounted for every VIP on the steps except three."

Burke watched him drink. "Let me guess—ID guys are good at guessing. You lost the Cardinal, Baxter, and the Malone woman."

Lieutenant Young looked at him quickly. "Where are they? They're not in the Cathedral, are they?"

"I'm afraid they are."

"Oh, Christ—sorry—shit. That's it. That's my job. Forget it. Forget it."

"Three out of about a hundred VIPs isn't bad."

"Don't joke! This is bad. Very bad."

"They're unharmed as far as I know," added Burke. "They also have a parish priest—Murphy. Not a VIP, so don't worry about that."

"Damn it. I lost three VIPs." He rambled on as he poured himself another glass. "Damn it, they should have sent the Secret Service. When the Pope came, the President sent the Secret Service to help us." He looked at Burke and the Monsignor and went on. "Most of the BSS was up by the reviewing stands. Byrd had all the good men. I got stuck with a handful of incompetents."

"Right." Burke moved to the door. "Get some competent men to stay with Monsignor Downes here. He's a VIP. I'm going to try to speak with the gunmen. They're VIPs, too."

Young glanced at Burke and said fiercely, "Why didn't you tell us something like this was going to happen, Burke?"

"You didn't ask." Burke left the office, descended the stairs, and found an elevator that took him into the basement. He came upon a worried-looking Hispanic custodian. "Sacristy," said Burke without preamble.

The man led him to a passage and pointed. Burke saw six TPU men standing along the walls with guns drawn. He held up his badge case and motioned the men to draw back from the sacristy. He unholstered his revolver, put it in his topcoat pocket, then walked down the short staircase to the opening of the passage. Burke put his head slowly around the corner and looked into the marble vaulted sacristy.

A TPU man behind him whispered, "Guy's got a Thompson at the top of those stairs."

Burke moved carefully into the sacristy, down the length of a row of vestment tables that ran along the wall to the right. At the end of the tables was another arched opening, and through it he could see a dimly lit polygon-shaped room of stone and brick.

Burke moved slowly toward the gates, keeping out of sight of the staircase opening. He heard muffled voices echoing down the staircase. Burke knew he had to speak with Finn MacCumail, and he had to have it together when he did. He leaned back against the marble wall to the side of the stairs and listened to his heart beat. He filled his lungs several times but couldn't find his voice. His hands clutched around the revolver in his pocket, and he pulled his hand free and steadied it against the wall. He looked at his watch. One minute. In one minute he would call for Finn MacCumail.

Maureen sat in the pew, her face in her hands, and Father Murphy and the Cardinal sat flanking her, keeping up a steady flow of soothing words. Baxter returned from the credence table, where a canteen of water had been placed. "Here."

She shook her head, then rose abruptly. "Let me alone. All of you. What do you know? You don't know the half of it. But you *will.*"

The Cardinal motioned to the other two, and they followed him across the sanctuary and stood beside the throne. The Cardinal said quietly, "She has to make peace with herself. She's a troubled woman. If she wants us, she'll come to us." He looked up at the altar rising from the sanctuary. "God has brought us together in His house, and we are in His hands now—us, as well as them. His will be done, not ours. We must not provoke these people and give them cause to harm us or this church."

Baxter cleared his throat. "We have an obligation to escape if a clear opportunity presents itself."

The Cardinal gave him a look of slight annoyance. "We are operating from different sets of standards, I'm afraid. However, Mr. Baxter, I'm going to have to insist that in my church you do as I say."

Baxter replied evenly, "There's some question, I think, concerning whose church this is at the moment, Your Eminence." He turned to Father Murphy. "What are your thoughts?"

Father Murphy seemed to vacillate, then said, "There's no use arguing about it. His Eminence is correct."

Baxter looked exasperated. "See here, I don't like being pushed about. We *must* offer some resistance, even if it's only psychological, and we must at least *plan* to escape if we're going to keep our sanity and self-respect. This may go on for days—weeks—and if I leave here alive, I want to be able to live with myself."

The Cardinal spoke. "Mr. Baxter, these people have treated us reasonably well, and your course of action would provoke retaliation and—"

"Treated us *well*? I don't give a damn *how* they treat us. They have no right to keep us here."

The Cardinal nodded. "You're right, of course. But let me make my final point, which is that I understand that much of the brashness of young men is a result of the proximity of young women—"

"I don't have to listen to this."

The Cardinal smiled thinly. "I seem to be annoying you. I'm sorry. Well, anyway, don't think for a moment that I doubt these people will kill me and Father Murphy as surely as they would you and Miss Malone. That's not important. What is important is that we not provoke them into the mortal sin of murder.

And also important to me is my obligation as guardian of this church. This is the greatest Catholic Cathedral in America, Mr. Baxter, Domus Ecclesiae, the Mother Church, the spiritual center of Catholicism in North America. Try to think of it as Westminster Abbey."

Baxter's face reddened. He drew a breath. "I have a duty to resist, and I will."

The Cardinal shook his head. "Well, we have no such duty to wage war," He moved closer to Baxter. "Can't you leave this in God's hands? Or, if you're not so inclined, in the hands of the authorities outside?"

Baxter looked the Cardinal in the eye. "I've made my position clear."

The Cardinal seemed lost in thought, then said, "Perhaps I *am* overly concerned about this church. It's in my trust, you see, and as with anyone else, material values figure into my calculations. But we *are* agreed that lives are not to be needlessly sacrificed?"

"Of course."

"Neither our lives"—he motioned around the Cathedral—"nor theirs."

"I'm not so certain about theirs," said Harold Baxter.

"All God's children, Mr. Baxter."

"I wonder."

"Come now."

There was a long silence, broken by Maureen Malone's voice as she crossed the sanctuary. "Let me assure you, Cardinal, that each one of these people was spawned in hell. I know. Some of them may seem like rational men and women to you—jolly good Irishmen, sweet talk, lilting brogues, and all that. Perhaps a song or poem later. But they're quite capable of murdering us all and burning your church."

The three men looked silently at her.

She pointed to the two clerics. "It may be that you don't understand real evil, only abstract evil, but you've got Satan in the sanctuary right now." She moved her outstretched hand and pointed to Brian Flynn, who was mounting the steps into the sanctuary.

Flynn looked at them and smiled. "Did someone mention my name?"

CHAPTER 23

B urke moved closer to the stairway opening, drew a deep breath, and called out, "This is the police! I want to speak with Finn MacCumail!" He heard his words echo up the marble stairway.

A voice with a heavy Irish accent called back, "Stand at the gate—hands on the bars! No tricks. I've got a Thompson."

Burke moved into view of the stairway and saw a young man, a boy really, kneeling on the landing in front of the crypt door. Burke mounted the steps slowly and put his hands on the brass gate.

Pedar Fitzgerald pointed the submachine gun down the stairs. "Stand fast!" he called back up the stairs. "Get Finn! There's a fellow here wants a word with him!"

Burke studied the young man for a moment, then shifted his attention to the layout. The stairs split to the left and right at the crypt door landing. Above the crypt door was the rear of the altar, from which rose a huge cross of gold silhouetted against the towering ceiling of the Cathedral. It didn't look to him as if anyone could get through the gates and up those stairs without being cut to pieces by overhead fire.

He heard footsteps on the left-hand stairs, and a tall figure emerged and stood outlined against the eerie yellow light com-

ing from the glass-paneled crypt doors. The figure passed beside
the kneeling man and moved deliberately down the dimly lit
marble stairs. Burke could not clearly see his features, but saw
now that the man was wearing a white collarless shirt and black
pants, the remains of a priest's suit. Burke said evenly, "Finn
MacCumail?" To an Irishman familiar with Gaelic history, as he
was, it sounded as preposterous as calling someone Robin Hood.

"That's right." The tall man kept coming. "Chief of the Fenians."

Burke almost smiled at this pomposity, but something in the
man's eyes held him riveted.

Flynn stopped close to the gates and stared at Burke. "And to
whom do I have the pleasure of speaking?"

"Chief Inspector Burke, NYPD, Commissioner's office." He
met the stare of the man's deep, dark eyes, then looked down at
his right hand and saw the large bronze ring.

Brian Flynn said, "I know who you are... *Lieutenant.* I have
an Intelligence section too. That's a bit galling, isn't it? Well," he
smiled, "if I can be Chief of the Fenians, you can be a Chief Inspector, I suppose."

Burke remembered with some chagrin the first rule of
hostage negotiating— never get caught in a lie. He spoke in a
slow, measured cadence. "I said that only to expedite matters."

"Admirable reason to lie."

The two men were only inches apart, but the gates had the
effect of lessening the intrusion into their zones of protected territory. Still, Burke felt uncomfortable but kept his hands on the
brass bars. "Are the hostages all right?"

"For the time being."

"Let me speak with them."

Flynn shook his head.

"There were shots fired. Who's dead?"

"No one."

"What is it you want?" Burke asked, though it didn't matter what the Fenians wanted, he thought, since they were not going to get it.

Flynn ignored the question. "Are you armed?"

"Of course. But I won't go against that Thompson."

"Some people would. Like Sergeant Tezik."

"He's been taken care of." Burke wondered how Flynn knew Tezik was crazy. He imagined that kindred spirits could recognize each other by the tone of their voices.

Flynn looked over Burke's shoulder at the sacristy corridors.

Burke said, "I've pulled them back."

Flynn nodded.

Burke said, "If you'll tell me what you want, I will see that your demands are passed directly to the top." He knew he was operating off his beat, but he knew also that he had to stabilize the situation until the Hostage Negotiator, Bert Schroeder, took over.

Flynn tapped his fingers on the bars, his bronze ring clanging against the brass in a nervous and, at the same time, unnerving way. "Why can't I speak directly to someone of higher rank?"

Burke thought he heard a mocking tone in his voice. "They are all out of communication. If you turn off the jamming device—"

Flynn laughed, then said abruptly, "Has anyone been killed?"

Burke felt his hands getting sticky on the bars. "Maybe in the riot...Police Commissioner Dwyer...died of a heart attack." He added, "You won't be implicated in that—if you surrender now. You've made your point."

"I haven't even begun to make my point. Were those people on the horse injured?"

"No. Your men saw the policewoman from the towers. The man was me."

Flynn laughed. "Was it, now?" He thought a moment. "Well, that makes a difference."

"Why?"

"Let's just say that it makes it less likely that you are working for a certain English gentleman of my acquaintance." Flynn considered, then said, "Are you wearing a transmitter? Are there listening devices in the corridors?"

"I'm not wearing a wire. I don't know about the corridors."

Flynn took a pencil-shaped microphone detector from his pocket and passed it over Burke's body. "I think I can trust you, even if you are an intelligence officer specializing in hunting Irish patriots like myself."

"I do my job."

"Yes. Too well." He looked at Burke with some interest. "The universal bloodhound. Dogged, nosy, sniffing about. Always wanting to know things. I've known the likes of you in London, Belfast, and Dublin." He stared at Burke, then reached into his pocket and pushed a piece of paper through the gate. "You're as good as anyone, I suppose. Here is a list of one hundred and thirty-seven men and women held by the British in internment camps in Northern Ireland and England. I want these people released by sunrise. That's 6:03 A.M.—New York time. I want them flown to Dublin and granted amnesty by the British and Irish governments plus asylum in the south if they want it. The transfer will be supervised by the International Red Cross and Amnesty International. When I receive word from these two organizations that this is accomplished, we will give you back your Cathedral and release the hostages. If this is not done by sunrise, I will throw Sir Harold Baxter from the bell tower, followed by, in random order, the Cardinal, Father Murphy, and Maureen Malone. Then I will burn the Cathedral. Do you believe me, Lieutenant Burke?"

"I believe you."

"Good. It's important that you know that each of my Fenians has at least one relative in internment. It's also important you know that nothing is sacred to us, not church or priests, not human life or humanity in general."

"I believe you will do what you say you will do."

"Good. And you'll deliver not only the message but also the essence and spirit of what I'm saying. Do you understand that?"

"I understand."

"Yes, I think you do. Now, for ourselves, our purpose is to be reunited with our kin, so we'll not trade their imprisonment for ours. We want immunity from prosecution. We will walk out of here, motor to Kennedy Airport by means of our own conveyances, and leave New York for various destinations. We have passports and money and want nothing from you or your government except a laissez-passer. Understood?"

"Yes."

Flynn leaned nearer the bars so that his face was very close to Burke's. "I know what's going through your mind, Lieutenant Burke—can we talk them out, or do we have to blow them out? I know that your government—and the NYPD—has a shining history of never having given in to demands made at gunpoint. That history will be rewritten before sunrise. You see, we hold all the cards, as you say—Jack, Queen, King, Ace, and Cathedral."

Burke said, "I was thinking of the British government—"

"That, for a change, is Washington's problem, not mine."

"So it is."

"From now on, communicate with me only through the telephone extension on the chancel organ. I don't want to see anyone moving down here."

Burke nodded.

"And you'd better get your command structure established before some of your cowboys try something."

Burke said, "I'll see that they don't."

Flynn nodded. "Stay close, Lieutenant, I'll be wanting you later." He turned and mounted the steps slowly, then disappeared around the corner of the right-hand staircase.

Burke stared up at the kneeling man with the Thompson, and the man jerked the barrel in a motion of dismissal. Burke took his hands off the brass gate and stepped down the stairs and out of the line of sight of the staircase. He wiped his sweaty palms across his topcoat and lit a cigarette as he walked to the corridor opening.

He was glad he wouldn't have to deal again with the man named Brian Flynn, or with the personality of Finn MacCumail, and he felt sorry for Bert Schroeder, who did.

Captain Bert Schroeder stood with his foot on the rim of the fountain in Grand Army Plaza, smoking a short, fat cigar. A light sleet fell on his broad shoulders and soaked into his expensive topcoat. Schroeder watched the crowd slowly trailing away through the lamplit streets around him. Some semblance of order had been restored, but he doubted if he would be able to pick up his daughter and make it to his family party.

The unit he had been marching with, County Tyrone, his mother's ancestral county, had dispersed and drifted off, and he stood alone now, waiting, fairly certain of the instinct that told him he would be called. He looked at his watch, then made his way to a patrol car parked on Fifth Avenue and looked in the window. "Any news yet?"

The patrolman looked up. "No, sir. Radio's still out."

Bert Schroeder felt a sense of anger at the undignified way the parade had ended but wasn't sure yet toward whom to direct it.

The patrolman added, "I think the crowd is thin enough for me to drive you someplace if you want."

Schroeder considered, then said, "No." He tapped a paging device on his belt. "This thing should still be able to receive a signal. But hang around in case I want you."

Schroeder's pager sounded, and he felt his heart pound in a conditioned response. He threw down his cigar and shut off the device.

The driver in the patrol car called out, "Somebody grabbed somebody, Captain. You're on."

Schroeder started to speak and found that his mouth was dry. "Yeah, I'm on."

"Give you a lift?"

"What! No...I have to...to call..." He tried to steady the pounding in his chest. He turned and looked up at the brightly lit Plaza Hotel on the far side of the square, then ran toward it. As he ran, a dozen possible scenarios flashed through his mind the way they always did when the call came—*hostages*—who? The Governor? The Mayor? Congressmen? Embassy people? But he pushed these speculations aside, because no matter what he imagined when the beeper sounded or the phone rang or the radio called his name, it always turned out to be something very different. All he knew for certain was that very shortly he would be bargaining hard for someone's life, or many lives, and he would do it under the critical eyes of every politician and police official in the city.

He bounded up the steps of the Plaza, ran through the crowded lobby, then down a staircase to the line of wall phones outside Trader Vic's. A large crowd was massed around the phones, and Schroeder pushed through and grabbed a receiver from a man's hand. "Police business! Move back!"

He dialed a special operator number and gave her a number

in Police Plaza. He waited a long time for a ring, and while he waited he lit another cigar and paced around to the extent of the phone cord.

He felt like an actor waiting for the curtain, apprehensive over his rehearsed lines, panicky that the ad libs would be disastrous. His heart was beating out of control now, and his mouth went dry as his palms became wet. He hated this. He wanted to be somewhere else. He loved it. He felt alive.

The phone rang at the other end, and the duty sergeant answered. Schroeder said calmly, "What's up, Dennis?"

Schroeder listened in silence for a full minute, then said in a barely audible voice, "I'll be at the rectory in ten minutes."

He hung up and, after steadying himself against the wall, pushed away from the phones and mounted the steps to the lobby, his body sagging, his face blank. Then his body straightened, his eyes came alive, and his breathing returned to normal. He walked confidently out the front doors and stepped into the police car that had followed him.

The driver said, "Bad, Captain?"

"They're all bad. Saint Pat's rectory on Madison. Step on it."

CHAPTER 24

Monsignor Downes's adjoining offices were filling rapidly with people. Burke stood by the window of the outer office sipping a cup of coffee. Mayor Kline and Governor Doyle came in looking very pale, followed by their aides. Burke recognized other faces as they appeared at the door, somewhat hesitantly, as though they were entering a funeral parlor. In fact, he thought, as people streamed in and exchanged subdued greetings the atmosphere became more wakelike, except that everyone still wore topcoats and green carnations—and there were no bereaved to pay condolences to, though he noticed that Monsignor Downes came close to filling that role.

Burke looked down into Madison Avenue. Streetlights illuminated the hundreds of police who, in the falling sleet, were clearing an area around the rectory. Police cars and limousines pulled up to the curb discharging police commanders and civilian officials. Lines were being brought in by the telephone company, and field phone wire was being strung by police to compensate for the lost radio communication. The machine was moving slowly, deliberately. Traffic was rolling; civilization, such as it was in New York, had survived another day.

"Hello, Pat."

Burke spun around. "Langley. Jesus, it's good to see someone who doesn't have much more rank than I do."

Langley smiled. "You making the coffee and emptying the ashtrays?"

"Have you been filled in?"

"Briefly. What a fucking mess." He looked around the Monsignor's office. "It looks like *Who's Who in the East* here. Has Commissioner Dwyer arrived yet?"

"That's not likely. He died of a heart attack."

"Christ. Nobody told me that. You mean that dipshit Rourke is in charge?"

"As soon as he gets here."

"He's right behind me. We put the chopper down in the courtyard of the Palace Hotel. Christ, you should have seen what it looked like from the air."

"Yeah. I think I would rather have seen it from the air." Burke lit a cigarette. "Are we in trouble?"

"We won't be invited to the Medal Day ceremonies this June."

"For sure." Burke tapped his ash on the windowsill. "But we're still in the game."

"You, maybe. You got a horse shot out from under you. I didn't have a horse shot out from under me. Any horses around?"

"I have some information from Jack Ferguson we can use when we're on the carpet." He took Langley's arm and drew him closer. "Finn MacCumail's real name is Brian Flynn. He's Maureen Malone's ex-lover."

"Ah," said Langley, "ex-lover. This is getting interesting."

Burke went on. "Flynn's lieutenant is John Hickey."

"Hickey's dead," said Langley. "Died a few years ago.... There was a funeral... in Jersey."

"Some men find it more convenient to hold their funeral before their demise."

"Maybe Ferguson was wrong."

"He saw John Hickey in Saint Pat's today. He doesn't make mistakes."

"We'll have the grave dug up." Langley felt chilled and moved away from the window. "I'll get a court order."

Burke shrugged. "You find a sober judge in Jersey tonight, and I'll dig it up myself. Anyway, Hickey's file is on the way, and Louise is checking out Brian Flynn."

Langley nodded. "Good work. The British can help us on Flynn."

"Right... Major Martin."

"Have you seen him?"

Burke inclined his head toward the double doors.

Langley said, "Who else is in there?"

"Schroeder and some police commanders, federal types, and people from the British and Irish consulates." As he spoke, Mayor Kline, Governor Doyle, and their aides went into the inner office.

Langley watched them, then said, "Has Schroeder begun his dialogue yet?"

"I don't think so. I passed on MacCumail's—Flynn's—demands to him. He smiled and told me to wait outside. Here I am."

Deputy Police Commissioner Rourke hurried across the room and into the inner office, motioning to Langley to follow.

Langley turned to Burke. "Listen for the sounds of heads rolling across the floor. You may be the next Chief of Intelligence—I have this vision of Patrick Burke captured for eternity in a bronze statue, on the steps of Saint Patrick's, astride a horse with flaring nostrils, charging up—"

"Fuck off."

Langley smiled and hurried off.

Burke looked at the people milling about the room. The Speaker of the House of Representatives, past and present governors, senators, mayors, congressmen. It *was* a veritable *Who's Who in the East,* but they looked, he thought, rather common and frightened at the moment. He noticed that all the decanters on the coffee table were empty, then fixed his attention on Monsignor Downes, still sitting behind his desk. Burke approached him. "Monsignor—"

The Rector of St. Patrick's Cathedral looked up.

"Feeling better?"

"Why didn't the police know this was going to happen?"

Burke resisted several replies, then said, "We *should* have known. It was all there if we had only... "

Langley appeared at the double doors and motioned to Burke.

Burke looked at the Rector. "Come with me."

"Why?"

"It's your church, and you have a right to know what's going to happen to it. Your Cardinal and your priest are in there—"

"Priests make people uncomfortable sometimes. They get in the way... unintentionally."

"Good. That may be what this group needs."

Monsignor Downes rose reluctantly and followed Burke into the inner office.

In the big room about forty men and women stood or sat, their attention focused around the desk where Captain Bert Schroeder sat. Heads turned as Burke and Monsignor Downes came into the room.

Mayor Kline rose from his chair and offered it to Downes, who flushed and sat quickly. The Mayor smiled at his own beneficence and good manners, then held his hands up for silence. He began speaking in his adenoidal voice that made everyone wince. "Are we all here? Okay, let's begin." He cleared his throat. "All right, now, we have all agreed that the City of New York is, under law, primarily responsible for any action taken in this matter." He looked at his aide, Roberta Spiegel. She nodded, and he went on. "So, to avoid confusion, we will all speak to the perpetrators with one voice, through one man...." He paused and raised his voice as though introducing a speaker. "The NYPD Hostage Negotiator...Captain Bert Schroeder."

The effect of the Mayor's delivery elicited some applause, which died away as it became apparent that it wasn't appropriate. Roberta Spiegel shot the Mayor a look of disapproval, and he turned red. Captain Schroeder rose and half acknowledged the applause.

Burke said softly to Langley, "I feel like a proctologist trapped in a room full of assholes."

Schroeder looked at the faces turned toward him and drew a deep breath. "Thank you, Your Honor." His eyes darted around the room. "I am about to open negotiations with the man who calls himself Finn MacCumail, Chief of the Fenian Army. As you may know, my unit, since it was started by Captain Frank Bolz, has concluded successfully every hostage situation that has gone down in this city, without the loss of a single hostage." He saw people nodding, and the terror of what he was about to undertake suddenly evaporated as he pictured himself concluding another successful case. He put an aggressive tone in his voice. "And since there's no reason to change tactics that have been so successful in criminal as well as political hostage situations, I will treat this as any other hostage situation. It will not be influenced by outside political considerations...but I do solicit your help and suggestions." He looked into the crowd and read expressions ranging from open hostility to agreement.

Burke said to Langley, "Not bad."

Langley replied, "He's full of shit. That man is the most political animal I know."

Schroeder went on. "In order to facilitate my job I'd like this room cleared of everyone except the following." He picked up a list written on Monsignor Downes's stationary and read from it, then looked up. "It's also been agreed that commanders of the field operations will headquarter themselves in the lower offices of the rectory. People connected with the negotiations who are not in this office with me will be in the Monsignor's outer office. I've spoken to the Vicar General by phone, and he's agreed that everyone else may use the Cardinal's residence."

Schroeder glanced at Monsignor Downes, then went on. "Telephones are being installed in the residence and . . . refreshments will be served in His Eminence's dining room. Voice speakers will be installed throughout both residences for paging and so that you may monitor my phone conversations with the perpetrators."

The room filled with noise as Schroeder sat down. The Mayor raised his hands for silence the way he had done so many times in the classroom. "All right. Let's leave the Captain to do his job. Everyone, Governor, ladies and gentlemen— please clear the room. That's right. Very good." The Mayor went to the door and opened it.

Schroeder mopped his brow and waited as the remaining people seated themselves. "All right. You know who I am. Everyone introduce themselves in turn." He pointed to the sole woman present.

Roberta Spiegel, a good-looking woman in her early forties, sat back in a rocking chair and crossed her legs, looking bored, sensual, and businesslike at the same time. "Spiegel. Mayor's aide."

A small man with flaming red hair, dressed in tweeds, said, "Tomas Donahue, Consul General, Irish Republic."

"Major Bartholomew Martin, representing Her Majesty's government in the...absence of Sir Harold Baxter."

"James Kruger, CIA."

A muscular man with a pockmarked face said, "Douglas Hogan, FBI."

A rotund young man with glasses said, "Bill Voight, Governor's office."

"Deputy Commissioner Rourke...Acting Police Commissioner."

A well-dressed man with a nasal voice said, "Arnold Sheridan, agent-in-charge, State Department Security Office, representing State."

"Captain Bellini, NYPD, Emergency Services Division."

"Inspector Philip Langley, NYPD, Intelligence Division."

"Burke, Intelligence."

Schroeder looked at Monsignor Downes, who, he realized, had not left. Schroeder considered for a moment as he sat at the man's desk with his gold-crossed stationery stacked neatly in a corner, then smiled. "And our host, you might say, Monsignor Downes, Rector of Saint Patrick's. Good of you to...come...and to let us use...Will you be staying?"

Monsignor Downes nodded hesitantly.

"Good," said Schroeder. "Good. Okay, let's start at the beginning. Burke, why the hell did you open negotiations? You know better than that."

Burke loosened his tie and sat back.

Schroeder thought the question may have sounded rhetorical, so he pressed on. "You didn't make any promises, did you? You didn't say anything that might compromise—"

"I told you what I said," interrupted Burke.

Schroeder stiffened. He glared at Burke and said, "Please repeat the exchange, and also tell us how he seemed—his state of
mind. That sort of thing."

Burke repeated what he had said earlier, and added, "He
seemed very self-assured. And it wasn't bravado. He seemed intelligent, too."

"He didn't seem unbalanced?" asked Schroeder.

"His whole manner seemed normal—except for what he was
saying, of course."

"Drugs—alcohol?" asked Schroeder.

"Probably had less to drink today than anyone here."

Someone laughed.

Schroeder turned to Langley. "We can't get an angle on this
guy unless we know his real name. Right?"

Langley glanced at Burke, then at the Acting Commissioner.
"Actually, I know who he is."

The room became quiet.

Burke stole a look at Major Martin, who seemed impassive.

Langley continued. "His name is Brian Flynn. The British
will certainly have a file on him—psy-profile, that sort of thing.
Maybe the CIA has something, too. His lieutenant is a man
named John Hickey, thought to have died some years ago. You
may have heard of him. He's a naturalized American citizen. We
and the FBI have an extensive file on Hickey."

The FBI man, Hogan, said, "I'll check."

Kruger said, "I'll check on Flynn."

Major Martin added, "Both names seem familiar. I'll wire
London."

Schroeder looked a bit happier. "Good. Good work. That
makes my job—our jobs—a lot easier. Right?" He turned to
Burke. "One more thing—did you get the impression that the
woman who fired at you was shooting to kill?"

Burke said, "I had the impression she was aiming for the horse. They probably have some discipline of firepower, if that's what you're getting at."

The policemen in the room nodded. Commissioner Rourke said, "Does anybody know anything about this group—the Fenians?" He looked at Kruger and Hogan.

Kruger glanced at Major Martin, then replied, "We have almost no funds to maintain a liaison section on Northern Irish affairs. It has been determined, you see, that the IRA poses no immediate threat to the United States, and preventive measures were not thought to be justified. Unfortunately, we are paying for that frugality now."

Douglas Hogan added, "The FBI thought it was the Provisional IRA until Major Martin suggested otherwise. My section, which specializes in Irish organizations in America, is understaffed and partly dependent on British Intelligence for information."

Burke nodded to himself. He was beginning to catch the drift. Kruger and Hogan were being petulant, taking an I-told-you-so line. They were also covering themselves, rehearsing for later testimony, and laying the groundwork for the future. Nicely done, too.

Commissioner Rourke looked at Major Martin. "Then you are...I mean...you are not..."

Major Martin smiled and stood. "Yes, I'm not actually *with* the consulate. I'm with British Military Intelligence. No use letting that get about, though." He looked around the room, then turned to Langley. "I told Inspector Langley that something was—what is the term?—coming down. But unfortunately—"

Langley said dryly, "Yes, the Major has been very helpful, as have the CIA and FBI. My own division did admirably too; and actually missed averting this act by only minutes. Lieutenant Burke should be commended for his resourcefulness and bravery."

There was a silence during which, Burke noticed, no one yelled "Hooray for Burke." It occurred to him that each of them was identifying his own objectives, his own exposure, looking for allies, scapegoats, enemies, and trying to figure how to use this crisis to his advantage. "I told Flynn we wouldn't keep him waiting."

Schroeder said, "I won't begin a dialogue until I clarify our position." He looked at Bill Voight, the Governor's aide. "Has the Governor indicated that he is willing to grant immunity from prosecution?"

Voight shook his head. "Not at this time."

Schroeder looked at Roberta Spiegel. "What is the Mayor's position regarding the use of police?"

Roberta Spiegel lit a cigarette. "No matter what kind of deal is concluded with London or Washington or anyone, the Mayor will enforce the law and order the arrest of anyone coming out of that Cathedral. If they don't come out, the Mayor reserves the right to send the police in to get them."

Schroeder nodded thoughtfully, then looked at Arnold Sheridan.

The State Department man said, "I can't speak for the administration or State at this time, and I don't know what the Attorney General's position will be regarding immunity from federal prosecution. But you can assume nobody in Washington is going along with any of those demands."

Schroeder looked at Tomas Donahue.

The Irish Consul General glanced at Major Martin, then said, "The Irish Republican Army is outlawed in the Irish Republic, and my government will not accept members of the IRA or offer them sanctuary in the unlikely event the British government decides to release these people."

Major Martin added, "Although I do not represent Her Majesty's government, I can assure you the government's position is as always regarding the IRA or whatever they're calling themselves today: Never negotiate, and if you do negotiate, never concede a single point, and if you do concede a point, never tell them you've conceded it."

Roberta Spiegel said, "Now that we know what uncompromising bastards we are, let's negotiate."

Commissioner Rourke said to Schroeder, "Yes, now all you have to do is talk them out, Bert. They've involved the Red Cross and Amnesty, so we can't easily lie to them. You've got to be very...very..." He couldn't come up with the word he wanted and turned to Captain Bellini, who had said nothing so far. "Captain, in the unlikely event Bert can't do it, is the Emergency Services Division ready to mount an...assault?"

Bellini shifted his massive frame in his small chair. The blue-black stubble on his face gave him a hard appearance, but the area under his eyes had gone very pale. "Yeah...yes, sir. When the time comes, we'll be ready."

Schroeder reached for the telephone. "Okay. I know where everyone's coming from. Right?"

Monsignor Downes spoke. "May I say something?"

Everyone looked at him. Schroeder took his hand off the receiver, smiled, and nodded.

Downes said softly, "No one has said anything about the hostages yet. Or about the Cathedral." There was a silence in the room and Monsignor Downes went on. "If, as I assume, your first responsibility is to the hostages, and if you make this clear to your superiors and to the people inside the Cathedral, then I don't see why a compromise can't be worked out." He looked around the room.

No one took it upon himself to explain the realities of international diplomacy to the Monsignor.

Schroeder said, "I haven't lost a hostage—or for that matter a building—yet, Monsignor. It's often possible to get what you want without giving anything in return."

"Oh...I didn't know that," said Monsignor Downes quietly.

"In fact," continued Schroeder assuringly, "the tack I am going to take is pretty much as you suggested. Stick around, you'll see how it's done." He picked up the telephone and waited for the police operator at the switchboard. He looked around the room and said, "Don't be disturbed if he seems to be winning a few rounds. You have to give them the impression they're scoring. By sunrise he'll tire—you ever go shark fishing? You let them run out the line until you're ready to reel them in." He said to the police operator, "Yes, get me the extension at the chancel organ." He put his elbows on the desk and waited. No one in the room moved.

CHAPTER 25

Governor Doyle put down the telephone and looked around the crowded outer office. People were jockeying for the newly installed phones, and a cloud of blue smoke hung over the elegant furnishings, reminding him of a hotel suite on election night, and that reminded him of the next election. He spotted Mayor Kline talking to a group of city and police officials and came up behind the Mayor, taking his arm in a firm grip. "Murray, I have to speak to you."

The Mayor let himself be propelled by the bigger man into the hallway and up to a landing on the staircase that led to the priests' rooms. The Mayor escaped the Governor's grasp and said, "What is it, Bob? I have things to do."

"I just spoke to Albany. The main concern up there is civil disobedience."

"I didn't think enough people lived in Albany to have a riot."

"No, *here*. In *Manhattan*. That mob outside could explode again...with all the drinking...."

The Mayor smiled. "What makes this Saint Patrick's night different from all other Saint Patrick's nights?"

"Look, Murray, this is not the time for your wisecracking. The seizure of this Cathedral may be just a prelude to a larger civil insurrection. I think you should call a curfew."

"*Curfew?* Are you crazy? Rush hour traffic is still trying to get out of Manhattan."

"Call it later, then." The Governor lowered his voice. "My analysts in Albany say that the only thing keeping this situation cooled down is the sleet. When the sleet stops, the bars will empty and there could be trouble—"

The Mayor looked incredulous. "I don't care *what* your analysts in Albany say. This is *Saint Patrick's Day* in New York, for God's sake. The biggest parade in the world, outside of the May Day Parade in Moscow, has just ended. The largest single party in New York—maybe in America—is just beginning. People plan this day all year. There are over a million people in midtown alone, jammed into bars, restaurants, and house parties. More liquor and food is consumed tonight than any other night of the year. If I called a curfew...the Restaurant Owners' Association would have me *assassinated.* They'd pour all the unconsumed beer into the Rockefeller Center skating rink and drown me in it. Shit, *you* try to enforce a curfew tonight."

"But—"

"And it's *religious.* What kind of an Irishman are you? That's all we need—a Jewish Mayor calling off Saint Patrick's Day. It'd be easier to call off *Christmas.* What kind of yo-yos are giving you advice in Albany? Fucking farmers?"

The Governor began pacing around the small landing. "Okay, Murray. Take it easy." He stopped pacing and thought a moment. "Okay, forget the curfew. But I *do* think you need the State Police and the National Guard to help keep order."

"No. No soldiers, no State Police. I have twenty thousand police—more than a full army division. Little by little we'll get them out on the street."

"The Sixty-ninth Regiment is mustered and in a position to lend a hand."

"Mustered?" Kline laughed. "Plastered is more like it. Christ, the enlisted men got off duty from the armory at two o'clock. They're so shitfaced by now they wouldn't know a rifle from their bootlaces."

"I happen to know that the officers and most of the noncoms are at a cocktail party in the armory right now, and—"

"What are you trying to pull?"

"Pull?"

"Pull."

The Governor coughed into his hand, then smiled good-naturedly. "All right, it's like this—you know damned well that this is the biggest disturbance to hit New York since the blackout of '77, and I have to show that I'm doing *something*."

"Fly to Albany. Let me run my city."

"*Your* city. It's my *state!* I'm responsible to *all* the people."

"Right. Where were you when we needed money?"

"Look...look, I don't need your permission to call out the National Guard or the State Police."

"Call your Attorney General and check on that." Mayor Kline turned and took a step toward the stairs.

"Hold on, Murray. Listen...suppose Albany foots the bill for this operation? I mean, God, this will cost the city *millions*. I'll take care of it, and I'll get Washington to kick in a little extra. I'll say it was an international thing, which it is—like the consulate protection money. Okay?"

The Mayor arrested his descent down the stairs and turned back toward the Governor. He smiled encouragingly.

The Governor went on. "I'll pay for it all if you let me send in my people—I need to show a state presence here—you understand. Okay? Whaddaya say, Murray?"

The Mayor said, "The money to be paid to the city within thirty days of billing."

"You got it."

"Including all overtime and regular time of all the city departments involved, including police, fire, sanitation, and other municipal departments for as long as the siege lasts, and all expenses incurred in the aftermath."

"All right...."

"Including costs of repair to municipal property, and aid to private individuals and businesses who sustain a loss."

The Governor swallowed. "Sure."

"But only the Sixty-ninth Regiment. No other guard units and no State Police— my boys don't get along with them."

"Let me send the State Police into the boroughs to fill the vacuum left by the reassignment to Manhattan."

The Mayor considered, then nodded and smiled. He stuck out his hand, and they shook on it. Mayor Kline said loudly, so that the people in the hallway below could hear, "Governor, I'd like you to call out the Sixty-ninth Regiment and the State Police."

Colonel Dennis Logan sat at the head table in the 69th Regiment Armory hall on Lexington Avenue. Over a hundred officers, noncommissioned officers, and civilian guests sat or stood around the big hall. The degree of intoxication ranged from almost to very. Logan himself felt a bit unsteady. The mood this year was not boisterous, Logan noticed, and there was a subdued atmosphere in the hall, a result of reports of the disturbance in midtown.

A sergeant came toward Logan with a telephone and plugged the phone into a jack. "Colonel, the Governor is on the line."

Logan nodded and sat up straight. He took the receiver, glanced at Major Cole, then said, "Colonel Logan speaking, sir. Happy Saint Patrick's Day to you, Governor."

"I'm afraid not, Colonel. A group of Irish revolutionaries has seized Saint Patrick's Cathedral."

The Colonel felt a heaviness in his chest, and every part of his body went damp, except his throat. "Yes, sir."

"I'm calling the Sixty-ninth Regiment to duty."

Colonel Logan looked around the hall at the scene spread out before him. Most of the officers and NCOs were wobbling, a few were slumped over tables. The enlisted men were home by now or scattered throughout every bar in the metropolitan area.

"Colonel?"

"Yes, sir."

"Full gear, riot-control equipment, weapons with live ammunition."

"Yes, sir."

"Assemble outside the Cardinal's residence on Madison for further orders. Don't delay."

"Yes, sir."

"Is the Sixty-ninth ready, Colonel?"

Logan started to say something rational, then cleared his throat and said, "The Fighting Irish are always ready, Governor."

"This is Captain Bert Schroeder of the New York Police Department." Schroeder reached out and turned on the switches that activated the speakers in both residences.

A voice with an Irish accent came into the room and echoed from the outer office, which quickly became still. "What took you so long?"

Burke nodded. "That's him."

Schroeder spoke softly, pleasantly, a tone designed to be soothing. "Things were a bit confused, sir. Is this—?"

"Finn MacCumail, Chief of the Fenians. I told Sergeant

Tezik and Lieutenant Burke I wanted to speak with a high rank-ing man. I'm only up to a captain now."

Schroeder gave his standard reply. "Everyone that you would want to speak to is present. They are listening to us from speak-ers. Can you hear the echo? We've all agreed that to avoid confusion I will do the speaking for everyone. They'll relay mes-sages through me."

"Who are *you*?"

"I have some experience in this."

"Well, that's interesting. Are there representatives of the Ir-ish, British, and American governments present?"

"Yes, sir. The Police Commissioner, the Mayor, and the Governor, too."

"I picked a good day for this, didn't I?"

Burke said to Schroeder, "I forgot to tell you, he has a sense of humor."

Schroeder said into the telephone, "Yes, sir. So let's get right down to business."

"Let's back up and establish the rules, Captain. Is everyone in contact with their capitals?"

"Yes, sir."

"Have Amnesty International and the Red Cross been con-tacted?"

"It's being done, sir."

"And you are the mouthpiece?"

"Yes, sir. It's less confusing. I think you'll find the arrange-ment acceptable." Schroeder sat at the edge of his chair. This was the most difficult part, persuading wild-eyed lunatics that it was better to speak to him than to the President of the United States or the Queen of England. "So, if we can proceed..."

"All right. We'll see."

Schroeder exhaled softly. "We have your demands in front

of us, and the list of people you want released from Northern Ireland. We want you to know that our primary concern is the safety of the hostages—"

"Don't forget the Cathedral. It's ready to be burned down."

"Yes. But our *primary* concern is human life."

"Sorry about the horse."

"What? Oh, yes. We are too. But no one—no human—has been killed, so let's all work to keep it that way."

"Commissioner Dwyer is feeling better, then?"

Schroeder shot a look at Burke and covered the mouthpiece. "What the hell did you tell him about Dwyer?"

"Rule number one. The truth."

"Shit!" Schroeder uncovered the mouthpiece. "The Commissioner's death was from natural causes, sir. You have not killed anyone." He stressed again, "Our goal is to protect lives—"

"Then I can burn down the Cathedral after I get what I want?"

Schroeder looked around the room again. Everyone was bent forward in their chairs, cigars and cigarettes discharging smoke into the quiet atmosphere. "No, sir. That would be arson, a felony. Let's not compound the problem."

"No problem here. Just do what you're told."

"Are the hostages safe?"

"I told Burke they were. If I say something, that's what I mean."

"I was just reassuring everyone here. There are a lot of people here...Mr. MacCumail, to hear what you have to say to them. The Rector of the Cathedral is here. He's very concerned about the Cardinal and the others. They're all counting on you to come through. Listen, is it possible to speak with the hostages? I'd like to—"

"Perhaps later."

"All right. Fine. Okay. Listen, I'd like to speak to you about that spotlight. That was a potentially dangerous act—"

"Not if you have the County Antrim shooting champion in the bell tower. Keep the spotlights off."

"Yes, sir. In the future, if you want something, just ask me. Try not to take things into your own hands. It's easier, sometimes, to ask."

"I'll try to remember that. Where exactly are you calling from?"

"I'm in the Rector's office."

"Good. Best not to get too far from the center of things."

"We're right here."

"So are we. All right, I have other things to see to. Don't be calling me every minute on some pretext. The next call I receive from you will inform me that the three governments and the two agencies involved are ready to begin working out the details of the transfer of prisoners."

"That may be some time. I'd like to be able to call you and give you progress reports."

"Don't make a nuisance of yourself."

"I'm here to help."

"Good. You can start by sending the keys to me."

"The keys?" He looked at Monsignor Downes, who nodded. Flynn said, "All the keys to the Cathedral—not the city. Send them now, with Lieutenant Burke."

Schroeder said, "I'm not sure I can locate any keys—"

"Don't be starting that bullshit, Captain. I want them within ten minutes or I raze the Altar of the Blessed Sacrament. Tell that to Downes and he'll produce all the keys he's got, and about a hundred he hasn't got."

Monsignor Downes came toward the desk, looking very agitated.

Schroeder said quickly into the phone, "All right. There was a misunderstanding. The Monsignor informs me he has a complete set of keys."

"I thought you'd find them. Also, send in corned beef and cabbage dinners for forty-five people. I want it catered by...hold on, let me check with my American friend here." There was a short silence, then Flynn said, "John Barleycorn's on East Forty-fifth Street. Soda bread, coffee and tea as well. And a sweet, if you don't mind. I'll pay the bill."

"We'll take care of that...and the bill, too."

"Captain, before this night is through there won't be enough money in the city treasury to buy you a glass of beer. I'll pay for the food."

"Yes, sir. One more thing. About the time limit...you've presented us with some complicated problems and we may need more time to—"

Flynn's voice became belligerent. "No extensions! The prisoners named had better be free in Dublin when the first light breaks through the windows of the Lady Chapel. Dawn or dead, Schaeffer."

"Schroeder. Look—"

"Whatever. Happy Saint Paddy's Day to you. *Erin go bragh*."

There was a click, and the sound of the phone hummed in the room. Captain Schroeder put down his telephone, shut off the speakers, and relit his cigar. He tapped his fingers on the desk. It had not gone well. Yet he felt he'd dealt with harder men than Finn MacCumail. Never as well spoken, perhaps, but crazier, certainly.

He kept reminding himself of two facts. One was that he'd never had a failure. The other was that he'd never failed to get an extension of a deadline. And much of his success in the first fact was a result of his success in the second. He looked up at the silent assembly. "This one is going to be rough. I like them rough."

Captain Joe Bellini stood at the window with his tunic open, his thumbs hooked into his gun belt. His fingers ran over his cartridge loops. He had a mental picture of his Emergency Services Division assaulting the big gray lady out there. He didn't like them rough; he didn't like them easy. He didn't like them at all.

Brian Flynn sat at the chancel organ beside the sanctuary and looked at the book resting on the keycover. "Schaeffer." He laughed.

John Hickey picked up the book, titled *My Years as a Hostage Negotiator,* by Bert Schroeder. "Schaeffer. Very good, Brian. But he'll be on to you eventually."

Flynn nodded. "Probably." He pushed back the rolltop cover of the keyboard and pressed on a key, but no sound came from the pipes across the ambulatory. "We need the key to turn this on," he said absently. He looked up at Hickey. "We don't want to hurt him too badly professionally. We want him in there. And toward the end, if we have to, we'll play our trump card against him—Terri O'Neal." He laughed. "Did ever a poor bastard have so many cards stacked against him without knowing it?"

CHAPTER 26

Flynn said, "Hello, Burke."

Burke stopped at the bottom of the sacristy stairs.

Flynn said, "I asked for you so you'd gain stature with your superiors."

"Thanks." Burke held up a large key-ring. "You want these?"

"Hand them through."

Burke climbed the steps and handed the keys through the bars.

Flynn produced the microphone sensor and passed it over Burke's body. "They say that technology is dehumanizing, but this piece of technology makes it unnecessary to search you, which always causes strained feelings. This way it's almost like trusting one another." He put the device away.

Burke said, "What difference would it make if I *was* wired? We're not going to discuss anything that I won't report."

"That remains to be seen." He turned and called out to Pedar Fitzgerald on the landing. "Take a break." Fitzgerald cradled his submachine gun and left. Flynn and Burke stared at each other, then Flynn spoke. "How did you get on to us, Lieutenant?"

"That's no concern of yours."

"Of course it is. Major Martin?"

Burke realized that he felt much freer to talk without a transmitter sending his voice back to the rectory. He nodded and saw a strange expression pass briefly over Flynn's face. "Friend of yours?"

"Professional acquaintance," answered Flynn. "Did the good Major tell you my real name?"

Burke didn't answer.

Flynn moved closer to the gate. "There is an old saying in intelligence work— 'It's not important to know who fired the bullet, but who paid for it.'" He looked at Burke closely. "Who paid for the bullets?"

"You tell me."

"British Military Intelligence provided the logistics for the Fenian Army."

"The British government would not take such a risk because of your petty war—"

"I'm talking about people who pursue their own goals, which may or may not coincide with those of their government. These people talk of historical considerations to justify themselves—"

"So do you."

Flynn ignored the interruption. "These people are monumental egotists. Their lives are meaningful only as long as they can manipulate, deceive, intrigue, and eliminate their enemies, real or imagined, on the other side or on their own side. They find self-expression only in situations of crisis and turmoil, which they often manufacture themselves. That's your basic intelligence man, or secret policeman, or whatever they call themselves. That's Major Bartholomew Martin."

"I thought you were describing yourself."

Flynn smiled coldly. "I'm a revolutionary. Counterrevolutionaries are far more despicable."

"Maybe I should get into auto theft."

Flynn laughed. "Ah, Lieutenant, you're an honest city cop. I trust you." Burke didn't answer, and Flynn said, "I'll tell you something else—I think Martin had help in America. He had to. Be careful of the CIA and FBI." Again Burke didn't respond, and Flynn said, "Who gains the most from what's happened today?"

Burke looked up. "Not you. You'll be dead shortly, and if what you say is true, then what does that make *you*? A pawn. A lowly pawn who's been played off by British Intelligence and maybe by the CIA and FBI, for their own game."

Flynn smiled. "Aye, I know that. But the pawn has captured the archbishop, you see, and occupies his square as well. Pawns should never be underestimated; when they reach the end of the board, they turn and may become knights."

Burke understood Brian Flynn. He said, "Assuming Major Martin is what you say he is, why are you telling me? Am I supposed to expose him?"

"No. That would badly compromise me, you understand. Just keep an eye on him. He wants me dead now that I've served his purpose. He wants the hostages dead and the Cathedral destroyed—to show the world what savages the Irish are. Be wary of his advice to your superiors. Do you understand?"

"I understand that you've gotten yourself in a no-win situation. You've been sucked into a bad deal thinking you could turn it around, but now you're not so sure."

"My goal is uncompromised. It's up to the British government to release my people. It will be their fault if—"

"For God's sake, man, give it up," Burke said, his voice giving way to impatience and anger. "Take a few years for aggravated assault, false imprisonment, whatever the hell you can work out with the DA."

Flynn gripped the bars in front of him. "Stop talking like a fucking cop! I'm a soldier, Burke, not a bloody criminal who makes deals with DAs."

Burke let out a long breath and said softly, "I can't save you."
"I didn't ask you to—but the fact that you mentioned it tells me
more about Patrick Burke, Irishman, than Patrick Burke, policeman, is willing to admit."

"Bullshit."

Flynn relaxed his grip on the bars. "Just take care of Major
Martin and you'll save the hostages and the Cathedral. I'll save
the Fenians. Now run along and bring the corned beef like a
good fellow, won't you? We may chat again."

Burke put a businesslike tone in his voice. "They want to
haul the horse away."

"Of course. An armistice to pick up the dead." He seemed
to be trying to regain control of himself and smiled. "As long as
they don't make corned beef out of it. One man with a rope and
an open vehicle. No tricks."

"No tricks."

"No, there have been enough tricks for one day." Flynn
turned and moved up the stairs, then stopped abruptly and said
over his shoulder, "I'll show you what a decent fellow I am,
Burke—everyone knows that Jack Ferguson is a police informer.
Tell him to get out of town if he values his life." He turned again
and ran up the stairs.

Burke watched him disappear around the corner on the landing. *I'm a soldier, not a bloody criminal.* It had been said without
a trace of anguish in his voice, but the anguish was there.

Brian Flynn stood before the Cardinal seated on his throne.
"Your Eminence, I'm going to ask you an important question."

The Cardinal inclined his head.

Flynn asked, "Are there any hidden ways—any secret passages into this Cathedral?"

The Cardinal answered immediately. "If there were, I wouldn't tell you."

Flynn stepped back and pointed to the towering ceiling at a point above the crypt where the red hats of the deceased archbishops of New York hung suspended by wire. "Would you like to have your hat hung there?"

The Cardinal looked at him coldly. "I am a Christian who believes in life everlasting, and I'm not intimidated by threats of death."

"Ah, Cardinal, you took it wrong. I meant I'd tell my people in the attic to take an ax to the plaster lathing until that beautiful ceiling is lying in the pews."

The Cardinal drew a short breath, then said softly, "To the best of my knowledge, there are no secret passages. But that doesn't mean there aren't any."

"No, it doesn't. Because I suspect that there are. Now, think of when you were first shown your new cathedral by the Vicar General. Surely there must be an escape route in the event of insurrection. A priest's hole such as we have in Ireland and England."

"I don't believe the architect considered such a thing. This is America."

"That has less meaning with each passing year. Think, Your Eminence. Lives will be saved if you can remember."

The Cardinal sat back and looked over the vast church. Yes, there were hollow walls with staircases that went somewhere, passages that were never used, but he could not honestly say that he remembered them or knew if they led from or to an area not controlled by these people. He looked out over the marble floor in front of him. The crypt lay below and, around the crypt, a low-ceilinged basement. But they knew that. He'd seen Hickey and Megan Fitzgerald descend through the bronze plate beside the altar.

Two thirds of the basement was little more than crawl space, a darkness where rats could scurry beneath the marble floor above. And above that darkness six million people passed every year to worship God, to meditate, or just to look. But the darkness below their feet stayed the same, until now—now it was seeping into the Cathedral and into the consciousness and souls of the people in the Cathedral. The dark places became important, not the sanctified places of light.

The Cardinal looked up at the figures standing tensely in the triforia and the choir loft, like sentinels on dark, craggy cliffs, guards on city walls. The eternal watchman, frightened, isolated, whispering, "*Watchman, what of the night?*"

The Cardinal turned to Flynn. "I can think of no way in and, by the same token, no way out for you."

"The way out for me will be through the front doors." He questioned the Cardinal closely about the suspected basement beneath the nave, passages between the basements outside the Cathedral, and the crawl space below.

The Cardinal kept shaking his head. "Nonsense. Typical nonsense about the church. This is a house of God, not a pyramid. There are no secrets here, only the mysteries of the faith."

Flynn smiled. "And no hoards of gold, Cardinal?"

"Yes, there is a hoard of gold. The body and blood of Christ that rests in the Tabernacle, the joy and goodwill and the peace and love that resides with us here— that is our hoard of gold. You're welcome to take some of that with you."

"And perhaps a few odd chalices and the gold on the altars."

"You're welcome to all of that."

Flynn shook his head. "No, I'll take nothing out of here but ourselves. Keep your gold and your love." He looked around the Cathedral and said, "I hope it survives." He looked at the Cardinal. "Well, perhaps a tour will refresh your memory. Come with me, please."

The Cardinal rose, and both men descended the steps of the sanctuary and walked toward the front of the Cathedral.

Father Murphy watched the Cardinal walk off with Flynn. Megan wasn't in sight, Baxter was sitting at the end of the pew, and John Hickey was at the chancel organ, speaking on the field phone. Murphy turned to Maureen. "You want desperately to do something, don't you?"

She looked at him. The catharsis of an escape from death made her feel strangely relaxed, almost serene, but the impulse for action still lay within her. She nodded slowly.

Father Murphy seemed to consider for a long time, then said, "Do you know any code—such as Morse code?"

"Yes. Morse code. Why?"

"You're in mortal danger, and I think you should make a confession, in the event something happens...suddenly...."

Maureen looked at the priest but didn't answer.

"Trust me."

"All right."

Murphy waited until Hickey put down the field phone and called out, "Mr. Hickey, could I have a word with you?"

Hickey looked over the sanctuary rail. "Use the one in the bride's room—wipe the seat."

"Miss Malone would like to make a confession."

"Oh," Hickey laughed. "That would take a week."

"This is not a joking matter. She feels her life is in mortal danger, and—"

"That it is. All right. No one's stopping you."

Father Murphy rose, followed by Maureen.

Hickey watched them move toward the side in the rail. "Can't you do it there?"

Murphy answered. "Not in front of everyone. In the confessional."

Hickey looked annoyed. "Be quick about it."

They descended the side steps and walked across the ambulatory to the confessional booth beside the bride's room. Hickey raised his hand to the snipers in the perches and called out to the two retreating figures. "No funny business. You're in the cross hairs."

Father Murphy showed Maureen into a curtained booth, then entered the archway beside it. He went through the priest's entrance to the confessional and sat in the small, dark enclosure, then pulled the cord to open the black screen.

Maureen Malone knelt and stared through the curtain at the dim shadow of the priest's profile. "It's been so long, I don't know how to begin."

Father Murphy said in the low, intimate whisper cultivated for the confessional, "You can begin by locating the button on the door frame."

"Excuse me?"

"There's a button there. If you press it, it buzzes in the upstairs hall of the rectory. It's to call a priest when confessions are not normally held, in case you have a need for instant forgiveness." He laughed softly at what Maureen thought must be an occupational joke in the rectory.

She said excitedly, "Do you mean we can communicate—"

"We can't get any signal back, and in any case we wouldn't want one. And I don't know if anyone will hear us. Quickly, now, signal a message—something useful to the people outside."

Maureen drew the curtain farther to cover her hand, then ran her fingers over the oak frame and found the button. She pressed it several times to attract someone's attention, then began in halting Morse code.

THIS IS MALONE. WITH FR. MURPHY.

What should she say? She thought back to her training—*Who, what, where, when, how many?*

OBSERVED 13-15 GUNMEN IN CATHEDRAL. SNIPER IN EACH
TRIFORIUM. ONE IN CHOIR LOFT. MAN AT SACRISTY STAIRS
WITH THOMPSON SUB. ONE OR TWO MEN/WOMEN IN EACH
TOWER. TWO OR MORE IN ATTIC. POSTS CONNECTED BY
FIELD PHONES. HOSTAGES ON SANCTUARY.

She stopped and thought of the snatches of conversation
she'd overheard, then continued in a faster, more confident signal.

VOTIVE CANDLES PILED IN ATTIC. BOMB? UNDER SANCTU-
ARY.

She stopped again and tried desperately to think—*Who,
what, where…?* She went on.

MACCUMAIL IS BRIAN FLYNN. JOHN HICKEY, LIEUTENANT.
MEGAN FITZGERALD THIRD IN COMMAND. OBSERVED MINES
ON DOORS, SNIPER RIFLES, AUTOMATIC RIFLES, PISTOLS,
M-72 ROCKETS, GAS MAS—

"Stop!" Murphy's voice came urgently through the screen.
She pulled her hand away from the buzzer.
Murphy said somewhat loudly, "Do you repent all your
sins?"
"I do."
The priest replied, "Say the rosary once."

Hickey's voice cut into the confessional. *"Once?* By God, I'd have her on her knees until Easter if we had that long. Come on out."

Maureen came out of the confessional as Father Murphy came through the archway. Murphy nodded to Hickey. "Thank you. Later I'd like the Cardinal to hear my confession."

Hickey's wrinkled face broke into a mocking smile. "Now, what have you done, Father?"

He stepped very close to Hickey. "I'll hear the confessions of your people, too, before this night is over."

Hickey made a contemptuous sound. "No atheists in cathedrals, eh, Padre?" He stepped back from the priest and nodded. "Someone once said, 'By night an atheist half believes in God.' Maybe you're right. By dawn they'll all turn to you as they see the face of death, with his obscene gaping grin, pressed against the pretty windows. But I'll not make a confession to any mortal man, and neither will Flynn nor that she-devil he sleeps with."

Father Murphy's face reddened. He went on, "I think Harold Baxter will want to make his peace as well."

"That heathen? In a Catholic church? Don't bet the poor-box money on it." Hickey turned and looked up at the solitary figure sitting in the pew on the sanctuary. "This whole operation may have been worth the while just to see that Protestant bastard on his knees in front of a Catholic priest. All right, let's get back to the corral."

Maureen said to Hickey, "I hope I live long enough to see how *you* face death." She turned and walked with the priest in silence to the communion rail. She said, "That man... There's something... wicked..."

The priest nodded. As they came up to the communion rail she said, "Do you think we got through?"

"I don't know."

"Do you know Morse code?"

He reached out and opened the gate in the rail. "No, but you'll write out those dots and dashes for me before I make my confession." He waved her through the rail absently. As she passed him she reached out and squeezed his hand. He suddenly came alert. "Wait!"

She turned on the steps. "What is it?"

He looked at Hickey, who was standing near the confessional watching them. He reached into his vestment and handed her a set of rosary beads. "Get back here and kneel at the rail."

She took the beads and glanced at Hickey. "Stupid of me—"

"My fault. Just pray he doesn't suspect." The priest walked into the sanctuary.

Maureen knelt at the rail and let the string of beads hang loosely from her hands. She turned. Her eyes rose over the Cathedral, and she peered into the dimly appreciated places. Dark figures like ravens stared down at her from the murky balconies. Megan was moving near the front doors like a shadow, and an unearthly stillness hung over the cold, gray towering stonework. She focused on John Hickey. He was staring at the confessional and smiling.

CHAPTER 27

Brian Flynn helped the Cardinal up into the bell room. The Cardinal looked at the torn copper louvers. Flynn said to Donald Mullins, "Have you formally met the Archbishop of New York?"

Mullins knelt and kissed the episcopal ring, then rose.

Flynn said, "Take a break, Donald. There's coffee in the bookstore."

Mullins went quickly down the ladder.

Flynn moved to the opening in the tower and looked out into the city. There was a long silence in the cold, drafty room. "That's incredible, you know...an armed revolutionary kneels in the dust and kisses your ring."

The Cardinal looked impatient. "Why are we up here? There can be no hidden passages up here."

Flynn said, "Have you had many dealings with Gordon Stillway?"

The Cardinal answered, "We planned the latest renovations together."

"And he never pointed out any curiosities to you? No secret—"

"I'm not in the habit of entertaining the same question more than once."

Flynn made an exaggerated bow. "Pardon me. I was only trying to refresh your memory, Your Eminence."

"What exactly do you want with me, Mr. Flynn?"

"I want you to speak with the negotiator, and I want you to
talk to the world. I'm going to set up a conference in that press
room so conveniently located in the subbasement below the sacristy. You will go on television and radio—"

"I'll do no such thing."

"Damn it, you've done enough talking on television and
radio to damage our cause. You've used your pulpit long
enough to speak out *against* the IRA. Now you'll undo that
damage."

"I spoke out against murder and mayhem. If that equals
speaking out against the IRA, then—"

Flynn's voice rose. "Have you seen a British internment
camp? Do you know what they do to those poor bastards in
there?"

"I've seen and heard reports, and I've condemned the British
methods in Ulster along with the IRA methods."

"No one remembers that." He put his face close to the Cardinal's. "You'll announce to the world that as an Irish-American,
and as a Catholic prelate, you are going to Northern Ireland to
visit the camps."

"But if you clear them out, who is there left to visit, Mr.
Flynn?"

"There are hundreds in those camps."

"And the ones to be released are the relatives of the men
and women with you. Plus, I'm sure, a good number of important leaders. The rest can stay so you can still claim some moral
justification for your bloody methods. I'm not as naïve as you
believe, and I won't be used by you."

Flynn let out a deep breath. "Then I won't guarantee the

safety of this church. I'll see that it's destroyed no matter what the outcome of the negotiations!"

The Cardinal moved near Flynn and said, "There is a price, Mr. Flynn, that each man must pay for each sin. This is not a perfect world, and the evildoers in it often escape punishment and die peacefully in their beds. But there is a higher court..."

"Don't try to frighten me with that. And don't be so certain that court would damn *me* and issue *you* wings. My concept of heaven and heavenly justice is a bit more pagan than yours. I picture Tirna-n'Og, where warriors are given the respect they no longer receive on earth. Your heaven has always sounded very effeminate to me."

The Cardinal didn't reply but shook his head.

Flynn turned away from him and looked into the blue city lights. After a time he said, "Cardinal, I'm a chosen man. I know I am. Chosen to lead the people of Northern Ireland out of British bondage."

He turned back to the Cardinal and thrust his right hand toward him. "Do you see this ring? This is the ring of Finn MacCumail. It was given me by a priest who wasn't a priest. A man who never was, in a place that never was what it seemed to be. A place sanctified by Druids a thousand years or more before the name Jesus Christ was ever heard in Erin. Oh, don't look so skeptical—you're supposed to believe in miracles, damn it."

The Cardinal looked at him sadly. "You've shut God's love out of your heart and taken into your soul dark things that should never be spoken of by a Christian." He held out his hand. "Give me the ring."

Flynn took an involuntary step back. "No."

"Give it to me, and we'll see if the Christian God, your true God, is effeminate."

Flynn shook his head and held up his hand balled into a fist.

The Cardinal dropped his outstretched arm and said, "I see my duty clearly now. I may not be able to save this church or save the lives of anyone in here. But before this night is over I'll try to save your soul, Brian Flynn, and the souls of the people with you."

Flynn looked down at the bronze ring, then at the Cardinal, and focused on the large cross hanging from his neck. "I wish sometimes that I'd gotten a sign from that God you believe in. But I never did. By morning one of us will know who's won this battle."

CHAPTER 28

Monsignor Downes stood at the window of his inner office, chain-smoking unfiltered cigarettes and staring out at the floodlit Cathedral through a haze of blue smoke. In his mind's eye he saw not only smoke but fire licking at the gray stone, reaching from the stained-glass windows and twining around the twin spires. He blinked his eyes and turned toward the people in the room.

Present now besides himself was Captain Schroeder, who probably wouldn't leave until the end, and sitting in his chairs were Lieutenant Burke, Major Martin, and Inspector Langley. Captain Bellini was standing. On the couch were the FBI man, Hogan, and the CIA man, Kruger—or was it the other way around? No, that was it. All six men were rereading a decoded message brought in by a detective.

Patrick Burke looked at his copy of the message.

—DER SANCTUARY.

MACCUMAIL IS BRIAN FLYNN. JOHN HICKEY, LIEUTEN-ANT. MEGAN FITZGERALD THIRD IN COMMAND. OBSERVED MINES ON DOORS, SNIPER RIFLES, AUTOMATIC RIFLES, PIS-TOLS, M-72 ROCKETS, GAS MAS—

Burke looked up. "D-E-R Sanctuary. Murder? Ladder? Under?"

Langley shrugged. "I hope whoever that was can send again. I have two men in the upstairs hall waiting to copy." He looked at the message again. "I don't like the way it ended so abruptly."

Bellini said, "I didn't like that inventory of weapons."

Burke said, "Malone or Baxter sent it. Either of them would know Morse code and know that this is the stuff we're looking for. Right? And if, as the Monsignor says, the buzzer is in the confessional, then we might rule out Baxter if he's, as I assume, of the Protestant persuasion."

Major Martin said, "You can assume he is."

The Monsignor interjected hesitantly. "I've been think-ing...perhaps Mr. Baxter *will* make a confession...so they can send again. Father Murphy will hear His Eminence's confession and vice versa—so we can expect, perhaps, three more mes-sages...."

"Then," said Martin, "we're out of sinners. They can't go twice, can they?"

Monsignor Downes regarded him coolly.

Bellini said, "Is that okay, Monsignor? I mean, to use the confessional to do that?"

Downes smiled for the first time. "It's okay."

Major Martin cleared his throat. "Look here, we haven't con-sidered that this message might be a ruse, sent by Flynn to make us believe he's well armed.... A bit subtle and sophisticated for the Irish...but it's possible."

Langley replied, "If we had the complete message, we might have a better idea of its authenticity."

Schroeder said to Langley, "I need information on the per-sonalities in there. Megan Fitzgerald. Third in command."

Langley shook his head. "I'll check the files, but I've never heard of her."

There was a period of silence in the room, while in the outer office men and women arrived and departed, telephones rang constantly, and people huddled in conversation. In the lower floors of the rectory police commanders coordinated crowd control and cordon operations. In the Cardinal's residence Governor Doyle and Mayor Kline met with government representatives and discussed larger issues around a buffet set up in the dining room. Phones were kept open to Washington, London, Dublin, and Albany.

One of the half-dozen newly installed telephones rang, and Schroeder picked it up, then handed it to the CIA man. Kruger spoke for a minute, then hung up, "Nothing on Brian Flynn or Megan Fitzgerald. Nothing on the Fenians. Old file on John Hickey. Not as good as yours." Two phones rang simultaneously, and Schroeder answered both, passing one to Hogan and one to Martin.

The FBI man spoke for a few seconds, then hung up and said, "Nothing on Flynn, Fitzgerald, or the Fenians. You have our file on Hickey. The FBI, incidentally, had an agent at his funeral checking out the mourners. That's the last entry. Guess we'll have to add a postscript."

Major Martin was still on the telephone, writing as he listened. He put the receiver down. "A bit of good news. Our dossier on Flynn will be Telexed to the consulate shortly. There's a capability paper on the Fenian Army as well. Your files on Hickey are more extensive than ours, and you can send a copy to London, if you will." He lit a cigarette and said in a satisfied tone, "Also on the way is the file on Megan Fitzgerald. Here's a few pertinent details: Born in Belfast, age twenty-one. Father deserted family—brother Thomas in Long Kesh for attacking a prison van. Brother Pedar is a member of the IRA. Mother hospitalized for a nervous breakdown." He added caustically, "Your typical Belfast family of five." Martin looked at Burke. "Her description—red hair, blue eyes, freckles, five feet seven inches, slender— quite good-looking according to the chap I just spoke to. Sound like the young lady who pegged a shot at you?"

Burke nodded.

Martin went on. "She's Flynn's present girl friend." He smiled. "I wonder how she's getting on with Miss Malone. I think I'm starting to feel sorry for old Flynn."

A uniformed officer stuck his head in the door. "Chow's here from John Barleycorn's."

Schroeder reached for the telephone. "All right. I'll tell Flynn that Burke is ready with his fucking corned beef." He dialed the operator. "Chancel organ." He waited. "Hello, this is Captain Schroeder. Finn MacCumail?..." He pushed the switches to activate all the speakers, and the next room became quiet.

"This is Dermot. MacCumail is praying with the Cardinal."

Schroeder hesitated. "Mr.... Dermot—"

"Just call me Hickey. John Hickey. Never liked these *noms de guerre*! Confuses everyone. Did you know I was in here? Have you got my file in front of you, Snider?"

"Schroeder." He looked down at the thick police file. Each man had to be played differently. Each man had his own requirements. Schroeder rarely admitted to having anyone's file in front of him as he negotiated, but it was equally important not to get caught lying to a direct question, and it was often convenient to play on a man's ego.

"Schroeder? You awake?"

Schroeder sat up. "Yes, sir. Yes, we knew you were in there. I have your file, Mr. Hickey."

Hickey cackled happily. "Did you read the part where I was caught trying to blow up Parliament in 1921?"

Schroeder found the dated entry. "Yes, sir. Quite"—he

looked at Major Martin, who was staring tight-lipped—"quite daring. Daring escape too—"

"You bet your ass, sonny. Now look at 1941. I worked with the Germans then to blow up British shipping in New York harbor. Not proud of that, you understand; but a lot of us did that in the Second War. Shows how much we hated the Brits, doesn't it, to throw in with the bloody Nazis."

"Yes, it does. Listen—"

"The Dublin government and the British government both sentenced me to death in absentia on five different occasions. Well, as Brendan Behan once said, they can hang me five times in absentia, too." He laughed.

There was some laughter from the adjoining office. No one in the inner office laughed. Schroeder bit his cigar. "Mr. Hickey—"

"What do you have for February 12, 1979? Read it to me, Schaeffer."

Schroeder turned to the last page and read. "Died of natural causes, at home, Newark, New Jersey. Buried...buried in Jersey City Cemetery...."

Hickey laughed again, a high, piercing laugh. Neither man spoke for a few seconds, then Schroeder said, "Mr. Hickey, first I want to ask you if the hostages are all right."

"That's a stupid question. If they weren't, would I tell *you*?"

"But they *are* all right?"

"There you go again. Same stupid question," Hickey said impatiently. "They're fine. What did you call for?"

Schroeder said, "Lieutenant Burke is ready to bring the food you ordered. Where—?"

"Through the sacristy."

"He'll be alone, unarmed—"

Hickey's voice was suddenly ill-tempered. "You don't have to reassure me. For my part I'd like you to try something, because quicker than you can make it up those stairs with a chaincutter or ram, the Cardinal's brains would be running over the altar, followed by a great fucking explosion that they'd hear in the Vatican, and a fire so hot it'd melt the brass balls off Atlas. Do you understand, Schroeder?"

"Yes, sir."

"And stop calling me sir, you candy-assed flatfoot. When I was a lad, if you looked at a constable cross-eyed he'd knock you into next week. Now you're all going round calling murderers sir. No wonder they picked New York for this. Fucking cops would rather bat softballs with a bunch of slum brats than bat heads. Also, while I'm on the subject, I don't like your voice, Schroeder. You sound mealy-mouthed. How the hell did you get picked for this job? Your voice is all wrong."

"Yes, sir ... Mr. Hickey .... What would you like me to call you ...?"

"Call me a son of a bitch, Schroeder, because that's what I am. Go on, you'll feel better."

Schroeder cleared his throat. "Okay ... you're a son of a bitch."

"Oh, yeah? Well, I'd rather be a son of a bitch than an asshole like you." He laughed and hung up.

Schroeder put down the receiver, took a long breath, and turned off the speakers. "Well ... I think ..." He looked down at Hickey's file. "Very unstable. Maybe a little senile." He looked at Burke. "You don't have to go if you ..."

"Yeah. I have to go. I damn well have to go. Where's the fucking food?" He stood.

Langley spoke. "I didn't like that part about the explosion."

Major Martin said, "I'd have been surprised if they hadn't set it up with explosives. That's their specialty."

Burke moved toward the door. "The Irish specialty is bull-shit." He looked at Martin. "Not subtle or sophisticated bull-shit, of course, Major. Just bullshit. And if they had as much gelignite and plastic as they have bullshit, they could have blown up the solar system." He opened the door and looked back over his shoulder. "Forty-five meals. Shit, I wouldn't want to have to eat every meal over the number of people they have in there."

Bellini called out at Burke's retreating figure. "I hope you're right, Burke. I hope to Christ you're right." He turned back to the people in the room. "*He* doesn't have to shoot his way in there."

Schroeder looked at Monsignor Downes, who appeared pale, then turned to Bellini and said irritably, "Damn it, Joe, stop that. No one is going to have to shoot his way into that Cathedral."

Major Martin was examining some curios on the mantelpiece. He said, as though to himself but loud enough for everyone to hear him, "I wonder."

CHAPTER 29

Flynn stood with Maureen on the landing in front of the crypt entrance. He found a key on the ring and opened the green, glass-paneled door. Inside, a set of stairs descended into the white-marbled burial chamber. He turned to Pedar Fitzgerald. "Somewhere in there may be a hidden passage. I'll be along shortly."

Fitzgerald cradled his submachine gun under his arm and moved down the stairs. Flynn shut the door and looked at the inscription in the bronze. *Requiescant In Pace.* "May they rest in peace," he said. Below the inscriptions were plaques bearing the names of the former archbishops of New York who were buried in the crypt. He turned to Maureen. "You remember how frightened we were to go down into Whitehorn Abbey's crypt?"

She nodded. "There have been too many graves in our lives, Brian, and too much running. God, look at you. You look ten years older than your age."

"Do I? Well...that's not just from the running. That's partly from not running fast enough." He paused, then added, "I was caught."

She turned her head toward him. "Oh...I didn't know."

"It was kept quiet. Major Martin. Remember the name?"

"Of course. He contacted me once, right after I'd gone to

Dublin. He wanted to know where you were. He said it would go easier on Sheila...and he said they would cancel the warrant for my arrest...Pleasant sort of chap, actually, but you knew he'd pull your fingernails out if he had you in Belfast."

Flynn smiled. "And what did you tell this pleasant chap?"

"I would have told him to go to hell except I thought he might actually go and find you there. So I told him to fuck off."

Flynn smiled again, but his eyes were appraising her thoughtfully.

She read the expression in his face. "I want you to understand that I never turned informer. Traitor, if you like, but never informer."

He nodded. "I believe you. If I didn't, I'd have killed you long ago."

"Would you?"

He changed the subject. "You're going to get people hurt if you try to escape again."

She didn't respond.

Flynn took a key from his pocket and held it out. "This is the key to the padlock on that chain. I'll open it now, and you can go."

"Not without the others."

"But you'd try to escape without the others."

"That's different."

He smiled and kept the key in front of her. "Ah, you're still a street fighter, Maureen. You understand that there's a price to pay—in advance—for a bit of freedom. Most men and women in this world would leave here quickly through the offered gate, and they wouldn't even entertain the thought of escaping with bullets whistling about their ears. You see, your values and requirements are reversed from ordinary people's. We changed you forever in those years we had you."

She remembered the way he had of interpreting for her all of her motives and actions, and how he had once had her so confused about who and what she was that she'd fallen into his power, willingly and gladly. She looked at him. "Shut up."

Flynn hesitated, then pocketed the key and shifted to another topic. "I chatted with the Cardinal. He believes in the ring, you know. You didn't believe because you thought that as a halfhearted Christian you shouldn't. But His Eminence is about as good a Christian as they make, you'll agree, and for that reason he believes."

She looked at the crypt door. "I never said I didn't believe in such things. I told you in Whitehorn Abbey on the evening I left that I couldn't understand why any power—good or evil—would pick *you* as their mortal emissary."

He laughed. "That's a terrible thing to say. You're a master of the low blow, Maureen. You'd be a bitch except you've got a good heart." He moved closer to her. "How do you explain the fact of Father Donnelly's disappearance? I've searched for that man—if man he was—over these past years, and no one has even heard of him."

She stared through a glass pane into the white, luminescent crypt and shook her head.

Flynn watched her, then put a different tone in his voice and took her arm in a firm grip. "Before I forget, let me give you one good piece of advice—don't provoke Megan."

She turned toward him. "The fact that I'm still breathing provokes her. Let me give *you* a piece of advice. If you get out of here alive, get as far from her as you can. She draws destruction like a lightning rod, Brian."

Flynn made no response and let go of her arm.

She went on. "And Hickey...that man is..." She shook her head. "Never mind. I see you've fallen in with a bad lot. We hardly know each other anymore, Brian. How can we give each other advice?"

He reached out and touched her cheek. There was a long silence on the crypt landing. Then from the sacristy corridor came the sound of footsteps and the squeaking of wheels on the marble floor. Maureen said suddenly, "If Major Martin caught you, how is it that you're alive?"

Flynn walked down the stairs and stood at the gate.

She followed. "Did you make a deal with him?"

He didn't answer.

"And you call yourself a patriot?"

He looked at her sharply. "So does Major Martin. So do you."

"I would never—"

"Oh, you'd make a deal. Popes, prime ministers, and presidents make deals like that, and it's called diplomacy and strategy. That's what this life is all about, Maureen—illusion and semantics. Well, I'm making no deals today, no accommodations, no matter what names the negotiator gives me for it to make it more palatable. That should make you happy, since you don't like deals."

She didn't reply.

He went on. "If you agree that the deal I made with Major Martin wasn't so awful, I'll put Sheila's name on the list of people to be released."

She looked at him quickly. "You mean, it's not—"

"Changes things a bit, doesn't it? Looking ahead, were you, to a tearful reunion with little Sheila? Now you've nothing whatsoever to gain from this. Unless, of course, you see my point in trafficking with the enemy."

"Why is it so important to you that I tell you that?"

A voice called out, "This is Burke. Coming in."

Flynn said to Maureen, "We'll talk again later." He shouted into the sacristy, "Come on, then." He drew back his jacket and adjusted the pistol in his waistband, then said to her, "I respect your abilities as a fighter enough to treat you like a man. Don't try anything, don't make any sudden moves, don't stand behind me, and keep silent until you're spoken to."

She answered, "If that was a compliment, I'm not flattered. I've put that behind me."

"Aye, like a reformed whore puts the streets behind her, but the urge is still there, I'll wager."

She looked at him. "It is now."

He smiled.

Burke appeared from the sacristy corridor, pushing a serving cart. He rolled the cart over the marble floor and stopped at the bottom stair below the gate.

"Do you know Miss Malone?" Flynn asked.

Burke nodded to her. "We've met."

"That's right," said Flynn. "Last evening at the Waldorf. I have a report on it. Seems so long ago, doesn't it?" He smiled. "I've brought her here to assure you we haven't butchered the hostages." He said to her, "Tell him how well you've been treated, Maureen."

She said, "No one is dead yet."

Burke replied, "Please tell the others that we are doing all we can to see that you're safely released." He put a light note in his voice. "Tell Father Murphy he can hear my confession when this is over."

She nodded and gave him a look of understanding.

Flynn was silent a moment, then asked, "Is the priest a friend of yours?"

Burke replied, "They're all friends of mine."

"Really?" He came closer to the gate. "Are you wired, Burke? Do I have to go through the debugging routine?"

"I'm clean. The cart is clean. I don't want to be overheard either." Burke came up the seven steps and was acutely aware of the psychological disadvantage of standing on a step eight inches below Flynn. "And the food's not drugged."

Flynn nodded. "No, not with hostages. Makes all the difference in the world, doesn't it?"

Maureen suddenly grabbed the bars and spoke hurriedly. "His real name is Brian Flynn. He has only about twelve gunmen—"

Flynn pulled the pistol from his waistband and pressed it hard against her neck. "Don't be a hero, Maureen. It isn't required. Is it, Lieutenant?"

Burke kept his hands in full view. "Easy now. Nice and easy. Miss Malone, don't say anything else. That's right."

Flynn spoke to her through clenched teeth. "That's good advice, lass. You don't want to jeopardize others, such as Lieutenant Burke, who's already heard too much." He looked at Burke. "She's impulsive and hasn't learned the difference between bravery and recklessness. That's my fault, I'm afraid." He grabbed her arm with his free hand and pulled her away from the gate. "Leave."

Maureen looked at Burke and said, "I've made a confession to Father Murphy, and I'm not afraid to die. We'll *all* make our confessions soon. Don't give in to these bastards."

Burke looked at her and nodded. "I understand."

She smiled, turned, and mounted the steps to the altar.

Flynn held the pistol at his side and watched her go. He seemed to be thinking, then said, "All right, how much do I owe you?"

Burke slowly handed a bill to Flynn.

Flynn looked at it. "Five hundred sixty-one dollars and twelve cents. Not cheap to feed an army in New York, is it?"

Flynn slipped the pistol into his waistband and counted out the money. "Here. Come closer."

Burke moved nearer the gate and took the bills and change.

Flynn said, "I deducted the sales tax on principle." He laughed. "Make certain you report that to the press, Lieutenant. They love that sort of nonsense."

Burke nodded. Brian Flynn, he decided, was not a complete lunatic. He had the uneasy feeling that Flynn was sharper than Schroeder, and a better performer.

Flynn looked down at the cart laden with covered metal dishes. "It wouldn't be Saint Paddy's Day without the corned beef, would it, Burke? Had yours?"

"No. Been busy."

"Well, come in and join us, then. Everyone would enjoy your company."

"I can't."

"Can't?" Flynn made a pretense of remembering something. "Ah, yes. Hostages will neither be given nor exchanged under any circumstances. Police will not take the place of hostages. But I'll not keep you prisoner."

"You seem to know a lot about this."

Flynn thrust his face between the bars, close to Burke's. "I know enough not to do anything stupid. I hope you know as much."

"I'm sure we've had more experience with hostage situations than you—see that *you* don't make any mistakes."

Flynn lit a cigarette and said abruptly, "So, I should formally introduce myself now that Miss Malone was thoughtful enough to tell you my name. I am as the lady said—as you might have known from other sources—Brian Flynn. Ring any bells?"

"A few. Back in the late seventies. Over there."

"Yes, over there. Over here now. Unlike John Hickey, I'm

not officially dead, only unofficially missing. All right, let's talk about our favorite subject. Is Major Martin present at your war councils?"

"Yes."

"Get him out of there."

"He's representing the British consulate for now."

Flynn forced a laugh. "Sir Harry will be distressed to hear that. Let me tell you that Martin will double-cross his own Foreign Office, too. His only loyalty is to his sick obsession with the Irish. Get him the hell away from the decision-making process."

"Maybe I'd rather have him close where I can see him."

Flynn shook his head. "You never see a man like that no matter how close he is. Get him out of the rectory, away from your commanders."

Burke said softly, "So your people on the outside can kill him?"

A slow smile passed over Flynn's face. "Oh, Lieutenant, you are the sharp one. Yes, indeed."

"Please don't do anything without talking to me first."

Flynn nodded. "Yes, I'll have to be straight with you. We may still be able to work together."

"Maybe."

Flynn said, "Look here, there's a lot of double-dealing going on, Burke. Only the New York police, as far as I can tell, have no ulterior motives. I'll count on you, Lieutenant, to do your job. You must play the honest broker and avert a bloodbath. Dawn tomorrow or—I promise you—this Cathedral will burn. That's as inevitable as the sunrise itself."

"You mean you have no control over that?"

Flynn nodded. "Very quick-witted of you. I control my people up to a point. But at dawn each man and woman in here will act on standing orders unless our demands have been met.

Without a word from me the prisoners will be shot or thrown from the bell tower, fires will be set, and other destructive devices will automatically engage."

Burke said, "You did a damned stupid thing to relinquish that kind of control. Stupid and dangerous."

Flynn pressed his face to the bars. "But you could do worse than dealing with me. If anything happened to me, you would have to deal with Hickey and the woman we call Grania, so don't you or Schroeder or anyone out there try to undermine me. Work with me and no one will die."

"Better the devil you know than the devils you don't know."

"Quite right, Lieutenant. Quite right. You may go."

Burke moved backward down a step, away from the gate. He and Flynn looked at each other. Flynn made no move to turn away this time, and Burke remembered the hostage unit's injunction against turning your back on hostage takers. "Treat them like royalty," Schroeder liked to say on television talk shows. "Never show them your back. Never use negative words. Never use words like death, kill, die, dead. Always address them respectfully." Schroeder would have had a stroke if he had heard this exchange.

Burke took another step backward. Schroeder had his methods, yet Burke was becoming convinced that this situation called for flexibility, originality, and even compromise. He hoped Schroeder and everyone else out there recognized that before it was too late.

He turned his back to Flynn, went down the steps past the serving cart, and moved toward the corridor opening, all the while aware of the deep, dark eyes that followed him.

CHAPTER 30

Patrick Burke made the long underground walk from the sacristy past the silent policemen in the corridors. He noticed that the Tactical Patrol Unit had been replaced by the Emergency Services Division. They wore black uniforms and black flak jackets, they carried shotguns, sniper rifles, automatic weapons, and silenced pistols, and they looked very unlike the public image of a cop, he thought. Their eyes had that unfocused look, their bodies were exaggeratedly relaxed, and cigarettes dangled from tight lips.

Burke entered the rectory's basement and made his way upstairs to the Monsignor's office suite, through the crowded outer office, and into the next room, shutting the door firmly behind him. Burke met the stares of the twelve people whom he had labeled in his mind the Desperate Dozen. He remained standing in the center of the room.

Schroeder finally spoke. "What took you so long?"

Burke found a chair and sat. "You told me to get the measure of the man."

"No negotiating, Burke. That's my job. You don't know the procedure—"

"Anytime you want me to leave, I'm gone. I'm not looking to get on the cover of *Time*."

Schroeder stood. "I'm a little tired of getting ribbed about that goddamned *Time* story—"

Deputy Commissioner Rourke cut in. "All right, men. It's going to be a long night." He turned to Schroeder. "You want Burke to leave after he briefs us?"

Schroeder shook his head. "Flynn has made him his errand boy, and we can't upset Mr. Flynn."

Langley broke in. "What did Flynn say, Pat?"

Burke lit a cigarette and listened to the silence for a longer time than was considered polite. "He said the Cathedral will more or less self-destruct at sunrise."

No one spoke until Bellini said, "If I have to take that place by force, you better leave enough time for the Bomb Squad to comb every inch of it. They've only got two mutts now—Sally and Brandy...." He shook his head. "What a mess...damn it."

Schroeder said, "No matter what type of devices they have rigged, they can delay them. I'll get an extension."

Burke looked at him. "I don't think you understood what I said."

Langley interjected. "What else did he say, Pat?"

Burke sat back and gave them an edited briefing, glancing at Major Martin, who stood against the fireplace in a classic pose. Burke had the impression that Martin was filling in the missing sentences.

Burke focused on Arnold Sheridan, the quintessential Wasp from State, tight smile, correct manners, cultivated voice that said nothing. He was assigned to the security section but probably found it distasteful to be even a quasi-cop. Burke realized that, as the man on the scene, Sheridan might sway the administration either way. Hard line, soft line, or line straddling. Washington could push London into an accommodation, and then, like dominoes, Dublin, Albany, and the City of New York would tumble into line. But as he looked at Sheridan he had no idea of what was going on behind those polite, vacant eyes.

Burke looked back at Schroeder as he spoke. This was a man who was an accomplished listener as well as a talker. He heard every word, remembered every word, even interpreted nuances and made analyses and conclusions but ultimately, through some incredible process in his brain, never really *understood* a thing that was said. Burke flipped a cigarette ash into a coffee cup. "I don't think this guy is a textbook case. I don't think he's going to bend in his demands or give extensions, Schroeder."

Schroeder said, "They all give extensions, Burke. They want to play out the drama, and they always think a concession will come in the next minute, the next hour, the next day. It's human nature."

Burke shook his head. "Don't operate on the premise that you'll get more time."

Major Martin interrupted. "If I may say something—Lieutenant Burke's analysis is not correct. I've dealt with the Irish for ten years, and they are dreadful liars, fakes, and bluffers. Flynn will give you extensions if you keep him hopeful that—"

Burke stood. "Bullshit."

The Irish Consul General stood also and said hesitantly, "Look here, Major, I...I think it's unfair to characterize the Irish..."

Martin forced an amiable tone into his voice. "Oh, sorry, Tomas. I was speaking only of the IRA, of course." He looked around the room. "I didn't mean to offend Irish Americans either. Commissioner Rourke, Mr. Hogan, Lieutenant Burke"—he looked at Schroeder and smiled—"or your better half."

Commissioner Rourke nodded to show there were no hard

feelings, and spoke. "Everyone is a little tense. Let's take it easy. Okay?" He looked at Burke. "Lieutenant, the Major has a lot of experience in these things. He's providing us with valuable information, not to mention insight. I know Irish affairs are your specialty, but this is not an Irish-American affair. This is different."

Burke looked around the room. "I'd like to make it an American affair for a few minutes. Specifically, I'd like to speak to the Commissioner, Captain Schroeder, Inspector Langley, Mr. Kruger, and Mr. Hogan—alone."

Commissioner Rourke looked around the room, unsure of what to say. Major Martin moved to the door. "I've got to get to the consulate." Tomas Donahue made an excuse and followed. Monsignor Downes nodded and left. Arnold Sheridan rose and looked at his watch. "I have to call State."

Bellini said, "You want me here, Burke?"

"It doesn't concern you, Joe."

Bellini said, "It better not." He left.

The Governor's aide suddenly looked alert. "Oh..." He stood. "I have to go...." He left.

Roberta Spiegel sat back in her rocker and lit another cigarette. "You can either go talk in the men's room—though that's no guarantee I won't follow—or you can talk here."

Burke decided he didn't mind her presence. He took Langley to the far end of the room and said quietly, "Did we hear from Jack Ferguson yet?"

Langley said, "We got through to his wife. She's sick in bed. She hasn't heard from him either."

Burke shook his head. He usually felt his first responsibility was to an informant who was in danger, but now he had no time for Jack Ferguson. Ferguson understood that—and understood, he hoped, that he was in danger. Burke moved to the center

of the room and addressed the remaining people. "I've dealt a
few cards from the bottom of the deck myself over the years,
but never have I seen a card game as stacked as this one. And
since I'm the one who almost got his head blown off this afternoon, I think you'll understand why I'm a little pissed off." He
looked at Kruger and Hogan. "You two have some explaining
to do." Burke took a long pull on his cigarette and continued.
"Consider this—we have here a well-planned, well-financed operation. Too much so, from what we know of the IRA, domestic
and foreign. I see here the hand of not so much the revolutionary but the counterrevolutionary—the government man." He
looked at Kruger and Hogan.

No one spoke.

"Brian Flynn has told me that Major Batholomew Martin
suggested an American operation to him and provided the necessary resources to carry it out. And if *that* is true, then I don't
think Martin could have pulled it off without the help of some
of your people—or at least without your well-known talent for
looking the other way when it suits you."

Langley stood. "Careful."

Burke turned. "Come off it, Langley. You had your suspi-
cions, too." He turned back to the people in front of him. "This
whole thing has been a staged performance, but I think it got
out of control because Brian Flynn wasn't playing his part as
written. Maybe he was supposed to knock over an armory or
blow a bank. But he got a better idea, and now we're all up to
our asses in the consequences."

Kruger stood. "I've never heard such paranoid nonsense—"

Hogan reached out and put his hand on Kruger's arm, then
sat forward. "Listen, Burke, what you say is not altogether un-
true." He paused, then went on. "The FBI *did* stand to gain
from this incident. Sure, when this is over they'll fire some peo-

ple at the top, but then the analysis will show how powerless we were to stop it. And maybe we'll become the beneficiaries of a little power and money." He leaned farther forward and put an aggrieved tone in his voice. "But to even *hint* that *we*—"

Burke waved his arm to cut off the disclaimers. "I have no real evidence, and I don't want any. All I want you to know is that Patrick Burke knows. And I almost got my fucking head blown off finding out. And if Flynn starts making public statements, people will tend to believe him, and your two outfits will be in trouble—again."

Hogan shook his head. "He won't make any public charges about outside help, because he's not going to admit to the Irish people that he worked with British Intelligence—"

Kruger looked at him sharply. "Shut up, Hogan."

Douglas Hogan waved his hand in dismissal. "Oh, for Christ's sake, Kruger, there's no use trying to play it coy." He looked at the four policemen in the room. "We had some knowledge of this, but, as you say, it got out of control. I can promise you, though, that no matter what happens, we will cover you...so long as you do the same. What's happened is past. Now we have to work at making sure we come out of this not only blameless but looking good." Douglas Hogan spread his hands out in front of him and said coaxingly, "We have been handed a unique opportunity to make some important changes in intelligence procedures in this country. A chance to improve our image."

Commissioner Rourke stood. "You people are...crazy."

Langley turned to the Commissioner. "Sir, I think we have no choice but to keep to the problem at hand. We can't change the series of events that brought us here, but we can try to ensure that the outcome won't be disastrous...as long as we work together."

The Commissioner looked at the FBI man, the CIA man, then at his two intelligence officers. He understood very clearly that their logic was not his logic, their world not his world. He understood, also, that anyone who could do what Kruger and Hogan had apparently done were dangerous and desperate men. He looked at Roberta Spiegel. She nodded to him, and he sat down.

Burke glanced around the room and said, "It's important that you all understand that Bartholomew Martin is a danger to any negotiated settlement. He means to see that the Cathedral is destroyed and that blood is shed." He looked at Rourke and Schroeder. "He is not your good friend." He stared at Kruger and Hogan. "The most Martin hoped for was an arms steal or a bank heist, but *Flynn* presented him with a unique opportunity to influence public opinion in America the way the IRA murder of Lord Mountbatten did in the British Isles. However, if Flynn walks out of the Cathedral with no blood shed and the IRA prisoners are released, he'll be a hero to a large segment of the Irish population, and no one will ever believe he meant to harm anyone or destroy the Cathedral—and Major Martin cannot allow that to happen." Burke turned again to Kruger and Hogan. "I want him neutralized—no, that's not like one of your famous euphemisms for murder. Don't look so uncomfortable. Neutralized—inoperative. Watched. I want a regular Foreign Office man representing the British government in New York, not Martin. I've given *you* a unique opportunity to save your own asses."

Kruger stared at Burke, unconcealed hostility in his eyes.

Hogan nodded. "I'll do what I can."

Roberta Spiegel said, "End of discussion." She looked at Schroeder. "Captain, you're on."

Schroeder nodded and turned on the speakers in the rectory

offices and in the Cardinal's residence. He placed the call through the switchboard and looked around the room while he waited. *New ball game for them,* he thought. But his ball game hadn't changed substantially. His only concern was the personality of Brian Flynn. His whole world was reduced to the electronic impulses between himself and Flynn. Washington, London, and Dublin could make it easier for him by capitulating, but they couldn't make it any more difficult than it already was. A voice in the earphone made him sit up. "Hello, Mr. Flynn? This is Captain Schroeder."

CHAPTER 31

B rian Flynn stood at the chancel organ and lit a cigarette as he cradled the receiver on his shoulder. "Schroeder, the corned beef was stringy. You didn't butcher the horse now, did you?"

The negotiator's voice came back with a contrived laugh in it. "No, sir. If there's anything else you want, please let us know."

"I'm about to do that. First of all, I'm glad you know my name. Now you know you're dealing with Ireland's greatest living patriot. Right?"

"Yes, sir . . . ."

"There'll be a monument erected to me someday in Dublin and in a free Belfast. No one will remember you."

"Yes, sir."

Flynn laughed suddenly. "I hear you writing, Schroeder. What are you writing? 'Megalomania'?"

"No, sir. Just keeping notes."

"Good. Now just listen and take notes on this. First..." Flynn leafed through Schroeder's autobiography as he spoke. " . . . . make certain you leave the Cathedral's floodlights on. It looks so grand bathed in blue light. Also, that will make it difficult for your ESD men to climb up the sides. I've people in skyscrapers with field glasses. If they see anything moving outside, they'll signal the towers or call me directly. Which brings me to point two. Don't interfere with my outside telephone lines. Point three, if the lights in here so much as flicker, I'll shoot everyone. Point four, no psy-warfare, such as your usual prank of running that silly armored car you own around the Cathedral. My men in the towers have M-72 rockets. Anyway, we've seen more armored cars than you've seen taxis, Schroeder, and they don't frighten us. Point five, no helicopters. If my men in the towers see one, they'll fire on it. Point six, tell your ESD people that we've planned this for a long time, and an attack would cost them dearly. Don't waste them. You'll need them next time." Flynn wiped a line of sweat from his forehead. "Point seven, I say again, no extensions. Plan to wrap it up by dawn, Schroeder. Point eight, I want a nice twenty-one-inch color television set. I'll tell you when I want Burke to bring it. Point nine, I want to see continuous news coverage until dawn. Point ten, I want to hold a news conference in the press room below the sacristy. Prime time, 10:00 P.M., live. Got all that?"

After a long silence Schroeder's voice came through, sounding strained. "Yes, sir. We'll try to accommodate you on all those points."

"You *will* accommodate me. What have you heard from Dublin, London, and Washington?"

"They're tied into their representatives, who are here in the Cardinal's residence. They're making progress."

"It's good to see allies working so well together. I hope they're all keeping their tempers as we are doing, Captain. What have you heard from Amnesty and the Red Cross?"

"They are willing to cooperate in any way possible."

"Good for them. Good people. Always there to lend a hand. How about immunity from prosecution for my people in here?"

Schroeder cleared his throat. "The U.S. Attorney General and the State Attorney General are discussing it. So far, all I can promise you is—"

"A fair trial," interrupted Flynn. "Wonderful country. But I don't want *any* trial at all, Schroeder."

"I can't make that promise at this time."

"Let me make something clear—at the same time you tell me those prisoners are being released, you'd better have a guarantee of immunity for us or it's no deal. I'll shoot the hostages and blow this place apart." Flynn could hear Schroeder's breathing in the earpiece.

Schroeder said softly, "Everything you ask for is being considered very carefully, but these things take time. All I'm concerned with at the moment is the safety—"

"Schroeder, stop talking to me as though I were some sort of criminal lunatic. Save that for your next case, if you have one. I'm a soldier, and I want to be spoken to as a soldier. The prisoners in here are being treated correctly. And your tone is very patronizing."

"I'm sorry. I didn't mean to offend you. I'm only trying to assure you of our good intentions. My job is to negotiate a settlement we can all live with, and—"

Flynn suddenly stood and said, "How do you call it negotiation if you don't intend to *give* anything?"

Schroeder didn't reply.

"Have you *ever* made any real concessions in all of your career as a hostage negotiator, Schroeder? Never. You're not even *listening* to me, for Christ's sake. Well, you'd damn well *better* listen, because when this Cathedral is in ruins and the dead are lying everywhere, you'll wish to God you paid more attention, and that you'd acted in better faith." "

I *am* listening. I *am* acting—"

"You'll be known, Captain Bert Schroeder, as the man who failed to save Saint Patrick's Cathedral and who has innocent blood on his hands. You'll never hold your head up again, and you'll not accept many talk-show invitations, I think."

Schroeder's voice came back, agitated for the first time that anyone who was listening could remember. "I haven't lied to you, have I? We haven't tried to use force, have we? You asked for food, we gave you food. You asked—"

"I paid for the fucking food! Now listen to me closely. I know you're only a middleman for a lot of bastards, but..." Flynn looked at Schroeder's picture on the cover of his book. It was an action shot, taken during a bank robbery that had turned into a hostage situation. Schroeder, unlike his predecessor, who always wore a baseball cap and Windbreaker, was dressed nattily in a three-piece pinstripe. The face and massive body suggested he was more the baseball-cap type, but Schroeder was reaching for his own style. Flynn studied the face on the cover. Good profile, firm jaw, erect carriage. But the eyes were unmistakably frightened. A bad picture. Flynn continued, "But I trust you, Schroeder—trust you to use your influence and your good offices. I want you to keep talking to me all night, Captain. I want you to carry my message to the people around you."

Schroeder's voice sounded surprised at the sudden expression of confidence. "Yes, sir. I'll do that. You can talk to me." Both men remained silent for a time, then Schroeder said, "Now I'd like to ask two favors of you."

Flynn smiled and flipped absently through the autobiography in front of him. "Go on."

"Well, for one thing, the jamming device is causing confusion in command and control, and we don't want an incident to occur because of a lack of communication. Also, it's causing interference with commercial radio and the sound portions of television broadcasts."

Flynn threw aside the book. "Can't have that. I'll think about it. What else?"

"I'd like to say a few words to each of the hostages."

"Maybe after the press conference."

"All right. That's fair. There is one other thing."

"There always is."

"Yes, well, since you and I are building a rapport—building confidence in each other—and I'm the only one talking to you, I wonder if you'd do the same for me. I mean, I spoke to Mr. Hickey before, and—"

Flynn laughed and looked around, but Hickey wasn't in sight. "John gave you a bit of a rough time, did he, Captain? He enjoys making unpleasant jokes. Well, just play along with him. He loves to talk—Irish, you know."

"Yes, but there could be a misunderstanding. You are the boss, and I want to keep my lines of communication open to *you*, and—"

Flynn dropped the receiver into its cradle and looked through a book of sheet music. He wanted to find something unchurchly that would take his mind away from the Cathedral. Of all the godforsaken places he'd ever found himself in, no place seemed more oddly forsaken than the Cathedral at this moment. Yet others, he knew, felt the presence of a divine spirit here, and he understood that the emptiness he felt was totally within himself. He found "The Rose of Tralee," turned the key into the organ, and played as he sang very softly.

> "The pale moon was rising above
> The green mountains,
> The sun was declining beneath
> The blue sea,
> As I strayed with my love to the
> Pure crystal fountain,
> That stands in the beauitful vale
> of Tralee...."

Bert Schroeder looked for a long time at the dead speaker, folded his hands on the desk, and thought. Flynn talked about immunity, which showed he thought of a future, and by implication his desire to keep his crime from being compounded was strong. He had no intention of killing anyone, least of all himself. More importantly, Flynn was beginning to depend on him. That always happened. It was inevitable as he came to realize that Schroeder's voice was the only one that mattered. Schroeder looked up. "I think I'm getting an angle on this guy."

Burke said, "It sounds like he has an angle on *you.*"

Schroeder's eyes narrowed, and he nodded reluctantly. "Yes, he seems to know something of my methods. I'm afraid the media has given my bureau too much coverage." He added, "I never sought publicity."

"You mean your autobiography was unauthorized? Christ, you should have at least waited until you retired before you released it." Burke smiled. "And now you've missed the big chapter. Catch it on the second printing. Talk to your agent about it." Burke put a conciliatory tone in his voice. "Look, Bert, I don't have all the answers, but—"

Schroeder stood. "No, you don't. And I'm tired of your sideline quarterbacking!"

No one spoke. Burke stood and moved toward the door.

Schroeder said, "Don't go far. Flynn may want coffee later."

Burke turned and said, "Up to this point we've had doublecrosses, incompetence, and some ordinary stupidity. And we've been damned lucky in spite of it. But if we don't get our act together by dawn, we're going to have a massacre, a desecration, and a lot of explaining to do."

Schroeder stared ahead and spoke placidly. "Just leave it to me."

CHAPTER 32

Father Murphy walked across the sanctuary and stood before the Cardinal's throne. "Your Eminence, I would like to make my confession."

The Cardinal nodded. "Take my hands."

Murphy felt the scrap of paper sticking to his palm. "No...I would like to go into the confessional."

The Cardinal stood. "We'll go into the Archbishop's sacristy."

"No..." Murphy felt a line of sweat collect on his brow. "They won't let us. We can go into the confessional where I heard Miss Malone's confession."

The Cardinal stared at him curiously, then nodded. "As you wish." He came down from the throne and walked toward the rear of the sanctuary, then descended the side steps that led into the ambulatory. Father Murphy glanced back at Maureen and Baxter. They nodded encouragingly, and he followed the Cardinal.

Leary leaned over the choir loft parapet, placed the cross hairs in front of the Cardinal's face, and led him as he walked from right to left across his magnified picture. Everyone in the triforia began shouting warnings to the two priests, shouting at Leary who they knew was about to fire, shouting for Flynn or Hickey.

The Cardinal seemed oblivious to the warnings. He stopped

at the archway that led to the priests' entrance to the confessional and waited for Father Murphy, who walked hesitantly across the ambulatory.

Leary centered his cross hairs on the gold cross that hung over the Cardinal's heart and took up the slack in the trigger.

Flynn suddenly appeared in front of the two priests with his arms raised and looked into the balconies. The shouting stopped. Leary straightened his body and stood with his rifle resting in the crook of his arm. Even from this distance Flynn could see that Leary had that distinctive posture of a hunter who had just been denied his quarry, motionless, listening, watching. Flynn saw Megan appear in the loft and move beside Leary, speaking to him as though she were soothing his disappointment. Flynn turned to the two priests. "What the hell do you think you're doing?"

The Cardinal answered evenly, "I'm going to hear a confession."

Flynn spoke between clenched teeth. "Are you *mad?* You can't come down from there without permission."

The Cardinal answered, "I don't need your permission to go anywhere in this church. Please stand aside."

Flynn fought down the anger inside him. "Let me tell you two something. Those people up there have standing orders to shoot.... All right, four of them may not be priest killers, but the fifth man would kill you. He would shoot his mother if that's what he's contracted to do. Just as you took your vows, he has taken his."

The Cardinal's face turned crimson; he began to speak, but Flynn cut him off. "That man has spent fourteen years as a sniper for a dozen different armies. By now he sees the world through cross hairs. His whole being is compressed into that solitary act. And he loves it—the sound of the gun, the recoil of the stock against his shoulder, the flash of the muzzle, the smell of burnt powder in his nostrils. It's like a sexual act to him—can you two understand *that?*"

Neither the Cardinal nor the priest answered. The Cardinal turned his head and looked up into the shadows of the choir loft, then turned back to Flynn. "It's hard to believe such a man exists. You should be careful he doesn't shoot *you.*" He stepped around Flynn and entered the wooden archway, then turned into the door of the confessional.

Father Murphy glanced at Flynn, then pushed aside the curtain and entered the confessional.

John Hickey stood some distance off near the Lady Chapel and watched silently.

Murphy knelt in the dark enclosure and began, "Bless me, Father..." He peered through a space in the curtain and saw Flynn walking away. He spoke in whispered tones to the Cardinal, making a hasty confession, then broke off abruptly and said, "Your Eminence, I'm going to use the call buzzer to send a coded message."

The dark outline of the Cardinal's profile behind the black screen stayed motionless as though he hadn't heard, then slowly the head nodded.

Murphy drew the curtain gently over the doorjamb and pressed the button in a series of alerting signals. He looked closely at the paper in his hand and squinted in the darkness. He began:

THIS IS FR. MURPHY.

Suddenly a hand flew through the curtain and grabbed his wrist. Hickey's voice filled the confessional. "While you're in there, Padre, confess to using the confessional for treachery." He flung the curtain aside, and Murphy blinked in the sudden light.

Hickey snatched the paper out of the priest's hand and pulled the curtain closed. "Go on, finish your damned confession. I'll finish the message."

Murphy slumped against the screen and spoke softly to the Cardinal. "I'm sorry...."

Hickey stood outside the booth and looked around. Flynn was gone. No one was paying any attention to him except Malone and Baxter on the sanctuary, who looked both angry and disheartened. Hickey smiled at them, then read the coded message, put his finger on the buzzer, and began to send. He repeated the salutation—.

THIS IS FR. MURPHY IN CONFESSIONAL WITH CARDINAL.

He continued, reproducing the halting wrist of a man who was sending for the first time. He modified the written message as he sent.

ESTIMATE OF FENIAN STRENGTH: NO MORE THAN EIGHT GUNMEN. ONE IN EACH OF EAST TRIFORIA. NONE IN WEST TRIFORIA. NONE IN CHOIR LOFT. ONE MAN AT SACRISTY STAIRS WITH THOMPSON—ONLY AUTO WEAPON SEEN. ONE MAN IN EACH TOWER. FIELD PHONES MALFUNCTIONING. HOSTAGES MOVED TO CRYPT. SAFE FROM FIRE.

He stopped and picked up the text of the message.

MACCUMAIL IS BRIAN FLYNN. JOHN HICKEY, LIEUTENANT. MEGAN THIRD IN COMMAND.

He improvised again.

NO MINES ON DOORS. GAS MASKS ARE OLD TYPE, INEFFECTIVE FILTERS.

He stopped and thought a moment. Then went on.

FENIANS LOYAL TO HICKEY. WILL NOT NEGOTIATE IN GOOD
FAITH. SUICIDAL TALK. BAXTER TO BE HANGED BEFORE
DAWN DEADLINE AS AN EXAMPLE. DO WHAT YOU MUST. WE
ARE NOT AFRAID. GOD BLESS YOU—FATHER MURPHY.

Hickey took his finger off the buzzer and smiled. The people
out there were a bit confused now...and frightened. Fright
led to desperation. Desperation led to reckless acts. Hickey put
himself in their place—discounting the possibility of negotiation, concerned over the hostages, underestimating the force
holding the Cathedral. The police would submit a plan to take
the Cathedral, and it would be accepted. And the politicians
would have the message to justify that use of force. The police
would burst through the doors, and they'd be met by explosions
and an unexpected volume of killing fire.

Hickey pictured it in his mind as he looked around
the Cathedral. Shattered marble, crumbling statues, dark red
blood running over the altars and floors, the dead lying
draped over the pews. The attic would be set aflame, and
the ceiling would fall into the nave, blowing their precious
stained glass into the streets. He saw dying bodies writhing
among the rubble and the flames. And when they thought
it was over, long after the last shot had been fired, as the
dawn streaked in through dusty shafts revealing the rescuers
and medics moving through the ruins, then the time bombs
would detonate, and the two main columns would tremble
and shudder and collapse in a deafening roar of granite and
marble, plaster and bronze, wood and concrete. The Cathedral would die, brick by brick, stone by stone, column by
column, wall by wall.... And in years to come when people

looked on the most magnificent ruin in America they would remember John Hickey's last mission on earth.

Maureen Malone sat very still in the pew and watched as Hickey sent his message. She turned to Harold Baxter. "Bastard!"

Baxter looked away from Hickey. "Yes, well, that's his prerogative, isn't it? But, no harm done. Especially if the first message was received."

"I don't think you understand," she said. "The people outside still believe we control that signal. Hickey is not sending them a rude message or something of that sort. He's reading from our message and sending a misleading intelligence report over our signatures."

Baxter looked at Hickey, and the comprehension of what she was saying came to him.

"And God only knows what he's telling them. He's mad, you know. Flynn is a paragon of rationality compared to Hickey."

"Hickey is not mad," said Baxter. "He's something far more dangerous than mad."

She looked down at the floor. "Anyway, I'll not apologize for trying."

"I'm not asking you to. But I think the next plan should be mine."

"Really?" She spoke with a frigid tone in her voice. "I don't think we have the time to wait for either your plan or your much discussed right moment."

He answered without anger. "Just give me a few more minutes. I think I know a way out of here."

Burke walked into the Monsignor's inner office, followed by Inspector Langley. A uniformed officer handed them each a copy of the decoded message. Burke sat on Schroeder's desk and

read the message. He looked around at the people present—
Schroeder, Commissioner Rourke, Roberta Spiegel, and
Bellini—the hard core of the Desperate Dozen, with Langley
and himself added or subtracted as the situation changed.

Captain Bellini looked up from his copy and spoke to Commissioner Rourke. "If this is accurate, I can take the Cathedral
with an acceptable risk to my people. If the hostages are in the
crypt, they have a fair chance of surviving... though I can't guarantee that." He looked at the message again. "They don't seem
to stand much chance with the Fenians anyway." He stood. "I'll
need a few more hours to plan."

Burke thought of Maureen's statement at the sacristy gate.
Twelve gunmen. Now Murphy said eight. He looked across the
room at Bellini. "And if it's not accurate?"

Bellini said, "How far off can they be? They're heads-up people. Right? They can count. Look, I'm not real anxious to do
this, but I feel a little better about it now."

Langley said, "We can't discount the possibility that one or
both of these messages are from the Fenians." He looked at his
copy and compared it to the earlier message, which he held in
his hand. "I'm a little confused. Something is wrong here." He
looked up. "Bellini, as an intelligence officer, I'd advise you not
to believe either of these."

Bellini looked distraught. "Well, where the hell does that put
me? Square fucking one, that's where."

Roberta Spiegel said, "Whether or not we believe either of
these messages, everybody in the Cardinal's residence and in the
next room is reading this last message, and they will come to
their own conclusions." She looked at Rourke. "This justifies a
preemptive attack, Commissioner. That's what's going through
their minds out there." She turned to Bellini. "Captain, be prepared to mount an attack at very short notice."

Bellini nodded distractedly.

The door opened, and Monsignor Downes came into the office. "Did someone want to see me?"

The five men looked at each other questioningly, then Roberta Spiegel said, "Yes, I asked to see you."

Downes remained standing.

The Mayor's aide thought a moment, then said, "Monsignor, neither the Mayor nor myself nor anyone wants to do anything that will harm this church or endanger the lives of the hostages. However—"

The Monsignor's body stiffened.

"However, if the police and my office and the people in Washington decide that negotiation is no longer possible and that there is a clear and immediate danger to the hostages... will you and the diocese stand behind our decision to send in the Emergency Services Division?"

Monsignor Downes stood motionless without answering.

Spiegel said to Bellini, "Give the Monsignor a copy of that message."

Downes took the paper and read it, then looked at Roberta Spiegel. "I'll have to check with the Vicar General. I cannot take the responsibility for this on my own." He turned and left the room.

Roberta Spiegel said, "Every time we uncover another layer of this problem I see how much we've underestimated Flynn. We're sandbagged pretty badly all around, and as the time slips by it's obvious that the easiest course of action is surrender— ours, not Flynn's."

Langley said, "Even surrender is not so easy. We may give in, but that doesn't mean Washington, London, or Dublin will."

Commissioner Rourke said to Bellini, "Captain, the only

thing we can do unilaterally, without anyone's permission except the Mayor's, is to attack."

Bellini answered, "That's always the easiest decision, sir—it's the execution that gets a little sticky."

Schroeder spoke up. "I get the feeling you've given up on the negotiations."

Everyone looked at him. Burke said, "Captain, you're still the best hope we've got. If there's any middle ground between our capitulation and an attack, I'm sure you'll find it. Brian Flynn said, however, that there was no middle ground, and I think he was telling us the truth. Dawn or dead."

Maureen watched Hickey as he spoke to the Cardinal and Father Murphy at the confessional. She said to Baxter, "He's questioning them about the buzzer and about the first message."

Baxter nodded, then stood. "Let's pace a bit and stretch our legs. We'll talk."

They began walking across the altar sanctuary toward the throne, a distance of forty feet, then turned and walked back. As they walked, Baxter inclined his head. "Look over there—at the brass plate."

Maureen glanced to the right of the altar. Beyond the sacristy staircase was the large brass plate through which Hickey and Megan Fitzgerald had descended with the suitcases.

Baxter looked over the length of the Cathedral. "I've been analyzing this building. When Hickey and Fitzgerald came up from that plate, they had earth on their hands and knees. So it must be mostly crawl space. There must be large areas that are unlit or badly lit. We have an area of almost a city block in which to disappear. If we can lift that plate quickly and drop into that space, they could never flush us out."

As they paced back toward the right side of the altar the plate came into view again. She said, "Even if we could raise the plate and drop below before we were shot, we wouldn't be free, and no one on the outside would know we were down there."

"We would know we weren't up *here*."

She nodded. "Yes, that's the point, isn't it?" They walked in silence for a few minutes, then Maureen said, "How do you plan to do it?"

Baxter outlined his plan.

Father Murphy and the Cardinal entered the sanctuary, and both Maureen and Baxter noticed that the two priests looked very pale. Father Murphy looked from Maureen to Baxter. "Hickey knows, of course."

The Cardinal spoke. "I would have had no objection to trying to signal the rectory." He looked at Murphy sharply, then at Baxter and Maureen. "You must keep me in-formed—beforehand—of your plans."

Baxter nodded. "We're about to do that, Your Eminence. We're considering an escape plan. We want you both to come with us."

The Cardinal shook his head and said emphatically, "My place is here." He seemed lost in thought for a moment, then said, "But I'm ready to give you my blessing." He turned to Father Murphy. "You may go if you choose."

Murphy shook his head and addressed Maureen and Baxter. "I can't leave without His Eminence. But I'll help you if I can."

Maureen looked at the three men. "Good. Let's work out the details and the timing." She looked at her watch. "At nine o'clock, we go."

CHAPTER 33

Captain Bellini said to Monsignor Downes as the Rector walked into the office, "Have you found the plans to the Cathedral yet?"

The Monsignor shook his head. "The staff is looking here and at the diocese building. But I don't believe we ever had a set on file."

Commissioner Rourke said to Langley, "What are you doing about finding the architect, Gordon Stillway?"

Langley lit a cigarette and took his time answering. He said finally, "Detectives went to his office on East Fifty-third. It was closed, of course—"

Rourke interrupted. "Are you getting a court order to go in?"

Langley noticed that the Deputy Commissioner was becoming more assertive. By midnight he'd probably try to give an order. Langley said, "Actually, someone already got in—without the benefit of a court order. No Cathedral blueprints. The detectives are trying to find a roster of employees. That's apparently missing also."

Monsignor Downes cleared his throat and said, "I don't approve of an assault...but it must be planned for, I suppose..." He looked at the bookcase and said, "Among those books you'll find about five that are pictorial studies of the Cathedral. Some have plans in them, very sketchy plans—for tourists to follow when they walk on the main floor. The interior pictures are very good, though, and may be helpful."

Bellini went to the bookcase and began scanning the shelves.

Burke stood. "There may be a set of blueprints in Stillway's apartment. No one's answering the phone, and the detective we have stationed there says no one's answering the door. I'm going over there now."

Schroeder stood also. "You can't leave here. Flynn said—"

Burke turned on him. "The hell with Flynn."

Roberta Spiegel said, "Go ahead, Lieutenant."

Langley ripped a page from his notebook. "Here's the address. Don't gain entry by illegal means."

Monsignor Downes said, "If you should find Gordon Stillway, remember he's a very old man. Don't excite him."

"I don't do anything illegal. I don't excite people." Burke turned and walked out into the adjoining office. A heavy cloud of blue smoke hung at face level over the crowded outer office. Burke pushed his way into the hall and went down the stairs. The rectory offices on the ground floor were filled with uniformed police commanders directing the field operations. Burke approached a captain sitting at a desk and showed his badge case. "I need a squad car and a maniac to drive it."

The captain looked up from a map of midtown. "Do you? Well, the area on the other side of the cordon is jammed solid with people and vehicles. Where is it you'd like to go in such a hurry, Lieutenant?"

"Gramercy Park. Pronto-like."

"Well, make your way to the IRT station on Lex."

"Bullshit." He grabbed a phone and went through the switchboard to the Monsignor's office. "Langley, is the helicopter still in the Palace courtyard? Good. Call and get it revved up."

Burke walked out of the rectory into Fifty-first Street and breathed in the cold, bracing air that made him feel better. The sleet was tapering off, but the wind was still strong. He walked into the deserted intersection of Fifty-first and Madison.

An eerie silence hung over the lamplit streets around the Cathedral, and in the distance he could see the barricades of squad cars, buses, and sanitation trucks that made up the cordon. Strands of communication wire ran over the sleet-covered streets and sidewalks. Sentries stood silhouetted against half-lit buildings, and National Guardsmen cruised by in jeeps, rifles pointed upward. Bullhorns barked in the wintry air, and policemen patrolled the sanitized area with shotguns. Burke heard their footsteps crunching in the unshoveled ice and heard his own quickening pace. As he walked, he thought of Belfast and, though he'd never been there, felt he knew the place. He turned up his collar and walked faster.

Across Madison Avenue a solitary figure on horseback rode slowly into the north wind. He stared at the rider, Betty Foster, as she passed beneath a streetlight. She didn't seem to notice him, and he walked on.

The wind dropped, and he heard in the distance, past the perimeter of the cordon, the sounds of music and singing. New York would not be denied its party. Burke passed the rear of the Lady Chapel, then approached the Cardinal's residence, and through the lace curtains on a groundfloor window he saw ESD men standing in a room. A lieutenant was briefing them, and Burke could see a chalkboard. *Win this one for the Gipper, lads.* Through another window on the corner Burke saw well-dressed men and women, the Governor and Mayor among them, crowded around what was probably a buffet. They didn't exactly look like they were enjoying themselves, but they didn't look as grim as the men around the chalkboard either.

In the intersection Burke turned and looked back at the Cathedral illuminated by its garden floodlights. A soft luminescence passed through the stained-glass windows and cast a colored shadow over the white street. It was a serene picture, postcard pretty: ice-covered branches of bare lindens and glistening expanses of undisturbed sleet. Perhaps more serene than it had ever been in this century—the surrounding area cleared of cars and people, and the buildings darkened....

Something out of place caught his eye, and he looked up at the two towers where light shone through the ripped louvers. In the north tower—the bell tower—he saw a shadow moving, a solitary figure circling from louver to louver, cold, probably edgy, watchful. In the south tower there was also a figure, standing motionless. Two people, one in each tower—the only eyes that stared out of the besieged Cathedral. So much depended on them, thought Burke. He hoped they weren't the panicky type.

The police command helicopter followed Lexington Avenue south. Below, Burke could see that traffic was beginning to move again, or at least what passed for moving traffic in Manhattan. Rotating beacons at every intersection indicated the scope of the police action below. The towering buildings of midtown gave way to the lower buildings in the old section of Gramercy Park, and the helicopter dropped altitude.

Burke could see the lamps of the small private park encircled by elegant town houses. He pointed, and the pilot swung the craft toward the open area and turned on the landing lights. The helicopter settled into a small patch of grass, and Burke jumped out and walked quickly toward the high wrought-iron fence. He rattled the bars of a tall gate but found it was locked. On the sidewalk a crowd of people stared back at him curiously. Burke said, "Is anyone there a keyholder?"

No one answered.

Burke peered between the bars, his hands wrapped around the cold iron. He thought of the zoo gate that morning, the ape house, the sacristy gate, and all the prisons he'd ever seen. He thought of Long Kesh and Crumlin Road, Lubianka and Dachau. He thought that there were too many iron bars and too many people staring at each other through them. He shouted with a sudden and unexpected anger, "Come on, damn it! Who's got a key?"

An elderly, well-dressed woman came forward and produced an ornate key. Without a word she unlocked the gate, and Burke slipped out quickly and pushed roughly through the crowd.

He approached a stately old town house across the street and knocked sharply on the door. A patrolman opened the door, and Burke held up his badge, brushing by him into the small lobby. A single plainclothesman sat in the only chair, and Burke introduced himself perfunctorily.

The man answered through a wide yawn, "Detective Lewis." He stood as though with some effort.

Burke said, "Any word on Stillway?"

The detective shook his head.

"Get a court order yet?"

"Nope."

Burke began climbing the stairs. When he was a rookie, an old cop once said to him, "Everybody lives on the top floor. Everybody gets robbed on the top floor. Everybody goes nuts on the top floor. Everybody dies on the top floor." Burke reached the top floor, the fourth. Two apartments had been made out of what was once probably the servants' quarters. He found Stillway's door and pressed the buzzer.

The detective climbed the stairs behind him. "No one home."

"No shit, Sherlock." Burke looked at the three lock-cylinders in a vertical row, ranging in age from very old to very new, showing the progression of panic with each passing decade. He turned to the detective. "Want to put your shoulder to that?"

"Nope."

"Me neither." Burke moved to a narrow staircase behind a small door. "Stay here." He went up the stairs and came out onto the roof, then went down the rear fire escape and stopped at Stillway's window.

The apartment was dark except for the yellow glow of a clock radio. There was no grate on the window, and Burke drew his gun and brought it through the old brittle glass above the sash lock. He reached in, unlatched the catch, and threw the sash up, then dropped into the room and moved away from the window in a crouch, his gun held out in front of him with both hands.

He steadied his breathing and listened. His eyes became accustomed to the dark, and he began to make out shadows and shapes. Nothing moved, nothing breathed, nothing smelled; there was nothing that wanted to kill him, and, he sensed, nothing that had been killed there. He rose, found a lamp, and turned it on.

The large studio apartment was in stark modern contrast to the world around it. Bone-white walls, track lighting, chromium furniture. The secret modern world of an old architect who specialized in Gothic restorations. *Shame, shame, Gordon Stillway.*

He walked toward the hall door, gun still drawn, looking into the dark corners as he moved. Everything was perfectly ordinary; nothing was out of place—no crimson on the white rug, no gore on the shiny chromium. Burke holstered his revolver and opened the door. He motioned to the detective. "Back window broken. Cause to suspect a crime in progress. Fill out a report."

The detective winked and moved toward the stairs.

Burke closed the door and looked around. He found a file cabinet beside a drafting table and opened the middle drawer alphabetized J to S. He was not too surprised to find that between St.-Mark's-in-the-Bouwerie and St. Paul the Apostle there was nothing but a slightly larger space than there should have been.

Burke saw a telephone on the counter of the kitchenette and dialed the rectory, got a fast busy-signal on the trunk line, dialed the operator, got a recording telling him to dial again, and slammed down the receiver. He found Gordon Stillway's bar in a shelf unit and chose a good bourbon.

The phone rang and Burke answered, "Hello."

Langley's voice came through the earpiece. "Figured you couldn't get an open line. What's the story? Body in the library?"

"No body. No Stillway. The Saint Patrick's file is missing, too."

Langley said, "Interesting..." He paused, then said, "We're having no luck in our other inquiries either."

Burke heard someone talking loudly in the background. "Is that Bellini?"

Langley said quietly, "Yeah. He's going into his act. Pay no attention."

Burke lit a cigarette. "I'm not having a good Saint Patrick's Day, Inspector."

"March eighteenth doesn't look real promising either." He drew a long breath. "There are blueprints in this city somewhere, and there are other architects, maybe engineers, who know this place. We could have them all by midmorning tomorrow—but we don't have that long. Flynn has thought this all out. Right down to snatching Stillway and the blueprints."

Burke said, "I wonder."

"Wonder *what*?"

"Hasn't it occurred to you that if Flynn had Stillway, then Stillway would be in the Cathedral where he'd do the most good?"

"Maybe he *is* in there."

Burke thought a moment. "I don't know. Flynn would tell us if he had the architect. He'd tell us he knows ways to blow the place by mining the hidden passages—if any. He's an intelligent man who knows how to get maximum mileage from everything he does. Think about it." Burke looked around the tidy room. A copy of the *New York Post* lay on the couch, and he pulled the telephone cord as he walked to it. A front-page picture showed a good fist-flying scene of the disturbance in front of the Cathedral at noon. The headline ran: DEMONSTRATION MARS PARADE. A subline said: BUT THE IRISH MARCH. The special evening editions would have better stuff than that.

Langley's voice came into the earpiece. "Burke, you still there?"

Burke looked up. "Yeah. Look, Stillway was here. Brought home the evening paper and..."

"And?"

Burke walked around the room holding the phone and receiver. He opened a closet near the front door and spoke into the phone. "Wet topcoat. Wet hat. No raincoat. No umbrella. No briefcase. He came home in the sleet, changed, and went out again carrying his briefcase, which contained, I guess, the Saint Patrick's file."

"What color are his eyes? Okay, I'll buy it. Where'd he go?"

"Probably went with somebody who had a good set of credentials and a plausible story. Somebody who talked his way into the apartment..."

Langley said, "A Fenian who got to him too late to get him into the Cathedral—"

"Maybe. But maybe somebody else doesn't want us to have the blueprints or Stillway . . . ."

"Strange business."

"Think about it, Inspector. Meanwhile, get a Crime Scene Unit over here, then get me an open line so I can call Ferguson."

"Okay. But hurry back. Schroeder's getting nervous."

Burke hung up and took his glass of bourbon on a tour around the apartment. Nothing else yielded any hard clues, but he was getting a sense of the old architect. Not the type of man to go out into the cold sleet, he thought, unless duty called. The phone rang. Burke picked it up and gave the operator Ferguson's number, then said, "Call back in ten minutes. I'll need to make another call."

After six rings the phone was answered, and Jack Ferguson came on the line, his voice sounding hesitant. "Hello?"

"Burke. Thought I'd get the coroner."

"You may well have. Where the hell have you been?"

"Busy. Well, it looks like you get the good-spy award this year."

"Keep it. Why haven't you called? I've been waiting for your call—"

"Didn't my office call you?"

"Yes. Very decent of them. Said I was a marked man. Who's on to me, then?"

"Well, Flynn for one. Probably the New York Irish Republican Army, Provisional Wing, for another. And I think you've outlived your usefulness to Major Martin— it *was* Martin you were playing around with, wasn't it?"

Ferguson stayed silent for a few seconds, then said, "He told me he could head off the Fenians with my help."

"Did he, now? Well, the only people he wanted to head off were the New York police."

Again, Ferguson didn't speak for a few seconds, then said, "Bastards. They're all such bloody bastards. Why is everyone so committed to this senseless violence?"

"Makes good press. What is your status, Jack?"

"Status? My status is I'm scared. I'm packed and ready to leave town. My wife's sister came and took her to her place. God, I wouldn't have waited around for anyone else, Burke. I should have left an hour ago."

"Well, why did you wait around? Got something for me?"

"Does the name Terri O'Neal mean anything to you?"

"Man or woman?"

"Woman."

Burke thought a moment. "No."

"She's been kidnapped."

"Lot of that going around today."

"I think she has something to do with what's happening."

"In what way?"

Ferguson said, "Hold on a moment. I hear someone in the hall. Hold on."

Burke said quickly, "Wait. Just tell me—Jack—Shit." Burke held the line. He heard Ferguson's footsteps retreating. He waited for the crash, the shot, the scream, but there was nothing.

Ferguson's voice came back on the line, his breathing loud in the earpiece. "Damned Rivero brothers. Got some señoritas pinned in the alcove, squeezing their tits. God, this used to be a nice Irish building. Boys would go in the basement and get blind drunk. Never looked at a pair of tits until they were thirty. Where was I?"

"Terri O'Neal."

"Right. I got this from a Boston Provo. He and some other lads were supposed to snatch this O'Neal woman last night if a man named Morgan couldn't pick her up in a disco. I assume

Morgan picked her up—it's easy today, like going out for a pack of cigarettes. You know? Anyway, now these Boston lads think it was part of what happened today, and they're not happy about what the Fenians did."

"Neither are we."

"Of course," added Ferguson, "it could all be coincidence."

"Yeah." Burke thought. *Terri O'Neal.* It was a familiar name, but he couldn't place it. He was sure it wasn't in the files, because women in the files were still rare enough to remember every one of them. "Terri O'Neal."

"That's what the gentleman said. Now get me the hell out of here."

"Okay. Stay put. Don't open the door to strangers."

"How long will it take to get a car here?"

"I'm not sure. Hang on. You're covered."

"That's what Langley told Timmy O'Day last summer."

"Mistakes happen. Listen, we'll have a drink next week...lunch—"

"Fuck lunch—"

Burke hung up. He stared at the telephone for several minutes. He had a bad taste in his mouth, and he stubbed out his cigarette, then sipped on the bourbon. The telephone rang, and he picked it up. "Operator, get me Midtown North Precinct."

After a short wait the phone rang, and a deep voice said, "Sergeant Gonzalez, Midtown North."

"This is Lieutenant Burke, Intelligence." He gave his badge number. "Do you have clear radio commo with your cars?"

The harried desk sergeant answered, "Yeah, the jamming isn't affecting us here."

Burke heard the recorder go on and heard the beep at four-second intervals. "You check me out after you hang up. Okay?"

"Right."

"Can you get a car over to 560 West Fifty-fifth Street? Apartment 5D. Pick up and place in protective custody—name of Jack Ferguson."

"What for?"

"His life is in danger."

"So is every citizen's life in this city. Comes with the territory. West Fifty-fifth? I'm surprised he's not dead yet."

"He's an informant. Real important."

"I don't have many cars available. Things are a mess—"

"Yeah, I heard. Listen, he'll want to go to the Port Authority building, but keep him in the station house."

"Sounds fucked up."

"He's involved with this Cathedral thing. Just do it, okay? I'll take care of you. *Erin go bragh, Gonzalez.*"

"Yeah, *hasta la vista.*"

Burke hung up and left the apartment. He went out into the street and walked back toward the park, where a crowd had gathered outside the fence. As he walked he thought about Ferguson. He knew he owed Ferguson a better shot at staying alive. He knew he should pick him up in the helicopter. But the priorities were shifting again. Gordon Stillway was important. Brian Flynn was important, and Major Martin was important. Jack Ferguson was not so important any longer. Unless... *Terri O'Neal.* What in the name of God was that all about? Why was that name so familiar?

CHAPTER 34

John Hickey sat alone at the chancel organ. He raised his field glasses to the southeast triforium. Frank Gallagher sat precariously on the parapet, reading a Bible; his back was to a supporting column, his sniper rifle was across his knees, and he looked very serene. Hickey marveled at a man who could hold two opposing philosophies in his head at the same time. He shouted to Gallagher, "Look lively."

Hickey focused the glasses on George Sullivan in the long southwest triforium, who was also sitting on the parapet. He was playing a small mouth organ too softly to be heard, except by Abby Boland across the nave. Hickey focused on her as she leaned out across the parapet, looking at Sullivan like a moon-struck girl hanging from a balcony in some cheap melodrama.

Hickey shifted the glasses to the choir loft. Megan was talking to Leary again, and Leary appeared to be actually listening this time. Hickey sensed that they were discovering a common inhumanity. He thought of two vampires on a castle wall in the moonlight, bloodless and lifeless, not able to consummate their meeting in a normal way but agreeing to hunt together.

He raised the glasses and focused on Flynn, who was sitting alone in the choir benches that rose up toward the towering brass organ pipes. Beyond the pipes the great rose window sat above his head like an alien moon, suffused with the night-lights of the Avenue. The effect was dramatic, striking, thought Hickey, and unintentionally so, like most of the memorable tableaux he had seen in his life. Flynn seemed uninterested in Megan or Leary, or in the blueprints spread across his knees. He was staring out into space, and Hickey saw that he was toying with his ring.

Hickey put down the glasses. He had the impression that the troops were getting bored, even claustrophobic, if that were possible in this space. Cabin fever— Cathedral fever, whatever; it was taking its toll, and the night was yet young. Why was it, he thought, that the old, with so little time left, had the most patience? Well, he smiled, age was not so important in here. Everyone had almost the same lifespan left...give or take a few heartbeats.

Hickey looked at the hostages on the sanctuary. The four of them were speaking intently. No boredom there. Hickey cranked the field phone beside him. "Attic? Status report."

Jean Kearney's voice came back with a breathy stutter. "Cold as hell up here."

Hickey smiled. "You and Arthur should do what we used to do when I was a lad to keep warm in winter." He waited for a response, but there was none, so he said, "We used to chop wood." He laughed, then cranked the phone again. "South tower. See anything interesting?"

Rory Devane answered, "Snipers with flak jackets on every roof. The area as far south as Forty-eighth Street is cleared. Across the way there are hundreds of people at the windows." He added, "I feel as though I'm in a goldfish bowl."

Hickey lit his pipe, and it bobbed in his mouth as he spoke. "Hold your head up, lad—they're watching your face through their glasses." He thought, *And through their sniper scopes.* "Stare back at them. You're the reason they're all there."

"Yes, sir."

Hickey rang the bell tower. "Status report."

Donald Mullins answered, "Status unchanged...except that more soldiers are arriving."

Hickey drew on his pipe. "Did you get your corned beef, lad? Want more tea?"

"Yes, more tea, please. I'm cold. It's very cold here."

Hickey's voice was low. "It was cold on Easter Monday, 1916, on the roof of the General Post Office. It was cold when the British soldiers marched us to Kilmainham Jail. It was cold in Stonebreaker's Yard where they shot my father and Padraic Pearse and fifteen of our leaders. It's cold in the grave."

Hickey picked up the Cathedral telephone and spoke to the police switchboard operator in the rectory. "Get me Schroeder." He waited through a series of clicks, then said, "Did you find Gordon Stillway yet?"

Schroeder's voice sounded startled. "What?"

"We cleaned out his office after quitting time—couldn't do it before, you understand. That might have tipped someone as dense as even Langley or Burke. But we had trouble getting to Stillway in the crowd. Then the riot broke."

Schroeder's voice faltered, then he said, "Why are you telling us this—?"

"We should have killed him, but we didn't. He's either in a hospital or drunk somewhere, or your good friend Martin has murdered him. Stillway is the key man for a successful assault, of course. The blueprints by themselves are not enough. Did you find a copy in the rectory? Well, don't tell me, then. Are you still there, Schroeder?"

"Yes."

"I thought you nodded off." Hickey saw Flynn moving toward the organ keyboard in the choir loft. "Listen, Schroeder, we're going to play some hymns on the bells later. I want a list of eight requests from the NYPD when I call again. All right?"

"All right."

"Nothing tricky now. Just good solid Christian hymns that sound nice on the bells. Some Irish folk songs, too. Give the city a lift. *Beannacht.*" He hung up. After uncovering the keyboard and turning on the chancel organ, he put his thin hands over the keys and began playing a few random notes. He nodded with exaggerated graciousness toward the hostages who were watching and began singing as he played. "In Dublin's fair city, where the girls are so pretty..." His voice came out in a well-controlled bass, rich and full, very unlike his speaking voice. " 'Twas where I first met my sweet Molly Malone..."

Brian Flynn sat at the choir organ and turned the key to start it. He placed his hands over the long curved keyboard and played a chord. On the organ was a large convex mirror set at an angle that allowed Flynn to see most of the Cathedral below—used, he knew, by the organist to time the triumphal entry of a procession or to set the pace for an overly eager bride, or a reluctant one. He smiled as he joined with the smaller organ below and looked at Megan, who had just come from the south tower. "Give us the pleasure of your sweet voice, Megan. Come here and turn on this microphone."

Megan looked at him but made no move toward the microphone. Leary's eyes darted between Flynn and Megan.

Flynn said, "Ah, Megan, you've no idea how important song is to revolution." He turned on the microphone. Hickey was going through the song again, and Flynn joined in with a soft tenor.

> "As she wheeled her wheelbarrow
> Through streets wide and narrow

Crying cockles, and mussels,
Alive, alive-o..."

John Hickey smiled, and his eyes misted as the music carried him back across the spans of time and distance to the country he had not seen in over forty years.

"She was a fishmonger,
And sure 'twas no wonder,
For her father and mother were
Fishmongers, too,
And they each wheel'd their barrow..."

Hickey saw his father's face again on the night before the soldiers took him out to be shot. He remembered being dragged out of their cell to what he thought was his own place of execution, but they had beaten him and dumped him on the road outside Kilmainham Jail. He remembered clearly the green sod laid carefully over his father's grave the next day, his mother's face at the graveside....

"And she died of a fever
And no one could save her,
And that was the end of sweet
Molly Malone,
But her ghost wheels her barrow..."

He had wanted to die then, and had tried to die a soldier's death every day since, but it wasn't in his stars. And when at last he thought death had come in that mean little tenement across the river, he found he was required to go on...to complete one last mission. But it would be over soon...and he would be home again.

CHAPTER 35

Bert Schroeder looked at the memo given him by the Hostage Unit's psychologist, Dr. Korman, who had been monitoring each conversation from the adjoining office. Korman had written: *Flynn is a megalomaniac and probably a paranoid schizophrenic. Hickey is paranoid also and has an unfulfilled death wish.* Schroeder almost laughed. What the hell other kind of death wish could you have if you were still alive?

How, wondered Schroeder, could a New York psychologist diagnose a man like Flynn, from a culture so different from his own? Or Hickey, from a different era? How could he diagnose *anybody* based on telephone conversations? Yet he did it at least fifty times a year for Schroeder. Sometimes his diagnoses turned out to be fairly accurate; other times they did not. He always wondered if Korman was diagnosing *him* as well.

He looked up at Langley, who had taken off his jacket in the stuffy room. His exposed revolver lent, thought Schroeder, a nice menacing touch for the civilians. Schroeder said to him, "Do you have much faith in these things?"

Langley looked up from his copy of the report. "I'm reminded of my horoscope— the language is such that it fits anybody...nobody's playing with a full deck. You know?"

Schroeder nodded and turned a page of the report and stared

at it without reading. He hadn't given Korman the psy-profiles on either man yet and might never give them to the psychologist. The more varying opinions he had, the more he would be able to cover himself if things went bad. He said to Langley, "Regarding Korman's theory of Hickey's unfulfilled death wish, how are we making out on that court order for exhumation?"

Langley said, "A judge in Jersey City was located. We'll be able to dig up Hickey...the grave, by midnight."

Schroeder nodded. *Midnight—grave digging.* He gave a small shudder and looked down at the psychologist's report again. It went on for three typewritten pages, and as he read Schroeder had the feeling that Dr. Korman wasn't all there either. As to the real state of mind of these two men, Schroeder believed only God knew that—not Korman or anyone in the room, and probably not the two men themselves.

Schroeder looked at the three other people remaining in the room—Langley, Spiegel, and Bellini. He was aware that they were waiting for him to say something. He cleared his throat. "Well...I've dealt with crazier people.... In fact, all the people I've dealt with have been crazy. The funny thing is that the proximity to death seems to snap them out of it, temporarily. They act very rational when they realize what they're up against—when they see the forces massed against them."

Langley said, "Only the two people in the towers have that visual stimulation, Bert. The rest are in a sort of cocoon. You know?"

Schroeder shot Langley an annoyed look.

Joe Bellini said suddenly, "Fuck this psycho-crap. *Where is Stillway?*" He looked at Langley.

Langley shrugged.

Bellini said, "If Flynn has him in there, we've got a real problem."

Langley blew a smoke ring. "We're looking into it."

Schroeder said, "Hickey is a liar. He knows where Stillway is."

Spiegel shook her head. "I don't think he does."

Langley added, "Hickey was very indiscreet to mention Major Martin over the phone like that. Flynn wouldn't have wanted Martin's name involved publicly. He doesn't want to make trouble between Washington and London at this stage."

Schroeder nodded absently. He was certain the governments wouldn't reach an accord anyway—or, if they did, it wouldn't include releasing prisoners in Northern Ireland. He had nothing to offer the Fenians but their lives and a fair trial, and they didn't seem much interested in either.

Captain Bellini paced in front of the fireplace. "I won't expose my men to a fight unless I know every column, pew, balcony, and altar in that place."

Langley looked down at the six large picture books on the coffee table. "Those should give you a fair idea of the layout. Some good interior shots. Passable floor plans. Have your men start studying them. Now."

Bellini looked at him. "Is that the best intelligence you can come up with?" He picked up the books in one of his big hands and walked toward the door. "Damn it, if there's a secret way into that place, I've got to know." He began pacing in tight circles. "They've had it all their way up to now...but I'll get them." He looked at the silent people in the room. "Just keep them talking, Schroeder. When they call on me to move, I'll be ready. I'll get those potato-eating Mick sons of bitches—I'll bring Flynn's balls to you in a teacup." He walked out and slammed the door behind him.

Roberta Spiegel looked at Schroeder. "Is he nuts?"

Schroeder shrugged. "He goes through this act every time a

situation goes down. He's getting himself psyched. He gets crazier as the thing drags on."

Roberta Spiegel stood and reached into Langley's shirt pocket and took a cigarette.

Langley watched her as she lit the cigarette. There was something masculine and at the same time sensuously feminine about all her movements. A woman who had an obvious power over the Mayor—although exactly what type of power no one knew for sure. And, thought Langley, she was much sharper than His Honor. When it came down to the final decision on which so many lives hung, *she* would be the one to make it. Roberta Spiegel, whose name was known to nobody outside of New York. Roberta Spiegel, who had no ambitions of elected office, no civil service career to worry about, no one to answer to.

Spiegel sat on the edge of Schroeder's desk and leaned toward him, then glanced back at Langley. She said, "Let me be frank while we three are alone—" She bit her lip thoughtfully, then continued. "The British are not going to give in, as you know. Bellini doesn't have much of a chance of saving those people or this Cathedral. Washington is playing games, and the Governor is—well, between us, an asshole. His Honor is—how shall I put it?—not up to the task. And the Church is going to become a problem if we give them enough time." She leaned very close to Schroeder. "So...it's up to you, Captain. More than any time in your distinguished career it's all up to *you*—and, if you don't mind my saying so, Captain, you don't seem to be handling this with your usual aplomb."

Schroeder's face reddened. He cleared his throat. "If you...if the Mayor would like me to step aside—"

She came down from the desk. "There comes a time when every man knows he's met his match. I think we've *all* met our match here at this Cathedral. We can't even seem to win a point. Why?"

Schroeder again cleared his throat. "Well...it always seems that way in the beginning. They're the aggressors, you understand, and they've had months to think everything out. In time the situation will begin to reverse—"

Spiegel slammed her hand on the desk. "They know that, damn it! That's why they've given us no time. *Blitzkrieg*, Schroeder, *blitzkrieg*. Lightning war. You know the word. They're not hanging around while we get our act together. Dawn or dead. That's the truest thing anyone's said all night."

Schroeder tried to control his voice. "Miss Spiegel...you see, I've had many years...let me explain. We are at a psychological disadvantage because of the hostages.... But put yourself in the *Cathedral*. Think of the disadvantages *they* must overcome. They don't want to die—no matter what they pretend to the contrary. That and that alone is the bottom line of their thinking. And the hostages are keeping them alive—therefore, they won't kill the hostages. Therefore, at dawn *nothing* will happen. *Nothing.* It never does. *Never.*"

Spiegel let out a long breath. She turned toward Langley and reached out not for another cigarette but for his pistol. She pulled it from his shoulder holster and turned to Schroeder. "See this? Men used to settle their arguments with this." She looked closely at the blue-black metal and continued. "We're supposed to be beyond that now, but I'll tell you something. There's more of this in the world than there are hostage negotiators. I'll tell you something else—I'd rather send Bellini in with his guns than wait around with my finger up my ass to see what happens at dawn." She dropped the pistol to her side and leaned over the desk. "If you can't get a firm extension of the dawn deadline, then we go in while we still have the cover of darkness—before that self-destruct response levels this block."

Schroeder sat motionless. "There is no self-destruct response."

Spiegel said, "God, I wish I had your nerves—it *is* nerves, isn't it?" She tossed the revolver back to Langley.

Langley holstered the gun. He looked at Spiegel. She got away with a great deal—the cigarettes, then the gun. She relieved him of his possessions with a very cavalier attitude. But maybe, he thought, it was just as well she didn't observe the cautious etiquette that men did in these situations.

Roberta Spiegel moved away and looked at the two police officers. "If you want to know what's really happening around you, don't listen to those politicians out there. Listen to Brian Flynn and John Hickey." She looked at a large wooden crucifix over Schroeder's head and then out through the window at the Cathedral. "If Flynn or Hickey say dawn or dead, they *mean* dawn or dead. Understand who you're dealing with."

Schroeder nodded, almost imperceptibly. For a split second he had seen the face of the enemy, but it disappeared again just as quickly.

There was a long silence in the room, then Spiegel continued softly, "They can sense our fear...smell it. They also sense that we're not going to give them what they want." She looked at Schroeder. "I wish the people out there could give you the kind of direction you should have. But they've confused your job with theirs. They expect miracles from you, and you're starting to believe you can deliver them. You can't. Only Joe Bellini can deliver them a miracle—a military miracle—none killed, no wounded, no damage. Bellini is looking better to the people out there. They're losing faith in the long hard road that you represent. They're fantasizing about a glorious successful military solution. So while you're stalling the Fenians, don't forget to stall the people in the other rooms, too."

CHAPTER 36

Flynn and Hickey played the organs, and George Sullivan played the pipes. Eamon Farrell, Frank Gallagher, and Abby Boland sang "My Wild Irish Rose." In the attic Jean Kearney and Arthur Nulty lay huddled together on a catwalk above the choir loft. The pipes of the great organ reverberated through the board on which they lay. Pedar Fitzgerald sat with his back against the crypt door. He half closed his tired eyes and hummed.

Flynn felt the lessening of the tensions as people lost themselves in reveries. He could sense a dozen minds escaping the cold stone fortress. He glanced at Megan and Leary. Even they seemed subdued as they sat on the choir parapet, their backs to the Cathedral, drinking tea and sharing a cigarette. Flynn turned away from them and lost himself in the thunderous organ.

Father Murphy knelt motionless before the high altar. He glanced at his watch.

Harold Baxter paced across the sanctuary floor, trying to appear restless while his eyes darted around the Cathedral. He looked at his watch. No reason, he thought, to wait the remaining minutes. They might never get an opportunity as good as this. As he passed by Father Murphy, he said, "Thirty seconds."

Maureen lay curled up on a pew, her face buried in her arms. One eye peered out, and she saw Baxter nod to her.

Baxter turned and walked back toward the throne. He passed close to the Cardinal and said, "Now."

The Cardinal stood, came down from the throne, and walked to the communion rail. He opened the gate and strode swiftly down the center aisle.

Father Murphy heard Baxter say, "Go." Murphy made the sign of the cross, rose quickly, and moved toward the side of the altar.

Flynn watched the movements on the sanctuary in the organ mirror as he played. He continued to play the lilting melody as he called out to Leary. "Turn around."

Leary and Megan both jumped down from the parapet and spun around. Leary raised his rifle.

Hickey's organ stopped, and Flynn's organ died away on a long, lingering note. The singing stopped, and the Cathedral fell silent, all eyes on the Cardinal. Flynn spoke into the microphone as he looked in the mirror. "Stop where you are, Cardinal."

Father Murphy opened the circuit-breaker box recessed into the side of the altar, pulled the switch, and the sanctuary area went dark. Baxter took three long strides, passed the sacristy staircase, and hit the floor, sliding across the marble toward the brass floorplate. Maureen rolled off the pew and crawled swiftly toward the rear of the sanctuary. Baxter's fingers found the grip on the brass plate and lifted the heavy metal until its hinges locked in place. Maureen pivoted, and her legs found the opening in the floor.

The four people in the triforia were shouting wildly. A shot rang out from the choir loft, and the shouting stopped. Four shots exploded in quick succession from the triforia.

Maureen dropped through the hole and fell to the earth floor below.

Baxter felt something—a spent bullet, a piece of marble—slam into his chest, and he rocked backward on his haunches.

The Cardinal kept walking straight head, but no one looked at him any longer.

Father Murphy crawled to the sacristy staircase and collided with Pedar Fitzgerald running up the steps. Both men swung wildly at each other in the partial darkness.

Baxter caught his breath and lunged forward. His arms and shoulders hung into the opening, and his feet slid over the marble trying to find traction.

Maureen was shouting, "Jump! Jump!" She reached up and grabbed his dangling arm.

Five more shots rang out, splintering marble and ringing sharply from the brass plate. Baxter felt a sharp pain shoot across his back, and his body jerked convulsively. Five more shots whistled through the dark over his head. He was aware that Maureen was pulling on his right hand. He tried to drop headfirst into the hole, but someone was pulling on his legs. He heard a shout very close to his ear, and the firing stopped.

Maureen was hanging from his arm, yelling up to him, "Jump! For God's sake, jump!"

Baxter heard his own voice, low and breathless. "Can't. Got me. Run. Run." Someone was pulling on his ankles, pulling him back from the hole. He felt Maureen's grip on his arm loosen, then break away. A pair of strong hands rolled him over on his back, and he looked into the face of Pedar Fitzgerald, who was kneeling above him, holding the submachine gun to his throat. In the half-light Baxter saw that there was blood spreading over Fitzgerald's neck and across his white shirt.

Fitzgerald looked down at him and spoke between labored

breaths. "You stupid son of a bitch! I'll kill you—you god-damned bastard." He pounded his fist into Baxter's face, then crawled over him to the hole and pointed the barrel of the gun down into the opening. He steadied himself and fired two long, deafening bursts into the darkness.

Baxter was dimly aware of a warm wetness seeping over the cold floor beneath him. His eyes tried to focus on the vaulted ceiling ten stories above his face, but all he saw were the blurry red spots of the Cardinals' hanging hats. He heard footsteps running toward the altar, coming up the stairs, then saw faces hovering over him— Hickey, then a few seconds later Flynn and Megan Fitzgerald.

Baxter turned his head and saw Father Murphy lying near the stairs, his hands pressed to his face and blood running between his fingers. He heard Megan's voice. "Pedar! Are you hit? Pedar?"

Baxter tried to raise his head to look for the Cardinal. Suddenly he saw Megan's shoe flying into his face, and a red flash passed in front of his eyes, followed by blackness.

Flynn knelt beside Pedar Fitzgerald and pulled the barrel of the gun out of the hole. He touched Fitzgerald's bloody neck wound. "Just grazed you, lad." He called to Megan. "Take him back to his post. Quickly."

Flynn lay prone at the edge of the opening and called down. "Maureen! Are you all right? Are you hit?"

Maureen knelt a few yards from the opening. Her body was trembling, and she took long breaths to steady herself. Her hands ran over her body, feeling for a wound.

Flynn called down again. "Are you hit?" His voice became anxious. "For God's sake, answer me."

She drew a deep breath and surprised herself by answering, "No."

Flynn's voice sounded more controlled. "Come back."

"Go to hell."

"Come back, Maureen, or we'll shoot Baxter. We'll shoot him and throw him down there where you can see him."

"They're all dead anyway."

"No, they're not."

"Let Baxter speak to me."

There was a pause, then Flynn said, "He's unconscious."

"Bloody murdering bastards. Let me speak to Father Murphy."

"He's...hurt. Wait. I'll get the Cardinal—"

"Go to hell." She knew she didn't want to hear any of their voices; she just wanted to run. She called back, "Give it up, Brian. Before more people are killed, give it up." Hesitantly she called, "Good-bye."

She drew away from the opening until her back came into contact with the base of a column. She stared at the ladder that descended from the opening. She heard someone speaking in half-whispered tones, and she had a feeling someone was ready to come down.

Flynn's voice called out again, "Maureen—you're not the kind who would run out on your friends. Their lives depend on you."

She felt a cold sweat break out over her body. She thought to herself, *Brian, you make everything so damned hard.* She stepped toward the opening but then hesitated. A new thought came into her mind. *What would Brian do?* He'd run. He always ran. And not out of cowardice but because he and all of them had long ago agreed that escape was the morally correct response to tight situations. Yet...he'd stayed with her when she was wounded. She vacillated between the column and the opening.

Flynn's voice cut into the dark basement. "You're a damned coward, Maureen. All right, then, Baxter's gone."

A shot rang out on the sacristy.

After the report died away he called out again. "Murphy is next."

Maureen instinctively moved back against the column. She put her face in her hands. "Bastards!"

Flynn yelled, "The priest is next!"

She picked up her head and wiped the tears from her eyes. She peered into the darkness. Her eyes adjusted to the half-light, and she forced herself to evaulate the situation calmly. To her right was the outer wall of the sacristy staircase. If she followed it she'd find the foundation wall, beyond which was freedom. That was the way she had to go.

She looked quickly back and saw a pair of legs dropping from the opening. More of the body was revealed as it descended the ladder—Hickey. Above Hickey's head another pair of legs appeared. Megan. Both of them held flashlights and pistols by their sides. Hickey turned his head and squinted into the blackness as he climbed down. Maureen crouched down beside the column.

Hickey's voice rolled through the black, damp air. He spoke as to a child. "Coming for you, darlin'. Coming to get you. Come to old John, now. Don't let the wicked Megan find you. Run to Mr. Hickey. Come on, then." He laughed and jumped down the last few steps, switched on the flashlight, and turned toward her.

Megan was right behind him, her fiery red features looking sinister in the overhead light.

Maureen drew a long breath and held it.

CHAPTER 37

Schroeder stood tensed with the phone to his ear. He looked up at Langley, the only person left in the office. "Goddamn it—they're not answering."

Langley stood at the window, staring intently at the Cathedral. On the other side of the double doors phones were ringing and people were shouting.

One of the doors burst open, and Bellini ran in looking more agitated than when he had last left. He shouted, "I have orders from fucking Kline to go in if you can't raise them!"

Schroeder looked up at him. "Get in here and close the door!" He yelled at the police operator, "Of course I want you to keep trying, you stupid ass!"

Bellini closed the door, walked to a chair, and fell into it. Sweat streamed down his pale face. "I...I'm not ready to go in...."

Schroeder said to Bellini impatiently, "How fucking long does it take to kill four hostages, Bellini? If they're dead already, Kline can damned well wait until you have at least a half-assed idea of how to hit the place."

Suddenly Flynn's voice came over the speaker. "Schroeder?"

Schroeder answered quickly, "Yes—" He controlled his voice. "Yes, sir. Is everything all right?"

"Yes."

Schroeder cleared his throat and spoke into the phone. "What is happening in there?"

Flynn's voice sounded composed. "An ill-advised attempt to escape."

Schroeder sounded incredulous. *"Escape?"*

"That's what I said."

"No one is hurt?"

There was a long pause, then Flynn said, "Baxter and Murphy are wounded. Not badly."

Schroeder looked at Langley and Bellini. He steadied his voice. "We're sending in a doctor."

"If they needed one, I'd tell you."

"I'm sending in a doctor."

"All right, but tell him before you send him that I'll blow his brains out."

Schroeder's voice became angry, but it was a controlled anger, contrived almost, designed to show that shooting was the one thing he wouldn't tolerate. "Damn you, Flynn, you said there'd be no shooting. You said—"

"It couldn't be helped, really."

Schroeder made his tone ominous. "Flynn, if you kill anyone—so help me God, if you hurt anyone, then we're beyond the let's-make-a-deal stage."

"I understand the rules. Calm down, Schroeder."

"Let me speak to each of the hostages. Now."

"Hold on." There was silence, then the Cardinal's voice filled the room. "Captain, do you recognize my voice?"

Schroeder looked at the other two men, and they nodded. He said, "Yes, Your Eminence."

The Cardinal spoke in a tone that suggested he was being coached and closely watched. "I'm all right. Mr. Baxter has received what they tell me is a grazing wound across his back and a ricochet wound in his chest. He's resting and seems all right. Father Murphy was also hit by a ricocheting bullet—in the face—the jaw. He's stunned but otherwise appears all right.... It was a miracle no one was killed."

The three men in the room seemed to relax. There were murmurs from the adjoining office. Schroeder said, "Miss Malone?"

The Cardinal answered hesitantly, "She is alive. Not wounded. She is—"

Schroeder heard the phone being covered at the other end. He heard muffled voices, an angry exchange. He spoke into the receiver, "Hello? Hello?"

The Cardinal's voice came back, "That's all I can say."

Schroeder spoke quickly, "Your Eminence, please don't provoke these people. You must not endanger your own lives, because you're also endangering other lives—"

The Cardinal replied in a neutral tone, "I'll pass that on to the others." He added, "Miss Malone is—"

Flynn's voice suddenly came on the line. "Good advice from Captain Courageous. All right, you see no one is dead. Everyone calm down."

"Let me speak to Miss Malone."

"She stepped out for a moment. Later." Flynn said abruptly, "Is everything set for my press conference?"

Schroeder's voice turned calm. "We may need more time. The networks—"

"I have a message for America and the world, and I mean to deliver it."

"Yes, you will. Be patient."

"That's not one of the Irish virtues, Schroeder."

"Oh, I don't know if that's true." He felt it was time for a more personal approach. "I'm half Irish myself, and—"

"Really?"

"Yes, my mother's people were from County Tyrone. Listen, I understand your frustrations and your anger—I had a great-uncle in the IRA. Family hero. Jailed by the English."

"For what? Being a bore like his nephew?"

Schroeder ignored the remark. "I grew up with many of the same hates and prejudices that you—"

"You weren't there, Schroeder. You weren't *there*. You were *here*."

"This won't accomplish anything," said Schroeder firmly. "You might make more enemies than friends by—"

"The people in here don't need any more friends. Our friends are dead or in prison. Tell them to let our people go, Captain."

"We're trying very hard. The negotiations between London and Washington are progressing. I see a light at the end of the tunnel—"

"Are you sure that light isn't a speeding train coming at you?"

Someone in the next room laughed.

Schroeder sat down and bit the tip off a cigar. "Listen, why don't you show us some good faith and release one of the wounded hostages?"

"Which one?"

Schroeder sat up quickly. "Well...well..."

"Come on, then. Play God. Don't ask anyone there. You tell me which one." "

The one that's the most badly wounded."

Flynn laughed. "Very good. Here's a counterproposal. Would you like the Cardinal instead? Think now. A wounded priest, a wounded Englishman, or a healthy Cardinal?"

Schroeder felt an anger rising in him and was disturbed that Flynn could produce that response. "Who's the more seriously hurt?"

"Baxter."

Schroeder hesitated. He looked around the room. His words faltered.

Flynn said, "Quickly!"

"Baxter."

Flynn put a sad tone in his voice. "Sorry. The correct response was to ask for a Prince of the Church, of course. But you knew that, Bert. Had you said the Cardinal, I would have released him."

Schroeder stared down at the unlit cigar. His voice was shaky. "I doubt that."

"Don't doubt me on things like that. I'd rather lose a hostage and make a point."

Schroeder took out a handkerchief and wiped his neck. "We're not trying to make this a contest to see who's got more nerve, who's got more...more..."

"Balls."

"Yes. We're not trying to do that. That's the old police image. We're rolling over for you." He glanced at Bellini, who looked very annoyed. He continued, "No one here is going to risk the lives of innocent people—"

"*Innocent?* There are no innocent civilians in war any more. We're all soldiers— soldiers by choice, by conscription, by implication, and by birth." Flynn drew a breath, then said, "The good thing about a long guerrilla war is that everyone gets a chance for revenge at least once." He paused. "Let's drop this topic. I want that television now. Send Burke."

Schroeder finally lit his cigar. "I'm sorry, he's temporarily out of the building."

"I told you I wanted him around. You see, Schroeder, you're not so accommodating after all."

"It was unavoidable. He'll call you soon." He paused, then

changed the tone of his voice. "Listen, along the same lines—I mean, we're building a rapport, as you said—can I ask you again to try to keep Mr. Hickey off the phone?"

Flynn didn't answer.

Schroeder went on, "I'm not trying to start any trouble there, but he's saying one thing and you're saying another. I mean, he's very negative and very... pessimistic. I just wanted to make you aware of that in case you didn't—"

The phone went dead.

Schroeder rocked back in his chair and drew on his cigar. He thought of how much easier it was dealing with Flynn and how difficult Hickey was. Then it hit him, and he dropped his cigar into an ashtray. *Good guy—bad guy.* The oldest con trick in the game. Now Flynn and Hickey were pulling that on *him.* "Sons of bitches."

Langley looked at Schroeder, then glanced at the note pad he'd been keeping. After each dialogue Langley felt a sense of frustration and futility. This negotiating business was not his game, and he didn't understand how Schroeder did it. Langley's instincts screamed at him to grab the phone and tell Flynn he was a dead motherfucker. Langley lit a cigarette and was surprised to see his hands shaking. "Bastards."

Roberta Spiegel took her place in the rocker and stared up at the ceiling. "Is anybody keeping score?"

Bellini stared out the window. "Can they fight as good as they bullshit?"

Schroeder answered, "The Irish are one of the few people who can."

Bellini turned back to the window, Spiegel rocked in her chair, Langley watched the smoke curl up from his cigarette, and Schroeder stared at the papers scattered on the desk. Phones rang in the other room; a bullhorn cut into the night air, and its echo drifted through the window. The mantel clock ticked loudly, and Schroeder focused on it. 9:17 P.M. At 4:30 he'd been marching in the parade, enjoying himself, enjoying life. Now he had a knot in his stomach, and life didn't look so good anymore. Why was someone always spoiling the parade?

CHAPTER 38

Maureen slid behind the thick column and watched Hickey as he stood squinting in the half-light. Megan came up behind him, swinging her big pistol easily by her side, the way other women swung a handbag—the way she herself had swung a pistol once.

Maureen watched them whispering to each other. She knew what they were saying without hearing a word: Which way has she gone? Should they split up? Fire a shot? Call out? Turn on the flashlights? She waited close-by, not fifteen feet away, because they'd never suspect she'd be this close, watching. To them she was a civilian, but they ought to have known her better. She was angry at their low regard of her.

Suddenly the flashlights came on, and their beams poked into the dark, distant places. Maureen pressed closer to the column.

Hickey called out, "Last chance, Maureen. Give up and you won't be hurt. But if we have to flush you out..." He let his voice trail off, the implied meaning more unnerving than if he had said it.

She watched them as they conferred again. She knew they expected her to go east toward the sacristy foundation. Flynn may even have heard the four of them discussing it. And that was the way she wanted to go but knew now she couldn't.

She prayed they wouldn't split up—wouldn't cut her off in both directions. She admitted, too, that she didn't want Megan to be away from Hickey... though perhaps if she *were* away from Hickey... Maureen slipped off her shoes, reached under her skirt, and slid off her panty hose. She twisted the nylon into a rope, wrapped the ends around her arms, and pulled it taut. She draped the nylon garrote over her shoulders and knelt, taking handfuls of earth and rubbing them across her damp face, her legs and hands. She looked down at her tweed jacket and skirt—dark but not dark enough. Silently she took them off, reversed them so the darker lining showed, and put them back on again. She buttoned the jacket over her white blouse and turned up the collar. All the while her eyes were fixed on Hickey and Megan.

Suddenly another pair of legs dropped into the hole, and a figure descended the ladder. Maureen recognized Frank Gallagher by the striped pants of his parade marshal's morning dress.

Hickey pointed toward the front of the Cathedral, and Gallagher drew a pistol and walked slowly west along the staircase wall toward the outer wall of the partially buried crypt. Hickey and Megan headed east toward the sacristy.

Maureen saw she had no way to go but south toward the crawl space beneath the ambulatory—the least likely place to find an exit, according to what Father Murphy knew of the layout. But as she watched Gallagher's flashlight moving slowly, she realized she could beat him to the end of the crypt, and from there she had more options. She moved laterally, to her left, parallel to Gallagher's course. Fifteen feet from the first column she came to another and stopped. She watched Gallagher's light almost directly opposite her. The shaft of light from the brass-plate opening was dimmer now, and the next column was somewhere in the darkness to her left.

She moved laterally again, running silently, barefoot, over the damp earth, hands feeling for pipes and ducts. The next column was irregularly spaced at about twenty-five feet, and she thought she'd missed it, then collided with it, feeling a sudden blow against her chest that knocked the wind out of her and made her give an involuntary gasp.

Gallagher's light swung out at her, and she stood frozen behind the column. The beam swung away, and she proceeded in a parallel course. She dashed toward the next column, counting her paces as she ran. At eight strides she stopped and felt in front of her, touching the stone column, and pressed against it.

She saw she was far ahead of Gallagher now, but his beam reached out and probed the place opposite her. The sanctuary floor above her ended a few feet beyond where she stood, and the steps that led to the communion rail sloped down to the crawl space below the main floor. She also saw, by the beam of light, the corner of the crypt where the wall turned away from her. She was no more than fifteen feet from it. She stooped down and passed her hands over the earth, finding a small piece of building rubble. She threw it back toward the last column she'd come from.

Gallagher's light swung away from her intended path toward the sound. She dashed forward, trying to judge the distance. Her hand hit the brick outer wall of the crypt, and she moved left toward the corner. Gallagher's light swung back. She ducked below the beam, then slid around the corner, bracing her back against the cold crypt. She sidestepped with her back against the wall, watching the beam of Gallagher's light as it passed off to her left. She felt for the nylon around her neck and swung it from her shoulders. She conjured up a picture of Frank Gallagher: pleasant looking, sort of vacuous expression. Big, too. She wrapped the nylon tightly around her hands and looped it.

The beam of light was growing in thickness and intensity, bobbing closer to the corner of the crypt. She could actually hear Gallagher's footsteps around the corner, could hear the tight-lipped nose-breathing she knew so well. *God,* she thought, *God, I never wanted to kill so badly.*

Discretion. When to run, when to fight. When in doubt, said Brian Flynn, run. Watch the wolves, he had said to her. They run from danger without self-recrimination. Even hunger wouldn't cloud their judgment. There'd be other kills. She steadied her hands and took a long breath, then swung the nylon around her shoulders and moved along the wall, to her right, away from Gallagher's approaching footsteps. *Next time.*

Something brushed across her face, and she stifled a yell as she swatted it away. Carefully she reached out and touched a hanging object. A pull chain. She reached up and found the light bulb, unscrewed it, and tossed it gently underhand into the crawl space in front of her. She pulled the chain, switching on the electricity. She thought, *I hope he sticks his fucking finger into it and burns.*

Gallagher came to the corner and knelt. He swung his light in a wide arc under the crawl space that began a few feet from the wall.

Maureen saw in the light in front of her the bottom of the steps that led down from the raised sanctuary above her. Farther back, in the crawl space, she saw the glowing red eyes of rats. She moved down the length of the crypt wall. It seemed to go on for a long way. Gallagher's light swung up from the crawl space and began probing the length of the wall.

She moved more quickly, stumbling over building rubble. After what she judged was about twenty-five feet her right hand felt the corner where the wall turned back toward the sacristy. The beam of light fell on her shoulder, and she froze. The light

played off her jacket, then swung away. She slid around the corner just as the light came back to reexplore the suspicious thing
it had picked out.

Maureen turned and kept her right shoulder to the wall as
she moved toward the sacristy foundation. She found another
light bulb and unscrewed it, then pulled the chain. Rats
squealed around her, and something ran across her bare feet.

The crypt wall turned in to meet the outer wall of the sacristy
staircase, and she judged that she was on the exact opposite side
of the staircase from where she'd come down through the brass
plate.

So far she had eluded them, gotten the better of them in a
game that was the ultimate hide-and-seek. Every Belfast alley
and factory park flashed through her mind. Every heart-thump-
ing, dry-throated crawl through the rubble came back to her,
and she felt alive, confident, almost exhilarated at the dangerous
game.

The ground rose, and she had to stoop lower until finally she
had to crawl on all fours. She felt to her front as she moved. A
rat scurried across her hand, another across her legs. Sweat ran
from her face and washed the dirt camouflage into her eyes and
mouth. Her breathing was so loud she thought Gallagher must
hear it clearly.

Behind her the beam of Gallagher's light probed in all directions. He could have no idea that he had actually been following
her... unless he had heard her or had seen her footprints, or had
found one of the empty light-sockets and guessed.... *Stick your
goddamned finger in one of them and fry.* She hoped he was as
frightened as she was.

She kept crawling until her hand came into contact with
cold, moist stone. She ran her fingers over the jagged surface,
then higher up, and she felt the rounded contour of a massive

column. Her hand slid down again, and she felt something soft and damp and drew away quickly. Cautiously she reached out again and touched the yielding, putty-like substance. She pulled a piece of it and brought it to her nose. "Oh, my God," she spoke under her breath. "Oh, you bastards. You really would do it."

Her knee bumped into something, and her hands reached down and felt the suitcase that they had carried down into the hole—a suitcase big enough to hold at least twenty kilos of plastic. Somewhere, probably on the other side of the staircase, was the other charge.

She wedged into the space between the stairway wall and the column's footing and took the nylon from around her shoulders. She found a half brick and held it in her right hand.

Gallagher came closer, his flashlight focused on the ground in front of him. She could see in the light the marks she had made when she had to crawl through the earth.

Gallagher's light swung up and focused on the column footing, then probed the space where she was hiding. He crawled closer and poked the light between the column and the wall.

For a long second the light rested directly on her face, and they stared at each other from less than a yard away. Gallagher's face registered complete surprise, she noticed. A stupid man.

She brought her hand down with the half brick in it and drove it between his eyes. The light fell to the floor, and she sprang out of her niche and wrapped the nylon garrote around his neck.

Gallagher thrashed over the earth floor like a wounded animal. Maureen hooked her legs around his torso and rode his back, holding the garrote like a set of reins, drawing it tightly around his neck with all the strength she could summon.

Gallagher weakened and fell forward on his chest, pinning

her legs beneath him. She pulled harder on the nylon, but there was too much give in it. She knew she was strangling him too slowly, causing him unnecessary suffering. She heard the gurgling coming from deep in his throat.

Gallagher's head twisted around at an unbelievable angle, and his face stared up at her. The fallen flashlight cast a yellow beam over his face, and she saw his bulging eyes and thick protruding tongue. His skin was split where she had hit him with the brick, and his nose was broken and bleeding. Their eyes met for a brief second.

Gallagher's body went limp and lay motionless. Maureen sat on his back trying to catch her breath. She still felt life in his body, the shallow breathing, the twitching muscles and flesh against her buttocks. She began tightening the garrote, then suddenly pulled it from his neck and buried her face in her hands.

She heard voices coming around the crypt, then saw two lights not forty feet away. She quickly shut off the flashlight and threw it aside. Maureen felt her heart beating wildly again as she groped for the fallen pistol.

The beam rose and searched the ceiling. A voice—Megan's—said, "Here's another missing bulb. Clever little bitch."

The other flashlight examined the ground. Hickey said, "Here are their tracks."

Maureen's hands touched Gallagher's body, and she felt him moving. She backed off.

Hickey called out, "Frank? Are you there?" His approaching light found Gallagher's body and rested on it.

Maureen crawled backward until she made contact with the base of the column. She turned and clawed at the plastic explosive, trying to pull it loose from the footing, feeling for the detonator that she knew was embedded somewhere.

The two beams of light came closer. Hickey shouted, "Maureen! You've done well, lass. But as you see, the hounds are onto the scent. We're going to begin probing fire if you don't give yourself up."

Maureen kept pulling at the plastic. She knew there would be no probing fire with plastic so close.

The sound of the two crawling people got closer. She looked back and saw two pools of light converging on Gallagher's body. Hickey and Megan were hovering over Gallagher now. Gallagher was trying to raise himself on all fours.

Megan said, "Here, I've found his light."

Hickey said, "Look for his gun."

Maureen gave one last pull at the plastic, then moved around the column until she ran into the foundation wall that separated her from the sacristy.

She put her right shoulder against the wall and crawled along it, feeling for an opening. Pipes and ducts penetrated the wall, but there was no space for her to pass through.

Hickey's voice called out again. "Maureen, my love, Frank is feeling a bit better. All is forgiven, darlin'. We owe you, lass. You've a good heart. Come on, now. Let's all go back upstairs and have a nice wash and a cup of tea."

Maureen watched as one, then two, then three flashlights started to reach out toward her.

Hickey said, "Maureen, we've found Frank's gun, so we know you're not armed. The game is over. You've done well. You've nothing to be ashamed of. Frank owes you his life, and there'll be no retributions, Maureen. Just call out to us and we'll come take you back. You've our word you won't be harmed."

Maureen huddled against the foundation wall. She knew Hickey was speaking the truth. Gallagher owed her. They wouldn't harm her while Gallagher was still alive; that was one of the rules. The old rules, Hickey's rules, her rules. She wondered about someone like Megan, though.

Her instincts told her that it was over—that she should give up while the offered amnesty was still in effect. She was tired, cold, aching. The flashlights came closer. She opened her mouth to speak.

CHAPTER 39

Inspector Langley was reading Monsignor Downes's appointment book. "I think the good Rector entertained the Fenians on more than one occasion.... Unwittingly, of course."

Schroeder looked at Langley. It would never have occurred to him to snoop through another man's papers. That's why he had been such a bad detective. Langley, on the other hand, would pick the Mayor's pocket out of idle curiosity. Schroeder said acidly, "You mean you don't suspect Monsignor Downes?"

Langley smiled. "I didn't say that."

Bellini turned from the window and looked at Schroeder. "You didn't have to eat so much shit, did you? I mean that business about rolling over and all that other stuff."

Schroeder felt his fright turning to anger. "For Christ's sake, it's only a ploy. You've heard me use it a dozen times."

"Yeah, but this time you *meant* it."

"Go to hell."

Bellini seemed to be struggling with something. He leaned forward with his hands on Schroeder's desk and spoke softly. "I'm scared, too. Do you think I *want* to send my men in there? Christ Almighty, Bert, I'm going in, too. I have a wife and kids. But Jesus, man, every hour that you bullshit with them is another hour for them to get their defenses tightened. Every hour shortens the time until dawn, when I *have* to attack. And I won't hit them at dawn in a last desperate move to save the hostages and the Cathedral, because they *know* I have to move at dawn if they don't have what they want."

Schroeder kept his eyes fixed on Bellini's but didn't reply.

Bellini went on, his voice becoming more strident. "As long as you keep telling the big shots you can do it, they're going to jerk me around. Admit you're not going to pull it off and let me...let me know in my own mind...that I *have* to go in." He said almost in a whisper, "I don't like sweating it out like this, Bert.... My men don't like this.... I have to *know*."

Schroeder spoke mechanically. "I'm taking it a step at a time. Standard procedures. Stabilize the situation, keep them talking, calm them down, get an extension of the deadline—"

Bellini slammed his hand on the desk, and everyone sat up quickly. "Even if you *could* get an extension of the deadline, how long would it be for? An hour? Two hours? Then I have to move in the daylight—while you stand here at the window smoking a cigar, watching us get massacred!"

Schroeder stood and his face twitched. He tried to stop himself from speaking, but the words came out. "If you have to go in, I'll be right next to you, Bellini."

A twisted smile passed over Bellini's face. He turned to Langley and Spiegel, then looked back at Schroeder. "You're on, Captain." He turned and walked out of the room.

Langley watched the door close, then said, "That was stupid, Bert."

Schroeder found his hands and legs were shaking, and he sat down, then rose abruptly. He spoke in a husky voice. "Watch the phone. I have to go out for a minute—men's room." He walked quickly to the door.

Spiegel said, "I took some cheap shots at him, too."

Langley looked away.

She said, "Tell me what a bitch I am."

He walked to the sideboard and poured a glass of sherry.

He had no intention of telling the Mayor's aide she was a bitch.

She walked toward him, reached out, and took the glass from his hand. She drank, then handed it back.

Langley thought, *She did it again!* There was something uncomfortably intimate and at the same time unnervingly aggressive about the proprietary attitude she had taken with him.

Roberta Spiegel walked toward the door. "Don't do anything stupid like Schroeder did."

He looked up at her with some surprise.

She said suddenly, "You married? Divorced...separated...single?"

"Yes."

She laughed. "Watch the store. See you later." She left.

Langley looked at the lipstick mark on his glass and put it down. "Bitch." He walked to the window.

Bellini had placed a set of field glasses on the sill. Langley picked them up and saw clearly the man standing in the belfry. If Bellini attacked, this young man would be one of the first to die. He wondered if the man knew that. Of course he did.

The man saw him and raised a pair of field glasses. They stared at each other for a few seconds. The young man held up his hand, a sort of greeting. The faces of all the IRA men Langley had ever known suddenly coalesced in this face—the young romantics, the old-guard IRA like Hickey, the dying Officials like Ferguson, the cold-blooded young Provos like most of them, and now the Fenians—crazier than the Provos—the worst of the worst.... All of them had started life, he was sure, as polite young men and women, dressed in little suits and dresses for

Sunday Mass. Somewhere something went wrong. But maybe they would get most of the worst crazies in one sweep tonight. Nip it in the bud here. He damn well didn't want to deal with them later.

Langley put down the glasses and turned from the window. He looked at his watch. Where the hell was Burke?

He had a sour feeling in his stomach. *Transference.* Somehow he felt he was in there with them.

Maureen watched the circle of light closing in on her and almost welcomed the light and Hickey's cajoling voice after the sensory deprivation she had experienced.

Hickey called out again. "I know you're frightened, Maureen. Just take a deep breath and call to us."

She almost did, but something held her back. A series of confused thoughts ran through her mind—Brian, Harold Baxter, Whitehorn Abbey, Frank Gallagher's ghostly face. She felt she was adrift in some foggy sea—with no anchor, misleading beacons, false harbors. She tried to shake off the lethargy and think clearly, tried to resolve her purpose, which was freedom. Freedom from Brian Flynn, freedom from all the people and things that had kept her feeling guilty and obligated all her life. *Once you're a hostage, you're a hostage the rest of your life.* She had been Brian's hostage long before he put a gun to her head. She had been a hostage to her own insecurities and circumstances all her life. But now for the first time she felt less like a hostage and less like a traitor. She felt like a refugee from an insane world, a fugitive from a state of mind that was a prison far worse than Long Kesh. *Once in, never out.* Bullshit. She began crawling again, along the foundation wall.

Hickey called out, "Maureen, we see you moving. Don't make us shoot."

She called back, "I know you don't have Gallagher's gun, because I have it. Careful I don't shoot *you*." She heard them talking among themselves, then the flashlights went out. She smiled at how the simplest bluffs worked when people were frightened. She kept crawling.

The foundation curved, and she knew she was under the ambulatory now. Somewhere on the other side of the foundation were the fully excavated basements beneath the terraces outside that led back to the rectory.

Beneath the thin layer of soil the Manhattan bedrock rose and fell as she crawled. The ceiling was only about four feet high now, and she kept hitting her head on pipes and ducts. The ducts made a noise when she hit them and boomed like a drum in the cold, stagnant air.

Suddenly the flashlights came on again, some distance off. Megan's voice called, "We found the gun, Maureen. Come toward the light or we shoot. Last chance."

Maureen watched the beams of light searching for her. She didn't know if they had Gallagher's gun or not, but she knew she didn't have it. She crawled on her stomach, commando style, pressing her face to the ground.

The lights began tightening around her. Hickey said, "I'm counting to ten. Then the armistice is over." He counted.

Maureen stopped crawling and remained motionless, pressed against the wall. Blood and sweat ran over her face; her legs and arms were studded with pieces of embedded stone. She steadied her breathing and listened for a sound from the basement that was only feet away. She looked for a crack of light, felt for a draft that might be coming from the other side, then ran her hands over the stone foundation. Nothing. She began moving again.

Hickey's voice called out, "Maureen, you're a heartless girl, making an old man crawl in the damp like this. I'll catch my death—let's go back up and have some tea."

The light beams were actually passing over her intermittently, and she froze when they did. They didn't seem to be able to pick out her blackened features in the darkness. She noticed that the stone wall turned again, then ended. Brick wall ran from the stone at right angles, and she suspected the brick wall was not a stress-bearing foundation but a partition behind which the foundation had disappeared. She rose to a kneeling position, reached for the top of the wall, and discovered a small space near the concrete ceiling. She pressed her face to the space but saw no light, heard no noise, and felt no air. Yet she was certain she was close to finding a way out.

A voice called out. Gallagher's. "Maureen, please don't make us shoot you. I know you spared my life—come on, then, be a good woman and let's all go back."

Again she knew they wouldn't shoot, if not because of the explosives then for fear of a ricochet among all this stone. She was suddenly angry at their small lies. What kind of idiot did they think she was? Hickey might be an old soldier, but Maureen knew more about war than Megan or Gallagher would live to learn. She wanted to scream an obscenity at them for their patronizing attitude. She moved along the wall and felt it curve farther inward. She judged from the configuration of the horseshoe-shaped ambulatory that she was now below the bride's room or confessional. Suddenly her hand came into contact with dry wood. Her heart gave a small leap. She faced the wall and knelt in front of it. Her hands explored the wood, set flush into the brick. She felt a rusty latch and pulled on it. A pair of hinges squeaked sharply in the still air. The flashlight beams came toward her.

Hickey called to her. "You're leading us a merry chase,

young lady. I hope you don't give your suitors as much trouble."

Maureen said under her breath, "Go to hell, you old bag of bones." She pulled slowly on the door. Cracks of light appeared around the edges, showing it to be about three feet square. She closed the door quickly, found a broken shard of brick, and threw it farther along the wall.

The light beams swung toward the noise. She pulled the door open a few inches and pushed her face to the small aperture. She blinked her eyes several times and focused on a fluorescent-lit hallway.

The hallway floor was about four feet below her—a beautiful floor, she thought, of white polished vinyl. The walls of the corridor were painted plasterboard; the ceiling a few feet above her head was white acoustical tile. A beautiful hallway, really. Tears ran down her face.

She swung the door fully open and rubbed her eyes, then pushed her hair away from her face. Something was wrong.... She put her hand out, and her fingers passed through a wire grill. A rat screen covered the opening.

CHAPTER 40

Burke walked into the Monsignor's inner office and looked at Langley, the sole person present, staring out the window. Burke said, "Everybody quit?"

Langley turned.

Burke said, "Where's Schroeder?"

"Relieving himself...or throwing up, or something. Did you hear what happened—?"

"I was briefed. Damned fools in there are going to blow it. Everyone's all right?"

"Cardinal said so. Also, you missed two good show-downs—Schroeder versus Spiegel and Schroeder versus Bellini. Poor Bert. He's usually the fair-haired boy, too." Langley paused. "I think he's losing it."

Burke nodded. "Do you think it's him, or is it us...or is it that Flynn is that good?"

Langley shrugged. "All of the above."

Burke went to the sideboard and noticed there was very little left in the decanters. He said, "Why did God let the Irish invent whiskey, Langley?"

Langley knew the drill. "To keep them from ruling the world."

Burke laughed. "Right." His voice became contemplative.

"I'll bet no Fenian has had a drink in forty-eight hours. Do you know a woman named Terri O'Neal?"

Langley concentrated on the name, then said, "No. I don't make it at all." He immediately regretted the common cop jargon and said, "I can't identify the name. Call the office."

"I called from downstairs. Negative. But they're rechecking. How about Dan Morgan?"

"No. Irish?"

"Probably Northern Irish. Louise is going to call back."

"Who are these people?"

"That's what I asked you." He poured the remainder of the brandy and thought a moment. "Terri O'Neal...I think I have a face and a voice, but I just can't remember...?"

Langley said, "Flynn's asked for a television in there. In fact, you're supposed to deliver it to him." Langley looked at Burke out of the corner of his eye. "You two get along real well."

Burke considered the statement for a few seconds. In spite of the circumstances of their meeting, he admitted that Flynn was the type of man he could have liked— if Flynn were a cop, or if he, Burke, were IRA.

Langley said, "Call Flynn now."

Burke went to the phone. "Flynn can wait." He made certain the speakers in the other rooms were not on, then turned on the voice box on the desk so that Langley could monitor. He dialed the Midtown North Precinct. "Gonzalez? Lieutenant Burke here. Do you have my man?" There was a long silence during which Burke found he was holding his breath.

"He's a prick," said Gonzalez. "Keeps screaming about police-state tactics and all that crap. Says he's going to sue us for false arrest. I thought you said he needed protection."

"Is he still there?"

"Yeah. He wants a ride to the Port Authority Terminal. I can't hold him a minute longer. If I get hit with a false arrest rap, I'm dragging you in with me—"

"Put him on."

"My pleasure. Wait."

Burke turned to Langley while he waited. "Ferguson. He's onto something. Terri O'Neal—Dan Morgan. Now he wants to run."

Langley moved beside Burke. "Well, offer him some money to stick around."

"You haven't paid him for today yet. Anyway, there's not enough money around to keep him from running."

Burke spoke into the telephone. "Jack—"

Ferguson's voice came into the room, high-pitched and agitated. "What the hell are you *doing* to me, Pat? Is this the way you treat a friend? For God's sake, man— "

"Cut it. Listen, put me on to the people you spoke to about O'Neal and Morgan."

"Not a chance. My sources are confidential. I don't treat friends the way you do. The intelligence establishment in this country—"

"Save it for your May Day speech. Listen, Martin has double-crossed all of us. He was the force behind the Fenians. This whole thing is a ploy to make the Irish look bad—to turn American public opinion against the Irish struggle."

Ferguson didn't speak for a while, then said, "I figured that out."

Burke pressed on. "Look, I don't know how much information Martin fed you, or how much information about the police and the Fenians you had to give him in return, but I'm telling you now he's at the stage where he's covering his tracks. Understand?"

"I understand that I'm on three hitlists—the Fenians', the Provos', and Martin's. That's why I'm leaving town."

"You have to stick. Who is Terri O'Neal? Why was she kidnapped by a man named Morgan? Whose show was it? Where is she being held?"

"That's your problem."

"We're working on it, Jack, but you're closer to it. And we don't have much time. If you told us your sources—"

"No."

Burke went on. "Also, while you're at it, see if you can get a line on Gordon Stillway, the resident architect of Saint Pat's. He's missing, too."

"Lot of that going around. I'm missing, too. Good-bye."

"No! Stick with it."

"Why? Why should I risk my life any further?"

"For the same reasons you risked it all along—peace."

Ferguson sighed but said nothing.

Langley whispered, "Offer him a thousand dollars—no, make it fifteen hundred. We'll hold a benefit dance."

Burke said into the phone, "We'd like to exonerate all the Irish who had nothing to do with this, including your Officials and even the Provos. We'll work with you after this mess is over and see that the government and the press don't crucify all of you." Burke paused, then said, "You and I as Irishmen"—he remembered Flynn's attempt to claim kinship—"you mad I want to be able to hold our heads up after this." Burke glanced at Langley, who nodded appreciatively. Burke turned away.

Ferguson said, "Hold on." There was a long silence, then Ferguson spoke. "How can I reach you later?"

Burke let out a breath. "Try to call the rectory. The lines should be clear later. Give the password...leprechaun.... They'll put you through."

"Leper is more like it, Burke. Make it leper. All right. If I can't get through on the phone, I won't come to the rectory—the cordon is being watched by all sorts of people. If you don't hear from me, let's have a standing rendezvous. Let's say the zoo at one."

Burke said, "Closer to the Cathedral."

"All right. But no bars or public places." He thought. "Okay, that small park on Fifty-first—it's not far from you."

"It's closed after dark."

"Climb the gate!"

Burke smiled. "Someday I'm going to get a key for every park in this town."

Ferguson said, "Join the Parks Department. They'll issue one with your broom."

"Luck." Burke spoke to Gonzalez. "Let him go." He hung up and took a deep breath.

Langley said, "Do you think this O'Neal thing is important enough to risk his life?"

Burke drained off the glass of brandy and grimaced. "How do people drink this stuff?"

"Pat?"

Burke walked to the window and looked out.

Langley said, "I'm not making any moral judgments. I only want to know if it's *worth* getting Jack Ferguson killed."

Burke spoke as if to himself. "A kidnapping is a subtle sort of thing, more complicated than a hit, more sinister in many ways—like hostage taking." He considered. "Hostage taking—that's a form of kidnapping. Terri O'Neal is a *hostage....*"

"Whose hostage?"

Burke turned and faced Langley. "I don't know."

"Who has to do what for whom to secure her release? No one has made any demands yet."

"Strange," agreed Burke.

"Really," said Langley.

Burke looked at Schroeder's empty chair. Schroeder's presence, in spite of everything, had been reassuring. He said half-jokingly, "Are you sure he's coming back?"

Langley shrugged. "His backup man is in another room with a phone, waiting like an understudy for the break of a lifetime.... " Langley said, "Call Flynn."

"Later." He sat in Schroeder's chair, leaned back, and looked at the lofty ceiling. A long crack ran from wall to wall, re-plastered but not yet painted. He had a mental image of the Cathedral in ruins, then pictured the Statue of Liberty lying on its side half submerged in the harbor. He thought of the Roman Coliseum, the ruined Acropolis, the flooded temples of the Nile. He said, "You know, the Cathedral itself is not that important. Neither are the lives of any of us. What's important is how we act, what people say and write about us afterward."

Langley looked at him appraisingly. Burke sometimes surprised him. "Yes, that's true, but you won't tell that to anybody today."

"Or tomorrow, if we're pulling bodies out of the rubble."

John Hickey's voice came to Maureen from not very far off. "So, what have we here? What light through yonder window breaks, Maureen?" He laughed, then said sharply, "Move back from there or we'll shoot you."

Maureen cocked her elbow and drove it into the rat screen. The wire bent, but the edges stayed fixed to the wall. She pressed her face to the grill. To her left the hallway ended about ten feet away. On the opposite wall toward the end of the passage were gray sliding doors—elevator doors—the elevator that opened near the bride's room above. She drove her elbow into the grill again, and one side of the frame ripped loose from the plaster-board. "Yes, yes...*please*..."

She could hear them behind her, scurrying over the rubble-strewn ground like the rats they were, faster, coming at the light source. Then John Hickey came out of the dark. "Hands on your head, darlin'."

She turned and stared at him, holding back the tears forming in her eyes.

Hickey said, "Look at you. Your pretty knees are all scratched. And what's that dirt all over your face, Maureen? *Camouflage?* You'll be needing a good wash."

He ran his flashlight over her. "And your smart tweeds are turned inside out. Clever girl. Clever. And what is *that* around your neck?" He grabbed the nylon garrote and twisted it. "My, what a naughty girl you are." He gave the garrote another twist and held it until she began to choke. "Once again, Maureen, you've shown me a small chink in our armor. What would we do without you?" He loosened the tension on the nylon and knocked her to the ground. His eyes narrowed into malignant slits. "I think I'll shoot you through the head and throw you into the corridor. That'll help the police make the decision they're wrestling with." He seemed to consider, then said, "But, on the other hand, I'd like you to be around for the finale." He smiled a black, gaping smile. "I want you to see Flynn die or for him to see you die."

In a clear flash of understanding she knew the essence of this old man's evil. "Kill me."

He shook his head. "No. I like you. I like what you're becoming. You should have killed Gallagher, though. You would have been firmly planted in the ranks of the damned if you had. You're only borderline now." He cackled.

Maureen lay on the damp earth. She felt a hand grab her long hair and pull her back across the floor into the darkness. Megan Fitzgerald knelt over her and put a pistol to her heart. "Your charmed life has come to an end, bitch."

Hickey called out, "None of that, Megan!"

Megan Fitzgerald shouted back. "You'll not stop me this time." She cocked the pistol.

Hickey shouted, "No! Brian will decide if she's to die—and if she's to die, he wants to be the one to kill her."

Maureen listened to this statement without any outward emotion. She felt numb, drained.

Megan screamed back. "Fuck you! Fuck Flynn! She'll die here and now."

Hickey spoke softly. "If you shoot, I'll kill you." Everyone heard the click of the safety disengaging from his automatic.

Gallagher cleared his throat and said, "Let her alone, Megan."

No one moved or spoke. Finally Megan uncocked her pistol. She turned on her light and shone it into Maureen's face. A twisted smile formed on Megan's lips. "You're old...and not very pretty." She poked Maureen's breast roughly with the muzzle of her pistol.

Maureen looked up through the light at Megan's contorted face. "You're very young, and you ought to be pretty, but there's an ugliness in you, Megan, that everyone can see in your eyes."

Megan spit at her, then disappeared into the dark.

Hickey knelt over Maureen and wiped her face with a handkerchief. "Well, now, if you want my opinion, I think you're very pretty."

She turned her face away. "Go to hell."

Hickey said, "You see, Uncle John saved your life again."

She didn't respond, and he went on. "Because I really want you to see what's going to happen later. Yes, it's going to be quite spectacular. How often can you see a cathedral collapsing around your head—?"

Gallagher made an odd gasping sound, and Hickey said to him, "Only joking, Frank."

She said to Gallagher, "He's not joking, you know—"

Hickey leaned close to her ear. "Shut up or I'll—"

"*What?*" She looked at him fiercely. "What can you do to me?" She turned toward Gallagher. "He means to see all of us dead. He means to see all your young friends follow him to the grave..."

Hickey laughed in a shrill, piercing tone.

The rats stopped their chirping.

Hickey said, "The little creatures sense the danger. They smell death. They know."

Gallagher said nothing, but his breathing filled the still, cold air.

Maureen sat up slowly. "Baxter? The others...?"

Hickey said in an offhand manner, "Baxter is dead. Father Murphy was hit in the face, and he's dying. The Cardinal is all right, though." He said in an aggrieved whisper, "Do you see what you've *done?*"

She couldn't speak, and tears ran down her face.

Hickey turned from her and played his light over the open hatchway.

Gallagher said, "We better put an alarm here."

Hickey answered, "The only alarm you'll hear from down here is from about a kilo of plastic. I'll have Sullivan come back and mine it." He glanced at Maureen. "Well, shall we go home, then?"

They began the long crawl back.

Hickey spoke as they made their way. "If I was a younger man, Maureen, I'd be in love with you. You're so like the women I knew in the Movement in my youth. So many of the revolutionary women in other movements are ugly misfits, neurotics and psychotics. But we've always been able to attract clearheaded, pretty lasses like yourself. Why is that, do you suppose?"

He said between labored breaths, "Well, don't answer me, then. Tired? Yes, me too. Slow down, Gallagher, you big ox. We've got some way to go yet before we can rest. We'll all rest together, Maureen. Soon this will be over...we'll be free of all our worries, all our bonds...before dawn...a nice rest...it won't be so bad...it won't, really.... We're going home."

CHAPTER 41

Schroeder came through the double doors of the Rector's inner office. "Look who's back. Did you call Flynn?"

"Not without you here, Bert. Feeling better?"

Schroeder came around the desk. "Please get out of my chair, Lieutenant."

Burke vacated the chair.

Schroeder looked at Burke as he sat. "Can you carry a TV set?"

"Why didn't he ask for a television right away?"

Schroeder thought. Flynn *wasn't* a textbook case in many respects. Little things like not immediately asking for a television...little things that added up...

Langley said, "He's keeping the Fenians isolated. Their only reality is Brian Flynn. After the press conference he'll smash the TV or place it where only he and Hickey can use it for intelligence gathering."

Schroeder nodded. "I never know if this TV business is part of the problem or part of the solution. But if they ask, we have to give." He dialed the switchboard. "Chancel organ." He handed the receiver to Burke, turned on all the speaker switches, then sat back with his feet on the desk. "On the air, Lieutenant."

A voice came over the speakers: "Flynn here."

"Burke."

"Listen, Lieutenant, do me a great favor, won't you, and stay in the damned rectory—at least until dawn. If the Cathedral goes, you'll want to see it. Tape all the windows, though, and don't stand under any chandeliers."

Burke was aware that more than two hundred people in the Cathedral complex were listening, and that every word was being taped and transmitted to Washington and London. Flynn knew this, too, and was playing it for effect. "What can I do for you?"

"Aren't you supposed to ask first about the hostages?"

"You said they were all right."

"But that was a while ago."

"Well, how are they *now?*"

"No change. Except that Miss Malone took a jaunt through the crawl space. But she's back now. Looks a bit tired, from what I can see. Clever girl that she is she found a hatchway from the crawl space into the hallway that runs past the bride's-room elevator." He paused, then went on, "Don't touch the hatch, however, as it's being mined right now with enough plastic to give you a nasty bump."

Burke looked at Schroeder, who was already on the other phone talking to one of Bellini's lieutenants. "I understand."

"Good. And you can assume that every other entrance you find will also be mined. And you can assume the entire crawl space is seeded with mines. You can also suspect that I'm lying or bluffing, but, really, it's not smart to call my bluff. Tell that to your ESD people."

"I'll do that."

Flynn said, "Anyway, I want the television. Bring it round to the usual place. Fifteen minutes."

Burke looked at Schroeder and covered the mouthpiece.

Schroeder said, "There's one waiting downstairs in the clerk's office. But you have to get something from him in return. Ask to speak to a hostage."

Burke uncovered the mouthpiece. "I want to talk to Father Murphy first."

"Oh, your friend. You shouldn't admit to having a friend in here."

"He's not my friend, he's my confessor."

Flynn laughed loudly. "Sorry, that struck me funny, somehow. That was no lady, that was my wife. You know?"

Schroeder suppressed a smirk.

Burke looked annoyed. "Put him on!"

Flynn's voice lost its humor. "Don't make any demands on me, Burke."

"I won't bring a television unless I speak to the priest."

Schroeder was shaking his head excitedly. "Forget it," he whispered. "Don't push him."

Burke continued, "We have some talking to do, don't we, Flynn?"

Flynn didn't answer for a long time, then said, "I'll have Murphy at the gate. See you in no-man's-land. Fifteen...no, fourteen minutes now, and don't be late." He hung up.

Schroeder looked at Burke. "What the hell kind of dialogue are you two carrying on down there?"

Burke ignored him and called through to the chancel organ again. "Flynn?"

Brian Flynn's voice came back, a bit surprised. "What is it?"

Burke found his body shaking with anger. "New rule, Flynn. You don't hang up until I'm through. Got it?" He slammed down the receiver.

Schroeder stood. "What the hell is wrong with you? Haven't you learned *anything*?"

"Oh, go fuck yourself." He wiped his brow with a handkerchief.

Schroeder pressed on. "Don't like being at the receiving end, do you? Messes up your self-image. These bastards have called me every name under the sun tonight, but you don't see me—"

"Okay. You're right. Sorry."

Schroeder said again, "What do you talk to him about down there?"

Burke shook his head. He was tired, and he was starting to lose his temper. He knew that if he was making mistakes because of fatigue, then everyone else was, too.

The phone rang. Schroeder answered it and handed it to Burke. "Your secret headquarters atop Police Plaza."

Burke shut off all the speakers and carried the phone away from the desk. "Louise."

The duty sergeant said, "Nothing on Terri O'Neal. Daniel Morgan—age thirty-four. A naturalized American citizen. Born in Londonderry. Father Welsh Protestant, mother Irish Catholic. Fiancée arrested in Belfast for IRA activities. May still be in Armagh Prison. We'll check with British—"

"Don't check *anything* with their intelligence sections or with the CIA or FBI unless you get the go-ahead from me or Inspector Langley."

"Okay. One of those." She went on. "Morgan made our files because he was arrested once in a demonstration outside the UN, 1979. Fined and released. Address YMCA on West Twenty-third. Doubt if he's still there. Right?" She read the remainder of the arrest sheet, then said, "I've put it out to our people and to the detectives. I'll send you a copy of the sheet. Also, nothing yet on Stillway."

Burke hung up and turned to Langley. "Let's get that television."

Schroeder said, "What was that all about?"

Langley looked at Schroeder. "Trying to catch a break to make your job and Bellini's a little easier."

"Really? Well, that's the least you can do after screwing up the initial investigation."

Burke said, "If we hadn't blown it, you wouldn't have the opportunity to negotiate for the life of the Archbishop of New York or the safety of Saint Patrick's Cathedral."

"Thanks. I owe you."

Burke looked at him closely and had the impression that he wasn't being completely facetious.

Maureen came out of the lavatory of the bride's room and walked to the vanity. Her outer garments lay draped over a chair, and a first-aid kit sat in front of the vanity mirror. She sat and opened the kit.

Jean Kearney stood to the side with a pistol in her hand and watched. Kearney cleared her throat and said tentatively, "You know... they still speak of you in the movement."

Maureen dabbed indifferently at her legs with an iodine applicator. She didn't look up but said listlessly, "Do they?"

"Yes. People still tell stories of your exploits with Brian before you turned traitor."

Maureen glanced up at the young woman. It was an ingenuous statement, without hostility or malice, just a relating of a fact she had learned from the storytellers—like the story of Judas. The Gospel according to the Republican Army. Maureen looked at the young woman's bluish lips and fingers. "Cold up there?"

She nodded. "Awfully cold. This is a bit of a break for me, so take your time."

Maureen noticed the wood chips on Jean Kearney's clothing. "Doing some carpentry in the attic?"

Kearney turned her eyes away.

Maureen stood and took her skirt from the chair. "Don't do it, Jean. When the time comes, you and—Arthur, isn't it?—you and Arthur must not do whatever it is they've told you to do."

"Don't say such things. We're loyal—not like you."

Maureen turned and looked at herself in the mirror and looked at the image of Jean Kearney behind her. She wanted to say something to this young woman, but really there was nothing to say to someone who had willingly committed sacrilege and would probably commit murder before too long. Jean Kearney would eventually find her own way out, or she'd die young.

There was a knock on the door, and it opened a crack. Flynn put his head in, and his eyes rested on Maureen; then he looked away. "Sorry. Thought you'd be done."

Maureen pulled on her skirt, then picked up her blouse and slipped into it.

Flynn came into the room and looked around. He fixed his attention on the bandages and iodine. "History does have a way of repeating itself, doesn't it?"

Maureen buttoned her blouse. "Well, if we all keep making the same mistakes, it's bound to, isn't it, Brian?"

Flynn smiled. "One day we'll get it right."

"Not bloody likely."

Flynn motioned to Jean Kearney, and she left reluctantly, a disappointed look on her face.

Maureen sat at the vanity and ran a comb through her hair.

Flynn watched for a while, then said, "I'd like to speak to you."

"I'm listening."

"In the chapel."

"We're perfectly alone here."

"Well...yes. Too alone. People would talk. I can't compromise myself—neither can you...."

She laughed and stood. "What would people talk *about*? Really, Brian...here in the bride's room of a cathedral.... What a lot of sex-obsessed Catholics you all still are." She moved toward him. "All right. I'm ready. Let's go."

He took her arms and turned her toward him.

She shook her head. "No, Brian. Much too late." His face had a look, she thought, of desperation...fright almost.

He said, "Why do women always say things like that? It's never too late; there are no seasons or cycles to these things."

"But there are. It's winter for us now. There'll be no spring—not in our lifetime."

He pulled her toward him and kissed her, and before she could react he turned and left the room.

She stood in the center of the bride's room, immobile for a few seconds, then her hand went to her mouth and pressed against her lips. She shook her head. "You fool. You damned fool."

Father Murphy sat in the clergy pews, a pressure bandage over the right side of his jaw. The Cardinal stood beside him. Harold Baxter lay on his side in the same pew. A winding bandage circled his bare torso, revealing a long line of dried blood across his back and a smaller spot of red on his chest. His face showed the result of Pedar Fitzgerald's blows. Megan's kick had swollen one eye nearly shut.

Maureen moved across the sanctuary and knelt beside the two men. They exchanged subdued greetings. Maureen said to Baxter, "Hickey told me you were dead and Father Murphy was dying."

Baxter shook his head. "The man's quite mad." He looked

around. Flynn, Hickey, and Megan Fitzgerald were nowhere to be seen. That, for some reason, was more unnerving than having them in his sight. He felt his hold on his courage slipping and knew the others were feeling that way also. He said, "If we can't escape...physically escape...then we have to talk about a way to survive in here. We have to stand up to them, keep them from dividing us and isolating us. We have to *understand* the people who hold us captive."

Maureen thought a moment, then said, "Yes, but they're hard people to know. I never understood Brian Flynn, never understood what made him go on." She paused, then said, "After all these years...I thought I'd have heard one day that he was dead or had a breakdown like so many of them, or ran off to Spain like so many more of them, but he just keeps going on...like some immortal thing, tortured by life, unable to die, unable to lay down the sword that has become so burdensome. ...God, I almost feel sorry for him." She had the uncomfortable feeling that her revelations about Brian Flynn were somehow disloyal.

The Cardinal knelt beside the three people. He said, "In the tower I learned that Brian Flynn is a man who holds some unusual beliefs. He's a romantic, a man who lives in the murky past. The idea of blood sacrifice—which may be the final outcome here—is consistent with Irish myth, legend, and history. There's this aura of defeat that surrounds the people here—unlike the aura of ultimate victory that is ingrained in the British and American psyche." The Cardinal seemed to consider, then went on. "He really believes he is a sort of incarnation of Finn MacCumail." He looked at Maureen. "He's still very fond of you."

Her face flushed, and she said, "That won't stop him from killing me."

The Cardinal answered, "He would only harm you if he thought you felt nothing for him any longer."

She thought back to the bride's room. "So what am I supposed to do? Play up to him?"

Father Murphy spoke. "We'll all have to do that, I think, if we're going to survive. Show him we care about him as a person...and I think at least some of us do. I care about his soul."

Baxter nodded slowly. "Actually, you know, it costs nothing to be polite...except a bit of self-respect." He smiled and said, "Then when everyone is calmed down, we'll have another go at it."

Maureen nodded quickly. "Yes, I'm willing."

The Cardinal spoke incredulously. "Haven't you two had enough?"

She answered, "No."

Baxter said, "If Flynn were our only problem, I'd take my chances with him. But when I look into the eyes of Megan Fitzgerald or John Hickey...Maureen and I spoke about this before, and I've decided that I don't want tomorrow's newspapers to speak of my execution and martyrdom, but I would want them to say, 'Died in an escape attempt.'"

The Cardinal said acidly, "It may read, 'A foolish escape attempt'...shortly before you were to be released."

Baxter looked at him. "I've stopped believing in a negotiated settlement. That reduces my options to one."

Maureen added, "I'm almost certain that Hickey means to kill us and destroy this church."

Baxter sat up with some difficulty. "There's one more way out of here...and we can all make it.... We *must* all make it, because we won't get another chance."

Father Murphy seemed to be struggling with something, then said, "I'm with you." He glanced at the Cardinal.

The Cardinal shook his head. "It was a miracle we weren't all killed last time. I'm going to have to insist that—"

Maureen reached into the pocket of her jacket and held out a small white particle. "Do any of you know what this is? No, of course you don't. It's plastic explosive. As we suspected, that's what Hickey and Megan carried down in those suitcases. This is molded around at least one of the columns below. I don't know how many other columns are set to be blown, or where they all are, but I do know that two suitcases of plastic, properly placed, are enough to bring down the roof." She fixed her eyes on the Cardinal, who had turned pale. She continued, "And I don't see a remote detonator and wire up here. So I have to assume it's set to go on a timer. What time?" She looked at the three men. "At least one of us has to get out of here and warn the people outside."

Brian Flynn strode up to the communion rail and spoke in an ill-tempered tone. "Are you plotting again? Your Eminence, please stay on your exalted throne. The wounded gentlemen don't need your comfort. They're comforted enough knowing they're still alive. Miss Malone, may I have a word with you in the Lady Chapel? Thank you."

Maureen stood and noticed the stiffness that had spread through her body. She walked slowly to the side steps, down into the ambulatory, then passed into the Lady Chapel.

Flynn came up behind her and indicated a pew toward the rear. She sat.

He stood in the aisle beside her and looked around the quiet chapel. It was unlike the rest of the Cathedral; the architecture was more delicate and refined. The marble walls were a softer shade, and the long, narrow windows were done mostly in rich cobalt blues. He looked up at one of the windows to the right of the entrance. A face stared back at him, looking very much like Karl Marx, and in fact the figure was carrying a red flag in one hand and a sledgehammer in the other, attacking the cross atop a church steeple. "Well," he said in a neutral tone, "you know you've arrived as a lesser demon when the Church sticks your face up in a window. Like a picture in the celestial post office. Wanted for heresy." He pointed up at the window. "Karl Marx. Strange."

She glanced at the representation. "You wish it was Brian Flynn, don't you?"

He laughed. "You read my black soul, Maureen." He turned and looked at the altar nestled in the rounded end of the chapel. "God, the money that goes into these places."

"Better spent on armaments, wouldn't you say?"

He looked at her. "Don't be sharp with me, Maureen."

"Sorry."

"Are you?"

She hesitated, then said, "Yes."

He smiled. His eyes traveled upward past the statue of the Virgin on the altar, to the apsidal window above it. "The light will break through that window first. I hope we're not still here to see it."

She turned to him suddenly. "You won't burn this church, and you won't kill unarmed hostages. So stop speaking as though you were the type of man who would."

He put his hand on her shoulder, and she slid over. He sat beside her and said, "Something is very wrong if I've given the impression I'm bluffing."

"Perhaps it's because I know you. You've fooled everyone else."

"But I'm not fooling or bluffing."

"You'd shoot me?"

"Yes . . . I'd shoot myself afterward, of course."

"Very romantic, Brian."

"Sounds terrible, doesn't it?"

"You should hear yourself."

"Yes...well, anyway, I've been meaning to speak with you again, but with all that's been going on...We have some time now." He said, "Well, first you must promise me that you won't try to escape again."

"All right."

He looked at her. "I mean it. They'll kill you next time."

"So what? Better than being shot in the back of the head—by you."

"Don't be morbid. I don't think it will come to that."

"But you're not sure."

"It depends on things out of my control now."

"Then you shouldn't have gambled with my life and everyone else's—should you? Why do you think the people out there will be rational and concerned about our lives if you're not?"

"They've no choice."

"No choice but to be rational and compassionate? You've developed quite a faith in mankind, I see. If people behaved like that, none of us would be here now."

"This sounds like the argument we never finished four years ago." He stared toward the windows for a while, then turned to her. "Would you like to come with me when we leave here?"

She faced him. "When you leave here it will be for the jail or the cemetery. No, thank you."

"Damn you.... I'm walking out of here as free and alive as I walked in. Answer the question."

"What's to become of poor Megan? You'll break her dear heart, Brian."

"Stop that." He held her arm tightly. "I miss you, Maureen." She didn't respond.

He said, "I'm ready to retire." He looked at her closely.

"Really I am. As soon as this business is done with. I've learned a good deal from this."

"Such as?"

"I've learned what's important to me. Look here, you quit when you were ready, and I'm doing the same. I'm sorry I wasn't ready when you were."

"Neither you nor I believe a word of that. 'Once in, never out.' That's what you and all of them have thrown up to me all these years, so I'm throwing it right back in your face. 'Once in—'"

"No!" He pulled her closer to him. "Right now I believe I'm going to get out. Why can't you believe it with me?"

She suddenly went limp and put her hand over his. She spoke in a despondent tone. "Even if it *were* possible—there are people who have plans for your retirement, Brian, and they don't include a cottage by the sea in Kerry." She slumped against his shoulder. "And what of me? I'm hunted by the Belfast IRA still. One can't do the kinds of things we've done with our lives and expect to live happily ever after, can we? When was the last time you heard a knock on the door without having a great thump in your chest? Do you think you can announce your retirement like a respected statesman and settle down to write your memoirs? You've left a trail of blood all over Ireland, Brian Flynn, and there are people—Irish and British—who want yours in return."

"There are places we could go—"

"Not on this planet. The world is very small, as a good number of our people on the run have found out. Think how it would be if we lived together. Neither of us could ever go out to buy a packet of tea without wondering if it would be the last time we'd see each other. Every letter in the mail could explode in your face. And what if there were...children? Think about that awhile."

He didn't reply.

She shook her head slowly. "I won't live like that. It's enough that I have to worry about myself. And it's a relief, to be honest with you, that I have no one else to worry about—not you, nor Sheila...so why should I want to go with you and worry about when they're going to kill you?...Why do you want to worry about when they're going to catch up with me?"

He stared at the floor between the pews, then looked up at the altar. "But...you would *like* to...I mean if it were possible...?"

She closed her eyes. "I wanted that once. I suppose, really, I still do. But it's not in our stars, Brian."

He stood abruptly and moved into the aisle. "Well...as long as you'd like to...that's good to know, Maureen." He said, "I'm adding Sheila's name to the list."

"Don't expect anything in return."

"I don't. Come along, then."

"Would you mind if I stayed here in the chapel?"

"I wouldn't, no. But...you're not safe here. Megan..."

"God, Brian, you speak of her as though she were a mad dog waiting to kill a sheep who's strayed from the fold."

"She's a bit...vindictive...."

"Vindictive? What have I ever done to her?"

"She...she blames you, in part, for her brother's capture.... It's not rational, I know, but she's—"

"Bloodthirsty. How in the name of God did you get mixed up with that savage? Is that what the youth of Northern Ireland's turning into?"

Flynn looked back toward the chapel opening. "Perhaps. War is all they've known—all Megan's known since she was a child. It's become commonplace, the way dances and picnics used to be. These young people don't even remember what downtown Belfast looked like before. So you can't blame them. You understand that."

She stood. "She goes a bit beyond war psychosis. You and I, Brian...*our* souls are not dead, are they?"

"We remember some of the life before the troubles."

Maureen thought of Jean Kearney. She pictured the faces of the others. "We started this, you know."

"No. The other side started it. The other side always starts it."

"What difference does it make? Long after this is over, our country will be left with the legacy of children turned into murderers and children who tremble in dark corners. We're perpetuating it, and it will take a generation to forget it."

He shook his head. "Longer, I'm afraid. The Irish don't forget things in a generation. They write it all down and read it again, and tell it round the peat fires. And in truth you, I, and Megan are products of what came long before the recent troubles. Cromwell's massacres happened only last week, the famine happened yesterday, the uprising and civil war this morning. Ask John Hickey. He'll tell you."

She took a long breath. "I wish you weren't so damned right about these things."

"I wish you weren't so right about us. Come along."

She followed him out of the quiet chapel.

CHAPTER 42

Flynn descended the sacristy steps and saw Burke and Pedar Fitzgerald facing each other through the gate. A portable television sat on the landing beside Burke.

Flynn said to Fitzgerald, "Bring the priest here in five minutes."

Fitzgerald slung the Thompson over his shoulder and left.

Burke looked at Flynn closely. He appeared tired, perhaps even sad.

Flynn took out the microphone detector and passed it over the television. "We're both suspicious men by temperament and by profession. God, it's lonely though, isn't it?"

"Why the sudden melancholy?"

Flynn shook his head slowly. "I keep thinking this won't end well."

"I can almost guarantee you it won't."

Flynn smiled. "You're a welcome relief from that ass Schroeder. You don't bother me with sweet talk or with talk of giving up."

"Well, now, I hate to say this after that compliment, but you *should* give it up."

"I can't, even if I wanted to. This machine I've put together has no real head, no real brain. But it has many killing appendages...inside and outside the Cathedral, each spring-loaded to act or react under certain conditions. I'm no more than the creator of this thing—standing outside the organism.... I suppose I speak for it, but not *from* it. You understand?"

"Yes." Burke couldn't tell if this pessimism was contrived. Flynn was a good actor whose every line was designed to create an illusion, to produce a desired response.

Flynn nodded and leaned heavily against the bars.

Burke had the impression that Flynn was fighting some inner struggle that was taking a great deal out of him.

After a time Flynn said, "Well, anyway, here's what I wanted to speak to you about. Hickey and I have concluded that Martin's abducted the resident architect of Saint Patrick's. Why, you ask? So that you can't plan or mount a successful attack against us."

Burke considered the statement. There'd certainly be more optimism in the rectory and Cardinal's residence if Gordon Stillway was poring over the blueprints with Bellini right now. Burke tried to put it together in his mind. The Fenians had missed Stillway; that was obvious by now. Maureen Malone wouldn't have found an unsecured passage if Stillway was in there, because Stillway, no matter how brave a man he might be, would have been spilling it all out after fifteen minutes with this bunch.

And it wasn't too difficult to believe that Major Martin had anticipated Stillway's importance and snatched him before the Fenians could get to him. But to believe all that, you had to believe some very nasty and cold-blooded things about Major Martin.

Flynn broke the silence. "Are you seeing it now? Martin doesn't want the police to move too fast. He wants to drag this out—he wants the dawn deadline to approach. He's probably already suggested that you'll get an extension of the deadline, hasn't he?"

Burke said nothing.

Flynn leaned closer. "And without a firm plan of attack you're ready to believe him. But let me tell you, at 6:03 A.M. this Cathedral is no more. If you attack, your people will be ripped up very badly. The only way this can end without bloodshed is on *my* terms. *You* believe that we've beaten you. So swallow all that goddamned Normandy Beach–Iwo Jima pride and tell the stupid bastards out there that it's finished and let's all go home."

"They won't listen to that."

"*Make* them listen!"

Burke said, "To the people out there the Fenians are no more the peers of the police and government than the New York street gang that calls itself the Pagans. They *can't* deal with you, Flynn. They're bound by law to arrest you and throw you in the slammer with the muggers and rapists, because that's all terrorists are— muggers, murderers, and rapists on a somewhat larger scale—"

"Shut up!"

Neither man spoke, then Burke said in a gentler tone, "I'm telling you what their position is. I'm telling you what Schroeder won't tell you. It's true we've lost, but it's also true we won't—can't—surrender. You could surrender... honorably... negotiate the best terms possible, lay down your guns—"

"No. Not one person in here can accept anything less than we've asked for."

Burke nodded. "All right. I'll pass it on.... Maybe we can still work something out that will save you and your people and the hostages and the Cathedral.... But the people in internment..." He shook his head. "London would never..."

Flynn also shook his head. "All or nothing."

Both men lapsed into a silence, each aware that he had said

more than he'd intended. Each was aware, too, that he had lost something that had been building between them.

Pedar Fitzgerald's voice came down the stairs. "Father Murphy."

Flynn turned and called back. "Send him down."

The priest walked unsteadily down the marble staircase, supporting his large frame on the brass rail. He smiled through the face bandages and spoke in a muffled voice. "Patrick, good to see you." He put his hand through the bars.

Burke took the priest's hand. "Are you all right?"

Murphy nodded. "Close call. But the Lord doesn't want me yet."

Burke released the priest's hand and withdrew his own.

Flynn put his hand to the bars. "Let me have it."

Burke opened his hand, and Flynn snatched a scrap of paper from him.

Flynn unfolded the paper and read the words written in pencil. *Hickey sent last message on confessional buzzer.* There followed a fairly accurate appraisal of the Cathedral's defenses. Flynn frowned at the first sentence: *Hickey sent last message...* What did that mean?

Flynn pocketed the paper and looked up. There was no anger in his voice. "I'm proud of these people, Burke. They've shown some spirit. Even the two holy men have kept us on our toes, I'll tell you."

Burke turned to Murphy. "Do any of you need a doctor?"

Murphy shook his head. "No. We're a bit lame, but there's nothing a doctor can do. We'll be all right."

Flynn said, "That's all, Father. Go back with the others."

Murphy hesitated and looked around. He glanced at the chain and padlock, then looked at Flynn, who stood as tall as he but was not as heavy.

Flynn sensed the danger and moved back. His right hand
stayed at his side, but the position of his fingers suggested he was
ready to go for his pistol. "I've been knocked about by priests
before, and I owe you all a few knocks in return. Don't give me
cause. Leave."

Murphy nodded, turned, and mounted the steps. He called
back over his shoulder, "Pat, tell them out there we're not
afraid."

Burke said, "They know that, Father."

Murphy stood at the crypt door for a few seconds, then
turned and disappeared around the turn in the staircase.

Flynn put his hands in his pockets. He looked down at the
floor, then lifted his head slowly until he met Burke's eyes. He
spoke without a trace of ruthlessness. "Promise me something,
Lieutenant—promise me one thing tonight.... "

Burke waited.

"Promise me this—that if they attack, you'll be with them."

"What—?"

Flynn went on. "Because, you see, if you know you're not involved on that level, then subconsciously you'll not see things
you should see, you'll not say things you should say out there.
And you'll not live so easily with yourself afterward. You know
what I mean."

Burke felt his mouth becoming dry. He thought of
Schroeder's foolishness. It was a bad night for rear-echelon people. The front line was moving closer. He looked up at Flynn
and nodded almost imperceptibly.

Flynn acknowledged the agreement without speaking. He
looked away from Burke and said, "Don't leave the rectory
again."

Burke didn't reply.

"Stay close. Stay close especially as the dawn approaches."

"I will."

Flynn looked past Burke into the sacristy and focused on the priests' altar in the small chapel at the rear that was directly below the Lady Chapel altar. There were arched Gothic windows behind this altar also, but these subterranean windows with soft artificial lighting behind them, eastward-facing windows, were suffused with a perpetual false dawn. He kept staring at them and spoke softly, "I've spent a good deal of my life working in the hours of darkness, but I've never been so frightened of seeing the sunrise."

"I know how you feel."

"Good.... Are they frightened out there?"

"I think they are."

Flynn nodded slowly. "I'm glad. It's not good to be frightened alone."

"No."

Flynn said, "Someday—if there's a day after this one—I'll tell you a story about Whitehorn Abbey—and this ring." He tapped it against the bars.

Burke looked at the ring; he suspected it was some sort of talisman. There always seemed to be magic involved when he dealt with people who lived so close to death, especially the Irish.

Flynn looked down at the floor. "I may see you later."

Burke nodded and walked down the steps.

CHAPTER 43

B rian Flynn stood beside the curtain entrance to the confessional and looked at the small white button on the jamb. *Hickey sent last message...* Flynn turned toward the sound of approaching footsteps.

Hickey stopped and looked at his watch. "Time to meet the press, Brian."

He looked at Hickey. "Tell me about this buzzer."

Hickey glanced at the confessional. "Oh, that. There's nothing to tell. I caught Murphy trying to send a signal on it while he was confessing—can you imagine such a thing from a *priest,* Brian? Anyway, I think this is a call buzzer to the rectory. So I sent a few choice words, the likes of which they've never heard in the good fathers' dormitory." He laughed.

Flynn forced a smile in return, but Hickey's explanation raised more questions than it answered. *Hickey sent last message...* Who sent the previous message or messages? He said, "You should have kept me informed."

"Ah, Brian, the burdens of command are so heavy that you can't be bothered with every small detail."

"Just the same—" He looked at Hickey's chalk-white face and saw the genial twinkle in his eyes turn to a steady burning stare of unmistakable meaning. He imagined he even heard a voice: *Don't go any further.* He turned away.

Hickey smiled and tapped his watch. "Time to go give them hell, lad."

Flynn made no move toward the elevator. He knew he had reached a turning point in his relationship with John Hickey. A tremor passed down his spine, and a sense of fear came over him unlike any normal fear he had ever felt. *What have I unleashed?*

Hickey turned into the archway beside the confessional, passing into the hallway of the bride's room. He stopped in front of the oak elevator door and turned off the alarm. Slowly he began to deactivate the mine.

Flynn came up behind him.

Hickey neutralized the mine. "There we are.... I'll set it again after you've gone down." He opened the oak door, revealing the sliding doors of the elevator.

Flynn moved closer.

Hickey said, "When you come back, knock on the oak door. Three long, two short. I'll know it's you, and I'll defuse the mine again." He looked up at Flynn. "Good luck."

Flynn stepped closer and stared at the gray elevator doors, then at the mine hanging from the half-opened oak door. *I'll know it's you, and I'll defuse the mine....* He looked into Hickey's eyes and said, "I've got a better idea."

Inspector Langley and Roberta Spiegel waited in the brightly lit hallway of the subbasement. With them were Emergency Service police and three intelligence officers. Langley checked his watch. Past ten. He put his ear to the elevator doors. He heard nothing and straightened up.

Roberta Spiegel said, "This bastard has all three networks and every local station waiting for him. Mussolini complex—keep them waiting until they're delirious with anticipation."

Langley nodded, realizing that was exactly how he felt waiting for Brian Flynn to step out of the gray doors.

Suddenly the noise of the elevator motor broke into the stillness of the corridor. The elevator grew louder as it descended from the hallway of the bride's room into the subbasement. The doors began to slide open.

Langley, the three ID men, and the police unconsciously straightened their postures. Roberta Spiegel put her hand to her hair. She felt her heart in her chest.

The door opened, revealing not Brian Flynn but John Hickey. He stepped into the hall and smiled. "Finn MacCumail, Chief of the Fenians, sends his respects and regrets." Hickey looked around, then continued. "My chief is a suspicious man— which is why he's stayed alive so long. He had, I believe, a premonition about exposing himself to the dangers inherent in such a situation." He looked at Langley. "He is a thoughtful man who didn't want to place such temptation in front of you— or your British allies. So he sent me, his loyal lieutenant."

Langley found it hard to believe that Flynn was afraid of a trap—not with four hostages to guarantee his safety. Langley said, "You're John Hickey, of course."

Hickey bowed formally. "No objections, I trust."

Langley shrugged. "It's your show."

Hickey smiled. "So it is. And to whom do I have the pleasure of speaking?"

"Inspector Langley."

"Ah, yes.... And the lady?" He looked at Spiegel.

Spiegel said, "My name is Roberta Spiegel. I'm with the Mayor's office."

Hickey bowed again and took her hand. "Yes. I heard you on the radio once. You're much more beautiful than I pictured you from your voice." He made a gesture of apology. "Please don't take that the wrong way."

Spiegel withdrew her hand and stood silent. She had the unfamiliar experience of being at a loss for a reply.

Langley said, "Let's go."

Hickey ignored him and called down the corridor, "And these gentlemen?" He walked up to a tall ESD man and read his name tag. "Gilhooly." He took the man's hand and pumped it. "I love the melody of the Gaelic names with the softer sounds. I knew Gilhoolys in Tullamore."

The patrolman looked uncomfortable. Hickey walked up and down the hallway shaking each man's hand and calling him by name.

Langley exchanged looks with Spiegel. Langley whispered, "He makes Mussolini look like a tongue-tied schoolboy."

Hickey shook the hand of the last man, a big flak-jacketed ESD man with a shotgun. "God be with you tonight, lad. I hope our next meeting is under happier circumstances."

Langley said impatiently, "Can we go now?"

Hickey said, "Lead on, Inspector." He fell into step with Langley and Spiegel. The three ID men followed. Hickey said, "You should have introduced those men to me. You ignored them—ignored their humanity. How can you get people to follow you if you treat them like jackstraws?"

Langley wasn't quite sure what a jackstraw was, and in any case chose not to answer.

Hickey went on. "In ancient days combatants would salute each other before battle. And a man about to be executed would shake his executioner's hand or even bless him to show mutual respect and compassion. It's time we put war and death on a personal basis again."

Langley stopped at a modern wooden door. "Right." He looked at Hickey. "This is the press room."

Hickey said, "Never been on television before. Do I need makeup?"

Langley motioned to the three ID men, then said to Hickey, "Before I take you in there, I have to ask you if you're armed."

"No. Are you?"

Langley nodded to one of the men who produced a metal detector and waved the wand over Hickey's body.

Hickey said, "You may find that British bullet I've been carrying in my hip since '21."

The metal detector didn't sound, and Langley reached out and pushed open the door. Hickey entered the room, and the sounds of conversation died abruptly. The press conference area below the sacristy was a long, light-paneled room with an acoustical tile ceiling. Several card tables were grouped around a long central conference table. Camera and light connections hung from trapdoors in the ceiling. Hickey looked slowly around the room and examined the faces of the people looking at him.

A reporter, David Roth, who had been elected the spokesman, rose and introduced himself. He indicated a chair at the head of the long table.

Hickey sat.

Roth said, "Are you Brian Flynn, the man who calls himself Finn MacCumail?"

Hickey leaned back and made himself comfortable. "No, I'm John Hickey, the man who calls himself John Hickey. You've heard of me, of course, and before I'm through you'll know me well enough." He looked around the table. "Please introduce yourselves in turn."

Roth looked a bit surprised, then introduced himself again and pointed to a reporter. Each man and woman in the press room, including, at Hickey's request, the technicians, gave his name.

Hickey nodded pleasantly to each one. He said, "I'm sorry I

kept you all waiting. I hope my delay didn't cause the representatives of the governments involved to leave."

Roth said, "They won't be present."

Hickey feigned an expression of hurt and disappointment. "Oh, I see.... Well, I suppose they don't want to be seen in public with a man like me." He smiled brightly. "Actually, I don't want to be associated with them either." He laughed, then produced his pipe and lit it. "Well, let's get on with it, then."

Roth motioned to a technician, and the lights went on. Another technician took a light reading near Hickey's face while a woman approached him with makeup. Hickey pushed her away gently, and she moved off quickly.

Roth said, "Is there any particular format you'd like us to follow?"

"Yes. I talk and you listen. If you listen without nodding off or picking your noses, I'll answer questions afterward."

A few reporters laughed.

The technicians finished the adjustments in their equipment, and one of them yelled, "Mr. Hickey, can you say something so we can get a voice reading?"

"Voice reading? All right, I'll sing you a verse from 'Men Behind the Wire,' and when I'm through, I want the cameras on. I'm a busy man tonight." He began to sing in a low, croaky voice.

> "Through the little streets of Belfast
> In the dark of early morn,
> British soldiers came marauding
> Wrecking little homes with scorn.
> Heedless of the crying children,
> Dragging fathers from their beds,
> Beating sons while helpless mothers
> Watch the blood flow from their heads—"

"Thank you, Mr. Hickey—"
Hickey sang the chorus—

> "Armored cars, and tanks and guns
> Came to take away our sons
> But every man will stand behind
> The men behind the wii-re!"

"Thank you, sir."
The camera light came on. Someone yelled, "On the air!"
Roth looked into the camera and spoke. "Good evening.
This is David—" Hickey's singing came from off camera:

> "Not for them a judge or jury,
> Or indeed a crime at all.
> Being Irish means they're guilty,
> So we're guilty one and a-lll—"

Roth looked to his right. "Thank you—"

> "Round the world the truth will echo,
> Cromwell's men are here again.
> England's name again is sullied
> In the eyes of honest me-nnn—"

Roth glanced sideways at Hickey, who seemed to have finished. Roth looked back at the camera. "Good evening, I'm David Roth, and we're broadcasting live...as you can see... from the press room of Saint Patrick's Cathedral. Not too far from where we now sit, an undisclosed number of IRA gunmen—"
"Fenians!" yelled Hickey.

"Yes... Fenians... have seized the Cathedral and hold four hostages: Cardinal— "

"They know all that!" shouted Hickey.

Roth looked upset. "Yes... and with us tonight is Mr. John Hickey, one of the... Fenians...."

"Put the camera on me, Jerry," said Hickey. "Over here— that's right."

Hickey smiled into the camera and began, "Good evening and Happy Saint Patrick's Day. I am John Hickey, poet, scholar, soldier, and patriot." He settled back into his chair. "I was born in 1905 or thereabouts to Thomas and Mary Hickey in a small stone cottage outside of Clonakily in County Cork. In 1916, when I was a wee lad, I served my country as a messenger in the Irish Republican Army. Easter Monday, 1916, found me in the beseiged General Post Office in Dublin with the poet Padraic Pearse, the labor leader James Connolly, and their men, including my sainted father, Thomas. Surrounding us were the Irish Fusiliers and the Irish Rifles, lackeys of the British Army."

Hickey relit his pipe, taking his time, then went on. "Padraic Pearse read a proclamation from the steps of the Post Office, and his words ring in my ears to this day." He cleared his throat and adopted a stentorian tone as he quoted: "'Irishmen and Irishwomen—in the name of God and the dead generations from which she receives her old tradition of nationhood, Ireland, through us, summons her children to her flag and strikes for freedom.'"

Hickey went on, weaving a narrative blend of history and fancy, facts and personal prejudices, interjecting himself into some of the more famous events of the decades following the Easter Monday rebellion.

Most of the reporters leaned forward in interest; some looked impatient or puzzled.

Hickey was serenely unaware of them or of the cameras and lights. From time to time he would mention the Cathedral to keep everyone's interest piqued, then would swing into a long polemic against the British and American governments or the governments of the divided Ireland, always careful to exclude the people of these lands from his wrath.

He spoke of his sufferings, his wounds, his martyred father, his dead friends, a lost love, recalling each person by name. He beamed as he spoke of his revolutionary triumphs and frowned as he spoke darkly of the future of an Ireland divided. Finally he yawned and asked for a glass of water.

Roth took the opportunity to ask, "Can you tell us exactly how you seized the Cathedral? What are your demands? Would you kill the hostages and destroy the Cathedral if—"

Hickey held up his hand. "I'm not up to that part yet, lad. Where was I? Oh, yes. Nineteen hundred and fifty-six. In that year the IRA, operating from the south, began a campaign against the British-occupied six counties of the North. I was leading a platoon of men and women near the Doon Forest, and we were ambushed by a whole regiment of British paratroopers backed by the murderous Royal Ulster Constabulary." Hickey went on.

Langley watched him from the corner, then looked around at the news people. They seemed unhappy, but he suspected that John Hickey was doing better with the public than with the media. Hickey had a hard-driving narrative style...a simplicity and almost crudeness—sweating, smoking, and scratching—not seen on television in a long time.

John Hickey—sitting now in fifty million American living rooms—was becoming a folk hero. Langley would not have been surprised if someone told him that outside on Madison Avenue vendors were hawking John Hickey T-shirts.

CHAPTER 44

Brian Flynn stood near the altar and watched the television that had been placed on the altar.

Maureen, Father Murphy, and Baxter sat in the clergy pews, watching and listening silently. The Cardinal sat nearly immobile, staring down at the television from his throne, his fingertips pressed together.

Flynn stood in silence for a long while, then spoke to no one in particular. "Long-winded old man, isn't he?"

Maureen looked at him, then asked, "Why didn't you go yourself, Brian?"

Flynn stared at her but said nothing.

She leaned toward Father Murphy and said, "Actually, Hickey seems an effective speaker." She paused thoughtfully. "I wish there were a way to get this kind of public platform without doing what they've done."

Murphy added as he watched the screen, "He's at least venting the frustrations of so many Irishmen, isn't he?"

Baxter glanced at them sharply. "He's not venting anyone's frustrations—he's inflaming some long-cooled passions. And I think he's embellishing and distorting it a bit, don't you?" No one answered, and he went on. "For instance—if he'd been ambushed by a regiment of British paras, he wouldn't be here to talk about it—"

Maureen said, "That's not the point—"

Flynn overheard the exchange and looked at Baxter. "Harry, your chauvinism is showing. Hail Britannia! Britannia rules the Irish. Ireland—first outpost of Empire and destined to be the last."

Baxter said to Flynn, "The man's a bloody demagogue and charlatan."

Flynn laughed. "No, he's *Irish.* Among ourselves we sometimes tolerate a poetic rearrangement of facts mutually understood. But listen to the man, Harry—you might learn a thing or two."

Baxter looked at the people around him—Maureen, Murphy, Flynn, the Fenians . . . even the Cardinal. For the first time he understood how little he understood.

Megan Fitzgerald walked up to the sanctuary and stared at the television screen.

Hickey, in the tradition of the ancient seanachies, interrupted his narrative to break into song:

> "Then, here's to the brave men of Ireland.
> At home or in exile away;
> And, here's to the hopes of our sire land,
> That never will rust or decay.
> To every brave down-trodden nation,
> Here's liberty, glorious and bright. But,
> Oh! Let our country's salvation,
> Be toasted the warmest, to-niiight!"

Megan said, "Bloody old fool. He's making a laughing-stock of us ranting like that." She turned to Flynn. "Why the hell did you send him?"

Flynn looked at her and said softly, "Let the old man have his day, Megan. He deserves this after nearly seventy years of war. He may be the world's oldest continuously fighting soldier." He smiled in a conciliatory manner. "He's got a lot to tell."

Megan's voice was impatient. "He's supposed to tell them that the British are the only obstacle to a negotiated settlement here. I've a brother rotting in Long Kesh, and I want him free in Dublin come morning."

Maureen looked up at her. "And I thought you were here only because of Brian."

Megan wheeled around. "Shut your damned mouth!"

Maureen stood, but Father Murphy pulled her quickly into the pew.

Flynn said nothing, and Megan turned and strode off.

Hickey's voice blared from the television. The Cardinal sat motionless staring at some point in space. Baxter looked away from everyone and tried to filter out Hickey's voice, concentrating on the escape plan. Father Murphy and Maureen watched the screen intently. Flynn watched also, but his thoughts, like Baxter's, were elsewhere.

John Hickey took out a flask and poured a dark liquid into his water glass, then looked up at the camera. "Excuse me. Heart medicine." He drained off the glass and let out a sigh. "That's better. Now, where was I? Right—1973—" He waved his arms. "Oh, enough of this. Listen to me, all of you! We don't want to hurt anyone in this Cathedral. We don't want to harm a Prince of the Roman Church—a holy man—a good man—or his priest, Father Murphy…a lovely man…." He leaned forward and clasped his hands together. "We don't want to harm one single altar or statue in this beautiful house of God that New Yorkers—Americans—love so dearly. We're not barbarians or pagans, you know."

He held his hands out in an imploring gesture. "Now listen to me...." His voice became choked, and tears formed in his eyes. "All we want is another chance for the young lives being wasted in British concentration camps. We're not asking for the impossible—we're not making any irresponsible demands. No, we're only asking— begging—begging in the name of God and humanity for the release of Ireland's sons and daughters from the darkness and degradation of these unspeakable dungeons."

He took a drink of water and stared into the camera. "And who is it who have hardened their hearts against us?" He thumped the table. "Who is it who'll not let our people go?" *Thump!* "Who is it that by their unyielding policy endangers the lives of the people in this great Cathedral?" He pounded the table with both fists. "The bloody fucking British—*that's* who!"

Burke leaned against the wall in the Monsignor's office and watched the screen. Schroeder sat at his desk, and Spiegel had returned to her rocker. Bellini paced in front of the screen, blocking everyone's view, but no one objected.

Burke moved to the twin doors, opened them, and looked into the outer office. The State Department security man, Arnold Sheridan, stood by the window in deep thought. Occasionally he would eye the British and Irish representatives. Burke had the impression that Sheridan was going to give them the unpleasant news from Washington that Hickey was scoring heavily and it was time to talk. An awkward, almost embarrassed silence lay over the office as Hickey's monologue rolled on. Burke was reminded of a living room he had sat in once where the adolescents and adults had somehow gotten themselves involved in watching an explicit documentary on teenage sex. Burke turned back to the inner office and stared at the screen.

Hickey's voice was choked with emotion. "Many of you may question the propriety of our occupation of a house of God, and it was, I assure you, the hardest decision any of us has ever made in our lives. But we didn't so much *seize* the Cathedral as we took *refuge* in it—claimed the ancient privilege of *sanctuary*. And what better place to stand and ask for God's help?"

He paused as though wrestling with a decision, then said softly, "This afternoon, many Americans for the first time saw the obscene face of religious bigotry as practiced by the Orangemen of Ulster. Right here in the streets of the most ecumenical city in the world, the ugliness of religious intolerance and persecution was made unmistakably clear. The songs you heard those bigots sing were the songs the little children are taught in homes, schools, and churches...." He straightened his posture; on his face was a distasteful look that melted into an old man's sadness. He shook his head slowly.

Schroeder turned away from the screen and said to Burke, "What's the latest with those Orangemen?"

Burke kept staring at the screen as he spoke. "They still say they're Protestant loyalists from Ulster, and they'll probably keep saying that until at least dawn. But according to our interrogators they all sound like Boston Irish. Probably IRA Provos recruited for the occasion." Given all the externals of this affair, Burke thought, psychological timing, media coverage, tactical preparations, political maneuverings, and last-ditch intelligence gathering—it was clear that Flynn would not extend the deadline and risk the tide turning against him.

Spiegel said, "It was a tactical blunder to let Hickey on television."

Schroeder said defensively, "What else could I do?"

Bellini interjected, "Why don't I grab him—then we'll use him to negotiate for the hostages."

Schroeder said, "Good idea. Why don't you go cold-cock him right now before they break for a commercial?"

Burke looked at his watch. 10:25 P.M. The night was slipping away so fast that it would be dawn before anyone realized it was too late.

Hickey looked around the press room. He noticed that Langley had disappeared. Hickey leaned forward and spoke to the cameraman. "Zoom in, Jerry." He watched the monitor. "Closer. That's it. Hold it." He stared at the camera and spoke in low tones that had the suggestion of finality and doom. "Ladies and gentlemen of America—and all the unborn generations who will one day hear my words—we are outnumbered two thousand to one by police and soldiers, besieged and isolated by our enemies, betrayed by politicians and diplomats, compromised and undermined by secret agents, and censured by the world press...." He placed his hand over his chest. "But we are not afraid, because we know that out there are friends who wish us success and Godspeed in our mission. And there are the men and women, old and young, in Long Kesh, Armagh, Crumlin Road—all the hellholes of England and Northern Ireland—who are on their knees tonight, praying for their freedom. Tomorrow, God willing, the gates of Long Kesh will be thrown open, and wives will embrace husbands, children will weep with parents, brothers and sisters will meet once more...."

The tears were running freely again, and he took out a big bandanna and blew his nose, then continued, "If we accomplish nothing else this night, we'll have made the world aware of their existence. And if we die, and others die with us, and if this great Cathedral where I sit right now is a smoldering ruin by morning, then it will only be because men and women of goodwill could not prevail against the repressive forces of darkness and inhumanity." He took a long breath and cleared his throat. "Till we meet again in a happier place...God bless you all. God bless America and Ireland and, yes, God bless our enemies, and may He show them the light. *Erin go bragh.*"

David Roth cleared his throat and said, "Mr. Hickey, we'd like you to answer a few specific questions...."

Hickey stood abruptly, blew his nose into the bandanna, and walked off camera.

Inspector Langley had returned; he opened the door, and Hickey moved quickly into the hall, followed by Langley and the three ID men. Langley came up beside Hickey and said, "I see you know when to quit."

Hickey put away his bandanna. "Oh, I couldn't go on any longer, lad."

"Yeah. Listen, you got your message across. You're way ahead. Now why don't you come out of there and give everyone a break?"

Hickey stopped in front of the elevator. His manner and voice suddenly became less teary. "Why the hell should we?"

Langley dismissed the three ID men. He took a notebook from his pocket and glanced at it. "Okay, Mr. Hickey, listen closely. I've just been authorized by representatives of the British and American governments to tell you that if you come out of the Cathedral now, the British will begin procedures to re-lease—quietly and at intervals—most of the people on your list, subject to conditions of parole— "

"*Most?* What kind of *intervals?* What kind of *parole?*"

Langley looked up from the notebook. "I don't know anything more than I'm telling you. I just got this over the phone. I'm only a cop, okay? And we're the only ones allowed to speak to you people. Right? So this is a little difficult but just listen and—"

"Pimp."

Langley looked up quickly. "What?"

"Pimp. You're pimping for the diplomats who don't want to make a direct proposition to us whores."

Langley flushed. "Look...look you—"

"Get hold of yourself, man. Steady."

Langley took a breath and continued in a controlled voice. "The British can't release all of them at once—not when you've got a gun to their heads—to everyone's heads. But it *will* be done. And also the State and U.S. Attorney General have agreed to allow all of you in there to post a low bond and go free awaiting trial—you understand what that means?"

"No, I don't."

Langley looked annoyed. "It means you can skip out on the fucking bail and get the hell out of the country."

"Oh...sounds dishonest."

Langley ignored the remark and said, "No one has been killed yet—that's the main thing. That gives us a lot of leeway in dealing with you—"

"It makes that much difference, does it? We've committed a dozen felonies already, terrified half the city, made fools of you, caused a riot, cost you millions of dollars, ruined your parade, and the Commissioner of Police has dropped dead of a heart attack. But you're willing to let bygones be bygones—give us a wink and run us off like Officer Muldoon stumbling onto a crap game in an alley—as long as no one's been killed. Interesting. That says a great deal about this society."

Langley drew another breath and said, "I won't make this offer again—for obvious reasons, no one will ever mention it over the telephone. So that's it." He slapped the notebook shut. "It's a fair compromise. Take it or leave it."

Hickey pressed the elevator button, and the doors opened. He said to Langley, "We wouldn't look very good if we compromised, would we? You'd look good, though. Schroeder would be booked solid on TV for a year. But we'd not have access to the airwaves so easily. All anyone would see or remember is us coming out the front doors of Saint Patrick's with our hands up. We'd do that gladly if the camps were emptied *first.* Then there's no way anyone could hide or steal our victory with diplomatic or journalistic babble."

"You'd be *alive,* for Christ's sake."

"Did you get my grave dug up yet?"

"Don't pull that spooky shit on me."

Hickey laughed.

Langley spoke mechanically, determined to deliver the last lines he had been instructed to say. "Use your power of persuasion with the people in there and your influence as a great Irish Republican leader. Don't tarnish with senseless death and destruction what you've already accomplished." He added his own thoughts. "You snowed about half of America tonight. Quit while you're ahead."

"I had a horse at Aqueduct this afternoon that quit while he was ahead.... But I'll pass your kind offer on to Mr. Flynn and the Fenians, and we'll let you know. If we never mention it, then you can assume we are holding fast to all our demands."

Hickey stepped into the elevator. "See you later, God willing." He pushed the button, and as the doors slid closed he called out, "Hold my fan mail for me, Inspector."

CHAPTER 45

Brian Flynn stood opposite the elevator's oak door, an M-16 rifle leveled at it. George Sullivan stood to the side of the door, listening. The elevator stopped, and Sullivan heard a soft rapping, three long and two short. He signaled in return, then defused the mine and opened the door.

John Hickey stepped out. Flynn lowered the rifle a half second too slowly, but no one seemed to notice.

Sullivan extended his hand. "Damned fine, John. You had me laughing and weeping at the same time."

Hickey smiled as he took Sullivan's hand. "Ah, my boy, it was a dream come true." He turned to Flynn. "You would have done even better, lad."

Flynn turned and walked into the ambulatory. Hickey followed. Flynn said as he walked, "Did anyone approach you?"

Hickey walked ahead to the chancel organ. "One fellow, that Inspector Langley. Gave us a chance to surrender. Promised us a low bail—that sort of thing."

"Did the British relay any information—any indication they would compromise?"

"The British? Compromise? They're not even *negotiating*." He sat at the keyboard and turned on the organ.

"They didn't get word to you through anyone?"

"You'll not hear from them." He looked at Flynn. "You've got to play the bells now, Brian, while we still have everyone's attention. We'll begin with—let's see— 'Danny Boy' and then do a few Irish-American favorites for our constituency. I'll lead, and you follow my tempo. Go on now."

Flynn hesitated, then moved toward the center aisle. Hickey began playing "Danny Boy" in a slow, measured meter that would set the tempo for the bells.

The four hostages watched Flynn and Hickey, then turned back to the television. The reporters in the Cathedral press room were discussing Hickey's speech. Baxter said, "I don't see that we're any closer to being let out of here."

Father Murphy replied, "I wonder...don't you think after this, the British...I mean..."

Baxter said sharply, "No, I don't." He looked at his watch. "Thirty minutes and we go."

Maureen looked at him, then at Father Murphy. She said, "What Mr. Baxter means is that he, too, thinks they were probably considering a compromise after Hickey's speech, but Mr. Baxter's decided that he doesn't want to be the cause of any compromise."

Baxter's face reddened.

Maureen continued. "It's all right, you know. I feel the same way. I'm not going to be used by them like a slab of meat to be bartered for what they want." She said in a quieter voice, "I've been used by them long enough."

Murphy looked at them. "Well...that's fine for you two, but I can't go unless my life is in actual danger. Neither can His Eminence." He inclined his head toward the Cardinal, who sat looking at them from his throne. Murphy added, "I think we all ought to wait...."

Maureen looked back at the Cardinal and saw by his face

that he was struggling with the same question. She turned to Father Murphy. "Even if Hickey's speech has moved the people out there toward a compromise, that doesn't move *Hickey* toward a compromise—does it?" She leaned forward. "He's a treacherous man. If you still believe he's evil and means to destroy us, destroy himself, the Fenians, and this church, then we *must* try to get out of here." She fixed her eyes on Murphy's. "Do you believe that?"

Murphy looked at the television screen. A segment of John Hickey's speech was being replayed. The volume was turned low, and Hickey's voice wasn't audible over the organ. Murphy watched the mouth moving, the tears rolling down his face. He looked into the narrow eyes. Without the spellbinding voice the eyes gave him away.

Father Murphy looked out over the sanctuary rail at Hickey playing the organ. Hickey's head was turned toward them as he watched himself on television. He was smiling at his image, then turned and smiled, a grotesque smile, at Father Murphy. The priest turned quickly back to Maureen and nodded.

Baxter looked up at the Cardinal's throne; the Cardinal bowed his head in return. Baxter glanced at his watch. "We go in twenty-seven minutes."

Flynn rode the elevator to the choir practice room, then stepped out into the loft. He walked up behind Leary, who was leaning over the parapet watching the hostages through his scope. Flynn said, "Anything?"

Leary continued to observe the four people on the sanctuary. At some point years ago he had realized that not only could he anticipate people's movements and read their expression, but he could also read their lips. He said, "A few words. Not too clear. Hard to see their lips." The hostages had reached a point in their relationships to each other where they communicated with fewer words, but their body language was becoming clearer to him.

Flynn said, "Well, are they or aren't they?"

"Yes."

"How? When?"

"Don't know. Soon."

Flynn nodded. "Warning shots first, then go for the legs. Understand?"

"Sure."

Flynn picked up the field phone on the parapet and called Mullins in the bell tower. "Donald, get away from the bells."

Mullins slung his rifle and pulled a pair of shooters' baffles over his ears. He snatched up the field phone and quickly descended the ladder to the lower level.

Flynn moved to a small keyboard beside the organ console and turned the switch to activate the nineteen keys that played the bells. He stood before the waist-high keyboard and turned the pages of bell music on the music desk, then put his hands over the big keys and joined with the chancel organ below.

The biggest bell, the one named Patrick, chimed a thunderous B-flat, and the sound crashed through the bell tower, almost knocking Mullins off his feet.

One by one the nineteen huge bells began tolling in their carillon, beginning at the first bell room where Mullins had been and running upward to a point near the top of the spire twenty-one stories above the street.

In the attic a coffee cup fell off a catwalk rail. Arthur Nulty and Jean Kearney covered their ears and moved to the Madison Avenue end of the Cathedral. In the choir loft and triforia the bells resonated through the stonework and reverberated in the floors. In the south tower Rory Devane listened to the steady chiming coming from the opposite tower. He watched as the activity on the rooftops slowed and the movement in the streets came to a halt. In the cold winter air the slow rhythmical sounds of "Danny Boy" pealed through the dark canyons of Manhattan.

The crowds around the police barricades began cheering, raising bottles and glasses, then singing. More people began moving outdoors into the avenues and side streets.

Television coverage shifted abruptly from the press room of the Cathedral to the roofs of Rockefeller Center.

In bars and homes all over New York, and all over the country, pictures of the Cathedral as seen from Rockefeller Center flashed across the screens, bathed in stark blue lighting. A camera zoomed in on the green and gold harp flag that Mullins had draped from the torn louvers.

The sound of the bells was magnified by television audio equipment and transmitted with the picture from one end of the continent to the other. Satellite relays picked up the signal and beamed it over the world.

Rory Devane slipped a flare into a Very pistol, pointed it up through the louvers, and fired. The projectile arched upward, burst into green light, then floated on a parachute, swinging like a pendulum in the breeze, casting an unearthly green radiance across the buildings and through the streets. Devane went to the eastward-facing louvers and fired again.

Remote cameras located in the streets, bars, and restaurants began sending pictures of men and women singing, cheering, crying. A kaleidoscope of images flashed across video screens—bars, street crowds, the green-lit sky, close-ups of tight-lipped police, the bell tower, long shots of the Cathedral.

The flares suddenly changed from the illumination type to signal flares, star bursts, red, white, blue, then the green, orange, and white of the Irish tricolor. The crowd reacted appropriately. All the while the rich, lilting melody of "Danny Boy" filled the air from the bell tower and filled the airwaves from televisions and portable radios.

> "O Danny Boy, the pipes, the pipes are calling
> From glen to glen, and down the mountain side,
> The summer's gone, and all the roses falling,
> 'Tis you, 'tis you, must go and I must bide...."

Finally, on each station, reporters after an uncommonly long period of silence began adding commentary to the scenes, which needed none.

In the sanctuary the hostages watched the television in fascinated silence. Hickey played the organ with intense concentration, leading Flynn on the bells. Both men glanced at each other from time to time across the hundred yards that separated them.

Hickey swung into "Danny Boy" for the third time, not wanting to break the spell that the bittersweet song had laid over the collective psyche of the Cathedral and the city. He laughed as tears rolled down his furrowed cheeks.

In the Cardinal's residence and in the rectory the only sound was the pealing of the bells rolling across the courtyard and resonating from a dozen television sets into rooms filled with people.

Burke stood in the Monsignor's inner office, where the original Desperate Dozen had reassembled along with some additional members whom Burke had labeled the Anguished Auxiliaries.

Schroeder stood to the side with Langley and Roberta Spiegel, who, Burke noticed, was becoming Langley's constant companion.

Langley stared at the screen and said, "If they'd had television on V-J day, this is what it would have looked like."

Burke smiled in spite of himself. "Good timing. Good theater...fireworks...really hokey, but Christ, it gets them every time."

Spiegel added, "And talk about your psychological disadvantages."

Major Martin stood in the rear of the room between Kruger and Hogan. He kept his head and eyes straight ahead and said in an undertone, "We've always underestimated the willingness of the Irish to make public spectacles of themselves. Why don't they suffer in silence like civilized people?"

The two agents looked at each other behind Martin's back but said nothing.

Martin glanced to either side. He knew he was in trouble. He spoke with a light tone in his voice. "Well, I suppose I've got to undo this—or perhaps in their typical Irish fashion they'll undo themselves if—Oh, sorry, Hogan...."

Douglas Hogan moved away from Martin.

Monsignor Downes found his diary buried under Schroeder's paperwork and drew it toward him, opening it to March 17.

He wrote, *10:35 P.M. The bells tolled tonight, as they've tolled in the past to mark the celebration of the holy days, the ends of wars, and the deaths of presidents.* He paused, then added, *They tolled for perhaps the last time. And people, I think, sensed this, and they listened and they sang. In the morning, God willing, the carillon will ring out a glorious Te Deum—or if it is God's will, they will ring no more.* Monsignor Downes put aside his pen and closed the diary.

Donald Mullins swung his rifle butt and smashed a hole in the thick, opaque glass of the lower section of the tower. He knocked out a dozen observation holes, the noise of the breaking glass inaudible through his shooters' baffles and the chiming of the bells. Mullins slung his rifle and took a deep breath, then approached a broken window in the east side of the tower room and stared out into the cold night.

He saw that Devane was alternating star bursts with parachute flares, and the clearing night sky was lit with colors under a bright blue moon. The anxiety and despair he had felt all evening suddenly vanished in the clarity of the night, and he felt confident about meeting his death here.

CHAPTER 46

Harold Baxter didn't consult his watch. He knew it was time. In fact, he thought, they should have gone sooner, before the bells and the fireworks, before Hickey's speech, before the Fenians had transformed themselves from terrorists to freedom fighters.

He took a long last look around the Cathedral, then glanced at the television screen. A view from the tallest building of Rockefeller Center showed the cross-shape of the blue-lit Cathedral. In the upper left corner sat the rectory; in the right corner, the Cardinal's residence. Within five minutes he would be sitting in either place, taking tea and telling his story. He hoped Maureen, the priest, and the Cardinal would be with him. But even if one or all of them were killed, it would be a victory because that would be the end of the Fenians.

Baxter rose from the pew and stretched nonchalantly. His legs were shaking and his heart was pounding.

Father Murphy rose and walked across the sanctuary. He exchanged quiet words with the Cardinal, then moved casually behind the altar and looked down the staircase.

Pedar Fitzgerald sat with his back to the crypt door, the Thompson pointed down the stairs toward the sacristy gate. He was singing to himself.

Father Murphy raised his voice over the organ. "Mr. Fitzgerald."

Fitzgerald looked up quickly. "What is it, Father?"

Murphy felt a dryness in his throat. He looked across the stairwell for Baxter but didn't see him. He said, "I'm . . . I'm hearing confessions now. Someone will relieve you if you want to—"

"I've nothing to confess. Please leave."

Baxter steadied his legs, took a deep breath and moved. He covered the distance to the right side of the altar in three long strides and bounded down the steps in two leaps, unheard over the noise of the organ. Maureen was directly behind him.

Father Murphy saw them suddenly appear on the opposite stairs and made the sign of the cross over Fitzgerald.

Fitzgerald sensed the danger and spun around. He stared at Baxter flying toward him and raised his submachine gun.

Father Murphy heard a shot ring out from the choir loft and dived down the stairs; he looked over his shoulder for the Cardinal but knew he wasn't coming.

Leary got off a single shot, but his targets were gone in less time than it took him to steady his aim from the recoil. Only the Cardinal was left, sitting immobile on his throne, a splash of scarlet against the white marble and green carnations. Leary saw Hickey climb across the organ and drop to the sanctuary beside the Cardinal's throne. The Cardinal stood, placing himself in Hickey's path. Hickey's arm shot out and knocked the Cardinal to the floor. Leary placed the cross hairs over the Cardinal's supine body.

Flynn continued the song on the bells, not wanting to alert the people outside that something was wrong. He watched the sanctuary in the mirror. He called out, "That will be all, Mr. Leary."

Leary lowered his rifle.

Baxter flew down the stairs, and his foot shot out, hitting

Fitzgerald full in the face. Fitzgerald staggered back, and Father Murphy grabbed his arm from behind. Baxter seized the submachine gun and pulled violently. Fitzgerald wrenched the gun back.

The sound of the chancel organ had died away, but the bells played on, and for a second they were the only sound in the Cathedral until the air was split by a burst of fire from the submachine gun. The muzzle flashed in Baxter's face, and he was momentarily blinded. Pieces of plaster fell from the vaulted ceiling above, crashing over the sacristy stairs.

Father Murphy yanked back on Fitzgerald's arm but couldn't break Fitzgerald's grip on the gun. Maureen ducked around Baxter and jabbed her fingers into Fitzgerald's eyes. Fitzgerald screamed, and Baxter found himself holding the heavy submachine gun. He brought the butt up in a vertical stroke but missed Fitzgerald's groin and solar plexus, hitting him a glancing blow across the chest.

Baxter swore, raised the butt again, and drove it horizontally into the young man's throat. Father Murphy released Fitzgerald, and he fell to the floor. Baxter stood over the fallen man and raised the gun butt over Fitzgerald's face.

Maureen shouted, "No!" She grabbed Baxter's arm.

Fitzgerald looked up at them, tears and blood running from his unfocused eyes. Blood gushed from his open mouth.

Brian Flynn watched Hickey and Megan moving across the sanctuary. Leary stood beside him, fingering his rifle and murmuring to himself. Flynn turned his attention back to the bells.

The four people in the triforia had barely taken in what had happened in the last fifteen seconds. They stared down into the altar sanctuary and saw the Cardinal lying sprawled on the floor and Hickey and Megan approaching the two stairwells cautiously.

Maureen held the Thompson, steadied herself, and pulled

back on the trigger. A deafening burst of automatic fire flamed out of the muzzle and slammed into the padlock and chain.

Murphy and Baxter crouched as bullets ricocheted back, cracking into the marble stairs and walls. Baxter heard footsteps on the sanctuary floor. "They're coming."

Maureen fired a long second burst at the gate, then swung the gun up at the right-hand staircase, placed Hickey in her sight, and fired.

Hickey's body seemed to twitch, then he dropped back out of view.

Maureen swung the gun around to the left and pointed it at Megan, who had stopped short on the first step, a pistol in her hand. Maureen hesitated, and Megan dived to the side and disappeared.

Baxter and Murphy ran down the stairs and tore at the shattered chain and padlock. Hot, jagged metal cut into their hands, but the chain began dropping away in pieces, and the padlock fell to the floor.

Maureen backed down the stairs, keeping the muzzle of the gun pointed up at the crypt door.

Police officers in the side corridors were shouting into the empty sacristy.

Baxter yelled to them. "Hold your fire! We're coming out! Hold it!" He tore the last section of chain away and kicked violently at the gates. "Open! Open!"

Father Murphy was pulling frantically on the left-hand gate, shouting, "No! They *roll*—!"

Baxter lunged at the right gate and tried to slide it along its track into the wall, but both gates held fast.

Flak-jacketed police began edging out into the sacristy.

Maureen knelt on the bottom stair, keeping the gun trained on the landing above. She shouted, "What's wrong?"

Baxter answered, "Stuck! Stuck!"

Murphy suddenly released the gate and straightened up. He grabbed at a black metal box with a large keyhole located where the gates joined and shook it. "They've locked it! The keys—they have the keys—"

Maureen looked back at them over her shoulder. She saw that the gate had its own lock, and she hadn't hit it even once. Baxter shouted a warning, and she spun around. She saw Hickey standing in front of the crypt door, his legs straddling Pedar Fitzgerald's body. Maureen raised the gun.

Hickey called down. "You can shoot me if you'd like, but that won't get you out of here."

Maureen screamed at him, "Don't move! Hands up!"

Hickey raised his hands slowly. "There's really no way out, you know."

She shouted, "Throw me the gate key!"

He made an exaggerated shrug. "I think Brian has it." He added, "Try shooting the lock out. Or would you rather use the last few rounds on me?"

She swore at him, spun around, and faced the gates. She shouted to Baxter and Murphy. "Move back!" She saw the police in the sacristy. "Get away!"

The police scattered back into the corridors. She pointed the muzzle at the boxlike lock that joined the gates and fired a short burst at point-blank range. The bullets ripped into the lock, scattering sparks and pieces of hot metal.

Baxter and Murphy yelled out in pain as they were hit. A piece of metal grazed Maureen's leg, and she cried out. She fired again, one round, and the rotating drum of .45-caliber bullets clicked empty. Murphy and Baxter seized the bars of the gates and pulled. The gates held fast.

Maureen swung back to find Hickey halfway down the steps,

a pistol in his hand. Hickey said, "You don't see that kind of craftsmanship today. Hands up, please."

Megan Fitzgerald knelt at the landing beside her brother. She looked down at Maureen, and their eyes met for a brief second.

Hickey's voice was impatient. "Hands on your heads! Now!"

Father Murphy, Baxter, and Maureen stood motionless.

Hickey called out to the police. "Stay in the corridors, or I'll shoot them all!" He shouted to the three people, "Let's go!"

They remained motionless.

Hickey pointed the pistol and fired.

The bullet whistled past Murphy's head, and he fell to the floor.

Maureen reversed the Thompson, grabbing its hot barrel in her hands, and brought it down savagely on the marble steps. The gunstock splintered and the drum flew off. She threw the mangled gun to the side, then stood erect and raised her arms.

Baxter did the same. Murphy stood and put his hands on his head.

Hickey looked at Maureen appreciatively. "Come on, then. Calm down. That's right. Best-laid plans and all that." He moved aside to let them pass.

Maureen stepped up to the landing and looked down at Pedar Fitzgerald. His throat was already beginning to swell, and she knew he would die unless he reached a hospital soon. She found herself cursing Baxter for botching it and injuring Fitzgerald so seriously, cursing Father Murphy for not remembering the gate's lock, cursing herself for not killing Hickey and Megan. She looked down at Megan, who was wiping the blood from her brother's mouth, but it kept flowing up from his crushed throat. Maureen said, "Sit him up or he'll drown."

Megan turned slowly and looked up at her. Her lips drew

back across her teeth, and she sprang up and dug her nails into Maureen's neck, shrieking, snarling.

Baxter and Murphy rushed up the remaining stairs and pulled the two women apart. Hickey watched quietly as the struggle and the shouting subsided, then said, "All right. Everyone feel better? Megan, sit the lad up. He'll be all right." He poked the pistol at the three hostages. "Let's go."

They continued up to the sanctuary. Hickey chatted amiably as he followed. "Don't feel too badly. Damned bad luck, that's all. Maureen, you're a terrible shot. You didn't come within a yard of me."

She turned suddenly. "I hit you! I hit you!"

He laughed, put his finger to his chest, and drew it away with a small drop of pale, watery blood. "So you did."

The hostages moved toward the pews. The Cardinal was slumped in his throne, his face in his hands, and Maureen thought he was weeping, then saw the blood running through his fingers. Father Murphy made a move toward the Cardinal, but Hickey shoved him away.

Baxter looked up into the triforia and choir loft and saw the five rifles trained on them. He was vaguely aware that the bells were still pealing, and the phone beside the chancel organ was ringing steadily.

Hickey called up to Gallagher. "Frank, get down here quickly and take Pedar's place." He pushed Baxter into a pew and said, as though complaining to a close friend, "Damned dicey operation I've gotten myself in, Harry. Lose one man and there's no one to replace him."

Baxter looked him in the eyes. "In school I learned that IRA stood for I Ran Away. It's a wonder anyone's stayed here."

Hickey laughed. "Oh, Harry, Harry. After this place explodes and they find your pieces, I hope the morticians put your stiff upper lip where your asshole was and vice versa." Hickey shoved Maureen into the pew. "And you—breaking up that gun—Like an old Celt yourself you were, Maureen, smashing your sword against a rock before dying in battle. Magnificent. But you're becoming a bit of a nuisance." He looked at Murphy. "And *you*, running out on your boss like that. Shame—"

Murphy said, "Go to hell."

Hickey feigned a look of shock. "Well, will you listen to this...?"

Murphy's hands shook, and he turned his back on Hickey.

Baxter stared at the television on the table. The scene had shifted back to the press room below. Reporters were speaking excitedly to their newsrooms. The gunfire, he knew, had undone the effects of Hickey's speech and the tolling bells. Baxter smiled and looked up at Hickey. He started to say something but suddenly felt an intense pain in his head and slumped forward out of the pew.

Hickey flexed his blackjack, turned, and grabbed Father Murphy by the lapel. He raised the black leather sap and stared into the priest's eyes.

Gallagher had come out of the triforium door and ran toward the sanctuary. "No!"

Hickey looked at him, then lowered the sap. "Cuff them." He moved to the television and ripped the plug from the outlet.

Maureen knelt over Baxter's crumpled body and examined the wound on his forehead. "Bloody bastards—" She looked at the choir loft where Flynn played the bells. Gallagher took her wrist and locked on a handcuff, then locked the other end to Baxter's wrist. Gallagher cuffed Murphy's wrist and led him to the Cardinal. Gallagher knelt, then passed the cuff through the arm in the throne and gently placed the cuff over the Cardinal's blood-streaked wrist. Gallagher whispered, "I'll protect you." He bowed his head and walked away.

Father Murphy slumped down on the top step of the raised platform. The Cardinal came down from the throne and sat beside him. Neither man spoke.

Megan came out of the stairwell carrying her brother in her arms. She stood in the center of the sanctuary looking around blankly. A blood trail led from the stairwell to where she stood, and the trail became a small pool at her feet. Hickey took Pedar from his sister's arms and carried the limp body down to the chancel organ. He propped Pedar Fitzgerald against the organ console and covered him with his old overcoat.

Gallagher unslung his rifle and went down to the crypt landing. He shouted to the police who were cautiously examining the gate. "Get back! Go on!" They disappeared to the sides of the sacristy.

Megan remained standing in the pool of blood, staring at it. The only sounds in the Cathedral were the pealing bells and the persistently ringing telephone.

Brian Flynn watched from the choir loft as he tolled the bell. Leary glanced at Flynn curiously. Flynn turned away and concentrated on the keyboard, completing the last bar of "Danny Boy," then began "The Dying Rebel." He spoke into the microphone. "Mr. Sullivan, the pipes, please. Ladies and gentlemen, a song." He began singing. Hesitantly, other voices joined him, and Sullivan's pipes began skirling.

> "The night was dark and the battle ended.
> The moon shone down O'Connell Street.
> I stood alone where brave men parted,
> Never more again to speak."

John Hickey picked up the ringing telephone.

Schroeder's voice came over the line, very nearly out of control. "What happened? What *happened*?"

Hickey growled, "Shut up, Schroeder! The hostages are not dead. Your men saw it all. The hostages are cuffed now, and there'll be no more escape attempts. End of conversation."

"Wait! Listen, are they injured? Can I send a doctor?"

"They're in reasonably good shape. If you're interested, though, one of my lads has been hurt. Sir Harold Baxter, knight of the realm, bashed his throat in with a rifle. Not at all sporting."

"God . . . listen, I'll send a doctor—"

"We'll let you know if we want one." He looked down at Fitzgerald. His throat was grotesquely bloated now. "I need ice. Send it through the gates. And a tracheal tube."

"Please . . . let me send—"

"No!" Hickey rubbed his eyes and slumped forward. He felt very tired and wished it would all end sooner than he had hoped.

"Mr. Hickey . . ."

"Oh, shut up, Schroeder. Just shut up."

"May I speak to the hostages? Mr. Flynn said I could speak to them after the press—"

"They've lost the right to speak with anyone, including each other."

"How badly are they hurt?"

Hickey looked at the four battered people on the sanctuary. "They're damned lucky to be alive."

Schroeder said, "Don't lose what you've gained. Mr. Hickey, let me tell you, there are a lot of people on your side now. Your speech was . . . magnificent, grand. What you said about your suffering, the suffering of the Irish—"

Hickey laughed wearily. "Yes, a traditional Irish view of history, which is at times in conflict with the facts but never inhibited by them." He smiled and yawned. "But everyone bought it, did they? TV is marvelous."

"Yes, sir, and the bells—did you see the television?"

"What happened to those song requests?"

"Oh, I've got some here—"

"Shove them."

After a short silence Schroeder said, "Well, anyway, it was really incredible, you know—I've never seen anything like that in this city. Don't lose that, don't—"

"It's already lost. Good-bye, Schroeder."

"Wait! Hold it! One last thing. Mr. Flynn said you'd turn off the radio jammer— "

"Don't blame your radio problems on us. Buy better equipment."

"I'm just afraid that without radio control the police might overreact to some perceived danger—"

"So what?"

"That almost happened. So, I was wondering when you were going to shut it off—"

"It will probably shut off when the Cathedral explodes." He laughed.

"Come on now, Mr. Hickey...you sound tired. Why don't you all try to get some sleep? I'll guarantee you an hour—two hours' truce—and send some food, and— "

"Or more likely it'll be consumed by the flames from the attic. Forty long years in the building—Poof—it'll be gone in less than two hours."

"Sir...I'm offering you a truce—" Schroeder took another breath, then spoke in a cryptic tone. "A police inspector gave you a...a status report, I believe...."

"Who? Oh, the tall fellow with the expensive suit. Watch that man, he's taking graft."

"Are you considering what he said to you?"

"As the Ulster Protestants are fond of saying, 'Not an inch!' Or would they now say centimeter? Inch. Yes, inch—"

"It's a fair solution to—"

"Unacceptable, Schroeder! Don't bother me with it again."

Schroeder said abruptly, "May I speak with Mr. Flynn?"

Hickey looked up at the loft. There was a telephone extension on the organ, but Flynn had not used it. Hickey said, "He's come to a difficult passage in the bells. Can't you hear it? Have a little consideration."

"We haven't heard from him in a long time. We expected him at the press conference. Is he...all right?"

Hickey found his pipe and lit it. "He's as well as any young man can be who is contemplating his imminent death, the sorrow of a lost love, the tragedy of a lost country, and a lost cause."

"*Nothing* is lost—"

"Schroeder, you understand Irish fatalism, don't you? When they start playing melancholy songs and weeping in their beers, it means they're on the verge of something reckless. And listening to your whimpering voice will not improve Brian Flynn's mood."

"No, listen, you're close—it's not lost—"

"Lost! Listen to the bells, Schroeder, and between their peals you'll hear the wail of the banshee in the hills, warning us all of approaching death." He hung up.

Megan was staring down at him from the sanctuary.

Hickey glanced at Pedar Fitzgerald. "He's dying, Megan."

She nodded hesitantly, and he looked at her. She seemed frightened suddenly, almost childlike. He said, "I can give him over to the police and he may live, but..."

She understood clearly that there would be no victory, no amnesty for them, or for the people in Northern Ireland, and that soon she and everyone in the Cathedral would be dead. She looked at her brother's blue-white face. "I want him here with me."

Hickey nodded. "Yes, that's the right thing, Megan."

Father Murphy shifted around on the throne platform. "He should be taken to a hospital."

Neither Megan nor Hickey answered.

Father Murphy went on, "Let me administer the sacrament—"

Hickey cut him off. "You've got a damned ritual for everything, don't you?"

"To save his soul from damnation—"

"People like you give eternal damnation a bad name." Hickey laughed. "I'll wager you carry some of that holy oil with you all the time. Never know when a good Catholic might drop dead at your feet."

"I carry holy oil, yes."

Hickey sneered. "Good. Later we'll fry an egg with it."

Father Murphy turned away. Megan walked toward Maureen and Baxter. Maureen watched her approach, keeping her eyes fixed steadily on Megan's.

Megan stood over the two cuffed people, then knelt beside Baxter's sprawled body and ripped the belt from his pants. She stood with her feet spread and brought the belt down with a whistling sound across Baxter's face.

Father Murphy and the Cardinal shouted at her.

Megan raised the belt again and brought it down on Maureen's upraised arms. She aimed the next blow at Baxter, but Maureen threw herself over his defenseless body and the belt lashed her across the neck.

Megan struck at Maureen's back, then struck again at her legs, then her buttocks.

The Cardinal looked away. Murphy was shouting at the top of his lungs.

Hickey began playing the chancel organ, joining with the bells. Frank Gallagher sat on the blood-smeared landing where Fitzgerald had lain and listened to the sounds of blows falling; then the sharp sounds were lost as the organ played "The Dying Rebel."

George Sullivan looked away from the sanctuary and played his bagpipe. Abby Boland and Eamon Farrell had stopped singing, but Flynn's voice called to them over the microphone, and they sang. Hickey sang, too, into the organ microphone.

"The first I saw was a dying rebel.
Kneeling low I heard him cry,
God bless my home in Tipperary,
God bless the cause for which I die."

In the attic Jean Kearney and Arthur Nulty lay on their sides, huddled together on the vibrating floor boards. They kissed, then moved closer. Jean Kearney rolled on her back, and Nulty covered her body with his.

Rory Devane stared out of the north tower, then fired the last flare. The crowds below were still singing, and he sang, too, because it made him feel less alone.

Donald Mullins stood in the tower below the first bell room, oblivious to everything but the pounding in his head and the cold wind passing through the smashed windows. From his pocket he took a notebook filled with scrawled poems and stared at it. He remembered what Padraic Pearse had said, referring to himself, Joseph Plunkett, and Thomas MacDonagh at the beginning of the

1916 uprising: "If we do nothing else, we shall rid Ireland of three bad poets." Mullins laughed, then wiped his eyes. He threw the notebook over his shoulder, and it sailed out into the night.

In the choir loft Leary watched Megan through his sniper scope. It came to him in a startling way that he had never once, even as a child, struck anyone. He watched Megan's face, watched her body move, and he suddenly wanted her.

Brian Flynn stared into the organ's large concave mirror, watching the scene on the altar sanctuary. He listened for the sound of Maureen's cries and the sound of the steady slap of the belt against her body, but heard only the vibrant tones of the chimes, the high, reedy wail of the bagpipes, the singing, and the full, rich organ below.

> "The next I saw was a gray-haired father,
> Searching for his only son.
> I said Old Man there's no use in searching
> Your only son to Heaven has gone."

He lowered his eyes from the mirror and shut them, listening only to the faraway chimes. He remembered that sacrifices took place on altars, and the allusion was not lost on him, and possibly some of the others understood as well. Maureen understood. He remembered the double meaning of sacrifice: an implied sanctification, an offering to the Deity, thanksgiving, purification.... But the other meaning was darker, more terrible—pain, loss, death. But in either case the understanding was that sacrifice was rewarded. The time, place, and nature of the reward was never clear, however.

> "Your only son was shot in Dublin
> Fighting for his Country bold.

He died for Ireland and Ireland only
The Irish flag green, white and gold."

A sense of overpowering melancholy filled him—visions of
Ireland, Maureen, Whitehorn Abbey, his childhood, flashed
through his mind. He suddenly felt his own mortality, felt it as
a palpable thing, a wrenching in his stomach, a constriction in
his throat, a numbness that spread across his chest and arms.

A confused vision of death filled the blackness behind his
eyelids, and he saw himself lying naked, white as the cathedral
marble, in the arms of a woman with long honey-colored hair
shrouding her face; and blood streamed from his mouth, over
his cold dead whiteness—blood so red and so plentiful that the
people who had gathered around remarked on it curiously. A
young man took his hand and knelt to kiss his ring; but the ring
was gone, and the man rose and walked away in disgust. And
the woman who held him said, *Brian, we all forgive you.* But that
gave him more pain than comfort, because he realized he had
done nothing to earn forgiveness, done nothing to try to alter
the course of events that had been set in motion so long before.

CHAPTER 47

B rian Flynn looked at the clock in the rear of the choir loft. He let the last notes of "An Irish Lullaby" die away, then pressed the key for the bell named Patrick. The single bell tolled, a deep low tone, then tolled again and again, twelve times, marking the midnight hour. St. Patrick's Day was over.

The shortest day of the year, he reflected, was not the winter solstice but the day you died, and March 18 would be only six hours and three minutes long, if that.

A deep silence lay over the acre of stone, and the outside cold seeped into the church, slowly numbing the people inside. The four hostages slept fitfully on the cool marble of the altar sanctuary, cuffed together in pairs.

John Hickey rubbed his eyes, yawned, and looked at the television he had moved to the organ console. The volume was turned down, and a barely audible voice was remarking on the new day and speculating on what the sunrise would bring. Hickey wondered how many people were still watching. He pictured all-night vigils around television sets. Whatever happened would happen live, in color, and few would be willing to go to sleep and see it on the replays. Hickey looked down at Pedar Fitzgerald. There were ice packs around his throat and a tube coming from his mouth that emitted a hissing sound. Slightly annoying, Hickey thought.

Flynn began playing the bells again, an Irish-American song this time, "How Are Things in Glocca Morra?"

Hickey watched the television. The street crowds approved of the selection. People were swaying arm in arm, beery tears rolling down red faces. But eventually, he knew, the magic would pass, the concern over the hostages and the Cathedral would become the key news story again. A lot of emotional strings were being pulled this night, and he was fascinated by the game of manipulation. Hickey glanced up at the empty triforium where Gallagher had stood, then turned and called back toward the sacristy stairs, "Frank?"

Gallagher called from the stairwell, "All quiet!"

Hickey looked up at Sullivan and Abby Boland, and they signaled in return. Eamon Farrell called down from the triforium overhead. "All quiet." Hickey cranked the field phone.

Arthur Nulty rolled over and reached out for the receiver. "Roger."

"Status."

Nulty cleared his throat. "Haven't we had enough bells, for God's sake? I can't hear so well with that clanging in my ears."

"Do the best you can." He cranked the phone again. "Bell tower?"

Mullins was staring through a shattered window, and the phone rang several times before he was aware of it. He grabbed it quickly. "Bell tower."

Hickey said, "Sleeping?"

Mullins moved one earpiece of the shooters' baffles and said irritably, "Sleeping? How the hell could anyone sleep with *that*?" He paused, then said, "Has he gone mad?"

Hickey said, "How are they behaving outside?"

Mullins trailed the phone wire and walked around the tower. "They keep coming and going. Mostly coming. Soldiers bivouacked in the Channel Gardens. Damned reporters on the roofs have been drinking all night. Could use a rip myself."

"Aye, time enough for that. At this hour tomorrow you'll be—where?"

"Mexico City...I'm to fly to Mexico City...." He tried to laugh. "Long way from Tipperary."

"Warm there. Keep alert." Hickey cranked again. "South tower."

Rory Devane answered. "Situation unchanged."

"Watch for the strobe lights."

"I know."

"Are the snipers still making you nervous, lad?"

Devane laughed. "No. They're keeping me company. I'll miss them, I think."

"Where are you headed tomorrow?"

"South of France. It's spring there, they tell me."

"So it is. Remember, a year from today at Kavanagh's in fair Dublin."

"I'll be there."

Hickey smiled at the dim memory of Kavanagh's Pub, whose front wall was part of the surrounding wall of Glasnevin Cemetery. There was a pass-through in the back wall where gravediggers could obtain refreshments, and as a result, it was said, many a deceased was put into the wrong hole. Hickey laughed. "Aye, Rory, you'll be there." He hung up and turned the crank again.

Leary picked up the phone in the choir loft. Hickey said, "Tell Brian to give the bells a rest, then." He watched Leary turn and speak to Flynn. Leary came back on the line. "He says he feels like playing."

Hickey swore under his breath. "Hold on." He looked at the television set again. The scenes of New York had been replaced by an equally dramatic view of the White House, yellow light coming from the Oval Office windows. A reporter was telling the world that the President was in conference with top advisers. The scene shifted to 10 Downing Street, where it was 5:00 A.M. A bleary-eyed female reporter was assuring America that the Prime Minister was still awake. A quick scene-change showed the Apostolic Palace in the Vatican. Hickey leaned forward and listened carefully as the reporter speculated about the closed-door gathering of Vatican officials. He mumbled to himself, "Saint Peter's next."

Hickey spoke into the phone. "Tell Mr. Flynn that since we can expect an attack at any time now, I suggest he stop providing them with the noise cover they need." He hung up and listened to the bells, which still rang. Brian Flynn, he thought, was not the same man who strode so cockily through this Cathedral little more than six hours before. Flynn was a man who had learned a great deal in those six hours, but had learned it too late and would learn nothing further of any consequence in the final six hours.

Captain Bert Schroeder was startled out of a half-sleep by the ringing telephone. He picked it up quickly.

Hickey's voice cut into the stillness of the office and boomed out over the speakers in the surrounding rooms, also startling some of the people there. "*Schroeder! Schroeder!*"

Schroeder sat up, his chest pounding, "Yes! What's wrong?"

Hickey's voice was urgent. "Someone's seized the Cathedral!" He paused and said softly, "Or was I having a nightmare?" He laughed.

Schroeder waited until he knew his voice would be steady. He looked around the office. Only Burke was there at the moment, sleeping soundly on the couch. Schroeder said, "What can I do for you?"

Hickey said, "Status report, Schroeder."

Schroeder cleared his throat. "Status—"

"How are things in Glocca Morra, London, Washington, Vatican City, Dublin? Anybody still working on this?"

"Of course. You can see it on TV."

"I'm not the public, Schroeder. *You* tell me what's happening."

"Well..." He looked at some recent memos. "Well...the Red Cross and Amnesty are positioned at all of the camps...waiting..."

"That was on TV."

"Was it? Well...Dublin...Dublin has not yet agreed to accept released internees—"

"Tell them for me that they're sniveling cowards. Tell them I said the IRA will take Dublin within the year and shoot them all."

Schroeder said emphatically, "Anyway, we all haven't agreed on terms yet, have we? So finding a place of sanctuary is of secondary importance—"

"I want to speak with all the governments directly. Set up a conference call."

Schroeder's voice was firm. "You know they won't speak to you directly."

"Those pompous bastards will be on their knees begging for an audience by six o'clock."

Schroeder put a note of optimism in his voice. "Your speech is still having favorable repercussions. The Vatican is—"

"Speaking of repercussions and concussions and all that, do you think—now this is a technical question that you should consider—do you think that the glass façade of the Olympic Tower will fall into the street when—"

Schroeder said abruptly, "Is Mr. Flynn there?"

"You have a bad habit of interrupting, Schroeder."

"Is Mr. *Flynn* there?"

"Of course he's here, you ass. Where else would he be?"

"May I speak to him, please?"

"He's playing the bells, for God's sake!"

"Can you tell him to pick up the extension beside the organ?"

"I told you, you don't interrupt a man when he's playing the *bells*. Haven't you learned anything tonight? I'll bet you were a vice cop once, busting into hotel rooms, interrupting people. You're the type."

Schroeder felt his face redden. He heard Hickey's voice echoing through the rectory and heard a few people laughing. Schroeder snapped a pencil between his fingers. "We want to speak with Mr. Flynn—privately, at the sacristy gate." He looked at Burke sleeping on the couch. "Lieutenant Burke wants to speak—"

"As you said before, it's less confusing to speak to one person. If I can't speak to the Queen, you can't speak to Finn MacCumail. What's wrong with *me*? By the way, what have you given up for Lent? Your brains or your balls? *I* gave up talking to fools on the telephone, but I'll make an exception in your case."

Schroeder suddenly felt something inside him come loose. He made a strong effort to control his voice and spoke in measured tones. "Mr. Hickey... Brian Flynn has a great deal of faith in me—the efforts I'm making, the honesty I've shown—"

The sound of Hickey's laughter filled the office. "He sounds like a good lad to you, does he? Well, he's got a surprise in store for *you*, Schroeder, and you won't like it."

Schroeder said, "We'd rather not have any surprises—"

"Stop using that imperial *we*. I'm talking about *you*. *You* have a surprise coming." Schroeder sat up quickly, and his eyes became more alert. "What do you mean by that? What does that mean? Listen, everything should be aboveboard if we're going to bargain in good faith—"

"Is Bellini acting in good faith?"

Schroeder hesitated. This use of names by these people was unsettling. These references to him personally were not in the script.

Hickey continued, "Where is Bellini now? Huddled around a chalk board with his Gestapo? Finding sneaky little ways to kill us all? Well, fuck Bellini and fuck you."

Schroeder shook his head in silent frustration, then said, "How are the hostages?" Hickey said, "Did you find Stillway yet?"

"Do you need a doctor in there?"

"Did you dig up my grave yet?"

"Can I send food, medicine—?"

"Where's Major Martin?"

Burke lay on the couch with his eyes closed and listened to the dialogue deteriorate into two monologues. As unproductive as the dialogue had been, it hadn't been as bizarre as what he was listening to now. He knew now, beyond any doubt, that it was finished.

Schroeder said, "What surprises does Flynn have planned for me?"

Hickey laughed again. "If I tell you, it won't be a surprise. I'll bet when you were a child you were an insufferable brat, Schroeder. Always trying to find out what people bought you for Christmas, sneaking around closets and all that."

Schroeder didn't respond and again heard the laughter from the next room.

Hickey said, "Don't initiate any calls to us unless it's to say we've won. I'll call you back every hour on the hour until 6:00 A.M. At 6:03 it's over."

Schroeder heard the phone go dead. He looked at Burke's still form on the couch, then shut off all the speakers and dialed again. "Hickey?"

"What?"

Schroeder took a deep breath and said through his clenched jaw, "You're a dead motherfucker." He put the phone down and steadied his hands against the desk. There was a taste of blood in his mouth, and he realized that he was biting into his lower lip.

Burke turned his head and looked at Schroeder. Their eyes met, and Schroeder turned away.

Burke said, "It's okay."

Schroeder didn't answer, and Burke could see his shoulders shaking.

CHAPTER 48

Colonel Dennis Logan rode in the rear of a staff car up the deserted section of Fifth Avenue, toward the Cathedral. He turned to his adjutant, Major Cole. "Didn't think I'd be passing this way again today."

"Yes, sir. It's actually March eighteenth."

Colonel Logan overlooked the correction and listened to the bells play "I'll Take You Home Again, Kathleen," then said, "Do you believe in miracles?"

"No, sir."

"Well, see that green line?"

"Yes, sir, the long one in the middle of the Avenue that we followed." He yawned.

"Right. Well, some years ago, Mayor Beame was marching in the parade with the Sixty-ninth. Police Commissioner Codd and the Commissioner for Public Events, Neil Walsh, were with him. Before your time."

Major Cole wished that this parade had been before his time. "Yes, sir."

"Anyway, it rained that morning after the line machine went by, and the fresh green paint washed away—all the way from Forty-fourth to Eighty-sixth Street. But later that morning Walsh bought some paint and had his men hand-paint the line right in front of the Cathedral."

"Yes, sir."

"Well, when we marched past with the city delegation, Walsh turns to Codd and says, 'Look! It's a miracle, Commissioner! The line's still here in front of the Cathedral!'"

Colonel Logan laughed at the happier memory and went on. "So Codd says, 'You're right, Walsh!' and he winks at him, then looks at Beame. 'Oh my gosh!' said the little Mayor. 'I always wanted to see a miracle. I never saw a miracle before!'" Logan laughed but refrained from slapping his or Cole's knee. The driver laughed, too.

Major Cole smiled. He said, "Sir, I think we've mustered most of the officers and at least half the men."

Logan lit a cigar. "Right . . . . Do they look sober to you?"

"It's hard to say, sir."

Logan nodded, then said, "We're not really needed here, are we?"

"That's difficult to determine, Colonel."

"I think the Governor is looking for high marks in leadership and courage, don't you?"

Major Cole replied, "The regiment is well trained in crowd and riot control, sir."

"So are twenty-five thousand New York police."

"Yes, sir."

"I hope to God he doesn't get us involved in an assault on the Cathedral."

The major replied, "Sir," which conveyed no meaning.

Colonel Logan looked through the window as the car passed between a set of police barriers and moved slowly past the singing crowds. "Incredible."

Cole nodded. "Yes, it is."

The staff car drew up to the rectory and stopped.

* * *

Captain Joe Bellini advised the newspeople that the press conference room might cave in if the Cathedral was blown up, and
they moved with their equipment to less vulnerable places outside the Cathedral complex as Bellini moved in. He stood in
the room beside a chalkboard. Around the tables and along the
walls, were sixty Emergency Service Division men, armed with
shotguns, M-16 rifles, and silenced pistols. In the rear of the
room sat Colonel Logan, Major Cole, and a dozen staff personnel from the 69th Regiment. A cloud of gray tobacco smoke
veiled the bright lights. Bellini pointed to a crude outline of
the Cathedral on the chalkboard. "So, Fifth Squad will attack
through the sacristy gates. You'll be issued steel-cut chainsaws
and bolt cutters. Okay?"

Colonel Logan stood. "If I may make a suggestion . . . Before,
you said your men had to control their fire. . . . This is your
operation, and my part is secondary, but the basic rules of
warfare . . . Well, anyway, when you encounter concealed enemy
positions that have a superior field of fire—like those triforia
and choir loft—and you know you can't engage them with
effective fire . . . then you have to lay down *suppressing* fire." Logan saw some signs of recognition. "In other words you flip
the switches on your M-16s from semiautomatic to full automatic—rock and roll, as the men say—and put out such an
intense volume of fire that the enemy has got to put his head
down. Then you can safely lead the hostages back down the sacristy stairs."

No one spoke, but a few men were nodding.

Logan's voice became more intense. He was suddenly giving
a prebattle pep talk. "Keep blasting those triforia, blast that
choir loft, slap magazine after magazine into those rifles, raking,

raking, raking those sniper perches, blasting away so long, so loud, so fast, and so hard that it sounds like Armageddon and the Apocalypse all at once, and no one—*no one*—in those perches is going to pick his head up if the air around him is filled with bullets and pulverized stone." He looked around the silent room and listened to his heart beating.

There was a spontaneous burst of applause from the ESD men and the military people. Captain Bellini waited until the noise died away, then said, "Yes, well, Colonel, that's sound advice, but we're *all* under the strictest orders not to blow the place apart—as you know. It's full of art treasures.... It's...well...you know..."

Logan said, "Yes, I understand." He wiped his face. "I'm not advocating air strikes. I mean, I'm only suggesting you increase your use of small-arms fire, and—"

"Such an intense degree of even small-arms fire, Colonel, would do"—Bellini remembered the Governor's words—"irreparable...irreparable damage to the Cathedral...the ceiling...the stonework...statues..."

One of the squad leaders stood. "Look, Captain, since when are art treasures more important than people? My mother thinks *I'm* an art treasure—"

Several people laughed nervously.

Bellini felt the sweat collecting under his collar. He looked at Logan. "Colonel, your mission..." Bellini paused and watched Logan stiffen.

Logan said, "My mission is to provide a tight cordon around the Cathedral during the assault. I know what I have to do."

Bellini almost smirked. "No, that's been changed. The Governor wants you to take a more active part in the assault." He savored each word as he said it. "The police will supply you with their armored personnel carrier. It's army surplus, and you'll be familiar with it." Bellini noticed that Major Cole had gone pale.

Bellini stepped closer to Logan. "You'll take the vehicle up the front steps with fifteen men inside—"

Logan's voice was barely under control. "This is *insane*. You can't use an armored vehicle in such a confined space. They might have armor-piercing ordnance in there. Good Lord, we couldn't maneuver, couldn't conceal the vehicle... These Fenians are guerrilla veterans, Captain. They know how to deal with tanks—they've seen more British armored cars than you've seen—"

"Taxis," said Burke as he walked into the press room. "That's what Flynn said to Schroeder. Taxis. Mind if Inspector Langley and I join you?"

Bellini looked tired and annoyed. He said to Logan, "Take it up with the Governor." Glancing at the wall clock, he said, "Everyone take ten. Clear out!" He sat down and lit a cigarette. The men filed out of the conference room and huddled in groups throughout the corridors.

Burke and Langley sat across from Bellini. Bellini said softly, "That fucking war hero is spooking my men."

Burke thought, *They should be spooked. They're going to get creamed.* "He means well."

Bellini drew on his cigarette. "Why are those parade soldiers in on this?"

Langley looked around, then said quietly, "The Governor needs a boost."

Bellini sipped on a cup of cold coffee. "You know... I discussed a lot of options for this attack with the Mayor and Governor. Ever notice how people who don't know shit about warfare all of a sudden become generals?" Bellini chain-lit another cigarette and went on in a voice that was becoming overwrought.

"So Kline takes my hand and squeezes it—Christ, I should've squeezed his and broken his fucking fingers. Anyway, he says, 'Joe, you know what's expected of you.' Christ Almighty, by this time I don't even know if I'm allowed to take my gun in there. But my adrenaline is really pumping by now, and I say to him, 'Your Honor, we have to attack *now*, while the bells are ringing.' Right? And he says—check this—he says, 'Captain, we have an obligation'—a moral something or other—'to explore every possible avenue of negotiation'—blah, blah, blah—'political considerations'— blah, blah—'the Vatican'—blah, blah. So I say...no, I didn't say it, but I should have...I should have said, 'Kline, you schmuck, do you want to rescue the hostages and save the fucking Cathedral, or do you want to make time with the White House and the Vatican?'"

He paused and breathed hard. "But maybe then I would have sounded like an asshole, too, because I don't really care about a pile of stone or four people I don't even know. My responsibility is to a hundred of my men who I do know and to their families and to myself and my wife and kids. Right?"

No one spoke for some time, then the telephone rang. Bellini grabbed it, listened, then handed it to Burke. "Some guy called the Leper. You hang out with classy people."

Burke took the receiver and heard Ferguson's voice. "Burke, Leper here."

Burke said, "How are you?"

"Cold, scared shitless, tired, hungry, and broke. But otherwise, well. Is this line secure?"

"No."

"Okay, I have to speak to you face to face."

Burke thought a moment. "Do you want to come here?"

Ferguson hesitated. "No...I saw people hanging around the

checkpoints who shouldn't see me. I'm very close to our rendezvous point. See you there."

Burke put down the receiver and said to Langley, "Ferguson's on to something."

Bellini looked up quickly. "Anything that can help me?"

Burke wanted to say, "Frankly, nothing can help you," but said instead, "I think so."

Bellini seemed to sense the lie and slumped lower in his chair. "Christ, we've never gone up against trained guerrillas...." He looked up suddenly. "Do I sound scared? Do I look scared?"

Burke replied, "You look and sound like a man who fully appreciates the problems."

Bellini laughed. "Yeah. I appreciate the hell out of the problems."

Langley seemed suddenly annoyed. "Look, you must have known a day like this would come. You've trained for this—"

"Trained?" Bellini turned on him. "Big fucking deal trained. In the army I was trained on how to take cover in a nuclear attack. The only instructor who made any sense was the one who told us to hold our helmets, put our heads between our legs, and kiss our asses good-bye." He laughed again. "Fuck trained." Bellini stubbed out his cigarette and breathed deeply. "Oh, well. Maybe Schroeder will pull it off." He smiled thinly. "He's got more incentive now." He pointed to a black bulletproof vest and a dark pullover sweater at the end of the table. "That's his."

Langley said, "Why don't you let him off the hook?"

Bellini shook his head, then looked at Burke. "How about you? What are *you* doing later?"

Burke said, "I'll be with you."

Bellini's eyes widened.

Langley looked at Burke quickly. "Like hell."

Burke said nothing.

Bellini said, "Let the man do what he wants."

Langley changed the subject and said to Bellini, "I have more psy-profiles for you."

Bellini lit a cigarette. "Put a light coat of oil on them and shove them up your ass."

Langley stiffened.

Bellini went on, enjoying the fact that no one could pull rank on him any longer. "Where's the architect, Langley? Where are the blueprints?"

Langley said, "Working on it."

"Terrific. Everybody is working on something—you, Schroeder, the Mayor, the President. Everybody's working. You know, when this started nobody paid much attention to Joe Bellini. Now the Mayor calls about every fifteen minutes asking how I'm making out. Calls me Joe. Terrific little guy."

Men started drifting back into the room.

Bellini leaned over the table. "They've got me cornered. When they start calling you by your first name, they've got you by the balls, and they're not going to let go until I charge up those fucking steps—holding not much more than my cock in one hand and a cross in the other—and get myself killed." He stood. "Believe me, Burke, it's all a fucking show. Everybody's got to play his part. You, me, the politicians, the Church, the bastards in the Cathedral. We *know* we're full of shit, but that's the way we learned how to play."

Burke stood and looked around at the ESD men, then looked closely at Bellini. "Remember, you're the good guys."

Bellini rubbed his temples and shook his head. "Then how come we're wearing black?"

CHAPTER 49

Patrick Burke stepped out of the rectory into the cold, gusty air. He looked at his watch. Nearly 1:00 A.M., March 18. They would still call it the St. Patrick's Day massacre or something catchy like that. He turned up his collar and walked east on Fifty-first Street.

At Park Avenue a city bus was drawn up to form a barricade. Burke walked around the bus, passed through a thin crowd, and crossed the avenue. A small group had congregated on the steps and terraces of St. Bartholomew's Episcopal Church, passing bottles and singing the songs that were being played on St. Patrick's bells. People were entering the church, and Burke recalled that many churches and synagogues had announced all-night prayer vigils. A news van was setting up cameras and lights.

Burke listened to the bells. Flynn—if it was Flynn playing—had a good touch. Burke remembered Langley's speculation about the John Hickey T-shirts. He envisioned a record jacket: St. Patrick's Cathedral—green star clusters—*Brian Flynn Plays the Bells.*

Burke passed by the church and continued east on Fifty-first Street. Between two buildings lay a small park. A fence and gate ran between the flanking structures, and Burke peered through the bars. Café tables and upturned chairs stood on the terraces beneath bare sycamores. Nothing moved in the unlit park. Burke grasped the cold steel bars, pulled himself up to the top, and dropped into the park. As he hit the frozen stone walk below, he felt a sharp pain shoot through his numb legs and swore silently. He drew his pistol and remained crouched. A wind shook the trees, and ice-covered twigs snapped and fell to the ground with the sound of breaking crystal.

Burke straightened up slowly and moved through the scattered tables, pistol held at his side. As he moved, the ice crackled under his shoes, and he knew that if Ferguson were there he would have heard him by now.

An overturned table caught his attention, and he moved toward it. A chair lay on its back some distance away. The ice on the ground was broken and scattered, and Burke knelt to get a closer look at a large dark blotch that on closer inspection looked like a strawberry Italian ice but wasn't.

Burke rose and found that his legs had become unsteady. He walked up the shallow steps to the next level of the terrace and saw more overturned furniture. In the rear of the park was a stone wall several stories high where a waterfall usually flowed. At the base of the wall was a long, narrow trough. Burke walked to the trough and stared down at Jack Ferguson lying in the icy water, his face blue-white, very much, Burke thought, like the color of the façade of the Cathedral. The eyes were open, and his mouth yawned as if he were trying to catch his breath from the shock of the cold water.

Burke knelt on the low stone abutment of the trough, reached out, and grabbed Ferguson's old trench coat. He pulled the body closer and saw, as the folds of the trench coat drifted apart, the two bullet-shattered knees poking out of the worn trousers—bone, cartilage, and ligaments, very white against the deeper color of bluish flesh.

He slipped his pistol into his pocket and pulled the small man easily onto the coping stone of the abutment. A small bullet hole showed like black palm ash in the center of Ferguson's forehead. His pockets had been rifled, but Burke searched the body again, finding only a clean, neatly pressed handkerchief which reminded him that he would have to call Ferguson's wife.

Burke closed Ferguson's eyes and stood, wiped his hands on his overcoat and blew into them, and then walked away. He righted an ice-covered chair, drew it up to a metal table, and sat. Burke took a long, deep breath and steadied his hands enough to light a cigarette. He drew on the cigarette, then took out his flask and opened it, but set it on the table without drinking. He heard a noise at the fence and looked out across the park. He drew his pistol and rested it in his lap.

"Burke! It's Martin."

Burke didn't answer. "Can I come up?"

Burke cocked his revolver. "Sure!"

Martin walked toward Burke, stopped, and looked past him at the low stone wall at the base of the waterfall. "Who's that?"

Burke didn't reply.

Martin walked up to the body and looked down into the frozen face. "I know this man . . . Jack Ferguson."

"Is it?"

"Yes. I've dealt with him—only yesterday, as a matter of fact. Official IRA. Marxist. Nice chap, though."

Burke said with no intonation in his voice, "The only good Red is a dead Red. Kill a Commie for Christ. Move here where I can see you."

"Eh?" Martin moved behind Burke's chair. "What did you say . . . ? See here, you didn't . . . did you?"

Burke repeated. "Here in front where I can see you."

Martin moved around the table.

Burke said, "Why are you here?"

Martin lit a cigarette. "Followed you from the rectory."

Burke was certain no one had followed him. "Why?"

"Wanted to see where you were going. You've been most un-helpful. I've been sacked from my consulate job, by the way. Is that your doing? People are starting to say the most incredible things about me. Anyway, I'm at loose ends now. Don't know what to do with myself. So I thought perhaps I could...well...lend you a hand...clear my name in the process.... Is that a gun? You can put that away."

Burke held the gun. "Who do you think killed him, Major?"

"Well, assuming it wasn't you..." He shrugged. "Probably his own people. Or the Provos or the Fenians. Did you see his knees? God, that's a nasty business."

"Why would the IRA want to kill him?"

Martin answered quickly and distinctly. "He talked too much."

Burke uncocked his revolver and held it in his pocket. "Where's Gordon Stillway?"

"Gordon...Oh, the architect." Martin drew on his cigarette. "I wish I were half as devious as you think I am."

Burke took a drink from his flask and said, "Look, the Cathedral is going to be stormed in the next few hours."

"Sorry it had to come to that."

"Anyway, I'm concerned now about saving as many lives as possible."

"I am, too. Our Consul General is in there."

"So far, Major, you've had it all your way. You got your Irish terrorism in America. We've had it pushed in our face. The point is made and well taken. So we don't need a burned-out Cathe-dral and a stack of corpses."

"I'm not quite sure I'm following you."

"It would help Bellini if he had the blueprints and the architect."

"Undoubtedly. I'm working on that also."

Burke looked at Martin closely. "Settle for what you've already got. Don't push it further."

"I'm sorry, I'm losing you again."

Burke stared at Martin, who put his foot on a chair and puffed on his cigarette. A gust of cold wind moved through the enclosed park and swirled around. Ice fell from the glistening trees, landing on Martin and Burke, but neither man seemed to notice. Martin seemed to reach a decision and looked at Burke. "It's not just Flynn, you see. My whole operation wasn't conceived just to kill Brian Flynn." Martin rubbed his chin with his gloved hand. "You see, I need more than Flynn's death, though I look forward to it. I also need a *lasting* symbol of Irish terrorism. I'm afraid I need the Cathedral to go down."

Burke waited a long time before he spoke. His voice was low, controlled. "It may become a symbol of Britain's unwillingness to negotiate."

"One gambles. But you see, London *did* offer a compromise, much to my surprise, and the Fenians, lunatics that they are, have not responded to it. And with the old man's speech and the bells and all that, it's the Fenians who are ahead, not me. Really, Burke, the only way I can influence public opinion, here and abroad, is if...well, if there's a tragedy. Sorry."

"It's going to backfire."

"When the dust clears, the blame will be squarely on the Irish. Her Majesty's government is very adept at expressing sorrow and pity for the loss of lives and property. Actually, the ruins of Saint Patrick's may have more value as a tourist attraction than the Cathedral did.... Not many good ruins in America...."

Burke's fingers scratched at the cold, blue steel of the revolver in his pocket.

Martin went on, his eyes narrowing and long plumes of vapor exhaling from his nose and mouth. "And, of course, the funerals. Did you see Mountbatten's? Thousands of people weeping. We'll do something nice for Baxter, too. The Roman Church will do a splendid job for the Cardinal and the priest. Malone . . . well, who knows?"

Burke said, "You're not tightly wrapped, you know that?"

Martin lit another cigarette, and Burke saw the match quivering in the dark. Martin spoke in a more controlled voice. "You don't seem to understand. One has to spread the suffering, make it more universal before you get a sense of outrage." Martin looked at his glowing cigarette. "One needs a magnificent disaster—Dunkirk, Pearl Harbor, Coventry, Saint Patrick's . . ." He knocked the ash from his cigarette and stared down at the gray smudge on the ice-covered table. ". . . And from those ashes rises a new dedication." He looked up. "You may have noticed the phoenix on the bronze ceremonial door of Saint Patrick's. It inspired me to name this Operation Phoenix."

Burke said, "Flynn may accept the compromise. He hinted as much to me. He may also make a public statement about how British treachery almost got everyone killed."

"He wouldn't admit that the greatest IRA operation since Mountbatten's murder was planned by an Englishman."

"He doesn't want to die quite as badly as you want him to die. He'll take what he's already gotten and come out of there a hero." Burke took another drink to fire his imagination. "On the other hand . . . there's still the possibility that he may destroy the place at dawn. So the Mayor and Governor want to carry out a preemptive strike. Soon. But they need encouragement. They won't move unless Bellini says he can bring it off. But Bellini won't say that unless he gets the blue-prints and the architect...."

Martin smiled. "Very good. It's hereditary, I see—I mean the ability to manufacture heaps of malarkey at the drop of a hat."

"If we don't have the architect, we won't attack. At 6:03 Flynn will call a time out, wait until the city is full of people and the morning TV shows are rolling, then magnanimously spare the Cathedral and hostages. No funerals, no bangs, not even a broken stained-glass window."

"At 6:03 something more dreadful will happen."

"One gambles."

Martin shook his head. "I don't know.... Now you've got me worried, Lieutenant. It would be just like that bastard to double-cross me...." He smiled. "Well, double-cross may not be the word.... These people are so erratic...you never know, do you? I mean, historically they always opt for the most reckless—"

Burke said, "You've got these Micks pretty well figured out, don't you, Major?"

"Well...no racial generalities intended, to be sure, but...I don't know..." He seemed to be weighing the possibilities. "The question is—do I gamble on an explosion at 6:03 or settle for a good battle before then...?"

Burke came closer to Martin. "Let me put it this way...." He breathed a long stream of cold fog in Martin's face. "If the Cathedral goes down"—he pulled his pistol, cocked it, and pressed it to Martin's temple—"then you're what we call a dead motherfucker."

Martin faced Burke. "If anything happened to me, you'd be killed."

"I know the rules." He tapped Martin on the forehead with the muzzle of the revolver, then holstered it.

Martin flipped his cigarette away and spoke in a businesslike tone. "In exchange for Stillway I want your word that you'll do everything you can to see that the assault is carried out before Flynn makes any overtures toward a compromise. You have his confidence, I know, so use that in any way you can—with him or with your superiors. And no matter what happens, you'll make certain that Flynn is not captured alive. Understood?"

Burke nodded.

Martin added, "You'll have Stillway and the blueprints in ample time, and to show you what a good sport I am, I'll give all this to you personally. As I said yesterday morning, you can look good with your superiors. God knows, Lieutenant, you need the boost."

Martin moved away from Burke and looked down at Ferguson's frozen body. He lit another cigarette and dropped the match carelessly on Ferguson's face. He looked at Burke. "You're thinking, of course, that like our late friend here, you know too much. But it's all right. I'm willing—obligated—to make an exception in your case. You're one of us—a professional, not an amateur busybody like Mr. Ferguson or a dangerous insurgent like Mr. Flynn. So act like a professional, Lieutenant, and you'll be treated like one."

Burke said, "Thank you for setting me straight. I'll do my best."

Martin laughed. "You can do your worst, if you like. I'm not counting only on you to see that things go my way. Lieutenant, there are more surprises inside and outside that Cathedral than even you suspect. And at first light, it will all unfold." He nodded his head. "Good evening." He turned and walked away at a leisurely pace.

Burke looked down at Ferguson. He bent over and picked the match from his face. "Sorry, Jack."

CHAPTER 50

The clock in the rear of the choir loft struck 3:00 A.M. Brian Flynn tolled the hour, then stood and looked at Leary sitting on the parapet, his legs swinging out into space three stories above the main floor. Flynn said, "If you nod off, you'll fall."

Leary answered without turning. "That's right."

Flynn looked around for Megan but didn't see her. He moved around the organ, picked up a rifle, and walked toward Leary.

Leary suddenly spun around and swung his legs into the choir loft. He said, "That's an old trick."

Flynn felt his body tense.

Leary continued. "Learned it in the army. You perch in a position that will get you hurt or killed if you fall asleep. Keeps you awake...usually."

"Interesting." He moved past Leary and entered the bell tower, then took the elevator down to the vestibule. He walked up the center aisle, his footsteps echoing in the quiet Cathedral. Sullivan, Boland, and Farrell were leaning out over the triforia. Hickey was asleep at the chancel organ. Flynn passed through the open gate of the communion rail and mounted the steps. The four hostages slept in pairs on opposite sides of the sanctuary. He glanced over at Baxter beside Maureen and watched the steady rise and fall of her chest, then looked up at where the Cardinal and Father Murphy lay cuffed to the throne, sleeping. Flynn knelt beside Maureen and stared down at her bruised face. He sensed that eyes were watching him from the high places, that Megan was watching from the dark, and that Leary's scope was centered on his lips. Flynn leaned over, his back to Leary, and positioned himself to block Leary's view of Maureen. He stroked her cheek.

She opened her eyes and looked up at him. "What time is it?"

"Late."

She said, "You've let it become late."

He said quietly, "I'm sorry...I couldn't help you..."

She turned her face away. Neither one spoke, then Maureen said, "This standoff with the police is like one of those games of nerve with autos racing toward each other, each driver hypnotized by the other's approach—and at one minute to dawn...is anyone going to veer off?"

"Bloody nonsense. This is war. Bloody stupid women, you think men play games of ego—"

"War?" She grabbed his shirt and her voice rose. "Let me tell *you* about *war*. It's not fought in churches with handcuffed hostages. And as long as you're talking about war, I'm still enough of a soldier to know they may not wait for dawn—they may be burrowing in here *right now,* and within the time it takes to draw your next breath this place could be filled with gunfire and you could be filled with bullets." She released his shirt. "War, indeed. You know no more about war than you do about love."

Flynn stood and looked at Baxter. "Do you like this man?"

She nodded. "He's a good man."

Flynn stared off at some point in the distance. "A good man," he repeated. "Someone meeting me for the first time might say that—as long as my history wasn't known." He stared down at her. "You don't like me much right now, but it's all right. I hope you survive, I even hope Baxter survives, and I hope you get on well together."

She lay on her back looking up at him. "Again, neither you nor I believe a word of that."

Flynn stepped away from her. "I have to go...." He looked over the sanctuary rail at Hickey and said suddenly, "Tell me about him. What's the old man been saying? What about the confessional buzzer?"

Maureen cleared her throat and spoke in a businesslike voice, relating what she had discovered about John Hickey. She added her conclusions. "Even if you win, he'll somehow make certain everyone dies." She added, "All four of us believe that, or we wouldn't have risked so much to escape."

Flynn's eyes drifted back to Hickey, then he looked around the sanctuary at the hostages, the bouquets of now-wilting green carnations, and the bloodstains on the marble below the high altar. He had the feeling he had seen this all before, experienced something similar in a dream or vision, and he remembered that he *had,* in Whitehorn Abbey. He shook off the impression and looked at Maureen.

Flynn knelt suddenly and unlocked the handcuff. "Come with me." He helped her up and supported her as he walked toward the sacristy stairs.

He was aware that Hickey was watching from the chancel organ, and that Leary and Megan were watching also, from the shadows of the choir loft. He knew that they were thinking he was going to let Maureen go. And this, he understood, as everyone who was watching understood, was a critical juncture, a test of his position as leader. Would those three in any way try to restrict his movements? A few hours before they wouldn't have dared.

He reached the sacristy stairs and paused, not hesitantly but defiantly, and looked up into the loft, then back at the chancel organ. No one made a sound or a movement, and he waited purposely, staring into the Cathedral, then descended the steps. He stopped on the landing beside Gallagher. "Take a break, Frank."

Gallagher looked at him and at Maureen, and Flynn could see in Gallagher's expression a look of understanding and approval. Gallagher's eyes met Maureen's; he started to speak but then turned and hurried up the stairs.

Flynn looked down the remaining steps at the chained gate, then faced Maureen.

She realized that Brian Flynn had reasserted himself, imposed his will on the others. And she knew also that he was going to go a step further. He was going to free her, but she didn't know if he was doing it for her or for himself, or to demonstrate that he could do anything he damned well pleased—to show that he was Finn MacCumail, Chief of the Fenians. She walked down the staircase and stopped at the gate. Flynn followed and gestured toward the sacristy. "Two worlds meet here, the worlds of the sacred and the profaned, the living and the dead. Have ever such divergent worlds been separated by so little?"

She stared into the quiet sacristy and saw a votive candle flickering on the altar of the priests' chapel, the vestment tables lining the walls, covered with neatly folded white and purple vestments of the Lenten season. Easter, she thought. *The spring. The Resurrection and the life.* She looked at Flynn.

He said, "Will you choose life? Will you go without the others?"

She nodded. "Yes, I'll go."

He hesitated, then drew the keys from his pocket. With a hand that was unsteady he unlocked the gate's lock and the chain's padlock, and began unwinding the chain. He rolled back the left gate and scanned the corridor openings but saw no sign of the police. "Hurry."

She took his arm. "I'll go, but not without you."

He looked at her, then said, "You'd leave the others to go with me?"

"Yes."

"Could you do that and live with yourself?"

"Yes."

He stared at the open gate. "I'd be imprisoned for a long time. Could you wait?"

"Yes."

"You love me?"

"Yes."

He reached out for her, but she moved quickly up the stairs and stopped halfway to the landing. "You'll not push me out. We leave together."

He stood looking up at her silhouetted against the light of the crypt doors. "I can't go."

"Not even for me? I'd go with you—for you. Won't you do the same?"

"I *can't*...for God's sake, Maureen...I *can't*. Please, if you love me, go. Go!"

"Together. One way or the other, *together.*"

He looked down and shook his head and, after what seemed like a long time, heard her footsteps retreating up the stairs.

He relocked the gate and followed, and when he walked up to the altar sanctuary, he found her lying beside Baxter again, the cuff locked on her wrist and her eyes closed.

Flynn came down from the sanctuary and walked to a pew

in the center of the Cathedral and sat, staring at the high altar. It struck him that the things most men found trying—leadership, courage, the ability to seize their own destiny—came easily to him, a gift, he thought, of the gods. But love—so basic an emotion that even unexceptional men were blessed with loving women, children, friends—that had always eluded him. And the one time it had not eluded him it had been so difficult as to be painful, and to make the pain stop he made the love stop through the sheer force of his will. Yet it came back, again and again. *Amor vincit omnia,* as Father Michael used to preach. He shook his head. *No, I've conquered love.*

He felt very empty inside. But at the same time, to his horror and disgust, he felt very good about being in command of himself and his world again.

He sat in the pew for a long time.

Flynn looked down at Pedar Fitzgerald, lying in a curled position at the side of the organ console, a blanket drawn up to his blood-encrusted chin. Flynn moved beside John Hickey, who lay slumped over the organ keyboard, and stared down at Hickey's pale, almost waxen face. The field phone rang, and Hickey stirred. It rang again, and Flynn grabbed it.

Mullins's voice came over the line. "I'm back in the bell room. Is that it for the bells, then?"

"Yes.... How does it look outside?"

Mullins said, "Very quiet below. But out farther...there're still people in the streets."

Flynn heard a note of wonder in the young man's voice. "They celebrate late, don't they? We've given them a Saint Patrick's Day to remember."

Mullins said, "There wasn't even a *curfew.*"

Flynn smiled. America reminded him of the *Titanic,* a three-hundred-foot gash in her side, listing badly, but they were still serving drinks in the lounge. "It's not like Belfast, is it?"

"No."

"Can you sense any anxiety down there...movement...?"

Mullins considered, then said, "No, they look relaxed yet. Cold and tired for sure, but at ease. No passing of orders, none of that stiffness you see before an attack."

"How are you holding up against the cold?"

"I'm past that."

"Well, you and Rory will be the first to see the dawn break."

Mullins had given up on the dawn hours ago. "Aye, the dawn from the bell tower of Saint Patrick's in New York. That needs a poem."

"You'll tell me it later." He hung up and picked up the extension phone. "Get me Captain Schroeder, please." He looked at Hickey's face as the operator routed the call. Awake, the face was expressive, alive, but asleep it looked like a death mask.

Schroeder's voice came through sounding slurred. "Yes..."

"Flynn here. Did I wake you?"

"No, sir. We've been waiting for Mr. Hickey's hourly call. He said...but I'm glad you called. I've been wanting to speak to you."

"Thought I was dead, did you?"

"Well, no.... You were on the bells, right?"

"How did I sound out there?"

Schroeder cleared his throat. "You show promise."

Flynn laughed. "Well, can it be you're developing a sense of humor, Captain?" Schroeder laughed self-consciously.

"Or is it that you're so relieved to be talking to me instead of Hickey that you're giddy?"

Schroeder didn't answer.

Flynn said, "How are they faring in the capitals?"

Schroeder's tone was reserved. "They're wondering why you haven't responded to what Inspector Langley related to you."

"I'm afraid we aren't very clear on that."

"I can't elaborate over the phone."

"I see.... Well, why don't you come to the sacristy gate, then, and we'll talk."

There was a long pause. "I'm not at liberty to do that.... It's against regulations."

"So is burning down a cathedral, which is what will happen if we don't speak, Captain."

"You don't understand, Mr. Flynn. There are carefully worked out rules...as I think you know.... And the negotiator cannot expose himself to...to..."

"I won't kill you."

"Well...I know you won't...but...Listen, you and Lieutenant Burke have...Would you like to speak with him at the gate?"

"No, I would like to speak with *you* at the gate."

"I..."

"Aren't you even curious to see me?"

"Curiosity plays no part—"

"Doesn't it? It seems to me, Captain, that you of all people would recognize the value of eyeball-to-eyeball contact."

"There's no special value in—"

"How many wars would have been avoided if the chiefs could have just seen the other man's face, touched each other, got a whiff of the other fellow's sweaty fear?"

Schroeder said, "Hold on."

Flynn heard the phone click, then a minute later Schroeder's voice came through. "Okay."

"Five minutes." Flynn hung up and poked Hickey roughly. "Were you listening?"

Flynn took Hickey's arm in a tight grip. "Someday, you old

bastard, you'll tell me about the confessional, and the things you've been saying to Schroeder and the things you've been saying to my people and to the hostages. And you'll tell me about the compromise that was offered us."

Hickey flinched and straightened up. "Let go! These old bones snap easily."

"I may snap the ones in your neck."

Hickey looked up at Flynn, no trace of pain in his face. "Careful. Be careful."

Flynn released his arm and pushed it away. "You don't frighten me."

Hickey didn't answer but stared at Flynn with undisguised malice in his eyes.

Flynn met his stare, then looked down at Pedar Fitzgerald. "Are you looking after him?"

Hickey didn't answer.

Flynn stared closely at Fitzgerald's face and saw it was white—waxy, like Hickey's. "He's dead." He turned to Hickey.

Hickey said without emotion, "Died about an hour ago."

"Megan..."

"When Megan calls, I tell her he's all right, and she believes that because she wants to. But eventually..."

Flynn looked up at Megan in the loft. "My God, she'll..." He turned back to Hickey. "We should have gotten a doctor...."

Hickey replied, "If you weren't so wrapped up in your fucking bells, you could have done just that."

Flynn looked at him. "*You* could have—"

"*Me?* What the hell do I care if he lives or dies?"

Flynn stepped back from him, and his mind began to reel.

Hickey said, "What do you see, Brian? Is it very frightening?" He laughed and lit his pipe.

Flynn moved farther away from Hickey into the ambulatory and tried to get his thoughts under control. He reevaluated each person in the Cathedral until he was certain he knew each one's motives...potential for treachery...loyalties and weaknesses. His mind focused finally on Leary, and he asked the questions he should have asked months ago: Why was Leary here? Why would a professional killer trap himself in a perch with no way out? Leary had to be holding a card no one even knew existed. Flynn wiped the sweat from his brow and walked up to the sanctuary.

Hickey called out, "Are you going to tell Schroeder about his darling daughter? Tell him for me—use these exact words—tell him his daughter is a dead bitch!"

Flynn descended the stairs behind the altar. Gallagher stood on the crypt landing, an M-16 slung across his chest. Flynn said, "There's coffee in the bookshop." Gallagher climbed the stairs, and Flynn went down the remaining steps to the gate. Parts of the chain had been pieced together, and a new padlock was clamped to it. He examined the gate's mangled lock; another bullet or two and it would have sprung. But there were only fifty rounds in the drum of a Thompson. Not fifty-one, but fifty.... And an M-72 rocket could take a Saracen, and the Red Bus to Clady on the Shankill Road went past Whitehorn Abbey...and it was all supposed to be haphazard, random, with no meaning...

Flynn stared into the sacristy. He heard men speaking in the side corridors, and footsteps approached from the center opening in the left wall. Schroeder stepped into the sacristy, looked around, turned toward Flynn, and walked deliberately up the stairs. He stood on the steps below the gates, his eyes fixed on Flynn's. A long time passed before Flynn spoke. "Am I as you pictured me?"

Schroeder replied stiffly, "I've seen a photo of you."

"And I of you. But am I as you *pictured* me?"

Schroeder shook his head. Another long silence developed, then Flynn spoke abruptly. "I'm going to reach into my pocket." Flynn took the microphone sensor and passed it over Schroeder. "This is a very private conversation."

"I will report everything said here."

"I would bet my life you don't."

Schroeder seemed perplexed and wary.

Flynn said, "Are they any closer to meeting our demands?"

Schroeder didn't like face-to-face negotiating. He knew, because people had told him, that his face revealed too much. He cleared his throat. "You're asking the impossible. Accept the compromise."

Flynn noticed the extra firmness in Schroeder's voice, the lack of sir or mister, and the discomfort. "What *is* the compromise?"

Schroeder's eyebrows rose slightly. "Didn't Hickey—"

"Just tell it to me again."

Schroeder related the offer and added, "Take it before the British change their minds about parole. And for yourselves, low bail is as good as immunity. For God's sake, man, no one has ever been offered more in a hostage situation."

Flynn nodded. "Yes.... Yes, it's a good offer—tempting—"

"Take it! Take it before someone is killed—"

"It's a little late for that, I'm afraid."

"What?"

"Sir Harold murdered a lad named Pedar. Luckily no one knows he's dead except Hickey and myself... and I suppose Pedar knows he's dead.... Well, when my people discover he's dead, they'll want to kill Baxter. Pedar's sister, Megan, will want to do much worse. This complicates things somewhat."

Schroeder passed his hand over his face. "God... listen, I'm sure it was unintentional."

"Harry bashed his throat in with a rifle butt. Could have been an accident, I suppose. It doesn't make the lad any less dead."

Schroeder's mind was racing. He swore to himself, *Baxter, you stupid bastard.*

"Look...it's a case of a POW trying to escape.... It's Baxter's duty to try.... You're a soldier..."

Flynn said nothing.

"Here's a chance for you to show professionalism...to show you're not a common crim—" He checked himself. "To show mercy, and—"

Flynn interrupted. "Schroeder, you are most certainly part Irish. I've rarely met a man more possessed of so much ready bullshit for every occasion."

"I'm serious—"

"Well, Baxter's fate depends mostly on what you do now."

"No. It depends on what *you* do. The next move is yours."

"And I'm about to make it." He lit a cigarette and asked, "How far are they along in their attack plans?"

Schroeder said, "That's not an option for us."

Flynn stared at him. "Caught you in a lie—your left eye is twitching. God, Schroeder, your nose is getting longer." He laughed. "I should have had you down here hours ago. Burke was too cool."

"Look—you asked me here for a private meeting, so you must have something to say—"

"I want you to help us get what we want."

Schroeder looked exasperated. "That's what I've been *doing.*"

"No, I mean *everything* we want. Your heart isn't in it. If the negotiations fail, you don't lose nearly as much as everyone in here does. Or as much as Bellini's ESD. They stand to lose fifty to a hundred men in an attack."

Schroeder thought of his imprudent offer to Bellini. "There will be no attack."

"Did you know Burke told me he'd go with Bellini? There's a man with a great deal to lose if you fail. Would you go with Bellini?"

"Burke couldn't have said that because Bellini's not going *anywhere*." Schroeder had the uneasy impression he was being drawn into something, but he had no intention of making a mistake this late. "I'll try to get more for you only if you give me another two hours after dawn."

Flynn ignored him and went on. "I thought I'd better give you a very personal motive to push those people into capitulation."

Schroeder looked at Flynn cautiously.

"You see, there's one situation you never covered in your otherwise detailed book, Captain." Flynn came closer to the gate. "Your daughter would very much like you to try harder."

"What...?"

"Terri Schroeder O'Neal. She wants you to try harder."

Schroeder stared for a few seconds, then said loudly, "What the hell are you talking about?"

"Lower your voice. You'll excite the police."

Schroeder spoke through clenched teeth. "What the *fuck* are you saying?"

"Please, you're in church." Flynn passed a scrap of paper through the bars.

Schroeder snatched it and read his daughter's handwriting: *Dad—I'm being held hostage by members of the Fenian Army. I'm all right. They won't harm me if everything goes okay at the Cathedral. Do your very best. I love you, Terri.*

Schroeder read the note again, then again. He felt his knees buckle, and he grabbed at the gate. He looked up at Flynn and tried to speak, but no sound came out.

Flynn spoke impassively. "Welcome to the Fenian Army, Captain Schroeder."

Schroeder swallowed several times and stared at the note.

"Sorry," said Flynn. "Really I am. You don't have to speak—just listen." Flynn lit another cigarette and spoke briskly. "What you have to do is make the strongest possible case for our demands. First, tell them I've paraded two score of well-armed men and women past you. Machine guns, rockets, grenades, *flamethrowers*. Tell them we are ready, willing, and able to take the entire six-hundred-man ESD down with us, to destroy the Cathedral and kill the hostages. In other words, scare the shit out of Joe Bellini and his heroes. Understand?" He paused, then said, "They'll never suspect that Captain Schroeder's report of seeing a great number of well-armed soldiers is false. Use your imagination—better yet, look up at the landing, Schroeder. Picture forty, fifty men and women parading past that crypt door— picture those machine guns and rockets and flamethrowers.... Go on, look up there."

Schroeder looked, and Flynn saw in his eyes exactly what he wanted to see.

After a minute Schroeder lowered his head. His face was pale, and his hands pulled at his shirt and tie.

Flynn said, "Please calm down. You can save your daughter's life only if you pull yourself together. That's it. Now...if this doesn't work, if they are still committed to an assault, then threaten to go public—radio, TV, newspapers. Tell Kline, Doyle, and all the rest of them you're going to announce that in all your years of hostage negotiating, that you, as the court of last resort for the lives of hostages, strongly and in no uncertain terms believe that neither an attack nor further negotiations can save this situation. You will declare, publicly, that therefore for the first time in your career you urge capitulation—for humanitarian as well as tactical reasons."

Flynn watched Schroeder's face but could see nothing revealed there except anguish. He went on, "You have a good deal of influence—moral and professional— with the media, the police force, and the politicians. Use every bit of that influence. You must create the kind of pressure and climate that will force the British and American governments to surrender."

Schroeder's voice was barely audible. "Time...I need time.... Why didn't you give me more time...?"

"If I'd told you sooner, you wouldn't have made it through the night, or you may have told someone. The only time left is that which remains until the dawn—less if you can't stop the attack. But if you can get them to throw open the prison gates...Work on it."

Schroeder pushed his face to the bars. "Flynn...please...listen to me.... "

Flynn went on. "Yes, I know that if you succeed and we walk out of here free, they'll certainly count us, and they'll wonder where all the flamethrowers are.... Well, you'll be embarrassed, but all's fair in love and war, and *c'est la guerre,* and all that rot. Don't even think that far ahead and don't be selfish."

Schroeder's head shook, and his words were incoherent. All that Flynn could make out was "Jail." Flynn said, "Your daughter can visit you on weekends." He added, "I'll even visit you."

Schroeder stared at him, and a choked-off sound rose in his throat.

Flynn said, "Sorry, that was low." He paused. "Look, if it means anything to you, I feel bad that I had to resort to this. But it wasn't going well, and I knew you'd want to help us, help Terri, if you understood the trouble she was in." Flynn's voice became stern. "She really ought to be more selective about her bunkmates. Children can be such an embarrassment to parents, especially parents in public life—sex, drugs, wild politics..."

Schroeder was shaking his head. "No...you don't have her. You're bluffing...."

Flynn continued. "But she's safe enough for the moment. Dan—that's her friend's name—is kind, considerate, probably a passable lover. It's the lot of some soldiers to draw easy duty—others to fight and die. Throw of the dice and all that. Then again, I wouldn't want to be in Dan's place if he gets the order to put a bullet in the back of Terri's head. No kneecapping or any of that. She's innocent, and she'll get a quick bullet without knowing it's about to come. So, are we clear about what you have to do?"

Schroeder said, "I won't do it."

"As you wish." He turned and began walking up the stairs. He called back. "In about a minute a light will flash from the bell tower, and my men on the outside will telephone Dan, and...and that, I'm afraid, will be the end of Terri Schroeder." He continued up the stairs.

"Wait! Listen, maybe we can work this out. Hold on! Stop walking away!"

Flynn turned slowly. "I'm afraid this is not negotiable, Captain." He paused and said, "It's awkward when you're involved personally, isn't it? Did you ever consider that every man and woman you've negotiated with or for was involved personally? Well, I'm not going to take you to task for your past successes. You were dealing with criminals, and they probably deserved the shoddy deals you got for them. You and I deserve a better deal. Our fates are intertwined, our goals are the same—aren't they? Yes or no, Captain? Quickly!"

Schroeder nodded.

Flynn moved down the stairs. "Good decision." He came close to the gate and put his hand out. Schroeder looked at it but shook his head. "Never."

Flynn withdrew his hand. "All right, then...all right...."

Schroeder said, "Can I go now?"

"Yes.... Oh, one more thing. It's quite possible you'll fail even if you dwell on the flamethrowers and threaten public statements and all that...so we should plan for failure."

Schroeder's face showed that he understood what was coming.

Flynn's voice was firm and businesslike. "If Bellini is to attack, in spite of everything you can do to stop it, then I'll give you another way to save Terri's life."

"No."

"Yes, I'm afraid you'll have to get down here and tell me when, where, how, that sort of thing—"

"No! No, I would never—never get police officers killed—"

"They'll get killed anyway. And so will the hostages and the Fenians and Terri. So if you want to at least save her, you'll give me the operational plans."

"They won't tell me—"

"Make it your business to know. The easier solution is to scare Bellini out of his fucking mind and get *him* to refuse. You've a great many options. I wish I had as many."

Schroeder wiped his brow. His breathing was erratic, and his voice was shaky. "Flynn...please...I'll move heaven and earth to get them to surrender—I swear to God I will—but if they don't listen—" He drew up his body. "Then I won't betray them. Never. Even if it means Terri—"

Flynn reached out and grabbed Schroeder by the arm. "Use your head, man. If they're repulsed once, they aren't likely to try again. They're not marines or royal commandos. If I beat them back, then Washington, the Vatican, and other concerned countries will pressure London. I can almost guarantee there'll be *fewer* police killed if I stop them in their tracks...stop them

before the battle gets too far along.... You *must* tell me if they've
got the architect and the blueprints...tell me if they will use gas,
if they're going to cut off the lights.... You know what I need.
And I'll put the hostages in the crypt for protection. I'll send a
signal, and Terri will be freed within five minutes. I won't ask
any more of you."

Schroeder's head shook.

Flynn reached out his other hand and laid it on Schroeder's
shoulder. He spoke almost gently. "Long after we're dead, after
what's happened here is only a dim memory to an uncaring
world, Theresa will be alive, perhaps remarried—children,
grandchildren. Step outside of what you feel now, Captain,
and look into the future. Think of her and think also of your
wife—Mary lives for that girl, Bert. She—"

Schroeder suddenly pulled away. "Shut up! For God's sake,
shut up...." He slumped forward, and his head rested against
the bars.

Flynn patted him on the shoulder. "You're a decent man,
Captain. An honest man. And you're a good father.... I hope
you're still a father at dawn. Well...will you be?"

Schroeder nodded.

"Good. Go on, then, go back, have a drink. Get yourself together. It'll be all right. No, don't go thinking about your gun.
Killing me or killing yourself won't solve anyone's problem but
your own. Think about Terri and Mary. They need you and love
you. See you later, Captain, God willing."

CHAPTER 51

Governor Doyle stood in a back room of the Cardinal's residence, a telephone in his hand. He listened to a succession of state officials: policemen, public relations people, legislators, the Attorney General, the commander of the state's National Guard. They spoke to him from Albany, from the state offices in Rockefeller Center, from their homes, and from their vacation hotels in warmer climates. All of these people, who normally couldn't decide on chicken or roast beef at a banquet, had decided that the time had come to storm the Cathedral. The Lieutenant Governor told him, frankly, if not tactfully, that his ratings in the polls were so low he had nothing to lose and could only gain by backing an assault on the Cathedral regardless of its success or failure. Doyle put the receiver into its cradle and regarded the people who were entering the room.

Kline, he noticed, had brought Spiegel, which meant a decision could be reached. Monsignor Downes took a seat beside Arnold Sheridan of the State Department. On the couch sat the Irish Consul General, Donahue, and the British Foreign Office representative, Eric Palmer. Police Commissioner Rourke stood by the door until Kline pointed to a chair.

Doyle looked at Bartholomew Martin, who had no official

status any longer but whom he had asked to be present. Martin, no matter what people were saying about him, could be counted on to supply the right information.

The Governor cleared his throat and said, "Gentlemen, Miss—Ms.—Spiegel, I've asked you here because I feel that *we* are the ones most immediately affected by this situation." He looked around the room. "And before we leave here, we're going to cut this Gordian knot." He made a slicing movement with his hand. "Cut through every tactical and strategic problem, political consideration, and moral dilemma that has paralyzed our will and our ability to *act!*" He paused, then turned to Monsignor Downes. "Father, would you repeat for everyone the latest news from Rome?"

Monsignor Downes said, "Yes. His Holiness is going to make a personal appeal to the Fenians, as Christians, to spare the Cathedral and the lives of the hostages. He will also appeal to the governments involved to show restraint and will place at their disposal the facilities of the Vatican where they and the Fenians can continue their negotiations."

Major Martin broke the silence. "The heads of state of the three governments involved are making a point of *not* speaking directly to these terrorists—"

The Monsignor waved his hand in a gesture of dismissal. "His Holiness would not be speaking as head of the Vatican State but as a world spiritual leader."

The British representative, Palmer, said, "Such an appeal would place the American President and the Prime Ministers of Ireland and Britain in a difficult—"

Monsignor Downes was becoming agitated by the negative response. "His Holiness feels the Church must do what it can for these outcasts because that has been our mission for two thousand years—these are the people who need us." He handed a sheet of paper to the Governor. "This is the text of His Holiness's appeal."

Governor Doyle read the short message and passed it to Mayor Kline.

Monsignor Downes said, "We would like that delivered to the people inside the Cathedral at the same time it's read on radio and television. Within the next hour— before dawn."

After everyone in the room had seen the text of the Pope's appeal, Eric Palmer said, "Some years ago, we actually did meet secretly with the IRA, and they made it public. The repercussions rocked the government. I don't think we're going to speak with them again—certainly not at the Vatican."

Donahue spoke with a tone of sadness in his voice. "Monsignor, the Dublin government outlawed the IRA in the 1920s, and I don't think Dublin will back the Vatican on this...."

Martin said, "As you know we've actually passed on a compromise to them, and they've not responded. The Pope can save himself and all of us a great deal of embarrassment if he withholds this plea."

Mayor Kline added, "The only way the Fenians can go to the Vatican is if I *let* them go. And I can't do that. I have to enforce the law."

Arnold Sheridan spoke for the first time, and the tone of his voice suggested a final policy position. "The government of the United States has reason to believe that federal firearm and passport laws have been violated, but otherwise it's purely a local affair. We're not going anywhere to discuss the release of Irish prisoners in the United Kingdom or immunity from prosecution for the people in the Cathedral."

Spiegel looked at Downes. "The only place negotiations can be held is right here—on the phone or at the sacristy gate. It is the policy of the police in this city to contain a hostage situation—not let it become mobile. And it is the law to arrest criminals at the first possible opportunity. In other words, the trenches are dug, and no one is leaving them under a truce flag."

The Monsignor pursed his lips and nodded. "I understand your positions, but the Church, which many of you consider so ironbound, is willing to try *anything*. I think you should know that personal appeals to all parties involved will be forthcoming from the Archbishop of Canterbury, the Primate of Ireland, and from hundreds of other religious leaders of every faith and denomination. And in almost every church and synagogue in this city and in other cities, all-night prayer vigils have been called. And at 5:00 A.M., if it's not over by then, every church bell in this city, and probably in the country, will begin ringing—ringing for sanity, for mercy, and for all of us."

Roberta Spiegel stood and lit a cigarette. "The mood of the people, notwithstanding bells and singing in the streets, is very hard line. If we take a soft approach and it explodes in our faces at 6:03, all of us will be out on our asses, and there'll be no all-night prayer vigils for us." She paused, then said, "So let's cut through the bullshit—or the Gordian knot—and decide how and when we're going to attack, and get our stories straight for afterward."

Cigarettes were being lit, and Major Martin was helping himself to the Cardinal's sherry.

The Governor nodded appreciatively. "I admire your honesty and perception, Ms. Spiegel, and—"

She looked at him. "This is why you asked us here, so let's get on with it, Governor."

Governor Doyle flushed but controlled his anger and said, "Good idea." He looked around. "Then we all agree that a compromise is not an option, that the Fenians won't surrender, and that they'll carry out their threats at dawn?"

There were some tentative nods.

The Governor looked at Arnold Sheridan and said, "I'm on my own?"

Sheridan nodded.

Doyle said, "But—off the record—the administration would like to see a hard-line approach?"

Sheridan said, "The message the government wants to convey is that this sort of thing will always be met by force—local force." Sheridan walked to the door. "Thank you, Governor, for the opportunity to contribute to the discussion. I'm sure you'll reach the right decision." He left.

Mayor Kline watched the door close and said, "We've been cut adrift." He turned to Donahue and Palmer. "You see, the federal system works marvelously— they collect taxes and pass laws, Mayor Kline fights terrorists."

Kline stood and began pacing. He stopped in front of Donahue and Palmer. "Do you understand that it is in my power, as the duly elected Mayor of this city, to order an assault on that Cathedral?"

Neither man responded.

Kline's voice rose. "It is my *duty*. And I don't have to answer to *anyone*."

Eric Palmer stood and moved toward the door. "We've offered all the compromises we can.... And if this is, as you indicate, a local matter, then there's no reason for Her Majesty's government to involve itself any further." He looked at Martin, who made no move to follow, then nodded to the others. "Good morning." He walked out.

Tomas Donahue stood. "I feel bad about all of this.... I've lived in this city for five years.... Saint Patrick's is my parish church.... I know the Cardinal and Father Murphy...." He looked at Monsignor Downes. "But there's *nothing* I can do." He walked to the door and turned back. "If you need me, I'll be in the consulate. God bless...." He left quickly.

Spiegel said, "Nice clean exits."

Governor Doyle hooked his thumbs on his vest pockets. "Well...there it is." He turned to Martin. "Major...won't you give us your thoughts.... As a man who is familiar with the IRA...what would be your course of action?"

Martin said without preamble, "It's time you discussed a rescue operation."

The Governor nodded slowly, aware that the phrase "rescue operation," as opposed to attack or assault, was a subtle turning point. The phraseology for the coming action was being introduced and refined. He turned abruptly to Monsignor Downes. "Are you willing to give your blessing to a rescue operation?"

The Monsignor looked up quickly. "Am I...? Well..."

Governor Doyle moved close to Downes. "Monsignor, in times of crisis it's often people like ourselves, at the middle levels, who get stuck holding the bag. And *we* have to act. Not to act is more immoral than to act with force." He added. "Rescue, we have to *rescue*—"

Monsignor Downes said, "But...the Papal plea..."

Mayor Kline spoke from across the room. "I don't want to see the Pope or the other religious leaders make fools of themselves. If God himself pleaded with these Fenians, it would make no difference."

The Monsignor ran his hands across his cheeks. "But why *me*...? What difference does it make what *I* say?"

Kline cleared his throat. "To be perfectly honest with you, Monsignor, I won't do a damned thing to rescue those people or save that Cathedral unless I have the blessing of a ranking member of the Catholic clergy. A Monsignor will do, preferably Irish like yourself. I'm no fool, and neither are you."

Monsignor Downes slumped into his chair. "Oh God..."

Rourke rose from his chair and walked to Downes. He knelt

beside the Monsignor's chair and spoke with anguish in his voice. "My boys are mostly Catholic, Father. If they have to go in here... they'll want to see you first... to make their confessions... to know that someone from the Church is blessing their mission. Otherwise, they'll... I don't know...."

Monsignor Downes put his face in his hands. After a full minute he looked up and nodded slowly. "God help me, but if you think it's the only way to save them..." He stood suddenly and almost ran from the room.

For a few seconds no one spoke, then Spiegel said, "Let's move before things start coming apart."

Mayor Kline was rubbing his chin thoughtfully. He looked up. "Schroeder will have to state that he's failed absolutely."

Governor Doyle said, "That should be no problem. He has." He added, "It would help also if we put out a news release—concurrent with the rescue—that the Fenians have made *new* demands in addition to the ones we were willing to discuss—" He stopped abruptly. "Damn it, there are *tapes* of every phone conversation.... Maybe Burke can—"

Kline interrupted. "Forget Burke. Schroeder is speaking in person to Flynn right now. That will give Schroeder the opportunity to state that Flynn has made a set of new demands."

The Governor nodded. "Yes, very good."

Kline said, "I'll have Bellini report in writing that he believes that there's a good chance of carrying out a rescue with a minimum loss of life and property."

Doyle said, "But Bellini's like a yo-yo. He keeps changing his mind—" He looked sharply at Rourke. "Will he write such a statement?"

Rourke's tone was anxious. "He'll carry out any orders to attack... but as for signing any statement... he's a difficult man. I

446   N E L S O N   D e M I L L E

know his position is that he needs more solid intelligence before
he says he *approves*—"

Major Martin said, "Lieutenant Burke tells me he's very close
to an intelligence breakthrough."

Everyone looked at Martin.

Martin continued. "He'll have at least the blueprints, perhaps the architect himself, within the next hour. I can almost
guarantee it." Martin's tone suggested that he didn't want to be
pressed further.

Kline said, "What we need from Inspector Langley are psy-
profiles showing that half the terrorists in there are psychotic."

Governor Doyle said, "Will these police officers cooperate?"

Spiegel answered. "I'll take care of Langley. As for Schroeder,
he's very savvy and politically attuned. No problem there. Regarding Bellini, we'll offer a promotion and transfer to wherever
he wants." Spiegel walked toward the telephone. "I'll get the media right now and tell them that the negotiations are reaching
a critical stage and it's absolutely essential they delay on those
Church appeals."

Doyle said almost smugly, "At least I know *my* man, Logan,
will do what he is told." He turned to Kline. "Don't forget, I
want a piece of this, Murray. At least one squad has to be from
the Sixty-ninth."

Mayor Kline looked out the window. "Are we doing the right
thing? Or have we all gone crazy?"

Martin said, "You'd be crazy to wait for dawn." He added,
"It's odd, isn't it, that the others didn't want to share this with
us?"

Roberta Spiegel looked up as she dialed. "Some rats have perceived a sinking ship and jumped off. Other rats have perceived
a bandwagon and jumped on. Before the sun rises, we'll know
which rats saw things more clearly."

* * *

Bert Schroeder sat at his desk in the Monsignor's office. Langley, Bellini, and Colonel Logan stood, listening to Mayor Kline and Governor Doyle tell them what was expected of them. Schroeder's eyes darted from Kline to Doyle as his thoughts raced wildly.

Roberta Spiegel sat in her rocker staring into the disused fireplace, absently twirling a brandy snifter in her hands. The room had grown cold, and she had Langley's jacket draped over her shoulders.

Major Martin stood at the fireplace, occupied with the curios on the mantel.

Police Commissioner Rourke stood beside the Mayor, nodding agreement at everything Kline and Doyle said, trying to elicit similar nodding from his three officers.

The Governor stopped speaking and looked at Schroeder a moment. Something about the man suggested a dormant volcano. He tried to gauge his reaction. "Bert?"

Schroeder's eyes focused on the Governor.

Doyle said, "Bert, this is no reflection on you, but if dawn comes and there's no compromise, no extension of the deadline—and there won't be—and the hostages are *executed* and the Cathedral *demolished* . . . well, it will be *you*, Bert, who'll get most of the public abuse. Won't it?"

Schroeder said nothing.

Mayor Kline turned to Langley. "And it will be *you*, Inspector, who will get a great deal of the official censure."

"Be that as it may—"

Bellini said heatedly, "We can handle criminals, Your Honor, but these are guerrillas armed with military ordnance—intrusion alarms, submachine guns, rockets, and . . . and

God knows what else. What if they have flamethrowers? Huh? And they're holed up in a national shrine. Christ, I still don't understand why the army can't—" The Mayor put a restraining hand on Bellini with a look of disappointment. "Joe...Joe, this is not like you."

Bellini said, "It sure as hell is."

Governor Doyle looked at Logan, who appeared uncomfortable. "Colonel? What's *your* feel?"

Colonel Logan came to a modified position of attention. "Oh...well...I am convinced that we should act without delay to mount an att—a rescue operation."

The Governor beamed.

"However," continued Logan, "the tactical plan is not sound. What you're asking us to do is like...like shooting rats in a china cabinet without breaking the china...or the cabinet...."

The Governor stared at Logan, his bushy eyebrows rising in an arc like squirrel tails. "Soldiers are often asked to do the impossible—and to do it well. National Guard duty is not all parades and happy hours."

"No, sir...yes, sir."

"Can the Fighting Irish hold up their end of the operation?"

"Of course!"

The Governor slapped Logan's shoulder soundly. "Good man."

The Mayor turned to Langley. "Inspector, you will have to come up with the dossiers we need on the Fenians."

Langley hesitated.

Roberta Spiegel fixed her eyes on him. "By no later than noon, Inspector." Langley looked at her. "Sure. Why not? I'll do some creative writing with the help of a discreet police psychologist—Dr. Korman—and come up with psy-profiles of the Fenians that would scare the hell out of John Hickey himself."

Major Martin said, "May I suggest, Inspector, that you also show a link between the death of that informer—Ferguson, I think his name was—and the Fenians? That will tidy up that business as well."

Langley looked at Martin and understood. He nodded.

Kline looked at Bellini. "Well, Joe... are you on our team?"

Bellini looked troubled. "I am... but..."

"Joe, can you honestly say that you're absolutely convinced these terrorists will not shoot the Cardinal and the others at dawn and then blow up Saint Patrick's Cathedral?"

"No... but—"

"Are you convinced your men cannot conduct a successful rescue operation?"

"I never said anything like that, Your Honor. I just won't sign anything.... Since when are people required to sign something like that?"

The Mayor patted his shoulder gently. "Should I get someone *else* to lead your men against the terrorists in a rescue operation, Joe? Or should I just let Colonel Logan handle the whole operation?"

Bellini's mind was filled with conflicting thoughts, all of them unhappy.

Spiegel snapped, "Yes or no, Captain? It's getting late, and the fucking sun is due at 6:03."

Bellini looked at her and straightened his posture. "I'll lead the attack. If I get the blueprints, then I'll decide if I'm going to sign anything."

Mayor Kline let out a deep breath. "Well, that's about it." He looked at Langley. "You'll of course reconsider your resignation."

Langley said, "Actually, I was thinking about chief inspector."

Kline nodded quickly. "Certainly. There'll be promotions for everyone after this."

Langley lit a cigarette and noticed his hands were unsteady. Kline and Doyle, he was convinced, were doing the right thing in attacking the Cathedral. But with the sure instincts of the politician, they were doing it for the wrong reasons, in the wrong way, and going about it in a slimy manner. But so what? That was how half the right things got done.

Mayor Kline was smiling now. He turned to Schroeder. "Bert, all we need from you is some more time. Keep talking to them. You're doing a hell of a job, Bert, and we appreciate it.... Captain?" He smiled at Schroeder the way he always smiled at someone he had caught not paying attention. "Bert?"

Schroeder's eyes focused on Kline, but he said nothing.

Mayor Kline regarded him with growing apprehension. "Now...now, Bert, I need a signed statement from you saying that it is your professional opinion, based on years of hostage negotiating, that you recommend a cessation of negotiations. Right?"

Schroeder looked around the room and made an unintelligible noise.

The Mayor seemed anxious but went on. "You should indicate that when you saw Flynn he made *more* demands...crazy demands. Okay? Write that up as soon as possible." He turned to the others. "All of you—"

"I won't do that."

Everyone in the room looked at Schroeder. Kline said incredulously, "What— what did you say?"

Roberta Spiegel stood quickly, sending the rocker sliding into Governor Doyle.

Doyle moved the rocker aside and approached Schroeder. "Those are true statements! And you haven't accomplished shit so far!"

Schroeder stood and steadied himself against the desk. "I've listened to all of you, and you're all crazy."

Spiegel said to Langley, "Get the backup negotiator."

Schroeder shouted, "No! No one can speak with Flynn but me.... He won't speak to anyone else.... You'll see he won't speak.... I'll call him now...." He reached for the telephone, but Langley pulled it away. Schroeder fell back in his chair.

Mayor Kline looked stunned. He tried to speak but couldn't get a word out.

Spiegel moved around the desk and looked down at Schroeder. Her voice was soft and dispassionate. "Captain, sometime between now and the time Bellini is ready to move, you will prepare a statement justifying our decision. If you don't, I'll see to it that you are brought up on departmental charges, dismissed from the force, and lose your pension. You'll end up as a bank guard in Dubuque—if you're lucky enough ever to get a gun permit. Now, let's discuss this intelligently."

Schroeder stood and took a deep breath. His voice had the control and tone of the professional negotiator again. "Yes, let's do that. I'm sorry, I became overwrought for a moment. Let's discuss what Brian Flynn really said to me, not what you'd have liked him to say." Schroeder looked at Bellini and Logan. "It seems those forty-five corned beef dinners were not a ruse—there were people to eat those dinners. I saw them. And flamethrowers...let me tell you about the flamethrowers...." He lit a cigar with shaking hands, then continued.

Schroeder went on in cool, measured tones, but everyone could hear an undercurrent of anxiety in his voice. He concluded, "Flynn has assembled what amounts to the largest, best-equipped armed force of trained insurgents this country has seen since the Civil War. It's too late to do anything except call Washington and tell them we've surrendered what is in our power to surrender...."

CHAPTER 52

Langley found Burke lying on a bed in a priest's room. "They've decided to hit the Cathedral!"

Burke sat up quickly.

Langley's voice was agitated. "Soon. Before the Pope's appeal—before the church bells ring and Monsignor Downes comes to his senses—"

"Slow down."

"Schroeder spoke to Flynn at the gate—said he saw forty or fifty armed Fenians— "

"Fifty?"

"But he didn't. I *know* he didn't."

"Hold on. Back up."

Langley paced around the small room. "Washington perceived a sinking ship. Kline and Doyle perceived a bandwagon. See? Tomorrow they'll both be heroes, or they'll be in Mexico wearing dark glasses and phony noses—"

Burke found some loose aspirin in the night table and chewed three of them.

Langley sat down on a chair. "Listen, Spiegel wants to see you." He briefed Burke quickly, then added, "You're the negotiator until they decide about Schroeder."

Burke looked up. "Negotiator?" He laughed. "Poor Bert. This was going to be his perfect game.... He really wanted this one." He lit a cigarette stub. "So"—he exhaled a stream of acrid smoke—"we attack—"

"No! We *rescue*! You have to call it a rescue operation now. You have to choose your words very carefully, because it's getting very grim and none of them is saying what they mean anymore—they never did anyway—and they lie better than we do. Go on, they're waiting for you."

Burke made no move to leave. "And Martin told them I would produce Stillway!"

"Yes, complete with blueprints. That was news to me—how about you?"

"And he never mentioned Terri O'Neal?"

"No—should he?" Langley looked at his watch. "Does it matter anymore?" Burke stared out the window into Madison Avenue. "Martin killed Jack Ferguson, you know."

Langley came up behind him. "No. The Fenians killed Jack Ferguson."

Burke turned. "Lots of phony deals going down tonight."

Langley shook his head. "Damned right. And Kline is passing out promotions like they were campaign buttons. Go get one. But you have to pay."

Langley began pacing again. "You have to sign a statement saying you think everything Kline and Doyle do is terrific. Okay? Make them give you a captain's pay. I'm going to be a chief inspector. And get out of ID. Ask for the Art Forgery Squad—Paris, London, Rome. Promise me you'll visit Schroeder in Dubuque—"

"Get hold of yourself."

Langley waved his arms. "Remember, Martin is in, Schroeder is out. Logan is in with Kline and Doyle but out with

Bellini—are you following me? Watch out for Spiegel. She's in
rare form—what a magnificent bitch. The Fenians are lunatics,
we're sane.... Monsignor Downes blesses us all.... What else?"
He looked around with wild darting eyes. "Is there a shower in
this place? I feel slimy. You still here? Beat it!" Langley fell back
on the bed. "Go away."

Burke had never seen Langley become unglued, and it was
frightening. He started to say something, then thought better of
it and left.

Burke walked beside Roberta Spiegel up the stairs. He listened
to her brisk voice as they moved. Martin was climbing silently
behind him.

Burke opened the stairshed door and walked onto the flat
rooftop of the rectory. A wind blew from the north, and frozen
pools of water reflected the lights of the tall buildings around
them. Spiegel dismissed a team of ESD snipers, turned up her
coat collar, and moved to the west side of the roof. She put her
hands on the low wrought-iron fence that ran around the roof's
perimeter and stared at the towering Cathedral rising across the
narrow courtyard.

The streets below were deserted, but in the distance, beyond
the barricades, horns blared, people sang and shouted, bagpipes
and other instruments played intermittently. Burke realized it
was after 4:00 A.M., and the bars had closed. The party was
on the streets now, probably still a hundred thousand strong,
maybe more, tenaciously clinging to the night that had turned
magic for them.

Spiegel was speaking, and Burke tried to concentrate on her
words; but he had no topcoat, and he was cold, and her words
were blowing away in the strong wind. She concluded, "We've
gotten our act together, Lieutenant, but before it comes apart,

we're going to move. And we don't want any more surprises. Understand?"

Burke said, "Art Forgery Squad."

Spiegel looked at him, momentarily puzzled, then said, "Oh...all right. Either that or shower orderly at the academy gym." She turned her back to the wind and lit a cigarette.

Burke said, "Where's Schroeder?"

Spiegel replied, "He understands we don't want him out of our sight and talking to the press, so rather than suffer the indignity of a guard, he volunteered to stick with Bellini."

Burke felt a vague uneasiness pass through him. He said, "And I'm the negotiator?"

Spiegel said, "In fact, yes. But for the sake of appearances, Schroeder is still on the job. He's not without his political connections. He'll continue his duties, with some modifications, of course, and later...he'll go on camera."

Martin spoke for the first time. "Captain Schroeder should actually go back to the sacristy and speak with Flynn again. We have to keep up appearances at this critical moment. Neither Flynn nor the press should sense any problem."

Burke cupped his hands and lit a cigarette, looking at Martin as he did. Martin's strategy was becoming clear. He thought about Schroeder hanging around Bellini, about Schroeder meeting Flynn again at the gate. He thought, also, that Flynn did not have fifty well-armed people, and therefore Schroeder was mistaken, stupid, or gullible, which seemed to be the consensus. But he knew Schroeder was none of these things. *When you have excluded the impossible,* said Sherlock Holmes, *whatever remains, however improbable, must be the truth.* Schroeder was lying, and Burke was beginning to understand why. He pictured the face of a young woman, heard her voice again, and placed her at a promotion party five or six years before. Almost hesitantly he made the final connection he should have made hours ago. Burke said to Spiegel, "And Bellini's working on a new plan of attack?"

Spiegel looked at him in the diffused light and said, "Right now Bellini and Logan are formulating plan B—escalating the response, as they say—based on the outside possibility that there is a powerful force in that Cathedral. They won't go in any other way. But we're counting on *you* to give us the intelligence we need to formulate a plan C, an infiltration of the Cathedral and surprise attack, using the hidden passages that many of us seem to believe exist. That may enable us to actually save some lives and save Saint Patrick's."

She looked out at the looming structure. Even from the outside it looked labyrinthine with its towers, spires, buttresses, and intricate stonework. She turned to Burke. "So, do you feel, Lieutenant Burke, that you've put your neck on a chopping block?"

"There's no reason why my neck shouldn't be where yours is."

"True," she said. "True. And yours is actually a little more exposed, since I understand you're going in with Bellini."

"That's right. How about you?"

She smiled unpleasantly, then said, "You don't *have* to go.... But it wouldn't be a bad idea... if you don't produce Stillway."

Burke glanced at Martin, who nodded slightly, and said, "I'll have him within... half an hour."

No one spoke, then Martin said, "If I may make another suggestion... let's not make too much of this architect business in front of Captain Schroeder. He's overwrought and may inadvertently let something slip the next time he speaks with Flynn."

There was a long silence on the rooftop, broken by the sounds of shoes shuffling against the frozen gravel and the wind rushing through the streets. Burke looked at Spiegel and guessed that she sensed Bert Schroeder had a real problem, was a real problem.

Spiegel put her hands in the pockets of her long coat and walked a few paces from Burke and Martin. For a few brief seconds she wondered why she was so committed to this, and it came to her that in those seven miserable years of teaching history what she had really wanted to do was make history; and she would.

Captain Joe Bellini rubbed his eyes and looked at the clock in the press conference room. 4:26 A.M. *The fucking sun is due at 6:03.* In his half-sleep he had pictured a wall of brilliant sunlight moving toward him, coming to rescue him as it had done so many times in Korea. *God,* he thought, *how I hate the sound of rifles in the night.*

He looked around the room. Men slept on cots or on the floor, using flak jackets for pillows. Others were awake, smoking, talking in low tones. Occasionally someone laughed at something that, Bellini guessed, was not funny. Fear had a special stink of its own, and he smelled it strongly now, a mixture of sweat, tobacco, gun oil, and the breath from labored lungs and sticky mouths.

The blackboard was covered with colored chalk marks superimposed on a white outline of St. Patrick's. On the long conference table lay copies of the revised attack plan. Bert Schroeder sat at the far end of the table, flipping casually through a copy.

The phone rang, and Bellini grabbed it. "ESD operations, Bellini."

The Mayor's distinctive nasal voice came over the line. "How are you holding up, Joe? Anxious to get rolling?"

"Can't wait."

"Good.... Listen, I've just seen your new attack plan.... It's a little excessive, isn't it?"

"It was mostly Colonel Logan's, sir," Bellini said.

"Oh...well, see that you tone it down."

Bellini picked up a full soft-drink can in his big hand and squeezed it, watching the top pop off and the brown liquid run over his fingers. "Approved or disapproved?"

The Mayor let a long time go by, and Bellini knew he was conferring, looking at his watch. Kline came back on the line. "The Governor and I approve...in principle."

"I thank you in principle."

Kline switched to another subject. "Is he still there?"

Bellini glanced at Schroeder. "Like dog turd on a jogger's sneakers."

Kline forced a weak laugh. "Okay, I'm in the state offices in Rockefeller Center with the Governor and our staffs—"

"Good view."

"Now, don't be sarcastic. Listen, I've just spoken to the President of the United States."

Bellini detected a note of self-importance in Kline's tone.

"The President says he's making definite progress with the British Prime Minister. He's also making noises like he might federalize the guard and send in marshals...." Kline lowered his voice in a conspiratorial tone. "Between you and me, Joe, I think he's putting out a smokescreen...covering himself for later."

Bellini lit a cigarette. "Who isn't?"

Kline's voice was urgent. "He's under pressure. The church bells in Washington are already ringing, and there are thousands of people marching with candles in front of the White House. The British Embassy is being picketed—"

Bellini watched Schroeder stand and then walk toward the door. He said into the phone, "Hold on." Bellini called to Schroeder, "Where you headed, Chief?"

Schroeder looked back at him. "Sacristy." He walked out the door.

Bellini watched him go, then said into the phone, "Schroeder just went to make a final pitch to Flynn. Okay?"

Kline let out a long breath. "All right...can't hurt. By the time he gets back you'll be ready to move—unless he has something very solid, which he won't."

Bellini remembered that Schroeder had never had a failure. "You never know."

There was a long silence on the line, then the Mayor said, "Do you believe in miracles?"

"Never actually saw one." He thought, *Except the time you got reelected.* "Nope, never saw one."

"Me neither."

Bellini heard a click on the line, followed by a dial tone. He looked across the quiet room. "Get up! Off your asses! Battle stations. Move out!"

Bert Schroeder stood opposite Brian Flynn at the sacristy gate. Schroeder's voice was low and halting as he spoke, and he kept looking back nervously into the sacristy. "The plan is a fairly simple and classical attack.... Colonel Logan drew it up.... Logan himself will hit the front doors with an armored carrier, and the ESD will hit all the other doors simultaneously with rams.... They'll use scaling ladders and break through the windows.... It's all done under cover of gas and darkness...everyone has masks and night scopes. The electricity will be cut off at the moment the doors are hit...."

Flynn felt the blood race through his veins as he listened. "Gas..."

Schroeder nodded. "The same stuff you used at the reviewing stands. It will be pumped in through the air ducts." He detailed the coordination of helicopters, snipers on the roofs, firemen, and bomb disposal men. He added, "The sacristy steps"—he looked down as though realizing he was standing in the very spot— "they'll be hit with steel-cut chain saws. Bellini and I will be with that squad.... We'll go for the hostages...if they're on the sanctuary..." He shook his head, trying to comprehend the fact that he was saying this.

"The hostages," said Flynn, "will be dead." He paused and said, "Where will Burke be?"

Schroeder shook his head, tried to go on, but heard his voice faltering. After some hesitation he slipped a sheaf of papers from his jacket and through the bars.

Flynn slid them under his shirt, his eyes darting between the corridor openings. "So there's nothing that the famous Captain Schroeder can do to stop this?"

Schroeder looked down. "There never was.... Why didn't you see that...?"

Flynn's voice was hostile. "Because I listened to you all night, Schroeder, and I think I half believed your damned lies!"

Schroeder was determined to salvage something of himself from the defeat and humiliation he had felt at the last confrontation. "Don't put this on *me*. You *knew* I was lying. You knew it!"

Flynn glared at him, then nodded slightly. "Yes, I knew it." He thought a moment, then said, "And I know you're finally speaking the truth. It must be a great strain. Well, I can stop them at the doors...if, as you say, they haven't discovered any hidden passages and they don't have the architect—" He looked suddenly at Schroeder. "They *don't* have him, do they?"

Schroeder shook his head. He drew himself up and spoke rapidly. "Give it up. I'll get you a police escort to the airport. I know I can do that. That's all they really want—they want you out of here!"

Flynn seemed to consider for a brief moment, then shook his head.

Schroeder pressed on. "Flynn—listen, they're going to hit you hard. You're going to *die*. Can't you grasp that? You can't delude yourself any longer. But all you have to do is say you're willing to take less—"

"If I wanted less, I would have asked for less. No more hostage negotiating, please. God, how you go on. Talk about self-delusion."

Schroeder drew close to the gate. "All right, I've done all I could. Now you release—"

Flynn cut him off. "If the details you've given me are accurate, I'll send a signal to release your daughter."

Schroeder grabbed at the bars. "What *kind* of signal? When? The phones will be cut off.... The towers will be under sniper fire—What if you're...dead? Damn it, I've given you the plans—"

Flynn went on. "But if you've lied to me about any part of this, or if there should be a change in plans and you don't tell me—"

Schroeder was shaking his head spasmodically. "No. No. That's not acceptable. You're not living up to your end."

Flynn turned and walked up the stairs.

Schroeder drew his pistol and held it close against his chest. It wavered in his hand, the muzzle pointing toward Flynn's back, but his hand shook so badly he almost dropped the gun. Flynn turned the corner and disappeared.

After a full minute Schroeder holstered the pistol, faced around, and walked back to the side corridor. He passed grim-faced men standing against the walls with slung rifles. He found a lavatory, entered it, and vomited.

CHAPTER 53

Burke stood alone in the small counting room close by the press room. He adjusted his flak jacket over his pullover and, after putting a green carnation in a cartridge loop, started for the door.

The door suddenly swung open, and Major Martin stood before him. "Hello, Burke. Is that what everyone in New York is wearing now?" He called back into the corridor, and two patrolmen appeared with a civilian between them. Martin smiled. "May I present Gordon Stillway, American Institute of Architects? Mr. Stillway, this is Patrick Burke, world-famous secret policeman."

A tall, erect, elderly man stepped into the room, looking confused but otherwise dignified. In his left hand he held a briefcase from which protruded four tubes of rolled paper.

Burke dismissed the two officers and turned to Martin. "It's late."

"Is it?" Martin looked at his watch. "You have fifteen full minutes to head off Bellini. Time, as you know, is relative. If you're eating Galway Bay oysters, fifteen minutes pass rather quickly, but if you're hanging by your left testicle, it drags a bit." He laughed at his own joke. "Bellini is hanging by his testicle. You'll cut him down—then hang him up there again after he's spoken to Mr. Stillway."

Martin moved farther into the small room and drew closer to Burke. "Mr. Stillway was kidnapped from his apartment by persons unknown and held in an empty loft not far from here. Acting on anonymous information, I went to the detectives in the Seventh Precinct and, *voilà,* Gordon Stillway. Mr. Stillway, won't you have a seat?"

Gordon Stillway remained standing and looked from one man to the other, then said, "This is a terrible tragedy...but I'm not quite certain what I'm supposed to— "

Martin said, "You, sir, will give the police the information they must have to infiltrate the Cathedral and catch the villains unawares."

Stillway looked at him. "What are you talking about? Do you mean they're going to attack? I won't have that."

Martin put his hand on Stillway's shoulder. "I'm afraid you've arrived a bit late, sir. That's not negotiable any longer. Either you help the police, or they go in there through the doors and windows and cause a great deal of death and destruction, after which the terrorists will burn it down and blow it up—or vice versa."

Stillway's eyes widened, and he let Martin maneuver him into a chair. Martin said to Burke, "You'd better hurry."

Burke came toward Martin. "Why did you cut it this close?"

Martin took a step back and replied, "I'm sorry. I had to wait for Captain Schroeder to deliver the attack plans to Flynn, which is what he's doing right now."

Burke nodded. Bellini's attack had to be canceled no matter what else happened. A new plan based on Stillway's information, if he had any, would jump off so close to 6:03 that it would probably end in disaster anyway. But Martin had delivered Stillway and therefore would be owed a great favor by Washington. He looked at Martin. "Major, I'd like to be the first to thank you for your help in this affair."

Martin smiled. "Now you're getting into the right spirit. You've been so glum all night, but you'll see—stick with me, Burke, and as I promised, you'll come out of this looking fine."

Burke addressed Stillway. "Are there any hidden passages into that Cathedral that will give the police a clear tactical advantage?"

Stillway sat motionless, contemplating the events that had begun with a sunny day and a parade, proceeded to his kidnapping and rescue, and ended with him in a subterranean room with two men who were obviously unbalanced. He said, "I have no idea what you mean by a clear tactical advantage." His voice became irritable. "I'm an architect."

Martin looked at his watch again. "Well, I've done my bit...." He opened the door. "Hurry now. You promised Bellini you'd be at his side, and a promise is sacred and beautiful. And oh, yes, later—if you're still alive—you'll see at least one more mystery unfold in that Cathedral. A rather good one." He walked out and slammed the door.

Stillway regarded Burke warily. "Who was he? Who are *you*?"

"Who are *you*? Are you Gordon Stillway—or are you just another of the Major's little jokes?"

Stillway didn't answer.

Burke extracted a rolled blueprint from the briefcase, unfurled it, and stared at it. He threw the blueprint on the table and looked at his watch. "Come with me, Mr. Stillway, and we'll see if you were worth the wait."

Schroeder walked into the press conference room and hurried toward a phone. "This is Schroeder. Get me Kline."

The Mayor's voice was neutral. "Yes, Captain, any luck?"

Schroeder looked around the nearly empty room. Rifles and flak jackets had disappeared, and empty boxes of ammunition and concussion grenades lay in the corner. Someone had scrawled on the chalkboard:

FINAL SCORE:
    CHRISTIANS AND JEWS————
    PAGANS AND ATHEISTS————

Kline's voice was impatient. "Well?"

Schroeder leaned against the table and fought down a wave of nausea. "No...no extension...no compromise. Listen..."

Kline sounded annoyed. "That's what eveyone's been telling you all night."

Schroeder drew a long breath and pressed his hand to his stomach. Kline was speaking, but Schroeder wasn't listening. Slowly he began to take in more of his surroundings. Bellini stood across the table with his arms folded, Burke stood at the opposite end of the room, two ESD men with black ski masks stood very near him, and an old man, a civilian, sat at the conference table.

The Mayor went on. "Captain, right now you are still very much a hero, and within the hour you will be the police department's chief spokesman." Schroeder examined Bellini's blackened face and thought Bellini was glaring at him with unconcealed hatred, as though he *knew*, but he decided it must be the grotesque makeup.

Kline was still speaking. "And you will not speak to a newsperson until the last shot is fired. And what's this I hear about you volunteering to go in with Bellini?"

Schroeder said, "I...I have to. That's the least I can do...."

"Have you lost your mind? What's wrong with you, anyway? You sound—have you been drinking?"

Schroeder found himself staring at the old man who, he now

noticed, was studying a large unrolled length of paper. His eyes passed over the silent men in the room again and focused on Burke, who seemed...almost sad. Everyone looked as though someone had just died. Something was wrong here—

"Are you drunk?"

"No...."

"Pull yourself together, Schroeder. You'll be on television soon."

"What...?"

"*Television!* You remember, the red light, the big camera.... Now you get clear of that Cathedral—get over here as soon as possible."

Schroeder heard the phone go dead and looked at the receiver, then dropped it on the table. He extended his arm and pointed at Gordon Stillway. "Who is *that?*"

The room remained silent. Then Burke said, "You know who that is, Bert. We're going to redraw the attack plans."

Schroeder looked quickly at Bellini and blurted, "No! No! You—"

Bellini glanced at Burke and nodded. He turned to Schroeder. "I can't believe you did that." He came toward Schroeder, who was edging toward the door. "Where're you going, ace? You going to tip your pal, cocksucker?"

Schroeder's head was shaking spasmodically.

Bellini drew closer. "I can't hear you, you shit! Your golden voice sounds like a toilet flushing."

Burke called out. "Joe—no hard stuff—just take his gun." Burke moved closer to the two men. The two ESD officers held their rifles at their hips, not understanding exactly what was going on but ready to fire if Schroeder made a move for his gun. Gordon Stillway looked up from his blueprints.

Schroeder found his voice. "No...listen...I have to talk

to Flynn...because...you see...I've got to try one more time—"

Bellini held out his hand. "Give me your gun—left hand—pinky in the trigger guard—nice and easy, and no one's going to get hurt."

Schroeder hesitated, then slowly reached into his jacket and carefully extracted the pistol with a hooked finger. "Bellini—listen—what's going on? Why—"

Bellini reached for the pistol with his left hand and swung with his right, hitting Schroeder a vicious blow to the jaw. Schroeder fell back against the door and slid down to the floor.

Burke said, "You didn't have to do that."

Bellini flexed his hand and turned to Burke. "You're right—I should've yanked his nuts out and shoved them up his nose." He looked back at Schroeder. "Tried to kill me, did you, scumbag?"

Burke saw that Bellini was contemplating further violence. "It had nothing to do with you, Bellini. Just cool out." He came up beside Bellini and put his hand on his shoulder. "Come on. You've got lots to do."

Bellini motioned to the ESD men. "Cuff this cocksucker and dump him in a closet somewhere." He turned to Burke. "You think I'm stupid, don't you? You think I don't know that you're all going to cover for that motherfucker, and as soon as the shit storm is over at dawn he's going to be the Mayor's golden boy again." He watched the ESD men carry Schroeder out and called after them, "Find some place with rats and cockroaches." He sat down and tried to steady his hands as he lit a cigarette.

Burke stood beside him. "Life is unfair, right? But someone handed us a break this time. Flynn thinks you're doing one thing, and you're going to do something else. So it didn't turn out so bad, right?"

Bellini nodded sulkily and looked at Stillway. "Yeah...

maybe…" He rubbed his knuckles and flexed his fingers again. "That hurt…but it felt so good." He laughed suddenly. "Burke, come here. Want to know a secret? I've been looking for an excuse to do that for five years." He looked at the ceiling. "Thank you, God." He laughed again.

The room began filling with squad leaders hastily recalled from their jump-off points, and Bellini watched them file into the room. The absolutely worst feeling in the whole world, Bellini thought, was to get yourself psyched out of your mind for a fight and have it postponed. The squad leaders, he saw, were in a bad mood. Bellini looked at Burke. "You better call His fucking Honor and explain. You can cover Schroeder's ass if you want, but even if you don't, it won't matter to Kline, because they'll still promote him and make him a national hero."

Burke took off his flak jacket and pullover. "I have to see Flynn and come up with a good reason why Schroeder isn't staying in touch with him."

Bellini moved to the head of the conference table and took a long breath. He looked at each of the twelve squad leaders and said, "Men, I've got some good news and some bad news. Thing is, I don't know which is which."

No one laughed, and Bellini went on. "Before I tell you why the attack is postponed, I want to say something…. The people in the Cathedral are desperate men and women…guerrillas…. This is combat…war…and the goal is not to apprehend these people at the risk of your own lives—"

A squad leader called out, "You mean shoot first and ask questions later, right?"

Bellini remembered the military euphemism for it. "Make a clean sweep."

CHAPTER 54

Father Murphy stood on the crypt landing, a purple stole around his neck. Frank Gallagher knelt before him, making a hasty confession in a low, trembling voice. Flynn waited just inside the large crypt door, then called out to Gallagher, "That's fine, Frank."

Gallagher nodded to the priest, rose, and moved into the crypt. Flynn handed him a sheet of paper and said, "Here's the part of the attack plan which deals with the sacristy gate." He briefed Gallagher, then added, "You can take cover here in the crypt while you keep the gates under fire." As Flynn spoke, Gallagher focused on the brownish blood that had flowed so abundantly from Pedar Fitzgerald's mouth. Father Murphy was standing in the center of the bloodstain, apparently without realizing it, and Gallagher wanted to tell the priest to move—but Flynn was clasping his hand. "Good luck to you, Frank. Remember, Dublin, seventeenth of March next."

Gallagher made an unintelligible noise, but he nodded with a desperate determination.

Flynn came out of the crypt and took Murphy's arm. He led the priest up the stairs, across the sanctuary, and down the side steps into the ambulatory. Father Murphy disengaged himself from Flynn and turned toward the chancel organ. John Hickey sat talking on the field phone, Pedar Fitzgerald's covered body at his feet. The priest knelt and pulled the coat back from Pedar's head. He anointed his forehead, stood, and looked at Hickey, who had hung up the receiver.

Hickey said, "Sneaked that in, did you? Well, where now is Pedar Fitzgerald's soul?"

Father Murphy kept staring at Hickey.

Hickey said, "Now, like a good priest, you'll ask me to confess, and you assume I'll refuse. But what if I do confess? Would my entire past life, including every sin, sacrilege, and blasphemy that you can imagine, be forgiven? Would I gain the kingdom of heaven?"

Murphy said, "You know you must repent."

Hickey slapped the top of the organ. "I *knew* there was a catch!"

Flynn took Murphy's arm and pulled him away. They passed beside the confessional, and Flynn paused to look at the small white buzzer. "That was clever, Padre. I'll give you that." Flynn looked back across the ambulatory at Hickey. "I don't know what messages you, Maureen, or Hickey sent, but you can be sure none of you accomplished anything beyond adding to the confusion out there."

Father Murphy replied, "I still *feel* better about it."

Flynn laughed and began walking. Murphy followed, and Flynn spoke as they walked. "You feel better, do you? My, what a big ego you have, Father." Flynn stopped in the transept aisle between the two south triforia. He turned and looked up at the triforium they'd just passed beneath and called up to Eamon Farrell. "I know you're devout, Eamon, but Father Murphy can't fly, so you'll have to miss this confession."

Farrell looked as though this were the one confession he didn't want to miss.

Father Murphy called up, "Are you sorry for all your sins?"

Farrell nodded. "I am, Father."

Murphy said, "Make a good act of contrition—you'll be in a state of grace, Mr. Farrell. Don't do anything to alter that."

Flynn was annoyed. "If you try any of that again, you'll not hear another confession."

Murphy walked away, and Flynn outlined the coming attack to Farrell. He added, "If we stop them, your son will be free at dawn. Good luck."

Flynn walked to the wide transept doors. The priest was staring at the two khaki-colored mines attached to the doors and four more can-shaped mines placed at intervals on the floor. Trip wires ran from them in all directions. "You see," said Flynn conversationally, "when the doors are smashed in, these two mines explode instantly, followed at fifteen-second intervals by the other four, producing, so to speak, a curtain of shrapnel of a minute's duration. Every doorway in here will be clogged with writhing bodies. The screams...wait until you hear the screams.... You wouldn't believe that men can make such noises. My God, it makes the blood run cold, Father, and turns the bowels to ice water."

Murphy continued to stare at the mines.

Flynn motioned overhead. "Look at these commanding views.... How in the world do they expect to succeed?" He led the priest to the small door in the corner of the transept and motioned Murphy to go first. They walked wordlessly up the spiral stairs and came out in the long triforium five stories above the main floor.

Abby Boland stood by the door, an M-16 rifle cradled in her arms. She had found a pair of overalls in a maintenance closet, and she wore them over her cheerleader's uniform. Flynn put his arm around her and walked her away from the priest as

he explained the coming attack and went through her assignments. Flynn looked across the nave at George Sullivan, who
was watching them. He took his arm from her shoulder and
said, "If we don't stop them . . . and if you determine in your own
mind that killing more of them won't help anything, then get
into the bell tower. . . . Don't try to cross the choir loft to get to
George. . . . Stay away from Leary and Megan. Understand?"

Her eyes darted to the choir loft, and she nodded.

Flynn continued. "The attic will take a while to fall in, and
the bombs won't damage the towers—they'll be the only things
left standing. George will be all right in the south tower."

"George and I understood we'd not see each other again after
this." She looked at Sullivan, who was still watching them.

"Good luck to you." Flynn moved toward the tower passage
and left her with Father Murphy.

After a few minutes Murphy rejoined Flynn, and Flynn
looked at his watch. "We don't have a great deal of time, so keep
these things short."

"How do you know how much time you've got? Am I to understand that you know the details of this attack?" He looked at
the sheaf of rolled papers in Flynn's hand.

Flynn tapped Murphy on the shoulder with the paper tube.
"Each man has a price, as you know, and it often seems pitifully
low, but did anyone ever consider that Judas Iscariot may have
needed that silver?" He laughed and indicated the spiral stairs.
They climbed three stories up into the tower, until they reached
the level that passed beside the attic. Flynn opened a large
wooden door, and they stepped onto a catwalk. Murphy peered
into the dimly lit expanse, then walked to a pile of chopped
wood and votive candles. He turned back and stared at Flynn,
who met his stare, and Murphy knew there was nothing to be
said.

Jean Kearney and Arthur Nulty moved out of the shadows and approached along a catwalk, their arms around each other. The expressions on their faces showed that they found the sight of Flynn and the priest to be ominous. They stopped some distance from the two men and looked at them, long plumes of breath coming from their mouths. Father Murphy was reminded of two lost souls who were not allowed to cross a threshold unless invited.

Flynn said, "The good Father wants to hear your sins."

Jean Kearney's face flushed. Nulty looked both embarrassed and frightened.

Flynn's eyebrows rose, and he let out a short laugh. He turned to the priest. "Self-control is difficult in times like these."

Murphy's face betrayed no anger or shock, but he let out a long, familiar sigh that Flynn thought must be part of the seminary training. Flynn motioned Murphy to stay where he was and strode across the catwalk. He handed Jean Kearney three sheets of paper and began briefing the two people. He concluded, "They'll come with the helicopters anytime after 5:15." He paused, then said, "Don't be afraid."

Jean Kearney answered, "The only thing we're afraid of is being separated." Nulty nodded.

Flynn put his arms around their shoulders and moved with them toward the priest. "Make Father Murphy a happy man and let him save your souls from the fires of hell at least." Flynn moved toward the door, then called back to Murphy. "Don't undermine the troops' morale, and no lengthy penances."

Flynn reentered the tower and waited in the darkness of a large, opaque-windowed room. He looked at his watch. According to Schroeder there were twenty minutes left until the earliest time the attack might begin.

He sat down on the cold, dusty floor, suddenly filled with

a sense of awe at what he had done. One of the largest civil disturbances in American history was about to end in the most massive police action ever seen on this continent—and a landmark was going to be deleted from the guidebooks. The name of Brian Flynn would enter history. Yet, he felt, all that was trivial compared to the fact that these men and women were willingly following him into death.

Abruptly he pivoted around, drew his pistol, and knocked out a pane of thick glass, then looked out at the night. A cold wind blew feathery clouds across a brilliant blue, moonlit sky. Up the Avenue dozens of flags hung from protruding staffs, swaying stiff and frozen in the wind. The sidewalks were covered with ice and broken glass, sparkling in the light. *Spring,* he thought. "Dear God, I'll not see the spring."

Father Murphy cleared his throat, and Flynn spun around. Their eyes met, and Flynn rose quickly. "That was fast."

Flynn began the climb up the winding stairs that gave way to a series of ladders. Murphy followed cautiously. He'd never been this high in either tower, and despite the circumstances he was eager in a boyish sort of way to see the bells.

They climbed into the lowest bell room, where Donald Mullins crouched behind the stonework that separated two louvers. He wore a flak jacket, and his face and hands were blackened with soot from a burned cork whose odor still hung in the cold room.

Father Murphy looked at the ripped louvers with obvious displeasure and then stared up at the bells hanging from their cross-beams. Flynn said nothing but looked out into the Avenue. Everything appeared as before, but in some vague, undefined way it was not. He said to Mullins, "Can you tell?"

Mullins nodded. "When?"

"Soon." Flynn gave him two sheets of paper. "They've got to

blind the eyes that watch them before the rest of the attack can proceed. It's all there in the order of battle."

Mullins ran a flashlight over the neatly typed pages, only vaguely interested in how Flynn came to have them. "My name here is Towerman North. Sounds like a bloody English lord or something." He laughed, then read, "If Towerman North cannot be put out with sniper fire, then high explosive and/or gas grenades will be fired into bell room with launchers. Helicopter machine gunners will be called in if Towerman North is still not neutralized...." He looked up. "Neutralized...God, how they've butchered the language here...."

Flynn saw that Mullins's smile was strained. Flynn said, "Try to keep us informed on the field phone.... Keep the receiver off the cradle so we can hear what's happening...."

Mullins pictured himself thrashing around on the floor, small animal noises coming from his mouth into the open receiver.

Flynn went on, "If you survive the snipers, you'll survive the explosion and the fire."

"That barely compensates me for freezing half to death."

Flynn moved to the west opening and stared down at the green and gold harp flag, glazed with ice, and ran his hand over it. He looked out at Rockefeller Center. Hundreds of windows were still lit with bright fluorescent light, and figures passed back and forth. He took Mullins's field glasses and watched. A man was eating a sandwich. A young woman laughed on the telephone. Two uniformed policemen drank from cups. Someone with field glasses waved to him. He handed the glasses back. "I never hated them before..."

Mullins nodded. "It's so maddeningly commonplace...but I've gotten used to it." Mullins turned to Father Murphy. "So, it's that time, is it?"

"Apparently it is."

Mullins came close to Murphy. "Priests, doctors, and undertakers give me worse chills than ever a north wind did."

Father Murphy said nothing.

Mullins's eyes stared off at some indeterminate place and time. He spoke in a barely audible voice. "You're from the north, and you've heard the caoine—the funeral cry of the peasants. It's meant to imitate the wail of a chorus of banshees. The priests know this but never seem to object." He glanced at Murphy. "Irish priests are very tolerant of these things. Well, I've heard the actual banshees' wail, Father, whistling through the louvers all night... even when the wind was still."

"You've heard nothing of the sort."

Mullins laughed. "But I have. I *have*. And I've seen the coach-a-bower. Immense it was and black-polished, riding over these rooftops, a red coffin mounted atop it, and a headless Dullahan madly whipping a team of headless horses... and the coach drew past this window, Father, and the coachman threw in my face a basin of cold blood."

Murphy shook his head.

Mullins smiled. "Well...I fancy myself a poet, you see... and I've license to hear things...."

Murphy looked at him with some interest. "A poet..."

"Aye." A faint smile played over his blue lips, but his voice was melancholy. "And some time ago I fell in love with Leanhaun Shee, the Gaelic muse who gives us inspiration. She lives on mortal life, as you may know, in return for her favor. That's why Gaelic poets die young, Father. Do you believe that?"

Murphy said, "They die young because they eat badly, drink too much, and don't dress well in winter. They die young because unlike most civilized poets they run off to fight in ill-conceived wars. Do you want to make your confession?"

Mullins knelt and took the priest's hands.

Flynn climbed down to the room below. A strong gust of wind came through the shattered windows and picked up clouds of ancient dust that had been undisturbed for a century.

Father Murphy came down the ladder. "This"—he motioned toward the broken windows—"this was the only thing that bothered him.... I suppose I shouldn't tell you that...."

Flynn almost laughed. "Well, one man's prank may be another's most tormenting sin, and vice versa." He jumped onto the ladder and descended to the spiral stairs, Father Murphy following. They came out of the tower into the subdued lighting and warmer air of the choir loft.

As Father Murphy moved along the rail he felt that someone was watching him. He looked into the choir pews that rose upward from the keyboard, and let out a startled gasp.

A figure stood above them, motionless in the shadows, dressed in a hooded monk's robe. A hideous, inhuman face peered out from the recesses of the cowl, and it was several seconds before Father Murphy recognized it as the face of a leopard. Leary's voice came out of the immobile face. "Scare you, priest?"

Murphy regained his composure.

Flynn said, "A bit of greasepaint would have done, Mr. Leary."

Leary laughed, an odd shrill laugh for a man with so deep a voice.

Megan rose from between the pews, dressed in a black cassock, her face covered with swirls of dull-colored camouflage paint, expertly applied, thought Flynn, by another hand.

She moved into the center aisle, and Flynn saw that it was an altar boy's robe and that it revealed her bare forearms. He saw also that her legs and feet were bare. He studied Megan's face and found that the paint did not make her features so impenetrable that he could not see the same signs he had seen in Jean Kearney. He said, "With death so near, Megan, I can hardly blame you."

She thrust her chin out in a defiant gesture.

"Well, if nothing else good comes of this, you've at least found your perfect mate."

Father Murphy listened without understanding at first, then drew in a sharp breath.

Megan said to Flynn, "Is my brother dead?"

Flynn nodded.

Her face remained strangely impassive. She motioned toward Leary as she fixed her deep green eyes on Flynn. "We won't let you surrender. There will be no compromises."

Flynn's voice was sharp. "I don't need either of you to explain my duty or my destiny."

Leary spoke. "When are they coming? How are they coming?"

Flynn told them. He said to Leary, "This may be your richest harvest."

"Long after you're all dead," said Leary, "I'll still be shooting."

Flynn stared up into the dark eyes that were as fixed as the mask around them. "Then what?"

Leary said nothing.

"I find it difficult, Mr. Leary, to believe you're prepared to die with us."

Megan answered, "He's as dedicated as you are. If we have to die, we'll die here together."

Flynn thought not. He had an impulse to warn Megan, but he didn't know what to warn her about, and it didn't seem to matter any longer. He said to her, "Goodbye, Megan. Good luck."

She moved back into the pews, beside Leary.

Murphy looked at the two robed figures. They stared back at him. He suspected they would snuff out his life from their dark perch with no more hesitation than a man swatting an insect. Yet... "I have to ask."

Flynn said, "Go ahead—make a feel of yourself again."

Murphy turned to him. "You're the feel who brought them here."

Megan and Leary seemed to sense what the discussion was about. Megan called out in a mocking voice, "Come up here, Father. Let us tell you our sins." Leary laughed, and Megan went on, "Keep you up nights, Father, and turn your face as scarlet as a cardinal's hat. You've never heard sins like ours." She laughed, and Flynn realized he had never heard the sound of her laugh.

Flynn took the priest's arm again and moved him into the south tower without resistance. They climbed the stairs and passed through a door into the long southwest triforium.

George Sullivan stood at the parapet staring down at the north transept door. Sullivan's kilts and tunic, thought Flynn, were incongruous with his black automatic rifle and ammunition pouches. Flynn called to him, "Confessions are being heard, George."

Sullivan shook his head without looking up and lit a cigarette. His mind seemed to be elsewhere. Flynn nudged him and indicated the empty triforium across the transept. "You'll have to cover Gallagher's sectors."

Sullivan looked up. "Why doesn't Megan go up there?"

Flynn didn't answer the question, and Sullivan didn't press him. Flynn looked out at Abby Boland. These personal bonds had always been the Fenian strength— but also the weakness.

Sullivan also glanced across the nave. He spoke almost self-consciously. "I saw she made a confession to the priest.... These damned women of ours are so guilty and ashamed.... I feel somehow betrayed..."

Flynn said lightly, "You should have told him your version."

Sullivan started to reply but thought better of it. Flynn extended his hand, and Sullivan took it firmly.

Flynn and Father Murphy walked together back into the south tower and climbed the ten stories into the louvered room where Rory Devane stood in the dark, his face blackened and a large flak jacket hanging from his thin shoulders. Devane greeted them affably, but the sight of the priest wearing the purple stole was clearly not a welcome one.

Flynn said, "Sometime after 5:15 snipers will begin pouring bullets through all eight sides of this room."

"The room will be crowded, won't it?"

Flynn went on. "Yet you have to stay here and engage the helicopters. You have to put a rocket into the armored carrier."

Devane moved to a west-facing opening and looked down. Flynn briefed Devane, then said, "Father Murphy is interested in your soul."

Devane looked back at the priest. "I made my confession this morning—right here in Saint Pat's, as a matter of fact. Father Bertero, it was. I've done nothing in the meanwhile I need to confess."

Murphy said, "If you say an act of contrition, you can regain a state of grace." He turned and dropped into the ladder opening.

Flynn took Devane's hand. "Good luck to you. See you in Dublin."

"Aye, Brian, Kavanagh's Pub, or a place close by the back wall."

Flynn turned and dropped down the ladder, joining Murphy on the next level. The two men left the south tower and made their way across the choir loft. They entered the bell tower, and Flynn indicated the spiral staircase. "I have to speak with Mullins again."

Murphy was about to suggest that Flynn use the field phone, but something in Flynn's manner compelled him not to speak. They climbed until they reached a level where the stairs gave way to ladders somewhere below the first bell room where Mullins was.

Flynn looked at the large room they were in. The tower here was four-sided, with small milky-glass windows separated by thick stone. Mullins had knocked holes in some of the panes in the event he had to change his location, and Flynn pulled off a thick triangle of glass and looked at it, then looked at Murphy. "A great many people watching this on television are morbidly fascinated with the question of how this place will look afterward."

Murphy said, "I don't need any more revelations from you tonight. As a priest nothing shocks me any longer, and I still cling to my faith in humanity."

"That is truly a wonder. I'm in awe of that...."

Murphy saw that he was sincere. "I observed how your people cared for each other, and for you.... I've heard some of their confessions.... There are hopeful signs amid all this."

Flynn nodded. "And Hickey? Megan? Leary? And me?"

"May God have mercy on all your souls."

Flynn didn't respond.

Murphy said evenly, "If you're going to kill me, do it quickly."

Flynn's face looked puzzled, then almost hurt. "No...why would you think that?"

Murphy automatically mumbled an apology but immediately felt it was unnecessary under the circumstances.

Flynn reached out and grabbed his arm. "Listen, I've kept my promise to you and let you run around doing your duty. Now I want a promise from you."

Father Murphy looked at him cautiously.

Flynn said, "Promise me that after this is finished, you'll see that all my people are buried together in Glasnevin with Ireland's patriots. You can have a Catholic ceremony, if that'll make you feel better.... I know it won't be easy.... It may take you years to convince those swine in Dublin.... They never know who their heroes are until fifty years after they're dead."

The priest looked at him without comprehension, then said, "I . . . won't be alive to . . ."

Flynn took the priest's big hand firmly as though to shake it, but slapped the end of a handcuff on his wrist and locked the other end around the ladder's rail.

Father Murphy stared at his tethered wrist, then looked at Flynn. "Let me loose."

Flynn smiled weakly. "You weren't even supposed to be here. Now just keep your wits about you when the bullets start to fly. This tower should survive the explosion."

Murphy's face went red, and he shouted again. "You've no right to do this! Let me go!"

Flynn ignored him. He pulled a pistol from his belt and jumped down into the ladder opening. "It may happen that Megan, Hickey . . . someone may come for you. . . ." He laid the pistol on the floor. "Kill them." He dropped down the ladder. "Good luck, Padre."

Murphy bent down and grabbed the pistol with his free hand. He pointed it at the top of Flynn's head. "Stop!"

Flynn smiled as he continued his climb down. "*Erin go bragh*, Timothy Murphy." He laughed, and the sound echoed through the stone tower.

Murphy shouted after him. "Stop! Listen...you must save the others too.... Maureen...For God's sake, man, she loves you...." He stared down into the dark hole and watched Flynn disappear.

Father Murphy threw the pistol to the floor and tugged at the cuffs, then sank to his knees beside the ladder opening. Somewhere in the city a church bell tolled, then another joined in, and soon he could hear the sounds of a dozen different carillons playing the hymn "Be Not Afraid." He thought that every bell in the city must be ringing, perhaps every bell in the country, and he hoped the others could hear them, too, and know they were not alone. For the first time since it had all begun, Father Murphy felt tears forming in his eyes.

CHAPTER 55

Brian Flynn came down from the tower and walked up the nave aisle, his footsteps echoing from the polished marble. He turned into the ambulatory and approached John Hickey, who stood on the raised platform of the chancel organ and watched him approach. Flynn walked deliberately up the steps and stood facing Hickey. After a short silence Hickey said, "It's 4:59. You let Murphy waste valuable time trying to save already damned souls. Does everyone know their orders at least?"

"Has Schroeder called?"

"No—that means either nothing is new or something is wrong." Hickey took out his pipe and filled it. "All night I've worried that my tobacco would run out before my life. It really bothered me.... A man shouldn't have to scrimp on his tobacco before he dies." He struck a match, and it sounded inordinately loud in the stillness. He drew deeply on his pipe and said, "Well, where's the priest?"

Flynn motioned vaguely toward the towers. "We've no grudge against him.... He shouldn't pay the price for being in the wrong place at the wrong time."

"Why not? That's why the rest of us are going to die." He flashed a look of feigned enlightenment. "Ah, I suppose playing God means you have to save a life for every ten score you take."

Flynn said, "Who *are* you?"

Hickey smiled with unrestrained glee. "Have I frightened you, lad? Don't be frightened, then. I'm just an old man who amuses himself by playing on people's fears and superstitions." Hickey stepped over the body of Pedar Fitzgerald and came closer to Flynn. He sucked noisily on his pipe, a pensive look on his face. "You know, lad, I've had more fun since I had myself buried than ever I did before I was interred. You get a lot of mileage out of resurrection—someone made a whole religion out of it once." He jerked a thumb toward the crucifix atop the altar and laughed again.

Flynn felt the old man's breath against his face. He put his right hand on the organ console. "Do you know anything about this ring?"

Hickey didn't look at it. "I know what you believe it is."

"And what is it *really*?"

"A ring, made of bronze."

Flynn slipped it from his finger and held it in his open palm. "Then I've held it too long. Take it."

Hickey shrugged and reached for it.

Flynn closed his hand and stared at Hickey.

Hickey's eyes narrowed into dark slits. "So, you want to know who I am and how I got here?" Hickey looked into the glowing bowl of his pipe with exaggerated interest. "I can tell you I'm a ghost, a thevshi, come from the grave to retrieve the ring and bring about your destruction and the destruction of the new Fenians—to perpetuate this strife into the next generation. There's the proper Celtic explanation you're looking for to make you feel better about your fears." He looked directly into Flynn's eyes. "But I can also tell you the truth, which is far more frightening. I'm *alive*. Your own dark soul imagined the thevshi, as it imagines the banshee, and the pooka, and the Far Darrig, and all the nightmarish creatures that walk the dark landscape of your mind and make you huddle around flickering peat fires. Aye, Brian, that's a fright, because you can't find sanctuary from those monsters you carry within you."

Flynn stared at him, examining the furrowed white face. Suddenly Hickey's eyes became benign, sparkling, and his mouth curled up in a good-natured smile. Hickey said, "You see?"

Flynn said. "Yes, I see. I see that you're a creature who draws strength from other men's weaknesses. It's my fault you're here, and it's my responsibility to see that you do no further harm."

"The harm is done. Had you stood up to me instead of wallowing in self-pity, you could have fulfilled your responsibility to your people, not to mention your own destiny."

Flynn stared at Hickey. "No matter what happens, I'll see you don't leave here alive." Flynn turned and walked to the sanctuary. He stood before the high throne. "Cardinal, the police will attack anytime after 5:15. Father Murphy is in a relatively safe place—we are not, and we will most probably die."

Flynn watched the Cardinal's face for a show of emotion, but there was none. He went on, "I want you to know that the people out there share in the responsibility for this. Like me they are vain, egotistical, and flawed. A rather sorry lot for products of so many thousands of years of Judeo-Christian love and charity, wouldn't you say?"

The Cardinal leaned forward in the throne. "That's a question for people who are looking for a path to take them through life. Your life is over, and you'll have all your answers very soon. Use the minutes left to you to speak to her." He nodded toward Maureen.

Flynn was momentarily taken aback. It was perhaps the last reply he expected from a priest. He stepped away from the throne, turned, and crossed the sanctuary.

Maureen and Baxter remained seated, cuffed together in the first pew. Without a word Flynn unlocked the handcuffs, then spoke in a distant voice. "I'd like to put you both in a less exposed place, but that isn't acceptable to some of the others. However, when the shooting starts, you won't be executed, because we may repel them and we'll need you again." He looked at his watch and continued in a dispassionate voice. "Sometime after 5:15 you'll see all the doors explode, followed by police rushing in. I know you are both capable of keeping a cool head. Dive between the pews behind you. As 6:03 approaches...if you're still alive...get out of this area no matter what's happening around you. That's all I can do for you."

Maureen stood and looked at him closely. "No one asked you to do anything for us. If you want to do something for everyone, get down those stairs right now and open the gates to them. Then go into the pulpit and tell your people it's finished. No one will stop you, Brian. I think they're waiting to hear from you."

"When they open the gates of Long Kesh, I'll open the gates here."

Her voice became angry. "The keys to the jails of Ulster are *not* in America, or in London or Dublin. They are in Ulster. Give me a year in Belfast and Londonderry, and I'll get more people out of jail than you've ever had released with your kidnappings, raids, assassinations—"

Flynn laughed. "A *year*? You wouldn't last a year. If the Catholics didn't get you, Maureen, the Prods would."

She drew a shallow breath and brought her voice under control. "Very well...it's not worth going into that again. But you've no right to con these people into dying. Your voice can break the spell of death that hangs over this place. Go on! Do it! Now!" She swung and slapped him on the face.

Baxter moved off to one side and looked away.

Flynn pulled Maureen to him and said, "All night everyone's been very good about giving me advice. It's odd, isn't it, how people don't pay much attention to you until you've set a time bomb ticking under them?" He released her arms. "You, for instance, walked out on me four years ago without much advice for my future. All the things you've said to me tonight could have been said then."

She glanced at Baxter and felt curiously uncomfortable that he was hearing all of this. She spoke in a low voice. "I said all I had to say then. You weren't listening."

· "You weren't speaking so loudly, either."

Flynn turned to Baxter. "And you, Harry." He moved closer to Baxter. "Major Bartholomew Martin needed a dead Englishman in here, and you're it."

Baxter considered this and accepted it in a very short time. "Yes...he's a sick man...an obsessed man. I suppose I always suspected..."

Flynn looked at his watch. "Excuse me, I have to speak to my people." He turned and walked toward the pulpit.

Maureen came up behind him and put her hand on his shoulder, turning him toward her. "Damn it, aren't you at least going to say good-bye?"

Flynn's face reddened, and he seemed to lose his composure, then cleared his throat. "I'm sorry...I didn't think you...Well—good-bye, then.... We won't speak again, will we? Good luck..." He hesitated, then leaned toward her but suddenly straightened up again.

She started to say something, but Gallagher's deep voice called out from the sacristy stairs, "Brian! Burke's here to see you!"

Flynn looked at his watch with some surprise.

Hickey called out from the organ, "It's a trap!"

Flynn hesitated, then looked at Maureen. She nodded slightly. He held her eyes for a moment and said, "Still trusting." He smiled and walked quickly around the altar and descended the stairs.

Burke stood at the gate in his shirt-sleeves, his shoulder holster empty and his hands in his pants pockets.

Flynn approached without caution and stood close to the gate. "Well?" Burke didn't answer, and Flynn spoke curtly. "You're not going to ask me to give up or— "

"No."

Flynn called up to Gallagher, "Take a break." He turned to Burke. "Are you here to kill me?"

Burke took his hands out of his pockets and rested them on the bars. "There's an implied white flag here, isn't there? Do you think I'd kill you like that?"

"You should. You should always kill the other side's commander when you have a chance. If you were Bellini, I'd kill you."

"There're still rules."

"Yes, I just gave you one."

A few seconds passed in silence, then Flynn said, "What do you want?"

"I just wanted to say I have no personal animosity toward you."

Flynn smiled. "Well, I knew that. I could see that. And I've none toward you, Burke. That's the hell of it, isn't it? I've no personal hatred of your people, and most of them have none toward me."

"Then why are we here?"

"We're here because in 1154 Adrian the Fourth gave Henry the Second of England permission to bring his army to Ireland. We're here because the Red Bus to Clady passes Whitehorn Abbey. That's why I'm here. Why are you here?"

"I was on duty at five o'clock."

Flynn smiled, then said, "Well, that's damned little reason to die. I'm releasing you from your promise to join the attack. Perhaps in exchange you'll decide to kill Martin. Martin set up poor Harry to be here—did you figure that out?"

Burke's face was impassive.

Flynn glanced at his watch. 5:04. Something was wrong. "Hadn't you better go?"

"If you like. Also, if you'd like, I'll stay on the phone with you until 6:03."

Flynn looked at Burke closely. "I want to speak to Schroeder. Send him down here."

"That's not possible."

"I want to speak to him! Now!"

Burke answered, "No one is intimidated by your threats anymore. Least of all Bert Schroeder." He exhaled a deep sigh. "Captain Schroeder put the muzzle of his gun in his mouth…"

Flynn grabbed Burke's arm. "You're lying! I want to see his body."

Burke pulled away and walked down into the sacristy, then looked back toward Flynn. "I don't know what pushed him off the edge, but I know that somehow you're to blame." Burke stood at the corridor opening. Barely three feet away stood a masked ESD man with a Browning automatic shotgun. Burke edged toward the opening and looked back at Flynn. He seemed to vacillate, then said, "Goodbye."

Flynn nodded. "I'm glad we met."

CHAPTER 56

Bellini stood close to the conference table in the press room, his eyes focused on four long, unrolled sheets of blueprints, their corners weighted with coffee cups, ashtrays, and grenade canisters. Huddled around him were his squad leaders. The first three blueprints showed the basement, the main floor, and the upper levels. The fourth was a cutaway drawing of a side view of the Cathedral. Now that they were all in front of him, Bellini was unimpressed.

Gordon Stillway was seated in front of the blueprints, rapidly explaining the preliminary details. Bellini's brow was creased. He looked around to see if anyone was showing signs of enlightenment. All he could read in the blackened, sweaty faces was impatience, fatigue, and annoyance at the postponement.

Burke opened the door and came into the room. Bellini glanced up and gave him a look that didn't convey much gratitude or optimism. Burke saw Langley standing by the rear wall and joined him. They stood side by side and watched the scene at the table for a few seconds, then Burke spoke without looking away from the conference table. "Feeling better?"

Langley's tone was cool. "I've never felt better in my life."

"Me too." He looked at the spot on the floor where Schroeder had fallen. "How's Bert?"

Langley said, "A police doctor is treating him for physical exhaustion." Burke nodded.

Langley let a few seconds go by. "Did Flynn buy it?"

Burke said, "His next move may be to threaten to kill a hostage if we don't show him Schroeder's body... with the back of his head blown away."

Langley tapped the pocket that held Schroeder's service revolver. "Well... it's important that Flynn believes the plans he has are the plans Bellini will use...." He inclined his head toward the squad leaders. "Lots of lives depend on that...."

Burke changed the subject. "What are you doing about arresting Martin?"

Langley shook his head. "First of all, he's disappeared again. He's good at that. Secondly, I checked with the State Department joker, Sheridan, and Martin has diplomatic immunity, but they'll consider expelling—"

"I don't want him expelled."

Langley glanced at him. "Well, it doesn't matter because I also spoke with our FBI buddy, Hogan, and he says Martin has happily expelled himself—"

"He's gone?"

"Not yet, of course. Not before the show ends. He's booked on a Bermuda flight out of Kennedy—"

"What time?"

Langley gave him a sidelong glance. "Departs at 7:35. Breakfast at the Southampton Princess—forget it, Burke."

"Okay."

Langley watched the people at the conference table for a minute, then said, "Also, our CIA colleague, Kruger, says it's their show. Nobody wants you poking around. Okay?"

"Fine with me. Art Forgery Squad, you say?"

Langley nodded. "Yeah, I know a guy in it. It's the biggest fuck-off job anyone ever invented."

Burke made appropriate signs of attentiveness as Langley painted an idyllic picture of life in the Art Forgery Squad, but his mind was on something else.

Gordon Stillway concluded his preliminary description and said, "Now, tell me again what precisely it is you want to know?"

Bellini glanced at the wall clock: 5:09. He drew a deep breath. "I want to know how to get into Saint Patrick's Cathedral without using the front door."

Gordon Stillway spoke and answered questions, and the mood of the ESD squad leaders went from pessimism to wary optimism.

Bellini glanced at the bomb disposal people. Their lieutenant, Wendy Peterson, the only woman present in the room, leaned closer to the blueprint of the basement and pulled her long blond hair away from her face. Bellini watched the woman's cold blue eyes scanning the diagram. There were seventeen men, one woman, and two dogs, Brandy and Sally, in the Bomb Squad, and Bellini knew beyond a doubt that they were all certifiable lunatics, including the dogs.

Lieutenant Peterson turned to Stillway. Her voice was low, almost a whisper, which was a sort of trademark of this unit, thought Bellini. Peterson said, "If you wanted to plant bombs—let's assume you didn't have a great deal of explosives with you but you were looking for maximum effect—"

Stillway marked two X's on the blueprints. "Here and here. The two big columns flanking the sacristy stairs." He paused reflectively and said, "About the time I was six years old they blasted the stairs through the foundation here and weakened the bedrock on which these columns sit. This is recorded information for anyone who cares to look it up, including the IRA."

Wendy Peterson nodded.

Stillway looked at her curiously. "Are you a bomb disposal person? What kind of job is that for a woman?"

She said, "I do a lot of needlepoint."

Stillway considered the statement for a second, then continued, "These columns are big, but with the type of explosives they have today, as you know, a demolition expert could bring them down, and half the Cathedral goes down with them... and God help you all if you're in there." He stared at Lieutenant Peterson.

Wendy Peterson said, "I'm not interested in the explosion."

Stillway again considered this obscure response and saw her meaning. He said, "But *I* am. There are not many like me around to rebuild the place...." He let his voice trail off.

Someone asked the question that had been on many people's minds all night. "*Can* it be rebuilt?"

Stillway nodded. "Yes, but it would probably look like the First Supernatural Bank."

A few men laughed, but the laughter died away quickly.

Stillway turned his attention back to the basement plans and detailed a few other idiosyncrasies on the blueprints.

Bellini rubbed the stubble on his chin as he listened. He interrupted: "Mr. Stillway, if we were to bring an armored personnel carrier—weighing about ten tons...give or take a ton—up the front steps, through the main doors—"

Stillway sat up. "*What?* Those doors are invaluable—"

"Could the floor hold the weight?"

Stillway tried to calm himself and thought a moment, then said reluctantly, "If you have to do something so insane...destructive...Ten tons? Yes, according to the specs the floor will hold the weight...but there's always some question, isn't there?"

Bellini nodded. "Yeah.... One other thing...they said—these Fenians said— they were going to set fire to the Cathedral. We have reason to believe it may be the attic.... Is that possible...?"

"Why not?"

"Well...it looks pretty solid to me—"

"Solid *wood.*" He shook his head. "What bastards..." Stillway suddenly stood. "Gentlemen—Miss—" He moved through the circle of people. "Excuse me if I don't stay to listen to you work out the details—I'm not feeling so well—but I'll be in the next room if you need me." He turned and left.

The ESD squad leaders began talking among themselves. The Bomb Squad people moved to the far end of the room, and Bellini watched them huddled around Peterson. Their faces, he noted, were always expressionless, their eyes vacant. He looked at his watch. 5:15. He would need fifteen to twenty minutes to modify the attack plan. It was going to be close, but the plan that was forming in his mind was much cleaner, less likely to become a massacre. He stepped away from the squad leaders and walked up to Burke and Langley. He hesitated a second, then said, "Thanks for Stillway. Good work."

Langley answered, "Anytime, Joe—excuse me—*Inspector.* You call, we deliver— architects, lawyers, hit men, pizza—"

Burke interrupted. "Do you feel better about this?"

Bellini nodded. "I'll take fewer casualties, the Cathedral has a fifty-fifty chance, but the hostages are still dead." He paused, then said, "Do you think there's any way to call off Logan's armored cavalry charge up Fifth Avenue?"

Langley shook his head. "Governor Doyle really has his heart set on that. Think of the armored car as one of those sound trucks they use in an election campaign."

Bellini found a cigar stub in his pocket and lit it, then

looked at his watch again. "Flynn expected to be hit soon after 5:15, and he's probably sweating it out right now. Picture that scene—good, *good.* I hope the motherfucker is having the worst time of his fucking life."

Langley said, "If he's not now, I expect he will be shortly."

"Yeah. Cocksucker." Bellini's mouth turned up in a vicious grin, and his eyes narrowed like little pig slits. "I hope he gets gut-shot and dies slow. I hope he pukes blood and acid and bile, until he—"

Langley held up his hand. "Please."

Bellini spun around and looked at Burke. "I can't believe Schroeder *told him*— "

Burke cut him off. "I never said that. I said I found the architect, and you should revise your attack. Captain Schroeder suffered a physical collapse. Right?"

Bellini laughed. "Of course he collapsed. I hit him in the face. What did you expect him to do—dance?" Bellini's expression became hard, and he made a contemptuous noise. "That cocksucker sold me out. He could have gotten a hundred men killed."

Burke said, "You forget about Schroeder, and I'll forget I heard you plant the idea in your squad leaders' heads about making a clean sweep in the Cathedral."

Bellini stayed quiet a minute, then said, "The attack is not going to be the way Schroeder told Flynn.... What's going to happen to his daughter?"

Langley took a file photo of Dan Morgan out of his pocket and laid it on a bridge table beside a snapshot of Terri O'Neal that he'd taken from Schroeder's wallet. "This man will murder her." He pointed to Terri O'Neal's smiling face.

The telephone rang, and Bellini looked at it. He said to the two men, "That's my buddy, Murray Kline. His Honor to you."

He picked up the extension on the bridge table. "Gestapo Head-quarters, Joe speaking."

There was a stammer on the other end, then the Mayor's voice came on, agitated. "Joe, what time are you moving out?"

Bellini felt a familiar heart-flutter at the sound of the military expression. Never again after today did he want to hear those words.

"Joe?"

"Yeah...well, the architect was worth the wait—"

"Good. Very good. What *time* are you jumping off?"

Jumping off. His heart gave another leap, and he felt like there was ice water in his stomach. "About 5:35—give or take."

"Can't you move it up?"

Bellini's voice had an insolent tone. "No!"

"I told you there are people trying to stop this rescue—"

"I don't get involved in politics."

Roberta Spiegel's voice came on the line. "Okay, forget the fucking politicians. The bombs, Bellini—"

"Call me Joe."

"You're leaving the Bomb Squad damned little time to find and defuse the goddamned *bombs,* Captain."

"Inspector!"

"Listen, you—"

"You listen, Spiegel—why don't you crawl around with the fucking dogs and help them sniff out the bombs? Brandy, Sally, and Robbie." He turned to Burke and Langley and smiled, a look of triumph on his face.

Langley winced.

Bellini continued before she could recover, knowing there was no reason to stop now. "They're short on dogs since your last fucking budget cuts, and they could use the help. You have your big nose into everything else."

There was a long silence on the line, then Spiegel laughed. "All right, you bastard, you can say what you want now, but later—"

"Yeah, later. I'd give my left arm for a guaranteed later. We move at 5:35. That's not negotiable—"

"Is Inspector Langley there?"

"Hold on." He covered the mouthpiece. "You want to talk to the Dragon Lady?" Langley's face flushed, and he hesitated before taking the phone from Bellini, who moved back to the conference table. "Langley here."

Spiegel said, "Do you know where Schroeder is? His backup negotiator can't locate him."

Langley said, "He's collapsed."

"Collapsed?"

"Yeah, you know, like fell down, passed out."

"Oh...well, get him inflated again and get him here to the state offices in Rockefeller Center. He has to do his hero act later."

"I thought he was supposed to be the fall guy."

She said, "No, you're a little behind on this.... We've rethought that. He's the hero now no matter what happens. He's got lots of good press contacts."

"Who's the fall guy?"

She went on, "You see, there are no such things as victory or defeat anymore— there are only public relations problems—"

"Who's the fall guy?"

Spiegel said, "That's you. You won't be alone, though...and you'll come out of it all right. I'll see to that."

Langley didn't answer.

She said, "Listen, Philip, I think you should be here during the assault."

Langley's eyebrows went up at the use of his first name. He

noted that her voice was pleasant, almost demure. "Rescue, You have to call it a rescue, Roberta." He winked at Burke.

Spiegel's voice was a little sharper. "Whatever. We—*I* want you up here."

"I think I'll stay down here."

"You get your ass up here in five minutes."

He glanced at Burke. "All right." He hung up and stared down at the phone. "This has been a screwy night."

"Full moon," said Burke. There was a lengthy silence, then Langley said, "Are you going in with Bellini?"

Burke lit a cigarette. "I think I should... to tidy up those loose ends... get hold of any notes the Fenians might have kept. There are secrets in that place... mysteries, as the Major said. And before Bellini starts blowing heads off... or the place goes up in smoke..."

Langley said, "Do what you have to do...." He forced a smile. "Do you want to change places with me and go hold Spiegel's hand?"

"No thanks."

Langley glanced nervously at his watch. "Okay... listen, tell Bellini to keep Schroeder locked in that room. At dawn we'll come for Schroeder and parade him past the cameras like an Olympic hero. Schroeder's in, Langley's out."

Burke nodded, then said, "That mounted cop... Betty Foster... God, it seems so long ago.... Anyway, make sure she gets something out of this... and if I don't get a chance to thank her later... you can..."

"I'll take care of it." He shook his head. "Screwy night." He moved toward the door, then turned back. "Here's another one for you to work out when you get in there. We lifted the fingerprints off the glass that Hickey used." He nodded toward the chair Hickey had sat in. "The prints were smudged, but Albany and the FBI say it's ninety percent certain it was Hickey, and we've got a few visual identifications from people who saw him on TV—"

Burke nodded. "That clears that up—"

"Not quite. The Jersey City medical examiner did a dental check on the remains they exhumed and..." He looked at Burke. "Spooky... really spooky..."

Burke said quickly, "Come off it, Langley."

Langley laughed. "Just kidding. The coffin was filled with dirt, and there was a note in there in Hickey's handwriting. I'll tell you what it said later." He smiled and opened the door. "Betty Foster, right? See you later, Patrick." He closed the door behind him.

Burke looked across the room. More than a dozen ESD leaders, completely clad in black, grouped in a semicircle around the table. Above them a wall clock ticked off the minutes. As he watched they all straightened up, almost in unison, like a football team out of a huddle, and began filing out the door. Bellini stayed behind, occupied with some detail. Burke stared at his black, hulking figure in the brightly lit room and was reminded of a dark rain cloud in a sunny sky.

Burke walked over to the conference table and pulled on a black turtleneck sweater, then slipped back into his flak jacket. He adjusted the green carnation he'd gotten from an ESD man who had passed out a basketful of them. Burke looked down at the blueprints and read the notations of squad assignments hastily scrawled across them. He said to Bellini, "Where's the safest place I can be during the attack?"

Bellini thought a moment, then said, "Los Angeles."

CHAPTER 57

Brian Flynn stood in the high pulpit, a full story above the main floor. He looked out at the Cathedral spread before him, then spoke into the microphone. "Lights."

The lights began to go out in sections: the sanctuary, ambulatory, and Lady Chapel lights first, the switches pulled by Hickey; then the lights in the four triforia controlled by Sullivan, followed by the choir-loft lights, and finally the huge hanging chandeliers over the nave, extinguished from the electrical panels in the loft. The vestibules, side altars, and bookstore darkened last as Hickey moved through the Cathedral pulling the remaining switches.

A few small lights still burned, Flynn noticed. Lights whose switches were probably located outside the Cathedral. Hickey and the others smashed the ones that were accessible, the sound of breaking glass filling the quiet spaces.

Flynn nodded. The beginning of the attack would be signaled when the last lights suddenly went out, a result of the police pulling the main switch in the rectory basement. The police would expect a dark Cathedral where their infrared scopes would give them an overwhelming advantage. But Flynn had no intention of letting them have such an advantage, so every votive candle, hundreds and hundreds of them, had been lit, and they shimmered in the surrounding blackness, an offering of sorts, he reflected, an ancient comfort against the terrors of the dark and a source of light the police could not extinguish. Also, at intervals throughout the Cathedral, large phosphorus flares were placed to provide additional illumination and to cause the police infrared scopes to white out. Captain Joe Bellini, Flynn thought, had a surprise in store for him.

Flynn placed his hands on the cool Carrara marble of the pulpit balustrade and blinked to adjust his eyes to the dim light as he examined the vast interior. Flickering shadows played off the walls and columns, but the ceiling was obscure. It was easy to imagine there was no roof, that the towering columns had been relieved of their burden and that overhead was only the night sky—an illusion that would be reality on the following evening.

The long black galleries of the triforia above, dark and impenetrable in the best of light, were nearly invisible now, and the only sense he had of anything being up there was the sound of rifles scraping against stone.

The choir loft was a vast expanse of blackness, totally shrouded from the murky light below as if a curtain had been drawn across the rail; but Flynn could feel the two dark presences up there more strongly than when he had seen them, as though they basked in blackness and flourished in the dark.

Flynn drew a long breath through his nostrils. The burning phosphorus exuded an overpowering, pungent smell that seemed to alter the very nature of the Cathedral. Gone was that strange musky odor, that mixture of stale incense, tallow, and something else that was indefinable, which he had labeled the Roman Catholic smell, the smell that never changed from church to church and that evoked mixed memories of childhood. *Gone, finally gone,* he thought. *Driven out.* And he was inordinately pleased with this, as though he'd won a theological argument with a bishop.

He lowered his eyes and looked over the flares and the dozens of racks of votive candles. The light seemed less comforting now, the candles burning in their red or blue glass like brimstone around the altars, and the brilliant white phosphorus like the leaping flames of hell. And the saints on their altars, he noticed, were moving, gyrating in obscene little dances, the beatific expressions on their white faces suddenly revealing a lewdness that he had always suspected was there.

But the most remarkable metamorphosis was in the windows, which seemed to hang in black space, making them appear twice their actual size, rising to dizzying heights so that if you looked up at them you actually experienced some vertigo. And above the soaring choir loft, atop the thousands of unseen brass pipes of the organ, sat the round rose window, which had become a dark blue swirling vortex that would suck you out of this netherworld of shadows and spirits—which was only, after all, the anteroom of hell—suck you, finally and irretrievably, into hell itself.

Flynn adjusted the microphone and spoke. He doubted his voice would break the spell of death, as she had said, and in any case he had the opposite purpose. "Ladies and gentlemen...brothers and sisters..." He looked at his watch. 5:14. "The time, as you know, has come. Stay alert...it won't be much longer now." He drew a short breath, which carried out through the speakers. "It's been my great honor to have been your leader.... I want to assure you we'll meet again, if not in Dublin, then in a place of light, the land beyond the Western Sea, whatever name it goes by...because whatever God controls our ultimate destiny cannot deny our earthly bond to one another, our dedication to our people...." He felt his voice wavering. "Don't be afraid." He turned off the microphone.

All eyes went from him to the doors. Rockets and rifles were at the ready, and gas masks hung loosely over chests where hearts beat wildly.

John Hickey stood below the pulpit and threw a rocket tube, rifle, and gas mask to Flynn. Hickey called out in a voice with no trace of fear, "Brian, I'm afraid this is goodbye, lad. It's been a pleasure, and I'm sure we'll meet again in a place of incredible light, not to mention heat." He laughed and moved off into the half-shadows of the sanctuary.

Flynn slung the rifle across his chest, then broke the seal on the rocket and extended the tube, aiming it at the center vestibule.

His eyes became misty, from the phosphorus, he thought, and they went out of focus, the clear plastic aiming sight of the rocket acting as a prism in the dim candlelight. Colors leaped all around the deathly still spaces before him like fireworks seen at a great distance, or like those phantom battles fought in his worst silent nightmares. And there was no sound here either but the steady ticking of his watch near his ear, the rushing of blood in his head, and the faraway pounding of his chest.

He tried to conjure up faces, people he had known from the past, parents, relatives, friends, and enemies, but no images seemed to last more than a second. Instead, an unexpected scene flashed into his consciousness and stayed there: Whitehorn Abbey's subbasement, Father Donnelly talking expansively, Maureen pouring tea, himself examining the ring. They were all speaking, but he could not hear the voices, and the movements were slow, as if they had all the time in the world. He recognized the imagery, understood that this scene represented the last time he was even moderately happy and at peace.

John Hickey stood before the Cardinal's throne and bowed. "Your Eminence, I have an overwhelming desire," he said matter-of-factly, "to slit your shriveled white throat from ear to ear, then step back and watch your blood run onto your scarlet robe and over that obscene thing hanging around your neck."

The Cardinal suddenly reached out and touched Hickey's cheek.

Hickey drew back quickly and made a noise that sounded like a startled yelp. He recovered and jumped back onto the step, pulled the Cardinal down from his throne, and pushed him roughly toward the sacristy stairs.

They descended the steps, and Hickey paused at the landing where Gallagher knelt just inside the doors of the crypt. "Here's company for you, Frank." Hickey prodded the Cardinal down the remaining stairs, pushing him against the gates so that he faced into the sacristy. He extended the Cardinal's right arm and handcuffed his wrist to the bars.

Hickey said, "Here's a new logo for your church, Your Eminence. Been a good while since they've come up with a new one." He spoke as he cuffed the other extended arm go a bar. "We've had Christ on the cross, Saint Peter crucified upside down, Andrew crucified on an X cross, and now we've got you hanging on the sacristy gates of Saint Patrick's. Lord, that's a natural. Sell a million icons."

The Cardinal turned his head toward Hickey. "The Church has survived ten thousand like you," he said impassively, "and will survive you, and grow stronger precisely because there are people like you among us."

"Is that a fact?" Hickey balled his hand into a fist but was aware that Gallagher had come up behind him. He turned and led Gallagher by the arm back to the open crypt doors. "Stay here. Don't speak to him and don't listen to him."

Gallagher stared down the steps. The Cardinal's outstretched arms and red robes covered half the grillwork. Gallagher felt a constriction in his stomach; he looked back at Hickey but was not able to hold his stare. Gallagher turned away and nodded.

Hickey took the staircase that brought him up to the right of the altar and approached Maureen and Baxter. They rose as he drew near.

Hickey indicated two gas masks that lay on the length of the pew that separated the two people. "Put those on at the first sign of gas. If there's one thing I can't stand, it's the sight of a woman vomiting—reminds me of my first trip to Dublin— drunken whores ducking into alleys and getting sick. Never forgot that."

Maureen and Baxter stayed silent. Hickey went on, "It may interest you to know that the plan of this attack was sold to us at a low price, and the plan doesn't provide much for your rescue or the saving of this Cathedral."

Baxter said, "As long as it provides for your death, it's a fine plan."

Hickey turned to Baxter. "You're a vindictive bastard. I'll bet you'd like to bash in another young Irishman's throat, now you've got the hang of it and the taste for it."

"You're the most evil, twisted man I've ever met." Baxter's voice was barely under control.

Hickey winked at him. "Now you're talking." He turned his attention to Maureen. "Don't let Megan or Leary shoot you, lass. Take cover between these pews and lie still in the dark. Very still. Here's your watch back, my love. Look at it as the bullets are whistling over your head. Keep checking it as you stare up at the ceiling. Sometime between 6:03 and 6:04 you'll hear a noise, and the floor will bounce ever so slightly beneath your lovely rump, and the columns will start to tremble. Out of the darkness, way up there, you will see great sections of ceiling falling toward you, end over end, as in slow motion, right onto your pretty face. And remember, lass, your last thoughts while you're being crushed to death should be of Brian—or Harry...any man will do, I suppose." He laughed as he turned away and walked toward the bronze plate on the floor. He bent over and lifted the plate.

Maureen called after him: "My last thought will be that God should have mercy on all our souls...and that your soul, John Hickey, should finally rest in peace."

Hickey threw her a kiss, then dropped down the ladder, drawing the bronze plate closed over him.

Maureen sat back on the pew. Baxter stood a moment, then moved toward her. She looked up at him and put out her hand. Baxter took it and sat close beside her so that their bodies touched. He looked around at the flickering shadows. "I tried to picture how this would end...but *this*..."

"Nothing is ever as you expect it to be.... I never expected you to be..."

Baxter held her more tightly. "I'm frightened."

"Me too." She thought a moment, then smiled. "But we made it, you know. We never gave them an inch."

He smiled in return. "No, we never did, did we?"

Flynn peered into the darkness to his right and stared at the empty throne, then looked out through the carved wooden screen to where the chancel organ keyboard stood on its platform beside the sanctuary. A candle was lit on the organ console, and for a moment he thought John Hickey was sitting at the keys. He blinked, and an involuntary noise rose in his throat. Pedar Fitzgerald sat at the organ, his hands poised over the keys, his body upright but tilted slightly back. His face was raised toward the ceiling as if he were about to burst into song.

Flynn could make out the tracheal tube still protruding from his mouth, the white dead skin, and the open eyes that looked alive as the flame of the candle danced in them. "Hickey," he said softly to himself, "Hickey, you unspeakable, filthy, obscene..." He glanced up into the choir loft but could not see Megan, and he concentrated again on the front doors.

5:20 came, then 5:25—

Flynn looked around the column to his rear and saw Maureen and Baxter huddled together. He watched them briefly, then turned back to the vestibule.

5:30.

A tension hung in the still, cold air of the Cathedral, a tension so palpable it could be heard in the steady beating chests, felt on the sweaty brows, tasted in the mouth as bile, seen in the dancing lights, and smelled in the stench of burning phosphorous.

5:35 came, and the thought began to take hold in the minds of the people in the Cathedral that it was already too late to mount an attack that would serve any purpose.

In the long southwest triforium George Sullivan put down his rifle and picked up his bagpipes. He tucked the bag under his arm, adjusted the three drone pipes over his shoulder, and put his fingers on the eight-holed chanter, and then put his mouth to the blowpipe. Against all orders and against all reason he began to play. The slow, haunting melody of "Amazing Grace" floated from the chanter and hummed from the drone pipes into the candlelit silence.

There was a very slight, almost imperceptible lessening of tension, a relaxing of vigilance, coupled with the most primitive of beliefs that if you anticipated something terrible, imagined it in the most minute detail, it would not happen.

BOOK V

Assault

For the great Gaels of Ireland
Are the men that God made mad,
For all their wars are merry,
And all their songs are sad.

G. K. Chesterton

B ellini stood at the open door of the small elevator in the basement below the Archbishop's sacristy. An ESD man stood on the elevator roof and shone a handheld spotlight up the long shaft. The shaft began as brick, but at a level above the main floor it was wood-walled and seemed to continue up, as Stillway had pointed out, to a level that would bring it through the triforium's attic.

Bellini called softly, "How's it look?"

The ESD man replied, "We'll see." He took a tension clamp from a utility pouch, screwed it tightly to the elevator cable at hip level, and then stepped onto it and tested its holding strength. He screwed on another and stepped up to it. Step by step, very quickly now, he began working his way up the shaft to the triforium level eight stories above.

Bellini looked back into the curving corridor behind him. The First ESD Assault Squad stood silently, laden with equipment and armed with silenced pistols and rifles that were fitted with infrared scopes.

On the floor just outside the elevator a communications man sat in front of a small field-phone switchboard that was connected by wire to the remaining ESD Assault Squads and to the state office in Rockefeller Center. Bellini said to the man,

"When the shit hits the fan, intersquad communication takes priority over His Honor and the Commissioner.... In fact, I don't want to hear from them unless it's to tell us to pull out."

The commo man nodded.

Burke came down the corridor. His face was smeared with greasepaint, and he was screwing a big silencer onto the barrel of an automatic pistol.

Bellini watched him. "This don't look like Los Angeles, does it, Burke?"

Burke stuck the automatic in his belt. "Let's go, Bellini."

Bellini shrugged. He climbed the stepladder and stood on the roof of the elevator, and Burke came up beside him in the narrow shaft. Bellini shone his light up the wall until it rested on the oak door that opened on the Archbishop's sacristy twenty feet above. He said to Burke in a quiet voice, "If there's a Fenian standing there with a submachine gun and he hears us climbing, there'll be a waterfall of blood and bodies dropping back on this elevator."

Burke shifted Bellini's light farther up and picked out the dim outline of the climbing man, now about one hundred feet up the shaft. "Or there may be an ambush waiting up there at the top."

Bellini nodded. "Looked good on paper." He shut off his light. "You got about one minute to stop being all asshole and get out of here."

"Okay."

Bellini glanced up at the dark shaft. "I wonder...I wonder if that door or any door in this place is mined?" Bellini was speaking nervously now. "Remember in the army...all the phony minefield signs? All the other bullshit psy-warfare...?" He shook his head. "After the first shot everything is okay...it's all the shit before.... Flynn's got me psyched out.... He understands...I'm sure he's crazier than me...."

Burke said, "Maybe Schroeder told him how crazy you really are... maybe Flynn's scared of *you*."

Bellini nodded. "Yeah..." He laughed, then his face hardened. "You know something? I *feel* like killing someone.... I have an *urge*... like when I need a cigarette... you know?"

Burke looked at his watch. "At least this one can't go into overtime. At 6:03 it's finished."

Bellini also checked his watch. "Yeah... no overtime. Just a two-minute warning, then a big bang, and the stadium falls down and the game is over." He laughed again, and Burke glanced at him.

The ESD climber reached the top of the shaft. He tied a nylon rope ladder to the pulley crossbeam and let the ladder fall. Bellini caught it before it hit the metal roof of the elevator. The communications man threw up a field-phone receiver, and Bellini clipped it to the shoulder of his flak jacket. "Well, Burke... here goes. Once you get *on* the ladder, you're not getting *off* the ladder so easy." He began climbing. Burke followed, and one by one the ten ESD men climbed behind them.

Bellini paused at the oak door of the Archbishop's sacristy and put his ear to it. He heard footsteps and froze. Suddenly the crack of light at the bottom of the door disappeared. He waited several more seconds, his rifle pointed at the door and his heart pounding in his chest. The footsteps moved away. His phone clicked, and he answered it quietly. "Yeah."

The operator said, "Our people outside report all the lights are going out in there—but there's... like candlelight... maybe flares lighting up the windows."

Bellini swore. The flares, he knew, would be white phosphorus. *Bastards.* Right from the beginning... right from the fucking beginning... He continued up the swaying ladder.

At the top of the shaft the climber sat on the crossbeam,

pointing his light farther up, and Bellini saw a small opening where the shaft wall ended a few feet from the sloping ceiling of the triforium attic. Bellini mumbled, "Caught a fucking break at least." He stood precariously on the crossbeam, eight stories above the basement, and stretched toward the opening, grabbing at the top of the wooden wall. He pulled himself up, squeezing his head and broad shoulders into the space, a silenced pistol in his hand. He blinked in the darkness of the half attic, fully expecting to be shot between the eyes. He waited, then turned on his light, cocking his pistol at the same time. Nothing moved but his pounding chest against the top edge of the wall. He slid down headfirst five feet to a beam that ran over the plaster lathing, breaking his fall with his outstretched arms and righting himself silently.

Burke's head and shoulders appeared in the opening, and Bellini pulled him through. One by one the First Assault Squad dropped into the small side attic behind the triforium.

Bellini crawled over the beams, sidled up to the wooden knee-wall and moved along it until he felt a small door Stillway had described. On the other side of the door was the southeast triforium, and in the triforium, he was certain, were one or more gunmen. He put a small audio amplifier to the door and listened. He heard no footsteps, no sound of life in the triforium, but somewhere in the Cathedral a bagpipe was playing "Amazing Grace." He mumbled to himself, "Assholes."

He backed carefully away from the wall and led his squad to the low, narrow space where the sloping roof met the stone of the outside wall. He unclipped the field phone from his jacket and spoke quietly to his switchboard below. "Report to all stations—First Squad in place. No contact."

* * *

The Second Assault Squad of ESD men climbed the rungs of the wide chimney, fire axes slung to their backs. They passed the steel door in the brick and continued up to the chimney pot.

The squad leader attached a khaki nylon rappelling line to the top rung and held the gathered rope in his hands. The cold night air blew into the chimney, making a deep, hollow, whistling sound. The squad leader stuck a periscope out of the chimney pot and scanned the towers, but the Fenians were not visible from this angle, and he pointed the scope at the cross-shaped roof. Two dormers faced him, and he saw that the hatches on them were open. "Shit." He reached back, and the squad commo man cranked the field phone slung to his chest and handed him the receiver. The squad leader reported, "Captain, Second Squad in position. The damned hatches are open now, and it's going to be tough crossing this roof if there're people leaning out those dormers shooting at us."

Bellini answered in a barely audible voice. "Just hold there until the towers are knocked out. Then move."

The Third Assault Squad climbed the chimney behind the Second Squad but stopped their ascent below the steel door. The squad leader maneuvered to a position beside the door, directing a flashlight on the latch. Slowly he reached out with a mechanical pincher and tentatively touched the latch, then drew it away. He called Bellini on the field phone. "Captain. Third in position. Can't tell if there are alarms or mines on the door."

Bellini answered, "Okay. When Second Squad clears the chimney, you open the door and find out."

"Right." He handed the phone back to the commo man hanging beside him, who said, "How come we never rehearsed anything like this?"

The squad leader said, "I don't think the situation ever came up before."

At 5:35 the ESD sniper-squad leader in Rockefeller Center picked up the ringing field phone on the desk in a tenth-floor office. Joe Bellini's voice came over the line, subdued but with no hesitation. He gave the code word. "Bull Run. Sixty seconds."

The sniper-squad leader acknowledged, hung up, drew a long breath, and pushed the office intercom buzzer in an alerting signal.

Fourteen snipers moved quickly to the seven windows that faced the louvered sections of the towers across Fifth Avenue and crouched below the sills. The intercom sounded again, and the snipers rose and threw open the sashes, then steadied their rifles on the cold stone ledges. The squad leader watched the second hand of his watch, then gave the final short signal.

Fourteen silenced rifles coughed, and the metallic sound of sliding operating rods clattered in the offices, followed by whistling sounds, then the coughs of another volley, breaking up into random firing as the snipers fired at will. Spent brass cartridge casings dropped silently on the plush carpets.

Brian Flynn looked down at the television sitting on the floor of the pulpit. The screen showed a close-up shot of the bell tower, the blue-lit shadow of Mullins staring out through the torn louvers. Mullins raised a mug to his lips. The scene shifted to another telescopic close-up of Devane in the south tower, a bored look on his face. The audio was tuned down, but Flynn could hear the droning voice of a reporter. The reporter gave the time. Everything seemed very ordinary until the camera panned back, and Flynn caught a glimpse of light from the rose window, which should have been dark. He realized he was seeing a video replay from early in the evening. Flynn reached for the field phone.

A dozen Fenian spotters in the surrounding buildings watched the Cathedral through field glasses.

One spotter saw movement at the mouth of the chimney. A second spotter saw the line of windows in Rockefeller Center open.

Strobe lights began signaling to the Cathedral towers.

Rory Devane knelt behind a stone mullion, blowing into his cold hands, his rifle cradled in the bend of his arms. His eye caught the flashing strobes, and then he saw a line of muzzle flashes in the building across the Avenue. He grabbed for the field phone, and it rang simultaneously, but before he could pick it up, shards of disintegrating stone flew into his face. The dark tower room was filled with sharp pinging sounds and echoed with the metallic clatter of tearing copper louvers.

A bullet slammed into Devane's flak jacket, sending him reeling back. He felt another round pass through his throat, but didn't feel the one that ricocheted into his forehead and fractured his skull.

Donald Mullins stood in the east end of the bell room staring out across the East River trying to see the predawn light coming over Long Island. He had half convinced himself that there would be no attack, and when the field phone rang he knew it was Flynn telling him the Fenians had won.

A strobe light flashed from a window in the Waldorf-Astoria, and his heart missed a beat. He heard one of the bells behind him ring sharply, and he spun around. Muzzle flashes, in rapid succession like popping flashbulbs, ran the width of the building across the Avenue, and more strobe lights flashed in the distance; but these warnings, which he had been watching for all night, made no impression on his mind. A series of bullets slammed into his flak jacket, knocked the breath out of him, and picked him up off his feet.

Mullins regained his footing and lunged for the field phone, which was still ringing. A bullet shattered his elbow, and another passed through his hand. His rifle fell to the floor, and everything went black. Still another round entered behind his ear and disintegrated a long swath of his skull.

Mullins staggered in blind pain and grabbed at the bell straps hanging through the open stairwell. He felt himself falling, sliding down the swinging straps.

Father Murphy huddled against the cold iron ladder in the bell tower, half unconscious from fatigue. A faint peal of the bell overhead made him look up, and he saw Mullins falling toward him. Instinctively he grabbed at the man before he passed through the opening in the landing.

Mullins veered from the gaping hole and landed on the floor, shrieking in pain. He lurched around the room, his hands to his face and his sense of balance gone along with his inner ear, blood running between his fingers. He ran headlong toward the east wall of the tower and crashed through the splintered glass, tumbling three stories to the roof of the northwest triforium.

Father Murphy tried to comprehend the surrealistic scene that had just passed before his cloudy eyes. He blinked several times and stared at the shattered window.

Abby Boland thought she heard a sound on the roof of the triforium's attic behind her and froze, listening.

* * *

Leary thought he heard the pealing of a bell from the tower and strained to listen for another.

Flynn was calling into the field phone, "South tower, north tower, answer."

In the chimney the commo men with the two squads answered their phones simultaneously and heard Bellini's voice. "Both towers clear. Move!"

The Second Squad leader threw the gathered rope up and out of the chimney and scrambled over the top into the cold air. They had gambled that by leaving on the blue floodlights that bathed the lower walls of the Cathedral, they wouldn't alert the Fenian spotters in the surrounding buildings or in the attic. But the squad leader felt very visible as he rappelled down the side of the chimney. He landed on the dark roof of the northeast triforium, followed by his ten-man Assault Squad. They moved quickly over the lower roof to a slender pinnacle that rose between two great windows of the ambulatory. The squad found the iron rungs in the stone that Stillway said would be there and climbed up to a higher roof, partially visible in the diffused lighting. Dropping onto the roof, they lay in the wide rain gutter where the wall met the sloping expanse of gray slate shingles, then began crawling in the gutter toward the closest dormer. The squad leader kept his eyes on the dormer as he moved toward it. He saw something poke out of the open hatchway, something long and slender like a rifle barrel.

The Third Assault Squad leader at the steel door watched the last dark form disappear from the chimney pot overhead and hooked his pinchers on the door latch, muttered a prayer, and lifted the latch, then slowly pushed in on the door, wondering if he was going to be blown up the chimney like soot.

Jean Kearney and Arthur Nulty stood in dormered hatchways, which were on opposite sides of the pitched roof, scanning the night sky for helicopters. Nulty, on the north slope of the roof, thought he heard a sound below. He looked straight down at the triforium roof but saw nothing in the dark. He heard a sound to his immediate right and turned. A long line of black shapes, like beetles, he thought, was crawling through the rain gutter toward him. He couldn't imagine how they got there without helicopters or without the spotters in the surrounding buildings seeing them climb the walls. Instinctively he raised his rifle and drew a bead on the first man, who was no more than twenty feet away.

One of the men shouted, and they all rose to one knee. Nulty saw rifles coming into firing position, and he squeezed off a single round. One of the black-clad men slapped his hand over his flak jacket, lost his balance and fell out of the rain gutter; he dropped three stories to the triforium roof below, making a loud thup in the quiet night.

Jean Kearney turned at the sound of Nulty's shot. "Arthur! What—?"

The dormer where Nulty stood erupted in flying splinters of wood, and Nulty fell back into the attic. He rose very quickly to his feet, took two steps toward Jean Kearney, his arms waving, then toppled over the catwalk and crashed to the plaster lathing below.

Kearney stared down at his body, then looked up at the dormer hatch and saw a man hunched in the opening. She raised her rifle and fired, but the man jumped out of view.

Kearney ran along the catwalk and dived across the wooden

boards, reaching a glowing oil lamp. She flung it up in an arc, and it crashed into a pile of chopped wood. She rolled a few feet farther and reached for the field phone, which was ringing.

Men were dropping into the attic from the open hatches, scrambling over the catwalks and firing blindly with silenced rifles into the half-lighted spaces. Bullets hit the rafters and floor around her with a thud.

Kearney fired back, and the noise of her rifle attracted a dozen muzzle flashes. She felt a sharp pain in her thigh and cried out, dropping her rifle. Blood gushed through her fingers as she held a hand under her skirt against the wound. With her other hand she felt on the floor for the ringing phone.

The woodpile was beginning to blaze now, and the light silhouetted the dark shapes moving toward her. They were throwing canisters of fire-extinguishing gas into the blazing wood, but the fire was growing larger.

She picked up her rifle again and shot into the blinding light of the fire. A man cried out, and then answering shots whistled past her head. She dragged herself toward the bell tower passage, leaving a trail of blood on the dusty floor. She reached another oil lamp and flung it into the pile of wood that lay between her and the tower, blocking her escape route.

She lay in a prone position, firing wildly into the flame-lit attic around her. Another man moaned in pain. Bullets ripped up the wood around her, and the windows in the peak behind her began shattering. The fires were reaching toward the roof now, curling around the rafters. The smell of burning wax candles mixed with the aroma of old, seasoned oak, and the heat from the fires began to warm her chilled body.

In the northeast triforium Eamon Farrell heard a distinct noise on the roof in the attic behind him. His already raw nerves had had enough. He held his breath as he looked down into the Cathedral at Flynn in the pulpit cranking the field phone. Sullivan and Abby Boland across from him were leaning anxiously out over the balustrades. Something was about to happen, and Eamon Farrell saw no reason to wait around to see what it was.

Farrell turned slowly from the balustrade, lay down his rifle, and opened the door in the knee wall behind him. He entered the dark attic and turned his flashlight on the steel door in the chimney. God, he was certain, had given him an escape route, and he had been right to keep it from Flynn and right to use it.

Carefully he approached the door, put the flashlight in his pocket, then lowered himself through the opening until his feet found an iron rung. He closed the door and stepped down to the next rung in the total darkness. His shoulder brushed something, and he gave a startled yelp, then reached out and touched a very taut rope.

He looked upward and saw a piece of the starlit sky at the mouth of the chimney, which was partly obscured by a moving shape. His stomach heaved as he became aware that he was not alone.

He heard someone breathe, smelled the presence of other bodies in the sooty space around him, pictured in his mind dangling shapes swinging on ropes in the darkness like bats, inches from him. He cleared his throat. "Wha—who...?"

A voice said, "It ain't Santa Claus, pal."

Farrell felt cold steel pressed against his cheekbone, and he shouted, "I surrender!" But his shout panicked the ESD man, and darkness erupted in a silent flash of blinding light. Farrell fell feet-first and then somersaulted into the black shaft, blood splattering over his flailing arms.

The Third Squad leader said, "I wonder where *he* was going?"

The squad moved silently through the chimney door and assembled in the dark attic over the bride's room.

Flynn turned off the television. He spoke into the pulpit microphone. "It's begun. Keep alert. Steady now. Watch the doors and windows. Rockets ready."

Bellini squatted at the door in the knee wall and listened to Flynn's voice through the public address system. "Yeah, motherfuckers, you watch the doors and windows." The First Squad knelt to the sides with rifles raised. Bellini put his hand to the latch, raised it, and pushed. The ESD men behind him converged on the door, and Bellini threw it open, rolling onto the floor into the dark triforium. The men poured through after him, diving and rolling over the cold floor, weapons pointing up and down the long gallery.

The triforium was empty, but on the floor lay a black morning coat, top hat, and a tricolored sash with the words Parade Marshal.

Half the squad crawled along the parapet, spacing themselves at intervals. The other half ran in a crouch to where the triforium turned at a right angle overlooking the south transept.

Bellini made his way to the corner of the right angle and raised an infrared periscope. The entire Cathedral was lit with candles and phosphorus flares and, even as he watched, the burning phosphorus caused the image to white out and disappear. He swore and lowered the periscope. Someone handed him a daylight periscope, and he focused on the long triforium across the transept. In the flickering light from below he could see a tall man in a bagpiper's tunic leaning over the balustrade and aiming a rifle at the transept doors across the nave. He shifted the periscope and looked down toward the dark choir loft but saw nothing, then scanned right to the long triforium across the nave and caught a glimpse of what looked like a woman in overalls. He focused on her and saw that her young face looked frightened. He smiled and traversed farther right to the short triforium across the sanctuary where the chimney was. It appeared empty, and he began to wonder just how many people Flynn had used to take the Cathedral and fuck up everyone's day.

Burke came up behind him, and Bellini whispered in his ear, "This is not going so bad." Bellini's field phone clicked, and he put it to his ear. The Third Squad reported to all points. "In position. One Fenian in chimney—KIA."

A voice cut in, and Bellini heard the excited shouts of the Second Squad leader. "Attic ablaze! Fighting fire! Three ESD casualties—one Fenian dead—one still shooting. Fire helicopters in position, but they won't come in until attic is secure. May have to abandon attic!"

Bellini looked up to the vaulted ceiling. He cupped his hand around the mouthpiece and spoke quickly. "You stay there and fight that fucking fire, you kill the fucking Fenian, and you bring those fire choppers in. You piss on that fire, you spit on that fire, but you do not leave that fire. Acknowledge."

The squad leader seemed calmer. "Roger, Roger, okay...."

Bellini put down the field phone and looked at Burke. "The attic is burning."

Burke peered up into the darkness. Somewhere above the dimly outlined ceiling, about four stories up, there was light and heat, but here it was dark and cold. Somewhere below there were explosives that could level the entire east end of the Cathedral. He looked at his watch and said, "The bombs will put the fire out."

Bellini looked at him. "Your sense of humor sucks, you know?"

* * *

Flynn stood in the pulpit, a feeling of impotence growing in him. It was ending too quietly, no bangs, not even whimpers, at least none that he could hear. He was becoming certain that the police had finally found Gordon Stillway, compliments of Bartholomew Martin, and they weren't going to come in through the doors and windows—Schroeder had lied or had been used by them. They were burrowing in right now, like rot in the timbers of a house, and the whole thing would fall with hardly a shot fired. He looked at his watch. 5:37. He hoped Hickey was still alive down there, waiting for the Bomb Squad in the darkness. He thought a moment, and the overwhelming conviction came over him that Hickey at least would complete his mission.

Flynn spoke in the microphone. "They've taken out the towers. George, Eamon, Frank, Abby, Leary, Megan—keep alert. They may have found another way in. Gallagher, watch the crypt behind you. Everyone, remember the movable blocks on the floor; watch the bronze plate on the sanctuary: scan the bride's room, the Archbishop's sacristy, the bookstore and the altars; keep an ear to the walls of the triforium attics—" Something made him look up to his right at the northeast triforium. "Farrell!"

No one answered.

Flynn peered into the darkness above. "Farrell!" He slammed his fist on the marble balustrade. "Damn it!" He cranked the field phone and tried again to raise the attic.

Bellini listened to the echoes of Flynn's voice die away from the speakers. The squad leader beside him said, "We have to move—now!"

Bellini's voice was cool. "No. Timing. It's like trying to get laid—it's all timing." The phone clicked, and Bellini listened to the Third Squad leader in the attic of the opposite triforium. "Captain, do you see anyone else in this triforium?"

Bellini answered, "I guess the guy called Farrell was the only one. Move into the triforium." He spoke to the operator. "Get me the Fourth Squad."

The Fourth Squad leader answered, and his voice resohated from the duct he was crawling through. "We jumped off late, Captain—got lost in the duct work. I think we're through the foundation—"

"*Think!* What the hell is wrong with you?"

"Sorry—"

Bellini rubbed his throbbing temples and brought his voice under control. "Okay... okay, we make up the time you lost by moving your time of last possible withdrawal from 5:55 to 6:00. That's fair, right?"

There was a pause before the squad leader replied, "Right."

"Good. Now you just see if you can find the block-square crawl space. Okay? Then I'll send the Bomb Squad in." He hung up and looked at Burke. "Glad you came?"

"Absolutely."

Flynn cranked the field phone. "Attic! Attic!"

Jean Kearney's voice finally came on the line, and Flynn spoke hurriedly. "They've taken out the towers, and they'll be coming through the roof hatches next—I can hear helicopters overhead. There's no use waiting for it, Jean—light all the fires and get into the bell tower."

Jean Kearney answered, "All right." She stood propped against a catwalk rail, supported by two ESD men, one of whom had the big silencer of a pistol pressed to her head. She shouted into the phone, "Brian—!" One of the men pulled the phone out of her hand.

She steadied herself on the rail, feeling lightheaded and nauseous from the loss of blood. She bent over and vomited on the floor, then picked her head up and tried to stand erect, shaking off the two men beside her. Hoses hung from hovering helicopters and snaked their way through the roof hatches, discharging billows of white foam over the flickering flames. She felt defeated but relieved that it was over. She tried to think about Arthur Nulty, but her thigh was causing her such pain that all she could think about was that the pain should go away and the nausea should stop. She looked at the squad leader. "Give me a pressure bandage, damn it."

The squad leader ignored her and watched the firemen coming through the hatches, taking over the hoses from his Assault Squad. He shouted to his men. "Move out! Into the bell tower!"

He turned back to Jean Kearney, noticing the tattered green Aer Lingus uniform; he looked at her freckled features in the subdued light and pointed at a smoldering pile of wood. "Are you *crazy?*"

She looked him in the eye. "We're loyal."

The squad leader listened to the sound of his men double-timing over the catwalks toward the tower passage. As he reached for the aid kit on his belt his eyes darted around at the firemen who were occupied with the large chemical hoses.

Jean Kearney's hand flew out and expertly snatched his pistol, put it to her heart, and fired. She back-pedaled, her arms swinging in wide circular motions until she toppled over to the dusty catwalk.

The squad leader looked at her, stunned, and then bent over and retrieved his pistol. "Crazy... crazy."

A thick mass of foam moved across the catwalk and slid over

Jean Kearney's body; the white billowing bubbles tinged with red.

Flynn used the field phone to call the choir loft. He spoke quickly to Megan. "I think they've taken the attic. They'll be coming through the side doors into the choir loft. Keep the doors covered so Leary can shoot."

Megan's voice was angry, nearly hysterical. "How the hell did they take the attic? What the bloody hell is going on, Brian? What the *fuck* is going wrong here?"

He drew a long breath. "Megan, when you've been on fifty missions, you'll know not to ask those questions. You just fight, and you die or you don't die, but you never ask—Listen, tell Leary to scan Farrell's post—I think they're also up there—"

"Who the hell ever said you were a military genius?"

"The British—it made them feel more important."

She hesitated, then said, "Why did you let Hickey do that to my brother?"

Flynn glanced at Pedar Fitzgerald's body propped up on the organ bench. "Hickey—like Mr. Leary—is a friend of yours, not mine. Ask Hickey when next you meet. Also, tell Leary to scan Gallagher's triforium—"

Megan cut in. "Brian...listen...listen..."

He recognized the tone of her voice, that childlike lilt she used when she became repentant about something. He didn't want to hear what she had to say and hung up.

Bellini scanned with the periscope as he reported to all points on the field phone. "Yeah...they're starting to look over their shoulders now. Man at the chancel organ...but he looks...dead...Still don't see Hickey.... Might be in the crawl space. Two hostages...Malone and Baxter...Murphy still missing...shit...Cardinal still missing—"

The Fifth Squad leader in the octagon room to the side of the sacristy gates cut in. "Captain, I'm looking at the gates with a periscope...bad angle...but someone—looks like the Cardinal—is cuffed to them. Advise."

Bellini swore softly. "Make sure it's him, and stand by for orders." He turned to Burke. "These Mick bastards still have some tricky shit up their shillelaghs— Cardinal's cuffed to the gates." He focused the periscope on Flynn in the pulpit directly below. "Smart guy.... Well, this potato-eating bastard is mine...but it's a tough shot.... Canopy overhead and a marble wall around him. He knows it's going down the tube, but he can't do shit about it. Cocksucker."

Burke said, "If the attic is secure and you get the bombs...you ought to try negotiating. Flynn will talk with twenty rifles pointing down at him. He's a lot of things, but stupid isn't one of them."

"Nobody told me nothing about asking him to surrender." Bellini put his face close to Burke's. "Don't get carried away with yourself and start giving orders, or I swear to God I'll grease you. I'm doing okay, Burke—I'm doing fine—I'm golden tonight—fuck you and fuck Flynn—let him squirm—then let him die."

The Fifth Assault Squad dropped one at a time from the duct opening and lay on the damp floor of the crawl space, forming a defensive perimeter. The squad leader cranked his field phone and reported, "Okay, Captain, we're in the crawl space. No movement here—"

Bellini answered, "You sure you're not in the fucking attic now? Okay, I'm sending the dogs and their handlers through the ducts with Peterson's Bomb Squad. When you rendezvous, move out. Be advised that Hickey may be down there—maybe others. Keep your head out of your ass."

Bellini signaled to Wendy Peterson. "Perimeter secure. Move through the ducts. Follow the commo wire and don't get lost."

She answered in a laconic voice that echoed in the ducts, "We're already moving, Captain."

Bellini looked at his watch. "Okay...it's 5:45 now. At 6:00—at 5:55 my people are getting the hell out of there, whether or not you think you got all the bombs. I suggest you do the same."

Peterson answered, "We'll play it by ear."

"Yeah, you do that." He hung up and looked at Burke. "I think it's time—before our luck turns."

Burke said nothing.

Bellini rubbed his chin, hesitated, then reached for the phone and called the garage under Rockefeller Center. "Okay, Colonel, the word is Bull—fucking—Run. Ready?"

Logan answered, "Been ready a while. You're cutting it close."

Bellini's voice was caustic. "It's past close—it's probably too damned late, but that doesn't mean you can't earn a medal."

Colonel Logan threw the field phone down from the commander's hatch of the armored carrier and called to the driver, "Go!"

The twenty thousand pounds of armor began rumbling up the ramp of the underground garage. The big overhead door rose, and the carrier slid into Forty-ninth Street, turned right, and approached Fifth Avenue at twenty-five miles per hour, then veered north up the Avenue gathering speed.

Logan stood in the hatch with an M-16 rifle, the wind billowing his fatigue jacket. He stared at the Cathedral coming up on his right front, then glanced up at the towers and roof. Smoke billowed over the Cathedral, and helicopters hovered, beating the smoke downward, thick hoses dropping into the attic hatches. "Good Lord..."

Logan looked into the silent predawn streets, empty except for the police posted in recessed doorways. One of them gave him a thumbs up, another saluted. Logan stood taller in the hatch; his mind raced faster than the carrier's engines, and his blood pounded through his veins.

The armored carrier raced up to the Cathedral. The driver locked the right-hand treads, and the carrier pivoted around, ripping up large slabs of the blacktop. The driver released the treads as the carrier pointed toward the front doors, and he gunned the engines. The vehicle fishtailed and raced across the wide sidewalk, bounced, and hit the granite steps, tearing away the stone as the treads climbed upward. The brass handrails disappeared beneath the treads, and the ten tons of armor headed straight for the ten tons of bronze ceremonial doors.

Logan made the sign of the cross, ducked into the hatch, and pulled the lid shut. The truck tires attached to the front of the carrier hit the doors, and the bolts snapped, sending the massive doors flying inward. The alarms sounded with a piercing ring. The carrier was nearly into the vestibule when the delayed mines on the doors began to explode, scattering shrapnel across the sides of the vehicle. The carrier kept moving through the vestibule and skidded across the marble floor to a stop beneath the choir loft overhang.

Harold Baxter grabbed Maureen and pulled her down beneath the clergy pews.

Brian Flynn raised a rocket launcher and took aim from the pulpit.

The rear door of the carrier dropped, and fifteen men of the 69th Regiment, led by Major Cole, scrambled over the door and began fanning out under the choir loft.

Frank Gallagher was speaking to the Cardinal when the sound of the exploding doors rolled through the Cathedral. For a moment he thought the bombs beneath him had gone off, then he recognized the sound for what it was. His chest heaved, and his body shook so badly that his rifle fell from his hands. He lost control of his nerves as he heard the reports of rifle fire in the Cathedral behind him. He let out a high-pitched wail and ran down the sacristy steps, falling to his knees beside the Cardinal. He grabbed at the hem of the red robe, tears streaming from his eyes and snatches of prayer forming on his lips. "God...O God...Father...Eminence...dear God..."

The Cardinal looked down at him. "It's all right, now. There...there..."

Colonel Logan rose quickly through the carrier hatch and rested his automatic rifle on the machine gun mount in front of him. He peered into the darkness as he scanned to his front, then saw a movement in the pulpit and zeroed in.

The First Squad, including Bellini and Burke, had risen up in unison from behind the balustrade, rifles raised to their shoulders.

Abby Boland saw the shadows appear along the ledge, black forms, eerie and spectral in the subdued light. She saw the tiny pinpoint flashes and heard the silencers cough like a roomful of old people clearing their throats. She screamed, "George!" Sullivan was intent on the transept doors opposite him but looked up when she screamed.

The Third Squad had burst out of the attic and occupied Farrell's triforium. They lined up along the parapet and searched the darkness for targets.

Brian Flynn steadied the M-72 rocket as a burst of red tracers streaked out of the commander's hatch of the carrier and cracked into the granite column behind him. He squeezed the detonator. The rocket roared out of the tube, sailed over the pews with a fiery red trail, and exploded on the sloping front of the armored carrier.

The carrier belched smoke and flame through ruptured seams, and the driver was killed instantly. Logan shot up from the hatch, flames licking at his clothing, and nearly hit the overhang of the loft. His smoking body fell back toward the blazing carrier, spread-eagled like a sky diver, and disappeared in clouds of black smoke and orange flame.

The First and Third ESD squads in the triforia were firing into the candlelit Cathedral, the operating mechanisms of their rifles slapping back and forth as the silencers wheezed, and spent brass piled up on the stone floors.

Abby Boland stood rigid for a split second as the scream died in her throat. She got off a single shot, then felt something rip the rifle from her hands, and the butt rammed her face. She fell to the floor, picked up a rocket, and stood again.

Sullivan fired a long automatic burst into Farrell's triforium and heard a scream. He shifted his fire to the triforium where Gallagher had been, but a single bullet hit him squarely in the chest. He tumbled to the floor, landing on his bagpipes, which emitted a sad wail that pierced the noises in the Cathedral.

Abby Boland saw him go down as she fired the rocket across the Cathedral.

Bellini watched the trail of red fire illuminating the darkness. It came toward him with a noise that sounded like a rushing freight train. "Duck!"

The rocket went high and exploded on the stonework above the triforium. The triforium shook, and the window above blew out of its stone mullions, sending thousands of pieces of colored glass raining down in sheets past the triforium to the sanctuary and pulpit below.

Bellini's squad rose quickly and poured automatic fire onto the source of the rocket.

Abby Boland held a pistol extended in both hands and fired at the orange flashes as the stonework around her began to shatter. The loud pop of a grenade launcher rolled across the Cathedral, and the top of the balustrade in front of her exploded. Her arms flew up and splattered blood and pistol fragments across her face. She fell forward, half blinded, and her mangled hands clutched at the protruding staff of the Papal flag. In her disorientation she found herself hanging out over the floor below. A burst of fire tore into her arms, and she released her grip. Her body tumbled head over heels and crashed into the pews below with a sharp splintering sound.

Pedar Fitzgerald's dead body took a half-dozen hits and lurched to and fro, then fell against the keyboard and produced a thundering dissonant chord that continued uninterrupted amid the shouting and gunfire.

Flynn crouched in the pulpit, fired long bursts at Farrell's triforium, then shifted his fire toward the vestibules where the men of the 69th Regiment had retreated from the burning carrier. Suddenly the carrier's gasoline exploded. Flames shot up to the choir loft, and huge clouds of black smoke rose and curled around the loft. The National Guardsmen retreated back farther through the mangled doors onto the steps.

Bellini leaned out of the triforium and sighted his rifle almost straight down and fired three shots in quick succession through the bronze pulpit canopy.

Flynn's body lurched, and he fell to his knees, then rolled over the pulpit floor. Bellini could see his body dangling across the spiral stairs. He took aim at the twitching form.

Burke hit Bellini's shoulder and deflected his shot. "No! Leave him."

Bellini glared at Burke for a second, then turned his attention to the choir loft. He saw a barely perceptible flash of light, the kind of muzzle fire that came from a combination silencer/flash suppressor and that could only be seen from head on. The light flashed again, but this time in a different place several yards away. Bellini sensed that whoever was in there was very good, and he had a very good perch, a vast sloping area completely darkened and obscured by rising smoke. Even as he watched he heard a scream from the end of the triforium, and one of his men fell back. He heard another moan coming from the opposite triforium. In a short time everyone was on the floor as bullets skimmed across the ledge of the balustrade a few feet above their heads. Burke sat with his back against the wall and lit a cigarette as the wood above him splintered. "That guy is good."

Bellini crouched across from him and nodded. "And he's got the best seat in the house. This is going to be a bitch." He looked at his watch. The whole thing, from the time Logan had hit the doors to this moment, had taken just under two minutes. But Logan was dead now, the National Guardsmen were nowhere to be seen, and he had lost some good people. The hostages might be dead, the people in the crawl space weren't reporting, and someone in the choir loft was having a good day.

Bellini picked up the field phone and called Fifth Squad in the corridor off the sacristy. "All the bastards are dead except one or two in the choir loft. You have to go for the Cardinal and the two hostages under the pews."

The squad leader answered, "How the hell do we rush that gate with the Cardinal hanging there?"

"Very carefully. Move out!" He hung up and said to Burke, "The sniper in the choir loft isn't going to be easy."

＊ ＊ ＊

The ESD men from the Fifth Assault Squad moved out of the octagon rooms on both sides of the sacristy gate and slid quickly along the walls, converging on the Cardinal.

The squad leader kept his back to the wall and peered carefully around the opening. His eyes met the Cardinal's, and both men gave a start; then the squad leader saw a man kneeling at the Cardinal's feet. Gallagher let out a surprised yell, and the squad leader did the same as he fired twice from the hip.

Gallagher rocked back on his haunches and then fell forward. His smashed face struck the bars, and he rolled sideways, sliding down the Cardinal's legs.

The Cardinal stared down at Gallagher lying in a heap at his feet, blood rushing from his head over the steps. He looked at the squad leader, who was staring at Gallagher. The squad leader turned and looked up at the top landing, saw no one, and gave a signal. ESD men with bolt cutters swarmed around the gates and severed the chain that tied them together. One of the men snapped the Cardinal's handcuffs while another one opened the gate lock with a key. So far no one had spoken a word.

The assault squad slid open the gates, and ten men ran up the stairs toward the crypt door.

The Cardinal knelt beside Gallagher's body, and a medic rushed out of a side corridor and took the Cardinal's arm. "Are you okay?" The Cardinal nodded. The medic stared down at Gallagher's face. "This guy don't look so good, though. Come on, Your Eminence." He tugged at the Cardinal's arm as two uniformed policemen lifted the Cardinal, steering him toward the corridor that led back to his residence.

One of the ESD men stood to the side of the crypt door and lobbed a gas canister down into the crypt. The canister popped, and two men wearing gas masks rushed in through the smoke. After a few seconds one of them yelled back, "No one here."

The squad leader took the field phone and reported, "Captain, sacristy gate and crypt secured. No ESD casualties, one Fenian KIA, Cardinal rescued." He added impulsively, "Piece of cake."

Bellini replied, "Tell me that after you get up those stairs. There's a motherfucker in the choir loft that can circumcise you with two shots and never touch your nuts."

The squad leader heard the phone click off. "Okay. Hostages under the pews— let's move." The squad split into two fire teams and began crawling up the opposite staircases toward the sanctuary.

Maureen and Baxter stayed motionless beneath the clergy pews. Maureen listened to the sounds of striking bullets echoing through the Cathedral. She pressed her face close to Baxter's and said, "Leary—maybe Megan—is still in the loft. I can't tell who else is still firing."

Baxter held her arm tightly. "It doesn't matter as long as Leary is still there." He took her wrist and looked at her watch. "It's 5:36. At 6:00 we run for it."

She smiled weakly. "Harry, John Hickey is a man who literally would not give you the right time of day. For all we know it's 6:03 right now. Then again, my watch may be correct, but the bombs may be set for right now. Hickey does not play fair—not with us nor with Brian Flynn."

"Why am I so bloody naïve?"

She pressed his arm. "That's all right. People like Hickey, Flynn...me...we're treacherous.... It's as natural as breathing...."

Baxter peered under the pews, then said, "Let's run for it."

"Where? This whole end of the Cathedral will collapse. The doors are mined. Leary's in the loft, and Gallagher is at the gate."

He thought a moment. "Gallagher owes you...."

"I wouldn't put myself at the mercy of any of them. We couldn't reach those stairs anyway. I won't be shot down by scum like Leary or Megan. I'm staying here."

"Then you'll be blown up by John Hickey."

She buried her face in her hands, then looked up. "Over the back of the sanctuary, keeping the altar between us and the choir loft. Into the Lady Chapel—the windows are about fifteen feet from the floor. Climb the chapel altar—one of us boosts the other up. We won't get that far, of course, but—"

"But we'll be heading in the right direction."

She nodded and began moving under the pews.

The Fifth Assault Squad crouched on the two flights of steps behind the high altar. The squad leader peered around the south side of the altar and looked to his left at the bronze floor-plate. He turned to the right, put his face to the floor, and tried to locate the hostages under the clergy pews, but in the bad light and at the angle he was looking he saw no one. He raised his rifle and called softly, "Baxter? Malone?"

They were both about to spring out toward the rear of the sanctuary but dropped to a prone position. Baxter called back, "Yes!"

The squad leader said, "Steps are clear. Cardinal's safe. Where is Father Murphy?"

Maureen peered across the sanctuary floor to the stairwell thirty feet away. "Somewhere in the towers, I think." She paused, then said, "Gallagher? The man who—"

The squad leader cut her off. "The bomb under us hasn't been found yet. You have to get out of there."

"What time is it?" Baxter asked.

The squad leader looked at his digital watch. "It's 5:46 and twenty seconds."

Maureen stared at the face of her watch. Ten minutes slow. "Bastard." She reset it and called back. "Someone's got to get the snipers in the loft before we can move."

The squad leader poked his head around the altar, looked up at the choir loft illuminated by candles and flares, and tried to peer into the blackness beyond. "He's too far away for us to get him or for him to get you."

Baxter shouted with anger in his voice, "If that were so, we wouldn't be here. That man is very good."

The squad leader said, "We're sitting on a *bomb,* and so far as I'm concerned it could go off *anytime.*"

Maureen called out to the squad leader, "Listen, two people planted the bombs, and they were down in the crawl space less than twenty minutes. They carried two suitcases."

The squad leader called back, "Okay—I'll pass that on. But you have to understand, lady, that the Bomb Squad could blow it—you know? So you have to make a break."

Maureen called back, "We'll wait."

"Well, we won't." The squad leader looked up at the triforium directly overhead where Bellini was, but saw no one at the openings. He called on the field phone. "Captain, Malone and Baxter are under the pews below you—alive." He passed on the information about the bombs and added, "They won't try to cross the sanctuary." Bellini's voice came over the line. "I don't blame them. Okay, in thirty seconds everyone fires into the loft. Tell them to run for it then."

"Right." He hung up and relayed the message to Maureen and Baxter.

Maureen called back, "We'll see—be careful—"

The squad leader turned and shouted to his men on the opposite stairs. "Heavy fire into the loft!" The men moved up the steps and knelt on the floor, firing down the length of the Cathedral. The squad leader moved the remainder of his squad around the altar and opened fire as the two triforia began shooting. The sound of bullets crashing into stone and brass in the loft rolled back through the Cathedral. The squad leader shouted to Malone and Baxter. "Run!"

Suddenly two rifles started firing rapidly from the choir loft with extreme accuracy. The ESD men on both sides of the altar began writhing on the cold sanctuary floor. Both teams pulled back to the staircases, dragging their wounded and leaving a trail of blood on the white marble.

The squad leader swore loudly and peered around the altar. "Okay, okay, stay there!" He glanced quickly up at the choir loft and saw a muzzle flash. The marble in front of him disintegrated and hit him full in the face. He screamed, and someone grabbed his ankles, dragging him back down the stairs.

Medics rushed up from the sacristy and began carrying away the wounded. The commo man cranked his field phone and reportd to Bellini in a shaky voice. "Hostages pinned down. This altar is the wrong end of a shooting gallery. We can't help them."

The Fourth Assault Squad moved slowly through the dark crawl space, the squad leader scanning his front with an infrared scope. The two dogs and their handlers moved with him. Behind the advancing line of men moved Wendy Peterson and four men of the Bomb Squad.

Every few yards the dogs strained at their leashes, and the Bomb Squad would uncover another small particle of plastic explosive without timers or detonators. The entire earth floor seemed to be seeded with plastic, and every colunm had a scrap of plastic stuck to it. A dog handler whispered to the impatient squad leader, "I can't stop them from following these red herrings."

Wendy Peterson came up beside the squad leader and said, "My men will follow up on these dogs. Your squad and I have to move on—faster—to the other side."

He stopped crawling, lay down an infrared scope, and turned his head toward her. "I'm moving like there were ten armed men in front of me, and that's the only way I know how to move when I'm crawling in a black fucking hole...Lieutenant."

The Bomb Squad men hurried up from the rear. One of them called, "Lieutenant?"

"Over here."

He came up beside her. "Okay, the mine on the corridor hatchway is disarmed, and we can get out of here real quick if we have to. The mine had a detcord running from it, and we followed it to the explosives around the main column on this side." He paused and caught his breath. "We defused that big mother—about twenty kilos of plastic—colored and shaped to look like stone—simple clock mechanism— set to go at 6:03—no bullshit about that." He held out a canvas bag and pressed it into Peterson's hands. "The guts."

She hunched over and lit a red-filtered flashlight, emptying the contents of the bag on the floor. Alarm clock, battery pack, wires, and four detached electric detonators. She turned on the clock, and it ticked loudly in the still air. She shut it off again. "No tricks?"

"No. We cut away all the plastic—no booby traps, no anti-intrusion devices. Very old techniques but very reliable, and top-grade plastic—smells and feels like that new C-5."

She picked off a clinging piece of plastic, kneading it between her thumb and forefinger, then smelled it.

The squad leader watched her in the filtered light and was reminded of his mother making cookie dough, but it was all wrong. "Really good stuff, huh?"

She switched off the light and said to the squad leader, "If the mechanism on the other one is the same, I'd need less than five minutes to defuse that bomb."

He said, "Good—now all you need is the other bomb. And *I* need about eight minutes to get the hell out of here and into the rectory basement. So at 5:55, no matter what's coming down, I say adios."

"Fair enough. Let's move."

He made no move but said, "I have to report the good news." He picked up the field phone. "Captain, the north side of the crawl space is clear of bombs."

Bellini answered, "Okay, very good." He related Maureen's information. "Move cautiously to the other side of the crypt. Hickey—"

"Yeah, but we can't engage him. We can move back to the hatchway, though, so you can have somebody drop concussion grenades through that bronze plate in the sanctuary. Then we'll move in and—"

Bellini cut him off. "Fifth Squad is still on the sacristy stairs. Took some casualties.... They're going to have trouble crossing the sanctuary floor—sniper up in the loft—"

"Well, blow him the fuck away and let's get it moving."

"Yeah...I'll let you know when we do that."

The squad leader hesitated, then said, "Well...we'll stay put...."

Bellini let a few seconds pass, then said, "This sniper is going to take awhile.... I'm not *positive* Hickey or anyone is down there.... You've got to get to the other column."

The squad leader hung up and turned to the dog handlers.

"Okay, drag those stupid mutts along, and don't stop until we get to the other side." He called to his men. "Let's go."

The three teams—ESD Assault Squad, Bomb Squad, and the dog handlers, twenty people in all—began moving. They passed the rear wall of the crypt and turned left, following the line of columns that would lead them to the main column flanking the sacristy stairs and what they hoped would be the last bomb.

They dropped from their hands and knees to a low-crawl position, rifles held out in front of them, the squad leader scanning with the infrared scope.

Peterson looked at her wristwatch as they moved. 5:47. If the mechanism on this side wasn't tricky, if there were no mines, if there were no other bombs, and if no one fired at them, then she had a very good chance of keeping St. Patrick's Cathedral from blowing up.

As she moved, though, she thought about triggers—all the ways a bomb could be detonated besides an electric clock. She thought about a concussion grenade that would set off an audio trigger, a flashlight that would set off a photo trigger, movement that would set off an inertial trigger, trip wires, false clocks, double or triple mechanisms, spring-loaded percussion mechanisms, remote mechanisms— so many nasty ways to make a bomb go off that you didn't want to go off. Yet, nothing so elaborate was needed to safeguard a time bomb until its time had come if it had a watchdog guarding it.

John Hickey knelt beside the main column, wedged between the footing and the sacristy stairwell, contemplating the mass of explosives packed around the footing and bedrock. His impulse was to dig out the clock and advance it to eternity. But to probe into the plastic in the dark might disconnect a detonator or battery connection. He looked at his watch. 5:47. Sixteen minutes to go. He could keep them away that long—long enough for the dawn to give the cameras good light. He grinned.

Hickey pushed himself farther back into the small space and peered up through the darkness toward the spot where the bronze plate sat in the ceiling. No one had tried to come through there yet, and as he listened to the shooting overhead, he suspected that Leary and Megan were still alive and would see to it that no one did. A bullet struck the bronze plate, and a deep resonant sound echoed through the dark. Four more bullets struck the plate in quick succession, and Hickey smiled. "Ah, Leary, you're showing off now, lad."

Just then his ears picked up the sound of whimpering. He cupped his ear and listened. Dogs. Then men breathing. He flipped the selector switch on his rifle to full automatic and leaned forward as the sound of crawling came nearer. The dogs had the scent of the massed explosives and probably of him. Hickey pursed his lips and made a sound. "Pssst!"

There was a sudden and complete silence.

Hickey did it again. "Pssst!" He picked up a piece of rubble and threw it.

The squad leader scanned the area to his front, but there was not even the faintest glimmer of light for the infrared scope to pick up and magnify.

Hickey said, "It's me. Don't shoot."

No one answered for several seconds, then the squad leader called out in a voice that was fighting to maintain control. "Put your hands up and move closer."

Hickey placed his rifle a few inches from the ground and held it horizontally. "Don't shoot, lads—please don't shoot. If you shoot...you'll blow us all to hell." He laughed, then said, "I, however, can shoot." He squeezed the trigger and emptied a twenty-round magazine across the ground in front of him.

He slapped another magazine into the well as the reports died away, and he heard screaming and moaning. He emptied another full magazine in three long bursts of grazing fire. He heard a dog howling, or, he thought, perhaps a man. He mimicked the howling as he reloaded and fired again.

The ESD snipers in both triforia were shooting down the length of the Cathedral into the choir loft, but the targets there—at least two of them—were moving quickly through the darkness as they fired. ESD men began to fall, dead and wounded, onto the triforium floors. An ESD man rose up beside Bellini and leaned out over the balustrade, putting a long stream of automatic fire into the loft. The red tracer rounds arched into the loft and disappeared as they embedded themselves into the woodwork. The organ keyboard was hit, and electrical sparks crackled in the darkness. The man fired again, and another stream of tracers struck the towering brass pipes, producing a sound like pealing bells. The tracer rounds ricocheted back, spinning and dancing like fiery pinwheels in the black space.

Bellini shouted to the ESD man and pulled at his flak jacket. "Too long! Down!"

All of a sudden the man released his rifle and slapped his hands to his face, then leaned farther out and rolled over the balustrade, crashing to the clergy pews below.

An ESD man with a M-79 grenade launcher fired. The small grenade burst against a wooden locker with a flash, and robes began to burn. Bellini picked up his bullhorn and shouted, "No grenades." The fire blazed for a few seconds, then began to burn itself out. Bellini crouched and held the bullhorn up. "Okay—First and Third squads—all together—two full magazines—automatic—on my command." He grabbed the rifle beside him and shouted into the bullhorn as he rose, "Fire!"

The remaining men in both triforia rose in unison and fired, producing a deafening roar as streams of red tracers poured into the black loft. They emptied their magazines, reloaded, fired again, then ducked.

There was a silence from the choir loft, and Bellini rose carefully with the bullhorn, keeping himself behind a column. He called out to the loft. "Turn the lights on and put your hands up, or we'll shoot again." He looked down at Burke sitting cross-legged beside him. "That's negotiating!" He raised the bullhorn again.

Leary knelt at the front of the loft in the north corner and watched through his scope as the bullhorn came up behind the column, diagonally across the Cathedral. He lay flat on top of the rail and leaned out precariously like a pool player trying to make a hard shot, putting the cross hairs of his scope over a small visible piece of Bellini's forehead. He fired and rolled back to the choir loft floor.

The bullhorn emitted an oddly amplified moan as Bellini's forehead erupted in a splatter of bone and blood. He dropped straight down, landing on Burke's crossed legs. Burke stared at the heavy body sprawled across him. Bellini's blackened temple gushed a small fountain of red...like a red rosebud, Burke thought abstractedly.... He pushed the body away and steadied himself against the parapet, drawing on his cigarette.

There was very little noise in the Cathedral now, he noted, and no sound at all from the survivors of the First Squad around him. Medics had arrived and were treating the wounded where they lay; they carried them back into the attic for the descent down the elevator shaft. Burke looked at his watch. 5:48.

Father Murphy listened to the sounds of footsteps approaching from below. His first thought was that the police had arrived;

then he remembered Flynn's words, and he realized it might be Leary or Megan coming for him. He picked up the pistol and held it in his shaking hand. "Who is it? Who's there?"

An ESD team leader from the Second Assault Squad two levels below motioned his fire team away from the open well. He raised his rifle and muffled his voice with his hand. "It's me.... Come on down...attic burning."

Father Murphy put his hand to his face and whispered, "The attic...oh...God ..." He called down. "Nulty! Is that you?"

"Yes."

Murphy hesitated. "Is... is Leary with you? Where's Megan?"

The team leader looked around at his men, who appeared tense and impatient. He called up the ladder well, "They're here. Come down!"

The priest tried to collect his thoughts, but his mind was so dulled with fatigue he just stared down into the black hole.

The team leader shouted, "Come down, or we're coming up for you!"

Father Murphy drew back from the opening as far as his cuffed wrist permitted. "I've got a gun!"

The team leader motioned to one of his men to fire a gas canister into the opening. The projectile sailed upward through the intervening level and burst on the ladder near Father Murphy's head. A piece of the canister struck him in the face, and his lungs filled with gas. He lurched back, then stumbled forward, falling through the opening. He hung suspended from his handcuffs, swinging against the ladder, his stomach and chest heaving as choked noises rose from his throat.

An ESD man with a submachine gun saw the figure dropping out of the darkness and fired from the hip. The body jerked, then lay still against the ladder. The ESD team moved carefully up to the higher level.

City lights filtered through the broken glass and cast a weak, shadowy illumination into the tower room. A cold wind blew away the smell of gas. An ESD man drew closer to the ladder, then shouted, "Hey! It's a priest."

The team leader dimly recalled some telephone traffic regarding the missing hostage, the priest. He cleared his throat. "Some of them were dressed as priests... right?"

The man with the submachine gun added, "He said he had a gun.... I heard it fall.... Something fell on the floor here...." He looked around and found the pistol. "See... and he called them by name...."

The man with the grenade launcher said, "But he's *cuffed*."

The team leader put his hands to his temples. "This is fucked up.... We might have fucked up...." He put his hand on the ladder rail and steadied himself. Blood ran down the rail and collected in a small pool around his fingers. "Oh... oh, no... no, no, *no*—"

The other half of the Second Squad from the attic made its way carefully down through the dark bell tower, then rushed into the long triforium where Abby Boland had been. They hit the floor and low-crawled down the length of the dark gallery, passing over the blood-wet floor near the flagstaff and turning the corner overlooking the north transept. Two men searched the triforium attic as the team leader reported on the field phone, 'Captain, northwest triforium secured. Anything you see moving up here is us."

A voice came over the wire. "This is Burke. Bellini is dead. Listen... send some men down to the choir loft level.... The rest of you stay there and bring fire down on that loft. There're about two snipers there—at least one of them is very accurate."

The team leader acknowledged and hung up. He looked back

at his four remaining men. "Captain got greased. Okay, you two stay here and fire down into the loft. You two come with me." He reentered the tower and ran down the spiral stairs toward the loft level.

One of the remaining two men in the triforium leaned out over the balustrade, steadying his rifle on the protruding flagstaff, which he noticed was splintered and covered with blood. He looked down and saw in the light of a flare a young woman's body lying in a collapsed pew.

"Jesus..." He looked into the dark loft and fired a short burst at random. "Flush those suckers out...."

A single shot whistled up out of the loft, passed through the wooden staff and punched into his flak jacket. He rose up off his feet, and his rifle flew into the air. The man lay stretched out on the floor for a few seconds, then rolled over on his hands and knees and tried to catch his breath. "Good God... Jesus H. Christ..."

The other man, who hadn't moved from his kneeling position, said, "Lucky shot, Tony. Bet he couldn't do it again."

The injured man put his hand under his flak jacket and felt a lump the size of an egg where his breast bones met. "Wow...fucking wow...." He looked at the other man. "Your turn."

The man pulled off his black stocking cap and pushed it above the balustrade on the tip of his rifle. A faint coughing sound rolled out of the choir loft, followed by a whistle and crack, then another, but the hat didn't move. The ESD man lowered the hat. "He stinks." He moved to a position several yards down the triforium and peered over the edge of the balustrade. The huge yellow and white Papal flag was no longer hanging from the staff but was stretched across the pews below, covering the body of the dead woman. The ESD man stared back at the staff and saw the two severed flag-ropes swaying. He ducked quickly and looked at the other man. "You're not going to believe this..."

Someone in the choir loft laughed.

An ESD man beside Burke picked up Bellini's bullhorn and began to raise it above the balustrade, then thought better of it. He pointed it upward from his kneeling position and called out, "Hey! You in the loft! Show's over. Nobody left but you. Come to the choir rail with your hands up. You won't be harmed." He shut off the bullhorn and said, "You'll be blasted into hamburger, motherfucker."

There was a long silence, then a man's voice called out from the loft. "You'll never take us." There were two sharp pistol shots, followed by silence.

The ESD man turned to Burke. "They blew their brains out." Burke said, "Sure."

The man considered for a moment. "How do we know?" he finally asked. Burke nodded toward Bellini's body.

The ESD man hesitated, then wiped Bellini's face and forehead with a handkerchief, and Burke helped him heft Bellini's body over the parapet.

Immediately there was a sound like a bee buzzing, followed by a loud slap, and Bellini's body was pulled out of their hands and crashed to the triforium floor behind them. An odd shrillish voice screamed from the loft, "Live ones! I want *live* ones!"

For the first time since the attack began Burke felt sweat forming on his brow.

The ESD man looked pale. "My God...."

The Second Squad leader led his remaining two men down the dark bell tower until they found the choir practice room. They searched it carefully in the dark and located the door that led out to the loft. The squad leader listened quietly at the door, then stood to the side and put his hand on the knob and turned it, but there was no alarm. The three men hugged the walls for a second before the squad leader pushed the door open, and they rushed the opening in a low crouch.

A shotgun exploded five times in the dark in quick succession, and the three men were knocked back into the room, their faces, arms, and legs ripped with buckshot.

Megan Fitzgerald stepped quickly into the room and shone a light on the three contorted bodies. One of the men looked up at the black-robed figure through the light and stared at her grotesquely made-up face, distorted with a repulsive snarl. Megan raised a pistol, deliberately shot each of the writhing figures in the head, then closed the door, reset the silent light alarm, and walked back into the loft. She called to Leary, who was moving and firing from positions all over the loft. "Don't let Malone or Baxter get away. Keep them pinned there until the bombs explode!"

Leary shouted as he fired, "Yeah, yeah. Just watch the fucking side doors."

A long stream of red tracers streaked out of the long northwest triforium and began ripping into the choir pews. Leary got off an answering shot before the last tracer left the muzzle of the ESD man's rifle, and the firing abruptly stopped.

Leary moved far back to the towering organ pipes and looked out at the black horizon line formed by the loft rail across the candle- and flare-lit Cathedral. It was strictly a matter of probability, he knew. There were thirteen hundred square feet of completely unlit loft and less than twenty police in a position to bring fire into the loft. And because of their overhead angle they couldn't bring grazing fire across the sloping expanse, but only direct fire at a specific point of impact, and that reduced the killing zone of their striking rounds. In addition, he and Megan had flak jackets under their robes, his rifle was silenced and the flash was suppressed, and they were both moving constantly. The ESD night scopes would be whited out as long as the phosphorus below kept burning, but he was firing into a lit area, and he could see their shapes when they came to the edge of the triforia. Probability. Odds. Skill. Vantage point. All in his favor. Always were. Luck did not exist. God did not exist. He called to Megan, "Time?"

She looked at her watch and saw the luminous minute hand tick another minute. "Fourteen minutes until 6:03."

He nodded to himself. There were times when he felt immortal and times when immortality only meant staying alive for just long enough to get the next shot off. Fourteen minutes. No problem.

Burke heard the field phone click and picked up the receiver from the floor. "Burke."

Mayor Kline's voice came through the earpiece. "Lieutenant, I didn't want to cut in on your command network—I've been monitoring all transmissions, of course, and not being there to see the situation, I felt it was better to let Captain Bellini handle it—but now that he's—"

"We appreciate that, sir." Burke noticed Kline's voice had that cool preciseness that was just a hair away from whining panic. "Actually, I have to get through to the crawl space, Mr. Mayor, so—"

"Yes—just a second—I was wondering if you could fill us in—"

"I just did."

"What? Oh, yes. Just one second. We need a situation report

from you as the ranking man in there—you're in charge, by the way."

"Thanks. Let me call you right back—"

"Fine."

He heard a click and spoke to the police operator. "Don't put that asshole through again." He dropped the receiver on the floor.

The Sixth Assault Squad of ESD rappelled from police helicopters into the open attic hatches. They ran across the foam-covered catwalks to the south tower and split up, one team going up toward Devane's position, the other down toward the triforium and choir loft levels.

The team climbing into the tower fired grenades ahead of them, moving up level by level until they reached the copper-louvered room where Devane had been posted. They looked for the body of the Fenian sniper in the dark, smoke-filled room but found only bloodstains on the floor and a gas mask lying in the corner.

The squad leader touched a bloodstain on the ascending ladder and looked up. "We'll go with gas from here."

The men pulled on gas masks and fired CS canisters to the next level. They moved up the ladder, floor by floor, the gas rising with them, into the narrowing spire. Above them they heard the echoing sounds of a man coughing, then the deep, full bellow of vomiting. They followed the blood trail on the rusty ladder, cautiously moving through the dark levels until they reached a narrow, tapering, octagonal room about fifteen stories above the street. The room had clover-shaped openings, without glass, cut into the eight sides of the stonework. The blood trail ended on the ladder, and the floor near one of the openings was smeared with vomit. The squad leader pulled off his gas mask and stuck his head and shoulders out of the opening and looked up.

A series of iron rungs ran up the last hundred feet of the tapering spire toward the copper cross on top. The squad leader saw a man climbing halfway up. The man lost his footing, then recovered and pulled himself up to the next rung. The squad leader dropped back into the small, cold room. He unslung his rifle and chambered a round. "These fucks blew away a lot of our people—understand?"

One of his men said, "It's not too cool to blow him away with all those people watching from Rockefeller Center."

The squad leader looked out the opening at the buildings across the Avenue. Despite orders and all the police could do, hundreds of people were at the windows and on the rooftops watching the climber make his way up the granite spire. A few people were shouting, making encouraging motions with their hands and bodies. The squad leader heard cheering and applauding and thought he heard gasps when the man slipped. He said, "Assholes. The wrong people are *always* getting the applause." He released the safety switch, moved toward the opening, and looked up. He shouted, "Hey, King Kong! Get your ass back here!"

The climber glanced down but continued up the spire.

The squad leader pulled his head back into the room. "Give me the rappelling line." He took the nylon rope and began hooking himself up. "Well, as the homicide detectives say, 'Did he fall or was he pushed?' That is the question."

The other half of the Sixth Assault Squad descended through the south tower and, following a rough sketch supplied by Gordon Stillway, located the door to the long southwest triforium. One of the men kicked the door in, and the other four rushed down the length of the long gallery in a crouch. An ESD man spotted a man dressed in kilts lying crumpled at the corner of the balustrade, a bagpipe sticking out from under his body.

Suddenly a periscope rose from the triforium across the transept, and a bullhorn blared. "Get down! The loft! Watch the loft!"

The men turned in unison and stared down at the choir loft projecting out at a right angle about thirty feet below them. A muzzle flashed twice, and two of the five men went down. The other three dove for the floor. "What the hell...?" The team leader looked wildly around the long dark gallery as though it were full of gunmen. "Where did that come from...the loft?" He looked at the two dead men, each shot between the eyes. "I never saw it.... I never heard anything...."

One of the men said, "Neither did they."

The fifteen men of the 69th Regiment had moved back into the Cathedral after the carrier had stopped burning, and they lay on the floor under the choir loft, sighting their rifles down the five wide aisles toward the raised sanctuary. Major Cole rose to one knee and looked over the pews with a pair of binoculars, then scanned the four triforia. Nothing seemed to be moving in the Cathedral, and the loudest sound was the striking of bullets from the Fenian sniper overhead. Cole looked at the smoking armored carrier beside him. The smell of burnt gasoline and flesh made his stomach heave.

A sergeant came up beside him. "Major, we have to do something."

The major felt his stomach heave again. "We are not supposed to interfere with the police in any way. There could be a misunderstanding...an accident..."

A runner came up the steps, moved through the battered

doors, and crossed the vestibule, finding Major Cole contemplating his watch. The runner crouched beside him. "From the Governor, sir."

Cole took the handwritten report without enthusiasm and read from the last paragraph. "Father Murphy still missing. Locate and rescue him and rescue the other two hostages beneath the sanctuary pews...." Cole looked up at the sergeant.

The sergeant regarded Cole's pale face. "If I found a way into that loft and zapped the sniper, you could dash up the aisle and grab the two hostages—" He smiled. "But you got to move quick because you'll be racing the cops for them."

Major Cole said stiffly, "All right. Take ten men into the loft." He turned to the runner. "Acknowledge message. Have the police command call their men in the triforia and tell them to hold fire on the loft for... five minutes." The runner saluted and moved off. Cole said to the sergeant, "Don't get anyone hurt."

The sergeant turned and led ten Guardsmen back into the south vestibule and opened the door to the spiral staircase. The soldiers double-timed up into the tower until they saw a large wooden door in the wall. The sergeant approached it cautiously and listened, but heard nothing. He put his hand on the knob and turned it slowly, then drew open the door a crack. There was complete blackness in front of him. At first he thought he wasn't in the loft, but then he saw in the distance candlelight playing off the wall of the long northern triforium above, and he recognized the empty flagstaff. He drew open the door, crouched with his rifle held out, and began walking in one of the cross aisles. The ten soldiers began following at intervals.

The sergeant slid his shoulder along the pew enclosure on his left as he moved, blinking into the darkness, listening for a sound somewhere in the cavernous loft. His shoulder slipped into an opening, and he turned, facing the wide aisle that ran up the center of the sloping loft. The entire expanse was pitch black, but he had a sense of its size from the massive rose window looming in the blackness, larger than a two-story house, glowing with the lights of Rockefeller Center across the Avenue. The sergeant took a step up the rising aisle, and he heard a sound like rustling silk in the pews above him.

A woman stood a few feet in front of him on the next higher step. The sergeant stared up at two points of burning green light that reflected the candlelight rising from the Cathedral behind him. The piercing eyes held him for a fraction of a second before he raised his rifle.

Megan screamed wildly and discharged a shotgun blast into his face. She jumped up on a pew and began firing down into the aisle below. The soldiers scrambled back along the aisle, buckshot pelting their helmets, flak jackets, and limbs as they retreated into the tower.

Leary shouted, "Keep them away, Megan! Keep me covered. I'm shooting like I never shot before. Give me time." He fired and moved, fired again and moved again.

Megan picked up her automatic rifle and fired quick bursts at the tower doors. Leary saw a periscope poking over the parapet in the southeast triforium and blew it away with a single shot. "I'm hot! God, I'm hot today!"

Burke heard the shotgun blasts from the loft, followed by the short, quick bursts of the M-16 and then the whistling of the sniper's rifle as rounds chipped away at the balustrade over his head.

The ESD man beside him said, "Sounds like the weekend commandos didn't capture the choir loft."

Burke picked up the field phone and spoke to the other three triforia. "At my command we throw everything we've got into the loft." He called the sacristy stairs. "Tell Malone and Baxter we're putting down suppressing fire again, and if they want to give it a try, this is the time to do it—there won't be another time."

Burke waited the remainder of the five minutes he had given the 69th, to be sure they were not going to try again to get into the loft, then put the field phone to his mouth. "Fire!"

Twenty-five ESD men rose in the four triforia and began firing with automatic rifles and grenade launchers. The rifles raked the loft with long traversing streams, while the launchers alternated their loads, firing beehive canisters of long needles, buckshot, high explosives, gas grenades, illumination rounds, and fire-extinguishing gas.

The choir loft reverberated with the din of exploding grenades, and thick black smoke mingled with the yellowish gas. The smoke and gas rose over the splintering pews, then moved along the ceiling of the Cathedral like an eerie cloud, iridescent in the light of the burning flares below.

Megan and Leary, wearing gas masks, knelt in the bottom aisle below the thick, protruding parapet that ran the width of the loft. Leary fired into the triforia, moved laterally, fired, and moved again. Megan sent streams of automatic fire into the sanctuary as she raced back and forth along the parapet.

Burke heard the sounds of the grenade launchers tapering off as the canisters were used up, and he heard an occasional exclamation when someone was hit. He stood and looked over the balustrade, through the smoke, and saw small flames flickering in the loft. From the field phone in his hand came excited voices as the other triforia called for medics. And still the firing from the loft went on. Burke grabbed an M-16 from one of the EDS men. "Goddamned sons of bitches—" He fired a full magazine without pause, reloaded and fired again until the gun overheated and jammed. He threw the rifle down savagely and shouted into the field phone, "Shoot the remaining fire-extinguishing canisters and get down."

The last of the canisters arched into the loft, and Burke saw the fires begin to subside. Impulsively he grabbed the bullhorn and shouted toward the loft, "I'm coming for you, cocksuckers. I'm—" He felt someone knock his legs out from under him, and he toppled to the floor as a bullet passed through the space where he had stood.

An ESD man sat cross-legged looking down at him. "You got to be cool, Lieutenant. There's nothing personal between them and us. You understand?"

Another man lit a cigarette and added, "They're giving it their best shot, and we're giving it our best shot. Today they got the force with them—see? And we don't. Makes you wonder, though.... I mean in a cathedral and all that..."

Burke took the man's cigarette and got control of himself. "Okay.... okay.... Any ideas?"

A man dabbing at a grazing wound across his jaw answered, "Yeah, offer them a job—my job."

Another man added, "Somebody's got to get *into* the loft through the towers. That's the truth."

Burke saw the dial of the other man's watch. He picked up the phone and called the sacristy stairs. "Did the hostages make it?"

The commo man answered, "Whoever's behind that M-16 up there wasn't shooting at you guys—it was raining bullets on the floor between the pews and the stairs—Christ, somebody up there has it in for these two."

"I'm sure it's not personal." Burke threw the phone down. "Still, I'm getting a little pissed off."

"What the hell is driving those two Micks on?" an ESD man asked. "Politics? I mean, I'm a registered Democrat, but I don't get *that* excited about it. You know?"

Burke stubbed out a cigarette and thought about Bellini. He looked down at the coagulated gore on his trousers that had been part of Bellini, those great stupid brains that had held a lot more knowledge than he had realized. Bellini would know what to do, and if he didn't, he would know how to inspire confidence in these semi-psychotics around him. Burke felt very much out of his element, unwilling to give an order that would get one more man killed; and he appreciated—really and fully appreciated—the reason for Bellini's erratic behavior all night. Unconsciously he rubbed at the stains on his trousers until someone said, "It doesn't come off."

Burke nodded. He realized now that he had to go to the loft, himself, and finish it one way or the other.

Maureen listened to the intense volume of fire dying away. The arm of the policeman who had fallen from the triforium above dangled between the pews, dripping blood into a large puddle of red. Through the gunfire she had thought she heard a sound coming from the pulpit.

Baxter said, "I think that was our last chance, Maureen."

She heard it again, a low, choked-off moan. She said, "We may have one more chance." She slid away from Baxter, avoiding his grasp, and rolled beneath the pews, coming out where they ended near the spiral pulpit staircase a few feet across a patch of open floor. She dove across the opening and flattened herself on the marble-walled steps, hugging the big column around which the steps circled. As she reached the top she noticed the red bloodstains on the top stairs. She looked into the pulpit and saw that he had dragged himself up to a sitting position, his back to the marble wall. His eyes were shut, and she stared at him for several seconds, watching the irregular rising and falling of his chest. Then she slid into the pulpit. "Brian."

He opened his eyes and focused on her.

She leaned over him and said quietly, "Do you see what you've done? They're all dead, Brian. All your trusting young friends are dead—only Leary, Megan, and Hickey are left—the bastards."

He took her hand and pressed it weakly. "Well...you're all right, then...and Baxter?"

She nodded, then ripped open his shirt and saw the bullet wound that had entered from the top of his shoulder. She moved her hands over his body and found the exit wound on his opposite hip, big and jagged, filled with bone splinters and marrow. "Oh, God..." She breathed deeply several times, trying to bring her voice under control. "Was it *worth* it?"

His eyes seemed clear and alert. "Stop scolding, Maureen."

She touched his cheek. "Father Murphy...Why did you...?"

He closed his eyes and shook his head. "We never escape what we were as children.... Priests awe me...." He drew a shallow breath. "Priests...cathedrals...you attack what you fear...primitive...self-protecting."

She glanced at her watch, then took him by his shoulders and shook him gently. "Can you call off Leary and Megan? Can you make them stop?" She looked up at the pulpit microphone. "Let me help you stand."

He didn't respond.

She shook him again. "Brian—it's over—it's finished—stop this killing—"

He shook his head. "I can't stop them.... You know that...."

"The bombs, then. Brian, how many bombs? Where are they? What time—?"

"I don't know...and if I did...I don't know...6:03...

sooner... later... two bombs... eight... a hundred.... Ask Hickey...."

She shook him more roughly. "You're a damned fool." She said more softly, "You're dying."

"Let me go in peace, can't you?" He suddenly leaned forward and took her hands in a surprisingly tight grip, and a spasm shook his body. He felt blood rising from his lungs and felt it streaming through his parted lips. "Oh... God... God, this is slow...."

She looked at a pistol lying on the floor and picked it up.

He watched her as she held the pistol in both hands. He shook his head. "No.... You've got enough regrets... don't carry that with you.... Not for me...." She cocked the pistol. "Not for you—for *me.* "

He held out his hand and pushed her arm away. "I *want* it to be slow...."

She uncocked the pistol and flung it down the steps. "All right... as you wish." She looked around the floor of the pulpit, and from among a pile of ammunition boxes she took an aid kit and unwrapped two pressure bandages.

Flynn said, "Go away.... Don't prolong this.... You're not helping...."

"You want it to be slow." She dressed both wounds, then extracted a Syrette of morphine from the kit.

He pushed her hand away weakly. "For God's sake, Maureen, let me die my way.... I want to stay clearheaded... to think...."

She tapped the spring-loaded Syrette against his arm, and the morphine shot into his muscle. "Clearheaded," she repeated, "clearheaded, indeed."

He slumped back against the pulpit wall. "Cold... cold... this is bad...."

"Yes...let the morphine work. Close your eyes."

"Maureen...how many people have I done this to...? My God...what *have* I done all these years...?"

Tears formed in her eyes. "Oh, Brian...always so late...always so late...."

Rory Devane felt blood collecting in his torn throat and tried to spit, but the blood gushed from his open wound again, carrying flecks of vomit with it. He blinked the running tears from his eyes as he moved upward. His hands had lost all sensation, and he had to look at them to see if they were grabbing the cold iron rungs.

The higher he climbed, the more his head throbbed where the ricochet had hit him, and the throbbing spread into his skull, causing a pain he wouldn't have believed possible. Several times he wanted to let go, but the image of the cross on the top drew him upward.

He reached the end of the stone spire and looked up at the protruding ornamental copper finial from which rose the cross. Iron spikes, like steps, had been driven into the bulging finial. He climbed them slowly, then threw his arms around the base of the cross and put his head down on the cold metal and wept. After a while he picked up his head and completed his climb. He draped his numb arms over the cross and stood, twenty-eight stories above the city.

Slowly Devane looked to his front. Across the Avenue, Rockefeller Center soared above him, half the windows lit and open, people waving at him. He turned to his left and saw the Empire State Building towering over the Avenue. He shifted his body around and looked behind him. Between two tall buildings he saw the flatland of Long Island stretching back to the horizon. A soft golden glow illuminated the place where the earth met the dark, starlit sky. "Dawn."

* * *

Burke knelt on the blood-covered floor of the triforium. The wounded had been lowered down the elevator shaft, and the dead, including Bellini, were laid out in the attic. Four ESD men of the First Assault Squad remained, huddled against the parapet. The sniper in the choir loft was skimming bullets across the top of the balustrades, but from what Burke could hear, few of the ESD men in the three other triforia were picking their heads up to return the fire. Burke took the field phone and called the opposite triforium. "Situation."

The voice answered, "Squad leader got it. Wounded evacuated down the chimney, and replacements moving up but—listen, what's the word from Rockefeller Center? It's late."

Burke had a vivid image of Commissioner Rourke throwing up in a men's room, Murray Kline telling everyone to be calm, and Martin, looking very cool, giving advice that was designed to finish off the Cathedral and everyone in it. Burke glanced at his watch. It would be slow going down that chimney. He spoke into the phone. "Clear out."

"I hear you."

Burke signaled the switchboard. "Did you get through to the towers or attic yet?"

The operator answered, "Attic under control. Upper parts of both towers are secure, except for some clown climbing the south tower. But down at the loft level everything's a fucking mess. Some weird bitch dressed like a witch or something is blasting away at the tower doors. Some ESD guys got wasted in the choir room. Army guys got creamed coming into the loft from the other tower. Very unclear. You want to speak to them? Tell them to try again?"

"No. Tell them to stand by. Put me through to the crawl space."

The operator's voice was hesitant. "We can't raise them. They were reporting fine until a few minutes ago—then I lost them." The man paused, then added, "Check the time."

"I know the fucking time. Everybody knows the fucking time. Keep trying the crawl space. Connect me with Fifth Squad."

An ESD man on the sacristy stairs answered, and Burke said, "Situation."

The man reported, "Sacristy behind me is filled with fresh Assault Squads, but only two guys at a time can shoot from behind the altar. We definitely cannot reach that bronze plate. We cannot reach the hostages, and they can't reach us. Christ, those two bastards up there can *shoot.*" He drew a deep breath. "What the hell is happening?"

"What's happening," Burke answered, "is that this end of the Cathedral will probably collapse in ten minutes, so send everyone back to the rectory basement except two or three men to keep contact with the hostages."

"Right."

Langley's voice came on the line. "Burke—get the hell out of there. Now." Burke answered, "Have the ESD and Bomb Squad send more people into the crawl space—Hickey must've nailed the others. There's at least one bomb left, and he's probably guarding it like a dog with a meaty bone. Get on it."

Langley said, "The bomb could blow *any* time. We can't send any more—"

Mayor Kline cut in, and his voice had the tone of a man speaking for the tape recorders. "Lieutenant, *on your advice,* I'll put one more Assault Squad and bomb team in there, but you understand that their chances—"

Burke ripped the wire out of the phone and turned to the man beside him. "Get everyone down the elevator shaft, and don't stop until you reach the basement of the Cardinal's residence."

The man slung his rifle. "You coming?"

Burke turned and moved around the bend in the triforium that overlooked the south transept. He stood and looked over the balustrade. The line of sight of the choir loft was blocked by the angle of the crossed-shaped building, and the ESD men had shot a line across the transept to the long triforium. Burke slipped into a rope harness and began pulling himself, hand over hand, across the hundred-foot-wide transept arm.

An ESD man on the far side reached out and pulled him over the balustrade. The two men walked quickly to the corner where Sullivan lay sprawled across his bagpipes, his kilts and bare legs splattered with blood. Both men crouched before they turned the corner, and Burke moved down the length of the triforium, passing six kneeling ESD snipers and two dead ones. He took a periscope and looked over the balustrade.

The choir loft was about three stories below, and from here he could see how huge and obscure it was, while the police perches were more defined by the candlelight playing off the window-like openings. Still, he thought, it was incredible that anyone in the loft had survived the volleys of fire, and he wondered why those two were so blessed.

He lowered the scope and moved farther to his right, then stood higher and focused the periscope on the floor below. The shattered front of the armored vehicle stuck out from under the loft, and he saw part of a body sprawled over it—Logan. Two blackened arms stuck straight out of what had been the driver's compartment. Major Cole and a few men knelt to the side of the carrier, looking grim but, he thought, also relieved that the day's National Guard exercises were nearly over.

A shot whistled out of the loft, and the periscope slapped Burke in the eye and flew out of his hands. Burke toppled and fell to the floor.

The ESD man beside him said, "You held it up too long, Lieutenant. And that was our last scope."

Burke rubbed his eye and brought his hand away covered with watery blood. He rose to one knee and looked at the man, who appeared blurry. "Any word from the towers?"

Before the man answered, a short staccato burst of fire rolled out of the loft, followed by another, and the man said, "That's the word from the towers—the witch wants nobody near her doors." He looked at his watch and said, "What a fucking mess.... We almost had it. Right?"

Burke looked at the ESD man across from him, who was a sergeant. "Any ideas?"

"The thing hinges on knocking out the loft so that Malone and Baxter can make it to the stairs and so the ESD people there can drop concussion grenades through the plate and turn that guy Hickey's brains to mashed potatoes. Then the bomb guys can get the bombs. Right?"

Burke nodded. This seemed to be the inescapable solution to the problem. The choir loft dominated the entire Cathedral, as it was meant to do for a different purpose. And Flynn had placed two very weird people up there. "What are our options for knocking out the loft?"

The ESD sergeant rubbed his jaw. "Well, we could bring new spotlights into the triforia, have helicopters machinegun through the rose window, break through the plaster lathing in the attic over the loft.... Lots of options...but all that ordnance isn't handy...and it takes time...."

Burke nodded again. "Yeah..."

"But the best way," said the sergeant, "is for somebody to

sneak into that loft from one of the towers. Once you're past the door, you've got space to maneuver, just like them, and you're as invisible as they are."

Burke nodded. The alternate answer was to get to the explosives through the crawl space and worry about the sniper and the hostages later. Then 6:03 wouldn't matter anymore. Burke picked up the field phone and spoke to the switchboard. "What's the situation in the crawl space?"

The operator answered, "The new ESD squad is in—found some survivors dragging wounded back. Dogs and handlers dead. Bomb Squad people all out of it except Peterson, who's wounded but still functioning. There's a crazy guy down there with an automatic weapon. The survivors say there's no way to get to any remaining bombs except through the bronze plate." The operator hesitated, then said, "Listen...Peterson said this guy could probably set off the bombs anytime he wants...so I'm signing off because I'm a little close to where the bombs are supposed to be. Commo is going to be broken until I get this switchboard set up someplace else. Sorry, Lieutenant." He added, "They're searching both towers and the attic for the radio jammer, and if they find it, you'll have radio commo. Okay? Sorry."

The phone went dead. Burke turned on a radio lying near his feet, and a rush of static filled the air. He shut it off.

The ESD commo man beside him said, "That's it. Nobody is talking to nobody now. We can't coordinate an attack on that loft if we wanted to—or coordinate a withdrawal...."

Burke nodded. "Looks like getting in was the easy part." He looked around the dark gallery. "Well, it's a big place. Looks pretty solid to me. The architect seemed to think this end would stand if the main columns over there went...."

One of the men asked, "Anybody guaranteeing that? Is anybody sure there aren't bombs under these columns?" He tapped one of the columns.

Burke responded, "Logically, they wouldn't have bothered with fires in the attic if the whole place was rigged to explode. Right?" He looked at the men huddled around him, but no one seemed relieved by his deductions.

The sergeant said, "I don't think logic has anything to do with how these cocksuckers operate."

Burke looked at his watch. 5:54. He said, "I'm staying...you're staying." He entered the south tower and began to climb down to the loft level.

Maureen looked at her watch, then said to Flynn, "I'm going back."

"Yes...no...don't leave...." His voice was much weaker now.

She wiped his brow with her hand. "I'm sorry...I can't stay here."

He nodded.

"Do you have much pain, Brian?"

He shook his head, but as he did his body stiffened.

She took another Syrette of morphine and removed the cap. With the blood he had lost, she knew this would probably kill him, but there would be no pain. She bent over and put her arm around his neck, kissing him on the lips as she brought the Syrette to his chest, near his heart.

Flynn's lips moved against hers, and she turned her head to hear. "No...no...take it away...."

She drew the Syrette back and looked at him. He had not opened his eyes once in the last several minutes, and she did not understand how he knew...unless it was that he just knew her too well. She held his hand tightly and felt the large ring pressing into her palm. She said, "Brian...can I take this...? If I leave here...I want to return it...to bring it home...."

He pulled his hand away and clenched his fingers. "No."

"Keep it, then—the police will have it."

"No.... Someone must come for it."

She shook her head and then kissed him again. Without a word she slid back toward the winding stairs.

He called to her, "Maureen...listen...Leary...I told him...not to shoot at you.... He follows orders.... You can tell when Megan is covering the tower door...then you can run...."

She lay still on the stairs, then said, "Baxter...?"

"Baxter is as good as dead.... You can go...go..."

She shook her head. "Brian...you shouldn't have told me that...."

He opened his eyes and looked at her, then nodded. "No, I shouldn't have...stupid.... Always doing the wrong thing...." He tried to sit up, and his face went white with pain. "Please...run...live..." His chest began to rise and fall slowly.

Maureen watched him, then slid slowly down the stairs and rolled quickly over the few feet of exposed floor and crawled between the pews, coming up beside Baxter.

Baxter said, "I wanted to follow you...but I thought perhaps..."

She took his hand and pressed it.

"He's dead?"

"No."

They lay side by side in silence. At 5:55 Baxter asked, "Do you think he could— or would—call off Leary and Megan?"

She said, "I didn't ask."

Baxter nodded. "I see.... Well, are you ready to run for it?"

"I'm not certain that's what I want to do."

"Then why did you come back here?"

She didn't answer.

He drew a short breath and said, "I'm going...."

She held his arm tightly and peered under the pew at the long expanse of blood-streaked white marble that seemed to radiate an incandescence of its own in the candlelight. She heard the staccato bursts of Megan's fire hitting the tower doors but no longer heard the sound of Leary's bullets striking in the Cathedral. "Leary is waiting for us."

"Then let's not keep him waiting." He began moving toward the end of the pew.

She kept a grip on his arm. "No!"

A policeman's voice called out from the sacristy stairwell behind the altar. "Listen, you're keeping two men here—I don't like to put it this way, but we'd rather be gone—you know?—so are you coming or not?" He thought he spoke just loud enough for them to hear, but the acoustics carried the sound through the Cathedral.

Two shots whistled out of the loft and cracked into the marble midway between the pews and the altar. Maureen slid beside Baxter and turned her face to him. "Stay with me."

He put his arm around her shoulders and called out to the stairwell. "Go on— there's no point in waiting for us."

There was no answer, and Maureen and Baxter edged closer to each other, waiting out the final minutes.

Wendy Peterson knelt behind the back wall of the crypt as a medic wound a bandage around her right forearm. She flexed her fingers and noticed that they were becoming stiff. *"Damn."*

The medic said, "You better go back." Another medic was tying a pressure bandage around her right heel.

She looked around the red-lit area. Most of the original

group had been left behind, dead from head wounds as a result of the ground-skimming fire. The rest were being evacuated, suffering from wounds in the limbs or buttocks or from broken clavicles where the flak jackets had stopped the head-on bullets. In the red light, pale faces seemed rosy, red blood looked black, and, somehow, the wounds seemed especially ugly. She turned away and concentrated on moving her fingers. "Damn it."

The new ESD squad leader assembled his men at the corner of the crypt and looked at his watch. "Eight minutes." He knelt down beside Peterson. "Listen, I don't know what the hell I'm supposed to be doing down here except collecting bodies because, let me tell you, there's no way to get that joker out of there, Lieutenant."

She moved away from the medics and limped to the edge of the vault. "You sure?"

He nodded. "I can't fire—right? He's got a gas mask, and concussion grenades are out. But even if we got him, there's not much time to defuse even one bomb, and we don't know how many there are. The damned dogs are dead, and there aren't any more dogs—"

"Okay...okay.... Damn it...we're so close."

"No," said the squad leader, "we are not close at all." Some of the men around him coughed nervously and pointedly. The squad leader addressed Peterson. "They said this was your decision...and Burke's decision." He picked up the field phone beside him, but it was still dead. "Your decision."

A voice called out from the dark, an old man's voice with a mocking tone. "Fuck you! Fuck all of you!"

A nervous young policeman shouted back, "Fuck you!"

The squad leader stuck his head around the crypt corner and shouted, "If you come out with your hands—"

"Oh, baloney!" Hickey laughed, then fired a burst of bullets at the red glow coming around the corner of the crypt. The gun-fire caused a deafening roar in the closed space and echoed far into the quarteracre of crawl space. Hickey shouted, "Is there a bomb squad lad there? Answer me!"

Peterson edged toward the corner. "Right here, Pop."

"*Pop*? Who are you calling Pop? Well, never mind—listen, these bombs have more sensitive triggers to make them blow than... than Linda Lovelace." He laughed, then said, "Terrible metaphor. Anyway, lass, to give you an example you'll appreciate professionally—I mean demolitions, not blowing—where was I? Oh, yes, I've lots of triggers—photosensitive, audio—all kinds of triggers. Do you believe that, little girl?"

"I think you're full of shit."

Hickey laughed. "Well, then send everyone away, darlin', and toss a concussion grenade at me. If that doesn't blow the bombs, then a demo man can come back and defuse them. *You* won't be able to with your brains scrambled, and I won't be able to stop him with *my* brains scrambled. Go on, lassie. Let's see what you're made of."

Wendy Peterson turned to the squad leader. "Give me a con-cussion grenade and clear out."

"Like hell. Anyway, you know we don't carry those things in spaces like this."

She unsheathed the long stiletto that she used to cut plastic and moved around the corner of the crypt.

The squad leader reached out and pulled her back. "Where the hell are you going? Listen, I thought of that—it's over sixty feet to where that guy is. *Nobody* can cover that distance without making some noise, and he'll nail you the second he hears you."

"Then cover me with noise."

"Forget it."

Hickey called out, "What's next, folks? One man belly-crawling? I can hear breathing at thirty-forty feet. I can smell a copper at sixty feet. Listen, gentlemen— and lady—the time has come for you to leave. You're annoying me, and I have things to think about in the next few minutes. I feel like singing—" He began singing a bawdy version of the British army song:

> "Fuck you aaa-lll, fuck you aaa-lll,
> The long and the short and the taa-lll.
> Fuck all the coppers, and fuck all their guns,
> Fuck all the priests and their bastard sons.
> S-o-oo, I'm saying good-bye to you all,
> The ones that appeal and appall.
> I stall and tarry,
> While you want to save Harry,
> But nevertheless fuck you aaa-lll."

Wendy Peterson put the stiletto back in its sheath and let out a long breath. "Let's go."

The procession began making its way back toward the open hatch to the corridor, moving with an affected casualness that disguised the fact that they were retreating at top speed. No one looked back except Wendy Peterson, who glanced over her shoulder once or twice. Suddenly she began running in a crouch, past the moving line of men, toward the open hatch.

John Hickey squeezed out of the tight space and sat down against the column footing, the mass of plastic explosive conforming to his back. "Oh...well..." He filled his pipe, lit it, and looked at his watch. 5:56. "My, it's late...." He hummed a few bars of "An Irish Lullaby," then sang softly to himself, "...too-ra-loo-ra-loo-ra, hush now don't you cry...."

* * *

The Sixth Squad leader climbed the iron rungs of the south spire alone, a nylon line attached to his belt. He moved quietly through the cold dark night to a point five feet below Rory Devane, who still clung to the arms of the cross. The ESD man drew his pistol. "Hey! Jesus! Don't move, or I'll blow your ass off."

Devane opened his eyes and looked down behind him.

The squad leader raised his pistol. "You armed?"

Devane shook his head.

The squad leader got a clear look at Devane's bloodied face in the city lights. "You're really fucked up—you know that?"

Devane nodded.

"Come on down. Nice and easy."

Devane shook his head. "I can't."

"Can't? You got up there, you bastard. Now get down. I'm not hanging here all fucking day waiting for you."

"I can't move."

The squad leader thought that about half the world was watching him on television, and he put a concerned expression on his face, then smiled at Devane good-naturedly. "You asshole. For two cents I'd jam this gun between your legs and blow your balls into orbit." He glanced at the towering buildings of Rockefeller Center and flashed a resolute look for the telescopic cameras and field glasses. He took a step upward. "Listen, sonny boy, I'm coming up with a line, and if you pull any shit, I swear to God, motherfucker, you're going to be treading air."

Devane stared down at the black-clad figure approaching. "You people talk funny."

The squad leader laughed and climbed up over the curve of the finial and wrapped his arms around the base of the cross. "You're okay, kid. You're an asshole, but you're okay. Don't move." He circled around to the side and pulled himself up until his head was level with Devane's shoulder, then reached out and looped a line around Devane's torso. "You the guy who fired the flares?"

Devane nodded.

"Real performer, aren't you, Junior? What else do you do? You juggle?" He tied the end of the long line to the top of the cross and spoke in a more solemn voice. "You're going to have to climb a little. I'll help you."

Devane's mind was nearly numb, but something didn't seem right. There was something incongruous about hanging twenty-eight stories above the most technologically advanced city in the world and being asked to climb, wounded, down a rope to safety. "Get a helicopter."

The squad leader glanced at him quickly.

Devane stared down into the man's eyes and said, "You're going to kill me."

"What the hell are you talking about? I'm risking my god-damned life to save you—shithead." He flashed a smile toward Rockefeller Center. "Come on. Down."

"No."

The squad leader heard a sound and looked up. A Fire Rescue helicopter appeared overhead and began dropping toward the spire. The helicopter dropped closer, beating the cold air downward. The squad leader saw a man in a harness edging out of the side door, a carrying chair in his hands. The squad leader hooked his arms over Devane's on the cross and pulled himself up so that they were face to face, and he studied the young man's frozen blue features. The blood had actually crystallized in his red hair and glistened in the light. The squad leader examined his throat wound and the large discolored mass on his forehead. "Caught some shit, did you? You should be dead—you know?"

"I'm going to live."

"They're stuffing some of my friends in body bags down there—"

"I never fired a shot."

"Yeah.... Come on, I'll help you into the sling."

"How can you commit murder—*here?*"

The squad leader drew a long breath and exhaled a plume of fog.

The Fire Rescue man was dangling about twenty feet above them now, and he released the carrying chair, which dropped on a line to within a few feet of the two men. The squad leader put his hands on Devane's shoulders. "Okay, Red, trust me." He reached up and guided the chair under Devane, strapped him in, then untied the looped rope. "Don't look down." He waved off the helicopter.

The helicopter rose, and Devane flew away from the spire, swinging in a wide arc through the brightening sky. The squad leader watched as the line was reeled in and Devane disappeared into the helicopter. The squad leader turned and looked back at Rockefeller Center. People were leaning from the windows, civilians and police, and he heard cheering. Bits of paper began sailing from the windows and floated in the updrafts. He wiped his runny eyes and waved toward the buildings as he began the climb down from the cross. "Hello, assholes—spell my name right. Hi, Mom—fuck you, Kline—I'm a hero."

Burke ran down the spiral stairs of the south tower until he reached a group of Guardsmen and police on the darkened choir loft level Burke said, "What's the situation?"

No one answered immediately, then an ESD man said, "We sort of ran into each other in the dark." He motioned toward a neat stack of about six bodies against the wall

"Christ...." Burke looked across the tower room and saw a splintered door hanging loosely from its hinges.

An ESD man said, "Stay out of the line of fire of that door."

"Yeah, I guessed that right away."

A short burst of rifle fire hit the door, and everyone ducked as the bullets ricocheted around the large room, shattering thick panes of glass. A National Guardsman fired a full magazine back through the door.

The steady coughing of the sniper's silencer echoed into the room, but Burke could not imagine what was left to fire at. He circled around the room and slid along the wall toward the door.

Wendy Peterson ran to the top step of the sacristy stairs behind the altar. Her breathing came hard, and the wound on her heel was bleeding. She called back to the crypt landing where the two remaining ESD men stood. "Concussion grenade."

One of the men shrugged and threw up a large black canister.

She edged out and glanced to her right. About thirty feet separated the hostages under the pews from the stairs. To her left, toward the rear of the sanctuary, five feet of floor separated her from the bullet-scarred bronze plate. How heavy, she wondered, was that plate? Which way did it hinge? Where was the handle? She turned back to the crypt landing. "The hostages?"

One of the men answered, "We can't help them. They have to make a break when they think they're ready. We're here in case they make it and are wounded... but they're not going to make it. Neither are we if we hang around much longer." He cleared his throat. "Hey, it's 5:57—can those bombs go before 6:03?"

She motioned toward the bronze plate. "What are my chances?"

The man looked down at the blood-streaked stairs and unconsciously touched his ear, which had been nicked by a shot from the loft—a shot fired from over a hundred yards away through the dim lighting. "Your chances of getting to the plate are good—fifty-fifty.

Your chances of opening it, dropping that grenade, waiting for it to go, then dropping in yourself, are a little worse than zero."

"Then we let the place go down?"

He said, "No one can say we didn't try." He ran his foot across the sticky blood on the landing. "Cut out."

She shook her head. "I'll hang around—you never know what might happen."

"I *know* what's going to happen, Lieutenant, and this is not the place to be when it happens."

Two shots struck the bronze plate and ricocheted back toward the Lady Chapel. Another shot struck the plaster ceiling ten stories above. Peterson and the two ESD men looked up at the black expanse and dodged pieces of falling plaster. A second later one of the Cardinal's hats that had been suspended over the crypt dropped to the landing beside one of the ESD men. The man picked it up and examined the tassled red hat.

Leary's voice bellowed from the loft. "Got a cardinal—on the wing—in the dark. God, I can't miss! I can't *miss!*"

The ESD man threw the hat aside. "He's right, you know."

Peterson said, "I'll talk to the hostages. You might as well go."

One of the men bounded down the stairs toward the sacristy gates. The other climbed up toward Peterson. "Lieutenant"—he looked down at the bloody, soiled bandages wrapped around her bare foot—"it takes about sixty seconds to make it to the rectory basement...."

"Okay."

The man hesitated, then turned and headed for the sacristy gates.

Peterson sat down on the top step and called out to Baxter and Malone, "How are you doing?"

Maureen called back, "Go away."

Peterson lit a cigarette. "It's okay...we have time yet....

Anytime you're ready...think it out." She spoke to them softly as the seconds ticked away.

Leary grazed a round over each of the four triforium balustrades, changed positions, fired at the statue of St. Patrick, moved laterally, picked out a flickering votive candle, fired, and watched it explode. He moved diagonally over the pews, then stopped and put two bullets through the cobalt blue window rising above the east end of the ambulatory. The approaching dawn showed a lighter blue through the broken glass.

Leary settled back into a bullet-pocked pew near the organ pipes and concentrated on the sanctuary—the stairwell, the bronze plate, and the clergy pews. He flexed his arm, which had been hit by shrapnel, and rubbed his cheek where buckshot had raked the side of his face. At least two ribs had been broken by bullets where they had hit his flak jacket.

Megan was firing at each of the tower doors, alternating the sequence and duration of each burst of automatic fire. She stood in the aisle a few feet below Leary and watched the two doors to her right and left farther down the loft. Her arms and legs were crusted with blood from shrapnel and buckshot, and her right shoulder was numb from a direct bullet hit. She suddenly felt shaky and nauseous and leaned against a pew. She straightened up and called back to Leary, "They're not even trying."

Leary said, "I'm bored."

She laughed weakly, then replied, "I'm going to blast those pews and flush those two out. You nail them."

Leary said, "In about six minutes half the Cathedral will fall in on them...or I'll get them if they make a break. Don't spoil the game. Be patient."

She knelt in the aisle and raised her rifle. "What if the police get the bombs?"

Leary looked at the sanctuary as he spoke. "I doubt they got Hickey.... Anyway, I'm doing what I was told—covering that plate and keeping those two from running."

She shouted as she took aim at the clergy pews. "I want to *see* her die—before I die. I'm going to flush them. You nail them. Ready?"

Leary stared, down at Megan, her silhouette visible against the candlelight and flares below. He spoke in a low, contemplative voice. "Everyone's dead, Megan, except Hickey and, I guess, Malone and Baxter. They'll all die in the explosion. That leaves only you and me."

She spun around and peered up into the blackness toward the place from which his voice had come.

He said, "You understand, I'm a professional. It's like I said, I only do what I'm told—never more, never less—and Flynn told me to make especially sure of you and Hickey."

She shook her head. "Jack...you can't.... Not after we..." She laughed. "Yes, of course.... I don't want to be taken.... Brian knew that.... He did it for me. Go on, then. Quickly!"

He raised a pistol, aimed at the dark outline, and put two bullets in rapid succession through her head. Megan's body toppled back, and she rolled down the aisle, coming to rest beside the Guard sergeant she had killed.

Burke stood in his stocking feet with his back to the wall just inside the tower door, a short, fat grenade launcher nestled in the bend of his elbow. He closed his eyes against the glare of the lights coming through the broken windows and steadied his breathing. The men in the tower room were completely still, watching him. Burke listened to the distant sound of a man and woman talking, followed by two pistol shots. He spun rapidly into the doorway and raced up the side aisle along the wall, then flattened himself in the sloping aisle about halfway up the loft. From farther back near the organ pipes came the sound of breathing. The breathing stopped abruptly, and a man's voice said, "I *know* you're there."

Burke remained motionless.

The man said, "I see in the dark, I smell what you can't smell, I hear *everything*. You're dead."

Burke knew that the man was trying to draw him into a panic shot, and he was not doing a bad job of it. The man was good. Even in a close-in-situation like this he was very cool.

Burke rolled onto his back, lifted his head, and looked out over the rail into the Cathedral. The cable that held the chandelier nearest the choir loft swayed slightly as it was being drawn up by the winch in the attic. The chandelier rose level with the loft, and Burke saw the Guardsman sitting on it, his rifle pointed into the loft. He looked, Burke thought, like live bait. *Live ones,* he wanted live ones. Burke's muscles tensed.

Leary fired, and the body on the chandelier jerked.

Burke jumped to his feet, pointed the grenade launcher at the direction of the sound, and fired its single beehive round. The dozens of needle darts buzzed across the quiet loft, spreading as they traveled. There was a sharp cry, followed immediately by the flash of a rifle that Burke saw out of the corner of his eyes as he turned and dove for the floor. A powerful blow on the back of his flak jacket propelled him headfirst into the wall, and he staggered, then collapsed into the aisle. Another shot ripped through the pews and passed inches over his head.

Burke lay still, aware of a pain in the center of his spine that began to spread to his arms and legs. Several more shots struck around him. The firing shifted to the doors, and Burke tried to crawl to another position but found that he couldn't move. He tried to reach the pistol in his belt, but his arm responded in short, spastic motions.

The firing shifted back toward him, and a round grazed his hand. His forehead was bleeding where he had crashed into the wall, and throbbing pains ran from his eyes to the back of his skull. He felt himself losing consciousness, but he could hear distinctly the sound of the man reloading his rifle. Then the voice said, "Are you dead, or do you just wish you were?"

Leary raised his rifle, but the persistent stabbing pain in his right leg made him lower it. He sat down in the center aisle, rolled back his trouser leg, and ran his fingers over his shin, feeling the tiny entry hole where the dart had hit him. He brought his hand around to his calf and touched the exit wound, slightly larger, with a splinter of bone protruding from the flesh. "Ah...shit...shit..."

He rose to his knee and emptied his rifle toward the doors and the side aisle, then ripped off his rubber mask and pulled the gas mask from around his neck. He tore off the long robe, using it to wipe his sniper rifle from end to end as he crawled down the center aisle. Leary placed the rifle in Megan's warm hands, reached into the front pew, and retrieved another rifle. He rose and steadied himself on the edge of the pew and slid onto the bench. Leary called out, "Martin! You out there?"

There was a silence, then a voice called back from the choir practice room. "Right here, Jack. Are you alone?"

"Yeah."

"Tell the police you're surrendering."

"Right. Come out here—alone."

Martin walked briskly into the choir loft, turned on a flashlight, and made his way through the dark into the center aisle. He stepped over Megan's body. "Hello, Jack." He approached Leary and edged into the pew. "Here, let's have that. That's a good lad." He took Leary's rifle and pistol, then called out, "He's disarmed."

ESD men began to move cautiously from both towers into the choir loft. Martin called to them. "It's all right—this man is an agent of mine." Martin turned to Leary and gave him a look of annoyance. "A bit early, aren't you, Jack?"

Leary spoke through clenched teeth. "I'm hit."

"Really? You look fine."

Leary swore. "Fitzgerald was starting to become a problem, and I had to do her when I had the chance. Then someone got into the loft, and I took a needle dart in the shin. Okay?"

"That's dreadful...but I don't see anyone in here.... You really should have waited."

"Fuck you."

Martin shone his light on Leary's shin. Like so many killers, he thought, Leary couldn't stand much pain. "Yes, that looks like it might hurt." He reached out and touched Leary's wound.

Leary let out a cry of pain. "Hey! God...that feels like there's still a needle in there."

"Might well be." Martin looked down at the sanctuary. "Malone and Baxter...?"

A policeman shouted from the side of the loft. "Stand up!"

Leary placed his hands on the pew in front of him and stood. He said to Martin, "They're both under the sanctuary pews there—"

The lights in the loft went on, illuminating the sloping expanse of ripped pews, bullet-pocked walls, burnt lockers, and scarred aisles. The towering organ pipes shone brightly where they had been hit, but above the pipes the rose window was intact. Leary looked around and made a whistling sound. "Like walking in the rain without getting wet." He smiled.

Martin waved his hand impatiently. "I don't understand about Baxter and Malone. They're dead, aren't they?"

The police stepped over the bodies in the aisle and moved up carefully into the pews, rifles and pistols raised.

Leary automatically put his hands on his head as he spoke to Martin. "Flynn told me not to kill her—and I couldn't shoot into the pews at Baxter without taking the chance of hitting her—"

"*Flynn*? You're working for *me*, Jack."

Leary pushed past Martin and hobbled into the aisle. "You give orders, he gives orders.... I do only what I'm told—and what I'm paid for—"

"But Flynn's money came from *me*, Jack."

Leary stared at Martin. "Flynn never bullshitted me. He told me this loft would be hell, and I knew it. You said it would be—how'd that go?—relatively without risk?"

Martin's voice was peevish. "Well, as far as I'm concerned you didn't fulfill your contract, I'll have to reconsider the nature of the final payment."

"Look, you little fuck—" Two ESD men covered the remaining distance up the aisle and grabbed Leary's upraised arms, pulling them roughly behind his back, then cuffing him. They pushed him to the floor, and he yelled out in pain, then turned his head back toward Martin as the police searched him. "If they got Hickey from below, they got the bombs anyway. If they didn't get him, you'll still get your explosion."

Martin noticed Burke moving toward him, supported by two ESD men. Martin cleared his throat. "All right, Jack—that's enough."

But Leary was obviously offended. "I lived up to my end. I mean, Christ, Martin, it's after six—and look around you—enough is enough—"

"Shut up."

Two ESD men pulled Leary to his feet. Leary said, "This leg...it feels funny...burns..."

Martin said nothing.

Leary stared at him. "What did you...? Oh...no..."

Martin winked at him, turned, and walked away.

An ESD man raised a bullhorn and called out into the Cathedral. "Police in the choir loft! All clear! Mr. Baxter—Miss Malone—run! Run this way!"

Baxter picked up his head and looked at Maureen. "Was that Leary?"

She forced a smile. "You're learning." She listened to the bullhorn call their names again. "I don't know..." She pressed her face against Baxter's, and they held each other tightly.

Wendy Peterson looked around the altar and stared up into the choir loft. It was completely lit, and she saw the police moving through the pews. Without looking at her watch she knew there were probably not more than three minutes left—less, if the bomb were set earlier, and she didn't remember one that was set for later than the threatened time.

She ran to the bronze plate, pulling the pin on the concussion grenade as she moved and calling back to the pews. "Run! Run!" She bent over and pulled up the heavy bronze plate with one hand.

Maureen stood, looking first at Wendy Peterson and then toward the illuminated expanse at the upper end of the Cathedral as Baxter came up beside her.

A bullhorn was blaring. "Run! Run this way!"

They began to run, but Maureen suddenly veered and dashed up the pulpit stairs, grabbing Flynn's arm and dragging him back down the steps. Baxter ran up behind her and pulled at her arm. She turned to him. "He's alive. *Please*..." He hesitated, then put Flynn over his shoulders, and they ran toward the communion rail.

Wendy Peterson watched silently until they reached a point in the center aisle where she thought they would be safe if the grenade detonated the bomb. She released the safety handle and flung the grenade into the hole with a motion that suggested *What the hell....* She dropped the plate back and stood off several feet, holding her hands over her ears.

The grenade exploded, ripping the bronze plate from its hinges and sending it high into the air. A shock wave rolled through the Cathedral, and the sanctuary trembled beneath her feet. Everything seemed to hang in suspension as she waited for a secondary explosion, but there was nothing except the ringing in her ears. She dropped through the smoke down the ladder.

Burke moved slowly toward Martin as the echoes of the shock wave passed through the loft.

Martin said, "Well, Lieutenant Burke, this is a surprise. I thought you'd be... well, somewhere else. You look terrible. You're walking strangely. Where are your *shoes?*" Martin checked his watch. "Two minutes... less, I think. Good view from here. Do you have cameras recording this? You won't see this again." He peered over Burke's shoulder at the sanctuary. "Look at all that metalwork, that marble. Magnificent. It's going to look exactly like Coventry in about three minutes." He patted the lapel of his topcoat as he turned back to Burke. "See? I've kept my carnation. Where's yours?" He looked anxiously into the sanctuary again. "What *is* that crazy woman up to? Turn around, Burke. Don't miss this."

Martin brushed past Burke and drew closer to the rail. He watched Baxter and Maureen approaching, accompanied by Major Cole and four Guardsmen. Brian Flynn's limp body was being carried on a stretcher by two of the Guardsmen. Martin said to Burke, "Governor Doyle will be pleased with his boys—Mayor Kline will be *furious* with you, Burke." Martin called down. "Harry, old man? Up here!" He waved. "Nicely done, you two."

Martin turned and looked back as Leary, almost unconscious, was being carried into the choir practice room. He said to Burke, "Ballistics will show that the rifle I took from him never fired a shot that killed anyone. He did kill that young woman sniper, though, the very moment he had—what do you call it?—the drop on her. Well, at least that's the way he's made it appear. He'll go free if he is tried." Martin looked back over his shoulder. "Good-bye, Jack. I'll see you later in the hospital." He called to an ESD squad leader. "Easy with that man—he works for me." Martin turned back to Burke as Leary disappeared into the choir room. "Your people are in an ugly mood. Well...the mysteries are unfolding now...Burke? Are you listening to me? Burke—" Martin looked at his watch, then at the sanctuary, and continued in a new vein. "The problem with you people is no fire discipline. Shoot first and ask questions later—great tradition. That's why Father Murphy is hanging dead from a ladder in the bell tower here—oh, you didn't know that, Burke?"

Martin walked to the edge of the loft and rested his hands on the parapet, looking straight down. Baxter and Malone were standing with their backs to him now. Flynn was lying near them on the floor, a National Guard medic crouched over him. Baxter, Martin noticed, had his arm around Maureen Malone's shoulder, and she was slumped against him. Martin said to Burke, "Come closer—look at this, Burke. They've made friends." He called down, "Harry, you old devil. Miss Malone. Get down, you two—there'll be a bit of falling debris." He turned to Burke behind him. "I feel rather bad about being the one who pushed for Baxter being on the steps.... If I had had *any* idea it would be so risky..."

Burke moved beside Martin and leaned on the rail. The feeling began to return to his legs and arms, and the numbness was replaced by a tingling sensation. He looked out into the Cathedral, focusing on the sanctuary. A dead ESD man lay in the clergy pews, and black smoke drifted out of the hole. Green carnations were strewn across the black-and-white marble floor, and hundreds of fragments of stained glass glittered where they'd fallen from above. Even from this distance he could see the blood splattered across the raised altar, the bullet marks everywhere. The police in the choir pews behind him fell silent and began to edge closer to the rail. The towers and attic had emptied, most of the police leaving the Cathedral through the only unmined exit—the damaged ceremonial doors. Some congregated in the two long west triforia, away from the expected area of destruction. They stared at the sanctuary, a block away, with a mesmerized fascination. Burke looked at his watch: 6:02, give or take thirty seconds.

Wendy Peterson shone her light into Hickey's face and poked his throat with her stiletto, but he was dead—yet there was no blood running from his nose, mouth, or ears, no protruding tongue or ruptured capillaries to indicate he had been killed by concussion. In fact, she thought, his face was serene, almost smiling, and he had probably died peacefully in his sleep and with no help from her or anyone else.

She set the light down pointing at the base of the column and switched on the lamp of her miner's helmet. "Photosensitive, my ass," she said aloud. "Bullshitting old bastard." She began speaking to herself, as she always did when she was alone with a bomb.

"Okay, Wendy, you silly bitch, one step at a time...." She drew a deep breath, and the oily smell of the plastic rose in her flaring nostrils. "All the time in the world..." She passed her hands gently over the dusty surface of the plastic, feeling for a place where the mechanism might be embedded. "Looks like stone.... Clever...all smoothed over...okay..." She slipped her wristwatch off and stuck it into the plastic. "Ninety seconds, Wendy, give or take.... Too late to clear out...stupid..." She was cutting with the stiletto, making a random incision into the plastic. "You get only two or three cuts now...." She thrust her right hand into the opening but felt nothing. The wound on her arm had badly stiffened her fingers. "Sixty seconds...time flies when you're..." She put her ear to the plastic and listened, but heard nothing except the blood pounding in her head. "...when you're having a good time.... Okay...cut here.... *Okay,* God? Careful...nothing here.... Where'd you put it, old man? Where's that ticking heart? Cut here, Wendy.... When you wish upon a star, makes no difference... *There... there,* that's it." She pushed back the plastic, enlarging the incision and revealing the face of a loudly ticking alarm clock. "Okay, clock time, 6:02. My time, 6:02—alarm time, 6:03.... You play fair, old man.... All right...." She wanted to yank the clock out, rip away the wires, or squash the crystal and advance the alarm dial, but that, more often than not, set the damned thing off. "Easy, baby...you've come so far now...." She thrust her hand into the plastic and worked her long, stiff fingers carefully through the thick, damp substance, feeling for anti-intrusion detonators as she dug toward the rear of the clock. "Go gently into this crap, Peterson.... Hand behind the clock...there...simple mechanism.... Where's the off switch? Come on...damn it...6:03—shit—*shit*— no alarm yet...few more seconds...steady, Wendy. Dear God, steady, *steady*..." The alarm rang loudly, and Wendy Peterson listened to it carefully, knowing it was the last sound she would ever hear.

* * *

A deep silence came over the Cathedral. Martin rested his folded arms on the rail as he stared into the sanctuary. He tapped his fingers on the watch crystal. "What time do you have, Burke? Isn't it late? What seems to be the problem?"

In the rectory and in the Cardinal's residence people have moved back from the taped windows. On all the rooftops around the Cathedral police and newspeople stood motionless. In front of televisions in homes and in the bars that had never closed, people watched the countdown numbers superimposed on the silent screen showing an aerial view of the Cathedral brightening slowly in the dawn light. In churches and synagogues that had maintained all-night vigils, people looked at their watches. 6:04.

Wendy Peterson rose slowly from the hole and walked to the middle of the sanctuary, blinking in the brighter lighting. She held something in both hands and stared at it, then looked slowly up at the triforia and loft. Her face was very pale, and her voice was slightly hesitant, but her words rolled through the silent Cathedral. "The detonating device..." She held up a clock connected by four wires to a large battery pack, from which ran four more wires. She raised it higher, as though it were a chalice, and in her other hand she held four long cylindrical detonators that she had clipped from the wires. White plastic still clung to the mechanism, and in the stillness of the Cathedral the ticking clock sounded very loud. She ran her tongue over her dry lips and said, "All clear."

No one applauded, no one cheered, but in the silence there was an audible collective sigh, then the sound of someone weeping.

The quiet was suddenly broken by the shrill noise of a long scream as a man fell headfirst from the choir loft. The body hit the floor in front of the armored carrier with a loud crack.

Maureen and Baxter turned and looked down at the awkwardly sprawled body, a splatter of blood radiating over the floor around the head. Baxter spoke in a whisper. "Martin."

Burke walked haltingly across the floor beneath the choir loft. The tingling in his back had become a dull pain. A stretcher was carried past him, and he caught a glimpse of Brian Flynn's face but couldn't tell if he was dead or alive. Burke kept walking until he came to Martin's body. Martin's neck was broken, his eyes were wide open, and his protruding tongue was half bitten off. Burke lit a cigarette and dropped the match on Martin's face.

He turned and looked absently at the huge, charred carrier and the blackened bodies on it, then watched the people around him moving, speaking quickly, going about their duties; but it all seemed remote, as though he were watching through an unfocused telescope. He looked around for Baxter and Malone but saw they were gone. He realized he had nothing to do at the moment and felt good about it.

Burke moved aimlessly up the center aisle and saw Wendy Peterson standing alone in the aisle and looking, like himself, somewhat at loose ends. Weak sunlight came through the broken window above the east end of the ambulatory, and she seemed, he thought, to be deliberately standing in the dust-moted shaft. As he walked past her he said, "Very nice."

She looked up at him. "Burke..."

He turned and saw she held the detonating mechanism. She spoke, but not really, he thought, to him. "The clock is working...see? And the batteries can't all have failed.... The connections were tight.... There're four separate detonators...but they never..." She looked almost appalled, he thought, as though all the physical laws of the universe that she had believed in had been revoked.

He said, "But you—you were—"

She shook her head. "*No.* That's what I'm telling you." She looked into his eyes. "I was about two seconds late.... It *rang*...I *heard* it ring, Burke.... I *did.* Then there was a strange sort of a feeling...like a presence. I figured, you know, I'm dead and it's not so bad. They talk about—in this business they talk about having an Angel on your shoulder while you work—you know? God Almighty, I had a regiment of them."

BOOK VI

Morning, March 18

And the Green Carnation withered,
as in forest fires that pass.

G. K. Chesterton

Patrick Burke blinked as he walked out through the ceremonial doors, down the center of the crushed steps between the flattened handrails, and into the thin winter sunlight.

The night's accumulation of ice was running from rooftops and sidewalks and melting over the steps of St. Patrick's into the littered streets. Burke saw on the bottom step the hand-lettered sign that the Fenians had stuck to the front doors, half torn, the words blurring over the soggy cardboard. The splatter of green paint from the thrown bottle bled out across the granite, and a long, barely visible trail of blood from the dead horse led into the Avenue. You wouldn't know what it all was, thought Burke, if you hadn't been there.

A soft south wind shook the ice from the bare trees along Fifth Avenue, and church bells tolled in the distance. Ambulances, police vehicles, and limousines splashed through the sunlit pools of water, and platoons of Tactical Police and National Guardsmen marched in the streets, while mounted police, half-asleep on their horses, moved in apparently random directions. Many of the police, Burke noticed, had black ribbons on their badges, most of the city officials wore black armbands, and many of the flags along the Avenue were at half-mast, as though this had all been thought out for some time, anticipated, foreseen.

Burke heard a sound on the north terrace and saw the procession of clergy and lay people who were completing their circle of the Cathedral walls, led by the Cardinal wearing a white stole. They drew abreast of the main doors and faced them, the Cardinal intoning, "Purify me with hyssop, Lord, and I shall be clean of sin. Wash me, and I shall be whiter than snow."

Burke stood a few yards off, listening as the assembly continued the rite of reconciliation for the profaned church, oblivious to the people swarming around them. He watched the Cardinal sprinkle holy water against the walls as the others prayed, and he wondered how so obscure a ritual could be carried out so soon and with such Roman precision. Then he realized that the Cardinal and the others must have been thinking about it all night, just as the city officials had rehearsed their parts in their minds during the long black hours. He, Burke, had never let his thoughts get much beyond 6:03, which was one reason why he would never be either the Mayor or the Archbishop of New York.

The procession moved through the portal two by two and past the smashed ceremonial doors into the Cathedral. Burke took off his flak jacket and dropped it at his feet, then walked slowly to the corner of the steps near Fiftieth Street and sat down in a patch of pale sunlight. He folded his arms over his knees and rested his head, falling into a half-sleep.

The Cardinal moved at the head of the line of priests who made up the Cathedral staff. A cross-bearer held a tall gold cross above the sea of moving heads, and the Litany of the Saints was chanted ss the line went forward through the gate of the communion rail.

The group assembled in the center of the sanctuary where Monsignor Downes awaited them. The altar was entirely bare of religious objects in preparation for the conclusion of the cleansing rite, and police photographers and crime lab personnel were hurrying through their work. The assembly fell silent, and people began looking around at the blood-splattered sanctuary and altar. Then heads began to turn out toward the ravaged Cathedral, and several people wept openly.

The Cardinal's voice cut off the display of emotion. "There will be time enough for that later." He spoke to two of the priests. "Go into the side vestibules where the casualties have been taken and assist the police and army chaplains." He added, "Have Father Murphy's body taken to the rectory."

The two priests moved off. The Cardinal looked at the sacristans and motioned around the sanctuary. "As soon as the police have finished here, make it presentable for the Mass that will be offered at the conclusion of the purification." He added, "Leave the carnations."

He turned to Monsignor Downes and spoke to him for the first time. "Thank you for your prayers, and for your efforts during this ordeal."

Monsignor Downes lowered his head and said softly, "I...they asked me to sanction your rescue...this attack..."

"I know all of that." He smiled. "More than once during the night I thanked God it wasn't I who had to deal with those...questions." The Cardinal turned and faced the long, wide expanse of empty pews. "God arises, His enemies are scattered, and those who hate Him flee before Him."

Captain Bert Schroeder walked unsteadily up the steps of St. Patrick's, a bandage covering the left side of his chalk-white jaw. A police medic and several Tactical Police officers escorted him.

Mayor Kline raced up to Schroeder, hand extended. "Bert! Over here! Bring him here, men."

A number of reporters had been let through the cordon, and they converged on Schroeder. Cameras clicked and newsreel microphones were thrust in his face. Mayor Kline pumped Schroeder's hand and embraced him, taking the opportunity to say through clenched teeth, "Smile, damn it, and look like a hero."

Schroeder looked distraught and disoriented. His eyes moved over the throng around him to the Cathedral, and he stared at it, then looked around at the people talking excitedly and realized that he was being interviewed.

A reporter called out, "Captain, is it true you recommended an assault on the Cathedral?"

Schroeder didn't answer, and Kline spoke up. "Yes, a rescue operation. The recommendation was approved by an emergency committee consisting of myself, the Governor, Monsignor Downes, Inspector Langley of Intelligence, and the late Captain Bellini. Intelligence indicated the terrorists were going to massacre the hostages and then destroy the Cathedral. Many of them were mentally unbalanced, as our police files show." He looked at each of the reporters. "There were no options."

Another reporter asked, "Who exactly was Major Martin? How did he die?" Kline's smile dropped. "That's under investigation."

There was a barrage of questions that Kline ignored. He put his arm around Schroeder and said, "Captain Schroeder played a vital role in keeping the terrorists psychologically unprepared while Captain Bellini formulated a rescue operation with the help of Gordon Stillway, resident architect of Saint Patrick's." He nodded toward Stillway, who stood by himself examining the front doors and making notes in a small book.

Kline added in a somber tone, "The tragedy here could have been much greater— " A loud Te Deum began ringing out from the bell tower, and Kline motioned toward the Cathedral. "The Cathedral stands! The Cardinal, Sir Harold Baxter, and Maureen Malone are alive. For this we should thank God." He bowed his head and after an appropriate interval looked up and spoke emphatically. "This rescue *will* be favorably compared to similar humanitarian operations against terrorists throughout the world."

A reporter addressed Schroeder directly. "Captain, did you find this man, Flynn— and the other one, Hickey—very tough people to negotiate with?"

Schroeder looked up. "Tough...?"

Mayor Kline hooked his arm through Schroeder's and shook him. "Bert?"

Schroeder's eyes darted around. "Oh...yes, yes I did—no, no, not...not any tougher than—Excuse me, I'm not feeling well.... I'm sorry...excuse me." He pulled loose from the Mayor's grip and hurried across the length of the steps, avoiding reporters. The newspeople watched him go, then turned back to Kline and began asking him about the large number of casualties on both sides, but Kline evaded the questions. Instead, he smiled and pointed over the heads of the people around him.

"There's the Governor crossing the street." He waved. "Governor Doyle! Up here!"

Dan Morgan stood near the window, his eyes focused on the television screen that showed the Cathedral steps, the milling reporters, police and city officials. Terri O'Neal sat on the bed, fully dressed, her legs tucked under her body. Neither person spoke nor moved.

The camera focused on Mayor Kline and Captain Schroeder, and a reporter was speaking from off camera commenting on Schroeder's bandaged jaw.

Morgan finally spoke. "It appears he didn't do what he was asked."

Terri O'Neal said, "Good."

Morgan let out a deep sigh and walked to the side of the bed. "My friends are all dead, and there's nothing good about that."

She kept looking at the television as she spoke in a hoarse whisper. "Are you going to kill...?"

Morgan drew his pistol from his belt. "No. You're free." He placed his hand on her shoulder as he pointed the silencer at the center of her head.

She put her face in her hands and began weeping.

He squeezed back on the trigger. "I'll get your coat...."

She suddenly took her face out of her hands and turned. She realized she was looking into the barrel of the pistol "Oh...no..."

Morgan's hand was shaking. He looked at her and their eyes met. The end of the silencer brushed her cheek, and he jerked the pistol away and shoved it in his belt. "There's been enough death today," he said. He turned and walked out of the bedroom. Terri O'Neal heard the front door open, then slam shut.

She found the cigarettes Morgan left behind, lit one, and stared at the television. "Poor Daddy."

Burke shifted restlessly, brought out of his short sleep by the noise around him and the pounding pain in his back. He rubbed his eyes and noticed that the injured eye was blurry again, and every inch of his body felt blurry; numb, he supposed, was a better word, numb except the parts that hurt. And his mind seemed numb *and* blurry, free-floating in the sunny light around him. He stood unsteadily, looked over the crowded steps, and blinked. Bert Schroeder and Murray Kline were holding court—and it was, he realized, just as he would have pictured it if he had allowed himself to think of the dawn. Schroeder surrounded by the press, Schroeder looking very self-possessed, handling questions like a pro—but as he watched he saw that the Hostage Negotiator was not doing well. He saw Schroeder suddenly break loose and make his way across the steps, through the knots of people like a broken-field runner, and Burke called out as he passed, "Schroeder!"

Schroeder seemed not to hear and continued toward the arched portal of the south vestibule. Burke came up behind him and grabbed his arm. "Hold on." Schroeder tried to pull away, but Burke slammed him against the stone buttress. "Listen!" He lowered his voice. "I know—about Terri—"

Schroeder looked at him, his eyes widening. Burke went on. "Martin is dead, and the Fenians are all dead or dying. I had to tell Bellini...but he's dead, too. Langley knows, but Langley doesn't give away secrets—he just makes you buy them back someday. Okay? So just shut your mouth and be very cool." He released Schroeder's arm.

Tears formed in Schroeder's eyes. "Burke...God Almighty...do you *understand* what I did...?"

"Yeah...yeah, I understand, and I'd really like to see you in the fucking slammer for twenty, but that won't help anything.... It won't help the department, and it won't help me or Langley. And it damn sure won't help your wife or daughter." He moved closer to Schroeder. "And don't blow your brains out, either.... It's a sin— you know? Hang around long enough in this job and someone will blow them out for you."

Schroeder caught his breath and spoke. "No...I'm going to retire—resign— confess...make a public—"

"You're going to keep your goddamned mouth shut. No one—not me or Kline or Rourke or the DA or anyone—wants to hear your fucking confession, Schroeder. You've caused enough problems—just cool out."

Schroeder hung his head, then nodded. "Burke...Pat... thanks...."

"Fuck you." He looked at the door beside him. "You know what's in this vestibule?"

Schroeder shook his head.

"Bodies. Lots of bodies. The field morgue. You go in there and you talk to those bodies—and say something to Bellini—and you go into the Cathedral and you make a confession, or you pray or you do anything you have to do to help you get through the next twenty-four hours." He reached out and opened the door, took Schroeder's arm, and pushed him into the vestibule, then shut the door. He stared down at the pavement for a long time, then turned at the sound of his name and saw Langley hurrying up the steps toward him.

Langley started to extend his hand, then glanced around quickly and withdrew it. He said coolly, "You're in a little trouble, Lieutenant."

Burke lit a cigarette. "Why?"

"*Why?*" He lowered his voice and leaned forward. "You pushed a British consulate official—a *diplomat*—out of the choir loft of Saint Patrick's Cathedral to his *death.* That's *why.*"

"He fell."

"Of course he fell—you pushed him. What could he do but fall? He couldn't *fly.*" Langley ran his hand over his mouth, and Burke thought he was hiding a smile. Langley regained his composure and said caustically, "That was very stupid— don't you agree?"

Burke shrugged.

Roberta Spiegel walked unnoticed through the crowd on the steps and came under the portal, stopping beside Langley. She looked at the two men, then said to Burke, "Christ Almighty, right in front of about forty policemen and National Guardsmen. Are you crazy?"

Langley said, "I just asked him if he was stupid, but that's a good question, too." He turned to Burke. "Well, are you stupid or crazy?"

Burke sat down with his back to the stone wall and watched the smoke rise from his cigarette. He yawned twice.

Spiegel's voice was ominous. "They're going to arrest you for *murder*. I'm surprised they haven't grabbed you yet."

Burke raised his eyes toward Spiegel. "They haven't grabbed me because you told them not to. Because you want to see if Pat Burke is going to go peacefully or if he's going to kick and scream."

Spiegel didn't answer.

Burke glared at her, then at Langley. "Okay, let me see if I know how to play this game. A file on Bartholomew Martin—right? He suffered from vertigo and fear of heights. Or how about this?—twenty police witnesses in the loft sign sworn affidavits saying Martin took a swat at a fly and toppled—No, no, I've got it—"

Spiegel cut him off. "The man was a *consulate official*—"

"Bullshit."

Spiegel shook her head. "No one can fix this one, Lieutenant."

Burke leaned back and yawned again. "You're Ms. Fixit in this town, lady, so you fix it. And fix me up with a commendation and captain's pay while you're about it. By tomorrow."

Spiegel's face reddened. "Are you *threatening* me?" Their eyes met, and neither turned away. She said, "And who's going to believe *your* version of anything that was discussed tonight?"

Burke stubbed out his cigarette. "Schroeder, who is a hero, will corroborate *anything* I say."

Spiegel laughed. "That's absurd."

Langley cleared his throat and said to Spiegel. "Actually, that's true. It's a long story.... I think Lieutenant Burke deserves...well, whatever he says he deserves."

Spiegel looked at Langley closely, then turned back to Burke. "You've got something on Schroeder—right? Okay, I don't have to know what it is. I'm not looking to hang you, Burke. I'll do what I can—"

Burke interrupted. "Art Forgery Squad. It would be a really good idea if I was in Paris by this time tomorrow."

Spiegel laughed. "Art Forgery? What the hell do you know about art?"

"I know what I like."

"That true," said Langley. "He does." He stuck his hand out toward Burke, "You did an outstanding job tonight, Lieutenant. The Division is very proud of you."

Burke took his hand and used it to pull himself up. "Thank you, Chief Inspector. I shall be clean of sin. Wash me, and I shall be whiter than snow."

Langley said, "Well...we'll just get you a commendation or something...."

Spiegel lit a cigarette. "How the hell did I ever get involved with cops and politicians? God, I'd rather be on the stroll in Times Square."

Burke said, "I thought you looked familiar."

She ignored him and surveyed the steps and the Avenue. "Where's Schroeder, anyway? I see lots of news cameras, but smiling Bert isn't in front of any of them. Or is he at a television studio already?"

Burke said, "He's in the Cathedral. Praying."

Spiegel seemed taken aback, then nodded. "That's *damned* good press. Yes, yes. Everyone's out here sucking up on the coverage, and he's in there praying. They'll eat it up. Wow... I could run that bastard for councilman in Bensonhurst..."

Stretcher-bearers began bringing the bodies out of the Cathedral, a long, silent procession, through the doors of the south vestibule, down the steps. The litters carrying the police and Guardsmen passed through a hastily assembled honor guard; the stretchers of the Fenians passed behind the guard. Everyone on the steps fell silent, police and army chaplains walked beside the stretchers, and a uniformed police inspector in gold braid directed the bearers to designated ambulances. The litters holding the Fenians were placed on the sidewalk.

Burke moved among the stretchers and found the tag marked Bellini, He drew the cover back and looked into the face, wiped of greasepaint—a very white face with that hard jaw and black stubble. He dropped the cover back and quickly walked a few steps off, his hands on his hips, staring down at his feet.

The bells had ended the Te Deum and began to play a slow dirge. Governor Doyle stood with his retinue, his hat in his hand. Major Cole stood beside him holding a salute. The Governor leaned toward Cole and spoke as he lowered his head in respect. "How many did the Sixty-ninth lose, Major?"

Cole looked at him out of the corner of his eye, certain that he had detected an expectant tone in the Governor's voice. "Five killed, sir, including Colonel Logan, of course. Three wounded."

"Out of how many?"

Cole lowered his salute and stared at the Governor. "Out of a total of eighteen men who directly participated in the attack."

"The *rescue*...yes..." The Governor nodded thoughtfully. "Terrible. Fifty percent casualties."

"Well, not quite fif—"

"But you rescued two hostages."

"Actually, they saved themselves—"

"The Sixty-ninth Regiment will be needing a new commander, Cole."

"Yes... that's true."

The last of the police and Guardsmen were placed in ambulances, and the line of vehicles began moving away, escorted by motorcycle police. A black police van pulled up to the curb, and a group of stretcher-bearers on the sidewalk picked up the litters holding the dead Fenians and headed toward the van.

An Intelligence officer standing beside the van saluted Langley as he approached and handed him a small stack of folded papers. The man said, "Almost every one of them had an identifying personal note on him, Inspector. And here's a preliminary report on each one." The man added, "We also found pages of the ESD attack plan in there. How the hell—?"

Langley took the loose pages and shoved them in his pocket. "That doesn't go in your report."

"Yes, sir."

Langley came up beside Burke sitting under the portal again, with Spiegel standing in front of him.

Burke said, "Where are Malone and Baxter?"

Spiegel answered, "Malone and Baxter are still in the Cathedral for their own protection—there may still be snipers out there. Baxter's in the Archbishop's sacristy until we release him to his people. Malone's in the bride's room. The FBI will take charge of her."

Burke said, "Where's Flynn's body?"

No one answered, then Spiegel knelt on the step beside Burke. "He's not dead yet. He's in the bookstore."

Burke said, "Is that the Bellevue annex?"

Spiegel hesitated, then spoke. "The doctor said be was within minutes of death...so we didn't...have him moved."

Burke said, "You're murdering him—so don't give me this shit about not being able to move him."

Spiegel looked him in the eye. "Everybody on both sides of the Atlantic wants him dead, Burke. Just like everyone wanted Martin dead. Don't start moralizing to me...."

Burke said, "Get him to Bellevue."

Langley looked at him sharply. "You know we can't do that now...and he knows too much, Pat.... Schroeder...other things.... And he's dangerous. Let's make things easy on ourselves for once. Okay?"

Burke said, "Let's have a look."

Spiegel hesitated, then stood. "Come on."

They entered the Cathedral and passed through the south vestibule littered with the remains of the field morgue that smelled faintly of something disagreeable—a mixture of odors, which each finally identified as death.

The Mass was beginning, and the organ overhead was playing an entrance song. Burke looked at the shafts of sunlight coming through the broken windows. He had thought that the light would somehow diminish the mystery, but it hadn't, and in fact the effect was more haunting even than the candlelight.

They turned right toward the bookstore. Two ESD men blocked the entrance but moved quickly aside. Spiegel entered the small store, followed by Burke and Langley. She leaned over the counter and looked down at the floor.

Brian Flynn lay in the narrow space, his eyes closed and his chest rising and falling very slowly. She said, "He's not letting go so easily." She watched him for a few seconds, then added, "He's a good-looking man...must have had a great deal of charisma, too. Very few are born into this sorry world like that.... In an-

other time and place, perhaps, he would have been...something
else.... Incredible waste..."

Burke came around the counter and knelt beside Flynn. He
pushed back his eyelids, then listened to his chest and felt for
his pulse. Burke looked up. "Fluid in the chest...heart is going...but it may take a while."

No one spoke. Then Spiegel said, "I can't do this...I'll get
the stretcher-bearers...."

Flynn's lips began to move, and Burke put his ear close to
Flynn's face. Burke said, "Yes, all right." He turned to Spiegel.
"Forget the stretcher...he wants to speak to her."

Maureen Malone sat quietly in the bride's room while four po-
licewomen tried to make conversation with her.

Roberta Spiegel opened the door and regarded her for a second, then said abruptly, "Come with me."

She seemed not to have heard and sat motionless.

Spiegel said, "He wants to see you."

Maureen looked up and met the eyes of the other woman.
She rose and followed Spiegel. They hurried down the side
aisle and crossed in front of the vestibules. As they entered the
bookstore Langley looked at Maureen appraisingly, and Burke
nodded to her. Both men walked out of the room. Spiegel said,
"There." She pointed. "Take your time." She turned and left.

Maureen moved around the counter and knelt beside Brian
Flynn. She took his hands in hers but said nothing. She looked
through the glass counter and realized there was no one else
there, and she understood. She pressed Flynn's hands, an overwhelming feeling of pity and sorrow coming over her such as she
had never felt for him before. "Oh, Brian...so alone...always
alone..."

Flynn opened his eyes.

She leaned forward so that their faces were close and said, "I'm here."

His eyes showed recognition.

"Do you want a priest?"

He shook his head.

She felt a small pressure on her hands and returned it. "You're dying, Brian. You know that, don't you? And they've left you here to die. Why won't you see a priest?"

He tried to speak, but no sound came out. Yet she thought she knew what he wanted to say and to ask her. She told him of the deaths of the Fenians, including Hickey and Megan, and with no hesitancy she told him of the death of Father Murphy, of the survival of the Cardinal, Harold Baxter, Rory Devane, and of the Cathedral itself, and about the bomb that didn't explode. His face registered emotion as she spoke. She added, "Martin is dead, also. Lieutenant Burke, they say, pushed him from the choir loft, and they also say that Leary was Martin's man.... Can you hear me?"

Flynn nodded.

She went on. "I know you don't mind dying...but I mind...mind terribly.... I love you, still.... Won't you, for me, let a priest see you? Brian?"

He opened his mouth, and she bent closer. He said, "...the priest..."

"Yes...I'll call for one."

He shook his head and clutched at her hands. She bent forward again. Flynn's voice was almost inaudible. "The priest...Father Donnelly...here..."

"What...?"

"Came here...." He held up his right hand. "Took back the ring...."

She stared at his hand and saw that the ring was gone. She looked at his face and noticed for the first time that it had a peaceful quality to it, with no trace of the things that had so marked him over the years.

He opened his eyes wide and looked intently at her. "You see...?" He reached for her hands again and held them tightly.

She nodded. "Yes...no...no, I don't see, but I never did, and you always seemed so sure, Brian—" She felt the pressure on her hand relax, and she looked at him and saw that he was dead. She closed his eyes and kissed him, then took a long breath and stood.

Burke, Langley, and Spiegel stood at the curb on the corner of Fifth Avenue and Fiftieth Street. The Sanitation Department had mobilized its huge squadrons, and the men in gray mingled with the men in blue. Great heaps of trash, mostly Kelly-green in color, grew at the curbsides. The police cordon that had enclosed two dozen square blocks pulled in tighter, and the early rush hour began building up in the surrounding streets.

None of the three spoke for some time. Spiegel turned and faced the sun coming over the tall buildings to the east. She studied the façade of the Cathedral, then said, "In class I used to teach that every holiday will one day have two connotations. I think of Yom Kippur, Tet. And after the Easter Monday Rising in 1916, that day was never the same again in Ireland. It became a different sort of holiday, with different connotations—different associations—like Saint Valentine's Day in Chicago. I have the feeling that Saint Patrick's Day in New York may never be the same again."

Burke looked at Langley. "I don't even *like* art—what the hell do I care if someone forges it?"

Langley smiled, then said, "You never asked me about the

note in Hickey's coffin." Langley handed him the note, and Burke read: *If you're reading this note, you've found me out. I wanted to spend my last days alone and in peace, to lay down the sword and give up the fight. Then again, if something good comes along— In any case, don't put me here. Bury me beneath the sod of Clonakily beside my mother and father.*

There was a silence, and they looked around for something to occupy their attention. Langley saw a PBA canteen truck that had parked beside the wrecked mobile headquarters. He cleared his throat and said to Roberta Spiegel, "Can I get you a cup of coffee?"

"Sure." She smiled and put her arm through his. "Give me a cigarette."

Burke watched them walk off, then stood by himself. He thought he might make the end of the Mass, but then decided to report to the new mobile headquarters across the street. He began walking but turned at the sound of an odd noise behind him.

A horse was snorting, thick plumes of fog coming from its nostrils. Betty Foster said, "Hi! Thought you'd be okay."

Burke moved away from the spirited horse. "Did you?"

"Sure." She reined the horse beside him. "Mayor make you nervous?"

Burke said, "That idiot.... Oh, the horse. Where do you *get* these names?"

She laughed. "Give you a lift?"

"No...I have to hang around...."

She leaned down from the saddle. "Why? It's over. *Over*, Lieutenant. You *don't* have to hang around."

He looked at her. Her eyes were bloodshot and puffy, but there was a determined sort of recklessness in them, brought on, he supposed, by the insanity of the long night, and he saw that she wasn't going to be put off so easily. "Yeah, give me a lift."

She took her foot from the stirrup, reached down, and helped him up behind her. "Where to?"

He put his arms around her waist. "Where do you usually go?"

She laughed again and reined the horse in a circle. "Come on, Lieutenant—give me an order."

"Paris," said Burke. "Let's go to Paris."

"You got it." She kicked the horse's flanks. "Gi-yap, Mayor!"

Maureen Malone rubbed her eyes in the sunlight as she came through the doors of the north vestibule flanked by FBI men, including Douglas Hogan. Hogan indicated a waiting Cadillac limousine on the corner.

Harold Baxter came out of the south vestibule surrounded by consulate security men. A silver-gray Bentley drew up to the curb.

Maureen moved down the steps toward the Cadillac and saw Baxter through the crowd. Reporters began converging first on Baxter and then around her, and her escort elbowed through the throng. She pulled away from Hogan and stood on her toes, looking for Baxter, but the Bentley drove off with a motorcycle escort.

She slid into the back of the limousine and sat quietly as men piled in around her and the doors slammed shut. Hogan said, "We're taking you to a private hospital."

She didn't answer, and the car drew away from the curb. She looked down at her hands, still covered with Flynn's blood where he had held them.

The limousine edged into the middle of the crowded Avenue, and Maureen looked out the window at the Cathedral, certain she would never see it again.

A man suddenly ran up beside the slow-moving vehicle and

held an identification to the window, and Hogan lowered the glass a few inches. The man spoke with a British accent. "Miss Malone..." He held a single wilted green carnation through the window. "Compliments of Sir Harold, miss." She took the carnation, and the man saluted as the car moved off.

The limousine turned east on Fiftieth Street and passed beside the Cathedral, then headed north on Madison Avenue and passed the Cardinal's residence, Lady Chapel, and rectory, picking up speed as it moved over the wet pavement. Ahead she saw the gray Bentley, then lost it in the heavy traffic. She said, "Lower the window."

Someone lowered the window closest to her, and she heard the bells of distant churches, recognizing the distinctive bells of St. Patrick's playing "Danny Boy," and she sat back and listened to them. She thought briefly of the journey home, of Sheila and Brian, and she recalled a time in her life, not so long ago, when everyone she knew was alive—parents, girl friends and boyfriends, relatives and neighbors— but now her life was filled with the dead, the missing, and the wounded, and she thought that most likely she would join those ranks. She tried to imagine a future for herself and her country but couldn't. Yet she wasn't afraid and looked forward to working, in her own way, to accomplish the Fenian goal of emptying the jails of Ulster.

The bells died in the distance, and she looked down at the carnation in her lap. She picked it up and twirled the stem in her fingers, then put it in the lapel of her tweed jacket.

Credit: Sandy DeMille

NELSON DEMILLE is a former U.S. Army lieutenant who served in Vietnam and is the author of sixteen acclaimed novels, including the #1 *New York Times* bestsellers *The Lion, The Gate House, Night Fall,* and *Plum Island.* His other *New York Times* bestsellers include *Wild Fire, Up Country, The Lion's Game, The Gold Coast, The Charm School, Word of Honor,* and *The General's Daughter,* which was a major motion picture starring John Travolta.

For more information, visit www.nelsondemille.net.

Fodor's

MAR 2024

P9-CCI-197

GREECE

7th Edition

Where to Stay and Eat for All Budgets

Must-See Sights and Local Secrets

Ratings You Can Trust

Fodor's Travel Publications   New York, Toronto, London, Sydney, Auckland
www.fodors.com

FODOR'S GREECE

Editors: Amy B Wang, Lisa Dunford, Constance Jones

Editorial Production: Bethany Cassin Beckerlegge

Editorial Contributors: Stephen Brewer, Elizabeth Carson, Jeffrey Carson, Shane Christensen, Angelike Contis, Ruth Craig, Robert Fisher, Wendy Holborow, Tania Kollias, Diane Shugart, Adrian Vrettos

Maps: David Lindroth, *cartographer*; Rebecca Baer and Bob Blake, *map editors*

Design: Fabrizio La Rocca, *creative director*; Guido Caroti, *art director*; Moon Sun Kim, *cover designer*; Melanie Marin, *senior picture editor*

Production/Manufacturing: Robert B. Shields

Cover Photo: (Wreck Beach, Zante): SIME s.a.s/eStockPhoto/PictureQuest.

Seventh Edition

ISBN: 1–4000–1651–7

ISBN-13: 978–1–4000–1651–8

ISSN: 0071–6413

SPECIAL SALES

This book is available at special discounts for bulk purchases for sales promotions or premiums. Special editions, including personalized covers, excerpts of existing books, and corporate imprints, can be created in large quantities for special needs. For more information, write to Special Markets/Premium Sales, 1745 Broadway, MD 6-2, New York, New York 10019, or e-mail specialmarkets@randomhouse.com.

AN IMPORTANT TIP & AN INVITATION

Although all prices, opening times, and other details in this book are based on information supplied to us at press time, changes occur all the time in the travel world, and Fodor's cannot accept responsibility for facts that become outdated or for inadvertent errors or omissions. So **always confirm information when it matters,** especially if you're making a detour to visit a specific place. Your experiences—positive and negative—matter to us. If we have missed or misstated something, **please write to us.** We follow up on all suggestions. Contact the Greece editors at editors@fodors.com or c/o Fodor's at 1745 Broadway, New York, NY 10019.

PRINTED IN THE UNITED STATES OF AMERICA

10 9 8 7 6 5 4 3 2 1

Be a Fodor's Correspondent

Your opinion matters. It matters to us. It matters to your fellow Fodor's travelers, too. And we'd like to hear it. In fact, we *need* to hear it.

When you share your experiences and opinions, you become an active member of the Fodor's community. That means we'll not only use your feedback to make our books better, but we'll publish your names and comments whenever possible. Throughout our guides, look for "Word of Mouth," excerpts of your unvarnished feedback.

Here's how you can help improve Fodor's for all of us.

Tell us when we're right. We rely on local writers to give you an insider's perspective. But our writers and staff editors—who are the best in the business—depend on you. Your positive feedback is a vote to renew our recommendations for the next edition.

Tell us when we're wrong. We're proud that we update most of our guides every year. But we're not perfect. Things change. Hotels cut services. Museums change hours. Charming cafés lose charm. If our writer didn't quite capture the essence of a place, tell us how you'd do it differently. If any of our descriptions are inaccurate or inadequate, we'll incorporate your changes in the next edition and will correct factual errors at fodors.com *immediately*.

Tell us what to include. You probably have had fantastic travel experiences that aren't yet in Fodor's. Why not share them with a community of like-minded travelers? Maybe you chanced upon a beach or bistro or bed-and-breakfast that you don't want to keep to yourself. Tell us why we should include it. And share your discoveries and experiences with everyone directly at fodors.com. Your input may lead us to add a new listing or highlight a place we cover with a "Highly Recommended" star or with our highest rating, "Fodor's Choice."

Give us your opinion instantly at our feedback center at www.fodors.com/feedback. You may also e-mail editors@fodors.com with the subject line "Greece Editor." Or send your nominations, comments, and complaints by mail to Greece Editor, Fodor's, 1745 Broadway, New York, NY 10019.

You and travelers like you are the heart of the Fodor's community. Make our community richer by sharing your experiences. Be a Fodor's correspondent.

Kaló taxídi! (Or simply: Happy traveling!)

Tim Jarrell, Publisher

CONTENTS

CONTENTS

ABOUT THIS BOOK

Our Ratings

Sometimes you find terrific travel experiences and sometimes they just find you. But usually the burden is on you to select the right combination of experiences. That's where our ratings come in.

As travelers we've all discovered a place so wonderful that its worthiness is obvious. And sometimes that place is so unique that superlatives don't do it justice: you just have to be there to know. These sights, properties, and experiences get our highest rating, Fodor's Choice ★, indicated by orange stars throughout this book.

Black stars highlight sights and properties we deem **Highly Recommended** ★, places that our writers, editors, and readers praise again and again for consistency and excellence.

By default, there's another category: any place we include in this book is by definition worth your time, unless we say otherwise. And we will.

Disagree with any of our choices? Care to nominate a place or suggest that we rate one more highly? Visit our feedback center at www.fodors.com/feedback.

Budget Well

Hotel and restaurant price categories from ¢ to $$$$ are defined in the opening pages of each chapter. For attractions, we always give standard adult admission fees; reductions are usually available for children, students, and senior citizens. Want to pay with plastic? **AE, D, DC, MC, V** following restaurant and hotel listings indicate whether American Express, Discover, Diner's Club, MasterCard, and Visa are accepted.

Restaurants

Unless we state otherwise, restaurants are open for lunch and dinner daily. We mention dress only when there's a specific requirement and reservations only when they're essential or not accepted—it's always best to book ahead.

Hotels

Hotels have private bath, phone, TV, and air-conditioning and operate on the European Plan (aka EP, meaning without meals), unless we specify that they use the Continental Plan (CP, with a Continental breakfast), Breakfast Plan (BP, with a full breakfast), or Modified American Plan (MAP, with breakfast and dinner) or are all-inclusive (AI, including all meals and most activities). We always

list facilities but not whether you'll be charged an extra fee to use them, so when pricing accommodations, find out what's included.

Many Listings
- ★ Fodor's Choice
- ★ Highly recommended
- ✉ Physical address
- ✛ Directions
- ⏏ Mailing address
- ☎ Telephone
- 🖷 Fax
- ⊕ On the Web
- ✎ E-mail
- 🎫 Admission fee
- ☉ Open/closed times
- ⚑ Start of walk/itinerary
- Ⓜ Metro stations
- 🚍 Credit cards

Hotels & Restaurants
- 🏨 Hotel
- 🛏 Number of rooms
- ☌ Facilities
- 🍽 Meal plans
- ✕ Restaurant
- ⚓ Reservations
- 🏛 Dress code
- ⚲ Smoking
- 🍸 BYOB
- ✕🏨 Hotel with restaurant that warrants a visit

Outdoors
- 🏌 Golf
- ⛺ Camping

Other
- ☺ Family-friendly
- 🔢 Contact information
- ⇨ See also
- ✉ Branch address
- ☞ Take note

Greece
(Ellada)

MACEDONIA

BULGARIA

Stavro
Sidirokastro
Serres
Philippi
Eleftheroupoli
Kilkis   Amfipoli
Edessa Gianitsa   Thessaloniki
Florina Alexandria
E86   E90 Nea
Kastoria   Thermi Apollonia
ALBANIA   Ptolemaïda   Veria Polygyros   Vatoped
Kozani   Katerini   Ormylia   Dafni
Siatista   Gulf of
Konitsa   Grevena Mount   Thermaïkos Kalithea
Delvinakio   Olympus   Paliouri
Metsovo Meteora   Elassona
Corfu   Kalambaka Tirnavos
Corfu   Igoumenitsa Ioanina   Agia
Paramythia   Trikala   Larissa Mount
E951   Pelion
Parga   Arta   Stavros Farsala Volos
Aliki   Karditsa   Skiathos
Preveza   Almiros Skopelos
Lamia   SPORA
Karpenissi   Sk
Lefkas
Vassiliki   Agrinio   Orhomenos EVIA
Delphi Arahova   K
Kephalonia Ithaki Nafpaktos Itea   Halkida
Messolongi E86 Galaxidi Livadia
Lixouri Sami   Patras   Gulf of Corinth Thebes
Diakofto   Megara Rafina
Killini E65   Corinth Piraeus Athens
Loutra Amalias Nemea   Glyfada
Zakynthos   Voula   Lav
Zakynthos Pyrgos Olympia Argos Mycenae Aegina
Kaïafas   Tripoli Nafplion Poros Souni
Andritsena   Tolo
Kyparissia PELOPONNESE Ermioni   Kyth
Hydra
Messini Sparta Leonidio   Spetses
Ionian Sea   Gargaliani Kalamata Mystras Geraki   Se
Pilos   Skala Kyparissi
Methoni   Koroni Gythio Monemvassia
Areopoli
M
Agia Pelagia
Kythira
Kythira

Mediterranean Sea

Hania

0
|_____| 100 miles
0
|_____| 150 km   CF

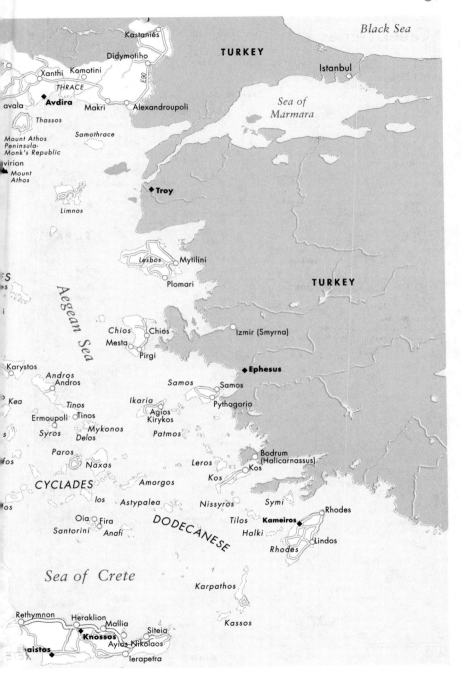

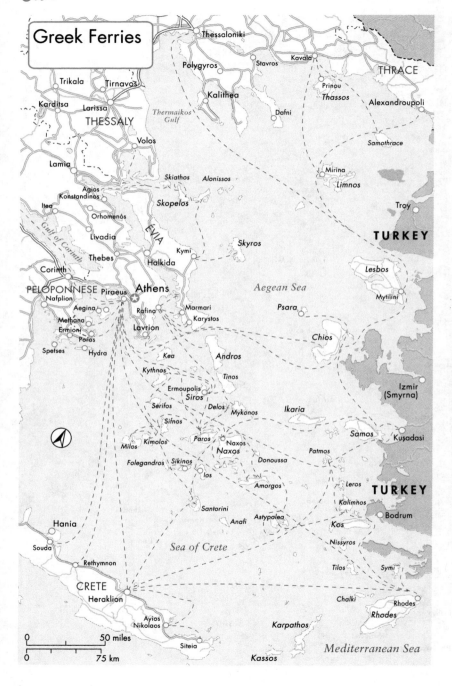

Greek Ferries

Thessaloniki

Trikala
Tirnavos
Karditsa
Larissa
THESSALY

Polygyros
Kalithea

Stavros
Kavala
Prinou
Thassos

THRACE

Alexandroupoli

Dafni

Samothrace

Volos

Lamia

Thermaikos Gulf

Agios Konstandinos
Itea
Orhomenós
Livadia
Gulf of Corinth
Thebes
Corinth
PELOPONNESE Piraeus
Nafplion
Aegina
Methana
Ermioni
Poros
Spetses
Hydra

Skiathos
Alonissos
Skopelos

EVIA

Kymi
Halkida

Skyros

Mirina
Limnos

Troy

TURKEY

Lesbos

Mytilini

Aegean Sea

Rafina
Lavrion

Marmari
Karystos

Psara

Chios

Kea

Andros

Kythnos
Ermoupolis
Siros

Tinos

Delos
Mykonos

Ikaria

Izmir (Smyrna)

Serifos
Sifnos

Paros

Milos
Kimolos
Folegandros
Sikinos
Ios

Naxos
Naxos

Donoussa

Amorgos

Samos

Kuşadasi

Patmos

Leros

TURKEY

Hania
Souda

Rethymnon

CRETE
Heraklion

Santorini
Anafi

Astypalea

Kalimnos

Kos

Bodrum

Nissyros

Sea of Crete

Tilos
Symi

Ayios Nikolaos

Siteia

Karpathos

Kassos

Chalki
Rhodes
Rhodes

Mediterranean Sea

0 ——— 50 miles
0 ——— 75 km

WHAT'S
WHERE

ATHENS	
	In Greece, all roads lead to Athens, the capital city that is both the birthplace of Western civilization and a bustling boomtown that re-created itself for the Olympic Games in 2004. Athenians take the juxtaposition of ancient splendor and cacophonous modernity with good-natured appreciation, and you would be wise to do likewise. Raise your eyes nearly anywhere and you're likely to be stopped in your tracks by the sight of the Acropolis, where Pericles rose to the heights of power and creative achievement, with the construction of the Parthenon and Propylaea. After a time-trip to the golden age of Greece, explore modern Athens's patchwork of neighborhoods to get a sense of the history of this gregarious city, its people, and what lies beyond the ubiquitous modern concrete facades. Take in a twilight view from Athenians' favorite "violet-crowned" aerie, Mt. Lycabettus, and drink in the twinkling lights of the metropolis that is home to more than 4 million souls, still growing and still counting. To leave the whirl of cars behind, stroll through the 19th-century Plaka district, where pastel-hue houses and vestiges of an earlier, simpler life keep beloved traditions intact. Pay a call on the Tomb of the Unknown Soldier in Syntagma Square—if you catch the changing of the Evzone Guard here, the sight of a soldier in 19th-century ceremonial garb parading in front of a funeral oration by Pericles will put the many layers of Athens perfectly in perspective.
ATTICA, THE SARONIC GULF ISLANDS & DELPHI 	Athens lies in a basin defined by three mountain masses: Mt. Hymettos to the east, Mt. Parnitha and Mt. Aigaleo to the west, and Mt. Pendeli to the north. East of Mt. Hymettos unfold the gently undulating hills of the Mesogeion. Scattered among and beyond these ranges are engaging sites and villages. Northwest of Athens are the ruins at Delphi, where the priestesses of antiquity uttered their enigmatic prophecies. The famous Marathon and monasteries such as Daphni lie just beyond the forbidding mountains guarding the passes into Athens. When Athenians want a break, they often make a quick crossing to the quirky islands in the Saronic Gulf—Aegina, Poros, Hydra, and Spetses. You're well advised to follow suit, and all the better if your island of choice is Hydra, where what's here (stone houses set above a welcoming harbor) and what's not (cars) provide a relaxing retreat. Back on the mainland, at the southern tip of Attica, the imposing Temple of Poseidon at Sounion still summons strong emotions in this land of seafarers.

WHAT'S WHERE

THE SPORADES 	Strung from Mt. Pelion to the center of the Aegean, the Sporades are distinct in character: sophisticated, tourist-addled Skiathos with its noted beaches (the crystal blue water is among the clearest in the Aegean) is closest to the mainland; due east is Skopelos, marked with dense pines, scenic villages, and lovely beaches. Farther east is rugged Alonnisos, the least developed, and a jumping-off point for the uninhabited islands. Fertile with oak and fruit trees, it can serve, at least for a spell, as your private paradise. Wild-nature lovers behold rugged Skyros as the jewel of the isles for its remoteness and stark beauty. The sight of a white village tumbling down a hillside—and that is exactly what will greet your eyes as you approach Skyros town—is just one of the visual delights of the Sporades. Evia almost touches the mainland, its vast coastline dotted with fishing villages, beaches, and occasional sites.
EPIRUS & THESSALY 	This remote region consists of two areas: to the west is the mountainous province of Epirus, bordered by Albania and the Ionian Sea, with the capital Ioannina to the west. The dense forests of Epirus were once the domain of Ali Pasha, a despot who carved a fiefdom in the region from 1788 until his downfall in 1821. Get a grasp on his exploits in lakeside Ioannina, with its mosques and impressive citadel. North of Ioannina are the remote villages of the Zagorohoria region, with stone Ottoman-era houses. In Dodona, south of Ioannina, the oldest oracle in Greece once made pronouncements from Zeus. Marking the threshold between Epirus and Thessaly is Metsovo, just beyond the lofty Katara Pass, which threads through the Mt. Pindos range. You can try some of Greece's best smoked cheeses here. Heading east, you descend into the realm of Thessaly, entering the Meteora, with its extraordinary eroded pinnacles of rock. The name means "to hang in midair," and the region's celebrated Byzantine monasteries—including frescoed Ayia Barbara and 800-year-old Ayios Stephanos—built atop these rocks seem to do just that, giving anyone fortunate enough to come upon them the impression that heaven may be within easy reach.

NORTHERN GREECE 	Macedonia to the west and Thrace to the east make up Northern Greece, which covers the Balkan frontier from Albania to Bulgaria and also touches Turkey. It is both a meeting point and a crossroads between Europe, the Mediterranean, and Asia—imbued with sights, sounds, and colors of a range of different cultures, their interaction over the centuries telling of successful commingling and fierce discord. Roman, Byzantine, and Ottoman rulers left their mark in sophisticated Thessaloniki (Greece's second-largest city), where churches and medieval monuments like the White Tower provide a dramatic backdrop for crowded markets and lively restaurants that serve some of the best food in Greece. Southwest of the city are the ancient sites of Pella, Vergina, and Dion, with their links to Alexander the Great. Also here is the home of the gods, Mt. Olympus, a solid, if ethereal, Greek realm, often shrouded in clouds and lightning as if to prove Zeus still holds sway. Southeast of Thessaloniki is the three-fingered peninsula of Chalkidiki, known as a region for pleasure seekers. It is also home to the monasteries of Mt. Athos, Greece's most solemn precinct; off-limits to women, these sanctuaries are an exclusive bastion as well.
CORFU 	There must be something special about a coastal island that is said to have been the inspiration for Prospero's island home in Shakespeare's *The Tempest*; moved Homer to call it a "beautiful and rich land"; and possibly sheltered Odysseus on his journey homeward. Corfu's strategic presence in the northern Ionian Sea at the entrance to the Adriatic has shaped its history. Corfu town, a little beauty of a city, retains evocative traces of its Venetian, French, and British occupiers, and activities from a simple stroll along the Esplanade to a visit to an outdoor market become special outings. Popularity may take its toll with summertime crowds, but no matter how clogged the roadways or how sophisticated the restaurants and resorts, nature still dominates the scene with a profusion of emerald mountains and bougainvillea-clad hillsides. Quiet, uncrowded beaches like those near Paleokastritsa are never far away, and Pontikonisi—according to legend, Odysseus's ship turned to stone—is an easy swim offshore. Even the gaudiness of the Achilleion, a villa built for Empress Elizabeth of Austria in Gastouri, is more than redeemed by its enchanting seaside gardens.

WHAT'S WHERE

NORTHERN PELOPONNESE 	This region—with Olympia, Mycenae, and Nafplion among its jewels—is blessed with rugged natural beauty and the intriguing remains of great kingdoms and empires of past eras. Separated from the north by a narrow isthmus, the Northern Peloponnese comprises the Argive peninsula, jutting into the Aegean, and runs westward past the isthmus and along the Gulf of Corinth to the Adriatic coast. Practically a stone's throw from the Corinth Canal spread the vestiges of the ancient city of Corinth, and just south of that is the superbly preserved 4th-century BC Theater at Epidauros. You can appreciate its perfect acoustics during the annual summer drama festival. Olympia hosted the games that originated here in 776 BC, and this sanctuary of Zeus and once-thriving city has lost none of its appeal; art lovers flock to the archaeological museum to marvel at the Hermes of Praxiteles. Even more ancient is the city of Mycenae—the fabled realm of Agamemnon—where you can explore the Lion Gate and other archaeological discoveries of Heinrich Schliemann. Mycenae's satellite, Tiryns, was also a center of wealth and power as early as the 17th century BC. Later empire builders—Byzantines, Venetians, and Turks—created the city of Nafplion, with its harmonious assemblage of medieval churches, Turkish mansions, stone stairs, fountains, tree-shaded plazas, and mighty offshore fortress.
SOUTHERN PELOPONNESE 	It's not that the southern realms of the Peloponnesian peninsula aren't endowed with their fair share of ancient splendors. The scant remains of Sparta—the city-state that made war and austerity its motto—are here, as are the hilltop Temple of Apollo at Bassae, the intact walls of Ancient Messene, and the even older Mycenaean ruins of Nestor's Palace. But medieval monuments of mellow stone make the most striking statements in this sun-drenched landscape of olive groves and mighty mountain ranges. Mystras, whose golden-hue palaces and monasteries adorn an herb-scented mountainside, saw the last hurrah of the Byzantine emperors in the 14th century. Monemvassia, another Byzantine stronghold, clings to a rock that seems to erupt from the sea; the town's narrow streets tempt you to linger for a night or two in a centuries-old house. Much of the region's charm has nothing to do with past civilizations, though. The pretty ports of Pylos and Methoni dispense a Greek tonic of blue sea, cloudless sky, and sandy beach (the beaches in this region are some of the finest and least developed in Greece). Gythion is the gateway to another world altogether—

the mysterious Mani, a wild region that plunges south across barren mountains to land's end and the entrance to the mythical Underworld. Tower houses jutting from the Mani's craggy landscape are reminders of the clan feuds of centuries past.

THE CYCLADES

These islands compose a quintessential, pristine Mediterranean archipelago, with ancient sites, droves of vineyards and olive trees, and stark whitewashed cubist houses, all seemingly crystallized in a backdrop of lapis lazuli. The six major stars in this island constellation in the central Aegean Sea—Andros, Tinos, Mykonos, Naxos, Paros, and Santorini—are well visited but still lure with a magnificent fusion of sunlight, stone, and sparkling aqua sea. They also promise culture and flaunt hedonism: ancient sites, Byzantine castles and museums, lively nightlife, shops, restaurants, and beaches simple and sophisticated. Mountainous Andros, the most northern of the main islands, is wealthy and dignified, good for anyone who appreciates history, museums, and quiet evenings. The too-fierce winds and too-few good beaches of Tinos are no deterrent to the hardy souls who come on pilgrimages to the Church of the Evangelistria and the island's 799 other churches and then stay on to explore the ornamented villages and fanciful dovecotes. On Mykonos, backpackers and jet-setters alike share the beautiful shores and the famous, Dionysian nightlife, but the old ways of life continue in fishing ports and along mazelike town streets. Uninhabited and ruin-strewn Delos, just a short boat trip away from Mykonos, is a sacred island that was once the religious center of the ancient world. Naxos, the greenest of the Cyclades, has the remains of Venetian fortifications as well as Mycenaean sites. Paros, west of Naxos and known for its golden sand beaches and fishing villages, as well as the pretty town of Naousa, takes the summer overflow crowd from Mykonos. There's no shortage of worldly pleasures on Santorini, the most southern of the islands, from shopping to yachting, but pastimes need be no more fancy than climbing up a snakelike staircase to the top of the 1,000-foot-cliffs encircling Santorini's flooded caldera or simply gazing out to sea across the cubes of Fira's Cycladic architecture (blindingly white except for colorful doors and shutters).

WHAT'S
WHERE

CRETE	To Greeks, Crete is the Megalonissi, the Great Island, where a sophisticated culture flourished 5,000 years ago, though its location in the eastern Mediterranean 175 km (108 mi) south of Athens did not discourage invasions from the mainland in ancient times. The largest and southernmost of the Greek islands seems to have a continent's worth of extraordinary sites and mysterious landscapes. Evidence of the brilliant Minoan civilization is abundant, most splendidly at the Palace of Knossos near Heraklion—the oldest throne in Europe still stands in the original throne room, adorned with legendary frescoes of griffins. Another notable Minoan remnant is the Palace of Phaistos, southwest of Heraklion, on a hill overlooking the sea. The island's cities, including Heraklion, with its excellent Archaeological Museum, in eastern Crete and Hania and Rethymnon in the west, are graced with vestiges of Venetian and Turkish conquerors. In all of Crete, you'll find the most development on the north shore, and for the most part the southern coast remains blessedly unspoiled. Western Crete is especially rugged, with inland mountains and the rough southern shoreline. The island's beaches include some of the finest in the world, and its soaring mountains and deep gorges are popular targets for international ramblers.
RHODES & THE DODECANESE	The Dodecanese (Twelve Islands) are the easternmost holdings of Greece, wrapped around the shores of Turkey and Asia Minor. Romans, Crusaders, Turks, and Venetians have left their architectural mark here, but most likely to hypnotize you are the landscape—from the rugged mountains of Patmos to the verdant fields of Kos and lush hillsides of Rhodes—and a way of life that, despite invasions of armies and sunseekers, remains essentially and delightfully Greek. Among the succession of remarkable visitors to these islands was St. John the Divine, who received the Revelation in a cave on Patmos, still a place of pilgrimage. For those with less spiritual goals, however, the easygoing island of Symi beckons with its unsullied villages and topaz coves. Everyone begins on the big island of Rhodes—including the medieval Knights of St. John, who, back in the 11th and 12th centuries, fled from Palestine to Rhodes, where they lavished their wealth on building palaces, churches, and loggias, many in Rhodes town. Today glitzy resort life is another attraction of the island. An ancient cult settled Kos and established the Asklepieion, the once-great healing center and medical school that produced the most famous physician of

all time, Hippocrates; now the island's beaches attract a cult of beachgoers.

THE NORTHERN ISLANDS

Each of these far-flung northern Aegean islands bordering Asia Minor is distinct. Lesbos, to the north, is dappled with mineral springs and a petrified forest. The Byzantine-Genoese castle, tile-roof houses, and cobblestone streets of Molyvos have attracted a number of artists to the island. Craggy Chios, off the tourist track, is extraordinary for its architecture; despite fires through the ages, some fortified villages, Byzantine monasteries, and stencil-walled houses remain. Samos, land of wine (Lord Byron loved the local vintages), honey, and mountain villages perched on ravines, is farthest south of the main islands. You can combine a visit to any of these islands with a day (or longer) trip to nearby Turkey. Throughout the Northern Islands, you'll find residents who go about their business as they have for centuries and greet visitors—fairly new arrivals in these parts—with a warm welcome.

QUINTESSENTIAL GREECE

The Greek Spirit

"Come back tomorrow night. We're always here at this time," is the gracious invitation that usually terminates the first meeting with your outgoing Greek hosts. The Greeks are open, generous, and above all, full of a frank, probing curiosity about you, the foreigner. They do not have a word for standoffishness, and their approach is direct: American? British? Where are you staying? Are you married or single? How much do you make? Thus, with the subtlety of an atomic icebreaker, the Greeks get to know you, and you, perforce, get to know them.

In many villages there seems to always be at least one English-speaking person for whom it is a matter of national pride and honor to welcome you and, perhaps, insist on lending you his only mule to scale a particular mountain, then offer a tasty dinner meal. This is the typically Greek, deeply moving hospitality which money cannot buy and for which, of course, no money could be offered in payment.

Worry Beads

Chances are that your host—no doubt, luxuriantly moustached—will greet you as he counts the beads of what appears to be amber rosaries. They are *komboloia* or "worry beads," a legacy from the Turks, and Greeks click them on land, on the sea, in the air to ward off that insupportable silence which threatens to reign whenever conversation lags. Shepherds do it, cops do it, merchants in their shops do it. More aesthetic than thumb-twiddling, less expensive than smoking, this Queeg-like obsession indicates a tactile sensuousness, characteristic of a people which has produced some of the Western world's greatest sculpture.

If you want to get a sense of contemporary Greek culture, and indulge in some of its pleasure, start by familiarizing yourself with the rituals of daily life. These are a few highlights—things you can take part in with relative ease.

Siestas

When does Greece slow down? In Athens, it seems never. But head out to the countryside villages and you'll find another tradition, the siesta—the only time Greeks stop talking and really sleep it seems. Usually after lunch and until 4 PM, barmen drowse over their bars, waiters fall asleep in chairs, and all good Greeks drift off into slumber wherever they are, like the enchanted courtiers of Sleeping Beauty. Then, with a yawn, a sip of coffee, and a large glass of ice water, Greece goes back to the business of the day.

Folk Music & Dance

It's a rare traveler to Greece who does not at some point in the trip encounter Greek song and folk dancing, sure to be vigorous, colorful, spontaneous, and authentic. The dances are many, often rooted in history or religion, or both: the *zeimbekiko,* a man's solo dance, is performed with a pantherlike grace and an air of mystical awe, the dancer, with eyes riveted to the floor, repeatedly bending down to run his hand piously across the ground. The music, played by *bouzoukia,* large mandolins, is nostalgic and weighted with melancholy. The most popular, however, of all Greek dances are the *kalamatianos* and *tsamikos.* The former is performed in a circle, the male leader waving a handkerchief, swirling, bounding, and lunging acrobatically. The latter, more martial in spirit, represents men going to battle, all to the sound of stamping, springing, and twisting cries of *opa!* No matter which dance you may decide to jump up and perform in, remember that plate-smashing is now verboten in most places. In lieu of flying pottery, however, a more loving tribute is paid—many places have flower vendors, whose blooms are purchased to be thrown upon the dancers as they perform.

WHEN TO GO

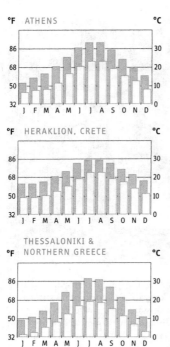

°F ATHENS °C

°F HERAKLION, CRETE °C

THESSALONIKI &
°F NORTHERN GREECE °C

The best time to visit Greece is late spring and early fall. In May and June the days are warm, even hot, but dry, and the seawater has been warmed by the sun. For sightseeing or hitting the beach, this is the time. Greece is relatively tourist free in spring, so if the beach and swimming aren't critical, April and early May are good; the local wildflowers are at their loveliest, too. Carnival, usually in February just before Lent, and Greek Easter are seasonal highlights. July and August (most locals vacation in August) are always busy—especially on the islands. If you visit during this peak, plan ahead and be prepared to fight the crowds. September and October are a good alternative to spring and early summer, especially in the cities where bars and cultural institutions reopen. Elsewhere, things begin to shut down in November. Transportation to the islands is limited in winter, and many hotels outside large cities are closed until April.

Climate

Greece has a typical Mediterranean climate: hot, dry summers and cool, wet winters. Chilliness and rain begin in November, the start of Greece's deceptive winters. Any given day may not be very cold—except in the mountains, snow is uncommon in Athens and to the south. But the cold is persistent, and many places are not well heated. Spring and fall are perfect, with warm days and balmy evenings. In the south a hot wind may blow across the Mediterranean from Africa. The average high and low temperatures for Athens and Heraklion and the average temperature for Thessaloniki are presented below.

🗂 Forecasts **National Observatory of Athens** ⊕ www.noa.gr. **Weather Channel Connection** ☎ 900/932-8437 95¢ per minute from a touch-tone phone ⊕ www.weather.com.

IF YOU LIKE

Ancient Civilizations

The sight greets you time and again in Greece—a line of solid, sun-bleached masonry silhouetted against a clear blue sky. If you're lucky, a cypress waves gently to one side. What makes the scene all the more fulfilling is the realization that a kindred spirit looked up and saw the same temple or theater some 2,000 or more years ago. Temples, theaters, statues, a stray Doric column or two, the fragment of a Corinthian capital: these traces of the ancients are thick on the ground in Greece, from the more than 3,000-year-old **Minoan Palace of Knossos** on the island of Crete to such relatively "new" monuments as the **Temple of Apollo** at Bassae (circa 420 BC) in the Peloponnese. During your travels you might clamber up the **Acropolis** to pay your homage to the **Parthenon;** step into the **Archaeological Museum in Piraeus** to see the Piraeus kouros, a 6th-century BC statue of Apollo; attend a performance at the 4th-century BC **Theater at Epidauros;** or climb through the ruins of the most sacred of ancient Greek sights, the **island of Delos.** You can have an experience like this every day in Greece, wherever you travel, from the mainland to islands as far flung as Kos, Santorini, and Rhodes. You can prepare yourself by reading up on mythology, history, and Greek architecture, but get used to the fact that coming upon these magnificent remnants of ancient civilizations is likely to send a chill up your spine every time you see them.

Sailing

Discovering Greece's geological jewels—many of them thickly scattered over the Aegean Sea like stepping stones between East and West—by yacht, boat, or caïque is a once-in-a-lifetime experience. You can "do" Greece in your own vessel according to your taste, pausing at will for scenery, swimming, or sightseeing, setting your own itinerary; signing up for an island voyage on a cruise ship is another popular option. Greece's jagged coasts let you explore a world of secluded hamlets, white chapels, and little villages reflected in blue water, as you ride out the sunny breeze that blows over the hills. Not that Zeus should set your schedule, but keep in mind the Aegean can be a great deal rougher than most people think during August, when the *meltemi,* the north wind, is a regular visitor to these waters.

If you are sailing directly from Italy or along the Dalmation Coast, **Corfu** is the first destination, a lush Ionian resort once the favorite of yachtsman King Paul of Greece. From here, yachters sometimes work their way down to **Messolonghi,** in the Gulf of Patras, where Byron died and where the sunsets can be unbelievable. South of the Peloponnese, few people fail to put in at **Crete**—the island where civilization is counted by the millennium. Sailing in a counterclockwise direction—old sea dogs maintain that this is the best way of covering the Aegean—you can enter the waters of **the Dodecanese** from the southwest. Another Mediterranean delight is **Rhodes,** with its ancient temples and medieval fortresses and wide range of discos. If you are looking for dreaminess, head west across the waters of the Dodecanese to **the Cyclades.** The islands here are all winners. Next could be the **Northern Islands,** including **Chios, Lesbos,** and **Samos.** Crossing the Gulf of Salonika to reach the Sporades requires good skill, but once you round **Cape Sounion**—give thanks to Poseidon at his incredible cliff-top temple here—you enter the hospitable waters of the **Saronic Gulf,** perhaps ending your odyssey in **Piraeus.**

IF YOU LIKE

Natural Wonders

Some countries have serene pastures and unobtrusive lakes, environments beautiful in a subtle way. Not Greece. Its landscapes seem put on Earth to astound outright, and often the intertwined history and spiritual culture are equally powerful. This vibrant modern nation is a land of majestic mountains whose slopes housed the ancient gods long before they nestled Byzantine monasteries or ski resorts. The country's sapphire-rimmed islands served as a cradle of great civilizations before they became playgrounds for sailors and beach lovers.

The Meteora, near Kalambaka, are indisputably amazing; these medieval monasteries perched precariously on top of eerily shaped pinnacles of rock command attention with their varied architecture, brilliant frescoes, and magnificent icons. There are no temples to the ancient gods on **Mt. Olympus,** but the majestic clustered summits reaching more than 9,700 feet into the heavens, impressive from any perspective, drew the Greeks' allegiance to the gods who were said to reside on the mountain. The craggy and heavily forested **Arcadian mountains** only recently isolated the Southern Peloponnese from the rest of Greece. To the south, three fingers of land dip into the Mediterranean; the most dramatic-looking of these peninsulas is **the Mani,** with its stark mountains and rocky coastlines. On Santorini, what may be the most beautiful settlements in the Cyclades straddle the wondrous **flooded caldera:** a crescent of cliffs, striated in black, pink, brown, white, and pale green, rising 1,100 feet. It may be from here that—while gazing out at the haunting, wine-color **Aegean Sea**—you decide you've found the sort of spectacle that drew you to Greece.

Alluring Towns & Villages

Historic, simple, famous, nondescript, or perfectly preserved: almost any Greek village seems to possess that certain balance of charm and mystique that takes your breath away. Here are some of the ones most worth your visit.

Reachable only by caïque, **Lalaria** on the island of Skiathos in the Sporades, has a polished limestone–and–marble beach that sets off the sparkling Aegean. Nearby grottoes call out for exploration. **Ia,** Santorini, is where you will find the cubical white houses you've dreamed of, and a sunset that is unsurpassed. The Greeks call the small city of **Nafplion** on the Gulf of Argos *oraia* (beautiful). The graceful mix of Greek, Venetian, and Turkish architecture helps make Nafplion perfect for strolling and lingering. **Monemvassia,** part ancient site, part living Byzantine town, has been called the Greek Gibraltar. Built on a rock jutting out from the Southern Peloponnese, its jumble of ruins next to shops and old churches disorients in a delightful way. **Hania** has a well-preserved Venetian quarter; narrow streets lined with Turkish houses enhance this captivating harbor-front town on the northern coast of Crete. **Rhodes town,** developed by the medieval Knights of St. John, is a gem, with its churches and Turkish buildings. Whitewashed buildings stenciled with exuberant traditional patterns create a unique effect in **Pirgi,** one of the defensive villages on Chios island founded by the Genoese in the 14th century. Finally, it's no wonder artists choose to live in **Molyvos,** on Lesbos island in the Northern Aegean: in summer flowers cascade down the balconies of the stone houses in this seaside town, and the red-tile roofs and cobblestoned streets are reminders of an earlier era.

GREAT ITINERARIES

ISLAND HOPPING

Fair warning: the danger of sailing through the Greek islands is that you will refuse to ever leave them. From these landfalls, some of the most justly famous, you can set off to find other idyllic retreats on your own.

Days 1–2: Mykonos

Jewel of the Cyclades, this very discovered island manages to retain its seductive charm. The main town is fascinating, despite the crowds in its narrow alleys. The beaches are world-renowned, and the spectacular temple ruins of Delos are only a short sail away. ⇨ *Mykonos in Chapter 9*.

Days 3–5: Crete

Despite the attractions of sea and mountains, it is still the mystery surrounding Europe's first civilization and empire that draws many travelers to Crete. Like them, you'll discover stunning testimony to the island's mysterious Minoan civilization, particularly at the legendary Palace of Knossos. Along these shores are blissful beaches as well as the enchanting Venetian-Turkish city of Hania. ⇨ *Chapter 10*.

Days 6–7: Rhodes

In one of the first Aegean playgrounds to be discovered by tourists, luxurious resorts are one draw; the magnificently preserved old town is another, with its 12th-century palaces and legendary harbor. ⇨ *Rhodes in Chapter 11*.

Days 8–10: Symi & Patmos

Only a short cruise from busy Rhodes, Symi is a world apart—quiet, undeveloped, and perfect for a retreat. Its main town, Chorio, is a treasury of neoclassical architecture. End your journey on a high note—

a day excursion to Patmos to visit its venerable monasteries and the site where St. John allegedly wrote his Revelation. ⇨ *Symi and Patmos in Chapter 11*.

BY PUBLIC TRANSPORTATION

- High-speed catamarans have halved travel time between Piraeus and Santorini.

- In summer, when ferries and boats run frequently, you should have little trouble moving from any of these islands to another.

- Except for Patmos and Symi, all are served by air as well.

GREAT ITINERARIES

HIGHLIGHTS OF GREECE

Among the pleasures of Greece are scrambling over time-burnished ruins, discovering an island you never want to leave, or simply lingering over a glass of ouzo on a taverna's terrace. To shorten this grand tour, visit the Meteora and Delphi as a long day trip or bypass Corfu. To do so, however, means foregoing the experience of rambling through mountain villages and island ports.

Days 1–2: Athens

The overture is your two-day tour of Athens. From the majestic Parthenon to hip Thission and edgy Psirri, the city remains a dazzling paradox—the word is Greek—of ancient and modern. ⇨ *Chapter 1.*

Day 3: Hydra

After your two days in Athens, hop the Flying Dolphin hydrofoil from Piraeus harbor for the 45-minute trip to this traffic-free island of stunning 19th-century stone mansions and idyllic seaside walks. ⇨ *The Saronic Gulf Islands in Chapter 2.*

Days 4–5: Nafplion

The charm continues in Nafplion, whose wide waterfront promenades, hilltop Venetian fortress, and maze of neoclassical houses make it the prettiest town in the Peloponnese. Classical ruins are abundant here, so explore Bronze Age Mycenae, the acropolis of Tiryns, or the great Theater at Epidauros. If a beach beckons, head to nearby Tolo or Porto Heli. ⇨ *Argolid & Corinthiad in Chapter 7.*

Day 6: Arcadia

The Arcadian mountains have many picturesque villages, but if you stay in Andrit-

sena, you will be well poised to visit the Temple of Apollo at Bassae in the clear light of early morning. ⇨ *Arcadia in Chapter 8.*

Day 7: Olympia

Explore the site where the ancient Olympic games were held in honor of Zeus. The god's Doric temple still dominates the sacred sanctuary as it has since the 5th century BC, though many of its broken columns now lie scattered under the noble pine trees. ⇨ *Achaea & Elis in Chapter 7.*

Days 8–10: Patras–Corfu

A travel day takes you north to the transportation hub of Patras, from where you can book a ferry ride for the 10-hour trip over Homer's "wine-dark" sea to the Ionian islands, the realm of Odysseus. On Corfu, stroll up Venetian arcaded streets and down the Esplanade in Corfu town; then ride a donkey through the lush green countryside. ⇨ *Corfu in Chapter 6, and Achaea & Elis in Chapter 7.*

Days 11–12: The Meteora

After taking the Igoumenítsa ferry back to the mainland, begin the scenic drive through the Pindos Mountains to the slate-roofed village of Metsovo. Then drop onto the Meteora plain, where Byzantine monasteries appear to float in midair atop their rocky pinnacles. ⇨ *Epirus & Thessaly in Chapter 4.*

Days 13–14: Thessaloniki

Head north to the city of Thessaloniki, which, like the mythical god Janus, is two-faced: a charming old town of churches, gardens, and monasteries backs into a vibrant modern town set along the bay.

Don't forget the treasures on view at the Archaeological Museum. ⇨ *Thessaloniki in Chapter 5.*

Day 15: Mt. Olympus

An easy excursion takes you to the village of Litochoro on Mt. Olympus. It's easy to see why the gods chose to inhabit these airy heights. ⇨ *Central Macedonia in Chapter 5.*

Day 16: Delphi

Next morning travel to Delphi, the "navel of the earth," to feast your eyes on the Temple of Apollo and the museum's celebrated *Charioteer* bronze. At sunset, when this spur of Mt. Parnassus is bathed in warm, deep purple light, ponder the Delphic Oracle's most famous pronouncement: "Know thyself." Overnight here, and then head back to Athens. ⇨ *Delphi in Chapter 2.*

BY PUBLIC TRANSPORTATION

- In peak season, more than 10 hydrofoils leave Piraeus's Zea Marina daily for Hydra; they also sail (but never on Sunday) for Nafplion. The metro and frequent buses make the run to Piraeus from Athens.

- Buses link Nafplion to Mycenae and Epidauros; the Nafplion-Argos bus goes to Tiryns.

- Take the bus to Tripoli to change for Andritsena in Arcadia. Express buses link Tripoli to Olympia and Patras, with its daily ferry—more frequent in high season—to Corfu.

- From Igoumenítsa, take the bus east to Ioannina; continue to Metsovo and on to Kalambaka to tour the Meteora; from Larissa—the hub of Thessaly—travel by train north to Thessaloniki.

- Heading back south, buses and trains stop at Litochoro for Mt. Olympus and continue on to Thebes, where you can make a bus connection for Delphi, which has frequent buses back to Athens.

GREAT ITINERARIES

THE GLORY THAT WAS GREECE: THE CLASSICAL SITES

Lovers of art, antiquity, and mythology journey to Greece to make a pilgrimage to its great archaeological sites. Here, at Delphi, Olympia, and Epidauros, the gods of Olympus were revered, Euripides' plays were first presented, and some of the greatest temples ever built still evoke the genial atmosphere of Greece's golden age (in spite of 2,500 years of wear and tear). Take this tour and you'll learn that it's not necessary to be a scholar of history to feel the proximity of ancient Greece.

Days 1–2: Athens

Begin at the beginning—the Acropolis plateau—where you can explore the greatest temple of Periclean Greece, the Parthenon, while drinking in heart-stopping views over the modern metropolis. After touring the ancient Agora, the Monument of Lysikrates, and the Odeon of Herod Atticus, finish up at the National Archaeological Museum (check opening hours). ⇨ *Chapter 1.*

Day 3: Sounion

Sun and sand, art, and antiquity lie southeast of Athens in Sounion. Here, the spectacular Temple of Poseidon sits atop a cliff 195 feet over the Saronic Gulf. Pay your own respects to the god of the sea at the beach directly below or enjoy the coves of the Apollo Coast as you head back west to the seaside resort of Vouliagmeni for an overnight. ⇨ *Attica in Chapter 2.*

Day 4: Eleusis & Corinth

Heading west of Athens, make a stop at Eleusis, home of the Sanctuary of Demeter and the haunted grotto of Hades, god of the Underworld. Past the Isthmus of Corinth—gateway to the Peloponnese—Ancient Corinth and its sublime Temple of Apollo beckon. Head south to the coast and Nafplion; en route, stop at a roadside stand for some tasty Nemean wine. ⇨ *Attica in Chapter 2 and Argolid & Corinthiad in Chapter 7.*

Days 5–6: Nafplion, Tiryns, Mycenae, Epidauros

Set up base in Nafplion—a stage set of Venetian fortresses, Greek churches, and neoclassical mansions—then set out to explore the mysteries of forgotten civilizations in nearby Tiryns, Mycenae, and Epidauros. North is Tiryns, where Bronze Age ramparts bear witness to Homer's "well-girt city." Farther north is Agamemnon's blood-soaked realm, the royal citadel of Mycenae, destroyed in 468 BC. Then take a day trip east to the famous ancient Theater at Epidauros, where a summer drama festival still presents the great tragedies of Euripides. ⇨ *Argolid & Corinthiad in Chapter 7.*

Days 7–8: Olympia & Bassae

After your third overnight in Nafplion, head west via either Argos (with helpful train connections) or Tripoli (by car on the E65) to Olympia—holiest site of the ancient Greek religion, home to the Sanctuary of Zeus, and birthplace of the Olympics. Walk through the olive groves of the sacred precinct; then get acquainted with Praxiteles' *Hermes* in the museum. Overnight here and then make a trip south to the remote Temple of Apollo at Bassae. ⇨ *Achaea & Elis in Chapter 7 and Arcadia in Chapter 8.*

Day 9: Delphi

Head north through verdant forests of the Elis region to Patras or nearby Rion for the ferry or bridge across the Corinthian Gulf; travel east along the coast and overnight in chic Galaxidi, with its elegant stone seafarers' mansions. The final day, set off to discover Delphi, whose noble dust and ancient ruins are theatrically set amid cliffs. Despite the tour buses, it is still possible to imagine the power of the most famous oracle of antiquity. From here, head back to Athens. ⇨ *Delphi in Chapter 2.*

BY PUBLIC TRANSPORTATION

- KTEL buses leave from the Platia Aigyptou, Liossion, and Odos Kifissou terminals in downtown Athens and connect to most of the major sites: southeast to Sounion along the coast, northwest to Delphi, and west to the Peloponnese.

- In some cases you will need to take the bus to the provincial capital (Corinth, Argos, Tripoli), then change to a local bus.

- Daily trains connect Athens's Peloponnisou station to Corinth and Argos, with bus connections to Nafplion and Olympia.

- Buses travel from Nafplion to Olympia via Argos and Tripoli.

ON THE
CALENDAR

The Greek calendar is filled with religious celebrations, cultural festivals, and civic occasions. Those events with roots in Byzantine Greece are especially intriguing, as they combine religious belief and national pride in a unique way. Shops may close early for local or national celebrations, and hotels may be booked during major events (such as Carnival at Patras). Verify the dates of events with the Greek National Tourism Organization (GNTO or EOT). For public holidays and major religious observances, *see* Holidays *in* Smart Travel Tips.

Carnival, or Apokreas, precedes Lent, so the dates vary each year. Towns and islands known to celebrate Carnival in style are Patras, Naousa, Veria, Kozani, Zante, Skyros, Xanthi, Mesta and Olimbi (on Chios), Galaxidi, Thebes, Poligiros, Thimiana, Lamia, Messinia, Soho, Serres, and Agiassos (on Lesbos); Karpathos, Heraklion, and Rethymnon on Crete; Amfissa, Efxinoupolis, and Ayia Anna on Evia.

The traditional activities preceding Easter are very moving, including funeral processions on Good Friday. Not only do they attest to the strength of the participants' faith, but they link modern Greece with its Byzantine roots, and the soldiers carrying the coffins illustrate the ties between church and government. Processions to churches on the night of Holy Saturday are a memorable sight. Following the midnight ceremony of the Resurrection, the congregations head homeward to feast, with the traditional red-dyed eggs and *mayiritsa* soup. More red-dyed eggs and roast lamb highlight the feasting on Easter Sunday. Seeing the rituals of Holy Week makes you understand the depth of meaning that the Easter greeting *Christos anesti,* "Christ is risen," and its response, *Alithos anesti,* "He has indeed risen," have for most Greeks.

ONGOING May–Sept.	**Folk dancing** is performed at the amphitheater on Filopappou Hill in Athens.
June–Sept.	The **Elliniko (Hellenic) Festival** presents ancient dramas, operas, music, and ballet, performed by nationally and internationally famous artists, in the 2nd-century Odeon of Herodes Atticus on the south slope of the Acropolis.
June–Oct.	**Folk dancing** performances are held in the theater in the old town of Rhodes on that island.

WINTER	
Dec. 31	New Year's Eve is the occasion for carol singing by children and the exchanging of gifts. On the island of Chios the day is marked by a contest for the best model boat.
Jan. 1	The Feast of St. Basil marks the beginning of the New Year. A special cake, the *Vassilopita,* is baked with a coin in it, which brings good luck to the finder.
Jan. 6	Epiphany, the day that marks the baptism of Christ, is celebrated by blessing the waters—marked by an official ceremony at Athens's harbor, Piraeus. Elsewhere, crosses are immersed in seas, lakes, and rivers.
Jan. 8	Gynaecocracy, in northeastern Greece, reverses the traditional roles of men and women: in the area around Serres, Kilkis, Xanthi, and Komotini, women spend the day at the cafés while the men do the housekeeping until evening.
3 weeks Feb.–mid-Mar.	Carnival, like Mardi Gras, celebrates the period before the beginning of Lent. The evenings are marked by parades, music, and dancing, and costumes are required. Carnival, more correctly known as Apokreas, runs three weeks before the beginning of Greek Lent (Clean Monday). So, depending on the date for Orthodox Easter (which changes annually), festivities usually begin in February.
SPRING	
Mar. 25	Independence Day commemorates the call for independence in 1821 by Germanos, the Metropolitan of Patras, which began the uprising in the Peloponnese that eventually freed Greece from Ottoman rule. Today it is marked by parades of the armed forces, especially in Athens.
Apr. 23	The Feast of St. George is a day for horse racing at Kaliopi on Limnos and at Pili on Kos. A three-day-long feast begins at Arachova, near Delphi; on Crete, at Assi Gonia, near Hania, a sheep-shearing contest follows the religious fiesta. Note that if St. George's Feast Day falls before Orthodox Easter Sunday, it is celebrated instead on Easter Monday.
Apr. or early May	Good Friday, Holy Saturday, and Easter Sunday are the most sacred days on the Orthodox calendar. The traditional candlelight funeral processions staged throughout the country on Good Friday are very powerful to watch.
May 21–23	The Anastenaria, a traditional fire-walking ritual with pagan roots and a Byzantine overlay, is performed in Ayia Eleni near Ayia Serres, and in Langada near Thessaloniki, where villagers dance on live embers while clasping icons of St. Constantine and St. Helen.

ON THE CALENDAR

SUMMER Mid-June–late Aug.	Lycabettus Theater presents a variety of performances in the amphitheater on Lycabettus Hill overlooking Athens.
Late June–early July	Navy Week, honoring the Greek navy, is celebrated in coastal towns. Fishermen at Plomari on Lesbos and Agria near Volos stage festivals, and at Volos the last day of Navy Week is marked by a reenactment of the mythical voyage of the ship *Argo,* with its crew led by Jason in search of the Golden Fleece.
July	The International Folk Festival, a two-week event held in Ioannina, features clarinet music, polyphonic singing, and the circle dances of Epirus.
July–Aug. weekends	The Epidauros Festival, world renowned for the excellence of the performances, is held in the ancient theater at Epidauros, known for its superb acoustics. Watching a classical comedy or tragedy in this peaceful rural setting sends chills down your spine—twilight falls, the audience quiets, and a play first performed 2,500 years ago begins. The Dodoni, Philippi, and Thassos festivals, like the better-known one at Epidauros, stage classical dramas in ancient theaters.
Aug.	The Epirotika Festival in Ioannina, Epirus, celebrates regional authors and artists with exhibitions, theatrical performances, and concerts.
Aug.	The Hippokrateia Festival on the island of Kos honors the father of medicine, a native son. Events include performances of ancient dramas and music, a flower show, and a costumed reenactment of the first swearing of the Hippocratic oath.
Aug.	At the Olympus Festival, a series of cultural events is held at the village of Litochoro near Olympus, in the well-preserved Frankish castle of Platamona.
FALL Mid-Sept.–Oct.	The International Trade Fair, held in mid-September in Thessaloniki, is a huge business event. It's followed by a series of festivals such as the Festival of Popular Song and the International Film Festival.
Oct.	The Dimitria Festival, which takes place in Thessaloniki, has exhibits of works by artists from all over Greece; it also showcases performances by Greek musicians.

SMART TRAVEL TIPS

Finding out about your destination before you leave home means you won't spend time organizing everyday minutiae once you've arrived. You'll be more streetwise when you hit the ground as well, better prepared to explore the aspects of Greece that drew you here in the first place. The organizations in this section can provide information to supplement this guide; contact them for up-to-the-minute details, and consult the A to Z sections that end each chapter for facts on the various topics as they relate to the country's many regions. Happy landings!

ADDRESSES

To make finding your way around as easy as possible, it's wise to learn to recognize letters in the Greek alphabet. Most areas have few road signs in English, and even those that are in English follow the official standardized transliteration code, resulting in odd spellings of foreign names. Sometimes there are several spelling variations in English for the same place: Agios or Ayios, Georgios or Yiorgos. Also, the English version may be quite different from the Greek, or even what locals use informally: Corfu is known as Kerkyra; island capitals are often just called Chora (town), no matter what their formal title; and Panepistimiou, a main Athens boulevard, is officially named Eleftheriou Venizelou, but if you ask for that name, no one will know what you're talking about. A long street may change names several times, and a city may have more than one street by the same name, so know the district you're headed for, or a major landmark nearby, especially if you're taking a taxi. In this guide, street numbers appear after the street name. Finally, there are odd- and even-numbered sides of the streets, but No. 124 could be several blocks away from No. 125.

AIR TRAVEL

BOOKING

Price is just one factor to consider when booking a flight: frequency of service and even a carrier's safety record are often just as important. Major airlines offer the greatest number of departures. Smaller airlines—including regional and no-frills airlines—usually have a limited number of flights daily. On the other hand, so-called low-cost airlines usually are cheaper, and their fares impose fewer restrictions.

When you book, look for nonstop flights and remember that "direct" flights stop at least once. Try to avoid connecting flights, which require a change of plane. Two airlines may operate a connecting flight jointly, so ask whether your airline operates every segment of the trip; you may find that the carrier you prefer flies you only part of the way. To find more booking tips and to check prices and make online flight reservations, log on to www.fodors.com.

CARRIERS

When flying internationally, you must usually choose between a domestic carrier, the national flag carrier of the country you are visiting, and a foreign carrier from a third country. You may, for example, choose to fly Olympic Airways to Greece. National flag carriers have the greatest number of nonstops. Domestic carriers may have better connections to your home town and serve a greater number of gateway cities. Third-party carriers may have a price advantage.

In Greece, when faced with a boat journey of six hours or more, consider flying. Olympic Airways has dominated the domestic market, with flights to more than 30 cities and islands. Alternative airlines providing cheaper fares (at times) and better service include Aegean Airlines.

Olympic Airways, the state-owned Greek carrier, has incurred criticism over the years for its on-time record, indifferent service, and aging aircraft. Three privatization attempts have failed since 2001, and there have been schedule cutbacks. The airline has a fleet of more than 44 aircraft, including A340-300 airbuses. Improved service and fewer cancellations, especially since the opening of Athens International Airport, have left more passengers pleasantly surprised. Olympic is rated among the top three carriers worldwide for safety.

Many European national airlines fly to Athens from the United States and Canada via their home country's major cities. Remember that these are often connecting flights that include at least one stop and may require a change of planes. Air France, British Airways, Delta, KLM, and Lufthansa all now operate code-share flights within Greece; British Airways has some direct flights to Crete.

▐ To & From Greece **Aegean** ☎ 210/626-1700 ⊕ www.aegeanair.com. **Air France** ☎ 800/237-2747 ⊕ www.airfrance.net. **Alitalia** ☎ 800/223-5730 ⊕ www.alitalia.it. **Austrian Airlines** ☎ 800/843-0002 ⊕ www.austrianair.com. **British Airways** ☎ 800/247-9297 ⊕ www.britishairways.com. **Delta** ☎ 800/241-4141 ⊕ www.delta.com. **El Al** ☎ 800/223-6700 ⊕ www.elal.com. **Finnair** ☎ 800/950-5000 ⊕ www.finnair.com. **Iberia Airlines** ☎ 800/772-4642 ⊕ www.iberia.com. **KLM Royal Dutch Airlines** ☎ 800/447-4747 ⊕ www.klm.com. **LOT Polish Airlines** ☎ 212/869-1074 ⊕ www.lot.com. **LTU International Airways** ☎ 210/323-0541 or 210/323-0542 ⊟ 210/324-1127 ⊕ www.ltu.com. **Lufthansa** ☎ 800/645-3880 ⊕ www.lufthansa.com. **Olympic Airways** ☎ 800/223-1226 outside New York, 212/735-0200 ⊕ www.olympic-airways.gr. **SAS Scandinavian Airlines** ☎ 800/221-2350 ⊕ www.scandinavian.net. **Swiss International Airlines** ☎ 800/221-4750 ⊕ www.swiss.com. **Thai Air** ☎ 800/426-5204 ⊕ www.thaiairways.com.

▐ From Australia & New Zealand **Singapore Airlines** ☎ 02/9350-0262 in Australia, 09/303-2129 in New Zealand ⊕ www.singaporeair.com. **Thai Airways** ☎ 02/9251-1922 in Australia, 09/377-3886 in New Zealand ⊕ www.thaiair.com.

▐ From the U.K. **British Airways** ☎ 0845/773-3377 ⊕ www.britishairways.com. **easyJet** ☎ 0870/600-0000 ⊕ www.easyjet.com. **Olympic Airways** ☎ 020/7409-3400.

▐ Within Greece **Aegean Airlines** ✉ Viltanioti 3, Kifissia, Athens ☎ 210/626-1700 or 801/11200 ⊟ 210/998-8300 ⊕ www.aegeanair.com. **Air France** ☎ 210/960-1100. **British Airways** ☎ 210/890-6666. **Delta Air Lines** ☎ 800/4412-9506. **El Al** ☎ 210/934-1120. **KLM Royal Dutch Airlines** ☎ 210/911-0100. **Lufthansa** ☎ 210/617-5200. **Olympic Airways** Main Athens ticket office and for prepaid tickets, ✉ Filellinon 15, near Syntagma Sq. ☎ 210/966-6666 reservations, 210/356-9111 airport arrival and departure information ⊟ 210/966-6111 ✉ Kotopouli 3, Omonia Sq. ☎ 210/926-7218 or 210/926-7219 ⊕ www.olympic-airways.gr.

CHECK-IN & BOARDING

Always **find out your carrier's check-in policy.** Plan to arrive at the airport about 2 hours before your scheduled departure time for flights within the United States and 2½ to 3 hours before international flights from the United States. You may need to arrive earlier if you're flying from one of the busier airports or during peak air-traffic times. To avoid delays at airport-security checkpoints, try not to wear any metal. Jewelry, belt and other buckles, steel-toe shoes, barrettes, and underwire bras are among the items that can set off detectors.

Any sharp objects, such as nail files or scissors, may be removed if you take them through airport security. Pack such items in luggage you plan to check.

Assuming that not everyone with a ticket will show up, airlines routinely overbook planes. When everyone does, airlines ask for volunteers to give up their seats. In return, these volunteers usually get a several-hundred-dollar flight voucher, which can be used toward the purchase of another ticket, and are rebooked on the next available flight out. If there are not enough volunteers, the airline must choose who will be denied boarding. The first to get bumped are passengers who checked in late and those flying on discounted tickets, so get to the gate and check in as early as possible, especially during peak periods.

Always **bring a government-issued photo ID** to the airport; even when it's not required, a passport is best.

In Greece, you need to show identification for both domestic and international flights. For domestic flights in Greece, arrive no later than 1 hour before departure time; for flights to the rest of Europe, 1½ hours; and for other international flights, 2 hours. If you get bumped because of overbooking, international carriers try to find an alternative route on another airline, but Olympic usually puts you on its next available flight, which might not be until the next day. (Under European Union law, you are entitled to receive up to €400 compensation for overbooking on flights shorter than 3,500 km [2,100 mi] and up to €600 for longer flights. In the past, Olympic Airways staff and traffic controllers have gone on strike for several hours a day; keep attuned to the local news. Check-in is straightforward and easy at Greece's larger airports, but on small islands, it sometimes gets confusing, since several airlines may use the same check-in counter, indicated by garbled announcements. Watch for movement en masse by the crowd.

If you have been wait-listed on an Olympic flight in Greece, remember that this list does not apply on the day of departure. A new waiting list goes into effect at the airport two hours prior to takeoff for domestic flights and three hours before international flights; you must be there to get a place.

CUTTING COSTS

The least-expensive airfares to Greece are often priced for round-trip travel and must usually be purchased in advance. Airlines generally allow you to change your return date for a fee; most low-fare tickets, however, are nonrefundable. It's smart to call a number of airlines and check the Internet; when you are quoted a good price, book it on the spot—the same fare may not be available the next day, or even the next hour. Always check different routings and look into using alternate airports. Also, price off-peak flights and red-eye, which may be significantly less expensive than others. Travel agents, especially low-fare specialists (⇨ Discounts & Deals), are helpful.

Consolidators are another good source. They buy tickets for scheduled flights at reduced rates from the airlines, then sell them at prices that beat the best fare available directly from the airlines. (Many also offer reduced car-rental and hotel rates.) Sometimes you can even get your money back if you need to return the ticket. Carefully read the fine print detailing penalties for changes and cancellations, purchase the ticket with a credit card, and confirm your consolidator reservation with the airline.

When you fly as a courier, you trade your checked-luggage space for a ticket deeply subsidized by a courier service. There are restrictions on when you can book and how long you can stay. Some courier companies list with membership organizations, such as the Air Courier Association and the International Association of Air Travel Couriers; these require you to become a member before you can book a flight.

Many airlines, singly or in collaboration, offer discount air passes that allow foreigners to travel economically in a particular country or region. These visitor passes usually must be reserved and purchased before you leave home. Information about passes often can be found on most airlines' international Web pages, which tend to be aimed at travelers from outside the carrier's home country. Also, try typing the name of the pass into a search engine, or search for "pass" within the carrier's Web site.

In October, at the end of the tourist season, you may find cheap seats to the rest of Europe, especially the United Kingdom, Germany, and Scandinavia, on planes carrying package tours that aren't completely full. Ask your local travel agent about the possibilities.

🔢 Consolidators **AirlineConsolidator.com** ☎ 888/468-5385 ⊕ www.airlineconsolidator.com; for international tickets. **Best Fares** ☎ 800/880-1234 ⊕ www.bestfares.com; $59.90 annual membership. **Cheap Tickets** ☎ 800/377-1000 or 800/652-4327 ⊕ www.cheaptickets.com. **Expedia** ☎ 800/397-3342 or 404/728-8787 ⊕ www.expedia.com. **Hotwire** ☎ 866/468-9473 or 920/330-9418 ⊕ www.hotwire.com. **Now Voyager Travel** ☎ 212/459-1616 ⊕ www.nowvoyagertravel.com. **Onetravel.com** ⊕ www.onetravel.com. **Orbitz** ☎ 888/656-4546 ⊕ www.orbitz.com. **Priceline.com** ⊕ www.priceline.com. **Travelocity** ☎ 888/709-5983, 877/282-2925 in Canada, 0870/111-7061 in the U.K. ⊕ www.travelocity.com.

🔢 Courier Resources **Air Courier Association/Cheaptrips.com** ☎ 800/211-5119 ⊕ www.aircourier.org or www.cheaptrips.com; $20 annual membership. **Courier Travel** ☎ 303/570-7586 🖷 313/625-6106 ⊕ www.couriertravel.org; $50 annual membership. **International Association of Air Travel Couriers** ☎ 308/632-3273 🖷 308/632-8267 ⊕ www.courier.org; $45 annual membership. **Now Voyager Travel** ✉ 1717 Ave. M, Brooklyn, NY 11230 ☎ 212/459-1616 🖷 718/504-4762 ⊕ www.nowvoyagertravel.com.

🔢 Discount Passes **FlightPass EuropebyAir**, ☎ 888/387-2479 ⊕ www.europebyair.com.

DOMESTIC FLIGHTS

The frequency of flights varies according to the time of year (with an increase between Greek Easter and November), and it is essential to book well in advance for summer or for festivals and holidays, especially on three-day weekends. Domestic flights are a good deal for many destinations. In summer 2005 the one-way economy Athens–Rhodes fare offered by Olympic was €60, excluding taxes; to Corfu, €60; to Santorini, €79; and to Heraklion, €58. Unless the flight is part of an international journey, the baggage allowance is only 33 pounds (15 kilograms) per passenger.

Scheduled (i.e., nonchartered) domestic air travel in Greece is provided predominantly by Olympic Airways, which operates out of Athens International Airport (Eleftherios Venizelos) in Spata. There is service from Athens to Alexandroupolis, Ioannina, Kastoria, Kavala, Kozani, Preveza, and Thessaloniki, all on the mainland; Kalamata in the Peloponnese; the Aegean islands: Astypalaia, Karpathos, Kassos, Kythira, Crete (Hania, Heraklion, and Sitia), Chios, Ikaria, Kos, Lesbos (listed as Mytilini in Greek), Limnos, Leros, Milos, Mykonos, Naxos, Paros, Rhodes, Samos, Skiathos, Syros, Skyros, Kastellorizo (only via Rhodes), and Santorini; Corfu (called Kerkyra in Greek), Kefalonia, and Zakynthos in the Ionian Sea. Flights also depart from Thessaloniki for Hania, Chios, Heraklion, Ioannina, Corfu, Limnos, Lesbos, Mykonos, Rhodes, Samos, and Santorini. You can also fly from Kozani to Kastoria on the mainland. Interisland flights, depending on the season, include the following: from Chios to Lesbos; from Karpathos to Kassos; from Santorini to Rhodes and Heraklion; from Rhodes to Karpathos, Kassos, Kastellorizo, and Mykonos, as well as Kos (summer only); between Kefalonia and Zakynthos (winter); and from Lesbos to Chios, Limnos, and Samos (winter).

For those traveling to Thessaloniki, a good alternative is Aegean Airlines, which has regular scheduled flights and sometimes even cheaper prices than Olympic. It also flies from Athens to Heraklion and Hania in Crete and to Rhodes. The company's planes also travel from Athens to Alexandroupolis, Ioannina, Kavala, Corfu, Lesbos, Rhodes, Santorini, Chios, Kos, and Thessaloniki. Planes depart Thessaloniki for Heraklion, Rhodes, Santorini, Alexandroupolis, Kavala, Corfu, Ioannina, Mykonos, Chios, Kos, and Lesbos. In summer, LTU International Airways operates several flights between points in Greece such as Rhodes and Kos or Athens and Samos.

Although weather is usually not an obstacle when flying throughout Greece, high winds may preclude planes from landing on some islands. Delays in domestic departures are not uncommon, and Olympic seldom offers much information to waiting passengers about the cause of delay or new departure times. Befriend a bilingual fellow passenger who can translate the announcements.

ENJOYING THE FLIGHT

State your seat preference when purchasing your ticket, and then repeat it when you confirm and when you check in. For more legroom, you can request one of the few emergency-aisle seats at check-in, if you're capable of moving obstacles comparable in weight to an airplane exit door (usually between 35 pounds and 60 pounds)—a Federal Aviation Administration requirement of passengers in these seats. Seats behind a bulkhead also offer more legroom, but they don't have underseat storage. Don't sit in the row in front of the emergency aisle or in front of a bulkhead, where seats may not recline. SeatGuru.com has more information about specific seat configurations, which vary by aircraft.

Ask the airline whether a snack or meal is served on the flight. If you have dietary concerns, request special meals when booking. These can be vegetarian, low-cholesterol, or kosher, for example. It's a good idea to pack some healthful snacks and a small (plastic) bottle of water in your carry-on bag. On long flights, try to maintain a normal routine, to help fight jet lag. At night, get some sleep. By day, eat light meals, drink water (not alcohol), and **move around the cabin** to stretch your legs. For additional jet-lag tips consult *Fodor's FYI: Travel Fit & Healthy* (available at bookstores everywhere).

If you smoke, inquire about your airline's policy. Most airlines, especially from the United States, are banning smoking throughout the plane. Olympic Airways does not allow smoking, nor do any airlines traveling within the EU. Even if you stop en route, the airport usually provides few places where you can smoke other than the cafés or bars or, as in Athens, specific areas designated for smokers.

To reduce swelling limbs, take off or loosen your shoes the minute you sit down (bring thick socks to pad around in), and try to keep your feet elevated. Get up and walk every two hours or do simple seat aerobics. Grab an available blanket when you first enter the plane, because compartments become chilly. Avoid sitting near the bathrooms; you will be jostled continuously by those waiting in line. To ward off talkative neighbors, order a headset even if you aren't planning to listen to the music, or carry a book. Note that most domestic Greek flights don't offer anything more than a beverage or snack.

FLYING TIMES

Flying time to Athens is 3½ hours from London, 9½ hours from New York, 12 hours from Chicago, 16½ hours from Los Angeles, and 19 hours from Sydney.

HOW TO COMPLAIN

If your baggage goes astray or your flight goes awry, complain right away. Most carriers require that you **file a claim immediately.** The Aviation Consumer Protection Division of the Department of Transportation publishes *Fly-Rights,* which discusses airlines and consumer issues and is available online. You can also find articles and information on mytravelrights.com, the Web site of the nonprofit Consumer Travel Rights Center.

Athens International Airport has customer information desks throughout the airport that operate on a 24-hour basis, as well as more than a dozen courtesy phones that put you through to the customer call center. You can also contact the Hellenic Civil Aviation Authority or the Quality Management Department, both at the airport.

🔃 Airline Complaints **Aviation Consumer Protection Division** ✉ U.S. Department of Transportation, Office of Aviation Enforcement and Proceedings, C-75, Room 4107, 400 7th St. SW, Washington, DC 20590 ☎ 202/366-2220 ⊕ airconsumer.ost.dot.gov. **Federal Aviation Administration Consumer Hotline** ✉ for inquiries: FAA, 800 Independence Ave. SW, Washington, DC 20591 ☎ 800/322-7873 ⊕ www.faa.gov.

🔃 Complaints at Athens Airport **Hellenic Civil Aviation Authority** ✉ Level 3, Room 607, main terminal bldg. ☎ 210/353-4157 weekdays 9-5, 210/353-4147 at other times. **Quality Management Department** ☎ 210/353-7240.

RECONFIRMING

Check the status of your flight before you leave for the airport. You can do this on your carrier's Web site, by linking to a flight-status checker (many Web booking services offer these), or by calling your carrier or travel agent. Always confirm international flights at least 72 hours ahead of the scheduled departure time. You do not need to reconfirm flights within Greece. Athens International Airport posts real-time flight information on its Web site (⊕ www.aia.gr).

AIRPORTS

Athens International Airport at Spata, 33 km (20 mi) southeast of the city center, opened in 2001 as the country's main airport. Officially named Eleftherios Venizelos, after Greece's first prime minister, the airport is user-friendly and high-tech. The main terminal building has two levels: upper for departures, ground level for arrivals. Unless you plan to avoid Athens altogether or to fly via your charter directly to the islands, the Athens airport is the most convenient because you can easily switch from international to domestic flights or get to Greece's main harbor, Piraeus, about a 50-minute drive south of the airport. Thessaloniki's airport has modern airport facilities for international

travelers, and the airport in Rhodes is undergoing a major upgrade and expansion.

Five major airports in Greece, listed below, service international flights. Airports on some smaller islands (Santorini, Syros, and Paros among them) take international charter flights during the busier summer months. Locals will sometimes refer to the airports with their secondary names, usually those of Greek statesmen, so these names—along with the three-letter airport codes—are also given. Information about airports other than Athens is given on the Olympic Airways Web site (⊕ www. olympic-airways.gr) and on the Civil Aviation Authority Web site (⊕ www.hcaa.gr).

🔃 Airport Information **Athens International Airport-Eleftherios Venizelos (ATH)** ✉ Spata ☎ 210/353-0000 flight information and customer service, 210/353-0445 tourist information, 210/353-0515 lost and found ⊕ www.aia.gr. **Heraklion International Airport-Nikos Kazantzakis (HER)** ✉ Heraklion, Crete ☎ 2810/397129. **Kerkyra (Corfu) Airport-Ioannis Kapodistrias (CFU)** ✉ Corfu town ☎ 26610/89600. **Rhodes International Airport (RHO)** ✉ Rhodes town ☎ 22410/83200. **Thessaloniki International Airport-Makedonia (SKG)** ✉ Mikras ☎ 2310/985000.

DUTY-FREE SHOPPING

Duty-free shopping allowances among European Union member countries were abolished in 1999, although there are still numerous merchandise offers for those traveling between EU countries by boat and plane. Duty-free sales for travel outside the EU remain business as usual (⇨ Customs & Duties).

Athens International Airport has more than 35 shops for duty-free shopping, from jewelry and designer clothing to books. Perfumes, cosmetics, and electronics are not worth buying; you can often find these for less money in your own country. What *are* cheaper are cigarettes, alcohol (including Greek ouzo and Metaxa brandy), good-quality ceramics, and CDs of Greek music. In other words, only buy a product that you can't get in your own country, and one that if sold in Greece carries the usual 19% value-added tax.

TRANSFERS

See Athens A to Z *in* Chapter 1 for information on transfers between the airport and Athens.

In Thessaloniki, municipal Bus 078 (€0.50) picks up travelers about every 40 minutes until 11:15 PM for the 45-minute ride (up to 90 minutes if there is traffic) into town; its final stop is the train station. The EOT office in the airport arrivals terminal has information. At other airports throughout Greece, especially on the islands, public transportation is infrequent or nonexistent; ask your hotel to make arrangements or take a taxi; rates are usually set to fixed destinations.

BIKE TRAVEL

Bike travel is catching on in Greece, and it's increasingly common to see cycling groups on flatter islands (80% of Greece is mountainous) or engaging in a mild form of mountain biking (descent only). The pleasures are that you will meet the locals and go slowly enough to enjoy the quirky details of Greek life. The downside is that roads are usually narrow and without bike lanes; Greek drivers don't have much experience with cyclists; spare parts may be hard to find away from major cities. The only place in Greece that has dedicated bike lanes, about 40 km (25 mi) of them, is the island of Kos in the Dodecanese. The best places to bike are secondary roads on islands, where you will also find bike rentals from April through October, with prices starting from €6.50 a day for a mountain bike. The best maps are by Road Editions and Anavasi, sold through the addresses below and at most bookstores.

🚲 Bike Maps **Anavasi** ✉ Stoa Arsakiou 6A, 10564 Athens ☎ 210/321-8104 ⊕ www.anavasi.gr Ⓜ Panepistimio. **Road Editions** ✉ Ippokratous 39, 10680 Athens ☎ 210/361-3242 📠 210/361-4681 ⊕ www.road.gr.

BIKES IN MOTION

If your bike is within your baggage weight allowance, it's free if you check it on the plane; otherwise, there is a fee ($100). Some airlines sell bike boxes, which are often free at bike shops, for about $15 (bike bags can be considerably more expensive). Ferries in Greece usually let you bring a bike on for free, though you may want to pay the small fee (varies) to store it in the bottom-deck luggage room during the journey. Trains and buses require a little more negotiation to ensure the bike travels on the same vehicle with you.

BOAT & FERRY TRAVEL

In a country with so many islands, ferries are important. Ships for the Ionian islands and Italy sail from ports on Greece's west coast, such as Patras and Igoumenitsa. Also on the west coast, the local ferry between Igoumenitsa and Corfu island runs many times daily in each direction. In Athens, ferries leave frequently from Piraeus, the main port 10 km (6 mi) south of downtown, for the Argo-Saronic islands, the Cyclades, the Dodecanese, and Crete. Shorter crossings to the Cyclades can be made from the other side of Attica; from Rafina to Andros, Tinos, and Mykonos; and from Lavrion to Kea and Kythnos. Some northern islands, like Thassos and Limnos, are more easily reached from Thessaloniki, and boats for the Sporades islands depart only from Agios Konstantinos and Volos on the northern mainland or Kimi on Evia island. When choosing a ferry, determine how many stops you'll make and the estimated arrival time. Sometimes a ferry that leaves an hour later for your destination gets you there faster. High-speed ferries are more expensive, with airplane seating, fare classes, and numbered seats. They'll get you where you're going more quickly, but lack the flavor of the older ferries with the open decks.

From Piraeus port, the quickest way to get into Athens, if you are traveling light, is to walk to the metro station and take an electric train to Omonia Square (€0.70) or Syntagma Square (€0.70, change at Monastiraki or Omonia to the Ethniki Aminas line), a 30-minute trip. Alternatively, you can take a taxi, which may take longer because of traffic; it will cost around €12, plus baggage and port surcharges. Often, drivers wait until they fill their taxi with debarking passengers headed in the same direction, which could take 25 minutes, plus the extra time accommodating everyone's route. It's faster to walk to the main street and hail a passing cab.

To get to Attica's main port, Rafina, take a KTEL bus, which leaves every half hour 5:30 AM to 9:30 PM from Aigyptou Square near Pedion Areos park in Athens. The fare is €1.55. The bus takes about an hour to get to Rafina; the port is slightly down the hill from the bus station.

Timetables change in winter and summer, and special sailings are often added around holiday weekends in summer when demand is high. In the Cyclades, Ionian, and Dodecanese, small ferry companies operate local routes that are not published nationally; passage can be booked through travel agents on the islands served. Boats may be delayed by weather conditions, especially when the northwestern winds called *meltemia* hit in August, so stay flexible—one advantage to not buying a ticket in advance. You usually can get on a boat at the last minute. Still, it is better to buy your tickets two to three days ahead if you are traveling between July 15 and August 30, when most Greeks vacation, if you need a cabin (good for long trips), or if you're taking a car. If possible, **don't travel by boat around August 15,** when most ferries are so crowded, the situation becomes comically desperate, although things have improved since strict enforcement of capacity limits. Reserve your return journey soon after you arrive.

Ticket prices don't vary because they're set by the government, and in most cases deck class (*triti thesi*) is good enough. First-class tickets are almost as expensive as flying.

If the boat journey will be more than a couple of hours, it's a good idea to take along water and snacks. Greek fast-food franchises operate on most ferries, and on longer trips boats have both cafeteria-style and full-service restaurants.

If your ship's departure is delayed for any reason (with the exception of force majeure), you have the right to stay on board in the class indicated on your ticket or, in case of a prolonged delay, to cancel your ticket for a full refund. If you miss your ship, you forfeit your ticket; if you cancel

in advance, you receive a partial or full refund, depending on how far in advance you cancel.

In advance of the lifting of domestic cabotage (transport in coastal waters within a country) restrictions in 2004, Greece's largest shipping operators ordered at least 20 new fast ferries from European and Asian shipyards. High-speed passenger-and-car catamarans have been brought in from Australia, halving travel time from Piraeus to Santorini from more than six to just over three hours. The end of cabotage restraints will increase competition in the Aegean and improve travelers' choices to popular destinations. Currently, the Greek merchant marine ministry issues licenses on a noncompetitive basis and sets fares and routes. When the market is liberalized, other EU ferry operators will be able to provide service between Greek ports. Already on the Adriatic crossing from Greece to Italy, used by more than one million travelers annually, competition is thriving after Italy, France, and Spain opened up routes to Greek ferries. The Adriatic crossing is also a main route for Greek trucks loaded with exports to the European Union.

FARES & SCHEDULES

You can buy tickets from a travel agency representing the shipping line you need, from the local shipping agency office, online through travel Web sites or direct from ferry companies, or at makeshift stands in front of the boat before departure (if tickets are still available). Except when paying at a travel agency, where you might be able to use a credit card (this will be discouraged), you pay cash. For schedules, any travel agent can call the port to check information for you, although they may not be as helpful about a shipping line for which they don't sell tickets. On islands the local office of each shipping line posts a board with departure times, or you can contact the port authority (*limenarchio*), where some English is usually spoken. Schedules are also posted online by the Merchant Marine Ministry (⊕ www.yen.gr), and the Greek National Tourism Organization (EOT) distributes weekly lists and ticket prices for boats leaving Athens. The English edition of *Kathimerini,* published as an insert to the *International Herald Tribune,* also lists daily departures from the capital. Or you can call for a recording, in Greek, of the day's domestic departures from major ports. At 1 PM, a new recording lists boats leaving the following morning.

🚩 **Agios Konstantinos Port Authority** ☎ 22350/31759. **Ferry departures** ☎ 1440. **Igoumenitsa Port Authority** ☎ 26650/22240 or 26650/22235. **Kimi Port Authority** ☎ 22220/22606. **KTEL bus to Rafina** ☎ 210/821-0872 ⊕ www.ktel.org. **Lavrion Port Authority** ☎ 22920/24125. **Patras Port Authority** ☎ 2610/341002 or 2610/341024. **Piraeus Port Authority** ☎ 210/412-4585 or 210/459-3000. **Rafina Port Authority** ☎ 22940/22300. **Thessaloniki Port Authority** ☎ 2310/531503 or 2310/531504. **Volos Port Authority** ☎ 24210/28888.

CATAMARANS & HYDROFOILS

Catamarans and hydrofoils, known as *iptamena delphinia* (flying dolphins), carry passengers from Piraeus to the Saronic Gulf islands (Aegina, Hydra, Poros, and Spetses), Cycladic islands, and eastern Peloponnesian ports, including Hermioni, Kyparissi, Kythera, Leonidion, Methana, Monemvassia, Nafplion, Neapolis, and Porto Heli. In summer there is additional service, including from Palia Epidauros to Aegina and Piraeus. You can also take hydrofoils from Agios Konstantinos or Volos to the Sporades islands. These boats are somewhat pricey and the limited number of seats means you should reserve (especially in summer), but they cut travel time in half. However, they often cannot travel if the sea is choppy, and cancellations are common. Tickets can be purchased through authorized agents or one hour before departure. Book your return upon arrival if you are pressed for time.

Hydrofoils for the Saronic Gulf islands depart from Gate E9, about 400 m (1,312 ft) from the Piraeus train station.

🚩 **Hellenic Seaways** ⊠ Akti Kondili and Aetolikou, 18535 Piraeus ☎ 210/419-9000 or 210/419-9200 for reservations ⊕ www.hellenicseaways.gr.

HYDROPLANES

A limited hydroplane service began operating in the Ionian in 2005, offering daily flights between Corfu and Paxos isle. At this writing, new routes were being introduced, including Corfu to Patras, Ioannina, and other Ionian islands. Prices are lower than regular airfare and higher than boat passage, or about €35 one-way (€60 round-trip) from Corfu to Paxos. Seaplane routes are also being considered for the eastern Aegean.

🚩 **AirSea Lines** ⊠ Poseidonos 18, Kallithea, 17674 Athens ☎ 210/940-2880 ⊠ Gouvia Marina, Corfu ☎ 26610/99316 ⊕ www.airsealines.com.

INTERNATIONAL FERRIES

You can cross to Turkey from the northeastern Aegean islands, from Lesbos to Dikeli, from Chios to Cesme, and from Samos to Kuşadası. Note that British passport holders must have £10 with them to purchase a visa on landing in Turkey, Australian citizens need $20 (American dollars) and U.S. citizens need $100; New Zealanders don't need a visa. You can purchase the visa beforehand, paying euros, at the Turkish Consulate in Athens (visa hours are weekdays 9 to 1).

There are frequent sails between Italy and Greece—at least five a day in summer from Brindisi, two each from Bari and Ancona, four to five a week from Trieste, and daily from Venice; all go to Corfu and/or Igoumenitsa and Patras (three a week call at the island of Kefalonia). Some of the shipping lines are Agoudimos/G.A. Ferries (Igoumenitsa to Brindisi via Corfu, Bari to Patras and Igoumenitsa), Anek Lines (Venice to Igoumenitsa, Corfu, and Patras; and Ancona to Igoumenitsa and Patras), Hellenic Mediterranean Lines (Patras to Brindisi, with stops at the Ionian islands), Minoan Lines (Venice to Igoumenitsa, Corfu, Patras; and Ancona to Igoumenitsa and Patras), Ventouris Ferries (Bari to Corfu, Igoumenitsa, and Kefalonia), Superfast Ferries (Ancona to Patras and Igoumenitsa; Bari to Igoumenitsa, Corfu, and Patras), My Way Ferries (Brinidisi to Igoumenitsa and Patras), Blue Star Ferries (Ancona to Patras and Igoumenitsa; Bari to Patras and Igoumenitsa), and Fragline Ferries (Brindisi to Corfu and Igoumenitsa).

Prices range widely, depending on when and how you travel, what kind of ship you're on, and what distance you travel. For Patras–Ancona in high season, passengers pay €49–€126 for the deck; €181–€454 for a deluxe outside cabin, depending on the shipping line and whether passage is one-way or round-trip. Children 4–12 usually receive a 50% discount, and those under 4 pay a small fee per passage if they don't occupy a berth or bed. Several companies offer family or group specials. When booking also consider when you will be traveling: an overnight sailing can be offset against hotel costs, and you will spend more on incidentals like food and drink when traveling during the day. To take your car from Patras to Ancona costs about €48–€174 in high season (€74–€118 in low season) and to Brindisi, €70 (€41 in low season), with a discount on the return.

Superfast Ferries, about one-third more expensive than conventional ferries, make the trip from Patras to Ancona in 19 hours, or Bari in 15 hours, and from Igoumenitsa to Bari in 9 hours. Blue Star Ferries make the crossing from Patras to Ancona in 21 hours, to Brindisi in 9. The ferries are outfitted with bars, a self-service restaurant, pool, two cinemas, casino, and shops. Book well in advance for summer and reconfirm shortly before sailing.
🚩 **Agoudimos/G.A. Ferries** ✉ Kapodistriou 2, 18531 Piraeus ☎ 210/412-6680 or 210/413-3583 🖨 210/422-0595 ⊕ www.agoudimos-lines.com. **Anek** ✉ Amalias 48, Syntagma, 10558 Athens ☎ 210/323-3481, 210/323-3819, 210/419-7430 international reservations 🖨 210/323-4137 ⊕ www.anek.gr. **Blue Star Ferries/Strintzis Lines** ✉ Karamanli 157, Pasalimani, 11673 Athens ☎ 210/891-9800 international reservations 🖨 210/891-9938 ✉ Agion Apostollon 145, 46100 Igoumenitsa ☎ 26650/23970 🖨 26650/22348 ⊕ www.bluestarferries.com. **Fragline Ferries** ✉ Rethymnou 5A, 10682 ☎ 210/821-4171 ⊕ www.fragline.gr. **Hellenic Mediterranean Lines** ✉ Pl. Loudovikou 4, 18510 Piraeus ☎ 210/422-5341 🖨 210/422-5317 ⊕ www.hml.gr. **Marlines** ✉ Akti Poseidonos 38, 18531 Piraeus ☎ 210/422-4950 or 210/411-0777 🖨 210/411-7780 ⊕ www.marlines.com. **Minoan Lines** ✉ Vas. Konstantinou 2, Pangrati, 11635 Athens ☎ 210/751-2356 🖨 210/752-0540 ⊕ www.minoan.gr. **My Way Ferries** ✉ Kifissias and

Gramou 71, Maroussi ☎ 210/805-6820 ⊕ www.maritimeway.com. **Superfast Ferries** ✉ Amalias 30, Syntagma, 10558 Athens ☎ 210/891-3252 🖨 210/891-9139 ✉ Othonos-Amalias 12, 26223 Patras ☎ 2610/622500 🖨 2610/623574 ✉ Agion Apostolon 147, Neo Limani, 46100 Igoumenitsa ☎ 26650/28150 🖨 26650/28156 ⊕ www.superfast.com. **Ventouris Ferries** ✉ Pireos and Kithiron 91, 18541 Piraeus ☎ 210/482-8001 through 210/482-8004 🖨 210/483-2909 ⊕ www.ventouris.gr.
🚩 **Turkish Consulate** ✉ Vasilissis Pavlou 22, Paleo Psyhiko, Athens ☎ 210/671-4828 🖨 210/677-6430.

BUSINESS HOURS

A new law passed in 2005 set uniform business hours (weekdays 9–9, Saturday 9–6) for retailers across Greece, although establishments in tourist resorts may remain open longer. For certain categories such as pharmacies, banks, and government offices, hours have always been standardized. Many small businesses and shops close for at least a week around mid-August, and most tourist establishments, including hotels, shut down on the islands and northern Greece from November until mid-spring. Restaurants, especially tavernas, often stay open on holidays; some close in summer or move to cooler locations. Christmas, New Year's, Orthodox Easter, and August 15 are the days everything shuts down, although, for example, bars work full force on Christmas Eve, since it's a very social occasion and not particularly family-oriented. Orthodox Easter changes dates every year, so check your calendar. On Orthodox Good Friday, shops open after church services, around 1 PM.

BANKS & OFFICES

Banks are normally open Monday–Thursday 8–2, Friday 8–1:30. Hotels also cash traveler's checks on weekends, and the banks at the Athens airport have longer hours.

Government offices are open weekdays from 8 to 2. For commercial offices, the hours depend on the business: large companies have adopted the 9–5 schedule, but some small businesses stick to the Mediterranean 8–2 workday.

CHURCHES & MONASTERIES

Your guess is as good as the locals' as to when churches and monasteries are open to the public; in numerous cases monasteries are merely ruins, no longer functioning or looked after. In cities, opening hours are fairly standard, but in rural areas, you may need to find the caretaker to unlock the church doors; he or she usually lives nearby. In such cases it is customary to light a candle or buy a postcard in remuneration. The best time to find churches unlocked is during services, especially Sunday morning; otherwise try from about 8 to noon and 5:30 to 7:30 on any day, unless otherwise noted. The hours for monasteries are dependent upon their keepers, but they are generally more likely to be open in the morning to early afternoon. Some monasteries may only admit the public at set times.

GAS STATIONS

All stations are open daily 7–7 (some close Sunday), and some pump all night in the major cities and along the National Road and Attica Highway. They do not close for lunch.

MUSEUMS & SIGHTS

The days and hours for public museums and archaeological sites are set by the Ministry of Culture; they are usually open Tuesday–Sunday 8:30 to 3, and as late as 7:30 in summer. (Summer hours are published on the ministry's Web site, www.culture.gr, in April or May.) Throughout the year arrive at least 30 minutes before closing time to ensure a ticket. Archaeological sites and museums close on January 1, March 25, the morning of Orthodox Good Friday, Orthodox Easter, May 1, and December 25–26. Sunday visiting hours apply to museums on Epiphany; Ash Monday, Good Saturday, Easter Monday, and Whitsunday (Orthodox dates, which change every year); August 15; and October 28. Museums close early (around 12:30) on January 2, the last Saturday of Carnival, Orthodox Good Thursday, Christmas Eve, and New Year's Eve. Throughout the guide, the hours of sights and attractions are denoted by the clock icon, ☉.

PHARMACIES

Pharmacies are open Monday, Wednesday, and Friday from about 8:30 to 3 and Tuesday, Thursday, and Friday from 8:30 to 2 and 5 until 8 or 8:30 at night. The pharmacy at Athens International Airport operates 24 hours. According to a rotation system, there is always at least one pharmacy open in any area; closed pharmacies post a list in their window of the nearest open establishment for Sundays and off-hours (⇨ Emergencies).

SHOPS

Department stores, shops, and supermarkets may stay open until 9 PM on weekdays and 8 PM on Saturday, but some merchants are sticking to the old business hours and continue to close on Monday, Wednesday, and Saturday afternoons. There are no Sunday trading hours, except for the last Sunday of the year and in tourist areas like Plaka in Athens and island or mainland resorts.

If it's late in the evening and you need an aspirin, soft drink, cigarettes, newspaper, or pen, look for the nearest street kiosk, called a *periptero*; these kiosks on street corners everywhere brim with all kinds of necessities. Owners stagger their hours, and many towns have at least one kiosk that stays open late, occasionally through the night. Neighborhood minimarkets also stay open late.

BUS TRAVEL

Organized bus tours can be booked together with hotel reservations by your travel agent. Many tour operators have offices in and around Syntagma and Omonia squares in Athens. Bus tours often depart from Syntagma or adjacent streets. Most chapters in this guide have information about guided tours.

It is easy to get around Greece on buses, which travel to even the most far-flung villages. The price of public transportation in Greece has risen steeply since 2000, but it is still cheaper than in other western European cities. Greece has an extensive, inexpensive, and reliable regional bus system (KTEL) made up of local operators. Each city has connections to towns and villages in its vicinity; visit the local KTEL office to check routes or use the fairly comprehensive Web site (⊕ www.ktel.org) to plan your trip in advance. Buses from Athens, however, travel throughout the country. The buses, which are punctual, span the range from slightly dilapidated and rattly to air-conditioned with upholstered seats. There is just one class of ticket. Board early, because Greeks have a very loose attitude about assigned seating, and ownership is nine-tenths' possession. Taking the bus from Athens to Corinth costs €6.60 and takes about 75 minutes; to Nafplion, €9.70, 2½ hours; to Patras, €13.90, 3 hours 10 minutes; and to Thessaloniki, €30, 7½ hours.

Although smoking is forbidden on KTEL buses, the driver stops every two hours or so at a roadside establishment; smokers can light up then. Drivers are exempt from the no-smoking rule; don't sit near the front seat if smoking bothers you.

In Athens, KTEL's Terminal A is the arrival and departure point for bus lines to northern Greece, including Thessaloniki, and to the Peloponnese destinations of Epidauros, Mycenae, Nafplion, and Corinth. Terminal B serves Evia, most of Thrace, and central Greece, including Delphi. To get into the city center, take Bus 051 from Terminal A (terminus at Zinonos and Menandrou off Omonia Square) or Bus 024 from Terminal B (downtown stop in front of the National Gardens on Amalias). Most KTEL buses to the east Attica coast—including those for Sounion, Marathon, and the ports of Lavrion and Rafina—leave from the downtown KTEL terminal near Pedion Areos park.

In Athens and Thessaloniki avoid riding city buses during rush hours. Buses and trolleys do not automatically stop at every station; you must hold out your hand to summon the vehicle you want. Upon boarding, validate your ticket in the canceling machines, at the front and back of buses (this goes for the trolleys and the subway train platforms, too). If you're too far from the machine and the bus is crowded, don't be shy: pass your ticket forward with the appropriate ingratiating

gestures, and it will eventually return, properly punched. Keep your ticket until you reach your destination, as inspectors who occasionally board are strict about fining offenders; a fine may cost you up to 40 times the fare. On intracity buses, an inspector also boards to check your ticket, so keep it handy.

CLASSES
The KTEL buses provide a comprehensive network of coverage within the country. That said, the buses are fairly basic in remoter villages and some of the islands—no toilets or refreshments. However, main intercity lines have preassigned seating and a better standard of vehicle.

CUTTING COSTS
If you are planning to take the bus, trolley, and metro several times in one day during your Athens stay, **buy a 24-hour ticket** for all the urban network (€3) or a single ticket (€1) valid for all travel completed within 90 minutes from the time it is first used. When assessing whether it's worth the money, remember that you must use a new ticket (€0.50–€0.70) for each leg of the journey for each method of transportation. A pass also saves you the hassle of validating your tickets numerous times. Students with ID qualify for half-price tickets. If you are staying for an extended period in the capital, **buy a weekly pass,** valid for seven days on all routes except the airport or X22 Saronida Express, or **buy a monthly pass,** available at the beginning of the month from downtown terminal kiosks and most metro stations (good value at €17.50 for unlimited bus and trolley travel; €35 if you also want to travel on the metro). You need a passport-size photograph of yourself for the pass. You can reduce regional bus fares if you **purchase a round-trip KTEL ticket,** which saves you about 15%.

FARES & SCHEDULES
In large cities, you can buy individual tickets for urban buses at terminal booths, convenience stores, or at selected *periptera* (street kiosks). KTEL tickets must be purchased at the KTEL station. On islands, in smaller towns, and on the

KTEL buses that leave from Aigyptou Square in Athens, you buy tickets from the driver's assistant once seated; try not to pay with anything more than a €5 bill to avoid commotion. Athens bus stops now have signs diagramming each route. It still helps if you can read some Greek, since most stops are only labeled in Greek. The Organization for Urban Public Transportation, north of the National Archaeological Museum, gives Athens route information and distributes maps (weekdays 7:30–3), but the best source for non-Greek speakers is EOT, which distributes information on Athens and KTEL bus schedules, including prices for each destination and the essential phone numbers for the regional ticket desks.

🚍 Athens Public Transportation **Organization for Urban Public Transportation** ⌧ Metsovou 15, Athens ☎ 185 ⊕ www.oasa.gr.

🚍 Regional Bus Service **Downtown KTEL terminal** ⌧ Aigyptou Sq., Mavromateon and Leoforos Alexandras, near Pedion Areos park ☎ 210/823-0179 for Sounion, Rafina, and Lavrion, 210/821-0872 for Marathon ⊕ www.ktel.org. **Terminal A** ⌧ Kifissou 100, Athens ☎ 210/512-4910 or 210/512-4911. **Terminal B** ⌧ Liossion 260, Athens ☎ 210/831-7153.

PAYING
Throughout Greece, you must pay cash for local and regional bus tickets. For bus tours, a travel agency usually lets you pay by credit card or traveler's checks.

RESERVATIONS
For KTEL, you can make reservations for many destinations free by phone; each destination has a different phone number. Reservations are unnecessary on most routes, especially those with several round trips a day. Book your seat a few days in advance, however, if you are traveling on holiday weekends, especially if you are headed out of Athens. In fact, because reservations sometimes get jumbled in the holiday exodus, it's best to go to the station and buy your ticket beforehand.

CAMERAS & PHOTOGRAPHY
The *Kodak Guide to Shooting Great Travel Pictures* (available at bookstores everywhere) is loaded with tips. The bright sunlight and endless color and variety of the Greek landscape seem to cry aloud to be photographed or filmed. The best light, especially when photographing the sea or panoramas, is in early morning or late afternoon, when haze clears up and the landscape is bathed in a honeyed glow. Use common sense when photographing locals; it's always better to elicit at least tacit approval. The people of the countryside, while friendly, are sometimes camera-shy, and if you want them on film, it is better to play at candid photography than to try to set up a pose. Photography of, or near, military establishments is strictly forbidden (indicated by a sign with an X-ed-out camera). In museums, flash photography is not allowed, and you might not be allowed to use a tripod at archaeological sites. It is considered rude to photograph people other than those in your party at nude beaches, where any camera is viewed with suspicion. Although you are obliged to photograph the Acropolis or whatever other ruin you're visiting, it will be your shots of the crystalline waters of some perfect beach that will make your friends ooh and aah every time.

🎞 Photo Help **Kodak Information Center** ☎ 800/242-2424 ⊕ www.kodak.com.

EQUIPMENT PRECAUTIONS
Don't pack film or equipment in checked luggage, where it is much more susceptible to damage. X-ray machines used to view checked luggage are extremely powerful and therefore are likely to ruin your film. Try to ask for hand inspection of film, which becomes clouded after repeated exposure to airport X-ray machines, and keep videotapes and computer disks away from metal detectors. Always keep film, tape, and computer disks out of the sun. Carry an extra supply of batteries, and be prepared to turn on your camera, camcorder, or laptop to prove to airport security personnel that the device is real.

In Greece, non-EU citizens should register valuable electronic equipment (e.g., laptop computers) with customs on entry, and then show the stamped passport page with the computer's serial number upon exit to prove they did not buy it in Greece. Although officials may never check you coming or going, it's good to follow this procedure to avoid last-minute trouble on departure.

FILM & DEVELOPING

Film is widely available; the most common brands are Kodak, Agfa, and Fujifilm. A roll of Kodak Gold color print film, 100 ASA (works well in strong light) costs about €4.50 for 36 exposures. Prices are higher at tourist shops; Agfa is usually the cheapest choice. The Advantix system is available in large cities and major resorts (from €5.65 for 200 Ultra, 24 exposures). Disposable cameras are good in a pinch (€10–€12). You can find 24-hour film-developing shops that provide satisfactory quality in all major towns and resort islands, but unless you're in a hurry, **develop your film at home,** where costs will be lower: a 24-print color roll costs about €11 to process.

VIDEOS

VHS tapes are widely available at photo and electronic shops. A 120-minute tape starts at €2.90. Greece uses the SECAM system, so tapes from the United States cannot be read by video players in Greece, and often vice versa.

CAR RENTAL

Because driving in Greece can be harrowing, car rental prices are higher than in the United States, and transporting a car by ferry hikes up the fare substantially, think twice before deciding on a car rental. It's much easier to take public transportation or taxis, which are among the cheapest in Europe. The exception is on large islands where the distance between towns is greater and taxi fares are higher; you may want to rent a car or a moped for the day for concentrated bouts of sightseeing.

In summer, renting a small car with standard transmission will cost you about €290 to €385 for a week's rental (including tax, insurance, and unlimited mileage). Four-wheel-drives can cost you anywhere from €80 to €97 a day, depending on availability and the season. Luxury cars are available at some agencies, such as Europcar, but renting a BMW can fetch a hefty price—anywhere from €98 per day

in low season to €120 a day in high season. This does not include the 19% V.A.T. (13% on the eastern Aegean islands). Convertibles ("open" cars) and minibuses are also available. Probably the most difficult car to rent, unless you reserve from abroad, is an automatic. Off-season, rental agencies are often closed on islands and in less-populated areas.

If you're considering moped or motorcycle rental, which is cheaper than a car, especially for getting around on the islands, try Motorent or Easy Moto Rent, both in Athens. On the islands, independent moped rentals are available through local agents.

🚗 Major Agencies **Alamo** ☎ 800/522-9696 ⊕ www.alamo.com. **Avis** ☎ 800/331-1084 ⊕ www.avis.com. **Budget** ☎ 800/472-3325 ⊕ www.budget.com. **Dollar** ☎ 800/800-6000 ⊕ www.dollar.com. **Hertz** ☎ 800/654-3001 ⊕ www.hertz.com. **National Car Rental** ☎ 800/227-7368 ⊕ www.nationalcar.com.

🚗 Athens Airport Agencies **Alamo** ☎ 210/353-3323 through 210/353-3324. **Avis** ☎ 210/353-0578 through 210/353-0579 ⊕ www.avis.gr. **Budget** ☎ 210/353-0553 through 210/353-0554 ⊕ www.budget.gr. **Europcar** ☎ 210/353-3321 ⊕ www.europcar.com. **Hertz** ☎ 210/353-4900 ⊕ www.hertz.gr. **SIXT Lion Rental** ☎ 210/353-0556 through 210/353-0576 ⊕ www.sixt.com.

🚗 Motorcycle Agencies **Easy Moto Rent** ✉ Athens ☎ 210/881-1993. **Motorent** ✉ Athens ☎ 210/923-4939.

CUTTING COSTS

You can usually reduce prices by reserving a car before you leave through a major rental agency. Or **opt for a midsize Greek agency and bargain for a price;** you should discuss when kilometers become free. These agencies provide good service, and prices are at the owner's discretion. It helps if you have shopped around and can mention another agency's offer.

Official rates in Greece during high season (July–September) are much cheaper if you rent through local agents rather than the large international companies. For example, a small car, such as the Fiat Seicento, will cost you about €290 for a week's rental (including tax, insurance, and unlimited mileage) as opposed to at least

€385 if you go through an international chain. Outside high season you can get some good deals with local agents; a car may cost you about €38 per day, all inclusive. Rates are cheaper if you book for three or more days.

For a good deal, book through a travel agent who will shop around. Do look into wholesalers, companies that do not own fleets but rent in bulk from those that do and often offer better rates than traditional car-rental operations. Prices are best during off-peak periods. Rentals booked through wholesalers often must be paid for before you leave home.

7 Local Agencies **Auto Europe Greece Car Rental** ✉ Alexandras 97, Ambelokipi, Athens ☎ 210/644-8242 📠 210/646-5468. **Fantastico Rent-a-Car** ✉ Michalakopoulou 62, Ilisia, Athens ☎ 210/778-3771 📠 210/778-4860 ✎ admin@fantastico-rentals.com. **Just Rent-A-Car** ✉ Syngrou 43, Athens ☎ 210/923-9104 or 210/923-8566 📠 210/924-7248. **Pappas Rent-A-Car** ✉ Amalias 44, Athens ☎ 210/322-0087 or 210/323-4772 📠 210/322-6472. **Swift Car Rental** ✉ Syngrou 50, Athens ☎ 210/923-3919 or 210/924-7006 📠 210/922-7922. **Thrifty Car Rental** ✉ Syngrou 25, Athens ☎ 210/924-3310 📠 210/924-3750.

7 Wholesalers **Auto Europe** ☎ 800/223-5555 or 207/842-2000 📠 207/842-2222 🌐 www.autoeurope.com. **Destination Europe Resources** (DER) ✉ 9501 W. Devon Ave., Rosemont, IL 60018 ☎ 800/782-2424 📠 800/282-7474. **Europe by Car** ☎ 800/223-1516 or 212/581-3040 📠 212/246-1458 🌐 www.europebycar.com. **Kemwel** ☎ 877/820-0668 or 800/678-0678 📠 866/726-6726 or 207/842-2124 🌐 www.kemwel.com.

INSURANCE

When driving a rented car you are generally responsible for any damage to or loss of the vehicle. Collision policies that car-rental companies sell for European rentals typically do not cover stolen vehicles. Before you rent—and purchase collision or theft coverage—see what coverage you already have under the terms of your personal auto-insurance policy and credit cards.

Rental agencies offer a full range of insurance: collision damage waiver costs about €11.30 to €19 a day, depending on the deduction and size of vehicle; personal in-

surance €4.25; and theft €4.50 to €8.60, depending on the car, though some companies include this in the rate.

REQUIREMENTS & RESTRICTIONS

In Greece your own driver's license is not acceptable unless you are a citizen of the European Union. For non-EU citizens, an International Driver's Permit (IDP) is necessary (⇨ Car Travel). To rent, you must have had your driver's license for one year and be at least 21 years old if you use a credit card (sometimes 23 if you pay cash); for some car categories, you must be 25. You need the agency's permission to ferry the car or cross the border (Europcar does not allow across-the-border rentals). A valid driver's-license is usually acceptable for renting a moped, but you will need a motorcycle driver's licence if you want to rent a larger bike.

SURCHARGES

Before you pick up a car in one city and leave it in another, ask about drop-off charges or one-way service fees, which can be substantial. Also inquire about early-return policies; some rental agencies charge extra if you return the car before the time specified in your contract while others give you a refund for the days not used. Most agencies note the tank's fuel level on your contract; to avoid a hefty refueling fee, return the car with the same tank level. If the tank was full, refill it just before you turn in the car, but be aware that gas stations near the rental outlet may overcharge. It's almost never a deal to buy a tank of gas with the car when you rent it; the understanding is that you'll return it empty, but some fuel usually remains.

CAR TRAVEL

Although road conditions are improving, driving in Greece still presents certain challenges. In Athens, traffic is mind-boggling most of the time and parking is scarce, although the situation is improving; public transportation or taxis are a much better choice than a rented car. If you are traveling quite a bit by boat, taking along a car increases ticket costs substantially and limits your ease in hopping on any ferry. On islands, you can always rent a taxi or a car for the day if you want to see something distant, and intradestination flights are fairly cheap. The only real reason to drive is if it's your passion, you are a large party with many suitcases and many out-of-the-way places to see, or you need the freedom to change routes and make unexpected stops not permitted on public transportation.

International driving permits (IDPs), required for drivers who are not citizens of an EU country, are available from the American and Canadian automobile associations. These international permits, valid only in conjunction with your regular driver's license, are universally recognized; having one may save you a problem with local authorities.

Regular registration papers and insurance contracted in any EU country or a green card are required, in addition to a driver's license (EU or international). EU members can travel freely without paying any additional taxes. If you are a non-EU member, you may import your vehicle duty-free for six months, but if you must leave the country without the car, customs "keeps" your car until your return; a Greek citizen must act as your guarantor. Cars with foreign plates are exempt from the alternate-day ban in Athens on driving in the center according to whether the license plate is odd or even.

The expansion and upgrading of Greece's two main highways, the Athens–Corinth and Athens–Thessaloniki highways (*ethniki odos*) and construction of an Athens beltway, the Attiki Odos, has made leaving Athens much easier. These highways (and the new Egnatia Odos, which goes east to west across northern Greece), along with the secondary roads, cover most of the mainland, but on islands, some areas (beaches, for example) are accessible via dirt or gravel paths. With the exception of main highways and a few flat areas like the Thessalian plain, you will average about 60 km (37 mi) an hour: expect some badly paved or disintegrating roads, stray flocks of goats, slowpoke farm vehicles, detours, curves, and near Athens and Thessaloniki, traffic jams. At the Athens

city limits, signs in English mark the way to Syntagma and Omonia squares in the center. When you exit Athens, signs are well marked for the National Road, usually naming Lamia for the north and Corinth or Patras for the southwest.

AUTO CLUB

The Automobile Touring Club of Greece, known as ELPA, operates a special phone line for tourist information that works throughout the country; the club also has several branch offices. If you don't belong to an auto club at home, you can join ELPA for €115, which gives you free emergency road service, though you must pay for spare parts. Membership lasts for a year and is good on discounts for emergency calls throughout the EU. Visit your local auto association before you leave for Greece; they can help you plan your trip and provide you with maps. They also can issue you an International Driver's Permit good for one year. Your local membership may qualify you for cheaper emergency service in Greece and abroad.

🇫 In Greece **Automobile Touring Club of Greece** (ELPA) ⊠ Mesogeion 395, Agia Paraskevi, Athens ☎ 210/606-8800 or 210/606-8838 🖷 210/606-8981 ⊕ www.elpa.gr ⊠ Patroon-Athinon 18, Patras 🖷🖷 2610/426416 or 2610/425411 ⊠ Papanastasiou 66, Heraklion, Crete 🖷🖷 2810/210581 or 2810/210654 ⊠ Vas. Olgas 230 and Aegeou, Thessaloniki ☎ 2310/426319 or 2310/426320 🖷 2310/412413. **Tourist Information Line** ☎ 174.

EMERGENCY SERVICES

You must put out a triangular danger sign if you have a breakdown. Roving repair trucks, manned by skilled ELPA mechanics, patrol the major highways, except the Attiki Odos, which has its own contracted road assistance company. They assist tourists with breakdowns for free if they belong to an auto club such as AAA or to ELPA; otherwise, there is a charge. The Greek National Tourism Office, in cooperation with ELPA, the tourist police, and Greek scouts, provides an emergency telephone line for those who spot a dead or wounded animal on the National Road.

🇫 **Automobile Touring Club of Greece** (ELPA) ☎ 10400 for breakdowns, 171 for a dead or hurt animal, 210/606-8800 outside Athens.

FROM THE U.K.

Though it is expensive, you can take a car to Greece (and at the same time greatly reduce your driving and save gasoline and hotel costs) by using the Paris–Milan and Milan–Brindisi car sleeper and then a car ferry to Corfu, Igoumenitsa, or Patras.

GASOLINE

Gas pumps and service stations are everywhere, and lead-free gas is widely available. However, away from the main towns, especially at night, open gas stations can be very far apart (⇨ Business Hours). **Don't let your gas supply drop to less than a quarter tank when driving through rural areas.** Gas costs about €1 a liter for unleaded ("ah-*mo*-lee-vdee"), €0.92 a liter for diesel ("*dee*-zel"). Prices may vary by as much as €0.10 per liter from one region to another. You aren't usually allowed to pump your own gas, though you are expected to do everything else yourself. If you ask the attendant to give you extra service (check oil and water or clean the windows), leave a small tip. International chains (BP, Mobil, Shell, and Texaco) usually accept credit cards; Greek-owned stations (Elinoil, EKO, Jetoil, and Revoil) usually do not unless they are in tourist areas.

IMPORTING YOUR CAR

Contact the Greek Consulate for a six-month duty-free license to import your car. When leaving Greece, you must get a customs stamp to take the car out of the country by contacting the Directorate for the Supervision and Control of Cars, or DIPEAK. There are no extensions; you either must leave the country with the car and return again after six months, under a new six-month permit, or leave the car in Greece for six months (no one can drive it), and then start anew.

🚗 Customs Stamps **Directorate for the Supervision and Control of Cars (DIPEAK)** ✉ Akti Kondili 32, 1st fl., 18545 Piraeus ☎ 210/462–7325 🖷 210/462–5182.

INSURANCE

In general, auto insurance is not as expensive as in other countries. You must have third-party car insurance to drive in Greece. If possible, get an insurance "green card" valid for Greece from your insurance company before arriving. You can also buy a policy with local companies; keep the papers in a plastic pocket on the inside right front windshield. To get more information, or to locate a local representative for your insurance company, call the Hellenic Union of Insurance Firms/Motor Insurance Bureau.

🚗 Insurance Bureau **Hellenic Union of Insurance Firms/Motor Insurance Bureau** ✉ Xenofontos 10, 10557 Athens ☎ 210/323–6733 🖷 210/333–4149.

ROAD CONDITIONS

Driving defensively is the key to safety in Greece, which is one of the most hazardous European countries for motorists. In the cities and on the highways, the streets can be riddled with potholes; motorcyclists seem to come out of nowhere, often passing on the right; and cars may even go the wrong way down a one-way street. In the countryside and on islands, you must watch for livestock crossing the road, as well as for tourists shakily learning to use rented motorcycles.

The many motorcycles and scooters weaving through traffic and the aggressive attitude of fellow motorists can make driving in Greece's large cities unpleasant—and the life of a pedestrian dangerous. Greeks often run red lights or ignore stop signs on side streets, travel the wrong way on one-way roads, or round corners without stopping. It's a good idea at night at city intersections and at any time on curvy country lanes to beep your horn to warn errant drivers.

In cities, you will find pedestrians have no qualms about standing in the middle of a busy boulevard, waiting to dart between cars; make eye contact so you can both determine who's going to slow. Rush hour in the cities runs from 7 to 10 AM and 2:30 to 3:30 PM on weekdays, plus 8 to 9 PM on Tuesday, Thursday, and Friday. Saturday mornings bring bumper-to-bumper traffic in shopping districts, and weekend nights guarantee crowding around nightlife hubs. In Athens, the only time you won't find traffic is very early morning and most of Sunday (unless you're foolish enough to go to a local beach at 4 PM in summer, which means you'll be caught in heavy end-of-weekend traffic when you return). Finally, perhaps because they are untrained, drivers seldom pull over for wailing ambulances; the most they'll do is slow down and slightly move over in different directions.

Highways are color-coded: green for the new, toll roads and blue for old, National Roads. Tolls range from €1.90 to €2.90. The older routes are slower and somewhat longer, but follow more scenic routes so driving is more enjoyable. The National Road can be very slick in places when wet—avoid driving in rain and on the days preceding or following major holidays, when traffic is at its worst as urban dwellers leave for villages.

ROAD MAPS
On the road map distributed by EOT, the National Roads are yellow and labeled with European road numbers, although these are not used on the roads themselves. For Athens, the best street guide, frequently updated, is *Athina-Pirea-Proastia* (Athens-Piraeus-Suburbs), published (in Greek only, unfortunately) by S. Kapranides and N. Fotis in conjunction with ELPA. The taxi driver's choice, it breaks down the capital into manageable sections and clearly depicts everything in each area from pedestrian zones and one-way streets to hotel and theater locations. It is sold at large bookstores for about €22. If you're driving around Greece and the islands, the Greek Road Editions regional maps are up-to-date and very good; seek them out. Athens is a good place to buy maps, but most islands sell decent road maps at tourist shops. Maps handed out by car-rental agencies are fairly decent (and are usually available in English).

RULES OF THE ROAD
International road signs are in use throughout Greece. You drive on the right, pass on the left, and yield right-of-way to all vehicles approaching from the right (except on posted main highways). Cars may not make a right turn on a red light. The speed limits are 120 kph (74 mph) on the National Road, 90 kph (56 mph) out-

side urban areas, and 50 kph (31 mph) in cities, unless lower limits are posted. The presence of traffic police on the highways has increased, and they are now much more diligent in enforcing speed limits or any other rules. However, limits are often not posted, and signs indicating a lower limit may not always be visible, so if you see Greek drivers slowing down, take the cue to avoid speed traps in rural areas.

In central Athens there is an odd-even rule to avoid traffic congestion. This rule is strictly adhered to and applies weekdays; license plates ending in odd or even numbers can drive into central Athens according to whether the date is odd or even. (The *daktylios*, as this inner ring is called, is marked by signs with a large yellow triangle.) This rule does not apply to rental cars, provided the renter and driver has a foreign passport. If you are renting a car, ask the rental agency about any special parking or circulation regulations in force. Although sidewalk parking is illegal, it is common. And although it's tempting as a visitor to ignore parking tickets, keep in mind that if you've surrendered your ID to the rental agency, you won't get it back until you clear up the matter. You can pay your ticket at the rental agency or local police station; fines start at €65 (for illegal parking) and can go as high as €290 (for running a red light). It never hurts to plead your case at the police station, especially if you have a reasonable argument. As a rule, police often give foreigners a break. However, they have become far stricter, regularly inspecting cars (which must have a fire extinguisher, emergency triangle, and first-aid kit) and introducing alcohol tests. The blood alcohol limit is 0.05, but police use their discretion when issuing citations; it is a criminal offense if you are over 0.08.

If you are involved in an accident, don't drive away. Accidents must be reported (something Greek motorists often fail to do) before the insurance companies consider claims. Try to get the other driver's details as soon as possible; hit-and-run is all too common in Greece. If the police take you in (they can hold you for 24 hours if there is a fatality, regardless of fault), you have the right to call your local embassy or consulate for help getting a lawyer.

The use of seat belts and motorcycle helmets is compulsory, though Greeks tend to ignore these rules, or comply with them by "wearing" the helmet on their elbows. Mobile phone use while driving a vehicle or motorbike is not legal, but it's very common.

CHILDREN IN GREECE

Greek parents, who dote on their children to the point of spoiling them, believe this is the natural order of things: you marry, have children, then shower them with attention. They will dote on your children, too, if you take them along. Couples traveling without children, on the other hand, are likely to be interrogated about this situation. Despite this fondness for little ones, organized child-care services are scarce. You'll have to make arrangements for special activities and babysitting on an ad hoc basis.

Locals are quite tolerant of children in public places: you often see youngsters running around in tavernas between the tables, and no one gives them a second glance until they step on the cat's tail. If your child is crying, other diners may try to cheer him or her up. About the only place you can't take kids is trendy nightclubs and upscale restaurants. Remember to bring a baby backpack for places where the stroller won't roll, such as archaeological sites. In terms of keeping your children happy, **don't overdo the ruins.** It's the sea that appeals to all ages. The Aegean is calm and warm, perfect for even the most timid child. You'll have a hard time coaxing your toddler out of the water and your teenager off the Jet Ski. However, keep in mind that kids want to be with other kids; **search out family beaches,** especially those with a café, where you can retire but still keep an eye on the brood. Whatever season you visit, your child will enjoy the local festivals with dancing, costumes, odd customs, and competitions: who wouldn't delight in seeing goatskin-clad masked men clanging their bells on Skyros or in flying a kite with hundreds of other kids on Clean Monday? Quick fixes for grouchy toddlers are the coin-operated rides (spaceships, trains) in many main squares and the ubiquitous big freezer boxes full of ice cream. In Athens, children are intrigued by the Changing of the Guard (Evzones in skirts), the ducks at the National Gardens, the rinky-dink amusement parks called *luna parks.* Most cities have scheduled activities for children from September through June, usually sponsored by the municipality, museums, and large stores. These events include storytelling, art shows, costume parties at Carnival time, and a special puppet "Theater of the Shadows," which features the beloved but sly Karagiozis. The Attica Zoological Park near Athens International Airport in Spata is a good trip for children.

The *Athens News* details upcoming activities for children in the capital, but if you can read Greek, the weekly *Athinorama* devotes an entire section to kids. These publications are available at newsstands throughout Greece. In the rest of the country, it's best to ask at the municipal tourist office or a travel agency.

As a destination for children, Greece falls short only in the sense that you will have to be more aware of your child's physical safety: beaches and hotel pools rarely have lifeguards, archaeological sites may be perched on unfenced cliffs, playgrounds sometimes have ill-maintained structures, busy island roads may have no sidewalks. If you're planning to rent bikes, **bring children's helmets.** Another concern: although Greek medical personnel will do their best to help you, if you are on a faraway island and your child has an accident or needs special equipment, there may be a delay in transporting him or her to the closest children's hospital. In general, however, such incidents are rare.

Be sure to plan ahead and involve your youngsters as you outline your trip. When packing, include things to keep them busy en route. On sightseeing days try to schedule activities of special interest to your children. If you are renting a car, don't forget to arrange for a car seat when you reserve. For general advice about traveling with children, consult *Fodor's FYI: Travel with Your Baby* (available in bookstores everywhere).

🗂 **Local Information Athens News** ✉ Christou Lada 3, 10237 Athens ☎ 210/323–3161 🖷 210/323–1384 ⊕ www.athensnews.gr. **Athinorama** ✉ Mesogeion 2–4, Athens Tower, 11527 Athens ☎ 210/745–0100 🖷 210/745–0211 ⊕ www.athinorama.gr.

FLYING

If your children are two or older, ask about children's airfares. As a general rule, infants under two not occupying a seat fly at greatly reduced fares or even for free. But if you want to guarantee a seat for an infant, you have to pay full fare. Consider flying during off-peak days and times; most airlines will grant an infant a seat without a ticket if there are available seats. When booking, confirm carry-on allowances if you're traveling with infants. In general, for babies charged 10% to 50% of the adult fare you are allowed one carry-on bag and a collapsible stroller; if the flight is full, the stroller may have to be checked or you may be limited to less.

Experts agree that it's a good idea to use safety seats aloft for children weighing less than 40 pounds. Airlines set their own policies: if you use a safety seat, U.S. carriers usually require that the child be ticketed, even if he or she is young enough to ride free, because the seats must be strapped into regular seats. And even if you pay the full adult fare for the seat, it may be worth it, especially on longer trips. Do **check your airline's policy about using safety seats during takeoff and landing.** Safety seats are not allowed everywhere in the plane, so get your seat assignments as early as possible.

When reserving, request children's meals or a freestanding bassinet (not available at all airlines) if you need them. But note that bulkhead seats, where you must sit to use the bassinet, may lack an overhead bin or storage space on the floor.

Look for planes in which each seat has its own TV, especially if it has a cartoon channel; this can make all the difference in the world on a transatlantic trek. Otherwise, bring *many* on-board activities.

As for intradestination flights, Olympic Airways says it provides bassinets for infants and baby food on every aircraft, as well as toys, but it is best to request such items when booking. One child under 2 accompanied by an adult and not occupying a separate seat usually pays only 10% of the adult fare. More than one infant under 2 and children 2–11 pay 60% of the adult fare. Make special arrangements for unaccompanied children when booking.

FOOD

Your child may be an adventurous eater, but toddlers and teenagers may balk at strange cuisine. At restaurants, children often enjoy Greek snacks called *mezedes*, which come in small portions and include bite-size meatballs (*keftedakia*), various croquettes, sausage chunks, and cheese or minced meat pastries called *pites*. Even picky eaters will nibble on french fries (try to get the kids to taste the roast potatoes first) and spaghetti with red sauce or just cheese (*macaronada*), available at all tavernas and restaurants. Cooks can also fry an egg for your child or make an omelet, plain or filled with ham and cheese. If you need to appease your child's hunger momentarily, try a bakery, which sells savory pies, sweet rolls, and chocolate croissants. When it comes to grilled sandwiches, or *tost,* let your child pick out the stuffings; they are sold everywhere. The best sandwich chain, Everest, is fast, cheap, and clean and also offers ice cream and pastries. A popular Greek hamburger chain with a decent salad bar, Goody's provides all the usual fast food, as do the international chains of McDonald's and Pizza Hut, found in larger cities. Even the smallest town has at least one pizza parlor.

LODGING

Most hotels in Greece allow children under a certain age to stay in their parents' room at no extra charge, but others charge for them as extra adults; be sure to find out the cutoff age for children's discounts and any extra charges like breakfast.

In off-season, you can often negotiate the price. Most hotels rated A-class and below have no special facilities (other than cots or roll-aways) for families, although a refrigerator in the room can make things easier and the hotel kitchen will accommodate parents who want to warm formula or baby food. Luxe-category resorts usually have a children's pool or playground, video arcade, billiard room or Ping-Pong tables, children's activity programs, and baby seats and children's meals in the restaurants. They can also usually arrange babysitting. If your family is on a budget, consider renting an apartment if you are staying longer than a week. It should include a kitchen with all necessary equipment, a small living area, and sometimes a separate bedroom. A supermarket and Laundromat are often nearby. Good choices are those on the beach.

In Athens, the receptionist or concierge at large hotels like the Athenaeum InterContinental and Athens Hilton maintain lists of babysitters; clients pay the sitter's taxi fare home at night. The Athens Hilton also offers a children's menu. Many resorts also cater to children; ask about any children's meal options or activity programs available when booking.

🛈 Best Choices **Athenaeum InterContinental** ✉ Syngrou 89–93, Athens ☎ 800/327–0200 reservations, 210/920–6000 Athens ⊕ www. intercontinental.com. **Athens Hilton** ✉ Vasilissis Sofias 46, Athens ☎ 800/445–8667 reservations, 210/728–1000 ⊕ www.athenshilton.com. **Grecotel Rethymna Beach** ✉ Rethymnon, Crete ☎ 28310/71002 ⊕ www.grecotel.gr. **Holiday Inn** ✉ Michalakopoulou 50, Athens ☎ 800/465–4239 reservations, 210/727–8000 ⊕ www.holidayinnathens.com.

SIGHTS & ATTRACTIONS

Places that are especially appealing to children are indicated by a rubber-duckie icon (🐤) in the margin.

SUPPLIES & EQUIPMENT

Disposable diapers (*panes,* pronounced "*pah*-nes") can be purchased throughout Greece in supermarkets, convenience stores, and pharmacies. A package of 28 Pampers Baby Dries costs €7.25; the 34-pack of Pampers Premiums jumps to €15.86. Although baby formula ("*for*-moo-la") is available in big supermarkets, you will also find a wide selection of good powder formulas in the pharmacy for

about €8.75 to €14 for a box that will last about 10 days. American formula is not that common, and premixed formula is unavailable. Children older than five months in Greece drink evaporated milk (*evapore,* "e-vah-po-*ray*") such as Noulac or Neslac, about €0.85 for a small can. Fruit creams and such, called *crema,* are about €6.75 for a 700-gram box (Nutricia), and a jar of Nestlé's beef and vegetable is €3.10.

TRANSPORTATION

Car seats are available at most rental agencies for a daily surcharge of about €2.70–€3.90. In Greece, car seats are not required, but that doesn't mean you shouldn't use one. By law, children under 10 are not allowed to sit in the front seat, although this is seldom enforced. School-age children receive a discount of at least 50% on city public transportation, KTEL buses, and trains. Neither bassinets nor special children's meals are available on trains.

COMPUTERS ON THE ROAD

Although major companies such as Toshiba, Canon, and Hewlett-Packard have representatives in Greece, computer parts, batteries, and adaptors are expensive in Greece and may not be in stock when you need them, so carry spares for your laptop. Your best bets are the national Plaisio and Germanos chains, although some camera shops carry computer equipment, too. Most upscale hotels now have modem connections in the rooms, and many can rent you a laptop.

Those who want to access their e-mail can visit one of the Internet cafés that have sprung up throughout Greece. Athens has more than 50, and you're sure to find at least one on most islands. Several, like Bits & Bytes and Cafe 4U, are open 24 hours; most do not accept credit cards. Besides coffee, they offer a range of computer services and charge about €3 per hour. A few establishments, including Athens Airport and Starbucks, have Wi-Fi service. If your cell phone works in Greece and you have a connection kit for your laptop, then you can buy a Vodafone Mobile Connect Card to get online.

🗗 **Internet Cafés** **Bits & Bytes** ✉ Akadimias 78, Athens ☎ 210/330-6590 ⊕ www.bnb.gr. **Cafe 4U** ✉ Ippokratous 44, Athens ☎ 210/361-1981 ⊕ www.cafe4u.gr. **Easy Internet Cafe** ✉ Syntagma Sq., Athens ⊕ www.easyinternetcafe-greece.gr. **Museum Internet Cafe** ✉ Patission 46, near the National Archaeological Museum, Athens ☎ 210/883-3418 ⊕ www.museumcafe.gr. **Skynet Centers** ✉ Apollonos 10, Athens ☎ 210/322-7551.

CONSUMER PROTECTION

Whenever possible, **pay with a major credit card** so you can cancel payment or get reimbursed if there's a problem, provided that you can provide documentation. This is the best way to pay, whether you're buying travel arrangements before your trip or shopping at your destination. Disgruntled consumers in Greece may lodge a complaint on the Consumers' Institute (INKA) hotline about everything from overpricing to poor service in taxis, hotels, restaurants, and archaeological sites. According to INKA, most complaints filed by foreign tourists concern museums and archaeological sites, banking services, road signs, and travel agencies and are related to overpricing, especially at restaurants and nightclubs. INKA provides legal advice and support as well as a complaints and information service. Learn your rights at the Citizens' Information Bureau set up by the Hellenic Foreign Ministry. Here, foreigners can lodge complaints and get suggestions for transactions with the state (always daunting) and information about their rights.

If you're doing business with a particular company for the first time, **contact your local Better Business Bureau and the attorney general's offices** in your own state and the company's home state, as well. Have any complaints been filed? Finally, if you're buying a package or tour, always **consider travel insurance** that includes default coverage (⇨ Insurance).

🗗 **BBBs** **Council of Better Business Bureaus** ✉ 4200 Wilson Blvd., Suite 800, Arlington, VA 22203 ☎ 703/276-0100 🖷 703/525-8277 ⊕ www.bbb.org.

🗗 **Local Resources** **Citizens' Information Bureau** ✉ Akadimias 3, Davaki Arcade, Athens ☎ 210/368-2700 ⊕ www.mfa.gr. **Consumers' Institute (INKA)**

✉ Akadimias 7, Athens ☎ 210/363-2443, 210/363-1721 hotline ⊕ www.inka.gr.

CRUISE TRAVEL & YACHTING

Cruises have always had a magical quality, even without the dramatic scenery of whitewashed Cycladic villages and ancient ruins balancing at the edge of sheer drops. Sailing into a harbor has an almost ceremonial feel that restores the grandeur lacking in air travel. And Greece, with its scores of islands scattered dotting the Aegean and Ionian seas, is an ideal cruise destination—perfect for travelers with a limited amount of time who wish to combine sightseeing with a relaxing vacation. This is especially true in spring and autumn, when the Aegean and Ionian climates are better suited for exploring hilltop ancient ruins than the sweltering heat of the summer months.

CRUISE TRAVEL

A cruise will spare the planning headaches of solitary island-hopping and the inconvenience of carting your luggage from one destination to the next. For budget-conscious travelers, cruises offer the advantage of controlled expenses: rates usually include everything except alcoholic drinks, shore excursions, and other extras (like hair salon or spa treatments). Prices start around €450 per person (double occupancy) for a three-day Aegean cruise. However, because one disadvantage is that port calls may be long enough only to allow time for a quick visit to one or two main attractions, cruises may be best for an overview, useful for planning a return trip to the more appealing island stops.

Three-day cruises of the Greek islands can be combined with a longer land tour—packages that several cruise companies are beginning to offer. Seven- or fourteen-day cruises usually have a larger geographic span; some concentrate on the eastern Mediterranean, covering an area that includes the Greek islands, Turkish coast, Cyprus, Israel, and Egypt, while others reach from Gibraltar to the Ionian isles, the western Peloponnese, and Athens. A day cruise of the Saronic isles, including Hydra and Poros or Spetses, is an excellent way to get a glimpse of island life and taste the sea air during a city break or land tour. You can choose cruises that start and end at the same port, or cruises that pick you up in one port and drop you off at another for the flight home. Some cruise packages include airfare and hotel stays.

The most popular Greek island destinations are Mykonos, Santorini, Patmos, Rhodes, Heraklion, and Corfu. Some cruise liners also make port calls near classical sites like Delphi and Olympia, or call at lesser-known destinations like Parga and Amorgos. A few cruises sail through the Corinth isthmus, a canal cut into the neck of the Peloponnese peninsula parallel to the *diolkos,* an ancient road along which boats were wheeled from the Corinthian Gulf to the Saronic Gulf.

CHOOSING A CRUISE

When deciding which type of cruise to book, there are two things to consider: the type of cruise and the type of ship. Some travelers revel in the glamour, luxury, and amenities of large cruise ships—essentially floating five-star resorts with organized daytime activities, pools, bars, and restaurants spread over several decks. Spas, fitness centers, cinemas, casinos, discos, and floor shows are not uncommon. As with large resorts, the cruise ship, rather than the destination, is the main attraction. Classic or midsize ships, which are more popular among Europeans than Americans, offer a range of amenities and comfortable accommodations but are not as flashy as the new megaships. Itineraries usually cover several ports, so you'll wake up at a new destination almost every day. A small ship or large yacht offers the greatest flexibility, including more opportunities for sightseeing, but is likely to be more expensive than a cruise on a midsize ship.

If you'd rather relax by the pool than trek through temples, opt for a cruise with more time at sea and fewer or shorter port calls. If you'd like time to explore each island destination, you'll want to choose a cruise where the boat spends the entire day in port and travels at night. Alternately, if the number of places you visit is more important than the time you spend in each

one, book a cruise with a full itinerary and one or two port calls a day.

For an overview of Greece's top sights, choose an itinerary that includes port calls in Piraeus for a shore excursion to the Acropolis and other sights in Athens; Mykonos, a sparkling Cycladic isle with a warren of whitewashed passages, followed by neighboring Delos, with its Pompeii-like ruins; Santorini, a stunning harbor that's actually a partially submerged volcano; Rhodes, where the Knights of St. John built their first walled city before being forced to retreat to Malta; and Heraklion, Crete, where you'll be whisked through a medieval harbor to the reconstructed Bronze Age palace at Knossos. Port calls at Katakolon and Itea mean excursions to Olympia and the Temple of Apollo at Delphi. Some cruises call at Epidauros and Nafplion, offering an opportunity for visits to the ancient theater and the citadel of Mycenae, or at Monemvasia or Patmos, the island where St. John wrote the book of Revelations.

BOOKING TIPS

When to go is as important as where to go. In July or August, the islands are crowded with Greek and foreign vacationers, so expect sights, beaches, and shops to be crowded. High temperatures could also limit time spent on deck. May, June, September, and October are the best months—warm enough for sunbathing and swimming, yet not so uncomfortably hot to make you regret the trek up Lindos.

Whether you book just a cruise, a combination cruise and land tour, or a cruise package with round-trip airfare, shop around for the best rates and confirm exactly what is and what isn't included in the price. At a minimum, rates include three meals a day, accommodations, activities, and entertainment, but not shore excursions and extras like alcoholic beverages. Make sure port taxes are included in the quoted price as well as ground transfers if you're also booking airfare. For packages, especially those that combine land tours, ask what type of accommodation is included and whether meals are, too. If you have special dietary requirements, inquire about vegan or kosher or low-salt menus.

Quoted prices are usually per person based on double occupancy, so if you're traveling alone, ask about the single supplement. Most cruise lines offer family and senior citizens' rates, and some offer discounts to customers who pay in full when booking. This may also apply to shore excursions and other extras. When you receive your tickets and other cruise documents, carefully check them against your booking. If there are discrepancies, contact your travel agent or the cruise company immediately.

Whether you research prices alone or go through a travel agent, you'll also want detailed information on the ship's accommodations. While no one intends to spend their holiday holed up in their room, its size is more important when you're at sea than on land. (And if you don't like your "hotel" you can't change it mid-sea.) So, when choosing a cabin category, carefully consider details—double bed or bunk beds, window size and view, floor and closet space—and amenities.

Finally, check the company's policy regarding cancellations and refunds, as well as optional insurance for cancellations. If you're purchasing airplane tickets separately, allow ample time for transfers at each end of the trip and consider additional insurance to cover the possibility of missing the cruise because of a flight delay.

MEALS, CLOTHES & CASH

Meals are usually served at specific times, but cruise lines try to accommodate travelers' preferences for early or late seating as well as for table size when they allocate seating assignments. Early seatings are better suited for families; if you like to linger over a meal, opt for a late seating.

What to pack is no more of a problem at sea than on shore. You'll need casual clothing for daytime; swimsuits and cover-ups for the pool and lounges; light, comfortable clothing and walking shoes for shore excursions; and a couple of formal and informal outfits for dinner; as well as a hat, and a light sweater, shawl, or windbreaker. Ask your travel agent or the cruise company for a program and dress code.

As with hotel stays, bar tabs, laundry bills, and other extras are charged to your cabin. Some companies require a deposit to cover incidentals when you book or when you board. Bills can be settled by credit card, personal check, or traveler's checks, although not all companies accept personal checks—so ask before you leave. If you're planning on paying cash, make sure you take along enough to cover shore expenses, too. Onboard expenses can run from €250 per person for a seven-day cruise, so if you're on a budget, monitor your expenses daily to avoid overspending.

CRUISE COMPANIES

Many major cruise lines call in the Greek islands. These cruises often call at ports outside Greece as well and may begin or end in Italy or Turkey.

Among the major lines sailing to the most popular Greek islands, Golden Star Cruises and Louis Hellenic Cruises offer three-day voyages mid-March through October that sail from Piraeus to Mykonos, Rhodes, Patmos, and Kuşadası in Turkey. Festival schedules cruises to different Greek islands and to Europe; Greek trips may include excursions to Ancient Olympia and Athens.

An alternative to cruising on a large ship is cruising on a yacht; companies such as Club Voyages and the Greek-based Vikings Yacht Cruises have information. For more information and exact itineraries contact a travel agency, preferably one that specializes in cruises. To learn how to plan, choose, and book a cruise-ship voyage, consult *Fodor's FYI: Plan & Enjoy Your Cruise* (available in bookstores everywhere).

🔗 Cruise Lines **Aegean Island Cruises** ✉ Akti Miaouli 87, 18538 Piraeus ☎ 210/429-1501 🖷 210/429-1511 ⊕ www.onedaycruises.gr. **Celebrity Cruises (Hellas)** ✉ Akadimias 31, 10672 Athens ☎ 210/360-9801 🖷 210/363-4271 ⊕ www.navigator.gr. **Costa Cruise Line** ☎ 800/462-6782 ⊕ www.costacruise.com. **Crystal Cruises** ☎ 800/804-1500 ⊕ www.crystalcruises.com. **Cunard** ☎ 800/728-6273 ⊕ www.cunard.com. **Epirotiki Cruise Lines** ✉ Akti Miaouli 87, 18538 Piraeus ☎ 210/429-1000 🖷 210/429-0042 ⊕ www.epirotikigroup.com. **Festival Cruises** ✉ 95 Madison Ave., Suite 609, New York, NY 10016 ☎ 212/779–

7168 📠 212/779-0948 🌐 www.festivalcruises.com. **Golden Star Cruises** ✉ Akti Miaouli 85, 18537 Piraeus ☎ 210/429-0650 reservations 📠 210/420-0660 🌐 www.goldenstarcruises.com. **Holland America Cruise Lines** 🌐 www.hollandamerica.com. **Louis Hellenic Cruises** ✉ Kanari 5-7, 18537 Piraeus ☎ 210/458-3400 📠 210/428-6140 🌐 www.louiscruises.com. **Orient Lines** ☎ 800/333-7300 🌐 www.orientlines.com. **Princess Cruises** ☎ 800/774-6237 🌐 www.princesscruises.com. **Royal Caribbean Cruises** ✉ Akadimias 31, 10672 Athens ☎ 210/360-9801 📠 210/363-4271 🌐 www.navigator.gr. **Seabourn Cruise Line** ☎ 800/929-9391 🌐 www.seabourn.com. **Silversea Cruises** ☎ 877/760-9052 🌐 www.silversea.com. **Star Clippers** ☎ 800/442-0551 🌐 www.starclippers.com. **Windstar Cruises** ☎ 800/258-7245 🌐 www.windstarcruises.com.

🔳 Cruises on Yachts **Club Voyages** ✉ 43 Hooper Ave., Atlantic Highlands, NJ 07716 ☎ 888/842-2122 or 732/291-8228 📠 732/291-4277. **Vikings Yacht Cruises** ✉ Artemidos 1, Glyfada 16674 ☎ 210/898-0729 or 210/894-9279 📠 210/894-0952 ✉ U.S. reservations, 4321 Lakemoor Dr., Wilmington, NC 28405 ☎ 800/341-8020 🌐 www.vikings.gr.

YACHTING

Life aboard a private yacht or sailboat is very different from that on a cruise ship. For starters, it's less formal. There's less space and simpler amenities, especially on sailboats where most of the day is spent on deck. You can either hire a boat with a few of your friends or, through a travel agency, join a party of people, but at such close quarters it's important to chose companions who understand the rules of life at sea.

Even with a skipper aboard, teamwork is essential. More sailing vacations—and friendships—have been ruined by arguments over depleted shower water than bad weather. But with compatible companions, a sailing vacation is unforgettable as you will experience the Greek islands in a completely different way as you discover pristine coves and sip ouzo beneath a star-filled sky. You can go from island to island, stopping to swim or fish wherever you please—if you don't happen to feel like going ashore one night to check out the nightlife, you can always stay on board and listen to the bouzouki

wailing across the water from in the little harbor where yo dropped anchor.

Deciding where to sail is largely a matter of personal taste. If you enjoy spending time at sea, you can chart a course to the eastern Aegean or the Dodecanese. If you'd like to island-hop, head for the Cyclades where even on a small sailboat you can go from Serifos to Sifnos or from Sifnos to Milos in just a couple of hours. Prefer a greener landscape? The Ionian is more like a pine-fringed lake than the open sea.

Yacht-rental agencies and travel agents have boats of all sizes and at all prices—if your budget is not too tight. Of course, when comparing the cost of a sailing holiday to a vacation on land, remember that the charter fees essentially cover hotel and ferry costs, and that you'll be spending less on restaurants since it's unlikely you'll be eating more than one meal a day ashore. A yacht offers more creature comforts; a sailboat is a more thrilling experience. If you don't know what type of cruiser to pick, the rental agent will be able to recommend one that's right for the size of your party and type of trip you're planning. In order to avoid an endless exchange of letters with an agency, it is best to give the following information in your first letter when you inquire to reserve a yacht: desired dates and period of charter and voyage; the number of passengers; and the type of craft you desire—auxiliary sailing yacht, motor yacht, or caïque. Even experienced sailors can find the Aegean challenging, so consider hiring a skipper. For local agencies, *see* Sailing & Windsurfing *in* Sports & the Outdoors.

Mooring and wintering facilities in Attica extend from Zea harbor in Piraeus to Lavrion, the closest sailing point for the Cyclades. There are roughly 90 yacht supply stations on the islands and mainland, and you can arrange to pick up a boat in Athens and drop it off in Rhodes or vice versa.

Below are two associations and a number of leading yachting outfitters. Two firms that organize highly sophisticated personalized yacht cruises and tours are Club ɔyages and Hellenic Adventures. Greece's largest and best-known charterers are Vernicos Yachts and Kiriacoulis Mediterranean (Sports & the Outdoors).

🇬🇷 Yachting Associations **Greek Yacht Brokers and Consultants Association** ✉ Filellinon 7, 10557 Athens ☎ 210/322-3221 🖷 210/322-3251. **Hellenic Professional Yacht Owners Association** ✉ A8 Zea Marina, 18536 Piraeus ☎ 210/428-0465 or 210/452-6335 🖷 210/428-0465.

🇬🇷 Yachting Outfitters **Alden Yacht Charters** ✉ 1909 Alden Landing, Portsmouth, RI 02840 ☎ 800/253-3654 or 401/683-4200 🖷 401/683-3668 ⊕ www.aldenyachts.com. **Club Voyages** ✉ 43 Hooper Ave., Atlantic Highlands, NJ 07716 ☎ 888/842-2122 or 732/291-8228 🖷 732/291-4277. **Cruise Med** ✉ 17280 Newhope St., Suite 18, Fountain Valley, CA 92708 ☎ 800/736-5717 🖷 714/641-0303 ⊕ www.cruisemed.com. **Exas Worldwide Yacht Charters, Inc.** ✉ 188 Reading Ave., Oaklyn, NJ 08107 ☎ 856/854-3891 🖷 856/854-3175 ⊕ www.exasyachts.com. **Greek Islands Cruise Center** ✉ 4321 Lakemoor Dr., Wilmington, NC 28405 ☎ 800/341-3030 or 910/350-0100 🖷 910/791-9400 ⊕ www.gicc.net. **Hellenic Adventures** ✉ 2940 Harriet Ave., Minneapolis, MN 55408 ☎ 800/851-6349 or 612/827-0937 🖷 612/827-0939 ⊕ www.hellenicadventures.com. **Huntley Yacht Vacations** ✉ 423 Jackson St., Suite 24, Port Townsend, WA 98368 ☎ 800/322-9224 or 360/379-6581 🖷 360/397-7910 ⊕ www.huntleyyacht.com. **Lynn Jachney Charters** ⌖ Box 302, Marblehead, MA 01945 ☎ 800/223-2050 or 781/639-0787 🖷 781/639-0216 ⊕ www.lynnjachneycharters.com. **The Moorings** ✉ 19345 U.S. 19 N, 4th fl., Clearwater, FL 33764 ☎ 888/952-8420 or 727/535-1446 ⊕ www.moorings.com. **Ocean Voyages** ✉ 1709 Bridgeway, Sausalito, CA 94965 ☎ 800/299-4444 or 415/332-4681 🖷 415/332-7460 ⊕ www.oceanvoyages.com. **SailAway Yacht Charters** ✉ 15605 S.W. 92nd Ave., Miami, FL 33157-1972 ☎ 800/724-5292 or 305/253-7245 🖷 305/251-4408 ⊕ www.1800sailaway.com.

CUSTOMS & DUTIES

When shopping abroad, keep receipts for all purchases. Upon reentering the country, **be ready to show customs officials what you've bought.** Pack purchases together in an easily accessible place. If you think a duty is incorrect, appeal the assessment. If you object to the way your clearance was handled, note the inspector's badge number. In either case, first ask to see a supervisor. If the problem isn't resolved, write to the appropriate authorities, beginning with the port director at your point of entry.

IN GREECE

Passing through Greek Customs is usually a painless procedure and certainly takes less time than retrieving your luggage. EU citizens can walk through, and even non-EU citizens arriving from a European city should quickly pass down the green lane. Look like a tourist and you won't have a problem. But if you have flown direct from the United States or Australia and are carting many shiny new suitcases and lots of boxes that look as if you've brought appliances for the relatives, you will be pulled over. In that case, it's better to politely bear the ordeal, which might just entail the opening of one bag.

You may bring into Greece duty-free: food and beverages up to 22 pounds (10 kilos); 200 cigarettes, 100 cigarillos, or 50 cigars; 1 liter of alcoholic spirits or 2 liters of wine; and gift articles up to a total of €175. For non-EU citizens, foreign banknotes amounting to more than $2,500 must be declared for re-export, but there are no restrictions on traveler's checks.

Only one per person of such expensive portable items as cameras, camcorders, computers, and the like is permitted into Greece. You should register these with Greek Customs upon arrival to avoid any problems when taking them out of the country again. Sports equipment, such as bicycles and skis, is also limited to one (pair) per person.

To bring in a dog or a cat, you need a health certificate issued by a veterinary authority and validated by the Greek Consulate and the appropriate medical authority (in the United States, the Department of Agriculture). It must state that your pet doesn't carry any infectious diseases and that it received a rabies inoculation no more than 12 months (for cats, six months) and no fewer than six days before arrival. Dogs must also have a veterinary certificate that indicates they have been wormed against echinococcus. For more information on Greek Customs, check with your local Greek Consulate or the Ministry of Foreign Affairs in Athens, which has more detailed information on customs and import/export regulations.

🛈 **Ministry of Foreign Affairs** ✉ Akadimias 3, Stoa Davaki, Athens ☎ 210/368-2700 Athens ⊕ www.mfa.gr.

IN THE U.S.

U.S. residents who have been out of the country for at least 48 hours may bring home, for personal use, $800 worth of foreign goods duty free, as long as they haven't used the $800 allowance or any part of it in the past 30 days. This exemption may include 1 liter of alcohol (for travelers 21 and older), 200 cigarettes, and 100 non-Cuban cigars. Family members from the same household who are traveling together may pool their $800 personal exemptions. For fewer than 48 hours, the duty-free allowance drops to $200, which may include 50 cigarettes, 10 non-Cuban cigars, and 150 ml of alcohol (or 150 ml of perfume containing alcohol). The $200 allowance cannot be combined with other individuals' exemptions, and if you exceed it, the full value of all the goods will be taxed. Antiques, which U.S. Customs and Border Protection defines as objects more than 100 years old, enter duty-free, as do original works of art done entirely by hand, including paintings, drawings, and sculptures. This doesn't apply to folk art or handicrafts, which are in general dutiable.

You may also send packages home duty free, with a limit of one parcel per addressee per day (except alcohol or tobacco products or perfume worth more than $5). You can mail up to $200 worth of goods for personal use; label the package PERSONAL USE and attach a list of its contents and their retail value. If the package contains your used personal belongings, mark it AMERICAN GOODS RETURNED to avoid paying duties. You may send up to $100 worth of goods as a gift; mark the package UNSOLICITED GIFT. Mailed items do not affect your duty-free allowance on your return.

To avoid paying duty on foreign-made high-ticket items you already own and will take on your trip, register them with a local customs office before you leave the country. Consider filing a Certificate of Registration for laptops, cameras, watches, and other digital devices identified with serial numbers or other permanent markings; you can keep the certificate for other trips. Otherwise, bring a sales receipt or insurance form to show that you owned the item before you left the United States.

For more about duties, restricted items, and other information about international travel, check out U.S. Customs and Border Protection's online brochure, *Know Before You Go.* You can also file complaints on the U.S. Customs and Border Protection Web site, listed below.

🛈 **U.S. Customs and Border Protection** ✉ For inquiries and complaints, 1300 Pennsylvania Ave. NW, Washington, DC 20229 ⊕ www.cbp.gov ☎ 877/227-5551, 202/354-1000.

DISABILITIES & ACCESSIBILITY

Many cruise ships to the Greek islands are equipped to accommodate people with disabilities, but access to archaeological sites throughout the country can present some difficulty, and most two-story museums do not have elevators, although some improvements were introduced in Athens for the 2004 Paralympic Games. Bathrooms, especially in restaurants, may be down a steep flight of stairs in the basement, and the frequently high-curbed and auto-packed sidewalks are difficult to negotiate in larger towns. Call ahead to find out exactly what obstacles you might face and to enlist extra help from staff. Public transportation in Greece is generally crowded, and few special provisions are available. The easiest solution is to use taxis to get between different points, or hire a taxi for the day; most hotels can arrange this. You may encounter stares—until recently Greeks with disabilities were encouraged to stay at home—but people usually lend a helping hand, since this is a country where hospitality is a time-honored virtue. Athens has some parking spaces to accommodate people with disabilities. Traveling with a companion or a group is advisable. For information on hotels and tourist sites catering to those with special needs, contact the Panhellenic Union of Paraplegic and Physically Challenged and the Greek

National Tourism Organization. The European Union publishes guides on accessible travel for 18 countries, including Greece, while specialist agencies like **Accessible Europe** (www.accessibleurope. com) organize tours for travelers who require special accessibility.

Ⓕ Local Source Panhellenic Union of Paraplegic and Physically Challenged ✉ Dimitsanis 3-5, Moschato, 18346 ☎ 210/483-2564 ⊕ www.pasipka.gr.

LODGING

Visitors will probably find it easier to manage in Greece's more modern resorts and hotels than in rented rooms; unfortunately, these are the more expensive establishments. A frequent problem even then is the bathroom, which seldom has a tub but a narrow, step-in shower with a ledge. Sometimes cheaper accommodations have the shower attached to one of the bathroom walls—that way you can sit while bathing, although the floor becomes wet and slippery. Think about requesting a spacious room near the elevator or on the ground floor. In better hotels, the rooms may be more manageable, but the multilevel public areas might not be accessible. The Athens hotels listed below have one or more rooms designed for travelers with disabilities.

Ⓕ Best Choices Athenaeum InterContinental ✉ Syngrou 89-93, Athens ☎ 800/327-0200 reservations, 210/920-6000 ⊕ www.intercontinental. com. **Hilton** ✉ Vasilissis Sofias 46, Athens ☎ 800/ 445-8667 reservations, 210/728-1000 ⊕ www. athenshilton.com. **Holiday Inn** ✉ Michalakopoulou 50, Athens ☎ 800/465-4239 reservations, 210/727-8000 ⊕ www.holidayinnathens.com. **Saint George Lycabettus** ✉ Kleomenous 2, Athens ☎ 210/729-0711 ⊕ www.sglycabettus.gr.

RESERVATIONS

When discussing accessibility with an operator or reservations agent, ask hard questions. Are there any stairs, inside *or* out? Are there grab bars next to the toilet *and* in the shower/tub? How wide is the doorway to the room? To the bathroom? For the most extensive facilities meeting the latest legal specifications, opt for newer accommodations. If you reserve through a toll-free number, consider also calling the hotel's local number to confirm the information from the central reservations office. Get confirmation in writing when you can.

SIGHTS & ATTRACTIONS

Because Greece's major attractions tend to be ancient ruins, and the government only recently has started building facilities with better access, it is hard for people in wheelchairs to negotiate several key sights. For example, the Acropolis requires that you walk up many steep steps at the Propylaea. However, an elevator added to the north side of the Acropolis should help people with mobility concerns. The bottom (and main) floor at the National Archaeological Museum is accessible, but many star exhibits are on the top floor, and the elevator can be slow and unreliable. On the other hand, the charming district of Plaka, where you can see the Monument of Lysicrates, the Tower of the Winds, and the Roman Agora, is largely accessible, except for the upper reaches of Anafiotika at the top of staircases or steep lanes. Two of the capital's best museums, the Benaki and the Goulandris Cycladic, are fully accessible. It depends—you can roll through the Old Town of Rhodes and much of the ruins at Nemea with a little help, see the Portara in Naxos from the harbor at sunset, and survey the ruins of Ancient Corinth and the Temple of Apollo at Delphi from the perimeter, but you might have trouble negotiating Akrotiri in Santorini or Knossos in Crete. Still, if you're really determined to see a particular sight, talk to the guards at the gate and see what they can suggest.

TRANSPORTATION

Only some Athens buses have a mechanism that lowers to lift wheelchairs. If you can walk a few steps, you can use the buses and the trains. Drivers and conductors are usually patient, since they often deal with local senior citizens who need extra time to mount the steps. There are no bathrooms on the buses, and those on the trains are cramped. In the Athens metro, stations have elevators to all platforms. In Greece it may be easier to rent a car and have a companion drive, or hire a taxi and driver for the day who can load and unload your wheelchair. Cars with hand controls are not available for rent. If you do find a space for people with disabilities, it's probably assigned to someone in the neighborhood (check for a license number on the sign). Especially in crowded Athens, Greeks leave their cars wherever they can, so park where it's most convenient for you, display your sign, and you probably won't have any problems. Airports are wheelchair-accessible, and Athens International Airport caters very well to people with disabilities.

The U.S. Department of Transportation Aviation Consumer Protection Division's online publication *New Horizons: Information for the Air Traveler with a Disability* offers advice for travelers with a disability, and outlines basic rights. Visit DisabilityInfo.gov for general information.

⌗ Information and Complaints Aviation Consumer Protection Division (⇨ Air Travel) for airline-related problems; ⊕ airconsumer.ost.dot.gov/publications/ horizons.htm for airline travel advice and rights. **Departmental Office of Civil Rights** ⊠ For general inquiries, U.S. Department of Transportation, S-30, 400 7th St. SW, Room 10215, Washington, DC 20590 ☎ 202/366-4648, 202/366-8538 TTY ☏ 202/366-9371 ⊕ www.dotcr.ost.dot.gov. **Disability Rights Section** ⊠ NYAV, U.S. Department of Justice, Civil Rights Division, 950 Pennsylvania Ave. NW, Washington, DC 20530 ☎ 800/514-0301, 202/514-0301 ADA information line, 800/514-0383 TTY, 202/514-0383 TTY ⊕ www.ada.gov. **U.S. Department of Transportation Hotline** ☎ 800/778-4838 or 800/455-9880 TTY for disability-related air-travel problems.

TRAVEL AGENCIES & TOUR OPERATORS

As a whole, the travel industry has become more aware of the needs of travelers with disabilities. In the United States, the Americans with Disabilities Act requires that travel firms serve the needs of all travelers. Some agencies specialize in working with people with disabilities.

⌗ Travelers with Mobility Problems Access Adventures/B. Roberts Travel ⊠ 1876 East Ave., Rochester, NY 14610 ☎ 800/444-6540 ⊕ www. brobertstravel.com, run by a former physical-rehabilitation counselor. **Flying Wheels Travel** ⊠ 143 W. Bridge St., Box 382, Owatonna, MN 55060 ☎ 507/

451-5005 ☏ 507/451-1685 ⊕ www. flyingwheelstravel.com.

DISCOUNTS & DEALS

Be a smart shopper and compare all your options before making decisions. A plane ticket bought with a promotional coupon from travel clubs, coupon books, and direct-mail offers or purchased on the Internet may not be cheaper than the least-expensive fare from a discount ticket agency. And always keep in mind that what you get is just as important as what you save.

In Athens a €12 ticket allows admission to all the sites and corresponding museums along the Unification of Archaeological Sites walkway for up to a week. You can buy the ticket at any of the sites, which include the Acropolis, Ancient Agora, Roman Agora, Temple of Olympian Zeus, Keramaikos, and Theater of Dionysus. Admission to many museums and archaeological sites is free on Sunday November through March. Entrance is usually free every day for EU students, half off for students from other countries, and about a third off for senior citizens.

DISCOUNT RESERVATIONS

To save money, look into discount reservations services with Web sites and toll-free numbers, which use their buying power to get a better price on hotels, airline tickets (⇨ Air Travel), even car rentals. When booking a room, always **call the hotel's local toll-free number** (if one is available) rather than the central reservations number—you'll often get a better price. Always ask about special packages or corporate rates.

When shopping for the best deal on hotels and car rentals, look for guaranteed exchange rates, which protect you against a falling dollar. With your rate locked in, you won't pay more, even if the price goes up in the local currency.

You may get up to a 15% discount when you book a hotel through a local Greek travel agent rather than reserve directly with the hotel (the agent often has special rates), and prices may be lower than booking through your country's travel agent. Contact agencies by fax; many now have

Web sites and e-mail addresses, making comparison shopping even easier.

🏨 Hotel Rooms **Accommodations Express** ☎ 800/444–7666 or 800/277–1064. **Hotels.com** ☎ 800/246–8357 🌐 www.hotels.com. **Steigen-berger Reservation Service** ☎ 800/223–5652 🌐 www.srs-worldhotels.com. **Turbotrip.com** ☎ 800/473–7829 🌐 w3.turbotrip.com.

PACKAGE DEALS

Don't confuse packages and guided tours. When you buy a package, you travel on your own, just as though you had planned the trip yourself. Fly/drive packages, which combine airfare and car rental, are often a good deal. In cities, ask the local visitor's bureau about hotel and local transportation packages that include tickets to major museum exhibits or other special events. If you **buy a rail/drive pass,** you may save on train tickets and car rentals. All Eurailpass holders get a discount on Eurostar fares through the Channel Tunnel and often receive reduced rates for buses, hotels, ferries, sightseeing cruises, and car rentals. Greek Flexipass Rail n' Fly includes two flight vouchers for selected air-travel routes within Greece and free or reduced fares on some ferries.

EATING & DRINKING

The biggest mistake you can make is to think Greek cuisine is all about moussaka and souvlaki. True, these are popular dishes, but you will be missing out if you don't try the staggering amount of regional specialties—from baked kid in a sealed oven in Metsovo to stuffed squash flowers or wild artichoke salad in Spata to the fluffy *kaltsounia* pastries of Crete. In the cities, a new breed of restaurant has emerged: trendy eateries that combine the best of Mediterranean cooking with elements from other international cuisines. In these posh eateries, of course, you don't get the full Greek experience—after all, this is the place where customers (and you can join them) still visit the taverna kitchen to peek into the cauldrons or to fussily select *their* fish to be barbecued. Red-mullet risotto on eggplant puree with a sprinkle of mastic is great, but nothing beats perfectly grilled octopus and a lus-cious homegrown-tomato salad served at sundown with a sip of chilled ouzo on a rickety beachside table.

Besides restaurants, Greece offers tavernas, informal places that serve classic Greek cooking, including *magirefta,* olive oil-based casseroles or oven-cooked dishes prepared in advance and served at room temperature. Every neighborhood has at least one taverna, and they range from tiny, tucked-away treasures to large, crowded urban haunts. Another kind of eatery is the *ouzeri* or *mezedopoleio,* somewhat like a tapas bar, where you sample appetizers. There are *psarotavernes,* fish tavernas, and *psistaries,* which offer grilled or spit-roasted meats.

On menus all over Greece you'll run into three categories of staple main courses: there are magirefta like moussaka, *pastitsio* (a baked dish of minced lamb and macaroni), or *yemista* (stuffed tomatoes or peppers), which usually has some ground lamb). Then there are *tis oras* ("of the hour"), with a subcategory called *sta karvouna,* or food that is cooked on the coals or grilled—like chops or steak. Finally, there is fish, of all kinds, which is outstanding (look for *tsipoura,* or gilt-head bream).

The restaurants we list are the cream of the crop in each price category. Properties indicated by an ✕🏠 are lodging establishments whose restaurant warrants a special trip. Although some prices have skyrocketed—a chicken pita sandwich at a chichi bar-restaurant, for example—dining in Greece, especially away from Athens and resorts such as Mykonos, is less expensive than in other EU countries. As a rule, if you see many Greek families eating somewhere, it's probably a safe bet in terms of the palate and the pocket.

CATEGORY	COST
$$$$	over €20
$$$	€16–€20
$$	€12–€15
$	€8–€11
¢	under €8

Prices, given in euros, are for one main course at dinner or, for restaurants that serve only mezedes (small dishes), for two mezedes.

MEALS & SPECIALTIES

Greeks don't really eat breakfast and few places serve that meal, unless it's a hotel dining room. You can pick up a cheese pie and rolls at a bakery or a sesame-coated bread ring called a *koulouri* sold by city vendors; order a *tost* ("toast"), a sort of dry grilled sandwich, usually with cheese or paper-thin ham slices, at a café; or dig into a plate of yogurt with honey. Local bakeries may offer fresh doughnuts in the morning. On islands in summer, cafés serve breakfast, from Continental to combinations that might include Spanish omelets and French coffee. Caffeine junkies can get a cup of coffee practically anywhere, but decaf is available only in bigger hotels.

Greeks eat their main meal at either lunch or dinner, so the offerings are the same. For lunch, heavyweight meat-and-potato dishes can be had, but you might prefer a real Greek salad (no lettuce, a slice of feta with a pinch of oregano, and ripe tomatoes) or souvlaki or grilled chicken from a taverna. For a light bite you can also try one of the popular Greek chain eateries such as Everest or Grigori's, found fairly easily throughout the country, for grilled sandwiches or spanakopita and *tiropita* (cheese pie); or Goody's, the local equivalent of McDonald's, where you'll get good-quality burgers at a fast-food outlet.

Coffee and pastries are eaten in the afternoon, usually at a café or *zaharoplastio* (pastry shop). The hour or so before restaurants open for dinner—around 7—is a pleasant time to have an ouzo or glass of wine and try Greek hors d'oeuvres, called mezedes, in a bar, ouzeri, or mezedopoleio. Dinner is often the main meal of the day, and there's plenty of food. Starters include *taramosalata* (a dip or spread made from fish roe) and *melitzanosalata* (made from smoked eggplant, lemon, oil, and garlic), along with the well-known yogurt, cucumber, and garlic *tzatziki*. A typical dinner for a couple might be two to three appetizers, an entrée, a salad, and wine. Diners can order as little or as much as they like, except at very expensive establishments. If a Greek eats dessert at all, it will be fruit or a modest wedge of a syrup-drenched cake like *revani* or semolina halvah, often shared between two or three diners. Only in fancier restaurants can diners order a tiramisu with an espresso. One option for those who want a lighter meal is the mezedopoleio.

In most places, the menu is broken down into appetizers (*orektika*) and entrées (*kiria piata*), with additional headings for salads (this includes dips like tzatziki) and vegetable side plates. However, this doesn't mean there is any sense of a first or second "course" as in France. The food arrives all at the same time, or as it becomes ready.

MEALTIMES

Breakfast is available until 10 at hotels and until early afternoon in beach cafés. Lunch is between 1:30 and 3:30 (and on weekends as late as 5), and dinner is served from about 8:30 to midnight, later in the big cities and resort islands. Most Greeks dine very late, around 10 or 11 PM. Unless otherwise noted, the restaurants listed in this guide are open daily for lunch and dinner.

PAYING

Credit cards are accepted in finer restaurants and some of the more upscale tavernas and fish tavernas. A credit card sign is usually posted in the window.

RESERVATIONS & DRESS

Reservations in Athens or Thessaloniki, as in major cities around the world, are usually recommended for more formal establishments and for "in" places, even on the more popular islands. Most informal establishments don't take reservations but will do their best to accommodate your party, jamming another table on the sidewalk if necessary. Though dress tends to be informal, Greeks do like to dress up when they go out. To be on the safe side, smart casual is best in order not to feel too underdressed. Bars, cafés, and family-run tavernas—especially near the beach—are more casual, and you might get away with wearing shorts. Reviews mention reservations only when they're essential or not accepted. Dress is mentioned only when men are required to wear a jacket or a jacket and tie.

WINE, BEER & SPIRITS

Ouzo is the national aperitif. Served in slim glasses and diluted with water or ice, which turns the liqueur milky white, ouzo is especially enjoyable on summer evenings and should be lingered over. In some parts of Greece, *raki,* which is clear and unflavored, or *tsipouro,* sometimes lightly flavored with aniseed, are drunk instead. Try a tiny sip undiluted first, and ask for mezedes with your drink. Greek wine is relatively inexpensive. Restaurants and tavernas often sell locally produced *kokkino* (red) and *aspro* (white) table wine from the barrel; many of them, purchased by the quarter, half, or full kilogram, are perfectly good. The regions that produce the best wines are the Peloponnese, Attica, northern regions such as Drama, and Santorini. For bottled wines, you might look for Boutari or Tsantalis from Naoussa, Carras Estate from Chalkidiki, and red wines from Nemea in the Peloponnese.

Many upscale restaurants and trendy tavernas now have extensive wine lists, including international imports, but the wine doesn't come cheap. Greece's wine industry has improved the quality of its offerings substantially, and with boutique wineries from regions all over the country producing quality vintages, there really is no need to pay more for imported labels. The origins of retsina, considered Greece's *vin du pays,* are uncertain. According to ancient authors, resin was added to preserve the wine or to seal wine containers. Whatever the original intent, the results can be splendid, so give it a chance. You might try it chilled first, with souvlaki or grilled fish.

You can buy alcohol at convenience shops, supermarkets, and liquor stores (*kaves*). Beer is also often available at kiosks and fast-food chains, even McDonald's. The most readily available beers are the local favorite Mythos, along with Amstel and Heineken. You can order wine and beer everywhere, at any time of day, and hard alcohol in restaurants, cafés, bars, and performance venues that have a hard-liquor license (ouzo counts as wine). Most places serve drinks until 2 or 3 AM on weekdays,

later on weekends. In most bars, if you order a straight drink, it's a generous portion, as much as a double. Keep in mind that if you want a martini, you must order a martini cocktail; otherwise, you'll get Martini and Rossi liqueur.

ECOTOURISM

Throughout the country, treat the environment with respect. Don't pick wildflowers; stay on the paths rather than tromping through vegetation; pick up your garbage (no matter what some Greeks do); be extremely careful with campfires and cigarettes, especially on hot windy days; and don't waste water, especially on the islands, which suffer from drought. To limit the amount of laundry detergent passing into the streams and sea, hotel guests can avoid turning in all their towels daily if they aren't dirty—many ecology-conscious hotels now have signs to this effect. Greece has many bird and animal species threatened with extinction, mostly due to the reduction of forest and marshland, so treat them with all due respect.

ELECTRICITY

To use electric-powered equipment purchased in the United States or Canada, **bring a converter and adapter.** The electrical current in Greece is 220 volts, 50 cycles AC. Wall outlets take Continental-type plugs with two round oversize prongs. If your appliances are dual-voltage, you'll need only an adapter; if not, you'll also need a step-down converter/transformer (United States and Canada). Appliances from Australia and New Zealand will only need the right adapter plug. Don't use 110-volt outlets marked FOR SHAVERS ONLY for high-wattage appliances such as blow-dryers. Most laptops operate equally well on 110 and 220 volts and so require only an adapter.

EMBASSIES

🇦🇺 Australia **Australia** ✉ Soutsou 37, at Tsochas 24, Ambelokipi, Athens ☎ 210/645-0404 🌐 www.ausemb.gr.

🇨🇦 Canada **Canada** ✉ Ioannou Genadiou 4, Kolonaki, Athens ☎ 210/727-3400 🌐 www.dfait-maeci.gc.ca.

📓 New Zealand **New Zealand Consulate** ⌧ Kifissias 268, Halandri, Athens ☎ 210/687-4700 or 210/687-4701 ✉ costas.costilinis@gr.pwcglobal.com.
📓 United Kingdom **United Kingdom** ⌧ Ploutarchou 1, Kolonaki, Athens ☎ 210/727-2600 ⊕ www.british-embassy.gr.
📓 United States **United States** ⌧ Vasilissis Sofias 91, Mavili Sq., Athens ☎ 210/721-2951 through 210/721-2959 ⊕ www.usembassy.gr.

EMERGENCIES

In cases of emergencies, locals are fairly helpful and will come to your aid. It's best to contact the police for more serious matters, even though responses can vary from mildly disinterested to efficient, depending on how serious they perceive your problem to be. If you must get to a hospital urgently, don't rely on ambulances, as they tend to get stuck in traffic (especially in Athens)—opt for a taxi instead. The *Athens News* and *Kathimerini* (the latter is inserted in the *International Herald Tribune*) have listings for pharmacies that are open late on a particular day. If you speak Greek, you can dial a recorded message listing the off-hours pharmacies.

The tourist police throughout Greece (numbers are given in each chapter) can provide general information and help in emergencies and can mediate in disputes.
📓 Coast Guard ☎ 108. **Duty Hospitals and Pharmacies** ☎ 1434. **Fire** ☎ 199. **Forest Service** ☎ 191 in case of fire. **National Ambulance Service (EKAV)** ☎ 166. **Off-hours Pharmacies** ☎ 107 in Athens, 102 outside Athens. **Police** ☎ 100. **Road Assistance** ☎ 104 ELPA. **S.O.S Doctors** ☎ 1016, a 24-hour private medical service. **Tourist Police** ⌧ Dimitrakopoulou 77, Athens ☎ 171 in Athens, 210/171 from outside Athens.
📓 Poison Center **Poison center** ☎ 210/779-3777.

ENGLISH-LANGUAGE MEDIA

In all major towns and on islands in summer, at least one kiosk or bookstore sells international publications. The kiosks are usually close to the main square. Shops in larger hotels also carry English-language media. U.K. papers include the *Times, Daily Mail,* the *Independent,* and the *Guardian,* as well as most tabloids; U.S. papers include the *Wall Street Journal* and *USA Today.* The *New York Times* is not

available, and Australian and Canadian papers are rare. On many islands, the papers are a day old because they have been shipped by ferry from Athens. Monday through Saturday the *International Herald Tribune* is available with a Greek news insert, and the local *Athens News* (a weekly newspaper) can be bought at most stands in Athens and throughout Greece. The international versions of *Time* and *Newsweek* are easy to find, as are commercial magazines ranging from *Wallpaper* to *Playboy.*

BOOKS

English-language books are easy to locate, but on a small island the selection may be limited to romance novels and spy thrillers, or dusty, secondhand volumes left behind in the lobby by hotel guests. You can purchase books at foreign-language bookstores, downtown kiosks, hotel shops, airports, flea markets, and sales held by nonprofit organizations. Children's picture books are also sold at toy stores such as Jumbo. New books, even paperbacks, are at least one-third more expensive than the price in their country of origin. An exception is English-language books printed in Greece, such as the Kedros translations of Greek novels, or history and museum guides; these are reasonably priced.
📓 Bookstores in Athens **Compendium** ⌧ Nikis 28, upstairs, Athens ☎ 210/322-1248, travel books, books on Greece, academic books, and used books. **Eleftheroudakis** ⌧ Nikis 20, Athens ☎ 210/322-9388 ⌧ Panepistimiou 17, Athens ☎ 210/325-8440, huge selection of Greek- and English-language books. **I Folia tou Vivliou** (Booknest) ⌧ Panepistimiou 25-29, in arcade and on 1st fl., Athens ☎ 210/323-1703, ample selection of British and American authors. **Papasotiriou** ⌧ Akadimias and Ippokratous, Athens ☎ 210/339-0637, mainstream fiction, cookbooks, foreign magazines, children's books, and books on history and politics. **Reymondos** ⌧ Voukourestiou 18, Athens ☎ 210/364-8188, great foreign-language books and magazines.

NEWSPAPERS & MAGAZINES

The weekly *Athens News,* which comes out on Friday, provides fairly neutral, good coverage of Greek events; a summary of the top international stories from the wires; financial information; and an arts section that reviews predominantly Athenian happenings. The paper offers good coverage on issues affecting foreign residents, including minority groups and migrant workers. It also prints useful information such as dates for pending bus strikes, ferry departure times, and addresses for all-night pharmacies and hospitals. A translated six-page version of the Greek paper *Kathimerini* appears as an insert in the *International Herald Tribune*. It also summarizes Greek news and includes more features and in-depth stories by Greek reporters, though these are harder to read because the translated pieces ignore conventions of United States and British journalism: leads are long, quotes are unattributed, and sentences often are convoluted and passive. Local English-language magazines come and go and are mostly mediocre; at press time, the best of the lot, *Odyssey,* an upscale bimonthly glossy written for the Greek diaspora, could be found at inner city kiosks and bookstores. *Inside Out,* a newer, monthly magazine, focuses on shopping, art gallery, and other listings, as well as restaurant reviews. Foreign magazines or newspapers usually have a small markup on the original price.

RADIO & TELEVISION

Athens has numerous radio stations (all are FM), and even islands have at least one local station. Those playing foreign music include trendy KLIK (88.0), rave-oriented Geronimo Groovy (88.9), and mainstream pop Kiss (92.9). Other foreign music stations include Rock FM (96.9), the retro Radio Gold (105.0), Kosmos (world music, 93.6), and Era 3 (90.9, with an English news broadcast at 9 AM), the only classical music on the dial. You can catch CNN Radio on the hour at Galaxy (92.0) or news bulletins from the BBC World Service on En Lefko (87.7). Public broadcasting's Filia (107 FM) offers programming in 12 languages, including foreign news and reports from the BBC World Service.

Your television choices include the top four private stations—Mega, Antenna, Alpha, and Star—and the public broadcasting network's ET-1 and NET. Throughout the day the private stations carry many American and some British serials that are subtitled rather than dubbed. The best shows seem to appear after midnight. Some stations run English-language soap operas in the afternoon. English-language documentaries are more likely to appear on the public stations. Cable and satellite TV, usually found in the better hotels, broadcast Euronews (in English), MTV, Filmnet, Discovery, and various French and Italian channels.

ETIQUETTE & BEHAVIOR

Greeks are friendly and openly affectionate. It is not uncommon, for example, to see women strolling arm in arm, or men kissing and hugging each other. Displays of anger are also quite common. You may see a man at a traffic light get out to verbally harangue an offending driver behind him, or a customer berating a civil servant and vice versa, but these encounters rarely become physical. To the person who doesn't understand Greek, the loud, intense conversations may all sound angry—but they're not. When you meet someone for the first time, it is customary to shake hands, but with acquaintances the usual is a two-cheek kiss hello and good-bye. One thing that may disconcert foreigners is that when they run into a Greek somewhere with another person, he or she usually doesn't introduce the other party, even if there is a long verbal exchange. If you can't stand it anymore, just introduce yourself, or at least acknowledge the person with a smile.

Greeks tend to stand closer to people than North Americans and northern Europeans, and they rely on gestures more when communicating. One gesture you should never use is the open palm, fingers slightly spread, shoved toward someone's face. The *moutza* is a serious insult. Another gesture you should remember, especially if trying to catch a taxi, is the Greek "no," which looks like "yes": a slight or exaggerated (depending on the sentiment) tipping back of the head, sometimes with the eyes closed and eyebrows raised. When you wave with your palm toward people, they may interpret it as "come here" instead of "good-bye"; and Greeks often wave good-bye with the palm facing them, which looks like "come here" to English speakers.

In some areas it still doesn't do to overcompliment a baby or a child, thought to provoke others' jealousy and thus bring on the evil eye. You will often see Greeks mock spitting, saying "ftou-ftou-ftou" to ward off harm, as an American might knock on wood after a threatening thought. (At baptisms, the godparent mock-spits three times to discourage Satan.) Although a woman who makes long eye contact with a man is interpreted as being interested in romance, in most cases, Greeks openly stare at anything that interests them, so don't be offended if you are the center of attention wherever you go.

When visiting a house for dinner, you can bring a small gift for the children—a foreign T-shirt, for example—or a box of pastries or sweets. Greeks often eat out of communal serving plates, so it's considered normal in informal settings to spear your tomato out of the salad bowl rather than securing an individual portion. Sometimes in tavernas you don't even get your own plate. Note that it is considered *tsigounia*, stinginess, to run separate tabs, especially because much of the meal is Chinese-style. Greeks either divide the bill equally among the party, no matter who ate what, or one person magnanimously treats. A good host insists that you eat or drink more, and only when you have refused a number of times will you get a reprieve; be charmingly persistent in your "no." When you plan to meet someone, be aware that Greeks have a loose sense of time. They may be punctual if meeting you on a street corner to go to a movie, but if they say they'll come round your hotel at 7 PM, they may show up at 8 PM. (Generally speaking, Greeks divide the day quite differently: morning ends at 1 or 2 PM, midday can stretch to 4 or 5, and for some, afternoon is 8 or 9 PM.)

Name days (the feast day of the saint after whom a person is named) are more important than birthdays in Greece, and the person who does the celebrating holds open house. If invited, you should take sweets, flowers, spirits, or a more personal gift if you know them well. (It's common in business circles to send a telegram to associates and clients on their name day.) You wish the reveler *chronia polla* ("*hron*-ya po-*la*"), or "many years."

Respect is shown toward elders; they are seldom addressed by their first name but called "Kiria" (Mrs./Ms.) and "Kirie" (Mr.) So-and-So. In country churches, and at all monasteries and nunneries, shorts are not allowed for either sex, and women may not wear pants. Usually, there is a stack of frumpy skirts that both men and women can don to cover their legs. In very strict places—the Patmos monastery, for example—women cannot reveal bare shoulders or too much cleavage. It's a good idea to carry large scarves for such occasions.

Most beaches are topless (and legally so), except those near the harbor or town center. The number of beaches where nude bathing is acceptable is slowly growing, although this is usually restricted to a beach's most remote edge. Watch to see what others do, and err on the conservative side.

Even if you make a mistake, it's unlikely Greeks will think you offensive. They're used to foreigners, don't expect you to know all the rules, and will probably chalk up the impropriety to *your* culture's strange dictates.

To help you decipher the complexity of Greek culture, read the excellent, entertaining *Exploring the Greek Mosaic,* by Benjamin Broome (Yarmouth, Maine: Intercultural Press, 1996), which thoughtfully analyzes Greece's social landscape and provides valuable insights, especially for those who want to do business in Greece.

BUSINESS ETIQUETTE
Business in Greece can be as informal as a meeting at a coffee shop in Kolonaki to the power-suit sect you'll see around Syntagma Square and Kifissias, where most international firms have offices. Many business conversations and much deal

making in the city take place on the run and over the cell phone, but when it comes to meetings, a formality in dress and setting do apply. Don't always expect punctuality—Greeks can be notoriously late—even though times are changing and Greeks must compete in a tougher economic climate since joining the EU.

GAY & LESBIAN TRAVEL

In Greece, homosexuality has been very much a part of life from antiquity to today. Indeed, many prominent figures of the country's cultural life (both past and present) are openly gay. You should be aware, however, of the special mentality of the Greek male vis-à-vis homosexuality. Sociological reports indicate a large portion of the population is bisexual, though this does not indicate a conscious recognition of being gay. Greek society remains conservative regarding open declarations and displays of homosexuality by either sex, although homosexual relations for men over 17 have been legal for many decades in Greece. The nearest thing to a gay scene in the Western sense of the word exists in Athens (around Makriyianni and Kolonaki), Thessaloniki, Mykonos, Rhodes, and Ios for men; for women, Athens and Eressos on Lesbos.

The weekly Greek-language entertainment magazine *Athinorama*, available at all kiosks, lists Athens's gay bars and dance clubs in its nightlife section. *To Kraximo* and *Greek Gay Guide* are publications available from kiosks in Omonia Square in Athens and near the Thessaloniki train station. The Gay and Lesbian Society in Athens provides resources for the gay community.

🔝 Local Resources **Gay and Lesbian Society (EOK)** ☎ 210/523-7333.

🔝 Gay- Lesbian-Friendly Travel Agencies **Different Roads Travel** ✉ 1017 N. LaCienega Blvd., Suite 308, West Hollywood, CA 90069 ☎ 800/429-8747 or 310/289-6000 (Ext. 14 for both) 🖷 310/855-0323 ✉ lgernert@tzell.com. **Kennedy Travel** ✉ 130 W. 42nd St., Suite 401, New York, NY 10036 ☎ 800/237-7433 or 212/840-8659 🖷 212/730-2269 ⊕ www.kennedytravel.com. **Now, Voyager** ✉ 4406 18th St., San Francisco, CA 94114 ☎ 800/255-6951 or 415/626-1169 🖷 415/626-8626 ⊕ www.nowvoyager.

com. **Skylink Travel and Tour/Flying Dutchmen Travel** ✉ 1455 N. Dutton Ave., Suite A, Santa Rosa, CA 95401 ☎ 800/225-5759 or 707/546-9888 🖷 707/636-0951; serving lesbian travelers.

HEALTH

Greece's strong summer sun and low humidity can lead to sunburn or sunstroke if you're not careful. A hat, long-sleeve shirt, and long pants or a sarong are essential for spending a day at the beach or visiting archaeological sites. Sunglasses, a hat, and sunblock are necessities, and insect repellent may keep the occasional horsefly and mosquito at bay. Drink plenty of water. Most beaches present few dangers, but keep a lookout for the occasional jellyfish and, on rocky coves, sea urchins. Should you step on one, don't break off the embedded spines, which may lead to infection, but instead remove them with heated olive oil and a needle.

Food is seldom a problem, but the liberal amounts of olive oil used in Greek cooking may be indigestible for some. Tap water in Greece is fine, and bottled spring water is readily available.

For minor ailments, go to the local pharmacy first, where the licensed staff can make recommendations for over-the-counter drugs. Most pharmacies are closed in the evenings and on weekends, but each posts the name of the nearest pharmacy open off-hours. Newspapers, including the *Athens News,* also carry a listing of pharmacies open late. Most state hospitals and rural clinics won't charge you for tending to minor ailments, even if you're not an EU citizen; at most, you'll pay a minimal fee. In an emergency you can call an ambulance (⇨ Emergencies), but waving down a taxi can be faster than waiting for an ambulance. Most hotels will call a doctor for you. In Athens, you can locate a doctor by calling S.O.S Doctors (⇨ Emergencies). For a dentist, check with your hotel, embassy, or the tourist police.

DIVERS' ALERT
Do not fly within 24 hours of scuba diving.

OVER-THE-COUNTER REMEDIES
All kiosks carry aspirin ("ah-spi-*ree*-nee"), but other drugs are only available at the

pharmacy ("far-ma-*kee*-oh"), though you often don't need a prescription. Condoms are available from kiosks, supermarkets, pharmacies, and sometimes vending machines in bar bathrooms or outside pharmacies. One aspirin substitute similar to Tylenol is Depon; other painkillers include Ponstan and Buscopan (good for menstrual cramps) and Salospir, which you can buy without prescription. Lomotil is widely available, and a good salve for sunburn is the inexpensive Bepanthol. The pharmacist will tell you what European medications equal yours and how to locate them. Many pharmacists also give shots and vaccinations. You will find a bigger selection of sunscreens at supermarkets and beauty stores such as Hondos Center or Sephora-Beauty Shop. All tourist areas have at least one store selling sunscreen, but it will be expensive. Two local brands sold outside Greece are Korres and Apivita, and a mastic-based line of cosmetics is also popular. But you can find everything from Coppertone and Nivea to Banana Boat.

PESTS & OTHER HAZARDS

In greener, wetter areas, mosquitoes may be a problem. You can burn coils ("spee-*rahl*") to discourage them or buy plug-in devices that burn medicated tabs ("pah-*steel*-ya"). Hotels usually provide these. The only poisonous snakes in Greece are the adder and the sand viper, which are brown or red, with dark zigzags. The adder has a V or X behind its head, and the sand viper sports a small horn on its nose. When hiking, wear high tops and don't put your feet or hands in crevices without looking first. If bitten, try to slow the spread of the venom until a doctor comes. Lie still with the affected limb lower than the rest of your body. Apply a tourniquet, releasing it every few minutes, and cut the wound a bit in case the venom can bleed out. Do NOT suck on the bite. Whereas snakes like to lie in the sun, the scorpion (rare) likes cool, wet places, in wood piles, and under stones. Apply Benadryl or Phenergan to minor stings, but if you have nausea or fever, see a doctor at once.

HOLIDAYS

January 1 (New Year's Day); January 6 (Epiphany); Clean Monday (first day of Lent); March 25 (Feast of the Annunciation and Independence Day); Good Friday; Greek Easter Sunday; Greek Easter Monday; May 1 (Labor Day); Pentecost; August 15 (Assumption of the Holy Virgin); October 28 (Ochi Day); December 25–26 (Christmas Day and Boxing Day).

Only on Orthodox Easter and August 15 do you find that just about *everything* shuts down. It's harder getting a room at the last minute on Easter and August 15 (especially the latter), and traveling requires stamina, if you want to survive on the ferries and the highways. On the other hand, the local rituals and rites associated with these two celebrations are interesting and occasionally moving (the Epitaphios procession on Good Friday).

INSURANCE

The most useful travel-insurance plan is a comprehensive policy that includes coverage for trip cancellation and interruption, default, trip delay, and medical expenses (with a waiver for preexisting conditions).

Without insurance you'll lose all or most of your money if you cancel your trip, regardless of the reason. Default insurance covers you if your tour operator, airline, or cruise line goes out of business—the chances of which have been increasing. Trip-delay covers expenses that arise because of bad weather or mechanical delays. Study the fine print when comparing policies.

If you're traveling internationally, a key component of travel insurance is coverage for medical bills incurred if you get sick on the road. Such expenses aren't generally covered by Medicare or private policies. U.K. residents can buy a travel-insurance policy valid for most vacations taken during the year in which it's purchased (but check preexisting-condition coverage). British and Australian citizens need extra medical coverage when traveling overseas.

Always **buy travel policies directly from the insurance company**; if you buy them from a cruise line, airline, or tour operator that goes out of business you probably won't be covered for the agency or operator's default, a major risk. Before making any purchase, review your existing health and home-owner's policies to find what they cover away from home.

▶ Travel Insurers In the United States: **Access America** ✉ 2805 N. Parham Rd., Richmond, VA 23294 ☎ 800/284-8300 📠 800/346-9265 or 804/673-1469 ⊕ www.accessamerica.com. **Travel Guard International** ✉ 1145 Clark St., Stevens Point, WI 54481 ☎ 800/826-1300 or 715/345-1041 📠 800/955-8785 or 715/345-1990 ⊕ www.travelguard.com.

▶ Insurance Information In Australia: **Insurance Council of Australia** ✉ Level 3, 56 Pitt St., Sydney, NSW 2000 ☎ 02/9253-5100 📠 02/9253-5111 ⊕ www.ica.com.au. In Canada: **RBC Insurance** ✉ 6880 Financial Dr., Mississauga, Ontario L5N 7Y5 ☎ 800/387-4357 or 905/816-2559 📠 888/298-6458 ⊕ www.rbcinsurance.com. In New Zealand: **Insurance Council of New Zealand** ✉ Level 7, 111–115 Customhouse Quay, Box 474, Wellington ☎ 04/472-5230 📠 04/473-3011 ⊕ www.icnz.org.nz. In the United Kingdom: **Association of British Insurers** ✉ 51 Gresham St., London EC2V 7HQ ☎ 020/7600-3333 📠 020/7696-8999 ⊕ www.abi.org.uk.

LANGUAGE

Greek is the native language not only of Greece but also of Cyprus, parts of Chicago, and Astoria, New York. Though it's a byword for incomprehensible ("it was all Greek to me," says Casca in Shakespeare's *Julius Caesar*), much of the difficulty lies in its different alphabet. Not all the 24 Greek letters have precise English equivalents, and there is usually more than one way to spell a Greek word in English. For instance, the letter delta sounds like the English letters "dh," and the sound of the letter gamma may be transliterated as a "g," "gh," or "y." Because of this the Greek for Holy Trinity might appear in English as Agia Triada, Aghia Triada, Ayia Triada, or even (if the initial aspiration and the "dh" are used) Hagia Triadha.

It seems complicated, but with a little time spent learning the alphabet and some basic phrases, you can acquire enough Greek to navigate—i.e., exchange greetings, find a hotel room, and get from one town to another. Many Greeks know English but appreciate a two-way effort. Only in isolated mountain villages might you not find someone who speaks at least a few words in English; in most cities and tourist areas, all Greeks know at least one foreign language. Note that if you ask directions, you will often get numerous opinions. It's best to use close-ended queries: "Is this the path to Galissas? Do I turn right at the stone church or left?" If you ask, "Where is Galissas?," a possible answer will be "Down a ways to the left and then you turn right by the baker's house, his child lives in Chicago, where did you say you went to school?"

If you only have 15 minutes to learn Greek, memorize the following: *yiá sou* (hello/good-bye, informal for one person); *yiá sas* (hello/good-bye, formal for one person and used for a group); *miláte angliká?* (do you speak English?); *den katalavéno* (I don't understand); *parakaló* (please/you're welcome); *signómi* (excuse me); *efharistó* (thank you); *ne* (yes); *óhee* (no); *pósso?* (how much?); *pou eéne. . . ?* (where is?), *. . . ee twaléta?* (. . . the toilet?), *. . . to tahidromío?* (. . . the post office?), *. . . to stathmó?* (. . . the station?); *kali méra* (good morning), *kali spéra* (good evening), *kali níhta* (good night). Also *see* Greek Vocabulary at the back of this guide.

LANGUAGE-STUDY PROGRAMS

There are language-study courses in Athens, but these require more of a time commitment than your one- or two-week vacation. Such programs, usually combined with sightseeing, are best booked from your country; check with your local university. The professional Athens Centre offers an intensive one-month program for all levels in a lovely old Pangrati house. You might meet local diplomats, classics students, or businesspeople out to master Greek. The center also runs one-month courses on the island of Spetses in July (about €2,000, including single-room accommodation). Both the Athens Centre and the Hellenic American Union offer longer courses as well, though the latter is geared more to Greeks learning English. Greek language courses are also offered by

College Year in Athens, a popular study-abroad program. Lingua Service Worldwide offers immersion courses in Athens and Hania throughout the year. Universities with Greek Studies programs are also a good source of information about course offerings.

🏛 **Athens Centre** ✉ Archimidou 48, Pangrati, 11636 Athens ☎ 210/701-2268 or 210/701-5242 🖷 210/701-8603 ⊕ www.athenscentre.gr. **College Year in Athens** ✉ Pl. Stadiou 5, Pangrati, 10024 Athens ☎ 210/756-0749 or 617/868-8200 in the U.S. 🖷 210/756-1497 ⊕ www.cyathens.org. **Hellenic American Union** ✉ Massalias 22, Kolonaki, 10679 Athens ☎ 210/368-0000 🖷 210/363-3174 ⊕ www.hau.gr. **Lingua Service Worldwide** ✉ 75 Prospect St., Suite 4, Huntington, NY 11743 ☎ 800/394-5327 or 631/424-0777 🖷 631/271-3441 ⊕ www.linguaserviceworldwide.com.

LODGING

Accommodations vary from luxury island resorts to traditional settlements that incorporate local architecture to inexpensive rented rooms peddled at the harbor. Family-run pensions and guesthouses outside Athens and Thessaloniki are often charming and comfortable; they also let you get better acquainted with the locals. Apartments with kitchens are available as well in most resort areas.

Although lodging is less expensive in Greece than in most of the EU and the United States, the quality tends to be lower. However, many hotels in Athens underwent massive renovations in anticipation of the 2004 Olympics, and new hotels have been built in the city; prices have risen dramatically. Often you can reduce the price by eliminating breakfast, by bargaining when it's off-season, or by going through a local travel agency for the larger hotels on major islands and in Athens and Thessaloniki. If you stay longer, the manager or owner will usually give you a better daily rate. An 8% government tax (6% outside the major cities) and 2% municipality tax are added to all hotel bills, though usually the rate quoted includes the tax; be sure to ask. If your room rate covers meals, another 2% tax may be added. Accommodations may be hard to find in smaller resort towns in winter and

at the beginning of spring. Remember that the plumbing in rooms and most low-end hotels (and restaurants, shops, and other public places) is delicate enough to require that toilet paper and other detritus be put in the wastebasket and not flushed.

The lodgings we list are the cream of the crop in each price category. We always list the facilities that are available—but we don't specify whether they cost extra: when pricing accommodations, always ask what's included and what costs extra: the usual items that may cost extra to your basic hotel room rate are breakfast, parking facilities, and even air-conditioning at some hotels.

Assume that hotels operate on the European Plan (EP, with no meals) unless we specify that they use the Continental Plan (CP, with a Continental breakfast), Breakfast Plan (BP, with a full breakfast), Modified American Plan (MAP, with breakfast and dinner), or the Full American Plan (FAP, with all meals). Also note that some resort hotels also offer half- and full-board arrangements for part of the year. All-inclusive resorts are also mushrooming; inquire when booking.

CATEGORY	ATHENS	ELSEWHERE
$$$$	over €200	over €160
$$$	€160-€200	€121-€160
$$	€100-€160	€91-€120
$	€60-€100	€60-€90
¢	under €60	under €60

Prices are for two people in a standard double room in high season, including taxes, and are given in euros.

APARTMENT & VILLA RENTALS

If you want a home base that's roomy enough for a family and comes with cooking facilities, **consider a self-catering apartment or furnished rentals including villas.** These can save you money, especially if you're traveling with a large group of people. Home-exchange directories list rentals (often second homes owned by prospective house swappers), and some services search for a house or apartment for you (even a castle if that's your fancy) and handle the paperwork. Some send an illustrated catalog; others send photographs only of specific properties, sometimes at a charge. Up-front registration fees may apply.

In Greece, luxury properties are limited and usually handled by international agents. Ploumis-Sotiropoulos in Athens handles upscale rentals, too. For more modest villas, you can go through package holiday companies in your country. You could also check the *Athens News* and *Kathimerini* classifieds under "Summer Holiday Rentals," which usually list seaside homes for long-term (weekly, monthly) rent; the papers' Web sites (⊕ www.athensnews.gr and ⊕ www.ekathimerini.com) have listings, too. Self-catering apartments are found in almost every tourist area; ask the local tourist police for a list.

🔏 International Agents **Hideaways International** ✉ 767 Islington St., Portsmouth, NH 03801 ☎ 800/843-4433 or 603/430-4433 🖷 603/430-4444 ⊕ www.hideaways.com, annual membership $185. **Sunisle Holidays** ✉ 2 Curtis Close, Rickmansworth, Hertfordshire, Great Britain ☎ 0871/222-1226 ⊕ www.sunisle.co.uk. **Villas and Apartments Abroad** ✉ 183 Madison Ave., Suite 201, New York, NY 10016 ☎ 800/433-3020 or 212/213-6435 🖷 212/213-8252 ⊕ www.vaanyc.com. **Villas International** ✉ 4340 Redwood Hwy., Suite D309, San Rafael, CA 94903 ☎ 800/221-2260 or 415/499-9490 🖷 415/499-9491 ⊕ www.villasintl.com.

🔏 Local Agents **Ploumis-Sotiropoulos** ☎ 210/364-3112 through 210/364-3119 🖷 210/363-8005 ⊕ www.ploumis-sotiropoulos.gr.

CAMPING

There are numerous campgrounds, most privately owned, throughout Greece. One or more can usually be found close to popular archaeological sites and beach resorts—they aren't intended for those who want to explore the wilds of Greece. Their amenities range from basic to elaborate, and those operated by the Greek National Tourism Office (EOT) are cushier than most. There is no such thing as a typical campground. You might find landscaped, lantern-lighted walkways between the tents and a restaurant, or a barren stretch with nary a shrub for shade. Your fellow campers run the gamut from Scandinavian families of four to Greek teenage ravers

juggling fire. In general, the atmosphere is loose and friendly.

The EOT distributes information on available campgrounds with site listings; the tourist organization also manages a number of campgrounds, including one in Athens (near Voula beach). "Free" camping is technically illegal, but such informal sites spring up annually, often around an island's nudist beaches. Usually there is some form of running water and a nearby taverna—ask around.

🔏 **Panhellenic Camping Association** ✉ Solonos 102, 10680 Athens 🖷 210/362-1560.

HOME EXCHANGES

If you would like to exchange your home for someone else's, join a home-exchange organization, which will send you its updated listings of available exchanges for a year and will include your own listing in at least one of them. It's up to you to make specific arrangements.

🔏 Exchange Clubs **HomeLink USA** ✉ 2937 N.W. 9th Terr., Wilton Manors, FL 33311 ☎ 800/638-3841 or 954/566-2687 🖷 954/566-2783 ⊕ www.homelink.org; $75 yearly for a listing and online access; $45 additional to receive directories. **Intervac U.S.** ✉ 30 Corte San Fernando, Tiburon, CA 94920 ☎ 800/756-4663 🖷 415/435-7440 ⊕ www.intervacus.com; $128 yearly for a listing, online access, and a catalog; $68 without catalog.

HOSTELS

No matter what your age, you can save on lodging costs by staying at hostels. In some 4,500 locations in more than 70 countries around the world, Hostelling International (HI), the umbrella group for a number of national youth-hostel associations, offers single-sex, dorm-style beds and, at many hostels, rooms for couples and family accommodations. Membership in any HI national hostel association, open to travelers of all ages, allows you to stay in HI-affiliated hostels at member rates; one-year membership is about $28 for adults; hostels charge about $10–$30 per night. Members have priority if the hostel is full; they're also eligible for discounts around the world, even on rail and bus travel in some countries.

Greek hostels run about €12 for a bed per night; some are quite loud and cater to a predominantly young crowd. Not all hostels fall under the jurisdiction of the Greek Youth Hostel Organization. Families with young children might do better to stay in a cheap hotel or rental room. Hostels (whether officially recognized or not) are operating in Athens and Thessaloniki on the mainland; Nafplion, Patras, and Olympia in the Peloponnese; Santorini; and Crete.

🛈 Organizations Hostelling International–USA ✉ 8401 Colesville Rd., Suite 600, Silver Spring, MD 20910 ☎ 301/495-1240 🖷 301/495-6697 ⊕ www. hiusa.org. **Hostelling International–Canada** ✉ 205 Catherine St., Suite 400, Ottawa, Ontario K2P 1C3 ☎ 800/663-5777 or 613/237-7884 🖷 613/ 237-7868 ⊕ www.hihostels.ca. **YHA England and Wales** ✉ Trevelyan House, Dimple Rd., Matlock, Derbyshire DE4 3YH, U.K. ☎ 0870/870-8808, 0870/ 770-8868, 0162/959-2600 🖷 0870/770-6127 ⊕ www.yha.org.uk.

🛈 In Greece Athens International Youth Hostel ✉ Victoros Ougo 16, Omonia Sq., 10438 Athens ☎ 210/523-2049 🖷 210/522-7952 ⊕ www. hostelbooking.com; membership costs about €10.50. **Greek Youth Hostel Organization** ✉ Damareos 75, Pangrati, 11633 Athens ☎ 210/751-9530 🖷 210/751-0616 ✉ y-hostels@otenet.gr.

HOTELS

The EOT authorizes the construction and classification of hotels throughout Greece. It classifies them into six categories: L (stands for deluxe), and A–E, which govern the rates that can be charged, though don't expect hotels to have the same amenities as their U.S. and northern European counterparts. Ratings are based on considerations such as room size, hotel services, and amenities including the furnishing of the room. Within each category, quality varies greatly, but prices don't. Still, you may come across an A-category hotel that charges less than a B-class, depending on facilities. The classifications can be misleading—a hotel rated C in one town might qualify as a B in another. For the categories L, A, and B, you can expect something along the lines of a chain hotel or motel in the United States, although the room will probably be somewhat smaller.

A room in a C hotel can be perfectly acceptable; with a D the bathroom may or may not be shared. Ask to see the room before checking in. You can sometimes find a bargain if a hotel has just renovated but has not yet been reclassified. A great hotel may never move up to a better category just because its lobby isn't the required size.

Official prices are posted in each room, usually on the back of the door or inside the wardrobe. The room charge varies over the course of the year, peaking in the high season when breakfast or half-board (at hotel complexes) may also be obligatory.

From mid-July to mid-August, it's harder to find hotels on the islands and near the beaches, just as it's more difficult to get a hotel near Peloponnese ski centers in winter and in Thessaloniki during the International Trade Fair in September. The rest of the time you can just walk in. A hotel may ask you for a deposit of up to 25% of the room rate. If you cancel your reservations at least 21 days in advance, you are entitled to a full refund of your deposit. If the room you booked is unavailable when you arrive, and you have proof of booking, the hotel must put you up in another hotel of at least the same category, in the same area, for the same length of time. If the hotel can't find you alternative lodging, it must reimburse you fully. Although a hotel is liable for damage to or theft of your valuables (unless it was your fault or the result of force majeure), it is only liable for up to €90 per customer, unless you can prove it assumed the safekeeping of your valuables. Just because these rights are guaranteed by the law doesn't mean you will automatically find compliance or a speedy resolution; contact tourist police if you have trouble.

EOT distributes lists of hotels for each region, although it does not make recommendations. Annual hotel directories are available at most English-language bookstores in Athens and Thessaloniki and at city kiosks in late spring. You can contact a hotel directly, go through a travel agent, or write one month in advance for reservations to the Hellenic Chamber of Hotels.

Unless otherwise noted, in this guide, hotels have air-conditioning (*climatismo*), room TVs, and private bathrooms (*banio*). Bathrooms mostly contain showers, though some older or more luxury hotels may have tubs. Beds are usually twins (*diklina*). If you want a double bed, ask for a *diplokrevati*. In upper-end hotels, the mattresses are full- or queen-size. This guide lists amenities that are available but doesn't always specify if there is a surcharge. **When pricing accommodations, always ask what costs extra** (TV, air-conditioning, private bathroom).

Use the following as a guide to making accommodation inquiries: to reserve a double room, *thelo na kleiso ena diklino*; with a bath, *me banio*; without a bath, *horis banio*; or a room with a view, *domatio me thea*.

If you need a quiet room (*isiho domatio*), get one with double-glazed windows and air-conditioning, away from the elevator and public areas, as high up (*psila*) as possible, and off the street. Check out the surroundings—is there a construction site nearby? A bar? Bus station? Airport? On Sunday and holy days, churches often broadcast the service over microphones in villages and small towns, and all ring their bells loudly. Even a braying donkey or crowing rooster can mar a bucolic setting at 5 AM. Sometimes older buildings are quieter due to their thicker walls, but if you're sensitive, the only guarantee for a peaceful night's sleep is a set of earplugs.

The very complete *Hellenic Traveling Pages*, a monthly publication available at most Greek bookstores, lists travel agencies; yacht brokers; bus, boat, and airplane schedules; and museum hours.

RESERVING A ROOM

🇬🇷 **Hellenic Chamber of Hotels** ✉ Stadiou 24, 10564 Athens ☎ 210/331-0022 through 210/331-0026 🖷 210/322-5449; open weekdays 8-2.
🇬🇷 **Guides** *Hellenic Traveling Pages* ✉ Info Publications, Pironos 51, 16341 Athens ☎ 210/994-0109 or 210/993-7551 🖷 210/993-6564.

RENTAL ROOMS

Most areas have pensions—usually clean, bright, and recently built. On islands in summer, owners wait for tourists at the harbor, and signs in English throughout villages indicate rooms available. The quality of rental rooms has improved enormously in recent years, with many featuring air-conditioning, a small TV set, or a small refrigerator—or all of these—in the room. Studios with a small kitchenette and separate living space are good choices for families. Around August 15, when it seems all Greeks go on vacation, even the most basic rooms are hard to locate, although you can query the tourist police or the municipal tourist office. In a pinch, owners may let you sleep on their roof for a small fee. On some islands the local rental room owners' association sets up an information booth. Few rooms are available in winter and early spring. Check the rooms first, for quality and location. Also, **make sure you feel comfortable with the owners if they live on the premises**; that inquisitive hostess feeding you warm goat milk may become overly chatty.

TRADITIONAL SETTLEMENTS

In an effort to provide tourist accommodations in traditional settings, the EOT has begun a restoration program, converting older buildings that reflect the local architecture into guesthouses. Some of the villages developed so far include Oia on Santorini; Vizitsa and Argalasti on Mt. Pelion; Mesta on Chios and nearby Psara island; Korischades in Evritania; Papingo in Epirus; Vathia in the Mani with its curious tower homes; and Monemvassia in the southern Peloponnese. EOT is devising a classification system for accommodations under the "rural tourism" category, including farmhouses and inns. These settlements and inns will be published in 2006 in a guide by Agrotouristiki, a private company in which EOT is the majority shareholder. The Greek Center for Rural Tourism also maintains lists of small inns, usually attached to farms, where you can stay and participate in activities from mushroom picking to rafting and cooking lessons.
🇬🇷 **Reservations & Information Agrotouristiki** ⊕ www.agrotour.gr. **Greek Center for Rural Tourism** ✉ Panepistimiou 10, 10671 Athens ☎ 210/364-4892 🖷 210/364-1653. **Greek Hotel and Cruise**

Reservation Center ☎ 800/736-5717 in the U.S., 714/641-3118 🖷 714/641-0303 ✉ Trigeta 48, 11745 Athens ☎ 210/937-0240 🖷 210/937-4400.

MAIL & SHIPPING

Letters and postcards take about 3 to 4 days to reach the United Kingdom, a week to 10 days for the United States, about 10 days for Australia and New Zealand. That's airmail. It takes even longer during August when postal staff is reduced, and during Christmas and Easter holidays. If what you're mailing is important, send it registered, which costs about €2.65 in Greece. For about €2.60, depending on the weight, you can send your letter "express"; this earns you a red sticker and faster local delivery. The post office also operates a courier service, EMS Express. Delivery to the continental United States takes about 2–3 days and costs €26.40. If you're planning on writing several letters, prepaid envelopes are convenient and cost €4.25 for five.

Post offices are open weekdays 7:30–2, although in city centers they may stay open in the evenings and on weekends. The main post offices in Athens and Piraeus are open weekdays 7:30 AM–9 PM, Saturday 7:30–2, and Sunday 9–1:30. The post offices at Athens International Airport and the Acropolis are open weekends, too. Throughout the country, mailboxes are yellow and sometimes divided into domestic and international containers; express boxes are red.

🗂 **Main post offices** ✉ Filonos 36, 18501 Piraeus ☎ 210/414-6101 ⊕ www.elta.gr ✉ Syntagma Sq. at Mitropoleos, Syntagma Sq., Athens ☎ 210/324-5970.

COURIERS

Within Greece, many services can get your items crosstown in a few hours or from a frontier island like Chios to Athens overnight. Costs depend on the distance covered and how fast you need your papers delivered. Rates start at about €5 for a simple intracity delivery.

🗂 Domestic Delivery **ACS** ✉ Leoforos Alexandras 23, Athens ☎ 210/646-0604 ⊕ www.acscourier.gr. **ELTA Courier** ✉ In most post office branches ☎ 800/118-3000 ⊕ www.eltacourier.gr.

OVERNIGHT SERVICES

Overnight service to the United States, United Kingdom, Canada, Australia, and New Zealand is now available almost everywhere in Greece. Outside cities, you usually need to take the package to the office yourself, and the reliability of the services varies. Overnight service from Athens to New York for documents up to 100 grams costs €25.

🗂 Major Services **DHL Worldwide Express** ✉ Filellinon 28, near Plaka, Athens ☎ 210/324-2327 office, 210/989-0000 24-hr customer service ⊕ www.dhl.gr; open weekdays 11-6, Saturday 11-3 (pickups only). **Federal Express** ✉ 31st km Varis-Koropiou Rd., Koropi ☎ 210/662-0222 ⊕ www.fedex.com/gr; open weekdays 9-6, Saturday 9-1:30.

POSTAL RATES

At this writing, airmail letters and postcards to destinations other than Europe and weighing up to 20 grams cost €0.65, and €1.15 for 50 grams (€0.60 and €1, respectively, to other European countries, including the United Kingdom).

RECEIVING MAIL

To receive letters when you're traveling around, have your mail addressed to "poste restante" and sent to any post office in Greece, where you can pick it up once you show your passport. Or have it mailed to American Express offices (Ermou 7, Athens 10563). The service is free for holders of American Express cards or traveler's checks. Other American Express offices are in Thessaloniki, Patras, Corfu, Rhodes, Santorini, Mykonos, Skiathos, and Heraklion in Crete.

🗂 **American Express** ✉ Ermou 7, 10563 Athens ☎ 210/322-3380 ⊕ www.americanexpress.com.

SHIPPING PARCELS

Send your important items registered. If sending a parcel, you must take it open to the post office for inspection. Bring brown butcher paper, tape, and string along, since the post office does not provide wrapping materials, although some cardboard packaging is sold at main branches. Packages take even longer to arrive than letters—"surface/air lift" means your parcel will need at least least two weeks to get to any destination.

MONEY MATTERS

Although costs have risen astronomically since Greece switched to the euro currency in 2002, the country will seem reasonably priced to travelers from the United States and Great Britain. Popular tourist resorts (including some of the islands) and the larger cities are markedly more expensive than the countryside. Though the price of eating in a restaurant has increased, you can still get a bargain. Hotels are generally moderately priced outside the major cities, and the extra cost of accommodations in a luxury hotel, compared to in an average hotel, often seems unwarranted.

Transportation is a good deal in Greece. Bus and train tickets are inexpensive, though renting a car is costly; there are relatively cheap—and slow—ferries to the islands, and express boats and hydrofoils that cost more. If your time is limited, domestic flights are a fair trade-off in cost and time saved, compared with sea and land travel.

Some sample prices: admission to archaeological sites: €3–€6; authentic Greek sponge: €8; a cup of coffee in a central city café: €2.60–€5 (Greek coffee is a little cheaper); beer: (500 ml) €2.80, in a bar €2.60–€6.50; soft drink: (can) €1.50, and in a café €2; spinach pie: €1.50; souvlaki: €1.90; grilled-cheese sandwich (tost): €2.60; taxi ride: about €25 from the airport to downtown Athens and €2.50 for a 2-km (1-mi) ride in the city center; local bus: €0.50; foreign newspaper: €2.50–€3.90.

Admission is free to most museums and archaeological sites on Sunday from November through March. Prices throughout this guide are given for adults. Substantially reduced fees are almost always available for children, students, and senior citizens. For information on taxes, *see* Taxes.

ATMS

ATMs are widely available throughout the country. Virtually all banks, including the National Bank of Greece (known as Ethniki), have machines that dispense money to Cirrus or Plus cardholders. You may find bank-sponsored ATMs at harbors and in airports as well. Other systems accepted include Visa, MasterCard, American Express, Diners Club, and Eurocard, but exchange and withdrawal rates vary, so shop around and check fees with your bank before leaving home. For use in Greece, your PIN must be four digits long. The word for PIN is pronounced "peen," and ATMs are called *alpha taf mi,* after the letters, or just *to mihanima,* "the machine." Machines usually let you complete the transaction in English, French, or German and seldom create problems, except Sunday night, when they sometimes run out of cash. For most machines, the minimum amount dispensed is €40. Sometimes an ATM may refuse to "read" your card. Don't panic; it's probably the machine. Try another bank.

CREDIT AND DEBIT CARDS

Should you use a credit card or a debit card when traveling? Both have benefits. A credit card allows you to delay payment and gives you certain rights as a consumer (⇨ Consumer Protection, *above*). A debit card, also known as a check card, deducts funds directly from your checking account and helps you stay within your budget. When you want to rent a car, though, you may still need an old-fashioned credit card.

Both types of plastic get you cash advances at ATMs worldwide if your card is properly programmed with your personal identification number (PIN). Both offer excellent, wholesale exchange rates. And both protect you against unauthorized use if the card is lost or stolen. Your liability is limited to $50, as long as you report the card missing. However, shop owners often give you a lower price if you pay cash rather than credit, because they want to avoid the credit card bank fees. Note that the Discover card is not widely accepted in Greece. The local Citibank, which issues Diners Club and MasterCard, can't cancel your cards but will pass on the message to the head offices of those cards.

Throughout this guide, the following abbreviations are used: **AE,** American Express; **DC,** Diners Club; **MC,** MasterCard; and **V,** Visa.

🔳 Reporting Lost Cards in the U.S. **American Express** ☎ 800/992-3404. **Diners Club** ☎ 800/234–

6377. **Discover** ☎ 800/347-2683. **MasterCard** ☎ 800/622-7747. **Visa** ☎ 800/847-2911.

🔲 Reporting Lost Cards in Greece **American Express** ☎ 00-800-44/127569 toll-free, 210/324-4975 through 210/324-4979. **Diners Club** ☎ 210/929-0200. **MasterCard** ☎ 210/929-0000. **Visa** ☎ 00-800-11/638-0304 toll-free.

CURRENCY

Greece's former national currency, the drachma, was replaced by the currency of the European Union, the euro (€), in 2002. Under the euro system, there are eight coins: 1 and 2 euros, plus 1, 2, 5, 10, 20, and 50 euro cents. Euros are pronounced "evros" in Greek; cents are known as "lepta." All coins have the euro value on one side; the other side has each country's unique national symbol. Greece's range from images of triremes to a depiction of the mythological Europa being abducted by Zeus transformed as a bull. Bills (banknotes) come in seven denominations: 5, 10, 20, 50, 100, 200, and 500 euros. Bills are the same for all EU countries.

CURRENCY EXCHANGE

For the most favorable rates, **change money through banks.** Although ATM transaction fees may be higher abroad than at home, ATM rates are excellent because they're based on wholesale rates offered only by major banks. You won't do as well at exchange booths in airports or rail and bus stations, in hotels, in restaurants, or in stores. To avoid lines at airport exchange booths, get a bit of local currency before you leave home.

Off Syntagma Square in Athens, the National Bank of Greece, Citibank, Alpha Bank, Commercial Bank, Eurobank, and Pireos Bank have automated machines that change your foreign currency into euros. When you shop, remember that it's always easier to bargain on prices when paying in cash instead of by credit card.

If you do use an exchange service, good options are American Express and Eurochange. Watch daily fluctuations and shop around. Daily exchange rates are prominently displayed in banks and listed in the *International Herald Tribune.* In Athens, around Syntagma Square is the best place to look. Those that operate after business hours have lower rates and a higher commission. You can also change money at post offices in even the most remote parts of Greece; commissions are lower than at banks, starting at about €2 for amounts up to €300. To avoid lines at airport exchange booths, **get a bit of local currency before you leave home.** At this writing the average exchange rate for the euro was €1.20 to the U.S. dollar, €1.42 to the Canadian dollar, €0.68 to the pound sterling, €1.60 to the Australian dollar, and €1.71 to the New Zealand dollar.

🔲 Exchange Services **International Currency Express** ✉ 427 N. Camden Dr., Suite F, Beverly Hills, CA 90210 ☎ 888/278-6628 orders 🖷 310/278-6410 ⊕ www.foreignmoney.com. **Travel Ex Currency Services** ☎ 800/287-7362 orders and retail locations ⊕ www.travelex.com.

🔲 Athens Exchange Services **American Express Travel Related Services** ✉ Ermou 7, Syntagma Sq. ☎ 210/322-3380; open weekdays 8:30-4, Saturday 8:30-1:30. **Eurochange** ✉ Karageorgi Servias 2, Syntagma Sq. ☎ 210/331-2462 ◷ Daily 8 AM-11 PM ✉ Omonias 10, Omonia Sq. ☎ 210/523-4816 ◷ Daily 8 AM-10 PM. **National Bank of Greece** ✉ Karageorgi Servias 2, Syntagma Sq. ☎ 210/334-8015; open Monday-Thursday 8-2 and 3:15-5:15, Friday 2:45-5:15, Saturday 9-3, Sunday 9-1; extended foreign exchange.

TRAVELER'S CHECKS

Traveler's checks are the best way to carry your money into Greece, keeping your funds safe until you change them into euros. As far as paying with checks, it depends on where you're headed. It's important to **remember that Greece is still a cash society, so plan accordingly.** If you're going to rural areas and small towns, go with cash; traveler's checks are best used in cities, though even in Athens most tavernas won't take them. Lost or stolen checks can usually be replaced within 24 hours. To ensure a speedy refund, buy your own traveler's checks—don't let someone else pay for them: irregularities like this can cause delays. The person who bought the checks should make the call to request a refund.

PACKING

Outside Athens, Greek dress tends to be middle of the road—you won't see torn jeans or extremely expensive suits, though locals tend to dress up for nightclubs and bouzoukià. In summer bring lightweight, casual clothing and good walking shoes. A light sweater or jacket, or a shawl, is a must for cool evenings, especially in the mountains. There's no need for rain gear in high summer, but don't forget sunglasses and a sun hat. Be prepared for cooler weather and some rain in spring and fall, and in winter add a warm coat.

Casual attire is acceptable everywhere except in the most expensive restaurants in large cities, but you should be prepared to dress conservatively when visiting churches or monasteries. It's not appropriate to show a lot of bare arm and leg; men wearing shorts must cover up as well, as must women in pants, in some stricter monasteries.

For dimly lighted icons in churches and moonless island walks, a small flashlight comes in handy. It's a good idea to bring zip-closing plastic bags, mosquito repellent for more verdant areas, moist towelettes, a roll of transparent tape, and a pocket calculator, all indispensable. A pair of opera glasses or binoculars can greatly enhance the appreciation of an archaeological site or give a better view of wall paintings in a church, for example.

In your carry-on luggage, pack an extra pair of eyeglasses or contact lenses and enough of any medication you take to last a few days longer than the entire trip. You may also ask your doctor to write a spare prescription using the drug's generic name, as brand names may vary from country to country. In luggage to be checked, **never pack prescription drugs, valuables, or undeveloped film.** And don't forget to carry with you the addresses of offices that handle refunds of lost traveler's checks. Check *Fodor's How to Pack* (available at online retailers and bookstores everywhere) for more tips.

To avoid customs and security delays, carry medications in their original packaging. Don't pack any sharp objects in your carry-on luggage, including knives of any size or material, scissors, nail clippers, and corkscrews, or anything else that might arouse suspicion.

To avoid having your checked luggage chosen for hand inspection, don't cram bags full. The U.S. Transportation Security Administration suggests packing shoes on top and placing personal items you don't want touched in clear plastic bags.

CHECKING LUGGAGE

You're allowed to carry aboard one bag and one personal article, such as a purse or a laptop computer. Make sure what you carry on fits under your seat or in the overhead bin. Get to the gate early, so you can board as soon as possible, before the overhead bins fill up.

Baggage allowances vary by carrier, destination, and ticket class. On international flights, you're usually allowed to check two bags weighing up to 70 pounds (32 kilograms) each, although a few airlines allow checked bags of up to 88 pounds (40 kilograms) in first class. Some international carriers don't allow more than 66 pounds (30 kilograms) per bag in business class and 44 pounds (20 kilograms) in economy. If you're flying to or through the United Kingdom, your luggage cannot exceed 70 pounds (32 kilograms) per bag. On domestic flights, the limit is usually 50 to 70 pounds (23 to 32 kilograms) per bag. In general, carry-on bags shouldn't exceed 40 pounds (18 kilograms). Most airlines won't accept bags that weigh more than 100 pounds (45 kilograms) on domestic or international flights. Expect to pay a fee for baggage that exceeds weight limits. Check baggage restrictions with your carrier before you pack.

Airline liability for baggage is limited to $2,500 per person on flights within the United States. On international flights it amounts to $9.07 per pound or $20 per kilogram for checked baggage (roughly $640 per 70-pound bag), with a maximum of $634.90 per piece, and $400 per passenger for unchecked baggage. You can buy additional coverage at check-in for about $10 per $1,000 of coverage, but it often excludes a rather extensive list of items, shown on your airline ticket.

Before departure, itemize your bags' contents and their worth, and label the bags with your name, address, and phone number. (If you use your home address, cover it so potential thieves can't see it readily.) Include a label inside each bag and **pack a copy of your itinerary.** At check-in, make sure each bag is correctly tagged with the destination airport's three-letter code. Because some checked bags will be opened for hand inspection, the U.S. Transportation Security Administration recommends that you leave luggage unlocked or use the plastic locks offered at check-in. TSA screeners place an inspection notice inside searched bags, which are re-sealed with a special lock.

If your bag has been searched and contents are missing or damaged, file a claim with the TSA Consumer Response Center as soon as possible. If your bags arrive damaged or fail to arrive at all, file a written report with the airline before leaving the airport.

It's a good idea to mark your bags with a bright ribbon or a similar marker, since few Greek airports check passengers' baggage claim checks against luggage upon exit. Baggage carts are limited at train stations and nonexistent at bus stations. In the smaller airports baggage carts are usually free but low in numbers. At Athens International Airport, baggage carts cost €1 and are found in the baggage claim area.

Always ask if your luggage is going through to the final destination; sometimes you have to pick up your bags and haul them through customs depending on where your plane stops (i.e., returning from Athens, you might have to get your luggage at the baggage claim in Chicago and clear customs because it's your first U.S. point of entry, then get back on the plane for Los Angeles).

⚑ Complaints U.S. Transportation Security Administration Contact Center ☎ 866/289-9673 ⊕ www.tsa.gov.

PASSPORTS & VISAS

When traveling internationally, carry your passport even if you don't need one. Not only is it the best form of ID, but it's also being required more and more. **Make two photocopies of the data page** (one for someone at home and another for you, carried separately from your passport). If you lose your passport, promptly call the nearest embassy or consulate and the local police.

U.S. passport applications for children under age 14 require consent from both parents or legal guardians; both parents must appear together to sign the application. If only one parent appears, he or she must submit a written statement from the other parent authorizing passport issuance for the child. A parent with sole authority must present evidence of it when applying; acceptable documentation includes the child's certified birth certificate listing only the applying parent, a court order specifically permitting this parent's travel with the child, or a death certificate for the nonapplying parent. Application forms and instructions are available on the Web site of the U.S. State Department's Bureau of Consular Affairs (⊕ travel.state.gov).

ENTERING GREECE

All U.S., Canadian, Australian, and New Zealand citizens, even infants, need only a valid passport to enter Greece for stays of up to 90 days. If you leave after 90 days and don't have a visa extension, you will be fined anywhere from €130 to €590 (depending on how long you overstay) by Greek airport officials, who are not flexible on this issue. Worse, you must provide *hartosima* (revenue stamps) for the documents, which you don't want to have to run around and find as your flight is boarding. U.K. citizens, like all EU nationals, need a passport but can stay indefinitely.

PASSPORT OFFICES

The best time to apply for a passport or to renew is in fall and winter. Before any trip, check your passport's expiration date, and, if necessary, renew it as soon as possible. (Some countries won't allow you to enter on a passport that's due to expire in six months or less, but this doesn't seem to be a problem in Greece.)

⚑ Canadian Citizens Passport Office ⊠ To mail in applications: 70 Cremazie St., Gatineau, Québec J8Y

3P2 ☎ 800/567-6868 or 819/994-3500 ⊕ www.ppt.gc.ca.

🇬🇧 **U.K. Citizens U.K. Passport Service** ☎ 0870/521-0410 ⊕ www.passport.gov.uk.

🇺🇸 **U.S. Citizens National Passport Information Center** ☎ 877/487-2778, 888/874-7793 TDD/TTY ⊕ travel.state.gov.

RESTROOMS

In Greece, be prepared to find everything from a ceramic hole in the floor at a public school to gleaming Italian fixtures in a nightclub. Restrooms are getting better and are downright luxurious in some nicer hotels, restaurants, and bars. But the standard of cleanliness and the state of repair vary tremendously. Out in the country, as a rule, the bathrooms tend to be worse, though you never know. The usually subterranean public toilets, such as those in parks and on main squares, are dirty, so go to a restaurant, hotel, or bar, or use one of the new, self-cleaning booths installed near parks and stadiums. In bus and train stations, attendants hand you a few sheets of toilet paper; leave €0.50 on their plate. You can walk into any large establishment, use their bathroom, and leave, especially if you are discreet. Also note that in Greece small waste bins are used for toilet paper and tampons, as a way of avoiding sewer blockages; it's best to abide by this rule. Always carry extra toilet paper, because many places don't provide any or it runs out. Gas stations don't have restrooms for the public, but on the highways you can stop at restaurant-convenience stores. You are expected to buy a snack or souvenir, but again, it's not necessary.

SAFETY

Greece is still one of the safest countries in Europe. Even Athens has a low crime rate, but the number of thefts, burglaries, and pickpocketing incidents at train and bus stations has gone up substantially in the past few years, and Greeks are starting to install alarms and lock their doors at night. You still see people sitting at cafés with their handbag carelessly dangling over chairs, or women and elderly people walking home late at night. If you take the normal precautions of carrying your money in a concealed security pouch, and if you avoid isolated places at night, you should have little problem. After hours, many ATMs require that you use your card to enter a locked glass vestibule; if the machine is unprotected, make sure it's well lighted. Leave immediately if someone suspicious starts lurking about. If you feel unsure about the safety of an area, ask your hotel before setting out. For example, crime has increased around Omonia Square in Athens, because of the large transient population that congregates there.

Don't wear a money belt or a waist pack, both of which peg you as a tourist. Distribute your cash and any valuables (including your credit cards and passport) between a deep front pocket, an inside jacket or vest pocket, and a hidden money pouch. Do not reach for the money pouch once you're in public.

Try to blend in with the Greeks: walk as if you know where you're going, and don't openly carry a map or a foreign newspaper.

LOCAL SCAMS

Men in Athens around Syntagma or Omonia squares should be careful of any stranger that tries to talk them into going to a local bar. Here, the unsuspecting foreigner will order drinks under the encouragement of hostesses hired by the establishment without realizing these cocktails are astronomically expensive. Hesitation in paying your whopping bill may result in uncomfortable encounters. Seek a policeman or call the tourist police (☎ 171).

WOMEN IN GREECE

If you carry a purse, choose one with a zipper and a thick strap that you can drape across your body; adjust the length so that the purse sits in front of you at or above hip level. (Don't wear a money belt or a waist pack.) Store only enough money in the purse to cover casual spending. Distribute the rest of your cash and any valuables between deep front pockets, inside jacket or vest pockets, and a concealed money pouch.

In general, women traveling alone are safe in Greece, though Greek men will try to talk to them, especially if they look foreign.

It's best to do as the Greek women do and ignore the amorous overtures, which are more annoying than threatening; responding will only be interpreted as a sign that you're interested. If you feel threatened, don't hesitate to shout; this will be enough to scare off most offenders. Greeks, especially in Athens, where people are out until all hours, will usually come to your aid. It's best to use common sense and avoid walking through parks or deserted parts of the city very late at night. If you are taking a taxi at night, the driver won't usually pick up a male passenger; if he does, he is obligated to ask your permission.

SENIOR-CITIZEN TRAVEL

Despite the dearth of facilities at hotels, museums, and archaeological sites for those with impaired movement, traveling in Greece can be quite pleasurable. Elders are treated with respect: most Greeks still take care of their parents at home, and crimes against the elderly are infrequent. Most Greeks—even taxi drivers—go out of their way to make sure older people receive good treatment.

To qualify for age-related discounts, **mention your senior-citizen status up front** when purchasing tickets—whether to enter a pay beach, see a movie, or visit an archaeological site. Greece does not have senior discounts for hotels or restaurants, but does for just about everything else, including admission fees and public transportation. When renting a car, **ask about promotional car-rental discounts,** which can be cheaper than senior-citizen rates.

🎓 Educational Programs **Elderhostel** ✉ 11 Ave. de Lafayette, Boston, MA 02111 ☎ 877/426–8056, 978/323–4141 international callers, 877/426–2167 TTY 📠 877/426–2166 ⊕ www.elderhostel.org. **Interhostel** ✉ University of New Hampshire, 6 Garrison Ave., Durham, NH 03824 ☎ 800/733–9753 or 603/862–1147 📠 603/862–1113 ⊕ www.learn.unh.edu.

SHOPPING

Because of hefty value-added taxes (13% or 19%, depending on the area), most items in Greece, especially electric appliances and clothing, cost more than in the United States and Canada, though Greece does have inexpensive shoes, furs, and leather goods. Good gift ideas are the natural Kalymnos sponges; flokati rugs made from long-haired goat wool; handicrafts such as embroidery, ceramics, and kilims; *komboloia* (worry beads) in plastic, wood, and onyx; and blue-and-white amulets that protect against *mati* (the evil eye). Objects made of fragrant olive wood—from bowls to sculptures—can be very attractive. Old jewelry and textiles, which are getting rather expensive, can still be a good deal and an adventure to track down. Leather bags and sandals and heavy wool sweaters (and fisherman's caps) are popular; some may be good buys, but some may soon fall apart. Take your time and inspect the seams and stitches before buying. Lightweight sundresses may look wonderful on the hanger in a store, but they're often made of flimsy fabrics—beware their transparency in the bright Greek sunlight.

Some of the goods you may want to purchase in Greece are inspired by the country's ancient civilization. Reproductions of early bronzes, Cycladic figurines, and Geometric, Corinthian, and Athenian vase paintings are ubiquitous. Some are poorly made and some feature rude subjects, but others are charming and even of museum quality. Certified museum copies are marked with a small seal, and are sold at museum shops as well as online (⊕ www. museumshop.gr).

What is cheaper in Greece is silver and gold jewelry, often original and unusual pieces. In some stores, chains are sold by the gram. Always bargain in tourist shops and with street vendors (except for sponges—prices are set by the government), and always get a receipt from shops. In an attempt to diminish tax fraud, the government heavily fines buyers who walk out of a store without proof of purchase. Most stores do not give you a cash refund, but they may give you a credit slip; they are liable if the item you purchased is defective. Pay attention when buying bargain items, since stores rarely allow exchanges or grant refunds during sales. Traditional sale periods run for about a month in January and July.

KEY DESTINATIONS

A delightful institution in Greece is the *laiki* (open-air market), which offers fresh produce at prices lower than in produce stores, as well as items sold by migrants, such as linen tablecloths (sold by the meter), caviar, and Russian lacquered dolls. Every town has a laiki, and big cities like Athens have several a day in different neighborhoods. In Athens, the main shopping areas are the Ermou pedestrian zone off Syntagma, the Stadiou–Panepistimiou corridor linking Syntagma and Omonia, and the ritzy Kolonaki district near the center. Plaka has mostly tourist shops, but their jewelers will go quite low on gold and silver prices. For icons, try the side streets around the Metropolitan Cathedral. In Thessaloniki, the longest shopping street is Tsimiski, and on the islands, shops are usually clustered off the main square and near the harbor.

SMART SOUVENIRS

Handicrafts such as flokati rugs, embroideries, hand-painted ceramics, icons, and wood paintings are all souvenirs worth seeking out in Greece. Knowing which of the numerous retailers in central Athens offer a good deal isn't easy, but it's definitely worth shopping around and bargaining down on the initial price you are offered. For quality ceramics, pottery ware, and icons, try the Center of Hellenic Tradition. The National Welfare Organization of Arts & Crafts shop Oikotechnia has a great selection of flokati rugs, worry beads, and other handicrafts.

🚩 Sources **Center of Hellenic Tradition** ✉ Mitropoleos 59, inside arcade, Plaka, Athens ☎ 210/321-3023. **Oikotechnia** ✉ Filellinon 14 Syntagma Sq., Athens ☎ 210/325-0240.

WATCH OUT

Note that the export of antiquities from Greece is forbidden. If any such articles are found in a traveler's luggage, they will be confiscated and the individual will be liable for prosecution. You are required to have an export permit (not normally given if the piece is of any value) for antiques and Byzantine icons, but replicas can be bought fairly cheaply, although even these require a certificate stating they are copies.

Many travel agencies or the Union of Official Guides can provide guides for individuals or groups, starting at about €90, including taxes for a four-hour tour of the Acropolis and its museum. Hire only those guides licensed by EOT, which means they have successfully completed a two-year state program. Travel agencies snatch up the best guides for their longer tours, so in general, those who freelance in high season at sights like the Acropolis and the National Archaeological Museum may be competent but are not of the same caliber. Talk to the guide a bit to see how articulate he or she is in English. Does the guide recite measurements in a monotone or enthusiastically give you all the juicy details of Zeus's peccadilloes? Trust your instincts and agree on the price and length of the tour beforehand.

🚩 **Union of Official Guides** ✉ Apollonos 9A, Plaka, Athens ☎ 210/322-9705 or 210/322-0090 📠 210/923-6884.

SPORTS & THE OUTDOORS

BIKING

Biking (⇨ Bike Travel) is no fun on crowded city streets but can be a pleasure on the islands and in the countryside. Resort areas usually have at least one bicycle rental shop, but helmets are seldom provided. Greek drivers still aren't used to seeing cyclists on the road, which can make bicycling occasionally nerve-racking. Most adventure travel agencies offer mountain-biking tours, and depending on the difficulty level, these may be your best bet.

BIRD-WATCHING

The Hellenic Ornithological Society arranges two- and three-day trips to important bird habitats, such as the Dounavi Delta, the Vikos Gorge, and the Messolonghi wetlands.

🚩 **Hellenic Ornithological Society** ✉ Vasiliou Irakleiou 24, Athens ☎ 210/822-7937 📠 210/822-8704 ⊕ www.ornithologiki.gr.

HIKING & MOUNTAIN BIKING

The country has plenty of rugged terrain for serious hiking and mountaineering. The Alpine Club of Athens arranges hikes in Attica and throughout the mainland to places like Evritania and Arcadia, as well as adventure camps for children in summer. The Hellenic Federation of Mountaineering & Climbing can supply details on refuges, mountain paths, and contact numbers for local hiking clubs. Treks throughout Greece are organized by adventure travel agencies, which also offer kayaking, rafting, mountain-biking, and camping trips. Anavasi publishes an excellent series of maps in print, CD-ROM, and GPS formats.

F Associations **Alpine Club of Athens** ⊠ Ermou 64 and Aiolou, 5th fl., Monastiraki, 10563 Athens ☎ 210/321-2355 or 210/321-2429 🖷 01/324-4789. **Anavasi** ⊠ Stoa Arsakiou 6A, 10564 Athens ☎ 210/321-8104 ⊕ www.anavasi.gr **M** Panepistimio. **Hellenic Federation of Mountaineering & Climbing** ⊠ Milioni 5, Kolonaki, 10673 Athens ☎ 210/364-5904 or 210/363-6617 🖷 210/364-2687 ⊕ www.sport.gov.gr.

F Adventure Travel Agencies **Cycle Greece** ⊠ Falirou 15, 11742 Athens ☎ 210/921-8160 ⊕ www.cyclegreece.gr. **F-Zein** ⊠ Ethnikis Antistaseos 103, Neo Psihiko, 15451 Athens ☎ 210/921-6285 or 210/923-0263 🖷 210/922-9995 ⊕ www.ezjourneys.gr. **Trekking Hellas** ⊠ Filellinon 7, 3rd fl., Syntagma Sq., 10557 Athens ☎ 210/331-0323 through 210/331-0326 🖷 210/324-4548 ⊕ www.trekking.gr ⊠ Tsimiski 71, 54622 Thessaloniki ☎ 2310/222128 🖷 2310/222129.

HORSEBACK RIDING
The helpful Hellenic Equestrian Federation provides a list of riding clubs throughout the country. Some resorts offer horseback riding, often in cooperation with the local club or riding center. The price is about €25 an hour per person.

F **Hellenic Equestrian Federation** ⊠ Dimitriou Ralli 37, Maroussi, 15124 Athens ☎ 210/614-1986 through 210/614-1988 🖷 210/614-1859 ⊕ www.equestrian.org.gr.

RAFTING & KAYAKING
Rivers in Greece run through some wild and beautiful scenery, especially in the mountains, and a trip on the water is one way to explore the countryside. The Alpin Club organizes trips, including transportation, guides, and equipment, to rivers throughout Greece; the price runs €115

for a weekend. Trekking Hellas and F-Zein (⇨ Hiking & Mountain Biking, *above*) also offer many white-water expeditions.

F **Alpin Club** ⊠ Adrianiou 42, Neo Psihiko, 11525 Athens ☎ 210/675-3514 or 210/675-3515 🖷 210/675-3516 ⊕ www.alpinclub.gr.

SAILING & WINDSURFING
Greece is a glorious place to sail or windsurf. The Hellenic Yachting Federation can provide lists of clubs with equipment and lessons available for both sailing and windsurfing. The best windsurfing beaches in Attica are Schinias, Varkiza, Vouliagmeni, Rafina, Loutsa, and Anavyssos, and in the rest of Greece: Ftelia in Mykonos; Prassonissi in Rhodes; Loutra Kaiafa in the Peloponnese; Mikri Vigla in Naxos; and New Golden Beach in Paros, the site of windsurfing world championships.

Those who have a diploma for sailing on the open sea can legally rent a sailboat (without a captain, if two people on board are licensed); rentals range from about €200 to €880 a day, depending on the size and age of the boat, season, and whether a skipper is included. Charter companies usually provide suggested sailing routes. Most have branch offices at designated marinas along each of these routes, and sometimes you can avoid Athens altogether by picking up your boat at these stations. Of the places listed below, Kyriacoulis Mediterranean Cruises runs a sailing school, Offshore Escape, with 8- and 10-week courses for beginners, as well as a refresher course for licensed sailors.

F **Ghiolman Yachts** ⊠ Filellinon 7, Syntagma, 10557 Athens ☎ 210/323-3696 or 210/323-0330 🖷 210/322-3251 ⊕ www.ghiolman.com. **Hellenic Yachting Federation** ⊠ Leoforos Poseidonos 51, Moschato, 18344 Athens ☎ 210/940-4825 🖷 210/940-4829 ⊕ www.eio.gr. **Kyriacoulis Mediterranean Cruises** ⊠ Alimou 7, Alimos, 17455 Athens ☎ 210/988-6187 through 210/988-6191 🖷 210/984-7296 ⊕ www.kiriacoulis.com. **Sun Yachting** ⊠ Leoforos Poseidonos 21, Kalamaki, 17455 Athens ☎ 210/983-7312 🖷 210/983-7528. **Vernicos Yachts** ⊠ Leoforos Poseidonos 11, Kalamaki, 17455 Athens ☎ 210/989-6000 🖷 210/985-0130 ⊕ www.vernicos.com.

SCUBA DIVING

Scuba diving is heavily restricted to protect underwater artifacts. It is forbidden to dive at night or remove anything from the sea floor. Areas where limited diving is permitted include Corfu, Chalkidiki, Mykonos, and Rhodes. A travel agent can steer you to a supervised dive trip, or you can call the Union of Diving Centers in Athens for advice on diving centers that best meet your needs. Some approved diving centers worth checking out are listed below. They may offer courses for various levels, equipment rentals and service, guides for hire, and trips of various lengths. Remember that any school dispensing diplomas should be recognized by the Greek state.

🎇 **Aegean Dive Center** ⊠ Pandoras 42 and Zamanou 53, 16674 Glyfada ☎ 210/894-5409 🖷 210/898-1120 ⊕ www.adc.gr. **Mediterranean Dive Center** ⊠ Vasilissis Pavlou 96, Kastella, 18533 Piraeus ☎ 210/412-5376, 6944/503-257 cell. **Scuba Diving Club of Vouliagmeni** ⊠ Leoforos Poseidonos, 16671 Ormos Vouliagmeni ☎🖷 210/896-1914. **Union of Diving Centers** ☎ 210/411-8909 or 210/411-9967.

TENNIS

There are tennis clubs in most large cities and island resorts. Call the Hellenic Tennis Federation for information on the clubs, from which you can rent courts by the hour (often included on EOT beaches), or check with your hotel concierge to help you find one that admits nonmembers.

🎇 **Hellenic Tennis Federation** ⊠ Ymittou 267, Pangrati, 11636 Athens ☎ 210/894-8900 🖷 210/865-2908.

STUDENTS IN GREECE

For students, Greece is an inexpensive destination. Not only are museums and archaeological sites free for EU members and cheaper for non-EU students (you must have an ISIC card), but student and youth rates are offered on public transportation as well as domestic and EU flights. Many travel agencies catering to students are on Filellinon and Nikis streets in Athens, off Syntagma Square.

Rented rooms and camping are the most inexpensive lodging—in summer, you can rent roof space if you've brought a sleep-

ing bag. Take advantage of souvlaki stands (the filling fast food of Greece), local tavernas, and the open-air market; convenience stores in tourist areas are wildly overpriced. Finally, watch expenditures in bars—in most, an alcoholic drink costs at least €8.

TRAVEL AGENCIES

To save money, **look into deals available through student-oriented travel agencies.** To qualify you'll need a bona fide student ID card. Members of international student groups are also eligible. A good agency to try, especially if you haven't managed to get your ISIC card and need a student pass for Greece, is International Student and Youth Travel Service.

🎇 In Greece **Himalaya** ⊠ Filellinon 4, 4th fl., 10557 Athens ☎ 210/322-5159 🖷 210/325-1474. **International Student and Youth Travel Service** ⊠ Nikis 11, 1st fl., 10557 Athens ☎ 210/323-3767 or 210/322-1267 🖷 01/322-1531. **USIT/ETOS Student and Youth Travel** ⊠ Filellinon 1, 10557 Athens ☎ 210/323-0483 or 210/323-8445 ⊕ www.usitetos.gr.

🎇 IDs & Services **STA Travel** ⊠ 10 Downing St., New York, NY 10014 ☎ 800/777-0112 24-hr service center, 212/627-3111 🖷 212/627-3387 ⊕ www.sta.com. **Travel Cuts** ⊠ 187 College St., Toronto, Ontario M5T 1P7, Canada ☎ 800/592-2887 in the U.S., 866/246-9762 or 416/979-2406 in Canada 🖷 416/979-8167 ⊕ www.travelcuts.com.

🎇 **Student Tours AESU Travel** ⊠ 3922 Hickory Ave., Baltimore, MD 21211 ☎ 800/638-7640 or 410/366-5494 🖷 410/366-6999 ⊕ www.aesu.com. **Contiki Holidays** ⊠ 801 E. Kastella Ave., 3rd fl., Anaheim, CA 92805 ☎ 888/266-8454 🖷 714/935-2579 ⊕ www.contiki.com.

TAXES

Taxes are always included in the stated price, unless otherwise noted. The Greek airport tax (€12 for travel within the EU and €22 outside the EU) is included in your ticket (as are a further €12.15 terminal facility charge and a €3.15 security charge), and the 8%–12% hotel tax rate (⇨ Lodging) is usually included in the quoted price.

VALUE-ADDED TAX

Value-added tax, 4.5% for books and about 19% (6%–13% on the Aegean islands) for almost everything else, called

FPA (pronounced "fee-pee-ah") by Greeks, is included in the cost of most consumer goods and services, except groceries. If you are a citizen of a non-EU country, you may get a V.A.T. refund on products (except alcohol, cigarettes, or toiletries) worth €117 or more bought in Greece from licensed stores that usually display a Tax-Free Shopping sticker in their window. Ask the shop to complete a refund form called a Tax-Free Check for you, which you show at Greek Customs.

Have the form stamped like any customs form by customs officials when you leave the country or, if you're visiting several European Union countries, when you leave the EU. Be ready to show customs officials what you've bought (pack purchases together, in your carry-on luggage); budget extra time for this. After you're through passport control, take the form to a refund-service counter for an on-the-spot refund, or mail it back in the pre-addressed envelope given to you at the store.

A refund service can save you some hassle, for a fee. Global Refund is a Europe-wide service with 190,000 affiliated stores and more than 700 refund counters—located at every major airport and border crossing. The service issues refunds in the form of cash, check, or credit-card adjustment, minus a processing fee. If you don't have time to wait at the refund counter, you can mail in the form instead.

V.A.T. Refunds Global Refund Canada Box 2020, Station Main, Brampton, Ontario L6T 3S3 800/993-4313 905/791-9078 www.globalrefund.com.

TAXIS

In Greece, as everywhere, unscrupulous taxi drivers sometimes try to take advantage of out-of-towners, using such tricks as rigging meters or tacking on a few zeros to the metered price. All taxis must display the rate card; it's usually on the dashboard, though taxis outside the big cities don't bother. Ask your hotel concierge or owner before engaging a taxi what the fare to your destination ought to be. It should cost between €20 and €25 from the airport (depending on the traffic) to the

Athens city center (this includes tolls) and about €12 from Piraeus port to the center. It does not matter how many are in your party (the driver isn't supposed to squeeze in more than four); the metered price remains the same. Taxis must give passengers a receipt if requested.

Make sure that the driver turns on the meter to Tarifa 1 (€0.30), unless it's between midnight and 5 AM, when Tarifa 2 (€0.60) applies. Remember that the meter starts at €1 and the minimum is €2.50. A surcharge applies when taking a taxi to and from the airport (€3) and from (but not to) ports and bus and train stations (€0.80). There is also a surcharge during holiday periods, about €0.30 and for each item of baggage if it's over 10 kilograms (22 pounds). If you suspect a driver is overcharging, demand to be taken to the police station; this usually brings them around. Complaints about service or overcharging should be directed to the tourist police; at the Athens airport, contact the Taxi Syndicate information desk. When calling to complain, be sure to report the driver's license number.

Taxi rates are inexpensive compared to fares in most other European countries, mainly because they operate on the jitney system, indicating willingness to pick up others by blinking their headlights or slowing down. Would-be passengers shout their destination as the driver cruises past. Don't be alarmed if your driver picks up other passengers (although he should ask your permission first). Drivers don't pick up anyone if you are a woman traveling alone at night. Each new party pays full fare for the distance he or she has traveled.

A taxi is free when a sign (ELEFTHERO) is up or the light is on at night. Once he indicates he is free, the driver cannot refuse your destination, so get in the taxi before you give an address. He also must wait for you up to 15 minutes, if requested, although most drivers would be unhappy with such a demand. Drivers are familiar with the major hotels, but it's good to know a landmark near your hotel and to have the address and phone written in

Greek. If all else fails, the driver can call the hotel from his mobile phone or a kiosk.

On islands and in the countryside, the meter may often be on Tarifa 2 (outside city limits). Do not assume taxis will be waiting at smaller island airports when your flight lands; often, they have all been booked by arriving locals. If you get stuck, try to join a passenger going in your direction, or call your hotel to arrange transportation.

When you're taking an early-morning flight, it's a good idea to reserve a radio taxi the night before (€2.50 surcharge, €1.50 for immediate response). These taxis are usually quite reliable and punctual; if you're not staying in a hotel, the local tourist police can give you some phone numbers for companies.

🔢 **Complaints in Athens Taxi Syndicate** ☎ 210/353-0575. **Tourist police** ☎ 171.

TELEPHONES

Greece's phone system has improved markedly. You can direct dial in most better hotels, but there is usually a huge surcharge, so use your calling card or a card telephone in the lobby or on the street. You can make calls from most large establishments, kiosks, card phones (which are everywhere), and from the local office of the Greek telephone company, known as OTE ("oh-*teh*").

Establishments may include several phone numbers rather than a central switchboard. Also, they now use cell (mobile) phones, indicated by an area code that begins with 69. Cell phone usage in Greece is very high and relatively cheap for those on contract with a carrier.

Doing business over the phone in Greece can be frustrating—the lines always seem to be busy, and English-speaking operators and clerks are few. You may also find people too busy to address your problem—the independent-minded Greeks are *not* very service-conscious. It is far better to develop a relationship with someone, for example a travel agent, to get information about train schedules and the like, or to go in person and ask for information face-to-face. Though OTE has updated its phone

system in recent years, it may still take you several attempts to get through when calling from an island or the countryside.

AREA & COUNTRY CODES

The country code for Greece is 30.

CELL PHONES

If your cell phone works in Greece and you decide to take it with you, ask your provider if it has a connection agreement with a Greek mobile carrier. If yes, manually switch your phone to that network's settings as soon as you arrive.

If you're traveling with a companion or group of friends and plan to use your cell phones to communicate with each other, buying a local prepaid connection kit (like Cosmote's What's Up, Vodafone's A La Carte and CU, or Tim's F2G or For All) is far cheaper for voice calls or sending text messages than using your regular provider.

DIRECTORY & OPERATOR ASSISTANCE

For Greek directory information, dial 11888; many operators speak English. In most cases you must give the surname of the shop or restaurant proprietor to be able to get the phone number of the establishment; tourist police are more helpful for tracking down the numbers of such establishments. For operator-assisted calls and international directory information in English, dial the International Exchange at ☎ 161. In most cases, there is a three-minute minimum charge for operator-assisted station-to-station and person-to-person connections.

Pronunciations for the numbers in Greek are: one ("*eh*-na"); two ("*dthee*-oh"); three ("*tree*-a"); four ("*tess*-ehr-a"); five ("*pen*-de"); six ("*eh*-ksee"); seven ("ef-*ta*"); eight ("och-*toh*"); nine ("eh-*nay*-ah"); ten ("*dtheh*-ka").

INTERNATIONAL CALLS

When dialing Greece from the United States or Canada, you would first dial 011, then 30, the country code. From continental Europe or the United Kingdom, you dial 0030. To call the United States or Canada from Greece, you dial 001 as the country code, and then the area code and number. The code for the United Kingdom is 0044, for Australia 0061, and for New Zealand 0064.

LOCAL CALLS

All telephone numbers in Greece have 10 digits. Area codes now have to be dialed even when you are dialing locally within a region. For cell phones, dial both the cell prefix (a four-digit number beginning with 69) and the telephone number from anywhere in Greece.

You can make local calls from the public OTE phones using phone cards, not coins, or from kiosks, which have metered telephones and allow you to make local or international calls. The dial ring will be familiar to English speakers: two beats, the second much longer than the first.

LONG-DISTANCE SERVICES

AT&T, MCI, and Sprint access codes make calling long-distance relatively convenient, but you may find the local access number blocked in many hotel rooms. First ask the hotel operator to connect you. If the hotel operator balks, ask for an international operator, or dial the international operator yourself. One way to improve your odds of getting connected to your long-distance carrier is to travel with more than one company's calling card (a hotel may block Sprint, for example, but not MCI). If all else fails, call from a pay phone. If you are traveling for a longer period of time, consider renting a cell phone from a local company.

You can also make international calls from card telephones or metered kiosk phones.

🗐 Long-Distance Carriers **AT&T** ☎ 800/225-5288. **MCI** ☎ 800/888-8000 or 800/444-3333. **Sprint** ☎ 800/877-7746.

🗐 Access Codes **AT&T Direct** ☎ 00/800-1311, 800/435-0812 in the U.S. **MCI WorldPhone** ☎ 00/800-1211, 800/444-4141 in the U.S. **Sprint International Access** ☎ 00/800-1411, 800/877-4646 in the U.S.

PHONE CARDS

Phone cards worth €3, €6, €12, or €24 can be purchased at kiosks, convenience stores, or the local OTE office and are the easiest way to make calls from anywhere in Greece. These phone cards can be used for domestic and international calls. Once

you insert the phone card, the number of units on the card will appear; as you begin talking, the units will go down. Once all the units have been used, the card does not get recharged—you must purchase another.

PUBLIC PHONES

OTE has card phones virtually everywhere, though some may not be in working order. If you want more privacy—the card phones tend to be on busy street corners and other people waiting to make calls may try to hurry you—use a card phone in a hotel lobby or OTE offices, though these tend to have limited hours. You can also use a kiosk phone. If you don't get a dial tone at first, you should ask the kiosk owner to set the meter to zero (Boreéte na to meetheneéste?).

TIME

Greek time is Greenwich Mean Time (GMT) plus 2 hours. To estimate the time back home, subtract 7 hours from the local time for New York and Washington, 8 hours for Chicago, 9 for Denver, and 10 for Los Angeles. Londoners subtract 2 hours. Those living in Sydney or Melbourne, add 8 hours. Greek Daylight Saving Time starts on the last Sunday in March and ends the last Sunday in October, different from the United States for one week a year. Stay alert—newspapers barely publicize the change.

TIPPING

How much to tip in Greece, especially at restaurants, is confusing. By law a 13% service charge is figured into the price of a meal (menus sometimes list entrées with and without service, to let you know their net cost—not to imply you have a choice of how much to pay). However, it is customary to leave an 8%–10% tip if the service was satisfactory. During the Christmas and Greek Easter holiday periods, restaurants tack on an obligatory 18% holiday bonus to your bill for the waiters.

The appropriate tip for maid service at your hotel depends on the quality of the service, the length of your stay, and the quality of the hotel. A service charge is included in the price of the room, but you might consider in $$$–$$$$ hotels leaving an additional €1 per night. Porters, found only at the more expensive hotels, should get €0.75 per bag; room-service waiters merit €1 per delivery. If a concierge has been very helpful, you can leave from €3 to €10. For restroom attendants €0.50 is appropriate. People dispensing programs at cinemas also get €0.40. On cruises, cabin and dining-room stewards get about €2 a day; guides receive about the same. For taxis, round up the fare to the nearest €0.50 or €1; during holidays, drivers legally receive a mandatory "gift"; the amount is posted in the cab during applicable days.

TOURS & PACKAGES

Because everything is prearranged on a prepackaged tour or independent vacation, you spend less time planning—and often get it all at a good price.

Operators that handle several hundred thousand travelers per year can use their purchasing power to give you a good price. Their high volume may also indicate financial stability. But some small companies provide more personalized service; because they tend to specialize, they may also be more knowledgeable about a given area.

BOOKING WITH AN AGENT

Travel agents are excellent resources. But it's a good idea to collect brochures from several agencies, as some agents' suggestions may be influenced by relationships with tour and package firms that reward them for volume sales. If you have a special interest, find an agent with expertise in that area. The American Society of Travel Agents (ASTA) has a database of specialists worldwide; you can log on to the group's Web site to find one near you.

Make sure your travel agent knows the accommodations and other services of the place being recommended. Ask about the hotel's location, room size, beds, and whether it has a pool, room service, or programs for children, if you care about these. Has your agent been there in person or sent others whom you can contact?

Do some homework on your own, too: local tourism boards can provide informa-

tion about lesser-known and small-niche operators, some of which may sell only direct.

BUYER BEWARE

Each year consumers are stranded or lose their money when tour operators—even large ones with excellent reputations—go out of business. So check out the operator. Ask several travel agents about its reputation, and try to **book with a company that has a consumer-protection program.** (Look for information in the company's brochure.) In the United States, members of the United States Tour Operators Association are required to set aside funds (up to $1 million) to help eligible customers cover payments and travel arrangements in the event that the company defaults. It's also a good idea to choose a company that participates in the American Society of Travel Agents' Tour Operator Program; ASTA will act as mediator in any disputes between you and your tour operator.

Remember that the more your package or tour includes, the better you can predict the ultimate cost of your vacation. Make sure you know exactly what is covered, and beware of hidden costs. Are taxes, tips, and transfers included? Entertainment and excursions? These can add up.

🔏 Tour-Operator Recommendations **American Society of Travel Agents** (⇨ Travel Agencies). **CrossSphere–The Global Association for Packaged Travel** ✉ 546 E. Main St., Lexington, KY 40508 ☎ 800/682-8886 or 859/226-4444 🖷 859/226-4414 ⊕ www.ntaonline.com. **United States Tour Operators Association** (USTOA) ✉ 275 Madison Ave., Suite 2014, New York, NY 10016 ☎ 212/599-6599 🖷 212/599-6744 ⊕ www.ustoa.com.

TRAIN TRAVEL

Fares are reasonable, and trains offer a good, though slow, alternative to long drives or bus rides. One of the most impressive stretches is the rack-and-pinion line between Kalavrita and Diakofto, which travels up a pine-crested gorge in the Peloponnese mountains. In fact, the leisurely Peloponnesian train is one of the more pleasant ways to see southern Greece. In central and northern Greece, the Pelion and Nestos routes cross breathtaking landscapes.

The main line running north from Athens divides into three lines at Thessaloniki, continuing on to Skopje and Belgrade; the Turkish border and Istanbul; and Sofia, Bucharest, and Budapest. The Peloponnese in the south is served by a narrow-gauge line dividing at Corinth into the Tripoli–Kalamata and Patras–Kalamata routes. Some sample fares: Athens–Corinth, €2.60; Athens–Nafplion, €4.80; Athens–Volos, €19.40.

The Greek Railway Organization (OSE) has two stations in Athens, side by side, off Diliyianni street west of Omonia Square: Stathmos Larissis and Stathmos Peloponnisou (⇨ Athens A to Z *in* Chapter 1 for more information). OSE buses for Albania, Bulgaria, and Turkey also leave from the Peloponnese station. The *Proastiakos* light-rail line (⊕ www.proastiakos. gr) linking the airport to Stathmos Larissis in Athens has been extended to Corinth; fares are €6 from Athens to Corinth and €8 from the airport to Corinth.

InterCity Express service from Athens to Thessaloniki is fast and reliable. The IC costs €45.20 (versus €14.10 for a regular train) but cuts the time by 90 minutes to about 4½ hours. The Athens–Patras IC train (3½ hours) costs €10 (compared to €5.30 and about 4 hours for a regular train). If you order your IC tickets no later than three days in advance, you can have them delivered to you in Athens by courier for a small fee.

CLASSES

All trains have both first- and second-class seating. On any train, it is best during high season or for long distances to travel first-class, with a reserved seat, as the difference between the first- and second-class coaches can be vast: the cars are cleaner, the seats are wider and plusher, and, most important, the cars are emptier. Without a reservation, in second class you sometimes end up standing among the baggage. The assigned seating of first class (*proti thesi*) is a good idea in July and August, for example, when the Patras–Athens leg is packed with tourists arriving from Italy. First class costs about 20% more than second class (*thefteri thesi*).

CUTTING COSTS

To save money, **look into rail passes.** But be aware that if you don't plan to cover many miles, you may come out ahead by buying individual tickets. Greece is one of 17 countries in which you can use Eurailpasses, which provide unlimited first-class rail travel, in all of the participating countries, for the duration of the pass. If you plan to rack up the miles in several countries, get a standard pass. These are available for 15 days ($588), 21 days ($762), one month ($946), two months ($1,338), and three months ($1,654).

If Greece is your only destination in Europe, consider purchasing a Greece Flexipass Rail 'n Fly. For $251 you get three days of first-class rail travel within a one-month period and two selected Olympic Airways flights, with an option to buy more flights at reduced rates.

If you're planning to make the Athens–Thessaloniki trip several times, buy an Intercity 6+1, which gives you seven trips for the price of six ($203 first class), and a discount on the next card when you return the old one. You can combine this with a Rail 'n Drive package offered by Hertz (⇨ Major Agencies *in* Car Rental, *above*). They will have a rental car waiting for you at any of the IC stations—Athens, Larissa, Thessaloniki, Volos—at lower prices.

The Balkan Flexipass covers first- and second-class train travel through Greece as well as Bulgaria, Romania, the Former Yugoslav Republic of Macedonia (FYROM), Turkey, and Yugoslavia (including Serbia and Montenegro); there are passes for 5, 10, or 15 travel days in a one-month period for about $175, $306, and $368, respectively (first-class). Youths pay about 50% less, senior citizens over 60 25% less. The pass is also good for some hotel and sightseeing discounts in Greece, Romania, and Yugoslavia.

In addition to standard Eurailpasses, ask about special rail-pass plans. Among these are the Eurail Youthpass (for those under age 26), the Eurail Saverpass (which gives a discount for two or more people traveling together), a Eurail Flexipass (which allows a certain number of travel days within a set period), the Euraildrive Pass and the Europass Drive (which combines travel by train and rental car). Whichever pass you choose, remember that you must **purchase your pass before you leave** for Europe.

Many travelers assume that rail passes guarantee them seats on the trains they wish to ride. Not so. You need to **book seats ahead even if you are using a rail pass**; seat reservations are required on some European trains, particularly high-speed trains, and are a good idea on trains that may be crowded—particularly in summer on popular routes. You also need a reservation if you purchase sleeping accommodations. On high-speed (IC) trains, you pay a surcharge.

🔂 Information and Passes **CIT Tours Corp.** ✉ 875 3rd Ave., New York, NY 10022 ☎ 800/248-8687 or 212/730-2400 in the U.S., 800/361-7799 in Canada ⊕ www.cit-tours.com. **DER Travel Services** ✉ 9501 W. Devon Ave., Rosemont, IL 60018 ☎ 800/782-2424 ᕕ 800/282-7474 information, 800/860-9944 brochures. **Rail Europe** ✉ 500 Mamaroneck Ave., Harrison, NY 10528 ☎ 877/257-2887 or 914/682-5172 ᕕ 800/432-1329 ✉ 2087 Dundas E, Suite 106, Mississauga, Ontario, Canada L4X 1M2 ☎ 800/361-7245 ᕕ 905/602-4198 ⊕ www.raileurope.com.

FARES & SCHEDULES

Note that any ticket issued on the train costs 50% more. The best, most efficient contact is OSE's general-information switchboard for timetables and prices. You can get train schedules and fares from EOT and from OSE offices. The Thomas Cook European Timetable is useful, too.

🔂 Train Information **Greek Railway Organization (OSE)** ✉ Karolou 1, near Omonia Sq., Athens ☎ 210/529-7006 or 210/529-7007 ✉ Sina 6, Athens ☎ 210/529-8910 ⊕ www.ose.gr. **InterCity Express** ☎ 210/529-7313; open Monday-Saturday 8-2:30. **OSE general information switchboard** ☎ 11100; open daily 7 AM-9 PM.

🔂 Train Timetables **Forsyth Travel Library** ᒌ Box 2975, Shawnee Mission, KS 66201-1375 ☎ 800/367-7984 ⊕ www.forsyth.com. **Thomas Cook, Timetable Publishing Office** ✉ Box 36, Thorpe Wood, Peterborough, Cambridgeshire PE3 6SB ⊕ www.thomascookpublishing.com.

FROM THE U.K.

There are two main routes to Greece by train from the United Kingdom: the overland route via Munich, Salzburg, Ljubljana, and Zagreb (about three days), or the more pleasant ride through Italy, then by ferry from Brindisi to Patras in the Peloponnese. In high summer, catch the train from London's Victoria Station to Dover for the crossing to Calais and the connecting service to Paris's Gare du Nord. You can also take the Eurostar service from Waterloo Station in London through the Channel Tunnel to the Gare du Nord. From the station, transfer to the Gare de Lyon for the train that runs via Switzerland to Milan. Switch there and travel through to Brindisi Maritime station, where you connect with the ferry to Patras (about 17 hours) and arrive the following day. From Patras there is bus and train service to Athens (total time London–Athens, about 2½ days). Given the many inexpensive deals available in summer, and taking into account food costs, it might be cheaper to fly from London.

PAYING

You can pay for all train tickets purchased in Greece with cash (euros) or with credit cards (Visa and MasterCard only).

RESERVATIONS

Reservations are a good idea in summer high season, when trains can be packed with travelers from other countries as well as from Greece.

TRANSPORTATION AROUND GREECE

Many of Greece's major highways have been resurfaced and extended, in particular the Athens–Thessaloniki and Athens–Patras highways and the Attiki Odos beltway skirting the capital's perimeter, so driving has become much easier. In the cities, driving remains a daunting exercise, and it's easier and cheaper to take taxis, especially for couples or families. Urban public transportation is also a good alternative, inexpensive, frequent, and operating until at least midnight. To travel throughout Greece's mainland, rely on KTEL buses, which operate an extensive network to even the most remote villages. Trains have fewer stops and are slower (except for the ICs between Athens and Patras or Athens and Thessaloniki) but are slightly cheaper. To get to an island, the ferry is usually the best bet, if the journey is 6 hours or less—especially with fast ferries that reduce travel time even further. Those pressed for time can take the more expensive hydrofoils to nearby islands or fly, usually with Olympic or Aegean Airlines. However, a 45-minute flight to Santorini beats the arduous ferry trip (4 to 12 hours), especially around August 15, when most Greeks vacation. For most islands, it's liberating to rent a motorbike for long-distance sightseeing not tied to bus schedules, but be extremely cautious and drive defensively.

TRAVEL AGENCIES

A good travel agent puts your needs first. Look for an agency that has been in business at least five years, emphasizes customer service, and has someone on staff who specializes in your destination. In addition, **make sure the agency belongs to a professional trade organization.** The American Society of Travel Agents (ASTA) has more than 10,000 members in some 140 countries, enforces a strict code of ethics, and will step in to mediate agent-client disputes involving ASTA members. ASTA also maintains a directory of agents on its Web site; ASTA's TravelSense.org, a trip-planning and travel-advice site, can also help to locate a travel agent who caters to your needs. (If a travel agency is also acting as your tour operator, *see* Buyer Beware *in* Tours & Packages.)

▮ Local Agent Referrals **American Society of Travel Agents** (ASTA) ⊠ 1101 King St., Suite 200, Alexandria, VA 22314 ☎ 800/965-2782 24-hr hotline, 703/739-2782 ⎙ 703/684-8319 ⊕ www. astanet.com and www.travelsense.org. **Association of British Travel Agents** ⊠ 68-71 Newman St., London W1T 3AH ☎ 020/7637-2444 ⎙ 020/7637-0713 ⊕ www.abta.com. **Association of Canadian Travel Agencies** ⊠ 130 Albert St., Suite 1705, Ottawa, Ontario K1P 5G4 ☎ 613/237-3657 ⎙ 613/237-7052 ⊕ www.acta.ca. **Australian Federation of Travel Agents** ⊠ Level 3, 309 Pitt St., Sydney, NSW 2000 ☎ 02/9264-3299 or 1300/363-416 ⎙ 02/

9264-1085 ⊕ www.afta.com.au. **Travel Agents' Association of New Zealand** ⊠ Level 5, Tourism and Travel House, 79 Boulcott St., Box 1888, Wellington 6001 ☎ 04/499-0104 ⎙ 04/499-0786 ⊕ www. taanz.org.nz.

VISITOR INFORMATION

Learn more about foreign destinations by checking government-issued travel advisories and country information. For a broader picture, consider information from more than one country.

Tourist police, stationed near the most popular tourist sites, can answer questions in English about transportation, steer you to an open pharmacy or doctor, and locate phone numbers of hotels, rooms, and restaurants. Also helpful are the municipal tourism offices. Finally, you can contact the Greek National Tourism Organization (GNTO, but known as EOT in Greece), which has offices throughout the world.

▮ EOT in Greece **EOT** ⊠ Tsochas 7, Ambelokipi, Athens ☎ 210/870-7000 ⊕ www.gnto.gr. ⊠ Athens International Airport, Spata ☎ 210/353-0445 or 210/354-5101 ⊠ Gorghikis Sxolis 46, Thessaloniki ☎ 2310/471027 ⊠ Thessaloniki International Airport, Thessaloniki ☎ 2310/471170 ⊠ Filopimenos 26, Patras ☎ 2610/620353.

▮ In the U.S. **Greek National Tourism Organization** ⊠ Olympic Tower, 645 5th Ave., New York, NY 10022 ☎ 212/421-5777 ⎙ 212/826-6940 ⊕ www. greektourism.com.

▮ Government Advisories **U.S. Department of State** ⊠ Bureau of Consular Affairs, Overseas Citizens Services Office, 2201 C St. NW, Washington, DC 20520 ☎ 888/407-4747 or 317/472-2328 for interactive hotline, 202/647-5225 ⊕ www.travel.state.gov. **Consular Affairs Bureau of Canada** ☎ 800/267-6788 or 613/944-6788 ⊕ www.voyage.gc.ca. **U.K. Foreign and Commonwealth Office** ⊠ Travel Advice Unit, Consular Directorate, Old Admiralty Bldg., London SW1A 2PA ☎ 0870/606-0290 or 020/7008-1500 ⊕ www.fco.gov.uk/travel.

WEB SITES

Do check out the World Wide Web when planning your trip. You'll find everything from weather forecasts to virtual tours of famous cities. Be sure to visit Fodors.com (⊕ www.fodors.com), a complete travel-planning site. You can research prices and book plane tickets, hotel rooms, rental cars, vacation packages, and more. In addition, you can post your pressing questions in the Travel Talk section. Other planning tools include a currency converter and weather reports, and there are loads of links to travel resources.

VISITOR INFORMATION

The U.S. Web site of the Greek National Tourism organization, ⊕ www.greektourism.com, is well laid out and packed with information and pictures; it has different content from the GNTO's broader site, ⊕ www.gnto.gr. You can also check out the official Web site of Athens (⊕ www.cityofathens.gr); the site of the Hellenic Ministry of Culture (⊕ www.culture.gr), which has basic information about museums, monuments, and archaeological sites; and the ministry's events site (⊕ www.cultureguide.gr), which lists cultural events throughout Greece. Packed full of everything you need to know about traveling by ferry are ⊕ www.greekferries.gr and ⊕ www.ferries.gr, which both let you book online.

SPECIAL INTEREST

The Hellenic Festival site, ⊕ www.hellenicfestival.gr, lists summer programs for the Athens Festival and the Festival of Epidauros. The site of the Athens Concert Hall, ⊕ www.megaron.gr, describes all the activities at this venue. A good resource guide to ancient Greece is ⊕ www.ancientgreece.com. A great site about all Greek coasts, ⊕ www.thalassa.gr, includes maps and information about water quality at beaches, sailing, and sea life. The Foundation for Environmental Education awards the Blue Flag designation to beaches, including those in Greece, that are clean, safe, and environmentally aware; ⊕ www.blueflag.org has details.

Athens

WORD OF MOUTH

"As we climb the Parthenon's hill at my very slow pace, stopping for photographs every minute, I feel the weight of all who have climbed before us. It brings tears to my eyes. Even now."
—nikki

"If you're staying at a hotel without an Acropolis view, have a leisurely dinner at a taverna in the Plaka with a vista as the sun sets and the lights come on. We sat on the roof at the Attalos at dusk and thought it was more impressive than just seeing the view at night."
—polly229

Updated by
Diane Shugart

IT'S NO WONDER THAT ALL ROADS LEAD to the fascinating and maddening metropolis of Athens. Lift your eyes 200 feet above the city to the Parthenon, its honey-color marble columns rising from a massive limestone base, and you behold architectural perfection that has not been surpassed in 2,500 years. Today this shrine of classical form, this symbol of Western civilization and political thought, dominates a 21st-century boomtown. To experience Athens fully is to understand the essence of Greece: tradition juxtaposed with modernity. While taking in the ancient monuments, you might bump into a smartly dressed lawyer chatting on her cell phone as she maneuvers around a priest in flowing robes heading for the ultramodern metro.

If you come to Athens in search of gleaming white temples, you may be aghast to find that much of the city has melded into what, viewed from your airplane window, appears to be a viscous concrete mass spreading across the Attica basin, from the beach towards the mountains. Amid the sprawl and squalor, though, you will witness startling beauty. Some is timeless, some the result of sprucing up done before the 2004 Olympics, when public squares and buildings throughout central Athens received face-lifts. Still, many of Athens's 4.5 million souls spend the day discussing the city's faults: the overcrowding, the traffic jams with their hellish din. Locals depend upon humor and flexibility to deal with the chaos; you should do the same. The rewards are immense if you take the time to catch the purple glow of sundown on Mt. Hymettus, light a candle in a Byzantine church beside black-shrouded grandmas while teens outside argue vociferously about soccer, or breathe in the tangy sea air while sipping a Greek coffee after a night at the coastal clubs.

Wander into less-touristy areas and you will often discover pockets of incomparable charm, in refreshing contrast to the dreary repetition of the modern facades. In lovely Athenian neighborhoods you can still delight in the pleasures of strolling. *Peripato,* the Athenians call it, and it's as old as Aristotle, whose students learned as they roamed about in his peripatetic school. This ancient practice survives in the modern custom of the evening *volta,* or stroll, taken along the pedestrianized Dionyssiou Areopagitou street skirting the base of the Acropolis. Along your way, be sure to stop in a taverna to observe Athenians in their element. They are lively and expressive, their hands fiddling with worry beads or gesturing excitedly. While often expansively friendly, they are aggressive and stubborn when they feel threatened, and they're also insatiably curious.

Amid the ancient treasures and the 19th-century delights of neighborhoods such as Anafiotika and Plaka, the pickax, pneumatic drill, and cement mixer have given birth to countless office buildings and modern apartments. Hardly a monument of importance attests to the city's history between the completion of the Temple of Olympian Zeus 19 centuries ago and the present day. That is the tragedy of Athens: the long vacuum in its history, the centuries of decay, neglect, and even oblivion. But within the last 150 years the Greeks have created a modern capital out of a village centered on a group of ruined marble columns. And since the late 1990s, inspired by the 2004 Olympics, they have gone far to

If you're planning a quick day in Athens before heading off elsewhere on the mainland or to an island, concentrate on the city's don't-miss classical sights, from the Acropolis to the National Archaeological Museum. In three days you can explore some key neighborhoods as well as monuments from the classical, Roman, and Byzantine periods; add two more days and you can take in some of the prettier suburbs, head to the beach, or check out new galleries.

If you have 1 day

Early in the morning, pay homage to Athens's most impressive monument, the Acropolis. Then descend through Anafiotika, the closest thing you'll find to an island village on the mainland. Explore the 19th-century quarter of Plaka, with its neoclassical houses, and stop for lunch at one of its many tavernas. Do a little bargaining with the merchants in the old Turkish bazaar around Monastiraki Square. Spend a couple of hours in the afternoon taking in the stunning collection of antiquities in the National Archaeological Museum (check to be sure it's open); then pass by Syntagma Square to watch the changing of the costumed Evzone guards in front of the Tomb of the Unknown Soldier. You can then window-shop or people-watch in the tony neighborhood of Kolonaki. Nearby, take the funicular up to Mt. Lycabettus for the sunset before enjoying a show at the Odeon of Herod Atticus, followed by dinner in the funky district of Psirri.

If you have 3 days

After a morning tour of the Acropolis, stop at the Acropolis Museum to view sculptures found on the site (note that the museum is in the process of moving to a new location below the Acropolis). Continue through Anafiotika and Plaka, making sure to stop at the Greek Folk Art Museum, the Roman Agora, and the Little Mitropolis church on the outskirts of the quarter. After a late lunch, detour to Hadrian's Arch and the Temple of Olympian Zeus, Athens's most important Roman monuments. In Syntagma Square, watch the changing of the Evzone guards, and then head to Kolonaki, followed by an ouzo on the slopes of Mt. Lycabettus at I Prasini Tenta, with its panorama of the Acropolis and the sea. Dine in a local taverna (Karavitis and Aphrodite are good choices), perhaps near the Panathenaic Stadium—in Pangrati, the National Gardens, or around the Temple of Zeus—which is lighted at night. On Day 2, visit the cradle of democracy, the ancient Agora, site of Greece's best-preserved Doric temple, the Hephaistion. Explore the Monastiraki area, including the tiny Byzantine Kapnikarea Church, which stands in the middle of the street. In Monastiraki you can snack on the city's best souvlaki, then hop the metro to Piraeus to explore its neighborhoods and feast on fish in Mikrolimano harbor. On the third day, start early for the National Archaeological Museum, breaking for lunch in one of the city's mezedopoleia. Swing through the city center, past the Old University complex, a vestige of King Otho's reign, to the Goulandris Cycladic and Greek Ancient Art Museum in Kolonaki or the more recent artifacts in the Benaki Museum down the street. Stroll through the National Garden. Complete the evening with ballet or pop music at the Odeon of Herod Atticus, a movie at a *therina* (open-air cinema), or, in winter, a concert at the Megaron Musikis/ Athens Concert Hall.

If you have
5 days

Spend your first three days as detailed above. On the fourth, see the Byzantine Museum, which houses Christian art from the 4th to the 19th century; then visit either the Goulandris Cycladic and Greek Ancient Art Museum or the Benaki Museum—whichever you missed on Day 3. Another option is to check out the city's contemporary art scene at Technopolis or Athinais. In the evening, splurge on a meal at Aristera-Dexia; then dance the *tsifteteli* (the Greek version of a belly dance) to Asia Minor blues in a rembetika club, or, if it's summer, visit the coastal stretch where the bars stay open until dawn. On the last day, elbow your way through the boisterous Central Market; then visit some of the many galleries that dot the area. Cut over to Kerameikos, Athens's ancient cemetery. After lunch in Thission, try a complete change from the urban pace: take the metro to the lovely suburb of Kifissia and view the grand homes from a horse-drawn carriage, shop, or relax in one of the many cafés. As an alternative, catch a bus near the Zappion hall entrance of the National Garden and head to one of the government-run beaches in Varkiza, Vouliagmeni, or Voula.

---

transforming Athens into a sparkling modern metropolis that the ancients would strain to recognize but would heartily endorse.

EXPLORING ATHENS

Although Athens covers a huge area, the major landmarks of the ancient Greek, Roman, and Byzantine periods are conveniently close to the modern city center. You can easily walk from the Acropolis to many other key sites, taking time to browse in shops and relax in cafés and tavernas along the way. The center of modern Athens is small, stretching from the Acropolis in the southwest to Mt. Lycabettus in the northeast, crowned by the small white chapel of Ayios Georgios. The layout is simple: three parallel streets—Stadiou, Eleftheriou Venizelou (familiarly known as Panepistimiou), and Akadimias—link two main squares, Syntagma (Constitution) and Omonia (Concord). Try to detour off this beaten tourist track: seeing the Athenian butchers in the Central Market sleeping on their cold marble slabs during the heat of the afternoon siesta may give you more of a feel for the city than seeing scores of toppled columns.

From many quarters of the city you can glimpse "the glory that was Greece" in the form of the Acropolis looming above the horizon, but only by actually climbing that rocky precipice can you feel the impact of the ancient settlement. The Acropolis and Filopappou, two craggy hills sitting side by side; the ancient Agora (marketplace); and Kerameikos, the first cemetery, form the core of ancient and Roman Athens. Preparations for the 2004 Olympics made these more accessible: Along the Unification of Archaeological Sites promenade, you can follow stone-paved, tree-lined walkways from site to site, undisturbed by traffic. Cars have also been banned or reduced in other streets in the historical center. In the National Archaeological Museum, vast numbers of artifacts illustrate the many millennia of Greek civilization; smaller museums such as the Goulandris Cycladic and Greek Ancient Art Museum and the Byzantine Museum illuminate the history of particular regions or periods.

Athens may seem like one huge city, but it is really a conglomeration of neighborhoods with distinctive characters. The Eastern influences that prevailed during the 400-year rule of the Ottoman Empire are still evident in Monastiraki, the bazaar area near the foot of the Acropolis. On the northern slope of the Acropolis, stroll through Plaka (if possible by moonlight), an area of tranquil streets lined with renovated mansions, to get the flavor of the 19th-century's gracious lifestyle. The narrow lanes of Anafiotika, a section of Plaka, thread past tiny churches and small, color-washed houses with wooden upper stories, recalling a Cycladic island village. In this maze of winding streets, vestiges of the older city are everywhere: crumbling stairways lined with festive tavernas; dank cellars filled with wine vats; occasionally a court or diminutive garden, enclosed within high walls and filled with magnolia trees and the flaming trumpet-shape flowers of hibiscus bushes.

Formerly run-down old quarters, such as Thission and Psirri, popular nightlife areas filled with bars and *mezedopoleia* (similar to tapas bars), are now in the process of gentrification, although they still retain much of their original charm, as does the colorful produce and meat market on Athinas. The area around Syntagma Square, the tourist hub, and Omonia Square, the commercial heart of the city about 1 km (½ mi) northwest, is distinctly European, having been designed by the court architects of King Otho, a Bavarian, in the 19th century. The chic shops and bistros of ritzy Kolonaki, the most modern neighborhood downtown, nestle at the foot of Mt. Lycabettus, Athens's highest hill (909 feet). Each of Athens's outlying suburbs has a distinctive character: in the north is wealthy, tree-lined Kifissia, once a summer resort for aristocratic Athenians, and in the south and southeast lie Kalamaki, Glyfada, and Vouliagmeni, with their sandy beaches, seaside bars, and lively summer nightlife. Just beyond the city's southern fringes is Piraeus, a bustling port city of waterside fish tavernas and Saronic Gulf views.

Except for August and major holidays, when many Athenians migrate to their ancestral villages outside the city, the streets are crowded. The best times to visit the city are late fall and spring, when you can avoid the oppressive heat and the hordes of package tourists at major archaeological sites; you can also enjoy the bustling nightlife in the center, because after June many restaurants and clubs shut down or relocate to the seaside. Holy Week of the Orthodox Easter, usually in April or May, is a chance to observe Greece's most sacred holiday, including mournful Good Friday processions accompanying Christ's bier, and the candlelit Easter midnight service, complete with fireworks. If you must come in summer, visit the sights in the early morning; then—as the Greeks do—take a nap or eat a leisurely lunch before continuing your explorations after 5 PM, when several museums and sites are still open.

Sights remain open in winter (November–April), usually 8:30–3, though in summer opening hours of major archaeological sites and museums are extended, sometimes to 7 PM, or roughly sunset. (Summer opening hours are set by the Hellenic Ministry of Culture every year and are usually announced sometime in April.) Most museums close one day a week, usually Monday. Throughout the year, arrive at least 45 minutes before closing times to ensure a ticket. The Hellenic Ministry of Culture's Web site (⊕ www.culture.gr) provides a good description of museums and archaeological sites. The best time to visit churches is during a service, especially on Sunday (dress conservatively). Otherwise, hours are not set in stone; try from about 8 AM to noon and 5:30 PM to 7:30 PM on any day, unless otherwise noted. For walking in Athens, city streets are considerably less crowded Saturday afternoon through Sunday.

A single €12 ticket gives you admission for a week to all sites, including the Acropolis, on the Unification of Archaeological Sites walkway. These include the ancient Agora, Roman Agora, Temple of Olympian Zeus, Kerameikos, and Theater of Dionyssos. You can buy this combined ticket at any of the sites.

The Acropolis, Filopappou & Environs

Ακρόπολη, Φιχοπάππου & περίχωρα

Described by the 19th-century French poet Alphonse de Lamartine as "the most perfect poem in stone," the Acropolis, or "High City," is a true testament to the golden age of Greece. Many of its structures were built from 461 to 429 BC, during the magical period when the intellectual and artistic life of Athens flowered at the height of the Athenian statesman Pericles's influence.

Archaeological evidence has shown that the flat-top limestone outcrop, 512 feet high, attracted settlers as early as Neolithic times because of its defensible position and its natural springs. It is believed to have been continuously inhabited throughout the Bronze Age and ever since. Over the years the Acropolis buildings have borne the damages of war as well as unscrupulous transformations into, at various times, a Florentine palace, an Islamic mosque, and a Turkish harem. The hazards of war continued up to 1944, when British paratroopers sited their bazookas between the Parthenon's columns. Since then, a more insidious enemy has arrived—pollution. The site is now undergoing conservation as part of an ambitious rescue plan launched in 1983. Since then, the Erechtheion temple has been completely restored and work on the Parthenon, Temple of Athena Nike, and Propylaea is due for completion by the end of 2006. A final phase of the unprecedented restoration project, involving additional sections of the Parthenon and massive landscaping works, is expected to last through 2020.

Despite the restoration work, a visit to the Acropolis can evoke the spirit of the ancient heroes and gods who were once worshipped there. See the buildings first and save the Acropolis Museum for last; familiarity with the overall setting will give the statues and friezes more meaning. The "Acropolis" neighborhood includes neoclassical buildings lining its main street, Dionyssiou Areopagitou; the centuries-old Odeon of Herod Atticus; the Dionyssos theater; and the Ilias LALAoUNIS Jewelry Museum. Nearby is Filopappou, a pine-clad summit that has the city's best

Café Culture On any street corner, at any time of day, you will see Athenians practicing the art of hanging out—sipping their coffees, debating the latest political debacle, or just watching the world go by. Walking in the city may seem difficult at times because of uneven pavements and cars parked on the sidewalk, but there is no shortage of places to stop: squares, *kafeneia* (traditional Greek coffeehouses), stylish cafés, or makeshift arrangements—two tables set up outside a dairy store—where you can sit for hours with an ouzo or the ubiquitous summer refreshment called frappé: instant Nescafé shaken with ice water, milk, and sugar to taste. The kafeneio is a cross between a living room, an office, a reading room, a club, and a gambling casino (backgammon is the favorite game of chance, played for very low stakes but with a passion that makes the Monte Carlo Casino seem like bingo in a church basement). The social life of the average Athenian takes place in the kafeneio—this is where the heart is; home is often just a place to sleep.

Classical Glories You don't have to look far in Athens to encounter perfection. Towering above all—both physically and spiritually—is the Acropolis, the ancient city of upper Athens and the stonied remains of one of the greatest civilizations the West has ever produced. Sooner or later, you will climb the hill to witness, close-up, monuments of beauty and grace that have not been surpassed in 2 millennia. Nowhere, in fact, has ancient allure been more elegantly expressed than in the six caryatids that support the porch of the Erechtheion. No matter that these maidens are copies (the originals are in the Acropolis's museum). When the setting sun bathes them in rosy hues, these great sculptures of the 5th century BC fire the imagination. The few friezes that remain in situ at the Parthenon, the loftiest point of the Acropolis, are enough to evoke the splendor with which this masterpiece of Doric architecture was once adorned. The ancient temples of Athens no longer serve their original purpose, but the Odeon of Herodes Atticus, a theater built into a hillside, still welcomes audiences to performances for part of the year. And at the National Archaeological Museum, a 3,500-year-old funeral mask is but one of the treasures reflecting centuries of artistic achievement. Pay a visit to the Hephaistion, the well-preserved Doric temple that graces the Agora, the marketplace and hub of everyday life in ancient Athens.

Nightlife Athens is a sociable, late-night town where people love to see and be seen, and the action goes on until morning: even at 3 AM central platias (squares) and streets are often crowded with revelers. Part of this is a function of Greek dinner preferences; 10 o'clock is not considered too late to start your evening meal. At *rembetika* clubs you can hear a form of blues imported from Asia Minor in the 1920s, while at bouzoukia joints popular singers belt out contemporary hits to the gyrating crowd. Sip cocktails by the sea or dance all night to house and hip-hop at the designer-decorated clubs on the coast. First-time visitors might want to check out a musical taverna, an institution as old as Greece itself. The entertainment, often featuring men (and occasionally women) dancing the extraordinary *zeimbekiko*, is sure to be vigorous, colorful, spontaneous, and Zorbaesque. Neither the increasingly European work hours nor changing bar curfews seem to slow the social pace—clubs and restaurants are usually packed.

view of the Acropolis, the Pnyx where the Athenian assembly met, and the tiny, rustic church of Ayios Dimitrios Loumbardiaris.

Wear a hat for protection from the sun and low-heel, rubber-sole shoes, as the marble on the Acropolis steps and near the other monuments is quite slippery. Bring plenty of water—you'll need it, and there are usually long lines at the on-site cantinas.

Numbers in the text correspond to numbers in the margin and on the Exploring Athens and Exploring Piraeus maps.

a good walk

If you see nothing else in Athens, you must visit the **Acropolis** ❶ ⌐. Even jaded Athenians, when overwhelmed by the city, feel renewed when they lift their eyes to this great monument. Take the metro to the Acropolis station, where the New Acropolis Museum is under construction. Follow the pedestrianized street Dionyssiou Aerogapitou, which traces the foothill of the Acropolis to its entrance at the Beulé Gate. Buildings include the architecturally complex Erechtheion temple, most sacred of the shrines of the Acropolis, and the Parthenon, which dominates the Acropolis and, indeed, the city skyline: it is the most architecturally sophisticated temple of its period. Time and neglect have given its marble pillars their golden-white shine, and the beauty of the building is made all the more stark and striking.

While on the outcrop, pause at the edge of the southern fortifications, where, on a clear day, you can see the coastline toward Sounion and the Saronic Gulf islands of Aegina and Salamina. Leave time for the **Acropolis Museum** ❷, which houses some superb sculptures from the Acropolis, including most of the caryatids and a large collection of colored statues of women dedicated to the goddess Athena. (When the New Acropolis Museum opens by the end of 2006, this collection will move there). As you exit the gate, detour right to the rock of **Areopagus** ❸, the ancient supreme court, from which St. Paul later preached to the Athenians.

Cross Dionyssiou Areopagitou to **Filopappou** ❹; before climbing the summit, via the footpaths crisscrossing the hill, stop at tiny **Ayios Dimitrios Loumbardiaris** ❺ church, and then have a coffee at the tourist pavilion. Descend Dionyssiou Areopagitou, past the **Odeon of Herod Atticus** ❻ and the Hellenistic **Theater of Dionyssos** ❼. Across the street is the controversial **New Acropolis Museum** ❽. The huge, modern museum will showcase the treasures of the Parthenon and will feature glass floors so that you can peer down into the ongoing archaeological excavations. Nearby is the **Ilias LALAoUNIS Jewelry Museum** ❾, with more than 3,000 pieces and a workshop where visitors can observe ancient techniques still used today.

TIMING   Such is the beauty of the Acropolis and the grandeur of the setting that a visit in all seasons and at all hours is rewarding. In general, the earlier you start out the better. By noon, the summer heat is blistering and the reflection of the light thrown back by the rock and the marble ruins almost blinding. An alternative, in summer, is to visit after 5 PM, when the light is best for taking photographs. In any season the ideal time might be the two hours before sunset, when occasionally the fabled violet light spreads from the crest of Mt. Hymettus (which the ancients called "violet-crowned") and gradually embraces the Acropolis. After dark the hill is spectacularly floodlighted, visible from many parts of the capital. A moonlight visit—sometimes scheduled by the authorities during full moons in summer—is highly evocative. In winter, if there are clouds trailing across the mountains, and shafts of sun lighting up the marble columns, the setting takes on an even more dramatic quality.

Depending on the crowds, the walk takes about four hours, including one spent in the Acropolis Museum. The Ilias LALAoUNIS Jewelry Museum is closed Tuesday, so you may want to take this tour another day.

What to See

① Acropolis. A survivor of war, the vagaries of religious change, and other Fodor'sChoice hazards, the massive Acropolis remains an emblem of the glories of classical Greek civilization. Even in its bleached and silent state, the Parthenon—the great Panathenaic temple that crowns the rise—has the power to stir the heart as few other ancient relics can. Seeing it bathed in the sunlight of the south, or sublimely swathed in moonlight, has caused more than a few people to marvel at the continuing vitality of this monument.

The term Akropolis (to use the Greek spelling) refers to the ancient Athenian "upper city" that occupies the tablelike hill. Foundations for a grand new temple honoring the city's patron, the goddess Athena, were laid after the victory at Marathon in 490 BC but were destroyed by Persians in 480–79 BC. After a 30-year building moratorium, ended by the peace treaty at Susa in 448 BC, Pericles undertook the ambitious project of reconstructing the temple on a titanic scale. Some scholars consider this extraordinary, enigmatic Athenian general to be the brilliant architect of the destiny of Greece at its height, while others conclude he was a megalomaniac who bankrupted the coffers of an empire and an elitist who catered to the privileged few at the expense of the masses.

The appearance of the buildings that composed the major portion of the Acropolis remained largely unaltered until AD 52, when the Roman emperor Claudius embellished its entrance with a flamboyant staircase. In the 2nd century Hadrian had his turn at decorating many of the shrines, and in 529 Justinian closed the philosophical schools, emphasizing the defensive character of the citadel and changing the temples into Christian churches.

You enter through the **Beulé Gate,** a late-Roman structure named for the French archaeologist Ernest Beulé, who discovered it in 1852. Made of marble fragments from the destroyed monument of Nikias on the south slope of the Acropolis, it has an inscription above the lintel dated 320 BC, dedicated by "Nikias son of Nikodemos of Xypete," who had apparently won a musical competition. Before Roman times, the entrance to the Acropolis was a steep processional ramp below the Temple of Athena Nike. This Sacred Way was used every fourth year for the Panathenaic procession, a spectacle that ended the festival celebrating Athena's remarkable birth (she sprang from the head of her father, Zeus); events included chariot races, athletic and musical competitions, and poetry recitals. Toward the end of July, all strata of Athenian society gathered at the Dipylon Gate of Kerameikos and followed a sacred ship as it was wheeled to the Acropolis. The ship was then anchored at the rocky outcrop below Areopagus, northwest of the Acropolis.

The **Propylaea** is a typical ancient gate, an imposing structure designed to instill proper reverence in worshippers as they crossed from the temporal world into the spiritual world of the sanctuary, for this was the main function of the Acropolis. Conceived by Pericles, the Propylaea was the masterwork of the architect Mnesicles. It was to have been the grandest secular building in Greece, the same size as the Parthenon. Construction was suspended during the Peloponnesian War, and it was never finished. The Propylaea was used as a garrison during the Turkish period; in 1656, a powder magazine there was struck by lightning, causing much damage; and the Propylaea was again damaged during the Venetian siege under Morosini in 1687.

The Propylaea shows the first use of both Doric and Ionic columns together, a style that can be called Attic. Six of the sturdier fluted Doric columns, made from Pendelic marble, correspond with the gateways of the portal. Processions with priests, chariots, and sacrificial animals entered via a marble ramp in the center (now protected by a wooden stairway), while ordinary visitors on foot entered via the side doors.

The slender Ionic columns (two-thirds the diameter of the Doric) had elegant capitals, some of which have been restored along with a section of the famed paneled ceiling, originally decorated with gold eight-pointed stars on a blue background. The well-preserved north wing housed the Pinakotheke, or art gallery, specializing in paintings of scenes from Homer's epics and mythological tableaux on wooden plaques. Connected to it was a lounge with 17 couches arranged around the walls so that weary visitors could enjoy a siesta. The south wing was a decorative portico (row of columns). The view from the inner porch of the Propylaea is stunning: the Parthenon is suddenly revealed in its full glory, framed by the columns.

The 2nd-century traveler Pausanias referred to the **Temple of Athena Nike** as the Temple of Nike Apteros, or Wingless Victory, for "in Athens they believe Victory will stay forever because she has no wings." Designed by Kallikrates, the minitemple was built in 427–424 BC to celebrate peace with Persia, with four Ionic columns at each portico end. The bas-reliefs on the surrounding parapet depicting the Victories leading heifers to be sacrificed must have been of exceptional quality, judging from the portion called "Nike Unfastening Her Sandal" in the Acropolis Museum. The best sections of the temple's frieze, which includes the Battle of Plataia with Greeks fighting the Persians, were whisked away to the British Museum two centuries ago and replaced with cement copies. In 1998 Greek archaeologists began the arduous task of dismantling the entire temple for conservation. The marble is being laser-cleaned to remove generations of soot; when the cleaning is finished, which the Ministry of Culture has announced will be by the end of 2006, the temple will be rebuilt on its original site. The temple's sculpted reliefs, on display in the Acropolis Museum, are scheduled to be moved to the New Acropolis Museum when it opens.

At the loftiest point of the Acropolis is the **Parthenon,** the architectural masterpiece conceived by Pericles and executed between 447 and 438 BC by the brilliant sculptor Pheidias, who supervised the architects Iktinos and Kallikrates in its construction. Although dedicated to the goddess Athena (the name Parthenon comes from the Athena Parthenos, or the virgin Athena) and inaugurated at the Panathenaic Festival of 438 BC, the Parthenon was primarily the treasury of the Delian League, an ancient alliance of cities. For the populace, the Erechtheion—*not* the Parthenon—remained Athena's holiest temple. Metal scaffolding around the Parthenon is part of an ongoing preservation project; several sections have been removed and all the scaffolding is expected to come down by the end of 2006 when this phase of renovation works is completed.

One of the Parthenon's features, or "refinements," is the way it uses *meiosis* (tapering of columns) and *entasis* (a slight swelling so that the column can hold the weight of the entablature), thus deviating from strict mathematics and breathing movement into the rigid marble. Architects knew that a straight line looks curved and vice versa, so they built the temple with all the horizontal lines somewhat curved. The columns, it has been calculated, lean toward the center of the temple; if they were to continue into space, they would eventually converge to create a huge pyramid.

Though the structure of the Parthenon is of marble, the inner ceilings and doors were made of wood. The original building was ornate, covered with a tile roof, decorated with statuary and marble friezes, and so brightly painted that the people protested, "We are gilding and adorning our city like a wanton woman" (Plutarch). Pheidias himself may have sculpted some of the exquisite, brightly painted *metopes* (the recessed spaces between the raised blocks on the frieze), but most were done by other artists under his guidance. The only ones remaining on site show scenes of battle: Athenians versus Amazons, and gods and goddesses against giants.

One of the most evocative friezes, depicting the procession of the Panathenaia, was 524 feet long, an extraordinary parade of 400 people, including maidens, magistrates, horsemen, and musicians, and 200 animals. To show ordinary mortals, at a time when almost all sculpture was of mythological or battle scenes, was lively and daring. About 50 of the best-preserved pieces of this panel, called the Parthenon Marbles by Greeks but known as the Elgin Marbles by almost everyone else, are in the British Museum in London; a few others can be seen in the Acropolis Museum. In the first decade of the 19th century, during the time of the Ottoman Empire, Lord Elgin, British ambassador in Constantinople, was given permission by the Sultan Selim III to remove stones with inscriptions from the Acropolis; he took this as permission to dismantle shiploads of sculptures. The removal remains controversial to this day: on one side, many argue that the marbles would have been destroyed if left on site; on the other side, a spirited long-term campaign aims to have them returned to Greece, to be appreciated in their original context. The New Acropolis Museum is being built with a special room for the marbles, in which they would be laid out in their original order; it will also have glass walls through which the temple the marbles once adorned will be clearly visible.

If the Parthenon is the masterpiece of Doric architecture, the **Erechtheion** is undoubtedly that of the more graceful Ionic order. A considerably smaller structure than the Parthenon, it outmatches all other buildings of the Greco-Roman world for sheer elegance and refinement of design and execution. More than any other ancient monument, this temple has its roots in the legendary origins of Athens. Here it was that the contest between Poseidon and Athena took place for the possession of the city. On this spot, the sea god dramatically plunged his trident into the rock and produced a spring of water; Athena created an olive tree, the main staple of Greek society. The panel of judges declared her the winner, and the city was named Athena. A gnarled olive tree outside the Erechtheion's west wall was planted where Athena's once grew, and marks said to be from Poseidon's trident can be seen on a rock wedged in a hole near the north porch. Completed in 406 BC, the Erechtheion was divided into two Ionic sanctuaries. The eastern one contained an olive-wood statue of Athena Polias, protector of the city, as well as a gold lamp that burned always, so large it was filled with fuel just once a year. The western part of the Erechtheion was dedicated to Poseidon-Erechtheus.

The most delightful feature of the Erechtheion, which has undergone extensive repair, is the south portico, facing the Parthenon, known as the **Caryatid Porch.** It is supported on the heads of six strapping but shapely maidens (caryatids) wearing delicately draped Ionian garments, their folds perfectly aligned to resemble flutes on columns. What you see today are copies; except for the caryatid dismantled by Lord Elgin, now in the British Museum, the originals were removed in 1977 to the Acropolis Museum to protect them from erosion caused by air pollution. One theory about the origin of the term "caryatid" is that the Athenians, to punish the people of Caryae in Laconia for collaborating with the Persians, seized the women of Caryae—Caryatids—and enslaved them. Because they were stunningly beautiful, the name came to be used for any attractive woman, including the maidens on the temple.

Once inaccessible to people with disabilities, the summit of the Acropolis can now be reached by elevator. Don't forget to ask the ticket takers for a copy of the free English-language guide to the site. It's packed with information, but workers usually don't bother to give it out unless asked. ✉ *Dionyssiou Areopagitou, Acropolis* ☎ *210/321–4172 or 210/321–0219* ⊕ *www.culture.gr* ✍ *Joint ticket for all Unification of Archaeological Sites €12* ☉ *Apr.–Oct., daily 8–sunset; Nov.–Mar., daily 8–2:30* Ⓜ *Acropolis.*

★ ❷ **Acropolis Museum.** Full of fabled objects of Attic art found on the Acropolis, this museum is unobtrusively snuggled in the southeast corner of the Acropolis site. Among the exhibits are legendary sculptures, plus the votive offerings to Athena. The displays are well executed, but their labeling in English is sketchy. The most notable displays of the museum are sculptures from the Archaic and classical periods, including, in Room IV, the *Rampin Horseman* and the compelling *Hound,* both by the sculptor Phaidimos. In Room I, the anguished expression of a calf being devoured by a lioness in a porous-stone pediment of the 6th century BC brings to mind Picasso's *Guernica*. Room II contains the charismatic *Calf-Bearer,* or *Moschophoros,* an early Archaic work showing a man named Rhombos carrying on his shoulders a calf intended to be sacrificed. A porous-stone pediment of the Archaic temple of Athena shows Heracles fighting against Triton—on its right side, note the rather scholarly looking "three-headed demon," bearing traces of the original red-and-black embellishment. In Rooms IV and V, take a good look at the exquisite *korai* (colored statues of women dedicated to the goddess Athena), with fascinating details of hair, clothing, and jewelry of the Archaic period. Room V also has striking pedimental figures from the Old Temple of Athena (525 BC), depicting the battle between Athena and the Giants. In Room VI is the 5th-century BC relief *Mourning Athena,* an example of the severe style favored in the classical period. In Room VIII, a superbly rendered slab by Pheidias from the eastern side of the Acropolis represents the seated Poseidon, Artemis, and Apollo. Incomparably graceful movement is suggested in *Nike Unfastening Her Sandal,* taken from the parapet of the Temple of Athena Nike. In a dimly lighted, air-conditioned glass case in Room IX are the badly damaged original caryatids, salvaged from the Erechtheion. This small museum is scheduled to close once the New Acropolis Museum is completed (the Culture Ministry has announced that it will be ready by the end of 2006); and the magnificent collection is moved. ✉ *Dionyssiou Areopagitou, Acropolis* ☎ *210/323–6665* ⊕ *www.culture.gr* 🎫 *Joint ticket for all Unification of Archaeological Sites* €12 ☉ *Apr.–Oct., daily 8–7:30; Nov.–Mar., Mon. 10–3, Tues.–Sun. 8:30–3* Ⓜ *Acropolis.*

❸ **Areopagus.** From this limestone rock, named after either Ares, the god of war, or the Arae, goddesses of vengeance, you have a good view of the Propylaea, the ancient Agora below, and the surrounding modern metropolis. This was once Athens's supreme judicial court, and legend says that Orestes was tried here for the murder of his mother, Clytemnestra. According to Pausanias, the accused stood at the Stone of Injury while the prosecutor pleaded his case at the Stone of Ruthlessness. From the outcrop, St. Paul delivered such a moving sermon on the "Unknown God" that he converted the senator Dionysius, who became the first bishop of Athens. Some of St. Paul's words (Acts 17:22–34) are written in Greek on a bronze plaque at the foot of the hill. The climb up is for the sure-footed. ✉ *Outside Acropolis's entrance, off Theorias, Acropolis* 🎫 *Free* ☉ *Daily* Ⓜ *Acropolis.*

❺ **Ayios Dimitrios Loumbardiaris.** A delightful grove borders this church, which derives its name from *loumbarda* (cannon). Here in 1656 on St. Dimitrios's Day, the congregation had gathered and on the Acropolis a Turkish garrison commander readied the cannons of the Propylaea to open fire during the final Te Deum of the service. The moment it started, a bolt of lightning struck the cannons, blowing up the Propylaea and killing the commander and many of his men. The stone church contains many icons and has an old-fashioned wood ceiling and roof. ✉ *At base of walkway to Filopappou hill, Filopappou* ☉ *Daily 7–7* Ⓜ *Thiseio.*

need a
break?
The little **Tourist Pavilion** (⊠ Filopappou hill, Filopappou ☎ 210/
923–1665) is a blissful hideaway far from the bustle of the
archaeological sites and the streets. It is landscaped and shaded by
overhanging pines, and the background music is provided by chirping
birds. The pavilion serves drinks, snacks, and a few hot dishes.

❹ **Filopappou.** This summit includes **Lofos Mousson** (Hill of the Muses),
whose peak offers the city's best view of the Parthenon, which appears
almost at eye level. Also there is the **Monument of Filopappus,** depicting a Syrian prince who was such a generous benefactor that the people accepted him as a distinguished Athenian. The marble monument
is a tomb decorated by a frieze showing Filopappus driving his chariot.
In 294 BC a fort strategic to Athens's defense was built here, overlooking the road to the sea. On the hill of the **Pnyx** (meaning "crowded"),
the all-male general assembly (Ecclesia) met during the time of Pericles.
Gathering the quorum of 5,000 citizens necessary to take a vote was
not always easy, as Aristophanes hilariously points out in his comedy
Ecclesiazusae (Women of the Assembly). Archers armed with red paint
were sent out to dab it on vote dodgers; the offenders were then fined.
Originally, citizens of the Ecclesia faced the Acropolis while listening to
speeches, but they tended to lose their concentration as they gazed upon
the monuments, so the positions of the speaker and the audience were
reversed. The speaker's platform is still visible on the semicircular terrace; from here, Themistocles persuaded Athenians to fortify the city
and Pericles argued for the construction of the Parthenon. Farther north
is the **Hill of the Nymphs,** with a 19th-century observatory designed by
Theophilos Hansen, responsible for many of the capital's grander edifices. He was so satisfied with his work, he had *servare intaminatum*
("to remain intact") inscribed over the entrance. ⊠ *Enter from Diony-
siou Areopagitou or Vasileos Pavlou, Acropolis* Ⓜ *Acropolis.*

☙ ❾ **Ilias LALAoUNIS Jewelry Museum.** Housing the creations of the internationally renowned artist Ilias Lalaounis, this private foundation also
operates as a study center. The 45 collections include 3,000 pieces inspired by subjects as diverse as the Treasure of Priam to the wildflowers of Greece; many of the works are eye-catching, especially the
massive necklaces evoking the Minoan and Byzantine periods. Besides
the well-made videos that explain jewelry making, craftspeople in the
workshop demonstrate ancient and modern techniques, such as chain
weaving and hammering. During the academic year the museum can
arrange educational programs in English for groups of children. The
founder also has several stores in Athens. ⊠ *Kallisperi 12, at Karyatidon,
Acropolis* ☎ *210/922–1044* ⊕ *www.lalaounis-jewelrymuseum.gr*
🖃 *€3, free Wed. after 3 and Sat. 9–11* ☉ *Sept.–mid-Aug., Mon. and
Thurs.–Sat. 9–4, Wed. 9–9, Sun. 11–4* Ⓜ *Acropolis.*

off the
beaten
path
NATIONAL MUSEUM OF CONTEMPORARY ART – When it's fully open
in 2007, this new museum in the former FIX beer brewery will be one
of the most important of the snazzy industrial-to-arts-space conversions
brightening the city's forbidding warehouse neighborhoods. Displayed
in three exhibition halls and in the rooftop garden will be works from

contemporary Greek and international artists. The permanent collection includes works by Ilya Kabakov, Gary Hill, Nan Goldin, George Hadjimichalis, Pavlos, and Allan Sekula; there is also an important collection of video art. Until renovation work is completed, the museum will host periodic exhibitions; consult local listings for upcoming events. ⊠ *Intersection of Kallirois and Franzt, Syngrou* ☎ *210/924–2111* 💷 *€3, free Thurs. after 5* ⊙ *Tues.–Sun. 11–7 during exhibitions;* Ⓜ *Syngrou-FIX.*

❽ **New Acropolis Museum.** After languishing for years in the small museum on the site of the Acropolis, the treasures of the Parthenon and other temples are set to have a spectacular new home. The Greek government is building a museum, designed by renowned architect Bernard Tschumi, at the foot of the Acropolis. With more than twice the space of the old museum, the new museum will allow sculptures that have been hidden in storage to be displayed for the first time. Its centerpiece will be a glassed-in rooftop room, built with the exact proportions of the Parthenon, with views of the temple itself. There, the Parthenon sculptures that Greece still owns (fewer than half of those that once graced the temple) will be arranged in their original order, with gaps left for the missing marbles. (Greece has long campaigned for the return of the Elgin Marbles, which once stood on the Parthenon and are now in the British Museum.) Another highlight of the museum will be glass floors that allow viewers to look into an ongoing archaeological dig. The museum is expected to be ready by the end of 2006. Once ready, the displays from the old museum will be restored and brought to the new space; eventually the old museum will close. ⊠ *Dionyssiou Areopagitou and Makriyianni, Acropolis* ⊕ *www.culture.gr* ☞ *Contact Acropolis Museum for updates on opening information* Ⓜ *Acropolis.*

❻ **Odeon of Herodes Atticus.** Hauntingly beautiful, this ancient theater was built in AD 160 by the affluent Herodes Atticus in memory of his wife, Regilla. Known as the Irodion by Athenians, it is nestled Greek-style into the hillside, but with typically Roman arches in its three-story stage building and barrel-vaulted entrances. The circular orchestra has now become a semicircle, and the long-vanished cedar roof probably covered only the stage and dressing rooms, not the 34 rows of seats. The theater, which holds 5,000, was restored and reopened in 1955 for the Elliniko Festival, or Hellenic Festival (formerly known as the Athens Festival). To enter you must hold a ticket to one of the summer performances, which range from the Royal Ballet to ancient tragedies and Attic comedies usually performed in modern Greek. Contact the Elliniko Festival box office for ticket information. ⊠ *Dionyssiou Areopagitou near intersection with Propylaion, Acropolis* ☎ *210/323–2771* ⊙ *Open only during performances* Ⓜ *Acropolis.*

❼ **Theater of Dionyssos.** It was on this spot in the 6th century BC that the Dionyssia festivals took place; a century later, dramas such as Sophocles's *Oedipus Rex* and Euripides's *Medea* were performed for the entire population of the city. Visible are foundations of a stage dating from about 330 BC, when it was built for 15,000 spectators as well as the assemblies formerly held on Pnyx. In the middle of the orchestra stood the altar to Dionyssos. Most of the upper rows of seats have been destroyed, but the lower levels, with labeled chairs for priests and dignitaries, remain. The fantastic throne in the center was reserved for the priest of Dionyssos: regal lions' paws adorn it, and the back is carved with reliefs of satyrs and griffins. On the hillside above the theater stand two columns, vestiges of the little temple erected in the 4th century BC by Thrasyllus the Choragus (the ancient counterpart of a modern impresario). ⊠ *Dionyssiou Areopagitou across from Mitsaion, Acropolis* ☎ *210/322–4625, 210/323–4482 box office* 💳 *€2, or with €12 joint ticket for all Unification of Archaeological Sites* ☉ *May–Oct., daily 8–7; Nov.–Apr., daily 8:30–2:30* Ⓜ *Acropolis.*

Plaka & Anafiotika

Πλάκα & Αναφιώτικα

One of Athens's prettiest neighborhoods, Plaka remains the last corner of 19th-century Athens, with Byzantine accents provided by churches. Second only to the Acropolis, the historical quarter is a must-see. During the 1950s and '60s, the area became garish with neon as nightclubs moved in and residents moved out, but locals, architects, and academicians joined forces in the early 1980s to transform a decaying neighborhood. Noisy discos and tacky pensions were closed, streets were changed into pedestrian zones, and old buildings were well restored. At night merrymakers crowd the old tavernas, which feature traditional music and dancing; many have rooftops facing the Acropolis. If you keep off the main tourist shopping streets of Kidathineon and Adrianou, you will be amazed at how peaceful the area can be, even in summer.

Above Plaka is Anafiotika, built on winding lanes that climb up the slopes of the Acropolis, its upper reaches resembling a tranquil village. In classical times it was abandoned because the Delphic Oracle claimed it as sacred ground. The buildings here were constructed by masons from Anafi island, who came to find work in the rapidly expanding Athens of the 1830s and 1840s. They took over this area, whose rocky terrain was similar to Anafi's, hastily erecting homes overnight and taking advantage of an Ottoman law that decreed that if you could put up a structure between sunset and sunrise, the property was yours. Ethiopians, imported as slaves by the Turks during the Ottoman period, stayed on after independence and lived higher up, in caves, on the northern slopes of the Acropolis.

a good walk

Take time to explore the side streets graced by old mansions under renovation by the Ministry of Culture. Begin your stroll at the **Monument of Lysikrates** ⑩ ➤, one of the few remaining supports (334 BC) for tripods (vessels that served as prizes) awarded to the producer of the best play in the ancient Dionyssia festival. Off the square on Galanou and Goura is the pretty church of **Ayia Aikaterini** ⑪. Take Herefondos to Plaka's central square, Filomoussou Eterias (or Platia Kidathineon), a great place to people-watch.

Up Kidathineon are three small but worthy museums: the **Greek Folk Art Museum** ⑫ has a rich collection ranging from 1650 to the present, including works by the beloved naive artist Theophilos Hatzimichalis. Across from the museum is the 11th- to 12th-century church of Sotira Tou Kottaki, in a tidy garden with a fountain that was the main source of water for the neighborhood until sometime after Turkish rule. The **Frissiras Museum** ⑬, in two neoclassical mansions, has a collection of paintings by top Greek and international contemporary artists, with a focus on the human figure. The tiny but delightful **Museum of Greek Children's Art** ⑭ surprises with the freshness of its exhibits. Nearby, the **Children's Museum** ⑮ makes a good stop for kids. Down the block and around the corner on Hatzimichali Aggelou is the **Center of Folk Art and Tradition** ⑯. Continue west to the end of that street, crossing Adrianou to Hill, then right on Epimarchou to the striking **Church House** ⑰ (on the corner of Scholeiou), once a Turkish police post and home to Richard Church, who led Greek forces in the War of Independence.

At the top of Epimarchou is **Ayios Nikolaos Rangavas** ⑱, an 11th-century church built with fragments of ancient columns. The church marks the edge of the **Anafiotika** ⑲ quarter, a village smack dab in the middle of the metropolis: its main street, Stratonos, is lined with cottages, occasional murals painted on the stones, and a few shops. Wind your way through the narrow lanes off Stratonos, visiting the churches Ayios Georgios tou Vrachou, Ayios Simeon, and Metamorphosis Sotiros. Another interesting church is 8th-century **Ayioi Anargyroi** ⑳, at the top of Erechtheos street. From the church, make your way to Theorias, which parallels the ancient *peripatos* (public roadway) that ran around the Acropolis. The collection at the **Kanellopoulos Museum** ㉑ spans Athens's history; nearby on Panos you'll pass the Athens University Museum (Old University), the city's first higher-learning institution.

Walk down Panos to the **Roman Agora** ㉒, which includes the Tower of the Winds and the Fethiye Mosque. Nearby visit the engaging **Museum of Greek Popular Musical Instruments** ㉓, where recordings will take you back to the age of *rembetika* (Greek blues). Also next to the Agora is Athens's only remaining **Turkish Bathhouse** ㉔, providing a glimpse into a daily social ritual of Ottoman times. On your way back to Syntagma Square, cut across Mitropolis (Cathedral) Square to the 12th-century Byzantine church known as **Little Mitropolis** ㉕, whose outer walls are covered with reliefs. Closer to Syntagma Square, on the corner of Pendelis and Mitropoleos, is the curious sight of **Ayia Dynamis** ㉖, a chapel peering out from between the cement columns of a Ministry building.

TIMING   Plaka is a delight any time of day, liveliest in the early evening or Sunday afternoons, when locals congregate at its outdoor cafés. Perhaps the best time to explore Anafiotika is a bit before sunset, when the haze is reduced and you can catch great views of the city. During Carnival, a three-week period preceding Orthodox Lent, costumed Athenians gather during evenings in Plaka for a stroll through the quarter, bopping one another with plastic clubs, showering confetti, and spraying foam at passersby: beware. If you want to visit the museums (some open only until mid-afternoon) or the churches (open 8 AM–noon and sometimes 5–7 PM), begin your excursion as early as possible. For planning ahead, check which museums are closed Monday. The walk, with

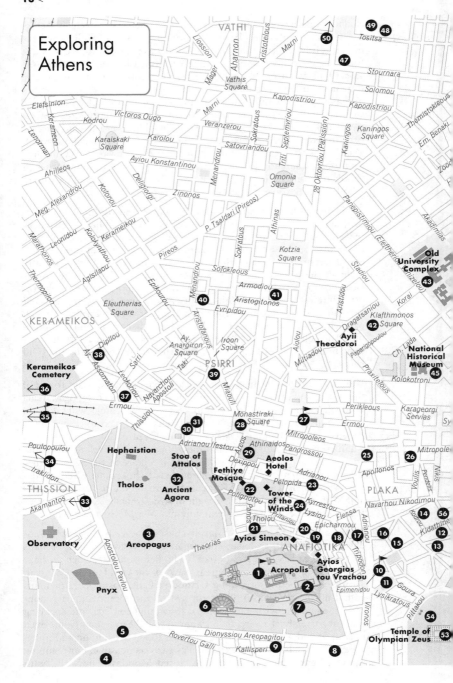

Exploring
Athens

VATHI

Tositsa

Stournara

Solomou

Kapodistriou

Kapodistriou

Aristotelous

Marni

Liossion

Aharnon

Mager

Vathis
Square

Victoros Ougo

Elefsinion

Kodrou

Karaiskaki
Square

Karolou

Kerameon

Lenormar

Ahilleos

Meg. Alexandrou

Kolonou

Marathonos

Leonidou

Agisilaou

Thermopilon

KERAMEIKOS

Eleutherias
Square

Kerameikos
Cemetery

36

Dipilou

38

Sairi

37

Leokoriou

Ermou

35

Ay. Assomaton

Poutopoulou

34

Iraklidon

THISSION

33

Akamantos

Observatory

Pnyx

5

4

Kolokynthou

Kerameikou

Epikourou

Menandrou

Aristofanous

Pireos

Menandrou

Satovriandou

Deligiorgi

Zinonos

Ayiou Konstantinou

Marni

Veranzerou

Sokratous

Triti Septemvriou

P. Tsaldari (Pireos)

Athinas

28 Oktovriou (Patission)

Omonia
Square

Kotzia
Square

Sofokleous

Armodiou

Aristogitonos

41

Evripidou

40

Ay.
Anargiron
Square

Iroon
Square

PSIRRI

39

Taki

Navarchou
Apostoli

Miaouli

Thissiou

Hephaistion

Stoa of
Attalos

Tholos

32

Ancient
Agora

30

31

Adrianou

Ifestou

Aeos

28

Monastiraki
Square

29

Dexippou

Fethiye
Mosque

Pandrossou

Athinaidos

Aeolos
Hotel

Adrianou

23

Pelopida

22

Tower
of the
Winds

24

Kyrrestou

Lysiou

Flessa

Epicharmou

20

19

18

17

Polignotou

Tholou

Adrianou

Theorias

21

Ayios Simeon

ANAFIOTIKA

Areopagus

3

Acropolis

1

Ayios Georgios
tou Vrachou

2

6

7

Dionyssiou Areopagitou

Rovertou Galli

Kallisperi

9

8

Panepistimiou (Eleftheriou)

Kaningos

Kaningos
Square

Themistokleous

Em. Benaki

Zoo

Akadimias

Old
University
Complex

43

Stadiou

Aristidou

Dragatsaniou

Klafthmonos
42   Square

Korai

Venizelou

Ch. Lada

National
Historical
Museum

45

Kolokotroni

Ayii
Theodoroi

Miltiadou

Aiolou

Papa rigopoulou

Praxitelous

Perikleous

Karageorgi
Servias

Sy

Mitropoleos

Ermou

27

25

26

Mitropole

Apollonos

PLAKA

Navarhou Nikodimou

14

56

Kodrou

Kidathine

12

16

15

13

10

11

Goura

Epimenidou

Vironos

Lysikratous

Pittakou

54

Temple of
Olympian Zeus

53

Tripodon

Nikis

Voulis

Pendelis

Mitropole

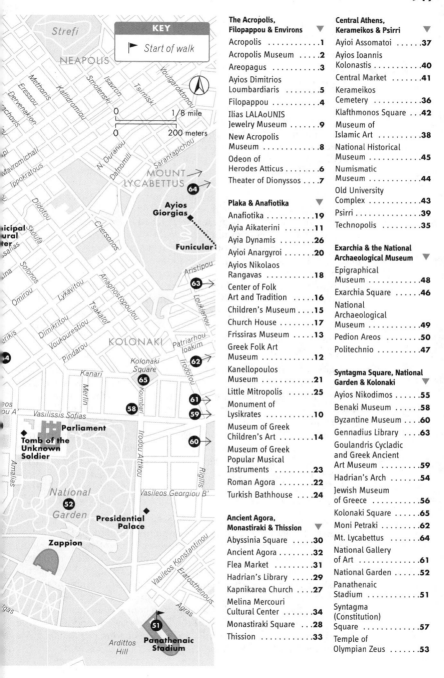

leisurely stops at one or two museums and time for a coffee break, takes about three hours.

What to See

★ ⓒ ⑲ **Anafiotika.** Set in the shadow of the Acropolis, this is the closest thing you'll find in Athens to the whitewashed villages of the Cycladic islands featured on travel posters of Greece. It is populated by many descendants of the Anafi stonemasons who arrived from that small island in the 19th century to work in the expanding capital. Anafiotika is an enchanting area of simple stone houses, many nestled right into the bedrock, most little changed over the years, others stunningly restored. Cascades of bougainvillea and pots of geraniums and marigolds enliven the balconies and rooftops, and the prevailing serenity is in blissful contrast to the cacophony of modern Athens. You seldom see the residents—only a line of washing hung out to dry, the lace curtains on the tiny houses, or the curl of smoke from a wood-burning fireplace indicate human presence. Perched on the bedrock of the Acropolis is **Ayios Georgios tou Vrachou** (St. George of the Rock), which marks the southeast edge of the district. One of the most beautiful churches of Athens, it is still in use today. **Ayios Simeon,** a neoclassical church built in 1847 by the settlers, marks the western boundary and contains a copy of a famous miracle-working icon from Anafi, Our Lady of the Reeds. The **Church of the Metamorphosis Sotiros** (Transfiguration), a high-dome 14th-century stone chapel, has a rear grotto carved right into the Acropolis. For those with children, there is a small playground at Stratonos and Vironos. ✉ *On northeast slope of Acropolis rock, Plaka* Ⓜ *Acropolis.*

⑪ **Ayia Aikaterini.** Built in the late 11th to early 12th century and enlarged in 1927, the church took its name in the 1760s when it was acquired by the Monastery of St. Catherine in the Sinai. Of the original structure, only the octagonal dome and central apse survive. The church is cruciform, its dome resting on a drum supported by four interior columns. The large sunken courtyard with royal palms and olive trees makes Ayia Aikaterini popular for baptisms and weddings; its choir is one of the city's best. ✉ *Off square on Galanou and Goura, Plaka* ☎ *210/ 322–8974* ⊙ *May–Oct., weekdays 7 AM–12:30 PM and 5:30–7, weekends 7 AM–12:30 PM and 5–10; Nov.–Apr., weekdays 7:30 AM–12:30 PM and 5–6:30, weekends 7 AM–12:30 PM and 5–10* Ⓜ *Acropolis.*

㉖ **Ayia Dynamis.** The "Divine Power" chapel, named for the Virgin Mary's supposed ability to help childless women conceive and topped by a dainty arch and bell, peeks out between the cement columns of the modern Ministry of Education and Religion. Its romantic history makes it worth mentioning: a Greek named Mastropavlis made cartridges here for the Turkish garrison, which had turned the church into a munitions works. At the same time, he secretly made ammunition for the Greek revolutionaries, which was smuggled to them by a courageous washerwoman. These were the first bullets fired at the Turks on the Acropolis when the War of Independence broke out in 1821. ✉ *On corner of Pendelis and Mitropoleos, Plaka* Ⓜ *Syntagma.*

㉑ Ayioi Anargyroi. According to legend, the church, also known as Metochion Panagiou Tafou, was built in the late 8th century by the empress Irene, an Athenian orphan and once the sole ruler of Byzantium, after the death of her husband. The Church of the Holy Sepulchre at Jerusalem, needing an outpost in Athens, acquired it in the 1700s and continues to occupy it today. The church has a gingerbread-like exterior, a delightful little garden containing fragments of ancient ruins, and a well that was used as a hiding place in troubled times. Today, it is the repository for the "divine light" or "Holy Fire" flown here from Jerusalem on Holy Saturday and then distributed with great fanfare to churches for the midnight resurrection services. ⊠ *Top of stairs where Erechtheos meets Prytaniou, Plaka.*

⑱ Ayios Nikolaos Rangavas. On the southeast side of this 11th-century Byzantine church rebuilt in the 18th century, you can see fragments of ancient columns and capitals incorporated into its walls, an example of the pragmatic recycling of the time. The church was the first to have a bell tower after the Greek revolution (bells were forbidden on Ottoman land). It is above the stairs off Prytaniou, a street named after the center of the ancient city where a sacred flame was kept burning. The best approach to the church is to walk up Epimenidou, down Thespidos, and left onto the Rangava path. ⊠ *Prytaniou 1, at top of Epimarchou, Plaka* ☎ *210/322–8193.*

⑯ Center of Folk Art and Tradition. Exhibits in the comfortable family mansion of folklorist Angeliki Hatzimichali include detailed costumes, ceramic plates from Skyros, handwoven fabrics and embroideries, and family portraits. ⊠ *Hatzimichali Aggelou 6, Plaka* ☎ *210/324–3972* 🎫 *Free* ☉ *Sept.–July, Tues.–Fri. 9–1 and 5–9, weekends 9–1.*

| need a break? |

Vyzantino (⊠ Kidathineon 18, Plaka ☎ 210/322–7368) is directly on Plaka's main square—great for people-watching and a good, reasonably priced bite to eat. Try the fish soup, roast potatoes, or baked chicken. **Glikis** (⊠ Aggelou Geronta 2, Plaka ☎ 210/322–3925) and its shady courtyard are perfect for a Greek coffee or ouzo and a *mikri pikilia* (a small plate of appetizers, including cheese, sausage, olives, and dips).

🖐 ⑮ Children's Museum. In the courtyard, you may see children forming melted chocolate in molds; upstairs in the neoclassical building, groups concoct toys out of recycled materials or learn to blow gigantic soap bubbles. The museum allows visitors up to the age of 12 to play freely and experiment; experienced staff encourage them to interact. Exhibits include the "family," where children take on the role of their parents; the kitchen, where they tackle food preparation; and the *horo katastrophis* ("destruction space"), where they are allowed to wreak havoc. Throughout the year, parents can sign children up for events such as a night at the museum, where they play, cook, and overnight in the room of their choice. The museum also runs a shop with toys and books. Often on weekdays the museum is booked for class trips, but staff will happily accommodate other children. ⊠ *Kidathineon 14, Plaka* ☎ *210/331–2995* ⊕ *www.hcm.gr* 🎫 *Free* ☉ *Sept.–July, Tues.–Sat. 10–2, Sun. 10–6.*

🔟 Church House. The striking, abandoned tower house with tiny windows, thick stone walls, and a tall chimney still bears traces of its past glory but remains in danger of collapse after a 1999 earthquake. Dating from the mid-18th century and used as a Turkish police post, the tower was bought after liberation by 19th-century historian George Finlay. He and his wife repaired the complex of buildings and lived here for half a century, while he wrote about Greek history, including what is considered the definitive work on the War of Independence. For many years, Church House served as a reference point among Athens's one-story buildings, a rare vestige of prerevolutionary Athens. Today the roof is in shambles, the Byzantine-style cornice has come loose, and cracks split the walls; officials are still discussing its preservation. ✉ *Corner of Epimarchou, Hill, and Scholeiou, Plaka* Ⓜ *Syntagma.*

🔟 Frissiras Museum. Two splendidly restored neoclassical mansions hold Greece's only museum of contemporary European painting, an eclectic and well-chosen collection of 3,000 pieces by Greek and international artists such as David Hockney, Dado, Pat Andrea, Andrea Martinelli, Costas Daoulas, Costas Papanikolaou, and Antonio Segui. Though the stylistic range is enormous, the pieces are all linked by a common theme: the human form. The works reflect subtly different cultural approaches to this universal subject: portraits by up-and-coming Greek artists share a distinctively folksy but ironic way of looking at the world. The Frissiras hosts competitions for young international painters and is gaining a reputation for spotting hot new talent. A small café, popular among art students, is a great place to pick up on the latest trends in contemporary Greek art. ✉ *Monis Asteriou 3 and 7, Plaka* ☎ *210/323–4678* ⊕ *www.frissirasmuseum.com* 🎫 *€6* ☾ *Wed.–Sun. 11–5; guided tours at 12:30 on weekends.*

🔟 Greek Folk Art Museum. Run by the Ministry of Culture, the museum focuses on folk art from 1650 to the present, with especially interesting embroideries, stone and wood carvings, Carnival costumes, and *Karaghiozis* (shadow player figures). Everyday tools—stamps for communion bread, spinning shuttles, raki flasks—attest to the imagination with which Greeks have traditionally embellished the most utilitarian objects. Don't miss the room of uniquely fanciful landscapes and historical portraits by beloved Greek naive painter Theophilos Hatzimichalis, from Mytilini. ✉ *Kidathineon 17, Plaka* ☎ *210/322–9031* ⊕ *www.culture.gr* 🎫 *€3* ☾ *Tues.–Sun. 10–2.*

🔟 Kanellopoulos Museum. The stately Michaleas Mansion, built in 1884, now showcases the Kanellopoulos family collection. It spans Athens's history from the 3rd century BC to the 19th century, with an emphasis on Byzantine icons, jewelry, and Mycenaean and Geometric vases and bronzes. Note the painted ceiling gracing the first floor. ✉ *Theorias and Panos, Plaka* ☎ *210/321–2313* ⊕ *www.culture.gr* 🎫 *€2* ☾ *Tues.–Sun. 8:30–3.*

need a break? Pause for a cool drink at the upscale **Nefeli Café** (✉ Panos 24, Plaka ☎ 210/321–2475), a large complex with an idyllic outdoor café shaded by awnings and draped with grapevines. It's perched below the Acropolis cliffs, looking down on Ayia Anna church. The casual **Cafe Dioscouri** (✉ Dioscouron and Mitroou, Plaka ☎ 210/321–9607) borders the pedestrian zone by the same name and has a view of the Hephaistion temple. If you're willing to pass up the view to soak up some atmosphere—and taste some delicious homemade, honey-drenched walnut cake—head for **Klepsydra**, a cozy café at the corner of Klepsidras and Thrasivoulou.

★ ㉕ **Little Mitropolis.** This church snuggles up to the pompous **Mitropolis** (on the northern edge of Plaka), the ornate Cathedral of Athens. Also called Panayia Gorgoepikoos ("the virgin who answers prayers quickly"), the chapel dates to the 12th century; its most interesting features are its outer walls, covered with reliefs of animals and allegorical figures dating from the classical to the Byzantine period. Look for the ancient frieze with zodiac signs and a calendar of festivals in Attica. Most of the paintings inside were destroyed, but the famous 13th- to 14th-century Virgin, said to perform miracles, remains. If you would like to follow Greek custom and light an amber beeswax candle for yourself and someone you love, drop the price of the candle in the slot. ✉ *Mitropolis Sq., Plaka* ☜ *Free* ☾ *Hrs depend on services, but usually daily 8–1* Ⓜ *Syntagma.*

➤ ⑩ **Monument of Lysikrates.** This monument was built by a *choregos* (theatrical producer) as the support for the tripod (a three-footed vessel used as a prize) he won for sponsoring the best play at the Theater of Dionyssos. It dates to 335–34 BC. Six of the earliest Corinthian columns are arranged in a circle on a square base, topped by a marble dome from which rise acanthus leaves. In the 17th century the monument was incorporated into a Capuchin monastery where Byron stayed while writing part of *Childe Harold*. The monument was once known as the Lantern of Demosthenes because it was incorrectly believed to be where the famous orator practiced speaking with pebbles in his mouth in an effort to overcome his stutter. A fresh-looking dirt track at the monument's base is a section of the ancient street of the Tripods, where sponsors installed prizes awarded for various athletic or artistic competitions. The street, one of the ancient city's grandest avenues, linked the Theater of Dionyssos with the Agora. ✉ *Lysikratous and Herefondos, Plaka* ⊕ *www.culture.gr* Ⓜ *Acropolis.*

☾ ⑭ **Museum of Greek Children's Art.** One of the few museums of its kind in the world, this small but attractive space displays exceptional children's art with the same dignity given to professional artwork. The results are surprisingly beautiful and thought-provoking, especially in exhibits that focus, for example, on the artwork of children in isolated mountain tribes or on specific themes such as children in the city. The museum also has many workshops and activities for children. ✉ *Kodrou 9, Plaka* ☎ *210/ 331–2621* ⊕ *www.childrensartmuseum.gr* ☜ *€2* ☾ *July–Sept., Tues.–Sat. 10–2, Sun. 11–2.*

☾ ㉓ **Museum of Greek Popular Musical Instruments.** An entertaining crash course in the development of Greek music, from regional *dimotika* (folk) to rembetika (blues), this museum has three floors of instruments.

Headphones are available so you can appreciate the sounds made by such unusual delights as goatskin bagpipes and discern the differences in tone between the Pontian lyra and Cretan lyra, string instruments often featured on World Music compilations. The museum, which has a lovely shaded courtyard, is home to the Fivos Anoyiannakis Center of Ethnomusicology. ⊠ *Diogenous 1–3, Plaka* ☎ *210/325–0198 or 210/325–4129* ⊕ *www.culture.gr* ⊠ *Free* ⊘ *Tues. and Thurs.–Sun. 10–2, Wed. noon–6* Ⓜ *Monastiraki.*

★ ㉒ **Roman Agora.** The city's commercial center from the 1st century BC to the 4th century AD, Roman market was a large rectangular courtyard with a peristyle that provided shade for the arcades of shops. Its most notable feature is the west entrance's Bazaar Gate, or **Gate of Athena Archegetis**, completed around AD 2; the inscription records that it was erected with funds from Julius Caesar and Augustus. Halfway up one solitary square pillar behind the gate's north side, an edict inscribed by Hadrian regulates the sale of oil, a reminder that this was the site of the annual bazaar where wheat, salt, and oil were sold. On the north side of the Roman Agora stands one of the few remains of the Turkish occupation, the **Fethiye (Victory) Mosque.** The eerily beautiful mosque was built in the late 15th century on the site of a Christian church to celebrate the Turkish conquest of Athens and to honor Mehmet II (the Conqueror). During the few months of Venetian rule in the 17th century, the mosque was converted to a Roman Catholic church; now used as a storehouse, it is closed to the public. Three steps in the right-hand corner of the porch lead to the base of the minaret, the rest of which no longer exists. The octagonal **Tower of the Winds (Aerides)** is the most appealing and well preserved of the Roman monuments of Athens, keeping time since the 1st century BC. It was originally a sundial, water clock, and weather vane topped by a bronze Triton with a metal rod in his hand, which followed the direction of the wind. Expressive reliefs around the octagonal tower personify the eight winds, called *I Aerides* (the Windy Ones) by Athenians. Note the north wind, Boreas, blowing on a conch, and the beneficent west wind, Zephyros, scattering blossoms. ⊠ *Pelopidas and Aiolou, Plaka* ☎ *210/324–5220* ⊕ *www.culture.gr* ⊠ *€2, or with €12 joint ticket for all Unification of Archaeological Sites* ⊘ *May–Oct., daily 8–7; Nov.–Apr., daily 8–3* Ⓜ *Monastiraki.*

㉔ **Turkish Bathhouse.** During Ottoman times, every neighborhood in Athens had a *hammam,* or public bathhouse, where men and women met to socialize among the steam rooms and take massages on the large marble platforms. Sunlight streaming through holes cut on the domed roofs and playing on the colorful tiled floors created a languorous atmosphere. This pretty, quirky little building, believed to date from the 15th century, is the only remaining Turkish bathhouse in Athens. It now functions as a museum and has been carefully restored, with all its original marble basins and platforms. ⊠ *Kyrrestou 8, Plaka* ☎ *210/324–4340* ⊠ *Free* ⊘ *Wed. and Sun. 10–2; opening days and hrs may increase, so call* Ⓜ *Monastiraki.*

Ancient Agora, Monastiraki & Thission

Αρχαία Αγορά, Μοναστηράκι & Θησείο

The Agora was once the focal point of community life in ancient Athens. It was the place where Socrates met with his students and where merchants squabbled over the price of olive oil. The Assembly met here first, before moving to the Pnyx, and locals gathered to talk about current events. The Agora became important under Solon (6th century BC), founder of Athenian democracy; construction continued for almost a millennium. Today, the site's sprawling confusion of stones, slabs, and foundations is dominated by the best-preserved Doric temple in Greece, the Hephaistion, built during the 5th century BC, and the impressive reconstructed Stoa of Attalos II, which houses the Museum of the Agora Excavations. You can still experience the sights and sounds of the marketplace in Monastiraki, the former Turkish bazaar area, which retains vestiges of the 400-year period when Greece was subject to the Ottoman Empire. On the opposite side of the Agora is another meeting place of sorts: Thission, a former red-light district. Although it has been one of the most sought-after residential neighborhoods since about 1990, Thission remains a vibrant nightlife district.

a good walk

Approach Monastiraki from the pedestrian street of Ermou, jammed from Syntagma Square to Aiolou with shops, cafés, sidewalk vendors, and wandering performers, including fire-eaters and hurdy-gurdy players. In the middle of the Kapnikareas intersection is striking **Kapnikarea Church** ㉗ ▶. Make your way to Pandrossou, an older shopping street that leads to **Monastiraki Square** ㉘, graced by the Tzistarakis Mosque and Panayia Pantassa church, exemplifying the East-West paradox that characterizes Athens. Walk up Areos, which during the Ottoman Empire was the Lower Bazaar, roofed and covered with vines. On the corner of Aiolou, you'll pass a nicely restored building, the former Aeolos Hotel, built in 1837 after Athens was made capital of Greece. Advertisements boasted that it had all European conveniences, including beds, at a time when guests in public lodging usually brought their blankets and slept on the floor. This area was the edge of the Upper Bazaar. You will arrive at what remains of **Hadrian's Library** ㉙, built in AD 132 and the intellectual center of its time. Return to the square and head west on Ifestou to **Abyssinia Square** ㉚, where junk dealers and antiques merchants gather; it's the perfect place to see a side of the city that is vanishing. It is also the heart of a rambunctious Sunday **flea market** ㉛.

After browsing through the market stalls, enter the **ancient Agora** ㉜ at the corner of Kinetou and Adrianou (the latter runs parallel to Ifestou). Be sure to visit the site's Museum of Agora Excavations, which offers a fascinating glimpse of everyday life in the ancient city. Exit at the site's opposite end onto Dionyssiou Areopagitou, crossing the boulevard to the **Thission** ㉝ quarter, a lively area with neoclassical homes overlooking trendy cafés. At the **Melina Mercouri Cultural Center** ㉞, exhibits recreate the streets of Athens during different epochs.

Those who want to escape Athens for a while may board the metro at the Thission station (at the end of Dionyssiou Areopagitou) or the Monastiraki station and take a ride to the northern suburb of **Kifissia,** once a summer resort for wealthy Athenians, evident in its tree-lined boulevards and grand villas.

TIMING   Monastiraki is at its best on Sunday mornings, when the flea market is in full swing; Ermou street, on the other hand, is most interesting Saturday mornings, when it's also most crowded. The ancient Agora has little shade, so in summer it's better to visit the site in early morning or, better, in late afternoon, so you can check out Thission's café scene afterward. Assuming you visit the Agora for about two hours, including a visit to the Museum of Agora Excavations, allow about four hours for the walk. You can spend an entire afternoon or evening in Kifissia. The trip takes about 40 minutes each way; the last train leaves Kifissia for Athens around midnight.

What to See

30 Abyssinia Square. Operating as a secondhand market since the early 20th century, the square hustles with activity all day long, with shop owners refinishing furniture and rearranging the bric-a-brac in their stalls. Weekend mornings, dealers flock from all over Greece to peddle an incredible array of goods, from old toasters to exquisite icons, while street musicians stroll amid the café tables, jostling their accordions and singing ballads of love and loss. ⊠ *Entrance off Ermou between Normanou and Kinetou, Monastiraki* Ⓜ *Monastiraki.*

need a break?   On Sunday afternoons, the best view of the vibrant spectacle of Abyssinia's flea market is from the red tables clustered on the street around **Café Abyssinia** (⊠ Kinetou 7, Monastiraki ☎ 210/321–7047), an old family-run favorite. As they've been doing for generations, all the market-goers come here to gossip, hear live music, and feast on couscous and chicken cooked with cumin.

★ **32 Ancient Agora.** This marketplace was the hub of ancient Athenian life. Besides administrative buildings, it was surrounded by the schools, theaters, workshops, houses, stores, and market stalls of a thriving town. Look for markers indicating the circular Tholos, the seat of Athenian government; the Mitroon, shrine to Rhea, the mother of gods, and the state archives and registry office ("mitroon" is still used today to mean registry); the Bouleterion, where the Council met; the Monument of Eponymous Heroes, the Agora's information center, where announcements such as the list of military recruits were hung; and the Sanctuary of the Twelve Gods, a shelter for refugees and the point from which all distances were measured.

Prominent on the grounds is the **Stoa of Attalos II,** a two-story building that holds the Museum of Agora Excavations. It was designed as a retail complex and erected in the 2nd century BC by Attalos, a king of Pergamum. The reconstruction in 1953–56 used Pendelic marble and creamy limestone from the original structure. The colonnade, designed for promenades, is protected from the blistering sun and cooled by breezes. The most notable sculptures, of historical and mythological figures from the 3rd and 4th centuries BC, are at ground level outside the museum. In the exhibition hall, chronological displays of pottery and objects from everyday life (note the child's terra-cotta potty) illustrate the settlement of the area from Neolithic times. There are such toys as knucklebones, and miniature theatrical masks carved from bone (Case 50); a *klepsydra* (a terra-cotta water clock designed to measure the time allowed for pleadings in court), and bronze voting discs (Cases 26–28); and, in Case 38, bits of *ostraka* (pottery shards used in secret ballots to recommend banishment), from which the word "ostracism" comes.

Take a walk around the site and speculate on the location of Simon the Cobbler's house and shop, which was a meeting place for Socrates and his pupils. The carefully landscaped grounds display a number of plants known in antiquity, such as almond, myrtle, and pomegranate. By standing in the center, you have a glorious view up to the Acropolis. **Ayii Apostoloi** is the only one of the Agora's nine churches to survive, saved because of its location and beauty. Inside, the dome and the altar sit on ancient capitals. Plans displayed in the narthex give an idea of the church's thousand-year-old history.

On the low hill called Kolonos Agoraios in the Agora's northwest corner stands the best-preserved Doric temple, the **Hephaistion,** sometimes called the Thission because of its friezes showing the exploits of Theseus. Like the other monuments, it is roped off, but you can walk around it to admire its 34 columns. It was originally dedicated to Hephaistos, god of metalworkers; metal workshops still exist in this area near Ifestou. The temple was converted to Christian use in the 7th century; the last services held here were a Te Deum in 1834, to celebrate King Otho's arrival, and a centenary Te Deum in 1934. Behind the temple, paths cross the northwest slope past archaeological ruins half hidden in deep undergrowth. Here you can sit on a bench and contemplate the same scene that Englishman Edward Dodwell saw in the early 19th century, when he came to sketch antiquities. ✉ *Three entrances: from Monastiraki on Adrianou; from Thission on Apostolou Pavlou; and descending from Acropolis on Ayios Apostoloi, Monastiraki* ☎ *210/321–0185* ⊕ *www.culture.gr* 🖭 *€4, or with €12 joint ticket for all Unification of Archaeological Sites* ☉ *May–Oct., daily 8–7; Nov.–Apr., daily 8–5; museum closes ½ hr before site* Ⓜ *Thiseio.*

㉛ **Flea market.** For Athenians, all the world's a stage. Just watching the social interplay between Greeks can provide hours of entertainment. The Sunday-morning market is a fitting setting in which to see lively haggling, and a fine destination in itself. Music blares from the carts pushing bootleg CDs, mingling with the twang of a bouzouki a prospective buyer is strumming. Peddlers shout to describe their wares: everything's for sale here, from gramophone needles to old matchboxes, from nose rings sold by young nomads to lacquered eggs and crisp white linens by the Pontian Greeks from the former USSR. Haggle, no matter how low the price. ✉ *Along Ifestou, Kynetou, and Adrianou, Monastiraki* Ⓜ *Monastiraki.*

㉙ Hadrian's Library. Built in AD 132, the extensively renovated remains of this public building (400 feet by 270 feet) are now accessible to the public. The east wall is supported by six attached Corinthian columns, and still standing are eight of the "one hundred splendid columns of Phrygian marble" mentioned by Pausanias, which apparently enclosed a cloistered court with a garden and pool. On the east side was the library itself, the intellectual center of its age, decorated with statues and murals under an alabaster and gold ceiling. Other areas were used for lectures and classes. On the west wall are traces of a fresco showing the outline of the Byzantine church Ayii Assomatoi, which stood next to it. ⊠ *Areos and Dexippou, Monastiraki* ⊙ *Tues.–Sun. 8:30–3* Ⓜ *Monastiraki.*

▶ **㉗ Kapnikarea Church.** It's said that the chapel was named for the *kapnikarious*, tax collectors who, during the Byzantine period, assessed residents for smoke coming from their chimneys; emanating smoke meant wealth enough to burn possessions. All pointy eaves and curvy arches, the church is really two adjoining chapels, one a cruciform structure of the 11th century, and the other a heavier 12th-century building of typical Byzantine raised brickwork, with a dome supported by four Roman columns. The latter was carefully restored by the University of Athens, of which it is now the official church. A prominent modern mosaic of the Virgin and Child adorns the west entrance, and the interior includes sentimental Western-style paintings installed before a 1930s decision that only traditional Byzantine icons and frescoes should appear in Greek churches. ⊠ *Kapnikareas and Ermou, Monastiraki* ☎ *210/322–4462* ⊙ *Mon., Wed., and Sat. 8–2; Tues., Thurs., and Fri. 8–12:30 and 5–7:30; Sun. 8–11:30* Ⓜ *Syntagma.*

off the beaten path

KIFISSIA – For a peaceful afternoon, hop on the metro for a 20- to 25-minute ride to this northern suburb. In ancient times, Herodes Atticus built his summer villa here to take advantage of cooler temperatures. The same appeal made Kifissia a summer resort for aristocratic Athenians at the turn of the 20th century. The streets north of the Kifissia station, with their verdant landscaping and ostentatious villas, evoke a gentler era. Walks on Dragoumi, Diligianni, Tatoi, Rangava, Pan, Tsaldari, Amalias, and Strofiliou are especially rewarding. After exploring the area, return to the 21st century and Kifissia's main street, Kassaveti, where young people flock to the cafés and shoppers to the boutiques and upscale malls, which also line Levidou, Kiriazi, and Kolokotroni streets. In shady Kefalari Square, decorated horse-drawn carriages await to take you on a ride along the quiet roads. In **Kifissia Park** (⊠ Between Kifissia metro station and Pl. Platanos), across from the metro station, the annual May flower show has dazzling plants (with experts standing by to give tips on proper plant care), competitions, and children's activities. Be sure to stop for a pastry or a *rizogalo* (rice pudding) at **Varsos** (⊠ Kassaveti 5 ☎ 210/801–2472), a Kifissia institution. The **Goulandris Natural History Museum** (⊠ Levidou 13 ☎ 210/808–6405 or 210/801–5870 ⊠ €3 ⊙ Sat.–Thurs. 9–2:30), good for kids, has displays of animal and plant life, fossils, and reconstructed prehistoric animals. The **Gaia**

Center (✉ Othonos 100 ☎ 210/801–5870 ☉ Sat.–Thurs. 9–2), an environmental research lab affiliated with the Goulandris Natural History Museum, contains well-done video and computer presentations on Greece's ecosystems, incorporating plenty of sound, light, and 3-D graphics. ✉ *Kifissia* Ⓜ *Kifissia.*

③④ Melina Mercouri Cultural Center. Installed in the former Poulopoulos hat factory built in 1886, the center gives a rare glimpse of Athens during the 19th century. You can walk through a reconstructed Athens street with facades of neoclassical homes that evoke the civilized elegance of the past, a pharmacy, printing press, dry goods store, *kafeneio* (coffeehouse), and dress shop, all painstakingly fitted out with authentic objects collected by the Greek Literary and Historical Archives. Throughout the year the center showcases temporary exhibitions, usually featuring contemporary Greek art. ✉ *Iraklidon 66, at Thessalonikis, Thission* ☎ *210/345–2150* 🎟 *Free* ☉ *Tues.–Sat. 9–1 and 5–9, Sun. 9–1* Ⓜ *Petralona.*

②⑧ Monastiraki Square. The square takes its name from the small **Panayia Pantanassa Church,** commonly called Monastiraki (Little Monastery). It once flourished as an extensive convent, perhaps dating to the 10th century, which stretched from Athinas to Aiolou streets. The nuns took in poor people, who earned their keep weaving the thick textiles known as *abas.* The buildings were destroyed during excavations and metro line construction that started in 1896. The convent's basic basilica form, now recessed a few steps below street level, was altered through a poor restoration in 1911, when the bell tower was added. The square's focal point, the 18th-century **Tzistarakis Mosque** (✉ Areos 1, Monastiraki ☎ 210/324–2066 🎟 €2 ☉ Wed.–Mon. 9–2:30), houses a ceramics collection that is beautifully designed, with the exhibits handsomely lighted and labeled. The mosque's creator, a newly appointed Turkish civil governor, knocked down a column from the Temple of Olympian Zeus to make lime for the mosque. Punished by the sultan for his audacity, he was also blamed by Athenians for an ensuing plague; it was believed the toppling of a column released epidemics and disasters from below the Earth. ✉ *South of Ermou and Athinas junction, Monastiraki.*

need a break? On Mitropoleos off Monastiraki Square are a handful of counterfront places selling souvlaki—grilled meat rolled in a pita with onions, *tzatziki* (yogurt-garlic dip), and tomatoes—the best bargain in Athens. Make sure you specify either a souvlaki sandwich or a "souvlaki plate," an entire meal. A contender for the best souvlaki in town is **Thanassis** (✉ Mitropoleos 69, Monastiraki ☎ 210/324–4705), which is always crowded with Greeks who come for the juicy meat and crunchy pitas. **Savvas** (✉ Mitropoleos 86, Monastiraki ☎ 210/321–3201) is a rival with nearby Thanassis for bragging rights to the best gyro—sandwiches of spicy spit-roasted meat.

③③ Thission. Have a snack in a turn-of-the-20th-century *ouzeri* (a publike eatery), listen to rock and roll in a bar that was once the Royal Stables, or sit down to a late supper after a show at the Odeon of Herodes Atticus. This vibrant neighborhood has become one of Athens's popular gathering places, rivaling upscale Kolonaki Square and the Psirri district. The main strip is the Nileos pedestrian zone across from the ancient Agora entrance, lined with cafés that are cozy in winter and have outdoor tables in summer. The rest of the neighborhood is quiet, an odd mix of mom-and-pop stores and dilapidated houses that are slowly being renovated; take a brief stroll along Akamantos (which becomes Galatias) around the intersections of Dimofontos or Aginoros, or down Iraklidon, to get a feel for the quarter's past. ⊠ *West of ancient Agora, Apostolou Pavlou, and Akamantos, Thission* Ⓜ *Thiseio.*

need a break?

It's a great concept: an old-style kafeneio complete with ouzo, Greek coffee, and *tavli* (backgammon games) for customers but with mod decor, designer lighting, hip music, and *freddo* (iced cappuccino). No wonder most people rolling the dice at **Kafeneio Thission** (⊠ Akamantos 2, Thission ☎ 210/347–3133) are not elderly gents but the under-40 set, who, when the weather warms up, spill out onto the sidewalk.

Central Athens, Kerameikos & Psirri

Αθήνα (κέντρο), Κεραμεικός & Ψυρρή

Downtown Athens is an unlikely combination of grit and beauty: the cavernous, chaotic Central Market, which replaced the bazaar in Monastiraki when it burned down in 1885, is 10 minutes from the elegant, neoclassical Old University complex. The surrounding area is filled with the remains of the 19th-century mansions that once made Athens world-renowned as a charming city. Some of these are crumbling into the streets; others, like the exquisite mansions that have been converted into the new Museum of Islamic Art, are regaining their lost loveliness. These buildings rub shoulders with incense-scented, 12th-century Byzantine churches as well as some of the city's most hideous 1970s apartment blocks, many of which are occupied by Greece's growing migrant population. The mix has become more heady as artists and fashionistas move to the neighborhoods of Psirri and Gazi and transform long-neglected warehouses into galleries, nightclubs, and ultrachic restaurants.

At the western edge of all this is the wide, green expanse of Kerameikos, the main cemetery in ancient Athens until Sulla destroyed the city in 86 BC. The name is associated with the modern word "ceramic": in the 12th century BC the district was populated by potters who used the abundant clay from the languid Iridanos River to make funerary urns and grave decorations. Kerameikos contains the foundations of two ancient monuments: the Dipylon Gate, where visitors entered the city, and the Sacred Gate, used for both the pilgrimage to the Eleusinian rites and for the Panathenaic procession in which the tunic for the statue of Athena was carted to the Acropolis. The area outside Kerameikos was settled by Turkish gypsies before the War of Independence, and then by Athens's Jewish community. The shops of the leading families lined Ermou; on Melidoni stands the Synagogue Beth Shalom, where congregants still worship.

a good
walk

To feel the buzz of the cutting-edge arts spaces sprouting up in Athens's roughneck former industrial district of Gazi, start at **Technopolis** ㉟ ▶, a foundry converted to an arts complex. Across the street, you'll reach the beginning of the Unification of Archaeological Sites walkway. Follow the pretty walkway up, where those interested in archaeology should visit **Kerameikos Cemetery** ㊱, the burial ground of ancient Athens's famous citizens. Continue east on Ermou to the intersection with Ayion Assomaton, where the 11th-century church of **Ayioi Assomatoi** ㊲ stands. Nearby, you can visit the **Museum of Islamic Art** ㊳, whose arrival in the neighborhood reinforces its rebirth as an arts community. The quirky, run-down neighborhood of **Psirri** ㊴, which gives you a different view of the city, starts here. After taking some time to explore its narrow streets, make your way to Evripidou and the oddest church in Athens, **Ayios Ioannis Kolonastis** ㊵, at the intersection with Menandrou.

Continue east on Evripidou, lined with aromatic shops selling herbs, nuts, olive oil soap, and household items, until you reach the **Central Market** ㊶, on the corner of Athinas. Hectic, crowded Athinas stretches from Omonia Square to Monastiraki and is replete with vendors of everything from canaries to garlic braids, but the 19th-century meat-and-fish market is the most entertaining spot. Evripidou ends at **Klafthmonos Square** ㊷ and what is perhaps the oldest church in Athens, Ayii Theodoroi. Cross Stadiou, walking up the Korai pedestrian zone to the **Old University complex** ㊸ on Panepistimiou. Then turn right and head a few blocks down to the impressive **Numismatic Museum** ㊹, ensconced in a neoclassical house. Alternately, continue along Stadiou towards Syntagma to the triangular Platia Kolokotroni, where a statue of the revolutionary war hero General Theodoros Kolokotronis astride his horse marks the entrance to the **National Historical Museum** ㊺.

TIMING Weekday mornings are the best time to take this approximately three-hour walk, including a short visit to one or two of the museums. The Central Market, which is closed Saturday afternoon and Sunday, bustles with pensioners inspecting the produce and cooks exchanging news with the fishmonger. Psirri is liveliest during Sunday afternoons and evenings, when the churches are illuminated and Athenians congregate in its bars and mezedopoleia. The Numismatic Museum is closed Monday, and the Vouros-Eftaxias Athens City Museum is closed several days—plan accordingly.

What to See

off the
beaten
path

ATHINAIS – Though this landmark arts complex in a converted silk factory is out of the way geographically, it's on every Athenian insider's radar and remains one of the best of a wave of arts spaces that have sprouted in Athens's old industrial district. The complex, still swathed in its original 1920s stonework, contains Greece's only **Museum of Ancient Cypriot Art,** with treasures dating back to the 9th century BC; a host of gallery spaces, whose exhibits rotate every six weeks; a concert hall; a theater; and a cinema that usually screens classic or art films. Athinais also has two excellent restaurants: the lush, sophisticated **Red,** considered one of the top restaurants in town, and the more affordable, highly regarded brasserie **Votanikos.** Bus tours frequently bring visitors here for lunch and a look at the museum, but the best time to visit is at night. See a movie or concert, stroll through the galleries and museum, have dinner, and finish off with a drink at the fashionable Boiler Bar. ✉ *Kastorias 34–36, Votanikos* ☎ *210/348-0000* ⊕ *www.athinais.com.gr* 🎫 *Free* ☉ *Museum and galleries daily 9* AM*–10* PM.

㊲ Ayioi Assomatoi. Named after the bodiless angels, the church dates to the 11th century. It was poorly rebuilt in 1880 but properly restored in 1959. Ayioi Assomatoi is in the form of a Greek cross, with a hexagonal dome and impressive exterior stonework. Some fragments of frescoes inside are probably from the 17th century, but art historians dispute the claim that an oil painting to the left of the entrance is by El Greco. ✉ *Ermou and Ayion Assomaton, Thission* Ⓜ *Monastiraki.*

㊵ Ayios Ioannis Kolonastis. St. John of the Column is undoubtedly the most unusual church in Athens. A Corinthian column, probably from a gymnasium dedicated to Apollo, protrudes from the tiled rooftop of the little basilica built around it in AD 565, and people with a high fever still come here to perform "curative" rituals that include tying a colored thread to the column and saying a special prayer. Mosaic floors that were unearthed here were probably part of an ancient temple to Asklepeios. ✉ *Evripidou 72, at intersection with Menandrou, Psirri* Ⓜ *Monastiraki.*

㊶ Central Market. The market runs along Athinas: on one side are open-air stalls selling fruit and vegetables at the best prices in town, although wily merchants may slip overripe items into your bag. At the corner of Armodiou, shops stock live poultry and rabbits. Across the street, in the huge covered market built in 1870, the surrealistic composition of suspended carcasses and shimmering fish on marble counters emits a pungent odor that is overwhelming on hot days. The shops at the north end of the market, to the right on Sofokleous, sell the best cheese, olives, halvah, bread, and cold cuts, including *pastourma* (spicy cured beef), available in Athens. Small restaurants serving the day's offerings dot the market; these stay open until the wee hours of the morning and are popular stops with weary clubbers heading home after long nights. ✉ *Athinas, Central Market* ☉ *Weekdays and Sat. morning* Ⓜ *Monastiraki.*

need a break?

"If you don't behave, I won't take you there," mothers in the Central Market used to say to unruly offspring about **Krinos** (✉ Aiolou 87, Central Market ☎ 210/321–6852). The lure is *loukoumades*—irresistible, doughnutlike fritters sprinkled with cinnamon and drizzled with a honeyed syrup based on a Smyrna recipe. Krinos has been serving the treat since it opened its doors in the 1920s; it is closed Sunday.

㊱ Kerameikos Cemetery. From the entrance of ancient Athens's cemetery, you can still see remains of the **Makra Teixoi** (Long Walls of Themistocles), which ran to Piraeus, and the largest gate in the ancient world, the

Dipylon Gate, where visitors entered Athens. The walls rise to 10 feet, a fraction of their original height (up to 45 feet). Here was also the **Sacred Gate,** used by pilgrims headed to the mysterious rites in Eleusis and by those who participated in the Panathenaic procession, which followed the Sacred Way. Between the two gates are the foundations of the **Pompeion,** the starting point of the Panathenaic procession. It is said the courtyard was large enough to fit the ship used in the procession. On the **street of Tombs,** which branches off the Sacred Way, plots were reserved for affluent Athenians. A number of the distinctive *stelae* (funerary monuments) remain, including a replica of the marble relief of Dexilios, a knight who died in the war against Corinth (394 BC); he is shown on horseback preparing to spear a fallen foe. From the terrace near the tombs, Pericles gave his celebrated speech honoring those who died in the early years of the Peloponnesian War, thus persuading many to sign up for a campaign that ultimately wiped out thousands of Athenians. To the left of the site's entrance is the **Oberlaender Museum,** whose displays include sculpture, terra-cotta figures, and some striking red-and-black-figured pottery. In 2003, the museum closed for expansion and renovation; when it reopens, displays are likely to include important finds from the excavation for the adjacent Kerameikos metro station. The extensive grounds of Kerameikos are marshy in some spots; in spring, frogs exuberantly croak their mating songs near magnificent stands of lilies. ⊠ *Ermou 148, Kerameikos, Monastiraki* ☎ *210/346–3552* ⊕ *www.culture.gr* 🖾 *Site and museum €2, or with €12 joint ticket for all Unification of Archaeological Sites* ☉ *May–Oct., daily 7:30–7; Nov.–Apr., daily 8:30–3.*

㊷ Klafthmonos Square. Public servants from the surrounding government offices lamented loudly here after being dismissed; hence, its name, the Square of Wailing. Behind the square at the corner of Evripidou and Aristidou is **Ayioi Theodorii,** a lovely mid-11th-century cruciform church, probably the oldest in Athens. The **Vouros-Eftaxias Athens City Museum** (⊠ Paparigoupoulou 7, Syntagma Sq. ☎ 210/324–6164 🖾 €5 ☉ Oct.–June, Mon., Wed., and Fri.–Sun. 9–1; July–Sept., Mon., Wed., and Fri.–Sat. 9–1), across from the square, was home to the teenage King Otho and his bride Amalia for seven years, while the royal palace was being built. The museum displays personal objects of the royal couple, as well as King Otho's throne. In a subbasement you can see a segment of the ancient city walls, and on the ground floor a model of Athens in 1842 shows how sparsely populated the new capital was. The first floor displays paintings by European artists who came to Athens, such as Edward Lear, Gasparini, and Dodwell. ⊠ *Off Stadiou between Paparigoupoulou and Dragatsaniou, Syntagma Sq.* Ⓜ *Panepistimiou.*

---

need a break?

As you sit gazing at the vast courtyard before you at **Polis** (⊠ Pesmazoglou 5, between Panepistimiou and Stadiou, upstairs in Stoa tou Vivliou, Syntagma Sq. ☎ 210/324–9588), you won't believe you're in the heart of downtown madness. Located on a rooftop over an arcade of bookstores, this café-bar serves light refreshments such as chicken salad pita and leek pie, cappuccino, and alcoholic drinks until late at night. The plaza is surrounded by buildings that cut off the city's sights and sounds, creating a seemingly secret enclave of white marble contrasting with shining blue sky.

㊳ **Museum of Islamic Art.** Antonis Benakis, founder of the city's outstanding Benaki Museum, spent much of his life in Alexandria, Egypt, where he amassed a celebrated collection of Islamic art. This collection is housed in a superbly renovated neoclassical mansion and is one of the few European museums devoted exclusively to Islamic art. The collection of 8,000 objects embraces ceramics, metalwork, jewelry, weaving, woodcarving, glassware, and engravings from the 4th century to modern times. Highlights include lustrous painted ceramics; a filigreed 10th-century gold belt from Samarra, Iraq; a section of a carved early Islamic throne, with stylized floral motifs; and a 14th-century universal astrolabe, the only known surviving piece of medieval astronomical equipment of its kind. Also on display is the marble-lined reception room of a 17th-century Egyptian mansion, transported from Cairo. ⊠ *Ayion Assomaton and Dipilou, Psirri* ☎ *210/325–1311* ⊕ *www.benaki.gr* ☜ *€5, free Thurs. afternoons* ⊙ *Tues. and Thurs.–Sun. 9–3, Wed. 9–9* Ⓜ *Monastiraki.*

㊺ **National Historical Museum.** After making the rounds of the ancient sites, you might think that Greek history ground to a halt when the Byzantine empire collapsed. A visit to this gem of a museum will fill in the gaps, often vividly, as with Lazaros Koyevina's copy of Eugene Delacroix's *Massacre of Chios*. Paintings, costumes, and assorted artifacts from small arms to flags and ship's figureheads are arranged in a chronological display tracing Greek history from the mid-16th century and the Battle of Lepanto through World War II and the Battle of Crete. A small gift shop near the entrance has unusual souvenirs, like a deck of cards featuring Greece's revolutionary heroes. ⊠ *Stadiou 13, Syntagma Sq.* ☎ *210/323–7617* ☜ *€3, free Sun.* ⊙ *Tues.–Sun. 9–2* Ⓜ *Syntagma.*

㊹ **Numismatic Museum.** Even those uninterested in coins might want to visit this museum for a glimpse of the former home of Heinrich Schliemann, who excavated Troy and Mycenae in the 19th century. He called his magnificent neoclassical house, designed for him by Ernst Ziller, the "Palace of Troy." Note the Pompeiian aesthetic in the ocher, terra-cotta, and blue touches; the mosaic floors inspired by Mycenae; and the dining-room ceiling painted with food scenes, under which Schliemann would recite the *Iliad* to guests. You can see more than 600,000 coins; displays range from the archaeologist's own coin collection to 4th-century BC measures employed against forgers to coins grouped according to what they depict—animals, plants, myths, famous buildings like the Lighthouse of Alexandria. Instead of trying to absorb everything, concentrate on a few cases—perhaps a pile of coins dug up on a Greek road, believed to be used by Alexander the Great to pay off local mercenaries. There is also a superb 4th-century BC decadrachm (a denomination of coin) with a lissome water goddess frolicking among dolphins (the designer signed the deity's headband). A silver didrachm (another denomination of coin) issued by the powerful Amphictyonic League after Philip II's death shows Demeter on one side and, on the other, a thoughtful Apollo sitting on the navel of the world. ⊠ *Panepistimiou 12, Syntagma Sq.*

☎ *210/364–3774* ⊕ *www.culture.gr* ▱ *€3* ⊙ *May–Oct., Tues. and Thurs.–Sun. 8–3, Wed. 8:30 AM–11 PM; Nov.–Apr., Tues. and Thurs.–Sun. 8:30–3, Wed. 8:30 AM–9 PM* Ⓜ *Syntagma or Panepistimiou.*

㊸ Old University complex. In the sea of concrete that is central Athens, this imposing group of marble buildings conjures up an illusion of classical antiquity. The three dramatic buildings belonging to the University of Athens were designed by the Hansen brothers in the period after independence in the 19th century and are built of white Pendelic marble, with tall columns and decorative friezes. In the center is the **Senate House** of the university. To the right is the **Academy,** flanked by two slim columns topped by statues of Athena and Apollo; paid for by the Austro-Greek Baron Sina, it is a copy of the Parliament in Vienna. Frescoes in the reception hall depict the myth of Prometheus. At the left end of the complex is a griffin-flanked staircase leading to the **National Library,** containing more than 2 million Greek and foreign-language volumes and now undergoing the daunting task of modernization. ⊠ *Panepistimiou between Ippokratous and Sina, Central Athens* ☎ *210/361–4301 Senate, 210/360–0209 Academy, 210/361–4413 Library* ⊕ *www.culture. gr* ⊙ *Senate and Academy weekdays 9–2; library Sept.–July, Mon.–Thurs. 9–8, Fri. 9–2* Ⓜ *Panepistimiou.*

> **need a break?**
>
> The spacious **Athinaiko Kafeneio** (⊠ Akadimias 50, entrance on Solonos in rear of Municipal Cultural Center, Central Athens ☎ 210/ 361–9265) beckons with good coffees, drinks, and tempting sweets. You can sit indoors or try the shady outdoor seating.

㊴ Psirri. At night, this quiet quarter becomes a whirl of theaters, clubs, and restaurants, dotted with dramatically lighted churches and lively squares. Defined by Ermou, Kerameikou, Athinas, Evripidou, Epikourou, and Pireos streets, Psirri has many buildings older than those in picturesque Plaka. Developers eager to renovate have initiated a flurry of building, and restaurants and bars are opening rapidly. Around the turn of the 20th century, the marginal mercantile area had an underground appeal and was home to the dispossessed, workers, and *manges,* or "tough guys." This was a place where a murder could take place over a misunderstood song request in a taverna, and it was the setting for a number of popular Greek novels.

If you're coming from Omonia Square, walk down Aiolou, a pedestrian zone with cafés and old shops as well as an interesting view of the Acropolis. Peek over the wrought-iron gates of the old houses on the narrow side streets between Ermou and Kerameikou to see the pretty courtyards bordered by long, low buildings, whose many small rooms were rented out to different families. In the Square of the Heroes, revolutionary fighters once met to plot against the Ottoman occupation. Linger on into the evening if you want to dance on tabletops to live Greek music, sing along with a soulful accordion player, hear salsa in a Cuban club, or watch the hoi polloi go by as you snack on updated or traditional *mezedes* (appetizers). ⊠ *Off Ermou, centered on Iroon and Ayion Anargiron squares, Psirri* ⊕ *www.psiri.gr* Ⓜ *Monastiraki.*

need a break? Late on weekend afternoons, Athenians, whether couples from Kolonaki or elderly women from Patissia, head for **Taki 13** (✉ Taki 13, Psirri ☎ 210/325–4707) for its unusual mezedes and live Greek music. The music often sets the crowd to dancing, or at least clapping and shouting enthusiastically as young gypsies shimmy between the tables.

▶ ㉟ **Technopolis.** Gazi, the neighborhood surrounding this former 19th-century-foundry–turned–arts complex, takes its name from the toxic gas fumes that used to spew from the factory's smokestacks. Today Gazi is synonymous with the hippest restaurants, edgiest galleries, and trendiest nightclubs in town. The smokestacks are now illuminated by red lights at night, pointing the way to art shows, performances, concerts, and happenings in Technopolis as well as to the rapidly expanding nightlife scene growing up around it. The city of Athens bought the disused foundry in the late 1990s and converted it to the "Art City" referred to by its Greek name. The transformation preserved all the original architecture and stonework, and work still continues: at this writing the complex includes six exhibition spaces and a large courtyard open to the public. The spaces regularly host shows of anything from comic-book art to trash sculpture to war photography, along with open-air jazz, rock and theater performances, rave nights, and parties. On permanent display in the small **Maria Callas Museum** (☉ Weekdays 9–5) are objects including the opera diva's personal photo albums, letters, and clothes. ✉ *Pireos 100, Gazi* ☎ *210/346–0981* ⊕ *www.culture.gr* 🎫 *Free* ☉ *9 AM–9 PM during exhibitions* Ⓜ *Thiseio.*

Exarchia & the National Archaeological Museum

Εξάρχεια & το Εθνικό Αρχαιολογικό Μουσείο

The bohemian neighborhood of Exarchia, mentioned in hundreds of Greek folk songs and novels, evokes strong feelings in every Athenian: this was the site of the most important events in the nation's recent history. Here, in 1973, the students of Athens Polytechnic rose up in protest against Greece's hated military dictatorship. The uprising was crushed and many students killed by tanks, but the protests were a turning point that led to the junta's fall the following year. Many of those students went on to become Greece's most prominent left-wing politicians; meanwhile, the neighborhood has remained a bastion of students and intellectuals, its many cafés and tavernas alive with political debate. Exarchia is not the most beautiful Athenian neighborhood—its walls are covered in graffiti decrying the latest Western imperialist outrage—but it is chock-full of old-fashioned bars, restaurants dishing up philosophical banter along with the food, used-book and -record stores, and spots for live rembetika, the Greek blues.

Even if all this holds no interest for you, Exarchia is home to a must-do of Greece: the stately National Archaeological Museum, with one of the most exciting collections of Greek antiquities in the world. Here are the sensational finds made by Heinrich Schliemann, discoverer of Troy and father of modern archaeology, in the course of his excavations of the royal tombs on the Homeric site of Mycenae in the 1870s. Here, too, are world-famous bronzes such as the *Jockey of Artemision* and a bronze of Poseidon throwing a trident (or is it Zeus hurling a thunderbolt?).

a good walk

Start with a coffee in **Exarchia Square** ㊻ ☞, where you can get a good feel for the hard-edged history of this old neighborhood. Then head down Stournari and turn right on 28 Oktovriou (Patission), looking into the grounds of the **Politechnio** ㊼, a national symbol of student resistance. If the National Archaeological Museum is closed, turn right up the wide pedestrian street of Tositsa, where you can walk around the cool courtyards and examine ancient marble inscriptions in the **Epigraphical Museum** ㊽. If it's a Saturday, you may want to walk a few blocks up bustling Kallidromiou, which on Saturday morning is transformed into one of the city's largest and most colorful markets, with vendors selling fruits, vegetables, herbs, flowers, and dry goods. Then head back down to the **National Archaeological Museum** ㊾, one of the most important museums in Greece. Two blocks up from the museum at the intersection of 28 Oktovriou (Patission) and Leoforos Alexandras is Athens's largest park, **Pedion Areos** ㊿, which provides visual relief from the urban sprawl.

TIMING   Try to visit the National Archaeological Museum after lunch, when most tour groups have departed; renovation is under way into 2007, so check in advance for temporary closings. If you hang on to your admission ticket, you can take a break at the pleasant although pricey garden café in front of the museum. Kallidromiou is at its liveliest during the Saturday-morning market and the Epigraphical Museum is closed Monday.

What to See

㊽ **Epigraphical Museum.** The ancient marble inscriptions here may constitute the world's most important collection of its kind; highlights include a 480 BC decree by the Assembly of Athens telling people to flee the city before the Persian invasion, a sacred law concerning worship on the Acropolis, and a stele with the Draconian laws on homicide. There's even a prototype voting machine from the 2nd century BC. ⊠ *Tositsa 1, Exarchia* ☎ *210/821–7637* ⊕ *www.culture.gr* ☞ *Free* ⊙ *Tues.–Sun. 8:30–3* Ⓜ *Panepistimiou.*

☞ ㊻ **Exarchia Square.** This square is worn around the edges, but you'll immediately feel its heartbeat, despite creeping gentrification and an unpopular redesign that replaced a patch of park with concrete. The many cafés are always full of students, anarchists, old-time left-wingers, and young, black-clad hipsters, who may be deconstructing Kazantzakis, fomenting rebellion, discussing the issues of the day, or just catching up on gossip. The streets leading off the square, especially Valtetsiou, are full of old tavernas serving up cheap, home-cooked classics to their regulars; movie theaters that never show anything but art and independent flicks; casual, friendly bars; and some of Athens's very best live music clubs. ⊠ *Intersection of Stournari and Themistokleous streets, Exarchia.*

need a break?

At chic **Diplo** (⊠ Themistokleous 70, Exarchia ☎ 210/330–1177), you can relax on lounges and listen to jazz, with a view of the square. The low-key **Floral** (⊠ Exarchia Sq., Exarchia ☎ 210/330–0938), spread out under shady trees and tents, is a café that's usually full of students. At **Rosalia** (⊠ Valtetsiou 58, Exarchia ☎ 210/330–2933), you can pick and choose from a tray of the day's specials brought to you at your table in a shaded garden.

㊾ National Archaeological Museum. By far the most important museum in Greece, this collection contains artistic highlights from every period of ancient Greek civilization, from Neolithic to Roman times. Be warned, however, that into 2007 the museum will be only partially open, with closed galleries marked by a red X on the floor plan by the main entrance. Underway is a grand-scale expansion and renovation that encompasses both a much-needed face-lift and a near doubling of gallery space; the plan will allow the museum to show works that have languished in storage for decades. The reorganized displays will be accompanied by enriched English-language information.

Fodor'sChoice
★

Holdings are grouped in five major collections: prehistoric artifacts (7th millennium BC to 1050 BC), sculptures, bronzes, vases and minor arts, and Egyptian artifacts. The museum's most celebrated display is the **Mycenaean Antiquities.** Here are the stunning gold treasures from Heinrich Schliemann's 1876 excavations of Mycenae's royal tombs: the funeral mask of a bearded king, once thought to be the image of Agamemnon but now believed to be much older, from about the 15th century BC; a splendid silver bull's-head libation cup; and the 15th-century BC Vaphio Goblets, masterworks in embossed gold. Mycenaeans were famed for their carving in miniature, and an exquisite example is the ivory statuette of two curvaceous mother goddesses with a child nestled on their laps.

Withheld from the public since they were damaged in the 1999 earthquakes, but not to be missed, are the beautifully restored **frescoes from Santorini,** delightful murals depicting daily life in Minoan Santorini. Along with the treasures from Mycenae, these wall paintings are part of the museum's Prehistoric Collection.

Other stars of the museum include the works of Geometric and Archaic art (10th–6th centuries BC), and kouroi and funerary stelae (8th–5th centuries BC), among them the stelae of the warrior Aristion signed by Aristokles, and the unusual *Running Hoplite* (a hoplite was a Greek infantry soldier). The collection of Classical art (5th–3rd centuries BC) contains some of the most renowned surviving ancient statues: the bareback *Jockey of Artemision,* a 2nd-century BC Hellenistic bronze salvaged from the sea; from the same excavation, the bronze *Artemision Poseidon* (some say Zeus), poised and ready to fling a trident (or thunderbolt?); and the *Varvakios Athena,* a half-size marble version of the gigantic gold-and-ivory cult statue that Pheidias erected in the Parthenon.

Some of the most moving displays are those of funerary architecture: the spirited 2nd-century relief of a rearing stallion held by a black groom, which exemplifies the transition from classical to Hellenistic style, the latest period in the museum's holdings. Among the most famous sculptures in this collection is the humorous marble group of a nude *Aphrodite* getting ready to slap an advancing Pan with a sandal, while Eros floats overhead and grasps one of Pan's horns.

Light refreshments are served in a lower ground-floor café, which opens out to a patio and sculpture garden. ✉ *28 Oktovriou (Patission) 44, Exarchia* ☎ *210/821–7717* ⊕ *www.culture.gr* ✆ *€6* ⊘ *Apr.–Oct. 15, Mon. 12:30–7, Tues.–Sun. 8:30–7; Oct. 16–Mar., Mon. 10:30–5, Tues.–Sun. 8:30–3. Closed Jan. 1, Mar. 25, May 1, Easter Sun., Dec. 25–26; open reduced hrs other holidays.*

☾ ㊿ **Pedion Areos.** In Athens's largest park, statues of war heroes from the 1821 revolution dot the many walkways and hidden corners, and in summer a small theater and cultural center stage performances. The park, once a firing range, was appropriately named for Ares, the god of war. It extends all the way to a section near the **Dikastiria** (courthouse complex) where at night several ouzeri are packed with Athenians taking advantage of the cool forest air. There are three **playgrounds:** two near the central entrance and one off Evelpidon. A small train for youngsters traverses the park, though its proprietor doesn't keep fixed hours. ✉ *Main entrance at 28 Oktovriou (Patission) and Leoforos Alexandras, Pedion Areos* ☎ *210/821–2239* ⊘ *Daily.*

㊼ **Politechnio.** In late 1973 students occupied this University of Athens building to protest the ruling junta. In response to their calls for resistance, many Greeks disobeyed military orders and showed their support by smuggling in supplies. On the night of November 16, snipers were ordered to fire into the courtyards while tanks rammed the gates: no one knows how many students were killed, because they were secretly buried in mass graves. The public was outraged, and less than a year later, the junta was toppled. Every year on November 17, students march from the Politechnio to the embassy of the United States, which supported the dictatorship. The building is still the site for frequent student demonstrations, especially since police are legally barred from entering its gates. At this writing, the building is closed indefinitely for extensive renovation; the School of Fine Arts has been permanently relocated to a disused factory on Pireos Street, a short distance from Gazi. ✉ *28 Oktovriou (Patission) 42, Exarchia* ☎ *210/772–4000* ⊘ *Late Aug.–July, offices weekdays 8–2; grounds daily.*

Syntagma Square, National Garden & Kolonaki

Πχατεία Συντάγματος, Εθνικός Κήπος & Κολωνάκι

Sooner or later, everyone passes through spacious Syntagma Square, which is surrounded by sights that span Athens's history from the days of Emperor Hadrian (Temple of Olympian Zeus) to King Otho's reign after the 1821 War of Independence (the National Garden and Parliament). Neighboring Kolonaki—the chic shopping district and one of the most fashionable residential areas—occupies the lower slopes of Mt. Lycabettus. Besides visiting its several museums, you can spend time window-shopping and people-watching, since cafés are busy from early morning to dawn.

a good walk

Begin at the site of the first modern Olympics (1896), the **Panathenaic Stadium** ⑤ ⌐ on Vasileos Konstantinou. You may want to detour right onto Irodou Attikou, which leads to the Presidential Palace, used by Greece's kings after the restoration of 1935 and now by the nation's head of state. Across the street from the stadium is the **National Garden** ㉒, a pet project of Queen Amalia. Bear right, past the neoclassical Zappion hall, where you exit onto Vasilissis Olgas, dominated by the **Temple of Olympian Zeus** ㉓, and around the corner on Amalias, **Hadrian's Arch** ㉔, which marks the spot where the ancient city ended and Hadrian's Athens began.

Off Amalias is the large Russian Orthodox church of **Ayios Nikodimos** ㉕ and, nearby, the **Jewish Museum of Greece** ㉖, which details the history of one of Greece's decimated communities. Amalias also passes above **Syntagma Square** ㉗ in front of Parliament and the Tomb of the Unknown Soldier, guarded by burly Evzone guards. Proceed up Vasilissis Sofias to the **Benaki Museum** ㉘ and the delightful **Goulandris Cycladic and Greek Ancient Art Museum** ㉙ to see hundreds of artifacts from the Cycladic civilization (3000–2000 BC). A few blocks up Vasilissis Sofias, the **Byzantine Museum** ㉠, in an 1848 mansion built by an eccentric French aristocrat, features a unique collection of icons.

Five minutes east of the museum is the **National Gallery of Art** ㉡, worth a visit for its special exhibits. Turn off Vasilissis Sofias onto Gennadiou, passing the 12th-century **Moni Petraki** ㉢, to **Gennadius Library** ㉣, containing one of the greatest collections on Greek subjects. Go left on Souidias (which becomes Spefsipou); at Ploutarchou, steps ascend to the funicular to the top of **Mt. Lycabettus** ㉤, three times the height of the Acropolis. The view from the top—pollution permitting—is one of the finest in Athens. You can see all the Attica basin, the harbor, and the islands of Aegina and Poros laid out before you. Minibus 060 from Kolonaki Square also stops at the funicular station. Walk or ride back to **Kolonaki Square** ㉥, which, especially on Saturday at noon, is crammed with chattering crowds of people who relax along the café-lined pedestrian zones or shop in the designer boutiques.

TIMING   Because most of the museums close around 3 PM—as do shops on Monday, Wednesday, and Saturday—plan your walk for mid-morning. The walk takes about four hours, but you may want to extend this to visit Mt. Lycabettus in the late afternoon, when the light produces the best view. Most of the sites are closed one day a week, though all are open Wednesday through Friday; choose your route accordingly.

What to See

⑤ **Ayios Nikodimos.** In 1780 the notoriously brutal Athens governor Hadji Ali Haseki pulled down this 11th-century convent chapel and used the stone to build a defensive wall around Athens. The church, built on the site of the chapel, was sold to the Russian government, who in 1852–56 modified it into a larger, cruciform building with a distinctive terra-cotta frieze; the separate tower was built to hold a massive bell donated by Tsar Alexander II. Note the displays of ornate Russian embroidery and the bright blues of the Pantocrator (Godhead) overhead. The female chanters of this Russian Orthodox church are renowned. ✉ *Fillelinon 21, Syntagma Sq.* ☎ *210/323–1090* Ⓜ *Syntagma.*

❺❽ **Benaki Museum.** Greece's oldest private museum, established in 1926 by
Fodor'sChoice an illustrious Athenian family, the Benaki was one of the first to place
★ emphasis on Greece's later heritage at a time when many archaeologists
were destroying Byzantine artifacts to access ancient objects. The collection (more than 20,000 items are on display in 36 rooms, and that's
only a sample of the holdings) moves chronologically from the ground
floor upward, from prehistory to the formation of the modern Greek
state. You might see anything from a 5,000-year-old hammered gold bowl
to an austere Byzantine icon of the Virgin Mary to Lord Byron's pistols
to the Nobel medals awarded to poets George Seferis and Odysseus Elytis.
Some exhibits are just plain fun—the re-creation of a Kozani (Macedonian town) living room; a tableau of costumed mannequins; a
Karaghiozi shadow puppet piloting a toy plane—all contrasted against
the marble and crystal-chandelier grandeur of the Benaki home. The mansion was designed by Anastassios Metaxas, the architect who helped restore the Panathenaic Stadium. The Benaki's gift shop, a destination in
itself, tempts with exquisitely reproduced ceramics and jewelry. The sec-
ond-floor café serves coffee and snacks, with a few daily specials, on a
veranda overlooking the National Garden. ✉ *Koumbari 1, Kolonaki*
☎ *210/367–1000* ⊕ *www.benaki.gr* ☑ *€6, free Thurs.* ☾ *Mon., Wed.,
Fri., and Sat. 9–5, Thurs. 9 AM–midnight, Sun. 9–3* Ⓜ *Syntagma.*

★ **❻⓪** **Byzantine and Christian Museum.** One of the few museums in Europe concentrating exclusively on Byzantine art displays an outstanding collection of icons, mosaics, and tapestries. Sculptural fragments provide an
excellent introduction to Byzantine architecture. The museum will be
closed periodically through 2006 to accommodate extensive renovations,
including the addition of a below-ground wing. When it reopens, much
of the collection will be displayed for the first time, including several
magnificent illuminated manuscripts. You will also be able to explore
the on-site archaeological dig of Aristotle's Lyceum. ✉ *Vasilissis Sofias
22, Kolonaki* ☎ *210/721–1027, 210/723–2178, or 210/723–1570*
⊕ *www.culture.gr* ☑ *€4* ☾ *Tues.–Sun. 8:30–3; call for periodic closings* Ⓜ *Evangelismos.*

**off the
beaten
path**

DESTE FOUNDATION, CENTER FOR CONTEMPORARY ART – Art
collector Dakis Joannou, who owns one of the world's largest
collections of modern art, opened this lively complex in a renovated
paper warehouse, a short taxi ride from downtown. His private
holdings range from Duchamp to Warhol to Koons, but the gallery
space is more often devoted to progressive exhibits designed to develop
audiences for contemporary art in Greece and to offer opportunities for
up-and-coming artists. The complex eschews the usual formality of
museums and instead casually mixes art, entertainment, new media,
and shopping. Included are the ground-floor Cosmos bar-restaurant, a
video projection room, an art shop, and a cybercafé. ✉ *Omirou 8, Neo
Psihiko* ☎ *210/672–9460* ⊕ *www.deste.gr* ☑ *Free* ☾ *Weekdays 8:30
AM–9 PM, Sat. noon–4. Closed 2 wks in Aug.*

FIRST CEMETERY OF ATHENS – This is Athens's equivalent of Paris's
Père-Lachaise, but it is whitewashed and cheerful rather than gloomy
and Gothic. The graves of the rich and famous are surrounded by
well-tended gardens and decorated with small photographs of the
departed, and birds chirp in the stately cypress and mandarin trees.
The main entrance off Anapafseos, which means "eternal rest," leads
to an open-air museum of mind-boggling funerary architecture: the
imposing temple dedicated to Heinrich Schliemann is adorned with
scenes from the Trojan War, and the touching marble *Sleeping
Maiden* sculpture by Yiannoulis Halepas marks the grave of Sophia
Afendaki. It was commissioned by her parents in the hope that some
day their young daughter would be awakened by a prince's kiss.
Perhaps the most visited grave is that of actress and national
sweetheart Aliki Vouyiouklaki; it is bedecked with lighted candles,
flowers, and fan letters left daily. The film star and politician Melina
Mercouri is also buried here, as is the popular, controversial former
prime minister Andreas Papandreou, who died in 1996.
⊠ *Anapafseos and Trivonianou, near Panathenaic Stadium, Pangrati*
☎ *210/923–6118 or 210/923–6720* ⊙ *May–Sept., daily 7:30 AM–8
PM; Oct.–Apr., daily 8–5* Ⓜ *Leoforos Vouliagmenis tram stop.*

❻❸ **Gennadius Library.** Book lovers who ascend the grand staircase into the
hallowed aura of the Reading Room may have difficulty tearing themselves away from this superb collection of material on Greek subjects,
from first editions of Greek classics to the papers of Nobel Laureate poets
George Seferis and Odysseus Elytis. The heart of the collection consists
of thousands of books donated in the 1920s by Greek diplomat John
Gennadius, who haunted London's rare-book shops for volumes connected to Greece, thus amassing the most comprehensive collection of
Greek books held by one man. He died bankrupt, leaving his wife to
pay off his debts, mostly to booksellers. The library's collection includes Lord Byron's memorabilia (including a lock of his hair); Heinrich Schliemann's diaries, notebooks, and letters; and impressionistic
watercolors of Greece by Edward Lear. Pride of place is given to the first
edition printed in Greek of Homer (the *Iliad* and the *Odyssey*). The Gennadius, which is under the custody of the American School of Classical
studies, is not a lending library. ⊠ *Souidias 61, Kolonaki* ☎ *210/721–
0536* ⊕ *www.ascsa.edu.gr* ⊙ *Mid-Sept.–mid-Aug., Mon.–Wed. and
Fri. 9:30–5, Thurs. 9:30–8, Sat. 9:30–2* Ⓜ *Evangelismos.*

❺❾ **Goulandris Cycladic and Greek Ancient Art Museum.** Funded by one of
FodorśChoice Greece's richest families, this museum has an outstanding collection of
★ 350 Cycladic artifacts dating from the Bronze Age, including many of
the enigmatic marble figurines whose slender shapes fascinated such artists
as Picasso, Modigliani, and Brancusi. Other collections focus on Greek
art from the Bronze Age through the 6th century AD. A glass corridor
connects the main building to the gorgeous adjacent Stathatos Mansion,
where temporary exhibits are mounted. ⊠ *Neofitou Douka 4 or Irodotou
1, Kolonaki* ☎ *210/722–8321 through 210/722–8323* ⊕ *www.cycladic.
gr* 🎫 *€3.50* ⊙ *Mon. and Wed.–Fri. 10–4, Sat. 10–3* Ⓜ *Evaneglismos.*

54 **Hadrian's Arch.** This marble gateway, built in AD 131 with Corinthian details, was intended both to honor the Hellenophile emperor Hadrian and to separate the ancient and imperial sections of Athens. On the side facing the Acropolis an inscription reads THIS IS ATHENS, THE ANCIENT CITY OF THESEUS, but the side facing the Temple of Olympian Zeus proclaims THIS IS THE CITY OF HADRIAN AND NOT OF THESEUS. ⊠ *Vasilissis Amalias at Dionyssiou Areopagitou, National Garden* ⊕ *www.culture. gr* ⊡ *Free* ☉ *Daily* Ⓜ *Acropolis.*

56 **Jewish Museum of Greece.** The museum's vivid memorabilia, on display in an elegantly renovated neoclassical building near Plaka, tells the story of the Jews in Greece from the 6th century BC to the Holocaust, when 87% of Greek Jews were killed; only about 5,000 remain today. The museum pays tribute to the diversity of the various Jewish communities with a collection organized according to periods and themes. These include the early history of the Romaniotes (Jews who espoused Greek culture and wrote Greek in the Hebrew script), many of whom lived in Halkida, one of Europe's oldest Jewish communities; the arrival of the Ladino-speaking Sephardic Jews after they were expelled from Spain during the Inquisition in 1492; the Jewish calendar and holidays; and religious items used in synagogues as well as in everyday domestic life. One room contains a reconstruction of the interior of the old Romaniote Synagogue of Patras, a community established by Jews from Syria in 323–281 BC. Ring the bell for admittance. ⊠ *Nikis 39, Plaka* ☎ *210/322–5582* ⊕ *www.jewishmuseum.gr* ⊡ *€3* ☉ *Weekdays 9–2:30, Sun. 10–2* Ⓜ *Syntagma.*

65 **Kolonaki Square.** To see and be seen, Athenians gather not on the square, officially called Filikis Eterias, but at the cafés on its periphery and along the Tsakalof and Milioni pedestrian zone. Glittery models, middle-aged executives, elegant pensioners—all congregate here for a quick coffee before work, for a drink after a hard day of shopping, or for foreign newspapers at the all-night kiosk. On the lower side of the square is the **British Council Library** (⊠ Kolonaki Sq. 17, Kolonaki ☎ 210/364–5768 ☉ Mon. and Thurs. 3–8; Tues., Wed., and Fri. 9:30–2:30; closed 3 wks in Aug.), which has some children's videos and a screening facility. ⊠ *Intersection of Patriarchou Ioakeim and Kanari, Kolonaki.*

> **need a break?** Enjoy a cappuccino and an Italian sweet standing at **Da Capo** (⊠ Tsakalof 1, Kolonaki ☎ 210/360–2497). This place is frequented by young trendsetters, especially on Saturday afternoons; people-watching is part of the pleasure.

62 **Moni Petraki.** Tucked into a sweet little park at Iassou, this church was built in the 12th century and decorated with paintings by Yiorgios Markos in the 18th century. ⊠ *Off Moni Petraki, Kolonaki* ☎ *210/721– 2402* ☉ *Mon.–Sat. 6 AM–noon, Sun. 6 AM–noon and 6:30–9:30* Ⓜ *Evangelismos.*

★ **64** **Mt. Lycabettus.** Myth claims that Athens's highest hill came into existence when Athena removed a piece of Mt. Pendeli, intending to boost the height of her temple on the Acropolis. While she was en route, a crone brought her bad tidings, and the flustered goddess dropped the rock in the middle of the city. Kids love the ride up the steeply inclined *teleferique* (funicular) to the summit, crowned by whitewashed **Ayios Georgios** chapel with a bell tower donated by Queen Olga. On a clear day, you can see Aegina island, with or without the aid of coin-operated telescopes. Built into a cave on the side of the hill, near the I Prasini Tenta café, is a small shrine to **Ayios Isidoros.** In 1859 students prayed here for those fighting against the Austrians, French, and Sardinians with whom King Otho had allied. From Mt. Lycabettus you can watch the sun set and then turn about to watch the moon rise over "violet-crowned" Hymettus as the lights of Athens blink on all over the city. ⊠ *Base: 15-min walk northeast of Syntagma Sq.; funicular every 10 mins from corner of Ploutarchou and Aristippou (take Minibus 060 from Kanari or Kolonaki Sq., except Sun.), Kolonaki* ☎ *210/722–7065* 🚃 *Funicular €4* ⊘ *Funicular daily 9* AM*–3* AM.

need a break?

The pricey café at the top of Mt. Lycabettus may be the most convenient place to stop, but persevere and you'll find a better deal and a more romantic, pine-scented setting at **I Prasini Tenta** (⊠ 5 mins down path that leaves from Ayios Giorgios or, if driving, turn left at fork when descending Mt. Lycabettus, Kolonaki ☎ 210/361–9447), an outdoor café where you can savor an ouzo and appetizers such as mushrooms stuffed with four cheeses, along with your Acropolis view.

⑥₁ National Gallery of Art. The permanent collections of Greek painting and sculpture of the 19th and 20th centuries (including the work of naive artist Theophilos) are still on display, but popular traveling exhibitions enliven the gallery. The exhibitions are usually major loan shows from around the world, such as an El Greco retrospective, Dutch 17th-century art, and an exhibit tracing the influence of Greece on works of the Italian Renaissance. ⊠ *Vasileos Konstantinou 50, Ilisia* ☎ *210/723–5857 or 210/723–5937* ⊕ *www.culture.gr* 🚃 *€6.50* ⊘ *Mon. and Wed. 9–3 and 6–9, Thurs.–Sat. 9–3, Sun. 10–2* Ⓜ *Evangelismos.*

☺ ⑤₂ National Garden. When you can't take the city noise anymore, step into this oasis completed in 1860 as part of King Otho and Queen Amalia's royal holdings. Here old men on the benches argue politics, police officers take their coffee breaks, and animal lovers feed the stray cats that roam among the more than 500 species of trees and plants, many labeled. At the east end is the neoclassical **Zappion hall,** built in 1888 and used for major political and cultural events: it was here that Greece signed its accession to what was then the European Community. Children appreciate the **playgrounds, duck pond, and small zoo** (⊠ East end of park, National Garden). The Hellenic Ornithological Society runs an **information kiosk** (⊠ Irodou Attikou entrance, near playground, National Garden 📠 210/381–1271 or 210/330–1167) dedicated to the park's birds. The society's activity program for children includes games geared to recognizing the park's winged visitors, drawing contests, and the making of swallow's nests to ensure sanctuary for homeless birds. The kiosk is open all year (though August depends on the volunteers), weekends 11–2:30. Youngsters ages 5–15 may settle into a good book at the **Children's Library** (☎ 210/323–6503 ☉ Sept.–July, Tues.–Sat. 8:30–2:30), a rustic, vine-covered stone cottage in a tranquil corner of the garden. Of its 4,000 books, only 60 are in English and French. It also has games and puzzles (some in English), a chess set, dominoes, crayons, and coloring books. ✉ *East of Vasilissis Amalias, between Vasilissis Olgas and Vasilissis Sofias, National Garden* ☎ *210/721–5019* ☉ *Daily 7* AM–*sunset* Ⓜ *Syntagma.*

need a break? Visit the romantic **Kafenedaki** (✉ National Garden), sometimes called Kipos, a cool spot with wrought-iron chairs and tables nestled under a bower of flowering vines. The café is next to a stone cottage inside the park's Irodou Attikou entrance (near Lykeiou). The menu is limited to a *poikilia* (variety) of mezedes, grilled "tost" (with ham and cheese), ice cream, apple cake, and drinks.

▶ **51** **Panathenaic Stadium.** Constructed by Lykourgus from 330 to 329 BC and used intermittently for Roman spectacles, the stadium was re-seated for the Panathenaic Games of AD 144 by Roman citizen Herodes Atticus of Marathon, a magistrate, senator, and wealthy patron of Athens. It later fell into ruin, and its marble was quarried for other buildings. By the mid-18th century, when it was painted by French artist Le Roy, it had become little more than a wheat field with scant remains and was later the midnight site of the secret rites of the witches of Athens. A blinding-white marble reconstruction of the ancient Roman stadium was rebuilt for the first modern Olympics, in April of 1896; that marble was meticulously cleaned and restored for the 2004 Olympics, when the stadium hosted the archery competition and marathon finish. Climb to the last row for a wonderful view of the Acropolis, or pretend to be a world-class athlete by running a lap around the stadium. ✉ *Near junction of Vasilissis Olgas and Vasileos Konstantinou, across from National Garden, Pangrati* ⊕ *www.culture.gr* ✉ *Free* ☉ *Daily 9–2 but can be viewed in its entirety without entering.*

★ **57** **Syntagma (Constitution) Square.** At the top of the city's main square stands **Parliament,** formerly the royal palace, completed in 1838 for the new monarchy. It seems a bit austere and heavy for a southern landscape, but it was proof of progress, the symbol of the new ruling power. The building's saving grace is the stone's magical change of color from off-white to gold to rosy mauve as the day progresses. Here you can watch the **changing of the Evzone guards** at the **Tomb of the Unknown Soldier**—in front of Parliament on a lower level—which takes place at intervals throughout the day. On Sunday the honor guard of tall young men don dress costume—a short white *foustanella* (kilt) with 400 neat pleats, one for each year of the Ottoman occupation, and red shoes with pompons—and still manage to look brawny rather than silly. A band accompanies a large troop of them in a memorable ceremony that leaves from the nearby barracks, arriving in front of Parliament by 11:15 AM. On a wall behind the Tomb of the Unknown Soldier, the bas-relief of a dying soldier is modeled after a sculpture on the Temple of Aphaia in

Exploring
Piraeus

Papastratou

Dragatsaniou

Akti Kondili

Metro
Alipedou

Mavromichali

Fokionos

Moutsopoulou

Dodekanissou

Samou

Athinon-Pireos

66

Omiridou Skilitsi

Navarinou
Gounari
Elth. Antistaseos
340 Syntagmatos
Peraiou

67

Vas. Georgiou A

Gr. Lambraki

Tsavella

Peace and
Friendship
Stadium

Akti Kallimasioti
Akti Poseidonos
Akti Miaouli

Iroon Politechniou

Veakio
Theater

72

KASTELLA

Vas. Pavlou

71

Akti Koundourou

Customs
House

Exhibition
Center

Hatzikiriakou

68

Akti Moutsopoulou

69

Akti Koundouriotou

Saronic
Gulf

Sp. Lambrou

Sahtouri

Akti Themistokleous

70

KEY

Start of walk

Aegina; the text is from the funeral oration said to have been given by
Pericles. Pop into the gleaming **Syntagma metro station** (⊠ Upper end
of Syntagma Sq. ☉ Daily 5 AM–midnight) to examine artfully displayed
artifacts uncovered during subway excavations. A floor-to-ceiling cross
section of earth behind glass shows finds in chronological layers, ranging from a skeleton in its ancient grave to traces of the 4th-century BC
road to Mesogeia to an Ottoman cistern. ⊠ *Vasilissis Amalias and
Vasilissis Sofias, Syntagma Sq.* Ⓜ *Syntagma.*

need a
break?

Since 1910, **Ariston** (⊠ Voulis 10, Syntagma Sq. ☎ 210/322–7626)
has been turning out arguably the city's best *tiropites* (cheese pies);
theirs are a little more piquant than usual and have a thicker pastry
crust. Avoid the tasteless variety often sold on the street and make a
pit stop here for the real thing, or try the equally good potato pies.
The establishment is open during shopping hours.

❺❸ **Temple of Olympian Zeus.** Begun in the 6th century BC, the temple was
completed in AD 132 by Hadrian, who also commissioned a huge gold-
and-ivory statue of Zeus for the inner chamber and another, only
slightly smaller, of himself. Only 15 of the original Corinthian columns
remain, but standing next to them may inspire a sense of awe at their

bulk, which is softened by the graceful carving on the acanthus-leaf capitals. The clearly defined segments of a column blown down in 1852 give you an idea of the method used in its construction. The site is floodlighted on summer evenings, creating a majestic scene when you round the bend from Syngrou. On the outskirts of the site to the north are remains of Roman houses, the city walls, and a Roman bath. ⊠ *Vasilissis Olgas 1, National Garden* ☏ *210/922–6330* ⊕ *www.culture.gr* ✉ *€2, or with €12 joint ticket for all Unification of Archaeological Sites* ⊙ *Tues.–Sun. 8:30–3* Ⓜ *Acropolis.*

Piraeus

Πειραιάς

To those who have seen the 1960 film *Never on Sunday,* the name Piraeus evokes images of earthy waterfront cafés frequented by free-spirited sailors and hookers, but many Athenians regard the port city (except for the Mikrolimano and Kastella neighborhoods) as merely low class. Neither image is correct: the restoration of older buildings and the addition of shopping centers and cafés have brought about a rejuvenation, both of place and community pride. Piraeus caters more to Greek families and young singles than to the rough-and-tumble crowd, and living in some parts of it carries a certain cachet these days. Also in its favor: the air pollution, noise level, and temperatures are considerably lower than they are in inner Athens.

Piraeus remains the port of Athens, 11 km (7 mi) southwest of the center, and is the third-largest city in Greece (after Athens and Thessaloniki), with a population of about 500,000. In 1834, after Greece gained independence from the Turks, the government offered land in Piraeus (at that point a mere wilderness) on favorable terms, and it was resettled by islanders from other parts of the country. The first factory was founded by Hydriots in 1847, and by the turn of the 20th century there were 76 steam-powered factories. After the 1920s Piraeus developed as an economic center, while Athens remained the cultural sphere. In the years following 1922, refugees from Asia Minor swelled the population, bringing with them rembetika music. In anticipation of a flood of visitors during the 2004 Olympics, the harbor district was given a general sprucing up, including a tree-lined promenade along the ancient walls surrounding the harbor, new parks, and the refurbishment of the old district of Kastella.

The fastest and cheapest way to get to Piraeus from central Athens is to take the electric train (Line 1, about 20–30 minutes, depending on whether you leave from Syntagma, Omonia, Monastiraki, or Thission station). The metro station is off Akti Kallimasioti on the main harbor. For those who don't have much time, take Bus 904, 905, or 909 opposite the Piraeus station directly to the Archaeological Museum rather than walking there; get off at the Fillelinon stop. If you're in a leisurely mood, you can instead take the tram from Syntagma, switching at Faliro from Line A to Line B, which terminates at Peace & Friendship Stadium, just a short walk to Kastella. The ride is slow, as the tram line winds through several outlying Athens neighborhoods before reaching the coast, but worth it once it zips along the beach.

a good walk

Start with a detour a few blocks from the metro to the **flea market** 66 ⌐, along Omiridou Skilitsi, and then stop for a coffee in one of the popular spots at the intersection with 34ou (which translates as 34th) Syntagmatos Pezikou, where Athenians come Sunday afternoons. If walking, turn left when exiting the metro, following Akti Kallimasioti to Akti Poseidonos. South of here is the Customs House and Port Authority—which processes passengers boarding boats going to other countries—and a modern exhibition center, where the Poseidonia Shipping Exhibition is held in June in connection with a biannual Nautical Week. Continuing on Akti Poseidonos, turn onto Vasileos Georgiou A' (A' translates as 1st), which passes the imposing 800-seat **Municipal Theater** 67 near Korai Square. Head south on Iroon Polytechniou, cutting through Terpsithea Square, and then go east on Harilaou Trikoupi to the **Archaeological Museum** 68 to see such rare finds as the Piraeus Kouros, a cult statue of Apollo from the 6th century BC. The street ends at the harbor of **Pasalimani** 69 (Zea Marina). To the west is the coastal road Akti Themistokleous, whose lantern-lined stretch has good views and reasonably priced seafood restaurants. Incorporated into the foundation of the **Hellenic Maritime Museum** 70, also on the road, are the original Long Walls of Themistocles, which ran all the way to Kerameikos Cemetery. To the east is the pretty, crescent-shape harbor of **Mikrolimano** 71, lined with seafood restaurants (a 10-minute walk from the Neo Faliro station for those who want to save their strength). Mikrolimano had lost favor with some Athenians because the harbor suffers from pollution, but the harbor is still crowded with yachts, and young people flock to its festive cafés on Sunday.

Above Mikrolimano is charming **Kastella** 72, terraces of 19th-century houses tucked up against the sloping hillside—an ideal spot for a walk before dinner on the harbor or a show at its Veakio Theater.

TIMING   On a day trip to Piraeus you can see the main sights, explore the neighborhoods around its three harbors, and have a seafood meal before returning to Athens. If you are taking an early-morning ferry or seeing a performance at the Veakio Theater, it makes good sense to stay in one of the seaside hotels. Note that the flea market is held only on Sunday, the Archaeological Museum is closed Monday, the Maritime Museum is closed Sunday and Monday, and the Municipal Theater is closed weekends.

What to See

★ 68   **Archaeological Museum.** Despite the impressive finds on display, this museum does not get many visitors—perhaps because of its drab exterior and its distance from the city center. That's too bad, because the museum's prize exhibits include four of the world's very few surviving classical bronze statues: the exquisitely made life-size **Piraeus Kouros** (probably a cult statue of Apollo from the late 6th century or early 5th century BC, and therefore the oldest known hollow-cast bronze statue); a 4th-century bronze of a pensive Athena, in a helmet decorated with griffins and owls; and two bronze versions of Artemis. Discovered in

1959, the works had been hidden in a warehouse during the 1st century BC, probably in anticipation of the 86 BC siege by Roman general Sulla, and were overlooked in the havoc that followed the sacking of Athens and Piraeus. Another exhibit is a broken bronze ram, probably from an ancient trireme, next to the sculpted marble eye that adorned the vessel's bow. One room contains unusual Mycenaean chariot figurines from a sanctuary near Methana, early Geometric vases, and musical instruments and writing tools from a 4th-century BC poet's grave. Stele are inscribed (in ancient Greek) with price regulations for tripe and other goodies like feet and lungs served at meat tavernas, then called *epthopoleia*. The collection of 5th- and 4th-century BC funerary steles and statues includes the urn of Lysis, about whom novelist Mary Renault wrote *The Last of the Wine*. The ground floor contains the 23-foot-high Kallithea funerary monument made in the late 4th century BC. The minitemple atop a high base embellished with reliefs contains statues of a rich Black Sea immigrant, his son, and a young slave. Showy grave monuments like this sparked a stern backlash and a 317 BC ruling that banned funerary architecture. ⊠ *Harilaou Trikoupi 31, at Fillelinon, Pasalimani* ☎ *210/452–1598* ⊕ *www.culture.gr* ▣ *€3* ☉ *Tues.–Sun. 8:30–3* Ⓜ *Piraeus.*

▶ ⑥⑥ **Flea market.** In the Monastiraki of Piraeus, outdoor stalls overflow on Sunday (from 8 until 2) with household items, electronic goods, and offbeat videocassettes, but throughout the week several interesting shops and stalls sell everything from antique Mytilini mirrors ("antique" at the flea market means from about 1850 on) to Thracian wedding gowns to 1950s furniture. The most rewarding stretch is along Omiridou Skilitsi between Ippodamias Square and Pilis street. On Navarinou, parallel to Akti Kallimasioti, another market sells cheese, cold cuts, dried fruit, bread, and nuts. It's good to buy provisions before taking a ferry, because the snack bars on board often have just a few items, and at high prices. ⊠ *Omiridou Skilitsi, parallel to metro tracks, near Pasalimani.*

🕙 ⑦⓪ **Hellenic Maritime Museum.** The 13,000 items on display include scale models and actual sections of triremes and famous boats, Byzantine flags, figureheads, documents, and uniforms. A section of the **Long Walls** is incorporated into the museum's foundation, and other well-preserved segments run along Akti Themistokleous, south of Zea Marina. ⊠ *Akti Themistokleous, Freattida Sq., Pasalimani* ☎ *210/451–6264 or 210/428–6959* ⊕ *www.culture.gr* ▣ *€1.50* ☉ *Sept.–July, Tues.–Fri. 9–2, Sat. 9–1:30.*

⑦② **Kastella.** Its neoclassical houses skillfully restored, this neighborhood behind Mikrolimano recalls a bygone era. In antiquity the hill was known as Mounichia and served as the acropolis of Piraeus. On the hill the **Veakio Theater** (⊠ Idis on Lofos Prof. Ilias, Kastella ☎ 210/419–4520) has a cultural festival late June through September, featuring visiting dance troupes, plays, and concerts. ⊠ *Behind Mikrolimano, Kastella.*

★ ⑦① **Mikrolimano.** The most touristy part of Piraeus, this graceful, small harbor is known to old-timers as **Turkolimano**. Sitting under the awnings by the sea and watching the water and the gaily painted fishing boats is the next best thing to hopping on a ferry and going to an island. In the high season, it is a good idea to have lunch here, as in the evening most of the many restaurants lining the harbor are packed. The hawkers in front of the restaurants are entertaining but can be aggressive. Don't be afraid to ask to see the prices on the menu or go to look at the fish stored in iced compartments. Be sure to specify how large a portion you want, and ask its price in advance. ⊠ *Akti Koumoudourou, Mikrolimano.*

67 **Municipal Theater.** The 800-seat theater was modeled after the Opéra Comique in Paris and finished in 1895. In the same building is the **Panos Aravantinos Decor Museum** (⊠ Ayios Konstantinou 2, near Pasalimani ☎ 210/419–4578 ☞ Free ☉ Sept.–July, Mon. 3–8, Tues.–Fri. 8–2), which displays sketches and models of the artist's theatrical sets. ⊠ *Iroon Polytechniou, near Pasalimani* ☎ *210/419–4584 information, 210/419–4550 box office* ☉ *Open only during performances.*

69 **Pasalimani (Zea Marina).** Once Athens's main naval base, lined with 196 boathouses big enough to hold one trireme, this small harbor is now a yachting marina with berths for more than 400 boats. The surrounding area has been rejuvenated, with the addition of many enticing cafés and pubs. There's a Greek National Tourism Organization (GNTO or EOT) office with maps, brochures, and timetables on the west side of the harbor close to the departure point for Saronic Gulf islands hydrofoils. ⊠ *Akti Moutsopoulou (western extension of Akti Koundouriotou), Pasalimani* Ⓜ *Piraeus.*

WHERE TO EAT

Whether you sample octopus and ouzo near the sea, roasted goat in a 100-year-old taverna, or cutting-edge cuisine in a trendy restaurant, dining in the city is just as relaxing as it is elsewhere in Greece: waiters never rush you, reservations are often unnecessary, and no matter how crowded, the establishment can always make room for another table. Athens's dining scene is experiencing a renaissance, with a particular focus on the intense flavors of regional Greek cooking. Quality has improved, both in preparation and presentation. International options such as classic Italian and French still abound—and a recent Greek fascination with all things Japanese means that sushi is served in every happening bar in town—but today, traditional and nouvelle Greek are the leading contenders for the Athenian palate. The most exciting new, upscale restaurants are contemporary playgrounds for innovative chefs offering a sophisticated mélange of dishes that pay homage to Greek cooking fused with other cuisines. Some of these have also incorporated sleek design, late-night hours, DJs, and adjoining lounges full of beautiful people, forming all-in-one bar-restaurants, renowned for both star Greek chefs and glitterati customers.

Traditional restaurants serve cuisine a little closer to what a Greek grandmother would make, but more formal, and with a wider selection than the neighborhood tavernas. Truly authentic tavernas have wicker chairs that inevitably pinch your bottom, checkered tablecloths covered with butcher paper, wobbly tables that need coins under one leg, and wine drawn from the barrel and served in small metal carafes. The popular hybrid—the modern taverna—serves traditional fare in more stylish surrounds; most are in the up-and-coming industrial-cum-artsy districts. If a place looks inviting and is filled with Greeks, give it a try. Mezedopoleia, sometimes called ouzeri, serve plates of appetizers—basically Levantine tapas—to feast on while sipping ouzo, though many now serve barrel and bottled wine as well.

In the last three weeks of August, when the city empties out and most residents head for the seaside, more than 75% of the restaurants and tavernas popular among the locals close, though bar-restaurants may reopen in different summer locations by the sea. Hotel restaurants, seafood restaurants in Piraeus, and tavernas in Plaka usually remain open. Most places serve lunch from about noon to 4 (and sometimes as late as 6) and dinner from about 9 to at least midnight.

As in most other cosmopolitan cities, dress varies from casual to fancy, according to the establishment. Although Athens is informal and none of the restaurants listed here requires a jacket or tie, you may feel more comfortable dressing up a bit in the most expensive places. Conservative casual attire (not shorts) is acceptable at most establishments.

Prices

WHAT IT COSTS In euros					
	$$$$	$$$	$$	$	¢
AT DINNER	over €20	€16–€20	€12–€15	€8–€11	under €8

Prices are for one main course at dinner, or for two *mezedes* (small dishes) at restaurants that serve only mezedes.

Acropolis & South

Ακρόπολη & προς τα νότια

$$$$ ✕ **Edodi.** There's no menu in this intimate, candlelit dining room. Instead, raw seasonal ingredients are brought theatrically to your table, chosen by you, then cooked to order according to your mood and tastes, which the waitstaff are quite skilled at gauging. Offerings are always changing, but the lobster with spicy Parmesan sauce is a perennial favorite. Other notable dishes have included a tart with feta, tomato, eggplant, and prosciutto, and a swordfish in a crust of potatoes in mustard sauce. Marinated fruit dominates the dessert list: plums stewed in wine and cinnamon, and mangos steeped in rum, served with caramel ice cream. Remember that Edodi has many devotees but only eight tables. ⊠ *Veikou 80, Koukaki* ☎ *210/921–3013* ⚑ *Reservations essential* ▤ *AE, DC, MC, V* ☉ *Closed Sun. and 2 wks in Aug. No lunch.*

$$$–$$$$ ✕ **Symposio.** Devoted clientele return for the rich, earthy cuisine of northern Epirus, where owner Vasilis Paparounas has his own farm. His organic vegetables, forest truffles, tender boar and venison, wild river crayfish, homemade cheeses, and unforgettable wild mushrooms (only available seasonally) are all flown in from the estate. Reserve a seat in the garden with an Acropolis view. Post-theater dinners can be just as

special as the performances at the nearby Odeon of Herodes Atticus. Ask the waiter to recommend a Greek vintage from the extensive wine list. ⊠ *Erechthiou 46, Makriyianni* ☎ *210/922–5321* ⚐ *Reservations essential* ▤ *AE, MC, V* ☻ *Closed Sun. and Aug. No lunch.*

$–$$$ ✕ **Strofi.** Walls lined with autographed photos of actors from the nearby Odeon of Herodes Atticus attest to Strofi's success with the after-theater crowd. Despite the many tourists, the dramatic rooftop garden views of the Acropolis still attract locals who have been coming here for decades. Start with a tangy *taramosalata* (fish roe dip) or velvety tzatziki, which perfectly complements the thinly sliced fried zucchini. Another good appetizer is *fava*, a puree of yellow split peas. For the main coarse, choose roast lamb with *hilopites* (thin egg noodles cut into small squares), rabbit *stifado* (a stew of meat, white wine, garlic, cinnamon, and spices), veal with eggplant, or kid goat prepared with oil and oregano. ⊠ *Rovertou Galli 25, Makriyianni* ☎ *210/921–4130 or 210/922–3787* ▤ *DC, MC, V* ☻ *Closed Sun. No lunch.*

Plaka

Πλάκα

$$$–$$$$ ✕ **Daphne's.** As attested to by the 206-page list of luminaries who have eaten here, celebrities and dignitaries visiting Athens are inevitably brought to dinner here. The appeal is almost ridiculously simple: take traditional, authentic but consistently well-made and well-presented Greek regional dishes; serve them in the immaculate, frescoed courtyard of a neoclassical mansion; hire top-notch, multilingual waitstaff; and have a good selection of Greek wines on hand; and they will come. Expect baked eggplant with cumin, tomatoes, and onions; lamb fricassee; stewed rabbit with *mavrodaphne,* a sweet red wine; and fresh grilled fish with olive oil and lemon. ⊠ *Lysikratous 4, Plaka* ☎ *210/322–7971* ⚐ *Reservations essential* ▤ *AE, MC, V.*

$–$$$ ✕ **I Palia Taverna tou Psarra.** Founded in 1898, this is one of the few remaining Plaka tavernas serving reliably good food as well as having the obligatory mulberry-shaded terrace. The owners claim to have served Brigitte Bardot and Laurence Olivier, but it's the number of Greeks who come here that testifies to Psarra's appeal. Oil-oregano octopus and marinated *gavros* (a small fish) are good appetizers. Simple, tasty entrées include rooster in wine, *arnaki pilino* (lamb baked in clay pots), and pork chops with ouzo. Can't make up your mind? Try the *ouzokatastasi* ("ouzo situation"), a plate of tidbits to nibble while you decide. ⊠ *Erechtheos 16, at Erotokritou, Plaka* ☎ *210/321–8733* ▤ *AE, MC, V.*

$–$$ ✕ **O Platanos.** Tourism hasn't seemed to blight this taverna—one of the **Fodor'sChoice** oldest in Plaka—at all, except on the now-multilingual menus rife with ★ amusing spelling. O Platanos remains a welcome sight compared with the many overpriced tourist traps in the area. The waiters are fast, but far from ingratiating, and the place is packed with Greeks. The shady courtyard is fine for outdoor dining. Don't miss the oven-baked potatoes, roasted lamb, fresh green beans in savory olive oil, and the exceptionally cheap but delicious barrel retsina. ⊠ *Diogenous 4, Plaka* ☎ *210/322–0666* ▤ *No credit cards* ☻ *Closed Sun.*

ON THE MENU

THE BEST OF ATHENS'S RESTAURANTS *have made enormous strides in quality and style since about 2002, thanks to Greek chefs who have studied at international culinary institutes. They returned home with a renewed interest in high-quality native ingredients combined with foreign techniques, particularly French and Asian. Indeed, you may have a hard time finding a traditional taramosalata (roe dip), as many chefs are eager to tweak Aegean-inspired cuisine into new forms. Expect newer-than-now house specialties at upscale restaurants, but remember: traditional Greek food can be sensational. You'll find out how sensational if you taste iman bayildi ("the cleric fainted"— presumably because the dish of eggplant with garlic and tomato was so delicious). Do try the hima, the house barrel wine; it's inexpensive and often quite good.*

If you can't understand the menu, just go to the kitchen and point at what looks most appealing, especially in tavernas, where not everything on the menu may be available at the time you order. In most cases, you don't need to ask—just walk to the kitchen (some places have food displayed in a glass case right at the kitchen's doorway), or point to your eye and then the kitchen; the truly ambitious can say (Bo-ro na dtho tee eh-he-teh steen koo-zee-na?), or "May I see what's in the kitchen?" When ordering fish, which is priced by the kilo, you will often go to the kitchen to pick out your fish, which is then weighed and billed accordingly. At some rustic places, like Margaro in Piraeus, you may wind up in the kitchen for another reason: when it's crowded, the staff asks you to prepare your own salad.

$–$$ ✕ **Taverna Xynos.** Stepping into the courtyard of this Plaka taverna is like entering a time warp back to Athens in the 1950s. In summer, tables move outside and a guitar duo drops by, playing ballads of yesteryear. Loyal customers say little has changed since then—although diners' demands have, making the setup seem somewhat dated. Start with the classic stuffed-grape-leaf appetizer, and then move on to the taverna's strong suit—dishes such as lamb *yiouvetsi* (baked in ceramic dishes with tomato sauce and barley-shape pasta), livers with sweetbreads in vinegar and oregano, and piquant *soutsoukakia,* meatballs fried, then simmered in a cinnamon-laced tomato sauce. This is one place where you could order the moussaka and not be disappointed. The entrance is down the walkway next to Glikis Kafenion. ✉ *Aggelou Geronda 4, Plaka* ☎ *210/ 322–1065* ▭ *No credit cards* ☉ *Closed weekends and July. No lunch.*

Monastiraki & Thission

Μοναστηράκι & Θησείο

$$$$ ✕ **To Spiti tou Pil Poul.** Take in a spectacular view of the Parthenon while browsing a menu that features *foie gras* topped with caramelized endives. Yes, the prices definitely tag "Mr. Pil Poul's House" as a restaurant for

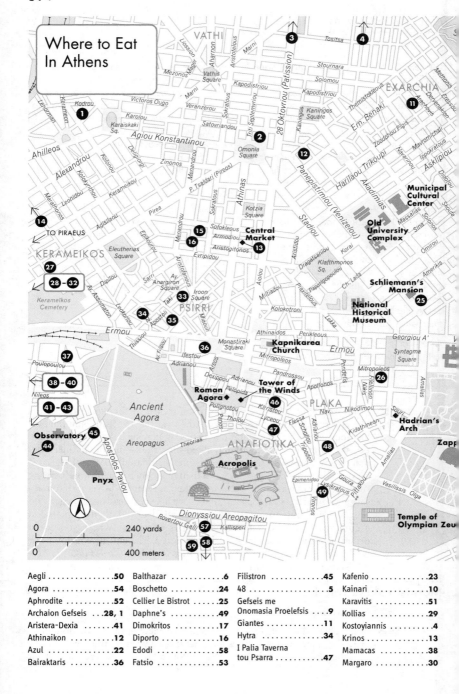

Where to Eat
In Athens

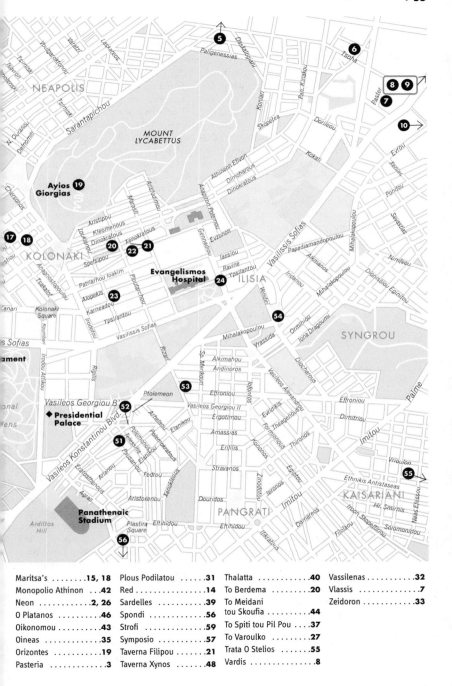

special occasions, but just stepping onto the marble terrace is enough to make it one. White linens and candlelight enhance the romantic aura of this beautifully restored neoclassical building at the edge of the Apostolou Pavlou promenade. A century ago, customers arrived on foot or in horse-drawn carriages for hat fittings, but today they drive up in SUVs to sample lobster with passion fruit or fish drizzled with champagne sauce, all served, with old-fashioned flourish, from silver platters. If you're just interested in soaking up the atmosphere, stake a spot in the lively ground floor cocktail lounge. ⊠ *Apostolou Pavlou 51 and Poulopoulou, Thission* ☎ *210/342–3665* ☰ *AE, MC, V* ☉ *Closed Mon.*

$–$$$ ✕ **Filistron.** In warm weather it's worth stopping by this place just to have a drink and enjoy the delightful, painterly scene from the roof garden—a sweeping view of the Acropolis and Mt. Lycabettus. In cooler weather, take a seat in the sunny, cheerful dining room off a pedestrian walkway. The long list of mezedes has classics and more unusual dishes: codfish croquettes with herb and garlic sauce; pork with mushrooms in wine sauce; grilled potatoes with smoked cheese and scallions; and an array of regional cheeses, washed down with a flowery white *hima* (barrel wine). The service is top-notch. ⊠ *Apostolou Pavlou 23, Thission* ☎ *210/346–7554 or 210/342–2897* ☰ *MC, V* ☉ *Closed 1 wk in Aug. No lunch.*

$–$$ ✕ **To Meidani tou Skoufia.** Bare stone, white paint, and rustic touches, such as a driftwood-framed mirror, belie the ultramodern approach of this *rakadiko,* a variation on the ouzeri that serves meze with raki, a clear spirit distilled from grape stems and skins. The menu may have changed but the quality of the food—and its flavor—hasn't, so order several dishes and share. Pick at morsels of roast lamb seasoned with fresh wild herbs, or succulent, tender pork. The menu features Greek favorites like smoky eggplant dip, chickpeas, and mint-spiked tzatziki. ⊠ *Troon 63, Ano Petralona* ☎ *210/341–2210* ☰ *No credit cards* ☉ *Closed Sun. and 1 wk in Aug. No dinner on Sun. in winter.*

¢–$$ ✕ **Oikonomou.** Plain whitewashed walls, rickety tables crammed into a small room in winter or onto the pavement in fair weather, and a couple of enormous *katsaroles* (stew pots) simmering just out of sight are the hallmarks of this classic taverna, which attracts a mixed crowd of regulars—mostly pensioners—and yuppies from the suburbs. They all come for the same thing: the home-cooked *magirefta* (dishes stewed in olive oil and tomatoes). Beef stewed with sweet pearl onions, eggplant in a cinnamon-flavored tomato sauce, and lemon-and-oregano flavored chicken are perennial favorites. Vegetarians can count on finding at least one meatless dish, like fresh green beans cooked with onions and diced tomatoes. Don't pass up the oven-roasted potatoes—a simple, yet satisfying feast when accompanied by boiled wild greens and feta. Wash it all down with a *kartoutso* (quarter kilo) of barrel wine. ⊠ *Troon 41 and Kydantidon, Ano Petralona* ☎ *210/346–7555* ☰ *No credit cards* ☉ *Closed Sun. dinner and mid-Aug.*

¢–$ ✕ **Bairaktaris.** After admiring the painted wine barrels and black-and-white stills of Greek film stars, go to the window case to view the day's magirefta—maybe beef *kokkinisto* (stew with red sauce) and *soutsoukakia* (oblong meatballs simmered in tomato sauce) spiked with cloves. Or sit down and order the gyro platter. Appetizers include small cheese pies with sesame seeds, tender mountain greens, and fried zucchini with a garlicky dip. Run by the same family for more than a century, this is one of the best places to eat in Monastiraki Square. ⊠ *Pl. Monastiraki 2, Monastiraki* ☎ *210/321–3036* ▤ *AE, MC, V.*

Central Athens, Psirri & Omonia Square

Αθήνα (κέντρο), Ψυρρή & Πλατεία Ομονοίας

$$$$ ✕ **Hytra.** Applying his French training to his Cretan background, chef Yiannis Baxevanis has created an imaginative menu that has caught the attention of the international press. If you find it hard to choose, sample the range of his culinary combinations—fish soup garnished with sea urchin, the classic lamb in egg-lemon sauce—with a tasting menu of 15 dishes. The wine list features an intriguing selection of vintages to accompany your meal, or you can stick with chilled raki, the traditional tipple of Crete. Don't let the understated bistro ambience fool you: this is one of the city's most fashionable eateries. ⊠ *Navarhou Apostoli 7, Psirri* ☎ *210/331–6767* ♺ *Reservations essential* ▤ *AE, DC, V* ☉ *Closed Sun. and June–Sept.*

$$$$ ✕ **Red.** Construction of the Athinais cultural complex set the stage for industrial-to-arts-space transformations throughout Athens; from the start, flamboyant Red led the way. Huge red divans, red banners suspended from the ceiling, candelabras, and antique mirrors fill the stone room. The menu is no less dramatic: try pigeon with cocoa pasta or bison with wasabi, quince, and lychee nuts. Less adventurous but equally delicious are the lobster risotto and grouper with wild mushrooms. In summer, dinner is served in the courtyard (painted a deep red). Combine dinner with a walk around Athinais's late-night galleries for an evening's entertainment. ⊠ *Athinais complex, Kastorias 34–36, Votanikos* ☎ *210/ 348–0000* ♺ *Reservations essential* ▤ *AE, MC, V* ☉ *Closed Sun. and 2 wks in Aug. No lunch.*

$$$–$$$$ ✕ **To Varoulko.** Not one to rest on his Michelin star, acclaimed chef Lefteris Lazarou is constantly trying to outdo himself, with magnificent results. Rather than use the menu, give him an idea of what you like and let him create your dish from what he found that day at the market. Among his most fabulous compilations are a crab salad studded with mango, grapes, and leeks; honey-laced mullet roe from Messolonghi on the Greek west coast, accompanied by cinnamony cauliflower puree; and lobster with wild rice, celery, and champagne sauce. Some dishes fuse traditional peasant fare like the Cretan *gamopilafo* ("wedding rice" flavored with boiled goat) with unusual flavors like bitter chocolate. The multilevel premises stand next to the Eridanos Hotel; in summer, dinner is served on a rooftop terrace with a wonderful Acropolis view. ⊠ *Pireos 80, Gazi* ☎ *210/522–8400* ♺ *Reservations essential* ▤ *AE, DC, V* ☉ *Closed Sun. No lunch.*

Fodor$Choice
★

$$–$$$$ ✕ **Archaion Gefseis.** The epicurean owners of "Ancient Flavors" combed through texts and archaeological records in an effort to re-create foods eaten in antiquity—not to mention how they were eaten, with spoon and knife only. Dishes like pancetta seasoned with thyme and squid cooked in its ink prove, if anything, the continuity between ancient and mod-

ern Greek cuisine. There's an undeniable kitsch factor in the setting: in a torch-lighted garden, waiters in flowing chitons serve diners reclining on couches. ✉ *Kodratou 22, Karaiskaki Sq., Metaxourgio* ☎ *210/523–9661* ⚓ *Reservations essential* ▤ *AE, MC, V* ☯ *Closed Sun.*

$–$$$ ✗ **Zeidoron.** This usually crowded Psirri hangout has decent mezedes, but the real draw is its strategic location. Metal tables line the main pedestrian walkway, great for watching all the world go by and for enjoying the sight of the neighborhood's illuminated churches and alleys. Small dishes include hot feta sprinkled with red pepper, grilled green peppers stuffed with cheese, crisp meatballs, pork in mustard and wine, eggplant baked with tomato and pearl onions, shrimp with ouzo, and an impressive array of dips and spreads. The wines are overpriced; opt for ouzo instead. ✉ *Taki 10, at Ayion Anargiron, Psirri* ☎ *210/321–5368* ▤ *No credit cards* ☯ *Closed Aug.*

★ **$–$$** ✗ **Athinaikon.** Choose among classic specialties at this mezedopoleio: grilled octopus, shrimp croquettes, broad beans in a decadent tomato sauce, swordfish souvlaki, and *ameletita* (sautéed lamb testicles). All goes well with the light barrel red. The decor is no-nonsense ouzeri, with marble tables, dark wood, and framed memorabilia. It's a favorite of attorneys and local office workers. ✉ *Themistokleous 2, Omonia Sq.* ☎ *210/383–8485* ▤ *No credit cards* ☯ *Closed Sun. and Aug.*

$–$$ ✗ **Maritsa's.** Brokers from the Athens Stock Exchange just a couple of doors down the street have made this mezedopoleio, an offshoot of the popular Kolonaki restaurant, their lunchtime haunt. Pick from classic taverna dishes—pickled octopus, grilled sardines, or deep-fried zucchini—and see if you can catch some insider gossip on the day's trading. ✉ *Sofokleous 17–19, Omonia* ☎ *210/325–1421* ▤ *MC, V.*

$–$$ ✗ **Oineas.** In cold weather, sit in the cozy interior dining room decorated with pastel posters from the 1960s and other mid-century Greek kitsch. In warm weather tables spill outside to the streets of vibrant Psirri. Cheerful Oineas is perfect for a group dinner: pass around bite-size *spanokopites* (spinach pies), slices of roasted red pepper and feta terrine, and tender beef chunks with a balsamic vinegar sauce. Or try a massive salad of bitter greens, sesame chicken, and shaved Parmesan. ✉ *Aisopou 9, Psirri* ☎ *210/321–5614* ▤ *V* ☯ *Closed 2 wks in Aug. No lunch.*

¢–$ ✗ **Diporto.** Through the years, everyone in Omonia has come here for lunch—butchers from the Central Market, suit-clad brokers from the nearby stock exchange, artists, migrants, and even bejeweled ladies who lunch; they're often sitting at the same tables when it gets crowded. Owner-chef Barba Mitsos keeps everyone happy with his handful of simple, delicious, and dirt-cheap dishes. There's always an exceptional *horiatiki* (Greek salad); other favorites are his buttery *gigantes* (large, buttery white beans cooked in tomato sauce), warming chickpea soup, and fried finger-size fish. Wine is drawn directly from the barrels lining the walls. ✉ *Theatrou and Sofokleous, Central Market* ☎ *No phone* ▤ *No credit cards* ☯ *No dinner.*

¢–$ ✗ **Neon.** The remodeled cafeteria in a landmark 1920s building is open until at least 2 AM and is an excellent choice when you're looking for something fast, filling, and inexpensive. Choose from the salad bar, made-to-order pasta and omelets, meat dishes, and sandwiches, as well as ice

GREEK FAST FOOD

THE SOUVLAKI IS THE ORIGINAL GREEK FAST FOOD: *spit-roasted or grilled meat, tomatoes, onions, and garlicky tzatziki wrapped in a pita to go. Greeks on the go have always eaten street food such as the endless variations of cheese pie, koulouri (sesame-covered bread rings), roasted chestnuts or ears of corn, and palm-size paper bags of nuts. But modern lifestyles and the arrival of foreign pizza and burger chains have cultivated a taste for fast food—and spawned several local brands definitely worth checking out.* **Goody's** *serves burgers and spaghetti as well as some salads and sandwiches. Items like baguettes with grilled vegetables or seafood salads are seasonal additions to the menu. At* **I Pitta tou Pappou** *you can sample several takes on the souvlaki: grilled chicken breast or pork-and-lamb patties, each served with a special sauce.* **Everest** *is tops when it comes to "tost"—oval-shape sandwich buns with any*

combination of fillings, from omelets and smoked turkey breast to fries, roasted red peppers, and various spreads. It also sells sweet and savory pies, ice cream, and desserts. Its main rival is **Grigoris,** *a chain of sandwich and pie shops that also runs the City Espresso Bars. If you want to sit down while you eat your fast food, look for a* **Flocafe Espresso Bar.** *Along with espresso, frappé, filtro (drip), and cappuccino, they also serve a selection of pastries and sandwiches, including brioche with mozzarella and pesto.*

cream and other desserts. ⊠ *Omonia Sq. and Dorou, Omonia Sq.* ☎ *210/522–3201* ▭ *No credit cards.*

Syntagma Square, National Garden & and Kolonaki

Πλατεία Συντάγματος, Εθνικός Κήπος & Κολωνάκι

$$$$ ✕ **Aegli.** Occupying a renovated landmark building in the lush Zappion Gardens, this innovative restaurant is lovely. The veranda overlooks the park's flowering trees and fountains and is wonderfully restful for a midday coffee or lunch. Acclaimed French-Greek chef Jean-Louis Capsalis delights with dishes that make the most of both branches of his heritage: begin with a salad of fresh crab and mint drizzled with lemon-infused olive oil, and then try grilled grouper with fresh spinach and sea-urchin juice or beef fillet with a ginger and coffee sauce. Save room for excellent desserts such as the cold strawberry soup with sweet wine sauce and orange confit. ⊠ *Zappion Gardens, National Garden* ☎ *210/336–9363* ⌂ *Reservations essential for dinner* ▭ *AE, DC, MC, V.*

$$$–$$$$ ✕ **Orizontes.** Have a seat on the terrace atop Mt. Lycabettus: the Acropolis glitters below, and beyond, Athens unfolds like a map out to the Saronic Gulf. It's tough to compete with such a view and, at times, the food and the service (or both) fail to match it. Standouts include a sumptuous tart of monkfish foie gras and sour apple, and Kobe beef crusted with Greek mountain herbs. No road goes this high: the restaurant is reached by cable car. ⊠ *Mt. Lycabettus, Kolonaki* ☎ *210/721–0701 or 210/722–7065* ⌖ *Reservations essential* ⊟ *AE, DC, MC, V.*

$$$–$$$$ ✕ **To Berdema.** Colanders and cheese graters double as wall decorations at this postmodern taverna that takes its food seriously. Sample the spicy, subtle Oriental-Greek cuisine of Istanbul's Greeks, distinctive for its piquant sauces flavored with chili and cinnamon. House specialties include fluffy deep-fried leek croquettes, slices of juicy spit-roasted meat served with hot tomato sauce and cooling yogurt dip, and delicious meatballs that marry pork, beef, and chicken. ⊠ *Spefsipou 8, Kolonaki* ☎ *210/722–4212* ⊟ *AE, MC, V* ⊘ *Closed mid-July–Aug.*

$$–$$$$ ✕ **Azul.** In this colorful jewel box of a restaurant, space may be cramped, but the food is superb. Start with mushrooms stuffed with nuts and *anthotiro* (soft, mild white cheese made from goat's and sheep's milk) or salmon and trout wrapped in pastry with champagne sauce. The spaghetti à la *nona* (godmother) with chamomile, Gorgonzola, and bacon is an unparalleled combination. Other memorable main dishes are beef fillet with raisins and cedar needles and chicken prepared with lemon leaves. In summer, Azul sets up tables outside in the pedestrian walkway. ⊠ *Haritos 43, Kolonaki* ☎ *210/725–3817* ⌖ *Reservations essential* ⊟ *AE, DC, MC, V* ⊘ *Closed Sun. Oct.–Apr. and last 2 wks in Aug. No lunch.*

$–$$$$ ✕ **Cellier Le Bistrot.** On the same spot occupied by Apotsos, an ouzeri that was a fixture on the Athenian social scene for decades, Cellier Le Bistrot has put its own imprint on the property. The upmarket bistro is just right for a casual lunch during a break in the day's shopping, as it is for dinner. Like the decor, the menu strikes a balance between the timeless and the contemporary: leather banquettes and mahogany surfaces around the room and flaky salmon with pasta on the plate. The service is as impeccable as the wine list, which is culled from the finest vintages from nearby Cellier, one of the city's top wine and liquor stores. ⊠ *Panepistimiou 10, in the arcade, Syntagma Sq.* ☎ *210/363–8525* ⊟ *AE, MC, V.*

$$ ✕ **Kafenio.** A Kolonaki institution, this ouzeri reminiscent of a French bistro is slightly fancier than the normal mezedopoleio, with cloth napkins, candles on the tables, and a handsome dark-wood interior. The enormous menu offers many unusual creations. The tender marinated octopus, fried eggplant, stuffed squash in egg-lemon sauce, and onion pie with fragrant dill are good choices. ⊠ *Loukianou 26, Kolonaki* ☎ *210/722–9056* ⊟ *No credit cards* ⊘ *Closed Sun. and 3 wks in Aug.*

$–$$ ✕ **Dimokritos.** As you mount a short but steep flight of steps off the street, you'll find yourself eye level with the display of pink taramosalata, eggplant dip, and other salads and spreads in the glass-front refrigerator by the kitchen. Take the opportunity to step inside and peek at what's simmering in the large baking trays and pots, then claim a table in the plain dining room. The decor in this modest, old-fashioned *estiatorio* (restaurant) amounts to nothing more than a framed print or two on the ocher-color walls. The menu might also lack imagination, but the food is reliably good and the service quick, with a slightly courtly manner. Try spinach pie encased in thin hand-rolled pastry, gigantes, boiled greens, and lemony beef casserole washed down with a carafe of house wine. ⊠ *Dimikritou 24, Kolonaki* ☎ *210/362–9468* ⊟ *No credit cards.*

$–$$ ✕ **Maritsa's.** Perched atop pretty, pedestrian Voukourestiou, this longtime Kolonaki favorite is popular with the Athenian smart set for its relaxed outdoor seating close to the shopping district and its consistent, classic Greek cuisine. The yogurty *anithosalata* (dill salad) is a delicious twist on typical tzatziki. Monkfish is stewed with lemon, herbs, mushrooms, and yellow peppers; chopped shrimp is wrapped in phyllo and served with a balsamic vinegar sauce. ⊠ *Voukourestiou 47, Kolonaki* ☎ *210/363–0132* ⊟ *AE, MC, V* ☎ *210/325–1421.*

$–$$ ✕ **Taverna Filipou.** This unassuming taverna is hardly the sort of place you'd expect to find in chic Kolonaki, yet its devotees include cabinet ministers, diplomats, actresses, and film directors. The appeal is simple, well-prepared Greek classics, mostly *ladera* (vegetable or meat casseroles cooked in an olive oil and tomato sauce), roast chicken, or fish baked in the oven with tomatoes, onions, and parsley. Everything's home-cooked, so the menu adapts to what's available fresh at the open-air produce market. In summer and on balmy spring or autumn evenings, choose a table on the pavement; in winter, seating is in a cozy dining room a few steps below street level. ⊠ *Xenokratous 19, Kolonaki* ☎ *210/721–6390* ⊟ *No credit cards* ☉ *Closed mid-Aug.*

¢–$ ✕ **Neon.** When this cafeteria opened on Syntagma, it was something of a gamble, but the concept caught on and other branches have since appeared around town. Load your tray at the salad bar or sandwich and bread counter, or queue for a made-to-order omelet or pasta dish. There's also a selection of meat dishes and magirefta to choose from at lunchtime. The dessert counter is impressive. ⊠ *Mitropoleos 3, Syntagma Sq.* ☎ *210/324–6873* ⊟ *No credit cards.*

Pangrati & Kaisariani

Παγκράτι & Καισαριανή

★ $$$$ ✕ **Spondi.** The star here is creative but flawless haute cuisine: artichoke terrine with duck confit and black ravioli with honeyed leek and shrimp are perfectly balanced appetizers. Splendid entrées include grilled sea bass with a fragrant rose-petal sauce and lamb so tender it falls from the bone, with couscous, raisins, and cumin. Don't skip dessert: try the daring but magnificent lotus flower filled with mandarin sorbet and banana-pineapple puree, with candied olives, vanilla oil, and a basil-saffron sauce. The white-linen dining room and bougainvillea-draped courtyard are more relaxed than Athens's other intensely designed temples to fancy food. ⊠ *Pirronos 5, Varnava Sq., Pangrati* ☎ *210/752–0658* ☎☎ *210/756–4021* ⚑ *Reservations essential* ⊟ *AE, DC, MC, V* ☉ *No lunch.*

$$–$$$ ✕ **Trata O Stelios.** The owner works directly with fishermen, guaranteeing that the freshest catch comes to the table. Just point to your preference and it will soon arrive in the way Greeks insist upon: grilled with exactitude, coated in the thinnest layer of olive oil to seal in juices, and accompanied by lots of lemon. Even those who scrunch up their nose at fish soup will be converted by this version of the dense yet delicate *kakkavia*. Stelios is also one of the few remaining places you can get real homemade taramosalata. Avoid the place during Sunday lunch; it's packed with Athenian families. ⊠ *Anagenniseos Sq. 7–9, off Ethnikis Antistaseos, Kaisariani* ☎ *210/729–1533* ☐ *No credit cards* ☉ *Closed 10 days at Orthodox Easter.*

$–$$ ✕ **Agora.** In summer, this café-restaurant's leafy garden is one of the best places to cool off after a morning poking around the National Art Gallery or the museums along Vasilissis Sofias. Relax on the shady wooden deck and choose from an impressive list of selections, including several pasta dishes and meat entrées such as pork fillets with a bread-crumb coating. But where the chef really goes to town is the dinner-size salads: try wholesome rye rusks on a bed of lettuce and topped with chopped fresh tomato, olives, and an overly generous dollop of *ksino-mizithra* (a soft, white goat cheese). End on a sweet note with creamy panna cotta or velvet-smooth chocolate souffle; if you can't make up your mind, share like Greek diners do. A word of caution: the waitstaff can be deft or disinterested, depending on the time of day, so go with the flow. ⊠ *Hatziyianni Mexi 6 and Ventiri 9, behind the Athens Hilton, Ilisia* ☎ *210/725–2252* ☐ *MC, V.*

$–$$ ✕ **Aphrodite.** This mezedopoleio's menu changes more often than the faces of its regulars, a mix of locals, politicians, and intellectuals who have elevated this cozy neighborhood square into a city insider's alter-native to Kolonaki. Sip the complimentary raki and crunch on bread sticks dipped in olive paste while deciding whether to order the day's special or a round of meze: roast red peppers stuffed with goat cheese, bite-size fried pies with a filling of wild greens, whole grilled squid, mar-inated anchovies, and a range of salads in season. In warm weather ta-bles go out on the *platia* (squares); in winter, seating is in a split-level dining room with a casual island ambience. ⊠ *Ptolemeon and Amynta 6, Pl. Proskopon, Pangrati* ☎ *210/724–8822* ☐ *MC, V.*

$–$$ ✕ **Fatsio.** Don't be fooled by the Italian name: the food at this old-fash-ioned restaurant is all home-style Greek. Walk past the kitchen and point at what you want before taking a seat. Favorites include a "souffle" that is actually a variation on baked macaroni-and-cheese, with pieces of ham and slices of beef and a topping of eggplant and tomato sauce. Quick service and good value for the money is the reason for Fatsio's endur-ing popularity among both elder Kolonaki residents and office work-ers seeking an alternative to fast food. ⊠ *Effroniou 5–7, off Rizari, Pangrati* ☎ *210/721–7421* ☐ *No credit cards* ☉ *Closed 1 wk mid-Aug. No dinner.*

★ **$–$$** ✕ **Karavitis.** The winter dining room is insulated with huge wine casks; in summer there is garden seating in a courtyard across the street (get there early so you don't end up at the noisy sidewalk tables). The clas-sic Greek cuisine is well prepared, including pungent tzatziki, *bekri meze* (lamb chunks in zesty red sauce), lamb ribs (when in season), *stam-naki* (beef baked in a clay pot), and melt-in-the-mouth meatballs. This neighborhood favorite is near the Panathenaic Stadium. ⊠ *Arktinou 35, at Pausaniou, Pangrati* ☎ *210/721–5155* ☐ *No credit cards* ☉ *Closed 1 wk mid-Aug. No lunch.*

Rouf & Gazi

Ρουφ & Γκάζι

$$$–$$$$
Fodor'sChoice
★
✕ **Aristera-Dexia.** Chef-owner Chrisanthos Karamolengos's stellar fusion cuisine and his conversion of industrial space into stylish surroundings have made him hugely influential on the local culinary scene. Popular dishes include pheasant sausage with parsnips in Madeira; pork tenderloin with apricot and ginger; shrimp rolls with a sesame-and-tomato paste sauce; and a Greek version of sushi—raw squid and trout roe on eggplant puree. The restaurant is divided by partitions (hence the name, "Left-Right") and a glass runway affords a peek below into Athens's best wine cellar. In summer, tables move outside and the menu switches to simpler taverna fare. Happily, prices drop accordingly. ⊠ *Andronikou 3, Rouf* ☎ *210/342–2380* ♨ *Reservations essential* ▭ *AE, MC, V* ⊘ *Closed Sun. No lunch.*

$$$–$$$$
✕ **Thalatta.** Walking into this charming renovated house off the factory-lined streets of Gazi feels like stumbling upon a wonderful secret. Owner Yiannis Safos, an islander from Ikaria, has transformed the space into a fresh, modern dining room with a colorful tile-paved courtyard. He fills the menu with fish pulled daily from the Aegean; ask about the selection, from sea urchins to clams. Perhaps try grilled octopus with pureed pumpkin and sun-dried tomatoes, monkfish carpaccio with wild fennel, or salmon with champagne sauce. Finish with homemade lemon sorbet—bits of zest are left in for added bite. ⊠ *Vitonos 5, Gazi* ☎ *210/ 346–4204* ♨ *Reservations essential* ▭ *MC, V* ⊘ *Closed Sun. No lunch.*

$$
✕ **Mamacas.** This first in the wave of modern tavernas springing up all over Athens helped to spark industrial Gazi's reincarnation as the chillest part of town. The clean white decor provides a refreshing visual counterpart to the surrounding warehouses. You may spot Greek models, pop stars, and other celebs, who remain after hours as the restaurant turns into a late-night bar. Amid all this modernity, the hearty, vibrant flavors of traditional food remain, albeit tweaked with contemporary sensibility, in dishes like pork with prunes, black-eyed-pea salad, and cuttlefish with spinach. ⊠ *Persofonis 41, Gazi* ☎ *210/346–4984* ▭ *MC, V* ⊘ *Closed Mon.*

$$
✕ **Sardelles.** Amid the bleak terrain of the city's long-defunct gasworks, the pure, simple lines of Greek island design come through in wooden kafeneion tables and 1950s-style metal-frame garden chairs picked up at auctions and painted dazzling white. Graze on cod cutlets or grilled fish drizzled with a mastic-flavor sauce as you watch the city's beautiful people flit from table to table exchanging air kisses and gossip. Sardines ("sardelles") in rock salt are the house speciality: accompany them with a salad of plump, juicy tomatoes and wash it all down with chilled *tsipouro*, a clear spirit distilled from grape stems and skins. ⊠ *Persofonis 15, Gazi* ☎ *210/347–8050* ▭ *No credit cards.*

$–$$
✕ **Monopolio Athinon.** Formerly a state-run store—a "monopoly," that sold goods such as matches and petroleum—this place has the feeling of a 1950s *oinomageirio* (workman's tavern serving barrel wine and magirefta). The emphasis is on small regional Greek dishes, with a few from Asia Minor, Sicily, and Morocco. The owners, an actor and his mother,

turn out some of the best *pites* (savory pies) in the city: try the traditional Cypriot *eliota*, crisp sesame-sprinkled pastry with olive-and-onion filling; the Cretan *souhli*, pie stuffed with meat, tomato, and cheese; and the tsoutsoukakia *Smyrnaikia* (Smyrna-style), spicy minced-beef patties filled with olives. ⊠ *Ippothontidon 10, at Keiriadon, Kato Petralona* ☎ *210/345–9172* ⊟ *No credit cards* ⊘ *Closed Mon. and July and Aug.*

Athens North & East

Αθήνα, βόρεια & ανατολική

In Exarchia, to the north of Kolonaki, many neighborhood tavernas dish up simple, home-cooked meals. At night, the area around Mavili Square comes alive with good bars and nightclubs. Ambelokipi starts around the north side of Mt. Lycabettus; it's densely packed with tavernas, pleasant restaurants, and small, friendly nightclubs. Pedion Areos, the city's largest park, lies on the north side of Leoforos Alexandras, about a 20-minute walk from central Athens. Judges and lawyers generally fill the lunch spots at the north end of the park, near the courthouse complex.

$$$$ ✕ **Balthazar.** With its airy neoclassical courtyard—paved with original painted tiles, canopied by huge date palms, and illuminated by colored lanterns—Balthazar truly feels like an oasis in the middle of Athens. This bar-restaurant attracts members of the art, media, and beautiful-people crowds. Come for dinner; stay to mingle as the DJ picks up the beat. Talented young chef Yiorgos Tsiktsiras keeps the quality and flavor high on the up-to-the-minute menu, with prices to match. Try the lime and avocado seviche or any one of the creative salads, then salmon with mango salsa, finishing off with homemade grape sorbet. ⊠ *Tsoha 27, at Soutsou, Ambelokipi* ☎ *210/644–1215* ⌂ *Reservations essential* ⊟ *AE, MC, V* ⊘ *Closed Sun. No lunch.*

$$$$
FodorsChoice
★ ✕ **48.** Thanks to a number of talented chefs who decided to tweak the classics, Greek cuisine is making food critics, domestic and international, sit up and take note. French-trained Christoforos Peskias is one of these chefs. Inspired by the setting—this cavernous space was previously home to an art gallery—he has created a menu with definite visual appeal. Rather than fusing Greek recipes with exotic ingredients, he has recreated ordinary dishes like *bakaliaros* (deep-fried cod) and the ubiquitous Greek salad with new ingredients. ⊠ *Armatolon and Klefton 48, between Leoforos Alexandras and Mt. Lycabettus, Ambelokipi* ☎ *210/641–1082* ⌂ *Reservations essential* ⊟ *AE, DC, V* ⊘ *Closed Sun.*

★ **$$$–$$$$** ✕ **Boschetto.** The thick greenery of a small urban park, the pampering of an expert maître d', and the flavors of Italian nouvelle cuisine may make you forget you're in the center of Athens. The specialty here is fresh pasta, such as shrimp cannelloni, green gnocchi with Gorgonzola sauce, and ravioli with duck livers and truffle zabaglione. Favorite entrées include succulent rooster, sweetbreads with al dente artichokes, and grilled buffalo steak with a sauce of coffee, figs, and mavrodaphne wine. End your meal with *crema cotta* (cooked cream) and the finest espresso in Athens. ⊠ *Evangelismos Park, near Hilton, Ilisia* ☎ *210/721–0893 or 210/722–7324* ⌂ *Reservations essential* ⊟ *AE, V* ⊘ *Closed Sun. and 2 wks in Aug. No lunch Oct.–Aug.*

$$–$$$ ✕ **Giantes.** The menu here definitely has a modern streak, but meals are served in a lovely flower-filled courtyard. The taverna is co-owned by one of Greece's foremost organic farmers, so almost everything is fresh and delicious, though a little pricier than the norm. The Byzantine pork and chicken with honey, raisins, and coriander are perennial favorites. After dinner here, see a show next door at the outdoor Riviera cinema, which specializes in classic movies and art flicks. ⊠ *Valtetsiou 44, Exarchia* ☎ *210/330–1369* ☐ *AE, DC, MC, V* ✆ *Closed Mon. and 1st 2 wks in Aug.*

$–$$$ ✕ **Vlassis.** Relying on traditional recipes from Thrace, Roumeli, Thes-
Fodor'sChoice   saly, and the islands, cooks whip up what may be the best Greek home-
★ style cooking in Athens. There's no menu: pick from the tray of 20 or so small dishes brought to your table. They're all good, but best bets include *tirokafteri* (a peppery cheese dip), *lahanodolmades* (cabbage rolls), *pastitsio* (baked minced meat and pasta with lamb liver), *katsiki ladorigani* (goat with oil and oregano), and the octopus stifado, which is tender and sweet with lots of onions. For dessert, order the halvah or a huge slice of *galaktobouriko* (custard in phyllo). ⊠ *Paster 8, Mavili Sq.* ☎ *210/646–3060* ⟁ *Reservations essential* ☐ *No credit cards* ✆ *Closed Aug.–mid-Sept. No dinner Sun.*

$$ ✕ **Kostoyiannis.** If you're looking for authenticity, this—one of the oldest and most popular tavernas in the area—is the place to go; it's liveliest late at night after the theatergoers arrive. The choice of Greek dishes is impressive—including shrimp salads, stuffed mussels, rabbit stifado, and sautéed sweetbreads. ⊠ *Zaimi 37, behind Archaeological Museum, Pedion Areos* ☎ *210/822–0624* ☐ *No credit cards* ✆ *Closed Sun. and late July–mid-Aug. No lunch.*

$–$$ ✕ **Kainari.** Handwoven throws and an odd collection of photographs and mementos adorn the walls of this cozy neighborhood taverna, where you'll rub elbows—literally—with businessmen, doctors, students, and other regulars. But what it lacks in space, it makes up for with an extensive menu combining daily specials (ask the fishmonger sipping ouzo at the next table) and favorites, like spicy grilled pancetta, twisted pites, and hand-cut fries cooked in olive oil. ⊠ *Xiromerou 20, behind Archaeological Museum, Erithros Stavros, Ambelokipi* ☎ *210/ 698–3011* ☐ *No credit cards* ✆ *Closed Sun. and Aug.*

¢–$$ ✕ **Pasteria.** Jars of pickled artichokes, olives, and other antipasto makings strive to create the look of a trattoria in this chain establishment, but the counters are too sleek and clean to really make it work. It doesn't matter: you're not here for the ambience but for a good, quick, inexpensive meal. Pick a booth or table, order your favorite pasta dish, then sit back and watch it whipped up by the short-order chef behind the glass-paneled kitchen. ⊠ *Patission 58 at Leoforos Alexandras, Pedion Areos* ☎ *210/825–0315* ☐ *MC, V.*

Piraeus & Kifissia

Πειραιάς & Κηφισιά

Not surprisingly, the port city of Piraeus, about 11 km (7 mi) southwest of central Athens, is full of seafood tavernas. Many of these are almost identical, dishing out overpriced, frozen-and-fried calamari and the like, but some old-time gems still serve simple, fresh, and often creative fish entrées in picturesque harbor settings. Piraeus is also starting to see a few haute seafood restaurants that combine fresh seafood with sophisticated and innovative preparations, fine wines, and those beautiful seaside settings, for truly special (but pricey) meals.

★ $$$$ ✕ **Vardis.** Many of the dishes on the seasonal French menu here have a Mediterranean touch, eschewing cream for olive oil. Starters might include pigeon cassoulet with foie gras in fig juice or octopus boiled in milk with hazelnut sauce. Especially good are the crayfish linguine, caramelized lamb cutlets with morel and porcini mushrooms, and salt-crust duck filled with foie gras and fragrant sherry sauce. One irresistible dessert is a Grand Marnier-and-forest berries soufflé. In summer, eat outside in the garden. This grand restaurant endowed with fin de siècle elegance—crystal chandeliers, floor-length snow-white linens, period chairs upholstered in cream brocade—is worth the ride to the northern suburb of Kifissia. ⊠ *Pentelikon Hotel, Diligianni 66, Kifissia* ☎ *210/623-0650 through 210/623-0656* ⌲ *Reservations essential* ☰ *AE, DC, MC, V* ☼ *Closed Sun. and Aug. No lunch.*

$$$$ ✕ **Vassilenas.** Longtime residents and frequent visitors rejoice in this family-run vestige of the good old days. The decor is minimal; in warm weather the operation moves to the upper terrace. Come here ravenously hungry—with friends—so you can do justice to the set menu of 16 dishes (€21 per person), brought in a steady stream to your table. Zesty shrimp *saganaki* (fried cheese) and fried monkfish or red mullet are two standouts, as is the dessert called *diples* (a deep-fried pastry served with walnuts and honey syrup). ⊠ *Etolikou 72, at Vitolion, Ayia Sofia, Piraeus* ☎ *210/461-2457* ☰ *No credit cards* ☼ *Closed Sun. and 3 wks in Aug. No lunch.*

$$$-$$$$ ✕ **Plous Podilatou.** Sleek and chic, with a seaside dining area decked out
Fodor's Choice in designer pastels, this restaurant evokes visions of the Riviera and is
★ utterly removed from the nearby clattering, shouting tavernas. It's tempting to dismiss Plous as pretentious when you see the prices, but venture in and taste the food—fresh, inventive, and bursting with flavor. The tender baby squid cooked with balsamic vinegar, honey, and rosemary is unforgettable, as are the grilled octopus with fennel and the delicious cuttlefish with white-beet risotto. ⊠ *Akti Erithros Stavros 42, Mikrolimano, Piraeus* ☎ *210/413-7910* ⌲ *Reservations essential* ☰ *AE, V.*

$$-$$$$ ✕ **Gefseis me Onomasia Proelefsis.** The name means "Flavors of Designated Origin," and all the produce comes hand-picked from regional farmers; meats and cheeses come from EU-certified producers, who adhere to top production standards. These dream ingredients are assembled into transcendent dishes by the inspired Nena Ismirnoglou, who spent two years at New York's Milos. Among her most memorable creations are a cucumber mousse topped with goat cheese and freshwater roe; Santorini fava with crisp beet chips, caramelized onions, and sundried tomatoes; and phyllo pouches filled with succulent veal and tomatoes, topped with spicy yogurt sauce. ⊠ *Kifissias 317, Kifissia* ☎ *210/800-1402* ⌲ *Reservations essential* ☰ *AE, V* ☼ *Closed Sun. No lunch.*

$$–$$$ ✕ **Kollias.** Relax on the jasmine-covered terrace and enjoy friendly
Fodor'sChoice   owner Tassos Kollias's creations. Flavors range from the humble to the
★   aristocratic: fried whole squid in its ink; sea urchin salad; lobster with
lemon, balsamic vinegar, and a shot of honey. He's known for bringing
in a high-quality catch, whether mullet from Messolonghi or oysters culled
by Kalymnos sponge divers, and prices are usually lower than at most
fish tavernas. For a fitting end to the meal, try fresh *loukoumades* (sweet
fritters) or *bougatsa* (custard in phyllo). Ask for directions when you
reserve—even locals get lost trying to find the obscure street. ⊠ *Stratigou
Plastira 3, near junction of Dramas and Kalokairinou, Tabouria, Piraeus*
☎ *210/462–9620 or 210/461–9150* ♲ *Reservations essential* ☰ *AE,
DC, MC, V* ✆ *Closed Aug. No lunch Mon.–Sat., no dinner Sun.*

$$ ✕ **Archaion Gefseis.** The original "Ancient Flavors" in central Athens was
such a hit that its owners opened a second restaurant in a pretty house
in Piraeus. Having scoured ancient texts to come up with the menu, they
present dishes that prove the remarkable continuity in what Greeks have
eaten over 2,500 years. Thyme-seasoned slices of grilled pork and bul-
ghur wheat with pine nuts come straight from the past, as do less-com-
mon combinations (such as sweet-and-sour sauces) that have been
reintroduced to Greece through fusion and exotic cuisines. ⊠ *Epi-
davrou 10, Mikrolimano, Piraeus* ☎ *210/413–8617* ♲ *Reservations es-
sential* ☰ *AE, MC, V* ✆ *Closed Sun.*

$–$$ ✕ **Margaro.** This popular, no-nonsense fish taverna serves five items,
along with excellent barrel wine: fried crayfish, fried red mullet, fried
marida (a small white fish), and huge Greek salads. Tables on the terrace offer a view of the busy port. If it's crowded, you may be asked
to go into the kitchen and prepare your own salad. ⊠ *Hatzikyriakou
126, by the Navy Officers Training School (Scholi Dokimon), Piraeus*
☎ *210/451–4226* ☰ *No credit cards* ✆ *Closed 15 days at Orthodox
Easter. No dinner Sun.*

WHERE TO STAY

As a result of the 2004 Olympics, Athens's hotels have risen both in quality and number of rooms. Nearly every hotel in town underwent a renovation before the games, with luxury hotels paying serious attention
to style and design and many adding spas, pools, and gyms. Concept
hotels like the Semiramis in Kifissia and Periscope in Kolonaki have not
escaped the notice of the international media. Athens's budget hotels—
once little better than dorms—now often have air-conditioning and
television, along with prettier public spaces. Perhaps best of all is the
increase in the number of good-quality, middle-rank family hotels, of
which there was long a shortage.

The most convenient hotels for tourists are in the city center. Some of
the older hotels in Plaka and near Omonia Square are comfortable and
clean, their charm inherent in their age. But along with charm may come
leaking plumbing, sagging mattresses, and other lapses in the details—
take a good look at the room. The thick stone walls of neoclassical buildings keep them cool in summer, but few of the budget hotels have
central heating, and it can be devilishly cold in winter. A buffet break-

fast is often served for a few euros extra: cold cuts and cheese, even poached eggs and other meat, but nothing cooked to order.

Prices

Along with higher quality have come higher hotel prices: room rates in Athens are not much less than in many European cities. Still, there are bargains to be had. The government, which awards hotel ratings (and therefore determines the official price), has announced it will switch to a star system to encourage hotels to upgrade. At this writing, Greek hotels were classified as Deluxe (L) and A through E according to amenities. Hotels that are part of an international chain or brand have already adopted the star classification system. Within each category, quality varies greatly, but prices usually don't. Still, you may come across an A-class hotel that charges less than a B-class, depending on facilities.

Paradoxically, you may get up to a 20% discount if you book the hotel through a local travel agent; it's also a good idea to bargain in person at smaller hotels, especially off-season. When negotiating a rate, bear in mind that the longer the stay, the lower the nightly rate, so it may be less expensive to spend six consecutive nights in Athens rather than staying for two or three nights at either end of your trip through Greece.

WHAT IT COSTS In euros				
$$$$	$$$	$$	$	¢
over €200	€160–€200	€100–160	€60–€100	under €60

Prices are for two people in a standard double room in high season, including tax.

Acropolis & South

Ακρόπολη & προς τα νότια

$$$$ 🏨 **Athenaeum InterContinental.** With a marble atrium lobby, central fountain, and private art collection, Athens's largest hotel provides a cool oasis on a busy city street. All rooms were refurbished in 2004, and standard rooms have marble floors in the sitting area, carpet under the bed, bright cobalt blue or vibrant green fabrics, and business-oriented conveniences like two phones and a work desk. The eighth- and ninth-floor club level has a private check-in, a lounge with an Acropolis view and a library, complimentary breakfast and evening cocktails, and private meeting rooms separate from the vast conference facilities. The hotel is on a main thoroughfare into the city at the edge of a residential, working-class neighborhood; an hourly shuttle runs to Syntagma Square, about 15 minutes away. ⊠ *Syngrou 89–93, Neos Kosmos, 11745* ☎ *210/920-6000* 🖷 *210/920–6500* ⊕ *www.intercontinental.com* ⇨ *543 rooms, 59 suites* ♣ *2 restaurants, room service, in-room safes, minibars, cable TV with movies, pool, health club, hair salon, spa, bar, shops, dry cleaning, laundry service, concierge floor, business services, convention center, parking (fee), no-smoking rooms* ☰ *AE, DC, MC, V.*

$$$$ 🏨 **Ledra Marriott.** The Ledra's main calling cards are its high-performance staff and its style. Comfortable rooms are furnished in warm reds and

oranges with feather duvets, overstuffed armchairs, marble bathrooms, and vast closet space. The fourth-floor executive lodgings are even more spacious and include a private check-in and lounge. The lobby piano bar sits below a spectacular 1,000-crystal chandelier; Kona Kai, the Polynesian restaurant, is excellent; and the Zephyros Café has a bountiful Sunday brunch. Enjoy a gorgeous Acropolis view from the rooftop pool. ⊠ *Syngrou 115, Neos Kosmos, 11745* ☎ *210/930–0000* 🖷 *210/935–8603* ⊕ *www.marriott.com* 🛏 *259 rooms, 11 suites* ♨ *3 restaurants, room service, in-room safes, minibars, cable TV with movies, in-room broadband, pool, 2 bars, shop, babysitting, laundry service, concierge, business services, travel services, no-smoking floors* ☰ *AE, DC, MC, V.*

$$$–$$$$ 🏨 **Herodion Hotel.** A good compromise between the area's budget venues and deluxe digs, this hospitable hotel is down the street from the Odeon of Herodes Atticus, where Hellenic Festival performances are held, and a few minutes from the Acropolis. Service is friendlier and more efficient here than at most other Plaka neighborhood hotels, while the marble in the renovated lobby lends a touch of grandeur. Rooms are done in light-wood furnishings and muted olive-color walls. The complimentary buffet breakfast is served in a peaceful, tree-shaded atrium; on the roof, there is a terrace with deck chairs and a Parthenon panorama. Take full advantage of the hotel's location and ask for a room with an Acropolis view. ⊠ *Rovertou Galli 4, Acropolis, 11742* ☎ *210/923–6832 through 210/923–6836* 🖷 *210/923–5851* ⊕ *www.herodion.gr* 🛏 *86 rooms, 4 suites* ♨ *Restaurant, coffee shop, room service, in-room safes, minibars, bar, shop, travel services* ☰ *DC, MC, V* ⊙| *BP.*

$–$$$ 🏨 **Philippos Hotel.** Just around the corner from its sister hotel, the Herodion, the Philippos shares its good qualities: a quiet location convenient to the Acropolis and friendly, efficient service. Modular dark-veneer beds (in smallish rooms) are offset by pale green carpets and draperies. You can sip a coffee in the light-filled atrium with comfortable couches and patio tables. Prices are kept down by details like the complimentary Continental (rather than full) breakfast, but the overall experience is just as positive. ⊠ *Mitseon 3, Makriyianni, 11742* ☎ *210/922–3611* 🖷 *210/922–3615* ⊕ *www.philipposhotel.gr* 🛏 *46 rooms, 2 suites* ♨ *Coffee shop, in-room safes, meeting rooms, travel services, no-smoking rooms* ☰ *MC, V* ⊙| *CP.*

$$ 🏨 **Acropolis View.** The Acropolis is a stone's throw away from this hotel tucked into a quiet neighborhood. About half of the simple, agreeable rooms—all with balconies—have Parthenon views. Or you can head up to the rooftop garden bar to enjoy a drink and the view. Front-desk staff in the homey lobby are quite efficient. ⊠ *Webster 10, Acropolis, 11742* ☎ *210/921–7303 through 210/921–7305* 🖷 *210/923–0705* ⊕ *www.acropolisview.gr* 🛏 *32 rooms* ♨ *Dining room, refrigerators, cable TV, bar; no smoking* ☰ *DC, MC, V* ⊙| *BP.*

$$ 🏨 **Austria Hotel.** The owners say it is 462 steps to the Acropolis from this hotel in the peaceful Filopappou neighborhood. There is a lovely Parthenon view from the roof terrace, and some room balconies face it as well. Compact, basic rooms, with beds, desks, and TVs, are clean and well maintained. ⊠ *Mouson 7, Filopappou, 11742* ☎ *210/923–5151*

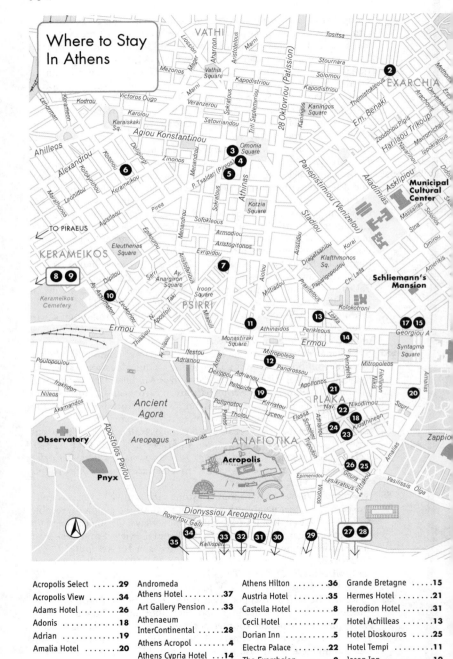

Where to Stay In Athens

or 210/922–0777 🖷 *210/924–7350* ⊕ *www.austriahotel.com* ⇱ *37 rooms* ⚐ *Dining room, room service, room TVs with movies, in-room data ports, bar, laundry service, travel services* ⊟ *AE, DC, MC, V* ⦿⃒ *CP.*

$–$$ ⚏ **Acropolis Select.** For only €10 more than many basic budget options, you get to stay in a slick-looking hotel with a lobby full of Philippe Starck–like furniture. Bright, comfortable rooms have cheery yellow spreads with an abstract red poppy design. Similar in color choice, the dramatic restaurant has daffodil-color walls and contemporary, scroll-back chairs in tomato red. About a dozen rooms look towards the Acropolis: ask for Rooms 401–405 for the best views. There are only 10 no-smoking rooms in the hotel, all on the fifth floor. The residential neighborhood of Koukaki, south of Filopappou Hill, is a 10-minute walk from the Acropolis. ⊠ *Falirou 37–39, Koukaki, 11742* 🕾 *210/921–1610* 🖷 *210/921–1610* ⊕ *www.acropoliselect.gr* ⇱ *72 rooms* ⚐ *Restaurant, room service, in-room safes, minibars, cable TV, gym, bar, business services, meeting room, no-smoking rooms* ⊟ *AE, DC, MC, V.*

$–$$ ⚏ **Art Gallery Pension.** A handsome house on a residential street, this pension is comfortably old-fashioned, with family paintings on the muted white walls, comfortable beds, hardwood floors, and ceiling fans. Many rooms have balconies with views of Filopappou or the Acropolis. A congenial crowd of visiting students and single travelers fills the place. In winter, lower rates are available to long-term guests, some of whom stay on for a few months. Rates with and without breakfast are available. Though the residential neighborhood, a 10-minute walk south of the Acropolis, lacks the charm of Plaka, it has many fewer tourists and the metro offers easy access to many of the city's sights. ⊠ *Erechthiou 5, Koukaki, 11742* 🕾 *210/923–8376 or 210/923–1933* 🖷 *210/923–3025* ⇱ *21 rooms, 2 suites* ⚐ *Dining room, in-room data ports, lounge, no-smoking rooms* ⊟ *No credit cards.*

¢ ⚏ **Marble House.** This popular pension has a steady, satisfied clientele—even in winter, when it has low monthly and weekly rates. Rooms are clean and quiet, with ceiling fans and rustic wooden furniture. Rooms with air-conditioning and private bath cost a few euros extra. The international staff is always willing to help out and the courtyard is a lovely place to relax. It is a little off the tourist circuit, but it's still possible to walk to most ancient sights (it's about 10 minutes from the Acropolis). It's also close to the metro and the Zinni stop on Trolley 1, 5, or 9 from Syntagma. ⊠ *Andreou Zinni 35, Koukaki, 11741* 🕾 *210/923–4058 or 210/922–6461* ⊕ *www.marblehouse.gr* ⇱ *16 rooms, 11 with bath* ⚐ *Dining room, fans, some kitchenettes, refrigerators; no a/c in some rooms, no room phones, no room TVs, no smoking* ⊟ *No credit cards.*

Plaka

Πλάκα

★ **$$$–$$$$** ⚏ **Electra Palace.** This is one of the nicest hotels in Plaka, with comfortable and simple, yet well-appointed rooms, ample storage space, and an excellent location on an attractive street close to area museums. Rooms from the fifth floor up have a view of the Acropolis–which you can also enjoy from the rooftop garden bar. Before setting out in the morning, fill up with one of the city's best buffet breakfasts—sausage, pancakes, and home fries. ⊠ *Nikodimou 18–20, Plaka, 10557* 🕿 *210/337–0000* 🖷 *210/324–1875* ⊕ *www.electrahotels.gr* ➯ *131 rooms, 19 suites* ᴧ *Restaurant, coffee shop, minibars, cable TV with movies, Wi-Fi, pool, laundry service, no-smoking floors* ⊟ *AE, DC, MC, V* ♜ *BP.*

$$–$$$
Fodor's Choice
★
Plaka Hotel. The Plaka is the most upscale in the family-owned chain that includes the hotels Hermes and Achilleas. Highly polished wood floors sparkle under guest-room beds, which have stylish wood headboards with burled inlays. Deep-blue velvet curtains rise to the ceiling and match the upholstery on the wood-arm easy chairs. The glassed-in breakfast room looks out over the bustling shopping thoroughfare of Ermou, Syntagma, and the Monastiraki metro. Some rooms offer views of the Acropolis, which can also be enjoyed from the roof garden. ⊠ *Kapnikareas 7, Plaka, 10556* 🕿 *210/322–2096 through 210/322–2098* 🖷 *210/322–2412* ⊕ *www.plakahotel.gr* ➯ *67 rooms* ᴧ *Dining room, in-room safes, minibars* ⊟ *AE, DC, MC, V* ♜ *BP.*

$$
Hermes Hotel. Athens's small, modestly priced establishments have generally relied on little more than convenient central locations to draw visitors. Not so at the Hermes: sunny yellow rooms with wardrobes and tufted comforters feel warm and welcoming. Breakfast is served in the cheerful dining room, and you can enjoy a sunset cocktail at the cozy roof-garden bar before setting off to sample the city's nightlife. CHAT tours has an office in the lobby and can help you arrange day trips. ⊠ *Apollonos 19, Plaka, 10557* 🕿 *210/323–5514* 🖷 *210/323–2073* ⊕ *www. hermeshotel.gr* ➯ *45 rooms* ᴧ *Dining room, in-room safes, some room TVs, travel services, no-smoking rooms* ⊟ *AE, MC, V* ♜ *BP.*

$
Adams Hotel. Favored by young people for its clean rooms and good value, this quiet hotel sits on a quiet Plaka side street across from Ayia Aikaterini church. Most of the rooms have balconies, and many, including all on the top floor, enjoy views of the Acropolis. If you're on a tight budget, you might consider one of the four rooms that have their private bath in the hall (€10 less). The knowledgeable owners, who also run the Meltemi Hotel in Paros, are especially helpful if this is your first time in Athens. ⊠ *Herefondos 6, at Thalou, Plaka, 10558* 🕿 *210/322–5381 or 210/324–6582* 🖷 *210/323–8553* ➯ *14 rooms* ᴧ *Bar, no-smoking floors* ⊟ *MC, V* ♜ *CP.*

$
Nefeli. The Nefeli has plain rooms in a great location—a quiet, pretty street in Plaka that's around the corner from the lively cafés of Platia Filomoussou Eterias and close to some of the city's best ancient sights and museums. The owners are polite and attentive, one reason guests keep returning to this no-frills pension. ⊠ *Hatzimichali Aggelou 2, Plaka, 10558* 🕿 *210/322–8044* 🖷 *210/322–5800* ➯ *18 rooms* ᴧ *No a/c* ⊟ *MC, V* ♜ *CP.*

¢–$
Adonis. If you're willing to sacrifice style, this small hotel's excellent location and clean rooms with balconies make it a good value. Gaze at the Acropolis from the rooftop dining room, then stroll through Plaka to explore the sacred rock and its temples. Most ancient sites are within easy walking distance, and what you can't reach on foot you can reach by metro, tram, trolley, or bus from nearby Syntagma Square. ⊠ *Ko-*

drou 3, Plaka, 10658 ☎ 210/324–9737 🖶 210/323–1602 🛏 26 rooms ⚷ Bar, Internet room ▭ No credit cards ⑪ CP.

★ ¢–$ 🖼 **Student and Travellers' Inn.** Wood floors, regular spruce-ups, and large windows make this spotless hostel cheerful and homey. The renovated house on an attractive and bustling street in Plaka has private rooms and shared dorm bedrooms. You pay extra for a private bathroom, but all rooms have a sink and mirror. There are also public computers with Internet access, and a small garden café. One caveat: the owners forbid food, drinks, or visitors in the rooms. The inn does not accept credit cards for payment, but a credit card number is required to make a reservation. ⊠ *Kidathineon 16, Plaka, 10658* ☎ 210/324–4808 🖶 210/321–0065 ⊕ *www.studenttravellersinn.com* 🛏 35 rooms, 14 with bath ⚷ Snack bar, Internet room; no a/c, no room phones, no room TVs ▭ No credit cards.

Monastiraki & Thission

Μοναστηράκι & Θησείο

$–$$ 🖼 **Adrian.** This comfortable pension offers friendly service and an excellent location in the heart of Plaka. Incurable romantics should ask for one of just three rooms looking towards the Acropolis; if you like being in the thick of things, enjoy the Acropolis view from the shaded roof garden and ask instead for one of the rooms with the spacious balconies overlooking the café-lined square. Some room rates include breakfast. ⊠ *Adrianou 74, Plaka, 10556* ☎ 210/325–0454 🖶 210/325–0461 ⊕ *www.douros-hotels.com* 🛏 22 rooms ⚷ Minibars, lounge, Internet room, no-smoking rooms ▭ MC, V.

$–$$ 🖼 **Cecil Hotel.** The owners here prove that with a little effort, it's perfectly possible to create a reasonably priced hotel that's still rich in beauty

Fodor'sChoice and character. The inside of this gracefully restored neoclassical town

★ house is painted in soft roses and ochers, with lavish molded architectural details in other pastels. The small but comfortable rooms have polished wood floors, high windows, chairs upholstered in folk prints, and, most importantly, soundproofing to buffer the noise of the busy commercial street below. The owner's friendly cat patrols the public spaces. Fuel up at the buffet breakfast, served in an airy dining room overlooking the historic though slightly gritty neighborhood between Monastiraki and the Central Market. ⊠ *Athinas 39, Monastiraki, 10554* ☎ 210/321–7079 🖶 210/321–8005 ⊕ *www.cecil.gr* 🛏 36 rooms ⚷ Lobby lounge ▭ AE, MC, V ⑪ BP.

$–$$ 🖼 **Jason Inn.** The cool marble lobby leads up to comfortable rooms furnished in warm peaches and pinks. All have mini-refrigerators, good-size closets, and safes. American buffet breakfast is included in the price, and the rooftop garden restaurant has an intriguing panorama spreading from the Acropolis to the ancient Kerameikos cemetery to the modern-day warehouse district of Gazi. Though it's on a run-down, seemingly out-of-the-way little corner, the Jason Inn is steps away from the buzzing nightlife districts of Psirri and Thission, not to mention the ancient Agora. ⊠ *Ayion Assomaton 12, Thission, 10553* ☎ 210/325–1106 🖶 210/324–3132 ⊕ *www.douros-hotels.com* 🛏 57 rooms ⚷ Restau-

rant, café, refrigerators, in-room safes, bar, no-smoking rooms ⊟ *AE, MC, V* ⛆ *BP.*

¢–$ ▦ **Hotel Tempi.** It's all about location for this bare-bones budget hotel just a short, pleasant stroll from Plaka, the Roman Agora, and Psirri's nightlife. Room windows have double-glazing to keep out the noise— an especially welcome feature on weekday mornings, when the shops on pedestrians-only Aiolou are open. Rooms at the lower end of the rate scale have shared baths, and several rooms have lovely views to the church of Ayia Irini, which is surrounded by a flower market most mornings. The friendly owners organize sightseeing tours around town. ☒ *Aiolou 29, Monastiraki, 10558* ☎ *210/321–3175* 🖷 *210/325–4179* ⤙ *24 rooms, 12 with bath* ☖ *Kitchen, lounge, laundry room; no room phones* ⊟ *AE, MC, V.*

Central Athens, Psirri & Omonia Square

Αθήνα (κέντρο), Ψυρρή & Πλατεία Ομονοίας

$$$ ▦ **Athens Acropol.** The Grecotel-owned Athens Acropol has a fresh, assured aesthetic that's style-conscious without being fussy. In the lobby, clusters of cylindrical light fixtures cast a glow on leather couches with beaded fuchsia cushions, and glass pots filled with growing bamboo. Spacious, quiet rooms are done in olive and cream, with pale patterned coffee tables, art deco-esque armchairs, and other retro details. ☒ *Pireos 1, Omonia Sq., 10552* ☎*210/528–2100* 🖷*210/523–1361* ⊕*www.grecotel. gr* ⤙ *164 rooms, 3 suites* ☖ *Restaurant, minibars, cable TV with movies, in-room broadband, gym, sauna, babysitting, dry cleaning, business services, car rental, no-smoking rooms* ⊟ *AE, DC, MC, V.*

$$–$$$ ▦ **Omonia Grand.** Though designers seem to have gone a bit overboard with neon art and urn-pattern wallpaper in the small lobby, never fear: the rooms, like those of its sister, the Athens Acropol, across the street, are comfortable and understated. Curvaceous lines and honey-color wood characterize the art deco–style furnishings. A fun lilac-and-silver color scheme and tapestry headboards enliven the suites. Double-glazed glass windows keep down the city noise. On street level, the Omonia Times restaurant—with windows looking out at the square—uses organic produce. ☒ *Pireos 2, Omonia Sq., 10552* ☎ *210/528–2100* 🖷 *210/523–4955* ⊕ *www.grecotel.gr* ⤙ *115 rooms, 3 suites* ☖ *Restaurant, café, room service, in-room safes, minibars, cable TV, dry cleaning, no-smoking rooms* ⊟ *AE, DC, MC, V.*

$–$$ ▦ **Dorian Inn.** The big, boxy Dorian Inn makes up for its lack of charm and intimacy with a friendly staff and spacious, modern rooms with sleek black headboards. The roof garden has a view of the city and a pool. The Omonia metro station, churches, and the Central Market are not far. ☒ *Pireos 15–17, Omonia Sq., 10552* ☎ *210/523–9782* 🖷 *210/522–6196* ⊕ *www.greekhotel.com/athens/dorianinn* ⤙ *146 rooms* ☖ *Restaurant, pool, no-smoking floor* ⊟ *AE, DC, MC, V.*

¢–$ ▦ **King Jason Hotel.** Like its sibling, the Jason Inn in Thission, this is a clean, modern, well-kept hotel in a central but down-at-the-heels area, made accessible by the metro a short walk away. Cheery rooms and helpful staff make up for the seedy surroundings. A hotel with these facilities—a sleek lobby, good room service, and complimentary breakfast buffet in a light-filled dining room—would cost twice as much in Plaka or Kolonaki. ⊠ *Kolonou 26, Omonia Sq., 10437* ☎ *210/523–4732* 🖷 *210/523–4906* ⊕ *www.douros-hotels.com* ⤙ *114 rooms* ⚬ *Dining room, room service, minibars, cable TV, in-room data ports, non-smoking rooms* ⊟ *AE, MC, V* ⧠ *BP.*

Syntagma Square & Kolonaki

Πλατεία Συντάγματος & Κολωνάκι

$$$$ 🖭 **Amalia Hotel.** Depending on your needs, the Amalia's best and worst feature is its location: right on one of Athens's biggest, busiest streets, directly across from Parliament. The minute you step outside, you're swept up in the noise and chaos of central Athens—fortunately, double-glazed windows and a view to the National Garden keep things peaceful inside. Although the rooms are fairly institutional, this place is a good deal for its convenience to the National Garden and transport; the airport shuttle is next door, the metro and tram just a few steps away. ⊠ *Amalias 10, Syntagma Sq., 10557* ☎ *210/323–7301* 🖷 *210/607–2135* ⊕ *www. amalia.gr* ⤙ *98 rooms, 1 suite* ⚬ *Restaurant, bar, cable TV, meeting rooms* ⊟ *AE, DC, MC, V.*

$$$$ 🖭 **Grande Bretagne.** Rest on custom-made silk ottomans in the lobby;
Fodor'sChoice drink tea from gold-leafed porcelain in the atrium; call your personal
★ butler 24 hours a day from your room—the landmark Grande Bretagne, built in 1842, stands head and shoulders above other luxury hotels in Athens. The guest list includes more than a century's worth of royals, rock stars, and heads of state. A massive renovation, completed in 2003, recaptured the original grandeur, restoring 19th-century oil paintings, antiques, and hand-carved details as they were a century earlier. ⊠ *Vasileos Georgiou A' 1, Syntagma Sq., 10564* ☎ *210/333–0000, 210/ 331–5555 through 210/331–5559 reservations* 🖷 *210/322–8034, 210/ 333–0910 reservations* ⊕ *www.grandebretagne.gr* ⤙ *290 rooms, 37 suites* ⚬ *3 restaurants, room service, minibars, cable TV, in-room broadband, 2 pools (1 indoor), health club, hair salon, spa, 3 bars, shop, babysitting, laundry service, concierge, car rental, travel services, no-smoking rooms* ⊟ *AE, DC, MC, V.*

★ **$$$$** 🖭 **King George II Palace.** A spacious lobby done in marble, mahogany, velvet, leather, and gold trim lures you into a world where antique crystal lamps and frosted glass shower stalls with mother-of-pearl tiles raise standards of luxury to dizzying heights. Each room is individually furnished with one-of-a-kind handcrafted furniture, antique desks, and raw silk upholstery. Heavy brocade curtains are no more than a decorative flourish: the rooms are soundproofed and their lighting calibrated to the natural light. At the Tudor Hall restaurant, savor Mediterranean delicacies and a view of the city skyline stretching from the Panathenaic Stadium to the Parthenon. ⊠ *Vasileos Georgiou A' 2, Syntagma Sq., 10564* ☎ *210/322–2210* 🖷 *210/325–0564* ⊕ *www.grecotel.gr* ⤙ *77 rooms, 25 suites* ⚬ *Restaurant, room service, minibars, cable TV with movies, in-room broadband, spa, 2 bars, lobby lounge, business services, meeting rooms, car rental, no-smoking rooms* ⊟ *AE, DC, MC, V.*

$$$–$$$$ 🏨 **St. George Lycabettus.** This small, luxurious hotel on the wooded
Fodor'sChoice slopes of Mt. Lycabettus, in upscale Kolonaki, is steps from Athens's mu-
★ seum row and designer shops. Most rooms have splendid views; all are
meticulously decorated. Each floor has its own theme, and rooms are de-
signed accordingly, with looks ranging from jewel-tone art nouveau to
sleek black-and-white minimalism to soothing neutrals with bamboo. The
rooftop pool bar and Le Grand Balcon restaurant have an unbeatable
panoramic view. Downstairs the postmodern 1970s-style lounge, Frame,
is one of the hottest nightspots in town. ⊠ *Kleomenous 2, Kolonaki, 10675*
☎ *210/729–0711 through 210/729–0719* 🖷 *210/729–0439 or 210/*
724–7610 ⊕ *www.sglycabettus.gr* 🛏 *162 rooms, 5 suites* ⚬ *2 restau-*
rants, in-room safes, cable TV with movies, in-room data ports, pool,
gym, bar, shop, dry cleaning, laundry service, business services, meeting
rooms, some pets allowed, no-smoking rooms ⊟ *AE, DC, MC, V.*

$$$ 🏨 **Athens Cypria Hotel.** This modest, friendly oasis in the city center is
a good bet for families. It has reasonable prices (considering the loca-
tion off Syntagma Square) and discounts for children up to 12 years old.
Cribs are provided free of charge. There are also several connecting family rooms. Modern, clean, simple blue-and-white rooms overlook a
quiet street, but if you'd like a view ask for one of the three rooms looking towards the Acropolis. Breakfast is an American-style buffet (with
eggs, not just cold meats). ⊠ *Diomias 5, Syntagma Sq., 10563* ☎ *210/*
323–8034 through 210/323–8038 🖷 *210/324–8792* 🖂 *diomeia@hol.*
gr 🛏 *71 rooms* ⚬ *Minibars, room TVs with movies, bar, babysitting,*
laundry service ⊟ *AE, MC, V* ⓘ *BP.*

$$ 🏨 **Hotel Achilleas.** Like its sisters, the Hermes and Plaka hotels, the Achil-
leas combines interesting design with the friendly, personal service that
comes from being family-run—and a price at the lower end of its cate-
gory. Black and white diamond tiles alternate down the center of the long,
sleek lobby lined by opposing black and white armchairs. The spicy mus-
tard-color guest-room walls contrast nicely with dusky blue bedding and
leopard-print curtains. The buffet breakfast is served in a stylish interior
courtyard. ⊠ *Lekka 21, Syntagma Sq., 10562* ☎ *210/322–5826, 210/*
322–8531, or 210/323–3197 🖷 *210/322–2412* ⊕ *www.achilleashotel.*
gr 🛏 *50 rooms* ⚬ *Dining room, in-room safes, minibars, cable TV, in-*
room data ports, no-smoking rooms ⊟ *AE, DC, MC, V* ⓘ *BP.*

¢–$ 🏨 **Hotel Dioskouros.** The real draws of Dioskouros over similarly cheap,
downtown spots are its amicable staff, central but quiet location at Plaka's
edge, and its shaded garden, where you can relax with a beer at the end
of the day. It's a students' and independent travelers' favorite. Many of
the basic rooms have space for the two twin beds and not much more.
⊠ *Pittakou 6, Syntagma Sq., 10558* ☎ *210/324–8165* 🖷 *210/321–9991*
⊕ *www.consolas.gr* 🛏 *18 rooms without bath* ⚬ *Dining room; no room*
TVs ⊟ *AE, DC, MC, V* ⓘ *CP.*

Athens North & East

Αθήνα, βόρεια & ανατολική

Bohemian Exarchia bumps up against posh Kolonaki on the northern
end, but they're a world apart in character. With many students, mod-

est hotels, and tavernas, Exarchia is perfect for younger and more bud-get-conscious travelers. Mavili Square is next to the U.S. Embassy, and the Megaron Musikis/Athens Concert Hall, about a 15-minute walk (or two metro stops) north of Syntagma Square. It has a handful of high-end business hotels, as well as some of Athens's best restaurants. Ilisia is southeast of Mt. Lycabettus.

$$$$ ⊞ **Athens Hilton.** The Hilton reflects the trend sweeping through most of Athens's high-end properties, whose recent revamps have left them with modern, clean-lined, and minimal design. The once-traditional lobby is now a vast expanse of white marble punctuated by sleek, mod benches. Rooms are fitted out in light wood, brushed metal, etched glass, and crisp white duvets. Facilities are business-oriented, with a stylish executive check-in lounge and huge conference rooms. Along with a spa, the hotel has the biggest hotel pool in Athens. It also boasts a branch of Milos, Manhattan's acclaimed Greek restaurant. ⊠ *Vasilissis Sofias 46, Ilisia, 11528* ☎ *210/728–1000, 210/728–1100 reservations* ⊕ *www. athens.hilton.com* ◂ *498 rooms, 19 suites* ♧ *4 restaurants, room service, in-room safes, minibars, cable TV with movies, in-room broadband, pool, wading pool, health club, hair salon, 2 bars, shops, babysitting, laundry service, business services, convention center, car rental, travel services, no-smoking rooms* ⊟ *AE, DC, MC, V.*

$$–$$$$ ⊞ **Andromeda Athens Hotel.** This small boutique hotel caters to business travelers, but all can relish the elegance and the meticulous service. A number of rooms and suites have been upgraded with furnishings by Philippe Starck and other world-class designers. All have ISDN connections and 12 stylish one- and two-room apartments operated by the hotel across the street have sound systems and kitchenettes. ⊠ *Timoleondos Vassou 22, Mavili Sq., 11521* ☎ *210/641–5000* 🖷 *210/646–6361* ⊕ *www.andromedaathens.gr* ◂ *21 rooms, 9 suites* ♧ *Restaurant, in-room fax, some kitchenettes, minibars, cable TV, in-room VCRs, in-room safes, in-room data ports, health club, spa, no-smoking rooms* ⊟ *AE, DC, MC, V.*

¢–$ ⊞ **Orion and Dryades.** These adjoined hotels in a residential area across from the park on craggy Lofos Strefis (Strefis Hill) have built up quite a student clientele by word-of-mouth. Their main selling point: cheap rates, which start at €25 for singles with shared baths and €35 for singles with en suite bathrooms. Orion is the humbler and cheaper, with smaller rooms and shared baths for every two rooms; its third-floor roof garden serves as the breakfast area for both hotels (Continental breakfast is €5; if you plan on eating breakfast, tell the owners the night before). Each hotel has a kitchen you may use, and most rooms have balconies. The nearby park has inexpensive ouzeri open in summer. ⊠ *Emmanuel Benaki 105, Exarchia, 11473* ☎ *210/382–7362, 210/330–2387, or 210/382–0191* 🖷 *210/380–5193* ◂ *Orion: 23 rooms without bath, Dryades: 15 rooms* ♧ *Some refrigerators, bar* ⊟ *V.*

¢ ⊞ **The Exarcheion.** Smack in the center of a lively, bohemian bar and café district, this hotel has been a fixture on the international backpacking circuit for years. Rooms are plain and slightly worn, but the fact that the National Archaeological Museum is just around the corner makes this a good value. ✉ *Themistokleous 55, Exarchia, 10683* ☎ *210/ 380–256* 🖷 *210/380–3296* 🛏 *49 rooms* 🍴 *Refrigerators* 🖃 *MC, V.*

Piraeus & Kifissia

Πειραιάς & Κηφισιά

The port town of Piraeus has not traditionally been known for its hotels, but does have a fair number of simple, decent lodgings—as well as a notable boutique property—good for when you've arrived by ferry late at night or must leave extremely early in the morning. Kifissia, a wealthy, leafy suburb about 16 km (10 mi) north of Athens, has a handful of small, high-end hotels that offer the option of a quieter, cooler, more relaxing stay at prices that, while still high, are lower than those of similar hotels in the center of Athens.

Staying along the coast outside Athens is a good way to beat the heat and smog of downtown in summer—however, extra traveling time may be a deterrent. For more information on nearby coastal lodging, *see* Vouliagmeni *in* Chapter 2.

★ **$$$$** 🖳 **Kefalari Suites.** Escape Athens's commotion among the two-tone neo-classical mansions and tree-lined boulevards of the posh Kefalari area in Kifissia. At this hotel with luxurious and imaginative theme suites, you can stay in the chateau-inspired Malmaison, with Louis XIV–like chairs and half canopy; the exotic Aqaba, with Moorish keyhole doorways and ironwork; or the more standard Boat House, with nautical-theme art and striped canvas curtains. The neighborhood is known for fine restaurants, but the suites do have kitchenettes. Other amenities include queen-size beds, verandas or balconies, and a sundeck with whirlpool tub. The breakfast includes cheese, cold cuts, cereal, yogurt, and cake. ✉ *23 km (14 mi) northwest of Athens, Pentelis 1, at Kolokotroni, Kifissia, 14562* ☎ *210/623–3333* 🖷 *210/623–3330* 🌐 *www.kefalarisuites. gr* 🛏 *13 suites* 🍴 *In-room data ports, some kitchenettes, minibars, cable TV, outdoor hot tub, no-smoking floor* 🖃 *AE, DC, MC, V* 🍴 *CP.*

$$$$ 🖳 **Semiramis Hotel.** For style-conscious travelers, a hotel like the Semiramis is a bigger draw than the destination city itself. When he decided to renovate his property in Kefalari, Kifissia's ritziest neighborhood, Dakis Ioannou, a noted collector of avant-garde art, gave designer Karim Rashid the room to let his imagination run wild. The result: a techie's playground rendered in a palette of 1960s pinks, oranges, and yellows. Gadgets galore, from fast Internet connections and plasma TVs to remote-controlled curtains and digital locks, combine with the artsy ambience to create a haven for the incurably cool. Even if you don't book a room, you can mingle with fashionable Athenians at the lounge bar—one of Kifissia's hottest meeting places. ✉ *Harilaou Trikoupi 48, Kifissia, 14562* ☎ *210/628–4400* 🖷 *210/628–4499* 🌐 *www. semiramisathens.com* 🛏 *42 rooms, 6 bungalows, 4 suites* 🍴 *Restaurant, minibars, cable TV, in-room broadband, pool, gym, lounge, no-smoking floor* 🖃 *AE, DC, MC, V.*

$$$–$$$$ 🖳 **Twentyone.** In the 1950s and '60s, wealthy Athenians decamped to the cool, tree-filled Kefalari district of Kifissia for summer, a practice that is being revived, in a manner, with the opening of a number of stylish hotels in the area. This design-conscious hotel takes its decorating cues—and a generous dose of hipness—from a wall mural by Georgia Sagri that continues from room to room. Internet access, slippers and bathrobes, and DVD players in the rooms complement the ambience created by glass-walled bathrooms and skylights in the split-level suites. ⊠ *Kolokotroni 21 and Mykonou, Kifissia, 14562* ☎ *210/623–3521* 🖷 *210/623–3821* ⊕ *www.twentyone.gr* ⇝ *17 rooms, 4 suites* ◔ *Restaurant, room service, cable TV, in-room DVD, in-room broadband, bar, business center, parking (free), no-smoking rooms* ▭ *AE, DC, MC, V.*

$$ 🖳 **Savoy.** Catching an early boat is really the only reason for staying in Piraeus, and in this respect the Savoy fits the bill perfectly, as its just a short walk from the port. Although renovated for the 2004 Olympics, it still hasn't shaken its slightly dated feel. Still, the rooms are clean and comfortable. ⊠ *Iroon Politechniou 93, Pasalimani, 18533 Piraeus* ☎ *210/428–4580* 🖷 *210/428–4588* ⊕ *www.savoyhotel.gr* ⇝ *68 rooms* ◔ *Restaurant, coffee shop, room service, cable TV, non-smoking rooms* ▭ *AE, MC, V.*

$ 🖳 **Castella Hotel.** Perched on the hill above the picturesque small harbor of Mikrolimano, just east of the main port, this is a good choice if you have an early boat to catch. Rooms are fairly large; some have a sea view, as does the flower-filled roof garden that overlooks the small harbor and the yacht club. ⊠ *Vasileos Pavlou 75, Mikrolimano, 18533 Piraeus* ☎ *210/411–4735* 🖷 *210/417–5716* ⇝ *32 rooms* ◔ *Restaurant, coffee shop, room service, some minibars* ▭ *AE, DC, MC, V.*

NIGHTLIFE & THE ARTS

Athenians take their amusement seriously: ancient Greek tragedies play in quarried amphitheaters; mega rock concerts ring out from huge halls; the latest nightclubs pound with the swaying bodies of the seriously chill; and gallery shows shine in renovated warehouses. Music is a big part of the scene. Many bars, tavernas, and clubs have live performances, in addition to the full schedule of festivals that bring international acts to the larger concert venues. Several of the former industrial districts are enjoying a renaissance, and large spaces have filled up with galleries, restaurants, and theaters—providing one-stop shopping for an evening's entertainment. June through September, the action moves outdoors: nightclubs open in seaside locations; movies are shown in garden theaters; and opera, ballet, and theater are staged in amphitheaters under the stars.

The Greek weekly *Athinorama* covers current performances, gallery openings, and films, as do the English-language newspapers *Athens News,* published Friday, and *Kathimerini,* inserted in the *International Herald Tribune,* available Monday through Saturday. The monthly English-language magazine *Insider* has features and listings on entertainment in Athens, with a focus on the arts. *Odyssey,* a glossy bimonthly magazine, also publishes an annual summer guide published in late June and sold at newsstands around Athens with the season's top performances and exhibitions.

Nightlife

Athens's world-famous nightlife starts late. Most bars and clubs don't get hopping until midnight and they stay open at the very least until 3 AM. Drinks are rather steep (about €6–€10), but generous. Often there is a cover charge on weekends at the most popular clubs, which also have bouncers. In summer many major downtown bars and clubs close their in-town location and move to the seaside. Ask your hotel for recommendations and summer closings. For a uniquely Greek evening, visit a club featuring rembetika music, a type of blues, or the popular *bouzoukia* (clubs with live bouzouki, a stringed instrument, music). Few clubs take credit cards for drinks.

Bars

Bars are the staple of Greek nightlife, with new establishments opening every week. They range from beautifully designed bar-restaurants with sleek patrons nibbling on sushi snacks to relaxed outdoor nightspots in parks below the Acropolis whose seats fill up with patrons of all ages. In addition, funky, edgy hangouts play everything from ethnic to house music. In summer, many bars open up into plant-filled courtyards or gardens; those that don't have that option usually close up from June to September. Unless otherwise noted, the bars listed here are open year-round.

★ **Balthazar.** Athenians of all ages come to escape the summer heat at this bar-restaurant in a neoclassical house with a lush garden courtyard and subdued music. ⊠ *Tsoha 27, Ambelokipi* ☎ *210/644–1215 or 210/645–2278.*

Bee. In this gay-friendly bar, upbeat music plays to the fashion-industry crowd. ⊠ *Miaouli and Themidos, Psirri* ☎ *210/321–2624.*

Central. Athens's beautiful people make an appearance here to see and be seen in the chic, creamy interior while enjoying cocktails and sushi. It's open day and night in Kolonaki Square; at night there's a hot club scene. ⊠ *Pl. Kolonakiou 14, Kolonaki* ☎ *210/724–5938.*

Folie. A congenial crowd of all ages gathers to dance to reggae, Latin, funk, and ethnic music. ⊠ *Eslin 4, Ambelokipi* ☎ *210/646–9852.*

Memphis. Gregarious is the word for this Athens classic. The music is predominantly 1980s, with some Gothic theme nights and occasional live bands. ⊠ *Ventiri 5, behind Hilton, Ilisia* ☎ *210/722–4104.*

Mommy. This bar-restaurant is a favorite of art-and-lifestyle magazine writers. Recline on retro pop-art sofas and nibble Chinese finger food. There are also sporadic theme and special-event nights. ⊠ *Delfon 4, Kolonaki* ☎ *210/361–9682.*

Fodor'sChoice **Parko.** With low-key music and a romantic park setting, Parko is a summer favorite. ⊠ *Eleftherias Park, Ilisia* ☎ *210/722–3784.*

★

Soul Garden. Popular Soul Garden is unquestionably hip but also friendly. Relax with a cocktail and snacks in the plant-filled, lantern-lighted courtyard; after 1 AM the dance floor inside picks up pace. ⊠ *Evripidou 65, Psirri* ☎ *210/331–0907.*

Stavlos. All ages feel comfortable at the bar in what used to be the Royal Stables. Sit in the courtyard or in the brick-wall restaurant for a snack like Cretan *kaltsounia* (similar to a calzone), or dance in the long bar. Stavlos often hosts art exhibits, film screenings, miniconcerts, and other happenings, as the Greeks call them, throughout the week. ⊠ *Iraklidon 10, Thission* ☎ *210/345–2502 or 210/346–7206.*

Bouzoukia

Many tourists think Greek social life centers on large clubs where live bouzouki music plays while patrons smash up the plates. Plate-smashing is now prohibited, but plates of flowers are sold for scattering over the performer or your companions when they take to the dance floor. Upscale bouzoukia line the lower end of Syngrou and stretch out to the south coast, where top entertainers command top prices. Be aware that bouzoukia food is overpriced and often second-rate. There is a per-person minimum (€30) or a prix-fixe menu; a bottle of whiskey costs around €200. For those who choose to stand at the bar, a drink runs about €15 to €20 at a good bouzoukia.

Fever. One of Athens's most popular bouzoukia showcases singers such as the dueling divas Anna Vissi and Kaiti Garbi. It's open Wednesday through Sunday. ⊠ *Syngrou 259, Neos Kosmos* ☎ *210/942–7580 through 210/942–7583.*

Rex. Over-the-top is the way to describe a performance at Rex—it's a laser-light show, multi–costume-change extravaganza, with headlining pop and bouzouki stars. ⊠ *Panepistimiou 48, Central Athens* ☎ *210/381–4591.*

Clubs

Nightclubs in Greece migrate with the seasons. From October through May, they're in vast, throbbing venues in central Athens and the northern suburbs; from June through September, many relocate to luxurious digs on the south coast. The same spaces are used from year to year, but owners and names tend to bounce around. With each seasonal reopening, clubs are completely refurbished with different decor, music, and themes—Asian minimalism and techno hip-hop DJs one season, colorful Moroccan embroideries and ethnic music the next, and who-knows-what the year after that. The seaside spots tend to capitalize on their stunning natural settings, with lots of white draperies, swimming pools, and a more relaxed atmosphere; but even reflect the latest trends in their annual reincarnations. The changes are part of the fun of clubbing in Athens, though also part of the confusion. Many clubs do at least keep the same name while moving around. Before heading out, check local listings or talk to your concierge. In summer, the best way to get to the clubs is by taxi—driving on the coastal road can be a nightmare. Just tell the taxi the name of the club; drivers quickly learn the location of the major spots once they open each year.

Most clubs charge a cover at the door and employ bouncers, aptly called "face-control" by Greeks because they tend to let only the most beautiful people in. One way to avoid both of these, since partying doesn't get going until after 1 AM, is to make an earlier dinner reservation at one of the many clubs that have restaurants as well. Some clubs, such as Central-Island and Akrotiri, have made a name for themselves with excellent food (for hefty prices). Dining at the club also assures you a table, helpful if you don't like standing all night. The only other way to guarantee a seat is to reserve a bar table, but beware—it requires purchasing a €100 bottle of whiskey.

Despite annual changes, the clubs listed below have kept the same identity or location for a few years and are among the city's top nightlife options.

Akrotiri Lounge. Luxurious Akrotiri has as much of a reputation for chef Christophe Clessienne's smart food as it does for its model-look-alike clientele, sea views, and a poolside dance floor. ⊠ *Vasileos Georgiou 11, Agios Kosmas, Kalamaki* ☎ *210/985–9147* ⊕ *www.akrotirilounge.gr.*
Central-Island. From September to May, Athens's beautiful people make an appearance at this designer-styled club to see and be seen while enjoying cocktails and sushi. From May to September, Central is closed in town; it reopens on the coast as Island, which is dreamily decked out in gauzy linens and directly overlooks the Aegean. ⊠ *Pl. Kolonaki 14, Kolonaki* ☎ *210/724–5938* ⊕ *www.island-central.gr* ⊠ *Island* ⊠ *16 km (10 mi) south of Athens, Limanakia Vouliagmenis, Varkiza* ☎ *210/ 965–3563 or 210/965–3564.*
Danza. A huge dance floor and a stream of guest DJs keep this club hopping year-round. Be warned: the truly cool don't cross the threshold until after 2 AM. ⊠ *Aristophanous 11, Psirri.*
★ **De stijl/Bo.** A seaside club that actually has a permanent address, Bo is in a huge old beachfront mansion. The beautiful tile floors don't seem any the worse for wear for having generations of club kids dance on them every night. The place is also open during the day for drinks and coffee, served on the terrace. ⊠ *8 km (5 mi) south of Athens, Konstantinou Karamanli 14, Voula* ☎ *210/895–9645.*
Plus Soda. Europe's top DJs spin at the dance temple of Athens. The club moves to the coast in summer, but locations vary each year. ⊠ *Ermou 161, Thission* ☎ *210/345–6187.*
Privilege. A champagne bar and 1930s-bordello decor attract an under-40 mainstream crowd. Face-control at the door can be daunting. ⊠ *Ayias Eleoussis and Kakourgodikiou, Psirri* ☎ *210/331–7801.*

Jazz & Blues Clubs

The jazz scene has built up momentum, and there are several venues from which to choose. Tickets to shows can be purchased at the clubs or major record stores.

Half Note Jazz Club. The original and best venue in town is the place for serious jazz sophisticates. It's a good idea to reserve a table ahead of time, especially for one near the stage; latecomers can always stand at the bar in back. ⊠ *Trivonianou 17, Pangrati* ☎ *210/921–3310 or 210/ 923–2460.*
House of Art. This laid-back venue hosts small, mostly blues, groups. ⊠ *Santouri 4, at Sarri, Psirri* ☎ *210/321–7678.*
Parafono. Leave the big names at other clubs and tap into the homegrown jazz circuit here instead. ⊠ *Asklippiou 130A, Exarchia* ☎ *210/644–6512* ⊕ *www.parafono.gr.*

Live-Music Bars

Alavastron. Ethnic music groups (Afro-Cuban, Indian, Peruvian) play to patrons at the few tables in this small bar. Be sure to order a glass of the potent *rakomelo* (raki with honey). ⊠ *Damareos 78, Pangrati* ☎ 210/756–0102.

Palenque Club. Look for announcements of salsa parties, live flamenco acts, and weekly tango lessons for the public here. This bar, named after an important Maya city, also hosts live musicians from Peru and Brazil. ⊠ *Farantaton 41, Ambelokipi* ☎ 210/748–7548 *or* 210/771–8090 ⊕ *www.palenque.gr.*

Rodon. Rock fans check the listings for the big names at Rodon. Blue jeans and anything black are the traditional attire here. ⊠ *Marni 24, Vathis Sq.* ☎ 210/524–7427.

Rembetika

The Greek equivalent of the urban blues, rembetika is rooted in the traditions of Asia Minor and was brought to Greece by refugees from Smyrna in the 1920s. It filtered up from the lowest economic levels to become one of the most enduring genres of Greek popular music, still enthralling clubgoers today. At these thriving clubs, you can catch a glimpse of Greek social life and even join the dances (but remember, it's considered extremely rude to interrupt a solo dance). The two most common dances are the *zeimbekikos,* in which the man improvises in circular movements that become ever more complicated, and the belly-dance-like *tsifteteli.* Most of the clubs are closed in summer; call in advance. Drink prices range from €5 to €8, a bottle of whiskey from €50 to €70, but the food is often expensive and unexceptional; it's wisest to order a fruit platter or a bottle of wine.

Anifori. This friendly, popular club plays both rembetika and *dimotika* (Greek folk music). It's open Friday through Sunday nights. ⊠ *Vasileos Georgiou A' 47, Pasalimani, Piraeus* ☎ 210/411–5819.

Boemissia. Usually crowded and pleasantly raucous, Boemissia attracts many young people, who quickly start gyrating in various forms of the tsifteteli. Doors are shut on Monday. ⊠ *Solomou 19, Exarchia* ☎ 210/384–3836 *or* 210/330–0865.

Mnisikleous. The authentic music of gravel-voiced Bobbis Tsertospopular, a popular *rembetis* (rembetika singer), draws audience participation Thursday through Sunday. ⊠ *Mnisikleous 22, at Lyceiou, Plaka* ☎ 210/322–5558 *or* 210/322–5337.

★ **Stoa ton Athanaton.** "Arcade of the Immortals" has been around since 1930, housed in a converted warehouse in the meat-market area. Not much has changed since then. The music is enhanced by an infectious, devil-may-care mood and the enthusiastic participation of the audience, especially during the best-of-rembetika afternoons (3:30–7:30). The small dance floor is always jammed. Food here is delicious and reasonably priced, but liquor is expensive. Make reservations for evening performances, when the orchestra is led by old-time rembetis greats. The club is closed Sunday. ⊠ *Sofokleous 19, Central Market* ☎ 210/321–4362 *or* 210/321–0342.

Taximi. At one time or other, most of Greece's greatest rembetika musicians have played at this old-time bar; many of their black-and-white pictures are on the smoke-stained walls. ⊠ *Isavron 29, at Harilaou Trikoupi, Exarchia* ☎ *210/363–9919.*

Tavernas with Music

Klimataria. At this century-old taverna, a guitarist (as well as an accordion player in winter) plays sing-along favorites much appreciated by the largely Greek audience. The price of this slice of old-style Greek entertainment is surprisingly reasonable. ⊠ *Klepsidras 5, Plaka* ☎ *210/324–1809 or 210/321–1215.*

Stamatopoulou Palia Plakiotiki Taverna. Enjoy good food and an acoustic band with three guitars and bouzouki playing old Athenian songs in an 1822 house. In summer the show moves to the garden. Greeks will often get up and dance, beckoning you to join them, so don't be shy. ⊠ *Lysiou 26, Plaka* ☎ *210/322–8722 or 210/321–8549.*

The Arts

Athens's energetic year-round performing arts scene kicks into a higher gear from June through September, when numerous stunning outdoor theaters host everything from classical Greek drama (in both Greek and English), opera, symphony, and ballet, to rock, pop, and hip-hop concerts. In general, dress for summer performances is fairly casual, though the city's glitterati get decked out for events such as a world premiere opera at the Odeon of Herodes Atticus. From October through May, when the arts move indoors, the Megaron Musikis/Athens Concert Hall is the biggest venue. Athenians consider the Megaron a place to see and be seen, and dress up accordingly.

Performances at outdoor summer venues, stadiums, and the Megaron tend to be priced between €20 to €120 for tickets, depending on the location of seats and popularity of performers. Mid-to-back-row seats in outdoor venues are usually quite affordable, with little sacrificed in the way of visibility. Visitors are often surprised at the number of theaters and art galleries in Athens, but both are very much part of a vibrant scene that has benefited from generous state support of the arts. Quantity doesn't always guarantee quality, so unless you have a very specific interest in local visual arts, stick with mainstream galleries like Rebecca Camhi, Bernier/Eliades, or the Frissiras Museum.

Concerts, Dance & Opera

Dora Stratou Troupe. The country's leading folk dance company performs Greek folk dances from all regions, as well as from Cyprus, in eye-catching authentic costumes. The programs change every two weeks. Performances are held Tuesday through Sunday from the end of May through September at 9:30 PM and Sunday at 8:15 PM at the Dora Stratou Theater. Tickets cost €13 and can be purchased at the box office before the show. ⊠ *Arakinthou and Voutie, Filopappou* ☎ *210/921–4650 theater, 210/324–4395 troupe's office* ☎ *210/324–6921* ⊕ *www.grdance.org.*

Megaron Musikis/Athens Concert Hall. World-class Greek and international artists take the stage at the Megaron Musikis to perform in concerts and opera from September through June. Information and tickets are available weekdays 10–6 and Saturday 10–4. Prices range from €18 to €90;

there's a substantial discount for students and those 8 to 18 years old. Tickets go on sale a few weeks in advance, and many events sell out within hours. On the first day of sales, tickets can be purchased by cash or credit card only in person at the Athens Concert Hall. From the second day on, remaining tickets may be purchased by phone, in person from the downtown box office (weekdays 10–4), and online. ⊠ *Vasilissis Sofias and Kokkali, Ilisia* ☎ *210/728–2333* 🖷 *210/728–2300* ⊕ *www.megaron. gr* ⊠ *Downtown box office* ⊠ *Omirou 8, Central Athens* ☎ *No phone.*

Philippos Nakas Conservatory. Inexpensive classical music concerts are held November through May at the conservatory. Tickets cost about €11. ⊠ *Ippokratous 41, Central Athens* ☎ *210/363–4000* 🖷 *210/360–2827.*

Festivals

August Moon Festival. Every year, on the night of the full moon in August (believed to be the brightest and most beautiful moon of the year), the Acropolis, Roman Agora, Odeon of Herodes Atticus, and sometimes other sites are open to the public for free. Performances of opera, Greek dance, and classical music take place amid the ancient columns by moonlight. If you're in Athens in August, this is a must-do. *Odeon of Herodes Atticus* ⊠ *Dionyssiou Areopagitou, Acropolis* ☎ *210/323–2771, 210/323–5582 box office.*

★ **Elliniko Festival.** The city's primary artistic event, the Hellenic Festival (formerly known as the Athens Festival), runs from June through September at the Odeon of Herodes Atticus. The festival has showcased performers such as Dame Kiri Te Kanawa, Luciano Pavarotti, and Diana Ross; such dance troupes as the Royal London Ballet, the Joaquin Cortes Ballet, and Maurice Béjart; symphony orchestras; and local groups performing ancient Greek drama. Usually a major world premiere is staged during the festival. The Odeon theater makes a delightful backdrop, with the floodlighted Acropolis looming behind the audience and the Roman arches behind the performers. The upper-level seats have no cushions, so bring something to sit on, and wear low shoes, since the marble steps are steep. For viewing most performances the Gamma zone is the best seat choice. Tickets go on sale two weeks before performances but sell out quickly for popular shows; they are available from the festival box office. Prices range from €16 to as high as €120 for the big names; student and youth discounts are available. *Odeon of Herodes Atticus* ⊠ *Dionyssiou Areopagitou, Acropolis* ☎ *210/ 323–2771, 210/323–5582 box office* ⊠ *Festival box office* ⊠ *Panepistimiou 39, Syntagma Sq.* ☎ *210/322–1459.*

Lycabettus Theater. A few Elliniko Festival events are held at the Lycabettus Theater, set on a pinnacle of Mt. Lycabettus. The specialty here is popular concerts; past performers have included B. B. King, Bob Dylan, Massive Attack, and Paco de Lucia. Since buses travel only as far as the bottom of the hill, and taxi drivers often won't drive to the top, buy a one-way ticket on the funicular and walk about 10 minutes to the theater. ⊠ *At top of Mt. Lycabettus, Kolonaki* ☎ *210/322–1459, 210/727–2233, 210/722–7209 theater box office.*

Petras Festival. The old rock quarry at Petroupoli (literally, "stone city") has been transformed into a stunning outdoor venue and is the home of a summer festival jam-packed with acts such as Stomp, Tierra Brava, and percussionists from around the world. ✉ *Varnali 76–78, Petroupoli* 📞 *210/501–2402 or 210/502–5250.*

Rockwave Festival. Every July Athens hosts the three-day outdoor rock festival at varying locations. The lineup has included such mega-acts as Sonic Youth, Garbage, Radiohead, Lou Reed, Patti Smith, Prodigy, and Sisters of Mercy. There's also bungee jumping, in-line skating, tattooing, and other extreme activities here. Tickets run about €30 for each day. *Box office ✉ Panepistimiou 42, in arcade, Syntagma Sq.* 📞 *210/360–8366.*

Vyronas Festival. Performances by well-known Greek musician Dimitris Mitropanos, international acts such as the Beijing Opera, and ancient Greek theater classics are staged in an old quarry, now the Theatro Vrahon. Shows begin around 9:30 PM. Buy tickets (€10–€15) at the theater before the show, or at any of the chain of Metropolis music stores. ✉ *Tatoulon, where Trolley 11 ends, Vyrona* 📞 *210/765–5748 or 210/765–3775.*

Film

Films are shown in original-language versions with Greek subtitles (except for major animated films), a definite boon for foreigners. Downtown theaters have the most advanced technology and most comfortable seats. Tickets run about €7. Check the *Athens News* or *Kathimerini* in the *International Herald Tribune* for programs, schedules, and addresses and phone numbers of theaters, including outdoor theaters. The Hellenic-American Union (www.hau.gr) and the British Council (www.britishcouncil.gr) screen films for free (screenings are usually published in local English-language media).

Unless theaters have air-conditioning, they close from June through September, making way for *therina* (open-air theaters), an enchanting, uniquely Greek entertainment that offers instant escapism under a starry sky. A feature of postwar Mediterranean countries that has survived only in Greece, open-air cinemas saw their popularity decline after the arrival of television. There's been a resurgence in their appeal, and about 75 now operate in the greater Athens area. They are usually set up in vine-covered lots or on rooftops; customers sit on lawn chairs at small tables, where they enjoy snacks and drinks ordered from the bar. In addition to current hits, many outdoor theaters show classic and art films—it's not at all unusual to find a central city summer cinema running a weeklong festival of movies by the Marx Brothers, Fritz Lang, or Jim Jarmusch. At some in-town places there's a mandatory low sound level at the second, later screening—a drag during comedies, when the laughter drowns out the next lines.

Attikon Renault. With its old-fashioned red-velvet and gold-trim embellishments, huge crystal chandelier, wide screen, enormous seats, and central location, this is the best theater in all of Athens. It screens world premieres and classic rereleases. ✉ *Stadiou 19, Syntagma Sq.* 📞 *210/ 322–8821.*

Cine Paris. Kitschy posters of old Greek movies are for sale in the lobby of this rooftop garden theater. It's close to many hotels, on Plaka's main walkway, but the place uses regular stereo instead of Dolby Digital sound. ✉ *Kidathineon 22, Plaka* 📞 *210/322–2071 or 210/324–8057.*

Cine Psirri. This neighborhood therina is far enough from apartment build-ings so that the sound isn't lowered during the second show. ⊠ *Sarri 40–44, Psirri* ☎ *210/321–2476 or 210/324–7234.*

Danaos 1 Ericsson. The spacious theater is not in the center city, but it does have comfortable seats, a great sound system, and current releases. ⊠ *Kifissias 109, 100 yds from Panormou metro, Ambelokipi* ☎ *210/ 692–2655.*

Dexameni. Sit in a bougainvillea-draped garden and see a film before or after checking out Kolonaki's chic restaurants and nightspots. ⊠ *Dex-ameni Sq., Kolonaki* ☎ *210/361–3942 or 210/360–2363.*

Elly. Frequent Elly for independent and art films that don't make it to Greece's more mainstream cinemas. ⊠ *Akadimias 64, Syntagma Sq.* ☎ *210/363–2789.*

Thission. Films at this open-air theater compete with a view of the Acrop-olis. It's on the Unification of Archaeological Sites walkway. ⊠ *Apos-tolou Pavlou 7, Thission* ☎ *210/342–0864 or 210/347–0980.*

Galleries

Athens's contemporary arts scene has been undergoing a revival, with a surge in interest in—and quality of—contemporary art. New galleries and art spaces open all the time, mostly in the former industrial districts of Gazi and Psirri. If you're interested in contemporary art, check out what's on at the Technopolis and Athinais arts complexes and at the Benaki Museum's new contemporary art exhibition space in Gazi. In 2006, the National Museum of Contemporary Art will complete its ren-ovation. Skim the arts listings of the *Athens News* and *Kathimerini* for the occasional "Cheap Art" shows where you can pick up original works by new artists at bargain prices.

Artower Agora. Works of up-and-coming Greek artists, with a focus on photographers, are shown at this warehouse gallery. ⊠ *Armodiou 10, Varvakeio Sq., Central Market* ☎ *210/324–9606.*

Athinais. Occupying a restored silk factory—still swathed in original, 1920s stonework—Athinais is one of the best of a wave of arts spaces sprout-ing up in Athens's old industrial district. The complex houses the Mu-seum of Ancient Cypriot Art, containing treasures dating back to the 9th century BC; a host of gallery spaces with rotating exhibits; a con-cert hall; a theater; two restaurants; and a cinema, which usually screens classic or art films. The best time to visit is at night: see a movie or con-cert, stroll through the galleries and museum, have dinner, and finish off with a drink at the au courant Boiler Bar. ⊠ *Kastorias 34–36, Votanikos* ☎ *210/348–0000* ⊕ *www.athinais.com.gr.*

Bernier/Eliades. Of the small contemporary art venues, this is consid-ered to be one of the best in town, representing artists such as Gilbert & George, George Hadjimichalis, Tony Cragg, and Juan Munoz. ⊠ *Ep-tahalkou 11, Thission* ☎ *210/341–3935* ⊕ *www.bernier-eliades.gr.*

Ileana Tounta Contemporary Art Center. This progressive gallery is set in a lovely garden space, with a sleek design that showcases the works of some of Greece's edgier artists. ⊠ *Klefton 48, at Armatolon, Ambelokipi* ☎ *210/643–9466* ⊕ *www.art-tounta.gr.*

Rebecca Camhi. Trailblazing Rebecca Camhi was Athens's first major gallery owner to open a warehouse art space in the inelegant Central

Market district; it sparked a trend. All of the city's art world comes to see her eclectic shows, which have included work by Nan Goldin and Konstantin Kakanias. ⊠ *Sofokleous 23, Central Market* ☎ *210/321–0448* ⊕ *www.rebeccacamhi.com.*

Technopolis. Chic galleries and restaurants fill a stunning, converted foundry in a former industrial neighborhood. It's a multipurpose arts-and-performance venue for everything from photography exhibits to music concerts. ⊠ *Pireos 100, Gazi* ☎ *210/346–0981.*

SPORTS & THE OUTDOORS

Beaches

Athenians leave the city in droves during the hotter months and head to the sea. The Greek National Tourism Organization can give you a full list of GNTO-run beaches, which have snack bars and beach umbrellas, chairs, dressing rooms, waterslides, banana rides or other children's activities, sports equipment for rent, occasionally windsurfing and waterskiing lessons, and various courts for basketball, tennis, and volleyball. Most are open from 8 AM to 8 PM from June through September; tickets run about €4–€8, with reduced rates for children.

You can join the beach volleyball games—or just watch—that begin in July at Palio Faliro, Schinias, and Palaia Fokaia beaches. The beaches near the Piraeus port often post signs warning of high pollution levels in the water: believe them. The most frequented beaches are at least 15 km (8 mi) outside of Athens; for more information, *see* Beaches *in* Excursions from Athens.

Bird-Watching

The **Hellenic Ornithological Society** (⊠ Emmanuel Benaki 53, Exarchia ☎🖷 210/381–1271 or 210/330–1167) runs a spring program in the National Garden and arranges two- and three-day trips to important bird habitats, like the Dounavi Delta, the Vikos Gorge, and the Messolonghi wetlands.

Health Clubs

Health clubs abound these days; there's little problem finding one near most hotels. The Athens Hilton and Athenaeum InterContinental have excellent facilities with saunas and pools that can be used by the general public for a fee.

The popular **Universal Studios** (⊠ Farantaton 4, Ambelokipi ☎ 210/771–5510 ⊠ 28 Oktovriou [Patission] 376, Patissia ☎ 210/211–0147) health clubs have modern weight machines and aerobics and step classes. One-day passes cost €11.

Hiking

The **Alpine Club of Athens** (⊠ Ermou 64 and Aiolou, 5th fl., Monastiraki ☎ 210/321–2355 🖷 210/324–4789) arranges day-trip hikes to such places as Evritania and Arcadia, ski trips, rock-climbing seminars, and adventure camps for children in summer.

F-Zein (⊠ Ethnikis Antistaseos 103, 2nd fl., Neo Psihiko ☎ 210/675–4300 🖷 210/672–9727 ⊕ www.ezjourneys.gr) runs hiking trips and also organizes kayaking, rafting, mountain biking, and camping expeditions for youngsters.

The **Hellenic Federation of Mountaineering and Climbing** (⊠ Milioni 5, Kolonaki ☎ 210/364–5904 🖷 210/364–2687) supplies details on mountain paths and refuges and has contact numbers for local hiking groups.

Try **Trekking Hellas** (⊠ Fillelinon 7, 3rd fl., Syntagma Sq., 10557 ☎ 210/331–0323 through 210/331–0326 🖷 210/323–4548 ⊕ www.trekking.gr) for adventure trips that include hiking, kayaking, and boating.

Sailing
Those who have certification for sailing on the open sea can legally rent a sailboat (without a captain, if two people on board are licensed). Depending on the boat's size, age, and whether or not a crew is included, rentals can range from about €200 to €17,000 a day. Charter companies usually will provide a list of suggested sailing routes. Most have branch offices at designated marinas along each of these routes, and sometimes you can avoid the capital altogether by picking up your boat at these stations.

Ghiolman Yachts (⊠ Fillelinon 7, Syntagma Sq. ☎ 210/322–8530 or 210/323–0330 🖷 210/322–3251 ⊕ www.ghiolman.com) is highly regarded for large-boat rentals.

The **Hellenic Yachting Federation** (⊠ Leoforos Poseidonos 51, Moschato ☎ 210/940–4825 🖷 210/940–4829 ⊕ www.eio.gr) provides a list (also available online) of local yachting clubs, where visitors can windsurf, sail, and take sailing lessons.

Kyriacoulis Mediterranean Cruises (⊠ Leoforos Poseidonos 51, Palio Faliro ☎ 210/988–6187 through 210/988–6191 🖷 210/984–7296 ⊕ www.kiriacoulis.com) charters yachts of all sizes to voyage throughout Greece and the Mediterranean.

Piraeus Sailing Club (⊠ Mikrolimano, Piraeus ☎ 210/417–7636 🖷 210/411–0287) holds sailing classes.

Vernicos Yachts (⊠ Leoforos Poseidonos 11, Alimos ☎ 210/985–0122 through 210/985–0128 🖷 210/985–0130 ⊕ www.vernicos.gr) has a huge fleet of new yachts and sailboats for charter.

Scuba Diving
Scuba diving is heavily restricted, to protect underwater artifacts, although there are about seven designated diving areas near Athens and another 15 within a radius of 100 km (60 mi). It is forbidden to dive at night and to remove anything from the sea floor. A travel agent can direct you to a supervised diving trip or a less-populated diving base.

Union of Diving Centers (⊠ Vasileos Pavlou 23, Kastella, Piraeus ☎ 210/411–8909 🖷 210/411–9967) can help you find the diving school or center that best fits your needs.

Tennis
The **Hellenic Tennis Federation** (⊠ Ymittou 267, Pangrati ☎ 210/756–3170 through 210/756–3172 🖷 210/756–3173) provides information

on tennis clubs where rental courts are available by the hour; several are near GNTO beaches.

SHOPPING

For serious retail therapy, most natives head to the shopping streets that branch off central Syntagma and Kolonaki squares. Syntagma is the starting point for popular Ermou, a pedestrian zone where large, international brands like Espirit and Marks & Spencer's have edged out small, independent retailers. You'll find local shops on streets parallel and perpendicular to Ermou: Mitropoleos, Voulis, Nikis, Perikleous, and Praxitelous among them. Poke around here for real bargains, like strings of freshwater pearls, loose semiprecious stones, or made-to-fit hats. Much ritzier is the Kolonaki quarter, with boutiques and designer shops on fashionable streets like Anagnostopoulou, Tsakalof, Skoufa, Solonos, and Kanari. Voukourestiou, the link between Kolonaki and Syntagma, is where you'll find Louis Vuitton, Ralph Lauren, and similar brands. In Monastiraki, coppersmiths have their shops on Ifestou. You can pick up copper wine jugs, candlesticks, cookware, and more for next to nothing. The flea market centered on Pandrossou and Ifestou operates on Sunday mornings and has practically everything, from secondhand guitars to Russian vodka. No matter how low the price, always bargain.

Two 2005 changes are transforming the city's retail scene: a law setting uniform shop hours (9 AM to 9 PM on weekdays and 9 AM to 6 PM on Saturday) and the arrival of shopping malls. Citylink, near Syntagma, is home to upscale boutiques like Ferragamo and Bally and the sprawling Attica department store. Three suburban megamalls are set to open in Maroussi, Piraeus, and Spata (near the airport) by the end of 2006.

Regardless, the souvenir shops in Plaka are usually open from early morning until the last tourist leaves. Originally set up by the government to provide employment for veterans, the sidewalk kiosks called *periptera* are the Greek version of a convenience store. Many of them have public phones, some metered for long-distance calls. Those in central squares are often open until very late and occasionally are open around the clock.

Antiques & Icons

Antiques are in vogue now, so the prices of these items have soared. Shops on Pandrossou sell small antiques and icons, but keep in mind that many of these are fakes. You must have government permission to export genuine objects from the ancient Greek, Roman, or Byzantine period.

Alekos Kostas. This *palaiopolio* (junk dealer) is especially popular among collectors of old radio sets and vintage toys, and carries wonderfully quirky items such as mechanized piggy banks. ⊠ *Pl. Abyssinia 3, Monastiraki* ☏ *210/321–1580.*

Kiritisis. Old coins, from Greece and around the world, are for sale at Kiritisis, along with stamps and medals. ⊠ *Areos 1, at Pandrossou, Monastiraki* ☏ *210/324–0544.*

Martinos. Serious antiques collectors should head here to look for items such as exquisite dowry chests, old swords, and Venetian glass. ⊠ *Pan-*

drossou 5, Monastiraki ☎ *210/321–3110* ✉ *Pindarou 24, Kolonaki* ☎ *210/360–9449.*

Nasiotis. With a little perseverance, you can make some interesting finds in this huge basement stacked with books, engravings, old magazines, and first editions. ✉ *Ifestou 24, Monastiraki* ☎ *210/321–2369.*

Pylarinos. Stamp and coin collectors love this packed shop, which also has a good selection of 19th-century engravings. ✉ *Panepistimiou 18, Syntagma Sq.* ☎ *210/363–0688.*

Clothing

Greece is known for its well-made shoes (most shops are clustered around the Ermou pedestrian zone and in Kolonaki), its furs (Mitropoleos near Syntagma), and its durable leather items (Pandrossou in Monastiraki). In Plaka shops you can find fishermen's caps—always a good present—and the natural wool undershirts and hand-knit sweaters worn by fishermen; across the United States these have surfaced at triple the Athens price.

★ **Afternoon.** Prices are lower than what you'll find abroad at this shop with an excellent collection of fashions by Greece's best new designers, including Sophia Kokosalaki, whose work has often graced the pages of *Vogue*. Look for labels from up-and-comers like Deux Hommes, Vasso Consola, and Pavlos Kyriakides. ✉ *Deinokratous 1, Kolonaki* ☎ *210/722–5380.*

Kaplan Furs. Despite animal rights campaigns, Mitropoleos is lined with fur shops. Kaplan has everything from pieced-together stoles to full-length minks, often from the northern city of Kastoria. ✉ *Mitropoleos 22–24, Syntagma Sq.* ☎ *210/322–2226.*

Me Me Me. Whether you're shopping around for a new cocktail dress or for funky accessories, this is the place to head for trendsetting creations by emerging Greek designers. ✉ *Haritos 19, Kolonaki* ☎ *210/722–4890.*

Occhi. Art and the latest clothes and accessories by young Greek designers are displayed side-by-side in this gallery-style shop. ✉ *Sarri 35, Psirri* ☎ *210/321–3298.*

Stavros Melissinos. A legendary poet and gentle soul, as well as shoemaker, Stavros outfits many tourists with his handmade sandals. The Beatles once visited his shop. ✉ *Ayias Theklas 2, Monastiraki* ☎ *210/321–9247.*

Gifts

Athens has great gifts, particularly handmade crafts. Better tourist shops sell copies of traditional Greek jewelry, silver filigree, Skyrian pottery, onyx ashtrays and dishes, woven bags, attractive rugs (including *flokati*, or shaggy goat-wool rugs), and little blue-and-white pendants designed as amulets to ward off the *mati* (evil eye).

An inexpensive but unusual gift is a string of *komboloi* (worry beads) in plastic, wood, or stone. You can pick them up very cheaply in Monastiraki or look in antiques shops for more expensive versions, with amber, silver, or black onyx beads. Reasonably priced natural sponges from Kalymnos also make good presents. Look for those that are unbleached, since the lighter ones tend to fall apart quickly. They're usually sold in front of the National Bank on Syntagma and in Plaka souvenir shops. The price is set by the government, so don't bother to bargain.

Baba. Greeks can spend hours heatedly playing *tavli* (backgammon). To take home a game set of your own, look closely for this hole-in-the-wall, no-name shop, which sells boards and pieces in all sizes and designs. ☒ *Ifestou 30, Monastiraki* ☏ *210/321–9994.*

Fodor'sChoice
★
Benaki Museum Gift Shop. The museum shop has excellent copies of Greek icons, jewelry, and folk art—at fair prices. ☒ *Koumbari 1, at Vasilissis Sofias, Kolonaki* ☏ *210/362–7367.*

Diplous Pelekys. Wool totes, pillow covers with hand-embroidered folk motifs, and, of course, pins featuring the Cretan double-headed axe (*diplous pelekys*) make excellent, and affordable, gifts. ☒ *Voulis 7 and Kolokotroni 3, Syntagma Sq.* ☏ *210/322–3783.*

Fresh Line. Among the solid shampoo cakes, body oils, and face packs are a tremendous number of Greek-made soaps that are sliced from big blocks or wheels as though they were cheese; you pay by weight. The strawberries-and-cream soap, Rea, contains real berries; the Orpheus and Eurydice soap for sensitive skin is made with vanilla, milk, and rice, just like Greek *rizogalo* (rice pudding). ☒ *Skoufa 10, Kolonaki* ☏ *210/364–4015.*

Goutis. One of the more interesting stores on Pandrossou, Goutis has an eclectic jumble of jewelry, costumes, embroidery, and old, handcrafted silver objects. ☒ *Dimokritou 40, Kolonaki* ☏ *210/361–3557.*

Ilias Kokkonis. This century-old store stocks any flag you've always wanted, large or small, from most any country. ☒ *Stoa Arsakeiou 8, enter from Panepistimiou or Stadiou, Omonia Sq.* ☏ *210/322–1189 or 210/322–6355.*

Korres. Natural beauty products blended in traditional recipes using Greek herbs and flowers have graced the bathroom shelves of celebrities like Nicole Kidman. In Athens they are available at most pharmacies for regular-folk prices. For the largest selection of basil-lemon shower gel, coriander body lotion, olive-stone face scrub, and wild-rose eye cream, go to the original Korres pharmacy behind the Panathenaic Stadium. ☒ *Eratosthenous and Ivikou, Pangrati* ☏ *210/722–2744.*

Mastiha Shop. Medical research lauding the healing properties of gummastic, a resin from trees only found in an area of Chios, has spawned a range of products, from chewing gum and cookies to cosmetics. ☒ *Panepistimiou 6, Syntagma Sq.* ☏ *210/363–2750.*

Riza. You can pick up wonderful lace, often handmade, in romantic designs at Riza. The shop also carries fabric at fair prices, and decorative items such as handblown glass bowls and brass candlesticks. ☒ *Voukourestiou 35, at Skoufa, Kolonaki* ☏ *210/361–1157.*

Tanagrea. Hand-painted ceramic pomegranates, a symbol of fertility and good fortune, are one of the most popular items in one of the city's oldest gift shops. ☒ *Voulis 26 and Mitropoleos 15, Syntagma Sq.* ☏ *210/322–3366.*

The Bead Shop. From pinhead-size "evil eyes" to 2-inch-diameter wood beads, you'll find a dizzying selection of beads to string your own *komboloi* or bracelet. ☒ *Pal. Benizelou 6, Mitropolis* ☏ *210/322–1004.*

The Shop. A plain or brightly colored olive-oil pourer, traditional *kafeneion* (coffeehouse) trays, and *fanaria* (birdcagelike contraptions in which to store fresh food): the Shop stocks items that embody Greek village life. Some of the aluminum pieces are handmade. ⊠ *Lysikratous 3, Plaka* ☎ *210/323–0350.*

Thiamis. Iconographer Aristides Makos creates beautiful hand-painted, gold-leaf icons on wood and stone. He also paints patron saints to order. ⊠ *Apollonos 12, Plaka* ☎ *210/331–0337.*

Handicrafts

Amorgos. Wood furniture, hand-carved and hand-painted by the shop's owners, has motifs from regional Greek designs. Needlework, hanging ceiling lamps, shadow puppets, and other decorative accessories are also for sale. ⊠ *Kodrou 3, Plaka* ☎ *210/324–3836.*

★ **Center of Hellenic Tradition.** The Center is an outlet for quality handicrafts—ceramics, weavings, sheep bells, and old paintings. Take a break from shopping in the center's Oraia Ellada café, in clear view of the Parthenon. ⊠ *Mitropoleos 59 and Pandrossou 36, Monastiraki* ☎ *210/321–3023, 210/321–3842 café.*

Lykeio Ellinidon. Resident weavers seated at two looms copy folk motifs from the costumes in the upstairs museum run by the Greek Women's Lyceum. This cozy shop stocks a range of handicrafts, starting at €5, and you can even custom-order a woven tapestry or bedcover. ⊠ *Dimokritou 7a, basement, Kolonaki* ☎ *210/361–1607.*

Oikotechnia. Craftspeople throughout Greece provide folk crafts for sale here by the National Welfare Organization: stunning handwoven carpets, flat-weave kilims, and tapestries from original designs. Hand-embroidered tablecloths and wall decorations make handsome presents; flokati rugs are also for sale. ⊠ *Filellinon 14, Syntagma Sq.* ☎ *210/325–0240.*

Jewelry

Prices are much lower for gold and silver in Greece than in many Western countries, and the jewelry is of high quality. Many shops in Plaka carry original pieces available at a good price if you bargain hard enough (a prerequisite). For those with more expensive tastes, the Voukourestiou pedestrian mall off Syntagma Square has a number of the city's leading jewelry shops.

Byzantino. Great values in gold, including certified copies of ancient Greek pieces and many original works designed in the on-site workshop, can be purchased here. ⊠ *Adrianou 120, Plaka* ☎ *210/324–6605.*

Elena Votsi. Elena Votsi designed jewelry for Gucci before opening her own boutique, where she sells exquisite creations in coral, amethyst, aquamarine, and turquoise. ⊠ *Xanthou 7, Kolonaki* ☎ *210/360–0936.*

Fanourakis. Original gold masterpieces can be had at these shops, where Athenian artists use gold almost like a fabric—creasing, scoring, and fluting it. ⊠ *Patriarchou Ioakeim 23, Kolonaki* ☎ *210/721–1762* ⊠ *Evangelistrias 2, Mitropolis* ☎ *210/324–6642* ⊠ *Panagitsas 6, Kifissia* ☎ *210/623–2334.*

Goulandris Cycladic Museum. Exceptional modern versions of ancient jewelry designs are available here. ⊠ *Neofitou Douka 4, Kolonaki* ☎ *210/724–9706.*

LALAoUNIS. A world-famous Greek jeweler experiments with his designs, taking ideas from nature, biology, and ancient Greek pieces—the last are sometimes so close to the original that they're mistaken for museum artifacts. ✉ *Panepistimiou 6, Syntagma Sq.* ☎ *210/361–1371* ✉ *Athens Tower, Sinopis 2, Ambelokipi* ☎ *210/770–0000.*

Pentheroudakis. Browse among the classic designs; there are even less-expensive trinkets, like silver worry beads that can be personalized with cubed letters in Greek or Latin and with the stone of your choice. ✉ *Voukourestiou 19, Kolonaki* ☎ *210/361–3187.*

★ **Sagianos.** For five generations, the Sagianos family's creations have adorned the fingers, necks, and ears of well-to-do Athenian matrons. The tradition continues, but with more modern, one-of-a-kind pieces inspired by ordinary objects like bar codes and buttons. ✉ *Makriyianni 3, Makriyianni* ☎ *210/362–5822.*

Xanthopoulos. Shop for traditional gold, silver, and jewels at this store. ✉ *Voukourestiou 4, Kolonaki* ☎ *210/322–6856.*

Zolotas. This jeweler, LALAoUNIS's main competitor, is noted for its superb museum copies. ✉ *Pandrossou 8, Plaka* ☎ *210/323–2413* ✉ *Stadiou 9, Syntagma Sq.* ☎ *210/322–1212.*

Local Delicacies

Bahar. One of the numerous spice shops lining Evripidou, Bahar carries culinary and pharmaceutical herbs. ✉ *Evripidou 31, Central Market* ☎ *210/321–7225.*

Cellier. Greek wine is going through a long-awaited renaissance, and the knowledgeable staff here can help you pick the bottles that show the best of what the new vintners have to offer. ✉ *Kriezotou 1, Syntagma Sq.* ☎ *210/361–0040.*

Central Market. Athenians come here for everything from live poultry and rabbits to fresh fruit and vegetables, and it's a good place to stop for picnic fixings. You can stock up on tasty local foods to bring home: packaged dried figs, packaged pistachios, *pastelli* (sesame-seed-and-honey candy), and all kinds of olives. ✉ *Athinas, Central Market.*

Gnision Esti. Homemade pasta flavored with artichokes, sugar-dusted almond cookies, and a dizzying array of pickled vegetables and preserves capture the flavor of Greek regional cuisine. ✉ *Christou Lada 2 and Anthimou Gazi, Syntagma Sq.* ☎ *210/324–4784.*

★ **Mesogeia.** Small, stylish Mesogeia is the place to go for award-winning olive oils from Crete; organic, elegantly packaged marinated vegetables grown in mountain villages; and delicious traditional spreads. ✉ *Niskis 52, Plaka* ☎ *210/322–9146.*

Matsouka. Roasted pistachio nuts, *pastokidono* (thick slices of quince jelly with whole almonds), and wafer-thin almond nougat make great gifts for foodie friends. ✉ *Karagiorgi Servias 3, Syntagma Sq.* ☎ *210/ 325–2054.*

Miseyiannis. For an inexpensive but interesting gift, pick up some freshly ground Greek coffee and the traditional pot to brew it, a *briki.* ✉ *Levendis 7, Kolonaki* ☎ *210/721–0136.*

Tyria Outra. Just outside the Central Market, this always-packed deli has an excellent selection of olives, cheeses, marinated grape leaves, and fresh halvah. ✉ *Sofokleous 17, Central Market* ☎ *210/322–1135.*

Music

Metropolis. Take your pick of a huge selection of all-Greek music, from rembetika to the latest Greek club hits, all by Greek artists. ✉ *Panepistimiou 54, Omonia Sq.* ☏ *210/380–8549.*

ATHENS A TO Z

To research prices, get advice from other travelers, and book travel arrangements, visit www.fodors.com.

AIR TRAVEL

The opening of Athens's sleek Eleftherios Venizelos International Airport has made air travel around the country much more pleasant and efficient. Greece is so small that few in-country flights take more than an hour or cost more than €200 round-trip. Aegean Airlines and Olympic Airways have regular flights between Athens, Thessaloniki, and most major cities and islands in Greece. For further information, *see* Air Travel *in* Smart Travel Tips.

AIRPORTS & TRANSFERS

For information about Eleftherios Venizelos International Airport near Athens, *see* Airports *in* Smart Travel Tips. The best way to get to the airport from downtown Athens is by metro or light rail. Single tickets cost €6 and include transfers (within 90 minutes of the ticket's initial validation; don't forget to validate the ticket again) to bus, trolley, or tram. Combined tickets for two (€10) and three (€15) passengers are also available; if you're making a stopover in Athens, opt for a round-trip ticket (€10), valid for trips to and from the airport made during a single 48-hour period.

In Athens three reliable express buses connect the airport with the metro (Ethniki Amyna station), Syntagma Square, and Piraeus. These buses are air-conditioned and have space for luggage. Express buses leave the arrivals level of the airport every 10 minutes and operate 24 hours a day. Bus E95 will take you to Syntagma Square (Amalias avenue); E94 goes to the bus terminus at the Ethniki Amyna metro stop (Line 3), which will get you into Syntagma within 10 minutes. Bus E96 takes the Vari–Koropi road inland and links with the coastal road, passing through Voula, Glyfada, and Alimo; it then goes on to Piraeus (opposite Karaiskaki Square).

The Attiki Odos and the expansion of the city's network of bus lanes has made travel times more predictable, and on a good day the E94 can get you to Ethniki Amyna in 40 minutes. Tickets to and from the airport cost €2.90 and are valid on all forms of transportation in Athens for 24 hours from the time of validation. Purchase tickets from the airport terminal, kiosks, metro stations, or even on the express buses. The Greek National Tourism Organization (GNTO, or EOT in Greece) dispenses schedules. You can also obtain brochures at the airport with bus schedules and routes.

Taxis (⇨ Taxis) are readily available at the arrivals level of the Athens airport; it costs an average of €22 to get into downtown Athens (including tolls). Limousine Service and Royal Prestige Limousine Service provide service to and from Athens; an evening surcharge of up to 50% often applies, and you should call in advance. Prices start at €80 for one-way transfer from the airport to a central hotel.

🔲Limousines **Limousine Service** ⊠Athens ☎210/970-6416 ⊕www.limousine-service. gr. **Royal Prestige Limousine Service** ⊠ Athens ☎ 210/988-3221 🖨🖨 210/983-0378.

BOAT & FERRY TRAVEL

Boat travel in Greece is common and relatively inexpensive. Every weekend thousands of Athenians set off on one- and two-hour trips to islands like Aegina, Hydra, and Andros, while in the summer ferries are weighed down with merrymakers on their way to Mykonos, Rhodes, and Santorini. Cruise ships, ferries, and hydrofoils from the Aegean and most other Greek islands dock and depart every day from Athens's main port, Piraeus, 10 km (6 mi) southwest of Athens. Ships for the Ionian islands sail from ports nearer to them, such as Patras and Igoumenitsa. Connections from Piraeus to the main island groups are good, connections from main islands to smaller ones within a group less so, and services between islands of different groups or areas—such as Rhodes and Crete—are less frequent.

Travel agents (⇨ Travel Agents) and ship offices in Athens and Piraeus have details. Boat schedules are published in *Kathimerini,* sold with the *International Herald Tribune*; EOT (⇨ Visitor Information) distributes boat schedules updated every Wednesday. You can also call a daily Greek recording (listed below) for ferry departure times. Timetables change according to seasonal demand, and boats may be delayed by weather conditions, so your plans should be flexible. Buy your tickets two or three days in advance, especially if you are traveling in summer or taking a car. Reserve your return journey or continuation soon after you arrive. For further information, *see* Boat & Ferry Travel *in* Smart Travel Tips.

To get to and from Piraeus harbor, you can take the green line metro (Line 1) from central Athens directly to the station at the main port. The trip takes 25–30 minutes. A taxi takes longer because of traffic and costs around €12–€15.

Athens's other main port is Rafina, which serves some of the closer Cyclades and Evia. KTEL buses run every 30 minutes between the port and the Mavromateon terminal in central Athens, from about 5:30 AM until 9:30 PM, and cost €2 (⇨ Bus Travel). At Rafina, the buses leave from an area slightly uphill from the port. The trip takes about one hour.

🔲**Ferry departures** ☎1440. **Piraeus** ⊠ Port Authority, Akti Miaouli, Piraeus ☎ 210/451-1311 through 210/451-1317. **Rafina** ☎ 22940/22300.

BUS TRAVEL TO & FROM ATHENS

Travel around Greece by bus is inexpensive, usually comfortable, and relatively fast. The journey from Athens to Thessaloniki takes roughly the same time as the regular train, though the InterCity Express train covers the distance 1¼ hours faster. To reach the Peloponnese, buses are speedier than trains. Information and timetables are available at tourist information offices. Make reservations at least one day before your planned trip, earlier for holiday weekends.

Terminal A is the arrival and departure point for bus lines that serve parts of northern Greece, including Thessaloniki, and the Peloponnese destinations of Epidauros, Mycenae, Nafplion, Olympia, and Corinth. Each destination has its own phone number; EOT offices distribute a list. Terminal B serves Evia, most of Thrace, and central Greece, including Delphi. EOT provides a phone list (⇨ Visitor Information). Tickets for these buses are sold only at this terminal, so you should call to book seats well in advance in high season or holidays.

To get to central city from Terminal A, take Bus 051 to Omonia Square; from Terminal B, take Bus 024 downtown. To get to the stations, catch Bus 051 at Zinonos and Menandrou off Omonia Square (for Terminal A) and Bus 024 on Amalias in front of the National Garden (for Terminal B). International buses drop their passengers off on the street, usually in the Omonia or Syntagma Square areas or at Stathmos Peloponnisou (train station).

🛈 **Terminal A** ⊠ Kifissou 100 ☎ 210/512-4910 or 210/512-4911. **Terminal B** ⊠ Liossion 260 ☎ 210/831-7096 for Delphi, 210/831-7173 for Livadia (Ossios Loukas via Distomo), 210/831-1431 for Trikala (Meteora).

BUS & TRAM TRAVEL WITHIN ATHENS

Athens and its suburbs are covered by a good network of buses, with express buses running between central Athens and major neighborhoods, including nearby beaches. During the day, buses tend to run every 15–30 minutes, with reduced service at night and on weekends. Buses run from about 5 AM to midnight. Main bus stations are at Akadimias and Sina and at Kaningos Square. Bus and trolley tickets cost €0.45. No transfers are issued; you validate a new ticket every time you change vehicles. If you're making several short stops, a 90-minute ticket (€1 for all modes of public transport and €0.70 for bus, trolley, and tram only) may be cheaper. Day passes for €3, weekly passes for €10, and monthly passes for €38 (€ 35 for metro, trolleys, and buses only and €17.50 for buses only) are sold at special booths at the main terminals. (Passes are not valid for travel to the airport or on the E22 Saronida Express.) Purchase individual tickets at terminal booths or at kiosks.

Maps of bus routes (in Greek) are available at terminal booths or from EOT. KTEL (Greece's regional bus system, made up of local operators) has an English-language Web site. The Web site of the Organization for Urban Public Transportation has an excellent English-language section. You can type in your starting point and destination and get a list of public transportation options for making the journey.

Orange-and-white KTEL buses provide efficient service throughout the Attica basin. Most buses to the east Attica coast, including those for Sounion (€3.70 for inland route and €4.10 on coastal road) and Marathon (€2.40), leave from the KTEL terminal.

A tram link between downtown Athens and the coastal suburbs was introduced in 2004. Line A runs from Syntagma to Glyfada; Line B traces the shoreline from Glyfada to the Peace & Friendship Stadium on the outskirts of Piraeus. Single tickets cost €0.60 or €0.40 for five stops and are sold at machines on the tram platforms.

🚊 **City trams** ⊕ www.tramsa.gr. **KTEL Buses** ✉ Pl. Aigyptou at corner of Mavromateon and Leoforos Alexandras near Pedion Areos park, Pedion Areos ☎ 210/821-0872, 210/821-3203 for Sounion, 210/821-0872 for Marathon ⊕ www.ktel.org. **Organization for Urban Public Transportation** ✉ Metsovou 15 Exarchia ☎ 185 ⊕ www.oasa.gr.

CAR RENTAL

If you are coming to Athens from abroad, especially the United States or Canada, and are planning to rent a car from a major international chain, it's almost always cheaper to book from your home country. Agencies are grouped around Syngrou and Syntagma Square in central Athens, and at the arrivals area of the airport. For further information, *see* Car Rental *in* Smart Travel Tips.

CAR TRAVEL

Greece's main highways to the north and the south link up in Athens; both are called Ethnikis Odos (National Road). Take the Attiki Odos, a beltway around Athens that also accesses Eleftherios Venizelos International Airport, to speed your travel time entering and exiting the city.

At the city limits, signs in English clearly mark the way to both Syntagma Square and Omonia Square in the city center. Leaving Athens, routes to the highways and Attiki Odos are well marked; signs usually name Lamia for points north, and Corinth or Patras for points southwest. From Athens to Thessaloniki, the distance is 515 km (319 mi); to Kalamata, 257 km (159 mi); to Corinth, 84 km (52 mi); to Lamia, 214 km (133 mi); to Patras, 218 km (135 mi); to Igoumenitsa, 472 km (293 mi).

DRIVING IN ATHENS Driving in Athens is not recommended unless you have nerves of steel; it can be unpleasant and even unsafe. It's fairly easy to get around the city with a combination of public transportation and taxis; save car rentals for excursions out of town. Red traffic lights are frequently ignored, and motorists often pass other vehicles while driving on hills and while rounding corners. Driving is on the right, and although the vehicle on the right has the right-of-way, don't expect this or any other driving rule to be obeyed. The speed limit is 50 kph (31 mph) in town. Traffic tends toward gridlock or heart-stopping speeding; parking in most parts of the city could qualify as an Olympic sport. Seat belts are compulsory, as are helmets for motorcyclists, though many natives ignore the laws. In downtown Athens do not drive in the bus lanes marked by a yellow divider; if caught, you may be fined.

Downtown parking spaces are hard to find, and the few downtown garages—including ones in vacant lots—are both expensive and perpetually full. The addition of parking meters and controlled parking zones at some point is expected to ease the situation in congested, high-traffic areas like Kolonaki, Syntagma, and Exarchia. Still, you're better off leaving your car in the hotel garage and walking or taking a cab. Gas pumps and service stations are everywhere, and lead-free gas is widely available. Be aware that all-night stations are few and far between.

For information about the Automobile Touring Club of Greece (ELPA), *see* Car Travel *in* Smart Travel Tips.

CHILDREN IN ATHENS

The concept of babysitting agencies hasn't really taken hold in Athens, in part because Greeks are used to taking their children almost everywhere, including restaurants and late-night cafés and cinemas. High-end hotel chains can arrange for staff to babysit children in your hotel for between €10 and €15 per hour.

DISABILITIES & ACCESSIBILITY

The concept of accessibility is still new in Greece, and Athens has long been an extremely difficult city for people with disabilities to negotiate. To host the 2004 Paralympic Games, for athletes with physical disabilities, the city had to make all of its new public buildings and infrastructure accessible; it also did some work to make older buildings at least partly accessible. Hotels in major chains have a handful of rooms equipped for wheelchairs, but most other hotels do not. Modern restaurants may have one accessible bathroom, but in most older tavernas, restaurants, and bars, the bathroom is downstairs. Elevators and entrances are often small and narrow; wheelchair ramps, when they exist, usually consist of a segment of staircase paved over to make a short, steep, and dangerous incline. Newer buses and trolleys have spaces designated for wheelchairs and those with disabilities, but not all are equipped with wheelchair lifts. In newer buildings, including the airport and metro stops, there is good accessibility. The EOT (⇨ Visitor Information) and the Panhellenic Union of Paraplegic and Physically Challenged can provide some information. For further information, *see* Disabilities & Accessibility *in* Smart Travel Tips.

Panhellenic Union of Paraplegic and Physically Challenged ⊠ Dimitsanis 3–5, Moschato, 18346 ☎ 210/483–2564 ⊕ www.pasipka.gr.

DISCOUNTS & DEALS

Athens's best deal is the €12 ticket that allows one week's admission to all the sites and corresponding museums along the Unification of Archaeological Sites walkway. You can buy the ticket at any of the sites, which include the Acropolis, ancient Agora, Roman Agora, Temple of Olympian Zeus, Kerameikos, and Theater of Dionyssos. Admission to almost all museums and archaeological sites is free on Sunday from mid-November through March. Entrance is usually free every day for EU students, half off for students from other countries, and about a third off for senior citizens.

EMBASSIES & CONSULATES

For embassies, *see* Embassies & Consulates *in* Smart Travel Tips.

EMERGENCIES

You can call an ambulance in the event of an emergency, but taxis are often faster. For car accidents, call the city police.

Ambulance ☎ 166. **City Police** ☎ 100. **Coast Guard** ☎ 108. **Fire** ☎ 199. **Tourist Police** ⊠ Dimitrakopoulou 77, Koukaki ☎ 171.

DOCTORS & DENTISTS Most hotels will call a doctor or dentist for you; you can also contact your embassy for referrals to either. For a doctor on call 2 PM–7 AM on Sunday and holidays, dial 105 (in Greek).

HOSPITALS Dial 106 (in Greek), check the *Athens News* or the English-language *Kathimerini,* or ask your hotel to check the Greek papers to find out which emergency hospitals are open; not all hospitals are open nightly. Hygeia Hospital is considered one of the best in Greece, as is its sister maternity hospital, Mitera; both have some English-speaking staff. Children go to Aglaia Kyriakou Hospital or Ayia Sofia Hospital. Note that children's hospitals answer the phone with "Pedon" and not the specific name of the institution.

🏥 **Aglaia Kyriakou Hospital** ✉ Levadias 3 and Thivon, Goudi ☎ 210/777–5611 through 210/777–5619. **Asklepion Hospital** ✉ Vasileos Pavlou 1, Voula ☎ 210/895–8301 through 210/895–8306. **Ayia Sofia Hospital** ✉ Mikras Asias and Thivon, Goudi ☎ 210/777–1811 through 210/777–1816. **Hygeia Hospital** ✉ Erythrou Stavrou 4, at Kifissias, Maroussi ☎ 210/686–7000 ⊕ www.hygeia.gr. **KAT Hospital** ✉ Nikis 2, Syntagma Sq. ☎ 210/801–4411, 166 for accidents. **Mitera** ✉ Erythrou Stavrou 6, at Kifissias, Maroussi ☎ 210/686–9000. **Ygeia** ✉ Erythrou Stavrou 4, at Kifissias, Maroussi ☎ 210/682–7940 through 210/682–7949.

LATE-NIGHT PHARMACIES There are no 24-hour pharmacies in Athens; a Greek-language phone recording (dial 107) lists pharmacies open on holidays and late at night, or you can check the listings in the English-language *Athens News* or *Kathimerini.* Each pharmacy posts in its window (in Greek) a list of establishments close by that are open during the afternoon break or late at night. Many pharmacies in the center have someone who speaks English, or try Thomas, near the Hilton, for convenience and spoken English.

🏥 **Late-night pharmacy hotline (in Greek)** ☎ 107. **Thomas** ✉ Papadiamantopoulou 6, near Hilton and Holiday Inn, Ilisia ☎ 210/721–6101.

ENGLISH-LANGUAGE MEDIA

English-language books, newspapers, and magazines are readily available in central Athens; international bookstores and kiosks in Kolonaki and Syntagma stock everything from the *Wall Street Journal* to *Wallpaper.* Local English-language publications include the weekly *Athens News,* which offers a mix of politics, features, travel, and style articles written by both Greek and international journalists; the English-language translation of the respected Greek broadsheet *Kathimerini,* sold as an insert with the *International Herald Tribune*; *Odyssey* magazine, a glossy bimonthly on politics, sports, travel, and events in Greece and among Greeks abroad; and *Insider,* a monthly magazine on lifestyle and entertainment in Athens, with a focus on shopping, art exhibits, restaurants, and nightlife.

BOOKSTORES Compendium carries travel books, books on Greece, academic books, and used books. For a huge selection of both Greek- and English-language books, check out Eleftheroudakis. I Folia tou Vivliou has an ample selection of British and American authors. Papasotiriou carries mainstream fiction, cookbooks, foreign magazines, children's books, and books on history and politics. Reymondos is the place to go for great foreign-language books and magazines.

🔲 Bookstores in Athens **Compendium** ✉ Nikis 28, upstairs, Athens ☎ 210/322-1248. **Eleftheroudakis** ✉ Nikis 20, Athens ☎ 210/322-9388 ✉ Panepistimiou 17, Athens ☎ 210/325-8440. **I Folia tou Vivliou** (Booknest) ✉ Panepistimiou 25-29, in arcade and on 1st fl., Athens ☎ 210/323-1703. **Papasotiriou** ✉ Akadimias and Ippokratous, Athens ☎ 210/339-0637. **Reymondos** ✉ Voukourestiou 18, Athens ☎ 210/364-8188.

LIBRARIES At the Hellenic-American Union, the library includes English-language books on Greek topics. Also try the British Council Library. Though it is not a lending library, the Gennadius Library at the American School of Classical Studies is interesting; call first, as hours change frequently.
🔲 **British Council Library** ✉ Kolonaki Sq. 17, Kolonaki ☎ 210/364-5768. **Gennadius Library, American School of Classical Studies** ✉ Soudias 61, Kolonaki ☎ 210/721-0536. **Hellenic-American Union** ✉ Massalias 22, Kolonaki ☎ 210/368-0000.

RADIO & TELEVISION For information, *see* English-language Media *in* Smart Travel Tips.

LANGUAGE

All Greeks are taught English in public school, and most retain at least a rudimentary knowledge. In Athens, you can expect to find decent English spoken in mid-range to high-end hotels, restaurants, shops, and most tourist sights. A fair number of taxi drivers speak some English; those that do are usually happy to show it off. Despite this, though, you may be surprised at some places where English does not seem to be spoken—at several offices of the Greek National Tourism Organization, for example.

INTERNET CAFÉS

For information, *see* Computers on the Road *in* Smart Travel Tips.

LODGING

APARTMENT & VILLA RENTALS Academics, businesspeople, and travelers who have fallen in love with Greece and decided to stay are all commonplace in Athens, which may account for the relative ease of finding short-term apartment and home rentals. Some hotels, such as the Andromeda Athens Hotel, offer studios and apartments for long-term stays. Otherwise, local agents can help you find anything from a tiny artist's studio to a seaside villa for periods ranging from a week to several months. Many travel agents in the United States can organize rentals in Greece.
🔲 Local Agents **Best Value Properties** ✉ Diadohou Pavlou 19c, Psihiko ☎ 210/671-7554. **Greek Real Estate Group** ✉ Dousmani 5, Suite 134, Glyfada ☎ 210/964-9514. **Helen's Real Estate** ✉ Stavraetou 7, Zografou ☎ 210/779-6536.

MAIL & SHIPPING

There are post offices all over Athens; ask your hotel how to get to the closest one. The city's two central post offices are in Syntagma Square and off Omonia Square; both are infamous for long lines and slow service. Avoid all post offices during the first week of the month, when Greeks line up to pay their utility bills. Post offices are open weekdays 8–2; some also open Saturday morning. If you want to mail a letter, you can do it from the yellow mailboxes outside post offices; there are separate boxes for international and domestic mail.

🚩 Post Offices **Omonia Square** ✉ Tritis Septemvriou 28, Omonia Sq. ☎ 210/522–4949 ⊗ Weekdays 7:30 ᴀᴍ–8 ᴘᴍ. **Syntagma Square** ✉ Corner of Mitropoleos and Filellinon, Suite 134, Syntagma Sq. ☎ 210/323–7573 ⊗ Weekdays 7:30 ᴀᴍ–8 ᴘᴍ, Sat. 7:30–2, Sun. 9–1:30.

METRO TRAVEL

Line 1 of the city's metro (subway) system, which dates from the 19th century, runs from Piraeus to the northern suburb of Kifissia, with several downtown stops. Downtown stations on Line 1 most handy to tourists include Platia Victorias, near the National Archaeological Museum; Omonia Square; Monastiraki, in the old Turkish bazaar; and Thission, near the ancient Agora and the nightlife districts of Psirri and Thission. Line 1 also has a stop at Irini, site of the Athens Olympic Sports Complex.

In 2000, the city opened Lines 2 and 3 of the metro, many of whose gleaming stations function as minimuseums, displaying ancient artifacts found on site. These lines are safe and fast but cover limited territory, mostly downtown. Line 2 cuts northwest across the city, starting from Syntagma Square station and passing through such useful stops as Panepistimiou (near the Old University complex and the Numismatic Museum); Omonia Square; the Stathmos Larissis stop next to Athens's train stations, and Acropolis, at the foot of the famous site. Line 3 runs from Monastiraki northeast to the Greek "Pentagon" (Ethnikis Aminas). The stops of most interest for visitors are Evangelismos, near the Byzantine Museum, Hilton Hotel, and National Gallery of Art, and Megaro Mousikis, next to the United States Embassy and concert hall. Extensions will eventually reach all the main suburbs; work will continue through 2007.

FARES &
SCHEDULES
The fare is €0.60 if you stay only on Line 1; otherwise, it's €0.70. A daily travel pass, valid for use on all forms of public transportation, is €3; it's good for 24 hours after you validate it. You must validate all tickets at the machines in metro stations before you board. Trains run between 5:30 ᴀᴍ and 11:30 ᴘᴍ. Maps of the metro, including planned extensions, are available in stations. There is no phone number for information about the system, so check the Web site, which has updates on planned extensions.

🚩 **Metro Information** ⊕ www.ametro.gr.

MONEY MATTERS

Since strikes and power outages are not uncommon in Greece, always keep extra cash on hand. Most banks and currency exchange offices are clustered around Syntagma and Omonia squares. Many change money only until 2 ᴘᴍ, even if they stay open later. Commissions tend to be between €2 and €3 but can be more at an exchange office rather than a bank. American Express cashes American Express traveler's checks free of commission.

🚩 Currency Exchange **American Express** ✉ Ermou 7, Syntagma Sq. ☎ 210/322–3380. **Eurochange** ✉ Karagiorgi Servias 2 and 4, Syntagma Sq. ☎ 210/331–2462 or 210/322–

0005. National Bank of Greece ⊠ Karagiorgi Servias and Stadiou, Syntagma Sq.
☎ 210/334–8015.

SIGHTSEEING TOURS

All travel agents in Athens offer the same handful of city and regional
tours: bus jaunts around the city, covering the major sights and including meals in scenic but tourist-infested Plaka tavernas; and one- to
three-day excursions to archaeological sites and cities outside Athens.
Small, custom-tailored tours that are nothing more than bus shuttles with
50 other people are starting to make an appearance.

BOAT TOURS For information about cruises to the Greek islands from Athens, *see* Cruise
Travel & Yachting *in* Smart Travel Tips.

BUS TOURS A basic four-hour bus tour includes a guided tour of the Acropolis and
National Archaeological Museum (when open); it also drives by most
other major sites and finishes up with lunch in a Plaka taverna. Reservations can be made through most hotels or any travel agency; many
agencies are clustered around Filellinon and Nikis streets off Syntagma
Square (⇨ Travel Agents). The tours run daily, year-round, and cost
around €45. Reserve at least a day in advance.

The "Athens Sightseeing Public Bus Line," or Bus 400, stops at all the
city's main sights, including the National Archaeological Museum,
Psirri, Kerameikos, Monastiraki, Syntagma, the Benaki Museum, the Panathenaic Stadium, Parliament, Acropolis, Temple of Olympian Zeus, and
National Art Gallery. Buses run every 30 minutes, from 7:30 AM to 9
PM and tickets cost €5. The full journey takes 90 minutes, but you can
hop on and off as you please. Bus 400 stops are marked by bright blue
waist-high pillars.

EXCURSION Most agencies (⇨ Travel Agents) offer excursions at about the same
TOURS prices, but CHAT is reputed to have the best service and guides. Common excursion tours include a half-day trip to the Temple of Poseidon at Sounion (€29); a half-day tour to the Isthmus and ancient Corinth
(€48); a full-day tour to Delphi (€76, €66 without lunch); a two-day
trip to Delphi (€116 including half-board—meaning breakfast and dinner—in first-class hotels); a three-day tour taking in Delphi and the
monasteries of Meteora with half-board in first-class hotels (€273);
a one-day tour to Nafplion, Mycenae, and Epidauros (€76, €66 without lunch); a two-day tour to Mycenae, Nafplion, and Epidauros
(€116 including half-board in first-class hotels); a four-day tour covering Nafplion, Mycenae, Epidauros, Olympia, and Delphi (€378
with half-board in first-class hotels); and a five-day "classical" tour
covering all major sights in the Peloponnese, as well as Delphi and Meteora (€492 with half-board in first-class hotels). Most tours run two
to three times a week, with reduced service in winter. It's best to reserve a few days in advance.

PERSONAL Major travel agencies (⇨ Travel Agents) can provide English-speaking
GUIDES guides to take you around Athens's major sights. The Union of Official
Guides provides licensed guides for individual or group tours, starting
at about €120, including taxes, for a four-hour tour of the Acropolis

and its museum. Hire only guides licensed by the EOT—they have successfully completed a two-year state program.

🎧 **Union of Official Guides** ✉ Apollonos 9A, Plaka ☎ 210/322-9705 or 210/322-0090 🖷 210/923-6884.

SPECIAL-
INTEREST TOURS
All travel agents offer an "Athens by Night" deal, which takes you around the monuments by moonlight and concludes with dinner and a floor show in Plaka (€47 includes dinner but not drinks). Amphitrion Holidays, part of the Amphitrion Travel group (⇨ Travel Agents), specializes in educational and offbeat tours for individuals in Athens and environs.

For organized adventure travel, contact Trekking Hellas. For horseback riding tours, the helpful Hellenic Equestrian Federation provides a list of Athens's riding clubs.

🎧 **Hellenic Equestrian Federation** ✉ Messinias 55, Goudi ☎ 210/748-6875 or 210/748-6876 🖷 210/778-1572. **Trekking Hellas** ✉ Filellinon 7, 3rd fl., Syntagma Sq. ☎ 210/331-0323 through 210/331-0326 🖷 210/324-4548 ⊕ www.trekking.gr.

WALKING TOURS
At Athenian Days, classicist Andrew Farrington and anthropologist Vassiliki Chryssanthopoulou create tailor-made walking tours of classical Athens for groups no larger than four. The lively, informative presentations conclude with a talk in a shady café and a take-home folder of information. Prices range from €50 to €70 per group.

🎧 **Athenian Days** ☎ 210/689-3828.

TAXIS

Most drivers in Athens speak basic English. Although you can find an empty taxi on the street, it's often faster to call out your destination to one carrying passengers; if the taxi is going in that direction, the driver will pick you up. Likewise, don't be alarmed if your driver picks up other passengers (although he should ask your permission first, and he will never pick up another fare if you are a woman traveling alone at night). Each passenger pays full fare for the distance he or she has traveled.

Taxi rates are still affordable compared to fares in other European capitals. Most taxi drivers are honest and hardworking, but a few con artists infiltrate the ranks at the airports and near popular restaurants and clubs frequented by foreigners. Get an idea from your hotel how much the fare should be, and if there's trouble, ask to go to a police station (most disagreements don't ever get this far, however). Make sure the driver turns on the meter and that the rate listed in the lower corner is 1, the normal rate before midnight; after midnight, the rate listed is 2.

Taxi drivers know the major central hotels, but if your hotel is less well known, show the driver the address written in Greek and make note of the phone number and, if possible, a nearby landmark. If all else fails, the driver can call the hotel from his mobile phone or a kiosk. Athens has thousands of short side streets, and few taxi drivers have maps, although newer taxis have GPS installed. Neither tipping nor bargaining is generally practiced; if your driver has gone out of the way for you, a small gratuity (10% or less) is appreciated.

FARES
The meter starts at €0.75, and even if you join other passengers, you must add this amount to your final charge. The minimum fare is €1.50.

The basic charge is €0.26 per kilometer (½ mi); this increases to €0.50 between midnight and 5 AM or if you go outside city limits. There are surcharges for holidays (€0.50), trips to and from the airport (€2), and rides to (but not from) the port, train stations, and bus terminals (€0.70). There is also a €0.29 charge for each suitcase over 10 kilograms (22 pounds), but drivers expect €0.29 for each bag they place in the trunk anyway. Waiting time is €7.10 per hour. Radio taxis charge an additional €1.30 for the pickup or €2.20 for a later appointment. Athina 1, Ermis, Hellas, Kosmos, and Parthenon are reliable radio taxi services.
🚖 Taxi Companies **Athina 1** ☎ 210/921-7942. **Ermis** ☎ 210/411-5200. **Hellas** ☎ 210/645-7000 or 210/801-4000. **Kosmos** ☎ 1300. **Parthenon** ☎ 210/532-3300.

TRAIN TRAVEL

The *proastiakos* ("suburban"), a light-rail network offering travelers a direct link from Athens airport to Corinth for €8, is introducing Athenians to the concept of commuting. The trains now serve the city's northern and eastern suburbs as well as western Attica. The Athens-to-Corinth fare is €6; lower fares apply for points in between. Upgrades are also being made to the segments linking Athens with Halkida and Thebes. If you plan on taking the train while in Athens, call the Greek Railway Organization (OSE) to find out which station your train leaves from, and how to get there. At this writing, Stathmos Peloponnisou, where the trains from the Peloponnese arrive, has been temporarily closed and operations transferred to the Ayii Anaryiri station. Trains from the north and international trains arrive at, and depart from, Stathmos Larissis, which is connected to the metro. If you want to buy tickets ahead of time, it's easier to visit a downtown railway office. For further information, *see* Train Travel *in* Smart Travel Tips.
🚆**Greek Railway Organization (OSE)** ☎210/529-7777 ⊕www.ose.gr. **OSE buses** ☎210/513-5768 or 210/513-5769. **Proastiakos** ☎ 210/529-7777 ⊕ www.proastiakos.gr. **Railway Offices** ✉ Karolou 1, Omonia Sq. ☎ 210/529-7006 or 210/529-7007 ✉ Sina 6, Kolonaki ☎ 210/529-8910 ✉ Filellinon 17, Syntagma Sq. ☎ 210/323-6747 ☉ Mon.-Sat. 8-2. **Stathmos Larissis** ☎ 210/529-8837. **Stathmos Peloponnisou** ☎ 210/529-8735.

TRANSPORTATION AROUND ATHENS

Many major sights, as well as hotels, cafés, and restaurants, are within a fairly small central area. It's easy to walk everywhere, though sidewalks are sometimes obstructed by parked cars. Most far-flung sights, such as beaches, are reachable by metro, bus, and tram. Check the Organization for Urban Public Transportation (OASA) Web site (⇨ Bus & Tram Travel within Athens) for English-language information on how to use public transport to get to sights around the city. OASA also answers questions about routes (usually only in Greek). The office, open weekdays 7:30–3, distributes maps of bus routes with street names in Greek; these are also distributed at the white ticket kiosks at many bus terminals.

The price of public transportation has risen steeply, but it is still less than that in other western European capitals. Riding during rush hours is definitely not recommended. Upon boarding, validate your ticket in the orange canceling machines at the front and back of buses and trolleys and in metro stations. Keep your tickets until you reach your destination, as inspectors occasionally pop up to check that they have been canceled and validated. They are strict about fining offenders, including tourists. You can buy a day pass covering the metro, buses, trolleys, and trams for €3, a weekly pass for €10, or, at the beginning of each month, a monthly pass for €38.

TRAVEL AGENTS

Several travel agents and tour services in Athens are listed below. Closer to Omonia, try Condor Travel, CHAT tours, or Pharos Travel and Tourism. ⧉ **American Express** ✉ Ermou 2, Syntagma Sq. ☎ 210/324–4975 🖨 210/322–7893. **Amphitrion Travel LTD** ✉ Syngrou 7, Central Athens ☎ 210/924–9701 🖨 210/924–9671 ✉ Deuteras Merachias 3, Pasalimani, Piraeus ☎ 210/411–2045 through 210/411–2049 🖨 210/417–0742 ⊕ www.amphitrion.gr. **CHAT** ✉ Stadiou 4, Syntagma Sq. ☎ 210/322–2886 🖨 210/323–5270. **Condor Travel** ✉ Stadiou 43, Central Athens ☎ 210/321–2453 or 210/321–6986 🖨 210/321–4296. **Dolphin Hellas** ✉ Syngrou 16, Makriyianni ☎ 210/922–7772 🖨 210/923–2101 ⊕ www.dolphin-hellas.gr. **Key Tours** ✉ Kallirois 4, Central Athens ☎ 210/923–3166 🖨 210/923–2008 ⊕ www.keytours.gr. **Magic Travel Service (Magic Bus)** ✉ Filellinon 20, Syntagma Sq. ☎ 210/323–7471 🖨 210/322–0219 ⊕ www.magic.gr. **Pharos Travel and Tourism** ✉ Triti Septemvriou 18, Patissia ☎ 210/523–3403 or 210/523–6142 🖨 210/523–3726. **Travel Plan** ✉ Christou Lada 9, Syntagma Sq. ☎ 210/323–8801 through 210/323–8804 🖨 210/322–2152 ⊕ www.travelplan.gr.

VISITOR INFORMATION

Greek National Tourism Organization (GNTO; EOT in Greece) offices generally close around 2 PM. The English-speaking tourist police can answer questions about transportation, steer you to an open pharmacy or doctor, and locate phone numbers of hotels and restaurants. The Web site of the city of Athens has a small but growing section in English. ⧉ **City of Athens Web site** ⊕ www.cityofathens.gr. **Greek National Tourism Organization (EOT)** ✉ Tsochas 7, Ambelokipi ☎ 210/870–7000 ✉ Eleftherios Venizelos International Airport, arrivals area ☎ 210/354–5101 ✉ EOT Bldg., 1st fl., Zea Marina, Pasalimani, Piraeus ☎ 210/452–2591 or 210/452–2586 ⊕ www.gnto.gr. **Tourist Police** ✉ Veikou 43, 4th fl., Koukaki ☎ 171.

Attica, the Saronic Gulf Islands & Delphi

2

EXCURSIONS FROM ATHENS

WORD OF MOUTH

"Choosing between Delphi or Sounion? Delphi has the temple ruins, the Roman amphitheater, the stunning views over the valley, the excellent museum. As for Sounion, it has the famed Temple of Poseidon with its stunning view. That's it."
—indytravel

"Not far from Delphi is beautiful Osios Loukas. This monastery, in its mountain setting, is picturesque enough, but the katholikon, or main sanctuary, is absolutely a dazzling sight. The first glimpse of this small church, filled with mosaics and light, stunned both me and my husband."
—smalt

Updated by
Diane Shugart

BOUNDED ON THREE SIDES BY SEA, Atikí (Attica) has an indented coastline fringed with innumerable sandy beaches and rocky inlets. Waterfront towns become the summer playgrounds for Athenians; nightclubs move seaward for the season and beach clubs have as many amenities as people. The coves and natural harbors are ideal for seafaring. Much of Attica is mountainous: on the stony foothills only a few shrubs grow in the poor soil; higher up, the feathery Aleppo pine of Attica (from which the resin is tapped to make retsina wine) is supplanted by dramatically tall fir trees. Several fertile plains here are well watered with rivers and seasonal streams. Separated from central Greece by mountains—Pateras, Kithairon, Pastra, and Parnitha—and bordered by the sea, Attica was easily defensible. Over all hangs the famed light, the purest of rays sharply delineating the exquisite configuration of mountains, sea, and plain that is Attica.

For true escape, you may need to head to the sun-gilt sea and the Saronic Gulf islands, which straddle the gulf between Athens and the Peloponnese. Aegina, Poros, Hydra, and Spetses are especially popular with Athenians, owing to their proximity and, especially in the case of the latter two, their beauty. Yet they all retain their distinct cultural traditions, best appreciated out of high season, when the isles are not inundated with mainlanders and tourists. Aegina, the closest Saronic island to the port of Piraeus, in ancient times was renowned for its bronze work; it eventually succumbed to the power of Athens and two millennia later played a pivotal role in the War of Independence. Tiny Poros, almost grazing the shores of the Peloponnese, was once the site of an imposing 6th-century BC Temple of Poseidon, now nothing more than a few columns and a pile of fragments. Extant proof of Hydra's and Spetses's prosperity in the 18th and 19th centuries are the stately, forbidding mansions built by the fleet-owning shipping magnates; they are now the playground of carefree European vacationers.

Delphi is a region immensely rich in mythological and historical allusions. The heart of ancient Greece, united under Athens in the 5th century BC, was the sacred precinct of Delphi. For the ancient Greeks, this site was the center of the universe, home to Apollo and the most sacred oracle, and today it remains a principal pilgrimage site. Nearby Mt. Parnassus is the destination for skiers, who stay in the mountain village of Arachova. Those who prefer the sea choose Galaxidi, a town of 19th-century stone mansions.

Exploring Attica, the Saronic Gulf Islands & Delphi

Athens lies in a basin defined by three mountain masses: Mt. Hymettos to the east, Mt. Aigaleo and Mt. Parnitha to the west, and Mt. Pendeli to the north. The bulk of Attica, which stretches southeast into the Aegean, lies east and north of the Athens basin. A tram line from Glyfada to downtown Athens, opened in 2004, allows travelers to enjoy the expansive sea views offered by a hotel on the coast while enjoying easy access to the city center. The Saronic Gulf Islands, whose ancient city-states rivaled Athens, are now virtually a part of the capital. Aegina is just 30 minutes from Piraeus by hydrofoil, and Spetses, the farthest, is just 90 minutes away. Cradled in the mountains, the Delphi region has terraced vineyards, steep cliffs, rocky mountain passes, and deep river gorges around Mt. Parnassus and Arachova. Past the modern town of Delphi, the landscape smooths as it sweeps down into a wide valley full of olive trees, ending at the waters of the Bay of Itea and the harbor-front town of Galaxidi.

About the Restaurants

Although not as common as they were a decade ago, a fair number of traditional Greek tavernas can be found in the market towns and villages of Attica, as well as along the backstreets of the Saronic Gulf Islands. Ask to see the *kouzina* (kitchen) to look at the day's offerings; you can even peer inside the pots. Informal but discreet and neat dress is appropriate at all but the very fanciest of restaurants, and unless noted, reservations are not necessary. Because fresh fish is expensive, and billed by weight, a meal for two may cost more than €50. Ask the price and weight of seafood before ordering, or stick to less-expensive choices like calamari, sardines (excellent grilled), or the finger-size *atherina* (silver smelts).

About the Hotels

Many of the hotels in Attica are resorts catering to package tourists or to Athenian families who move to the coast for summer. In the last two decades, many have been built of reinforced concrete slabs, with spindly metal balconies and diverse facilities, but the decor, which varies little from one to the next, tends to be a modern "Greek island" look: simple pine furnishings, single beds, tile floors, and, at most, a colorful bedspread. Rooms in even the lowest price categories usually have air-conditioning, a small TV set, and a mini refrigerator. Be forewarned: a few of the large resort hotels require you to take half-board in high season. A travel agent can often negotiate a better hotel price and eliminate the half-board requirement, but Web specials are available, too. The southeastern coast of Attica, from Glyfada to Sounion, underwent a major pre-Olympic 2004 overhaul. Existing hotels were completely renovated and a number of new ones built (prices rose, too).

Delphi and Arachova have a number of appealing small lodging establishments, with fresh, cheerful rooms and public spaces, but elsewhere these picturesque, cozy, family-owned country inns and pensions are rare. Note also that many hotels close in late fall and reopen usually around Easter Week, except in Delphi and Arachova, where high season (with top prices) is during ski season, and weekdays are about half the price of weekends. Accommodations on the Saronic Gulf islands range from elegant 19th-century mansions, usually labeled as traditional settlements, to spare rental rooms overlooking a noisy waterfront. Ask at small hotels if solar water heaters are used in summer; if so, find out when it's best to bathe—otherwise you may be forced to choose between taking a freezing cold shower or not bathing at all.

Numbers in the text correspond to numbers in the margin and on the Attica & the Saronic Gulf Islands map.

If you have 3 days

A three-day trip means concentrating on the essentials, which means exploring 🏛 **Delphi** ⑲ ►, with stunning mountain scenery, a world-famous archaeological site, and an excellent museum. Touring the sights can easily take up two days. Be sure to leave Athens early (it's a three- to four-hour trip), especially in summer when it's best to see the ruins before it gets too hot. A third day could be spent hiking on Mt. Parnassus, with a night in the mountain village of 🏛 **Arachova** ⑱, or head to the sea and the pretty port town of 🏛 **Galaxidi** ⑳.

2

If you have 6 days

Begin by spending the first morning of your six-day tour heading toward 🏛 **Delphi** ⑲; stop at the Byzantine monastery of **Osios Loukas** ⑰ before driving on to spend two nights in and around the ancient city. The third day, drive west to explore the archaeological site at Rhamnous or the ancient sanctuary at **Amphiareion** ⑧ before reaching 🏛 **Marathon** ⑦. Wake up and continue down the coast, passing through **Brauron** ⑤. Poseidon's temple is your destination in 🏛 **Sounion** ④. Drive up the eastern coast of Attica and catch the ferry in Piraeus. Two days pass very quickly on the island of 🏛 **Aegina** ⑬.

If you have 9 days

Take a break from ancient Greece and visit the Byzantine **Monastery of Kaisariani** ① ► and the Vorres Museum at **Paiania** ⑥ before driving south along the coast. 🏛 **Vouliagmeni** ③ has swank seaside lodging that attracts Athenians, or you could press on to the rugged, cliff-top 🏛 **Sounion** ④. Next day, foray north to **Brauron** ⑤ and walk through the Sanctuary of Artemis; then drive on to the plain of 🏛 **Marathon** ⑦. Spend a night or two exploring the sights in the area, maybe with a side trip to the ancient city of **Phyle** ⑩. On Day 4, leave Attica and start your journey to the mountainous area around 🏛 **Delphi** ⑲, where you stay for two nights. On your way back past Athens to the port of Piraeus, stop at the **Eleusis** ⑫. The last three days, relish the leisurely life of the Saronic Gulf islands. On 🏛 **Aegina** ⑬ you can snack on the island's famous pistachios and visit the Temple of Aphaia. 🏛 **Hydra** ⑮ is where the European jet set escapes to lounge in beautiful old mansion-hotels set on car-free streets. 🏛 **Spetses** ⑯ is quieter, with a long shoreline and pine-forested hills.

WHAT IT COSTS In euros					
	$$$$	**$$$**	**$$**	**$**	**¢**
RESTAURANTS	over €25	€21–€25	€16–€20	€10–€15	under €10
HOTELS	over €200	€161–€200	€121–€160	€80–€120	under €80

Restaurant prices are for one main course at dinner or, for restaurants that serve only *mezedes* (small dishes), for two mezedes. Hotel prices are for two people in a standard double room in high season, including taxes.

Timing

As elsewhere in Greece, services in these areas are greatly reduced December through March, except in Delphi and Arachova, which are refuges for skiers who usually flock to Mt. Parnassus up north. The Saronic Gulf islands explode into activity in July and August (when Arachova closes down), so be prepared to go head to head with the crowds and the heat; a better time to visit is April to June, when wildflowers carpet the arid hillsides of Attica and the Marathon plain and hills leading to Rhamnous, or in fall, September and October.

ATTICA

ΑΤΤΙΚΗ

Want to escape from the cacophony of Athens? Head for the interior of Attica, with its rustic inns, local wineries, small towns, and rolling hills. It is believed that recorded history began near here, in the towns of the Boeotian plain, although where legend leaves off and fact begins is often a matter of conjecture (witness Thebes, home of the luckless Oedipus). Historians can be sure that since the first millennium BC, the story of Attica has been almost inextricably bound to that of Athens, the most powerful of the villages that lay scattered over the peninsula. By force and persuasion Athens brought these towns together, creating a unit that by the 5th century BC had become the center of an empire.

Northeast of Mt. Pendeli, between the slopes and the sea, lies the fabled plain of Marathon, its flat expanse now dotted with small agricultural communities and seaside resorts, where many Athenians have summer homes. Attica includes such sites as the Temple of Poseidon, spectacularly perched on Cape Sounion, and, up the coast and around the northern flank of Mt. Pendeli, the enchanting, rural archaeological site at the Amphiareion. It takes in the Fortress of Phyle, on the slopes of Mt. Parnitha; the Sanctuary of Demeter and Kore at Eleusis; and the Monastery of Daphni.

It is in the small towns of the interior of Attica that the soul of Attica lies. This once quiet and undulating landscape has changed significantly since the construction of the Eleftherios Venizelos (Athens International Airport) in Spata. The many olive groves and vineyards once gracing this region made way for increased development, as new highways give these once-remote towns almost immediate access to Athens.

Monastery of Kaisariani

Μονή Καισαριανής

★ ⌐ ❶ 6 km (4 mi) east of Athens center.

The Monastery of Kaisariani lies on the slopes of Mt. Hymettos, the eastern "wall" of Athens, which yields the sun each morning and catches

2

Beaches

There's little that compares with the feeling of diving off the rocks into pristine waters at some secluded cove—or dancing until daybreak by the water at one of Greece's trendy beachfront clubs. Even driving up Mt. Parnassus slopes or hiking down Mt. Parnitha, the shore is rarely more than an hour away, so make sure to include time for a swim in your itinerary. Attica's paying beaches have everything from showers and changing cabins to restaurants, bars, water-sports rentals, and water parks. Often there's at least a taverna on the beach, so you can sip ouzo and pick at a meze while the kids splash around just steps away. Varkiza's broad sandy bay and Vouliagmeni's sheltered waters are the place to head for a cooling dip after a morning of sightseeing or shopping. On Aegina, Hydra, Poros, or Spetses, pack a picnic, hire a water taxi, and set off to explore a remote beach.

Ancient Sites

The ancient Greeks believed Delphi was the center of the world and today thousands of visitors continue to flock to the site daily. The stunning natural setting—backed by sheer rock with an open vista extending across the Corinthian Gulf to the northern Peloponnese—is definitely part of the ruin's mystique. The Temple of Poseidon on Sounion is equally awe-inspiring. Its proud profile etched against the Aegean's Technicolor sunsets have made it one of Greece's most photographed monuments. In July and August visit these and other archaeological sites, like the island of Aegina's Temple of Aphaia, as early in the day as possible since there is little shade and the heat can be withering, and you may avoid the crowds.

Great Flavors

The cuisine of Attica mixes that of Athens, central Greece, and the Peloponnese. Local ingredients predominate, with fresh fish becoming scarcer and more expensive in the past few years. Since much of Attica's vegetation is used to support herds of grazing sheep and the omnivorous goat, the meat of both animals is also a staple in many country tavernas. Rural tavernas serve big *tapsia* (pans) of *pastitsio* (layers of pasta, meat, and cheese laced with cinnamon) or *papoutsakia* (sliced eggplant with minced meat or with tomatoes and onion)—all tasty, inexpensive meals. Regional cuisine in Delphi and Arachova relies heavily on meats, including game, as do the smaller Attica villages such as Paiania and Pikermi. However, even in these areas vegetarians will be able to put together an unforgettable meal of wild greens, pies, homemade noodles cooked in fresh tomato sauce, *fasolia* (baked broad beans), and an astonishing number of thick dips listed on menus under salads. On the Saronic Gulf islands and in the coastal town of Galaxidi, fresh fish and seafood courses dominate. Aegina is famous for its pistachios.

Nightlife

Perhaps it is the daytime heat through so many months of the year; perhaps it is an excess of energy; perhaps it is their intense sociability, unrequited during the workday—whatever the reason, Greeks love going out at night. For dancing, the clubs at most large resort hotels are usually open to outsiders as well as patrons, but more popular are the Athens dancing clubs that move to rented space on the coastal road, especially south of the capital from Glyfada to Vouliagmeni, and at eastern beach towns like Porto Rafti and Nea Makri. Of the islands, Hydra and Spetses offer the most sophisticated bars and clubs. Clubs and addresses change annually, so ask around. Many have Greek music and dancing starting at midnight; some are open only in the area's high season.

---

its last purple shadows at night. Denuded of its pine forests in the destructive years during World War II, the mountain has since been successfully reforested by the Athenian Friends of the Trees Society and is fragrant with the scent of pine, olive, and eucalyptus trees. Painter Edward Dodwell spent some days here in the beginning of the 19th century and commented, "But no view could equal that from Hymettos, in rich magnificence or attractive charms." The location is surely spectacular, even if the views of the Acropolis, Piraeus, and the Saronic Gulf are now slightly spoiled by urban sprawl.

An ascent on *kalderimia,* natural cobblestone paths, brings you to a glen of pine, almond, poplar, cypress, and plane trees, fed by a copious flow of water. The exquisite medieval buildings of the walled monastery surround a central court and include the *katholikon* (or main church, built in a cross-in-a-square shape), a refectory, cells, and a bathhouse, all restored in 1957 and 2003. Most of the frescoes (except for those in the narthex, which have been credited to Ioannis Ipatos, a 17th-century Peloponnesian artist) are from the 17th and 18th centuries and are in the Cretan style. There are wonderful frescoes of the Virgin Mary with the archangels Michael and Gabriel and a series painted on the arches depicting the life of Christ. The oldest paintings, dating from the 14th century, are in the side chapel of St. Anthony and show the Virgin Mary at prayer.

The grounds of the monastery are worth a walk; an herb garden thrives, especially in April through June, when wildflowers form a lovely coat of color over the hills. A spring feeds the ram's-head fountain to the left of the monastery's entrance; the original is in the Acropolis Museum and was part of a Roman sarcophagus. To the right just after the courtyard, a path leads to the *aghiasmos,* or sacred fountain, coming from the sacred spring that is the source of the famed Illissos River. It has also been identified as the site of the ancient temple dedicated to Aphrodite (the backdrop for the jealous lovers in Ovid's *Ars Amatoria,* or *The Art of Love*), although no traces remain. Amazingly, this spring supplied the water for all of Athens until the Marathon Dam was built (1925–31). Greeks come to fill bottles with water from the fountains, reputed to aid conception of healthy children, and mothers often sprinkle its water on the heads of sick children. Make your way up the stone steps beside the monastery, past the picnic tables and up the hill, to the **Chapel of the Ascension,** an open, simple structure that looks more like a cave than a chapel. Icons of various sizes line its stone walls, and a small altar provides a place for worshippers to light a candle. ⊠ *Mountain road starting at Ethnikis Antistaseos, 6 km (4 mi) east of Athens center* ☎ *210/ 723–6619* ⊕ *www.culture.gr* 🖾 *€2* ☉ *Tues.–Sun. 8:30–3; grounds daily sunrise–sunset.*

en route | Up the hill from the Monastery of Kaisariani (9 km [5½ mi]), the Monastery of Asteriou dates to the 11th century. A nearby path descends 1½ km (about 1 mi) to the chapel of Byzantine Ayios Ioannis Theologou above the suburb of Goudi. On this pleasant detour, enjoy another view of Athens, the *mesogeia* (interior) of Attica, and the Marathon plain, and take a closer look at—and scent of—the tiny aromatic shrubs (sage and thyme, mostly) that still lure the bees of Mt. Hymettos, giving that special flavor to its famous honey. No Athenian would consider a visit to Kaisariani complete without a stop at one of its fine tavernas, like Masa and Taverna tis Bomenas.

Glyfada

Γλυφάδα

❷ *21 km (13 mi) south of Monastery of Kaisariani, 17 km (10½ mi) south-east of Athens.*

A palm-fringed coastal promenade, parks, beautiful villas, golf courses, shopping, and seaside dining have always made Glyfada a popular destination for both young and old. Since the relocation of the former international airport from here to Spata, it's much quieter and less touristy. Athenians come to swim, stroll, and spend quiet moments gazing at the sea. A tram link to downtown Athens and Piraeus (change at Neo Faliro) has eased traffic. On summer weekends trams operate through the night to serve clubbers who come to enjoy the nightlife that has moved here from Athens to escape the heat. Glyfada has several fine hotels and, with Athens city center just a tram ride away, makes a good base for travelers who like being near the beach.

Glyfada hosts a **summer concert festival** with Greek and ethnic music and theater performances at the carved-marble open-air theater Aixoni in August and September. Program and ticket information can be obtained from the Glyfada town hall. ⊠ *Aixoni, Hydras 11* ⊠ *Town hall, Saki Karagiorga 2* ☎ *210/891–2330.*

Beaches

Attica's southwestern coast is mainly rock, with some short, sandy stretches in Glyfada and Voula that have been made into public pay beaches. Along with snack bars, changing rooms, beach umbrellas, and rental water-sport equipment for windsurfing and waterskiing, there are gardens, parking, and playgrounds. These beaches have received Blue Flags for cleanliness from the European Union despite their proximity to Athens. Most are open from 8 AM to 8 PM in summer, and entry fees are generally from €4 to €15. At some beaches, fees go up on weekends, and at others, you may have to pay extra for a lounge chair or parking. In July and August, when temperatures climb past 100°F (38°C), public beaches often stay open until midnight. Farther south or east along the coast, accessible by tram, there are open or free beaches from Flisvos up to Glyfada's Asteria.

The town of **Alimos** (⊠ 10 km [6 mi] south of Athens, 5 km [3 mi] north of Glyfada ☎ 210/981–3315) has the nearest developed beach to Athens. It has umbrellas and lounge chairs and is packed in summer.

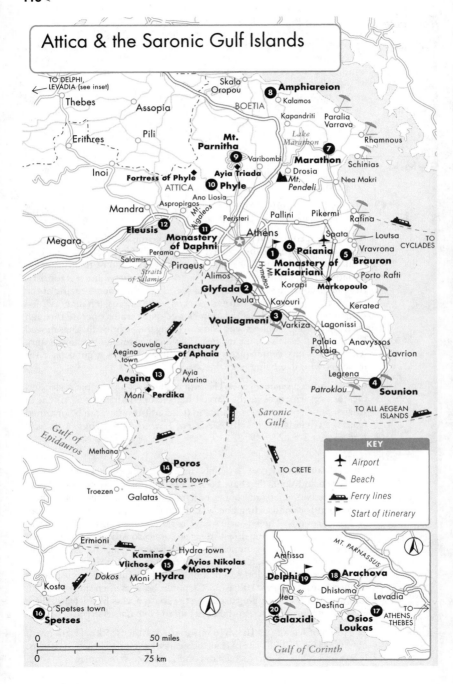

Attica & the Saronic Gulf Islands

TO DELPHI, LEVADIA (see inset) ←

Thebes

Assopia

Skala Oropou

8 **Amphiareion**

BOETIA

Kalamos

Kapandriti

Paralia Varrava

Lake Marathon

7

Rhamnous

Erithres

Pili

Mt. Parnitha

9 Varibombi

Marathon

Schinias

Inoi

Fortress of Phyle ◆

Ayia Triada ◆

Drosia

Mt. Pendeli ▲

Nea Makri

ATTICA

10 **Phyle**

Mandra

Ano Liosia

Aspropirgos

Mt. Aigaleos

Peristeri

Pallini

Pikermi

Rafina

Eleusis **12**

Monastery of Daphni **11**

Athens ✈

Spata

Loutsa

Vravrona

TO CYCLADES

Megara

Perama

Piraeus

1 **6** **Paiania**

Monastery of Kaisariani

5 **Brauron**

Salamis

Straits of Salamis

Alimos

Glyfada **2**

Mt. Hymettos

Koropi

Markopoulo ◆

Porto Rafti

Voula

Kavouri

Vouliagmeni **3**

Varkiza

Kerated

Souvala

Aegina town

Sanctuary of Aphaia ◆

Kavouri

Palaia Fokaia

Lagonissi

Anavyssos

Lavrion

Aegina **13**

Ayia Marina

Legrena

4 **Sounion**

Moni ◆ **Perdika**

Patroklou

TO ALL AEGEAN ISLANDS

Gulf of Epidauros

Methana

Saronic Gulf

TO CRETE

KEY

✈ Airport

🏖 Beach

🚢 Ferry lines

▶ Start of itinerary

Poros **14**

Poros town

Troezen

Galatas

Ermioni

Kamina ◆ Hydra town

Vlichos ◆

15 ◆ **Ayios Nikolas Monastery**

Kosta

Dokos

Moni ◆ **Hydra**

Spetses town

16 **Spetses**

0   50 miles

0   75 km

Amfissa

MT. PARNASSUS

Delphi **19**

18 **Arachova**

48

Dhistomo

Levadia

Itea

Desfina

TO ATHENS, THEBES

20

Galaxidi

Osios Loukas **17**

Gulf of Corinth

Asteria Seaside (⊠ 15 km [9 mi] south of Athens ☎ 210/894–5676) in Glyfada really stands out. The sprawling, upmarket complex, built around a fine sand beach, has private bungalows and landscaped grounds shaded by elegant pergolas. Facilities include lounge chairs, umbrellas, pools, lockers, changing rooms, showers, trampolines, a playground, a self-service restaurant, three bars, and water sports. Keep going all day and night at the trendy Balux pool bar and club where you can sip cocktails, sway to the live music, or book a Pilates session.

Voula A (☎ 210/895–9632 ⊠ 3 km (2 mi) south of Glyfada, Voula) is a favorite of the younger set (music is broadcast over the outdoor sound system). It has a wooden pavilion, beach bar, waterslides, and white-canvas umbrellas above comfortable wood lounge chairs. **Voula B** (☎ 210/895–9590 ⊠ 2 km [1 mi] south of Glyfada, Voula) is managed by the same company as Voula A, but it's a quiet and green area, with a sandy shore and calm shallow waters that attract families and a slightly older crowd.

Where to Stay & Eat

$$$$ ✕ **Septem.** Crisp white linens, colored crystal, and gleaming silverware seem slightly decadent set on tables along the sea's edge, but as part of a minimalist decor they compliment the gorgeous surrounds. Chef Jean-Yves Carattoni's light Mediterranean cuisine only adds to Septem's cachet as a haunt of Athen's beautiful people. Try green risotto with grilled octopus, or lobster tails seasoned with coriander and served on a tomato tart, with a glass of perfectly chilled white wine from the extensive list. Linger over dinner just long enough for things to heat up on the dance floor at Balux at the beach club next door. ⊠ *Vas. Georgiou II 58, next to Asteria Seaside beach* ☎ *210/894–1620* ⚒ *Reservations essential* ▭ *AE, DC, MC, V* ☉ *Closed Nov.–Apr. No lunch.*

$$$$ ✕ **Smaragdi.** Established in 1908, this once-humble fish taverna was the favorite place of Athenian couples, in real life and in Greek movies. In recent years, it has spruced up its image—and raised prices, accordingly— but truth is you can't dine any closer to the water without getting your toes wet. Go around sunset and nibble on fried atherina, washed down with ouzo. ⊠ *Leoforos Karamanli 10 (an extension of Poseidonos), Voula* ☎ *210/965–7404* ⚒ *Reservations essential* ▭ *DC, MC, V.*

$$–$$$$ ✕ **Aioli.** Dishes at this bistro are Mediterranean with a twist; for example, juicy slices of freshly cooked beet and small artichokes are accompanied by the restaurant's namesake, aioli, the classic French garlic mayonnaise. The menu is short, yet satisfies a range of tastes. Try the fresh pasta or fish of the day, which is grilled to a crust with coarsely grated salt and filled with pine nuts. If you're up for dessert, the caramelized apple is worth the few extra calories. ⊠ *Artemidos 9, near Pl. Esperidon* ☎ *210/894–0181* ⚒ *Reservations essential* ▭ *DC, MC, V* ☉ *Closed Sun. and 10 days in Aug. No lunch Sun.–Fri.*

$$–$$$$ ✕ **Theodoros & Eleni.** Share a platter of steamed mussels covered in a thin feta sauce, deep-fried battered shrimp rolled in sesame seeds, or *saganaki* (any dish fried in a small pan with cheese) cubes while you wait for your fish—perfectly grilled and served with the classic Greek olive-oil-and-lemon dressing on the side. Attentive service is part of the homeyness of this understated restaurant housed in a small, suburban villa with outdoor seating in the shaded garden. ⊠ *Kondili 8* ☎ *210/898–3140* ♣ *Reservations essential* ☰ *DC, MC, V* ☉ *No dinner Sun.*

$ ✕ **George's Steak House.** When all you really want is a burger, head to George's. The menu's limited to steaks (George learned how to carve a T-bone from a visiting American), fries, salads, and *biftekia* (thick, grilled, hamburger-like patties of ground beef and pork). The service is fast, so don't be disappointed if all the tables are taken when you arrive; there's a continuous stream of diners coming and going. ⊠ *Konstantinoupoleos 4* ☎ *210/894–6020* ☰ *No credit cards.*

$$ ▦ **Blazer Suites.** The late availability of breakfast service suggests this all-suites hotel doesn't just cater to executives. The service is friendly and personal—adding to the hotel's clublike panache. Here you can relax with home comforts and conveniences like a well-equipped kitchenette, separate living and sleeping quarters, a second TV, and stereo. Blazer Suites' location, a short walk from Glyfada's shopping and restaurants, makes it easy for you to combine sightseeing with languid days by the pool or nearby beach. ⊠ *Leoforos Karamanli 1, 16673 Voula* ☎ *210/965–8801* ⊕ *www.blazersuites.gr* ⇨ *28 suites* ♣ *Restaurant, room service, kitchenettes, cable TV, pool, bar, laundry services, Internet room, meeting rooms, free parking* ☰ *AE, DC, MC, V* ⍩ *BP.*

$–$$ ▦ **Emmantina.** Carpeted rooms are simply furnished with beds, bedside tables, and built-in vanities with chairs, in a blue-and-yellow color scheme. Double-glazed windows and balcony doors eliminate any noise from the main road. A covered bar provides a shady place for refreshment next to the rooftop pool. Late into the night the popular Vinilio disco pulses with dance music and neon lights. A bonus: the hotel provides free airport transport. ⊠ *Leoforos Poseidonos 33, 16675* ☎ *210/898–0683* 🖷 *210/894–8110* ⊕ *www.emmantina.com* ⇨ *80 rooms* ♣ *Restaurant, cable TV, in-room broadband, pool, 2 bars, Internet room, business services, meeting rooms, airport shuttle, free parking* ☰ *AE, DC, MC, V* ⍩ *CP.*

$ ▦ **Palmyra Beach.** Poised at the edge of the Glyfada seafront, the Palmyra Beach is 150 feet from an open beach and just a short walk from the district's shopping, restaurants, and nightlife—close enough not to miss a thing, yet away from the bustle. Under the same management as the Emmantina on the opposite side of Poseidonos, it shares the same competent service and extras like free airport transfer. All rooms have balconies, some overlooking the beach. ⊠ *Leoforos Poseidonos 70, 16675* ☎ *210/898–1183* ⊕ *www.palmyra.gr* ⇨ *58 rooms* ♣ *Restaurant, room service, cable TV, in-room broadband, pool, bar, laundry services, Internet room, meeting rooms, airport shuttle, free parking* ☰ *AE, DC, MC, V* ⍩ *BP.*

$ ▦ **Zina Hotel.** All the spacious apartments at the family-friendly Zina can sleep at least four and have double-glazed windows and balconies. It's in a quiet area with lots of trees and flowers, just a short walk from the large Lambrakis playground, and a few minutes further from the beach. With a fully equipped kitchenette and bus to downtown Athens a few steps away, it's a good choice for travelers who want to combine beach time with sightseeing. The penthouse has a sweeping view over all of Glyfada. ✉ *Evangelistrias 6, 16674* ☎ *210/960–3872* 🖷 *210/960–4004* 🛏 *19 apartments* 🗄 *Kitchenettes, laundry facilities* ▤ *V.*

Nightlife

Glyfada is renowned as a summer party spot, since some of Athens's most popular clubs close up shop downtown and move here in summer. Places seem to change their name and style each season to keep up with trends; ask at your hotel for the latest information. Most clubs have a cover charge that includes a drink (€10–€25); if you're a large party, take a tip from the Greeks and share a bottle (whiskey, vodka) to save on the cost of ordering single drinks.

Balux (✉ Vas. Georgiou II 58 ☎ 210/894–1062) is on the golden sands at Asteria Seaside beach, and is one of the hottest clubs—a favorite of Greek celebrities. The music at **Bebek** (✉ Leoforos Poseidonos 3, Voula ☎ 210/ 981–3950) is mainstream, with occasional theme nights. **Cubanita** (✉ Waterfront, Diadochou Pavlou ☎ 210/898–3092), a bar-restaurant with resident DJ, is the place for clubbers who love a Latin beat. **De Stijl** (✉ Leoforos Poseidonos 4, Voula ☎ 210/895–2403) is always drawing a glamorous crowd; you do have to look the part to get in and enjoy those Greek dance hits. A huge and impressive club, **Envy Seaside** (✉ Paralia Agiou Kosma, Hellenikon ☎ 210/985–2994) throws sunset dance parties on Sunday. From Psyrri, its base in winter, **Mao** (✉ Waterfront, Diadochou Pavlou ☎ 210/894–1620) moves to a man-made beachfront "peninsula" for summer where hip clubbers sip drinks and dance around a lagoon.

Sports & the Outdoors

Yachts can be rented year-round, but May, June, September, and October are less expensive than summer, and, even better, the *meltemi* (brisk northern winds) are not blowing then. Many yacht brokers charter boats and organize scuba tours and flotilla cruises in small, rented sailboats around the islands.

In a seaside suburb between Glyfada and Athens, **Vernicos Yachts** (✉ Leoforos Poseidonos 11, Alimos ☎ 210/989–6000 🖷 210/985–0130 ⊕ www.vernicos.com) hosts weeklong cruises and charters boats.

Vouliagmeni

Βουλιαγμένη

❸ *8 km (5 mi) southwest of Glyfada, 25 km (16 mi) south of Athens.*

A classy seaside residential suburb, Vouliagmeni is the most prestigious address for an Athenian's summer home or business. It's coveted for the large yacht harbor and the scenic promontory, Laimos Vouliagmenis, which is covered with umbrella pines and includes an area called Kavouri, with several seaside fish tavernas. Much like Glyfada, Vouliagmeni can serve as a convenient base from which to explore Attica, but it is far less crowded.

Beaches

Here beaches are quieter, and even cleaner, than the beaches farther north toward Athens. The only free area beach is **Kavouri** (✉ Western shore of Vouliagmeni headland), which extends south from Voula B to Vouliagmeni. The upscale beach on Laimos Vouliagmenis promontory, **Asteras Beach** (⊠ Apollonos 40 ☎ 210/890–2000), belongs to the hotel Astir Palace Vouliagmenis but is open to the public from 8:30 to 6:30. Its more exclusive location has always commanded a hefty fee, which means the green lawns and sandy stretch are usually not so crowded.

Akti Vouliagmenis (⊠ 2 km [1 mi] west of Vouliagmeni ☎ 210/896–0906) has elegant wooden lounge chairs, umbrellas, and shiny cabanas. **Yabanaki** (⊠ 5 km [3 mi] east of Vouliagmeni, Varkiza ☎ 210/897–2414) has beach-club amenities—water sports, bars, restaurants, a children's water park, and cabins where you can take a nap—spread across 25 acres. Varkiza's sandy beach park is open 8 to 7:30. The broad bay is popular with windsurfers.

The part salt, part spring-fed waters of the **lake at Vouliagmeni** (⊠ 2 km [1 mi] southeast of town ☎ 210/896–2237) are reputed to have curative powers, thus are popular with older Greeks. The lake is open 6:30 AM to 8 PM; facilities include lockers and showers, and there's a pleasant snack bar. Most of the lake has a gradual slope and sandy bottom (although caution is recommended, as it deepens suddenly in parts).

en route
South of Vouliagmeni the road threads along a rocky and heavily developed coastline dotted with inlets where intrepid bathers swim off the rocks, after leaving their cars in the roadside parking areas and scrambling down to the inviting *limanakia* (coves), below. (If you're not driving, you can take the E22 Saronida Express from the Akadimias terminal in central Athens.) If you are a good swimmer and want to join them, take along your snorkel, fins, and mask so you can enjoy the underwater scenery, but avoid the stinging sea urchins (you won't have to be reminded a second time) clustered on rocks. Stop at **Georgiadis Bakery** (⊠ 5 km [3 mi] southeast of Vouliagmeni, Varkiza ☎ No phone) to pick up a snack. Athenians flock here for the *piroshki,* a Russian turnover filled with spicy ground meat, but leave carrying bags filled with all types of baked goods, from baguettes and hearty peasant loaves to honey-drenched cakes.

Where to Stay & Eat

$$$$ ✕ **Island.** Claim a place at the bar and observe the fashionable exchange air kisses while casting an eye around to see who's watching. People come in waves: some early for drinks, some late for dancing, and some flowing from the bar to the restaurant to the disco in this complex. Palm trees, bamboo, flowering shrubs, and staggered terraces create an elegant and slightly exotic backdrop for one of the city's hottest summer hangouts. The restaurant's imaginative Mediterranean cuisine, using ingredients such as saffron and feta, comes at a price, but you can sample some of these flavors at the bar for less. ⊠ *On Athens–Sounion coastal road, 3 km (2 mi) southeast of Vouliagmeni, Varkiza* ☎ *210/965–3563* ⌦ *Reservations essential* ☰ *V.*

$$$–$$$$ ✕ **Apaggio.** High-quality, traditional Greek seafood, with a view of the Saronic Gulf—what could be better? The menu is always changing. If

you're lucky you may find dishes such as *sinagrida* (snapper) made Rhodes-style (with white sauce and mushrooms); codfish croquettes, a specialty of Andros; seafood *saganaki* (a dish cooked in a small pan with cheese, tomato, and peppers) crammed with mussels, shrimp, and crayfish; or a fried mix of squid and other shellfish. More than 70 Greek labels show up on the wine list. You're also welcome to stop just for an ouzo or coffee from noon until late. ⊠ *On coastal road to Sounion, 17 km (10½ mi) south of Vouliagmeni, at 41-km (25½-mi) mark, Lagonissi* ☎ *22910/26261* ▭ *AE, DC, V* ☉ *Closed weekdays Oct.–Apr.*

$$–$$$$ ✕ **Garbi.** Athenians flock year-round to share a seafood platter and bottle of white wine or feast on *kakavia,* the Greek fisherman's version of bouillabaisse. There's meat on the menu, but most opt for the fresh grilled fish and a selection of appetizers with subtle influences from the cuisine of Istanbul Greeks. But it's not just the food that attracts locals to this family-run restaurant: there are also elegant wood-beam ceilings and a superb view of the coast, all just 30 minutes from downtown Athens. ⊠ *3 km (2 mi) west of Vouliagmeni, Liou 21, Kavouri* ☎ *210/896–3480* ⌃ *Reservations essential weekends* ▭ *DC, MC, V.*

$–$$ ✕ **I Remvi.** The last of the fish tavernas lining the coastal road in Palaia Fokaia, this is the smallest, the cheapest, and the most romantic. *Remvi* means "daydreaming," easy to do as you sit at little tables with checkered tablecloths sipping potent barreled wine and gazing out to sea. The family-run place keeps expanding its delicious menu—the fish soup, made with the freshest bream, sweet onions, carrots, and potatoes, is worth the wait. Seafood appetizers like crab salad and fried calamari are a good lead-in to the superbly fresh fish, served by the kilo. ⊠ *On Athens–Sounion coastal road, 34 km (21 mi) south of Vouliagmeni, Palaia Fokaia* ☎ *22910/36236* ▭ *V.*

$$$$ ▢ **Astir Palace Vouliagmeni.** Staying here carries quite a cachet with Athenians—and has since the resort first opened in the 1960s. The secluded resort spans 80 acres of pine-covered promontory extending into the Saronic Gulf. Accommodations are in three separate facilities: the Arion, an exclusive club-hotel and spa featuring chic, secluded bungalows with spacious rooms; the Nafsika, a resort and convention center built into the hillside; and, the cliff-top Aphrodite, with balconies overlooking the sea. Rack rates start at €350, and go up to €6,000 for a suite, but you might be able to find a promotional price. The Astir is owned by the National Bank of Greece and the civil service mentality is often evident in the hotel staff's attitude. ⊠ *Apollonos 40, 16671* ☎ *210/890–2000* 🖷 *210/896–2582* ⊕ *www.astir-palace.com* ⇖ *485 rooms, 76 bungalows, 35 suites* ♨ *3 restaurants, minibars, cable TV, 4 tennis courts, indoor pool, 3 saltwater pools, gym, massage, spa, beach, boating, parasailing, waterskiing, bar, shops, helipads* ▭ *AE, DC, MC, V.*

$$$$

Fodor'sChoice

★   ▢ **The Margi.** A sculptural stone fireplace in the lobby, a rich brown leather headboard in one guest room, an antique dressing table in another: no detail escapes notice at Margi, an upscale boutique hotel. Individually furnished rooms exude elegance, with marble baths and sweeping views of Vouliagmeni Bay. Soothing creams, scented candles, and soft earth tones make your room a private haven in which to relax or work. Even though you are so near the beach, the intimate, greenery-filled pool courtyard might

entice you: have a drink at the cabana bar, sample sushi from an upholstered wicker chaise, or read by lamplight in the covered outdoor living
room. ⊠ *Litous 11, 16671* ☎ *210/896–2061* 🖷 *210/896–0229* ⊕ *www.*
themargi.gr ➴ *90 rooms, 7 suites* ♿ *2 restaurants, room service, in-*
room safes, minibars, cable TV with movies, in-room DVD, some in-room
broadband, pool, 2 bars, dry cleaning, laundry service, Internet room, busi-
ness services, no-smoking rooms ⊟ *AE, DC, MC, V* ⏸❘ *BP.*

$$$ ⚃ **Vouliagmeni Suites.** These suites prove you can't judge a book by its
cover: the austere facade gives way to lounges and guest rooms filled
with decorator touches chosen to make different statements: breezy
whites and gauzy fabrics say romance in one, vivid colors and bold prints
to strike a more playful note in another. Set back from the busy seafront,
the property commands a sweeping view of Vouliagmeni Bay—especially
enticing at sunset from the rooftop Jacuzzi. ⊠ *Panos 8, 16671* ☎ *210/*
896–4901 ⊕ *www.grecotel.gr* ➴ *36 suites* ♿ *Restaurant, snack bar, in-*
room safes, refrigerators, cable TV, pool, gym, outdoor hot tub, bar ⊟ *AE,*
DC, MC, V.

¢–$$ ⚃ **Stefanakis Hotel and Apartments.** Sacrifice style for value: here you get
a good location, balconies, friendly service, and a generous breakfast
buffet (at an extra cost with the apartments). Guest rooms have twin
beds and mini refrigerators, and the apartments—in a separate building—have two bedrooms and a kitchenette. There's a pool, too, but Varkiza's wonderful sand beach and café-lined waterfront are just a short
walk away. Regular bus service runs from Varkiza to downtown Athens
and sights like Sounion. ⊠ *3 km (2 mi) east of Vouliagmeni, Aphrodi-*
tis 17, 16672 Varkiza ☎ *210/897–0528* 🖷 *210/897–0249* ➴ *40 rooms,*
12 apartments ♿ *Some kitchens, refrigerators, pool, bar; no room TVs*
⊟ *MC, V* ☼ *Closed Nov.–mid-Apr.* ⏸❘ *BP.*

Sounion

Σούνιο

❹ *50 km (31 mi) southeast of Vouliagmeni, 70 km (44 mi) southeast of*
Athens.

Poised at the edge of a rugged 195-foot cliff, the Temple of Poseidon
hovers between sea and sky, its "marble steep, where nothing save the
waves and I may hear mutual murmurs sweep" unchanged in the centuries since Lord Byron penned these lines. Today the archaeological site
at Sounion is one of the most photographed in Greece. The coast's raw,
natural beauty has attracted affluent Athenians, whose splendid summer villas dot the shoreline around the temple. There's a tourist café by
the temple, and a few minimarts on the road, but no village proper. Arrange your visit so that you enjoy the panorama of sea and islands from
this airy platform either early in the morning, before the summer haze
clouds visibility and the tour groups arrive, or at dusk, when the promontory has one of the most spectacular sunset vantage points in Attica.

In antiquity, the view from the cliff was matched emotion for emotion
by the sight of the cape (called the "sacred headland" by Homer) and
its mighty temple when viewed from the sea—a sight that brought joy

to sailors, knowing upon spotting the massive temple that they were close to home. Aegeus, the legendary king of Athens, threw himself off the cliff when he saw his son's ship approaching flying a black flag. The king's death was just a Greek tragedy born of misunderstanding: Theseus had forgotten to change his ship's sails from black to white—the signal that his mission had succeeded. So the king thought his son had been killed by the Minotaur. To honor Aegeus, the Greeks named their sea, the Aegean, after him.

Fodor's Choice
★
Although the columns at the **Temple of Poseidon** appear to be gleaming white from a distance in the full sun, when you get closer you can see that they are made of gray-veined marble, quarried from the Agrileza valley 2 km (1 mi) north of the cape, and have 16 flutings rather than the usual 20. Climb the rocky path that roughly follows the ancient route, and beyond the scanty remains of an ancient *propylon* (gateway), you enter the temple compound. On your left is the *temenos* (precinct) of Poseidon, on your right a *stoa* (arcade) and rooms. The temple itself (now roped off) was commissioned by Pericles, the famous leader of Greece's golden age. It was probably designed by Ictinus, the same architect who designed the Temple of Hephaistos in the ancient Agora of Athens, and was built between 444 and 440 BC. The people here were considered Athenian citizens, the sanctuary was Athenian, and Poseidon occupied a position second only to Athena herself. The badly preserved frieze on the temple's east side is thought to have depicted the fight between the two gods to become patron of Athens.

The temple was built on the site of an earlier cult to Poseidon; two colossal statues of youths, carved more than a century before the temple's construction (perhaps votives to the god), were discovered in early excavations. Both now reside at the National Archaeological Museum in Athens. The 15 Doric columns that remain stand sentinel over the Aegean, visible from miles away. Lord Byron had a penchant for carving his name on ancient monuments, and you can see it and other graffiti on the right corner pillar of the portico. The view from the summit is breathtaking. In the slanting light of the late-afternoon sun, the landmasses to the west stand out in sharp profile: the bulk of Aegina backed by the mountains of the Peloponnese. To the east, on a clear day, one can spot the Cycladic islands of Kea, Kythnos, and Serifos. On the land side, the slopes of the acropolis retain traces of the fortification walls. ✉ *Cape of Sounion* ☎ *22920/39363* ⊕ *www.culture.gr* 🎫 *€4* ⊗ *Daily 8 AM–dusk.*

Beaches

If you spend the morning and have lunch on the beach below **Sounion,** you may also want to take a swim. The sandy strip becomes uncomfortably crowded in summer.

On your approach to the Temple of Poseidon, there is a decent beach at **Legrena** (✉ 4 km [2½ mi] north of Sounion, before the turnoff for Haraka). From there you can catch a small boat across to the uninhabited isle of Patroklos; the service operates daily and leaves approximately every 10 minutes. The broad sand beach at **Anavyssos** (✉ 13 km [8 mi] northwest of Sounion) is at this writing free. It's slated for development into an organized, paying beach with more amenities.

Where to Stay & Eat

$$$–$$$$ ✕ **Theodoros-Eleni.** More than two-thirds of the diners here are returning customers, which says a lot about this taverna run by a Greek-British husband-and-wife team. Like their taverna in Glyfada, the menu is built around fresh fish and seafood, with marvelous additions like a twisted spanakopita, spinach pie made with homemade phyllo, and boiled salads in season. ⊠ *Off Athens–Sounion coastal road, 3 km (2 mi) south of Sounion, Legrena* ☎ *22920/51936* ▤ *MC, V.*

$–$$ ✕ **Akroyiali.** The Trikaliotis family runs a packed house on weekends when locals stop in for the fresh white and saddled bream, pandora, and red mullet caught by fishing caïques. There are just a few appetizers—*taramosalata* (fish roe salad), octopus, shrimp salad—and a small selection of wines on the menu. ⊠ *On beach below Temple of Poseidon* ☎ *22920/39107* ▤ *No credit cards* ☉ *No dinner weekdays Nov.–Feb.*

$$$$ 🏨 **Grecotel Cape Sounio.** Set amid the verdant pine forest of Sounion National Park, all bungalows are built as in amphitheater seating—to embrace the coast and maximize sea vistas. Floor-to-ceiling sliding glass doors open onto walk-on terraces, many facing southeast toward the Temple of Poseidon; some have private pools. If you don't want to leave the comfort of your bungalow or villa, just order from the 24-hour room service menu. The octagonal glass-wall spa and fitness center overlook the sea, and on the two bays below the hotel is a private beach, with water-sports rentals available. ⊠ *Athens–Sounion coastal road at 67-km (42-mi) mark, 19500 Poseidonios* ☎ *22920/39010* 🖷 *22920/39011* ⊕ *www.grecotel.gr* ⊅ *154 bungalows* ⚭ *Restaurant, café, room service, 3 tennis courts, pool, health club, spa, boating, parasailing, 2 bars, children's programs (ages 4–11)* ▤ *AE, DC, MC, V* ⦿ *BP.*

Brauron

Βραυρώνα

❺ *45 km (28 mi) north of Sounion, 40 km (25 mi) southeast of Athens.*

The **Sanctuary of Artemis** rises on the site of an earlier shrine, at Brauron in a waterlogged depression at the foot of a small hill. Found here are a 5th-century BC temple and a horseshoe-shape stoa. Today it's off the beaten track, but the sanctuary was well known in antiquity: Aristophanes mentions the dance in *Lysistrata,* and in Euripides' drama *Iphigenia in Tauris,* Iphigenia arrives at Brauron with an image of the goddess stolen from Tauris. Here the virgin huntress was worshipped as the protector of childbirth. Every four years the Athenians celebrated the Brauronia, an event in which girls between ages 5 and 10 took part in arcane ceremonies, including a dance in which they were dressed as bears. The museum next to the site contains statues of these little girls, as well as many votive offerings. Those without cars could take the metro from downtown Athens to Ethniki Amyna (Line 3) and then switch to Bus 304 or 316 and ride to the end; the site is a 1-km (½-mi) walk from there. ⊠ *Off Markopoulo highway* *at foot of hill near fork in road to northern Loutsa* ☎ *22990/27020* ⬚ *€3* ⊙ *Museum and site Tues.–Sun. 8–3.*

Beaches

Kakia Thalassa (✉ 14 km [9 mi] south of Brauron, Keratea), with its public playground, ball courts, and open-air cinema, lends itself to being a relaxed, family outing. This sheltered cove with a sand beach is at the end of a country road that winds through pines past the imposing Keratea Monastery. Reserve one of the tables on the rocks overlooking the water at the beachfront taverna, Kapetan Christos. It's the perfect perch from which to watch both the sunset and the children playing on the sand. On the way from Brauron, you could pick up a tin of honey sold roadside by local producers whose hives dot the surrounding hills.

The coast road north from Brauron, which skirts an extensively (and poorly) developed coastline, leads to a pleasant beach at **Loutsa** (✉ 8 km [5 mi] north of Brauron) framed by a backdrop of umbrella pines. With safe shallow waters perfect for small children, it gets extremely congested and noisy in July and August. The port of **Rafina** (✉ 15 km [9 mi] north of Brauron) has become more developed as the ferry and hydrofoil routes to the Cyclades that depart from here have become more popular. If you have some time to kill before catching your ferry, Rafina has a number of good tavernas on and near the harbor worth the visit. The beach here is a little less crowded in summer than Loutsa.

Where to Stay & Eat

$$$–$$$$ ✕ **Ioakeim.** Start with succulent octopus stewed in red wine, or broad beans baked in tomato sauce, and a salad of boiled wild samphire while deciding whether to follow with grilled sardines, calamari, or the day's catch. Friendly service and a familial staff has made this fish restaurant a favorite among locals. ✉ *Harbor front, Rafina* ☎ *22940/23421* ▭ *No credit cards* ⊙ *Closed Tues.*

$$–$$$$ ✕ **O Xipolitos.** No longer a closely guarded secret of Athenians with summer homes in Loutsa and nearby Rafina, this simple fish taverna draws raves from food critics for its superb grilled fish. Munch on homemade *tirokafteri,* a spicy dip made with soft white cheese, and salad while waiting for the main course. ✉ *8 km (5 mi) north of Brauron, G. Papandreou 1, at 25 Martiou, Paralia Loutsas* ☎ *22940/28342* ▭ *No credit cards.*

$$$$ ▦ **Club Med Mare Nostrum.** This sprawling resort and thalassotherapy center has the amenities and "holiday village" spirit of the Club Med brand. Rejuvenate at the spa—the subtle lighting on the ceiling of the indoor saltwater pool has a starlike effect. Treatments include sauna, *hamam* (Turkish steam bath), seaweed and mud wraps, and massage— Swedish, reflexology, and shiatsu. Superior rooms, on the third level of the main building, have carpeting instead of terracotta tile. Regular rates don't include spa services, but you can select a package that does. ✉ *Above Brauron (Vravrona) Bay, 19003* ☎ *22940/71000, 801/118– 0200 toll-free* 🖷 *22940/47790* ⊕ *www.clubmed.com* ⤳ *300 rooms, 125 bungalows, 3 suites* ♿ *2 restaurants, miniature golf, 3 tennis courts, pool, gym, spa, waterskiing, volleyball, bar* ▭ *AE, DC, MC, V* ⦿ *FAP.*

¢–$$ 🖫 **Hotel Avra.** Strategically located at the Rafina port, this is a perfect hotel for a stay over when you have an early ferry to catch or arrive late from the islands, although for the same reason it's not recommended for a longer stay—at least not at the height of summer when the harbor is congested and Rafina is packed with Athenians who have holiday homes there. Request a room with a sea view since about a third face towards the town. ⊠ *South of square on seaside, 19009 Rafina* ☎ *22940/22780* 🖷 *22940/23320* ⤴ *84 rooms, 16 suites* ♨ *Restaurant, room service, bar* ▭ *MC, V* ❯Ⓞ❮ *BP.*

Paiania

Παιανία

⑥ *40 km (25 mi) northwest of Brauron via Markopoulo, 18 km (11 mi) east of Athens.*

Paiania was the birthplace of the famous orator Demosthenes, and although there's not much to see of the ancient town now, people come to visit a unique art museum. The **Vorres Museum** displays folk art and an intriguing collection of contemporary Greek art in a building that's a rare specimen of traditional local architecture. Ion Vorres owns, operates, and even lives in the museum. He has salvaged many treasures and incorporated them beautifully: a stack of millstones transformed into sculptures embedded in a wall; polished marble wellheads emerging from a flower bed; oak tables fashioned from monastery doors; commemorative plates bestowed by returning sea captains on their loved ones; paintings of historic moments such as the opening of the Corinth canal. The modern gallery and sculpture courtyard are dedicated to post–World War II works, including those by Yiannis Moralis, Yiannis Tsarouchis, Nikos Hadjikyriakos-Ghikas, Pavlos, and Spyros Vassiliou. When he's not busy in his museum, Vorres wears the hat of mayor. Those without cars can take Bus A5 from Akadimias in Athens; in Ayia Paraskevi transfer to Bus 308 and get off in Paiania's main square. The museum is about 328 feet farther. ⊠ *Diadochou Konstantinou 1* ☎ *210/664–2520 or 210/664–4771* ⊕ *www.culture.gr* 🖃 *€4.40* ☉ *Sept.–July, weekdays by appointment, weekends 10–2.*

♺   The **Koutouki cave,** discovered in 1926 by a shepherd who had lost his goat, has been rigged with paths, lights, and sound to show off the stalagmites and stalactites—one is called the Statue of Liberty. Cavernous vaults, narrow corridors, and rainbow-color walls formed at the rate of half an inch a year. Guides leading the 20-minute tours do speak English. High on the eastern slopes of Hymettos, the way is connected to Paiania village by a good paved road. ⊠ *Above Paiania on road to cemetery, 4 km (2½ mi) north of town* ☎ *210/664–2108* 🖃 *€4.50* ☉ *Daily 9–4.*

off the beaten path   **MESOGEIA –** Forsake the coast to explore more of the *mesogeia*, or interior. Although the bare hilly country has been spoiled some by cement-box dwellings, there are also farmhouses, stands of olive trees, and vineyards in the interior and Mt. Hymettos hovers to the west. The area is still blanketed in part by sweet-smelling thyme and sage, food for the bees, whose hives in blue boxes are a familiar sight along many a country road. In October look for *mustalevria,* grape must jelly—a Greek delicacy since ancient times. For a taste of bucolic kitsch, stop at the *vlahika* (a barbecue taverna originally established by shepherds, often nomadic Vlachs) in **VARI,** – where waiters dressed as shepherds will flag you towards a taverna serving lamb roast on the spit.

Follow the lead of oenophiles from Athens, who drive here with large, empty wicker-covered bottles to fill with the local retsina and musty red wines (empty water bottles serve the same purpose).

MARKOPOULO – is home of Kourtaki, the most popular bottled retsina, and a town also famed for its barrel wine and country bread. As they garner attention for winning awards for interesting wines beyond retsina, local wineries like **MEGAPANOS ESTATE** (⊠ Odos Amorgos, off Pikermi–Spata road, Pikermi ☎ 210/603–8038) – have opened to the public. Here you get to taste wines from the dry, full-bodied red xinomavro grapes and whites like the fruity moschofilero and sharp savatiano. Sleek, modern facilities complement the tasting room's rustic style; it's open daily by appointment.

Where to Eat

$–$$$ ✕ **Kyra Elli.** A lively outdoor seating area allows you to enjoy coffee by the pool and playground, or you can sip a glass of local wine inside the bright, conservatory-like taverna while listening to live popular Greek music and *rembetika* (music similar to the blues in lyrical content but set to acoustic sound of the bouzouki). Juicy grilled chicken, tender lamb chops, and a good fillet are perennial favorites. December to February, hare and partridge are often added to the menu. For dessert, taste the *ravani,* a rich semolina cake laced with brandy and cinnamon and topped with almonds, or the special ice creams. ⊠ *Lavriou 76* ☎ *210/664–5024* ▭ *No credit cards* ☉ *No dinner Mon.*

$–$$ ✕ **Tou Skorda to Hani.** Good, solid fare, reasonable prices, and friendly service have kept Athenians coming back for the past 30 years. This is definitely not a taverna for vegetarians; the menu is built around game from quail to wild boar. Other specialties include spicy, homemade, peasant-style sausages and goat cooked slowly in a clay pot or *gastra* on a fire. ⊠ *21-km (13-mi) mark Leoforos Marathonos, 5 km (3 mi) east of Paiania, Pikermi* ☎ *210/603–9240* ▭ *No credit cards* ☉ *Closed Tues. and Apr.–Sept.*

Marathon

Μαραθώνας

❼ *31 km (19 mi) northeast of Paiania, 42 km (26 mi) northeast of Athens.*

Today Athenians enter the fabled plain of Marathon to enjoy a break from the capital, visiting the freshwater lake created by the dam, or sunning at the area's beaches. When the Athenian *hoplite* (foot soldier), assisted by the Plataians, entered the plain in 490 BC, it was to crush a numerically superior Persian force. Some 6,400 invaders were killed fleeing to their ships, while the Athenians lost 192 warriors. This, their proudest victory, became the stuff of Athenian legends; the hero Theseus was said to have appeared himself in aid of the Greeks, along with the god Pan. The Athenian commander Miltiades sent a messenger, Pheidippides, to Athens with glad tidings of the victory; it's said he ran the 42 km (26 mi) hardly taking a breath, shouted *Nenikikame!* ("We won!"), then dropped dead of fatigue (more probably of a heart attack)—the inspiration for the marathon race in today's Olympics. To the west of the Marathon plain are the quarries of Mt. Pendeli, the inexhaustible source for a special marble that weathers to a warm golden tint.

The 30-foot-high **Marathon Tomb** is built over the graves of the 192 Athenians who died in the 490 BC battle against Persian forces. At the base, the original gravestone depicts the Soldier of Marathon, a hoplite, which has been reproduced here (the original is in the National Archaeological Museum in Athens). This collective tomb, which contains the cremated remains of the national heroes, was built to honor them. The battle is plotted on illustrated panels, supplemented by a three-dimensional map of local landmarks. ⊠ *5 km (3 mi) south of Marathon* ☎ *22940/55055* 🎟 *Combined ticket with Archaeological Museum €3* ☉ *Tues.–Sun. 8:30–3.*

About 1½ km (1 mi) north of the Marathon Tomb is the smaller burial mound of the Plataians killed in the same battle, as well as the **Archaeological Museum.** Five rooms contain objects from excavations in the area, ranging from Neolithic pottery from the cave of Pan to Hellenistic and Roman inscriptions and statues (labeled in English and Greek). Eight larger-than-life sculptures came from the gates of a nearby sanctuary of the Egyptian gods and goddesses. In the center of one of the rooms stands part of the Marathon victory trophy—an Ionic column that the Athenians erected in the valley of Marathon after defeating the Persians. ⊠ *Plataion 114, approximately 6 km (4 mi) south of Marathon* ☎ *22940/55155* 🎟 *Combined ticket with Marathon Tomb €3* ☉ *Tues.–Sun. 8:30–3.*

The archaeological site at **Rhamnous,** an isolated, romantic spot on a small promontory, overlooks the sea between continental Greece and the island of Euboia. From at least the Archaic period, Rhamnous was known for the worship of Nemesis, the great leveler, who brought down the proud and punished the arrogant. The site, excavated during many years, preserves traces of temples from the 6th and 5th centuries BC. The smaller temple from the 6th century BC was dedicated to Themis, goddess of Justice. The later temple housed the cult statue of Nemesis, envisioned as a woman, the only cult statue remains left from the high classical period. Many fragments have turned up, including the head, now in the British Museum. The acropolis stood on the headland, where ruins of a fortress (5th and 4th centuries BC) are visible. As you wander over this usually serene, and always evocative, site you discover at its edge little coves where you can enjoy a swim. For those going by public transportation, take a KTEL bus from Athens toward the Ayia Marina port, get off at the Ayia Marina and Rhamnous crossroads, and follow the signs on the flat road, about 3 km (2 mi). Or take a taxi from

Marathon village. ⊠ *15 km (9 mi) northeast of Marathon* ☎ *22940/ 63477* 🖃 *€2, free Sun. Nov.–Apr.* ☉ *Tues.–Sun. 8:30–3.*

Lake Marathon is a huge man-made reservoir formed by the **Marathon Dam** (built by an American company in 1925–31). It claims to be the only dam faced with marble. You may be astonished by the sight of all that landlocked water in Greece and want to contemplate it over a drink or snack at the café on the east side. At the downstream side is a marble replica of the Athenian Treasury of Delphi. This is a main source of water for Athens, supplemented with water from Parnitha and Boeotia. ⊠ *8 km (5 mi) west of Marathon, down side road from village of Ayios Stefanos.*

Youngsters tired of trekking through museums may appreciate the distraction of the **Attica Zoological Park.** Spread across 32 acres, the zoo is home to 46 mammal species, 28 types of reptiles, and 304 birds, from a jaguar and wallaby to a brown bear and snowy owl. Take the Spata exit if you're coming from the airport or the Rafina exit if you're coming from the direction of Eleusis. ⊠ *Yalou, Spata* ☎ *210/663–4726* 🖃 *€11* ☉ *Daily 9–dusk.*

Beaches

The best beach is the long, sandy, pine-backed stretch called **Schinias** (⊠ 10 km [6 mi] southeast of Marathon). It's crowded with Athenians on the weekend, and is frequently struck by strong winds in summer. The coves at **Rhamnous** (⊠ 8 km [5 mi] northeast of Marathon), about 2,000 feet from the approach, are cozy and remote. These are favorite swimming spots of nudists and free campers, although this is forbidden. Beware of spiny sea urchins when swimming off the rocks. **Paralia Varnava** (⊠ 10 km [6 mi] northeast of Marathon), less crowded than Schinias, is reached from Varnavas village.

Where to Stay & Eat

$–$$ ✕ **Argentina.** While living in South America, owner Nikos Milonas learned how to carve beef, how high to fire up the grill, and exactly how to time a perfect medium-rare steak. The meat-loving population of Greece has been benefiting from his expertise ever since. Salad and home fries round out the menu. On a clear day you get a peek at the sea from the large veranda. ⊠ *Vitakou 3, Kalentzi, about 1½ km (1 mi) after dam crossing* ☎ *22940/66476* 🍴 *Reservations essential* ▤ *AE, V* ☉ *Closed Mon. and 3 wks in Aug. No lunch weekdays. No dinner Sun.*

$–$$ ✕ **O Hondros.** On the busy main harbor road of the resort community of Nea Makri, O Hondros ("the fat one") is a good choice if you're seeking more variety than the standard meat or seafood tavernas. Try the grilled green peppers filled with feta cheese, vegetable rolls, and grilled chicken with parsley. ⊠ *5 km [3 mi] south of Marathon, Leoforos Poseidonos and Masaioi, Nea Makri* ☎ *22940/50430* ▤ *No credit cards.*

$ ✕ **Kali Kardia.** For more than 35 years, Egre's taverna—as it's known locally—has been a family favorite. The menu is fairly simple, yet there's something about the juicy biftekia and potato-chip-shape fries that brings folks back. The move from a side street near the harbor to a residence with a pretty garden behind the town hall hasn't changed this homey taverna's prices, service, or food. ⊠ *Kosti Palama 12* ☏ *22940/ 23856* 🍽 *No credit cards* ⊙ *Closed weekdays Oct.–Apr. No dinner weekdays May–Sept.*

¢–$ ✕ **Tehlikidis.** Introduced to Greece by repatriated Greeks from the Black Sea region, the *peinirli* is the local version of the calzone. The boat-shape pieces of thick, hand-tossed dough are topped with ham, cheese, bacon, egg, onions, sausage, or ground beef, then drizzled with butter and baked in a wood-burning oven. The classic peinirli, originally a workman's snack, is here topped with *kasseri*, a sharp local cheese. ⊠ *19 km (12 mi) west of Marathon, Argonafton 4, Drosia* ☏ *210/622–9002* 🍽 *No credit cards* ⊙ *No lunch Sun.*

¢–$$ 🏨 **Cabo Verde.** Spacious rooms with sea views that include Evia Island's profile across the strait are this hotel's main assets. It's small enough to provide personal service, but large enough to have a pool and sauna. The marina, the beach, and the handful of tavernas that comprise the seaside village of Mati are just steps away. A children's playground is close by as well. ⊠ *7 km (4½ mi) south of Marathon, Poseidonos 41, 19009 Mati* ☏ *22940/33111, 2810/220088 reservations* 🖷 *2810/ 220785* ⊕ *www.caboverde.gr* 🛏 *32 rooms, 3 suites* ⚐ *Restaurant, café, pool, sauna, bar* 🍽 *MC, V* ⊙ *Closed Nov.–Mar.*

¢–$$ 🏨 **Marathon Beach Hotel.** A friendly staff and a beachfront location in Nea Makri, 5 km [3 mi] south of Marathon, make this a good value. The furnishings are unexceptional, but between the swimming pool, beach, and open-air café, who's spending time indoors? For €10 you can have breakfast and for €15, half-board. ⊠ *Poseidonos 12, 19005 Nea Makri* ☏ *22940/91301* 🖷 *22940/95307* ✉ *hotelmb@otenet.gr* 🛏 *166 rooms* ⚐ *2 restaurants, café, tennis court, 2 bars, pool, wading pool* 🍽 *AE, MC, V* ⊙ *Closed Nov.–Mar.*

Sports

Every year in early November, the **Athens Classic Marathon** is run over roughly the same course taken in 490 BC by the courier Pheidippides, when he carried to Athens the news of victory over the Persians. The 42-km (26-mi) race, open to men and women of all ages, starts in Marathon and finishes at the Panathenaic Stadium in Athens. You can apply and pay your entry fee either online or by mail. Even if you don't have the stamina for the race, cheer on the runners at the end of the route in Athens—the runners represent many ages, nationalities, and physiques. Those who finish the course sprint triumphantly into the stadium, where the first modern Olympics were held in 1896. ⊠ *SEGAS, Race Organizers, Syngrou 137, 17121 Syngrou Athens* ☏ *210/935–1888, 210/935–8489, or 210/934–8106* 🖷 *210/935–8594 or 210/934–2980* ⊕ *www.athensclassicmarathon.gr.*

Amphiareion

Αμφιαράειον

❽ *26 km (16 mi) northwest of Marathon, 49 km (31 mi) northeast of Athens.*

Cradled in a hidden valley at a bend in the road, the **Sanctuary of Amphiaraos** is a quiet, well-watered haven, blessed with dense pines and other foliage. It is startlingly different from the surrounding countryside, where overgrazing, fires, and development have destroyed most of the trees. Amphiaraos was the Bronze Age king of Argos and, according to Aeschylus, one of the six champions who joined Polyneices in his bid to regain the throne of Thebes. As with other mortal heroes, he was transformed after death into a healing divinity. In the sanctuary dedicated to his cult are the remains of a miniature theater, a 4th-century BC Doric temple, the long stoa, and the **Enkimiterion** (literally, "dormitory"), where patients stayed awaiting their cure. They would sacrifice a ram, then lie down wrapped in its skin, waiting for a dream, which resident priests would interpret for the prescribed cure, usually involving baths in the healing waters. It was customary for patients to thank the gods by throwing coins into the water, which priests retrieved to melt into votives they could sell. Between the dormitory and altar, look for the relatively well-preserved remains of a water clock similar to the one at the Ancient Agora of Athens. If you don't have a car to get here, it's easiest to take a KTEL bus to Skala Oropou and then a taxi. The guards can help you call a taxi for the return. ✉ Oropos ☎ 22950/62144 🔊 €2 🕙 Tues.–Sun. 8:30–3.

Mt. Parnitha

Όρος Πάρνηθα

❾ 53 km (33 mi) southwest of Amphiareion, 33 km (20½ mi) northwest of Athens.

The summit of Mt. Parnitha, Attica's highest mountain, has a splendid view of the plain of Athens cradled by Mt. Pendeli and Mt. Hymettos. The high slopes are a protected national park. Lovely nature walks thread through the Mt. Parnitha massif. In April and May the forest blooms with wildflowers, red poppies, white crocuses, purple irises, and numerous species of orchid. Many Athenians come year-round, especially on Sunday, to enjoy the clean air, but some are equally attracted by the gaming tables at the Regency Casino Mont Parnes.

Outdoors

There are 12 marked hiking trails, with varying degrees of difficulty, on Mt. Parnitha. Several start from the chapel of Ayia Triada, including a two-hour walk to the **Cave of Pan** (there is a map behind the church). One of the milder, and most pleasant, hikes follows a marked trail from Ayia Triada through the national park to **Ayios Petros** at Mola. The path leads past the Skipiza spring, providing along the way spectacular views of western Attica and the town of Thebes. The 6-km (4-mi) walk takes about two hours, and you might even spot deer darting among the trees. A 3-km (2-mi) ascent from Ayia Triada (approximately 40 minutes) leads to the **Bafi Refuge** (✉ 5th fl., Ermou 64, Monastiraki, 10563 Athens ☎ 210/246–9050 refuge, 210/321–2429 club 🖷 210/324–4789 club), run by the Alpine Club of Athens, where basic board and lodging are available. The refuge has a fireplace and kitchen; water is piped in from a nearby spring. From Bafi, one trail turns south, tracing the fir and pine woods along the Houni ravine, skirting the craggy Flambouri peak—a favorite nesting place of the park's raptors. This trail intersects with another path leading to the **Flambouri Refuge** (✉ Filadelfias 126, 13671 Aharnes ☎ 210/246–1528 or 210/246–6466), a basic hikers' hut run by the Aharnes Alpine Club.

Phyle

Φυλή

⑩ *16 km (10 mi) south of Mt. Parnitha, 31 km (19 mi) northwest of Athens.*

Evidence of the livestock-based economy in the area of Phyle (Fili) is everywhere: in the dozens of whole lambs, pigs, and goats strung up in front of butcher shops; in the numerous tavernas lining the main street; in the many window displays of fresh sheep yogurt. Beyond the nearby village of Khasia, the road climbs Mt. Parnitha.

The Athenians built several fortresses on the ancient road between Mt. Parnitha and Thebes, including the untended 4th-century BC **Fortress of Phyle** (✉ On a high bluff west of the road to Thebes, 10 km [6 mi] north of Phyle), now in ruins. The road looping back and around the flank of Mt. Parnitha climbs slowly through rugged, deserted country along the ancient road northwest to Thebes. Here the fortress watched over the passes between Attica and Boeotia, offering a dramatically beautiful vista, with the fortress's rugged rectangular masonry scattered about the site. Fragments of the wall still stand; it was made of blocks, each up to 9 feet high, and was reinforced with five towers (two are still visible). When it snows on Mt. Parnitha, the road up to the fortress may be closed, so check with your hotel about weather conditions on the mountain.

Monastery of Daphni

Μονή Δάφνης

⑪ *35 km (22 mi) southwest of Phyle, 11 km (7 mi) west of Athens.*

Sacked by Crusaders, inhabited by Cistercian monks, and desecrated by Turks, the Monastery of Daphni remains one of the most splendid Byzantine monuments in Greece. Dating from the 11th century, the golden age of Byzantine art, the church contains a series of miraculously preserved mosaics without parallel in the legacy of Byzantium: powerful portraits of figures from the Old and New Testaments, images of Christ and the Virgin Mary in the *Presentation of the Virgin,* and, in the golden dome, a stern *Pantokrator* ("ruler of all") surrounded by 16 Old Testament prophets who predicted his coming. The mosaics, made of chips of four different types of marble, are set against gold.

Daphni means "laurel tree," which was sacred to Apollo, whose sanctuary once occupied this site. It was destroyed in AD 395 after the antipagan edicts of the emperor Theodosius, and the Orthodox monastery was probably established in the 6th century, incorporating materials of Apollo's sanctuary in the church and walls. Reoccupied by Orthodox monks only in the 16th century, the Daphni area has since been host to a barracks and mental institution. At this writing, the monastery is closed while undergoing long-term restoration; officials hope it will be reopened by mid-2006. Based on some of the mosaic work that has been shown privately, it will be well worth the wait. ✉ *End of Iera Odos, Haidari* ☎ *210/581–1558* ⊕ *www.culture.gr.*

Eleusis

Ελευσίνα

🔟 *11 km (7 mi) west of the Monastery of Daphni, 22 km (14 mi) west of Athens.*

The growing city of Athens co-opted the land around Eleusis, placing shipyards in the pristine gulf and steel mills and petrochemical plants along its shores. It is hard to imagine that there once stretched in every direction fields of corn and barley sacred to the goddess Demeter, whose realm was symbolized by the sheaf and sickle.

The **Sanctuary of Demeter** lies on an east slope, at the foot of the acropolis, hardly visible amid modern buildings. The legend of Demeter and her daughter Persephone explained for the ancients the cause of the seasons and the origins of agriculture. It was to Eleusis that Demeter traveled in search of Persephone after the girl had been kidnapped by Hades, god of the underworld. Zeus himself interceded to restore her to the distraught Demeter but succeeded only partially, giving mother and daughter just half a year together. Nevertheless, in gratitude to King Keleos of Eleusis, who had given her refuge in her time of need, Demeter presented his son Triptolemos with wheat seeds, the knowledge of agriculture, and a winged chariot so he could spread them to mankind. Keleos built a *megaron* (large hall) in Demeter's honor, the first Eleusinian sanctuary.

The worship of Demeter took the form of mysterious rites, part purification and part drama, and both the Lesser and the Greater Eleusinian rituals closely linked Athens with the sanctuary. The procession for the Greater Eleusinia began and ended there, following the route of the Sacred Way. Much of what you see now in the sanctuary is of Roman construction or repair, although physical remains on the site date back to the Mycenaean period. Follow the old Sacred Way to the great *propylaea* (gates) and continue on to the Precinct of Demeter, which was strictly off-limits on pain of death to any but the initiated. The *Telesterion* (Temple of Demeter), now a vast open space surrounded by battered tiers of seats, dates to 600 BC, when it was the hall of initiation. It had a roof supported by six rows of seven columns, presumably so the mysteries would be obscured, and it could accommodate 3,000 people. The museum, just beyond, contains pottery and sculpture, particularly of the Roman period. Although the site is closed at night, you can see the sacred court and propylae from a distance thanks to special lighting by Pierre Bideau, the French expert who also designed the new lighting for the Acropolis in Athens. ✉ *Eleusis* ☎ *210/554–6019* 🖃 *€4* ⏱ *Tues.–Sun. 8:30–3.*

THE SARONIC GULF ISLANDS

ΝΗΣΙΑ ΣΑΡΩΝΙΚΟΥ ΚΟΛΠΟΥ

The Saronic Gulf islands are the aristocracy of the Greek isles. They're enveloped in a patrician aura that is the combined result of history and their more recent cachet as the playgrounds of wealthy Athenians. Aegina's pretty country villas have drawn shipping executives, who commute from the island to their offices in Piraeus. Here pine forests mix with groves of pistachio trees, a product for which Aegina is justly famous. Water taxis buzz to Poros, more like an islet, from the Peloponnese, carrying weary locals eager to relax on its beaches and linger in the island cafés. The island's rustic clay-tile roofs have a cinematic beauty that has inspired poets, writers, and musicians who have lived here. Hydra and Spetses are farther south and both ban automobiles. Hydra's stately mansions, restaurants, and boutiques cater to the sophisticated traveler. Spetses has both broad forests and regal, neoclassical buildings. Rather than being spoiled by tourism, all four islands have managed to preserve their laid-back attitude, well suited to the hedonistic lifestyle of weekend pleasure-seekers arriving by yacht and hydrofoil.

Aegina

Αίγινα

🔞 *30 km (19 mi) south to Aegina town from the port of Piraeus.*

Although it may seem hard to imagine, by the Archaic period (7th–6th centuries BC) Aegina was a mighty maritime power. It introduced the first silver coinage (marked with a tortoise) and established colonies in the Mediterranean. By the 6th century BC, Aegina had become a major art center, known in particular for its bronze foundries—worked by such sculptors as Kallon, Onatas, and Anaxagoras, and its ceramics, which were exported throughout the Mediterranean world. This powerful island, lying so close off the coast of Attica, could not fail to come into conflict with Athens. As Athens's imperial ambitions grew, Aegina became a thorn in its side. In 458 BC Athens laid siege to the city, eventually conquering the island. In 455 BC the islanders were forced to migrate from the island, and Aegina never again regained its former power.

After 1204 the island was a personal fiefdom of both Venice and Spain; in 1451 it was claimed fully by Venice. After it was devastated and captured by Barbarossa, the pirate, in 1537, it was repopulated with Albanians. Morosini recaptured Aegina for Venice in 1654, and it was not ceded to Turkey until 1718. In the 19th century, it experienced a remarkable rebirth as an important base in the War of Independence, briefly holding the seat of government for the fledgling Greek nation (1826–28). The first modern Greek coins were minted here. At this time many people from the Peloponnese, plus refugees from Chios and Psara, emigrated to Aegina, and many of the present-day inhabitants are descended from them.

The eastern side of Aegina is rugged and sparsely inhabited today, except for Ayia Marina, a former fishing hamlet now given over mainly to package tours. The western side of the island, where Aegina town lies, is more fertile and less mountainous than the east; fields are blessed with grapes, olives, figs, almonds, and, above all, the treasured pistachio trees. Idyllic seascapes, and a number of beautiful courtyard gardens, make Aegina town attractive. A large population of fishermen adds character to the many café-taverna hybrids serving ouzo and beer with pieces of grilled octopus, home-cured olives, and other mezedes along the waterfront. Much of the ancient city lies under the modern. Although some unattractive modern buildings mar the harborscape, a number of well-preserved neoclassical buildings and village houses are found on the backstreets. Boats and hydrofoils from Piraeus dock (35 minutes) at Souvala, a sleepy fishing village on the island's northern coast, and at the main port in Aegina town.

As you approach from the sea, your first view of Aegina town takes in the sweep of the harbor, punctuated by the tiny white chapel of **Ayios Nikolaos.** ⊠ *Harbor front, Aegina town.*

During the negotiations for Greece during the War for Independence, Ioannis Kapodistrias, the first president of the country, conducted meetings in the medieval **Markelon Tower.** ⊠ *Town center, Aegina town.*

The **Archaeological Museum** is small, but it was the first to be established in Greece (1829). Finds from the Temple of Aphaia and excavations throughout the island, including early-and middle-Bronze Age pottery, are on display. Among the archaic and classical pottery is the distinctive Ram Jug, depicting Odysseus and his crew fleeing the Cyclops, and a 5th-century BC sphinx. Also notable is a Hercules sculpture from the Temple of Apollo. ⊠ *Harbor front, 100 ft from ferry dock, Aegina town* ☎ *22970/22248* ⊕ *www.culture.gr* ✉ *€3* ☉ *Tues.–Sun. 8:30–3.*

need a break?

A must in Aegina is to have a bite to eat in the *psaragora* (fish market). A small dish of grilled octopus at the World War II-era **agora** (market; ⊠ Pan Irioti, Aegina town ☎ 22970/27308) is perfect with an ouzo. Inside, fishermen gather mid-afternoon and early evening, worrying their beads while seated beside glistening octopus hung up to dry—as close to a scene from the film *Zorba the Greek* as you are likely to see in modern Greece.

The haunting remains of the medieval **Palaiachora** (Old Town), built in the 9th century by islanders whose seaside town was the constant prey of pirates, are set on the rocky, barren hill above the monastery. Capital of the island until 1826, Palaiachora has the romantic aura of a mysterious ghost town, a miniature Mistras that still has more than 20 churches. They are mostly from the 13th century, and a number of them have been restored and are still in use. They sit amid the ruins of the community's houses abandoned by the inhabitants in the early 19th century. Pick up a booklet on the island from the Aegina Tourist Police that provides a history of settlement and directs you to several of the most interesting churches. Episkopi (often closed), Ayios Giorgios, and Meta-morphisi have lovely but faded (by dampness) frescoes. The frescoes of the church of Ayioi Anargyroi are especially fascinating because they are of pagan subjects, such as the mother goddess Gaia on horseback and Alexander the Great. The massive Ayios Nektarios Monastery, 1 km (½ mi) west of Palaiachora, is one of the largest in the Balkans. ⊠ *5 km (3 mi) south of Aegina town center.*

The small port of **Ayia Marina** has many hotels, cafés, restaurants, and a beach. ⊠ *11 km (7 mi) east of Aegina town, via small paved road below Sanctuary of Aphaia.*

From the **Temple of Aphaia,** perched on a promontory, you have superb views of Athens and Piraeus across the water—with binoculars you can see both the Parthenon and the Temple of Poseidon at Sounion. This site has been occupied by many sanctuaries to Aphaia; the ruins visible today are those of the temple built in the early 5th century BC. Aphaia was apparently a pre-Hellenic deity, whose worship eventually converged with that of Athena. The temple, one of the finest extant examples of Archaic architecture, was adorned with an exquisite group of pedimental sculptures that are now in the Munich Glyptothek. Twenty-five of the original 32 Doric columns were either left standing or have been reconstructed. The museum opens at 9, 11, noon, and 1 (for 15 minutes only) for no extra fee. The exhibit has many fragments from the once brilliantly colored temple interior and inscriptions of an older temple from the 6th and 5th centuries BC, as well as drawings that show a reconstruction of the original building. From Aegina town, catch the bus for Ayia Marina on Platia Ethniyersias, north of where the ferries dock; ask the driver to let you off at the temple. A gift and snack bar is a comfortable place to have a drink and wait for the return bus to Aegina town or for the bus bound for Ayia Marina. ⊠ *13 km (8 mi) east of Aegina town, Ayia Marina* ☎ *22970/32398* 🎟 *€4* ☻ *Apr.–Nov., daily 8:15–7; Dec.–Mar., daily 8:15–5.*

Follow the lead of the locals and visiting Athenians, and for an excursion, take a bus (a 20-minute ride from Platia Ethniyersias, the main Aegina town bus station) to the pretty village of **Perdika** to unwind and eat lunch at a seaside taverna. Here there's a small beach and a wildlife sanctuary sponsored by the Friends of the Strays of Aegina and Angistri, that also has a gift shop in town. Places to eat in Perdika have multiplied over the years but are still low key and charmingly decorated, transporting you light-years away from the bustle of much of modern Greece. Try O Nondas, the first fish taverna after the bus station, for a meal on the canopied terrace overlooking the little bay and the islet of Moni. Antonis, the famous fish tavern, draws big-name Athenians year-round. Other interesting cafés include the inviting Remetzo; the Kioski, in a little stone building; and mainstream bar Cafe Aigokeros, which attracts a slightly bohemian crowd. There's also a small sand cove with shallow water safe for young children to swim in. ⊠ *22 km (14 mi) south of Aegina town.*

MONI – In summer, caïques make frequent trips of 10 minutes from Perdika harbor to this little islet, inhabited only by birds and relocated *kri-kri* (Cretan goats). Trails are good for hiking, after which a swim off a little sand beach in the marvelously clear water is most welcome. If you want to stay for a few hours, it is best to make an appointment for your boatman to return for you (pay him when he does). A small snack bar operates in summer, although you would be better off bringing a picnic lunch.

Beaches

There are no broad coasts, and most beaches on Aegina are slivers of sand edging the coastal roads. Aegina town's beaches are pleasant enough, though crowded, as are Ayia Marina's. The **Aegina Water Park** (⊠ 4 km [2½ mi] south of town center, Faros ☎ 22970/25664) has a children's pool and waterslides, as well as a wade-up bar serving snacks and drinks. There's a good swimming spot at the sandy beach of **Marathonas** (⊠ 13 km [8 mi] south of Aegina town). After Marathonas, **Aiginitissa** (⊠ 17 km [11 mi] south of Aegina town) is a large, sandy bay lined with umbrellas and wood lounge chairs. **Klima** (⊠ 19 km [12 mi] south of Aegina town) is a semi-secluded beach, with a finely pebbled bay that has crystal-clear waters. Turn left at the intersection just before entering Perdika.

Where to Stay & Eat

$–$$$$ ✕**Antonis.** Use fresh, quality ingredients and prepare them with care: this is the secret of Antonis's enduring success. Even the humble Greek salad is memorable thanks to hand-selected, perfectly ripe tomatoes, sweet onions, and goat's-milk feta. Bite-size pies are made fresh, with hand-rolled phyllo and filled with soft white cheese or chopped wild greens. If you're dining on fish, let the staff help you choose from the day's catch. Discreetly attentive, the service seems like true hospitality, especially when a platter of complimentary fruit in season arrives just as you finish your meal. Reserve ahead for weekends. ⊠ *Waterfront, Perdika* ☎ *22970/61443* ⊟ *MC, V.*

$–$$$ ✕**Taverna O Kyriakos.** Look out over the water as you enjoy some of the freshest seafood on the island. Order the red mullet, or sargus—all expertly grilled. *Magirefta* (prepared dishes) such as oven-roasted lamb and beef *kokkinisto* (slow-cooked in tomato sauce) are even cheaper options. Excellent appetizers include eggplant salad, zucchini pie, and *bourekakia* (small meat pies). ⊠ *Marathonas beach, 5 km (3 mi) northeast of Aegina town, Marathonas* ☎ *22970/24025* ⊟ *No credit cards* ☉ *Closed Dec. and Jan., and weekdays Oct., Nov., Feb., and Mar.*

$–$$ ✕**Taverna O Kostas.** Hollowed-out wine barrels used for displaying wines and serving food are more kitsch than antique, but they match the lightheartedness of this country tavern. Cooks showily prepare saganaki over live flames by the table as waiters pull wine from the barrels lining the walls. The menu is solid Greek fare, slightly tweaked for non-Greek palates in search of a "genuine" taverna experience. Yes, it's touristy, but it's also fun. ⊠ *Aegina–Alones road, Ayia Marina* ☎ *22970/32424* ⊟ *No credit cards.*

$–$$ ✕ **To Maridaki.** The gracious owner does his best to make you feel welcome at this crowded waterfront restaurant. In addition to the large selection of fresh fish (try the fried *koutsomoures,* sweet baby red mullet), he also serves grilled octopus and grilled meats—souvlaki, beef patties heavy on the onions, and pork chops. Magirefta include *pastitsio* (layers of pasta and meat topped with béchamel sauce), peppers stuffed with rice, delicious okra stewed with tomatoes, and moussaka. Be sure to have a nibble of the homemade *tiropites* (phyllo-crust cheese pies). ✉ *Leoforos Dimokratias between town hall and Panagitsa church, Aegina town* ☎ *22970/25869* ▭ *AE, DC, MC, V.*

¢–$$ ✕ **Vatsoulia.** Ask a local which is the best restaurant in Aegina, and the response is invariably Vatsoulia. In summer the garden is a pleasant oasis, scented with jasmine and honeysuckle; in winter, nestle inside the cozy dining room. Start with eggplant in garlic sauce or zucchini croquettes. Continue with taverna classics such as veal in red sauce; thick, juicy grilled pork chops; or moussaka enlivened with cinnamon and a wonderfully fluffy béchamel. In winter try the hare stew. A 10-minute walk from Aegina town center gets you to this rustic taverna. ✉ *Aphaias 75, Aegina town* ☎ *22970/22711* ✍ *Reservations essential* ▭ *AE, MC, V* ⊙ *Closed Mon. No lunch.*

$ ✕ **Ela Mesa.** It's hardly surprising to find fish and seafood dominating the menu of a waterfront taverna, but at Ela Mesa these ingredients come together in inventive dishes like golden shrimp *bourekia* (wrapped in phyllo, deep-fried, and served in a cream base) and *midopilafo* (mussel risotto). Crisp, deep-fried zucchini puffs are a variation on the fried, sliced zucchini. ✉ *Pl. Christou Panagouli, Souvala* ☎ *22970/53158* ▭ *AE, MC, V.*

$ 🏨 **Hotel Apollo.** Take advantage of the beachside location by relaxing on the restaurant terrace or renting a boat to water-ski. Steps lead down from the sundeck to the sand. Spartan guest rooms at this white, block-shape hotel all have balconies and sea views. TVs and refrigerators are available for rent. The town center of the overdeveloped Ayia Marina is a 10-minute walk from the hotel; a bus stop is 750 feet from the hotel. ✉ *Ayia Marina beach, 18010 Ayia Marina* ☎ *22970/32271 through 22970/32274, 210/323–4292 winter in Athens* 📠 *22970/32688* 🌐 *www.apollo-hotel.de* ⇆ *107 rooms* ♖ *Restaurant, miniature golf, tennis court, saltwater pool, waterskiing, Ping-Pong; no a/c in some rooms, no room TVs* ▭ *AE, DC, MC, V* ⊙ *Closed Nov.–Mar.* 🍴 *BP.*

¢–$ 🏨 **Eginitiko Archontiko.** This jewel of a pension was once the home of the legendary Zinovia, whose literary salons attracted such luminaries as Kazantzakis and the island's own *ayios* (saint), Nektarios. Original painted walls and ceilings in the salon and the suite have been carefully preserved and fitted out with brass beds and simple wood furniture; you can even stay in Kazantzakis's room with its lovely balcony. The sunporch is an ideal place to enjoy breakfast in winter; the roof garden, with its many pots, is perfect in summer. It's only 300 feet from the port, opposite the Markelon Tower. Breakfast costs €10 extra with some rate plans. ✉ *Thomaidou 1, at Ayiou Nikolaou, 18010 Aegina town* ☎ *22970/24968* 📠 *22970/24156* 🌐 *www.lodgings.gr* ⇆ *12 rooms, 1 suite* ♖ *Dining room* ▭ *AE, DC, MC, V.*

¢–$ ⬚ **Hotel Brown.** A late-19th-century sponge factory was converted to a hotel in 1959 and renovated in 2002; the result is a pastiche of styles easily compensated for by a beachfront location just minutes from the town center. Some of the spare rooms have sea views, but no balconies; those in the garden bungalows are arranged around an interior courtyard and open onto terraces. ✉ *Harbor road, 18010 Aegina town* 🕿 *22970/22271* ⊕ *www.hotelbrown.gr* ⬦ *28 rooms* ⌂ *Dining room, refrigerators* ▭ *MC, V* ⍾ *BP.*

¢–$ ⬚ **Rastoni.** Quiet and secluded, the hotel's Zen quality is heightened by the landscaped Mediterranean garden with its pistachio trees, wood pergolas and benches, and rattan armchairs where you can curl up with a book or just spend the day staring out at sea. Rooms have the same sleek, minimalist feel, plus private verandas with panoramic views. Rastoni overlooks the beach and the Kolonna promontory, a short walk (about 900 feet) north of the center. Breakfast costs €5 extra. ✉ *Dimitriou Petriti 31, 18010 Aegina town* 🕿 *22970/27039* ⊕ *www.rastoni.gr* ⬦ *11 studios* ⌂ *Kitchenettes, refrigerators* ▭ *AE, MC, V.*

¢–$ ⬚ **To Petrino Spiti.** Owner Elpida Thanopoulou lives adjacent to the Stone House, a delightful compound of buildings constructed in the traditional village methods. She keeps an eagle eye on the operation, making sure the rooms are spotlessly clean. All the rooms have beautiful, traditional pine furniture, folk crafts, and paintings, as well as fully equipped kitchens, ceiling fans, and spare beds. The studio apartments on the second floor have excellent views of the sea and nearby Angistri ground floor rooms open onto the garden. A suite, formed by two adjoining studios, is furnished with family heirlooms. This quiet area of Aegina town is set a little back from the harbor and Ayios Nikolaos church. ✉ *Stratigou Petriti 5, 18910 Aegina town* 🕿 *22970/23837 through 22970/23838, 210/867–9787 in Athens* ⬦ *12 apartments* ⌂ *Fans, kitchens; no a/c, no room TVs* ▭ *No credit cards.*

¢ ⬚ **Pension Rena.** Come home to the handmade lace curtains and the wood and marble furnishings lovingly tended by proprietor Rena Kappou. All rooms have a refrigerator and a balcony. The breakfast of homemade sweet breads, jams, and fresh juice is served family-style in the dining room or courtyard. With an advance request, Rena will cook dinner for you. Her specialties: *yiouvetsaki* (meat baked in ceramic dishes with tomato sauce and barley-shape pasta) and *kasseropita* (a pie made from kasseri cheese). It's a 10-minute walk from the town harbor. ✉ *Parodos Ayias Irinis, Faros, 18010 Aegina town* 🕿 *22970/24760 or 22970/22086* 🖷 *22970/24244* ⊕ *www.pensionrena.gr* ⬦ *8 rooms* ⌂ *Dining room, refrigerators* ▭ *AE, MC, V* ⍾ *BP.*

Festivals

St. George's Day is celebrated at **Ayios Giorgios** (✉ Paliochora, 5 km [3 mi] south of Aegina town center) on April 23 (or the day after Easter if April 23 falls during Lent); feasting and dancing follow a liturgy at the church.

Two of the most important festivals held at **Ayios Nektarios Monastery** (✉ 6 km [4 mi] southeast of Aegina town) are Whitmonday, or the day after Pentecost (the seventh Sunday after Easter), and the November 9 saint's day, when the remains of Ayios Nektarios are brought down from the monastery and carried in a procession through the streets of town, which are covered in carpets and strewn with flowers.

On the Assumption of the Virgin Mary, August 15—the biggest holiday of summer—a celebration is held at **Chrysoleontissa** (⊠ 6 km [4 mi] east of Aegina town), a mountain monastery.

On September 6 and 7, the feast of the martyr Sozon is observed with a two-day *paniyiri* (saint's day festival), celebrated at **Ayios Sostis** (⊠ 22 km [14 mi] south of Aegina town, Perdika).

On the feast day of St. Nicholas, December 6, **Ayios Nikolaos** (⊠ Waterfront, Aegina town), the small chapel on the Aegina town harbor, and the large twin-towered church in the town center hold festive celebrations.

Nightlife

Greek bars and clubs frequently change names so it's sometimes hard to keep up with the trends. The ever-popular **Avli** (⊠ Pan Irioti 17, Aegina town ☎ 22970/26438) serves delicious appetizers in a small courtyard that goes from café-bistro by day to bar (playing Latin rhythms) by night. **Perdikiotika** (⊠ Aphaias 38, Aegina town ☎ 22970/23443) is a club in an 1860 building that was once a combination bank-produce store; the original safe and painted ceiling depicting Hermes remain. The music is world beat. On the outskirts of Aegina town, **On The Beach** (⊠ 2 km [1 mi] north of center, Aegina town ☎ No phone) draws an early crowd with its sunset cocktails and chill-out music, before notching up the music to a beach party tempo.

The Outdoors

Aegina is one of the best islands for hiking, since the interior is gently undulating, older dirt trails are often still marked by white paint markings, and the terrain has many landscapes. Those who are ambitious might want to hike from Aegina town to the Temple of Aphaia or on the unspoiled eastern coast from Perdika to Ayia Marina, two routes described in detail in Gerald Thompson's *A Walking Guide to Aegina,* available at Kalezis gift shop.

Shopping

Aegina's famous pistachios, much coveted by Greeks, can be bought from stands along the town harbor. They make welcome snacks and gifts. A treat found at some of the Aegean town bakeries behind the harbor is *amigdalota,* rich almond cookies sprinkled with orange flower water and powdered sugar. If you want to have a picnic lunch on the island or on the ferryboat while en route to another Saronic island, check out the luscious fruit displayed on several boats in the center of the harbor.

Close to the Markelos Tower is **Ergastiri** (⊠ Pileos 7, Aegina town ☎ 22970/23210), a small shop that carries an eye-catching selection of unusual ceramic plates, pitchers, and cups in vivid colors. Outstanding examples of glass candle holders are suspended from the ceiling, in imitation of Orthodox church candles. Finely crafted cobalt blue beads, *mati* (evil-eye amulets), make excellent conversation pieces to bring home as gifts.

Kalezis (✉ Dimokratias 35, Aegina town ☎ No phone) is a gift shop in the middle of the Aegina waterfront that also sells guidebooks, English-language paperbacks, and international newspapers.

Poros

Πόρος

⑭ *22 km (14 mi) south of Aegina town.*

The island of Poros sits due south of Aegina, separated from the Peloponnese by a narrow strait. Actually composed of two closely linked islands—the smaller Sferia, closer to the mainland, and the hillier Kalavria—they are divided by a small canal. The unusual geography provided settlers sufficient protection to spread their settlement along the coast rather than build it in the amphitheatrical style typical of Greek island ports. As the ferry approaches Sferia, you get your first glimpse of Poros town, spread over a pair of rocky hills and dominated by its eye-catching clock tower. A number of pebbled and sandy beaches can be found on the southwest coast of Kalavria. Known for its pine forests and sandy beaches, Poros quite often gets overlooked by those flocking to Hydra or Spetses, but this small, verdant island is certainly worth exploring. As you sail through the narrow straits of Poros and head on toward Hydra, the monastery on the piney hillside to your left is the 18th-century Zoodochos Pighi, or "life-giving spring."

Ongoing excavations of the Sanctuary of Poseidon have revealed the floor of a triangular structure as well as coins, pottery, and other artifacts displayed at the **Archaeological Museum** ✉ *Main street, Poros town* ☎ *22980/ 23276* 🖼 *€2* ☉ *Tues.–Sun. 8:30–3.*

The ruins of the important **Sanctuary of Poseidon** are at the approximate center of the island. Demosthenes took refuge here after fleeing Athens in 322 BC in the wake of the Macedonian takeover. The orator died at the temple by taking his own life, and was initially buried there, although his body was later transferred to Athens. Many of the blocks from the temple were carried off in the 18th century to build the monastery on nearby Hydra, but it's worth visiting the temple for the view alone. ✉ *5 km (3 mi) northeast of Poros town.*

off the
beaten
path

LEMONODASSOS – Hire a fishing boat from the port at Poros town to take you across the channel to mainland Lemonodassos (15 minutes, about €10), literally lemon woods. This dense grove, with more than 20,000 lemon trees, was first planted in the 18th century. A short hike up a gentle citrus-scented slope leads past a small spring and ends at a taverna. Youngsters love the donkey ride up the hill.

Beaches

Neorio (✉ 2 km [1 mi] west of Poros town) beach has many tavernas and water-sports facilities. West of Neorio, pine trees virtually hug the shore at the pretty bays, **Agapi** and **Apothikes** (✉ 3 km [2 mi] west of Poros town).

Not far from the Sanctuary of Poseidon, the quiet, pebbled beach of **Vagionia** (⊠ 10 km [6 mi] north of Poros town) is one of the prettiest on the island.

Where to Stay & Eat

$–$$$ ✕ **Kathestos.** Seasonal ingredients dictate the menu here, but there's usually a selection of plain grilled fish or seafood and home-cooked vegetable-base dishes simmered in an olive oil and tomato sauce. Try the *bakaliaros plaki,* cod cooked in a slow oven with fresh tomatoes, onions, and parsley. ⊠ *Harbor road, Poros town* ☎ *22980/24770* ▤ *No credit cards.*

$–$$$ ✕ **Oasis Tavern.** Fresh and delicious lobster pasta is the house specialty at this friendly, casual taverna that has been operating in the center of town since 1965. Family recipes and quality ingredients are menu staples. There's an emphasis on seafood dishes and a large selection of appetizers. Enjoy views across the Peloponnese as you sit near the water's edge. ⊠ *Past town hall, at far end of ferry dock, Poros town* ☎ *22980/ 22955* ▤ *MC, V.*

¢–$$ ▦ **Sto Roloi.** As the name "at the clock" suggests, this 200-year-old island house is below the clock tower, in the oldest part of town. Many details have been lovingly preserved, from the postwar tiles and pink geometric motifs on the ground floor to the simple island furnishings. The three apartments all have their own style. The striking terrace apartment (more expensive, accommodating up to five guests) on the second floor has superb harbor views from a balcony, a master bedroom with a queen bed, and a luxurious bathroom—complete with steam room and hydro-massage tub. At nearby Anemone there's another apartment and a villa for rent. Let the owner know when you're arriving and she will meet you at the dock. ⊠ *Karra 13, at Hatzopoulou, 18020 Poros town* ☎ *22980/25808* ☎☎ *210/963–3705 in Athens* ⊕ *www.storoloi-poros.gr* ⤴ *3 apartments, 1 studio, 1 villa* ♿ *Kitchens* ▤ *MC, V.*

Hydra

Ύδρα

🕒 *28 km (18 mi) south of Poros town port.*

As the full length of Hydra stretches before you when you round the easternmost finger of the Northern Peloponnese, your first reaction might not, in fact, be a joyful one. Gray, mountainous, and barren, the island has the gaunt look of a saintly figure in a Byzantine icon. But as the island's curved harbor—one of the most picturesque in all of Greece—comes into view, delight will no doubt take over. Because of the nearly round harbor, the town is only visible from a perpendicular angle, a quirk in the island's geography that often saved the island from attack since passing ships completely missed the port.

Although there are traces of an ancient settlement, the island was sparsely inhabited until the Ottoman period. Hydra took part in the Greek Revolution (1821) and by the early 19th century the island had developed an impressive merchant fleet, creating a surge in wealth and exposing traders to foreign cultures. Their trade routes stretched from the mainland to Asia Minor and even America.

In the middle of the 20th century the island became a haven for artists and writers like Canadian singer-songwriter Leonard Cohen and the Norwegian novelist Axel Jensen. In the early 1960s, an Italian starlet named Sophia Loren emerged from Hydra's harbor waters in the Hollywood flick *A Boy and a Dolphin*. Even though the harbor is flush with bars and boutiques, today Hydra seems as fresh and innocent as when it was "discovered". The two- and three-story, gray and white houses with red tile roofs, many built from 1770 to 1821, climb the steep slopes around Hydra town harbor. The noble port and houses have been rescued and placed on the Council of Europe's list of protected monuments, with strict ordinances regulating construction and renovation.

Although Hydra has a landmass twice the size of Spetses, only a fraction is habitable and after a day or so on the island, faces begin to look familiar. All motor traffic is banned from the island (except for several rather noisy garbage trucks). When you arrive by boat, mule tenders in the port will rent you one of their fleet to carry your baggage—or better yet, you—to your hotel, for around €10. Mule transport is the time-honored and most practical mode of transport up to the crest; you may see mules patiently hauling anything from armchairs and building materials to cases of beer.

Impressed by the architecture they saw abroad, shipowners incorporated many of the foreign influences into their *archontika*, old, gray-stone mansions facing the harbor. The forbidding, fortresslike exteriors are deliberately austere, the combined result of the steeply angled terrain and the need for buildings to blend into the gray landscape. One of the finest examples of this Hydriot architecture is the **Lazaros Koundouriotis Mansion**, built in 1780 and beautifully restored in the 1990s as a museum. The interior is lavish, with hand-painted ceiling borders, gilt moldings, marquetry, and floors of black-and-white marble tiles. Some rooms have pieces that belonged to the Koundouriotis family, who played an important role in the War for Independence; other rooms have exhibits of costumes, jewelry, wood carvings, and pottery from the National Museum of Folk History. ⊠ *On a graded slope over the port, on west headland, Hydra town* ☎ 22980/52421 ✑ €3 ☉ *Mar.–Oct., Tues.–Sun. 10–4:30.*

Hydra Historical Archives and Museum has a collection of historical artifacts and paintings dating back to the 18th century. A small first-floor room contains figureheads from ships that fought in the 1821 War for Independence. There are old pistols and navigation aids, as well as portraits of the island's heroes and a section devoted to local costume, including the dark *karamani*, pantaloons worn by Hydriot men. ⊠ *On east end of harbor, Hydra town* ☎ 22980/52355 ✑ €3 ☉ *Daily 9–4:30 and 7–9.*

Founded in 1643 as a monastery, the **Church of the Dormition** has since been dissolved and the monks' cells are now used to house municipal offices and a small ecclesiastical museum. The church's most noticeable feature is an ornate, triple-tier bell tower made of Tinos marble, likely carved in the early 19th century by traveling artisans. There's also an exquisite marble iconostasis in the main church. ⊠ *Along central sec-*

tion of harbor front, Hydra town 🕾 *No phone* 🎨 *Donations accepted* ⊙ *Daily 7–2 and 4:30–8:30.*

Kaminia, a small fishing hamlet built around a shallow inlet, has much of Hydra town's charm but none of its bustle—except on Orthodox Good Friday, when the entire island gathers here to follow the funerary procession of Christ. On a clear day, the Peloponnese coast is plainly visible across the water and spectacular at sunset. Take the 15-minute stroll from Hydra town west; a paved coastal track gives way to a staggered, white path lined with fish tavernas. ⊠ *1 km (½ mi) west of Hydra town.*

From Kaminia, the coastal track continues to **Vlichos,** another pretty village with tavernas, a historic bridge, and a rocky beach on a bay. It's a 5-minute water-taxi ride from the Hydra town port or a 40-minute walk (25 minutes past Kaminia). ⊠ *6 km (4 mi) west of Hydra town.*

off the beaten path

HYDRA'S MONASTERIES – If you're staying for more than a day, you have time to explore Hydra's monasteries. Hire a mule for the ascent up Mt. Klimaki, where you can visit the **Profitis Ilias Monastery** (about two hours on foot from Hydra town) and the embroidery workshop at the nearby nunnery of **Ayia Efpraxia.** Experienced hikers might be tempted to set off for the **Zourvas Monastery** at Hydra's tip. It's a long and difficult hike, but its rewards include spectacular views and a secluded cove for a refreshing dip. An alternative: hire a water taxi to Zourvas.

The convent of **Ayios Nikolaos Monastery** is to the southeast of Hydra town, after you pass between the monasteries of Agios Triadas and Agias Matronis (the latter can be visited). Stop here for a drink and a sweet (a donation is appropriate), and to see the beautiful 16th-century icons and frescoes in the sanctuary. When hiking wear sturdy walking shoes and, because of the heat, start out early in the morning in summer. Your reward: stunning vistas over the island (resplendent with wildflowers and herbs in spring), the western and eastern coasts, and nearby islets on the way to area monasteries.

Beaches

Beaches are not the island's main attraction; the only sandy stretch is a private beach belonging to a hotel near Mandraki. There are small, shallow coves at Kaminia and Vlichos, west of the harbor. At **Hydronetta** (⊠ Western edge of harbor, Hydra town) the gray crags have been blasted and laid with cement to form sundecks. Sunbathing and socializing at the beach bars take priority over swimming, but diving off the rocks into the deep water is exhilarating. Water taxis (about €10) ferry bathers from Hydra town to pebble beaches on the island's **northern coast,** including **Bisti** and **Ayios Nikolaos,** where there are sun beds and umbrellas.

Where to Stay & Eat

$$–$$$$ ✕ **Enalion.** A charming young trio of owners—Fanis, Kostas, and Alexandros—imbues the place with energy and attentive service. Their light, imaginative approach to Mediterranean cuisine includes dishes like *skordopitakia* (garlic bread with tomato and shrimp), and a good selection

of vegetarian options, including vegetable tarts. All go perfectly with a glass of house wine and the accompanying tunes of Greek music. ⊠ *6 km (4 mi) west of Hydra town, 100 ft from beach, Vlichos* ☎ *22980/ 29680* ☰ *AE, DC, MC, V* ☉ *Closed Dec.–Mar.*

★ **$–$$$$** ✕ **Kondylenia's.** In a whitewashed fisherman's cottage on a promontory overlooking the little harbor of Kaminia, the restaurant is irresistibly charming (if a little pricey). Peek into the kitchen below the terrace to see what's cooking: a whole fish may be char-grilling. When available, order *kritamos* (rock samphire), vegetation which grows on the island's rocky coast, or share an order of fresh-caught grilled squid. ⊠ *3 km (2 mi) west of Hydra town, on headland above harbor, Kaminia* ☎ *22980/ 53520* ☰ *MC, V* ☉ *Closed Nov.–Mar.*

$–$$ ✕ **Iliovasilema.** There's more to recommend this taverna than the spectacular *iliovasilema* (sunset). Try the terrific *tiropitakia* and *spanakopitakia* (little cheese pies and little spanakopita), sardine salad, or mushrooms grilled with sun-dried tomatoes. For your main dish, don't pass up the sea urchin spaghetti cooked in fresh seawater. Walking back is extra romantic if it's a clear moonlit night. ⊠ *6 km (4 mi) west of Hydra town, harbor front, Vlichos* ☎ *22980/52067* ☰ *MC, V.*

$–$$ ✕ **Kyria Sofia.** The oldest restaurant in Hydra is decorated in bright green, original woodwork inside. It also has an outdoor terrace with half a dozen tables that quickly get snapped up by those who have discovered this little gem. Leonidas lived in New York for many years, and he's more than happy to share his culinary stories as he serves your meal. For tasty appetizers try the small cheese pies with cinnamon and fresh salads. ⊠ *Miaouli 62, past Miranda Hotel, Hydra town* ☎ *22980/53097* ☰ *No credit cards* ☉ *Closed mid-Jan.–mid-Mar. No lunch.*

$–$$ ✕ **Manolis.** Open throughout the year, Manolis is a favorite among Athenians with holiday homes on the island. The food is simple and solid: a typical mixture of *tis oras* (barbecued meat prepared to order), and mostly meatless magirefta. In summer, seating is in a small shaded courtyard. ⊠ *Sahtouri, Hydra town* ☎ *22980/29631* ☰ *No credit cards.*

$–$$ ✕ **To Geitoniko.** Christina and her husband, Manolis, cook home-style Greek dishes in a cozy old Hydriot house with stone floors and wooden ceilings. Try the octopus *stifado* (stew) with pearl onions, or beef with quince. Grilled meats and fresh fish are also available. Scrumptious desserts include halvah, baklava, and Hydriot delicacies like almond-honey cookies. It's a good idea to arrive before 9 PM for dinner; there are only 20 tables under the vine-covered pergola outside and they fill up. ⊠ *Spiliou Harami, opposite Pension Antonis, Hydra town* ☎ *22980/ 53615* ☰ *No credit cards* ☉ *Closed Nov.–Feb.*

★ **$$–$$$$** ✕🛏 **Bratsera.** An 1860 sponge factory was transformed into this posh hotel, with doors made out of old packing crates still bearing the "Piraeus" stamp. Hints of the building's rustic past are visible in the Hydriot gray stonework, exposed-timber ceilings, and wide plank floors. Some guest rooms have four-poster ironwork beds, others have cozy lofts, and all are decorated with portraits and engravings. The restaurant operates in the oleander- and bougainvillea-graced courtyard, and its kitchen, which specializes in European cuisine, is considered one of the island's best. Bar tables spill out poolside, next to the restaurant tables, and quiet Greek music plays on weekends. ✉ *On left leaving port, near Hydra Tours office, 18040 Hydra town* ☎ *22980/53971 through 22980/53975, 22980/52794 restaurant, 210/721–8102 winter in Athens* 🖶 *22980/53626, 210/722–1619 winter in Athens* ⊕ *www.bratserahotel. com* 🛏 *19 rooms, 4 suites* ♿ *Restaurant, room service, refrigerators, pool, bar* 🚮 *AE, DC, MC, V* ⊘ *Closed Nov.–Mar.* ⦿ *BP.*

$$–$$$ 🏨 **Orloff.** Built in 1798 by Catherine the Great for Count Orloff, who came to Greece with a Russian fleet to try to dislodge the Turks, this archontiko retains its splendor. The thick white walls and white linens are offset by cornflower blue on the deep window wells and matching blue guest-room carpets. Antiques in the public (and some private) rooms have been carefully chosen—curvaceous walnut sofas, chairs, dining sets, and highboys; old paintings and lithographs; and gilt mirrors. Superior rooms are suites with sitting areas; all rooms have views of the town or the courtyard shaded by a mulberry tree. ✉ *Rafalia 9, 350 ft from port, 18040 Hydra town* ☎ *22980/52564, 22980/52495, 210/522–6152 winter in Athens* 🖶 *22980/53532, 210/522–7265 winter in Athens* ⊕ *www.orloff.gr* 🛏 *5 rooms, 4 suites* ♿ *Dining room, minibars, concierge* 🚮 *AE, MC, V* ⊘ *Closed Nov.–late Mar.* ⦿ *BP.*

$–$$ 🏨 **Angelica Hotel.** A beautifully restored small island villa with white walls, pale red stonework around the entry, and a red barrel-tile roof has been converted into a warm pension clustered among other Hydra town buildings. Angelica's compact rooms have tall ceilings and basic beds with boldly striped covers; many lead onto a lovely open terrace, where you can enjoy the homemade buffet breakfast. It's a three-minute walk from the port. A sign of the hotel's popularity is its annex, with slightly cheaper rates, and an independent villa for rent that sleeps six. Eight suites in an adjacent building are being renovated at this writing. ✉ *Miaouli 42, 18040 Hydra town* ☎ *22980/53202 or 22980/53264* 🖶 *22980/53542* ⊕ *www. angelica.gr* 🛏 *14 main hotel rooms, 5 annex rooms, 8 suites, 1 apartment, 1 villa* ♿ *Dining room, refrigerators* 🚮 *AE, MC, V* ⦿ *BP.*

★ $–$$ 🏨 **Miranda.** Art collectors might feel right at home among the interesting 18th- and 19th-century furniture and art (Oriental rugs, wooden chests, nautical engravings) at the Miranda. In July and August a ground-floor gallery hosts local exhibits and international artists. This traditional Hydriot home was built in 1821 by a Captain Danavasi and is now classified by the Ministry of Culture as a national monument. The two suites on the top floor have huge balconies, sea views, and graceful ceiling frescoes done by Venetian painters. The large breakfast is served in the interior courtyard, full of fragrant lemon blossoms, jasmine, and bougainvillea. ✉ *Miaouli, 2 blocks inland from port center, 18040 Hydra town* ☎ *22980/52230, 22980/53953, 210/804–3689 winter in Athens* 🖶 *22980/53510* ✎ *mirandahydra@hol.gr* 🛏 *12 rooms, 2 suites* ♿ *Minibars; no room TVs* 🚮 *MC, V* ⊘ *Closed Nov.–Feb.* ⦿ *BP.*

Festivals

Status as a weekend destination has made Hydra a popular venue for all sorts of events, from international puppet festivals to open-air performances by British theater troupes. Exhibits, concerts, and performances are usually held in July and August and details are available from the **Municipal Cultural Center** (✉ Main street, Hydra town ☎ 22980/52210).

The island celebrates its crucial role in the War of Independence with the **Miaoulia,** which takes place the third week of June. Festivities include military parades and dancing, and culminate in a reenactment of the night Admiral Miaoulis loaded a vessel with explosives and sent it upwind to the Turkish fleet. Naturally, the model enemy's ship goes down in flames.

On **Megali Paraskevi** (Good Friday) of Orthodox Easter, a mournful procession of parishioners holding candles follows the *epitaphios* (funeral bier) as it winds its way from Hydra town to Kaminia harbor, where the bier is set afloat, illuminated by several fishing boats; youth dive in to retrieve it. Greek Orthodox Holy Week ends at midnight on the eve of Easter with **Anastasi** (Resurrection Mass) liturgies. There's joyful singing of hymns, exploding fireworks, and churches competing to see who can raise the Resurrection cross highest.

Nightlife

Bars often change names, ownership, and music—if not location—so check with your hotel for what's in vogue. Housed in the ground floor of an early-19th-century mansion, **Amalour** (⊠ Tombazi, behind port, Hydra town ☎ 22980/53125) attracts a mature crowd who sip beverages and listen to live music—jazz and the latest Greek hits. Hydra's hot dance spot is **Heaven** (⊠ Up hill from harbor, Hydra town ☎ 22980/52716). The disco is built onto the cliff, with amazing harbor views and a cooling breeze on those warm summer nights. The trendy **Nautilus Bar** (⊠ West of the harbor, Hydra town ☎ 22980/53563) hosts Greek music jam sessions.

The bar **Pirate** (⊠ South end of harbor, Hydra town ☎ 22980/52711) has been a fixture of the island's nightlife since the late 1970s. It got a face-lift, added some mainstream dance hits to its rock music-only playlist, and remains popular and raucous. The **Saronicos** (⊠ Harbor front, Hydra town ☎ 22980/52589) goes wild after midnight and is ideal for diehard partygoers. The club's easy to spot: there's a fishing boat "sofa" out front.

The minuscule **Ydronetta** (⊠ West of Hydra town, on the way to Kaminia, past Kanoni ☎ 22980/53125) has an enchanting view from its perch above the harbor. It's jammed during the day and it is *the* place to enjoy an ouzo or fruity long drink at sunset.

Shopping

A number of elegant shops (some of them offshoots of Athens stores) sell fashionable and amusing clothing and jewelry, though you won't save much by shopping here. Worth a visit is the stylish store of local jewelry designer **Elena Votsi** (⊠ Ikonomou 3, Hydra town ☎ 22980/53342). Exquisite handmade pieces are more work of art than accessory. Her designs sell well in Europe and New York.

Sports

Explore the sea with diving instructor Alexander Agapakis and his professional staff at the **Hydra Diving Center** (⊠ 66 ft from port, before post office ☎☎ 22980/53900 ⊕ www.divingteam.gr). They arrange snorkeling, scuba lessons, and boat excursions. Licensed divers can rent equipment.

Spetses

Σπέτσες

16 *24 km (15 mi) southwest of Hydra town port.*

In the years leading up to the revolution, Hydra's great rival and ally was the island of Spetses. Lying at the entrance to the Argolic Gulf, off the mainland, Spetses was known even in antiquity for its hospitable soil and verdant pine-tree-covered slopes. The pines on the island today, however, were planted by a Spetsiot philanthropist dedicated to restoring the beauty stripped by the shipbuilding industry in the 18th and 19th centuries. There are far fewer trees than there were in antiquity, but the island is still well watered, and the many prosperous Athenians who have made Spetses their second home compete to have the prettiest gardens and terraces. The island shows evidence of continuous habitation through all of antiquity. From the 16th century, settlers came over from the mainland and, as on Hydra, they soon began to look to the sea, building their own boats. They became master sailors, successful merchants, and, later, in the Napoleonic Wars, skilled blockade runners, earning fortunes that they poured into building larger boats and grander houses. With the outbreak of the War of Independence in 1821, the Spetsiots dedicated their best ships and brave men (and women) to the cause.

By most visitors' standards, the Spetses town is small—no larger than most city neighborhoods—yet it's divided into districts. Kastelli, the oldest quarter, extends towards Profitis Ilias and is marked by the 18th-century Ayia Triada church, the town's highest point. The area along the coast to the north is known as Kounoupitsa, a residential district of pretty cottages and gardens with pebble mosaics in mostly nautical motifs. A water taxi ride here from Kosta, across the channel on the mainland, takes about 15 minutes. Ships dock at the modern harbor, **Dapia,** in Spetses town. This is where the island's seafaring chieftains met in the 1820s to plot their revolt against the Ottoman Turks. A protective jetty is still fortified with cannons dating from the War of Independence. Today, the town's waterfront strip is packed with cafés; and the navy-blue-and-white color scheme adopted by Dapia's merchants hints of former maritime glory. The harbormaster's offices, to the right as you face the sea, occupy a building designed in the simple two-story, center-hall architecture typical of the period and this place.

The 1914 **Hotel Poseidonion** was the scene of glamorous, Athenian society parties and balls in the era between the two world wars, and was once the largest resort in the Balkans and southeastern Europe. The hotel's public rooms retain the era's elegance. ☒ *West side of Dapia, Spetses town* ☎ *22980/72308.*

In front of a small park is **Bouboulina's House,** where you can take a 45-minute guided tour (available in English) and learn about this interesting heroine's life. Laskarina Bouboulina was the bravest of all Spetsiot revolutionaries, the daughter of a Hydriot sea captain, and the wife—then widow—of two more sea captains. Left with a considerable inheritance and nine children, she dedicated herself to increasing her already substantial fleet and fortune. On her flagship, the *Agamemnon,* the largest in the Greek fleet, she sailed into war against the Ottomans at the head of the Spetsiot ships. Her fiery temper led to her death in a family feud many years later. It's worth visiting the mansion just for the architectural details, like the the carved-wood Florentine ceiling in the main salon. Hours are unpredictable, but are posted along with tour times on the door. ⊠ *Behind Dapia, Spetses town* ☎ *22980/72416* ⊕ *www.bouboulinamuseum-spetses.gr* ⊡ *€4.*

A fine late-18th-century archontiko, built in a style that might be termed Turko-Venetian, contains Spetses's **museum.** On display are articles from the period of Spetses's greatness during the War for Independence, including Bouboulina's bones and a revolutionary flag. A small collection of ancient artifacts is mostly ceramics and coins. ⊠ *Archontiko Hatziyianni-Mexi, 600 ft south of harbor, Spetses town* ☎ *22980/ 72994* ⊡ *€3* ⊙ *Tues.–Sun. 8:30–3.*

Spetses actually has two harbors; the **Paleo Limani** (Old Harbor), also known as Baltiza, slumbers in obscurity. As you stroll the waterfront, you might imagine it as it was in its 18th- and 19th-century heyday: the walls of the mansions resounding with the noise of shipbuilding and the streets humming with discreet whisperings of revolution and piracy. Today, the wood keels in the few remaining boatyards are the backdrop for trendy bars, cafés, and restaurants. ⊠ *Waterfront, 1½ km (1 mi) southeast of Dapia, Spetses town.*

The promontory is the site of the little 19th-century church, **Ayios Mamas** ⊠ *Above harbor, Spetses town.* On the headland sits **Ayios Nikolaos,** the current cathedral of Spetses, and a former abbey. Its lacy white-marble bell tower recalls that of Hydra's port monastery, and it was here that the islanders first raised their flag of independence. ⊠ *On road southeast of the waterfront, Spetses town.*

Anargyios and Korgialenios School is known as the inspiration for the school in John Fowles's *The Magus.* It was established in 1927 as an English-style boarding school for the children of Greece's Anglophilic upper class. ⊠ *½ km (¼ mi) west of Dapia, Spetses town.*

Walk along the coast to **Analipsi,** the old fisherman's village. At Easter, instead of setting off fireworks at midnight to celebrate the resurrection, local tradition dictates that a boat is set afire and put out to sea. Excavations here unearthed pottery shards and coins from the 7th century. ⊠ *1 km (½ mi) south of Spetses town.*

Beaches
Water taxis at Dapia make scheduled runs to the most popular outlying beaches, but can also be hired for trips to more remote coves. The beach at **Ayia Marina** (⊠ 2 km [1 mi] southeast of Spetses town) is the home of the elegant Paradise Bar. You can hire a horse-drawn buggy from town to arrive in style. **Scholes** (⊠ 3 km [2 mi] southeast of Spet-

ses town center, in front of the Anargyios and Korgialenios School) is a triangular patch of sand beach that draws a young crowd with its beach volleyball courts, water sports, and bars.

Spetses's best beaches are on the west side of the island. **Ayioi Anargyroi** (⊠ 4 km [2½ mi] west of Spetses town) is clean and cosmopolitan, with umbrellas and lounge chairs. The gently sloped seabed has deep waters suitable for snorkeling, waterskiing, and other water sports (rentals available). Pine trees, tavernas, and umbrellas line **Ayia Paraskevi** (⊠ 5 km [3 mi] west of Spetses town). Sheltered, with a mostly sandy shore, the beach is accessible by road, although most bathers prefer to make the trip by water taxi. **Zogeria** (⊠ 9 km [5½ mi] west of Spetses town), a pine-edged cove with deep sapphire waters, is best reached by water taxi. A gorgeous natural setting more than makes up for the lack of amenities—there's just a tiny church and a modest taverna. On a clear day you can see all the way to Nafplio.

Where to Stay & Eat

★ **$$–$$$$**   ✕ **Patralis.** Sit on a seaside veranda and savor seafood mezedes and fresh fish—fried, grilled, or baked. *Psari a la Spetses* is a flaky swordfish or tuna steak baked with garlic-laced vegetables. The house specialties are the fish soup, *astakomakaronada* (lobster with spaghetti), and a kind of paella stuffed with mussels, shrimp, and crayfish. Magirefta include stuffed peppers and tomatoes; oven-baked lamb; and *papoutsakia* (literally, "little shoes"), sliced eggplant with minced meat or with tomatoes and onion. They make a mean baked apple for dessert, and the service is especially friendly. ⊠ *Kounoupitsa, near Spetses Hotel, Spetses town* ☎ *22980/72134* ▤ *MC, V* ☉ *Closed Nov. and Dec.*

$–$$$ ✕ **Exedra.** Called Sioras or Giorgos by locals (all three names are on the sign), this waterside taverna is in the Old Harbor, where the yachts pull up. House specialties are fish á la *Spetsiota* (baked with fresh tomato and wine); a dish called Argo: shrimp and lobster baked with feta; and mussels saganaki. Magirefta include the hard-to-find *gouronopoulo kokkinisto* (suckling pig slow-cooked in tomato sauce). Fresh fish is always available, and you can also order meats such as souvlaki and even schnitzel. ⊠ *At edge of Old Harbor, Spetses town* ☎ *22980/73497* ▤ *MC, V* ☉ *Closed Nov.–Feb.*

$ ✕ **Lazaros.** A boisterous local crowd fills the small tables and old family photos and barrels of retsina line the walls. In summer you can eat outside in the courtyard. A small selection of well-prepared dishes includes some daily specials, such as goat in lemon sauce, chicken kokkinisto, grilled meats, and, occasionally, fresh fish at good prices. Tasty appetizers include homemade tzatziki and taramosalata, *mavromatika* (black-eyed pea salad), garlic potatoes, and tender marinated beets. Order the barrel retsina (priced by the kilo). ⊠ *Kastelli, 900 ft up hill from harbor, Spetses town* ☎ *22980/72600* ▤ *No credit cards* ☉ *Closed mid-Nov.–mid-Mar. No lunch.*

★ **$$–$$$$**   ▥ **Nissia Traditional Residences.** The plain, rather austere facade of this restored 1920s industrial complex conceals a village of self-contained villas arranged around a quad with a swimming pool in the center. Each apartment is named after an island; cheery white rooms, with wood and built-in furniture, have splashes of a primary color on the pillows and upholstery—bright blue check, red-and-white stripe, or lemon yellow. Even the studios (which overlook the garden) seem roomy, and sea-view apartments have spacious sitting areas with fireplaces. Aristocratic walnut dining sets, love seats, and beds furnish the huge, splurge-worthy, two-story Presidential Residences. ⊠ *Kounoupitsa, 1,500 ft west of Dapia, 18050 Spetses town* ☎ *22980/75000 through 22980/75011, 210/346–2879, 210/342–1279 in Athens* 🖹 *22980/75012, 210/346–5313 in Athens* ⊕ *www.nissia.gr* ⤶ *14 studios, 5 maisonettes, 12 suites* △ *Restaurant, kitchens, cable TV, pool, meeting room* ⊟ *AE, DC, MC, V.*

\$\$–\$\$\$ 🏨 **Spetses Hotel.** Enjoy both privacy—surrounded by greenery, beach, and water—and proximity to town, just a short walk. Here waiters bring drinks to your lounge chair in the sand. Blue-carpeted rooms have wood-veneer beds covered in plaid spreads. Balconies have either a sea or a town view. Breakfast can be taken in bed, on your balcony, or in the terrace restaurant. The staff can help you arrange excursions to mainland sights. ⊠ *Beachfront, 1 km (½ mi) west of Dapia, 18050 Spetses town* ☎ *22980/72602 through 22980/72604, 210/821–3126 winter in Athens* 🖹 *22980/72494, 210/821–0602 winter in Athens* ⊕ *www.spetses-hotel.gr* ⤶ *77 rooms* △ *Restaurant, room service, minibars, cable TV, in-room data ports, beach, bar, laundry service, meeting rooms* ⊟ *MC, V* ☉ *Closed Nov.–Mar.* ⊠| *BP.*

★ ¢–\$\$ 🏨 **Niriides Apartments.** Old-fashion wood shutters and beds with wrought-iron frames are just the right accents to set off the cool white, minimalist interiors of these apartments a short walk from the main harbor. The four-bed apartments are a good value, especially in the off-season. ⊠ *Dapia, 18050 Spetses town* ☎ *22980/73392 210/984–1851 winter in Athens* 🖹 *22980/29596, 210/984–1746 winter in Athens* ⊕ *www.niriides-spetses.gr* ⤶ *8 apartments* △ *In-room safes, kitchenettes, cable TV, in-room data ports* ⊟ *D, MC, V* ⊠| *BP.*

Festival

Spetses puts on an enormous harbor-front reenactment of a **War of Independence naval battle** for one week in early September, complete with costumed fighters and burning ships. Book your hotel well in advance if you wish to see this popular event. There are also concerts and exhibitions the week leading up to it.

Nightlife

For the newest "in" bars, ask your hotel or just stroll down to the Old Harbor, which has the highest concentration of clubs.

Bratsera (⊠ Waterfront, Spetses town ☎ No phone) is a popular mainstream bar in the middle of Dapia. Surviving many years and with ever bigger dimensions, including a seaside patio, is **Club Figaro** (⊠ Old Harbor, Spetses town ☎ No phone). International rhythms play earlier in the evening; late at night, it's packed with writhing bodies, and when the music switches to Greek at midnight, as the Greeks say, *ginete hamos*—chaos reigns.

Sports

The lack of cars and the predominantly level roads make Spetses ideal for bicycling. One good trip is along the coastal road that circles the island, going from the main town to Ayia Paraskevi beach.

Ilias Rent-A-Bike (✉ Ayia Marina road, by Pl. Analipsis, Spetses town ☎🖨 6973/886407) rents well-maintained bikes and equipment.

DELPHI & ENVIRONS

ΔΕΛΦΟΙ

The region of Delphi is steeped in history: it was in Thebes, according to legend, and so described by Sophocles in *Oedipus Rex,* that the infant Oedipus was left by his father, Laios, on a mountainside to die after an oracle predicted he would murder his father and marry his mother. Some shepherds, ignorant of the curse, rescued him, and he was raised by the king of Corinth. The saga unfolded when, as a young man, Oedipus was walking from Delphi and met his father, Laius, King of Thebes, near the Triple Way. The latter, having struck Oedipus with his whip in order to make room for his chariot to pass, was in turn attacked and accidentally killed by the young man, who did not recognize his father, not having seen his parents since his birth. Journeying to Thebes, he solved the riddle of the terrible Sphinx and, as a reward, was offered the throne and the hand of Jocasta (who was, unbeknownst to him, his mother). When they discovered what had happened, Oedipus blinded himself and Jocasta hanged herself.

The preferred route from Athens follows the National Road to the Thebes turnoff, at 74 km (46 mi). Take the secondary road south past Thebes and continue west through the fertile plain—now planted with cotton, potatoes, and tobacco—to busy Levadia, capital of the province of Boeotia. If you detour in Levadia by following the signs for the *piges* (hot springs), you come to the banks of the ancient springs of Lethe and Mnemosyne, or Oblivion and Remembrance (these springs are about a 10-minute walk from the main square); in antiquity the Erkinas (Hercyne) gorge was believed to be the entrance to the underworld. Today, the plane- and maple-tree-shaded river is spanned by an old stone arch bridge built in Ottoman times. Almost halfway between Levadia and Delphi, the Triple Way (where the roads from Delphi, Daulis, and Levadia meet) is where Oedipus fatefully met his father.

If you turn south toward Dhistomo at the junction, you can visit the monastic complex at Osios Loukas and its Byzantine architecture. The National Road continues to Mt. Parnassus, where the formerly quiet mountain village of Arachova is now a successful confluence of traditional Greek mountain village and Athenian-style cafés, thanks to the proximity of ski lifts. The sublime ruins at Delphi are captivating whether you have little knowledge of ancient Greece or have long awaited a chance to see where the Pythian priestesses uttered their cryptic prophecies. After the Acropolis of Athens, Delphi is the most powerful ancient site in Greece. Its history reaches back at least as far as the Mycenaean period; in Homer's *Iliad* it is referred to as Pytho. Southwest of the Delphi ruins on the coast, picturesque Galaxidi now caters to wealthy Athenians who have restored many of the mansions once owned by shipbuilders.

Osios Loukas

Όσιος Λουκάς

★ ⓱ *150 km (93 mi) northwest of Athens.*

The monastic complex at Osios Loukas, still inhabited by a few monks, is notable for both its exquisite mosaics and its dramatic stance, looming on a prominent rise with a sweeping view of the Elekonas peaks and the sparsely inhabited but fertile valley. The outside of the buildings is typically Byzantine, with rough stonework interspersed with an arched brick pattern. It is especially beautiful in February when the almond branches explode with a profusion of delicate oval pinkish-white blooms.

Luke (Loukas) the Hermit, not the evangelist who wrote a book of the New Testament, was a medieval oracle who founded a church at this site and lived here until his death in AD 953. He was probably born in Delphi, after his family fled from Aegina during a raid of Saracen pirates. This important monastery was founded by the emperor Romanos II in AD 961, in recognition of the accuracy of Loukas's prophecy that Crete would be liberated by an emperor named Romanos. The katholikon, a masterpiece of Byzantine architecture, was built in the 11th century over the tomb of Luke. It follows to perfection the Byzantine cross-in-a-square plan under a central dome and was inspired by Ayia Sophia in Constantinople; in turn, it was used as a model for both the Monastery of Daphni and Mystra churches. Impressive mosaics in the narthex and in portions of the domed nave are set against a rich gold background and done in the somber but expressive 11th-century hieratic style by artists from Thessaloniki and Constantinople. Particularly interesting are the reactions evident on the faces of the apostles, which range from passivity to surprise as Christ washes their feet in the mosaic of *Niptir,* to the far left of the narthex.

In the second niche of the entrance is a mosaic showing Loukas sporting a helmet and beard, with his arms raised. The engaging *Nativity, Presentation in the Temple,* and the *Baptism of Christ* mosaics are on the curved arches that support the dome. Two priceless icons from the late 16th century, *Daniel in the Lion's Den* and *Shadrach, Meshach, and Abednego in the Flames of the Furnace,* by Damaskinos, a teacher of El Greco, were stolen a few years back from the white marble iconostasis in the little apse and have been replaced with copies. The tomb of Osios Loukas is in the crypt of the katholikon; his relics, formerly in the Vatican, were moved here in 1987, making the monastery an official shrine. A highlight of the complex is the Theotokos (Mother of God), a small communal church dedicated to the Virgin Mary, on the left as you enter. On the periphery is the monks' cells and a refectory. To visit you must wear either long pants or a skirt. Bring a small flashlight to help see some of the frescoes. ⊠ *On rise above valley* ☎ *22670/22797* ⌨ €3 ⊙ *May–mid-Sept., daily 8–2 and 4–7; mid-Sept.–Apr., daily 8–5.*

Arachova

Αράχωβα

18 *24 km (16 mi) northwest of Osios Loukas, 157 km (97 mi) northwest of Athens.*

Arachova's gray-stone houses with red-tile roofs cling to the steep slopes of Mt. Parnassus, the highest mountain in Greece after Mt. Olympus. The last decade brought a boom to this once-quiet region, which in winter is transformed into a busy ski resort. Weekends attract sophisticated Athenians heading for the slopes: hotel prices soar and rooms are snapped up; cobblestone streets fill with jeeps carrying skis aloft; and village taverns get crowded after dark as people warm their weary bones before the fires. Unlike other Greek destinations, in summer there are hardly any Greek tourists in Arachova and not everything may be open.

If you're lucky enough to be in Arachova for the festival on **St. George's Day**—April 23 (or the Monday after Easter if April 23 falls during Lent)—you're in for the time of your life. St. George, the dragon slayer, is the patron saint of Arachova, and the largest church on the top of the highest hill in town is dedicated to him. So, naturally, the festival here lasts three days and nights, starting with a procession behind the generations-old silver icon from the church, in which the villagers don the local costumes, most of them ornately embroidered silken and brocaded heirlooms that testify to the rich cultural heritage of the town. The festival is kicked off in fine form with the race of the *yeroi*, the old men of the town, who are astonishingly agile as they clamber up the stone steps without so much as a gasp for air. The following days are filled with athletic contests, cooking competitions, and, at night, passionate dancing in the tavernas until long after the goats go home.

Where to Stay & Eat

$–$$ ✕ **Taverna To Agnandi.** Warm yourself at your choice of several fireplaces in this old house, and look out at the excellent views of the mountains. *Tirokafteri,* a piquant cheese spread, is the perfect accompaniment to the stone-ground country bread to start. Follow with a sampling of the large purplish Amphissa olives, *fava* (mashed yellow split peas, lemon, and raw onions), or the potent *skordalia* (potato-garlic spread). Meat dominates the entrées: rooster in tomato sauce, and stuffed lamb shank, for example. ✉ *Delfon, next to town hall* ☎ *22670/32114* ▬ *No credit cards* ☉ *Closed June–Aug.*

$ ✕ **Dasargiris.** Arachova's oldest taverna still draws gargantuan crowds—causing occasional staff surliness—simply because of the amazing food. Lamb with oregano and beef in a red sauce are both served with *hilopites,* the thin egg noodles cut into thousands of tiny squares, for which the area is known. Sample the fried *formaella* (a mild local sheep's-milk cheese); the *hortopites* (pastries filled with mountain greens); grilled beef patties stuffed with formaella or Gouda cheese; or the *splinandera* (a tasty mix of various lamb organs), which Greek customers swear by. At Easter the cook makes an unforgettable roast lamb and egg-lemon soup. ✉ *Delfon 56* ☎ *22670/31291* ▬ *No credit cards* ☉ *Closed Aug.*

¢–$ ✕ **Karathanassis.** In winter, skiers descend from the slopes and head straight here to fortify themselves for a night of clubbing with a plate of boiled goat served in its broth. Other house specials are a delicious vegetable soup and tender lamb cooked in a clay pot. Whet your appetite with grilled peasant sausages and home fries, washed down with wine or *tsipouro* (liquor made from grapes) from the taverna's private stock. ⊠ *Arachova–Delphi Rd.* ☏ *22670/31360* ⊟ *No credit cards.*

$–$$$ ▦ **Hotel Anemolia.** At this hotel on a bluff above the road to Delphi, at the western edge of Arachova, most of the large guest rooms have a view of the plain of Amphissa from their balconies; on a clear day you may be able to see as far as the Peloponnese. The eight suites have fireplaces and minibars but no balconies. Enjoy après-ski among the rustic furnishings and country antiques in the large lobby sitting area with a fireplace, or swim year-round in the heated, covered pool. Rates, which fall dramatically off-season, include one American-style breakfast per room; dinner is included in some plans. A new wing with 25 rooms is scheduled to open in 2006. ⊠ *Arachova–Delfon road, 32004* ☏ *22670/ 31640* ☐ *22670/31642* ⊕ *www.cybex.gr/appl/anemolia* ⇘ *55 rooms, 8 chalet-style suites* ⚭ *Restaurant, room service, indoor pool, Internet room, conference center* ⊟ *AE, DC, MC, V* ◉ *BP.*

¢–$$$ ▦ **Guesthouse Generali.** This enchanting century-old building has been lovingly restored by husband-and-wife owners Stamatis and Zinovia. Detailed effort has gone into the romantic decor of the seven, varying-size rooms (six with fireplaces); yours may have a hand-sewn linen half canopy draped over the bed, for example. The small indoor pool (no children permitted) and the sauna are rare treasures. To get here from the center, walk down the steps next to Agnandi tavern and past the church. A breakfast-brunch buffet (service from 8 AM to 1 PM) is available for €15 per person. ⊠ *Behind local school and church of Panayia, 32004* ☏ *22670/31529* ☐ *22670/32287* ⊕ *www.generalis-xenon.com* ⇘ *7 rooms* ⚭ *Dining room, refrigerators, pool, hot tub, sauna, some pets allowed; no room TVs* ⊟ *No credit cards.*

¢–$ ▦ **Arachova Inn.** Small, efficient, yellow-and-peach-tone guest rooms have a view of the lower town and valley. The sitting rooms and dining areas display a few local handicrafts and have rustic wood furnishings. In winter the dining room, where the buffet breakfast is served, and the lounges are warmed by fires in the hearths. The staff members at this simple establishment are quite friendly. ⊠ *Arachova–Delphi road, 32004* ☏ *22670/ 31353* ☐ *22670/31134* ⇘ *42 rooms* ⚭ *Restaurant, room service, pool, gym, sauna, recreation room, meeting room; no a/c in some rooms* ⊟ *AE, DC, MC, V* ◉ *BP.*

¢–$ ▦ **Guesthouse Maria.** Simple and affordable, this rustic inn is housed in a restored 1800 building on a quiet lane off the main road. The rooms' decor is as spare as the austere stone exterior, but perfectly captures local flavor thanks to well-placed accents like hand-loom wool throws, wooden spindles hung on the wall, and woven curtains embroidered with folk motifs. The three studios have mini refrigerators and a hot plate. ⊠ *Off Delfon, near village center, 32004* ☏ *22670/31803* ⇘ *4 rooms, 3 studios* ⚭ *Some refrigerators; no room phones* ⊟ *No credit cards.*

Nightlife

On winter weekends Arachova streets are jammed with Athenians who come almost as much for the nightlife as for the skiing. Clubs change frequently, but favorites remain. The rowdy **Snow Me** (✉ Pl. Lakka ☎ 22670/31197) is a split-level club with young things dancing on the bar and a doorman to keep out the unhip. **Emboriko** (✉ Delfon ☎ 22670/32467) is where an older crowd of politicians, journalists, and artists mingle anonymously. The bar is action-packed; two quieter, rear sections serve light food. At **Petra** (✉ Pl. Lekka ☎ 22670/31056) quiet foreign and Greek music plays in small rooms with fireplaces and dart boards.

Sports & the Outdoors

HIKING Arachova and its environs are made for exploring on foot, either by simply walking a country lane to see where it leads or picking up one of the hiking trails like the E4 through Parnassus National Park or the ancient footpath down the mountain. The 8,061-foot summit of **Mt. Parnassus** (✉ 28 km [17 mi] north of Arachova) is now easily accessible, thanks to roads opened up for the ski areas. The less hardy can drive to within 45 minutes of the summit. You can motor up to the **refuge** (✉ Alpine Club of Athens, Ermou 64, 5th fl., Monastiraki, 10563 Athens ☎ 210/321–2355 or 210/321–2429 📠 210/324–4789), run by the Alpine Club of Athens, at 6,201-foot high to spend the night and then walk to the summit in time to catch the sunrise—the best time to be on Mt. Parnassus.

SKIING Rental equipment is available at local shops in Arachova and at the **Parnassos Ski Center** (✉ 28 km [17 mi] north of Arachova ☎ 22340/22694, 22340/22695, 22670/31692 in Arachova ⊕ www.parnassos-eot.gr), just 40 minutes from Arachova. The Fterolakka area has good restaurants and several beginners' runs. The Kelaria area has more challenging runs. A daily ski pass costs about €20 on weekends, €15 weekdays.

Shopping

Arachova was known even in pre-ski days as a place to shop for wool, and stores selling rugs and weavings line the main street. The modern mass-produced bedspreads, *flokati* (woolen rugs, sometimes dyed vivid colors), and kilim-style carpets sold today are reasonably priced. If you poke into dark corners in the stores, you still might turn up something made of local wool; anything that claims to be antique bears a higher price.

Also look for local foodstuffs like the delicious Parnassus honey; the fiery *rakomelo,* a combination of anise liqueur and honey, is served in most of the bars and cafés.

Delphi

Δελφοί

▶ ⑲ *10 km (6 mi) west of Arachova, 189 km (118 mi) northwest of Athens.*

Nestled in the mountain cliffs, modern Delphi is perched dramatically on the edge of a grove leading to the sea, west of an extraordinary ancient site. A stay in town can prove most memorable—especially if you come at *Pascha* (Easter). The hospitable people of modern Delphi take

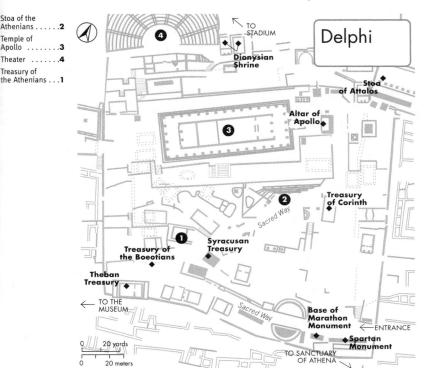

great pride in their town. They maintain a tradition of comfortable, small hotels and a main street thick with restaurants and souvenir shops. Ancient Delphi, the home of famous oracle in antiquity, can be seen from the town's hotels or terraced village houses. It's easily reached from almost any point in the central town, at most a 5- to 10-minute walk. When the archaeological site is first seen from the road, it would appear that there is hardly anything left to attest to the existence of the ancient religious city. Only the Treasury of the Athenians and a few other columns are left standing, but once you are within the precincts, the plan becomes clearer and the layout is revealed in such detail that it is not impossible to conjure up a vision of what the scene must have once been when Delphi was the holiest place in all Greece.

At first the settlement probably was sacred to Gaia, the mother goddess; toward the end of the Greek Dark Ages (circa 1100–800 BC), the site incorporated the cult of Apollo. According to Plutarch, who was a priest of Apollo at Delphi, the oracle was discovered by chance, when a shepherd noticed that his flock went into a frenzy when it came near a certain chasm in the rock. When he approached, he also came under a spell and began to utter prophecies, as did his fellow villagers. Eventually a *Pythia,* an anointed woman over 50 who lived in seclusion, was the one who sat on the three-footed stool and interpreted the prophecy.

On oracle day, the seventh of the month, the Pythia prepared herself by washing in the Castalian Fountain and undergoing a purification involving barley smoke and laurel leaves. If the male priests of Apollo determined the day was propitious for prophesying, she entered the Temple of Apollo, where she drank the Castalian water, chewed laurel leaves, and presumably sank into a trance. Questions presented to her received strange and garbled answers, which were then translated into verse by the priests. A number of the lead tablets on which questions were inscribed have been uncovered, but the official answers were inscribed only in the memories of questioners and priests. Those that have survived, from various sources, suggest the equivocal nature of these sibylline emanations: perhaps the most famous is the answer given to King Croesus of Lydia, who asked if he should attack the Persians. "Croesus, having crossed the Halys River, will destroy a great realm," said the Pythia. Thus encouraged, he crossed it, only to find his *own* empire destroyed.

During the 8th and 7th centuries BC, the oracle's advice played a significant role in the colonization of southern Italy and Sicily (Magna Graecia) by Greece's Amphictyonic League. By 582 BC the Pythian Games had become a quadrennial festival similar to those held at Olympia. Increasingly an international center, Delphi attracted supplicants from beyond the Greek mainland, including such valued clients as King Midas and King Croesus, both hailing from wealthy kingdoms in Asia Minor. During this period of prosperity many cities built treasure houses at Delphi. The sanctuary was threatened during the Persian War but never attacked, and it continued to prosper, in spite of the fact that Athens and Sparta, two of its most powerful patrons, were locked in war.

Delphi came under the influence first of Macedonia and then of the Aetolian League (290–190 BC) before yielding to the Romans in 189 BC. Although the Roman general Sulla plundered Delphi in 86 BC, there were at least 500 bronze statues left to be collected by Nero in AD 66, and the site was still full of fine works of art when Pausanias visited and described it a century later. The emperor Hadrian restored many sanctuaries in Greece, including Delphi's, but within a century or two the oracle was silent. In AD 385 Theodosius abolished the oracle. Only in the late 19th century did French excavators begin to uncover the site of Apollo.

Start your tour of the old Delphi in the same way the ancients did, with a visit to the **Sanctuary of Athena.** Pilgrims who arrived on the shores of the Bay of Itea processed up to the sanctuary, where they paused before going on to the Ancient Delphi site. The most notable among the numerous remains on this terrace is the **Tholos** (Round Building), a graceful 4th-century BC ruin of Pendelic marble, the purpose and dedication of which are unknown, although round templelike buildings were almost always dedicated to a goddess. By the second millennium BC, the site was already a place of worship of the earth goddess Gaia and her daughter Themis, one of the Titans. The gods expressed themselves through the murmuring of water flooding from the fault, from the rustle of leaves, and from the booming of earth tremors. The Tholos remains one of the purest and most exquisite monuments of antiquity. Theodoros, its architect, wrote a treatise on his work: an indication in itself of the exceptional architectural quality of the monument. Beneath the Phaedriades, in the cleft between the rocks, a path leads to the **Castalian Fountain,** a spring where pilgrims bathed to purify themselves before continuing. (Access to the font is prohibited because of the danger of falling rocks.) On the main road, beyond the Castalian Fountain, is the modern entrance to the sanctuary. ✉ *Below road to Arachova, before Phaedriades* 🎫 *Free.*

Fodor'sChoice
★
After a square surrounded by late-Roman porticoes, pass through the main gate to **Ancient Delphi** and continue on to the **Sacred Way,** the approach to the Altar of Apollo. Walk between building foundations and bases for votive dedications, stripped now of ornament and statue, mere scraps of what was one of the richest collections of art and treasures in antiquity. Thanks to the 2nd-century AD writings of Pausanias, archaeologists have identified treasuries built by the Thebans, the Corinthians, the Syracusans, and others—a roster of 6th- and 5th-century BC powers. The **Treasury of the Athenians,** on your left as you turn right, was built with money from the victory over the Persians at Marathon. The **Stoa of the Athenians,** northeast of the treasury, housed, among other objects, an immense cable with which the Persian king Xerxes roped together a pontoon bridge for his army to cross the Hellespont from Asia to Europe.

The **Temple of Apollo** visible today (there were three successive temples built on the site) is from the 4th century BC. Although ancient sources speak of a chasm within, there is no trace of that opening in the earth from which emanated trance-inducing vapors. Above the temple is the well-preserved **theater,** which seated 5,000. It was built in the 4th century BC, restored in about 160 BC, and later was restored again by the Romans. From a sun-warmed seat on the last tier, you see a panoramic bird's-eye view of the sanctuary and the convulsed landscape that encloses it. Also worth the climb is the view from the **stadium** still farther up the mountain, at the highest point of the ancient town. Built and restored in various periods and cut partially from the living rock, the stadium underwent a final transformation under Herodes Atticus, the Athenian benefactor of the 2nd century AD. It lies cradled in a grove of pine trees, a quiet refuge removed from the sanctuary below and backed by the sheer, majestic rise of the mountain. Markers for the starting line inspire many to race the length of the stadium. ✉ *Road to Arachova, immediately east of modern Delphi* ☎ *22650/82312* ⊕ *www.culture. gr* 🎫 *€6* ☼ *Apr.–Oct., daily 7:30–7; Nov.–May, daily 8:30–2:45.*

★ The **Delphi Museum** contains a wonderful collection of art and architectural sculpture, principally from the Sanctuaries of Apollo and Athena Pronoia. Visiting the museum is essential to understanding the site and sanctuary's importance to the ancient Greek world, which considered Delphi its center. (Look for the copy of the *omphalos,* or Earth's navel, a sacred stone from the adytum of Apollo's temple.) Curators have used an additional 15,000 square feet of museum space, opened in 2004, to create contextual, cohesive exhibits. You can now view all the pediments from Apollo's temple together and new exhibits include a fascinating collection of 5th-century BC votives.

One of the greatest surviving ancient bronzes on display commands a prime position in a spacious hall, set off to advantage by special lighting: the *Charioteer* is a sculpture so delicate in size (but said to be scaled to life) it is surprising when you see it in person for the first time. Created in about 470 BC, the human figure is believed to have stood on a terrace wall above the Temple of Apollo, near which it was found in 1896. It was part of a larger piece, which included a four-horse chariot. Scholars do not agree on who executed the work, although Pythagoras of Samos is sometimes mentioned as a possibility. The donor is supposed to have been a well-known patron of chariot racing, Polyzalos, the Tyrant of Gela in Sicily. Historians now believe that a sculpted likeness of Polyzalos was originally standing next to the charioteer figure. The statue commemorates a victory in the Pythian Games at the beginning of the 5th century BC. Note the eyes, inlaid with a white substance resembling enamel, the pupils consisting of two concentric onyx rings of different colors. The sculpture of the feet and of the hair clinging to the nape of the neck is perfect in detail.

Two life-size Ionian *chryselephantine* (ivory heads with gold headdresses) from the Archaic period are probably from statues of Apollo and his sister Artemis (she has a sly smirk on her face). Both gods also figure prominently in a frieze depicting the Gigantomachy, the gods' battle with the giants. These exquisitely detailed marble scenes, dated to the 6th century BC, are from the Treasury of the Siphnians. The *caryatids* (supporting columns in a female form) from the treasury's entrance have been repositioned to offer a more accurate picture of the building's size and depth. The museum's expansion also allowed curators to give more space to the *metopes,* marble sculptures depicting the feats of Greece's two greatest heroes, Heracles and Theseus, from the Treasury of the Athenians. ✉ *East of Ancient Delphi* ☎ *22650/82312* ⊕ *www.culture.gr* 🎫 *€6, Ancient Delphi and museum €9* ⊘ *Apr.–Nov., weekdays 6:45 AM–7:30 PM, weekends 8:30–3; Dec.–Mar., daily 9:30–3:30.*

Where to Stay & Eat

★ **$–$$** ✕ **Epikouros.** Nothing in the uncluttered restaurant design detracts from the view of alpine slopes from the large, open veranda. Even in the colder months, a clear canopy protects the seating area and allows diners to look out year-round. Start with *horta,* freshly boiled greens drizzled with local olive oil and lemon, or the Greek salad with generous chunks of feta. The house specialty is a must: the wild boar stifado is cooked with plenty of baby onions and fresh tomato sauce, fragrantly seasoned with bay leaves and cinnamon. *Soutzoukakia,* oval-shape meatballs in tomato sauce, served with fries or rice is an interesting alternative for timid palates. ✉ *Friderikis 33, at Vas. Pavlou* ☎ *22650/83250* ▭ *AE, MC, V.*

$–$$ ✕ **Panayota.** Don't judge by the plain exterior—the meat here is all organic and local, and the hilopites are made by the owner's hands. Chef Christo serves traditional recipes with flair; make sure to try *arni sta klimata* (oven-baked lamb on vine branches). Even the light salads and sautéed vegetables are a treat because of the fresh crispness of the vegetables and top-notch olive oil. ✉ *Ayios Giorgios, Ano Arachova* ☎ *22670/32735* ▭ *No credit cards* ⊘ *Closed Mon.–Wed. June–Aug.*

¢–$$ ✕ **Iniochos.** Local specialties and small dishes, such as zucchini cro-
quettes, roast feta, and the *bekri* ("drunk's") meze, a meat appetizer meant
to be consumed slowly with wine, are served here at the favorite restau-
rant in Delphi. Residents stop by late at night to have a nightcap or a
snack—fried formaella cheese, *sfongato* (country vegetable omelet), or
a sweet baklava—and to sing along to pianist Yiannis's amazing reper-
toire of old Greek songs. In winter warm yourself at the fireplace in the
dining room; in summer eat on the enormous veranda overlooking the
valley of Delphi. ✉ *Friderikis 19, at Vas. Pavlou* ☎ *22650/82710*
⚐ *Reservations essential* 🖃 *AE, DC, MC, V.*

¢–$ ✕ **Lekaria.** Escape the noise and the crowds of the main street, and
climb up a side lane to dine on typical Greek taverna food in a covered
courtyard with lots of plants. You can have your *loukaniko* (a spicy Greek
sausage) flambéed with brandy table-side. Less dramatic but no less tasty
is the *soutzoukakia*. Or you might choose *briam*, thinly sliced eggplant,
carrots, potatoes, and fresh chopped tomatoes drizzled with olive oil
and cooked in a slow oven. For dessert, follow the Greeks' lead and have
sliced apples sprinkled with cinnamon. ✉ *Apollonos 33* ☎ *22650/*
82864 🖃 *MC, V.*

¢–$ ✕ **Taverna Vakchos.** Owner Andreas Theorodakis and his family keep a
watchful eye on the kitchen and on the happiness of his customers. Choose
to eat in the spacious dining room or out on the large flower-bedecked
sheltered veranda with a stunning valley view. The menu is heavy on
meat dishes, either grilled to order or simmered in the oven, but vege-
tarians can put together a small feast from boiled wild greens, savory
pies, and other meatless Greek classics. Seasonal dishes include game
such as hare and, if you're really lucky, venison. ✉ *Apollonos 31*
☎ *22650/83186* 🖃 *No credit cards.*

★ $–$$$$ ⊡ **Acropole.** Feel completely secluded, though you're in the heart of the
action as you look out over a sea of olive trees from your balcony. Carved
Skyrian pine furniture and traditional linens and paintings decorate the
simple, attractive public and private rooms. Guest rooms on the upper
floor have a sloping cathedral ceiling in pine as well. You may want to
ask for one of the rooms with a fireplace for cold evenings. The light
breakfast is fresh yogurt drizzled with local honey. ✉ *Filellinon 13, 33054*
☎ *22650/82675 through 22650/82677* 🖷 *22650/83251* ⊕ *www.delphi.*
com.gr 🛏 *42 rooms* ⚒ *Dining room, some minibars, cable TV, bar* 🖃 *AE,*
DC, MC, V ⦿| *BP.*

$–$$$$ ⊡ **Amalia.** Thirty-five acres of gardens spread down the mountainside,
helping the low-lying Amalia blend seamlessly with the olive groves and
pines of surrounding Delphi. Breathtaking views of Itea port seen from
various public verandas, the rooms, and the poolside bar add to the hotel's
appeal. An open, central hearth in the lobby sitting area is complemented
by modern furnishings and a multihue blue-gray slate floor blocked off
in large, varied squares. Comfortable contemporary rooms have wood-
veneer furnishings and balconies. ✉ *Apollonos 1, 33054* ☎ *22650/82101,*
210/607–2000 in Athens 🖷 *22650/82290, 210/607–2135 in Athens*
⊕ *www.amalia.gr* 🛏 *184 rooms* ⚒ *Restaurant, coffee shop, cable TV,*
pool, bar, shops, meeting rooms 🖃 *AE, DC, MC, V* ⦿| *BP.*

$ 🏨 **Hotel Vouzas.** Ask for a room with a view of the gorge that the hotel sits above; the intimate public living room, with a fireplace, also has a great view. A fantastic large veranda, where breakfast is served half the year, overlooks the olive groves, and the Pleistos River. Despite the unexceptional rooms, the hotel fills up on winter weekends with Athenians who come to challenge the Mt. Parnassus ski slopes 30 minutes away. They leave fortified by the large buffet breakfast; half-board is also available. This is the closest hotel (about 1,600 feet) to the archaeological site of Ancient Delphi. ⊠ *Friderikis 1, at Vas. Pavlou, 33054* 🕾 *22650/ 82232 through 22650/82234, 210/984–6861 in Athens* 🖷 *22650/ 82033, 210/982–3772 in Athens* ⇆ *58 rooms, 1 suite* ♻ *Restaurant, minibars, bar* 🖃 *MC, V* ⊠ *BP.*

$ 🏨 **Pythia Art.** The Art hotel attracts style-conscious weekenders from Athens with painted ceiling recesses and bright colors. The modern sofas in the lounge are in bold contrast to the ancient stone exterior. Soothing earth tones in the clean-line, contemporary guest rooms evoke nature. Continental breakfast is served in the dining room, but you can order light meals from 24-hour room service. ⊠ *Friderikis 6, at Vas. Pavlou, 33054* 🕾 *22650/82328* ⇆ *27 rooms, 1 suite* ♻ *Dining room, room service, bar* 🖃 *MC, V* ⊠ *CP.*

★ ¢–$ 🏨 **Apollo.** This lovely little hotel is owned and operated by a congenial husband-and-wife team ("She's the decorator; I do the public relations," says he). The *saloni* (living room) here has traditional wall hangings and old prints among its carefully selected furnishings. The cheerful rooms have light-wood beds set off by blue quilts and striped curtains; many have wood-post balconies with black-iron railings. The same warm honey-color woodwork is seen on the first-level French doors. ⊠ *Friderikis 59B, at Vas. Pavlou, 33054* 🕾 *22650/82244* 🖷 *22650/ 82455* ⇆ *21 rooms* ♻ *Dining room, minibars; no a/c, no room phones, no room TVs* 🖃 *MC, V* ⊙ *Closed weekdays Dec.–mid-Mar.* ⊠ *BP.*

★ ¢ 🏨 **Villa Filoxenia.** This charming corner house is owned—and decorated—by the same couple who own the Apollo. Woven bedcovers and rugs, hand-carved end tables, and copper pans recreate the feel of a traditional mountain home. Standard guest rooms, suites with fireplaces and balconies, and studios with kitchenettes suit different travelers' needs. Breakfast, brought to your room, is a selection of home-baked goods with generous servings of local honey, cheese, and sliced ham. ⊠ *Friderikis 15, at Vas. Pavlou, 33054* 🕾 *22650/83114* 🖷 *22650/ 82455* ⇆ *16 studios, 12 rooms, 4 suites* ♻ *Dining room, minibars; no room phones* 🖃 *MC, V* ⊙ *Closed weekdays Dec.–mid-Mar.* ⊠ *BP.*

Festivals

Sit in the ancient stadium of Delphi under the stars and watch everything from the National Beijing Opera Theater's the *Bacchae* to the tragedies of Aeschylus and Euripides, and even folk and traditional music improvisations at the **Summer Arts Festival** (⊠ Stadium, Ancient Delphi 🕾 210/331–2781 through 210/331–2785), organized by the European Cultural Centre of Delphi in July. The festival is in conjunction with an annual symposium. All performances, which begin around 8:30 PM, are open to the public and charge a small fee.

EASTER WEEK IN DELPHI

ORTHODOX EASTER WEEK *is the most important holiday in Greece, and Delphians celebrate it with true passion. The solemn Good Friday service in Ayios Nikolaos church and the candlelight procession following it, accompanied by the singing of haunting hymns, are one of the most moving rituals in all of Greece. By Saturday evening, the mood is one of eager anticipation as the townspeople are decked out in their nicest finery and the earnest children are carrying lambades, beautifully decorated white Easter candles. At midnight the lights of the cathedral are extinguished, and the priest rushes into the sanctuary shouting Christos anesti! (Christ is risen). He lights one of the parishioner's candles with his own and the flame is passed on, one to the other, until the entire church is illuminated with candlelight, which is reflected in the radiant faces of the congregation. Firecrackers are set off by the village schoolboys outside to punctuate the exuberance of the moment. After the liturgy is finished, each person tries to get his or her candle home while still lighted, a sign of good luck for the following year, whereupon the sign of the cross is burned over the door. Then the Easter fast is broken, usually with mayiritsa (Easter soup made with lamb) and brilliantly red-dyed hard-boiled eggs. On Easter Sunday, the entire village works together to roast dozens of whole lambs on the spit. It is a joyous day, devoted to feasting with family and friends, but you are welcome and may be offered slices of roast lamb and glasses of the potent dark red local wine. In the early evening, a folk-dance performance is held in front of the town-hall square, followed by communal dancing and free food and drink.*

Galaxidi

Γαλαξείδι

 35 km (22 mi) southwest of Delphi.

Sea captains' homes with classic masonry, and an idyllic seaside location reminiscent of an island, have steadily attracted outsiders recognizing Galaxidi's potential. The heyday of the harbor town was in the 19th century—thanks to shipbuilding and a thriving mercantile economy—but after the invention of steamships it slipped into decline. Today the old town is classified a historical monument and undergoes continual renovation and restoration. If you are a shore person rather than a mountain person, Galaxidi is a good alternative to Delphi as a base for the region. Stroll Galaxidi's narrow streets with their elegant stone mansions and squares with geraniums and palm trees, and then take a late-afternoon swim in one of the pebbly coves around the headland to the north, dine along the waterfront, and enjoy the stunning mountain backdrop over the sea. If you walk to the far side of the sheltered harbor, Galaxidi appears, reflected in the still waters.

If you happen to be in Galaxidi at the start of Greek Orthodox Lent, **Kathara Deftera** (Clean Monday), duck. Locals observe the holiday with flour fights in the town's streets. The common baking flour is tinted with food dye and by the end of the day everyone and everything in sight—buildings, cars, shrubs—is dusted with a rainbow of colors that match spring's bright palette. The custom has pagan roots: every year the dead were thought to be allowed to leave Hades for a day and return to Earth; if they had a good time, a good crop was assured.

Peek into **Ayios Nikolaos** (⊠ Old town). The cathedral, named after the patron saint of sailors (Nicholas), possesses a beautiful carved 19th-century altar screen. The little **Nautical Museum** has a collection of local artifacts from ships and the old sea captains' houses. ⊠ *Mousiou 4* 🖅 *Free* ☉ *Weekdays 9:30–1:30, weekends 9:30–2.*

Where to Stay & Eat

$–$$ ✕ **To Barko tis Maritsas.** Inside an 1850 captains' *kafeneio* (coffeehouse), this waterfront restaurant is decorated with a nautical theme. Not to be missed are the pies—zucchini with dill, and spinach—as well as the eggplant dip flavored with grated walnut. Fresh fish is always plentiful, but mussels are what Galaxidi is known for—here they're served in a saganaki, steamed, and in a pilaf. Homemade sweets include the regional *amigdalopasta* (cake made with almonds and topped with *kaimaki*, rich clotted cream–base ice cream). ⊠ *Akti Ianthis 34, on waterfront* 🕾 *22650/41059* ⌘ *Reservations essential* 🖃 *MC, V.*

¢–$$ ✕ **O Tassos.** Locals and tourists pack O Tasso's waterfront terrace, the first you see as you approach from the center; they're drawn in year-round by the quality of the seafood. Farm-raised crawfish, *karavidhes*, are simply boiled and sprinkled with lemon—a true delicacy. Crispy fried calamari and whole fish, such as char-grilled snapper, are fresh as can be. Complete the feast with boiled greens and garlic-potato sauce, a large village salad, and a carafe of local wine. ⊠ *Akti Ianthis 69, at far end of harbor on waterfront* 🕾 *22650/41291* 🖃 *V.*

¢–$ ✕ **O Bebelis.** The wine barrel by the front door is the first hint that this cozy *ouzeri* (bar serving mezedes), tucked into a side street off the harbor, is a place for the *meraklis*, someone who savors life's every moment. Sit back, order the house wine, and pick at little treats laid before you like home-cured olives, stuffed onions, steamed mussels, and other seasonal small dishes prepared and served by the genial owner's mother. ⊠ *N. Mama, near start of harbor* 🕾 *22650/41677* 🖃 *No credit cards.*

¢–$ ✕ **O Dervenis.** Look inland, to O Dervenis, for some of the best small mezedes in town. It will be tough choosing an appetizer from among the homemade tzatziki, the spinach pie made with feta and *kefalograviera* (a soft cheese), the marinated octopus, and the *gavros* (resembles a large anchovy). Other options include minced meat wrapped in fresh vine leaves (tender enough to use only the first few weeks of summer), and a local specialty, *avgopita* (egg pie). Contemplate your selection in the covered garden courtyard. ⊠ *N. Gourgouris, next to old girls' school* 🕾 *22650/41177* 🖃 *No credit cards.*

¢–$ ✕ **Omilos.** Relax on the shiplike deck as the Bay of Itea stretches before you, the peaks of Mt. Parnassus tower in the distance, and the little gray-stone houses of Delphi topped with rose-slate roofs cluster on inland slopes. If you want really fresh fish, watch as one of the staff casts a line and hauls in your *sargos* or *tsipoura* (respectively, bream or panfish). Have it grilled to a golden brown and lightly embellished with oil, lemon, and oregano. Sunset is a particularly attractive time here, but the place is open early morning to late at night. After your meal, swim off the pebble beach. ⊠ *Old Yacht Club, main harbor entrance* ☎ 22650/42111 ☰ *No credit cards.*

¢–$ ⊡ **Galaxa Hotel.** A 180-year-old, blue-and-white captain's house has been transformed into a first-rate hotel. The Galaxa has simple rooms in bright robin's-egg blue and white as well, and photos of antique ship reproductions hang on the walls. Six rooms have the coveted sea view, but if yours doesn't, you have an excuse to sit longer in the terrace garden, which is also a bar. A full breakfast includes juice, eggs, homemade breads and marmalades, and local honey. Want to see a bit of the area? The hotel's owners will happily arrange an excursion on their boat. ⊠ *Eleftherias 8, near John Kennedy road, 33052* ☎ *22650/41620 through 22650/41625* 🖷 *22650/42053* 🛏 *10 rooms* ♨ *Boating, bar; no TV in some rooms* ☰ *AE, DC, MC, V* ❙○❙ *BP.*

★ ¢–$ ⊡ **Villa Ianthia.** Superb hospitality is the main reason you won't want to leave Villa Ianthia after you're welcomed into the hotel over an Italianate *tapeto marmo* (marble carpet). The reception room, graced by a stained-glass window, is the perfect setting for enjoying cocktails and popular piano melodies on weekends. Rooms are spacious and simply furnished in classic, slightly rustic style, with original art on the walls. Look to the sea or Mt. Parnassus over the wrought-iron railing of your small balcony. The breakfast buffet—served until noon—is laden with breads, homemade marmalades, and various baked treats prepared fresh daily. ⊠ *Anexartisias, opposite town hall, 33052* ☎ *22650/42433* 🖷 *22650/42434* ✉ *oianthia_corp@yahoo.gr* 🛏 *10 rooms, 2 suites* ♨ *Minibars* ☰ *MC, V* ❙○❙ *CP.*

★ ¢   ⊡ **Hotel Ganimede.** Elegant spaces take full advantage of the 19th-century sea captain's house in a lush garden. Unpretentious antiques are interspersed with Arachova weavings, small sculptures, and paintings, giving each room personality. There's one single available (€36). In winter a blazing fire beckons from the sitting room. Have the optional breakfast (€8) there, or in the courtyard in summer: the homemade marmalades (apricot, fig, and tangerine), breads, cakes, and cheese scones are delicious. ⊠ *N. Gourgouris 20, 33052* ☎ *22650/41328* 🖷 *22650/41664* ⊕ *www.gsp.gr/ganimede.gr* 🛏 *5 rooms, 2 studios, 1 suite* ♨ *Dining room, some in-room hot tubs, some kitchenettes* ☰ *MC, V* ⊙ *Closed Nov.–Dec. 20.*

EXCURSIONS FROM ATHENS A TO Z

To research prices, get advice from other travelers, and book travel arrangements, visit www.fodors.com.

BIKE & MOPED TRAVEL

On the islands of Aegina and Spetses, many people rent scooters, mopeds, and bicycles from shops along the harbor, but extreme caution is advised: the equipment may not be in good condition, roads can be narrow and treacherous, and many drivers scorn your safety. Wear a helmet, and drive defensively.

BOAT & FERRY TRAVEL

The islands of Poros and Spetses are so close to the Peloponnese mainland that you can drive there, park, and ferry across the channel in any of a number of caïques (price negotiable), but to get to them from Athens or to visit the other Saronic Gulf islands, you must take to the sea in a ferry.

Saronikos Ferries carries you and your car from the main port in Piraeus (near Platia Karaiskaki, Gate C) to Aegina (1½ hours) and Poros (2 hours, 20 minutes) or you alone—no cars allowed—to Hydra (3 hours, 15 minutes) and Spetses (4 hours, 25 minutes). The Consortium Poseidon also travels to Aegina and Poros. You can get a weekly boat schedule from the EOT. There are approximately a half dozen departures per day, and fares range from about €5 per person for Aegina to about €11 for Spetses. Car rates are usually four times the passenger rate. Ferries are the leisurely and least-expensive way to travel. Most people now prefer the speedier Hellenic Seaways hydrofoils (no cars allowed) that also depart from Piraeus. You can get to Aegina in 40 minutes (€9), to Poros in 1 hour (€14), to Hydra in 90 minutes (€16), and to Spetses (€22) in just under 2 hours. There are about a half dozen departures daily; but make reservations ahead of time; boats fill quickly. You can also reserve through a travel agent.

From a small port, Rafina has grown into a bustling harbor with connections to the Cyclades and the northeastern Aegean island of Limnos. The additional travel time to reach Rafina pays off in shorter sea journeys, via Blue Star Ferries, especially to Andros, Tinos, Mykonos, and Syros.

🚢 **Blue Star Ferries** ☎ 210/891-9800 ⊕ www.bluestarferries.com. **Consortium Poseidon** ☎ 210/417-5382 or 210/417-1395. **Hellenic Seaways** ☎ 210/419-9000 or 210/419-9200 ⊕ www.hellenicseaways.gr. **Saronikos Ferries** ☎ 210/417-1190, 210/411-7341, or 210/412-4585.

BUS TRAVEL

Places close to Athens can be reached with the blue city bus lines (€0.45): Bus A16 from Platia Eleftherias for Daphni; Bus 224 from Vassilisis Sofias or Akadimias, coupled with a 25-minute walk, for Kaisariani; Bus A2, A3, or B3 from Platia Syntagma for Glyfada; Bus A2 to Voula; Bus A2 to Glyfada, then connect with Bus 114, 115, or 116 to Vouliagmeni; Bus A2 or A3 to Glyfada, then connect with Bus 115, 116, or 149 for Varkiza. For the rest of the destinations, if you can't rent a car, the next most efficient mode of travel is the regional KTEL bus system in combination with taxis. The extensive network serves all points in Attica from Athens, and local buses connect the smaller towns and villages at least daily.

FARES & SCHEDULES   KTEL buses for eastern Attica leave hourly from their main station in downtown Athens (Platia Aigyptou at the corner of Mavromateon and Leoforos Alexandras). You can also catch this bus from Platia Klathmonos or on Filellinon. KTEL buses depart regularly for Marathon (€2.35), Rhamnous (€3.23), and Amphiareion (€2.64). The Greek National Tourism Organization (EOT) distributes a list of bus schedules.

KTEL buses servicing western Attica depart from Terminal B in Athens. To Delphi (via Arachova), there are six departures, beginning at 7:30 AM. The journey takes about three hours and costs €10.20. Four buses daily make the 4-hour trip to Galaxidi, starting at 7:30 AM; the fare is €12.20. Buses depart hourly from 5:50 AM to 8:30 PM for Dhistomo near Osios Loukas; the journey takes 2½ hours and costs €9.55. Note that the prices above are one-way fares. To get to Terminal B from downtown Athens, catch Bus 024 on Amalias in front of the National Gardens. Tickets for these buses are sold only at this terminal, so you should call to book seats well in advance during high season or holidays.

🚌 **Athens Main** Terminal A ✉ Pl. Aigyptou, Athens ☎ 210/512-4910. **Athens Terminal B** ✉ Liossion 260, Athens ☎ 210/831-7179. **KTEL Amphiareion** ☎ 210/823-0179. **KTEL Delphi & Arachova** ☎ 210/831-7096 or 210/831-7173. **KTEL Marathon** ☎ 210/821-0872. **KTEL Osios Loukas** ☎ 210/831-7173. **KTEL Rahmnous** ☎ 210/821-0872. **KTEL Sounion** ☎ 210/821-3203.

CAR RENTALS
Local and international agencies have offices in downtown Athens—most are on Syngrou Avenue—as well as at the arrival level at Eleftherios Venizelos–Athens International Airport, in Spata.

CAR TRAVEL
Points in Attica can be reached from the main Thessaloniki–Athens and Athens–Patras highways, with the National Road (Ethnikos Odos) the most popular route, especially since it has been extended and linked to the new Attica Highway (Attiki Odos). From the Peloponnese, you can drive east via Corinth to Athens, or from Patras, cross the Corinthian Gulf via the Rio–Antirrio bridge, the longest cable suspension bridge in Europe, to visit Delphi first. Most of the roads when you get off the new highway are two-lane secondary arteries; a few of them (notably from Athens to Delphi and Itea, and Athens to Sounion) have been upgraded so are good quality, not to mention spectacularly scenic. Expect heavy traffic to Delphi in summer and ski season and to and from Athens on weekends. Cars are not allowed on Hydra and Spetses.

EMERGENCIES
Keep in mind that hailing a cab may be faster than calling and waiting for an ambulance. The Automobile Touring Club of Greece (ELPA) assists tourists with breakdowns free of charge if they belong to AAA or to ELPA; otherwise, there is a charge. Patients are admitted to regional hospitals according to a rotating system; call the duty hospital number, or in an emergency, an ambulance.

🚑 **Ambulance** ☎ 166. **Duty Hospitals and Clinics** ☎ 1434. **ELPA** ✉ Mesogeion 395, Ayia Paraskevi ☎ 104 in emergency, 210/606-8800 ⊕ www.elpa.gr. **Fire** ☎ 199. **Forest Fires** ☎ 191. **Police** ☎ 100. **Tourist Police** ☎ 22970/27777 in Aegina, 171 in Attica, 22650/82900 in Delphi, 22980/52205 on Hydra, 22980/22462 on Poros, 22980/73100 on Spetses.

MEDIA

The English-language weekly newspaper *Athens News* carries entertainment listings for the towns around Athens (and for the Athens clubs that moved to the southern Attica seashore for summer). The daily English language–edition of the Greek newspaper *Kathimerini* is inserted in the *International Herald Tribune*.

SPORTS & THE OUTDOORS

The Alpine Club of Athens organizes advanced skiing classes for the experienced and snowboarding classes for children on Mt. Parnassus. Contact the Hellenic Skiing Federation for more information about skiing Mt. Parnassus.

For a booklet on Greece's hiking refuges and information on hiking paths, including the E4 and E6 trails, and on local hiking groups, contact the Greek Federation of Mountaineering Associations. Hiking expeditions are run by Trekking Hellas. F-Zein arranges all kinds of sports-adventure travel, including hiking, rafting, mountain climbing and biking, and canyoning.

⛰ Hiking **F-Zein** ✉ Ethnikis Antistaseos 103, Neo Psyhiko, Athens ☎ 210/921-6285 or 210/923-0263 🖷 210/922-9995 ⊕ www.ezjourneys.gr. **Greek Federation of Mountaineering Associations** ✉ Milioni 5, Kolonaki, Athens ☎ 210/364-5904 or 210/363-6617 🖷 210/364-4687. **Trekking Hellas** ✉ 3rd fl., Filellinon 7, Syntagma, Athens ☎ 210/331-0323 through 210/331-0326 🖷 210/323-4548 ⊕ www.trekking.gr.

⛷ Skiing **Alpine Club of Athens** ✉ 5th fl., Ermou 64, Monastiraki, Athens ☎ 210/321-2355 or 210/321-2429 🖷 210/324-4789. **Hellenic Skiing Federation** ✉ 8th fl., Karageorgi Servias 7, Syntagma, Athens ☎ 210/321-2355 🖷 210/324-4789.

TRAVEL AGENCIES

Full-service agencies, like those listed below, handle hotel reservations, transportation tickets, and tours.

🐬 **Dolphin Hellas** For Attica ✉ Leoforos Syngrou 16, Syngrou, Athens ☎ 210/922-7772 ⊕ www.dolphin-hellas.gr. **Kastalia Travel & Tourism** ✉ Vas. Pavlou 9, Delphi ☎ 22650/82212. **Saronic Gulf Travel** ✉ Waterfront, Poros town ☎ 22980/24800.

TOURS

Most agencies run tour excursions at about the same prices, but CHAT and Key Tours have the best service and guides, plus comfortable air-conditioned buses. Taking a half-day trip to the breathtaking Temple of Poseidon at Sounion (€30) avoids the hassle of dealing with the crowded public buses or paying a great deal more for a taxi. A one-day tour to Delphi with lunch costs €79, but the two-day tour (€116) gives you more time to explore this wonder. A full-day cruise from Piraeus, with either CHAT or Key Tours, visits three nearby islands—Aegina, Poros, and Hydra—and costs around €80 (including buffet lunch on the ship).

The Union of Attica Winemakers has a booth at Athens airport where you can pick up a map with a wine tour route that encompasses its 30-odd members.

🚌 **CHAT** ✉ Xenofontos 9, Syntagma, Athens ☎ 210/322-2886 or 210/323-0827 🖷 210/323-5270 ⊕ www.chatours.gr. **Key Tours** ✉ Kallirois 4, Syntagma, Athens ☎ 210/

923-3166 or 210/923-3266 🖨 210/923-2008 ⊕ www.keytours.gr. **Union of Attica Winemakers** ☎ 210/353-1315.

VISITOR INFORMATION

The Greek National Tourism Organization offices in Athens may have information on excursions outside the city. For more detailed information, consult with municipal tourist offices and tourist police offices. Arachova's office is open from December to March only.

🚩 **Aegina Tourist Office** ✉ Town Hall, Aegina ☎ 22970/22220. **Aegina Tourist Police** ✉ Leonardou Lada 11, Aegina town ☎ 22970/27777. **Arachova Tourist Office** ✉ Arachova-Delfon road, Arachova ☎ 22670/31692. **Attica Tourist Police** ✉ Dimitrakopoulou 77, Koukaki, Athens ☎ 171. **Delphi Tourist Office** ✉ Friderikis 12, at Vas. Pavlou, Delphi ☎ 22650/82900. **Delphi Tourist Police** ✉ Angelos Sikelianou 3, Delphi ☎ 22650/82220. **Hydra Tourist Police** ✉ Port, Hydra town ☎ 22980/52205. **Poros** ✉ Dimosthenous, off Pl. Iroon, Poros town ☎ 22980/22462. **Spetses** ✉ Hatziyianni-Mexi, near museum, Spetses town ☎ 22980/73744.

The Sporades

3

SKIATHOS, SKOPELOS, ALONISSOS, SKYROS & EVIA

WORD OF MOUTH

"Skopelos is absolutely divine. About the biggest entertainment was watching the ferry boats come in—it's a wonderful place to just relax, unwind, and let the world go by."

—joyce

"Try Skiathos: it's very Euro-centric (as opposed to Yank), beaches are world-class, and a variety of nightlife abounds."

—adrian

"We went to Santorini but liked Skiathos better. Great beaches, typical Greek town, great, cheap tavernas, plenty of nightlife in town, some touring spots. I'd go back in a heartbeat."

—mary

By Lea Lane

Updated by
Shane
Christensen

LIKE EMERALD BEADS SCATTERED ON SAPPHIRE satin, the verdant Sporades islands of Skiathos, Skopelos, and Alonissos, and a nearby host
of tiny, uninhabited islets, are resplendent with pines, fruit trees, and
olive trees. The lush countryside, marked with sloping slate roofs and
wooden balconies, strongly resembles that of the Pelion peninsula to which
the islands were once attached. Only on Skyros, farther out in the
Aegean, will you see a windswept, treeless landscape, or the cubistic architecture of the Cyclades. Sitting by itself east of Evia, Skyros is neither geographically nor historically related to the other Sporades. Evia
itself—Greece's second-largest island (after Crete) and not technically
part of the Sporades—offers a vast, elongated strip of coast.

The Sporades have changed hands constantly throughout history, and
wars, plunder, and earthquakes have eliminated all but the strongest ancient walls. A few castles and monasteries remain, but these islands are
now geared more for having fun than for sightseeing. Skiathos is the
most touristy, to the point of overkill, while less-developed Skopelos has
fewer beaches and much less nightlife, but a main town that is said to
be the most beautiful in the Sporades. Owing to natural disasters—a
plague on its grapevines, an earthquake that ruined its lovely acropolis—the second half of the 20th century was hard on Alonissos. Yet the
island's pristine setting is so stunning that nature lovers and romantic
couples flock here in ever greater numbers. Late to attract tourists, Skyros is the least traveled of the Sporades. It's also the most remote and
quirky, with well-preserved traditions. Evia presents a curious mix of
mainland and island culture. A seaside escape for harried Athenians, it
remains a favorite for sunseekers of all nationalities.

The Sporades are (with the exception of Skyros) quite easily reached from
the mainland; even so, many parts remain idyllic. They may be close to
each other yet they remain different in character, representing a spectrum of Greek culture, from towns with screaming nightlife to hillsides
where the tinkle of goat bells may be the only sound for miles. Quintessential Greek-island delights beckon: sun, sand, and surf, with memorable
dining under the stars. Almost all restaurants have outside seating,
often under leafy trees, where you can watch the passing Greek dramas
of daily life: lovers arm-in-arm, stealing a kiss; animated conversations
between restaurateur and patron that may last for the entire meal; fishermen cleaning their bright yellow nets and debating and laughing as
they work. Relax and immerse yourself in the blue and green watercolor
of it all.

Exploring the Sporades

Bustling with tourists, Skiathos sits closest to the mainland; it has a pretty
harbor area and the liveliest nightlife, international restaurants and
pubs, and resort hotels. Due east is Skopelos, covered with dense, fragrant pines, where you can visit scenic villages, hundreds of churches,
and lovely beaches. Farther east in the Aegean, though still close by, rugged
and rural Alonissos is surrounded by a National Marine Park. The least
progressive of the islands, it is the most naturally beautiful and has a
fascinating old hill town.

Some visitors return year after year to mythical Skyros, southeast of the other islands, for its quiet fishing villages, expansive beaches, and stunning cubist rabbit warren of a town that seems to spill down a hill. As a current citadel of Greek defense Skyros also has the bonus of an airport. Evia—not really part of the Sporades but so near them it seems to be—is closer to the mainland than the Sporades, and is connected by a bridge. The island offers plenty of beaches, fishing villages, and touristy towns.

Regular air shuttles and boat service have brought the aptly named Sporades ("scattered ones") closer together. The islands are connected by ferry and sometimes hydrofoil, although some are infrequently scheduled, especially November to April. A number of uninhabited islands in the Sporades archipelago can also be visited by chartered boat. If you are taking it easy, you can generally just jump on a caïque and island-hop. If time is limited and you want to do something in particular, it's best to plan your schedule in advance. Olympic Airways offers a weekly flight to Skyros from Athens. Flying Dolphin hydrofoils and Olympic flight timetables are available from travel agents; for regular ferries, consult the EOT in Athens.

About the Restaurants

By the water or in the heart of a rural village, in a simple taverna or a more upscale restaurant, dining in Evia and the Sporades is as much about savoring the day as consuming the fresh island food. Greeks here, as on the mainland, love to eat and drink, share and talk. To facilitate these pleasures, tavernas are tucked throughout the islands, and pastry shops offer afternoon respite with refreshing frappés, tall glasses of cold, sweetened coffee and milk. If in doubt, eat where the locals do; few tourist hangouts are as good, and prices decrease the farther you get from views or water. Although you may not have many elegant meals in the Sporades, you'll eat fabulously and meet wonderful people along the way.

About the Hotels

Accommodations reflect the pace of tourism on each particular island: Skopelos has a fair number of hotels, Skiathos and Evia a huge number; there are not many hotels on Alonissos, and Skyros has even fewer. Most hotels close from October or November to April or May, as noted in the listings in this chapter. Reservations are a good idea, though you may learn about rooms in pensions and private homes when you arrive at the airport or ferry landing. The best bet, especially for those on a budget, is to rent a converted room in a private house—look for the Greek National Tourism Organization (EOT or GNTO) license displayed in windows. Owners meet incoming ferries to tout their location, offer rooms, and negotiate the price. However, at the height of summer in July and August, island-hopping without reservations might be risky, especially on Evia, which fills with weekenders driving across the bridge from the Athens area.

In Skyros most people take lodgings in town or along the beach at Magazia and Molos: you must choose between being near the sea or the town's bars and eateries. Accommodations are basic, and not generally equipped

You could get around Skiathos, Skopelos, and Alonissos in three days, since there are daily ferry connections between them. Traveling between these islands and Skyros requires advance planning, since ferries and flights to Skyros are much less frequent. Also, make sure that you are arriving and leaving from the correct harbor; some islands, such as Evia and Skopelos, have more than one from which to depart. Five days can be just enough for touching each island in summer; off-season you need more days to accommodate the ferry schedule. Eight days would be more than enough to see all the islands and still enjoy a delightfully relaxed sojourn.

3

Numbers in the text correspond to numbers in the margin and on the Sporades map.

If you have 3 days

Inveterate island-hoppers might spend one night on each of three islands, although your trip might be more comfortable if you plant yourself on one. On **Skiathos** ❶ ☞ –❺, by day take in the beautiful but crowded beaches and the museum or perhaps Evangelistria Monastery, and at night join the fun at a taverna or restaurant and then a bustling nightclub. Day people should stay on **Skopelos** ❻–❾ to explore the numerous monasteries and churches. If you want to escape civilization as much as possible, head for **Alonissos** ❿–❸. Or you could drive to Evia, spend some time there, and then take a ferry from its harbor at Kimi to **Skyros** ❹–❾, for its slower pace and shopping. Or drop the rental car in Evia, ferry over to Skyros, and fly back to Athens from there.

If you have 5 days

You can rush through every island with a well-thought-out schedule or be selective and come away with the essence of a few of these distinctive islands. Fly to **Skyros** ❹ ☞ –❾ from Athens. Spend three or four relaxing days there and then take a day or two to explore Evia. Alternatively, base yourself in the main group of Skiathos, Skopelos, and Alonissos. If you like it lively, spend three days and nights on **Skiathos** ❶–❺; then head for **Skopelos** ❻–❾ and stay there for two nights. You can take a day cruise from Skopelos to see **Alonissos** ❿–❸ and some of the uninhabited islands, with deserted beaches, ancient monasteries, and wildlife reserves. If natural beauty and peaceful surroundings are your thing, split the nights between the latter two islands, and consider a day cruise into the National Marine Park.

If you have 8 days

This is long enough to explore all of the Sporades at a relaxed pace. Start in **Evia** ☞ and spend a night or two visiting Halkidha and Eretria before heading to Kimi for the boat to **Skyros** ❺–❿. Alternatively, you can fly from Athens direct to Skyros. Enjoy the handicrafts and dramatically set Skyros town, and plan ahead so that you can catch the weekly hydrofoil to **Alonissos** ❿–❸. Spend a night or more there or at least visit it as part of a cruise from **Skopelos** ❻–❾. Its unspoiled beauty captivates nature lovers, and its part-destroyed hilltop village is haunting. Stay several nights and perhaps rent a car to explore the inland forests and out-of-the-way churches. If you seek a lively club and social scene, spend your last couple of nights on **Skiathos** ❶–❺; from here you might leave time to go on to the Pelion peninsula on the mainland.

with television sets. In Skiathos tourists are increasingly renting private apartments, villas, and minivillas with kitchen facilities. Local island travel agents (⇨ Travel Agents *in* The Sporades A to Z) can help you sort out the possibilities.

Rates fluctuate considerably from season to season; the August high-season prices listed in the lodging chart may drop by more than half between October and May. Always negotiate off-season.

WHAT IT COSTS In euros					
	$$$$	**$$$**	**$$**	**$**	**¢**
RESTAURANTS	over €20	€16–€20	€12–€15	€8–€11	under €8
HOTELS	over €160	€121–€160	€91–€120	€60–€90	under €60

Restaurant prices are for one main course at dinner, or for two *mezedes* (small dishes) at restaurants that serve only mezedes. Hotel prices are for two people in a standard double room in high season, including taxes.

Timing

Winter is least desirable, as the weather turns cold and rainy; most hotels, rooms, and restaurants are closed, and ferry service is minimal. If you do go from November through April, book in advance and leave nothing to chance. The same advice applies to July and August peak season, when everything is open but overcrowded, except on Skyros and Alonissos. The *meltemi,* the brisk northerly summer wind of the Aegean, keeps things clearer and cooler than on the mainland even on the hottest days. Late spring and early summer are ideal, as most hotels are open, crowds have not arrived, the air is warm, and the roadsides and fields of flowers are incredible; September is also mild, and the beach crowds have returned to work.

SKIATHOS

ΣΚΙΑΘΟΣ

Part sacred (scores of churches), part profane (active nightlife), the hilly, wooded island of Skiathos is the closest of the Sporades to the Pelion peninsula. It covers an area of only 42 square km (16 square mi), but it has some 70 beaches and sandy coves. A jet-set island 25 years ago, today it teems with European—mostly British—tourists on package deals promising sun, sea, and late-night revelry. Higher prices and a bit of Mykonos' attitude are part of the deal, too.

In winter most of the island's 5,000 or so inhabitants live in its main city, Skiathos town, built after the War of Independence on the site of the colony founded in the 8th century BC by the Euboean city-state of Chalkis. Like Skopelos and Alonissos, Skiathos was on good terms with the Athenians, prized by the Macedonians, and treated gently by the Romans. Saracen and Slav raids left it virtually deserted during the early Middle Ages, but it started to prosper during the later Byzantine years.

Beaches The Sporades have a huge number of beaches, both pebbly and sandy, and with a bit of research and adventuresome spirit you can find one you like—from those crowded with people, water sports, and music to secluded coves accessible only by boat. Of all the islands, Skiathos is perhaps best for major beaches—the star location being Koukounaries, whose golden sands are famous throughout Greece.

3

Cruising Alonissos is the gateway to the National Marine Park, which comprises all of Alonissos's satellite islands, some of which are off-limits. Found here is one of the last preserves of the endangered monk seal. Nature lovers can make excursions from Skopelos to Psathoura and Kyra Panayia in the National Marine Park. On the other islands, you can hop on a tour or taxi boat and explore the natural beauty of the coastline and islets. With some of the clearest waters in the Aegean and hundreds of protected coves, the Sporades (excluding Skyros) are ideal for yachting, especially the uninhabited islands. Mooring can be arranged at the ports at each island.

Festivals Skyros's *Apokries* pre-Lenten Carnival revelry relates to pre-Christian fertility rites and is famous throughout Greece. Young men dressed as old men, maidens, or "Europeans" roam the streets. The pre-Lenten Carnival traditions of Skopelos, although not as exotic as those of Skyros, parody the expulsion of the once-terrifying Barbary pirates. August 15 is the Panayia (Festival of the Virgin), celebrated on Skyros at Magazia beach and on Skopelos in Skopelos town; its cultural events continue to late August. Skiathos hosts cultural events in summer, including a dance festival in July. Evia holds a drama festival all summer long, in Halkidha.

The islands all celebrate feast days in honor of their patron saints, with banquets, carnivals, processions from the church, costumes, folk dancing, fireworks, and revelry late into the night. Skiathos's feast day is July 26, in honor of St. Paraskevi; on Skopelos it is February 25, in honor of St. Riginosi. On the numerous feast days in the Pelion peninsula, there is dancing until late at night. And if you are lucky enough to happen by a wedding party on any of the islands, you may be invited to join in the fun—eating, dancing, and feeling part of the family in no time.

Great Flavors Ask your waiter for suggestions about local specialties—you won't go wrong with the catch of the day on any of the islands. Octopus and juicy prawns, grilled with oil and lemon or baked with cheese and fresh tomatoes, are traditional dishes. Alonissos and Skyros especially are noted for spiny lobster, which is almost as sweet as the North Atlantic variety. Sadly, only on Skyros will you find barrel wine; the small amount produced elsewhere is savored at home. Desserts are simple—puddings, spoon sweets (such as preserved figs or cherries), and pastries.

Hiking All the islands are wonderful for walking, especially in spring, when Greece's wildflowers are unsurpassed. For those who like isolated beauty and smaller scale, Skyros and Alonissos are special. Alonissos has made quite a name for itself among Greek hikers, with 17 clearly marked trails. Some of the islands' monasteries and more remote refuges are only accessible on foot and often are linked by marked trails. Evia offers an exhilarating mountain climb up Mt. Ochi. You can buy walkers' maps in souvenir shops and tourist offices in the main towns.

When the Crusaders deposed their fellow Christians from the throne of Constantinople in 1204, Skiathos and the other Sporades became the fief of the Ghisi, knights of Venice. One of their first acts was to fortify the hills on the islet separating the two bays of Skiathos Harbor. Now connected to the shore, this former islet, the Bourtzi, still has a few stout walls and buttresses shaded by some graceful pine trees.

Nine idyllic islets lush with pines and olive groves surround Skiathos, and two lie across the main harbor, with safe anchorage and a small marina. You can sail over, or hire a caïque, to swim and sun on the isolated beaches.

Skiathos Town

Σκιάθος (Πόλη)

► ❶ *8 km (5 mi) east of Troullos.*

Though the harbor is picturesque from a distance—especially from a ferry docking at sunset, when a purple light casts a soft glow and the lights on the hills behind the quay start twinkling like faint stars—Skiathos town close-up has few buildings of any distinction. Many traditional houses were burned by the Germans in 1944, and postwar development has pushed up cement apartments between the pleasant, squat, red-roof older houses. Magenta bougainvillea, sweet jasmine, and the casual charm of brightly painted balconies and shutters camouflage most of the eyesores as you wander through the narrow lanes and climb up the steep steps that serve as streets. Activity centers on the waterfront or on Papadiamantis, the main drag: banks, travel agents, telephones, post offices, police and tourist police stations, plus myriad cafés, fast-food joints, postcard stands, tacky souvenir shops, tasteful jewelry stores, and rent-a-car and -bike establishments. Shops, bars, and restaurants line the cobbled side streets, where you can also spot the occasional modest hotel and rooms-to-rent signs. The east side of the port, where the larger boats and Flying Dolphin hydrofoils dock, is not as interesting. The little church and clock tower of Ayios Nikolaos watch over it from a hill reached by steps so steep they're almost perpendicular to the earth.

Papadiamantis Museum is devoted to one of Greece's finest writers, Alexandros Papadiamantis (1851–1911), who wrote passionately about traditional island life and the hardships of his day. Skiathos plays a part in his short stories; his most famous novel, *The Murderess*, has been translated to English. Three humble rooms with his bed, the low and narrow divan where he died, some photos, and a few personal belongings are all that is exhibited. ⊠ *Right of Papadiamantis at fork* ☎ *24270/ 23843* 🖾 *Free* ⊘ *Tues.–Sun. 9:30–1:30 and 5–8:30.*

The **Bourtzi** (⊠ End of causeway extending from the port) is a piney islet that was once a fortress. It divides the harbor and now is a cultural center with periodic events and activities. In July and August, art and antiquities exhibitions and open-air performances are held here. West of the waterfront is the fishing port and the dock where caïques depart for round-the-island trips and the beaches. The sidewalk is filled with cafés and *ouzeris* (casual bars) catering more to people-watchers than serious culinary aficionados. At the far end of the port, beginning at the square around the 1846 church of Trion Hierarchon, fancier restaurants spread out under awnings, overlooking the sea. A few good restaurants and bars are hidden on backstreets in this neighborhood, many of them serving foreign foods.

Beaches

Skiathos is known for its beaches, but as has happened so many times before, popularity has a way of spoiling special places. Since the arrival of English expatriates in the early 1960s, the beautiful, piney 14-km (9-mi) stretch of coast running south of town to famed, gold-sand Koukounaries has become one almost continuous ribbon of villas, hotels, and tavernas. One beach succeeds another, and in summer the asphalted coast road carries a constant stream of cars, buses, motorbikes, and pedestrians buzzing beach to beach, like frenzied bees sampling pollen-laden flowers. To access most beaches, you must take little, usually unpaved, lanes down to the sea. Along this coast, the beaches, **Megali Ammos, Vassilias, Achladia, Tzaneria, Vromolimnos,** and **Platania,** all offer water sports, umbrellas, lounge chairs, and plenty of company.

Where to Stay & Eat

★ **$$–$$$**   ✕ **The Windmill.** Views from the outdoor platforms of the 1880 mill–turned–elegant restaurant are spectacular. White terraces have dark, rough-hewn wood rails and small balconies poke out from the mill building. Open only for dinner, the Windmill serves creative dishes like Thai fish cakes with sweet chili sauce, duck with a honey-and-orange sauce, and a number of vegetarian options. Be prepared to climb up to— and descend from—the hill above Ayios Nikolaos for one of the island's best restaurants. Follow signs to the top of the short but steep staircase. ⊠ *Above clock tower* ☎ *24270/24550* ⚊ *Reservations essential* ▤ *MC, V* ⊘ *Closed mid-Oct.–mid-May. No lunch.*

¢–$$$ ✕ **Don Quijote Tapas Bar Restaurant.** A chic rooftop terrace overlooks the harbor and enjoys a certain solitude from the bustle below. One of the few tapas bars in Greece, Don Quijote serves an impressive selection of hot and cold tapas (Spanish appetizers), such as baked feta in foil, avocado with prawns, fried calamari, chorizo, and Spanish tortillas. Paella is also available as either a vegetarian or a seafood dish. The staff provides calm, friendly service. ⊠ *East harbor* ☎ *24270/21600* ▤ *MC, V* ⊘ *Closed Nov.–Apr.*

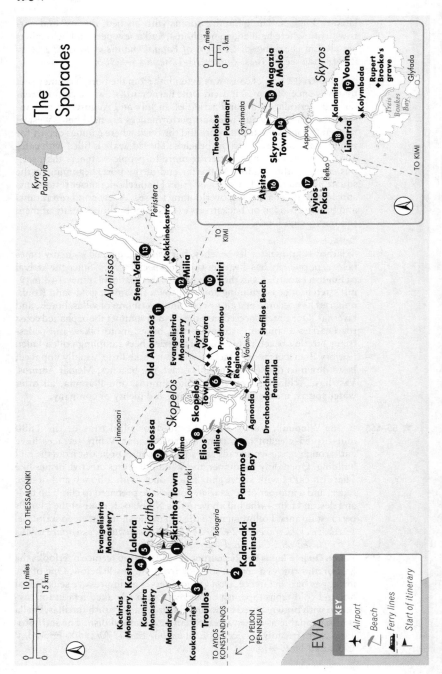

The Sporades

KEY
✈ Airport
🏖 Beach
⚓ Ferry lines
▲ Start of itinerary

¢–$$ ✕ **Asprolithos.** The Asprolithos kitchen is surprisingly ambitious, and it's easier to list what's *not* on the menu. Choices range from traditional Greek dishes like moussaka to more contemporary entrées, such as shrimp and artichokes in a cheese sauce. Dine in a delightful open-air atrium filled with plants and flowers. An extensive wine selection accompanies the menu. ✉ *Mavroyiali at Korai* ☏ *24270/23110 or 24270/ 21016* 🖃 *MC, V* ⊘ *No lunch.*

★ ¢–$$ ✕ **Ta Psarädika.** You can't get any closer to the fish market than this old port taverna, and the fresh seafood dishes prove it. Fish is caught daily by local fishermen expressly for the restaurant, which is family-owned and run. Locals love the tripe soup in winter, but you might want to sit at an outside table, sip the local wine, and stay with the mezedes and finny creatures. ✉ *Far end of old port* ☏ *24270/23412* 🖃 *AE, MC, V* ⊘ *Closed Dec. and Jan.*

¢–$ ✕🖼 **Fresh.** The warm, inviting owners, Astergios and Spyros, can be counted on to entertain while imparting their in-depth knowledge of Skiathos. Many of the simple studios with modern furnishings have great views of the harbor. For Greek food—*pastitsio* (pasta with aromatic meat sauce and béchamel), moussaka—reasonable prices, and great service, don't pass up the casual boardwalk café (¢), also fun for people-watching. ✉ *Portside, 37002* ☏ *24270/21998* ⤶ *10 studios* ⚭ *Restaurant, kitchens, cable TV* 🖃 *AE, DC, MC, V* ⊘ *Closed Nov.–Apr.* ℃ *CP.*

★ ¢ ✕🖼 **Mouria Hotel and Taverna.** A wonderful choice for budget travelers, Mouria first opened in 1830 as a market and taverna and is today an inn and restaurant run by the great-grandchildren of the original owners. Guest rooms, some of which can accommodate up to six people, have air-conditioning as well as access to kitchen and laundry facilities. Ask for a room with a balcony overlooking the courtyard, where Papadiamantis once came to write stories. The reasonably priced taverna (¢–$$) serves traditional Greek food and fish brought in from the hotel's own boat. ✉ *Areti Ioannou (behind National Bank), 37002* ☏ *24270/ 23069* 🖷 *24270/23859* ⤶ *12 rooms* ⚭ *Restaurant, laundry facilities; no room phones* 🖃 *MC, V.*

$ 🖼 **Alkyon.** Don't be disappointed by the boxy exterior and the lack of architectural embellishments—this is a discreet, light-filled hotel with many rooms offering lovely views of the new harbor. It's just enough away from the motion and commotion of Skiathos's main artery to provide some tranquillity, but it's also within easy walking distance of terrific nightlife. The rooms are comfortable and sunny (all come with private balconies), and the lounge areas are spacious and inviting. ✉ *New Harbor, 37002* ☏ *24270/22981 through 24270/22985* 🖷 *24270/21643* ⊕ *www.greekhotel.com* ⤶ *89 rooms* ⚭ *Snack bar, kitchenettes, pool, lounge; no room TVs* 🖃 *AE, MC, V* ⊘ *Closed Nov.–Mar.*

Nightlife

Skiathos is filled with night owls, and for good reason. Bars for all tastes line main and side streets, from pubs run by Brits to quintessential Greek bouzouki joints in beach tavernas. Most of the nightlife in Skiathos town is centered along the waterfront and on Papadiamantis, Politechniou, and Evangelistrias streets. The most active season, as you might expect, is June through August, when nightclubs catering to all tastes open in the New Port.

MUSIC &
NIGHTCLUBS Start your night with a drink at **Rock n' Roll** (⌧ Old Port ☎ 24270/22944 ☉ Closed Oct.–Apr.), which has more than 100 cocktails to choose from and a DJ after 9:30 PM. Another popular bar, **Kentavros Bar** (⌧ Papadiamantis Sq. ☎ 24270/22980 ☉ Closed Oct.–Apr.), entertains a young professional crowd with rhythm and blues, funk, soul, and rock starting at 9:30 PM. For late-night action along a row of hopping clubs, the hottest club at this writing was **Kahlua** (⌧ Tasos Antonaros (in the New Port) ☎ 24270/23205 ☉ Closed Oct.–Apr.), which has indoor and outdoor dancing and is open in summer until 3 AM.

Sports & the Outdoors

FISHING The Aegean is rich with fresh seafood, but overfishing and such scurrilous practices as dynamiting and bottom trawling have greatly diminished the once-abundant resources of the Sporades. It is now illegal to fish with scuba equipment. You can hire fishing boats to seek what remains, and what remains tastes wonderful; look for rental signs on the boats at the ports.

SAILING For multiday charters with or without crew, contact **Active Yachts** (⌧ Portside ☎ 0030/697–2245391 ☉ Closed Oct.–Apr.), which also rents motorboats by the day.

SCUBA DIVING Popular beaches often have diving-equipment rental and instructors on hand. Skiathos is the only island with a scuba-diving school, the **Dolphin Diving Center** (⌧ Porto Nostos Beach (off bus stop 12) ☎ 24270/21599 ⎙ 24270/22525 ⊕ www.ddiving.gr ☉ Closed Nov.–Apr.). Single or multiple dives, as well as full-certification programs, are offered.

Shopping

Tourist shops generally close in the off-season, except in the rare instance that the owners are local. The only stores likely to stay open year-round are food shops operated by islanders. Call ahead to confirm a shop is open.

ANTIQUES &
CRAFTS The **Archipelago** (⌧ Near Papadiamantis Museum ☎ 24270/22163) is the most stunning shop on the island. Browse here among the antiques, pottery, jewelry made from fossils, and embroideries. **Galerie Varsakis** (⌧ Trion Hierarchon ☎ 24270/22255) has kilims, embroideries, jewelry, icons, and hundreds of antiques, set off by the proprietor's surrealistic paintings. **Loupos and His Dolphins** (⌧ Papadiamantis Sq. ☎ 24270/23777) is two adjacent shops that sell museum copies of Byzantine jewelry, ceramics made in Volos, furniture, and antiques. **Skia** (⌧ Behind National Bank, off Papadiamantis ☎ 24270/21728) sells original paintings, sculptures, and ceramics handcrafted by the owners, Milena and Vladislav.

JEWELRY **Odysseus Jewelry** (⌧ Papadiamantis ☎ 24270/24218) sells gold and silver pieces. **Seraïna** (⌧ Near Papadiamantis Museum ☎ 24270/22039) sells jewelry, ceramic plates, and lamp shades. **Simos** (⌧ Papadiamantis ☎ 24270/22916) has unique silver and gold designs.

Kalamaki Peninsula

Καλαμάκι (χερσόνησος)

2 *6 km (4 mi) south of Skiathos town.*

The less-developed area on the south coast of Skiathos is the Kalamaki peninsula, where the British built their first villas. Some are available for rent in summer, many above tiny, unfrequented coves. Access here is by boat only, so you can usually find your own private beach to get away from the crowds. Motor launches run at regular intervals to the most popular beaches from Skiathos town, and you can always hire a boat for a private journey.

Where to Stay

$$$$ ☒ **Skiathos Princess.** Flanking virtually the whole of Platania Bay below Ayia Paraskevi, Skiathos Princess has all the expected amenities of a luxury resort. The hotel is owned by an international organization that has worked hard to improve the resort's quality. Tile-floor rooms have marble bathrooms and patios or balconies—most with sea views. The Princess offers spa services and a poolside bar. ☒ *8 km (5 mi) from Skiathos town, 37002 Ayia Paraskevi* ☎ *24270/49731* 🖷 *24270/49740* ⊕ *www.vi-hotels.com/princess* 🛏 *131 rooms, 25 suites, 2 apartments* ⚑ *Restaurant, in-room safes, refrigerators, pool, wading pool, hair salon, hot tub, massage, sauna, 2 bars, meeting rooms, airport shuttle, no-smoking rooms* ▤ *AE, MC, V* ☉ *Closed Nov.–Apr.* ⓧ *BP.*

$$$ ☒ **Atrium.** On a picturesque pine hill above Platanias beach, with stone and ocher walls, terra-cotta tiles, and sloping roofs, the Atrium resembles a Mt. Athos monastery. There's nothing monastic, however, about its stylish interior, understated antiques, nooks for conversation, TV room, backgammon, and top-floor pool and bar. Ask for a room with a sea view, and prepare for the climb up from the beach at Ayia Paraskevi. Cars and mopeds are available for hire from the hotel on request. ☒ *8 km (5 mi) from Skiathos town, 37002 Platanias* ☎ *24270/49345 or 24270/49376* 🖷 *24270/49444* ⊕ *www.atriumhotel.gr* 🛏 *75 rooms, 6 suites* ⚑ *Restaurant, in-room safes, refrigerators, cable TV, pool, billiards, Ping-Pong, bar, shop* ▤ *AE, DC, MC, V* ☉ *Closed mid-Oct.–Apr.*

Troullos

Τρούλλος

3 *4 km (2½ mi) west of Kalamaki peninsula, 8 km (5 mi) west of Skiathos town.*

On the coast road west of Kalamaki peninsula lies Troullos Bay, a resort area. Continue west and you come to Koukounaries beach—famous, beautiful, and unfortunately overcrowded.

The dirt road north of Troullos leads to beaches and to the small, and now deserted, **Kounistra Monastery** (☒ *4 km [2½ mi] north of Troullos*). It was built in the late 17th century on the spot where an icon of the Virgin miraculously appeared, swinging from a pine tree. The icon spends most of the year in the church of Trion Hierarchon, in town, but on November 20 the townspeople parade it to its former home for the celebration of the Presentation of the Virgin the following day. You can enter the deserted monastery church any time, though its interior has been blackened by fire and its 18th-century frescoes are hard to see.

Beaches

Though **Koukounaries** (⊠ 4 km [2½ mi] northwest of Troullos, 12 km [8 mi] west of Skiathos town) has been much touted as Greece's best beach, photos displaying it must either have been taken a long time ago or on a brilliant, deserted winter's day. All summer it is so packed with umbrellas, beach chairs, and blistering tourists that you can hardly see the sand. The multitudes can be part of the fun, however: think of this as an international Greek island beach party. Water activities abound, with waterskiing, sailing (laser boats), paddleboats, and banana-boat rides all available. The beach can only be reached from its ends, as a lagoon separates it from the hinterland.

Around the island's western tip are **Ayia Eleni and Krasa** (⊠ 1 km [½ mi] west of Koukounaries beach, 13 km [8 mi] west of Skiathos town), facing Pelion peninsula, which looms close by. These beaches are also known as Big and Little Banana, perhaps because sun worshippers—mainly gay men on Little Banana—often peel their clothes off. Rocky coves provide some privacy.

Mandraki (⊠ 5 km [3 mi] northwest of Troullos Bay, 12 km [8 mi] west of Skiathos town) has privacy because the beach is a 25-minute walk from the road. Sometimes called Xerxes's Harbor, this is where the Persian king stopped on his way to ultimate defeat at the battles of Artemisium and Salamis. The reefs opposite are the site of a monument Xerxes supposedly erected as a warning to ships, the first such marker known in history.

Megalos Aselinos and Mikros Aselinos (⊠ 7 km [4½ mi] north of Troullos, 8 km [5 mi] west of Skiathos town), north of Mandraki beach, can be reached by car or bike.

Where to Stay & Eat

★ **$$$$** ☒ **Aegean Suites.** In a league of its own on Skiathos, this luxurious boutique hotel pampers guests with refined service and gracious accommodations. The 20 suites are separated by a series of stairs, and they and the poolside restaurant peer over the Aegean sea near Troullos. Each accommodation has a separate living room, bedroom, and balcony and is uniquely decorated with original Greek artwork. The beach lies close by, and come night there is no reason to stray far from the outdoor candlelit restaurant, Pelagos, operated primarily for guests of the hotel. Expect outstanding service. ⊠ *Megali Ammos Beach* 🕭 *(winter address: Santikmos Hotels & Resorts, 40 Ag. Konstantinou Str., Aethrio Centre, office A40, 15124 Maroussi, Athens)* ☎ *24270/24069* 🖷 *24270/ 24070* ⊕ *www.aegeansuites.com* ⌁ *20 suites* ⌂ *Restaurant, in-room safes, minibars, cable TV, in-room DVD, Wi-Fi, pool, exercise equipment, massage, sauna* ⊟ *AE, D, MC, V* ⊗ *Closed Nov.–Apr.* ⍟ *BP.*

$ ☒ **Troullos Bay.** This homey beachfront hotel invites reading, chatting, and relaxing in bamboo chairs around the lobby's (usually unlighted) fireplace. Bedrooms have wood furniture, striped duvets, tile floors, and colorful prints. Most rooms have balconies and views of the pretty beach. The restaurant, decorated with bamboo and chintz, serves a combination of Greek and international good food and opens onto the lawn near the sand's edge. This hotel is ideal for those who prefer a quiet and peaceful environment. ⊠ *Troullos, 37002 Troullos Bay* ☎ *24270/ 49390* 🖶 *24270/49218* 🛏*43 rooms* 🔊 *Restaurant, beach, boating, parasailing, waterskiing, bar* 🚪 *MC, V* ⊘ *Closed Nov.–Apr.*

Sports & the Outdoors

Skiathos's **Skiathos Riding Center** (⊠ Bus stop 25 near Koukounaries ☎ 24270/49548 ⊕ www.skiathos-riding.com ⊘ Closed Oct.–Apr.) offers one- to two-hour mountain-trail outings on horseback for beginners and experienced riders. There are also donkey rides for kids.

Kastro

Κάστρο

❹ *13 km (8 mi) northeast of Troullos, 9 km (5½ mi) northeast of Skiathos town.*

Also known as the Old Town, Kastro perches on a forbidding promontory high above the water and accessible only by steps. Skiathians founded this former capital in the 16th century when they fled from the pirates and the turmoil on the coast to the security of this remote cliff—staying until 1829. Its landward side was additionally protected by a moat and drawbridge, and inside the stout walls they erected 300 houses and 22 churches, of which only two remain. The little Church of the Nativity has some icons and must have heard many prayers for deliverance from the sieges that left the Skiathians close to starvation.

You can drive or take a taxi or bus to within 325 feet of the Old Town, or wear comfortable shoes for a walk that's mostly uphill. Better, take the downhill walk back to Skiathos town; the trek takes about three hours and goes through orchards, fields, and forests on the well-marked paths of the interior.

Four kilometers (2½ mi) southwest of Kastro is the deserted **Kechrias monastery,** an 18th-century church covered in frescoes and surrounded by olive and pine trees. Be warned: the road to Kechrias from Skiathos town and to the beach below is tough going; stick to a four-wheel-drive vehicle.

Lalaria

Λαλάρια

❺ *2 km (1 mi) east of Kastro, 7 km (4½ mi) north of Skiathos town.*

Fodor'sChoice
★

The much-photographed, lovely Lalaria beach, on the north coast, is flanked by a majestic, arched limestone promontory. The polished limestone and marble add extra sparkle to the already shimmering Aegean. There's no lodging here, and you can only reach Lalaria by taking a boat from the old port in Skiathos town, where taxi and tourist boats are readily available. In the same area lie **Skoteini (Dark) Cave, Galazia (Azure) Cave,** and **Halkini (Copper) Cave.** If taking a tour boat, you can stop for an hour or two here to swim and frolic. Bring along a flashlight to turn the water inside these grottoes an incandescent blue.

★   The island's best-known and most beautiful monastery, **Evangelistria,** sits on Skiathos's highest point and was dedicated in the late 18th century to the Annunciation of the Virgin by monks from Mt. Athos. It encouraged education and gave a base to revolutionaries, who pledged an oath to freedom and first hoisted the blue-and-white flag of Greece here in 1807. Looming above a gorge, and surrounded by pines and cypresses, the monastery has a high wall that once kept pirates out; today it encloses a ruined refectory kitchen, the cells, a small museum library, and a magnificent church with three domes. A gift shop sells the monastery's own Alypiakos wine, olive oil, preserves, and icons. It's close to Lalaria, but it's also about a 10-minute drive, or an hour's walk, from Skiathos town. ⊠ *2 km (1 mi) south of Lalaria, 5 km (3 mi) north of Skiathos town* ☎ *No phone* 🖅 *Donations accepted* ⊙ *Daily 9–7.*

---

need a break?   A couple of miles south of Evangelistria Monastery, the dirt road veers off toward the north and northwest of the island. Follow this track for a quick repast; about 2 km (1 mi) on, an enterprising soul has set up a café and snack bar, **Platanos** (⊠ Off main road south of Evangelistria Monastery ☎ No phone ⊙ Closed Oct.–Apr.), where you can stare at the astounding view of the harbor for as long as you like.

Pelion Peninsula

Πήλιο

3 hrs by ferry, 1½ hrs by hydrofoil, east of Skiathos town, on mainland.

An incredibly charming landscape of stone churches, elegant houses adorned with rose arbors, and storybook town squares lies across the water from Skiathos on the mainland, about 320 km (200 mi) northeast of Athens. Pelion peninsula looms large in myth and legend. Jason and the Argonauts are said to have embarked from the port of ancient Iolkos, once set opposite modern Volos, on the northwestern tip of the peninsula, to make good a vague claim to the Golden Fleece. Mt. Pelion, still thickly wooded with pine, cypress, and fruit trees, was the home of the legendary Centaurs, those half-man–half-horse beings notorious for lasciviousness and drunkenness. Here, too, on a cypress-clad hill overlooking Volos, was the site of the wedding banquet of the nymph Peleus and the mortal Thetis. Uninvited, the goddess of discord, Eris, flung a golden apple between Athena and Aphrodite, asking Prince Paris of Troy to decide who was the fairest (and thereby giving Homer one heck of a plot).

Today the peninsula is much more peaceful, dotted with no fewer than 24 lovely villages. As you leave Volos (having explored its waterfront esplanade and splendid archaeological museum), you ascend along serpentine roads into the cooler mountains, enjoying great views over Volos Bay. Some roads wind down to beautiful white-sand or roundstone beaches, such as Horefto and Milopotamos. Nestled among the forests are villages such as Tsangarades, Milies (with the beautifully frescoed Ag Taxiarchis church), and Vyzitsa, while high above Volos is exquisite Portaria, whose *kokkineli* (fresh red wine) has to be consumed on the spot, as it does not stand up well to transport. Neither visitors nor locals complain of this. Separated from Portaria by a deep ravine is Makrynitsa, incredibly rich in local color. The village square is straight out of fairyland: the large, paved terrace overhangs the town and gulf below, yet feels intimate thanks to a backdrop of huge plane trees that shade a small Byzantine church and a lulling fountain.

Most of the Pelion villages have archetypal Greek houses—replete with bay windows, stained glass, and ornamentation—whose elegance cannot be bettered. To get to Pelion from Skiathos by car, take the three-hour ferry down to Volos; you can also board the hydrofoil and rent a car in Pelion. There is daily train service to Volos from Athens's Stathmos Larissa station (this ride takes six hours).

For information on the Pelion peninsula and accommodations in the lovely government-renovated village inns, contact the **EOT** (✉ Riga Fereous, Volos ☎ 24210/23500), open weekdays 7–2:30.

SKOPELOS

ΣΚΟΠΕΛΟΣ

This triangular island's name means "a sharp rock" or "a reef"—a fitting description for the terrain on its northern shore. It's an hour away from Skiathos by hydrofoil and is the second largest of the Sporades. Most of its 122 square km (47 square mi), up to its highest peak on Mt. Delfi, are covered with dense pine forests, olive groves, and orchards. On the south coast, villages overlook the shores, and pines line the pebbly beaches, casting jade shadows on turquoise water. Although this is the most populated island of the Sporades, with two major towns, Skopelos remains peaceful and absorbs tourists into its life rather than giving itself up to their sun-and-fun needs. It's not surprising that ecologists claim it's the greenest island in the region.

Legend has it that Skopelos was settled by Peparethos and Staphylos, colonists from Minoan Crete, said to be the sons of Dionysos and Ariadne, King Minos's daughter. They brought with them the lore of the grape and the olive. The island was called Peparethos until Hellenistic times, and its most popular beach still bears the name Stafilos. In the 1930s a tomb believed to be Staphylos's was unearthed, filled with weapons and golden treasures (now in the Volos museum on the Pelion peninsula).

The Byzantines were exiled here, and the Venetians ruled for 300 years, until 1204. In times past, Skopelos was known for its wine, but today its plums and almonds are eaten rather than drunk, and incorporated into the simple cuisine. Many artists and photographers have settled on the island and throughout summer are part of an extensive cultural program. Little by little, Skopelos is cementing an image as a green and artsy island, still unspoiled by success.

Skopelos Town

Σκόπελος (Πόλη)

❻ *11 km (7 mi) southeast of Glossa.*

Pretty Skopelos town, the administrative center of the Sporades, over-looks a bay on the north coast. On a steep hill below, scant vestiges of the ancient acropolis and medieval castle remain. The town works hard to stay charming—building permits are difficult to obtain, signs must be in native style, pebbles are embedded into the walkways. Three- and four-story houses rise virtually straight up the hillside, reached by flag-stone steps, where women sit chatting and knitting by their doorways. The whitewashed houses look prosperous and cared for, their facades enlivened by brightly painted or brown timber balconies, doors, and shut-ters. Flamboyant vines and potted plants complete the picture. Interspersed among the red-tile roofs are several with traditional gray fish-scale slate—too heavy and expensive to be used much nowadays.

Off the waterfront, prepare for a breath-snatching climb up the almost perpendicular steps in Skopelos town, starting at the sea wall. You will encounter many churches as you go. The uppermost, the 11th-century Ayios Athanasios, was built on a 9th-century foundation. At the top you're stand-ing within the walls of the 13th-century castle, erected by the Venetian Ghisi lords who held all the Sporades as their fief. It in turn rests upon polygonal masonry of the 5th century BC, as this was the site of one of the island's three ancient acropoli. Once you've admired the view and the stamina of the old women negotiating the steps like mountain goats, wind your way back down the sea-wall steps by any route you choose. Wher-ever you turn, you may spy a church; Skopelos claims some 360, of which 123 are in the town proper. Curiously, most of them seem to be locked, but the exteriors are striking—some incorporating ancient artifacts, Byzan-tine plates or early Christian elements, and slate-capped domes.

A few of Skopelos's 40 monasteries—dazzling white and topped with terra-cotta roofs—are perched on the nearby mountainside, circling in tiers to the shore. Most offer spectacular views of the town; some are deserted, but others are in operation and welcome you to visit (dress appropriately: no bare legs or arms, and women must wear skirts). You can drive or go by bike, but even by foot, with a good walking guide, you can visit them all in a few hours.

★ For a glimpse of the interior of a Skopelan house, visit the **Folk Art Museum**, a 19th-century mansion with period furniture and traditional tools. Check out the example of an elaborate women's festive costume: silk shirt embroidered with tiny flowers, velvet coat with wide embroi-dered sleeves, and silk head scarf. Even today, women in the villages dress this way for special occasions. ✉ *Hatzistamat* ☎ *24240/23494* 🎟 *€2* 🕓 *May–Sept., daily 10–10.*

Evangelistria Monastery was founded in 1676 and completely rebuilt in 1712. It contains no frescoes but has an intricately carved iconostasis and an 11th-century icon of the Virgin with Child, said to be miraculous. ⊠ *On mountainside opposite Skopelos town, 1½ km (1 mi) to the northeast* ☎ *24240/23230* ⌷ *Free* ☉ *Daily 9–1 and 3–5.*

★ The **Prodromou** (Forerunner), dedicated to St. John the Baptist, now operates as a convent. Besides being of an unusual design, its church contains some outstanding 14th-century triptychs, an enamel tile floor, and an iconostasis spanning four centuries (half carved in the 14th century, half in the 18th century). The nuns sell elaborate woven and embroidered handiwork; opening days and hours vary. ⊠ *2½ km (1½ mi) east of Skopelos town.*

The tiny port of **Agnonda** has many tavernas along its pebbled beach. It is named after a local boy, Agnonas, who returned here from Olympia in 546 BC wearing the victor's wreath. ⊠ *5 km (3 mi) south of Skopelos town.*

The road from the beach at Stafilos runs southwest through the rounded **Drachondoschisma Peninsula,** where St. Reginos dispatched the dragon. ⊠ *5 km (3 mi) south of Skopelos town.*

Beaches

Most beaches lie on the sheltered coast, south and west of the main town, and are reached from the road by footpath. The water in this area is calm, and pines grow down to the waterfront. Scattered farms and tavernas, houses with rooms for rent, and one or two pleasant hotels line the road to the beach at **Stafilos** (⊠ 8 km [5 mi] southeast of Skopelos town), the closest to town and the most crowded. Prehistoric walls, a watchtower, and an unplundered grave suggest that this was the site of an important prehistoric settlement. **Velania** (⊠ 1 km [½ mi] east of Stafilos), reachable by footpath, takes its name from the *valanium* (Roman bath) that once stood here, which has since disintegrated under the waves. It's a nude beach today.

Where to Stay & Eat

¢–$$ ✕ **Alexander Garden Restaurant.** When you've had enough of the waterfront, follow the signs up to this little garden restaurant in the hills. A 200-year-old well in the center of the elegant terrace produces its own natural spring water. Here, none of the main dishes are prefab; your order is cooked just for you. Especially recommended are *orektika* (appetizers) such as fried eggplant or zucchini, served with *tzatziki* (garlic and yogurt dip) or *tirosalata* (cheese dip). ⊠ *Odhos Manolaki; turn inland after corner shop Armoloi* ☎ *24240/22324* ⊟ *MC, V* ☉ *No lunch.*

¢–$$ ✕ **Molos.** The best of the cluster of tavernas near the ferry dock, Molos serves excellent grilled meat, stuffed grape leaves, meatballs, and *magirefta* (dishes cooked ahead in the oven, and often served at room temperature.) It's one of the few places in town open for lunch, especially delightful at an outdoor table. ⊠ *Waterfront* ☎ *24240/22551* ⊟ *No credit cards* ☉ *Closed Nov.–Mar.*

$ ✕ **Perivoli.** Locals come here to have an elegant meal in a candlelit garden. The menu is not only varied but imaginative and delicious. Suggestions include rolled pork with mushrooms in wine sauce, seafood risotto, and any of the beef fillets. Make sure to leave room for dessert, as the *amigdalopita* (almond cake with chocolate and fresh cream) is a winner. The secret is out, though—this place is usually crowded. Follow the signs up from Platia Platanos (aka Souvlaki Square). ⊠ *Off Pl. Platanos* ☎ *24240/23758* ▭ *MC, V* ☉ *Closed Oct.–May. No lunch.*

¢–$ ✕ **Mihalis.** Come here for the delicious *Skopelitiki tiropita* (Skopelos cheese pie), or splurge on *rizogalo* (rice pudding). Bougainvillea lines the walls of the courtyard, where you hear the warble of canaries. Opposite stands a barbershop that embodies the charm of another era. ⊠ *East side of port, 3 blocks inland from bank* ☎ *24240/22014* ▭ *No credit cards.*

★ ☾ $$$ 🏨 **Skopelos Village.** Each spacious bungalow sleeps from two to six people and has a balcony or patio, kitchen, large bedroom(s), and living room. The design is traditional northern Greek, with white stucco exterior and interior walls, orange barrel-tile roofs, and rustic pine beds. The central courtyard has a sparkling pool, and taverna tables sit poolside. The hotel lies next to the beach and is about a 15-minute walk from the town center. ⊠ *1 km (½ mi) west of center, 37003* ☎ *24240/23011 or 24240/ 23012* 🖷 *24240/22958* ⊕ *www.skopelosvillage.gr* ↝ *36 suites* ☾ *Restaurant, room service, in-room safes, kitchens, pool, tennis court, bar, playground, no-smoking rooms* ▭ *MC, V* ☉ *Closed Nov.–Apr.*

☾ $$ 🏨 **Alkistis.** Amid a grove of olive trees stand four buildings of cheerful apartments with kitchenettes, housekeeping, and a pool bar. The exteriors are pastel-contemporary, but the lounges and dining terraces are more traditional, though airy and bright. Geared toward families or couples with cars, it makes an agreeable alternative to a beach or town hotel. Room TVs are provided upon request. ⊠ *2 km (1 mi) southeast of town on road to Stafilos, 37003* ☎ *24240/23006 through 24240/23009* 🖷 *24240/22116* ⊕ *www.skopelosweb.gr/alkistis* ↝ *25 apartments* ☾ *Restaurant, grocery, kitchenettes, pool, wading pool, bar, playground; no room TVs* ▭ *No credit cards* ☉ *Closed Oct.–May.*

¢ 🏨 **Pension Sotos.** This cozy, restored old Skopelete house on the waterfront is inexpensive and extremely casual. Tiny rooms look onto one of the hotel's two courtyard terraces. Breakfast is not offered, although you are welcome to bring your own food and use the communal kitchen. ⊠ *Waterfront, 37003* ☎ *24240/22549* 🖷 *24240/23668* ↝ *12 rooms* ☾ *No a/c in some rooms, no room phones, no TVs in some rooms* ▭ *No credit cards.*

The Outdoors

A big caïque captained by a knowledgeable local guide makes day cruises from Skopelos to Alonissos and the National Marine Park. The tour includes a visit to Patitiri, the port of Alonissos, and to the island of Kyra Panayia, where you can walk, swim, snorkel, and visit a post-Byzantine monastery. You can make reservations at Madro Travel (⇨ Travel Agents *in* The Sporades A to Z).

Nightlife

Nightlife on Skopelos is more sedate than it is on Skiathos. There is a smattering of cozy bars playing music of all kinds, and each summer at least one nightclub operates (look for advertisements). The *kefi* (good mood) is to be found at the western end of the waterfront, where a string of bar-nightclubs come to life after midnight. Take an evening stroll; most bars have tables outside, so you really can't miss them.

Virtually all bars and clubs are closed in the off-season.

At **Anatoli** (✉ Old Kastro ☎ 24240/22851), tap into a truly Greek vein with proprietor Giorgo Xithari, who strums up a storm on his bouzouki and sings *rembetika,* traditional Greek acoustic blues (without the benefit of a microphone). Sometimes other musicians join in, sometimes his sons, and with enough ouzo, you might, too.

Venture into the back alleys and have a drink at **Ionos Blue Bar** (✉ Skopelos town ☎ 24240/23731), which offers cool jazz and blues. **Mercurius** (✉ Skopelos town ☎ 24240/24593), along the waterfront, is an artsy jazz bar with a candlelit terrace and unbeatable sea view. **Platanos Jazz Club** (✉ Next to ferry dock, Skopelos town ☎ 24240/23661), on the eastern part of the harbor, is atmospheric and quietly popular.

Shopping

The town's tiny shops are tucked into a few streets behind the central part of the waterfront. Handicrafts include loom-woven textiles made by nuns. There are numerous clothing stores throughout the alleyways of Skopelos town. Most, however, don't restrict themselves just to selling clothes but offer a hodgepodge of other accessories, so it's fun to browse. Local honey, prunes, almonds, and candy are especially delicious. Take home a box of *hamalia* (sugar and almond paste) or *rozethes* (plum sweets).

Most, but not all, stores stay open year-round, but many have reduced hours.

CLOTHING **Mythos** (✉ Behind port, next to post office ☎ 24240/23943) sells fashionable Greek and international styles for women. Try **Pragmata** (✉ Behind port, above Verdo Bldg. ☎ 24240/22866) for clothes, shoes, and other accessories.

LOCAL CRAFTS **Archipelago** (✉ Waterfront ☎ 24240/23127), the sister shop of Archipelago on Skiathos, has modern ceramics and crafts, great jewelry, handbags, and a wonderful selection of pricey antiques. **Armoloi** (✉ Waterfront ☎ 24240/22707), one of the neatest shops, displays ceramics made by local potters, tapestries, embroideries, and bags crafted from fragments of old Asian rugs and kilims. Try **Ploumisti** (✉ Waterfront ☎ 24240/22059) for kilims, bags, hand-painted T-shirts, and jewelry. **Yiousouri** (✉ Waterfront ☎ 24240/23983) sells decorative ceramics.

Panormos Bay

Όρμος Πανόρμου

❼ *6 km (4 mi) west of Skopelos town, 4 km (2½ mi) northwest of Agnonda.*

Due northwest of Agnonda is Panormos Bay, the smallest of the ancient towns of Peparethos, founded in the 8th century BC by colonists from Chalkis. A few well-concealed walls are visible among the pine woods on the acropolis above the bay. With its long beach and its sheltered inner cove ideal for yachts, this is fast becoming a holiday village, although so far it retains its quiet charm. Inland, the interior of Skopelos is green and lush, and not far from Panormos Bay traditional farmhouses called *kalivia* stand in plum orchards. Some are occupied; others have been turned into overnight stops or are used only for feast-day celebrations.

Look for the outdoor ovens, which baked the fresh plums when Skopelos was turning out prunes galore. This rural area is charming, but the lack of signposts makes it easy to get lost, so pay attention.

Beaches

Pebbly **Milia** (⊠ 2 km (1 mi) north of Panormos Bay) Skopelos's longest beach, is considered by many to be its best. Though still secluded, Milia Bay is up and coming—parasols and recliners are lined across the beach ready and waiting for the summer crowd. There's an enormous taverna, thankfully ensconced by pine trees; the food is only decent, but cold drinks and ice cream are a luxury in the noonday sun. No matter what, Milia is breathtaking, and if you want to minimize the distance between you and the deep blue sea, locate the owner of one of the villas for rent right on the beach. They're well tended and a few short strides from the water's edge. Next door and accessible through the Adrina Beach Hotel, **Adrina Beach** has gorgeous turquoise water and a feeling of seclusion. Dassia, the verdant islet across the bay, was named after a pirate who drowned there—a woman.

Where to Stay

★ $$$$ 🏨 **Adrina Beach.** Atop a picture-book cove, this terraced hotel has uninterrupted views of Panormos Bay from every level. Outside there is multihued bougainvillea; indoors, the blue and white is carried throughout, complemented by terra-cotta floors. Plates adorn the walls, *amphorae* (large clay vessels that usually held wine) the corners. The only fly on the baklava might be the many stairs between the private beach, pool, taverna area, and your room, and the steep walk back from the little town. ⊠ 1 km (½ mi) northwest of Panormos Bay, 37003 Adrina 📞 24240/23371 or 24240/23373 📠 24240/23372 🌐 www.adrina.gr 🛏 45 rooms, 10 suites ⚂ Restaurant, snack bar, refrigerators, pool, gym, massage, beach, bar, playground 🖃 AE, DC, MC, V ⊗ Closed Nov.–Apr. ⦿❘ BP.

$ 🏨 **Panormos Beach.** The owner's attention to detail shows in the beautifully tended flower garden, the immaculate rooms with pine furniture and handwoven linens, the country dining room, and the entrance case displaying his grandmother's elaborate costume. The lobby even looks like a little museum decorated with antiques and traditional clothes. This exceptionally peaceful hotel is a five-minute walk from the beach. ⊠ Beachfront, 37003 📞 24240/22711 📠 24240/23366 🌐 www.panormosbeach-hotel.gr 🛏 34 rooms ⚂ Snack bar, refrigerators; no room TVs 🖃 No credit cards ⊗ Closed Nov.–Apr.

Elios

Έλιος

❽ 10 km (6 mi) north of Panormos Bay, 25 km (16 mi) west of Skopelos town.

Residents of Klima who were dislodged in 1965 by the same earthquake that devastated Alonissos now live here. The origin of its name is more intriguing than the village: legend has it that when St. Reginos arrived in the 4th century to save the island from a dragon that fed on humans, he demanded, "Well, where in *eleos* (God's mercy) is the beast?"

Klima (⊠ 3 km [2 mi] north of Elios) means "ladder," and in this village Kato (Lower) Klima leads to Ano (Upper) Klima, clinging to the mountainside. Some houses destroyed in the 1965 earthquake have not been restored and are still for sale. If you crave an island retreat, this could be your chance.

Where to Stay

$ ▥ **Zanétta.** These simple, peaceful apartments are surrounded by pine trees and close to the sea. Two-bedroom apartments host four people and the three bedrooms can accommodate six. The white hotel with yellow trim and red barrel-tile roof is about a five-minute walk from the water. ⊠ *Hovolo Beach, 37005* ☎ *24240/33140* 🖷 *24240/33717* ⊕ *www.skopelosweb.gr/zanetta* 🛏 *16 apartments* ♨ *Snack bar, kitchens, tennis court, pool* 🖃 *MC, V* ⊗ *Closed Nov.–Apr.*

> **en route** | **Loutraki** is the tiny port village where the ferries and hydrofoils stop to and from Skiathos, and it is not very charming. Three hundred yards from the port are the remains of the **acropolis of Selinous,** the island's third ancient city. Unfortunately, everything lies buried except the walls.

Glossa

Γχώσσα

❾ *38 km (23 mi) northwest of Skopelos town, 14 km (8 mi) northwest of Elios, 3 km (1½ mi) northwest of Klima.*

Delightful Glossa is the island's second-largest settlement, where whitewashed, red-roof houses are clustered on the steep hillside above the harbor of Loutraki. Venetian towers and traces of Turkish influence remain; the center is closed to traffic. This is a place to relax, dine, and enjoy the quieter beaches. Just to the east, have a look at Ayios Ioannis monastery, dramatically perched above a pretty beach. There's no need to tackle the series of extremely steep steps to the monastery, as it is not open to visitors.

Where to Eat

★ ¢–$ ✕ **Restaurant Agnanti.** If in Glossa, make time to stop at this restaurant in a beautifully restored home. With breathtaking views of the sea below, creative dishes, and reasonable prices, the restaurant has stayed true to the spirit that first gave it its renown. Fresh produce and local wines underscore the high quality. Begin with a sun-dried tomato-and-smoked-cheese salad, and move on to the lemon chicken, pork with plums, or goat in a tomato sauce. ⊠ *Above bus stop, on left side of Agiou Riginou* ☎ *24240/33076* 🖃 *MC, V* ⊗ *Closed Nov.–Apr.*

ALONISSOS

ΑΛΟΝΝΗΣΟΣ

In the clearest waters of the Aegean, Alonissos is the unspoiled Greece. Barter was still the usual method of trade until the late 1960s, when tourism finally catapulted this serene island into the 20th century, sort of. Nature has conspired to keep Alonissos underpopulated and undeveloped. Although the island—once called Evoinos ("good wine")—was famous for its wine in past centuries, the vines were ruined by a phylloxera plague in the 1950s, and many residents left. Rocky terrain prevented construction of an airport, so big-time package tourism never got off the ground. As a relative backwater the island may lack chic beaches and hot nightclubs, but the upside is huge: forest walks, caves, boat trips to islands and nature preserves, and beaches where jet-skiing and parasailing are unknown. There are a few hotels, several rooms to rent, some nice tavernas, and a cheerful laid-back pace. Europeans love it, but most of the tourists and daytrippers are nature lovers rather than party people.

Lush with pine, oak, fruit trees, and mastic and arbutus bushes, hilly Alonissos has small, fertile plains, a steep northwestern coastline, and an east coast with pebbled beaches. The center of the island submerged long ago, perhaps in a cataclysmic earthquake, leaving only islets and a rock called Psathoura. The surrounding islands are some of the last preserves of the endangered monk seal. Of the approximately 500 living monk seals throughout the world, about 10% make their home here, closely monitored by scientists.

Alonissos hardly gets more than a line or two in the history books, and because of its different names—Ikos and Liadromia—researchers find it difficult to trace. Peleus, Achilles' father, once lived on the island; Philip of Macedon coveted it; the Venetians erected a fortress here. Its waters cover dozens of fascinating shipwrecks, not to mention a ruined city or two, but little else is known of its past. While Skiathos and Skopelos were sending merchant fleets to the Black Sea and Egypt in the 18th and early-19th centuries, sailors from Alonissos were probably plundering them. When the Sporades and Greece gained independence, the pirates turned to fishing. Today their descendants are still fishing, farming, and herding sheep.

Most of the 3,000 or so inhabitants (half that in winter) live in and around the port of Patitiri, hurriedly developed to house victims of the 1965 earthquake that devastated the hilltop capital. Many fishing families live in Steni Vala, farther northeast. On a conical hill 600 feet above the port is haunting Old Alonissos, or Chora. Its tiny houses, deserted after the earthquake, have been restored by Athenians and Europeans who bought them for next to nothing and thus are somewhat resented by the resettled villagers in the port areas below. Chora comes to life in summer, but for much of the year it seems almost a ghost town, aside from an occasional cat and a few stalwart year-rounders.

To explore beyond Patitiri and Old Alonissos, you can either rent a motorbike or car, or take a caïque, which can also carry you to the neighboring islets. The roads to the various beaches have fairly decent dirt surfaces. The road from Patitiri to Steni Vala is now paved; north of Steni Vala are virtually no signs of habitation. Roads in the island's interior are just dirt tracks, where hikers, bikers, and shepherds sporadically wend their ways.

Patitiri

Πατητήρι

 11 km (7 mi) southwest of Steni Vala.

Patitiri ("wine press") was once a wine-making center, but today it's the island's main port, set in a pretty cove flanked by white, pine-clad cliffs. Along the diminutive waterfront are tavernas and cafés, a couple of hotels, the boat agency, and a gas station. Most of the buildings are modern and drab, built to house and serve the refugees from Old Alonissos, the half-destroyed old capital up the hill. But the backstreet houses have flower-filled boxes, and the sun twinkling on the blue Aegean keeps things cheery. Nearby, 4 km (2½ mi) north of Patitiri, is Votsi, a tiny harbor set among cliffs—a perfect spot to sit in a taverna, watch the fishing boats come in, and sip ouzo. Some people swim off the rocks there.

Patitiri is the gateway to the **National Marine Park,** which comprises the waters and all the islands (some off-limits to visitors) in the vicinity. The Hellenic Society for the Study and Protection of the Monk Seal is charged with researching and preserving the species. Scientists are always on the lookout for orphans, and they track the mature seals, too. A daylong guided boat tour of the park is a must for nature lovers. While watching for the winsome but elusive monk seals, look for other wildlife, flora, and fauna. Gulls, terns, warblers, falcons, herons, kingfishers, and migrant birds all fill the air at different times of the year. Jellyfish colonies look like bunches of iridescent balloons bobbing with the waves, and groups of playful dolphins love to dive in wakes of boats.

Travel agencies and the tourist office in Patitiri book excursions to the park, or inquire portside; many small boats also make a daily trip. Most day trips, which cost about €45 including lunch, visit Psathoura and Kyra Panayia island and its Byzantine monastery and allow you to swim in Ayios Petros and Ayios Dimitrios Bay. **Albedo Travel** (⇨ Travel Agents *in* The Sporades A to Z) operates a beautiful mahogany motor-sailer called the *Odyssey* a couple of times per week.

Beaches

Pick one of the **beaches** and claim it. The rocky outcroppings and coves throughout the coast are quiet havens tucked among cliffs, and you can easily clamber from rocky ledges to the calm and sparkling turquoise water. Most beaches are on the east coast. As you go north from Patitiri, unpaved roads take you to swimming areas with some facilities, including **Hrysi Milia, Kokkinokastro, Tzórtzi, Yialo,** and, farther north, **Aglos Dimitrios,** a nudist beach. At the tip of Alonissos, the deserted beach at **Gerakas** is good for snorkeling.

Accessible by water taxi from Patitiri, **Kalamakia** is on a picturesque stretch of Alonissos's eastern coast. There's not much of a beach here, but there are a couple of the island's best fish restaurants. At **Margarita** (☎ 24240/ 65738 ☉ Closed Oct.–Apr.), the morning catches come off the boat docked in front. Choose your fish from the refrigerated case and have it weighed and priced before you order.

| off the |
| beaten |
| path |

ISLETS – Surrounding Alonissos and reachable by authorized taxi or tour boats leaving from Patitiri, the small islands are special for many reasons; excursions to them can also be arranged from Skiathos or Skopelos. **Peristera** ("pigeon") is the closest. It has a tiny shepherd population, the ruins of a castle, and a few delightful sandy beaches that the caïques buzz along. Southeast is **Skantzoura,** which has marble beaches, a monastery, and the submerged ruins of the ancient town of Skandyle. Bring binoculars, and if you're lucky you may spot an Eleanora falcon or a rare Aegean seagull with white wings and a black hood. The biggest in the island group is **Kyra Panayia** (Pelagos), which has sometimes been identified as ancient Alonissos. Here, too, there is a monastery (16th century) and traces of a Neolithic settlement. Its two bays, Planitis and Ayios Petros, are often filled with flotillas—groups of yachts usually chartered by visitors.

Yioura, to the northeast, was once used as a place of exile for undesirable politicos. Unusual flora and a rare species of wild goat thrive here, and the most impressive of the island's caves, crammed with colorful stalactites and stalagmites, is said to be where Homer's Cyclops lived. Recent excavations show remains from 3000 BC, including pottery and hooks made of bone. This local civilization is not found in any other part of Greece. Excavations were going on at this writing—check if the cave is open. **Psathoura,** the most northerly of the Sporades, has a 26-meter (85-ft) lighthouse built in 1895; it is said to have the brightest beacon in the Aegean, and for good reason. The islet is so low in the water it can hardly be seen until you're on top of it. Near its harbor are the ruins of yet another sunken city—perhaps ancient Ikos?

Where to Stay & Eat

$–$$$ ✕ **Argo.** In this quiet restaurant, set in a garden on a cliff overlooking the rocky east coast, any meal is a pleasure, but brunch is especially delightful. At dinner the romantic scene is all flowers, tiles, breezes, and, on some nights, moonlight, sparkling silver on the Aegean. While the menu changes daily, there is always tasty fresh fish and lobster (€80). ⊠ *Next to Paradise Hotel* ☎ *24240/65141* 🖃 *AE, DC, MC, V* ☺ *Closed Nov.–Apr.*

¢–$ ✕ **Flisvos.** Outdoor tables sit across the road from the restaurant, under a shady awning next to the water. A waiter may well sit down at your table to help you decide what to order—the swordfish souvlaki is delicious, as is *tiropita alonnisou* (a deep-fried cheese pie formed of swirls of pastry). Freshly made pizza and pasta add an Italian accent to the usual taverna food. It's open at 7 AM—a rarity here—and is a great place to wait for a boat. ⊠ *Agora at the waterfront* ☎ *24240/65307* 🖃 *No credit cards* ☺ *Closed Oct.–May.*

$ ✕ **To Kamaki.** Locals love this basic ouzeri, renowned for its fresh calamari, baked mussels, shrimp or tuna salads, and large portions of assorted seafood appetizers. June to August the boats leave a daily haul of fish and shellfish. Outdoor tables beckon, but the one drawback is

a stream of motorbikes going by out front. ✉ *Ikion Dolopon* ☎ *24240/
65245* ▤ *MC, V* ⊘ *Closed Nov.–Mar.*

$ ⊞ **Haravgi.** You can watch harbor comings and goings from the balconies
of this simple, clean, convenient hotel set in a garden and near swimming areas and tavernas. All the rooms share the spectacular view of
the sparkling waters below. ✉ *On waterfront, 37005* ☎ *24240/65090*
🛏 *24240/65189* ⤹ *18 rooms* ⚖ *Café, refrigerators, bar; no room
phones* ▤ *No credit cards* ⊘ *Closed Nov.–Apr.* ⦿ *BP.*

★ $ ⊞ **Paradise Hotel.** Although the rooms and balconies here are small and
simple, the hotel's view of the sea is breathtaking and the flower garden, set amid pines and rocks, is lovely. Guests often hang out at the
friendly bar or shady terrace beside the sparkling pool, or walk down
a flight of stairs to swim in secluded coves. ✉ *Above port, 37005*
☎ *24240/65160 or 24240/65213* 🛏 *24240/65161* ⊕ *www.paradise-
hotel.gr* ⤹ *31 rooms* ⚖ *Fans, pool, wading pool, bar; no a/c, no room
TVs* ▤ *MC, V* ⊘ *Closed mid-Oct.–Apr.* ⦿ *CP.*

Nightlife

Surprisingly, Alonissos has lots of little bars and cafés, some with live
music. When you get here ask the locals which is best at the moment.
Cactus Bar (✉ South side of harbor ☎ 24240/66054) serves cocktails,
coffee, and sweets and has an excellent location on the waterfront, with
a candlelit terrace and magical view of the port's bobbing boats and illuminated rocks. **To Koutouki** (✉ Top of town, near National Bank
☎ 24240/65832) offers live traditional music and dancing.

The Outdoors

You can take any number of fascinating walks and hikes on Alonissos:
into Old Alonissos, through the countryside around Patitiri, past seaside fishing villages onto secluded beaches, among hilltop monastery
settlements, through forests, and along the rocky, remote terrain.
Albedo Travel employs expert English-speaking guides to lead hiking
trips in summer; a number include boat trips, lunch, and the chance to
swim. You can also travel to the National Marine Park on a chartered
boat tour; they are offered roughly four times per week in summer. Information is also available at Albedo Travel (⇨ Travel Agents *in* The
Sporades A to Z).

Old Alonissos (Chora)

Παλιά Αλόννησος (Χώρα)

❶ *3 km (2 mi) west of Patitiri.*

FodorsChoice
★

Despite its still-ravaged state, in many ways this traditional village,
which was once the island capital, is the most spectacular in all the Sporades. The destruction caused by the 1965 earthquake has not all been
repaired. The government moved villagers to the harbor area, and today
Old Alonissos has been repopulated by Europeans (mostly English and
German) who cherish its beauty. The original town dates from the 10th
century, when the population sought safety above the sea. Ruins of walls
from the 15th-century Byzantine-Venetian fortress still crown the peak,

and the little chapel called Tou Christou, with a fish-scale roof, is especially charming.

The town seems frozen in time, its scale intimate and compelling. (Indeed, until the earthquake, all goods were hauled up by mule.) Narrow cobblestone paths are lined with whitewashed stone buildings hung with ornate, colorfully painted wooden balconies dripping with vines. Wildflowers turn cracks into beauty spots, and old pots stand guard by ancient doorways. Each corner offers quirky angles, sharp shadows in the sunshine, and glimpses of blue sea beyond as you navigate the mud and stone streets.

At the top of Old Alonissos is a 360-degree view of the Aegean, cove beaches set within cliffs, and medieval watchtowers, and on the clearest days you can see as far as Mt. Olympus in northern Greece, 177 km (110 mi) away. A few charming restaurants, a couple of transient boutiques, and a tiny museum, midway in the maze of buildings, make up the tourist attractions. In addition, in a small plaza is a memorial to 11 Greek patriots executed by Germans in World War II.

To contemplate it all, you might decide to stay here rather than in the port below. If you can't hack the steep 25-minute hike up the ecological trail from Patitiri to Old Alonissos—through forest, fields of mustard and poppies, lemon orchards, and olive groves—you can forego the exercise and take the island's single bus or a taxi.

Where to Stay & Eat

¢–$$ ✕ **Astrofengia.** At this restored family house you can enjoy a delightful garden and the stunning view (the name means "starlight"). From the varied, innovative menu choose one of the many organic salads, the three-cheese pie, or the tasty hummus. ⊠ *Before entrance to Old Alonissos, take path to left as soon as you get off bus* ☎ *24240/65182* ▤ *No credit cards* ⊘ *Closed Oct.–May. No lunch.*

¢ ▥ **Fantasia House.** This simple inn is centrally located near the bus and taxi stops, which means you don't have to hike all the way up steep alleys to get a good night's sleep. The studio rooms are clean and comfortable, and all have views of the sea, which shimmers far below. ⊠ *On main street, 37005* ☎ *24240/65186* ⇥ *10 rooms* ♨ *No a/c, no room phones, no room TVs* ▤ *No credit cards* ⊘ *Closed Nov.–Apr.*

Shopping

A number of small shops have mushroomed throughout the old town of Alonissos, particularly in the Kastro area. Tourist shops generally close in the off-season, except in the rare instance that the owners are local. The only stores likely to stay open year-round are food shops operated by islanders. Call ahead to confirm a shop is open.

The most interesting shop in town is **Gorgona** (⊠ Old Town ☎ 24240/66108), with three floors of antiques from throughout Greece, as well as handmade jewelry. Owner-architect Elma Bezou also rents out traditional houses in the old town. **Hyronax** (⊠ Old Town ☎ 24240/66287) sells traditional clothes and gifts, including silver and gold jewelry.

Milia

Μηλιά

12 *3 km (2 mi) northeast of Chora.*

This charming, secluded area of Alonissos has a number of little swimming coves offering varying degrees of privacy. At **Kokkinokastro** (⊠ 2 km [1 mi] northeast of Milia), where the red cliffs and pebble beach contrast with the surrounding pines and water, you can find traces of an acropolis—shards, tombs, walls—as well as a Ghisi fortress. Some experts think Kokkinokastro was also the site of the ancient city of Ikos.

Where to Stay

$$–$$$ ⌸ **Milia-Bay.** You might have thought that hotels of this class no longer
Fodor's Choice exist, but intimate, friendly Milia-Bay is individually attentive to guest needs.
★ Self-catering villa-apartments face the sea, placing you close to uninhabited islands and spectacular marine life. Red-clay tile floors are offset by wood furnishings and crisp white-and-blue striped upholstery. A pool bar, where a homemade snack or dish of the day is available, adds to the sense of serenity. On a clear day you can see all the way to Skyros. ⊠ *Above Milia beach, 37005* ☎ *24240/66032 or 24240/66035, 210/895–0794 in Athens* 🖷 *24240/66037, 210/895–3591 in Athens* ⊕ *www.milia-bay.gr* 🗨 *6 studios, 9 one-bedroom apartments, 4 two-bedroom apartments* ⚐ *Kitchenettes, cable TV, pool, bar* ⊟ *MC, V* ⊙ *Closed Nov.–Mar.*

Steni Vala

Στενή Βάλα

13 *3 km (2 mi) northeast of Kokkinokastro.*

A tiny fishing village, Steni Vala is flanked by two beautiful beaches and is the headquarters of the Hellenic Society for the Study and Protection of the Monk Seal (not open to the public). The town can be reached by car or boat, and there are wonderful walking trails leading from the town that afford spectacular views of the islands of Peristera and Adelfia. Steni Vala has a few good tavernas and shops selling traditional handicrafts.

Where to Eat

$$$ ✕ **Steni Vala.** Seafood served here is caught daily by the owner in nearby waters. Fresh catches may include mackerel, blacktail, mullet, cod fish, and lobster. The Greek specialties, such as cheese pie, are great, too. Sit overlooking the fjordlike harbor from the terrace or in the large dining room. This is a great place to eat before or after a day on the water, as it lies within easy walking distance of terrific beaches. ⊠ *Harborside* ☎ *24240/65590* ⊟ *MC, V* ⊙ *Closed Nov.–Apr.*

SKYROS

ΣΚΥΡΟΣ

Even among these unique isles, Skyros stands out. Its rugged terrain looks like a Dodecanese island, and its main town, occupied on and off for the last 3,300 years and filled with mythical ghosts, looks Cycladic. It has military bases, and an airport with periodic connections to Athens, yet it remains the most difficult ferry connection in the Sporades. With nothing between it and Lesbos, off the coast of Turkey, its nearest neighbor is the town of Kimi, on the east coast of Evia.

Surprisingly beguiling, this southernmost of the Sporades is the largest (209 square km [81 square mi]). A narrow, flat isthmus connects Skyros's two almost equal parts, whose names reflect their characters—*Meri* or *Imero* ("tame") for the north, and *Vouno* (literally, "mountain," meaning tough or stony) for the south. The heavily populated north is virtually all farmland and forests. The southern half of the island is forbidding, barren, and mountainous, with Mt. Kochilas its highest peak (2,598 feet). Its western coast is outlined with coves and deep bays dotted with a series of islets.

Skyros has a role in the legends of the *Iliad:* before the Trojan War, Theseus, the deposed hero-king of Athens, sought refuge in his ancestral estate on Skyros. King Lykomedes, afraid of the power and prestige of Theseus, took him up to the acropolis one evening, pretending to show him the island, and pushed him over the cliff—an ignominious end. In ancient times, Timon of Athens unearthed what he said were Theseus's bones and sword, and placed them in the Theseion—more commonly called the Temple of Hephaistion—in Athens, in what must be one of the earliest recorded archaeological investigations.

Until Greece won independence in 1831, the population of Skyros squeezed sardine-fashion into the area under the castle on the inland face of the rock. Not a single house was visible from the sea. Though the islanders could survey any movement in the Aegean for miles, they kept a low profile, living in dread of the pirates based at Treis Boukes bay on Vouno.

Strangely enough, although the island is adrift in the Aegean, the Skyrians have not had a seafaring tradition, and they have looked to the land for their living. Their isolation has brought about notable cultural differences from the other Greek islands, such as pre-Christian Carnival rituals. Today there are more than 300 churches on the island, many of them private and owned by local families. An almost-extinct breed of pony resides on Skyros, and exceptional crafts—carpentry, pottery, embroidery—are practiced by dedicated artisans whose creations include unique furniture and decorative linens. There are no luxury accommodations or swank restaurants: this idiosyncratic island makes no provisions for mass tourism, but if you've a taste for the offbeat, you may feel right at home.

Skyros Town

Σκύρος (Χωριό)

▶ **14** *10 km (6 mi) north of Linaria.*

Fodor'sChoice ★

As you drive south from the airport, past brown, desolate outcroppings with only an occasional goat as a sign of life, Skyros town suddenly looms around a bend. It resembles a breathtaking imaginary painting by Monet,

Cézanne, or El Greco: blazing white, cubist, dense, and otherworldly, cling-ing, precariously it seems, to the precipitous rock beneath it and topped gloriously by a fortress-monastery. This town more closely resembles a village in the Cyclades than any other you'll find in the Sporades.

Called *Horio, Hora,* and *Chora* ("town") by the locals, Skyros town is home to 90% of the island's 3,000 inhabitants. The impression as you get closer is of stark, simple buildings creeping up the hillside, with a tangle of labyrinthine lanes winding up, down, and around the tiny houses, Byzantine churches, and big squares. As you stroll down from the ruins and churches of the Kastro area, or explore the alleyways off the main drag, try to peek discreetly into the houses. Skyrians are house-proud and often leave their windows and doors open to show off. In fact, since the houses all have the same exteriors, the only way for families to dis-tinguish themselves has been through interior design. Walls and coni-cal mantelpieces are richly decorated with European- and Asian-style porcelain, copper cooking utensils, wood carvings, and embroideries. Wealthy families originally obtained much of the porcelain from the pi-rates in exchange for grain and food, and its possession was a measure of social standing. Then enterprising potters started making exact copies, along with the traditional local ware, leading to the unique Skyrian style of pottery. The furniture is equally beautiful, and often miniature in order to conserve interior space.

Farther up the hill, the summit is crowned with three tiny cubelike churches with blue and pink interiors, and the ruined Venetian cistern, once used as a dungeon. From there you have a spectacular view of the town and surrounding hills. The roofs are flat, the older ones covered with a dark gray shale that has splendid insulating properties. The house walls and roofs are interconnected, forming a pattern that from above looks like a magnified form of cuneiform writing. Here and there the shieldlike roof of a church stands out from the cubist composition of white houses that fills the hillside—with not an inch to spare.

Most commercial activity takes place in or near Agora (the market street), familiarly known as Sisifos, as in the myth, because of its frus-trating steepness. Found here are the town's pharmacies, travel agen-cies, shops with wonderful Skyrian pottery, and an extraordinary number of tiny bars and tavernas but few boutiques and even less kitsch. In the summer heat, all shops and restaurants close from 2 PM to 6 PM, but the town comes alive at night.

The **Apokries,** pre-Lenten Carnival revelry, on Skyros relates to pre-Chris-tian fertility rites and is famous throughout Greece. Young men dressed as old men, maidens, or "Europeans" roam the streets teasing and tor-menting onlookers with ribald songs and clanging bells. The "old men" wear elaborate shepherd's outfits, with masks made of baby-goat hides and belts dangling with as many as 40 sheep bells.

The best way to get an idea of the town and its history is to follow the sinuous cobbled lanes past the mansions of the old town to the *kastro,* the highest point, and the 10th-century fortified **Monastery of St. George,** which stands on the site of the ancient acropolis and Bronze Age settlement. Little remains of the legendary fortress of King Lykomedes, portrayed in Skyros's two most colorful myths, though lower down on the north and southwest face of the rock are the so-called Pelasgian bastions of immense rectangular fitted blocks, dated to the classical period or later.

A white marble lion, which may be left over from the Venetian occupation, is in the wall above the entrance to the monastery. This classical symbol is a reminder of when Skyros was under Athenian dominion and heavily populated with Athenian settlers to keep it that way. This part of the castle was built on ancient foundations (look right) during the early Byzantine era and reinforced in the 14th century by the Venetians. The monastery itself was founded in 962 and radically rebuilt in 1600. Today it is inhabited by a sole monk.

Unfortunately, the once splendid frescoes of the Monastery of St. George are now mostly covered by layers of whitewash, but look for the charming St. George and startled dragon outside to the left of the church door. Within, the ornate iconostasis is considered a masterpiece. The icon of St. George on the right is said to have been brought by settlers from Constantinople, who came in waves during the Iconoclast Controversy of the 9th century. The icon has a black face and is familiarly known as Ayios Georgis o Arapis ("the Negro"); the Skyrians view him as the patron saint not only of their island but of lovers as well. ⊠ *1 km (½ mi) above waterfront.*

Take the vaulted passageway from the St. George's Monastery courtyard to the ruined church of **Episkopi**, the former seat of the bishop of Skyros, built in 895 on the ruins of a temple of Athena. This was the center of Skyros's religious life from 1453 to 1837. You can continue up to the summit from here. ⊠ *Above St. George's Monastery.*

The tiny **archaeological museum** (on the way to Magazia beach as you begin to descend from the town) contains finds, mostly from graves dating from Neolithic to Roman times. Weapons, pottery, and jewelry are represented. ⊠ *Pl. Rupert Brooke (at far end of Sisifos)* ☎ 22220/91327 ▭ €2 ☉ *Tues.–Sun. 8:30–3.*

★ The **Faltaits Historical and Folklore Museum** has an outstanding collection of Skyrian decorative arts. Built after independence by a wealthy family that still owns it, the house is far larger than the usual Skyros dwelling, and it's almost overflowing with rare books, costumes, photographs, paintings, ceramics, local embroideries, Greek statues, and other heirlooms. The embroideries are noted for their flamboyant colors and vivacious renderings of mermaids, hoopoes (the Skyrians' favorite bird), and human figures whose clothes and limbs sprout flowers. A hand-written copy of the Proclamation of the Greek Revolution against the Ottoman empire is among the museum's historical documents. The informative guided tour is well worth the extra euros. ⊠ *Pl. Rupert Brooke* ☎ 2222/091232 ▭ €2, tour €5 ☉ *Daily 10–2 and 6–9.*

It'd be hard to miss the classical bronze statue, *To Brook,* dedicated to the English poet Rupert Brooke. Every street seems to lead either to it or to the Kastro, and the statue stands alone with a 180-degree view of the sea behind it. In 1915, Brooke was 28, on his way to the Dardanelles to fight in World War I when he died of septicemia on a French hospital ship off Skyros. Brooke was a socialist, but he became something of a paragon for war leaders such as Churchill. ⊠ *Pl. Rupert Brooke.*

Beaches

Around the northern end of the island is a dirt road to **Theotokos** (⊠ 15 km [9 mi] northwest of Skyros town). The large Greek air base near the northern tip of the beach is off-limits.

Where to Stay & Eat

¢–$$ ✕ **Margetis Taverna.** A vest-pocket taverna wedged in among shops on the main drag, Margetis is known locally as the best place for fish on the island. It's popular, so get there early (8–8:30). Though fish and lobster are always pricey, they are worth it here, as is the roast pork loin, lamb, or goat chops. Try the flavorful barrel wine, sit outside under the big tree, and watch the folks walk by. ⊠ *Agora* ☎ 22220/91311 ⊟ *No credit cards* ⊘ *No lunch.*

★ ¢–$ ✕ **Papous Ki'Ego.** "My Grandfather and I," as the name translates in English, serves terrific Greek cuisine in an eclectic dining room decorated with hanging spoons, bottles of wine and ouzo, and whole heads of garlic. The proud grandson suggests that diners order a selection of mezedes and share with others at the table. The best include fried pumpkins with yogurt, *tzatziki* (garlic dip), zucchini croquettes, and meatballs doused with ouzo and served flambé. If you want a single dish, the baby goat served as a casserole tastes delicious. ⊠ *Agora* ☎ 22220/93200 ⊟ *MC, V* ⊘ *Closed Nov. and Dec. No lunch.*

$$–$$$ ✕▥ **Nefeli.** This superb little hotel is decorated in Cycladic white and soft green trim, with a brilliant sparkling pool and elegant bar terrace. The three buildings reflect unique styles, including modern, traditional, and antique, and the guest rooms have handsome furniture and sophisticated amenities. The suites come with hydro-massage baths. Nefeli's restaurant ($–$$) serves organic food from its own Skyros farm, with outstanding service; breakfast is served à la carte. The hotel lies about a five-minute walk from the town center and the beach. ⊠ *Plageiá, 34007* ☎ 22220/91964 🖷 22220/92061 ⊕ *www.skyros-nefeli.gr* ⇆ 4 *apartments, 7 studios, 8 rooms, 2 suites* ⚐ *Restaurant, room service, some kitchens, minibars, cable TV, saltwater pool, bar, playground, laundry services* ⊟ *AE, DC, MC, V.*

Nightlife

Skyros town's bars are seasonal affairs, offering loud music in summer. **Apokalypsis** (⊠ Next to post office) plays hits from the '60s and '70s. **Calypso** (⊠ Agora) is the oldest bar-club and plays mostly jazz and blues. **Stone** (⊠ South of Skyros town) is popular with the disco crowd.

Shopping

Want to buy something really unusual for a shoe lover? Check out the multithonged *trohadia*, worn along with pantaloons by Skyrian men as part of their traditional costume. Skyrian pottery is both utilitarian and decorative. Although you will see it all over town, the best places to shop are all on Agora. Skyrian furniture can be shipped anywhere.

Tourist shops generally close in the off-season, except in the rare instance that the owners are local. The only stores likely to stay open year-round are food shops operated by islanders. Call ahead to confirm a shop is open.

CLOTHING You can find the conversation-stopping trohadia at the **Argo Shop** (⊠ Off Pl. Rupert Brooke ☏ No phone).

FURNITURE The workshop of **Lefteris Avgoklouris** (⊠ About 100 yds from Pl. Rupert Brooke on right side of road heading down hill ☏ 22220/91106), a carpenter with flair, is open to visitors. Ask around to find other master carpenters and craftspersons who make original furniture and other artistic handicrafts.

POTTERY The best store selling Skyrian handmade ceramics and imports is **Srgastiri** (⊠ Agora ☏ 22220/91559).

Magazia & Molos

Μαγαζιά & Μώλος

⑮ *1 km (½ mi) northeast of Skyros town.*

Coastal expansions of the main town, these two resort areas are the place to stay if you love to swim. Magazia, where the residents of Horio used to have their storehouses and wine presses, and Molos, a bit farther north, where the small fishing fleet anchors, are both growing fast. You can sunbathe, explore the isolated coastline, and stop at sea caves for a swim. Nearby are rooms to rent and tavernas serving the day's catch and local wine. From here, Skyros town is only 15 minutes away, along the steps that lead past the archaeological museum to Platia Rupert Brooke.

At the August 15 **Panayia** (Festival of the Virgin) on the beach at Magazia, children race on the island's domesticated small ponies, similar to Shetland ponies.

Beaches

From **Molos** to **Magazia** is a long, sandy beach. A short walk south of Magazia, **Pourias** offers good snorkeling, and nearby on the cape is a small treasure: a sea cave turned into a chapel. North of Molos, past low hills, fertile fields, and the odd farmhouse, a dirt road leads to the beach at **Palamari.**

Where to Stay

$–$$ ⊡ **Skiros Palace.** With a big freshwater pool and a gorgeous, isolated beach, this is a water lover's dream. Separate white, low-rise cubist buildings have arched windows and flat roofs. Rooms decorated with traditional Aegean furnishings offer simple wood beds, chairs, desks, and verandas; upstairs rooms also have air-conditioning. The hotel offers breakfast for an additional charge. ⊠ *North of Molos, 34007 Girismata* ☏ *22220/91994 or 22220/92212* ☏ *22220/92070* ⊕ *www.skiros-palace.gr* ⊅ *80 rooms* ⬧ *Restaurant, cafeteria, refrigerators, pool, beach, no-smoking rooms; no a/c in some rooms, no room TVs* ▤ *AE, MC, V* ☉ *Closed Oct.–June.*

¢–$ ⊡ **Paliopirgos Hotel.** Just above Magazia, the small Cycladic-style hotel bathed in white boasts stunning views of the blue-green water below.

Maria Makris is the perfect host at breakfast (provided for an additional charge) in the roof garden; in the evening, sip a cocktail in the same spot, and watch the sun set and the moon rise. Rooms at this intimate hotel are pristinely decorated, each with a small, well-equipped kitchen area, a single and double bed, and a balcony with a sea view. It's a five-minute walk to both the beach at Magazia and the town center. ✉ *Beachfront, 37007 Magazia* ☎ *22220/91014 or 22220/92964* 🖷 *22220/92185* ⌨ *9 rooms* ♢ *Bar, kitchenettes* ▤ *MC, V* ☾ *Closed Nov.–Mar.*

Nightlife

For late-night dancing, the best club is **Skiropoulo** (✉ On beach before Magazia ☎ No phone ☾ Closed Oct.–Apr.). Music is Western at first and, later on, Greek. A laser lighting system illuminates the rocks of the acropolis after the sun has gone down. The club can be reached from Platia Rupert Brooke by descending the steps past the archaeological museum.

Atsitsa

Ατσίτσα

🔟 *14 km (9 mi) west of Molos.*

On the northwest coast, pine forests grow down the rocky shore at Atsitsa. The beaches north of town—Kalogriá and Kyra Panayia—are sheltered from the strong northern winds called the *meltemi.*

On July 27, the chapel of **Ayios Panteleimon** (✉ On dirt road south of Atsitsa) holds a festival in honor of its patron saint.

Skyros Centre was founded in 1978 in this remote area. It was the first and remains the foremost center for holistic vacations. Participants come for a two-week session and can take part in activities as diverse as windsurfing, creative writing with well-known authors, art, tai chi, yoga, massage, dance, drama, and psychotherapy. Courses also take place in Skyros town, where participants live in rooms in villagers' houses. Skyros's courses are highly reputed. Contact the London office well in advance of leaving for Greece. ✉ *Atsitsa coast* ⌂ *Prince of Wales Rd. 92, London NW5 3NE, U.K.* ☎ *207/267–4424 or 207/284–3065* 🖷 *207/284–3063* 🌐 *www.skyros.co.uk.*

The Outdoors

Experienced hikers can take the 6-km (4-mi) walk around the headland from Atsitsa to Ayios Fokas, but the trek takes skill to negotiate at times and can be hazardous in bad weather.

Ayios Fokas

Άγιος Φωκάς

🔢 *5 km (3 mi) south of Atsitsa, 12 km (8 mi) west of Skyros town.*

The road south from Atsitsa deteriorates into a rutted track, nerve-wracking even for experienced motorbike riders. At Ayios Fokas there are three lovely white-pebbled beaches and a small taverna where Kyria Kali serves her husband's just-caught fish with her own vegetables, homemade cheese, and bread. She also rents out a couple of very basic rooms without electricity or plumbing.

Beaches
The **beaches** south of Ayios Fokas are most accessible from the Linaria–Horio main road. South of **Pefko** the dirt road becomes smooth and paved again.

Linaria

Λιναριά

⑱ *8 km (5 mi) southeast of Ayios Fokas, 10 km (6 mi) south of Skyros town, 40 km (25 mi) northeast of Kimi on Evia by boat.*

All boats and hydrofoils to Skyros dock at the tiny port of Linaria because the northeast coast is either straight, sandy beach, or steep cliffs. A bus to Skyros town meets arrivals. To get to the otherwise inaccessible sea caves of Pentekáli and Diatryptí, you can take a caïque from here. This dusty area offers scenes of fishermen tending their bright-yellow nets and not much more.

Vouno

Βουνό

⑲ *Via Loutro, 5 km (3 mi) northwest of Linaria; access to southern territory starts at Ahilli, 4 km (2½ mi) south of Skyros town.*

In the mountainous southern half of Skyros, a passable dirt road heads south at the eastern end of the isthmus, from Aspous to Ahilli. The little Bay of Ahilli (from where legendary Achilles set sail with Odysseus) is a yacht marina. Some beautiful, practically untouched beaches and sea caves are well worth the trip for hard-core explorers.

Thorny bushes warped into weird shapes, oleander, and rivulets running between sharp rocks make up the landscape; only goats and rare Skyrian ponies can survive this desolate environment. Many scholars consider the beautifully proportioned, diminutive horses to be the same breed as the horses sculpted on the Parthenon frieze. They are, alas, an endangered species, and only about 100 survive.

Pilgrims to **Rupert Brooke's grave** should follow the wide dirt road through the Vouno wilderness down toward the shore. As you reach the valley, you can catch sight of the grave in an olive grove on your left. He was buried the same night he died on Skyros, and his marble grave was immortalized with his prescient words, "If I should die think only this of me:/ That there's some corner of a foreign field/ That is forever England." Restored by the British Royal Navy in 1961, the grave site is surrounded by a stout wrought-iron and cement railing. You also can arrange for a visit by taxi or caïque in Skyros town.

Beaches
The beach of **Kalamitsa** is 4 km (2½ mi) along the road south from Ahilli. Three tavernas are at this old harbor. The inviting, deserted **Kolymbada** beach is 5 km (3 mi) south of Kalamitsa.

EVIA

EYBOIA

► In any other country, an island as large and beautiful as Evia would be a prime tourist attraction. Yet it is often ignored by travelers to Greece, who tend to think of it not as an island but a suburb, as it is only 80 km (50 mi) north of Athens. Athenian day-trippers and weekenders do crowd in, ironically, to get away from crowds back home. Lying to the south and west of the Sporades, and connected to the almost contiguous mainland by bridge and frequent ferry service, Evia is the second-largest island in the country, after Crete. It has sandy beaches, fertile valleys, wooded mountains, and some pretty villages—just what tourists think of as pleasantly Greek.

Long and narrow, with mountains running north to south, the island has good roads and varied terrain, with steep cliffs in the east and beach resorts in the west. Some towns along the main route are touristed and commercialized, while others, off the beaten track, remain peaceful and basically unchanged. A tour of the highlights of Evia could be done in a couple of days, as an easy island getaway from Athens, by ferry or car. This tour begins in Karystos in the south, one of the ferry and hydrofoil ports, and ends in the north coast, characterized by fishing villages and miniresorts; you may also start where the boats port (in Marmari, Eretria, Kimi, Aedipsos) or you can cross the bridge to and from the mainland at Halkidha.

Karystos

Κάρυστος

90 km (56 mi) southeast of Halkidha.

In a valley below Mt. Ochi on the Karystian Bay, Karystos is one of the most popular southeastern resorts in Evia, a one-hour boat ride from the mainland port of Rafina. This neoclassical town was designed in a grid pattern by a Bavarian architect named Bierbach, commissioned by King Otho. Ancient ruins are scattered through the area, and a Byzantine church is worth visiting. On the coast below Karystos are beaches; tucked among them is the lighthouse that marks the Cava d'Oro, the strait between Evia and Andros.

Explore the remains of a 14th-century Venetian castle called the **Bourtzi** (⊠ Near Karystos harbor). Its walls were filled with marble quarried near here, confiscated from an earlier temple to Apollo.

The russet ruins of a 14th-century Franco-Turkish fortress were built with the colorful stone that gave the town its earlier name, **Castel Rosso** (⊠ 4 km [2½ mi] northeast of Karystos, Myli). An aqueduct behind it once carried spring water by tunnel to the Bourtzi.

To climb the 4,610-foot **Mt. Ochi** (⊠ 4 km [2½ mi] northeast of Karystos, Myli), take the path from Myli in the lush slopes above the town to the bizarre half-hewn marble columns lying like felled logs among the rocks. Near the summit is a structure called the Dragon's House, thought to be a temple of Hera. The mountain was a quarry site in the Roman era, and the Dragon's House, which is unlike anything Greek, may have been erected by workers from Asia Minor.

Where to Stay & Eat

¢ ✕ **Kavo d'Oro.** The Gold Cave taverna has outdoor dining and local wine to go along with the hearty home-style Greek meals. Try meat stews, vegetables cooked in olive oil, great stuffed grape leaves, and freshly cooked eggplant. ☒ *Parados Sachtouri* ☎ *22240/22326* ▭ *No credit cards* ☉ *Closed Oct.–Dec.*

$-$$ 🏨 **Apollon Suites Hotel.** Shining white and modern throughout, this all-suite hotel's accommodations have separate living areas overlooking palm-studded lawns, a terraced pool, and the beach beyond. For families or friends traveling together, it's an especially good value. ☒ *Beachside, 34001* ☎ *22240/22045 or 22240/22048* 🖷 *22240/22049* ⊕ *www.apollonsuiteshotel.com* ⤵ *36 suites* ⌂ *Restaurant, grocery, kitchens, pool, bar, meeting rooms* ▭ *AE, MC, V* ☉ *Closed Nov.–Mar.* ⎜⊘⎜ *BP.*

Marmari

Μαρμάρι

10 km (6 mi) northwest of Karystos, 80 km (50 mi) southeast of Halkidha.

The port of Marmari, rapidly sprouting mediocre hotels and summer homes, is connected by ferry to Rafina on the mainland. The road north goes inland along the middle of the island, providing glimpses of Frankish watchtowers and bisecting tiny villages inhabited by Greeks of Albanian origin. Their ancestors were brought here forcibly by the Venetians during the 14th century and later by the Turks, to supplement the declining local population. Many still speak their own Greek dialect, and Albanian at home.

en route | **Villages.** On the drive from Marmari to Eretria you pass several interesting hamlets. Stira, set amid streams and forests, has an ancient citadel. Nea Stira, on a bay, has beaches with changing facilities and mysterious, huge blocks of stone. In this wooded area, fossils of prehistoric animals have been discovered. Aliveri, along with Byzantine churches and an old tower, also has a major power plant belching smoke.

Eretria

Ερέτρια

65 km (40 mi) northwest of Marmari, 15 km (9 mi) southeast of Halkidha.

In ancient times Eretria was Evia's second city—a major maritime power, with a school of philosophy, founded in the 3rd century BC by one of Plato's pupils. Today, drab, dusty Eretria is regarded just as a place where people board the 30-minute ferry to the mainland. Neither its interesting ruins nor its jewel of a museum is even signposted.

West of the acropolis are the ruins of a temple, a palace, and Eretria's **ancient theater.** It has two vaulted passageways—one leading to, the other under, the orchestra—no doubt used for deus ex machina effects and spectral apparitions. ⊠ *North of town museum.*

The **museum** amid cypress trees was opened in collaboration with the Swiss School of Archaeology, which is responsible for digging at Eretria. It has beautifully exhibited finds from the area—including magnificent Black Figure vases, ex-votos galore, and children's toys and jewelry. Ask the guard to take you to the **House of the Mosaics,** a five-minute walk away, to view the 4th-century BC treasures. ⊠ *Odos Archaio Theatrou* ☎ *22290/62206* 🖼 *€2* ◷ *Tues.–Sun. 8–3.*

Kimi

Κύμη

40 km (25 mi) northeast of Eretria, 50 km (31 mi) northeast of Halkidha.

Kimi, the ferry port for Skyros, is a fishing village that sits high on a plateau, overlooking its harbor. It has stone houses; a busy main square; pine, fir, and mulberry trees everywhere; and good beaches (follow the secondary roads).

In a traditional house is a charming little **folk museum,** which has displays of memorabilia, costumes, and historical artifacts. Probably the dried-fig capital of Greece, Kimi was once known for its silk production and was an important port in the late 19th century. The museum has a good deal of Victoriana and some diaphanous silk garments. On the first floor you will find photos and documents of George Papanicolaou, the renowned locally born doctor who developed the Pap test technique to detect cervical cancer. ⊠ *On road to port* ☎ *2222/022011* 🖼 *€1.50* ◷ *Daily 10–1 and 6–8:30.*

Where to Eat

¢–$ ✕ **Skyros.** Here, the succulent seafood is dressed simply with lemon. Locals feast on the grilled shrimp and octopus, washed down with local wine. Outside tables overlook the waterfront, and this is a good place to lunch while you wait for your ferry to Skyros. ⊠ *Harborside* ☎ *24240/22624* ▭ *No credit cards* ◷ *Closed Nov.–Apr.*

Halkidha

Χαλκίδα

50 km (31 mi) southwest of Kimi, 90 km (56 mi) northeast of Athens.

Halkidha (Chalkis), Evia's largest town, has been linked by a bridge to the mainland since the 5th century BC. It was a major producer of weaponry, and its metalwork can be seen at Olympia, Delphi, and other ancient sites. Changing direction several times a day, the ocean current that rushes through the 50-yard channel between the mainland and the island perplexes scientists and often confounded travel plans before the bridge was built. Halkidha is still a major commercial center; cement factories blight its southern suburbs. That Orthodox Greeks, Muslims, and Jews live and work together here reflects the importance of Evia on trade routes through the centuries. Though the town may have more urban problems than blessings, the waterfront is a nice place to pass the time if you're waiting for a connecting bus.

off the
beaten
path

STENI – Head 30 km (19 mi) northeast from Halkidha's extended suburbs and look for signs to Steni, a pretty village with clear mountain springs, halfway up Mt. Dirfis, Evia's highest mountain. At 5,725 feet, it's a challenge to hikers, a boon to botanists because of its many unique species, and to ordinary mortals a place of glorious views. You can drive a good way up it. ⊠ *Nearly at end of road from Nea Artaki (just north of Halkidha) to Kambia.*

Where to Stay & Eat

$ ✕ **Tsaf.** Sit in a traditional ouzeri on the main square and try all types of seafood (especially shellfish). The *pikilia* (assorted mezedes) is grandiose, while the *kidonia* oysters are heartily recommended. Accompanied by a drizzle of lemon juice and an ice-cold ouzo, raw clams make the perfect summer meal. ⊠ *Papanastasiou 3* ☎ *22210/80070* 🚭 *No credit cards.*

$$$ 🏨 **Best Western Lucy.** Time has taken its toll, yet the 1950s design of the waterfront promenade's first hotel imbues it with a charm that might qualify as "retro chic." Guest rooms are simple but comfortable, with double beds and small desks; most of them have a panoramic view of the water, the fortress, and Evia's old bridge. ⊠ *Leoferos Voudouri 10, 34100* ☎ *22210/23831 through 22210/23835* 🖷 *22210/22051* ⊕ *www. lucy-hotel.gr* ↩ *80 rooms, 12 suites* ⚑ *Restaurant, minibars, cable TV, bar, meeting rooms, no-smoking rooms* 🚭 *AE, DC, MC, V* ¶❘ *CP.*

en route

On the coast going north from Halkidha, the road runs parallel to a river shaded by enormous plane trees. One of them is so huge it takes 27 men to encircle its trunk.

Aedipsos

Αιδηψός

80 km (50 mi) northwest of Halkidha, 30 km (19 mi) northwest of Limni.

Head to the fishing village of Aedipsos, via the coastal road full of spectacular views, for hot springs that have been soothing aches and pains since antiquity—the likes of Aristotle and Plutarch have sung their praises. Take a whiff of the sulfurous vapors and a peek at the yellow rocks, and then take a dip. There are about 80 springs around Aedipsos with temperatures of 85°F–145°F (29°C–63°C), many of which flow into the sea near public beaches. Of the area therapeutic spas, Thermae Sylla, with state-of-the-art facilities, is the best. Some hotels have the bubbling waters piped right into their private rooms. A ferry departs from Aedipsos and leads to Arkitsa, the National Road, and to Athens.

Where to Stay

$$$–$$$$ 🖼 **Thermae Sylla Spa Wellness Hotel.** Combine the advantages of a health spa and the pleasures of a resort, and you get Thermae Sylla. A mere 50 yards from the beach, the spa emphasizes thalassotherapy, while the two restaurants serve fresh products from the hotel's own farm. Ultimately, what makes this hotel so special is that Aedipsos's noted sulfur springs are set right on the grounds. Enormous rooms soothe you with a neutral and earth-tone palette. ⊠*Beachfront* ⬧*Patision 345B, 111 44 Athens* ☎ *22260/60100, 210/211–0601 in Athens* ⓐ *22660/22055, 210/211–0603 in Athens* ⊕*www.thermaesylla.gr* ⤳*103 rooms, 5 suites* ♿*2 restaurants, pool, wading pool, gym, sauna, spa, windsurfing, parasailing, waterskiing, 4 bars, no-smoking rooms* ☰ *AE, DC, MC, V* ◎*MAP.*

THE SPORADES A TO Z

To research prices, get advice from other travelers, and book travel arrangements, visit www.fodors.com.

AIR TRAVEL

CARRIERS Olympic Airways flies daily in summer to Skiathos from Athens International Airport. The trip takes 50 minutes; the fare is €60 one way. In summer there are also weekly Olympic Airways flights from Athens to Skyros Airport. The flight takes 35 minutes; the fare is €40 one way. Alonissos, Skopelos, and Evia have no air service.

🚹 **Olympic Airways** ☎ 80111/44444 within Greece, 210/966–6666 in Athens ⊕ www. olympicairlines.gr.

AIRPORTS

Skiathos Airport handles direct charter flights from many European cities.
🚹 **Athens International Airport** ⊠ Spata ☎ 210/353–0000. **Skiathos Airport** ⊠ 1 km [½ mi] northeast of Skiathos town ☎ 24270/22049. **Skyros Airport** ⊠ 11 km [7 mi] northwest of Skyros town ☎ 22220/91600.

BOAT & FERRY TRAVEL

Ferry travel to Skiathos, Skopelos, and Alonissos requires that you drive or take a bus to Ayios Konstandinos, located a couple of hours north of Athens near Volos. Altogether, there are at least two or three ferries per day (regular, or the fast Flying Dolphin hydrofoils) in summer from Ayios Konstandinos to Skiathos, Skopelos, and Alonissos; fewer in winter. Tickets are available from several travel agents on the dock. The fast ferry costs €23 to Skiathos and takes one hour; the fare is higher to continue on to Skopelos (€27) or Alonissos (€31). The regular ferry takes twice as long and costs half as much.

Getting to Skyros is equally tricky. You must drive or take a bus to Kimi and then catch one of the two daily ferries, or the weekly hydrofoil, to Skyros. You can buy ferry tickets at the Kimi dock when you get off the bus; the trip to Skyros takes two hours and costs €8.30.

BETWEEN THE ISLANDS Regular ferries connect Skiathos, Skopelos, and Alonissos; between Skyros and the other Sporades there is no regular boat service. The once-per-week Flying Dolphin hydrofoil that travels from Kimi, on Evia, to all the Sporades is by far the quicker, more reliable way to travel between the islands. Because schedules change frequently, check the times listed outside travel agencies in each of the port towns; the agents sell tickets.

Connecting through Kimi is the easiest way to get between Skyros and the other islands (the alternative is to fly through Athens). However, there is only one ferry per week from Kimi to Alonissos. If you miss this ferry, you can take a bus from Kimi to Halkidha and connect to the bus to Ayios Konstandinos; you may have to wait a few hours in Ayios Konstandinos for the ferry to Alonissos. This ends up being a full-day trip. ⚑**Flying Dolphin** ☎ 21041/99000 ⊕ www.hellenicseaways.gr. **Port Authority** ☎ 24240/ 65595 in Alonissos, 22350/31759 in Ayios Konstandinos, 22220/22606 in Kimi, 24270/ 22017 in Skiathos town, 24240/22180 in Skopelos town, 22220/91475 in Skyros town.

BUS TRAVEL
From central Athens, buses to Ayios Konstandinos, the main port for the Sporades (except Skyros), cost €11.50 and take about 2½ hours. Buses from Athens to Kimi, on Evia island (the only port where boats depart for Skyros), cost €11 and take 2½ hours. For those connecting to Ayios Konstandinos from Halkidha, on Evia island, the bus costs €8 and takes 1½ hours. Check the **KTEL** (⊕ www.ktel.org) site for schedules.

A Ceres Lines bus leaves Syntagma (Constitution) Square in Athens to meet Flying Dolphin at Ayios Konstandinos. Ask for information when you book. Bus fare from Athens to Ayios Konstandinos is €11.50.

FARES & SCHEDULES Buses on Skiathos leave Skiathos town to make the beach run as far as Koukounaries every 30 minutes from early morning until 11:30 PM. Buses on Skopelos run six times a day from Skopelos town to Glossa and Loutraki, stopping at the beaches. Alonissos has one bus that makes the trip from Patitiri to Alonissos town (Chora) and back from 9 AM to 2 PM only. Skyros buses carry ferry passengers between Linaria and Horio, stopping in Molos in summer. All cities on Evia are serviced with frequent buses. For information contact the KTEL bus station. ⚑**Athens to Ayios Konstandinos** ☎ 210/831-7147 in Athens. **Athens to Skyros** ☎ 210/ 831-7163 in Athens. **Ceres Lines bus** ☎ 210/428-0001, 210/428-3555 in Pireas. **KTEL bus station** ☎ 22210/22026 in Halkidha.

CAR TRAVEL
To get to Skiathos, Skopelos, and Alonissos by car you must drive to the port of Ayios Konstandinos (Ayios) and from there take the ferry. The drive to Ayios from Athens takes about two hours. For high-season travel you might have to reserve a place on the car ferry a day ahead.

For Skyros you must leave from the port of Kimi on Evia. From Athens, take the Athens–Lamia National Road to Skala Oropou and make the 30-minute ferry crossing to Eretria on Evia (every half hour in the daytime). No reservations are needed. Because it is so close to the mainland, you can skip the ferry system and drive directly to Evia over a short land bridge connecting Ayios Minas on the mainland with Halkidha. From Athens, about 80 km (50 mi) away, take the National Road 1 to the Schimatari exit, and then follow the signs to Halkidha. Beware that weekend crowds can slow traffic across the bridge.

ROAD
CONDITIONS
The road networks on all four islands are so rudimentary that cars are not really needed, but it's not a bad idea to rent one for a day to get a feel for the island, then use the bus or a scooter thereafter. Car rentals usually cost €30–€40 per day, while scooters cost about €15–€20. Four-wheel drives, cars, scooters, and motorbikes can be rented everywhere. If you rent a scooter, however, be extra cautious: many of those for hire are in poor condition. The locals are not used to the heavy summer traffic on their narrow roads, and accidents provide the island clinics with 80% of their summer business. Check with the travel agencies for rental information.

EMERGENCIES

The most efficient way to get to a medical center is to ask a taxi driver to take you to the nearest facility. Emergency services are listed by island.

📳 Alonissos **Police** ☎ 24240/65205 in Patitiri. **Medical Center** ☎ 24240/65208.

📳 Evia **Police** ☎ 22260/22456 in Aedipsos, 22290/61111 in Eretria, 22210/87000 in Halkidha, 22240/22262 in Karystos, 22220/22555 in Kimi, 22240/31333 in Marmari. **Medical Center** ☎ 22260/55311 in Aedipsos, 22290/62222 in Eretria, 22210/21901 in Halkidha, 22240/22207 in Karystos, 22220/46202 in Kimi, 22240/31300 in Marmari.

📳 Skiathos **Tourist Police** ☎ 24270/23172 in Skiathos town. **Medical Center** ☎ 24270/22222 in Skiathos town.

📳 Skopelos **Police** ☎ 24240/33333 in Glossa, 24240/22235 in Skopelos town. **Medical Center** ☎ 24240/22222 in Skopelos town.

📳 Skyros **Police** ☎ 22220/91274 in Skyros town. **Medical Center** ☎ 22220/92222 in Skyros town.

SPORTS & THE OUTDOORS

BOATING
In Skiathos, small motorboats can be rented at the Marine Center. Boats can also be rented at the Marine Center in Alonissos.

📳 **Marine Center–Alonissos** ✉ Near Elinoil gas station on waterfront ☎ 24240/65206. **Marine Center–Skiathos** ✉ Near airport runway ☎ 24270/22888 or 24270/21178 🖷 24270/23262.

TAXIS

Taxis wait at the ferry landings on all the islands. Even Alonissos has three. They are unmetered, so negotiate your fare in advance.

TRANSPORTATION AROUND THE SPORADES

On all islands, caïques leave from the main port for the most popular beaches, and interisland excursions are made between Skiathos, Skopelos, and Alonissos. You can also hire a caïque (haggle over the price) to tour around the islands; they are generally the preferred way to get around by day. For popular routes, captains have signs posted showing their destinations and departure times. On Skyros, check with Skyros Travel for caïque tours. In Alonissos, day trips are organized to the many smaller islands in the vicinity.

TRAVEL AGENTS

Travel agents on the islands handle hotel booking, private room rental, car rental, and transportation tickets. Anything and everything on Alonissos can be arranged at Albedo Travel, including boat trips to the National Marine Park from Patitiri. Alonissos Travel & Tourism Agency also arranges boat tours and hiking excursions on Alonissos. Skyros Travel has a virtual monopoly on hydrofoil tickets. Thalpos Holidays rents villas and has a number of boat excursions that start from the island of Skopelos.

7 **Albedo Travel** ⊠ Patitiri Alonissos ☎ 24240/65804 ⊕ www.albedotravel.com. **Alonissos Travel & Tourism Agency** ⊠ Near waterfront, Alonissos ☎ 24240/61588 or 24240/66000 🖶 24240/65511. **Creator Tours** ⊠ New Port, Skiathos ☎ 24270/22385 or 24270/21384 🖶 24270/21136 ⊕www.creatortours-skiathos.gr. **Madro Travel** ⊠Waterfront, Skopelos town ☎ 24240/22145 ⊕ www.madrotravel.com. **Skyros Travel** ⊠ Agora, Skyros town ☎ 22220/91123 or 22220/91600 🖶 22220/92123. **Thalpos Holidays** ⊠ Paralia Skopelou, Skopelos town ☎ 24240/22947 ⊕ www.holidayislands.com.

VISITOR INFORMATION

The Greek National Tourism Organization is the authority on the Sporades. Contact the tourist police in Skiathos town for information on the island. In Skopelos, try the Skopelos Municipality.

7 **Greek National Tourism Organization (GNTO or EOT)** ⊠ Tsoha 7, Athens ☎ 210/870-7000 ⊕ www.gnto.gr. **Alonissos official Web site** ⊕ www.alonissos.gr/en. **Skiathos Municipality** ⊠ Odhos Papadhiamndiou, Skiathos town ☎ 24270/23300 ⊕ www.n-skiathos.gr. **Skopelos Municipality** ⊠ Waterfront, Skopelos town ☎ 24240/22205 ⊕ www.skopelosweb.gr. **Skyros official Web site** ⊕ www.skyros.gr.

Epirus & Thessaly

IOANNINA, METSOVO &
THE METEORA MONASTERIES

4

214 <

Updated by
Adrian Vrettos

STARK MOUNTAINS, LUSH FORESTS, SWIFT RIVERS, and remote villages marked with unique customs, language, and architecture distinguish the province of Epirus, which is bordered by Albania and the Ionian Sea. Epirus means "the mainland," standing in contrast to the neighboring islands of Corfu, Paxi, and Lefkas, strung along the coast. The land changes abruptly from the delicately shaded green of the idyllic olive and orange groves near the shore to the tremendous solidity of the bare mountains inland. This was the splendid massive landscape that came to cast its spell over Lord Byron, who traveled here to meet tyrant Sinan Ali Pasha (1741–1822). The Epirote capital of Ioannina still bears many vestiges of this larger-than-life figure, who seems to have stepped from the pages of *The Arabian Nights*.

Going back in time, and taking an easy trip southwest of Ioannina, you can visit Dodona, the site of the oldest oracle in Greece. North of Ioannina, in the mountainous region known as Zagorohoria, or the Zagori, dozens of tiny, unspoiled villages contain remnants of the Ottoman period, and outdoor activities such as hiking are abundant.

The route east from Ioannina leads to the thriving traditional village of Metsovo in the Pindos Mountains and over the Katara Pass on one of the most dramatic roads in Greece. It ends in the fertile province of Thessaly, where, on the edge of the plain, the Byzantine-era monasteries of Meteora seem to float in midair, built atop bizarrely shaped pinnacles that tower over the town of Kalambaka. At this spiritual center of Orthodox Greece, the quiet contemplation of generations of monks is preserved in wondrously frescoed buildings. Nearby, spectacular mountain passes reveal shepherd villages with richly costumed women speaking the Vlach vernacular.

As you view these extraordinary rock-pinnacle monasteries—today one of Greece's most famous attractions—it's easy to credit the story about the original ascent's being achieved by way of a rope fastened to an eagle's leg, whose nest lay atop one of the rocks. The Meteora is a destination for those eager to discover a vanished way of life that demanded rigorous labor as well as religious fervor.

Exploring Epirus & Thessaly

The region consists of two areas: the mountainous province of Epirus, with appealing traditional villages such as Metsovo and its lakeside capital, Ioannina, to the west; and the Thessalian plain, an agricultural heartland with the Meteora at its edge. The mountainous Zagorohoria region, north of Ioannina in Epirus, is becoming very popular for its access to outdoor activities and for its stone-built towns, which have fine examples of Ottoman architecture. In Thessaly, what was once a lake is now a large, open, fertile plain with cotton, apples, and cherries among other produce cultivated in abundance. In contrast to most of the Thessalian landscape, the area around Kalambaka and the monasteries of the Meteora is rugged and steep.

About the Restaurants & Hotels

In restaurants, ask what's cooking, because many menus change seasonally and may include delightful specials that aren't listed. Informal

Although distances in this region may seem small, often the mountain roads that connect sights cannot be negotiated swiftly; a tour of the region should take this into account.

Numbers in the text correspond to numbers in the margin and on the Epirus & Thessaly map.

4

If you have 3 days

Take a morning flight from Athens to 🚏 **Ioannina** ❶ ⛳ and spend the late morning in the citadel, visit the island in the afternoon, and stay overnight. The next day make your way to 🚏 **Kalambaka** ❺ and spend the night there. Spend a full day touring the monasteries at the **Meteora** ❻, returning to Ioannina for the night.

If you have 5 days

Start with 🚏 **Ioannina** ❶ ⛳ and visit **Dodona** ❷ in the morning to see the ancient oracle of Zeus. See the citadel in the afternoon and the nearby island that night. The next morning stop at the Perama Cave on your way to 🚏 **Metsovo** ❹; spend the day exploring Metsovo. Be sure to get a taste of the Metsovone cheese and grab a bottle of Katogi wine. In the morning, move on to 🚏 **Kalambaka** ❺ to make the trek along the monastery route of the **Meteora** ❻. After staying overnight in either Kalambaka or Kastraki, on your last day return to Ioannina and visit sights you may not have been able to fit in on your first day, such as the Pavlos Vrellis Museum of Greek History in nearby Bizani and the Kostas Frontzos Museum of Epirote Folk Art and the old bazaar in town.

If you have 7 days

Base yourself in 🚏 **Ioannina** ❶ ⛳ for two nights, taking time to visit the island, citadel, and museums of the city. Rent a car or hire a taxi to visit the Perama Cave or the Pavlos Vrellis Museum of Greek History in Bizani. On Day 3, drive on to explore mountain villages in the 🚏 **Zagorohoria Region** ❸ northwest of Ioannina; spending at least one night in one of the traditional homes in villages like Megalo Papingo. Continue by driving to 🚏 **Kalambaka** ❺. Get there in the evening and be up early to visit the monasteries of the **Meteora** ❻. If you're an avid walker, and want to explore some of the best countryside in all of Greece, add a second night in the Zagorohoria Region; if you're more interested in the monasteries, spend two nights instead near Meteora. Head back west on Day 6 and stop to spend the night at the traditional village of 🚏 **Metsovo** ❹. Midday on the next day, return to Ioannina for your last night and move on from there to Athens or Thessaloniki.

dress is usually appropriate throughout this area, though Greeks may well be clad in the latest fashions, whether the clothing is comfortable or not.

Rooms are usually easy to find in Ioannina and, except at the best hotels, are simply decorated. Reservations might be necessary for Kalambaka, which is packed with tour groups in late spring and summer, and in Metsovo during ski season or the town's July 26 festival. In these two towns, private rooms are likely to be far cheaper than comparable hotel rooms—look for advertisements as you arrive. Off-season, prices drop drastically from those listed here, and you should always try to negotiate. In some cases, prices will skyrocket for Greek Easter and Christmas.

WHAT IT COSTS In euros					
	$$$$	$$$	$$	$	¢
RESTAURANTS	over €20	€16–€20	€12–€15	€8–€11	under €8
HOTELS	over €160	€121–€160	€91–€120	€60–€90	under €60

Restaurant prices are for one main course at dinner or, for restaurants that serve only *mezedes* (small dishes), for two mezedes. Hotel prices are for two people in a standard double room in high season, including taxes.

Timing

As in all of Greece, places are more likely to be open in the morning than in the afternoon, and museums and sites often close Monday; hours vary in summer and winter. Ioannina is easy to visit year-round, but excursions to the countryside are best May through October, when most places are open. Metsovo can be blissfully cool even in high summer (especially at night), making the town *panagyri* (saint's day festival) for Ayia Paraskevi, held July 26, quite pleasant, but the heat is oppressive elsewhere in this region at this time. The mountain roads to Metsovo are often blocked and impassable December to March; if you get there, however, the small ski center will be open. Keep in mind that the Meteora monasteries are open different days. They attract considerably fewer people in winter, when you might find an enhanced sense of spirituality in their windy isolation. You do need to plan ahead, since many accommodations are closed in winter.

EPIRUS

ΗΠΕΙΡΟΣ

Ancient Epirus was once a huge country that stretched from modern-day Albania (an area the Greeks still call Northern Epirus and one in which Greek is still spoken by large communities) to the Gulf of Arta and modern Preveza. The region is bordered by the Ionian Sea to the west, the islands of Lefkadha to the south, and Corfu to the north. Inland it is defined by a tangle of mountain peaks and upland plains, and the climate is markedly Balkan.

Despite the region's geographical barriers, it has been invaded many times. Its hinterland character has made it the perfect hideout for rebels and the home of disparate peoples. In ancient times the province was ruled by a king, the last being the famous Pyrrhus (319 BC–272 BC), who united the tribes of Epirus and began an expansionist policy that mimicked that of Alexander the Great. Pyrrhus's territorial gains came through overwhelming loss of lives, giving rise to the expression "Pyrrhic victory."

4

Great Flavors In Ioannina's lakeside and island restaurants you can sample dishes with ingredients culled from the lakes: frogs' legs, eel, crayfish, and turtles. Epirote kitchens also produce delicious tried-and-true recipes, such as *moschato kokkinisto* (a tomato-base veal stew with carrots, onions, and peas), lamb in lemon sauce, and *lathera* (stove-top vegetable stew made with artichoke hearts, beans, okra, and tomatoes). For Greeks, Metsovo brings to mind the costly but delectable smoked Metsovone cheese and Katogi red wine pressed from French Bordeaux grapes grown locally. Metsovites (Metsovo locals) are known for their meat specialties, too, such as *kontosouvli* (lamb or pork kebab), boiled goat, *trahanas* soup (made from cracked wheat boiled in milk and dried), and sausages or meatballs stuffed with leeks. *Pites* (pies, *pita*, pie singular) are pastry envelopes filled with local and seasonal produce, from savory meats and vegetables to sweet dairy creams and honey. Those with a penchant for sweets will savor *bougatsa*, a local custard served fresh at breakfast time at many places. For dessert, *galaktobouriko*, a creamy custard encased in phyllo dough and soaked with brandy-spiked citrus syrup, is a treat when served fresh from the oven; other treats include *kataifi Ioanniotiko* (shredded wheat pastry, Ioannina style), especially good when served with ice cream and baked apples.

Spiritual Culture All around Greece are signs of the importance of religion over the ages, from the tumbled ruins of the temples of the ancients to sprawling medieval monastic complexes. Ioannina in Epirus retains some of its heritage from the days when the Ottoman Turks held sway; the Aslan Mosque, now a museum, preserves reminders of the days when Greeks, Turks, and Jews lived side by side. The Synagogue of Ioannina continues to stand, though no longer in use. On nearby Nissi, Ayios Nikolaos ton Filanthropinon, a Byzantine monastery, has bold, expressive frescoes. South of Ioannina is the sanctuary to Zeus Naios and the Dodona Oracle; here the decisions of Zeus were believed to rustle through the leaves of the Sacred Oak. Kalambaka in Thessaly is the gateway to one of Greece's greatest expressions of religious dedication: the Byzantine monasteries at Meteora, which sit atop eroded pinnacles of rock. The religious life here was strict but still permitted the creation of magnificent frescoes and icons that celebrated faith. Although the region's religious sanctuaries represent different faiths, things sometimes overlap a bit: the church of the Dormition of the Virgin in Kalambaka, for example, appears to have been built on the site of a temple to Apollo, with ancient mosaics under the current floor.

Although invaded by Normans in 1080, Epirus gained in importance after the influx of refugees from Constantinople and the Morea beginning in 1205 and was made a despotate, a principality ruled by a despot. Ioannina was subsequently made the capital of Epirus and fortified by Michalis Angelos, the first despot. In 1345 the Serbs captured Epirus and established a monarchy from 1348 to 1386. In 1431 Ioannina surrendered to the Ottomans and Epirus remained a part of its empire until it became part of Greece in 1913, almost 100 years after Greece's liberation from the Turks. The cultural influence from its Ottoman occupation is evident. Besides this influence, Metsovo and the surrounding area contain the largest concentration of the non-Greek population known as the Vlachs, nomadic shepherds said to be descendants of legionnaires from garrisons on the Via Egnatia, one of the Roman Empire's main east–west routes. The Vlachs speak a Romance language related to Italian and Romanian.

This section includes—in geographical succession—the capital of the province, Ioannina, with its rich Ottoman heritage; nearby Dodona, most ancient of Greek oracles; and the traditional Vlach mountain village of Metsovo to the west, perhaps the most accessible village and a good base for exploring.

Ioannina

Ιωάννινα

▶ ❶ *305 km (189 mi) northwest of Athens, 204 km (126 mi) west-south-west of Thessaloniki.*

On the rocky promontory of Lake Pamvotis lies Ioannina, its fortress punctuated by mosques and minarets whose reflections, along with those of the snowy peaks of the Pindos range, appear in the calm water. The lake contains tiny Nissi, or "small island," where nightingales still sing and fishermen mend their nets. Although on first impression parts of the city may seem noisy and undistinguished, the old quarter preserves a rich heritage. Outstanding examples of folk architecture remain within the castle walls, and in the neighborhoods surrounding them; Ioannina's historic mansions, folk houses, seraglios, and bazaars are a reminder of the city's illustrious past. Set at a crossroads of trading, the city is sculpted by Balkan, Ottoman, and Byzantine influences. Thanks to a resident branch of the Greek national university, today the lively provincial capital city (population 100,000) has a thriving contemporary cultural scene (and a proliferation of good restaurants and lively bars). Things get particularly lively the first two weeks of July, when the city's International Folk Festival takes place.

The name Ioannina was first documented in 1020 and may have been taken from an older monastery of St. John. Founded by Emperor Justinian in AD 527, Ioannina suffered under many rulers: it was invaded by the Normans in 1082, made a dependency of the Serbian kingdom in 1345, and conquered by the Turks in 1431. Above all, this was Ali Pasha's city, where, during its zenith, from 1788 to 1821, the despot carved a fiefdom from much of western Greece. His territory extended from the Ionian Sea to the Pindos range and from Vaona in the north to Arta in the south. The Turks ended his rule in 1821 by using deception to capture him; Ali Pasha was then shot and decapitated.

Tree-lined **Dionyssiou Skylosofou,** which circles the citadel along the lake, is ideal for a late-afternoon stroll. The street was named for a defrocked Trikala bishop who led an ill-fated uprising against the Turks in 1611 and was flayed alive as a result. A moat, now filled, ran around the south-

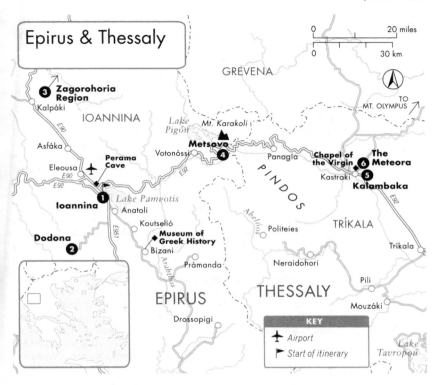

Epirus & Thessaly

GREVENA

0   20 miles
0   30 km

3 Zagorohoria Region
Kalpáki

IOANNINA

Lake Pigón   Mt. Karakoli

TO MT. OLYMPUS

Asfáka
Votonóssi
Metsovo
4
Panagía
Chapel of the Virgin 6 The Meteora

Perama Cave
Eleousa
E90
E92

Kastraki
Kalambaka 5

Ioannina 1
Lake Pamvotis
Anatoli

P I N D O S

TRÍKALA

Dodona
2
Koutselió
E961
Politeies

Museum of Greek History
Bizani

Tríkala

Prámanda
Neraidohori

Pili

EPIRUS
Drossopigi

THESSALY
Mouzáki

Lake Tavropoú

KEY
✈ Airport
▶ Start of itinerary

west landward side, and today the walls divide the old town—with its rose-laden pastel-color houses, overhanging balconies, cobblestone streets, and birdsong—from the new. ✉ *Lakeside end of Odhos Averoff.*

One of Ioannina's main attractions is the **Kastro** (Castle), with massive, fairly intact stone walls that once dropped into the lake on three sides; Ali Pasha completely rebuilt them in 1815. The city's once-large Romaniote Jewish population, said to date from the time of Alexander the Great, lived within the walls, alongside Turks and Christians. The Jews were deported by the Nazis during World War II, to meet their deaths at extermination camps; of the 4,000-odd inhabitants around the turn of the 20th century, fewer than 100 remain today. The area inside the walls is now a quiet residential area. Outside the citadel walls, near the lake, a **monument** at Karamanli and Soutsou streets commemorates the slaughter of the Jewish community. ✉ *Lakeside end of Odhos Averoff.*

The collections in the remarkably well-preserved **Aslan Mosque,** now the **Municipal Museum,** recall the three communities (Greek, Turkish, Jewish) that lived together inside the fortress from 1400 to 1611. The vestibule has recesses for shoes, and inscribed over the doorway is the name of Aslan Pasha and THERE IS ONLY ONE GOD, ALLAH, AND MUHAMMED IS HIS PROPHET. The mosque retains its original decoration and *mihrab,* a niche that faces

Mecca. Exhibited around the room are a walnut and mother-of-pearl table from Ali Pasha's period, ornate inlaid *hamam* (Turkish bath) shoes on tall wooden platforms, clothes chests, and a water pipe. There is also a collection of 18th- and 19th-century guns. ⊠ *North end of citadel* ☎ *26510/ 26356* 🖃 *€4* ⊙ *Nov.–Apr., daily 8–3; May–Oct., daily 7–8.*

Within the larger citadel is the **fortress,** called *Its Kale* by the Turks, where Ali Pasha built his palace; these days the former palace serves the city as the **Byzantine Museum.** The museum's small collection of artworks, actually almost all post-Byzantine, includes intricate silver manuscript Bible covers, wall murals from mansions, and carved wooden benediction crosses covered in lacy silver, gathered from all over the countryside of Epirus. It's carefully arranged in the front half of the museum with good English translations. The second half of the museum houses an important collection of icons and remarkable iconostases, painted by local masters and salvaged from 16th- and 17th-century monasteries. The most interesting section is devoted to silver works from Ali Pasha's treasury from the seraglio. Nearby is the **Fethiye (Victory) Mosque,** which purports to contain Ali Pasha's tomb. ⊠ *Eastern corner of citadel* ☎ *26510/39580* 🖃 *€3* ⊙ *Tues.–Sun. 8–5.*

The dignified **Synagogue of Ioannina,** active during the days of the Romaniote Jewish community but no longer in regular use, is a couple of blocks inside the citadel gate. Generally it is only open for religious services on holidays, but a tour can be arranged by making a reservation with guides Sam Cohen and Avram Zivolis (only Greek and Hebrew spoken). ⊠ *Ioasaf Eliyia 18b, at Ioustianou* ☎ *26510/28541, 26510/ 26801 for tours* 🖃 *Free* ⊙ *Tours by appointment, otherwise closed except for religious holidays.*

Vestiges of 19th-century Ioannina remain in the **old bazaar.** On Anexartisias are some Turkish-era structures, such as the Liabei arcade across from the bustling municipal produce market and, on Filiti, a smattering of the copper-, tin-, and silversmiths who fueled the city's economy for centuries. Some workshops still have wares for sale. ⊠ *Around the citadel's gates at Ethnikis Antistasios and Averoff.*

> **need a break?**
>
> **Filistrou** (⊠ Andronikou Paleologou 20 ☎ 26510/72429), an intimate café on a main street near the citadel area, occupies a 200-year-old residence with a colorful folk interior with decorated ceilings. Pamper yourself with some of the most unique drinks in Greece. Try *salepi* and other Arab herbal drinks with a splash of alcohol, or stop by in the late evening for Metaxa brandy and a *visino* (a spoon sweet made up of black cherries preserved in syrup, eaten by the spoonful or added to a beverage). For breakfast, try the thick strained yogurt topped with chestnut-color honey and chopped walnuts. The café is open September to June, daily 11–11.

The **Archaeological Museum** is the best in the area but is, at this writing, closed for refurbishment, possibly until 2007. Some works in the museum have been loaned to museums in the area, and others are in storage. When the museum reopens, it will have multimedia technology and contemporary exhibition space. ⊠ *Pl. 25 Martiou* ☎ *26510/33357, 26510/ 35498, 26510/25490 for updates on renovation* ⊕ *www.culture.gr.*

The small **Kostas Frontzos Museum of Epirote Folk Art,** in a restored Ottoman house, has a collection of richly embroidered local costumes, rare woven textiles made by the nomadic tent-dwelling Sarakatsanis, ceramics, and cooking and farm implements. ⊠ *Odos Michail Angelou 42* ☎ *26510/20515 or 26510/23566* 🎫 *€3* ☽ *Mon. and Wed. 9–2 and 5:30–8; Tues., Thurs., and Fri. 9–2; weekends 10–3:30.*

The waterfront square, **Platia Mavili,** is lined with smart cafés that fill with travelers having breakfast or waiting for the next boat to the nearby island. In the evening the *molos* (seawall) is *the* place to hang out—the youth of Ioannina while away the hours here over frappés or long drinks. The *volta* (ritual evening promenade) is still a favorite way of passing the time and keeping up to date with all the action and gossip, but these days people carry an added accessory—the modern *kinito* (cellular telephone). At night the area is especially gregarious, with vendors selling corn, halvah, and cassettes of Epirote clarinet music.

Lake Pamvotis remains picturesque despite the fact that the water level is so low (the streams that feed it are drying up) it's become too polluted for swimming. Still, it has the longest rowing course in Greece, and teams from all over the Balkans use it for training. The Valkaniadia rowing championships are periodically hosted here.

Look back at the outline of the citadel and its mosques in a wash of green as you take the 10-minute ride from the shore toward the small island of **Nissi.** The whitewashed lakeside island village was founded in the late 16th century by refugees from the Mani (in the Peloponnese). No outside recreational vehicles are allowed, and without the din of motorcycles and cars, the village seems centuries away from Ioannina. Ali Pasha once kept deer here for hunting. With its neat houses and flower-trimmed courtyards, pine-edged paths, runaway chickens, and reed-filled backwater, it's the perfect place to relax, have lunch, visit some of the monasteries (dress appropriately and carry a small flashlight to make it easier to see the magnificent frescoes), and have a pleasant dinner. Frogs' legs, eel, and carp take center stage, although traditional taverna food can also be found. ⊠ *Ferry below citadel, near Pl. Mavili* 🚢 *Ferry €1.50* ☽ *May–Sept., ferry daily on the ½ hr 6:30 AM–midnight; Oct.–Apr., daily on the hr 6:30 AM–10 PM.*

The main attraction on Nissi is the 16th-century Pandelimonos Monastery, now the **Ali Pasha Museum.** Ali Pasha was killed here in the monks' cells on January 17, 1822, after holding out for almost two years. In the final battle, Ali ran into an upstairs cell, but the soldiers shot him through its floorboards from below. (The several bullet holes in the floor were newly drilled because the floor had to be replaced.) A wax version of the assassination can be seen at the Pavlos Vrellis Museum of Greek History in Bizani, south of Ioannina. A happier Ali Pasha, asleep on the lap of his wife, Vasiliki, can be seen in the museum's famous portrait. Here also is the crypt where Vasiliki hid, some evocative etchings and paintings of that era, an edict signed by Ali Pasha with his ring seal (he couldn't write), and his magnificent narghile, a water pipe, standing on the fireplace. The community-run museum is generally open as long as boats are running; if the doors are shut, ask around to be let in. The local ticket taker will give a brief tour of the museum in Greek and broken English (supplemented by an English-language printed guide). A tour is free, but do leave a tip. ⊠ *On Nissi, take left from boat landing and follow signs* ☎ *26510/ 81791* 🖼 *€0.60* ⊙ *Daily 10–10.*

Agios Nikolaos ton Filanthropinon has the best frescoes of Nissi's several monasteries. The monastery was built in the 13th century by an important Byzantine family, the Filanthropinos, and a fresco in the northern exonarthex (the outer narthex) depicts five of them kneeling before St. Nikolaos (1542). Many of the frescoes are by the Kontaris brothers, who later decorated the mighty Varlaam in Meteora. Note the similarities in the bold coloring, expressiveness, realism, and Italian influence—especially in the bloody scenes of martyrdom. Folk tradition says the corner crypts in the south chapel were the meeting places of the secret school of Hellenic culture during the Ottoman occupation. A most unusual fresco here of seven sages of antiquity, including Solon, Aristotle, and Plutarch, gives credence to this story. It is not really feasible, however, that the school would have been kept a secret from the Ottoman governors for long; more likely, the reigning Turkish pasha was one who allowed religious and cultural freedom (as long as the taxes were paid). ⊠ *On island, follow signs* ☎ *No phone* 🖼 *€1* ⊙ *Daily 8–8.*

★ ⊙ The **Pavlos Vrellis Museum of Greek History** displays a collection of historical Epirote figures from the past 2,500 years in more than 30 settings (streets, mountains, caves, churches, and more); look for the tableau of Ali Pasha's murder. All the figures were sculpted in wax by artist Pavlos Vrellis, a local legend who embarked on this endeavour at the ripe age of 60. His studio is on the premises. ⊠ *11 km (7 mi) south of Ioannina, Ethnikos Odos Ioanninon–Athinon road, Bizani* ☎ *26510/92128* ⊕ *www. vrellis.org* 🖼 *€5* ⊙ *May–Oct., daily 9:30–5; Nov.–Apr., daily 10–4.*

> **off the beaten path**
>
> **PERAMA CAVE** – The cave's passageways, discovered in the early 1940s by locals hiding from the Nazis, extend for more than 1 km (½ mi) under the hills. You learn about the high caverns and multihue limestone stalagmites during the 45-minute guided tour; one begins about every 15 minutes. Printed English-language information is available. Be prepared for the many steps you must walk up on the way out. You can catch Bus 8 from Ioannina's clock tower to get here. ⊠ *E92, 4 km (2½ mi) north of Ioannina* ☎ *26510/81521* 🖼 *€6* ⊙ *May–Oct., daily 8:30–7; Nov.–Apr., daily 8:30–5.*

Where to Stay & Eat

$$$ ✕ **Es Aei.** A set menu that changes every three months with the seasons

FodorśChoice and an emphasis on vegetarian dishes and organic produce reflect the

★ philosophy of innovative owners Manos Chronakis and Haris Stavrou. In this 200-year-old house in the historic center adjacent to the citadel, the Greek *pikilia* (variety plate) has been mastered. Choose between various vegetables or meats and add a salad. Dishes may contain in-

THE REIGN OF ALI PASHA

BORN IN THE 1740S in Tepeline, Albania, Ali Pasha rose to power by unscrupulous means. The most notorious ruler of Epirus employed assassins to carry out his plots of murder and brigandage. He was made pasha of Trikala in 1787 and a year later seized Ioannina, then the largest town in Greece. For the next 33 years, Ali pursued his ambition: to break from the Ottoman Empire and create his own kingdom. He paid only token tribute to the sultan and allied himself according to his needs with the French, the British, and the Turks. In 1797 he collaborated with Napoléon; the next year he seized Preveza from the French; and by 1817 he was wooing the British and Admiral Nelson, who gave him Parga.

Historical accounts focus on the fact that he had an insatiable libido and combed the countryside looking for concubines, accumulating a harem numbering in the hundreds. He attacked the Turkish Porte ("Sublime Porte" [or gate] of the sultan's palace, where justice was administered; by extension, the Ottoman government), and he brutalized his Greek subjects. Ali's most infamous crime was perhaps the drowning of Kyra Frosini, his son's mistress, and 16 other women, by tying them in stone-laden bags and dumping them in Lake Pamvotis. Apparently, Ali was in love with Frosini, who rejected him, and, spurred on by his son's wife, he had Frosini killed on charges of infidelity. He regretted his deed and ordered that 250 pounds of sugar be thrown into the lake to sweeten the water Frosini would drink. A superstition persists that Frosini's ghost hovers over the lake on moonlit nights.

gredients direct from the couple's small farm in Tzoumerka. Eventually, produce will be sold upstairs at the folklore exhibition center. ⊠ *Koundouriotou 50* ☎ *26510/34571* ▤ *No credit cards* ☉ *Closed July and Aug.*

$$–$$$
Fodor'sChoice
★
✕ **Gastra.** Mr. Vassilis has run this friendly traditional taverna for more than 30 years. Here you can discover how Greek grandmothers cooked before the comforts of electricity were introduced to Epirus. The *gastra* is basically a large container with hot coals placed on the iron lid over the pot. Your meal (of lamb, chicken, or goat) roasts very slowly in its own juices, resulting in tender, juicy meat with a crispy outer skin. ⊠ *Leoforos Kostaki 16a, 7 km (4½ mi) north of Ioannina on the way to the airport, Eleousa* ☎ *26510/61530* ⚠ *Reservations essential* ▤ *No credit cards* ☉ *Closed Mon.*

$–$$
✕ **Ithaki.** Among the many restaurants on the trendy lakeside street, Ithaki stands out. You can eat traditional Ioanniotika fare, such as vegetable pies, frogs' legs, and fried Metsovitiko cheese, while enjoying the view of Pamvotis lake with the mosque of Kaplan Pasha reflecting in its waters. The speciality of the house is the spit-roasted *kontosouvli* (tender pork), and the tasty homemade baklava. ⊠ *Stratigou Papagou 20a* ☎ *26510/74730* ▤ *MC, V.*

¢–$ ✕ **Ivi.** Old-fashioned and no-nonsense, this Ioannina landmark serves excellent *magirefta* (dishes precooked in an oven or on the stove). Open from 5 AM, it's the place to head to after a long night out on the town. Tripe soup and *mageiritsa* (sheep's liver and intestine) are some unusual dishes. Vegetarians could try the leeks sautéed and baked with celery or the green bean ragout. There's usually a fish entrée such as grilled *kolios* (mackerel), *bakaliaros* (fried cod), or *galeos* (shark) with *skordalia* (garlic-potato sauce). ⊠ *Pl. Neomartiros Yoryiou 4* ☎ *26510/73155* ⊟ *No credit cards* ⊙ *Closed every other Sun.*

$$$ ✕⊡ **Epirus Palace.** Indulging oneself in the city of Ali Pasha seems entirely fitting, and you can do so in style at this stunning, lavish hotel, opened in 1999 by the innovative brothers Natsis. Some of the exquisite furniture, highlighted with gold and silver, was handmade for the hotel. Rooms are spacious, and the marble bathrooms are luxurious. For a more international taste of Greece, dine at the sophisticated à la carte hotel restaurant, which prides itself on its *loukoulia gevmata* (sumptuous feast). ⊠ *7 km (4½ mi) south of Ioannina, Ethnikos Odos Ioanninon–Athinon Rd., 45221* ☎ *26510/93555* ⊟ *26510/92595* ⊕ *www.epiruspalace.gr* ↩ *51 rooms, 2 suites* ⚶ *3 restaurants, minibars, cable TV, in-room data ports, pool, 2 bars, convention center, meeting rooms, some no-smoking rooms* ⊟ *AE, D, MC, V* ⦿❘ *BP.*

$$$ ⊡ **Du Lac.** Built in traditional Ioannina style, the hotel's two ocher-color buildings sit on ample, landscaped grounds opposite the lake to the south of the old town. The Du Lac attracts business conferences, but its children's pool and quiet setting make it popular with families, too. Rooms are large, carpeted, individually climate-controlled, and decorated in sunny tones, with prints or photographs of old Ioannina on the wall. Some rooms have balconies that face the lake or the city. ⊠ *Akti Miaouli and Ikkou, 45221* ☎ *26510/59100* ⊟ *26510/59200* ⊕ *www.dulac.gr* ↩ *119 rooms, 10 suites* ⚶ *Restaurant, cafeteria, cable TV, in-room data ports, pool, wading pool, bar, meeting rooms* ⊟ *AE, D, MC, V* ⦿❘ *BP.*

★ $ ⊡ **Kastro Hotel.** A restored neoclassical mansion is the more popular of only two accommodation options within the walls of the citadel, so make reservations well in advance. Wooden beams, painted wooden ceilings, two fireplaces (in the sitting and breakfast rooms), and cast-iron beds are thoroughly delightful. Thick stone walls keep things cool in summer. The owners and staff are very helpful, and breakfast (additional, upon request) is homemade jams, ham, cheese, fruit, and local honey. ⊠ *Andronikou Paleologou 57, 45332* ☎ *26510/22866* ⊟ *26510/22780* ⊕ *www.epirus.com/hotel-kastro* ↩ *7 rooms* ⚶ *Fans, some pets allowed; no a/c, no phones* ⊟ *MC, V.*

¢ ⊡ **Filyra.** When architect-owner Periklis Papadias opened his lodging within an old Jewish mansion in 2001, he planted his own *filyra*, or lime tree, in the courtyard. The studio apartments come with kitchenware and a dining table. Only one has a double bed (ask for the *diplo*); other rooms have from two to four twin beds. This is a great reasonable option in a prime location—inside the citadel walls. ⊠ *Andronikou Paleologou 18, 45221* ☎ *26510/83560* ⊟ *26510/83567* ✉ *ppapadia@tee.gr* ↩ *5 studios* ⚶ *Kitchenettes* ⊟ *No credit cards.*

¢ 🏨 **Pension Dellas.** Evangelos Dellas inherited this island lakeshore establishment from his parents; its welcoming hospitality is a delightful change from hotels in town. The pension is immaculate, sunny, and quiet, with two balconies overlooking the lake and sunset. Make the boat ride to the island village from Platia Mavili yourself or call to be picked up in the family boat. ☒ *Nissi, 45444* 📞 *26510/81494 or 26510/89894* 🛏 *4 rooms* ⚗ *Restaurant, bar, some pets allowed; no room phones* 🚭 *No credit cards.*

Nightlife & the Arts

BARS & CAFÉS   Even in a relatively small city like Ioannina, the *magazia* (club-cafés) are always changing names and owners; they may close for winter and open elsewhere for summer, usually under the stars. Karamanli, adjacent to the citadel, is lined with trendy *mezedopolia* (Greek-style tapas bars) and smart pubs. **Club Preview** (☒ Giosif Eligia and Aetorrahis 📞 26510/64522), by the Kastro, is a popular club open late—but closed June through August—with lots of loud foreign music. **Iperokeanios** (☒ Pl. Mavili 10 📞 06510/33781), by the citadel near Giosif Eligia and Aetorrahis, is one of the hippest coffee shops along the seawall; it serves ice cream and sweets. If it's full, try the adjacent Ploton. The waterfront music taverna **Kyknos** (☒ Stratigou Papagou 📞 26510/75557), very popular with students, is a good place to hang out for the night or to charge your batteries before clubbing.

The **Web** (☒ Pirsinella 21 📞 26510/74115 or 26510/26813) is the place to check your e-mail as you socialize with other tourists and locals and sip coffee or a strong drink until late at night.

FESTIVALS   The local tourist office can provide information about festivals, including a bazaar in September. The **International Folk Festival,** showcasing the region's music and dancing, takes place in July. For those seeking the haunting *klarino* (clarinet) music and graceful circle dances of Epirus such as the *pogonisios* and *beratis,* this is a fascinating event. Local groups also perform eerie polyphonic singing, another unique folk tradition rooted in Epirus.

Shopping

Ioannina has long been known throughout Greece for its silver craftsmanship and for its jewelry, copper utensils, and woven items. You can find delicate jewelry items on the island of Nissi, but there are also many silver shops on Odhos Averoff (the better place for larger items, like trays, glasses, and vases), near Platia Yoryious Georgiou. Avoid the shinier and brighter items in stores near the entrance to the citadel.

Doublis (☒ Pl. Neom. Grigoriou 📞 26510/79287) is one of the better arts-and-crafts shops in this area; a careful eye can discern some prizes amid the typical tourist paraphernalia.

Antique collectors consider **Papazotos Zikos** (☒ Andronikou Paleologou 2, inside the citadel 📞 26510/83103), one of the must-go-to shops; it has a large collection of Ali Pasha's original belongings.

Dodona

Δωδώνη

 22 km (14 mi) southwest of Ioannina.

Said to be the oldest in Greece, the **Dodona Oracle** flourished from at least the 8th century BC until the 4th century AD, when Christianity succeeded the cult of Zeus. Homer, in the *Iliad,* mentions "wintry Dodona," where Zeus's pronouncements, made known through the wind-rustled leaves of a sacred oak, were interpreted by priests "whose feet are unwashed and who sleep on the ground." The oak tree was central to the cult, and its image appears on the region's ancient coins. Here Odysseus sought forgiveness for slaughtering his wife's suitors, and from this oak the Argonauts took the sacred branch to mount on their ship's prow. According to one story, Apollo ordered the oracle moved here from Thessaly; Herodotus writes that it was locally believed a dove from Thebes in Egypt landed in the oak and announced, in a human voice, that the oracle of Zeus should be built. The oracle had its ups and downs. Consulted in the heroic age by Heracles, Achilles, and all the best people, it went later into a gentle decline, because of its failure to equal the masterly ambiguity of Delphi.

As you enter the archaeological site of Dodona, you pass the **stadium** on your right, built for the Naïa games and completely overshadowed by the **theater** on your left. One of the largest and best preserved on the Greek mainland, the theater once seated 17,000; it is used for summer presentations of ancient Greek drama. Its building in the early 3rd century BC was overseen by King Pyrrhus of Epirus. The theater was destroyed, rebuilt under Philip V of Macedon in the late 3rd century, and then converted by the Romans into an arena for gladiatorial games. Its retaining wall, reinforced by bastions, is still standing. East of the theater are the foundations of the **bouleuterion** (headquarters and council house) of the Epirote League, built by Pyrrhus, and a small rectangular temple dedicated to Aphrodite. The remains of the **acropolis** behind the theater include house foundations and a cistern that supplied water in times of siege.

The remains of the **sanctuary of Zeus Naios** include temples to Zeus, Dione (goddess of abundance), and Heracles; until the 4th century BC there was no temple. The Sacred Oak was here, surrounded by abutting cauldrons on bronze tripods. When struck, they reverberated for a long time, and the sound was interpreted by soothsayers. Fragments of oracular questions and answers from as early as the 8th century have been recovered. In the 4th century BC, a small temple was built near the oak, and a century later the temple and oak were enclosed by a stone wall. By King Pyrrhus's time, the wall had acquired Ionic colonnades. After a 219 BC Aeolian attack, a larger Ionic temple was built, and the surrounding wall was enhanced by a monumental entrance. The oak tree currently on the site was planted by archaeologists; the original was probably cut down by Christians in the 4th century AD.

Two buses leave daily (except Thursday) from Ioannina's Bizaniou Station, one at 7 AM and the other at 4 PM. The most efficient way to get here from Ioannina is with a rented car or a taxi; the driver will wait an hour at the site. Negotiate with one of the drivers near Ioannina's clock tower or ask your hotel to call a radio taxi service. Hours may be reduced from October to May. ⊠ *Signposted off E951, near Dodona* ☎ *26510/82287* ⊕ *www.culture.gr* ⊠ €3 ☉ *Daily 8–5.*

The Ioannina tourist office has information about summer presentations of **Ancient Greek drama** (Tourist office ⊠ Dodonis 39, Ioannina ☎ 26510/41868 or 26510/46662) at Dodona.

Zagorohoria Region

Ζαγοροχώρια (περισχή)

★ ❸ *40 km (25 mi) to 65 km (41 mi) north of Ioannina.*

One of the most beguiling and untamed sections of Greece is the region of Zagorohoria (pronounced zah-go-ro-*hor*-ee-ah), also known as Zagori or Zagoria, which comprises 46 villages to the north and northwest of Ioannina. Here you can see *arhontika* (stone mansions with walls and roofs made of gray slate from surrounding mountains), winding cobbled streets, graceful arched Turkish bridges, churches with painted interiors, *kalderimi* (old mule trails), and forests of beech, chestnut, and pine. If you have only a day to spare, rent a car or bargain with a taxi driver in Ioannina to transport you to some of the many villages connected by well-paved roads. If you opt to spend the night in one of the villages, you have the chance to truly soak up the local color, get a look at the interiors of some of the Ottoman-style living quarters, and partake of some excellent food. Wonderful hikes are another pleasure for those who choose to stay and explore awhile.

Some of the more accessible villages, such as Megalo, Mikro Papingo, and Monodendri, are likely to be packed with travelers in July and August, particularly on weekends and major holidays. Book ahead or, better yet, stay in some of the (even) lesser-known villages.

Kipi, 40 km (25 mi) north of Ioannina in the central Zagori, is famous for its three-arch packhorse bridge, and a fascinating folklore museum is run by the community. **Tsepelovo,** 5 km (3 mi) northeast of Kipi, is one of the most authentic villages. Perched on the slopes of Mt. Tymphai, at 3,960 feet, it was built using the gray-brown rock that makes up most of the surroundings.

A must-see village, **Monodendri,** 44 km (27 mi) north of Ioannina, is a well-preserved settlement perched on the rim of a gorge on the boundary of the Vikos–Aoos National Park. There's a stunning vista from the abandoned 15th-century monastery, Agia Paraskevi. In **Ano Pedina,** 8 km (5 mi) east of Monodendri, you can visit a restored convent.

Papingo, 59 km (37 mi) north of Ioannina, has delightful architecture— many houses are still topped with the silvery blue slate that used to be so common throughout Epirus—varied scenery, and friendly locals, although it was among the first villages here "discovered" by wealthy Greeks. **Megalo Papingo** (Big Papingo), 3 km (2 mi) southeast of Papingo, is near the river Voidomatis, which has excellent rafting and canoeing. **Mikro Papingo** (Little Papingo), below some limestone rocks, is really small—the population is fewer than 100—but appealing.

Konitsa, a pretty market town 65 km (41 mi) north of Ioannina, served by bus, makes a good base for exploration in northern Zagorohoria. It's an ideal place to enjoy some of the many outdoor activities which include hiking, rafting, and paragliding. In town are the famous single-arch stone bridges of Aoos and Klidonia. Other places of interest in the town include the Palace of Chamko (Ali Pasha's mother) and the mosque of Sultan Suleiman. The Stomio Monastery, built in 1774, nestles at the entrance of the Aoos Gorge.

Where to Stay & Eat

$$–$$$ ✕ **Tsoumanis.** There are two tavernas with the name Tsoumanis in town; choose the one just up from the main square that is run by Nick Tsoumanis and his wife. The menu changes throughout the year, ensuring that everything you eat is fresh and in season and all the ingredients are local. The lamb gastra seems to be a favorite of the locals who dine there, as are the potatoes covered with a thick layer of cheese, somewhat like au gratin. Not to be missed are the soups, perfect for warming your spirits in the mountain air. ⊠ *Off main square, Megalo Papingo* ☎ *26530/41893* ☱ *MC, V.*

¢–$ ✕ **Ouzeri Nikos Tsoumanis.** Irresistible mezedes and a potent *tsipouro* (a liquor made from grapes) help you leave the cares of the real world behind. Order a drink and you are also served with an appetizer platter consisting of anything from salted anchovies, fried zucchini, meatballs, baked giant beans, and sliced tomatoes (it's a potluck and usually changes with each drink you order). ⊠ *Main square, Megalo Papingo* ☎ *26530/41893* ☱ *No credit cards.*

¢ ✕☲ **Panorama.** True to the traditional style of Konitsa, and to the pension's name, Panorama has eye-catching views of the surrounding countryside. Rooms, all of which are in the simple stone-and-wood Epirote style, have a balcony and a fireplace. A homey breakfast helps build up your energy for the ensuing outdoor activities, which Panagiotis Mourechidis, the owner, will help you organize. With a *kotopita* (chicken pie) and the usual tasty meat dishes served, the in-house taverna is a good option for a hearty dinner washed down with a strong ruby-red house wine. ⊠ *Follow signs from main Sq., 44100 Konitsa* ☎ *26550/23135* ☲ *26550/23135* ⊕ *www.konitsapanorama.com* ⇥ *18 rooms* ⌂ *Pool, refrigerators, bar* ☱ *V* ¶◯| *CP.*

☾ ¢–$ ☲ **Zarkada.** Most of the rooms in this pension in the heart of the picturesque Monodendri village are equipped with fireplaces—an essential luxury during the long and cold winter nights. Three of the rooms have saunas and another seven have hot tubs. The friendly Mr. Zarkada is more than happy to help you arrange outdoor activities. Like most of the places to stay in the area, Zarkada has its own taverna serving sumptuous, local savory pies and roasted meats. ⊠ *Off main square, 44004 Monodendri* ☎ *26530/71305* ☲ *26530/71505* ⊕ *www.monodendri.com* ⇥ *18 rooms* ⌂ *Some in-room hot tubs, refrigerators, bar, playground* ☱ *MC, V.*

Sports & the Outdoors

Hiking is one of the real pleasures of the Zagorohoria Region, but trails can be challenging. Your safest bet is to go with a guided walk; a number of outfitters schedule gorge hikes and other activities (⇨ Sports & the Outdoors *in* Epirus & Thessaly A to Z, *below*). Make sure you have proper footwear, hiking gear, food and water, and emergency supplies and provisions, and *never* hike in heavy rains or go far in groups of fewer than four. Staff at most hotels can provide basic maps and put you in touch with local guides or trekking clubs. One of the best hiking maps of Zagori is by **Anavasi** (☎ 210/729–3541 ⊕ www.mountains.gr). It's GPS compatible and includes shorter and longer walks in the area.

★ If you're a physically fit hiker, you may want to hike at least part of the steep and long **Vikos Gorge.** To get to the gorge, you follow a precipitous route from the upper limestone table lands of Monodendri down almost 3,300 feet to the clear, rushing waters of the Voidomatis trout stream (no swimming allowed) as it flows north into Albania. It's a strenuous but exhilarating eight-hour hike on which you are likely to see dramatic vistas, birds of prey, waterfalls, flowers and herbs, and hooded shepherds tending their flocks.

Metsovo

Μέτσοβο

❹ *100 km (62 mi) south of northern part of Zagorohoria Region, 58 km (36 mi) east of Ioannina, 293 km (182 mi) northwest of Athens.*

The traditional village of Metsovo cascades down a mountain at about 3,300 feet above sea level, below the 6,069-foot Katara Pass, which is the highest in Greece and marks the border between Epirus and Thessaly. Even in summer, the temperatures may be in the low 70°sF, and February's average highs are just above freezing. Early evening is a wonderful time to arrive. As you descend through the mist, dazzling lights twinkle in the ravine. Stone houses with gray slate roofs and sharply projecting wooden balconies line steep, serpentine alleys. In the square, especially after the Sunday service, old men—dressed in black flat caps, dark baggy pants, and wooden shoes with pom-poms—sit on a bench, like crows on a tree branch. Should you arrive on a religious feast day, many villagers will be decked out in traditional costume. Older women often wear dark blue or black dresses with embroidered trim every day, augmenting these with brightly colored aprons, jackets, and scarves with floral embroidery on holidays.

Although most such villages are fading away, Metsovo, designated a traditional settlement by the Greek National Tourism Organization (GNTO or EOT), has become a prosperous community with a growing population. In winter it draws skiers headed for Mt. Karakoli, and in summer it is—for better or worse—a favorite destination for tourist groups. For the most part Metsovo has preserved its character despite the souvenir shops selling "traditional handicrafts" that may be imports and the slate roofs that have been replaced with easy-to-maintain tile.

The natives are descendants of nomadic Vlach shepherds, once believed to have migrated from Romania but now thought to be Greeks trained by Romans to guard the Egnatia Highway connecting Constantinople and the Adriatic. Metsovo became an important center of finance, commerce, handicrafts, and sheepherding, and the Vlachs began trading farther afield—in Constantinople, Vienna, and Venice. Ali Pasha abolished the privileges in 1795, and in 1854 the town was invaded by Ottoman troops led by Abdi Pasha. In 1912 Metsovo was freed from the Turks by the Greek army. Many important families lived here, including the Averoffs and Tositsas, who made their fortunes in Egyptian cotton. They contributed to the new Greek state's development and bequeathed large sums to restore Metsovo and finance small industries. For example, Foundation Baron Michalis Tositsa, begun in 1948 when a member of the prominent area family endowed it (although he was living in Switzerland), helped the local weaving industry get a start.

The Vlach language is so related to Latin that it was used during World War II to communicate with occupying Italian forces, and villagers still speak it among themselves. In winter, while the village lies buried in snow, shepherds move their flocks from the mountains to the lowlands around Trikala; their wives, nicknamed the "white widows," tend to their hearths in isolation. The shepherds' numbers are dwindling, however (they herd about 15,000 sheep today), as many have turned to tourism for their livelihoods.

For generations the Tositsa family had been one of the most prominent in Metsovo, and to get a sense of how Metsovites lived (and endured the arduous winters in style), visit their home, a restored late-Ottoman-period stone-and-timber building that is now the **Tositsa Museum** of popular art and local Epirote crafts. Built in 1661 and renovated in 1954, this typical Metsovo mansion has carved woodwork, sumptuous textiles in rich colors on a black background, and handcrafted Vlach furniture. In the stable are the gold-embroidered saddle used for special holidays and, unique to this area, a fanlight in the fireplace, ensuring that the hearth would always be illuminated. The goatskin bag on the wall was used to store cheese. Wait for the guard to open door prior to the tour. Guides usually speak some English. ✉ *Up stone stairs to right off Tositsa (main road) as you descend to main town Sq.* ☏ 26560/41084 ⊕ *www.epcon.gr/metsovo* ◫ €3 ☯ *By guided tour, every ½ hr May–Oct., Fri.–Wed. 9–1:30 and 4–6; Nov.–Apr., Fri.–Wed. 9–1:30 and 3–5.*

The freely accessible 18th-century church of **Agia Paraskevi** has a flamboyantly decorated altar screen that's worth a peek. Note that July 26 is its saint's day, entailing a big celebration in which the church's silver icon is carried around the town in a morning procession, followed by feasting and dancing. ✉ *Main Sq.*

The **Averoff Gallery** displays the outstanding personal art collection of politician and intellectual Evangelos Averoff (1910–90). The 19th- and 20th-century paintings depict historical scenes, local landscapes, and daily activities. Most major Greek artists, such as Nikos Ghikas and Alekos Fassianos, are represented. One painting known to all Greeks is Nikiforos Litras's *Burning of the Turkish Flagship by Kanaris,* a scene from a decisive battle in Chios. Look on the second floor for Pericles Pantazis's *Street Urchin Eating Watermelon,* a captivating portrait of a young boy. Paris Prekas's *The Mosque of Aslan Pasha in Ioannina* depicts what Ioannina looked like in the Turkish period. ⊠ *Main Sq.* ☎ *26560/ 41210* ⊕ *www.epcon.gr/metsovo* ⊡ *€3* ⊙ *Mid-June–mid-Sept., Wed.–Mon. 10–6.30; mid-Sept.–mid-June, Wed.–Mon. 10–4..* Call in advance to visit the **winery.** Don't leave without a few bottles of the exquisite, full-bodied, musky red Katogi-Averoff wine. It's about a 45-minute walk, however. ⊠ *Eastern edge of village, in Upper Aoos Valley* ☎ *26560/41010* ⊡ *Free* ⊙ *Weekdays 8:30–3:30.*

The small **ski resort,** which has one chairlift, nestles in the slopes of Mt. Karakoli. ⊠ *1½ km (1 mi) north of village* ☎ *26560/41206.*

> **off the beaten path**

AYIOS NIKOLAOS MONASTERY – Visit a restored 14th-century monastery, about a 30-minute walk into the valley (with the trip back up about an hour). The *katholikon* (main church) is topped by a barrel vault, and what may have once been the narthex was converted to a *ginaikonitis* (women's gallery). Two images of the *Pantocrator* (Godhead), one in each dome—perhaps duplicated to give the segregated women their own view—stare down on the congregation. You can also see the monks' cells, with insulating walls of mud and straw; the abbot's quarters; and the school where Greek children were taught during the Turkish occupation. The keepers will give you a closely guided tour in English and explanation of the unusual 18th-century frescoes created in Epirote style. ⊠ *Down into valley via footpath (follow signs near National Bank of Greece; turn left where paving ends)* ⊡ *€1* ⊙ *May–Oct., daily 9–7; Nov.–Apr., daily 9–1.*

Where to Stay & Eat

$–$$ ✕ **Taverna Metsovitiko Saloni.** A large fireplace, Metsovo costumes on the walls, old photos, and carved wooden furniture enliven the dining room. Try the vegetable pies, especially the *kolokithopita* (zucchini pie) made from *bobota* (corn flour), an unusual crust in Greece but an Epirote favorite; in addition, the *saganaki* (fried cheese) made with four Metsovo cheeses is a winner. Savor the large wine selection (good local choices are Katogi and Zitsa), tender lamb *yiouvetsi* (baked in tomato-wine sauce), and desserts including Metsovitiko baklava and thick sheep yogurt with pastry, honey, and walnuts. ⊠ *Tositsa 10, above post office* ☎ *26560/ 42142* ☷ *No credit cards.*

★ ¢–$$ ✕ **To Paradosiako.** The name means "traditional," and that's what this comfortable spot decorated with colorful weavings and folk crafts is. Vasilis Bissas, the chef-owner, has revived many of the more esoteric regional specialties. Try the *fileta tou dasous* (fillet of the forest)—a choice beef fillet stuffed with cheese, ham, tomato, mushrooms, and "wood-cutters' potatoes" (potato slices baked with bacon and four kinds of cheese). "Grandmothers' bread" is toasted and stuffed with cheese, bacon, tomato, peppers, and onions, then baked in the oven. Accompany your meal with the house wine, guaranteed to be a well-searched-out regional speciality, or choose the heady local red Katogi. ⊠ *Tositsa 44* ☎ *26560/42773* ▭ *No credit cards* ◯ *No lunch.*

$ ✕🍴 **Galaxias.** A great place to rest your mountain-weary feet, this small hotel is blessed with a restaurant (next door) that serves choice local cuisine. In summer you sit outside in the garden, in winter inside by the fireplace. Select the local specialties such as leek pie with a corn pastry, veal with noodles from Metsovo, or boiled goat. Start with half a kilo of house barrel wine, *miso kilo hima*. The guest rooms are designed in typical Metsovo style: simple, with the splash of color on a *kourelou*, or traditional rug. Some bathrooms have tubs, others showers; still others have their own fireplaces. ⊠ *Above main square, 44200* ☎ *26560/ 41202 or 26560/41123* 🖷 *26560/41124* ⊕ *www.metsovo.com/ galaxyhotel/* 🛏 *10 rooms* ⚖ *Restaurant, some pets allowed; no a/c* ▭ *AE, MC, V.*

★ ¢–$ 🍴 **Bitouni.** Local craftsmen created the elegantly carved wooden ceilings in this traditional-style Metsovo mansion. A large fireplace in the main reception room warms the cozy hotel. Six luxury suites have panoramic views of the surrounding mountains. Soothe your weary travelers muscles in the on-site sauna. Two brothers, fluent in English, run this friendly establishment and three times a week mother Bitouni makes a mean vegetable pie. ⊠ *On main street leading up from the central Sq. 44200* ☎ *26560/41217* 🖷 *26560/41545* ⊕ *www.hotelbitouni.com* 🛏 *18 rooms, 6 suites* ⚖ *Dining room, sauna, bar; no a/c* ▭ *AE, MC, V* ¶◯ *CP.*

¢ 🍴 **Hotel Olympic.** For budget-level lodging (approximately €30 for two), this hotel is a fine choice. Like most other places in Metsovo, the Olympic is family owned, so you get that homey feel; it's also traditionally designed, so you get a clean, simple room. Wood and stone make the country living complete. Ask for a room with a view. The owners also run the taverna 5F on the main square, where you can grab a quick snack before a hike around town. ⊠ *Main square, behind Agia Paraskevi, 44200* ☎ *26560/41337 or 26560/41383* 🖷 *26560/41837* ⊕ *www.metsovo. com/olympichotel* 🛏 *20 rooms* ⚖ *Bar; no a/c* ▭ *AE, MC, V* ¶◯ *CP.*

Shopping

Metsovo is famous throughout Greece for its expensive smoked cheeses. You can try them at one of the *tiropolio* (cheese shops) in the main square. You may even be able to get a taste before you buy. Metsovo is also known for its fabrics, folk crafts, and silver. Although many of the "traditional" arts and crafts here are imported, low-quality imitations, with a little prowling and patience you can still make some finds, especially if you like textiles and weavings. Some of them are genuine antiques that cost a good deal more than the newer versions, but they are far superior in quality. Everything's available on the main square. **Aris Talaris** (⊠ Hotel Egnatia, Arvantinou 20 ☎ 26560/41901) has two shops: one sells quality silver jewelry made in Talaris's own workshop, and the other displays gold pieces. The Metsovo silver-work trade is one of the oldest trades in the region; members of the Talaris family have been silversmiths for many generations. Near the Hotel Egnatia, the shop of **Vangelis Balabekos** (⊠ Arvantinou ☎ 26560/41623) sells traditional clothing from Epirus and other areas of Greece.

THESSALY

ΘΕΣΣΑΛΙΑ

Though Thessaly, with part of Mt. Olympus within its boundaries, is the home of the immortal gods, a Byzantine site holds pride of place: Meteora, the amazing medieval monasteries on top of inaccessible needles of rock. The monasteries' extraordinary geological setting stands in vivid contrast to the rest of Thessaly, a huge plain in central Greece, almost entirely surrounded by mountains: Pindos to the west, Pelion to the east, Othrys to the south, and the Kamvounian range to the north. It is one of the country's most fertile areas and has sizable population centers in Lamia, Larissa, Trikala, and Volos. Thessaly was not ceded to Greece until 1878, after almost five centuries of Ottoman rule; today vestiges of this period remain. Kalambaka and Meteora are in the northwest corner of the plain, before the Pindos Mountains. The best time to come here is spring, especially to the Meteora monasteries, when the mountains are still snow covered and blend harmoniously with the green fields, the red poppies, and the white and pink flowering fruit trees.

Kalambaka

Καλαμπάκα

❺ *71 km (44 mi) east of Metsovo, 154 km (95 mi) southwest of Thessaloniki.*

Kalambaka may be dismissed as one more drab modern town, useful only as a base to explore the fabled Meteora complex north of town. Yet an overnight stay here, complete with a taverna dinner and a stroll in the main squares, provides a taste of everyday life in a provincial Thessalian town. This will prove quite a contrast to an afternoon spent at nearby Meteora, where you can get acquainted with the glorious history and architecture of the Greek Orthodox Church. Invariably, you return to modern Kalambaka and wind up at a poolside bar to sip ouzo and contemplate the asceticism of the Meteora monks. If you'd rather stay in a more attractive place slightly closer to the monasteries, head to Kastraki, a hamlet with some attractive folk-style houses about 2½ km (1 mi) north of Kalambaka.

Burned by the Germans during World War II, Kalambaka has only one building of interest, the centuries-old cathedral church of the **Dormition of the Virgin.** Patriarchal documents in the outer narthex indicate that it was built in the first half of the 12th century by Emperor Manuel Comnenos, but some believe it was founded as early as the 7th century, on the site of a temple of Apollo (classical drums and other fragments are incorporated into the walls, and mosaics can be glimpsed under the present floor). The latter theory explains the church's paleo-Christian features, including its center-aisle *ambo* (great marble pulpit), which is usually to the right of the sanctuary; its rare *synthronon* (four semicircular steps where the priest sat when not officiating) east of the altar; and its Roman-basilica style, originally adapted to Christian use and unusual for the 12th century. The church has vivid 16th-century frescoes, work of the Cretan monk Neophytos, son of the famous hagiographer Theophanes. The marble baldachin in the sanctuary, decorated with crosses and stylized grapes, probably predates the 11th century. The courtyard outside the church provides welcome respite under the cool shade of a eucalyptus tree. Behind the church you can stroll through a small necropolis: boxes upon boxes of bones that have been disinterred and washed in accordance with Orthodox tradition. ⊠ *North end of town, follow signs from Pl. Riga Fereou* ☎ *24320/24297* ⊕ *www.culture.gr* ◙ *€2* ⊙ *Daily 8–1 and 4–8.*

Where to Stay & Eat

★ **$$** ✕ **Estiatorio Meteora.** At this spot on the main square, a local favorite since 1925, the Gertzos family serves food prepared by the matriarch, Ketty. Meteora is known for hearty main courses—try Ketty's special wine-and-pepper chicken, veal or pork *stifado* (stew)—and some specialties from Asia Minor, including *tzoutzoukakia Smyrneika,* aromatic meatballs in a red sauce laced with cumin. All customers are ushered through the kitchen to place their order. Do try the local wine with your meal. Call ahead if you want lunch; it's served only several, varying days a week. ⊠ *Ekonomou 4, on Pl. Dimarchiou* ☎ *24320/22316* ▤ *No credit cards* ⊙ *Closed Feb.*

$ ✕ **Paradissos.** When a Greek woman cooks with *meraki* (good taste and mood), the world does indeed feel like *paradissos* (paradise). Owner Kyriakoula Fassoula serves up meat dishes cooked *tis oras* (to order), such as grilled pork and lamb chops. Vegetarians can choose from delectable eggplant *papoutsakia* ("little shoes"), fried zucchini with garlic sauce, and various boiled greens. Complimentary fruit is served for the finale, but it would be a shame to pass up the flaky baklava. ⊠ *On main road to Meteora across from Spania Rooms, Kastraki* ☎ *24320/22723* ▤ *No credit cards.*

🐣 **¢–$** ✕ **O Kipos Tou Ilia.** This simple taverna with a traditional Greek menu and a waterfall in the garden attracts everyone from visiting royalty to Olympic medal–winners. Kids get their own *paithika piata* (kids' plates). Unusual appetizers include spicy fried feta with peppers and grilled mushrooms. Among the main dishes are beef *stamna* (baked in a covered clay pot with herbs, potatoes, and cheese), rabbit with onions, and vegetable croquettes. ⊠ *Trikalon, at terminus of Ayia Triada, before entrance to Kalambaka* ☎☎ *24320/23218* ▤ *V.*

$$$ ▥ **Amalia.** A low-lying, clay-color complex outside Kalambaka (on the road to Trikala), this hotel has spacious, handsome public rooms that somehow avoided the generic stamp. Relax in the sitting room, with a fireplace (in the bar and in the restaurant), striking antiques, and floral murals, or enjoy the poolside bar, with glistening blue tiles and rustic rafters. Grounds are beautifully landscaped and blissfully quiet. Rooms are done in soothing colors and have large beds and prints; some also have balconies. ⊠ *14 km [9 mi] along Ethnikos Odos Trikalon–Ioanninon Rd., 42200* ☎ *24320/72116 or 24320/72117* 🖷 *24320/72457* ⊕ *www.amalia.gr* ⇨ *170 rooms, 2 suites* ♿ *Restaurant, cafeteria, pool, bar, meeting rooms* ▤ *AE, DC, MC, V* ⊘I *CP.*

$$ ⌷ **Hotel Divani.** A few minutes from the center of town, this hotel has optimal views of the Meteora rocks from the rooms' balconies. Its large open spaces, quiet corners, and private garden encourage relaxation. The exterior is plain, as are the rooms, but they're shielded from outside noise. The professional reception staff will arrange and negotiate a price for a leisurely taxi ride to the monasteries. ✉ *Ethnikos Odos Trikalon 1, 42200* ☏ *24320/23330* 🖷 *24320/23638* ⊕ *www.divanis.gr* ⤸ *163 rooms, 1 suite* ♦ *Restaurant, cable TV, indoor pool, outdoor pool, sauna, 2 bars, conference center* ▭ *AE, DC, MC, V* ⊓ *BP.*

$ ⌷ **Hotel Antoniadis.** A pink exterior encapsulates pastel rooms with carpeting and modern wooden furniture. Many rooms at this reliable in-town hotel have a view of the Meteora monasteries, as does the rooftop pool and bar. ✉ *Trikalon 148, 42200* ☏ *24320/24387 or 24320/23419* 🖷 *24320/24319* ✍ *antoniadishotel@altecnet.gr* ⤸ *80 rooms* ♦ *Restaurant, pool, bar* ▭ *V.*

★ ¢–$ ⌷ **Doupiani House.** Reside in a traditional stone-and-wood hotel set amid vineyards in the upper reaches of the idyllic village of Kastraki. Each room—with a luxurious carved double bed, oak floors, and cupboards—has a balcony with panoramic views of both Meteora and Kastraki. Vivacious owner Toula Naki serves breakfast (extra charge, but the produce is local) around the pergola in the large garden, which is perfumed with the scent of roses, jasmine, and honeysuckle. If you have enough stamina, you can walk to the monasteries from here; Thanassis Naki will happily provide you with his excellent homemade area hiking maps. ✉ *Kastrakiou, left off main road to Meteora, near Cave Camping, 42200 Kastraki* ☏☏ *24320/77555 or 24320/75326* ✍ *doupiani-house@kmp.forthnet.gr* ⤸ *11 rooms* ▭ *MC, V.*

¢ ⌷ **Hotel Edelweiss.** Every room is spotless, with bare white walls (ok, so you may feel a little like you're in a hospital), but many of them have balcony views. Do request one looking out over the pool and the towering Meteora rocks beyond. The bar attracts a lively local crowd, and the hotel runs a Western-and-Greek popular music club next door. ✉ *Eleftherios Venizelou 3, 42200* ☏ *24320/23966 or 24320/23884* 🖷 *24320/24733* ✍ *edelweis@hol.gr* ⤸ *60 rooms* ♦ *Restaurant, pool, 2 bars, dance club* ▭ *MC, V* ⊓ *CP.*

Nightlife

Kalambaka isn't the most cosmopolitan city, but you may find some fun places for ice cream or coffee along the main drag, Trikalon. Platia Dimoula is all abuzz on weekends as locals descend from the surrounding villages. **Arena** (✉ Pl. Dimoula ☏ 24320/77999) is an Internet bar and café open from around 10 AM until late night.

| en route | On the road to the Meteora monasteries, which begins outside of Kalambaka in Kastraki, you pass the 12th-century **Chapel of the Virgin** (✉ At Doupiani), where the monks first gathered. On St. George's Day (celebrated on April 23 or on the Tuesday following Easter, whichever comes first) you can spot, about 8 km (5 mi) outside Kastraki, what looks like a clothesline hung with brightly colored fabrics set high up in a crevice. According to legend, a woodcutter who lost his leg promised to give St. George all his wife's |

clothing if he was healed—which he was. On St. George's Day, women offer scarves or other items of clothing and young men scale the rocks to hang them up for the saint. Some local women have set up shop and sell homemade jams, olive oil, and other delicacies during much of the year.

The Meteora

Μετέωρα

❻ *3 km (2 mi) north of Kalambaka, 178 km (110 mi) southwest of Thes-*
Fodor'sChoice *saloniki.*
★

The name Meteora comes from the Greek word *meteorizome* ("to hang in midair"), and the monasteries, perched on a handful of strangely shaped rock pinnacles that rise 984 feet above the Peneus Valley, seem to do just that. Their lofty aeries imbue them with an otherworldly quality; the azure heavens seem close enough to touch while the valley of worldly distractions remains far below. Looming between the Pindos range and the Thessalian plain, the rocks remain an enigma. Some geologists say a lake that covered the area 30 million years ago swept away the soil and softer stone as it forced its way to the sea. Others believe the Peneus River slowly carved out the towering pillars, now eroded by wind and rain. Legend has a more colorful story—these rock needles were supposedly meteors hurled by an angry god.

By the 9th century AD ascetic hermits were inhabiting the rocks' crevices. On Sundays and holidays they gathered at Stagi (present-day Kalambaka) and Doupiani, and they eventually formed religious communities. With Byzantine power on the wane and an increase in religious persecution from invading foreigners, the monks retreated to the inaccessible rocks. In 1336 they were joined by two monks from Mt. Athos, Abbot Gregorios of Magoula and his companion, St. Athanasios. The abbot returned to Athos, but he commanded St. Athanasios to build a monastery here. Notwithstanding the legend that says that the saint flew up to the rocks on the back of an eagle, St. Athanasios began the backbreaking task of building the Megalo Meteoro (1356–72) using pulleys and ropes to haul construction material. The monks themselves had to endure a harrowing ride in a swinging net to reach the top.

Despite St. Athanasios's strictness of rule, the monastery attracted many devotees, including, in 1371, John Urosh of Serbia, who relinquished accession to the throne to become a monk, using the name Ioasaph. His royal presence brought contributions to the monasteries, and the congregation grew quickly. By the 16th century the Meteora had at least 20 smaller settlements and 13 monasteries, which were embellished with frescoes and icons by such great artists as Theophanis Strelitzas, a monk from Crete. The larger monasteries prospered on revenues from estates in Thessaly and eastern Europe; during the late Byzantine period, they served as bastions of Christianity against Turkish domination.

The monastic communities eventually disappeared for several reasons: some of the wealthy monasteries were plagued by bitter power struggles. Monasticism as a vocation gradually lost its appeal, causing even grand communities to dwindle. Smaller, poorer monasteries could not afford to maintain the old buildings; many of their structures were neglected or abandoned. After the Greco-Turkish War of 1919–22, the already diminished monastic lands and revenues were appropriated by the state on behalf of refugees from Asia Minor, another blow to the few remaining monasteries.

Only six monasteries are open to the public. The architecture was restricted by the space available and buildings rise from different levels. Some are whitewashed; others display the pretty Byzantine pattern of stone and brick, the multiple domes of the many churches dominating the wooden galleries and balconies that hang precariously over frightening abysses. The days of jointed ladders, pulled up in an emergency, are no more, and the nets are strictly limited to hauling up supplies. A comfortable road winds ingeniously through the sandstone labyrinth close to the cliff.

When visiting you are expected to dress decorously: men must tuck up long hair and wear long pants, women's skirts (no pants allowed) should fall to the knee, and both sexes should be sure to cover their shoulders. Some monasteries provide appropriate coverings at their entrances. Opening hours vary depending on the season, but information can be readily confirmed in Kalambaka by your hotel receptionist. All monasteries can be visited in a single journey from Kalambaka—a 21-km (13-mi) round-trip by car. A bus leaves Kalambaka for Megalo Meteoro five times daily (once daily in winter). Megalo Meteoro and Varlaam are the two most rewarding monasteries to visit. You can hike along the footpaths between monasteries, but you'd better be in good shape, because there are many steps up to most monasteries. It also helps to buy a map of the monasteries in Kalambaka. Once on the monastery circuit, there are just a few overpriced concession stands; if you plan to make a day of it, stock up on picnic goods in town. Many people visit the monasteries on guided tours, so you may run into crowds.

The monastery of **Ayios Nikolaos Anapafsas** seems impossibly crammed atop its narrow rock. The katholikon, or main church, was built in 1388 and was later expanded; the monastery itself dates from the end of the 15th century. Because of the rock's peculiar shape, the katholikon faces north rather than the usual east. Its superb 16th-century frescoes are the work of Theophanis Strelitzas. Though conservative, his frescoes are lively and expressive: mountains are stylized, and plants and animals are portrayed geometrically. Especially striking are the treatments of the Temptation, the scourging of Christ, and a scene of Adam naming the animals. The serpent is in the form of the legendary basilisk, which could kill with a mere look or a breath. The rock's small area precluded the construction of a cloister, so the monks studied in the larger-than-usual narthex. Visitors are admitted in small groups. ⊠ *Along monastery route, about 3 km (2 mi) northeast of Kalambaka* ☎ *24320/22375* ⊕ *www.culture. gr* 🎫 *€2* ☯ *Apr.–Oct., Sat.–Thurs. 9–5; Nov.–Mar., Sat.–Thurs. 9–1.*

The inaccessible **Ayia Moni** monastery has been deserted since an 1858 earthquake. Locals believe the area is haunted. ⊠ *Along monastery route, across from Agios Nikolaos monastery.*

Because of its breathtaking location, the compact monastery of **Ayia Barbara,** with its colorful gardens in and around red- and gray-stone walls, is the favorite for picture-taking. Abandoned in the early 1900s, it stood empty until nuns moved in some years ago and restored it. The monastery's founding in 1288 by the monks Nicodemus and Benedict has yet to be confirmed, but it is known that 156 years later the monastery was restored for the first time. The main church, dedicated to the Transfiguration, has well-preserved frescoes dating from the mid-16th century. Most depict gory scenes of martyrdom, but one shows lions licking Daniel's feet during his imprisonment. ☒ *Along monastery route, across vertiginous bridges from Ayia Moni area* ☎ *24320/22649* ⊕ *www. culture.gr* ▨ *€2* ☉ *Apr.–Oct., daily 9–6; Nov.–Mar., daily 9–2.*

The highest and most powerful monastery is **Megalo Meteoro,** or the Church of the Metamorphosis (Transfiguration). Founded by St. Athanasios, the monk from Athos, it was built of massive stones on the highest rock, 1,361 feet above the valley. As you walk toward the entrance, you see the chapel containing the cell where St. Athanasios once lived. This monastery had extensive privileges and held jurisdiction over the others for centuries; an 18th-century engraving in its museum depicts it towering above the other monasteries.

The sanctuary of the present church was the chapel first built by St. Athanasios, later added to by St. Ioasaph. The rest of the church was erected in 1552 with an unusual transept built on a cross-in-square plan with lateral apses topped by lofty domes, as in the Mt. Athos monasteries. To the right of the narthex are the tombs of Ioasaph and Athanasios; a fresco shows the austere saints holding a monastery in their hands. Also of interest are the gilded iconostasis, with plant and animal motifs of exceptional workmanship; the bishop's throne (1617), inlaid with mother-of-pearl and ivory; and the 15th-century icons in the sanctuary. The expressiveness and attention to color and detail of these icons have led art historians to conclude they may also be the work of Theophanis Strelitzas. In the narthex are frescoes of the Martyrdom of the Saints, gruesome scenes of persecution under the Romans. A chamber stacked with skulls and bones of monks is opposite.

The refectory now houses the treasury, with miniatures, golden bulls, historic documents, and elaborately carved crucifixes, including one that the monk Daniel labored over for 10 years. The front of this crucifix shows 10 scenes with several figures each, and representations of 24 single figures. Portable icons include the Virgin, by Tzanes, another well-known artist. The adjacent kitchen is blackened by centuries of cooking. From November to March the monastery may close early. ☒ *Along monastery route, past intersection for Varlaam monastery* ☎ *24320/22278* ▨ *€2* ⊕ *www.culture.gr* ☉ *Wed.–Mon. 9–6.*

The monks from **Varlaam,** which sits atop a ravine and is reached by a climb of 195 steps, were famous for their charity. Originally here were the Church of Three Hierarchs (14th century) and the cells of a hermitage started by St. Varlaam, who arrived shortly after St. Athanasios. Two brothers from the wealthy Aparas family of Ioannina rebuilt the church in 1518, incorporating it into a larger katholikon called Agii Pandes (All Saints). A church document relates how it was completed in 20 days, after the materials had been accumulated atop the rock over a period of 22 years. The church's main attraction, the 16th-century frescoes—mostly of ascetic subjects, including scenes from the life of John the Baptist and a disturbing Apocalypse with a yawning hell's mouth—completely covers the walls, beams, and pillars. The frescoes' realism, the sharp contrasts of light and dark, and the many-figured scenes show an Italian influence, though in the portrayal of single saints they follow the Orthodox tradition (the West had no models to offer). Note the Pantocrator peering down from the dome. These are the work of Frangos Katellanos of Thebes, one of the most important 16th-century hagiographers.

Other buildings include the infirmary, a chapel to Sts. Cosmas and Damien, and the refectory, now a sacristy, which displays the manuscript Gospel Book of the Byzantine emperor Constantine Porphyrogennetus, bearing his signature. There are large storerooms and an ascent tower with a net and a winch. Until the 1920s the only way to reach most of the monasteries was by retractable ladder or net. A bishop of Trikala subsequently decreed that steps be cut to allow access to all the monasteries, and today the ropes are used only for hauling up supplies. ⊠ *Along monastery route, 328 ft southwest of intersection for Megalo Meteoro* ☎ *24320/22277* ⊕ *www.culture.gr* 🖃 *€2* ☉ *May–Oct., Fri.–Wed. 9–4; Nov.–Apr., Sat.–Wed. 9–3.*

The least-visited site, along the eastern route, is **Ayios Stephanos,** the oldest monastery. According to an inscription that was once on the lintel, the rock was inhabited before AD 1200 and was the hermitage of Jeremiah. By the beginning of the 14th century, the inhabitants lived together in an organized monastic community. After the Byzantine emperor Andronicus Paleologos stayed here in 1333 on his way to conquer Thessaly, he made generous gifts to the monks, which funded the building of a church in 1350. A permanent bridge has replaced the movable one that once connected the monastery with the hill opposite. Today Ayios Stephanos is an airy convent, where the nuns spend their time painting Byzantine icons, writing, or studying music; some are involved in the community as doctors and professors. The katholikon has no murals but contains a carved wooden baldachin and an iconostasis depicting the Last Supper. You can also visit the **old church of Ayios Stephanos,** with late-15th-century frescoes, as well as a **small icon museum.** ⊠ *Along eastern monastery route (from main road at intersection for Kalambaka, bear right at fork)* ☎ *24320/22279* ⊕ *www.culture.gr* 🖃 *€2* ☉ *Apr.–Oct., Tues.–Sun. 9–1:30 and 3:30–5.30; Nov.–Mar., Tues.–Sun. 9:30–2 and 3–5.*

need a break? Although you may stop anywhere on the circuit, the stretch approaching Ayia Triada from Ayios Stephanos has the best views for a midday **picnic.** Just hike a few yards off the road to a spot overlooking the valley and unpack.

Of all the monasteries, **Ayia Triada** seems the most primitive and remote; if pressed for time, you may want to skip this one. James Bond fans will recognize the monastery from the 1981 movie *For Your Eyes Only*. According to local legend, the monk Dometius was the first to arrive in 1438; the main church, dedicated to the Holy Trinity, was built in 1476, and the narthex and frescoes were added more than 200 years later. Look for the fresco with St. Sisois gazing upon the skeleton of Alexander the Great, meant to remind the viewer that power is fleeting. In the early 1980s thieves stole precious antique icons, which have never been recovered. The iconostasis has one icon (1662) that depicts Christ in local costume; another scene, of three angels, symbolizes the Holy Trinity. The apse's pseudo-trefoil window and the sawtooth decoration around it and beneath other windows lend a measure of grace to the structure. There are also the monks' cells, a chapel dedicated to St. John the Baptist, a small folk museum, a kitchen, a refectory, and cisterns. Ayia Triada is best known for its view, with Ayios Stephanos and Kalambaka in the south and Varlaam and Megalo Meteoro to the west. A footpath near the entrance (red arrows) descends to Kalambaka, about 3 km (2 mi) away. ⊠ *Along eastern monastery route, 656 ft north of Ayios Stefanos* ☎ *24320/22220* ⊕ *www.culture.gr* ⊠ *€2* ⊗ *Fri.–Wed. 9–12:30 and 3–5.*

EPIRUS & THESSALY A TO Z

To research prices, get advice from other travelers, and book travel arrangements, visit www.fodors.com.

AIR TRAVEL

Ioannina is a 70-minute flight from Athens and a 50-minute flight from Thessaloniki. From June through August, Olympic Airlines usually has two or three flights daily from Athens to Ioannina and about five flights per week from Thessaloniki to Ioannina. In other months, two flights daily leave Athens for Ioannina and about four flights per week depart Thessaloniki for Ioannina. Aegean Airlines has one flight per day to Ioannina from Athens. AirSea Lines flies regularly to Corfu from Ioannina in their seaplanes.

🛪 Carriers **Aegean Airlines** ⊠ Othonos 10, Athens ☎ 210/331-5502, 210/331-5503, 801/112-0000 for local charge countrywide, 210/353-4294 airport ⊕ www.aegeanair. com ⊠ Pirsinella 11, Ioannina ☎ 26510/64444, 26510/65200, 26510/65201 Ioannina airport. **AirSea Lines** ⊠ Spyrou Lambrou 36, Ioannina ☎ 26510/49800 ⊕ www.airsealines. com. **Olympic Airlines** ⊠ Spirou Katsadima 6, Ioannina ☎ 26510/23120, 801/114-4444 for local charge countrywide ⊕ www.olympicairlines.com ⊠ Ioannina airport, Ioannina ☎ 26510/22355.

AIRPORTS

The Ioannina airport is 8 km (5 mi) north of town.

🛪 **Ioannina airport** ⊠ 8-km- [5-mi-] mark on Ethnikos Odos Ioanninon-Trikalon Rd. ☎ 26510/83310 or 26510/83320.

BUS TRAVEL

About nine buses a day make the seven-hour trip from Athens's Terminal A (Kifissou) to Ioannina's main Zosimadon station. Some buses take the longer route east through Kalambaka and Trikala rather than the usual southern route to the Rion–Antirion ferry over the suspension bridge which is the largest in Europe. From Athens's dismal Terminal B (Liossion), seven buses leave daily for the five-hour journey to Kalambaka. Most routes require you to hop on a different bus for the final leg from Trikala, but one morning bus goes direct. From Thessaloniki the bus takes you via Konitsa to Ioannina in a little over seven hours.

Around three KTEL buses leave Ioannina daily for Metsovo (about one hour) and two buses for Kalambaka (two hours); frequencies are the same in the opposite direction. Buses for Dodona leave from Ioannina's smaller, Bizaniou station. The several-times-weekly bus heading for Melingi village passes the ancient site. Other bus options drop you off 1 km (½ mi) or ½ km (¼ mi) from the site; ask for information based on the day you want to go. On Sunday, service is reduced for all towns. Regular bus service runs from Ioannina's main terminal to the towns in the Zagorohoria.

🚌 **Zosimadon station** Main terminal ⊠ Between Sina and Zosimadou, Ioannina ☎ 26510/27442 for Metsovo and Kalambaka, 26510/25014 for Dodona. **Bizaniou station** Smaller station ⊠ Bizaniou 21, Ioannina ☎ 26510/25014 for Dodona. **KTEL information** ⊕ www.ktel.org. **Terminal A** ⊠ Kifissou 100, Athens ☎ 210/512-4910, 210/512-9363 for Ioannina. **Terminal B** ⊠ Liossion 260, Athens ☎ 210/831-1434 for Trikala Kalambaka and Meteora.

CAR RENTALS
🚗 **Avis** ⊠ Dodonis 96, Ioannina ☎ 26510/46333 for city and airport ⊕ www.avis.com. **Budget** ⊠ Dodonis 109, Ioannina ☎ 26510/43901 or 6932/641943 ⊕ www.budget.com. **Hertz** ⊠ Pirsinella 11, Ioannina ☎ 26510/38911 ⊕ www.hertz.com ⊠ Airport, Ioannina ☎ 26510/27400. **Tomaso** ⊠ Dodonis 42, Ioannina ☎ 26510/66900 ⊕ www.tomaso.gr.

CAR TRAVEL
A rented car is by far the best way to explore the region, and one is essential to go beyond the main sights. Driving to Kalambaka or Ioannina from Athens takes the greater part of a day. To reach Ioannina take the National Road west past Corinth in the Peloponnese, crossing the magnificent Rion–Antirion bridge. The total trip is 445 km (276 mi). For Kalambaka, take the National Road north past Thebes; north of Lamia there's a turnoff for Trikala and Kalambaka (a total of 330 km [204 mi]). The drive from Thessaloniki takes around five hours and winds you over the mountains and river valleys of Kozani and Grevena on the National Road.

The road from Ioannina to Metsovo to Kalambaka is one of the most scenic in northern Greece, but it traverses the famous Katara Pass, which is curvy and possibly hazardous, especially December through March (snow chains are necessary). If you have a few people, it might be more relaxing and almost as economical to hire a taxi to drive you around, at least for a day.

EMERGENCIES
🚑 Ioannina **Emergencies** ☎ 100, 171 for tourist police. **Panepistimiako General Hospital** ⊠ Panepistimiou ☎ 26510/99111. **Police** ☎ 26510/25673, 0651/26431 tourist police. 🚑 Kalambaka **Health Center** ☎ 24320/22222. **Police** ☎ 24320/76500.

🔏 Metsovo **Health Center/First Aid** ☎ 26560/41111, 26560/41112, or 26560/41071. **Police** ☎ 26560/41233.

SPORTS & THE OUTDOORS

HIKING &
WALKING

In Ioannina, contact the Greek Alpine Club for walking-tour information. It can organize treks to the Pindos Mountains. Aris Talaris can arrange excursions, in his eight-seater minibus, around the Metsovo area, Kalambaka, and the Zagorohoria, as well as hiking trips to the Vikos Gorge, mainly during summer season. Metsovo Alpine Club has information on hiking trails and the nearby ski center.

Robinson Expeditions in Ioannina specializes in outdoor tours and can make arrangements for single travelers or groups to hike the Vikos Gorge; other programs are hang-gliding, rafting, kayaking, and studying nature. The company also schedules rock-climbing excursions around the Meteora. For alternative adventures and extreme sports, contact Trekking Hellas and No Limits (both for the Zagorohoria) and Ecoexperience (for Metsovo).

🔏 **Aris Talaris** ✉ Hotel Egnatia, Arvantinou 20, Ioannina ☎ 26560/41263 or 26560/41900 🖷 26510/75060. **Ecoexperience** ✉ Metsovo ☎ 26560/41770 or 26560/41719 ⊕ www.ecoexperience.gr. **Greek Alpine Club** ✉ Despotatou Ipirou 2, Ioannina ☎ 26510/22138. **Metsovo Alpine Club** ☎ 06560/41249. **No Limits** ✉ Central square, Konitsa ☎ 26550/23777 ⊕ www.nolimits.com.gr. **Robinson Expeditions** ✉ Mitropoleos 23, Ioannina ☎ 26510/74989 or 26510/29402 🖷 26510/25071 ⊕ www.robinson.gr. **Trekking Hellas** ✉ Nap. Zerva 7, Ioannina ☎ 26510/71703 ⊕ www.trekking.gr.

TAXIS

In Ioannina your hotel reception desk should be able to help you negotiate with a taxi driver, especially if you want a tour. You can find taxis at the local bus station and in the central square and at other spots around town. If you see a cab along the street, step into the road and shout your destination. The driver will stop if he or she is going in your direction. You can also phone for a taxi. In smaller towns you can ask the hotel reception desk for help; taxi ranks are normally in the main square.

🔏 Radio Taxis **Ioannina** ☎ 26510/46777, 26510/46778, 26510/46779, or 26510/46780. **Kalambaka** ☎ 24320/22310 or 24320/22822.

TOURS

CHAT and Key Tours have similar guided trips to Meteora and northern Greece from Athens. A two-day, one-night tour to Delphi and Meteora with lodging and half-board costs €138. In Metsovo, Kassaros Travel has summer tours (€15 includes picnic) that explore the rugged countryside in an off-road vehicle; in winter, try the snowmobile tour for about €100.

🔏 **CHAT** ✉ Stadiou 4, Athens ☎ 210/322-2886 ⊕ www.chatours.gr. **Kassaros Travel** ✉ Kassaros Hotel, Triantafyllou Tsoumaka 3, Metsovo ☎ 26560/41800, 26560/41346, 26560/41662, or 6944/383131 🖷 26560/41262. **Key Tours** ✉ Kallirois 4, Athens ☎ 210/923-3166 ⊕ www.keytours.com.

TRAIN TRAVEL

Locals normally prefer to travel by bus, because trains generally take longer. However, train travel makes sense on the Athens Larissis Station–Kalambaka route if you take the express Intercity (five hours). It costs around the same as a bus—about €19.10 for the train and €18.10 for the bus. Investing in a first-class seat (*proti thesi*) for €26 means more room and comfort. The nonexpress train is agonizingly slow (at least eight hours) and requires a change at Palaiofarsalo.

📋 **OSE Railway** ✉ Larissis Station, Theodorou Deliyanni 31, Athens ☎ 210/513–1601 ⊕ www.ose.gr ✉ Pindou and Kondyli, Kalambaka ☎ 24320/22451.

TRAVEL AGENTS

📋 **Daskalopoulos Yiannis Tour World** ✉ 28th Oktovriou 13, Ioannina ☎🖨 26510/21222. **Robinson Travel Agency** ✉ 8th Merarhias 10, Ioannina ☎ 26510/29402 or 26510/74989 🖨 26510/25071.

VISITOR INFORMATION

The Greek National Tourism Organization (GNTO or EOT) in Ioannina is open weekdays 7:30–2:30 and 5:30–8, Saturday 9–1 in July and August; hours vary other months. Mornings are always best. In summer a tourist information booth is usually erected in the main square of Kalambaka, but it's best to visit the town hall for information.

📋 **Greek National Tourism Organization** ✉ Dodonis 39, 45332 Ioannina ☎ 26510/41868 or 26510/46662 🖨 26510/49139 ⊕ www.eot.gr. **Kalambaka Municipality** ✉ Vlahava and Trikalon, Kalambaka ☎ 24320/22339 or 24320/22346.

Northern Greece

THESSALONIKI, CHALKIDIKI & THE ALEXANDER THE GREAT SITES

WORD OF MOUTH

"To the east of Thessaloniki is Philippi of Biblical fame. To the southwest is Vergina, which has the grave of Alexander the Great's father, and the ruins of the ancestral palace. . . . Thessaloniki itself has some interesting ruins to see. We went through there coming and going and the traffic is crazy, second only to Athens."

—Robert_Brandywine

"Northern Greece is nice too. When I was there we drove up north to Thessaloniki and the surrounding areas . . . and climbed Mt. Olympus on the way back down south, which was an experience I'll never forget (and, I've actually never met someone else who said they did this!)."

—Karen

www.fodors.com/forums

By Lea Lane

Updated by
Tania Kollias

BOTH A MEETING POINT AND A CROSSROADS for Europe, the Mediterranean, and Asia, this region is imbued with the sights, sounds, and colors of cultures that have blended harmoniously and clashed violently by turns. The area called Northern Greece in this guide borders Albania, the Former Yugoslav Republic of Macedonia (FYROM), Bulgaria, and Turkey. Here vast, fertile plains overflow with the remnants of the powerful civilizations that vied for control: temples and fortifications built by Athens and Sparta, rough-hewn Macedonian tombs, the arches and rotundas of imperial Rome, the domes of Byzantium, and the minarets and *hamams* (baths) of the Ottomans. Thessaloniki was once home to Alexander the Great and the crossroads of the ancient world; today it is Greece's second city, brimming with antiquities, street markets, and myriad cosmopolitan flavors. In Northern Greece, you can stroll empty beaches and hike virgin trails through wildflowers, experience the meditative majesty of ancient monasteries, and head for the pleasure-oriented seaside resorts. From the frescoed tomb of Philip II of Macedon to Zeus's mythical throne atop Mt. Olympus, Northern Greece is full of surprises.

Some 6,000 years ago the first inhabitants lived in Thessaloniki. The region was established as the state of Macedonia in the 8th century BC, and an illustrious monarchy was ensconced by about the 7th century BC. Macedonian King Philip II (382–336 BC) and his son Alexander the Great conquered all of Greece except Sparta, and all of Persia as well. After Alexander's death, his brother-in-law Cassander established Thessaloniki as the capital (316 BC), naming it for his new bride, Alexander's half-sister and daughter of the much-married Philip, who had named her after his famous *nike* (victory) in Thessaly, where her mother had been one of his prizes. The Romans took Macedonia as Alexander's successors squabbled, and by 146 BC, the rest of Greece had fallen under Roman rule. After the assassination of Julius Caesar, Marc Anthony defeated Brutus and Cassius at the battles of Philippi in Macedonia in 42 BC. Under Pax Romana, St. Paul twice traveled through on his way to Corinth.

The second great flowering of Greek and Macedonian culture came during the Byzantine Empire (circa AD 312–1453), when the center of Greek civilization shifted from Athens to Constantinople (today Istanbul). Thessaloniki became the second most important city in the empire and it remained so during the Ottoman domination that lasted from the fall of Constantinople until the 1912–13 Balkan Wars. Macedonia was then united with the rest of Greece, and the 1923 Treaty of Lausanne established the present borders of Thrace. The region saw two more battles: in 1941 Mussolini's troops invaded Northern Greece but were pushed back into Albania, causing the German army to intervene and fight its way through the country; and at the end of World War II, Epirus and Macedonia were the principal arenas for the Greek Civil War (1946–49) between the Communists and Royalists.

The collapse of Yugoslavia rekindled age-old ethnic and religious animosities. Northern Greeks are especially resentful of the Former Yugoslav Republic of Macedonia's insistence on calling itself "Macedonia," and for the largely Slav and Albanian populace's attempt to usurp ancient Greek symbols. Since 1993, the European Union and United Nations recognize the republic's name as Macedonia until an agreement with Greece can be reached.

Despite the tensions, Northern Greece is flourishing. Now a regional hub; the highway connecting Macedonia with more remote regions of Thrace has been upgraded, and the Greek section of a transcontinental highway is underway. Thessaloniki is in every sense a Balkan city, especially with the influx of immigrants from the area from the 1990s. It is home to the country's largest university, and hotels were built and upgraded to cater to 2004 Olympics events that took place in the area. The city hosts a European Cup soccer match in June 2006, ahead of the International Association of Athletics Federations' World Cup in Athens in September.

Exploring Northern Greece

A delightful geographic mix awaits you: in the mountains, from snow-covered Mt. Olympus in the west to the mineral-rich eastern ranges, forests of pine, spruce, juniper, oak, and chestnut abound, and ski resorts and centers for climbing beckon. Cosmopolitan Thessaloniki lies in the strategic center of Macedonia, nestled gracefully in the wide but protective arms of the Thermaic Gulf and buttressed on its inland side by a low-lying mountain range around which the Axios River flows south to the Aegean. This is a vast, fertile plain of grain, vegetables, and fruit. In the lowlands of Chalkidiki the turquoise sea laps at miles of white-sand beach along coastal inlets. You don't have to travel far from Thessaloniki to find these pleasures: the famed three-fingered peninsulas, with their vistas of mountain and sea, and tipped by famed Mt. Athos monasteries, are only a few hours away by car on good highways.

About the Restaurants

Multicultural Thessaloniki is known for its excellent Greek restaurants; Thessalonicans also love to experiment, and many restaurants with international cuisine are opening. Neighborhoods in other cities and towns center on tavernas and casual bars, in which you may be encouraged to go to the kitchen and choose your meals from the pots. In most villages, pastry shops offering traditional sweets, and cafés pouring dark, strong coffee, are bustling at all hours.

Even at the best restaurants dress is usually casual (neat and dark clothes are favored for evening). Although at higher-priced establishments reservations are possible, nothing is guaranteed. You can arrive around 8, earlier than most Greeks like to eat dinner (many places do not open before then)—but it's much more fun to come at 9 or 10 and mix with the locals. Even if the restaurant is very crowded, the management will usually manage to squeeze you in somewhere or you can sit at the bar while you wait for a table.

About the Hotels

Thessaloniki's hotels are geared mostly to the practical needs of transient businesspeople, with little emphasis on capturing the spirit of the place. City accommodation is fairly pricey compared to regional towns,

Thessaloniki's central location in Macedonia makes it a perfect base for a short itinerary; the ancient sites are within a couple of hours by car or bus. For a trip of five days, a car rented in Thessaloniki simplifies sightseeing and allows time for serendipitous pleasures.

Numbers in the text correspond to numbers in the margin and on the Exploring Thessaloniki and Northern Greece maps.

5

If you have 3 days

Starting in ⊞ **Thessaloniki** ❶–❷❸ ▶, spend a day exploring both the old and the new city, not missing the Archaeological Museum and the White Tower. Take a long promenade on the boardwalk and join Thessalonicans for coffee by the sea. Spend your second day visiting the famous Alexander the Great sites—**Pella** ❷❹ and **Vergina** ❷❺—and then head back to Thessaloniki for nightlife. On the third day, relax, visit a museum or shop in the morning, and then drive out to have lunch near Mt. Olympus and explore **Dion** ❷❻; you could also spend the entire day in the mountain area.

If you have 5 days

Follow the three-day itinerary above, with the option of spending the third night in the village of Litochoro on the slopes of ⊞ **Mt. Olympus** ❷❼. The next morning drive to the Chalkidiki area, and spend the day outdoors, overnighting in **Ouranoupolis** ❷❽. If you are male and have made arrangements in advance, you could stay the fourth night at **Mt. Athos** ❷❾, otherwise return to Thessaloniki for the night and spend Day 5 further delving into museums, historic areas, and shops before you depart.

and if you're driving, parking is a major consideration. September, October, and November are especially crowded due to festivals and trade fairs; reserve ahead. The selection of hotels elsewhere in Northern Greece varies from exclusive seaside resorts in Chalkidiki to modest, family-managed, hostel-like housing on the slopes of Mt. Olympus. Throughout the area, hotels are usually small, somewhat spartan affairs, with charm that comes mainly from their surroundings. Some resorts, particularly in Chalkidiki, close for winter (generally November through April, but dates vary with weather). Always ask about discounts, which are common (for Internet booking, extended stays, off-season stays, etc.). High season in Thessaloniki is September, during the major trade fair.

WHAT IT COSTS In euros				
	$$$$	$$$	$$	$	¢
RESTAURANTS	over €20	€16–€20	€12–€15	€8–€11	under €8
HOTELS	over €160	€121–€160	€91–€120	€60–€90	under €60

Restaurant prices are for one main course at dinner or, for restaurants that serve only *mezedes* (small dishes), for two mezedes. Hotel prices are for two people in a standard double room in high season, including taxes.

Timing

Thessaloniki has interesting events and cultural activities throughout the year, and all seasons can claim their special treats. Travel throughout Northern Greece is best from May through October. The advent of spring brings a profusion of wildflowers, and the golden harvest season is a mellow time of wheat, wine, and olives. Fall months are also busy with people attending business events and festivals. July and August are most crowded but best for sunning, swimming, and chatting with northern Europeans and Greek families on holiday. Weather and demand can influence open hours; venues may move seasonally to other locations, restaurants, bars, and clubs change ownership or close, and the culture ministry announces new operating hours for museums and sites each year—often within weeks of the change. Winter hours, which can begin in September, October, or November until April, May, or June, are nearly always shorter.

THESSALONIKI

ΘΕΣΣΑΛΟΝΙΚΗ

At the crossroads of East and West, where North blends into South, Thessaloniki (accent on the "ni") has seen the rise and fall of many civilizations: Macedonian, Hellenic, Roman, Byzantine, Ottoman, and that of the Jews and the modern Greeks. Each of its successive conquerors has plundered, razed, and buried much of what went before. In 1917 a great fire destroyed much of what was left, but the colorful past can still be seen and sensed. The vibrant city with close to 1.5 million inhabitants today—also known as Thessalonike, Saloniki, Salonika or Salonica—has a spacious, orderly layout that is partly a result of French architect Ernest Hébrard, who rebuilt the city after the fire.

The town is fairly centralized and easy to get used to. Whether you're in Ano Polis (Upper City) or along the bay, short walks here are well rewarded; you may come across parks, squares, old neighborhoods with narrow alleyways and gardens, courtyards draped with laundry, neoclassical mansions, and some of the more than 50 churches and 40 monasteries. Thessaloniki's early Christian and Byzantine monuments, with their distinctive architecture and magnificent mosaics, are UNESCO World Heritage Sites. The ever-changing nature of the city continues and neighborhoods like Ladadika, a former warehouse district (which got its name from the olives and olive oil or *ladi* stored here), have been recycled into pedestrian zones of restaurants and clubs. The neighborhood is filled with young and old, strolling by fountains, snapping fingers to the music in the air, and savoring mezedes and microbrewery beers at tables spilling onto the stone squares.

The appeal of Thessaloniki lies in part in its warmth, accessibility, and languid pace. The afternoon *mesimeri*, or siesta, is still sacrosanct (don't ever call some people between 3 and 5 PM). Take your time exploring in-town archaeological sites and Byzantine treasures, making sure to stop for café-style people-watching. The two walks suggest routes for exploring highlights. The best, however, is simply to wander through the streets

Great Flavors

The cosmopolitan, multiracial character of Thessaloniki—building on its historic Byzantine and Ottoman influences—has created a multifaceted cuisine of sometimes subtle sophistication; many Greeks feel Thessaloniki has the best food in the country. It is distinguished by its liberal use of fragrant Levantine spices, including hot red peppers from Florina called *florines* and sweet peppers known as *boukova*. Traditional Thracian and Macedonian cooks adapt to the seasons: in winter, rich game such as boar and venison is served, and in summer, there are mussels and other seafood from the Aegean, and fruits and vegetables from the fertile plains. Wheat, corn, rye, and barley grown in this breadbasket of Greece yield especially fine baked goods. The relatively cooler climate here is reflected in rich chicken soups, roast chicken, stuffed vegetables, and stewed lamb and pork.

5

Thessaloniki is especially known for its *mezedes,* or small portions of food; every little *ouzeri* (casual bar serving ouzo and mezedes) or taverna has at least one prized house recipe. Leisurely lunches consisting of a multitude of little plates are the focal point of a typical Thessaloniki day. Specialties include *medhia* (mussels), which come from farms outside the bay and are served in different styles including *saganaki* (fried in a pan with tomatoes, peppers, and feta) and *achnista* (steamed in broth with herbs). Also look for *soutzoukakia* (Anatolian-style meatballs in tomato sauce, seasoned with cumin). *Amiletita* (lambs' testicles) are tender and flavorful, a delicacy for those who give them a try. *Peinerli* (an open-faced boat of bread filled with cheese and ham) is a Black Sea specialty brought here by the Pontii, Greeks who emigrated from that area. Along the coast, informal restaurants specialize in barbecued chicken.

Meals are complemented by generous amounts of wine, ouzo, and *tsipouro,* the local version of grappa. Try the excellent barrel or bottled local wines, especially reds under labels such as Naoussa or Porto Carras or a little bottle of Mavromatina retsina, considered the best bottled version in Greece. Throughout the city, little shops and cellars specialize in a Macedonian treat called a submarine (or *ipovrihio*), a spoonful of sweets such as *visino* (black) cherries in syrup, dipped in a glass of ice water.

Monasteries

Monks got to Northern Greece long before tour groups, and the sites they chose for their monasteries are the most beautiful locations throughout the cities and countryside. Some of the most impressive monastic complexes in the world are at the Ayion Oros (Holy Mountain) of Mt. Athos, on the forested easternmost peninsula of Chalkidiki. Only men can visit and stay overnight, but boat tours give you a view of the buildings, some of which are right by the water or on the rocky slopes near the shore. The remains of the early Christian Zygou Monastery are outside Ouranoupolis.

Urban Culture

Thessaloniki, Greece's second-largest city, has a rich multicultural heritage that testifies to the contributions of the many civilizations that moved through and dominated the area. The Romans carried away much of the early

Macedonian-Hellenistic heritage, and their temples became Byzantine churches when the empire faded. The Ottoman Turks, in turn, converted churches into mosques and built their own distinctive public buildings and handsome mansions. A fire destroyed much of the city in 1917 and a modern metropolis sprang up in its wake, but neighborhoods such as the Old Turkish Quarter and the Ano Polis (Upper City) remain worlds unto themselves. Interesting churches and excellent museums, including the Archaeological Museum and the Byzantine Museum, illuminate the history of the city. Thessaloniki is European or Balkan rather than Middle Eastern, a vital crossroads of culture, and a fascinating contrast to Athens.

responding to whatever you encounter. It is hard to get lost, since the entire city slopes downhill to the bay, where you can always align yourself with the White Tower and the city skyline.

Kentro & Ladadika

Κέντρο & Λαδάδικα

Exploring the area from the White Tower west along the seaside to Platia Aristotelous (Aristotelous Square) reveals icons of the city's history: grand monuments of Emperor Galerius, artifacts from the Neolithic period through the Roman occupation housed in the archaeological museum, and prominent churches, as well as the city's most important landmark, the tower itself. The lively shopping streets, bustling markets, and cafés of the Kentro (City Center) and adjacent areas reward you with the unexpected encounters and sensual treats of a great city.

a good walk

Begin at the **White Tower ❶** ▶, taking in the city's expanse from the rooftop. Walk east on the seaside promenade, Leoforos Nikis, until you see the dramatic bronze statue of Alexander the Great and his horse, Bucephalus. Meander through the lovely park to the north, with its cafés and children's playground, to get to the renowned **Archaeological Museum ❷**, with finds dating from prehistoric Greece to Alexander's Macedonia. The **Byzantine Museum ❸** is across Tritis Septemyriou to the east of the museum. Head across the enormous square called H.A.N.T.H. toward the city center to the beginning of the city's fanciest shopping street, Tsimiski. Stay on the north side until you reach the beautiful pedestrian Dimitriou Gounari, a street lined with delightful shops and cafés. It crosses Tsimiski and leads you north directly to the **Arch of Galerius ❹**. Even if the **Rotunda ❺** is closed, try to explore the narrow streets surrounding the area, rich with cluttered junk and antiques shops; on Wednesday you can see the eclectic street market. Pass by delightful **Ayios Panteleimon ❻** before crossing Egnatia Odos to the south side of the street and continue west to the lovely 14th-century **Church of the Metamorphosis ❼**. Continuing west on Egnatia Odos, turn right and walk a half block up Ayias Sofias to the oldest Byzantine church in the city, the 5th-century **Panagia Achiropiitos ❽**. Next head south again on Ayias Sofias for a short downhill walk to reach the 8th-century church of **Ayia Sofia ❾**.

To get to a more contemporary part of the city center, walk west on Ermou, which leads to **Modiano Market** ⑩, with its myriad fresh foods. Take a look at the evocative **Memorial to Grigoris Lambrakis** ⑪, west of the market on Eleftherias Venizelou. Walk south towards the waterfront until you reach Ayiou Mina, a small street north of Tsimiski. Turn west to visit the **Jewish Museum of Thessaloniki** ⑫, documenting the long history of the Jews in this area. If you've made an appointment to visit the **Monastiriotou Synagogue** ⑬, walk north on Ionos Dragoumi and turn left on Egnatia Odos and then right on Syngrou. Otherwise continue west from the Jewish Museum to the **Museum of Greek Musical Instruments** ⑭, which has more than 200 instruments of all sizes and shapes dating from the Bronze Age to the present century. You can quit now and reward yourself at one of Ladadika's cafés.

TIMING   Leave most of a day for this walk, depending on your speed. Plan to spend at least an hour at the Archaeological Museum. The best time to see smaller Byzantine churches is during a service, especially early morning on Sunday, because they may be closed most of the time. If you visit on Sunday, dress conservatively and be quiet and respectful of congregants; do not walk around with your guidebook in hand. Otherwise, hours are not set in stone; try from about 8 AM to noon and 5:30 to 7:30 on any day, except where noted.

What to See

❹ **Arch of Galerius.** The imposing *kamára* (arch) is one of a number of monuments built by Galerius around AD 305, during his reign as co-emperor of Diocletian's divided Roman Empire. It commemorated the Roman victory over Persia in AD 297, and you can still see scenes of those battles on the badly eroded bas-reliefs. Originally, the arch had four pediments and a dome and was intended to span not only the Via Egnatia, the ancient Roman road, but also a passageway leading north to the Rotunda. Only the large arches remain. ⌧ *Egnatia Odos, Pl. Sintrivaniou, Kentro.*

❷ **Archaeological Museum.** The unpretentious, single-story white structure
Fodor'sChoice   gives no hint from the outside of the treasures within. A superb collec-
★   tion of artifacts from Neolithic times, sculptures from the Archaic, classical, and Roman eras, and remains from the Archaic temple at Thermi, all reside under this roof. Objects discovered during construction of the Egnatia and Thessaloniki–Skopje highways were added in 2005 to the collection displayed in eight galleries. Start off in Gallery 4, which traces the ancient city's history. The Sindos gallery contains finds from 121 Archaic and early classical tombs in nearby Sindos, including many objects made of gold. ⌧ *Manoli Andronikou 6, H.A.N.T.H., Kentro* ☎ *2310/830538 or 2310/861306* ⊕ *www.culture.gr* ⌦ *€4, combined ticket with Byzantine Museum €6* ☾ *May–Sept., Mon. 1–7:30, Tues.–Sun. 8–7:30; Oct.–Apr., Mon.–Sun. 8:30–3.*

★ ❾ **Ayia Sofia.** The founding date of this church, a UNESCO World Heritage Site and the focal point of the city's Easter and Christmas celebrations, has been the subject of disagreements over the centuries. Ecclesiastics think it was built after the first Council of Nicea (AD 325), when Jesus was de-

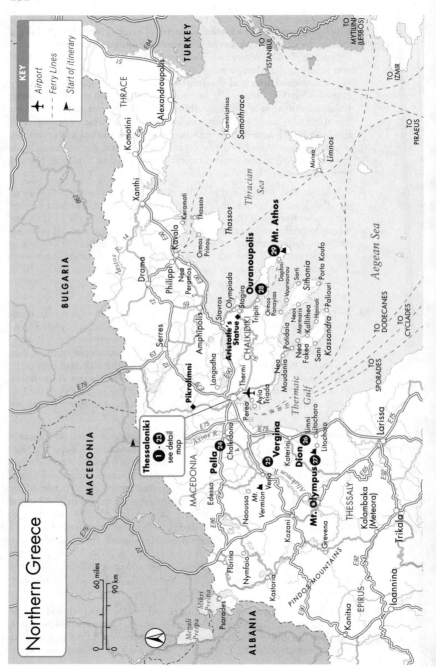

Northern Greece

KEY

- ✈ Airport
- --- Ferry Lines
- ▲ Start of itinerary

BULGARIA

TURKEY

MACEDONIA

MACEDONIA

ALBANIA

THRACE

THESSALY

EPIRUS

PINDOS MOUNTAINS

Thracian Sea

Aegean Sea

Thermaic Gulf

CHALKIDIKI

Sithonia

Kassandra

Thassos

Samothrace

Limnos

TO MYTILINI (LESBOS)

TO IZMIR

TO ISTANBUL

TO PIRAEUS

TO DODECANES

TO CYCLADES

TO SPORADES

Thessaloniki ❶ - ㉓
see detail map

Pikrolimni ◆

Aristotle's Statue ◆

Ouranoupolis ㉘

Mt. Athos ㉙

Pella ㉔

Vergina ㉖

Dion ㉗

Mt. Olympus ㉗

Alexandroupolis

Komotini

Xanthi

Kavala

Drama

Serres

Amphipolis

Stavros

Olympiada

Stagira

Tripiti

Ormos Panayias

Daphni

Vourvourou

Sarti

Neos Marmaras

Porto Koufo

Paliouri

Hanioti

Kallithea

Sani

Nea Fokea

Potidaia

Nea Moudania

Nea Triada

Ayia Triada

Perea

Thermi

Langadha

Philippi

Nea Peramos

Keramoti

Thassos

Ormos Prinou

Kamariotissa

Mirina

Edessa

Naoussa

Mt. Vermion

Veria

Kozani

Grevena

Katerini

Litochoro

Litochoro

Limni

Nymfaio

Florina

Kastoria

Psarades

Mikri Prespa

Megali Prespa

Kalambaka (Meteora)

Trikala

Ioannina

Konitsa

Larissa

Chalkidona

Axios R.

Aliakmon R.

Aspros R.

Nestos R.

0   60 miles

0   90 km

E75

E79

E90

E92

E65

E86

E75

clared a manifestation of Divine Wisdom; other church historians say it was contemporaneous with the magnificent church of Ayia Sofia in Constantinople, completed in AD 537, on which it was modeled. From its architecture the church is believed to date to the late 8th century, a time of transition from the domed basilica to the cruciform plan. The rather drab interior contains two superb mosaics: one of the Ascension and the other of the Virgin Mary holding Jesus in her arms. This latter mosaic is an interesting example of the conflict in the Orthodox Church (AD 726–843) between the iconoclasts (icon smashers, which they often literally were) and the iconodules (icon venerators). At one point in this doctrinal struggle, the Virgin Mary in the mosaic was replaced by a large cross (still partly visible), and only later, after the victory of the iconodules, was it again replaced with an image of the Virgin Mary holding baby Jesus. The front gate is a popular meeting spot. ⊠ *Ermou and Ayias Sofias, Kentro* ☎ *2310/270253* ⊗ *May–Oct., Mon.–Sun. 7 AM–1 and 6–8; Nov.–Apr., Mon.–Sun. 7 AM–1 and 5–7.*

★ ❻ **Ayios Panteleimon.** A prime example of 14th-century Macedonian religious architecture, Ayios Panteleimon is an eye-catching church that draws you in to take a closer look. Restored in 1993 after an earthquake in 1978, the facade reveals the ornamental interplay of brick and stonework, and a dome displays typically strong upward motion. ⊠ *Iasonidou and Arrianou, near Egnatia Odos, Kentro* ⊗ *Mon.–Thurs. 9–noon and 4:30–6:30, Fri. 8 PM–10:30 PM, Sat. 9–noon, Sun. 7–10 AM.*

★ ♻ ❸ **Byzantine Museum.** Awarded the Council of Europe's 2005 Museum Prize, much of the country's finest Byzantine art—priceless icons, frescoes, sculpted reliefs, jewelry, glasswork, manuscripts, pottery, and coins—is on exhibit here. Ten rooms contain striking treasures, notably an exquisite enamel-and-gold "woven" bracelet (Room 4), and an enormous altar with piratic skull-and-crossbones. A mezzanine (Room 7) shows how early pottery was made. Check the Web site for the museum's changeable winter hours. ⊠ *Leoforos Stratou 2, Kentro* ☎ *2310/ 868570* ⊕ *www.mbp.gr* 🎫 *€4, combined ticket with Archaeological Museum €6* ⊗ *June–Sept., Mon. 1–7:30, Tues.–Sun. 8–7:30; Oct.–May closes earlier.*

❼ **Church of the Metamorphosis.** This sunken church, part of which is below ground level, is an example of 14th-century Macedonian church architecture, with a decorative mix of brick and stonework and a dome thrusting upward. ⊠ *Egnatia Odos, Kentro.*

Egnatia Odos. It was during the Byzantine period that Thessaloniki came into its own as a commercial crossroads, because the Via Egnatia, which already connected the city to Rome (with the help of a short boat trip across the Adriatic), was extended east to Constantinople. Today Egnatia Odos virtually follows the same path; it is Thessaloniki's main commercial thoroughfare, although not as upscale as the parallel Tsimiski, two blocks to the south. ⊠ *City points southwest to northeast, Kentro.*

⓬ **Jewish Museum of Thessaloniki.** Among the displays in this museum dedicated to the history of the local Jewish community are tombstones from the city's ancient necropolis, which was on the grounds now inhabited

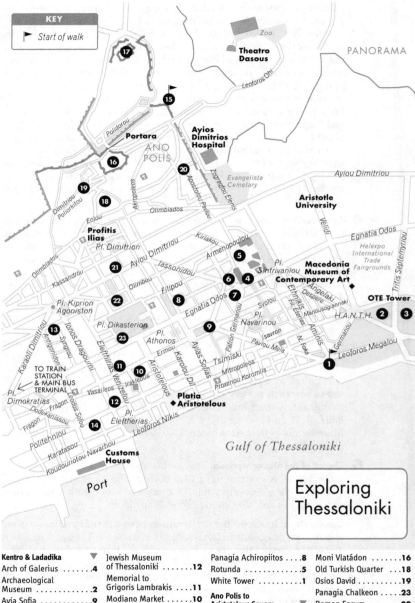

Exploring
Thessaloniki

by the Aristotle University. Also on exhibit are objects rescued from the 32 synagogues that existed around the city, some of which were destroyed by the Nazis. The neoclassical building is one of the few Jewish structures that were spared in the great fire of 1917. ⊠ *Ayiou Mina 13, Kentro* ☎ *2310/ 250406 or 2310/250407* ⊕ *www.jmth.gr* ⊠ *Free* ⊙ *Aug. 16–July 14, Tues., Fri., and Sun. 11–2, Wed. and Thurs. 11–2 and 5–8; July 15–Aug. 15, Mon., Tues., and Fri. 11–2, Wed. and Thurs. 11–2 and 5–8.*

Macedonia Museum of Contemporary Art. A large and expanding permanent collection of Greek and foreign works, as well as important temporary shows, are on exhibit. ⊠ *Egnatia 154, Helexpo, Kentro* ☎ *2310/ 240002 or 2310/281212* ⊕ *www.culture.gr* ⊠ *€3* ⊙ *Tues.–Sat. 10–2 and 6–9, Sun. 11–3.*

⑪ Memorial to Grigoris Lambrakis. If you've read the 1966 novel *Z* by Vassilis Vassilikos (or seen the 1969 Costas-Gavras film about the murder of Lambrakis, a leftist member of Parliament, by rightists in 1963), this monument is especially moving. The murder precipitated the events leading to the 1967–74 dictatorship of the colonels. A dramatic bronze head and arm, above which flutters a sculpted dove, marks the spot. ⊠ *Corner of Ermou and El. Venizelou, Kentro.*

⑩ Modiano Market. Overhauled in 1922 by Jewish architect Eli Modiano, this old landmark is basically a rectangular building with a glass roof and pediment facade. Inside, the rich aromas of food—fish, meats, vegetables, fruits, breads, and spices—compete with music and the noisy, colorful market characters, from the market owners to the bargain hunters. In the little tavernas nearby, ouzo and mezedes are sold at all hours. It is worth a visit—as is the generally cheaper **open-air market** (on the north side of Ermou)—even if you have no intention of buying anything. ⊠ *Block bounded by Aristotelous, Ermou, Irakliou, and Komninon, Kentro* ⊙ *Mon., Wed., and Sat. 8:30–2:30; Tues., Thurs., and Fri. 8:30–1:30 and 5:30–8:30.*

⑬ Monastiriotou Synagogue. The foundations for the city's only existing pre-Holocaust synagogue were laid in 1925, and construction spanned two years. The synagogue became the center of the Jewish ghetto during the Nazi occupation; the building survived because the Red Cross used it as a warehouse after the community was deported to concentration camps. Today the synagogue is open only for major events. If you want to visit and find it closed, contact the community center and someone will open it for you. ⊠ *Syngrou 51, Kentro* ☎ *2310/275701 community center* ⊙ *Community center weekdays 8–3:30; synagogue by arrangement.*

⑭ Museum of Greek Musical Instruments. A handsomely renovated building holds more than 200 ancient to modern instruments that are stunningly displayed with dramatic lighting (and thorough labeling in Greek and English). Some are reproductions modeled after those seen in ancient vase paintings, sculptures, and manuscripts. The unique collection includes fantastically shaped instruments that are works of art in their own right. The oldest instrument on display is a triangular psaltery, copied from an exquisite sculpture of one of the Cycladic idols that dates to 2800 BC. Other exhibits include a five-string lyre with a sound box made from a tortoise shell, Pan pipes, an ancient guitar, and wind instruments. The museum's conference center often hosts talks and concerts. ⊠ *Katouni 12–14, Ladadika* ☎ *2310/555265* ▭ *Free* ☉ *May–Sept., Wed.–Mon. 10–2 and 5–7; Oct.–Apr., Wed.–Mon. 10–4.*

❽ **Panagia Achiropiitos.** The name *Achiropiitos* means "made without hands" and refers to the icon representing the Virgin that miraculously appeared in this 5th-century Byzantine church during the 12th century. An early example of the basilica form, the church has marvelous arcades, monolithic columns topped by elaborate capitals, and exquisite period mosaics of birds and flowers. It is the second-oldest church in Thessaloniki and probably the oldest in continuous use in the eastern Mediterranean. An inscription in Arabic on a column states that "Sultan Murat captured Thessaloniki in the year 1430," which was the year the church was converted temporarily into a mosque. ⊠ *Ayias Sofias 56, Kentro.*

Pinacothiki (Municipal Art Gallery). Nestled amid lush gardens, the art gallery has a distinctive icon collection from the Byzantine and post-Byzantine periods, engravings that highlight the development of the craft of icon making in Greece, and a representative collection of modern Greek art. One section shows the work of three generations of Thessalonican artists, documenting modern art in the city from the turn of the 20th century to 1967. The museum building, the 1905 Villa Mordoh, draws from neoclassical, Renaissance, and art nouveau styles. ⊠ *Vasilissis Olgas 162, at 25 Martiou, east of Kentro, Depot* ☎*2310/425531* ⊕*www.thessalonikicity. gr* ▭ *Free* ☉ *Tues.–Fri. 9–1 and 5–9, Sat. 5–9, Sun. 9–1.*

★ ❺ **Rotunda.** Also known as Ayios Giorgios, this brickwork edifice has become a layered monument to the city's rich history. Built in AD 306, it was probably intended as Roman emperor Galerius's mausoleum. However, when he died in Bulgaria, his successor refused to have the body brought back. Under Theodosius the Great, the Byzantines converted the Rotunda into a church dedicated to St. George, adding the impressive 4th-century AD mosaics of early saints. The Ottomans made it a mosque (the minaret still stands). It was restored after damage suffered in a 1978 earthquake, and is undergoing restoration at this writing. Once a month and on major holidays a liturgy is held here, as are occasional art exhibits and concerts. ⊠ *Dimitriou Gounari off Pl. Sintrivaniou, Kentro* ☎ *2310/968860* ☉ *May–Oct., Tues.–Sun. 8–7:30; Nov.–Apr., Tues.–Sun. 8–3.*

★ ⚑ ❶ **White Tower.** Formidable sea walls and intermittent towers encircling the medieval city were erected in the 15th century on the site of earlier walls. In 1866, with the threat of piracy diminishing and European commerce increasingly imperative, the Ottoman Turks began demolishing them. The city's most famous landmark, and a symbol of Macedonia, the White Tower is the only medieval defensive tower left standing along the seafront (the other remaining tower, the Trigoniou, is in the Upper City). During the 19th century this was an infamous prison and execution site that became known as the Bloody Tower. In the future, the tower is expected to hold permanent exhibits as the Thessaloniki City Museum. ⊠ *Leoforos Nikis and Pavlou Melas, Kentro* ☎ *2310/267832* ⊕ *www. culture.gr* ▭ *€2* ☉ *Tues.–Sun. 8:30–3.*

Ano Polis to Aristotelous Square

Άνω Πόλη ως την Πλατεία Αριστοτέλους

Ano Polis, where many fortified towers once bristled along the city's upper walls, is what remains of 19th-century Thessaloniki. It's filled with timber-frame houses with their upper stories overhanging the steep streets. The views of the modern city below and the Thermaic Gulf are stunning, but other than Byzantine churches, there are few specific places of historical interest. It's an experience in itself to navigate the steps, past gossipy women, grandfathers playing backgammon in smoky cafés, and giggling children playing tag in tiny courtyards filled with sweet-smelling flowers, stray cats, and flapping laundry.

Getting here can be a chore, as taxi drivers often try to avoid the cramped, congested streets and fear missing a fare back down. Have your hotel find a willing driver, or take a local bus. Bus 23 leaves from the terminal at Platia Eleftherias (two blocks west of Aristotelous Square, on the waterfront side), every 10 to 15 minutes and follows an interesting route through the narrow streets of Ano Polis. Or you can stroll the 30 minutes north from the White Tower, along Ethnikis Aminis, to get to Ano Polis.

a good walk

Start this excursion with the superb aerial city view from the **Tower of Trigoniou** ⑮ ▐; then walk west along the inside of the seaward wall (the wall should be to your right). Walk a few yards past the second *portara* (large open gateway), and to your left is the entrance to the grounds of **Moni Vlatádon** ⑯ and its tiny chapel dedicated to Sts. Peter and Paul. The **Eptapyrghion** ⑰ is north along Eptapyrghiou. Backtrack to the Tower of Trigoniou and continue west along Eptapyrghiou to the first wide street on your left, Dimitriou Poliorkitou, and take the broad flight of stairs to the beginning of the **Old Turkish Quarter** ⑱ toward the sea. Follow Dimitriou Poliorkitou west, bearing left, and take the winding descent to the left and then to the right until you come to the doors of the 5th-century **Osios David** ⑲.

Turn right and continue down the narrow cobblestone street to the first intersection. Below a strange tin "palace" of the self-proclaimed King of the Greeks, follow Akropoleos to the small Platia Romfei; walk east along Kryspou, Aiolou, Malea, and Kodrou to Irodotou, in order to see the beautiful frescoes in the exceptional 14th-century **Ayios Nikolaos Orfanos** ⑳.

Walk downhill on Apostolou Pavlou, the legendary path Apostle Paul took to the Upper City to address the Thessalonians, and cross busy Kassandrou; passing by modern Turkey's founder Ataturk's House. Turn right onto Ayiou Dimitriou, which can be crowded, noisy, and not very attractive, so you may choose to walk along a more pleasant parallel street. Continue west about six blocks until you reach **Ayios Dimitrios** ㉑, a church dedicated to Thessaloniki's patron saint and where he was martyred. Forge on downhill, one block south from the church, to the excavation of the ancient **Roman Forum** ㉒. Walk west on Olimbou and turn left at the second corner onto short, diagonal Tositsa street, and you enter the city's prime junk, antiques, and roaming-peddler promenade. Browse through here and make your way down to **Panagyia Chalkeon ㉓**, one of the oldest churches in the city, on the southwest corner of immense Platia Dikasterion, cross to the south side of Egnatia Odos; a half block east, take a right on Aristotelous and end your walk by the waterfront at Aristotelous Square. This is the village square of the city center; stop for a drink and postcard-writing session at one of its many *kafeneia* (traditional coffeehouses) before you take a well-deserved Greek siesta.

TIMING This tour should take a few hours, at least. You will want to spend some time at Ayios Dimitrios. Finding yourself gazing at evocations of the city's rich past, both artistic and historic, and taking in the flea markets—especially if you get caught up in haggling over a trinket—can easily mean an exploration of this district can take a whole day.

What to See

Ano Polis (Upper City). This elevated northern area of the city gained its other name, Ta Kastra (The Castles), because of the castle of Eptapyrghion and the fortified towers that once dominated the walls. The area within and just outside the remains of the walls is like a village unto itself, a pleasing jumble of the rich, the poor, and the renovated. Rustic one-story peasant houses, many still occupied by the families that built them, sit side by side with houses newly built or restored by the wealthier class. As the area continues to be upgraded, tavernas, café-bars, and restaurants spring up to serve visitors, both Greek and foreign, who flock there for a cool evening out.

Ataturk's House. The soldier and statesman who established the Turkish republic and became its president, Ataturk (Mustafa Kemal) was born here in 1881. He participated in the city's Young Turk movement, which eventually led to the collapse of the sultanate and the formation of the modern Turkish state. The modest pink house is decorated in Ottoman style; you can explore the small museum with personal photos and clothing dating from the leader's early life in Thessaloniki. To get in, ring the bell at the **Turkish Consulate** (✉ Ayiou Dimitriou 151 ☎ 2310/248452) down the block and show your passport; you'll be given an escorted tour. ✉ *Apostolou Pavlou 17, at Ayiou Dimitriou, Kentro* 🖂 *Free* ☉ *Daily 10–5.*

★ ㉑ **Ayios Dimitrios.** Magnificent and covered in mosaics, this five-aisle basilica is Greece's largest church and a powerful tribute to the patron saint of Thessaloniki. It was rebuilt and restored from 1926 to 1949 with attention to preserving the details of the original; the marks left by a fire can still be seen throughout. In the 4th century, during the reign of Emperor Galerius, the young, scholarly Dimitrios was preaching Christianity in the coppersmith district, in contravention of an edict. He was arrested and jailed in a room in the old Roman baths, on the site of the present church. While he was incarcerated in AD 303, Dimitrios gave a Christian blessing to a gladiator friend named Nestor, who was about to fight Galerius's champion, Lyaios. When Nestor fought and killed Lyaios, after having made Dimitrios's blessing public, the enraged Galerius had Nestor executed on the spot and had Dimitrios speared to death in his

THE JEWS OF THESSALONIKI

FOR CENTURIES THESSALONIKI *provided a safe refuge for Jews from around the world, and the Jewish community grew to be the largest in the Balkans. Today a Jewish presence exists in the city, as shown in the Jewish Museum of Thessaloniki and synagogues such as Monastiriotou, even though the community numbers only 1,500.*

The original Jewish population of Thessaloniki, with whom the apostle Paul argued while proselytizing on his visit in AD 49, were called Romaniote. They were Greek-speaking and traced their origins to Alexander the Great's mission to Jerusalem in 333 BC. There were more arrivals throughout the 14th and 15th centuries from places such as Hungary, Portugal, Sicily, and North Africa; 20,000 Sephardic Jews came here after all Jews were expelled from Spain in 1492. During Ottoman rule, these Jews helped turn the city into a vibrant commercial center,

contributing to its development through the mid-1900s. By the first decade of the 20th century, the community owned more than 50 synagogues and 20 religious schools. The Great Fire of 1917 destroyed much of Thessaloniki, leaving 700,000 citizens homeless, including many of the 50,000 Jews.

At the start of World War II, the community numbered 56,000. The Germans, who occupied the city from 1941 through 1944, deported most of the city's Jews to concentration camps. Almost 95% of the Jewish population perished. The city dedicated a square in memory of the Holocaust victims in 1986, and a memorial was created in 1997 at the Jewish Cemetery in Stavroupolis. The **Jewish Community** *(⊠ Tsimiski 24, Kentro ☎ 2310/275701 ⊕ www.jct.gr) is tiny but very active.*

cell. His Christian brethren were said to have buried him there. A church was built on the ruins of this bath in the 5th century but was destroyed by an earthquake in the 7th century. The church was rebuilt, and gradually the story of Dimitrios and Nestor grew to be considered apocryphal until the great 1917 fire burned down most of the 7th-century church and brought to light its true past. The process of rebuilding uncovered rooms beneath the apse that appear to be baths; the discovery of a reliquary containing a vial of bloodstained earth helped confirm that this is where St. Dimitrios was martyred. You enter through a small doorway to the right of the altar. The church's interior was plastered over when the Turks turned it into a mosque, but eight original mosaics remain on either side of the altar. Work your way through the crypt, containing sculpture from the 3rd to 5th century AD and Byzantine artifacts, or peruse the parish women's crafts cooperative. ⊠ *Ayiou Dimitriou 97, Kentro* ☎ *2310/270591* 🎫 *Free* ☉ *Mon. 12:30–7, Tues.–Sat. 8–8, Sun. 11–8.*

⓴ Ayios Nikolaos Orfanos. Noted frescoes here include the unusual *Ayion Mandilion* in the apse, which shows Jesus superimposed on a veil sent to an Anatolian king, and the *Niptir,* also in the apse, in which Jesus is washing the disciples' feet. The artist is said to have depicted himself in the right-hand corner wearing a turban and riding a horse. The 14th-century church, which became a dependency of the Vlatádon monastery in the 17th century, has an intriguing mix of Byzantine architectural styles and perhaps the most beautiful midnight Easter service in the city. ⊠ *Irodotou (entrance), Pl. Kallithea and Apostolou Pavlou, Ano Polis* ⊙ *Tues.–Sun. 8:30–3.*

⑰ Eptapyrghion. In modern times, this Byzantine fortress—its name means "the seven towers"—was an abysmal prison, closed only in 1988. There's not much to see here except wall ruins and a small museum that documents the building's history. The area is an untended green space, not an unpleasant place to sit and survey Thessaloniki below. The surrounding tavernas accommodate throngs of locals in the evening. ⊠ *Eptapyrghiou, Ano Polis.*

need a break?

Rest your feet and step back in time at the **Café Bazaar** (⊠ Papamarkou 34, Kentro ☎ 2310/241817), an art deco café and restaurant on a street parallel to Ermou, on Platia Athonos. This area was the Jewish quarter prior to the 1917 fire. After that, a French architect built numerous shops known as the bazaar.

⑯ Moni Vlatádon. The Vlatades Monastery, shaded with pine and cypress, is a cruciform structure that displays a mixture of architectural additions from Byzantine times to the present. It's known for its Ecumenical Foundation for Patriarchal Studies, the only one in the world. The small central church to the right of the apse has a tiny **chapel dedicated to Sts. Peter and Paul,** which is seldom open. It is believed to have been built on the spot where Paul first preached to the Thessalonians, in AD 49. Go through the gate entrance to get a panoramic view of the city of Thessaloniki. ⊠ *Eptapyrghiou 64, Ano Polis.*

★ ⑱ Old Turkish Quarter. During the Ottoman occupation, this area, probably the most picturesque in the city, was considered the best place to live. In addition to the superb city views, in summer it catches whatever breeze there is. Once the home of some of the poorest families in Thessaloniki, the area is rapidly gentrifying, thanks to European Union development funds (which repaired the cobblestones), strict zoning and building codes, and the zeal of young couples with the money to restore the narrow old houses. The most notable houses are on Papadopolou, Kleious, and Dimitriou Poliorkitou streets. ⊠ *South of Dimitriou Poliorkitou, Ano Polis.*

need a break?

A tree shades the terrace and blue, multipane storefront of the **Tsinari Ouzeri** (⊠ Papadopoulou 72, at Kleious, Ano Polis ☎ 2310/284028), the last remaining Turkish-style coffeehouse (opened in 1850) and the only one to have survived the fire of 1917. During the 1920s it became the social hub for the refugees from Asia Minor who lived here. Now a café and *ouzeri* (a bar where appetizers are sold), it is especially popular before siesta time (3:30–4). Try the thick, black coffee, or have an ouzo and share delicious appetizers such as eggplant puree or charcoal-grilled sardines.

⑲ **Osios David** (Blessed David). This entrancing little church with a commanding
Fodor'sChoice view of the city was supposedly built about AD 500 in honor of Galerius's
★ daughter, who was secretly baptized while her father was away fighting.
It was later converted into a mosque, and at some time its west wall—the
traditional place of entrance (in order to look east when facing the altar)—
was bricked up, so you enter Osios David from the south. No matter; this
entirely suits the church's rather battered magic. You can still see the ra-
diantly beautiful mosaic in the dome of the apse, which shows a rare beard-
less, somewhat Orphic Jesus, as he seems to have been described in the
vision of Ezekiel: Jesus is seen with a halo and is surrounded by the four
symbols of the Evangelists—clockwise, from top left, are the angel, the
eagle, the lion, and the calf. To the right is the prophet Ezekiel and, to the
left, Habakuk. To save it from destruction, the mosaic was hidden under
a layer of calfskin during the iconoclastic ravages of the 8th and 9th centuries. Plastered over while a mosque, it seems to have been forgotten until
1921, when an Orthodox monk in Egypt had a vision telling him to go
to the church. On the day he arrived, March 25 (the day marking Greek
independence from the Ottomans), an earthquake shattered the plaster
revealing the mosaic to the monk—who promptly died. ⊠ *Timotheou 7,
near intersection of Dimitriou Poliorkitou and Ayia Sofia, Ano Polis*
☎ *2310/221506* ⊘ *Mon.–Sat. 9–noon and 6–8.*

★ ㉓ **Panagia Chalkeon.** The name *Chalkeon* comes from the word for copper, and the beautiful "Virgin of the Copper Workers" stands in what
is still the traditional copper-working area of Thessaloniki. Completed
in 1028, this is one of the oldest churches in the city displaying the domed
cruciform style and is filled with ceramic ornaments and glowing mosaics. Artisans and workers frequently drop by during the day to light
a candle to this patron of physical laborers. The area around Panagia
Chalkeon has many shops selling traditional copper crafts at low prices.
⊠ *Chalkeon 2, southwest corner of Pl. Dikasterion, Kentro.*

Platia Athonos. A warren of side streets around a tiny square with a fountain is filled with tavernas and crafts stores. The area is frequently referred to but rarely appears on street maps, as everyone knows where
it is. *East of Aristotelous, between Gennadiou and Karolou Dil, between
Egnatia and Ermou.*

㉒ **Roman Forum.** The forum in the ancient agora, or market, dates back to
the end of the 2nd century AD. The small amphitheater here, which hosted
public celebrations and athletic and musical contests in ancient times,
is now often the site of romantic concerts on balmy summer evenings.
⊠ *Between Olimbou and Filipou, behind Pl. Dikasterion, Kentro*
☎ *2310/221266* ⊠ *Free* ⊘ *May–Oct., Mon.–Sun. 8–7; Nov.–Apr.,
Mon.–Sun. 8–5.*

➤ ⑮ **Tower of Trigoniou.** From this survivor of the city walls, you can see the
city spread out below you in a graceful curve around the bay, from the
suburbs in the east to the modern harbor in the west and, on a clear
day, even Mt. Olympus, rising near the coastline at the southwest reaches
of the bay. There is, however, little of historic interest to see within the
walls. ⊠ *Eptapyrghiou, Ano Polis.*

off the beaten path

PIKROLIMNI – Literally "sour lake," Pikrolimni is an organized thalassotherapy center spa, where sulfur-rich clay waters are purported to do wonders for the body. There are common pools (one for men and one for women) filled with this medicinal clay water (€15) and spa services. The center has 31 rooms (€60 for a double) for overnighting, plus a bar, tavern, and mini-soccer, and basketball courts. ⊠ *23 km (37 mi) north of Thessaloniki, Kilkis* ☎ *23410/ 29971 through 23410/29973* ⊕ *www.pikrolimnispa.gr.*

Where to Eat

★ **$$$$** ✕ **Miami.** More reminiscent of a white-and-blue Cycladic beach house than of Miami in South Florida, this *psarotaverna* (seafood taverna) has a patio that juts right into the sea. They've been serving quality mezedes and traditional seafood here since 1945. The wine list has more than 300 choices, most of them regional. The restaurant is 15 minutes from the city center; you can take Bus 5 from Megalou Alexandrou on the Faliro neighborhood waterfront. Reservations are essential on weekends. ⊠ *Thetidos 18, Nea Krini* ☎ *2310/447996* ⊕ *www.miami.gr* ⊟ *AE, DC, MC, V.*

★ **$$-$$$** ✕ **Krikelas.** The original Krikelas opened in seaside Kalamaria in 1940 and it remains today a standby for old-fashioned cooking. Local wines and game dishes figure prominently on the menu. Try the homemade cheese and the mixed grill, *garides saganaki* (pan-seared prawns with tomatoes and feta), or the *lagos stifado* (rabbit stew). Leave room for Asia Minor–influenced sweets such as *dandourma,* an ice cream concoction mixed with milk and cherry syrup. ⊠ *Salaminos 6, Ladadika* ☎ *2310/501600* ⊟ *AE, DC, MC, V* ⊙ *Closed July and Aug.*

★ **$$** ✕ **Aristotelous Ouzeri.** Behind a wrought-iron gate opening to a stoa, artists, scholars, and businesspeople pack marble-topped tables. This convivial place epitomizes the quality and spirit of Thessaloniki dining, down to the traditional spoon-sweet desserts. Once you sample the calamari *gemista* (stuffed with cheese), fried eggplant with garlic, or crispy fried smelts, you'll understand why no one is in a hurry to leave. The entrance is on the east side of Aristotelous, between Irakliou and Tsimiski. Be warned: address numbers repeat at the square of the same name down the street. ⊠ *Aristotelous 8, Kentro* ☎ *2310/230762* ⊟ *AE, MC, V.*

★ **$$** ✕ **Ouzeri Melathron.** "Ouzo's Mansion" was established as Greece's first ouzeri franchise (1993). Unlike the fare in many other such restaurants, everything here is freshly cooked and precisely managed; the chefs are trained in a style that is essentially Mediterranean, with some French and Turkish influences. Pick from insolently named items, such as "transvestite lamb" (it's chicken), on the exhaustive menu, or try snails in butter. Don't forget to order a kilo of house wine. There are also outlets in other cities, such as Lamia, Larissa, Karditsa, Komotini, and Varkiza. ⊠ *El. Venizelou 23, at Ermou, in Stoa Ermeion, Kentro* ☎ *2310/ 220043* ⊟ *MC, V.*

$-$$
Fodor'sChoice
★

✕ **O Loutros.** Diners at this side-street Thessaloniki institution rub shoulders with lawyers, students, out-of-towners, and workers from the Bezesteni market. The trendy-yet-traditional digs are opposite an old Turk-

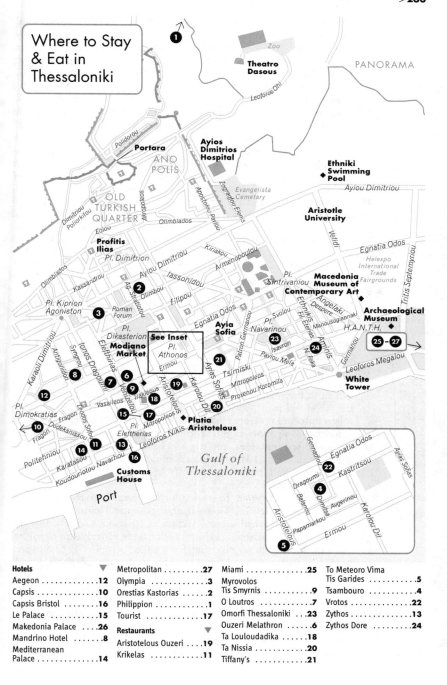

Where to Stay & Eat in Thessaloniki

Hotels ▼		
Aegeon	12	
Capsis	10	
Capsis Bristol	16	
Le Palace	15	
Makedonia Palace	26	
Mandrino Hotel	8	
Mediterranean Palace	14	

Metropolitan	27	
Olympia	3	
Orestias Kastorias	2	
Philippion	1	
Tourist	17	
Restaurants ▼		
Aristotelous Ouzeri	19	
Krikelas	11	

Miami	25	
Myrovolos Tis Smyrnis	9	
O Loutros	7	
Omorfi Thessaloniki	23	
Ouzeri Melathron	6	
Ta Louloudadika	18	
Ta Nissia	20	
Tiffany's	21	

To Meteoro Vima Tis Garides	5	
Tsambouro	4	
Vrotos	22	
Zythos	13	
Zythos Dore	24	

ish bath (*loutra* means "baths"). Try grilled *koutsomoura* (baby red mullets), grilled eggplant, mussels in rice pilaf, or smelt or shrimp sautéed in a casserole with cheese and peppers. Do sample the owner's own retsina, which comes straight from the barrel, and check if they have the exquisite *kazandibi*, a marvelous flan with a slightly burned top, sweetened with a hint of rose water. Live bouzouki music caps an evocative, sultry evening. ✉ *M. Kountoura 5, Kentro* ☎ *2310/228895* ▭ *AE, MC, V.*

$–$$ ✗ **Omorfi Thessaloniki.** The friendly staff at "Beautiful Thessaloniki" and a menu that incorporates around 120 reasonably priced dishes from all over Greece make this a popular choice. Start with the *tsipouro* (a potent spirit made from grapes) and a few mezedes—oven-cooked octopus with olive oil, for example—and keep adding as your mood strikes; that's how the Greeks do it. ✉ *Pl. Navarinou 6, Kentro* ☎ *2310/270714* ▭ *No credit cards* ⊙ *Closed Mon. and 1–2 wks in Aug. No dinner Sun.*

$–$$ ✗ **Ta Nissia.** You're in the city here, even though the furnishings may make you feel as if you've been transported to some Cycladic isle. More than 70 wines and 150 menu items give you plenty of options, such as stuffed squid with cheese and herbs, turkey with ouzo sauce, and veal with smoked eggplant. Reservations are accepted from November through April. ✉ *Proxenou Koromila 13, Kentro* ☎ *2310/285991* ▭ *MC, V* ⊙ *Closed Sun. and July and Aug.*

$–$$ ✗ **Tsambouro.** One of the favorites in Platia Athonos, this spot is particularly lively at lunchtime, when the pedestrian walkways are clustered with tables of gregarious (and ravenous) groups attracted by the terrific food and reasonable prices. Good picks are the grilled octopus, as tender and flavorful as lobster; fried *marides* (smelt); and retsina and barrel wine. ✉ *Vagdamali 4, Kentro* ☎ *2310/281435* ▭ *No credit cards.*

★ $–$$ ✗ **Vrotos.** Some of the most delicious and innovative appetizers in Thessaloniki are served at this little ouzeri run by the Vrotos family. You can sit in the noisy interior, decorated with old movie posters, or at the tables out front, all jammed with the cognoscenti. A strong Anatolian influence is evident in the terrific mezedes: try the cheese spread made with Roquefort, eggplant, and walnuts; the *bougiourdi* (feta and other cheeses, tomatoes, and peppers baked in a clay pot); and *prassopita* (leek pie). ✉ *Mitropolitou Gennadiou 6, Pl. Athonos, Kentro* ☎ *2310/223958* ▭ *No credit cards* ⊙ *Closed 3 wks in Aug., Sun. June–Aug. No dinner Sun.*

★ $ ✗ **Myrovolos Tis Smyrnis.** To see a colorful spectacle, go to this beloved hangout—also called Tou Thanassi, after its owner, Thanassis—on a Saturday afternoon when a cross section of Salonika's society fills the Modiano Market. Roaming gypsy musicians even provide entertainment. The food here is equally diverting, from grilled octopus (sliced off specimens hanging nearby) and stuffed squid to *media saganaki* (mussels with cheese-and-tomato sauce). If you do plan to come on Saturday, make a reservation; it's the only day they are accepted. ✉ *Komninon 32, Modiano Market, Kentro* ☎ *2310/274170* ▭ *No credit cards.*

★ $ ✗ **Ta Louloudadika.** Location is everything here: on a lively cul-de-sac across from the *louloudadika* (flower market), this fish restaurant and ouzeri has outdoor seating amid the lunchtime street action. The gold interior with folk accents is mellow, perfect for an ouzo and mezedes. But the food is not an afterthought—crisp calamari rings, sweet morsels of rosy *karavides* (crayfish), and tender stuffed *soupies* (cuttlefish) are some of the delicacies that draw faithful diners. There's live Greek music Wednesday through Saturday night. ⊠ *Komninon 20, Kentro* ☎ *2310/225624* 🚭 *MC, V* ⊘ *No dinner Sun.*

$ ✕ **Tiffany's.** Paneled walls, lighting sconces, long tables, and sidewalk dining: this local downtown favorite has some elements of a Parisian bistro. Its grilled meats and stews are the essence of Northern Greece: simple, tasty, and traditional. ⊠ *Iktinou 3, south of Ayia Sofia church, Kentro* ☎ *2310/274022* 🚭 *AE, MC, V.*

$ ✕ **Zythos Dore.** Crowded and lots of fun, Zythos Dore café has a great view of the White Tower as well as a good buzz. Columns tower above tile floors and there are plenty of choices: Greek and international food, bottled or barrel beers, and wine from around the world. Have a drink or a big-deal meal. Zythos, in hip Ladadika, follows the same concept and is one of the best places to hang out in the former warehouse district. ⊠ *Tsiroyiannis 7, Kentro* ☎ *2310/279010* 🚭 *DC, MC, V* ⊠ *Zythos Katouni 5, Ladadika* ☎ *2310/540284* 🚭 *V.*

¢–$ ✕ **To Meteoro Vima Tis Garides.** This casual, friendly place in the midst of busy Modiano Market is known for great *garides* (prawns), served in many different ways, and its humor; the name translates as "the meteoric step of the prawn." Other traditional fare is on the menu, too. Order your ouzo and a selection of mezedes and take in the bustle of market life. ⊠ *Irakliou 31, Modiano Market, Kentro* ☎ *2310/279867* 🚭 *No credit cards* ⊘ *Closed mid-July–mid-Aug.*

Where to Stay

$$$$ 🏨 **Capsis.** One of the best-managed venues in the city was renovated in 2005 and is stylish and sophisticated, with inlaid marble halls and rooms done in soothing tones. King-size beds and 24-hour room service are some pampering touches. Some rooms are specially designed for travelers with mobility concerns. The view from the popular rooftop restaurant sweeps the city. This old standby near the train station hosts a lot of business conventions, so book well ahead. ⊠ *Monastiriou 18, Platia Dimokratias, 54629* ☎ *2310/521321* 🖷 *2310/510555* ⊕ *www.capsishotel.gr* ⥂ *415 rooms, 7 suites* ⇘ *2 restaurants, room service, IDD phones, minibars, room TVs with movies, some in-room DVD/VCR, pool, 2 bars, babysitting, laundry service, Internet room, business services, meeting rooms, car rental, parking (fee)* 🚭 *AE, DC, MC, V* ⦿ *BP.*

$$$$ 🏨 **Capsis Bristol.** An elegant retreat with a touch of history, this exquisite
Fodor'sChoice   boutique hotel occupies one of the few buildings that survived the great
★   fire of 1917 untouched. During Ottoman rule the structure served as the city's post office. A mixture of handmade furniture, hand-picked antiques, and works of art makes this place special. The rooms are named after important Macedonian personalities such as Alexander the Great, Perseus, and Aristotle. Ask about half-price summer discounts. The Capsis Bristol straddles the Ladadika and Kentro neighborhoods, near the waterfront. ⊠ *Oplopiou 2, at Katouni, Ladadika, 54625* ☎ *2310/*

506500 🖷 *0310/515777* 🌐 *www.capsishotel.gr* 🛏 *16 rooms, 4 suites* ⚐ *Restaurant, IDD phones, minibars, cable TV with movies, in-room data ports, bar, babysitting, laundry service, business services, meeting rooms* 🚬 *AE, DC, MC, V* ⦿ *CP.*

★ **$$$–$$$$** 🏨 **Makedonia Palace.** You might see a rock star or the president of Albania here; it's that kind of place. Inside you get a real sense of being in Greece, with its mosaics, murals, and artifacts. The luxury Grecotel chain has installed state-of-the-art amenities (mini-stereos, dual-voltage outlets, multimedia convention center) behind a '70s-era facade. This waterfront landmark, southeast of the White Tower, has stunning sunset and Mt. Olympus views. There are playgrounds on either side of the building. The rooftop bar and restaurant serve excellent international food. ✉ *Alexandrou 2, at Megalou, Faliro, 54640* ☎ *2310/897197* 🖷 *2310/897211* 🌐 *www.grecotel.gr* 🛏 *260 rooms, 24 suites* ⚐ *2 restaurants, IDD phones, minibars, cable TV with movies, in-room DVD/VCR, in-room broadband, in-room data ports, 2 pools, wading pool, health club, hair salon, 3 bars, lobby lounge, shop, babysitting, playground, laundry service, business services, convention center, free parking* 🚬 *AE, DC, MC, V.*

$$$ 🏨 **Le Palace.** Although it's on one of the city's main thoroughfares, this updated art deco gem is a well-kept secret among savvy business travelers and Greek tourists. The lounge and restaurant are popular with neighborhood people as well. Rooms in its five stories have high ceilings, wooden floors, and smartly designed bathrooms. ✉ *Tsimiski 12, at El. Venizelou, Kentro, 54624* ☎ *2310/257400* 🖷 *2310/256589* 🌐 *www.lepalace.gr* 🛏 *53 rooms, 4 suites* ⚐ *Restaurant, room service, IDD phones, cable TV, in-room data ports, lounge, business services, meeting room* 🚬 *AE, DC, MC, V* ⦿ *CP.*

★ **$$$** 🏨 **Mediterranean Palace.** From the abundance of amenities at this six-story hotel near the port and Ladadika, it's easy to see that the Mediterranean Palace caters to business travelers. Besides a phone in the bathroom and soundproof windows, rooms have wireless Internet service and, on request and for a fee, an in-room PC and fax. The chandeliers, black marble-top tables, and richly upholstered furniture are meant to evoke aristocratic 1930s Thessaloniki. Everything is bright and shining, and the polish extends to exemplary service. Ask about rates that include an American-style buffet breakfast. ✉ *Salaminos 3, at Karatasou, Ladadika, 54626* ☎ *2310/552554* 🖷 *2310/552622* 🌐 *www. mediterranean-palace.gr* 🛏 *118 rooms, 7 suites* ⚐ *Restaurant, IDD phones, in-room safes, cable TV with movies, in-room broadband, in-room data ports, Wi-Fi, hair salon, bar, lobby lounge, babysitting, laundry service, business services, meeting rooms, car rental, parking (fee), no-smoking rooms* 🚬 *AE, DC, MC, V.*

$$$ 🏨 **Olympia.** Location counts at this hotel on a corner close to the flea market, copper market, Roman Forum, and Ayios Dimitrios. Well maintained and modern, it's simple but professionally managed. The bar, which has cable TV, is open 24 hours. On this site back in 1931, the Olympia public baths were opened; the hotel wing was added in 1964. ✉ *Olimbou 65, at Papageorgiou, Kentro, 54631* ☎ *2310/235421* 🖷 *2310/ 276133* 🌐 *www.olympia.com.gr* 🛏 *111 rooms* ⚐ *Restaurant, cafete-*

ria, room service, IDD phones, in-room data ports, bar, business services, meeting rooms, car rental, travel services, free parking ⊟ *AE, DC, MC, V* ⏀ *CP.*

★ **$–$$** ⊡ **Aegeon.** One of the friendliest-looking of the hotels along busy and central Egnatia's hotel strip, Aegeon is within striking distance of the train station, port, city center, and Ladadika districts. Folk art decorates the walls, and wooden furniture sit atop ceramic tile floors. Small, soundproof rooms have spacious bathrooms. ⊠ *Egnatia 19, Kentro, 54630* ☎ *2310/522921* 🖷 *2310/522922* ⊕ *www.aegeon-hotel.gr* ⤳ *59 rooms* ⚐ *Dining room, snack bar, room service, some refrigerators, cable TV with movies, in-room data ports, parking (fee)* ⊟ *AE, DC, MC, V* ⏀ *CP.*

$ ⊡ **Metropolitan.** Locals love this updated 1960s hotel near the bay in the southeast; it's within walking distance of major museums, the White Tower, and the Trade Fair grounds. Rooms on its eight floors are simple and well maintained, with floral drapes and spreads. The friendly staff can help organize a trip to Vergina and surrounding sites; the owner himself is incredibly helpful. ⊠ *Vasilissis Olgas 65, at Fleming, 1½ km (1 mi) southeast of center, Faliro, 54642* ☎ *2310/824221* 🖷 *2310/849762* ⊕ *www.metropolitan.gr* ⤳ *116 rooms, 7 suites* ⚐ *Restaurant, room service, some refrigerators, cable TV, some in-room data ports, bar, 2 Internet rooms, meeting rooms, car rental, travel services, parking (fee)* ⊟ *AE, DC, MC, V* ⏀ *BP.*

$ ⊡ **Philippion.** Want complete seclusion? The Philippion sits amid the lovely forest of Seih-Sou on a hilltop overlooking Thessaloniki. The city center is a 15- to 30-minute ride on the hotel shuttle bus (operating from morning until about midnight), depending on traffic. The airport is an easy 15-minute drive away. ⊠ *Dasos Seih-Sou, 5 km (3 mi) northeast of center, Ayios Pavlos, 56610* ☎ *2310/203320* 🖷 *2310/218528* ⊕ *www.philippion.gr* ⤳ *88 rooms, 4 suites* ⚐ *Restaurant, coffee shop, room service, IDD phones, minibars, cable TV, pool, bar, business services, meeting rooms, free parking* ⊟ *AE, DC, MC, V* ⏀ *BP.*

★ **$** ⊡ **Tourist.** A high-ceilinged, turn-of-the-20th-century building houses a modest family-run, three-story hotel that's quite popular with regular foreign visitors—from business-trippers to families. Rooms have high ceilings, and wainscotting figures prominently among the old-fashioned elegance. Three of the 10 single rooms have private bathrooms that are outside the room. Book in advance; the location, just west of Aristotelous Square, is prime. ⊠ *Mitropoleos 21, at Komninon, Kentro, 54624* ☎ *2310/270501* 🖷 *2310/226865* ⊕ *www.touristhotel.gr* ⤳ *37 rooms* ⚐ *Refrigerators, cable TV with movies, in-room broadband, in-room data ports* ⊟ *AE, DC, MC, V* ⏀ *CP.*

★ **¢–$** ⊡ **Mandrino Hotel.** This budget option comes with unexpected amenities, such as an Internet station and no-smoking rooms. The Mandrino Hotel is quite central, along busy Egnatia, near Ayios Dimitrios, Ladadika, and Aristotelous Square. Rooms are nondescript but entirely adequate; go for those in the rear of the building, which are quieter. In a building quirk, the hot water is on the right. Booking through the hotel's Web site may get you a 25% discount on the going rate. ⊠ *Antigonidon 2, at Egnatia, Kentro, 54630* ☎ *2310/526321 through 2310/526325* 🖷 *2310/526321* ⊕ *www.mandrino.gr* ⤳ *72 rooms* ⚐ *Dining room,*

room service, minibars, cable TV, in-room data ports, bar, lobby lounge, Internet room, business services, parking (fee), no-smoking floors ▭ AE, MC, V ⫐ CP.

¢–$ ⌷ **Orestias Kastorias.** Blink and you may miss this circa-1920 hotel on a quiet, narrow street leading from the Roman Forum to Ayios Dimitrios church. Front rooms have balconies and views of the ancient ruins. The decor in this three-story walk-up is spare—Formica and wood-look vinyl flooring are the norm. ✉ *Agnostou Stratiotou 14, Kentro, 54631* ☎ *2310/276517* 🖷 *2310/276572* ⊕ *www.okhotel.gr* ⇶ *37 rooms* ⌂ *Some fans, cable TV, in-room data ports; no a/c in some rooms* ▭ *MC, V.*

Nightlife & the Arts

Nightlife

Thessaloniki's nightlife is one of its true assets. Bars, pubs, breweries, discos, and clubs in the city center fill the streets with young people in search of fun. In summer, most clubs close, as their clients flock to the beaches of Chalkidiki, which functions as an outer suburb of the city. The discos on the road to the airport go in and out of fashion and change names (and concept) from one season to the next, so ask at your hotel for the newest and best. There's no local English-language periodical, but flick through the listings in the free entertainment weeklies *city* and *About;* the live-act titles, ads, bar names, or categories (Irish pub, chill-out bar, etc.), and film titles are often in English.

BARS & CLUBS When you hear locals talking about Paralia, they are referring to the road that lines the city center's waterfront, Leoforos Nikis. The cafés and bars here buzz at all hours of the day and night. Walk east along Proxenou Koromila, one block up from the waterfront to find more intimate, cool bars. Pedestrian Katouni street in Ladadika is lined with cafés and bars; this neighborhood is Thessaloniki's answer to Athens's Psyrri and Thissio nightlife areas. The club district Sfageia is a short hike or cheap taxi ride southwest of the train station, along 26th Oktovriou street. Restaurants may have live *rembetika* (lyrical music with words akin to the blues) and other Greek music.

A premier coffee bar, **Balkan** (✉ Proxenou Koromila 3, near Aristotelous Sq., Kentro ☎ 2310/265050) has excellent taped music in addition to great java and luscious chocolate cookies. You can also order alcoholic
★ beverages, European-style entrées, and salads. **Taj Mahal** (✉ Pavlou Mela 30, Kentro ☎ 2310/263686) capitalizes on the Arabian Nights trend: lounge on Indian seats, listen to ethno-pop music, eat Eastern mezedes)—or try an apple-flavor smoke on the *nargileh* (hookah). One of a chain popular in Athens, Rhodes, and Mykonos, this branch is open daily from 10 AM until late.

Odos Oneiron (✉ Vaiou 3, Ladadika ☎ 2310/555036) is a taverna with live rembetika. It moves to Chalkidiki each summer.

FodorsChoice **Mylos** (✉ Andreadou Georgiou 25, Sfageia ☎ 2310/525968), in a for-
★ mer mill on the southwest edge of the city, has become perhaps the best venue in Greece for jazz, folk, and pop acts, both Greek and foreign.

This not-to-be-missed complex of clubs, bars, and ouzeri-tavernas, as well as art galleries and a concert stage, exemplifies how a respectful architectural conversion can become a huge success. The lively place buzzes with the young and hip as early as 11 PM. **Vilka** (✉ 26th Oktovriou 58, Sfageia) is a gallery, café, bar, restaurant, and shop complex in a former industrial space. A palm tree–lined courtyard filled with comfy chairs creates an upmarket, discreet vibe. **Wooloomooloo** (Casa la Femme; ✉ 26th Oktovriou 61, Sfageia ☎ 2310/540607) is a great place to dance to the latest club music into the wee hours of the morning.

CASINO Next to the airport is the large and elaborate **Regency Casino Thessaloniki** (✉ 12th km Ethnikos Odos, Thessaloniki–Airport road, Aerodromio ☎ 2310/491234 ⊕ www.thessaloniki.regencycasino.hyatt.com)—open 24 hours. You must be 23 and have valid identification, such as a passport, to enter (€6 after 8 PM).

The Arts
Thessaloniki is an outstanding town for all things cultural: large orchestras and string trios, drama and comedy, and performances by international and local favorites are all part of the scene. For current happenings or information about festivals in the city or area, check with your hotel or the Greek National Tourism Organization (GNTO or EOT). The **Culture Ministry** (✉ Tsimiski 62, Kentro ☎ 2310/253600 ⊕ www.cultureguide.gr) produces the *Culture Guide of Thessaloniki,* available online, around town, and from their office.

CONCERTS The **Megaron Moussikis Thessaloniki** (Thessaloniki Concert Hall; ✉ 25th Martiou and Paralia, Kalamaria ☎ 2310/895800, 2310/895938, 2310/895939 box office) is a large venue that hosts local and international orchestras (including the Municipal Orchestra of Thessaloniki) and classical, folk, and jazz nights, as well as seminars and lectures.

The live music club **Ydrogeios** (✉ 26th Oktovriou 33, Sfageia ☎ 2310/516515) presents concerts in different genres from September to May, and the venue's jazz café hosts various local and international acts Thursday to Saturday.

FESTIVALS *Anastanarides* (fire dancers) are a famous part of Northern Greece. On May 21, the feast day of Sts. Constantine and Eleni, religious devotees in the villages of Langadha (25 km [15 mi] north of Thessaloniki) and Ayia Eleni (80 km [50 mi] northeast of Thessaloniki) take part in a three-day rite called the *pirovassia* (literally, "fire dancing"), in which, unharmed, they dance barefoot over a bed of hot coals while holding the saints' icons. Although assumed to be of pre-Christian origin, the tradition adopted its Christian aspects around 1250 in the eastern Thracian village of Kosti. At this time the villagers are said to have rescued the original icons from a burning church.

Apokriés, or Carnival celebrations, mark the period preceding Lent and end the night before Clean Monday, the beginning of Lent. These costume-and-parade affairs are particularly colorful (and often bawdy) in Northern Greece. You are welcome to join in the fun in Thessaloniki and other towns. Sohos, 32 km (20 mi) northeast of Thessaloniki, hosts a festive event in which people cavort in animal hides with sheep bells around their waists and phallic headdresses. In Naoussa, 112 km (70 mi) to the west of Thessaloniki, some participants wear *foustanellas* (short, pleated white kilts), special masks, and chains of gold coins across their chests, which they shake to "awaken the Earth." The whole town dons costumes and takes to the streets behind the brass marching bands that have a tradition of playing New Orleans–style jazz.

St. Dimitrios's feast day is celebrated on October 26, but its secular adjunct, the **Dimitria Festival,** has developed into a major series of cultural events that include theater, dance, art exhibits, and musical performances that take place from September to December at venues around Thessaloniki.

More than 1,000 participants from Greece and some 30 countries descend on the **International Trade Fair** (⊠ Egnatia 154, north of the Archaeological Museum, Kentro ☎ 2310/291115 ⊕ www.helexpo.gr) to promote their wares—from gadgets to tourism products. An important event in Greek politics, the prime minister traditionally makes the annual state-of-the-economy speech from the fair, which is held in mid-September at the Helexpo fairgrounds.

FILM A must-do in summer, especially for film-lovers, is to see a movie at an open-air cinema. There are usually two showtimes (around 8 and 11 PM, the later one usually at lower volume, depending on the neighborhood). Call ahead to see what's playing—some screen oldies and foreign films (subtitled in Greek), others run the latest Hollywood movies subtitled or dubbed). **Alex** (⊠ Ayias Sofias and Olimbou, Kentro ☎ 2310/ 269403) is the most central.

In November the best films by new directors from around the world are screened and awards given at the **International Film Festival** (⊠ Olympion Bldg., Pl. Aristotelous 10, Kentro ☎ 2310/378431 or 210/870–6000 Athens ⊕ www.filmfestival.gr). Films are subtitled or simultaneously translated; screening tickets are hard to come by.

THEATER Performances are in Greek, although there are occasional visits by English-speaking groups. The **Kratiko Theatro** (State Theater; ⊠ Opposite the White Tower, Kentro ☎ 2310/223404) presents plays, ballets, and special performances of visiting artists year-round. **Theatro Dasous** (Forest Theater; ⊠ In Seih-Sou forest, Ayios Pavlos ☎ 2310/218092 or 2310/245307) stages theatrical performances in foreign languages in summer, as well as other events, such as concerts.

Children's stages put on well-known plays for kids, usually on Sunday mornings from September to May. They are likely in Greek, but depending on the play and the age of your tot, it might not matter. **Sofouli** (⊠ Trapezoundos 5, at Sofouli, Kalamaria ☎ 2310/423925) has three performances on Sunday.

Sports & the Outdoors

Beaches
Beaches in Thessaloniki and its suburbs are on water too polluted to be recommended, even though you may see locals swimming there. The near-

est safe beaches are in Perea and Ayia Triada, south of the city past the airport, about 15 and 25 km (10 and 15 mi, over half an hour by bus) away, respectively, from the city center.

🕙 **Waterland** is an alternative to the beach. This water park has wave pools, waterslides, children's pools, and restaurants. Follow the signs and turn right toward Souroti; from there it's about another 6 km (4 mi). "Waterland" buses leave from the KTEL office at Monastiriou 69; the trip takes about half an hour. ☒ *1st exit past the airport off the Thessaloniki–Chalkidiki road, Tagarades* ☎ *23920/72025 through 23920/ 72029, 23920/72030* ☐ *€12.50* ☉ *May 25–June 14 and Aug. 16–Sept. 15, daily 10–6; June 15–July 14, daily 10–7; July 15–Aug. 15, daily 10–8.*

Sailing

The bay is a safe harbor for sailors, with a dramatic backdrop of mountains, the hilltop old city, and the more modern city skyline. You can hire a skippered-only 40-foot sailboat for seven to eight people from the **Nautical Athletic Club of Kalamaria** (☒ Mikro Emvolo, Kalamaria ☎ 2310/454111).

Spectator Sports

BASKETBALL Thessaloniki has some of the best basketball teams in the country and fans here are as rabid as those in NBA championship cities in the United States. **Aris** (☒ Alexandrio Arena, Lambraki 2, Helexpo, Kentro ☎ 2310/ 265600 office, 2310/273495 stadium ⊕ www.arisbc.gr) plays at the domed athletic center within the Helexpo International Trade Fairgrounds. **Iraklis** (☒ Ivanofio Stadium, Ayiou Dimitriou 159B, P. Tsaldari, Ano Polis ☎ 2310/246006 ⊕ www.iraklisbasket.bluefans.info) has its own large sports complex north of the university, near Kaftantzoglio Stadium. **PAOK** (☒ PAOK Sports Arena, Antoni Tritsi 12, Pylaia ☎ 2310/ 472551 ⊕ www.paokbc.gr) plays in Pylaia, an eastern suburb.

SOCCER Greeks enjoy soccer—and arguing about it—enormously. Aris, Iraklis (the oldest soccer club in Greece, founded in 1908), and PAOK play their seasons in spring and fall. Thessalonki was a venue city for 2004 Olympics soccer matches and for a 2006 European Cup meet.

Aris (☒ Cleanthis Vikelidis Stadium, Papanastasiou 154, Harilaou ☎ 2310/325044, 2310/325001, 2310/305402 ⊕ www.arisfc.gr) plays about 1 km (½ mi) north of the seafront amusement park. **Iraklis** (☒ Kaftantzoglio Stadium, Ayiou Dimitriou 159, P. Tsaldari, Ano Polis ☎ 2310/ 968018, 2310/219719 stadium, 2310/478800 office ⊕ www.iraklis-fc. gr) is *the* main soccer club of Thessaloniki; they play north of Aristotle University. The home stadium for **PAOK** (☒ Toumba Stadium, Mikras Asias 1, Toumba ☎ 2310/950950 ⊕ www.paokfc.gr) is several blocks east of the Helexpo International Trade Fairgrounds.

Shopping

Among the best buys in Thessaloniki are folk arts and crafts, leather, and jewelry. If it's traditional handmade objects, antiques, and souvenirs you're after, Platia Athonos is the place to go. You might want to take home a long-handled, demitasse coffee pot or nautical bric-a-brac.

Handmade copper items can be picked up near the Panayia Chalkeon church or at the Bezesteni market, off Egnatia at Eleftherios Venizelou. Is it handmade jewelry your heart is set on? Head to Aristotelous Square. Don't forget to sample the city's legendary sweets and pastries where and whenever possible.

The government has made efforts to harmonize shop opening hours, but the afternoon siesta is still observed by many small establishments. Hours are generally from about 9 to 1:30 or 2; stores reopen in the evenings on Tuesday, Thursday, and Friday. Many shops close for a few weeks in July or August.

Antiques

Antiques shops on Mitropoleos between Ayias Sofias and the White Tower are perfect for leisurely browsing; look also on the streets around Platia Athonos.

One block west of the Roman Forum, **Tositsa** is the best junk, antiques, and roaming-peddler street in the city, with good finds from brass beds to antique jewelry. The *paliatzidiko* (flea market) here has a marvelous jumble of fascinating, musty old shops, with the wares of itinerant junk collectors spread out on the sidewalks, intermingled with small, upscale antiques shops.

On Wednesday the narrow streets surrounding the Rotunda are taken over by a **bazaar** with knickknacks and the occasional interesting heirloom, antique, or folk art piece for sale.

Books

The following bookstores are rich with beautifully illustrated children's books on ancient Greek heroes and myths. **Ianos** (✉ Aristotelous 7, Kentro ☎ 2310/277164) draws travelers because of its stock of foreign-language books. **Malliaris** (✉ Dimitriou Gounari 39, Kentro ☎ 2310/277113 ✉ Aristotelous 10, Kentro ☎ 2310/262485) carries a large stock of books in English and other foreign languages. **Molho** (✉ Tsimiski 10, west of El. Venizelou, Kentro ☎ 2310/275271), the city's oldest bookshop, sells a wide selection of newspapers and magazines in myriad languages and specializes in English and French books.

Clothing

Thessalonicans are noted for being tastefully and stylishly dressed. Clothing here is high quality (but notice that sizes are a lot smaller than their American counterparts). The best shopping streets are Tsimiski, with its brand-name boutiques, Mitropoleos, Proxenou Koromila, Mitropolitou Iosif, Karolou Dil, and P. P. Germanou. Cheaper children's clothing (normally extortionate) can be found on Syngrou, south of Egnatia.

Greek Souvenirs

Platia Athonos has shops with traditional, handmade items; craftspeople themselves own many of the stores on the narrow streets between Aristotelous and Ayias Sofias. The streets around Panayia Chalkeon have shops selling copper items. Try at the Archaeological Museum for Macedonian-focused souvenirs.

MUSIC IN THESSALONIKI

Thessaloniki was known as the City of Refugees because it was one of the major destinations for the thousands of displaced Asia Minor refugees during the population exchange starting in 1923. Greeks became a majority in Thessaloniki (surpassing the Turks and Jews) and brought along their music, a form of rembetika similar to the blues in lyrical content but set to plaintive minor chord music highlighted by the bouzouki. You can still hear it at tavernas and ouzeries, often on weekends. Pontic, an ethnic music style rarely heard elsewhere in Greece, was brought along with another group of refugees, from the Black Sea Coast. Traditional instruments such as kemence (a form of lyra, a string instrument), bagpipe, and diaouli (large drum) accompany a staccato rhythm. The music is usually quite loud, as it is now accompanied by heavily amped keyboards and guitars.

Many songs have been written about Thessaloniki, mostly nostalgic tunes of longing. You may want to purchase some of this music, so that you, too, can reminisce. Greece's premier composer (and bouzouki player), Vassilis Tsitanis, wrote "Omorfi Thessaloniki" ("Beautiful Thessaloniki"); grab a version of the song interpreted by Glykeria. Dimitris Mitropanos has composed two of the most gut-wrenching tunes; ask for "S'anazito sti Saloniki" ("I'm Looking for You in Salonica") and "Ladadika," written about the old district. For something more contemporary, try "Genithika sti Saloniki" ("I Was Born in Salonica") by Dionysius Savvopoulos, the Greek Bob Dylan. Kristi Stassinopoulou, on the musical edge, performs what she calls a "Balkan ethno-trance" or "Greek techno folk psychedelia." Don't leave a music store without buying something by Savinna Yiannatou, whose Judeo-Spanish folk songs are spine-chillingly sublime.

★ **Alexandra Theodossiou** (✉ Papamarkou 43,, Pl. Athonos, Kentro ☎ 2310/265039) is a lively ceramics shop. **Ergastirio Kouklis** (Doll Workshop; ✉ Mitropolitou Gennadiou 2, Kentro ☎ 2310/236890) displays dolls artistically designed by Artemis Papadopoulou. **Mastihashop** (✉ Karolou Dil 15, Kentro ☎ 2310/250205 ⊕ www.mastihashop.com) carries products containing mastic—a tree resin produced on the Aegean island of Chios. Everything from face cream to preserves and sweets come in extremely attractive, easy-to-pack tins.

Music

Music shops are on pedestrian and bohemian Gounari, south of the Rotunda. **Blow Up** (✉ Aristotelous 8, Kentro ☎ 2310/233255 or 2310/276394) is central and carries a wide selection. **Studio 52** (✉ Dimitriou Gounari 46, Kentro ☎ 2310/271301 or 2310/251178) is the city's all-time favorite music store, with a huge number of CDs.

Sweets

Thessaloniki is well known for its food, including a vast array of Balkan and Eastern-oriented pastries and desserts. Every neighborhood in Thessaloniki seems to claim the city's best sweet shop; most of these—unusual for Greece—have Web sites. Sit down, sample, and decide which you think is best.

With eight outlets in Thessaloniki, **Agapitos** (✉ Tsimiski 53, between Ayias Sofias and Karolou Dil, Kentro ☎ 2310/235935 ⊕ www.agapitos. gr) aptly translates as "loved one." The oldest son of a venerable Thessaloniki family owns this chain. **Averof** (✉ Vasilissis Georgiou 11, Kentro ☎ 2310/814284 ⊕ www.averof.gr) is the only patisserie in Thessaloniki that creates kosher pastries, a fact that makes friendly owner Marios Papadopoulos proud.

★ Sample Thessaloniki's fabled Anatolian sweets at central **Hatzi.** (✉ El. Venizelou 50, Kentro ☎ 2310/279058). Specialties include the must-be-burned *kazandibi,* a kind of flan; *trigono,* a cream-filled confection; and *kataïfi* (a well-known Eastern dessert that looks a bit like shredded wheat) served with *kaïmaki* (real cream that's sweetened and iced). Choose a beverage—like iced coffee, granita, or *boza* (a thick, sweet, millet-and-corn drink)—and people-watch from the pedestrian side street that faces the gardens of Panagia Chalkeon church.

CENTRAL MACEDONIA

ΚΕΝΤΡΙΚΗ ΜΑΚΕΔΟΝΙΑ

Ancient ruins, mountains, beachfront resorts, and sacred sanctuaries lie within easy reach of Thessaloniki in Central Macedonia. Pella, Vergina, and Dion are three major archaeological sites associated with Alexander the Great and his father, Philip II, heroes of the ages. An attractive village, Litochoro, sits beneath the peaks of Mt. Olympus. The region of Chalkidiki is best known as Thessaloniki's summer playground with its beaches and resorts, including Ouranoupolis and its offshore islands. Holy Mt. Athos is a male-only monastic peninsula of natural and spiritual beauty.

In the 7th century BC the Dorian Makednoi (Macedonian) tribe moved out of the Pindos mountains (between Epirus and Macedonia), settled in the fertile plains below, and established a religious center at the sacred springs of Dion at the foot of Mt. Olympus. Perdikkas, the first king of the Macedonians, held court at a place called Aigai, now known to have been at Vergina; and in the 5th century BC, the king of that time, Archelaos (413–399), moved his capital from Aigai to Pella, which was then on a rise above a lagoon leading to the Thermaic Gulf.

In 359 BC, after a succession of kings and near anarchy exacerbated by the raids of barbarian tribes from the north, the 23-year-old Philip II was elected regent. Philip II pulled the kingdom together through diplomacy and marital alliances and then began expanding his lands, taking the gold mines of the Pangeon mountains and founding Philippi there. In 356 BC, on the day that Alexander the Great was born, Philip II was said to have simultaneously taken the strategic port of Potidea in Chalkidiki, received news of his horse's triumph in the Olympic Games, and learned of a general's victory against the Illyrians. That was also the day the temple of Artemis at Ephesus was destroyed by fire, which later prompted people to say that the goddess was away on that day, tending to Alexander's birth. In 336 BC, Philip II was assassinated in Vergina at a wedding party for one of his daughters. (His tomb there was discovered in 1977 by the Greek archaeologist Manolis Andronikos.) Alexander, then 20, assumed power, and within two years he had gathered an army to be blessed at Dion, before setting off to conquer the Persians and most of the known world.

Pella

Πέλλα

★ ㉔ *40 km (25 mi) west of Thessaloniki.*

Pella was Alexander's birthplace and the capital of the Macedonian state in the 4th century. The modern-day village is not the most alluring, nor is there anywhere to stay. The ancient village ruins and its museum—both best known for their intricate, artful, beautifully preserved floor mosaics, mainly of mythological scenes—are on either side of the main road toward Edessa (where waterfalls invite a possible further trip). It's best to first get an overview at the **Archaeological Museum,** which contains a model of the 4th-century BC dwelling that stood across the road, as well as fascinating artifacts of Neolithic, Bronze, and Iron Age settlers, some as old as the 7th century BC. Note also the unique statuette of a horned Athena (apparently influenced by Minoan Crete), the statue of Alexander sprouting the horns of Pan, and the adorable sleeping Eros (Cupid), reproductions of which can be bought at the gift shop. Descriptions are sparse, but the attendants, pointedly not experts, are happy to share what they know.

In 1914, two years after the Turks' departure, the people who lived on the land were moved to a village north of here, and excavations of the **archaeological site** began. These include portions of the walls; the sanctuaries of Aphrodite, Demeter, and Cybele; the marketplace; cemetery; and several houses. In 1987, on a small rise to the north, the remains of the **palace** came to light; at present they are still excavating. If coming by train, get off at Edessa and take the KTEL bus to the site. If coming by bus, get off the Thessaloniki–Edessa KTEL bus at the site. ✉ *Off E86, Thessaloniki–Edessa Rd.* ☎ *23820/31160* ⊕ *www.culture.gr* 🎟 *€6* ☉ *Tues.–Sun. 8–7:30, Mon. noon–7:30.*

Vergina

Βεργίνα

㉕ *40 km (25 mi) south of Pella, 135 km (84 mi) southwest of Thessaloniki.*

Fodor'sChoice
★

Some of antiquity's greatest treasures await you at the Royal Tombs of Vergina, opened to the public in 1993, 16 years after their discovery. Today the complex, including a museum, is a fitting shrine to the original capital of the kingdom of Macedonia, then known as Aigai. The entrance is appropriately stunning: you walk down a white sandstone ramp into the partially underground structure, roofed over by a large earth-covered dome approximately the size of the original tumulus. Here on display are some of the legendary artifacts from the age of Philip II of Macedonia (382–336 BC).

For years both archaeologists and grave robbers had suspected that the large mound that stood on this site might contain something of value, but try as they might, neither of these groups was successful in penetrating its secret. Locals still remember playing ball on the mound as children. Professor Manolis Andronikos, who discovered the tombs, theorized in his book *The Royal Tombs of Vergina* that one of Alexander's successors, wanting to protect Philip's tomb from robbers, had it covered with broken debris and tombstones to make it appear that the grave had already been plundered, and then built the tumulus so that Philip's tomb would be near the edge rather than the center. When Andronikos discovered it, on the final day of excavation, in 1977, he had been trying one of the last approaches, with little hope of finding anything—certainly not the tomb of Philip II, in as pristine condition as the day it was closed.

This was the first intact Macedonian tomb ever found—imposing and exquisite, with a huge frieze of a hunting scene, a masterpiece similar to those of the Italian Renaissance but 1,800 years older, along with a massive yet delicate fresco depicting the abduction of Persephone (a copy of which is displayed along one wall of the museum). Two of the few original works of great painting survive from antiquity. On the left are two tombs and one altar that had been looted and destroyed in varying degrees by the time Andronikos discovered them. Macedonian Tomb III, on the right, found intact in 1978, is believed to be that of the young Prince Alexander IV, Alexander the Great's son, who was at first kept alive by his "protectors" after Alexander's death and then poisoned (along with his mother) when he was 14. To the left of Tomb III is that of Philip II. He was assassinated in the nearby theater, a short drive away; his body was burned, his bones washed in wine, wrapped in royal purple, and put into the magnificent, solid gold casket with the 16-point sun, which is displayed in the museum. His wife, Cleopatra (not the Egyptian queen) was later buried with him.

The tombs alone would be worth a special trip, but the golden objects and unusual artifacts that were buried within them are equally impressive. Among these finds, in practically perfect condition and displayed in dramatic dimmed light, are delicate ivory reliefs, elegantly wrought gold laurel wreaths, and Philip's crown, armor, and shield. Especially interesting are those items that seem most certainly Philip's: a pair of greaves (shin guards), one shorter than the other—Philip was known to have a limp. To the right of the tombs there's a gift shop that sells books and postcards; the official gift shop is outside the entrance gate (across from Philippion restaurant), on the same side of the road. Macedonian souvenirs available here are scarce elsewhere.

The winding road to the **site of Philip's assassination** goes through rolling countryside west of modern Vergina, much of it part of the vast royal burial grounds of ancient Aigai. On the way you pass three more **Macedonian tombs** of little interest, being rough-hewn stone structures in typical Macedonian style; the admission to the Royal Tombs includes these. The **palace** itself is nothing more than a line of foundation stones that shows the outline of its walls. It was discovered by French archaeologists in 1861 but not thought to have any particular significance; ancient Aigai was then thought to be somewhere near Edessa. In the field below are the remnants of the **theater,** discovered by Andronikos in 1982. It was on Philip's way here, to attend the wedding games that were to follow the marriage of his daughter to the king of Epirus, that he was murdered and where his son, Alexander the Great, was crowned.

To get to Vergina by bus, go from Thessaloniki KTEL main terminal to Veria, and take a bus to the site from there. If going by train, get off at Veria station. A local "blue" bus takes passengers from the outlying station into town, where you can take the KTEL bus. Be attentive if coming by car, the route is not well marked from Pella. ⊠ *Off E90, near Veria* ☎ *23310/92347* ⊕ *www.culture.gr* 💰 *€8* ⊙ *June–Oct., Mon. noon–7, Tues.–Sun. 8–7; Nov.–May, Tues.–Sun. 8:30–3.*

off the beaten path

BOUTARI WINERY – If you happen to hear the call of Dionysus, give in to the temptation. The Boutari vineyards are known for dry reds. Call ahead to book a tour, which takes you through the cellars. You can also taste the wine and make your own purchases. The winery is closed two weeks in August. ⊠ *40 km (25 mi) northwest of Vergina, Stenimachos, Naoussa* ☎ *23320/41666* ⊕ *www.boutari.gr* 💰 *Tour €3* ⊙ *Daily 9–3.*

Where to Stay & Eat

$

Fodor'sChoice
★

✕ **Philippion.** Choose from traditional foods such as moussaka or try the highly recommended fresh pasta, such as cannelloni stuffed with spinach and cheese. The regional vegetables are especially delicious, and fresh frozen yogurt is made from local fruits. Self-serve cafeteria style lunch is available, but this is also a taverna-restaurant. Reservations are not necessary, but be warned tour buses do stop here. ⊠ *Outside archaeological site* ☎ *23310/92892* ⊕ *www.filippion.gr* ⊟ *AE, MC, V.*

$$$

🏨 **Dimitra.** On a quiet street a five-minute walk from the ancient archaeological site at Vergina is the village's luxury lodging. This beautiful two-story hotel was built in 2003. Each of the 10 spacious studio suites has its own elegant, classic style and high-quality features, such as a fireplace, piano, or PC. Dimitra's parents, the owners, may offer to give you a private viewing of an oil painting of the hotel's namesake. Consider making this a base for area excursions; discounts are available for extended stays. ⊠ *Athinas 5, 59031* ☎ *23310/92900* 🖷 *23310/ 92901* ✍ *zisseka@yahoo.com* 📶 *10 suites* ⚑ *Dining room, room service, BBQs, kitchenettes, minibars, lounge, babysitting, laundry service, business services, some pets allowed* ⊟ *No credit cards* ⚐ *BP.*

¢

🏨 **Vergina Pension.** Between the modern and ancient village sits a two-story, pine-furniture-and-crisp-sheets accommodation like those found all over the country. It's got all the basics covered and has wraparound balconies and plants in the unusually wide corridors. The dining room–snack bar is enormous; you can start the day with a Continental breakfast for €10. ✉ *Aristotelous 55, 59031* ☎ *23310/92510* 🖷 *23310/ 92511* 🛏 *10 rooms* ⚬ *Snack bar, some refrigerators, bar, laundry service, some pets allowed; no room phones* ⊟ *No credit cards.*

Dion

Δίον

❷❻ *90 km (56 mi) south of Vergina, 87 km (54 mi) southwest of Thessa-*
FodorsChoice *loniki.*
★

At the foothills of Mt. Olympus lies ancient Dion. Even before Zeus and the Olympian gods, the mountain was home to the Muses and Orpheus, who entranced the men of the area with his mystical music. The story says that the life-giving force of Dion came from the waters in which the murderers of Orpheus (the women of Mt. Olympus, jealous for attention from their men) washed their hands on the slopes of the sacred mountain to remove the stain of their own sin. The waters entered the earth and rose, cleansed, in the holy city of Dion. (Zeus is *Dias* in Greek, it's he for whom the city was named.)

Ancient Dion was inhabited from as early as the classical period (5th century BC) and last referred to as Dion in the 10th century AD according to the archaeological findings. Start at the **museum** to see the videotape (in English) prepared by the site's renowned archaeologist, Dimitris Pandermalis, which describes the excavations, the finds, and their significance. (His efforts to keep the artifacts in the place where they were found have established a trend for decentralization of archaeological finds throughout Greece.) The second floor contains a topographical relief of the area and the oldest surviving pipe organ precursor—the 1st-century BC hydraulis. The basement learning area has an Alexander mosaic, model of the city, and ancient carriage shock absorbers. Labels are very basic. ✉ *Adjacent to archaeological site* ☎ *23510/53206* ⊕ *www. culture.gr* 🖾 *€3* ⊙ *Mon. 12:30–7:30, Tues.–Sun. 8–7.*

Unearthed ruins of various buildings include the villa of Dionysos, public baths, a stadium (the Macedonian Games were held here), shops, and workshops. The road from the museum divides the diggings at the archaeological site into two areas. On the left is the **ancient city** of Dion itself, with the juxtaposition of public toilets and several superb floor mosaics. On the right side are the **ancient theaters** and the **Sanctuaries of Olympian Zeus, Demeter, and Isis.** In the latter, which is a vividly beautiful approximation of how it once looked, copies of the original statues, now in the museum, have been put in place.

Today a feeling of peace prevails at Dion, at the foot of the mountain of the gods. Few people visit this vast, underrated city site. The silence is punctuated now and then by goats, their bells tinkling so melodically you expect to spy Pan in the woods at any moment. Springs bubble up where excavators dig, and scarlet poppies bloom among the cracks— this is the essence of Greece.

Dion is about a 1½-hour journey from Thessaloniki; buses leave every half hour or so for Katerini, where you can take the local "blue" bus to the Dion site (€1). From Katerini, you could also hop on the connecting route to Litochoro at the base of Mt. Olympus (€6.50), which has good dining and lodging options, and take a taxi (around €7) to the site. If coming by train get off at Katerini, 17 km (27 mi) south of the site, then take a bus or a taxi to the site or to Litochoro (the isolated Litochoro railway station is outside town). Winter hours are unpredictable. ✉ *7 km (4 ½ mi) north of Litochoro off E75/1A, Thessaloniki–Athens Rd.* ☎ *23510/53484* ⊕ *www.culture.gr* ▣ *€4* ☉ *May–Oct., daily 8–5; Nov.–Apr. reduced hrs.*

Where to Stay & Eat

★ **$–$$$** ✕ **Dionysos.** Excellent food and true Greek *filoxenia* (hospitality) await at the combination tourist shop, café, and three-meal-a day restaurant. Recommended are the *loukanika* (sausages); rolled, spiced, and spit-roasted meat; and the saganaki. If you want to try the specialty of the area, *katsikaki sti souvla* (roasted goat on a spit), order at least a day ahead. The house barrel wine, *krasi hima,* is locally produced, and the owners serve homemade tsipouro liquor. ✉ *Village center, directly opposite museum* ☎ *23510/53276* ▤ *No credit cards.*

$–$$
Fodor'sChoice
★

▣ **Safeti.** The mauve-color Safeti, opened in 2005, is a most welcome addition to Dion, and Greece in general. Four gorgeous, modern suites—one of which has a hot tub, another, a fireplace—upstairs make good use of chrome, light wood, ceramic tiles, and leather furniture. Downstairs, crafts and products all enterprisingly made by the Safeti family (most right on-site) are for sale: organic preserves, liqueurs, and pasta; loom-made rugs; dolls and bags; mosaics; and copper pots. Full breakfast, made with ingredients right from the garden, is available. ✉ *Opposite ancient Dion museum, on main road, 60100* ☎ *23510/46272 or 694/7720343 cell* 🖶 *23510/46273* 🛏 *4 suites* ☾ *In-room safes, some in-room hot tubs, kitchens, microwaves, cable TV with movies, in-room data ports, 3 shops, laundry service, business services* ▤ *MC, V.*

Mt. Olympus

Όρος Όλυμπος

★ ㉗ *17 km (10 mi) southwest of Dion, 100 km (62 mi) southwest of Thessaloniki.*

To understand how the mountain must have impressed the ancient Greeks and caused them to shift their allegiance from the earth-rooted deities of the Mycenaeans to those of the airy heights of Olympus, you need to see the mountain clearly from several different perspectives. On its northern side, the Olympus range catches clouds in a turbulent, stormy bundle, letting fly about 12 times as many (surely Zeus-inspired) thunder-and-lightning storms as anywhere else in Greece. From the south, if there is still snow on the range, it appears as a massive, flat-topped acropolis, much like the one in Athens; its vast, snowy crest hovering in the air, seemingly capable of supporting as many gods and temples as the ancients could have imagined. As you drive from the sea to Mt.

Olympus, this site appears as a conglomeration of thickly bunched summits rather than as a single peak. The truly awe-inspiring height is 9,570 feet.

Litochoro is the lively town (population 7,000, plus a nearby army base) nestled at the foot of the mountain and is the modern address for Olympus these days. Souvenir shops, restaurants, local-specialty bakeries (stock up before a hike), and hotels vie for customers. Litochoro is 1½ hours by KTEL bus from Thessaloniki (almost every half hour from Thessaloniki and hourly from nearby Katerini). The isolated Litochoro train station is hard to access, about 5 km (3 mi) from the town near the seaside. Better to take the train to Katerini and then a bus from there.

Where to Stay & Eat

★ **$-$$** ✕ **To Pazari.** Take the opportunity to gorge on fresh seafood at cheap prices at this taverna that also serves fresh local meat dishes. Accompany the blow-out with super-soft village bread and a killer garlic-eggplant salad (dip), along with the house white. The fish soup in winter is also a specialty. Follow the signs 100 yards past the main square and up to the left around the corner. ✉ *25th Martiou, Litochoro* ☎ *23520/ 82540 or 23520/84185* ▭ *MC, V.*

$ ✕ **Olympos.** If it's the familiar you crave, try Olympos, right on the square beside the National Bank. Everything is homemade or grilled, from veal schnitzel and burgers to spaghetti, breakfast omelets, and traditional Greek dishes. You can eat in or get it packed to take out on the trail. ✉ *Kentriki Pl., Litochoro* ☎ *23520/84282* ▭ *No credit cards.*

★ ☺ **$$$$** 🏨 **Dion Palace Beauty & Spa Resort.** Enjoy excellent views of the sea or the peaks at the Dion Palace. Proximity to the beach, Mt. Olympus, and the archaeological site at Dion are the big draws here. There's also a luxury spa, as well as many activities for kids. Water sports are available through a private operator. KTEL buses on the Thessaloniki-bound Katerini–Litochoro route (Camping Mitikas stop; go through the camp ground) run every hour in summer, from about 6 AM–9:30 PM. ✉ *Limni Litochoro, 6 km (4 mi) northeast of Litochoro, 60200 Gritsa* ☎ *23520/ 61431 through 23520/61434* 🖷 *23520/61435* ⊕ *www.dionpalace.com* ◱ *187 rooms, 9 suites* ☺ *3 restaurants, dining room, grocery, room service, IDD phones, in-room safes, minibars, cable TV, in-room data ports, 2 tennis courts, pool, indoor pool, wading pool, gym, spa, beach, 4 bars, recreation room, shop, playground, business services, 2 convention centers, meeting rooms* ▭ *AE, DC, MC, V* ⏏ *BP.*

★ **¢-$** 🏨 **Olympus Mediterranean.** You get good value for the price at this spa hotel built in 2004. Rooms on each of its four floors are done in a different style, such as traditional or modern. Some rooms have a fireplace and/or hot tub; all have balconies. There's an indoor pool and beauty treatment rooms in the basement. Follow signs up and left from the main square (not far); it's hidden beside To Pazari taverna. ✉ *Dionyssou 5, 60200 Litochoro* ☎ *23520/81831* 🖷 *23520/83333* ✎ *olympus-med@acn.gr* ◱ *20 rooms, 3 suites* ☺ *Café, dining room, room service, in-room safes, some in-room hot tubs, minibars, cable TV, indoor pool, hot tub, spa, bar* ▭ *DC, MC, V* ⏏ *BP.*

¢ 🖩 **Villa Drosos.** A gated garden, a location near a park, and outdoor pool make Drosos very appealing for young families. The hotel faces Ayios Giorgios churchyard in a quiet area about a five-minute walk (200 yards) from the main road. Continental breakfast is available. ⊠ *Archelaou 20, 60200 Litochoro* ☎ *23520/84561 or 23520/84562* 🖶 *23520/84563* 🖢 *13 rooms* ⚲ *Cafeteria, ice-cream parlor, snack bar, room service, BBQs, minibars, refrigerators, in-room data ports, pool, bar, travel services, some pets allowed* ⊟ *V.*

★ ¢ 🖩 **Villa Pantheon.** You know you're somewhere special when you see this family-run establishment at the trailhead for Mt. Olympus; views stretch to the sea and the mountains. Townfolk recommend this as the best hotel in town. All the suites (with three or four beds) have fireplaces. Breakfast is à la carte and optional, unless you stay four or more days, then it's included. Reservations are a must, especially on weekends and holidays. From the square it's a 10-minute walk up Enipeos past the Aphrodite Hotel. Continue slightly left after the juncture, turn up Ayiou Dimitriou, and keep going over the bridge; the hotel's on the right. ⊠ *Ayiou Dimitriou terma (end), 60200 Litochoro* ☎ *23520/83931* 🖶 *23520/83932* 🖢 *4 rooms, 8 suites* ⚲ *Dining room, kitchenettes, minibars, cable TV with movies and video games, in-room broadband, in-room data ports, bar, recreation room* ⊟ *MC, V.*

Sports & the Outdoors

Mt. Olympus has some of the most beautiful nature trails in Europe. Hundreds of species of wildflowers and herbs bloom in spring, more than 85 of which are found only on this mountain. There are basically three routes to Zeus's mountain top, all beginning in Litochoro. The most-traveled road is via Prionia; the others are by Diastavrosi (literally, "crossroads") and along the Enipeos. You can climb all the way on foot or take a car or negotiate a taxi ride to the end of the road at Prionia (there's a taverna) and trek the rest of the way (six hours or so) up to snow-clad Mytikas summit—Greece's highest peak at 9,570 feet. The climb to Prionia takes about four hours; the ride, on a bumpy gravel road with no guardrails between you and breathtakingly precipitous drops, takes little less than an hour, depending on your nerves. If you can manage to take your eyes off the road, the scenery is magnificent. The trail is snow-free from about mid-May until late October.

During your Mt. Olympus hike, you could take a lunch break or stay overnight at **Spilios Agapitos.** The refuge is run by the daughter of Kostas Zolotas, the venerable English-speaking guru of climbers. To bunk down for the night costs €10 per person; there are blankets but no sheets. Bring your own flashlight, towel, and soap. The restaurant is open 6 AM–9 PM. It's 6 km (4 mi), about 2½–3 hours, from Prionia to Refuge A. From here it's 5 km (3 mi), about 2½–3 hours, to the Throne of Zeus and the summit. The trail is easygoing to Skala summit (most of the way), but the last bit is scrambling and a bit hair-raising. Some people turn back. ⊠ *Refuge A* ☎ *23520/81800* ⊙ *Mid-May–Oct.; overnight guests must arrive by 8 PM.*

If you plan to hike up Mt. Olympus, be sure to take a map; the best are produced by **Anavasi** (⊠ Arsakiou arcade 6A, Omonia Sq. Athens 🖶☎ 210/321–8104 ⊕ www.mountains.gr).

Ouranoupolis

Ουρανούπολη

28 *110 km (68 mi) east of Thessaloniki, 224 km (189 mi) north and east of Mt. Olympus.*

Meaning "heaven's city" in Greek, Ouranoupolis (also spelled Ouranopolis) is an appealing cul-de-sac on the final point of land that separates the secular world from the sacred sanctuaries of Mt. Athos. The village, noted for its rug and tapestry weaving, is particularly entrancing because of the bay's aquamarine waters, and the town is full of families on holiday in summer. The narrow village beaches can become overcrowded. There are many pensions and rooms-to-let around town, but the hotels on an islet or slightly outside the main town are quietest.

Ouranoupolis was settled by refugees from Asia Minor in 1922–23, when the Greek state expropriated the land from Vatopedi monastery on Mt. Athos. The settlement, known as Prosforion, was until then occupied by farming monks, some of whom lived in the Byzantine **Tower of Prosforion**, its origins dating from the 12th century. The tower subsequently became the abode of Joice and Sydney Loch, a couple who worked with Thessaloniki's noted American Farm School to help the refugees develop their rug-weaving industry. The tower was burned, altered, and restored through the centuries. It is rather a breezy and open place to take in the view on a sweltering day. ⊠ *Main square, waterfront* ☎ *23770/71389 or 23770/71651* 🎫 *€2* ☉ *June–Oct., Mon.–Sun. 9–5.*

off the beaten path
SMALL ISLANDS – Floating on the Proviakas Bay's turquoise waters are tiny emerald islands which are reachable from Tripiti via a 15-minute caïque or ferry ride that runs every half hour or so in summer—and by small outboard motorboats, which you can rent by the day. All the islets have glorious white-sand beaches, and two— **Gaidoronisi** (part of the Drenia group) and the fishing hamlet of **Amouliani town**—have places to eat. ⊠ *Tripiti, 6 km (4 mi) north of Ouranoupolis.*

en route
If you make your own way to Ouranoupolis via Route 16, do stop at **Aristotle's Statue** in Stagira (watch for the blink-and-miss road sign), the region of this remarkable man's birthplace. Aristotle's theories and inventions are recreated in engaging hands-on exhibits around a grassy knoll with a surveying view. ⊠ *West of modern village* ☎ *No phone* ⊠ *€1.*

Where to Stay & Eat

$–$$
Fodor's Choice
★
✕ **Kritikos.** The owner is a local fisherman, and everything served is catch-of-the-day. Don't confuse this modern, cream-hue restaurant with the eponymous snack bar up the road. Here the family cooks traditional village recipes—the seafood pasta is sublime—and Macedonian specialties, such as *melitzana horiatiki* (an eggplant, tomato, feta, garlic and olive oil salad). The *kolokithokeftedes* (zucchini-and-potato croquettes) are enormous. The owner's efforts received a citation in the country's top-

10 "best of" *Alpha Guide,* yet the place remains unpretentious and very well priced for what you get. They even produce their own wine and tsipouro. ⊠ *Main road, away from the tower* ☎ *23770/71222* ⊟ *DC, MC, V.*

★ $$$–$$$$ 🏨 **Agionissi Resort.** A private boat transports you from Ouranoupolis to the secluded islet of Amouliani, which still has a village of 500 fishing families. Rooms in bungalows are modern and uncluttered, with white walls, dark wooden furniture, and area rugs. The restaurant has marvelous seafood and an impressive selection of wines from Chalkidiki and Mt. Athos. The pool bar has a view of Mt. Athos from its terrace. The resort's three beaches have been awarded the European eco-label Blue Flag for water cleanliness. Half-board is available. ⊠ *5-min boat ride from Ouranoupolis, 1½ km (1 mi) outside village, 63075 Amouliani Island* ☎ *23770/51102* 🖷 *23770/51180* ⊕ *www.papcorp.gr* ⤳ *70 rooms* ᗒ *Restaurant, room service, IDD phones, in-room safes, minibars, cable TV, tennis court, saltwater pool, exercise equipment, spa, beach, dock, fishing, mountain bikes, horseback riding, Ping-Pong, 2 bars, library, shop, playground, laundry service, business services, travel services* ⊟ *AE, MC, V* ⊗ *Closed Nov.–Apr.* ⑩ *BP.*

$$$–$$$$ 🏨 **Xenia Ouranoupolis.** A low-lying, early-1960s design makes this tranquil retreat almost invisible among the tamarisk and olive groves. The rooms, too, make the most of nature, with French doors framing the sea. A private white-sand beach beckons only yards away; the location attracts many families and seniors. The restaurant is noted for its seafood and local specialties. Xenia guests can avail themselves of facilities—like the tennis court, spa, and horseback riding—at sister property Agionissi Resort. ⊠ *Waterfront, 63075* ☎ *23770/71412* 🖷 *23770/71362* ⊕ *www.papcorp.gr* ⤳ *20 rooms, 20 bungalows* ᗒ *Restaurant, snack bar, room service, in-room safes, minibars, cable TV, saltwater pool, wading pool, beach, dock, fishing, volleyball, 2 bars, library, shop, playground, laundry service, business services, meeting room, travel services, free parking* ⊟ *AE, MC, V* ⊗ *Closed Nov.–Mar.* ⑩ *BP.*

$$$ 🏨 **Skités.** Find peace and privacy on a bluff off a gravel road south of
Fodor'sChoice town. Each of the small, pleasant rooms in this charming complex of
★ garden bungalows has its own entrance. The staff works to make you feel comfortable and the restaurant's home-style meals change daily, with a focus on vegetarian dishes. Sea views from the terrace are lovely. Stays can include three meals a day, with half-board another option. In the evening there are often cultural events to enjoy, such as classical music concerts, poetry readings, and theatrical presentations. ⊠ *1 km (½ mi) south of town, c/o Pola Bohn, 63075* ☎ *23770/71140 or 23770/71141* 🖷 *23770/71322* ⊕ *www.skites.gr* ⤳ *21 rooms, 4 apartments* ᗒ *Restaurant, some kitchens, minibars, some in-room data ports, pool, beach, dock, boating, 2 bars, laundry service, business services, meeting room, some pets allowed; no room TVs* ⊟ *MC, V* ⊗ *Closed Nov.–Apr.* ⑩ *BP.*

¢ 🏨 **Acrogiali.** Built in 1935, this is the town's first hotel, and the only one across the street from the beach. The three-story building is nothing special to look at, but it has been modernized (2002), and the sea view rooms are just fine for basic beach holidays. The same family also runs an off-beach hotel around the corner. ⊠ *Beach road, 63075* ☎ *23770/*

71201 ✆ *15 rooms* 🏠 *Refrigerators, boating, laundry service, travel services, some pets allowed* 🖃 *No credit cards.*

Mt. Athos

Όρος Άθως

★ ㉙ *50 km (31 mi) southeast of Ouranoupolis, 120 km (74 mi) southeast of Thessaloniki.*

The third peninsula of Chalkidiki, Mt. Athos is called *Ayion Oros* (Holy Mountain) in Greek, although it does not become a mountain until its southernmost point (6,667 feet). The peninsula is prized for its pristine natural beauty, seclusion (no women allowed), and spirituality; its monasteries contain priceless illuminated books and other treasures.

The Virgin Mary, it is said, was brought to Athos by accident from Ephesus, having been blown off course by a storm, and she decreed that it be venerated as her own special place. This story has since become the rationale for keeping it off-limits to all women but the Virgin herself. Hermits began settling here and formed the first monastery in the 10th century. By the 14th century, monasteries on the 650-square-km (250-square-mi) peninsula numbered in the hundreds. In 1924 the Greek state limited the number of monasteries, including Russian, Bulgarian, and Serbian Orthodox, to 20, but a number of hermitages and separate dependencies called *skités* also exist. The semiautonomous community falls under the religious authority of the Istanbul-based Orthodox Ecumenical Patriarch.

Men who want to visit Mt. Athos should contact the **Holy Executive of the Holy Mt. Athos Pilgrims' Bureau** at least six months in advance of arrival. You must obtain a written permit (free) from this office, which issues 10 permits a day for non-Orthodox visitors, and 100 permits a day for Orthodox visitors (Greek or foreign). You will need to pick it up in person, presenting your passport. Enquire about making reservations for a specific monastery, which must be done in advance, noting however, that some might be closed for renovations. The permits are valid for a four-day visit on specific dates, which may be extended by authorities in Karyes. When you arrive at Ouranoupolis, you also need to pick up a *diamonitirio,* or residence permit (€35); ask at the Thessaloniki bureau for more information. The boat departs Ouranoupolis for Daphni on the peninsula at 9:45 AM; it's a two-hour sail. Local transport takes you the last 13 km (8 mi) to Karyes and to monasteries beyond from there. Mt. Athos is a place of religious pilgrimage: proper attire is long pants and shirts with sleeves at least to mid-arm; wearing hats inside the monasteries is forbidden. Video cameras and tape recorders are banned from the mountain, but taking photographs is allowed. ⊠ *Egnatia 109, Kentro, Thessaloniki* ☎ *2310/252578* 🖷 *2310/222424* ☉ *Weekdays 9–2, Sat. 10–noon.*

Both men and women can take one of the three-hour boat tours around the edge of Athos peninsula; **Ouranoupolis Port Authority** (☎ 23770/71248 or 23770/71249) can help you find a boat. **Athos Sea Cruises** ●

(✉ Near tower on main road, Ouranoupolis ☎ 23770/71370 or 23770/71606) sails for the Mt. Athos area from May to October at 10 AM (€16), with an additional afternoon departure in July and August.

NORTHERN GREECE A TO Z

To research prices, get advice from other travelers, and book travel arrangements, visit www.fodors.com.

AIR TRAVEL

There are direct flights to Thessaloniki from London, Brussels, Frankfurt, Stuttgart, Munich, Zurich, and Vienna, with good connections from the United States. Olympic Airlines and other international carriers fly from Athens to Thessaloniki. There are usually at least five daily flights to and from Athens; flying time is 40–45 minutes. Domestic carriers including Aegean Air connect Thessaloniki with a number of other cities as well as Mykonos, Santorini, Crete, Rhodes, Corfu, Limnos, Chios, and Lesbos.

🛪 Carriers **Aegean Air** ✉ Leoforos Nikis 1, Port, Thessaloniki ☎ 2310/239225, 801/112-0000 reservations, 2310/476470 airport ⊕ www.aegeanair.com. **Olympic Airlines** ✉ Kountouriotou 3, Kentro, Thessaloniki ☎ 2310/368311 or 2310/368666 ⊕ www.olympicairlines.com.

AIRPORTS

Thessaloniki Macedonia International Airport (SKG) is at Mikras, 13 km (8 mi) southeast of the city center on the coast; it's about a 20-minute drive. Bus 78 to and from the airport originates at the KTEL bus terminal, stops at the train station, and makes a stop at Aristotle Square (along Egnatia).

🛪 Airport Information **Thessaloniki Macedonia International Airport** ✉ 16th km (10th mi) Ethnikos Odos, Thessaloniki–Perea Rd., Mikras ☎ 2310/473212.

BOAT & FERRY TRAVEL

Hellenic Seaways, Nel, Minoan, and other sea lines connect Thessaloniki to Chios, Lesbos, Limnos, Samos, Heraklion (Crete), Kos, Rhodes, Skiathos, Skopelos, Alonnisos, Naxos, Mykonos, Paros, Santorini, and Tinos. Buy tickets at the Karacharisis Travel and Shipping Agency, Zorpidis Travel Services (Sporades and Cyclades islands only), or Polaris Travel Agency. Connections from Thessaloniki to Rhodes, Kos, and Samos should be confirmed at Karacharisis Travel and Shipping Agency. You can connect to Piraeus from Kavala, 136 km (85 mi) east of Thessaloniki. In summer you should reserve a month in advance. City port authorities, GNTO/EOT offices, and the Greek Travel Pages online have ferry schedules.

🛪 **Greek Travel Pages** ⊕ www.gtp.gr. **Karacharisis Travel and Shipping Agency** ✉ Kountouriotou 8, Port, Thessaloniki ☎ 2310/513005 🖷 2310/532289. **Kavala Port Authority** ☎ 2510/224967 or 2510/223716. **Polaris Travel Agency** ✉ Egnatia 81, Kentro, Thessaloniki ☎ 2310/276051, 2310/278613, 2310/232078 🖷 2310/265728 ✉ Kountouriotou 19, Port, Thessaloniki ☎ 2310/548655 or 2310/548290. **Thessaloniki Port Authority** ☎ 2310/531504 through 2310/531507. **Zorpidis Travel Services** ✉ Salaminos 4, at Kountouriotou, Port, Thessaloniki ☎ 2310/555995 ⊕ www.zorpidis.gr.

BUS TRAVEL

The trip to Thessaloniki from Athens takes about seven hours, with one rest stop (and no access to onboard toilets). Buy tickets at least one day in advance at Athens's Terminal A or at the Thessaloniki ticket office, which sells departure tickets to Athens; one-way fare is about €30.

Intercity KTEL buses connect Thessaloniki with locations throughout Greece. There are small ticket-office terminals (*praktorio*) for each line and separate ticket offices and telephone numbers for each destination. You can browse the KTEL Web site to get an idea of timetables, or call KTEL Thessaloniki Main Terminal, but it's often best to make ticket inquiries in person. The KTEL main terminal is on Thessaloniki's southwestern outskirts, off the National Road (Ethnikos Odos). It has left-luggage storage.

🚩 **KTEL Main Terminal** ✉ Giannitson 194, Menemeni, Thessaloniki ☎ 2310/595408, 2310/510834 lost and found ⊕ www.ktel.org. **KTEL Chalkidiki Terminal** For Chalkidiki-bound buses) ✉ Kifissias 33, at Egeou, Kalamaria, Thessaloniki ☎ 2310/316555. **KTEL Katerini station** ✉ Katerini ☎ 23510/46720 or 23510/23313. **KTEL Katerini "blue bus" station** For Dion site ✉ Katerini ☎ 23510/37600. **KTEL Litochoro depot** ✉ Litochoro ☎ 23520/81271. **KTEL Monastiriou ticket office** ✉ Monastiriou 69, West Thessaloniki, Thessaloniki ☎ 2310/555777. **KTEL reservations** ☎ 2310/595411 or 2310/595435 Athens, 2310/595428 Litochoro, 2310/595432 Veria. **KTEL Veria station** ✉ Veria ☎ 23310/22342 or 23310/23334.

BUS TRAVEL WITHIN THESSALONIKI

Buses are frequent and the routes practical. Bus 1 plies the route from the train station to the main KTEL Main Terminal; Bus 78 goes from the KTEL Main Terminal to the train station and the airport; Bus 39 from Platia Dikasterion (at Aristotelous and Egnatia, in the city center) goes to the KTEL Chalkidiki Terminal (for Ouranoupolis, etc). Tickets cost €0.45 and are purchased at bus company booths, and at some kiosks (*periptera*) or corner stores; not on the bus.

🚩 **Organization of Public Transport of Thessaloniki (O.A.S.T.H.)** ✉ Papanastasiou 90, West Thessaloniki ☎ 2310/981250, 2310/981202 lost and found.

CAR RENTALS

🚩 Agencies **Akon car rental** ✉ Main road, Ouranoupolis ☎ 23770/71644 🖶 23770/71645. **Avis** ✉ Thessaloniki Macedonia International Airport ☎ 2310/473858 ⊕ www.avis.com. **Budget** ✉ Aggelaki 15, H.A.N.T.H., Kentro, Thessaloniki ☎ 2310/254031 ⊕ www.budget.com. **Hertz** ✉ Thessaloniki Macedonia International Airport ☎ 2310/473952 ⊕ www.hertz.com ✉ El. Venizelou 1, Kentro, Thessaloniki ☎ 2310/224906.

CAR TRAVEL

Driving to Greece from Europe through the Former Yugoslav Republic of Macedonia is possible but often time-consuming owing to many border problems. The Athens–Thessaloniki part of the Ethnikos Odos (National Road), the best in Greece, is 500 km (310 mi) and takes five to seven hours. The roads in general are well maintained and constantly being improved and widened throughout the region. A good four-lane highway that begins in Athens goes to the border with Turkey; watch for closures as the new Egnatia Highway (linking Igoumenitsa and Europe in the west to Turkey and points east) is under phased construction. You can get information from the Greek Automobile Touring Club (ELPA). Posted speed limits are up to 120 kph (75 mph), and vehicles regularly use the shoulder as an extra lane.

Driving in Thessaloniki is not recommended because of the congestion, frequent traffic jams, and scarcity of parking. Walking and taking a local bus or taxi are much easier on the nerves. But having a car to get out of town and explore the smaller villages is helpful.

Greek Automobile Touring Club (ELPA) ⊠ Vasilissis Olgas 228–230, Kalamaria, Thessaloniki ☎ 2310/426319 or 2310/426320, 10400 road assistance ⊕ www.elpa.gr.

CONSULATES

Australian Consulate ⊠ Archaeologikou Mousiou 28, Faliro, 54641 Thessaloniki ☎ 2310/827494 ⊕ www.ausemb.gr. **British Consulate** ⊠ Aristotelous 21, Kentro, 54624 Thessaloniki ☎ 2310/278006 ⊟ 2310/283868 ⊕ www.british-embassy.gr. **Canadian Consulate** ⊠ Inside Le Palace Hotel, Tsimiski 12, Kentro, 54624 Thessaloniki ☎ 2310/256350 ⊟ 2310/256351 ⊕ www.dfait-maeci.gc.ca. **United States Consulate** ⊠ Tsimiski 43, Kentro, 54623 Thessaloniki ☎ 2310/242900, 2310/24905 through 2310/24907 ⊟ 2310/242927 ⊕ www.usconsulate.gr.

EMERGENCIES

Lists of late-night pharmacies and hospitals on emergency duty are published in newspapers and posted in the windows of all pharmacies. In Thessaloniki, you can also contact your consulate (⇨ Consulates) for information on hospitals, doctors, and dentists. The European Union emergency hotline has English-speakers.

Emergency Services **Ambulance** ☎ 166. **European Union Hotline** ☎ 112. **Police** ☎ 100. **Thessaloniki Tourist Police** ⊠ 4th fl., Dodekanissou 4, Platia Dimokratias, Thessaloniki ☎ 2310/554871.

Hospitals **Ahepa Hospital** ⊠ Kyriakidi 1, Kentro, Thessaloniki ☎ 2310/993111. **Ippokration Hospital** ⊠ Konstantinoupoleos 49, Kentro, Thessaloniki ☎ 2310/892000.

ENGLISH-LANGUAGE MEDIA

Newspapers and magazines are sold at the international press kiosks on Egnatia Odos and Ayias Sofias, Aristotelous Square and Tsimiski, Ionos Dragoumi and Leoforos Nikis by the entrance to the port, and the newsstand at Ayias Sofias 37.

INTERNET CAFÉS

Internet cafés are found near most key spots in Thessaloniki. Meganet, open 24 hours, has about 70 machines and a youthful, tourist-wise staff, along with good music, coffee, and croissants. E-Global has Internet outlets around town.

e-Global ⊠ Egnatia 117, Kentro, Thessaloniki ☎ 2310/949595 ⊠ Vasilissis Olgas 16, Faliro, Thessaloniki ☎ 2310/887711. **Meganet** ⊠ Pl. Navarinou 5, Kentro, Thessaloniki ☎ 2310/269591 or 2310/250331.

Sports & the Outdoors

Trekking Hellas runs hiking, rafting, mountain biking, and other outdoor excursions in the region, including some great trips up the mythical Mt. Olympus by foot (or bike) from Litochoro. Hellenic Alpine Club can help with information on hiking Mt. Olympus. Oreivatein is a good online resource for area mountains and hiking.

🏃 **Hellenic Alpine Club** ✉ Thessaloniki ☎ 2310/278288. **Oreivatein** ⊕ www.oreivatein. com. **Trekking Hellas** ✉ 3rd fl., Alexandros Bldg., Giannitson 31, West Thessaloniki, Thessaloniki ☎ 2310/523522 ⊕ www.trekking.gr.

TAXIS

Lefkos Pyrgos, Makedonia, and Euro are some taxi companies in Thessaloniki. If you try to hail one off the street, you may be expected to call out your destination—the drivers are excellent lip-readers. Enquire about tailored trips: sites such as Vergina, Pella, and Dion can be covered within a few hours, cost should be €50–€100. Lefko has a special-needs taxi (van) service for those with disabilities, as well as regular taxi service. You can take the Litochoro Taxi to Dion, get picked up from Litochoro train station, Katerini bus station, and so on. It is a private taxi, not a company, as are the others in Litochoro.

🚖 **Euro** ☎ 2310/866866 or 2310/551525. **Lefko** ☎ 2310/861050. **Lefkos Pyrgos** (White Tower) ☎ 2310/214900. **Litochoro Taxi** ☎ 6977/320853 cell. **Makedonia** ☎ 2310/550500.

TOURS

Dolphin Hellas leads organized tours of Northern Greece that begin in Athens and take in the ancient archaeological sites. Like other agencies, the company also arranges tailored tours and books hotels and car rental. Going through an agency often nets a cheaper rate than those quoted to individual walk-ins. Major tour operator Zorpidis runs half-day tours to Vergina–Pella from Thessaloniki, and even arranges honeymoon trips. Velas Tours can also set you up at a thalassotherapy spa near Thessaloniki. To hire a sightseeing guide, contact the Thessaloniki Tourist Guide Association.

🏛 **Dolphin Hellas** ✉ Main office, Athanassiou Diakou 16, at Syngrou, Acropolis, Athens ☎ 210/922-7772 through 210/922-7775 ⊕ www.dolphin-hellas.gr. **Thessaloniki Tourist Guide Association** ☎☎ 2310/546037. **Velas Tours** ✉ Egnatia 6, Kentro, Thessaloniki ☎ 2310/512032 or 2310/518015 ⊕ www.velastours.gr. **Zorpidis Travel** Main location ✉ 1st fl., Egnatia 76, Kentro, Thessaloniki ☎ 2310/244400 ⊕ www. zorpidis.gr ✉ For flights and tours ✉ Aristotelous 27, Kentro, Thessaloniki ☎ 2310/282600 ✉ For ferries ✉ Salaminos 4, at Kountouriotou, West Thessaloniki ☎ 2310/555995.

TRAIN TRAVEL

Out of some 10 Athens–Thessaloniki trains per day, three are express (4½ hours). Make reservations in advance at Athens Larissis Station (Stathmos Larissis) south office (far-left facing, not the main entrance ticket booths, which are for same-day tickets only), or in Thessaloniki. The fastest Intercity will set you back €50; other express options begin at €33. The standard train fare begins at around €14. A €40 ticket can be purchased that is good for 10 days' (nonexpress) travel in the center and north of the country (i.e., from Larissis Station). Thessaloniki station has a left-luggage office.

🚆 **OSE Larissis Station** ✉ Theodorou Deliyanni, Athens ☎ 1110, 1440 departures recording ⊕ www.ose.gr. **OSE Thessaloniki Train Station** ✉ Monastiriou 28, West Thessaloniki, Thessaloniki ☎1110, 2310/599068 lost and found ⊕ www.ose.gr ✉ Aristotelous 18, Kentro, Thessaloniki ☎ 2310/598120.

VISITOR INFORMATION

In Thessaloniki, the Greek National Tourism Organization (GNTO or EOT) central regional office on Tsimiski is open May–September 15, weekdays 9:30–9:30 and weekends 9–3; September–April, weekdays 9–3—but unscheduled breaks and closures are common. There's also a branch at the airport. OTE Directory Assistance is useful for finding oft-changing addresses and phone numbers; most operators speak English.
🏠 **Greek National Tourism Organization (GNTO/EOT)** ✉ Tsimiski 136, at Dagli, Kentro, Thessaloniki ☎ 2310/221100 or 2310/252170 ⊕ www.mintour.gr. **OTE Directory Assistance** ☎ 11888.

Corfu

6

"I loved Corfu. . . . it's quite different from the dry islands with the white houses that you see in photos. It is lush with greenery and olive trees, for one thing, and also it has such a varied history (various empires owned it at one time or another) that you can go into Corfu town, sit under a Venetian-style arcade, eat Greek food, and hear a discussion about a game of cricket."

—elaine

"I recommend spending a full day in Corfu town itself. It's not a very big town, but there's lots to see and plenty of opportunities for just relaxing in cafés and people-watching."

—Xenos

By Lea Lane
Updated by Wendy Holborow

THE IONIAN ISLANDS ARE ALL LUSH AND LOVELY, but Kerkyra (Corfu) is the greenest and, quite possibly, the prettiest of all Greek islands—emerald mountains, ocher and pink buildings, shimmering silver olive leaves. The turquoise waters lap rocky coves and plants like bougainvillea, scarlet roses, and wisteria spread over cottages. Homer's "well-watered gardens" and "beautiful and rich land" were Odysseus's last stop on his journey home. Corfu is also said to be the inspiration for Prospero's island in Shakespeare's *The Tempest*. This northernmost of the major Ionian islands has, through the centuries, inspired other artists, as well as conquerors, royalty, and, of course, tourists.

Today more than a million—mainly British—tourists visit every year, and in summer crowd the evocative capital city of Corfu town (population 100,000). As a result, the town is increasingly filled with stylish restaurants and hotels but also package resorts and clogged roadways, blighting areas of its beauty. Still, the entire island has gracefully absorbed its many layers of history and combines neoclassical villas and extensive resorts, horse-drawn carriages and Mercedes—simplicity and sophistication—in an alluring mix.

Corfu's proximity to Europe, 72 km (45 mi) from Italy and 2 km (1 mi) or so from Albania, and its position on an ancient trade route, assured a lively history of conquest and counter-conquest. In classical times, Corinth colonized the northern Ionian islands, but Corfu, growing powerful, revolted and allied itself with Athens, a fateful move that triggered the Peloponnesian War. Subjection followed: to the tyrants of Syracuse, the kings of Epirus and of Macedonia, in the 2nd century BC to Rome, and from the 11th to the 14th century to Norman and Angevin kings. Then came the Venetians, who protected Corfu from Turkish occupation and provided a 411-year period of development. Napoléon Bonaparte took the islands after the fall of Venice. "The greatest misfortune which could befall me is the loss of Corfu," he wrote to Talleyrand, his foreign minister. Within two years he'd lost it to a Russo-Turkish fleet.

For a short time the French regained and fortified Corfu from the Russians, and their occupation influenced the island's educational system, architecture, and cuisine. Theirs was a Greek-run republic—the first for modern Greece—which whetted local appetites for the independence that arrived later in the 19th century. In 1814 the islands came under British protection; roads, schools, and hospitals were constructed, and commercialism developed. Corfu was ruled by a series of eccentric lord high commissioners. Nationalism finally prevailed, and the islands were ceded to Greece in 1864.

Through the years, Corfu has attracted a great many artists, writers, patrons of the arts, poets, and musicians. Celebrated Greek poet Dionysios Solomos (1798–1857) penned his poem *Hymn to Freedom* while in residence. The ode was set to music by another prominent Corfiot, Nikolaos Mantzaros (1795–1872) and became Greece's national anthem. Lord Guilford endowed Corfu with its university in 1823—the first university in modern Greece. Among Corfu's more modern celebrities were the Durrell brothers: Lawrence, who wrote *Prospero's Cell*—one of the most beloved of tributes to Corfu—and Gerald, whose fond memories of growing up in Corfu inspired his delightful *My Family and Other Animals*.

Indeed, when you look at Corfu in total, it's hard to believe that any island so small could generate a history so large. The classical remains have suffered from the island's tempestuous history and also from earthquakes; architecture from the centuries of Venetian, French, and British rule is most evident, leaving Corfu with a pleasant combination of contrasting design elements. And although it was bombed during the Italian and Nazi occupation in World War II, the town of Corfu remains one of the loveliest in all of Greece, every nook and cranny tells a story, every street meanders to a myth. The island's northeast section has become geared to tourism, but there are inland farming villages that seem undisturbed by the civilizations that have come and gone. Corfu today is a vivid tapestry of cultures; a sophisticated weave, where charm, history, and natural beauty blend.

Exploring Corfu

Corfu lies strategically in the northern Ionian Sea at the entrance to the Adriatic, off the western edge of Greece. The lush, mountainous landscape seems more classic European than Greek, and indeed some geologists believe it is the top of a submerged mountain range that broke off from the mainland. It is moderated by westerly winds, scored with fertile valleys, and punctuated by enormous, gnarled olive trees, planted over the course of 400 years by the Venetians. Figs, oranges, and grapes grow abundantly in the clear light and mild climate.

The island, which is about 64½ km (40 mi) long and up to 29 km (18 mi) wide, with 201 km (125 mi) of sparkling, indented coastline, is small enough to cover completely in a few days. Roads vary from gently winding to spiraling, but they're generally well marked. The focus is Corfu town, but historic attractions are nearby, valley farming villages are spread inland, and a series of coastal villages and towns are separated by mountains, coves, or beaches. Within a couple of turns the verdant landscape can vary from flatland to rocky outcrop to mountains, but the clear blue sea is a constant.

About the Restaurants

The food and prices at some Corfu town restaurants are as European as they are Greek, although inexpensive tavernas and typical Greek cuisine exist in the island villages. As elsewhere in Greece, the demand for fresh fish often exceeds the supply. Lobster and seafood are often priced by the kilo, and injudicious ordering can easily produce an expensive meal in a moderate restaurant. To be sure, ask the price before ordering a dish, even if the waiter recommends it.

About the Hotels

Corfu has town bed-and-breakfasts in renovated Venetian town houses and sleek resorts with children's camps and spas. The explosion of tourism in recent years has led to prepaid, low-price package tours, and

Corfu is often explored in a day by people off a cruise ship on a tour of the Greek islands. Two days allows enough time to visit Corfu town and its nearby environs and most famous sites. With four days you can spend time exploring the island's other historic sites and natural attractions along both coasts. Six days allows you time to get a closer look at the museums, churches, and forts and perhaps even take a day trip to Albania.

Numbers in the text correspond to numbers in the margin and on the Corfu Town and Corfu maps.

6

**If you have
2 days**

On the first day meander along the narrow, cobbled lanes of ⊞ **Corfu town** ❶–❶❺ ⌐; have a bite at one of the cafés along the Liston; and then take in the view at the rooftop café of the Cavalieri Hotel. The next day venture out of town, south to the former summer estate of Greece's royal family, Mon Repos, which is now a museum. Drive 1 km (½ mi) farther to **Kanoni** ❶❻, where you can see the most famous vista on Corfu, that of the island of Pontikonisi. Return to Corfu town for the night.

**If you have
4 days**

Because Corfu is small, you could make day trips to outlying villages and return to accommodations in Corfu town if you wish. Alternatively, follow the two-day itinerary and then on the third day visit Achilleion palace in **Gastouri** ❶❼. You could spend the night at the hilltop ⊞ **Pelekas** ❶❽ or farther north at the seaside ⊞ **Paleokastritsa** ❶❾. Don't forget to see the ruins of Angelokastro in the mountains at Lakones. On the fourth day, cross the island and take the coast road northeast around the bay, through a string of highly developed resort towns set among olive groves and beaches. Schedule your drive so you can stop for a meal at one of the excellent tavernas in **Agni** ❷❶. The pretty coastal road now leads north to the most mountainous part of the island and historic ⊞ **Kassiopi** ❷❷. Spend the night there so you can explore the northern beaches of Roda and Sidari, or head into the mountains to stay near ⊞ **Ano Korakiana** ❷❶.

**If you have
6 days**

Follow the four-day itinerary above, but take more time in the place of your choice. ⊞ **Corfu town** ❶–❶❺ is worth a second or third day—to shop, sightsee, visit museums, sit in the courtyards, and absorb the pace of Corfiot life. Serious beach enthusiasts might stay longer at ⊞ **Paleokastritsa** ❶❾. Nature lovers might want to spend an afternoon hiking around Mt. Pantokrator, make a day trip from ⊞**Pelekas** ❶❽ to bird-watch the Korisia lake, or take a short boat ride from the north side of the island to the wild and lovely Diapontia islands. If you're interested in ancient civilizations, you may want to go on a day-long boat tour from Corfu town to the archaeological site at Butrint, Albania. Then again, you may just want to spend the extra days relaxing at a café in the Corfiot sun.

---

the largest hotels often cater to groups. These masses can get rowdy and overwhelm otherwise pleasant surroundings, mainly in towns along the southeast coast. Budget accommodation is scarce, though it can be found with effort; the Greek National Tourism Organization (GNTO or EOT) can often help.

WHAT IT COSTS In euros					
	$$$$	$$$	$$	$	¢
RESTAURANTS	over €20	€16–€20	€12–€15	€8–€11	under €8
HOTELS	over €200	€160–€200	€120–€160	€80–€120	under €80

Restaurant prices are for one main course at dinner or, for restaurants that serve only *mezedes* (small dishes), for two mezedes. Hotel prices are for two people in a standard double room in high season including taxes.

Timing

The best times to enjoy Corfu are April through June, September, and October, when the weather is at its finest, crowds are smallest, and sites, dining, and lodging are up and running. These months are still considered off-season, so bargain; prices can be considerably lower than during the peak months of July and August. Unlike on most of the other Greek isles, winter months in Corfu can be rainy and cool, and although summers are not quite as hot as on some of the more southern islands, overcrowding and humidity can make things uncomfortable.

Festivals are held throughout the year, especially around the Greek Orthodox holidays. Worth noting are Carnival, with a parade on the last Sunday before Lent; and Holy Week, including Easter Sunday and the breaking of crockery on Holy Saturday. Bands accompany the processions carrying the remains of St. Spyridon, Corfu's patron saint, held four times a year: Palm Sunday, Holy Saturday, August 11, and the first Sunday in November. The Corfu Arts Festival is in September.

Visiting attractions and participating in activities early or late in the day can help you to avoid heat and long lines (remember "only mad dogs and Englishmen go out in the noonday sun"). Be sure to check on times and schedules, and watch out for the mid-afternoon closings. Greeks eat lunch and dinner quite late by American standards, so if you don't mind being unfashionable, you can lunch at noon and dine at seven without having to battle for tables, saving precious time for seeing the sights or lazing around.

CORFU TOWN

ΠΟΛΗ ΤΗΣ ΚΕΡΚΥΡΑΣ

★ *34 km (21 mi) west of Igoumenitsa, 41 km (26 mi) south of Lefkimmi.*

This lovely capital and cultural, historical, and recreational center is off the middle of the island's east coast. All ships and planes lead to Corfu town, on a narrow strip of land hugged by the Ionian Sea. Though beguilingly Greek, much of Corfu's old town displays the architectural styles of many of its conquerors—molto of Italy's Venice, a soupçon of France, and more than a tad of England. A multisight ticket (€8), available at any of the sights, includes admission to the Archeological Museum, the Museum of Asiatic Art, the Byzantine Museum, and the Old Fortress.

Great Flavors

Corfiot food specialties, which tend to reflect the island's Venetian heritage, are served at most restaurants and tavernas. Those worth a try are *sofrito* (veal cooked in a sauce of vinegar, parsley, and plenty of garlic) served with rice or potatoes; *pastitsada* (a derivation of the Italian dish *spezzatino*—layers of beef and pasta, called *macaronia* in Greek, cooked in a rich and spicy tomato sauce and topped off with béchamel sauce); *bourdetto* (firm-flesh fish stewed in tomato sauce with lots of hot red pepper); and *bianco* (whole fish stewed with potatoes, herbs, black pepper, and lemon juice).

Corfu doesn't have many vineyards, but if you find a restaurant that has its own barrel wine, try it—you'll rarely be disappointed. Two drinks that are legacies of the British are *tsitsibira* (ginger-beer), often drunk while watching cricket, and the bright-orange liqueur made from kumquats, which the colonists first planted on the island. Locals say the liqueur, available at any tourist shop, is an aphrodisiac. Bottled water can and should be bought everywhere—Corfu's tap water is *not* one of its pleasures.

Hiking

Corfu's verdant, varied interior, especially the area around Mt. Pantokrator, is excellent hiking terrain. There are trails to the summit from the villages of Strinylas, Spartylas, and Old Perithia. The fully marked Corfu Trail, created in 2002, runs 220 km (137 mi) from the northern to southern tip of the island, winding through Corfu's most beautiful scenery, from the lake at Korisia and the west-coast beaches to Mt. Pantokrator; it also passes through small villages and near monasteries. It takes about 10 days to hike the entire trail (there are hotels and tavernas along the way), but it's possible to explore small chunks of it in a day or two.

Water Sports

Sand and pebble beaches and coves edge the island, but the west coast has the widest sand beaches for sunning and swimming. Snorkeling and diving are best in the many rocky inlets and grottos on the northwest coast, and Paleokastritsa and Ermones have diving schools where you can take lessons and rent equipment. The winds on the west coast are best for windsurfing, although the water on the east coast is calmer. Sailboards are available, and paddleboats and rowboats can be rented at many beaches. Waterskiing, water polo, parasailing, jet skiing, and other water activities are sponsored by resorts throughout the island.

Calm waters in the coves and bays make boating popular. You can moor boats at the new port in Corfu town, and at Paleokastritsa on the west coast. Motorboats and sailboats can be rented at the old port in Corfu town; in Paleokastritsa, Kondokali, and Kassiopi; and on the northeast coast. To charter a yacht or sailboat without a crew, you need a proficiency certificate from a certified yacht club. Corfu has customs and health authorities, passport control, supply facilities, and exchange services, and it is one of the few official entry-exit ports in Greece.

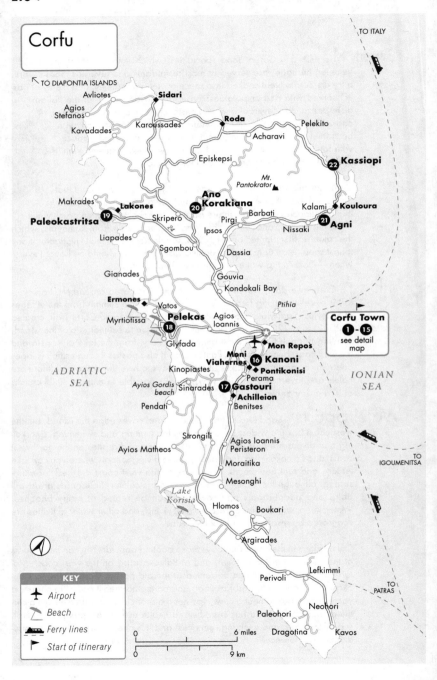

Corfu

TO ITALY

TO DIAPONTIA ISLANDS

Avliotes
Sidari
Agios
Stefanos
Kavadades
Karoussades
Roda
Pelekito
Acharavi
Episkepsi
Mt.
Pantokrator ▲
22 Kassiopi
Makrades
Lakones
Ano Korakiana **20**
Kalami **Kouloura**
Paleokastritsa 19
Skripero
Barbati
21 Agni
Liapades
Pirgi
Nissaki
Ipsos
Sgombou
Dassia
Gianades
Gouvia
Kondokali Bay
Ptihia
Ermones
Vatos
Pelekas
Agios
Ioannis
Corfu Town
1 - 15
see detail map
Myrtiotissa
18
Glyfada
Mon Repos
IONIAN SEA
Mani Viahernes **Kanoni 16**
Kinopiastes
Pontikonisi
ADRIATIC SEA
Ayios Gordis beach
Sinarades
Perama
17 Gastouri
Pendati
Achilleion
Benitses
Strongili
Agios Ioannis
Peristeron
Ayios Matheos
Moraitika
TO
IGOUMENITSA
Mesonghi
*Lake
Korisia*
Hlomos
Boukari
Argirades
TO
PATRAS
Perivoli
Lefkimmi
Paleohori
Neohori
Dragotina
Kavos

KEY
✈ *Airport*
⊿ *Beach*
⛴ *Ferry lines*
▶ *Start of itinerary*

0   6 miles
0   9 km

a good
walk

Arriving from mainland Greece by ferry, you dock at the new port, adjacent to the **New Fortress** ❶ ▶, with its British citadel. East of the fortress is the area of Velissariou, one of Corfu town's main streets, and the western edge of the historical center. Here is the former **Jewish Quarter** ❷, with its old synagogue. From Velissariou, go southeast toward Voulgareos, turn left on G. Theotoki, and go left about 10 minutes to Platia Theotoki. Ahead is the ornate, marble, 17th-century **Town Hall** ❸. Note the elaborate Venetian design, popular throughout the town. Adjacent is the neoclassical **Catholic Church of Ayios Iakovos** ❹, more commonly known as the Cathedral of San Giacomo. Go north on Theotoki to Filarmonikis, four blocks through the medieval area of **Campiello** ❺—narrow winding streets filled with artisans' shops and restaurants—to the **Orthodox Cathedral** ❻. From the cathedral, look up to see the nearby red bell tower of the **Church of St. Spyridon** ❼, dedicated to the island's patron saint. Head north to the waterfront to explore the fascinating **Byzantine Museum** ❽; then backtrack to the cathedral area.

Southeast from the museum, in Kapodistriou, is the historic **Corfu Reading Society** ❾, with its grand outside staircase. From here go south two blocks to Ayios Ekaterinis. East are the colonnade of the **Palace of St. Michael and St. George** ❿ and the arcades of the Liston area. Along the central path is the **Statue of Count Schulenburg** ⓫, hero of the siege of 1716. The southern half of the **Esplanade** ⓬ has a Victorian bandstand, Ionic rotunda, and a statue of Ioannis Kapodistrias, a Corfu resident and the first president of modern Greece. Relax awhile, and then cross over the bridge to the **Old Fortress** ⓭ on the northeastern tip of Corfu town. In the southern section of the fort is the Church of St. George, with views of Albania.

If you have the time and enjoy walking, go south along Leoforos Dimokratias and the water, about 10 minutes. Past the Corfu Palace hotel, and the gardens of the Garitsa neighborhood, take the first right to the **Archaeological Museum** ⓮. Farther south along Garitsa Bay, about 10 minutes more, brings you to the **Tomb of Menekrates** ⓯, two blocks west on Menekratous. Stroll back to the old town center along the waterfront and enjoy the breeze.

TIMING
This walk encompasses the highlights of Corfu town and views beyond and can take half a day or more, depending on how long you wander in the medieval section and how far south you go along the bay. Linger a bit here and there as you explore and let yourself feel the slightly languid pace of daily life.

What to See

⓮ **Archaeological Museum.** Examine finds from ongoing island excavations; most come from Kanoni, the site of Corfu's ancient capital. The star attraction is a giant relief of snake-coiffed Medusa, depicted as her head was cut off by the hero Perseus—at which moment her two sons, Pegasus and Chrysaor, emerged from her body. The 56-foot-long sculpture once adorned the pediment of the 6th-century BC Temple of Artemis at Kanoni and is one of the largest and best-preserved pieces of Archaic sculpture in Greece. ⊠ *Vraila 1, off Leoforos Dimokratias, past Corfu Palace hotel* ☎ *26610/30680* ⌂ *€3* ⊘ *Tues.–Sun. 8:30–3.*

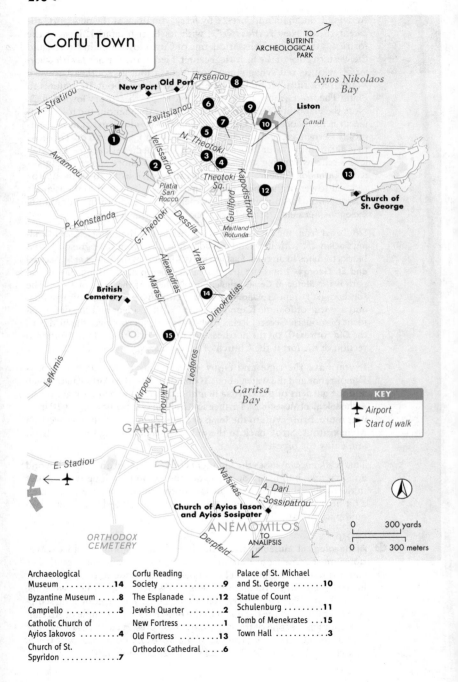

Corfu Town

TO
BUTRINT
ARCHEOLOGICAL
PARK

X. Stratirou

New Port   Old Port

Arseniou   8

Ayios Nikolaos
Bay

Zavitsianou   6

Velissariou

9

Liston

Canal

N. Theotoki   7

10

1

5

2

3   4

Theotoki Sq.

11

Platia
San
Rocco

Kapodistriou

12

13

Church of
St. George

Avramiou

P. Konstanda

G. Theotoki   Dessila

Prosalendou

Maitland
Rotunda

Alexandras

Vrala

Marasli

British
Cemetery

14

Dimokratias

15

Lefkimis

Kirpou

Aikinou

Leoforos

Garitsa
Bay

GARITSA

KEY
✈ Airport
⚑ Start of walk

E. Stadiou

✈

Nafsikas

A. Dari
I. Sossipatrou

Church of Ayios Iason
and Ayios Sosipater

ANEMOMILOS

ORTHODOX
CEMETERY

Derpfeld

TO
ANALIPSIS

0   300 yards
0   300 meters

British Cemetery. Flowers—rare orchids and lilies, cultivated cyclamens, snowdrops, tulips, and hundreds of wildflowers—bloom in this overgrown cemetery established in 1814, as do fascinating stories told by the stone angels, Celtic crosses, and quirky inscriptions atop the nearly 600 memorials. Along the cypress-lined paths (Greeks believe the pointed trees help guide souls to heaven) are tombs of the British colonizers, soldiers who died during the Crimean and two world wars, and more recently, Brits who so fell so in love with Corfu that they were buried here years after they'd returned home. ⊠ *Kolokotroni 22* 🖾 *Free* ☉ *Daily 9–dusk.*

8 **Byzantine Museum.** Panagia Antivouniotissa, an ornate church dating from the 16th century, houses an outstanding collection of Byzantine religious art. More than 85 icons from the 13th to the 17th century hang on the walls as the ethereal sounds of Byzantine chants are piped in overhead. Watch for works by the celebrated icon painters Tzanes and Damaskinos; they are perhaps the best-known artists of the Cretan style of icon painting, with unusually muscular, active (and sometimes viscerally gruesome) depictions of saints. Their paintings more closely resemble Renaissance art—another Venetian legacy—than traditional, flat orthodox icons. ⊠ *Arseniou Mourayio* ☎ *26610/38313* 🖾 *€2* ☉ *Tues.–Sun. 8:30–3.*

5 **Campiello.** Narrow, winding streets and steep stairways make up the Campiello, the large, traffic-free medieval area of the town. Balconied Venetian buildings are mixed among multistory, neoclassical 19th-century ones built by the British, with laundry often hanging between them. Small cobbled squares centered with wells, high-belfry churches, and alleyways that lead nowhere and back, with artisans' shops along the way, add to an utterly lovely urban space. ⊠ *West of the Esplanade, northeast of New Fortress.*

4 **Catholic Church of Ayios Iakovos.** Built in 1588 and consecrated 50 years later, this elegant cathedral was erected to provide a grand place of worship for Corfu town's Catholic occupiers. If you use the Italian name, San Giacomo, locals will know it. Bombed by the Nazis in 1943, the cathedral's neoclassical facade of pediments, friezes, and columns was practically destroyed, and then rebuilt, but the bell tower remains intact. ⊠ *Pl. Dimarcheiou next to Town Hall* ☎ *No phone.*

Church of Ayios Iason and Ayios Sosipater. The suburb of Anemomilos is crowned by the ruins of the Paleopolis church and by the 11th-century Church of Ayios Iason and Ayios Sosipater. It was named after two of St. Paul's disciples, St. Jason and St. Sosipater, who brought Christianity to the island in the 1st century. The frescoes are faded, but the icons are beautiful, and the exterior is dramatic among the unspoiled greenery. This is one of only two Byzantine churches on the island; the other is in the northern coastal village of Ayios Markos. ⊠ *Anemomilos at south end of Garitsa Bay* ☎ *No phone.*

7 **Church of St. Spyridon.** Built in 1596, this church is the tallest on the island, thanks to its distinctive red-domed bell tower, and is filled with silver treasures. The patron saint's internal remains—smuggled here after the fall of Constantinople—are contained in a silver reliquary and carried in procession four times a year, along with his mummified body,

Fodor'sChoice
★

which can be seen through a glass panel. His slippered feet are actually exposed so that the faithful can kiss them. The saint was not a Corfiot but originally a shepherd from Cyprus, who became a bishop before his death in AD 350. His miracles are said to have saved the island four times: once from famine, twice from the plague, and once from the hated Turks. During World War II, a bomb fell on this holiest place on the island but didn't explode. Maybe these events explain why it seems every other man on Corfu is named Spiros. If you keep the tower in sight you can wander as you wish without getting lost around this fascinating section of town. ⊠ *Agiou Spyridon* ☎ *No phone.*

❾ Corfu Reading Society. The oldest cultural institution in modern Greece, the Corfu Reading Society was founded in 1836. The building, filled with the archives of the Ionian islands, has a stunning exterior staircase leading up to a loggia. ⊠ *Kapodistriou* ☎ *26610/39528* 🎫 *Free* ☉ *Weekdays 9:15–1:45 and 5:30–8, Sat. 9:15–1:45.*

⓬ The Esplanade. Central to the life of the town, this huge, open parade ground on the land side of the canal is, many say, the most beautiful *spianada* (esplanade) in Greece. It is bordered on the west by a street lined with seven- and eight-story Venetian and English Georgian houses, and arcades, called the **Liston.** The name refers to a list that the Venetians kept of lucky upper-class townspeople who were allowed to walk and linger here. Today, happily, its beauty can be enjoyed by all. Cafés spill out onto the passing scene, and Corfiot celebrations, games, and trysts occur in the sun and shadows. Sunday cricket matches, a holdover from British rule, are sometimes played on the northern half of the Esplanade, which was once a Venetian firing range. On the southern half is an ornate **Victorian bandstand** and a **statue of Ioannis Kapodistrias,** a Corfu resident and the first president of modern Greece. He was also, unfortunately, the first Greek president to be assassinated, in 1831. The restored **Ionic rotunda** was built in honor of Sir Thomas Maitland, the not-much-loved first British lord high commissioner who was appointed in 1814 when the island became a protectorate of Britain. ⊠ *Between Old Fortress and old town.*

❷ Jewish Quarter. This twist of streets was home to the area's Jewish population from the 1600s until 1940, when the community was decimated, most sent to Auschwitz by the occupying Nazis. Fewer than 100 of 5,000 Jews survived. At the southern edge of the ghetto, a 300-year-old synagogue with an interior in Sephardic style still proudly stands. ⊠ *Parados 4, off Velissariou, 2 blocks from New Fortress.*

▶ **❶ New Fortress.** Built in 1577–78 by the Venetians, the New Fortress was constructed to strengthen town defenses only three decades later than the "old" fortress. The French and the British subsequently expanded the complex to protect Corfu town from a possible Turkish invasion. You can wander through the maze of tunnels, moats, and fortifications, and the moat (dry now) is the site of the town's marketplace. A classic British citadel stands at its heart. At the top, there is an exhibition center as well as the trendy Morrison Café, which has stunning views by day and international DJs spinning cool, ambient tunes at night. The best time to tour is early morning or late afternoon. ⊠ *Solomou on promontory northwest of Old Fortress* ☎ *26610/27370* 🖭 *€2* ⊙ *June–Oct., daily 9 AM–9:30 PM.*

★ ⑬ **Old Fortress.** Corfu's entire population once lived within the walls of the Old Fortress, or Citadel, built by the Venetians in 1546 on the site of a Byzantine castle. Separated from the rest of the town by a moat, the fort is on a promontory mentioned by Thucydides. Its two heights, or *korypha* ("bosom"), gave the island its Western name. Standing on the peaks, you have a gorgeous view west over the town and east to the mountainous coast of Albania. Inside the fortress, many Venetian fortifications were destroyed by the British, who replaced them with their own structures. The most notable of these is the quirky **Church of St. George,** built like an ancient Doric temple on the outside and set up like a Greek Orthodox church on the inside. In summer there are folk-dancing performances in the fortress, and in August sound-and-light shows tell the fortress's history. ⊠ *On northeastern point of Corfu town peninsula* ☎ *26610/48310* 🖭 *€4* ⊙ *Weekdays 8–7, weekends 8:30–3.*

❻ **Orthodox Cathedral.** This small, icon-rich cathedral was built in 1577. It is dedicated to St. Theodora, the island's second saint. Her headless body lies in a silver coffin by the altar; it was brought to Corfu at the same time as St. Spyridon's remains. Steps lead down to the harbor from here. ⊠ *Southwest corner of Campiello, east of St. Spyridon* ☎ *26610/39409.*

❿ **Palace of St. Michael and St. George.** Admire Ming pottery in an ornate colonial palace as Homer's Ionian sea shimmers outside the windows. This elegant, colonnaded 19th-century Regency structure houses the **Museum of Asiatic Art,** a notable collection of Asian porcelains and Sino-Japanese art, as well as the **Municipal Art Gallery,** which displays work by Corfiot artists and depictions of the island's history and famous figures. The building was constructed as a residence for the lord high commissioner and headquarters for the order of St. Michael and St. George; it was abandoned after the British left in 1864 and precisely renovated about a hundred years later by the British ambassador to Greece. Before entering the galleries, stop at the Art Café in the shady courtyard, where you may have trouble tearing yourself away from the fairy-tale view of the lush islet of Vido and the mountainous coast of Albania. ⊠ *North end of the Esplanade* ☎ *26610/30443 Museum of Asiatic Art, 26610/48690 Municipal Art Gallery* 🖭 *€3* ⊙ *Tues.–Sun. 8:30–3.*

Fodor's Choice
★

⑪ **Statue of Count Schulenburg.** The hero of the siege of 1716, an Austrian mercenary, is immortalized in this statue. The siege was the Turks' last (and failed) attempt to conquer Corfu. ⊠ *Along central path of the Esplanade.*

⑮ **Tomb of Menekrates.** Part of an ancient necropolis, this site held funerary items that are now exhibited in the Archaeological Museum. ⊠ *South around Garitsa Bay, to right of obelisk dedicated to Sir Howard Douglas.*

❸ **Town Hall.** The rich marble, 17th-century Town Hall was built as a Venetian loggia and converted in 1720 into Greece's first modern theater—a far cry from the classic amphitheater pioneered in Epidaurus. A second story was added by the British before it became a grand town hall early in the 20th century. Note the sculpted portraits of Venetian dignitaries over the entrance—one is actually a lion, the symbol of Venice. ⊠ *Pl. Theotoki* ☎ *26610/40401* ☎ *Free* ☉ *Weekdays 9–1.*

off the beaten path

BUTRINT ARCHEOLOGICAL PARK – A UNESCO World Heritage Site across the Corfu Straits in southern Albania, the Butrint Archaeological Park contains remarkably well preserved remains from more than 3,000 years of civilization—from the Bronze Age to the Ottoman Empire. The ruins spread over 16 square km (10 square mi) of pristine hills and lakes. Highlights in the ancient city of Butrint (mentioned in the *Aeneid*) include a Hellenistic Greek theater and Roman baths; there are also Byzantine chapels and Venetian fortresses. During Albania's years of communist rule and domestic turbulence, the site was cut off from tourists and archaeologists. Today the site is open to the public and the government is slowly allocating money for its protection and study. Tour operators such as Petrakis Lines and Cruises organize day trips from Corfu town to Butrint. For about €60, you get a half-hour boat trip to and from Albania, a 40-minute bus ride to Butrint, a guided tour of the site, lunch in the Albanian town of Saranda, and all international port fees. A passport, but not a visa, is necessary for the trip. *Petrakis Lines and Cruises* ⊠ *Venizeloua 9, new port, Corfu town* ☎ *26610/31649 or 26610/38690.*

Where to Eat

★ **$$–$$$$** ✕ **To Dimarcheio.** Menu items like marinated salmon with fennel and veal carpaccio reflect the chef's classic French training. But ask the waiter what else is in the kitchen, and he may reel off a list of hearty village favorites that includes a rich *sofrito* (veal cooked in a sauce of vinegar, parsley, and plenty of garlic), *pastitsada* (a derivation of the Italian dish *spezzatino*—layers of beef and pasta, called *macaronia* in Greek, cooked in a rich and spicy tomato sauce and topped off with béchamel sauce), and pork stewed with celery, leeks, and wine. You won't go wrong choosing from among them. In June you can sit beneath a jacaranda tree's electric-blue flowers; year-round the outdoor tables of the Town Hall restaurant overlook the comings and goings at that elegant building. ⊠ *Pl. Dimarcheiou* ☎ *26610/39031* ☱ *AE, DC, MC, V.*

$–$$$$ ✕ **Aegli.** More than 100 different dishes, both local and international, are on the menu. Start with a plate of baked artichokes, then move on to perfectly executed Corfiot classics such as spicy swordfish *bourdetto* (firm-flesh fish stewed in tomato sauce with lots of hot red pepper), or the more unusual *arnaki kleftiko* (lamb cooked as the *kleftes,* War of Independence fighters, liked it), with onions, olives, mustard, and feta cheese. Tables in front, with comfortable armchairs and spotless tablecloths, overlook the nonstop parade on the Esplanade at Liston. Aegli keeps late hours, serving drinks and sweets midnight until 2 AM. ⊠ *Kapodistriou 23, Liston* ☎ *26610/31949* ☱ *AE, MC, V.*

$$$ ✕ **Venetian Well.** Tables organized around a 17th-century well, a staff that tiptoes past lingering lovers—the scene is as delicious as the food.

In a Venetian building, on the most charming little square in the old town, operatic and traditional music overhead accompanies the Greek and international specialties. Creative entrées include crepes with spinach and green tea sauce, and wild boar. ⊠ *Pl. Kremasti across from Church of the Panagia* ☎ *26610/44761* ⌲ *Reservations essential* ☰ *MC, V* ⊙ *No lunch Sun.*

$–$$$ ⨉ **Gerekos.** One of the island's most famous seafood tavernas, Gerekos always has fresh fish. Opt for a table on the terrace and try the whitefish *me ladi* (cooked in olive oil, garlic, and pepper). ⊠ *Kondokali Bay, 6 km (4 mi) north of Corfu town* ☎ *26610/91281* ⌲ *Reservations essential* ☰ *AE, V.*

★ **$–$$$** ⨉ **Rex Restaurant.** A friendly Corfiot restaurant in a 19th-century town house, Rex has been a favorite for nearly 100 years, and with good reason. Classic local specialties such as a hearty and meaty pastitsada, *stifado* (meat stewed with sweet onions, white wine, garlic, cinnamon, and spices), and *stamna* (lamb baked with potatoes, rice, beans, and cheese) are reliably delicious. Dishes such as rabbit stewed with fresh figs and chicken with kumquats are successful twists on the regional fare. Outside tables are perfect for people-watching on the Liston. ⊠ *Kapodistriou 66, west of Liston* ☎ *26610/39649* ☰ *AE, D, MC, V.*

¢–$$ ⨉ **Bellisimio.** Contrary to its Italian sounding name, this is a traditional, family-run Greek taverna where owner Stavros invites you into the kitchen to look at the available food. Here you can relax, away from the bustling crowds, on a quiet square and eat traditional favorites such as *briam* (a mixture of eggplant, zucchini, and potatoes in olive oil and tomato sauce). Only Corfiot wine is sold, in order to keep prices affordable. ⊠ *Pl. Lemonia off N. Theotoki* ☎ *26610/41112* ☰ *No credit cards* ⊙ *Closed Nov.–Apr. and Sun. Sept.–July. No lunch Sun. in Aug.*

Where to Stay

$$$$ ⊡ **Corfu Imperial.** A deluxe resort complex—run by top Greek chain Grecotel—juts into Komeno Bay atop a 14-acre peninsula. Luxury rooms, bungalows, and villas focus on comfortable elegance, with balconies and sea views. The seven suites, all different, have large living rooms and bathrooms with whirlpool tubs, and the Presidential Suite additionally has a dining room and a dramatic view across the Ionian Sea to the shores of Albania. Though extensive, the property blends harmoniously with the lush landscape of olive, palm, and cypress trees and colorful gardens. ⊠ *Komeno Bay, 10 km (6 mi) north of Corfu town, 49100* ☎ *26610/88400* ☎☎ *26610/91481* ⊕ *www.grecotel.gr* ⨠ *178 rooms, 120 bungalows, 7 suites, 4 villas* ⌂ *2 restaurants, snack bar, cable TV, 2 tennis courts, pool, hair salon, beach, boating, waterskiing, 3 bars, shops, babysitting, children's programs (ages 4–12), laundry service, meeting rooms* ☰ *AE, DC, MC, V* ⊙ *Closed Nov.–Apr.*

★ **$$$$** ⊡ **Corfu Palace.** Overlook the bay outside the town center from spacious rooms decorated with Louis XIV–style furniture. Every room has a seaview balcony and huge marble bathrooms. The two restaurants both have seating in the lush gardens adjacent to the sprawling pool, and once a week there's a barbecue. You can book a tennis court at the nearby Corfu Tennis Club and hire facilities at the Corfu Yacht Club. Three days a week a shuttle runs to Glyfada on the west coast. ✉ *Leoforos Dimokratias 2, 49100* ☎ *26610/39485* 🖷 *26610/31749* ⊕ *www. corfupalace.com* ⟷ *101 rooms, 11 suites* ♢ *2 restaurants, room service, minibars, cable TV, indoor pool, saltwater pool, spa, 2 bars, shops, babysitting, convention center* ▭ *AE, DC, MC, V.*

$$$ 🏠 **Daphnila Bay.** Yet another dazzling member of the Grecotel chain, the Daphnila Bay has as its star attraction the impressive Elixir Thalasso Spa, which specializes in thalassotherapy and aromatherapy. Guest rooms are large and brightly decorated with spacious balconies; the public lounges are an elegant mix of sophisticated high-tech design with traditional folk elements. The property is in the midst of an olive grove and surrounded by verdant pines, which sweep down to the edge of a beach. ✉ *11 km (7 mi) north of Corfu town, 49100 Dassia* ☎ *26610/ 91520* 🖷 *26610/91026* ⊕ *www.grecotel.gr* ⟷ *126 rooms, 134 bungalows, 2 suites* ♢ *3 restaurants, tennis court, 2 pools (1 indoor), health club, spa, beach, bar, babysitting* ▭ *AE, D, MC, V* ☾ *Closed Nov.–Mar.*

$$–$$$ 🏠 **Kontokali Bay.** When you tire of exploring the streets and museums in town, this hotel is a fine place to relax away from it all. The pastel guest rooms, with modern wood appointments, are cheerful and sunlit, with balconies facing the sea, the mountains, or the lake. Umbrellas and chaise lounges wait for you on the two beaches. A buffet and a grill restaurant serve Greek and Italian cuisine, or you might order a snack from the beach bar. ✉ *Kondokali Bay, 6 km (4 mi) north of Corfu town, 49100* ☎ *26610/90500 through 26610/ 90509, 26610/99000 through 26610/99002* 🖷 *26610/91901* ⊕ *www. kontokalibay.com* ⟷ *152 rooms, 82 bungalows* ♢ *3 restaurants, room service, in-room safes, minibars, cable TV, 2 tennis courts, pool, wading pool, gym, massage, beach, dock, boating, waterskiing, 2 bars, dance club, children's programs (ages 2 and up), laundry service, Internet room, business services, meeting rooms* ▭ *AE, DC, MC, V* ☾ *Closed Nov.–Mar.*

$ 🏠 **Cavalieri Hotel.** Ask for a room on the fourth or fifth floor, with a number ending in 2, 3, or 4, for a breathtaking view of the Old Fort near the Liston. The building is swank yet graceful and chock-full of history—it was built in the 18th century and is a landmark of old Corfu. Rooms have polished wood furniture and old brass fixtures, though the bathrooms are a little cramped. The highlight is the roof garden, where, over a drink at sunset, you have the most glorious view in town. Be warned though, the service is not always top-notch. ✉ *Kapodistriou 4, 49100* ☎ *26610/39041* 🖷 *26610/39283* ⊕ *www.cavalieri-hotel.com* ⟷ *50 rooms* ♢ *Restaurant, room service, minibars, bar* ▭ *AE, DC, MC, V.*

¢–$ 🏠 **Hotel Bella Venezia.** This colorful two-story Venetian town house in the center of town was operated as a hotel as early as the 1800s. The large lobby has a marble floor; a rich, polished wood ceiling; and chandeliers. The high-ceiling rooms are small but have elegant furniture, and some with canopy beds. Enjoy the buffet breakfast in the huge garden. There are no views, but because of that it's a good value. ✉ *Zambelli 4, behind Cavalieri Hotel, 49100* ☎ *26610/20707 or 26610/44290* 🖷 *26610/20708* ⟷ *32 rooms* ♢ *Snack bar, refrigerators, lobby lounge* ▭ *AE, DC, MC, V* ❍ *BP.*

¢ ▦ **Hotel Hermes.** The bare-bones Hermes is popular with backpackers because it has clean rooms, comfortable beds (a double, two twins, or a single), and cheap rates (as little as €28 for a double). The nearby daily produce market is convenient for stocking up for picnics, but noisy in the mornings. ⊠ *G. Markora 14, 49100* ☎ *26610/39268* ⟿ *25 rooms* ⚫ *No a/c, no room TVs* ⊟ *MC, V* ⦿ *BP.*

Nightlife & the Arts

Corfiots love music, from the traditional string bouzouki to classical. Sunday concerts are held at the bandstand on the Esplanade in summer, and brass bands can often be heard throughout the town.

Past the Commercial Center, 3 km (2 mi) west of town is a string of discos that really don't start swinging until after midnight. They have names like Privilege, Omega, and Apocalypsis, and they throb with the latest Euro-pop and dance hits. Incredibly loud sound systems and futuristic designs are just what the young flesh-baring crowd wants for dancing into the wee hours. Most of the clubs charge €10 cover, which includes the first drink. Greek clubs come and go by the minute, so be sure to ask the concierge and locals for the current hot spots.

BARS & CLUBS For sunsets with your ouzo and *mezedes* (appetizers), try the **Aktaion Bar** (⊠ South of Old Fortress) on the water. The rooftop bar at the **Cavalieri Hotel** (⊠ Kapodistriou 4 ☎ 26610/39041) is hard to beat for views.

Hip but relaxed **Cofineta** (⊠ Liston, north end) has cane chairs out on the cobblestones and a good view not of nature, but of decked-out promenade strollers. At **Ekati** (⊠ Alykes Potamou) crowds are sophisticated and older, but the volume of the live music is nevertheless high for this *skiladiko* (roughly, "dog party"). Chichi is the club tone, with excessive baubles and Paris designer labels in evidence. Ekati is at the end of the disco strip west of the center.

Have a drink from the bar at **Internet Cafe Netoikos** (⊠ Kalokeretou 12–14 ☎ 26610/47479) while you do business online from 10 AM to midnight every day except Sunday, when the place opens at 6 PM. At the top of the New Fortress, **Morrison Café** (⊠ Solomou, on northwest town promontory) overlooks the water and has Corfu's best DJ, who favors cool acid jazz. It stays open long after the rest of the fortress is closed to the public.

FILM Corfu town's **Feinikas** (⊠ Akadimias) is said to be the oldest outdoor cinema in Greece. It shows undubbed international movies in a pretty courtyard from June to September.

Shopping

Corfu town has myriad tiny shops. Increasingly, designer boutiques, shoe shops, and accessory stores are opening up in every nook and cranny of the town. For traditional goods head for the narrow streets of the Campiello where olive wood, lace, jewelry, and wine shops abound. For perishable products such as liqueurs and candies, you may do better checking out the supermarkets than buying in the old town. Most of the shops listed below are in the Campiello and are open May to October, from 8 AM until late (whenever the last tourist leaves); they're generally closed September to April. Stores in outlying shopping areas tend to close Monday, Wednesday, and Saturday afternoons at 2:30 PM, and all day Sunday.

Alexis Traditional Products. For locally made wines and spirits, including kumquat liqueur and marmalade, go to Alexis Traditional Products. Traditional sweets, local olive oil, olives, and olive oil soap—as well as honey, herbs, and spices—are also sold. ⊠ *Solomou 10–12, Spilia* ☎ *26610/21831.*

Katafigio. You can take a replica of your favorite museum artifact home with you from this shop. There's also a display of chess sets, some of which have pieces depicting ancient Greek heroes. ⊠ *N. Theotoki 113* ☎ *26610/43137.*

Mironis Olive Wood. Bowls, sculptures, wooden jewelry, and much more are crammed into two tiny family-run shops. Smaller items are made as you watch. ⊠ *Filarmonikis 27* ☎ *26610/40621* ⊠ *Agiou Spyridon 65* ☎ *26610/40364.*

Nikos Sculpture and Jewellery. Nikos makes original gold and silver jewelry designs, and sculptures in cast bronze; they're expensive but worth it. ⊠ *Paleologou 50* ☎ *26610/31107* ⊠ *N. Theotoki 54* ☎ *26610/32009* ⊕ *www.nikosjewellery.gr.*

Rolandos. Visit the talented artist Rolando and watch him at work on his paintings and handmade pottery. ⊠ *N. Theotoki 99* ☎ *26610/45004.*

SOUTH CORFU

ΝΟΤΙΑ ΚΕΡΚΥΡΑ

Outside Corfu town, near the suburb of Kanoni, are several of Corfu's most unforgettable sights, including the lovely view of the island of Pontikonisi. The palace and grounds of Mon Repos nearby were once owned by Greece's royal family and are open to the public as a museum. A few villages south of Benitses, and some on the island's southern tip, are standardly overrun with raucous package-tour groups. If you seek a hard-drinking, late-night crowd, and beaches chockablock with activities and tanning bodies, head there. If you're looking for more solitary nature in the south, take a trip to Korisia.

Kanoni

Κανόνι

16 *5 km (3 mi) south of Corfu town.*

At Kanoni, the site of the ancient capital, you may behold Corfu's most famous view, which looks out over two beautiful islets. Keep in mind that though the view *of* the islets has sold a thousand postcards, the view *from* the islets is that of a hilly landscape built up with resort hotels and summer homes and of the adjacent airport, where planes take off directly over the churches. The little island of **Moni Viahernes** is reached by causeway and has a tiny, pretty convent. **Pontikonisi,** or Mouse Island, has tall cypresses guarding a 13th-century chapel. Legend has it that the island is really Odysseus's ship, which Poseidon turned to stone here: the reason why Homer's much-traveled hero was shipwrecked on Phaeacia (Corfu) in the *Odyssey.* June to August a little motorboat runs out to Pontikonisi every 20 minutes.

The island's only casino is in the sleek and curving hotel, **Corfu Holiday Palace.** The nearly 5,500 square feet of gaming space is open daily noon–3 AM. ⊠ *Kanoni* ☎ 26610/46941.

�},} The royal palace of **Mon Repos** is surrounded by gardens and ancient ruins. It was built in 1831 by Sir Frederic Adam for his wife, and it was later the summer residence of the British lord high commissioners. Prince Philip, the duke of Edinburgh, was born here. After Greece won independence, it was used as a summer palace for the royal family of Greece, but it was closed when the former king Constantine fled the country in 1967, after which the Greek government expropriated it. Throughout the '90s, the estate was tangled in an international legal battle after Constantine petitioned to have the property returned; the Greek government finally paid him a settlement and opened the fully restored palace as a museum on the island's rich history. After touring the palace, wander around the extensive grounds, which include ruins of temples from the 7th and 6th centuries BC as well as the small but lovely beach that was once used exclusively by the Greek royal family and is now open to the public. Ask museum officials for maps and information; the pamphlets are free and useful but aren't handed out unless requested. Opposite Mon Repos are ruins of Ayia Kerkyra, the 5th-century church of the Old City. ⊠ *1 km (½ mi) north of Kanoni, near Mon Repos beach* ☎ *26610/41369* 🎟 *€3* ⊘ *Tues.–Sun. 8:30–7.*

Gastouri

Γαστούρι

⑰ *19 km (12 mi) southwest of Corfu town.*

The village of Gastouri, still lovely despite the summer onrush of day-trippers, is the site of the **Achilleion.** Although in remarkably bad taste (Lawrence Durrell called it "a monstrous building"), the palace is redeemed by lovely gardens stretching to the sea. Built in the late 19th century by the Italian architect Rafael Carita for Empress Elizabeth of Austria, this was a retreat for her to nurse her health and her heartbreak over husband Franz Josef's numerous affairs. Elizabeth named the palace after her favorite hero, Achilles, whom she identified with her son. After she was assassinated, Kaiser Wilhelm II bought it and lived here until the outbreak of World War I, during which he still used it as a summer residence. After the armistice, the Greek government received it as a spoil of war.

The interior contains a pseudo-Byzantine chapel, a pseudo-Pompeian room, and a pseudo-Renaissance dining hall, culminating in a vulgar fresco called *Achilles in His Chariot.* One of the more interesting furnishings is Kaiser Wilhelm II's saddle seat, used at his desk. On the terrace, which commands a superb view over Kanoni and the town, is an Ionic peristyle with a number of statues in various degrees of undress. The best is *The Dying Achilles*. In 1962 the palace was restored, leased as a gambling casino, and later was the set for the casino scene in the James Bond film *For Your Eyes Only*. The casino has since moved to the Corfu Holiday Palace. The exhibits on the ground floor contain mementos and portraits. ⊠ *Main St.* ☎ *26610/56210* 🖼 *€6* ☉ *June–Aug., daily 8–7; Sept.–May, daily 9–4.*

The freshwater lagoon of **Korisia** (⊠ 17 km [10 mi] southwest of Gastouri) was created by the Venetians, who flooded a former marshland to create this scenic, wildlife-rich lake spreading more than 3 square km (2 square mi). The sand dunes between Lake Korisia and the Ionian Sea are awash with flowers in April and May. This is one of the few beaches on Corfu where you can escape crowds and development, though there's a small beach bar.

Where to Stay & Eat

$$$$ ✕ **Taverna Tripas.** Taken in the right spirit, this most famous (and most touristed) of Corfu's tavernas can be fun. The festivity kicks in when the live music and local dancers fill the courtyard (patrons join in, too), and it's not uncommon to see Greek politicians and their retinues dining here. The fixed menu has a choice of tasty *mezedakia* (small appetizers); the pastitsada and beef *kokkinisto* (roasted in a clay pot with garlic and tomatoes) are especially good. Wash it all down with lots of barrel retsina. ⊠ *2 km (1 mi) northwest of Gastouri, Kinopiastes* ☎ *26610/56333* ⊕ *www.tripas.gr* 🍴 *Reservations essential* ▭ *No credit cards* ☉ *No lunch.*

$$$$ ▦ **Marbella Hotel.** In an olive grove near the emerald waters of Agios Ioannis south lies the deluxe Marbella Hotel complex and bungalows. The spacious, sophisticated Mediterranean-style accommodation has amazing views of the sea or the garden from balconies which adjoin the rooms. Single rooms are available, and prices drop almost by half off-season. The Marbella is on the coast road between Benitses and Moraitika. ⊠ *10 km (6 mi) south of Gastouri, 49084 Agios Ioannis Peristeron* ☎ *26610/71183* 🖨 *26610/71189* ⊕ *www.marbella.gr* 🛏 *396 rooms* ♺ *5 restaurants, minibars, cable TV, saltwater pool, wading pool, health club, hair salon, jet skiing, parasailing, waterskiing, archery, Ping-Pong, shops, children's programs (ages 4–12), Internet room, car rental, free parking* ▭ *AE, D, MC, V* ☉ *Closed Nov.–Apr.* ⑩ *MAP.*

$$ ▦ **San Stefano.** Close to Achilleion palace and 900 feet from the beach, this modern hotel commands a hill overlooking the water in 35 acres of garden. Rooms have standard hotel furniture and balconies from which to savor the coastline vistas. Bungalows have kitchenettes with refrigerators. It's hard to get bored here, with so many land and water sports, pools and the beach, and tennis. ⊠ *1 km (½ mi) south of Gastouri, 49084 Benitses* ☎ *26610/71123* 🖨 *26610/71124 or 26610/72272* ⊕ *www.ellada.net/sanstef* 🛏 *216 rooms, 4 suites, 39 bungalows* ♺ *2 restaurants, some kitchenettes, 2 tennis courts, pool, wading pool, beach, boating, waterskiing, Ping-Pong, 3 bars, shop, children's programs (ages 5–12),* *playground, business services, meeting rooms, some pets allowed* ⊟ *AE, DC, MC, V*⋅⊙ *Closed Nov.–Mar.*

$–$$ 🏨 **Aeolos Beach Hotel.** Gardens and olive groves create peace at the southeast end of the island, and tunnel access leads to a small pebbled beach. The rooms are basic: family rooms may have a double bed and two singles and not much else; studio and one-bedroom apartments have kitchens. The property's spread-out design is beautiful, but not suitable for people with walking difficulties. Live evening entertainment includes music and folk dancing. ⊠ *13 km (8 mi) south of Corfu town, 3 km (2 mi) north of Gastouri, 49100 Perama* 🕾 *26610/331326* 🖥 *26610/40420* ⊕ *www.aeolosbeach.gr* 🛏 *73 rooms, 124 apartments, 83 bungalow* ⚹ *2 restaurants, tennis court, 2 pools, wading pool, beach, archery, billiards, Ping-Pong, 4 bars, Internet room, children's programs (ages 4-12), beach* ⊟ *AE, D, MC, V* ⊙ *Closed Nov.–Apr.* ❚◎❙ *MAP.*

WEST-CENTRAL CORFU

ΔΥΤΙΚΗ-ΚΕΝΤΡΙΚΗ ΚΕΡΚΥΡΑ

The agricultural Ropa Valley divides the sandy beaches and freshwater lagoon of the lower west coast past Ermones from the dramatic mountains of the northwest. Hairpin bends take you through orange and olive groves, over the mountainous spine of the island to the rugged bays and promontories of the coast. The road descends to the sea, where two headlands near Paleokastritsa, 130 feet high and covered with trees and boulders, form a pair of natural harbors.

Pelekas

Πέλεκας

⑱ *11 km (7 mi) northwest of Gastouri, 13 km (8 mi) west of Corfu town.*

Inland from the coast at Glyfada is Pelekas, a hilltop village that overflows with tourists because of its much-touted lookout point, called **Kaiser's Throne.** German kaiser Wilhelm II enjoyed the sunset here when not relaxing at Achilleion palace. The rocky hilltop does deliver spectacular views of almost the entire island and sea beyond.

North across the fertile Ropa Valley is the resort town of **Ermones** (⊠ 8 km [5 mi] north of Pelekas), with pebbly sand beaches, heavily wooded cliffs, water with plentiful fish, large hotels, and a backdrop of green mountains. The Ropa River flows into the Ionian Sea there.

Beaches

The beach at **Pelekas** has soft, golden sand and clear water but is developed and tends to be crowded. There's a huge resort hotel next to it. Free minibuses regularly transport people to the beach from the village, which is a long and steep walk otherwise. The large, golden beaches at **Glyfada** (⊠ 2 km [1 mi] south of Pelekas) are the most famous on the island. Though the sands are inevitably packed with sunbathers—some hotels in Corfu town run daily beach shuttles to Glyfada—many still come. Sun beds, umbrellas, and water sports equipment is available for rent and there are several tourist resorts.

The isolated **Myrtiotissa** (✉ 3 km [2 mi] north of Pelekas) beach, between sheer cliffs, is noted for its good snorkeling and nude sunbathing. Backed by olive and cypress trees, this sandy stretch was called by Lawrence Durrell in *Prospero's Cell* (with debatable overenthusiasm) "perhaps the loveliest beach in the world." Alas, summer crowds are the norm.

Where to Stay & Eat

$$$–$$$$ ✕ **Spiros and Vassilis.** Escape the in-town tourist hordes and venture to a timeless restaurant on farmland belonging to the Polimeri family. Steak, as well as frogs' legs and escargots, is a big winner on the classic French menu. An extensive wine list and truly efficient, discreet service add to the pleasure. ✉ *9 km (6 mi) west of Corfu town on road to Pelekas, Agios Ioannis* ☎ *26610/52552 or 26610/52438* ▤ *AE, D, MC, V* ⊘ *No lunch.*

¢–$$ ✕ **Jimmy's.** Only fresh ingredients and pure local olive oil are used at this family-run restaurant serving traditional Greek food. Try *tsigareli*, a combination of green vegetables and spices, or some of Jimmy's own Corfiot meat dishes. There's a nice choice of vegetarian dishes and of sweets. The place opens early in the morning for breakfasts and stays open all day. ✉ *Pelekas* ☎ *26610/94284* ▤ *MC, V* ⊘ *Closed Nov.–Apr.*

★ $$$ ▦ **Pelekas Country Club.** The old family mansion of Nikos Velianitis, amid 200 acres of olive and cypress trees, forms the kernel for this idyllic retreat. Seven impeccably furnished bungalows and four state-of-the-art suites are decorated with antiques and family heirlooms from England and Russia and have large verandas overlooking the gardens. Olive Press House and the François Mitterrand Suite are recommended. Breakfast treats include fresh-squeezed fruit juices and homemade jams served in the mansion dining room. ✉ *Kerkyra–Pelekas road, 49100* ☎ *26610/52239 or 26610/52917* ▤ *26610/52919* ⊛ *www.country-club.gr* ⇅ *7 bungalows, 4 suites* ⚹ *Dining room, some kitchenettes, tennis court, pool, horseback riding, bar; no a/c in some rooms* ▤ *No credit cards* ❢❙ *BP.*

$ ▦ **Levant Hotel.** Guest rooms have small balconies to enjoy the breathtaking views (and sunsets) over the Adriatic Sea and across silver-green olive groves. The neoclassical Levant retains a touch of romance in the traditional Corfiot style: canopies hang over the beds in comfortable rooms. Start off your day with a soul-warming breakfast served on the main terrace. This hotel is under Kaiser Wilhelm II's favorite lookout point. ✉ *Near Kaiser's Throne, 49100* ☎ *26610/94230 or 26610/94335* ▤ *26610/94115* ⊛ *www.levanthotel.com* ⇅ *25 rooms* ⚹ *Restaurant, room service, minibars, pool, bar, meeting room* ▤ *MC, V* ❢❙ *BP.*

Paleokastritsa

Παλαιοκαστρίτσα

⑲ *21 km (13 mi) north of Pelekas, 25 km (16 mi) northwest of Corfu town.*

Identified by archaeologists as the site of Homer's city of the Phaeacians, this spectacular territory of grottoes, cliffs, and turquoise waters has a big rock named Kolovri, which resembles the mythological ship that brought Ulysses home. The natural beauty and water sports of Paleo, as Corfiots call it, have brought hotels, tavernas, bars, and shops to the hillsides above the bays, and the beaches swarm with hordes of people on day trips from Corfu town. You can explore the quiet coves in peace with a pedal boat or small motorboat rented from the crowded main beach. There are also boat operators that go around to the prettiest surrounding beaches; ask the skipper to let you off at a beach that appeals to you and to pick you up on a subsequent trip.

Paleokastritsa Monastery, a 17th-century structure, is built on the site of an earlier monastery, among terraced gardens overlooking the Adriatic Sea. Its treasure is a 12th-century icon of the Virgin Mary, and there's a small museum with some other early icons. Note the Tree of Life motif on the ceiling. Be sure to visit the inner courtyard (go through the church), built on the edge of the cliff, dappled white, green, and black by the sunlight on the stonework, vine leaves, and habits of the hospitable monks. Under a roof of shading vines you look precipitously down to the placid green cove and the torn coastline stretching south. ⊠ *On northern headland* ☎ *No phone* 🖾 *Donations accepted* ⊘ *Daily 7–1 and 3–8.*

The village of **Lakones** is on the steep mountain behind the Paleokastritsa Monastery. Most of the current town was constructed in modern times, but the ruins of the 13th-century **Angelokastro** also loom over the landscape. The fortress was built on an inaccessible pinnacle by a despot of Epirus during his brief rule over Corfu. The village sheltered Corfiots in 1571 from attack by Turkish wannabe conquerors. Look for the chapel and caves, which served as sanctuaries for hermits. The road to this spot was reputedly built by British troops in part to reach Lady Adam's favorite picnic place, the Bella Vista terrace (there's a café there now). Kaiser Wilhelm also came here to enjoy the magnificent view of Paleokastritsa's coves. ⊠ *5 km (3 mi) northeast of Paleokastritsa.*

Where to Stay & Eat

$–$$$ ✕ **To Vrakos** (The Rock). Overlooking the rock of the bay in Paleokastritsa, where Homer's wine-dark sea touches forest-green mountains, the view here is one of those Greek keys that explain all. As for the food, the lobster and spaghetti is delicious, and the house salad is a tasty mix of rocket lettuce, spinach, and cabbage with mushrooms and croutons. The prices are reasonable considering the fantastic views. ⊠ *North end of beach* ☎ *26630/41233* 🖃 *AE, MC, V* ⊘ *Closed Nov.–May.*

¢ 🏠 **Casa Lucia.** The stone buildings of an olive press have been converted into individually decorated guest cottages, each overlooking a tranquil garden filled with hibiscus, olive trees, and bougainvillea. Cottages have two to five beds with colorful stripe linens and a few antiques, and most have their own small kitchens and courtyard. Tai chi and yoga sessions are held out in the garden by the pool. ⊠ *Corfu–Paleokastritsa road, 13 km (8 mi) northwest of Corfu town, 49083 Sgombou* ☎ *26610/91419* ⊕ *www.casa-lucia-corfu.com* ⇨ *10 cottages* ⚿ *Some kitchens, pool; no a/c, no room phones, no room TVs* 🖃 *AE, D, MC, V.*

NORTH CORFU

ΒΟΡΕΙΑ ΚΕΡΚΥΡΑ

The main roads along the northeast coast above Corfu town are crowded with hotels, gas stations, touristy cafés, and shops. But head inland a bit and there are more peaceful settings—dusty villages where olives, herbs, and home-brewed wine are the main products, and where goats roam the squares and chickens peck at the roadsides. Steep Mt. Pantokrator ("ruler of all"), and at 2,970 feet the highest peak on Corfu, forms the northeast lobe of the island. The northern coastal area is replete with pretty coves, and it has the longest sand beach in Corfu, curving around Roda to Archaravi.

Ano Korakiana

Άνω Κορακιανά

★ ⑳ 6 km (4 mi) east and north of Paleokastritsa, 19 km (12 mi) north of Corfu town.

Corfiots call this beautiful village Little Venice, for its narrow lanes winding through old Venetian houses painted in fading peach and ocher. Instead of watery canals, they're set against the silvery-green olive-tree-covered slopes of Mt. Pantokrator, and filled with gardens of pomegranate and lemon trees and brilliantly colored flowers. Life is quiet but happy here: old men bring their chairs out to the square, where they can drink coffee and gossip while looking out to the sea; heavenly aromas drift out from the bakeries, said to make the island's best bread; and some afternoons the town marching band strikes up a tune in the square.

Where to Eat

$$$ ✕ **Etrusco.** Hidden in the old mansion of a tree-filled village is one of
Fodor'sChoice   the best restaurants in Greece. Etrusco is run by the Italian-Corfiot
★   Botrini family, whose passion for both cuisines, combined with flawless technique and creativity, results in truly memorable dinners. Chef Ettore Botrini delights with dishes like homemade *pappardelle* (flat pasta with rippled edges) with duck and truffles, and medallions of fish cooked in Triple Sec and sesame seeds. For starters try the extraordinary home-cured meats and marinated fish—particularly delicious is the salmon in aromatic oil and poppy seeds. Ettore's wife, Monica, prepares the desserts; her terrine of peaches and white chocolate is sublime. ⊠ *1 km (½ mi) east of Ano Korakiana, Kato Korakiana* ☎ *26610/93342* ⌲ *Reservations essential* ▭ *MC, V* ⊘ *No lunch.*

Agni

Αγνή

㉑ 7 km (4½ mi) north of Ano Korakiana, 28 km (17 mi) north of Corfu town.

Tiny, clear-water Agni is little more than a scenic fishing cove. Like the rest of Corfu's coast, it has good swimming, and you can rent small boats to go exploring on your own. What makes it a don't-miss destination is its three outstanding restaurants, all lining the pretty harbor. If you're doing a drive around Corfu's north coast, try to stop at Agni for lunch or dinner—or both.

The harbor town at **Kouloura** (✉ 3 km [2 mi] south of Agni) is on a U-shape bay enclosed by cypress, eucalyptus, and palm trees and has a small shingle beach with close views of the Albanian coastline. This coastline is part of Corfu immortalized by the Durrell brothers—much of Lawrence Durrell's writing of *Prospero's Cell* was done in what is now a taverna called the White House, south in Kalami. Donkeys still plod the roads, cafés serve local wine, and life here on the lower slopes of Mt. Pantokrator holds its sweet charm, even when besieged by tourists in July and August.

Where to Eat

$$$–$$$$ ✕ **Taverna Agni.** The quintessential island taverna, Taverna Agni sits on a white-pebble beach near shallow turquoise waters, with cypress-covered mountains as backdrop. The food—stuffed zucchini flowers, chicken cooked in champagne, grilled fish caught earlier that day—is just as much a reason to stop here as the setting. ✉ *North end of Agni beach* ☎ *26630/91142* ⊕ *www.agni.gr* ⌂ *Reservations essential* ▤ *MC, V* ⊘ *Closed Nov.–Apr.*

$$$–$$$$ ✕ **Toula's.** Of the Agni restaurants, Toula gets the most creative with the abundant fresh seafood and seasonal produce. Many declare the fragrant shrimp pilaf to be the best they've ever tasted—cooked with lots of garlic, parsley, and chili, and a secret spice Toula refuses to reveal. The pasta with lobster or prawns is also excellent, as are simpler dishes, like fresh grilled bream and mussels cooked in broth. ✉ *Waterfront* ☎ *26630/91350* ▤ *MC, V* ⊘ *Closed Nov.–Apr.*

¢–$$ ✕ **Taverna Nicholas.** Which Corfiot village dishes are available at Taverna Nicholas depends on what produce has been brought down from the mountains, and what fish out of the sea, that day. Likely as not, there will be an exemplary sofrito, cod with garlic sauce, and chicken in white wine with freshly picked herbs. The simple, whitewashed beachfront terrace restaurant has been serving food for several generations. ✉ *South end of Agni cove* ☎ *26630/91243* ▤ *AE, MC, V* ⊘ *Closed Nov.–mid-Apr.*

Kassiopi

Κασσιόπη

㉒ *8 km (5 mi) northwest of Agni, 36 km (23 mi) northeast of Corfu town.*

North around Mt. Pantokrator, Kassiopi occupies a promontory between two bays, where the wind can blow hard in late summer. It was an important town during Roman times, with a shrine to Zeus that Nero and other emperors visited; Tiberius had a villa here. A church with a 17th-century icon and frescoes now occupies what was probably the site of Zeus's shrine, on the western side of the harbor.

During the Byzantine era this settlement rivaled Corfu town, but the town declined when Kassiopi's fortress, built by the Angevins, was destroyed by the Venetians. Now the fishing village has discovered the tourist trade and has become a busy resort; its harbor front has been taken up by tavernas, shops, and bars catering to charter groups.

On the north coast, **Roda** (⊠ 8 km [5 mi] northwest of Kassiopi), a growing resort community, has pebble beaches and plenty of tourists, and though some spots farther west are less crowded, the roads to them are not as passable. Its narrow beach, which adjoins the beach at Archaravi, has especially calm and shallow waters and a campsite, so it's popular with local families. The remains of a 5th-century Doric temple were found here.

Sidari (⊠ 12 km [8 mi] northwest of Kassiopi) has archaeological remains dating back to 7000 BC but today is crowded with families splashing in the calm waters. To the west, unique striated cliffs are constantly being eroded into tunnels and caves, most notably the "tunnel of love." Think carefully: legend has it that if you take a boat through this narrow channel, you will be able to marry whoever was in your thoughts at the time.

off the beaten path

DIAPONTIA ISLANDS – Even with a four-wheel drive and a map of dirt roads, it can still be tough to find a stretch of truly pristine coastal spot on cosmopolitan Corfu. Less than 7 km (4½ mi) northwest of Corfu, the three tiny Diapontia islands look more like the lush, untouched landscape evoked by Homer and Shakespeare. All three have beaches where you won't see anything at all beyond dreamlike water, white sand, and hilltops where wild herbs and flowers wave in the breeze. The island of **Othonoi** also has a few ruined Venetian castles, and a cave said to be the spot where Calypso held Odysseus captive. Verdant **Erikoussa** has excellent fishing and a thickly wooded inland. **Mathraki,** where the year-round population rarely exceeds 100, has long, solitary, stunningly beautiful beaches. Each makes a memorable day trip. If you want to stay longer, each also has a handful of small hotels; there are also tavernas at the harbors where boats dock from Corfu. Boats for the Diapontia islands leave three times a week from Agios Stefanos. *San Stefano Travel:* ⊠ *18 km (11 mi) northwest of Kassiopi, Agios Stefanos* ☎ *26630/51910.*

Where to Stay & Eat

$–$$$ ✕ **Petrinos.** For a warm welcome from friendly staff, come to Petrinos. Specialities of the house include mushrooms stuffed with lobster in a champagne-and-cream sauce. A separate bar area for a nightcap ends the evening. ⊠ *Kassiopi* ☎ *26630/81760* ▤ *MC, V* ☉ *Closed Nov.–Mar.*

¢ 🏨 **Apraos Bay Hotel.** On the northern tip of the island sits this small, brick-red Venetian-style hotel. Rooms are fresh and airy, with white tile floors and white bedding offset by dark lacquer furniture. French doors open out onto private balconies and a fantastic view of the sea and the Albanian coast. The hotel has access to a private beach and nearby Kassiopi has all the action anyone could want. ⊠ *2 km (1 mi) north of Kassiopi, 49100 Apraos* ☎ *26630/98137* 🖶 *26630/98331* ✐ *apraos@otenet. gr* ⇥ *16 rooms* ⚘ *Restaurant, pool, beach, piano bar, recreation room; no room phones, no room TVs* ▤ *MC, V* ☉ *Closed Nov.–Mar.*

Nightlife
Kostas Bar (✉ North end ☎ 26630/81955) has authentic Greek dancing, and occasional guest appearances by belly dancers, followed by disco music.

CORFU A TO Z

To research prices, get advice from other travelers, and book travel arrangements, visit www.fodors.com.

AIR TRAVEL
Olympic Airlines and Aegean Airlines both have two to three flights a day from Athens to Corfu town. Fares change, but the hour-long flight starts at about €180 round-trip. AirSea Lines has connections to the islands of Paxos and Lefkas and to Ioannina on the mainland. The airline plans to expand to the whole Ionian region and to Brindisi in Italy. Between April and October many charter flights arrive in Corfu directly from the United Kingdom and northern Europe.

🛫 Carriers **Aegean Airlines** ☎ 210/998-8350, 210/998-8300 in Athens ⊕ www.aegeanairlines.gr. **AirSea Lines** ☎ 26610/99316 ⊕ www.airsealines.com. **Olympic Airlines** ☎ 26610/38694, 26610/38695, 26610/49484, or 26610/49485 ⊕ www.olympicairlines.com.

AIRPORTS
Corfu Airport is northwest of Kanoni, 3 km (2 mi) south of Corfu town. A taxi from the airport to the town center costs around €6; there is no airport bus. Taxi rates are on display in the arrivals hall.

🛫 **Corfu Airport** ☎ 26610/89600.

BOAT & FERRY TRAVEL
There are no ferries from Piraeus to Corfu town; you need to drive to Patras or to the northwestern city of Igoumenitsa, to catch one of the daily ferries for Corfu. You can buy tickets at the ports, or book in advance through the ferry lines or travel agents. For the most up-to-date information on boat schedules, call the port authority in the city of departure or check the Greek ferry information Web site.

Ferries from Patras to Corfu town (six to seven hours) generally leave around 11 PM or midnight. The ferries are run by Minoan, ANEK, and Blue Star lines and tickets cost about €25 per person, €70 per car, and €40 per person for a cabin. Kerkyra Lines and Cruises runs ferries between Igoumenitsa and Corfu town (two hours); tickets are €8 per person and €32 per car. Petrakis Lines and Cruises hydrofoils go from Igoumenitsa to Corfu town (45 minutes) on Sunday and Corfu town to Igoumenitsa on Tuesday (€12). International ferries between Greece and Italy stop in Corfu town at least several times a week; check with Minoan Lines.

🚢 Boat & Ferry Lines **ANEK Lines** ✉ Amalias 54, Athens ☎ 210/419-7420 ⊕ www.anekferry.com. **Blue Star Ferries** ✉ Amalias 54, Athens ☎ 210/891-9800 ⊕ www.bluestarferries.com. **Corfu Port Authority** ☎ 26610/32655. **Greek ferry info** ⊕ www.greekferries.gr. **Igoumenitsa Port Authority** ☎ 26650/22235. **Kerkyra Lines and Cruises** ✉ Eleftheriou Venizelou 32, Corfu town ☎ 26610/23874. **Minoan Lines** ✉ Thermopylon 6, Piraeus ☎ 210/414-5700 ⊕ www.minoan.gr. **Patras Port Authority** ☎ 2610/341002. **Petrakis Lines and Cruises** ✉ Venizeloua 9, new port, Corfu town ☎ 26610/31649.

BUS TRAVEL

KTEL buses leave Athens Terminal A for Corfu town (10 hours, €35 one-way), via Patras and the ferry, three or four times a day. The inexpensive local bus network covers Corfu island, with reduced service Sunday, holidays, and off-season service. Green KTEL buses leave for long-distance destinations from the Corfu town terminal near the new port. Blue local buses (with destinations including Kanoni and Gastouri) leave from Platia San Rocco. You can get timetables and information at both bus depots and in the English-language news magazine *The Corfiot*.

🚍 **Corfu local buses** ⊠ Pl. San Rocco, Corfu town ☎ 26610/31595. **KTEL Corfu buses** ⊠ Avramiou, Corfu town ☎ 26610/39862 or 26610/30627 ⊠ Terminal A, Kifissou 100, Athens ☎ 210/512–4190 or 210/512–9443.

CAR & MOTORBIKE RENTALS

You need a car to get to some of Corfu's loveliest and most inaccessible places and the gentle climate and rolling hills make Corfu ideal motorbike country. As on all Greek islands, exercise caution with regard to steep, winding roads and fellow drivers equally unfamiliar with the terrain.

Corfu town has several car-rental agencies, most clustered around the ports. There's a gamut of options, ranging from international chains offering luxury four-wheel drives to local agencies offering cheap deals on basic wheels. Prices can range from €25 a day for a Fiat 127 (100 km [62 mi] minimum) to €80 a day for a four-wheel jeep with extras. Expect additional charges of around €15 for insurance, delivery, and so forth. It's definitely worth it to shop around: chains have a bigger selection, but the locals will usually give a cheaper price. Don't be afraid to bargain, especially if you want to rent a car for several days. In Corfu town, Ocean Car Hire has good bargains, and Reliable Rent-a-Car has dozens of options. Other agencies include Top Cars and Olympus Rent-a-Car.

A 50cc motorbike can be rented for about €25 a day and €110 a week, a 125cc motorbike for about €30 a day and €160 a week, but you can bargain, especially if you want it for longer. Helmets are rarely provided, and then only on request. Check the lights, brakes, and other mechanics before you accept a machine. Be warned and be careful. In Corfu town, try Easy Rider; rentals are available in even the most remote villages.

🚗 **Easy Rider** ⊠ Eleftheriou Venizelou 50, Corfu town ☎ 26610/43026. **Ocean Car Hire** ⊠ New port, Corfu town ☎ 26610/44017 ⊕ www.oceancar.gr. **Olympus Rent-a-Car** ⊠ National Stadium 29, Corfu town ☎ 26610/36147. **Reliable Rent-a-Car** ⊠ Donzelot 5, Corfu town ☎ 26610/35740. **Top Cars** ⊠ Donzelot, Corfu town ☎ 26610/35237 ⊕ www.topcars.gr.

CAR & MOTORBIKE TRAVEL

The best route from Athens is the National Road via Corinth to Igoumenitsa (472 km [274 mi]), where you take the ferry to Corfu. In winter, severe weather conditions often close the straits at Rion–Antirion, and the ferries from Igoumenitsa can also stop running.

There is little or no system to Greek driving, and "Depend on the other guy's brakes" best expounds the basic philosophy of many drivers. The road surfaces deteriorate as the tourist season progresses, and potholes abound.

EMERGENCIES

In Corfu town there's always one pharmacy open 24 hours; call the 24-hour information line to find out which one.

Hospital ⊠ Andreadi, Corfu town ☎ 26610/45811. **Police** ⊠ Alexandras 19, Corfu town ☎ 100. **24-Hour Pharmacy Information** ☎ 107.

ENGLISH-LANGUAGE MEDIA

The monthly English news magazine *The Corfiot,* written mostly by and for ex-pats, has information on events; restaurant reviews; and bus, boat, and plane schedules. It's available at newsstands and at English-language bookshops, the largest of which is Lykoudis, which also has memoirs and novels related to the island. Lykoudis also runs a kiosk that sells English-language periodicals, from *Financial Times* to *Seventeen.*

English-Language Bookstores Lykoudis ⊠ Pl. Polimnias Skaramgka, Corfu town ☎ 26610/39845 🔲 Kiosk ⊠ Kapodistria 11, Corfu town ☎ No phone.

SPORTS & THE OUTDOORS

The Companion Guide to the Corfu Trail and *The Second Book of Corfu Walks: The Road to Old Corfu,* written by Hilary Whitton Paipeti, editor of *The Corfiot,* both give information on hiking the Corfu Trail, Mt. Pantokrator, and other parts of the island. These are available at Corfu's English-language bookstores. Aperghi Travel provides hiking information and maps, arranges lodging and transportation along the Corfu Trail, and hosts 7- and 14-day Corfu Trail hiking tours. Lemonhouse Walks leads guided walking tours tailored to your needs.

Hiking Aperghi Travel ⊠ Polyla Lakovou 1, Corfu town ☎ 26610/48713 ⊕ www.travelling.gr/corfutrail. **Lemonhouse Walks** ⊠ Pelekas ☎ 26610/94840 ⊕ www.lemonhouse.com.

TAXIS

Taxis are available 24 hours a day, and rates, which are set by the government, are reasonable—when adhered to. Many drivers speak English and know the island in a very special way. If you want to hire a cab and driver on an hourly or daily basis, negotiate the price before you travel. In Corfu town, taxis wait at Platia Sarokou, Platia Theotoki, the Esplanade, and the ports.

Corfu Taxis ☎ 26610/33811, 26610/30383, or 26610/39911.

TOURS

Many travel agencies run half-day tours of Old Corfu town, and tour buses go daily to all the sights on the island; All-Ways Travel is reliable. Charitos Travel has more than 50 tours of the island and can create custom tours for groups of five or more. International Tours arranges hiking, mountain biking, horseback riding, jeep trips, and other such excursions around the island. Cosmic Travel has east-coast boat trips as well as sunset and moonlight cruises from Kassiopi. Petrakis Lines

and Cruises has boat day trips to Albania, the Ionian island of Cephalonia, and other nearby islands.

All-Ways Travel ✉ G. Theotoki 34, Corfu town ☎ 26610/33955 ⊕ www.allwaystravel.
com. **Charitos Travel** ✉ Arseniou 35, Corfu town ☎ 26610/44611 ⊕ www.charitostravel.
gr. **Cosmic Travel** ✉ Kassiopi ☎ 26630/81624 ⊕ www.cosmic-kassiopi.com. **International Tours** ✉ Eleftheriou Venizelou 32, Corfu town ☎ 26610/39007 or 26610/38107.
Petrakis Lines and Cruises ✉ Ethnikis Antisaseos 4, Corfu town ☎ 26610/31649.

TRAVEL AGENCIES

For boat and air tickets and for hotel reservations, All-Ways Travel is
an established travel agency with a solid reputation.

All-Ways Travel ✉ G. Theotoki 34, Corfu town ☎ 26610/33955 ⊕ www.allwaystravel.
com.

VISITOR INFORMATION

Corfu Tourist Police ✉ Kapodistriou 1, Corfu town ☎ 26610/30265. **Greek National
Tourism Organization (GNTO or EOT)** ✉ Pl. San Rocco, Corfu town ☎ 26610/20733
⊕ www.gnto.gr.

Northern Peloponnese

NAFPLION, PATRAS & OLYMPIA

7

Updated by
Stephen
Brewer

HANGING LIKE A LARGE LEAF from the stem of the Corinthian isthmus, the Peloponnese is graced by astounding and imposing ruins that are matched with equally varied and beautiful scenery. Massive mountains covered with low evergreen oak and pine trees surround coastal valleys and loom above rocky shores and sandy beaches. Over the millennia this rugged terrain nourished kingdoms and empires and witnessed the birth of modern Greece. The region is named for Pelops, son of the mythical Tantalos, whose tragic descendants, including Atreus and Agamemnon, dominate the half-legendary Mycenaean centuries. Traces of these lost realms—ruined Bronze Age citadels, Greek and Roman temples and theaters, and the fortresses and settlements of the Byzantines, Franks, Venetians, and Turks—attest to the richness of the land.

The Northern Peloponnese comprises the Argive peninsula, jutting into the Aegean, and runs westward past the isthmus and along the Gulf of Corinth to Patras and the Adriatic coast. It is divided into seven nomes (provinces): Argolid (east), Corinthia (northeast), Achaea (northwest), Elis (northwest), Messinia (southwest), Laconia (southeast), and Arcadia (north center). The oldest region is the fertile Argive plain (Argolid), the heart of Greece in the late Bronze Age and the home of the heroes of Homer's *Iliad*. A walk through the Lion Gate into Mycenae, the citadel of Agamemnon, brings the Homeric epic to life, and the massive walls of nearby Tiryns glorify the age of might. The thriving market town of Argos, the successor to Mycenae and Tiryns, engaged in a long rivalry with Sparta. Corinth, the economic superpower of the 7th and 6th centuries BC, dominated trade and established colonies abroad. Although eclipsed by Athens, Corinth earned a reputation for ostentatious wealth and loose living. Today modern Corinth is a bustling, if unremarkable, regional center. Not far from Corinth is Epidauros, the sanctuary of Asklepios, god of healing, where in summer Greek dramas are re-created in the ancient theater, one of the finest and most complete to survive. Olympia, the sanctuary of Zeus and site of the ancient Olympic Games, lies on the western side of the Peloponnese.

By the 13th century, the armies of the Fourth Crusade (in part egged on by Venice) had conquered the Peloponnese after capturing Constantinople in 1204. But the dominion of the Franks was brief, and Byzantine authority was restored under the Palaiologos dynasty. Soon after Constantinople fell in 1453, the Turks, taking advantage of an internal rivalry, crushed the Palaiologoi and helped themselves to the Peloponnese. In the following centuries the struggle between the Venetians and the Ottoman Turks was played out in Greece. The two states alternately dominated the Northern Peloponnese until the Ottomans ultimately prevailed as Venetian power declined in the early 1700s. The Turkish mosques and fountains and the Venetian fortifications of Nafplion recall this epic struggle. The Peloponnese played a key role in the Greek War of Independence; after the Turks withdrew in 1828, Nafplion was the capital of Greece from 1829 to 1834 (after which the capital was moved to Athens). An insurrection of the garrison at Nafplion helped bring about the abdication of King Otto in 1862, and in 1874, Heinrich Schliemann, the enigmatic amateur archaeologist, began his exca-

The eastern and western portions of the Northern Peloponnese are easily divided into two separate three-day itineraries; a six-day tour catches the region's highlights, and a thorough exploration requires about nine days. Those with less time should consider investigating either the eastern or western half only; for travelers entering Greece from Italy, the Vouraikos Gorge and Olympia are options, and for those entering Greece through Athens, Nafplion and the Argolid are only a short hop away. One thing to keep in mind: people usually wind up asking themselves why they didn't allot more time to this fascinating area of Greece.

7

Numbers in the text correspond to numbers in the margin and on the Northern Peloponnese, Nafplion, Mycenae, and Ancient Olympia maps.

If you have 3 days

The wealth of interesting sites on either side of the Northern Peloponnese will keep the intrepid occupied for at least three days: start with a day in lovely ⬚ **Nafplion** ❺ –⓲ ⚑ followed by a day spent exploring some of the highlights of the Argolid—**Mycenae** ㉑ –㉛ and **Tiryns** ⓳. A third day near Nafplion will allow a visit to the theater at **Epidauros** ❷, or you can make the excursion west to **Olympia** ㊵ –㊲. For those entering Greece from Italy and with only a couple of days to spare, try spending a day in ⬚ **Olympia** ㊵ –㊲, a day enjoying the train ride along the picturesque **Vouraikos Gorge** ㉟ en route to **Kalavrita** ㊱, and a day clambering over the parapets of the Frankish **Chlemoutsi Castle** ㊴ and relaxing on a nearby beach.

If you have 6 days

Spend three days in ⬚ **Nafplion** ❺ –⓲ ⚑ and use the city as a base to explore the Argolid. You can get to Nafplion by boat, train, or car, and can rent transportation. The city itself is appealing, and from there you can easily explore nearby **Mycenae** ㉑ –㉛, **Tiryns** ⓳, **Epidauros** ❷, and **Argos** ⓴. On the fourth day drop down through the mountains of the central Peloponnese to ⬚ **Olympia** ㊵ –㊲, where you can spend the night. Then head around the top of the peninsula, passing **Chlemoutsi Castle** ㊴ and taking some time out to enjoy a swim at one of the spectacular beaches nearby. You can spend the night in ⬚ **Patras** ㊳ or continue on to a more scenic place, such as ⬚ Diakofto or ⬚ **Kalavrita** ㊱, entry points for the ⬚ **Vouraikos Gorge** ㉟, before getting your last dose of ruins in **Ancient Corinth** ㉝. Remember that this trip can be easily reversed if you are coming from Italy and arriving in Patras.

If you have 9 days

Starting at the isthmus, journey south toward Nafplion, visiting **Isthmia** ❶ ⚑, **Ancient Corinth** ㉝, and **Epidauros** ❷ en route. Spend five nights in ⬚ **Nafplion** ❺ –⓲, using it as a base for daily excursions. You'll want to spend at least one day exploring the beautiful city itself. The five major archaeological sites north of Nafplion—**Tiryns** ⓳, **Argos** ⓴, **Mycenae** ㉑ –㉛, **Ancient Nemea** ㉜, and **Ancient Corinth** ㉝ —could easily occupy two or even three days, and you might also want to relax at one of the nearby beaches. Olympia beckons the Peloponnesian traveler sooner or later, but don't rush. There's plenty to see en route from the Argolid, including the alluring beauty of the **Vouraikos Gorge** ㉟, which you can enjoy on an overnight stop in ⬚ Diakofto or ⬚ **Kalavrita** ㊱.

You might want to spend a little time taking in the big-city scene of 🖼 **Patras** ㊳ and then press on to nearby sights such as the best-preserved Frankish castle in the Peloponnese, **Chlemoutsi Castle** ㊴, with a stop at the beautiful beach at **Kalogria.** Finally, take a languid trip through the verdant province of Elis to impressive, ancient 🖼 **Olympia** ㊵–㊾, where the Olympic Games were first held almost three millennia ago.

---

vations of Mycenae, which led to the discovery of the Acropolis and the Treasury of Atreus.

A large portion of Greece's emigrants to the United States in the 20th century (12%–25% of the male population) have roots in the Peloponnese (their family names are often identified with an ending in *poulos,* meaning "son of"); almost all dreamed of returning to their Greek villages when they had raised their families and had accumulated a sufficient *ekonomies* (nest egg). Quite a number of them have done just that, so if you find yourself unable to convey what you need through phrasebook Greek and body language in one of the remote villages here, an elderly *Helleno-Americanos* (Greek-American) may be called upon to assist. Time seems to have stood still in the smaller towns here, and even in the cities you'll encounter a lifestyle that remains more traditionally Greek than that of some of the more developed islands. The joy of exploring this region comes as much from watching life transpire in an animated square as it does from seeing the impressive ruins.

Most of the Peloponnese is mountainous and rural, with farms and olive groves on the hillsides and in the valleys. However, Patras, in Achaea on the far northwest of the Peloponnese, is the third-largest city in Greece. A modern port (and your port of entry if you're arriving in Greece by boat from Italy) and hub for business and trade, Patras has long been known for its wine and festive pre-Lenten Carnival season. Although modern concrete-block buildings now deface most of the larger Peloponnese towns, Nafplion has maintained its traditional architectural heritage, which is largely inspired by Venetian, Ottoman, and German neoclassical trends. Many people also head to holiday resorts such as Porto Heli and Tolo, attracted by sand and sea. But knowing travelers venture to this region for far more than suntans. After all, the "cyclopean" walls at Tiryns, the Lion Gate and beehive tombs at Mycenae, the theater in Epidauros, and the world-famous sculptures at Olympia are some of the once-in-a-lifetime wonders to be seen and relished here.

Exploring the Northern Peloponnese

The gods of ancient Greece blessed the Northern Peloponnese with natural beauty, and forgotten civilizations left behind their mysteries. The region includes several distinct geographical areas: on the eastern side are the Argolid plain and the Corinthiad, where Tiryns and Epidauros are. Here, too, the ruined city of Mycenae, with giant tombs to the heroes of Homer's *Iliad,* stands sentinel over the plain, where warriors once assembled en route to Troy. Nearby Nafplion, with its ancient Greek,

Venetian, and Turkish edifices jutting into the Bay of Argos, is the most beautiful city in Greece. On the western side are the provinces of Achaea and Elis, home of Ancient Olympia and the scattered remains of the ancient Olympic stadium, and the bustling port city of Patras. The easiest way to get around the Northern Peloponnese is by car, on the region's well-maintained and well-marked roads. Corinth, Nemea, Tiryns, Argos, and Epidauros are within easy reach of Nafplion, and when it comes time to venture farther, it's easy to get to other parts of the Peloponnese via the E65, a four-lane highway.

About the Restaurants

One of the simplest pleasures of Greece is a late dinner of traditional food with good Greek wine, preferably *varelisio* (from the barrel). From late April until as late as early November, you can expect to enjoy this experience outdoors. In the small towns here, any restaurant that pretends to offer more than this should be viewed with suspicion. The same goes for a big bill—no need to pay one, since you can usually enjoy a meal of such staples as lamb or moussaka for about €10 a person, even in larger cities. Dress is casual and reservations unnecessary, although you might be asked to wait for a table, if you're dining with the majority at 9 PM or later. Expect to pay quite a bit for most fresh fish and seafood; a single portion is usually about €15. Never settle for frozen fish, which may not even be from Greek waters. Look for red wines from the region around Nemea, between Corinth and Argos, and try Patras's sweet *mavrodaphne,* a heavy dessert wine. Another favorite in Patras is *dendoura,* a clove liqueur served after dinner as a digestive.

Most restaurants in the Northern Peloponnese are open year-round, as they cater to locals. Only in beach resorts, such as Tolo and Porto Heli, do restaurants close seasonally. In towns and cities, Greeks usually begin arriving for dinner long after tourists have finished their meals—at 10 or even later.

About the Hotels

Those accustomed to traveling in the United States and Europe should not expect to find such amenities as Internet connections everywhere they go, though air-conditioning and televisions are increasingly common, even in inexpensive hotels; unless otherwise noted, expect hotel amenities to include telephones, televisions, and air-conditioning.

Hotels in Nafplion, Patras, and other large towns and cities tend to be open year-round. In beach resorts, such as Tolo and Porto Heli, many hotels close in late October and reopen in late March or early April. A few resort-type hotels in beach towns cater to an international clientele, and there are business-style hotels in Patras. In Nafplion, many old houses have been converted to pleasant small hotels, and in Patras and Nafplion you are likely to find the region's more luxurious and expensive lodgings. Overall, though, lodging is a good value, and even in high season you can usually manage to find a clean and pleasant room for two, with breakfast, for €50 or even less.

	WHAT IT COSTS In euros				
	$$$$	$$$	$$	$	¢
RESTAURANTS	over €20	€16–€20	€12–€15	€8–€11	under €8
HOTELS	over €160	€121–€160	€91–€120	€60–€90	under €60

Restaurant prices are for one main course at dinner or, for restaurants that serve only *mezedes* (small dishes), for two mezedes. Hotel prices are for two people in a standard double room in high season, including taxes.

Timing

As in much of Greece, late April and May provide optimum conditions for exploration—hotels, restaurants, and sites have begun to extend their hours but the hordes of travelers have not yet arrived. September and October are also excellent times because the weather is warm but not oppressive, the sea is at its balmiest, and the throngs of people have gone home. In summer, morning and early-evening activity will avoid the worst of the heat, which can be a formidable obstacle. Remember that on Monday many state museums and sites are closed. During off-season (November–April), many are free on some Sundays. An advantage of visiting the Northern Peloponnese in summer is the chance to attend a performance of classical Greek drama at the theater at Epidauros; performances run from July through September.

ARGOLID & CORINTHIAD

ΑΡΓΟΛΙΔΑ & ΚΟΡΙΝΘΙΑ

Ancient Tiryns and Mycenae gaze over the plain of Argos, which dominates the Argolid, and nearby Epidauros hosts audiences from around the world who come to see drama performed in its classical theater. The city of Argos lies in the center of the plain; nearby is the city of Nafplion. Behind the mountains that surround the plain on all sides (except the south) is the Corinthiad, a more hilly region, with ancient Corinth as its principal site.

Isthmus

Ισθμός

75 km (47 mi) southwest of Athens, 7 km (4½ mi) southeast of Corinth.

More of a pit stop than a town, the isthmus is where the Peloponnese begins. Were it not for this narrow neck of land less than 7 km (4½ mi) across, the waters of the Gulf of Corinth and the Saronic Gulf would meet and would make the Peloponnese an island; hence the name, which means "Pelops's island." The tragic myths and legends surrounding Pelops and his family—Atreus, Agamemnon, Orestes, and Electra, among others—provided the grist for poets and playwrights from Homer to Aeschylus and enshroud many of the region's sites to this day.

7

Archaeological Sites

The concentration of classical ruins in the Northern Peloponnese is more dense than anywhere else in the world. Ancient Corinth, Ancient Nemea, Mycenae, Argos, Tiryns, and Epidauros are all within a short drive of one another, near the city of Nafplion. This delightful city, with Byzantine, Venetian, and Turkish roots, makes an ideal base from which to explore the well-preserved ruins of ancient Greece. At some point you will also want to travel west to see the magnificent remains of the ancient city of Olympia, with the Temple of Zeus and the remnants of the Olympic stadium. You can view the finds from the sites in archaeological museums in Nafplion, Argos, Olympia, and elsewhere.

Beaches

The beaches along the western coast of the Peloponnese are considered to be some of the best in Greece and are generally less crowded than those in other areas. Excellent stretches near Kastro, under Chlemoutsi Castle, include Katakolo and Spiantza. Closer to Patras is Kalogria, a 6-km (4-mi) stretch of sand bordered by pine forests. Along the Gulf of Corinth are some beaches with spectacular views of the opposite shore, but some are of pebbles rather than sand. Xylokastro, near Corinth, starts out pebbly but becomes sandy farther from town. The popular areas are well equipped for water sports: paddleboats can be hired, and you can arrange windsurfing lessons at small operations at many beaches, such as Tolo. In some resorts, such as Porto Heli, waterskiing and jet-skiing are popular diversions.

City Pleasures

Nafplion is the favorite Greek city of many seasoned travelers, probably because it is graciously endowed with a magnificent setting on the Gulf of Argos, imposing remains, shady parks, lively squares, an animated waterfront, and street after street of old houses, churches, and mosques. A stroll on the promenade takes you around the peninsula on which the city is built, with views of the cliffs. Nafplion also has many good hotels and restaurants and is an excellent base from which to explore the nearby classical ruins. Should you want to take a well-deserved break from high-minded sightseeing, a number of good beaches are nearby.

Shopping

Olympia has many shops specializing in big-ticket gold jewelry—some nice, others gaudy. Nafplion has an excellent selection of stores selling high-quality gold jewelry, especially around Constitution Square and on Staikopoulou. Patras is the best bet for fashion, especially downtown around Korinthou and Maizonas streets. Folk crafts are the highlights in the smaller villages—with a bit of poking around, you can find outstanding examples of strikingly colored old weavings, especially *tagaria* (shepherd's shoulder bags), which command a higher price than the newer versions. They make wonderful wall hangings.

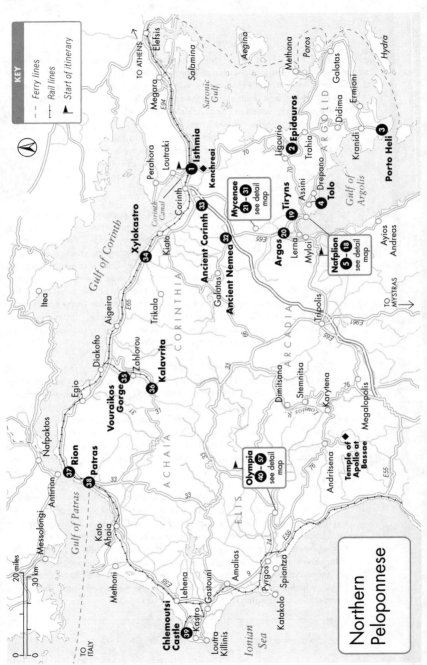

KEY

--- *Ferry lines*
—|— *Rail lines*
▲ *Start of itinerary*

TO ATHENS

Aegina

Salamina

Saronic Gulf

Megara

E94

Elefsis

Perahora

Loutraki

1 ◆ **Isthmia**

Kenchreai

Corinth Canal

Corinth

Xylokastro

34

Kiato

33 **Ancient Corinth**

Galatas

32 **Ancient Nemea**

E65

Aigeira

Ilea

Diakofto

Trikala

CORINTHIA

Zahlorou

35 **Vouraikos Gorge**

36 **Kalavrita**

Egio

Nafpaktos

Antirrion

Messolongi

37 **Rion**

38 **Patras**

Gulf of Patras

Kato Ahaia

Methoni

ACHAIA

33

33

39 **Chlemoutsi Castle**

Kastro

Loutra Killinis

Lehena

Gastouni

TO ITALY

Ionian Sea

Amalias

Pyrgos

Spiantza

Katakolo

ELIS

40–57 ▲ **Olympia** see detail map

74

E55

Lonsios R.

ARCADIA

Andritsena

◆ **Temple of Apollo at Bassae**

76

Karytena

Megalopolis

Stemnitsa

Dimitsana

E65

E961

Tripolis

TO MYSTRAS →

Gulf of Corinth

993

E65

33 **Ancient Corinth**

Ligourio

70

70

2 ● **Epidauros**

Trahia

A R G O L I D

Didima

Drepano

Assini

Ermioni

Kranidi

Methana

Poros

Galatas

Hydra

3 ● **Porto Heli**

Gulf of Argolis

4 ● **Tolo**

19 **Tiryns**

Mycenae see detail map **21–31**

20 **Argos**

Lerna

Myloi

Nafplion see detail map **5–18**

Ayios Andreas

20 miles
30 km

Northern Peloponnese

For the ancient Greeks the isthmus was strategically important for both trade and defense; Corinth, with harbors on either side of the isthmus, grew wealthy on the lucrative east–west trade. Ships en route from Italy and the Adriatic to the Aegean had to sail around the Peloponnese, so in the 7th century BC a paved roadway called the Diolkos was constructed across the isthmus, over which ships were hauled using rollers. You can still see remnants near the bridge at the western end of the modern canal. Nero was the first to begin cutting a canal, supposedly striking the first blow, with a golden pickax, in AD 67, a task he then turned over to 6,000 Jewish prisoners. But the canal project died with Nero the following year, and the roadway was used until the 13th century. The modern canal, built 1882–93, was cut through 285 feet of rock to sea level. The impressive sight is a fleeting one if you are speeding by on the highway, so keep a sharp lookout. A well-marked turnoff leads to the tourist area, which has many restaurants (best avoided) and souvenir shops, as well as an overlook above the canal.

▶ ❶ **Isthmia,** an ancient sanctuary dedicated to Poseidon, 1 km (½ mi) west of the canal, isn't much to look at today, but in antiquity it was an important place. From 580 BC, this was the site of the Isthmian Games, biennial athletic and musical competitions on a par with those at Nemea, Delphi, and Olympia. Little remains of the ancient city, since its buildings were dismantled for stone to repair the Isthmian wall and to build a large fortress. Better preserved are the remains of the fortress, called the **Hexamilion,** and of the **wall** (east of the sanctuary is a stretch that rises more than 20 feet). The remains of a **Roman bath** include some good mosaics. A museum near the site entrance contains objects uncovered in excavations over the years. ⊠ *Off Hwy. 94* ☎ *0741/37244* ⊕ *www. culture.gr* ≦ *€2* ⊘ *May–Oct., daily 8–7; Nov.–Apr., daily 8–3.*

Epidauros

Επίδαυρος

❷ *62 km (38 mi) south of the isthmus, 25 km (15 mi) east of Nafplion.*

Fodor'sChoice
★

The Sanctuary of Asklepios remains world renowned for one thing: the **Theater at Epidauros,** the best-preserved Greek theater anywhere because it was covered up sometime in antiquity and had to be dug out. Built in the 4th century BC with 14,000 seats, the theater was never remodeled in antiquity, and because it was rather remote, the stones were never quarried for secondary building use. The extraordinary qualities of the theater were recognized even in the 2nd century AD. Pausanias of Lydia, the 2nd-century AD traveler and geographer, wrote, "The Epidaurians have a theater in their sanctuary that seems to me particularly worth a visit. The Roman theaters have gone far beyond all the others in the world . . . but who can begin to rival Polykleitos for the beauty and composition of his architecture?" In addition, the acoustics of his theater are so perfect that even from the last of the 55 tiers every word can be heard. Test this fact out during the **summer drama festival,** with its outstanding productions.

The condition of the rest of the **Sanctuary of Asklepios,** dedicated to the god of healing and the most important healing center in the ancient world, does not match the theater but is in the midst of a decades-long restoration project. Some copies of its sculptures are in the **site museum,** but the originals are in the National Archaeological Museum in Athens. An exhibit of ancient medical implements is of interest, as are detailed models of the sanctuary and blueprints. Heading south from the isthmus on Highway 70, don't take the turnoffs for Nea Epidauros or Palaio Epidauros; follow the signs that say "Ancient Theatre of Epidauros." ✉ *Off Hwy. 70 near Ligourio* ☎ *27530/23009* ⊕ *www.culture.gr* 🎫 *€6* ☉ *May–Oct., daily 8–7:30; Nov.–Apr., daily 8–5.*

Where to Eat

★ ¢–$$ ✕ **Leonidas.** Seating in a rear garden in summer and in front of a fire in winter adds to the pleasure of dining at this friendly taverna. The grilled pork chops are excellent, as are the moussaka and the stuffed vine leaves in egg-lemon sauce. Dessert choices are brandy-and-cinnamon-laced *revani* (semolina cake) or luscious *kataifi* (shredded dough filled with chopped pistachio nuts) topped with *kaimaki* (clotted cream). The owner may walk you around to show off his photos of celebs who have dined here. Many actors and audience members dine here on performance nights, so reserve in advance on those days. ✉ *Epidauros main Rd.* ☎ *27530/22115* 🖃 *V.*

The Arts

The **Festival of Ancient Drama** (✉ Off Hwy. 70 near Ligourio) in the theater at Epidauros offers memorable performances from late June through August, Friday and Saturday only, at 9 PM. All productions are of ancient Greek drama in modern Greek, many presented by the national theater troupe. Actors are so expressive (or often wear ancient masks to signal the mood) that you can enjoy the performance even if you don't know a word of Greek. Get to the site early (and bring a picnic lunch or have a drink or a light meal at the excellent Xenia Café on-site), because watching the sun set behind the mountains and fields of olives and pines is unforgettable. The festival sells tickets a short time before performance days at the theater.

You can buy tickets through the **Athens and Epidaurus Festival Box Office** (✉ Panepistimiou 39, in arcade, Athens ☎ 210/928–2900 ☉ Weekdays 8:30 AM–4 PM) or purchase tickets online at (⊕ www.hellenicfestival. gr). Tickets are also available at the box office of the **Theatre of Epidaurus** (☎ 27530/22026 ☉ June–Sept., Mon.–Thurs. 9–2 and 7 PM–8 PM, Fri. and Sat. 9:30–9:30). Tickets are €17–€40. Many tour operators in Athens and Nafplion offer tours that include a performance at Epidauros. On the days of performances, four or five buses run between Nafplion and the theater; there's service to Nafplion after the play. Look for those that say THEATER or EPIDAUROS, not NEA EPIDAUROS or ARCHEA EPIDAUROS.

Porto Heli

Πόρτο Χέλι

❸ *54 km (33 mi) south of Epidauros, 81 km (50 mi) southeast of Nafplion.*

A booming but undistinguished summer resort favored by Germans on
package tours, Porto Heli is well supplied with tavernas, restaurants,
souvenir shops, and discos. If you're in search of traditional Greek culture, look elsewhere. Even the beach isn't particularly remarkable. In
fact, the only reason to venture out here is to take in the stark mountain scenery on the drive from Nafplion or Epidauros and to see, on the
south side of the bay, the **submerged ruins of the ancient city of Halieis.**

Where to Stay

$$$ 🏨 **Porto Heli.** If you're eager for a resort experience, you won't do much
better than this modern, well-kept hotel, which caters to package tours
with water sports at the nearby beach, a big swimming pool, and a buf-
fet breakfast. The reasonably large, white and pastel stucco rooms have
modern furnishings and marble floors. Many have balconies facing the
sea. ✉ *Beach road, 21300* ☎ *27540/53400* 📠 *27540/51549* ⊕ *www.
akshotels.com* 🛏 *214 rooms, 10 suites* ⚐ *Restaurant, miniature golf,
2 tennis courts, pool, wading pool, windsurfing, video game room,
playground* ☐ *MC, V* ⦿ *BP.*

Sports & the Outdoors

Although its beach is not as good as others in the vicinity, Porto Heli's
circular bay offers sheltered water for swimming, windsurfing, waterskiing,
and other aquatic sports and is a safe harbor for sailboats. Waterskiing
lessons are given at the **Porto Heli hotel** (✉ Beach Rd. ☎ 27540/53400).

The beach at **Kosta** (✉ South of Porto Heli) is more pleasant and less
crowded than those at Porto Heli.

Tolo

Τολό

❹ *77 km (48 mi) northwest of Porto Heli, 11 km (7 mi) southeast of Naf-
plion.*

A resort center close to Nafplion, Tolo is not unattractive, but the only
reason to spend time here instead of in Nafplion is to party with young
backpackers and lie on the jam-packed beach with the package tour groups
who fill the larger hotels. If you do stay in Tolo, it's easy to join orga-
nized excursions to Mycenae and even Olympia. There is frequent bus
service from Nafplion's KTEL station to Tolo, but if you decide to by-
pass the resort altogether, you won't be missing much.

If you make a beach excursion to nearby Kastraki Beach, also fit in a
bit of history: ancient **Asine** was an important Mycenaean city, although
all that remains are an ancient wall and ramparts in the lower town and
Geometric and Hellenistic traces on the acropolis. It lies on a small penin-

sula that forms the left arm of the Bay of Tolo; the wildflowers here are lovely in spring. At the peninsula's tip is an odd bit of military history: a shattered but still legible mosaic made by Italian soldiers during World War II and dedicated to Il Duce—Mussolini. ⊠ *Near Kastraki Beach, 1 km (½ mi) inland* ☎ *27520/27502* ⊕ *www.culture.gr* ⊠ *Free* ⊘ *Tues.–Sun. 8–2:30.*

Beach

Before Tolo, near the Bronze Age and classical site of Asine, the road takes a sharp turn to the fine **Kastraki Beach** (listed on signs as Paralia Asinis). It has a number of small hotels, is less crowded than Tolo, and offers *pedalos* (rafts with foot pedals), canoes, and Windsurfers for rent.

Where to Stay & Eat

¢–$ ✕ **Akroyiali.** Matriarch Anastasia Moutzouris still cooks up good traditional Greek fare at this beach taverna, which has been here for decades. In summer, you can eat at the tables right on the beach. Appetizers include fried eggplant slices, tender broad beans, marinated octopus, and grilled squid. For a main course, there are fresh fish, as well as *soutzoukakia* (spicy meatballs, Smyrna style), souvlakia, tomatoes and peppers stuffed with rice accented with wild *rigani* (oregano), and grilled chicken. The barrel wine (white and red) is light but potent. ⊠ *Aktis 10* ☎ *27520/59789* ⊟ *No credit cards* ⊘ *Closed Dec.*

¢ ✕🏨 **Hotel Taverna Romvi.** The only restaurant (¢–$) in town to rival Akroyiali also rents pleasant, airy, and very well-priced rooms, all with balconies and half of them overlooking the sea. The shady terrace next to the beach is a good place to linger over a lunch of assorted *mezedes* (appetizers) and fresh fish. You can also try a simple dish of pork, chicken, or lamb, served grilled, seasoned with mountain herbs and lemon, and nicely accompanied by the house's barrel wine. ⊠ *Aktis 32, 21056* ☎ *27520/59331* 🖷 *27520/59890* ⊕ *www.hotel-romvi.gr* ⇋ *20 rooms* ⌂ *Restaurant, refrigerators; no room TVs* ⊟ *MC, V* ⊘ *Closed Nov.–mid-Apr.* �◎| *BP.*

$ 🏨 **Tolo Hotel.** This tidy hotel is especially pleasant because of its hanging-over-the-beach location and a staff that's fluent in several languages and exceptionally helpful. All the units are straightforward in their furnishings and well kept—ask for one with a sea view, in which balconies hover directly over the sand. Rooms facing the main road can be noisy in high season. If the hotel is full or if you require a little extra space, ask about accommodations in one of the other Skalidis properties. ⊠ *Bouboulinas 15, 21056* ☎ *27520/59248* 🖷 *27520/59689* ⊕ *www. hoteltolo.gr* ⇋ *36 rooms in main hotel, 15 rooms in annex across the street* ⌂ *Restaurant, some kitchenettes, cable TV, bar* ⊟ *MC, V* ⊘ *Closed Nov.–Feb.* ◎| *BP.*

Nafplion

Ναύπλιο

▶ *65 km (40½ mi) south of Corinth, 11 km (7 mi) northwest of Tolo.*

Fodor'sChoice
★

Oraia (beautiful) is the word Greeks use to describe Nafplion. The town's old section, on a peninsula jutting into the Gulf of Argos, mixes

Greek, Venetian, and Turkish architecture; narrow streets, often just broad flights of stone stairs, climb the slopes beneath the walls of Acronafplia; statues honoring heroes preside over tree-shaded plazas surrounded by neoclassical buildings; and the Palamidi fortress—an elegant display of Venetian might from the early 1700s—guards the town. The Greeks are right: Nafplion is beautiful. It deserves at least a leisurely day of your undivided attention, and you may want to spend several days or a week here and use the city as the base from which to explore the many surrounding sights.

Little is known about ancient Nafplion, although Paleolithic remains and Neolithic pottery have been found in the vicinity. The town grew in importance in Byzantine times, and it was fought over by the Byzantines and the Frankish crusaders. It has been held by the duke of Athens, the Venetians, and the Turks. In the War of Independence, the Greeks liberated the town, and it briefly became the national capital. During World War II, German troops occupied Nafplion from April 1941 until September 1944. Today Nafplion is once again just a provincial city, busy only in the tourist season and on weekends when Athenians arrive to get away from city pressures.

a good walk

Nafplion is well designed for strolling. If you're ambitious and eager to get your bearings, you might start by climbing the hill of the **Palamidi** ❺ ▶, the elegant Venetian fortress that sits atop its 700-foot peak (take a taxi up the road or tackle the 800-step climb skyward)—an on-a-clear-day-you-can-see-forever view of the Nafplion peninsula and the surrounding Argive plain will be your reward. Once you explore the fort, head back down to relax at the foot of the fort in a pleasant series of tree-shaded parks and squares, including **Kolokotronis Park,** Kapodistria Square, Staikopoulou Park, and Three Admiral Square. As you head north along Syngrou street, another park awaits, with statues that include one of local heroine Bouboulina (⇨ Miniature triangular park, below). You'll pass the large **Palace of Justice** ❻. Turn the corner on which Bouboulina's pedestal sits and walk one block from the harbor along Sophoni street to the **Peloponnesian Folklore Foundation Museum** ❼. Then walk south and turn right on Amalias or on Vasileos Konstantinou to reach **Syntagma (Constitution) Square** ❽, the center of the old town. The latter street is more picturesque, with older buildings; the more commercial Amalias is lined with butcher shops and grocery stores. Immediately to the left as you enter Syntagma from Vasileos Konstantinou street is the **old mosque** ❾. Walking from the mosque (now an art gallery) along the south side of Syntagma, you continue past the Mycenaean-style **National Bank** ❿, a quite fitting overture to the town's **Archaeological Museum** ⓫, on the west side of Syntagma; just beyond it is the formidable government building that occupies another mosque, this one known as the **Turkish mosque** ⓬.

Westward you'll find the **Church of the Virgin Mary's Birth** ⓭, an elaborate post-Byzantine structure. Continuing north, you come to quayside and Philhellenes Square and the **St. Nicholas Church** ⓮. From St. Nicholas westward along the quayside (called Akti Miaouli) is an unbroken chain of restaurants, most just average, and, farther along, better patis-

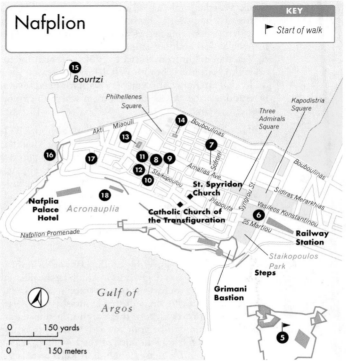

series. It is pleasant in the afternoon for postcard writing, an iced coffee or ouzo, and conversation. From the quay, you can embark on a boat trip out to the miniature fortress of the **Bourtzi** 🅕 in the harbor. Or you can continue walking along the waterfront promenade to the **Five Brothers** 🅖 bastion, and then follow the winding Kostouros street up to **Psaromachalas** 🅗, the picturesque fishermen's quarter. Return to the Five Brothers to continue on the promenade that follows the sea along the south side of the Nafplion peninsula, or instead, go through the tunnel that looks like a James Bond movie set from the parking lot off Kostouros street and take the elevator to the Nafplia Palace hotel and the top of the **Acronafplia** 🅘 fortress. The hotel bar is an excellent place to enjoy a sunset.

Timing

A full exploration of this lovely town takes an entire day; a quick tour, with some omissions, could be done in three hours. While the above itinerary will show you all the main sights, you can get a good sample of Nafplion by following your nose through its winding streets and charming squares. Note that although this walk begins at the Palamidi, you might want to save the climb up to the fort as a special expedition—it's a great spot at sunset.

What to See

⓲ Acronafplia. Potamianou street, actually a flight of stone steps, ascends from St. Spyridon Square toward this imposing hilltop of ruined fortifications, which the Turks once called Its Kalé (Three Castles). Until the Venetian occupation, it had two castles: a Frankish one on the eastern end and a Byzantine one on the west. The Venetians added the massive Castello del Torrione (or Toro for short) at the eastern end around 1480. (If you have trouble locating the Toro, look under the now-deserted Xenia Hotel, which was built on part of it.) During the second Venetian occupation, the gates were strengthened and the huge Grimani bastion was added (1706) below the Toro. The Acronafplia is accessible from the elevator on the west side or by the road from the east side, near the Naplia Palace hotel, which sits on the ruins of the Frankish fort. Most of the remains of fortifications can be explored free of charge on overgrown paths that provide stupendous views over Nafplion and the sea.

⓫ Archaeological Museum. To say that this red-stone building, built in 1713 to serve as the storehouse for the Venetian fleet, is "well constructed" is an understatement; its arches and windows are remarkably well proportioned. It has housed the regional archaeological museum since 1930, and holds artifacts from such sites as Mycenae, Tiryns, Asine, and Dendra. As of this writing, the museum is closed for restoration until further notice. ⊠ *West side of Syntagma Sq.* ☏ *27520/27502* ⊕ *www. culture.gr* ⛀ *Free.*

off the beaten path

AYIA MONI – Before or after exploring Nafplion, drive out the Epidauros road and turn right after 1 km (½ mi) to visit the Byzantine convent and church of Ayia Moni, a place of Christian devotion with a pagan twist. It was built in 1149 by Leo, the bishop of Argos and Nafplion, and an inscription on the west gate expresses the possibility that the Virgin will reward him by absolving him of his sins. In the monastery garden is a fountain said to be the spring Kanathos, where Hera annually renewed her virginity. Admission to the convent is free, but it is generally closed; ring the bell, and the nuns may admit you. They also sell beautiful embroidery.

⓯ Bourtzi. The sight of the Bourtzi, Nafplion's pocket-size fortress in the middle of the harbor, is captivating. Built in 1471, the Bourtzi (or Castelli) was at first a single tower, on a speck of land generously called St. Theodore's Island. Francesco Morosini is said to have massacred the Turkish garrison when he recaptured it for Venice in 1686. A tower and bastion were then added, giving the building the shiplike appearance it has today. In 1822, after the Bourtzi was captured in the War of Independence, it was used to bombard the Turks defending the town. In the unsettled times following the revolution, the government retreated to the Bourtzi for a while; after 1865, it was the residence of the town executioners; and from 1930 until 1970 it was run as a hotel. During the day the Bourtzi is no longer menacing; a tree blooms bright red in its courtyard in spring. Extending from the extreme end of the quay is a large breakwater, the west mole, built by the Turks as the anchor point for a large chain that could be drawn up between it and the Bourtzi, blocking the harbor completely. Some tour boats now circle the island. Boats leave on no fixed schedule from the eastern end of Akti Miaouli; the trip costs about €10. ⊠ *In harbor.*

Catholic Church of the Transfiguration. In the 19th century King Otho returned this Venetian-built church to Nafplion's Catholics. It is best known for the wooden arch erected inside the doorway in 1841, with the names carved on it of philhellenes who died during the War of Independence (Lord Byron is number 10). Note also the evidence of its use as a mosque by the Turks: the mihrab (Muslim prayer recess) behind the altar and the amputated stub of a minaret. The church has a small museum and an underground crypt in which can be found sculptural work commemorating the defeat of the Turks at the hands of the Greeks and philhellenes. ⊠ *Zigomala, 2 blocks south of St. Spyridon.*

Church of Ayios Georgios. On Plapouta street is a square whose showpiece is this church, a Byzantine-era monument set at an angle, with five domes dating from the beginning of the 16th century and a Venetian arcade and campanile. Inside is the throne of King Otho. Around the square are several **neoclassical houses**—the one opposite the church is exceptional. Note the palmette centered above the door, the pilasters on the third floor with Corinthian capitals, the running Greek-key entablature, and the end tiles along the roofline. Nafplion has many other neoclassical buildings; keep your eyes open and don't forget to look up once in a while. ⊠ *Plapouta, 2 blocks west of Syngrou.*

⑬ **Church of the Virgin Mary's Birth.** The church rises next to an **ancient olive tree**, where, according to tradition, St. Anastasios, a Nafpliote painter, was killed in 1655 by the Turks. Anastasios was supposedly engaged to a local girl, but he abandoned her because she was immoral. Becoming despondent as a result of spells cast over him by her relatives, he converted to Islam. When the spell wore off, he cried out, "I was a Christian, I am a Christian, and I shall die a Christian." A Turkish judge ordered that he be beheaded, but a mob stabbed Anastasios to death. A local tradition holds that he was hanged on this olive tree and that it never again bore fruit. The church, a post-Byzantine three-aisle basilica, was the main Orthodox church during the Venetian occupation. It has an elaborate wooden reredos carved in 1870. ⊠ *West of Syntagma Sq.*

⑯ **Five Brothers.** Above the harbor at the western edge of town are the ruins of a fortification known as the Five Brothers, the only remaining part of the wall built around Nafplion in 1502. The name comes from the five guns placed here by the Venetians; there are five here today, all from around 1690 and all bearing the winged lion of St. Mark. ⊠ *Near promontory of peninsula.*

need a break?

Beyond the Five Brothers, near the promontory of the peninsula, a few pleasant cafés and bars line the seaside promenade that follows the southern edge of the peninsula. These are good places to sit with an ouzo and watch the sun set behind the mountains across the gulf; some establishments have created little swimming areas alongside the tables, so it's not unusual to see patrons bobbing around in the water.

Kolokotronis Park. The centerpiece of this park is a bronze equestrian statue surrounded by four small Venetian cannons, which commemorates the revolutionary hero Theodore Kolokotronis (1770–1843). ✉ *Syngrou and Sidiras Merarkhias.*

Miniature triangular park. This contains, inevitably, a monument to **Admiral Konstantinos Kanaris,** a revolutionary hero; across from its far end is the **bust of Laskarina Bouboulina.** Twice widowed by wealthy shipowners, she built her own frigate, the *Agamemnon.* Commanding it herself, along with three small ships captained by her sons, Bouboulina blockaded the beleaguered Turks by sea, cutting off their supplies. **Bouboulina's pedestal** sits on the corner. ✉ *Syngrou, north of Three Admiral Sq.*

Nafplion Promenade. This promenade around the Nafplion peninsula is paved with reddish flagstones and graced with an occasional ornate lamppost. Here and there a flight of steps goes down to the rocky shore below. (Be careful if you go swimming here, because the rocks are covered with sea urchins, which look like purple-and-black porcupines and whose quills can inflict a painful wound.) Before you reach the very tip of the peninsula, marked by a ship's beacon, there is a little shrine at the foot of a path leading up toward the Acronafplia walls above. Little Virgin Mary, or **Ayia Panagitsa** (✉ End of promenade), hugs the cliff on a small terrace and is decorated with icons. During the Turkish occupation it hid one of Greece's secret schools. Other terraces, like garden sanctuaries, have a few rosebushes and the shade of olive and cedar trees. Along the south side of the peninsula, the promenade runs midway along the cliff—it's 100 feet up to Acronafplia, 50 feet down to the sea. All along there are magnificent views of the cliff on which the Palamidi sits and the slope below, known as the Arvanitia.

❿ National Bank. This structure displays an amusing union of Mycenaean and modern Greek architectural elements with concrete. (The Mycenaeans covered their tholos tombs (circular vaults) with mounds of dirt; the bank's ungainly appearance may explain why.) Take a look at the **sculptures** (✉ Square next to National Bank) of a winged lion of St. Mark (which graced the main gate in the city's landward wall, long since demolished) and of Kalliope Papalexopoulou (a leader of the revolt against King Otho), whose house once stood in the vicinity. ✉ *South of Syntagma Sq.*

❾ Old mosque. Immediately to the left as you enter Syntagma Square from Vasileos Konstantinou street is this venerable mosque. It was formerly used for various purposes: as a school, a courthouse, municipal offices, and a movie theater. (The writer Henry Miller, who did not care for Nafplion, felt that the use of the building as a movie theater was an example of the city's crassness.) ✉ *Syntagma Sq.*

❻ Palace of Justice. The gracelessness of this building is magnified by its large size. This monumentality makes it useful as a landmark, however, since the telephone-company (OTE) office and pay phones are in the next building. Nearby, across Syngrou street from the KTEL bus station, is a **square** with a statue honoring Nikitaras the Turk-Killer, who directed the siege of Nafplion during the War of Independence. ✉ *Syngrou, 2 blocks down from Kapodistria Sq.*

★ ▶ ❺ **Palamidi.** Seen from the old part of Nafplion, this fortress, set on its 700-feet peak, is elegant, with the red-stone bastions and flights of steps that zigzag down the cliff face. A modern road lets you drive up the less-precipitous eastern slope, but if you are in reasonable shape and it isn't too hot, try climbing the stairs. Most guidebooks will tell you there are 999 of them, but 892 is closer to the mark. From the top you can see the entire Argive plain and look across the gulf to Argos or down its length to the Aegean.

Built in 1711–14, the Palamidi comprises three forts and a series of free-standing and connecting defensive walls. The name is taken from the son of Poseidon, Palamedes, who, legend has it, invented dice, arithmetic, and some of the Greek alphabet. Sculpted in gray stone, the lion of St. Mark looks outward from the gates. The Palamidi fell to the Turks in 1715 after only eight days. After the war, the fortress was used as a prison, its inmates including the revolutionary war hero Theodore Kolokotronis; a sign indicates his cell. On summer nights the Palamidi is illuminated with floodlights, a beautiful sight from below. ⊠ *Above town* ☎ *27520/28036* 🔲 *€3* 🕙 *May–Oct., weekdays 8:30–7, weekends 8:30–2:30; Nov.–Apr., weekdays 8:30–3, weekends 8:30–2:30.*

need a break? For a respite, head to the pleasant series of tree-shaded **Staikopoulou squares** (⊠ At foot of Palamidi). A tranquil café welcomes the weary, benches give your less-than-bionic feet a break, and children will appreciate the playground and duck pond. At the west end of the area, the Nafpliotes have reconstructed the Venetian Gateway, which originally guarded the entrance to the Palamidi; it commemorates the Venetian recapture of the city in 1487. Standing amid Byzantine and classical ruins, the gateway invites contemplation of the passage of time.

❼ **Peloponnesian Folklore Foundation Museum.** This exemplary small museum focuses on textiles and displays outstanding costumes, handicrafts, and household furnishings. Many of the exhibits are precious heirlooms that have been donated by Peloponnesian families. The gift shop has some fascinating books and a good selection of high-quality jewelry and handicrafts, such as weavings, kilims, and collector folk items such as *roka* (spindles) and wooden *koboloi* (worry beads). ⊠ *Vasileos Alexandrou 1, on block immediately north of Amalias, going up Sofroni* ☎ *27520/28947* ⊕ *www.culture.gr* 🔲 *€4* 🕙 *Mar.–Jan., Wed.–Mon. 9–3; shop daily 9–2 and 6–9.*

⓱ **Psaromachalas.** The fishermen's quarter is a small district of narrow, alleylike streets running between cramped little houses that huddle beneath the walls of Acronafplia. The old houses, painted in brownish yellow, green, and salmon red, are embellished with additions and overhangs in eclectic styles. The walk is enjoyable, but you may feel like a voyeur scrutinizing the private lives of the locals. The pretty, miniature white-washed chapel of **Ayios Apostoli** (⊠ Off parking lot of Psaromachalas) has six small springs that trickle out of the side of Acronafplia. ⊠ *Along Kostouros.*

⑭ St. Nicholas Church. Built in 1713 for the use of sailors by Augustine Sagredo, the prefect of the Venetian fleet, this church near the waterfront has a facade and belfry that are recent additions. Inside, the church is furnished with a Venetian reredos and pulpit, and a chandelier from Odessa. ⊠ *Off Philhellenes Sq.*

St. Spyridon Church. This one-aisle basilica with a dome (1702), west of Ayios Georgios, has a special place in Greek history, for it was at its doorway that the statesman Ioannis Kapodistrias was assassinated in 1831 by the Mavromichalis brothers from the Mani, the outcome of a long-running vendetta. The mark of the bullet can be seen next to the Venetian portal. On the south side of the square, opposite St. Spyridon, are two of the four Turkish fountains preserved in Nafplion. A third is a short distance east (away from St. Spyridon) on Kapodistria street, at the steps that constitute the upper reaches of Tertsetou street. ⊠ *Terzaki, St. Spirdonas Sq., Papanikolaou.*

⑧ Syntagma (Constitution) Square. The center of the old town is one of Greece's prettiest *platias* (squares), distinguished by glistening, multicolor marble paving bordered by neoclassical and Ottoman-style buildings. In summer the restaurants and patisseries on the square—a focal point of Nafpliote life—are boisterous with the shouts and laughter of children and filled with diners well into the evening. ⊠ *Along Amalias and Vasileos Konstantinou.*

⑫ Turkish mosque. Now known as the Vouleftiko (Parliament), this mosque was where the Greek National Assembly held its first meetings. The mosque is well built of carefully dressed gray stones. Legend has it that the lintel stone from the Treasury of Atreus was used in the construction of its large, square-domed prayer hall. ⊠ *Staikopoulou next to Archaeological Museum and behind National Bank.*

Beaches

The closest sandy beach to Nafplion is **Karathona,** about 3 km (2 mi) south of town by road; the pine-backed sands are favored by Greek families with picnic baskets and serviced by buses. This is an ideal spot for kids, since the waters remain shallow far out into the bay. The resort town of Tolo is a short bus ride (€0.90) from the main station; service every hour) or a reasonably priced taxi ride (about €15); beware, though, that the beach at Tolo is packed solid with sunburnt northern Europeans in the warm months.

In Nafplion, **Arvanitia Beach** (⊠ South side of town, nestled between Acronafplia and the Palomides), is not really a beach but a seaside perch made of smooth rocks and backed by fragrant pines. This is a good place for a quick plunge after a day of sightseeing. Changing cabins, shaded cabanas, a snack bar, and an ouzeri are on the premises. You can walk to Arvanitia by following the seaside promenades south of town, and, if you're up for a hike, from there follow a dirt track that hugs the coastline past several coves that are nice for swimming.

Where to Stay & Eat

It's a Nafplion tradition to have dessert at one of the cafés on Syntagma Square or the *zacharoplasteia* (patisseries) on the harbor. Lingering over an elaborate ice-cream concoction or after-dinner drink is a memorable way to wrap up an evening. Tempting, too, is the traditional Italian *gelato* (ice cream) at the Antica Gelateria di Roma (corner of Farmakopoulou and Komninou).

$–$$ ✕ **Arapakos.** Nafplion locals are demanding when it comes to seafood, so it's a credit to this attractive, nautical-theme taverna that locals pack in to enjoy expert preparations of fresh catches. The kitchen sends out such traditional accompaniments as *tzatziki* (yogurt garlic dip) and oven-roasted vegetables of the season, as well as grilled lamb chops and chicken fillets. ⊠ *Bouboulinas 79* ☎ *27520/2767* ▭ *No credit cards.*

★ **¢–$$** ✕ **Paleo Archontiko.** Seating here is in the ground floor of an old stone mansion or on the narrow street in front. Tassos Koliopoulos and his wife, Anya, oversee the ever-changing menu, which highlights such specialties as beef *stifado* (casserole slow-cooked with tomatoes and small onions) and *krassato* (rooster in wine sauce). It's not unusual for a musician to wander by and serenade the diners, another reason the place is wildly popular with locals (it's best to reserve on weekends and in high season). ⊠ *Siokou and Ipsilantou, behind Commercial Bank, 1 block from Epidauros Hotel* ☎ *27520/22449* ▭ *No credit cards.*

¢–$ ✕ **Kanakarakis.** A quiet lane behind the waterfront is the site for this local favorite, which occupies a beautiful, high-ceiling, wood-beamed room. Choose among delicious mezedes such as *saganaki* (fried cheese); eggplant salad; and *pites* (pies) filled with wild greens, chicken, pumpkin, and cheese. Main dishes include moist grilled chicken and lamb *souvla* ("on a spit"). Save room for desserts; the kataifi (shredded wheat pastry) and *karidopita* (rich walnut cake) are luscious. ⊠ *Vasileos Olgas 18* ☎ *27520/25371* ▭ *No credit cards.*

¢–$ ✕ **Ta Fanaria.** Staikopoulou street is one long outdoor dining room, with dozens of tourist-oriented tavernas serving night and day, and this popular place is leagues ahead of its neighbors. The kitchen concentrates on excellent preparations of such staples as *ladera* (vegetables cooked in olive oil), charcoal-grilled lamb ribs, and *imam bayilda* (eggplant stuffed with onions), and serves them beneath a grape arbor in a quiet lane next to the restaurant. ⊠ *Staikopoulou 13* ☎ *27520/27141* ▭ *V.*

$$$$ ⬠ 🖼 **Amphitryon Hotel.** Sea views fill every window here. The airy, stylish, and contemporary guest rooms all open to teakwood decks. Open-air lounges make the most of sea breezes. Though the old city is just a few steps away, you may feel like you're mid-sea on a ship, a pretty swanky one: mattresses are remote controlled to conform to the shape of your body, drapes open at the push of a button, bathrooms are equipped with Jacuzzis, and some showers double as steam cabinets. As of this writing, guests may use the pools at the sister hotel, the Nafplia Palace, while the Amphitryon installs its own. ⊠ *Spiliadou, 21100* ☎ *27520/70700* 📠 *27520/28783* ⊕ *www.amphitryon.gr* ⌨ *42 rooms, 3 suites* ⚒ *Restaurant, room service, in-room fax, in-room safes, in-room hot tubs, minibars, cable TV, in-room DVD, in-room broadband, bar* ▭ *AE, MC, V* ⧖ *BP.*

$$$$ 🖼 **Nafplia Palace.** An elevator whisks you up to the extensive grounds of this dramatic and very expensive hotel, built on the ruins of the Frankish fortification atop Acronafplia. Public spaces tend to be cavernous and austere, but the delightful pine-scented terraces and swimming pools seem to hang in midair, high above the city and bay. Spacious rooms (under renovation) in the main building have exposed stonework, terraces, marble bathrooms, and separate dressing areas. Rooms and suites in the "villas" wing are even snazzier, with sumptuous bathrooms and chic modern furnishings; some have private pools. ☒ *Acronafplia, 21100* ☎ *27520/28981 through 27520/28985* 🖶 *27520/ 28783* ⊕ *www.helioshotels.gr* ⤷ *80 rooms, 4 suites* 🍴 *2 restaurants, snack bar, room service, minibars, cable TV, in-room DVD in some rooms, in-room broadband in some rooms, 2 pools, bar* ▤ *AE, MC, V* ⌘ *BP.*

$$ 🏨 **King Othon II.** The family that owns the King Othon I also operates this "branch" in a neighboring mansion. Rooms at this second lodging are larger and have the same high ceilings and ornate, neoclassical detailing. Many are set up like suites, with separate sitting areas; a number have sea views. Breakfast is served on a rear terrace. ☒ *Spiliadou 5, 21100* ☎ *27520/97790* ⤷ *10 rooms* 🍴 *Minibars* ▤ *AE, MC, V* ⌘ *BP.*

★ $ 🏨 **Hotel Latini.** This handsomely restored old house feels like a well-appointed private home. Just off the waterfront in the center of town, there are views of the bay and palm trees in an adjoining square. The top-floor suite is especially commodious, with sloping ceilings and two balconies, but all guest rooms are graciously appointed and have sparkling bathrooms. An elaborate breakfast is served in a pleasant room opening onto a narrow lane of the old town. ☒ *Othonos 47, 21100* ☎ *27520/ 96470* 🖶 *27520/96471* ✉ *latini@altecnet.gr* ⤷ *9 rooms, 1 suite* 🍴 *Minibars* ▤ *AE, MC, V* ⌘ *BP.*

$ 🏨 **King Othon I.** This gracious neoclassical mansion has decorative rosette ceilings and a curving wooden staircase leading to the upper floor. The high-ceilinged rooms are pleasantly decorated in a turn-of-the-20th-century style; those on the ground floor are a bit small, as are bathrooms throughout. Breakfast is served in the lovely garden at the side of the house. ☒ *Farmakopoulou 4, 21100* ☎ *27520/27585* 🖶 *27520/ 27595* ⤷ *11 rooms* 🍴 *Refrigerators* ▤ *AE, MC, V* ⌘ *BP.*

¢–$ 🏨 **Byron.** A great deal of charm prevails here, from the simply but tastefully decorated rooms, with Turkish carpets and the odd sloping ceiling, to the outdoor patio set atop an old Turkish *hamam* (bath). The staff is quite welcoming, and the location at the top of the old town, up the street from the church of Ayiou Spiridona, is delightful (though you might want to call ahead and ask for directions on the easiest way to reach the hotel with your baggage). Breakfast is an additional €6. ☒ *Platonos 16, Pl. Kapodistriou, 21100* ☎ *27520/22351* 🖶 *27520/26338* ⊕ *www.byronhotel.gr* ⤷ *14 rooms, 4 studios* 🍴 *In-room safes, minibars* ▤ *AE, MC, V.*

¢ 🏨 **Epidauros.** The owner of this simple hotel brims with pride over his establishment, one of the first hotels in Nafplion, which occupies a former merchant prince's home and an adjoining building. Rooms are spartan, but breezy balconies provide a nice perch above the pedestrian lanes of the old town, and Syntagma Square is a block away. ☒ *Kokinou 2, 21100* ☎ *27520/27541* ⤷ *35 rooms, 25 with bath* 🍴 *No room phones* ▤ *No credit cards.*

¢ 🏨 **Tirins Hotel.** Run by the same owners as the Epidauros, the surroundings at this hotel are no-frills but sparkling clean. The appeal is the location near the seafront—in the center of the old town. Breakfast is not served, which is a good excuse to sit at a nearby café and watch the morning routine in Nafplion. ⊠ *Othonos 41, 21100* 🖼🖼 *27520/ 27541* 🗪 *12 rooms* ♢ *No room phones* ▤ *No credit cards.*

Nightlife

BARS & DISCOS **Paleo Lichnari** (⊠ Bouboulinas 39), a restaurant-club along the eastern end of the waterfront, presents live Greek *rembetika* (urban blues) and popular music every weekend and some weeknights in summer; it's frequented by vacationing Greeks who usually arrive after midnight.

Shopping

Many stores in Nafplion sell tacky reproductions of bronzes, frescoes, and vase paintings, which your family, friends, and coworkers will probably stash away and soon forget. But a number of tasteful shops sell fine-quality merchandise, including smart sportswear. For antiques and woven goods, such as colorful *tagaria* (shepherds' shoulder bags), head toward the end of Vassilos Konstantinou street near the bus station; several shops here also sell dried herbs and natural honey.

★ **Agynthes** (⊠ Siokou 10 🖼 27520/21704 or 27520/22380), showcases handwoven and naturally dyed woolens, cotton, and silks, some of which have been fashioned into chic scarves and other apparel. **Helios** (⊠ Siokou 4 🖼 27520/22329), carries a distinctive line of stylish bric-a-brac for the home, along the lines of brass lanterns and candlesticks. The **Komboloi Museum** (⊠ Staikopoulou 25 🖼 27520/21618 🗩 €2), in an old Nafpliote home, has a shop on the ground floor that sells antique and new worry beads and attractive beaded key chains. The museum's exhibits of historic worry beads are fascinating. **Odyssey** (⊠ Syntagma Sq. 🖼 No phone) is the best place in Nafplion for newspapers and books in English; the owners are very helpful if you ★ need advice or directions. The **Peloponnesian Folklore Foundation Museum Shop** (⊠ Vasileos Alexandrou 1, on block immediately north of Amalias, going up Sofroni 🖼 27520/28947) stocks an appealing array of merchandise that includes jewelry, candlesticks, and other gift items. **To Kobologaki T'Anaplioy** (⊠ Palpouta 19 🖼 27520/23990) carries a large selection of amber beads, strung into stunning necklaces and bracelets.

Tiryns

Τίρυνθα

★ ⑲ *5 km (3 mi) north of Nafplion.*

Partly obscured by citrus trees are the well-preserved ruins of the Mycenaean acropolis of Tiryns, more than 3,000 years old. Some people skip the site, but if you see this citadel before touring Mycenae, you can understand those rambling ruins more easily. Homer describes Tiryns as "the wall-girt city," and Pausanias, writing in the 2nd century AD, gave the cyclopean walls his highest praise: "Now the Hellenes have a mania for admiring that which is foreign much more than that which is in their own land . . . whilst they bestow not a word on the treasure-house of

Minyas or the walls of Tiryns, which nevertheless are fully as deserving of admiration." The modern writer Henry Miller was repelled by the place, as he records in *The Colossus of Maroussi:* "Tiryns is prehistoric in character. . . . Tiryns represents a relapse. . . . Tiryns smells of cruelty, barbarism, suspicion, isolation." Today the site seems harmless, home to a few lizards who timidly sun themselves on the Bronze Age stones. Archaeological exploration of the site, which still continues, shows that the area of the acropolis was occupied in Neolithic times, about 7,000 years ago.

The citadel makes use of a long, low outcrop, on which was set the circuit wall of gigantic limestone blocks of the type called "cyclopean" because the ancients thought they could have been handled only by the giant cyclops—the largest block is estimated at more than 15 tons. Via the **cyclopean ramp** the citadel was entered on the east side, through a gate leading to a narrow passage between the outer and inner walls. You could then turn right, toward the residential section in the **lower citadel,** or to the left toward the **upper citadel** and **palace.** The heavy **main gate** and **second gate** blocked the passage to the palace and trapped attackers caught between the walls. After the second gate, the passage opens onto a rectangular **courtyard,** whose massive left-hand wall is pierced by a **gallery of small vaulted chambers,** or casemates, opening off a **long, narrow corridor** roofed by a **corbeled arch.** (The chambers were possibly once used to stable horses, and the walls have been worn smooth by the countless generations of sheep and goats who have sheltered there.) This is one of the famous galleries of Tiryns; another such gallery at the southernmost end of the acropolis also connects a series of five casemates with sloping roofs.

An elaborate entranceway leads west from the court to the upper citadel and palace, at the highest point of the acropolis. The complex included a colonnaded **court;** the great *megaron* (main hall) opened onto it and held the royal throne. Surviving fragments suggest that the floors and the walls were decorated, the walls with frescoes (now in the National Archaeological Museum in Athens) depicting a boar hunt and women riding in chariots. Beyond the megaron, a large **court** overlooks the houses in the lower citadel; from here, a long **stairway** descends to a small **postern gate** in the west wall. At the excavated part of the lower acropolis a significant discovery was made: two parallel **tunnels,** roofed in the same way as the galleries on the east and south sides, start within the acropolis and extend under the walls, leading to **subterranean cisterns** that ensured a continuous water supply.

From the palace you can see how Tiryns dominated the flat, fertile land at the head of the Gulf of Argos. Pioneering German archaeologist Heinrich Schliemann (1822–90), in his memoirs, waxed rhapsodic when recalling this scene: "The panorama which stretches on all sides from the top of the citadel of Tiryns is peculiarly splendid. As I gaze northward, southward, eastward, or westward, I ask myself involuntarily whether I have elsewhere seen aught so beautiful . . . " The view would have been different in the Late Bronze Age: the ancient shoreline was nearer to the citadel, and outside the walls there was an extensive settlement. Profitis Ilias, the prominent hill to the east, was the site of the Tiryns cemetery. ✉ *Off road to Argos, on low hill past suburbs of Nafplion* ☎ *27520/22657* ⊕ *www.culture.gr* 🎫 *€3* ⊙ *May–Oct., daily 8–7; Nov.–Apr., daily 8:30–3.*

Argos

Άργος

❷⓿ *12 km (7½ mi) northwest of Nafplion, 7 km (4½ mi) northwest of Tiryns.*

On the western edge of the Argive plain, amid citrus groves, is the city of Argos (population 21,000), the economic hub of the region. The fall of Mycenae and Tiryns at the close of the Late Bronze Age proved favorable for Argos. Under King Pheidon, Argos reached its greatest power in the 7th century BC, becoming the chief city in the Peloponnese. In the mid-5th century BC, it consolidated its hold on the Argive plain by eradicating Mycenae and Tiryns. But like Corinth, Argos was never powerful enough to set its own course, following in later years the leadership of Sparta, Athens, and the Macedonian kings. Twice in its history, women are said to have defended Argos: once in 494 BC when Telesilla the poetess (who may be mere legend) armed old men, boys, and women to hold the walls against the Spartans; and again in 272 BC when Pyrrhus, king of Epiros, who was taking the city street by street, was felled from above by an old woman armed with a tile.

Remains of the classical city are scattered throughout the modern one, and you can see in a small area the extensive **ruins** of the Roman bath, *odeon* (a roofed theater), and agora, or market. The theater is especially striking, and its well-preserved seats climb a hillside. ✉ *Tripoleos* 🎫 *Free* ⊙ *Tues.–Sun. 8:30–3.*

The **Archaeological Museum** houses a small but interesting collection of finds from the classical city. ✉ *Off main square, Ayios Petros* ☎ *27510/ 68819* ⊕ *www.culture.gr* 🎫 *€2* ⊙ *Tues.–Sun. 8:30–3.*

The **Kastro,** a Byzantine and Frankish structure, incorporates remnants of classical walls and was later expanded by the Turks and Venetians. It's quite a hike to get to, but your reward will be an unsurpassed view of the Argolid plain. Nestle yourself into a ruined castle wall to guard against the fierce wind and ponder the mysteries of the long-lost Mycenaean civilization. ✉ *On top of hill above town* 🎫 *Free* ⊙ *Daily 8–6.*

Shopping

On Saturday morning the main square is transformed into a huge household-merchandise and produce market (dwarfing that at Nafplion). It's more fun than yet another tourist shop, and you can often find good souvenirs, such as wooden stamps used to impress designs on bread loaves, at prices that haven't been inflated. Argos is also well known throughout Greece for its ouzo.

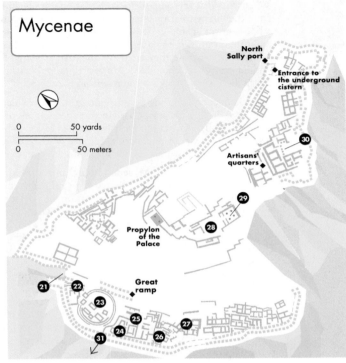

Mycenae

Μυκήνες

9 km (5½ mi) north of Argos, 21 km (13 mi) north of Nafplion.

The ancient citadel of Mycenae, which Homer described as "rich in gold," stands on a low hill, wedged between sheer, lofty peaks but separated from them by two deep ravines. The gloomy, gray ruins are hardly distinguishable from the rock beneath; it's hard to believe that this kingdom was once so powerful that it ruled a large portion of the Mediterranean world, from 1500 BC to 1100 BC. This is one site that should be seen after you have read a concise historical and mythological summary—only then will the setting come to life. The major archaeological artifacts from the dig are in the National Archaeological Museum in Athens, so seeing these first will also add to your appreciation. The most famous object from the treasure found here is the so-called Death Mask of Agamemnon, a golden mask that 19th-century archaeologist Heinrich Schliemann found in the last grave he excavated. He was ecstatic, convinced this was the mask of the legendary king—but it is now known that this is impossible, since the mask dates from an earlier period.

When you visit this site, make sure that you are adequately protected from the sun by wearing long sleeves and a hat (there is no shade), carry a bottle of water, and wear sturdy walking shoes. The ground is uneven and often confusing to navigate; every week paramedics carry out people who fell because they were not adequately geared for the climb. If you have physical limitations, it's best to go only as far as the plateau by the Lion Gate and view the rest from there.

In their uncompromising severity, these ruins provide a fitting background to the horrors perpetrated by three generations of the cursed family of Atreus. The saga seems more legend than history—but Schliemann's belief in Homer was triumphantly vindicated when he discovered the royal town of Mycenae, which became infamous as Agamemnon's realm.

In the 17th century BC, Mycenae began an extraordinary period of growth in wealth and power that was to influence all of the eastern Mediterranean. The Mycenaean civilization, at first heavily influenced by that of Minoan Crete, spread throughout Greece, and by 1350 BC the Mycenaean culture was predominant, not only on the mainland and in the Aegean but also on Crete. Clay tablets inscribed with Mycenaean Greek writing (called Linear B) have provided information about the society. At its height, the culture centered on palaces, from which kings or princes governed feudally, holding sway over various bakers, bronze workers, textile and perfumed-oil manufacturers, masons, potters, and shepherds. There were merchants, priests and priestesses, possibly a military leader, nobles, and, perhaps, slaves. The dwellings of the elite were decorated with wall paintings depicting processions of ladies, hunting scenes, ox-hide shields, heraldic griffins, and such religious activities as priestesses bearing stalks of grain.

From the list of deities who received offerings, it seems that the Mycenaeans worshipped familiar classical deities, but the bizarre figurines found in a shrine at Mycenae (now in the Nafplion archaeological museum)—along with models of coiled snakes—are scarcely human, let alone godlike in the style of classical statuary. Mycenaeans usually buried their dead in chamber tombs cut into the sides of hills, but rulers and their families were interred more grandly, in shaft graves at first and later in immense tholos tombs—circular vaults, a hallmark of Mycenaean architecture, made by overlapping successive courses of stones while reducing the diameter of the opening, until it was closed with a single stone on top. The tholos was built into a hillside, like a chamber tomb, entered by a long passage, or *dromos,* and covered with a mound of earth. Doors at the end of the dromos allowed the tomb to be opened and reused—not a bad feature, since the average life expectancy of a Mycenaean was about 36 years.

Massive fortification walls and gateways, also Mycenaean specialties, were necessary defenses in a culture whose economy of agriculture and trade was supplemented by occasional raiding and intercity warfare. The Mycenaeans had widespread trade contacts—their pottery has been found in Cyprus, southern Italy, Egypt, and the Levant. Wrecks of trading ships apparently headed toward Greece have yielded ox-hide-shape bronze ingots, aromatic resin, logs of ebony and ivory, and blue glass for jewelry. But the heyday of the Mycenaeans did not last long. Drought, earthquake, invasion, and economic collapse have all been suggested individually and in combination for their fall. Around 1250 BC, arrangements were made to secretly secure the water supplies at Mycenae itself as well as at Tiryns and Athens. Coincidence? Sometime around 1200 many sites, but not all, seem to have suffered some destruction. It is unclear whether this was an uprising, invasion, or earthquake. Recovery and rebuilding took place, but it is likely that the palaces were no longer used, and it is certain that a major shift in political and economic administration was under way. By 1100 BC, when there may have been another round of destruction, Greece was heading into a Dark Age. Writing became a lost art, connections beyond the Aegean were nearly severed, and many sites were abandoned.

★ ㉑ In 1841, soon after the establishment of the Greek state, the Archaeological Society began excavations of the **ancient citadel,** and in 1874 Heinrich Schliemann began to work at the site. Today the citadel is entered from the northwest through the famous **Lion Gate.** The triangle above the lintel depicts in relief two lions, whose heads, probably of steatite, are now missing. They stand facing each other, their forepaws resting on a high pedestal representing an altar, above which stands a pillar ending in a uniquely shaped capital and abacus. Above the abacus are four sculptured discs, interpreted as representing the ends of beams that supported a roof. The gate was closed by a double wooden door sheathed in bronze. The two halves were secured by a wooden bar, which rested in cuttings in the jambs, still visible. The holes for the pivots on which it swung can still be seen in both sill and lintel.

㉒ Inside on the right stands the **Granary,** so named for the many *pithoi* (clay storage vessels) that were found inside the building and held carbonized wheat grains. Between it and the Lion Gate a flight of steps used to lead to the top of the wall. Today you see a broad ramp leading steeply up to the palace; the staircase is modern. Beyond the granary is the grave cir-
㉓ cle, made up of six **stone slabs,** encircled by a row of upright stone slabs interrupted on the northern side by the entrance. Above each grave stood a vertical stone stele. The "grave goods" buried with the dead were personal belongings including gold face masks, gold cups and jewelry, bronze swords with ivory hilts, and daggers with gold inlay, now in the National Archaeological Museum of Athens. South of the stone slabs lie the re-
㉔ ㉕ ㉖ mains of the **House of the Warrior Vase,** the **Ramp House,** the **Cult Cen-**
㉗ **ter,** and others; farther south is the **House of Tsountas** of Mycenae.

The palace complex covers the summit of the hill and occupies a series of terraces; people entered through a monumental gateway in the north-
㉘ west side and, proceeding to the right, beyond it, came to the **Great Court-yard** of the palace. The ground was originally covered by a plaster coating above which was a layer of painted and decorated stucco. East
㉙ of the Great Courtyard is the **throne room,** which had four columns supporting the roof (the bases are still visible) and a circular hearth in the center. Remains of an **Archaic temple** and a **Hellenistic temple** can be seen north of the palace, and to the east on the right, on a lower level, are the **workshops** of the artists and craftsmen employed by the king.

THE HOUSE OF ATREUS

MYCENAE WAS FOUNDED by Perseus, son of Zeus and Danae, and the Perseid dynasty provided many of its rulers. After the last of them, Eurystheus (famous for the labors he imposed on Hercules), the Mycenaeans chose Atreus, son of Pelops and Hippodamia, as their ruler. But Atreus hated his brother, Thyestes, so much that he offered Thyestes his own children to eat, thereby incurring the wrath of the gods. Thyestes pronounced a fearful curse on Atreus and his progeny.

Menelaus, one son of Atreus, was married to the beautiful Helen and ruled her lands. It was this Helen who was abducted by Paris, beginning the Trojan War. Atreus's heir, the renowned and energetic Agamemnon, was murdered on his return from the Trojan War by his wife, Clytemnestra, and her lover, Aegisthus (Thyestes's surviving son). Also murdered by the pair was Agamemnon's concubine, Cassandra, the mournful prophetess whom Agamemnon had brought back with him.

Orestes and his sister Electra, the children of Agamemnon, took revenge for the murder of their father, and Orestes became king of Mycenae. Another daughter of Agamemnon, Iphigenia, was brought to be sacrificed because someone—Agamemnon or one of the men in the forces of Menelaus—had offended the goddess Artemis by bragging about his hunting skills or killing a sacred animal. Various versions of Iphigenia's fate exist. During the rule of Orestes's son, Tisamenus, the descendants of Hercules returned and claimed their birthright by force, thus satisfying the wrath of the gods and the curse of Atreus.

The works of Homer and the classical plays of Aeschylus, Sophocles, and Euripides are good sources for anyone who wants to delve further into the saga of this tragic family.

---

30 On the same level, adjoining the workshops to the east, is the **House of the Columns,** with a row of columns surrounding its central court. The remaining section of the east wall consists of an addition made in around 1250 BC to ensure free communication from the citadel with the subterranean reservoir cut at the same time. ✉ 9 km (5½ mi) north of Argos ☎ 27510/76585 ⊕ www.culture.gr ▣ Combined ticket with Treasury of Atreus €6 ⊗ Daily 8:30–7.

On the hill of Panagitsa, on the left along the road that runs to the citadel, lies another Mycenaean settlement, with, close by, the most imposing
31 example of Mycenaean architecture, the **Treasury of Atreus.** Its construction is placed around 1250 BC, contemporary with that of the Lion Gate. Like the other tholos tombs, it consists of a passageway built of huge squared stones, which leads into a domed chamber. The facade of the entrance had applied decoration, but only small fragments have been preserved. Traces of bronze nails suggest that similar decoration once existed inside. The tomb was found empty, already robbed in antiquity, but it must at one time have contained rich and valuable grave goods. Pausanias wrote that the ancients considered it the Tomb of Agamemnon, its other name. ✉ Across from citadel of Mycenae ▣ Combined ticket with Mycenae €6 ⊗ Daily 8:30–7.

Where to Eat

¢–$ ✕ **To Mykinaiko.** At this pleasant, family-run restaurant in the modern village, where summer seating is on the front terrace, always ask what has been cooked up as specials that day. You might try *lachanodolmades* (cabbage rolls) in a tart egg-lemon sauce, *papoutsakia* (eggplant "shoes" filled with tomatoes and garlicky ground beef, topped with béchamel), or spaghetti embellished only with tomato-meat sauce and topped with local *kefalograviera* cheese. Sample the barrel wine from nearby Nemea, especially the potent dark red, known as the Blood of Hercules to the locals. ⊠ *Main Rd.* ☎ *27510/76724* ⊟ *AE, MC, V.*

Ancient Nemea

Αρχαία Νεμέα

32 *18 km (11 mi) north of Mycenae.*

The ancient storytellers proclaimed that it was here Hercules performed the first of the Twelve Labors set by the king of Argos in penance for killing his own children—he slew the ferocious Nemean lion living in a nearby cave. Historians are interested in Ancient Nemea as the site of a sanctuary of Zeus and the home of the biennial Nemean games, a Pan-hellenic competition like those at Isthmia, Delphi, and Olympia (today there is a society dedicated to reviving the games).

The main monuments at the site are the **temple of Zeus** (built about 330 BC to replace a 6th-century BC structure), the **stadium**, and an **early Christian basilica** of the 5th–6th centuries AD. Several columns of the temple still stand. An extraordinary feature of the stadium, which dates to the last quarter of the 4th century BC, is its vaulted tunnel and entranceway. The evidence indicates that the use of the arch in building may have been brought back from India with Alexander, though arches were previously believed to be a Roman invention. A spacious **museum** displays finds from the site, including pieces of athletic gear and coins of various city-states and rulers. Around Nemea, keep an eye out for roadside stands where local growers sell the famous red Nemean wine of this region. ⊠ *North of E65 near modern village of Nemea* ☎ *27460/22739* ⊕ *www.culture.gr* ⊡ *Site €3, site and museum €4* ⊙ *May–Oct., Tues.–Sun. 8–7; Nov.–Apr., Tues.–Sun. 8:30–3.*

| en route | As the road (E65) emerges from the hills onto the flatter terrain around Corinth, the massive rock of **Acrocorinth** peaks on the left. The ancient city sat at the foot of this imposing peak, its long walls reaching north to the harbor of Lechaion on the Gulf of Corinth. |

Ancient Corinth

Αρχαία Κόρινθος

★ **33** *35 km (22 mi) northeast of Ancient Nemea, 81 km (50 mi) southwest of Athens.*

West of the isthmus, the countryside opens up into a low-lying coastal plain around the head of the Gulf of Corinth. Modern Corinth, near the coast about 8 km (5 mi) north of the turnoff for the ancient town, is a regional center of some 23,000 inhabitants. Concrete pier-and-slab is the preferred architectural style, and the city seems to be under a seismic curse: periodic earthquakes knock the buildings down before they have time to develop any character. Corinth was founded in 1858 after one of these quakes leveled the old village at the ancient site; another flattened the new town in 1928; and a third in 1981 destroyed many buildings. Most tourists avoid the town altogether, visiting the ruins of Ancient Corinth and moving on. Anyone interested in folklore will certainly want to stop at the notable **Folk Museum** to views exhibits including rare examples of 300 years of bridal and daily wear, old engravings, and dioramas. ✉ *Town wharf, Corinth* ☎ *27410/25352* ⊕ *www.culture. gr* ✆ *€2* ☉ *Tues.–Sun. 8:30–1:30.*

Ancient Corinth, at the base of the massive Acrocorinth peak (1,863 feet), was blessed: it governed the north–south land route over the isthmus and the east–west sea route. The fertile plain and hills around the city (where currants named for Corinth are grown) are extensive, and the Acrocorinth served as a virtually impregnable refuge. It had harbors at Lechaion on the Gulf of Corinth and at Kenchreai on the Saronic Gulf. In the 5th century BC, Corinth was a wealthy city with a reputation for luxury and vice, including a Temple of Aphrodite with more than 1,000 sacred prostitutes. These facts are emphasized too often today—amid all the titillation, the real story of Corinth is lost.

The city came to prominence in the 8th century BC, becoming a center of commerce and founding the colonies of Syracuse in Sicily and Kerkyra on Corfu. The 5th century BC saw the rise of Athens as the preeminent economic power in Greece, and Athenian "meddling" in the Gulf of Corinth and in relations between Corinth and her colonies helped bring about the Peloponnesian War. After the war, Corinth made common cause with Athens, Argos, and Boetia against Sparta, later remaining neutral as Thebes and then Macedonia rose to power.

In the second half of the 4th century BC, Corinth became active once more; in 344 BC the city sent an army to rescue Syracuse, which was threatened by local tyrants allied with the Carthaginians. Timoleon, the aristocrat who led the army, was in self-imposed exile after killing his own brother, who had plotted to become tyrant of Corinth. Corinthian opinion was divided as to whether Timoleon was the savior of the city or merely a murderer, so no one objected to Timoleon's appointment to this dangerous mission (he wasn't present at the time). The Corinthian statesman Teleclides understood the challenge facing Timoleon perfectly, saying, "We shall decide that he slew a tyrant if he is successful; that he slew his brother if he fails." The tyrants were suppressed and Carthaginian armies expelled from Sicily; Timoleon, declared a hero, retired to a small farm outside Syracuse, where he died two years later.

Corinth was conquered by Philip II of Macedon in 338 BC, but it was named the meeting place of Philip's new Hellenic confederacy. After Philip was assassinated, Alexander immediately swooped down on Corinth to meet with the confederacy, to confirm his leadership, and to forestall any thoughts of rebellion.

After the death of Alexander, the climate continued to be profitable for trade, and Corinth flourished. When the Roman general Flamininus defeated Macedonia in 198–196 BC, Corinth became the chief city of the Achaean confederacy, and in fact the chief city of Greece. Eventually the confederacy took up arms against Rome, attacking with more impetuosity than training, and was crushed. The Romans under Lucius Mummius marched to Corinth and defeated a second Greek army, and Pausanias wrote: ". . . Two days after the battle he took possession in force and burnt Corinth. Most of the people who were left there were murdered by the Romans, and Mummius auctioned the women and children." Corinth was razed in 146 BC and its wealth sent back to Rome, and for the next century the site was abandoned.

In 44 BC, Julius Caesar refounded the city, and under the Pax Romana, Corinth became wealthy and prospered as never before; its population (about 90,000 in 400 BC) was recorded as 300,000 plus 450,000 slaves. It was the capital of Roman Greece, equally devoted to business and pleasure, and was mostly populated by freedmen and Jews. The apostle Paul lived in Corinth for 18 months during this period (AD 51–52), working as a tent maker or leather worker, making converts where he could, and inevitably making many enemies as well. He preached to both pagans and Jews, causing the Jewish priests to drag him before the Roman proconsul, although he was acquitted.

The city received imperial patronage from Hadrian, who constructed an aqueduct from Lake Stymfalia to the city, and Herodes Atticus made improvements to its civic buildings. Corinth survived invasions but was devastated by earthquakes and began a long decline with further invasions and plague. After 1204, when Constantinople fell to the Fourth Crusade, Corinth was a prize sought by all, but it eventually surrendered to Geoffrey de Villehardouin (the subsequent prince of Achaea) and Otho de la Roche (soon to be duke of Athens). Corinth was captured by the Turks in 1458; the Knights of Malta won it in 1612; the Venetians took a turn from 1687 until 1715, when the Turks returned; and the city finally came into Greek hands in 1822.

The ancient city was huge. Excavations, which have gone on since 1896, have exposed ruins at several locations: on the height of Acrocorinth and on the slopes below, the center of the Roman city, and northward toward the coast. Most of the buildings that have been excavated are from the Roman era; only a few from before the sack of Corinth in 146 BC were rehabilitated when the city was refounded.

The **Glauke Fountain** is past the parking lot on the left. According to Pausanias, "Jason's second wife, Glauke (also known as Creusa), threw herself into the water to obtain relief from a poisoned dress sent to her by Medea." Beyond the fountain is the **museum,** which displays examples of the pottery decorated with friezes of panthers, sphinxes, bulls, and such, for which Corinth was famous; some mosaics from the Roman period; and marble and terra-cotta sculptures. The remains of a temple (Temple E) adjoin the museum, and steps lead from there left toward the **Temple of Apollo.**

Seven of the original 38 columns of the Temple of Apollo are still standing, and the structure is by far the most striking of Corinth's ancient buildings, as well as being one of the oldest stone temples in Greece (mid-6th century BC). Beyond the temple are the remains of the **North Market**, a colonnaded square once surrounded by many small shops. South of the Temple of Apollo is the main Forum of ancient Corinth. A row of shops bounds the Forum at the far western end. East of the market is a series of small temples, and beyond is the Forum's main plaza. A long line of shops runs lengthwise through the Forum, dividing it into an **upper (southern)** and **lower (northern) terrace,** in the center of which is the bema (large podium), perhaps the very one where the Roman proconsul Gallio refused to act on accusations against St. Paul.

The southern boundary of the Forum was the **South Stoa**, a 4th-century building, perhaps erected by Philip II to house delegates to his Hellenic confederacy. There were originally 33 shops across the front, and the back was altered in Roman times to accommodate such civic offices as the council hall, or *bouleuterion,* in the center. The road to Kenchreai began next to the bouleuterion and headed south. Farther along the South Stoa were the entrance to the **South Basilica** and, at the far end, the **Southeast Building,** which probably was the city archive.

In the lower Forum, below the Southeast Building, was the **Julian Basilica,** a former law court; under the steps leading into it were found two starting lines (an earlier and a later one) for the course of a footrace from the Greek city. Continuing to the northeast corner of the Forum, you approach the facade of the **Fountain of Peirene.** Water from a spring was gathered into four reservoirs before flowing out through the arcadelike facade into a drawing basin in front. Frescoes of swimming fish from a 2nd-century refurbishment can still be seen. The Lechaion road heads out of the Forum to the north. A colonnaded courtyard, called the **Peribolos of Apollo,** is directly to the east of the Lechaion Road, and beyond it lies a **public latrine,** with toilets in place, and the remains of a **Roman-era bath,** probably the Baths of Eurykles described by Pausanias as Corinth's best known.

Along the west side of the Lechaion road is a large basilica entered from the Forum through the **Captives' Facade,** named for its sculptures of captive barbarians. West of the Captives' Facade the row of **northwest shops** completes the circuit.

Northwest of the parking lot is the **Odeon,** cut into a natural slope, which was built during the AD 1st century, but it burned down around 175. Around 225 it was renovated and used as an arena for combats between gladiators and wild beasts. North of the Odeon is the **Theater** (5th century BC), one of the few Greek buildings reused by the Romans, who filled in the original seats and set in new ones at a steeper angle. By the 3rd century they had adapted it for gladiatorial contests and finally for mock naval battles.

North of the Theater, inside the city wall, are the **Fountain of Lerna** and the **Asklepieion,** the sanctuary of the god of healing with a small temple (4th century BC) set in a colonnaded courtyard and a series of dining rooms in a second courtyard. Terra-cotta votive offerings representing afflicted body parts (hands, legs, breasts, genitals, and so on) were found in the excavation of the Asklepieion, and many of them are displayed at the museum. A stone box for offerings, complete with copper coins, was found at the entrance to the sanctuary. Off the lower courtyard are the drawing basins of the Fountain of Lerna. ✉ *Off E94, 7 km (4 mi) west of Corinth* ☎ *27410/31207* 🌐 *www.culture.gr* 🎫 *€4* ⏲ *May–Oct., daily 8–7; Nov.–Apr., daily 8–5.*

Looming over ancient Corinth, the limestone **Acrocorinth** was one of the best naturally fortified citadels in Europe, where citizens retreated in times of invasions and earthquakes. The climb up to Acrocorinth is worth the effort for both the medieval fortifications and the view, one of the best in Greece. The entrance is on the west, guarded by a moat and outer gate, middle gate, and inner gate. Most of the fortifications are Byzantine, Frankish, Venetian, and Turkish—but the right-hand tower of the innermost of the three gates is apparently a 4th-century BC original. On the slope of the mountain is the Sanctuary of Demeter, which you can view but not enter. ✉ *Take road outside ticket office in Ancient Corinth, where taxis often wait for visitors (about €5 for trip up and back); at the tourist pavilion, 3½ km (2 mi) beyond, walk 10 mins to Acrocorinth gate* ☎ *27410/31207* 🌐 *www.culture.gr* 🎫 *€6* ⏲ *May–Oct., daily 8–7; Nov.–Apr., daily 8–5.*

Xylokastro

Ξυλόκαστρο

㉞ *34 km (21 mi) west of Ancient Corinth.*

Xylokastro, a pleasant little town, is perfect if you want to soak your feet after trudging around Ancient Corinth. The road west of town that climbs up Sithas Valley also climbs up to Ano Trikala, an alpine landscape where the peak (second highest in the Peloponnese) stays covered with snow into June.

Beach

A wide, paved promenade along the shore, with a beautiful view of the mountains across the gulf, leads to a good if somewhat pebbly **beach** (✉ Beyond east end of town).

ACHAEA & ELIS

ΑΧΑΪΑ & ΗΛΕΙΑ

Achaea's wooded mountains guard the mountains of Arcadia to the south and mirror the forbidding mountains of central Greece on the other side of the Corinthian gulf. Those who venture into Achaea may find their way to Patras, a teeming port city. Elis, farther to the south, is bucolic and peaceful. This is a land of hills green with forests and vegetation, and it is not surprising that the Greeks chose this region as the place in which to hold the Olympic Games.

Vouraikos Gorge

Φαράγγι του Βουραϊκού

★ ㉟ *Diakofto, the coastal access point: 47 km (29 mi) west of Xylokastro; Kalavrita: 25 km (15 mi) south of Diakofto.*

The Vouraikos Gorge is a fantastic landscape of towering pinnacles and precipitous rock walls that you can view on an exciting train ride. In addition, a road goes directly from Diakofto to Kalavrita; the spectacular 25-km (15-mi) drive negotiates the east side of the gorge.

Diakofto is a peaceful seaside settlement nestled on a fertile plain with dramatic mountains as a background; the village straggles through citrus and olive groves to the sea. If you're taking a morning train up the gorge, plan on spending the night in Diakofto, maybe enjoying a swim off one of the pebbly beaches and a meal in one of several tavernas. After dinner, take a stroll on Diakofto's main street to look at the antique train car in front of the train station, then take a seat at an outdoor table at one of the cafés surrounding the station square and enjoy a *gliko* (sweet). This is unembellished Greek small-town life.

The *Kalavrita Express,* an exhilarating narrow-gauge train ride, makes a dramatic 25-km journey (15-mi) journey between Diakofto and Kalavrita. Italians built the railway between 1889 and 1896 to bring ore down from Kalavrita, and these days a diminutive train, a cabless diesel engine sandwiched between two small passenger cars, crawls upward, clinging to the rails in the steeper sections with a rack and pinion, through and over 14 tunnels and bridges, rushing up and down wild mountainside terrain. Beyond the tiny hamlet of Zakhlorou, the gorge widens into a steep-sided green alpine valley that stretches the last 11 km (7 mi) to Kalavrita, a lively town of about 2,000 nestled below snowcapped Mt. Helmos. The *Kalavrita Express* makes the round-trip from Diakofto four times daily. The trip takes about an hour, and the first train leaves at 7 AM. Comings and goings are well timed so you can do some exploring; in a day's outing, for example, you can alight at Zakhlorou, make the trek to Mega Spileo, continue on to Kalavrita, explore that town, and return to Diakofto by the last train of the day. ⊠ *Diakofto* ☎ *210/323–6747* ✉ *€8 round-trip* ⊙ *Call ahead for schedule.*

Forty-five minutes into its trip, the *Kalavrita Express* pauses at the stream-laced mountain village of Zakhlorou, from where you can hike up a steep path through evergreen oak, cypress, and fir to the monastery of **Mega Spileo** (altitude 3,117 feet). This hour-long trek (one-way) along a rough donkey track gives you superb views of the Vouraikos valley and distant villages on the opposite side. The occasional sound of bells is carried on the wind from flocks of goats grazing on the steep slopes above. It's also possible to take a cab from the village, though they are not always at hand; if you're driving, the monastery is just off the road between Diakofto and Kalavrita and is well marked. The monastery, founded in the 4th century and said to be the oldest in Greece, has been burned down many times, most recently in 1934. It once had 450 monks and owned vast tracts of land in the Peloponnese, Constantinople (now Istanbul), and Macedonia, making it one of the richest in Greece. Mega Spileo sits at the base of a huge (360-foot-high) curving cliff face and incorporates a large cavern (the monastery's name means "large cave"). You can tour the monastery to see a charred black-wax-and-mastic icon of the Virgin, supposedly painted by St. Luke, found in the cave after a vision of the shepherdess Euphrosyne led some monks there in AD 362. Also on display are ornate vellum manuscripts of early gospels and the preserved heads of the founding monks. Modest dress is required; wraps are available at the entrance. ⊠ *Zakhlorou* 🖼 *€2* ☉ *Daily 8–6.*

Where to Stay & Eat

¢ ✕ **Kostas.** This *psitaria* (grill house) is run by a hospitable Greek-Australian family. Grilled chicken is the main attraction, but *horta* (boiled wild greens), huge *horiatiki* (village) salads with a nut-flavor feta cheese, and stuffed zucchini are other reasons to enjoy a meal on the large terrace in warm months or the cozy dining room in winter. ⊠ *Main road coming into town opposite National Bank, Diakofto* 🕿 *26910/43228* ▭ *No credit cards.*

¢ 🏠 **Chris-Paul Hotel.** Rooms in this appealing hotel, just around the corner from the train station, are attractive and well maintained. Each has a balcony overlooking the surrounding orchards. There's a pool in the garden, and the congenial bar and terrace are perfect for a cocktail before dinner. Breakfast is €5 extra, but you'll do better walking over to one of the cafés near the station. ⊠ *Clearly signposted, in orchard close to train station, 25100 Diakofto* 🕿 *26910/41715* 🖷 *26910/42128* ⊕ *www.chrispaul-hotel.gr* ⇘ *24 rooms* ♿ *Pool, bar* ▭ *DC, MC, V.*

¢ 🏠 **Romantzo Hotel.** If you want to spend the night in a romantic setting, the mountain village of Zakhlorou is your place. This aptly named inn is really just a basic refuge. The small, extremely modest rooms have baths and balconies from which you can enjoy the views over the wooded valley. The hotel's restaurant across the way prepares hearty country fare and serves an à la carte breakfast—handy if you're using the hotel as a base for an early-morning hike to the monastery of Mega Spileo. ⊠ *Next to railroad station platform, 25001 Zakhlorou* 🕿🕿 *26920/22758* ⇘ *9 rooms* ♿ *No a/c, no room phones, no room TVs* ▭ *No credit cards.*

⬭ **en route** If you're driving from Diakofto to Kalavrita, make a stop at **Tetramythos vineyards** (⊠ 5 km [3mi] south of Diakofto, Ano Diakofto 🕿 26910/97224). The winery attributes the high quality and refined flavor of its reds and whites to the location of its vineyards on the northern slopes of Mt. Helmos, which protects the grapes from hot winds. The winery operates tours and gives tastings year-round, weekdays 9–4, and weekends 9–7.

Kalavrita

Καλάβρυτα

③⑥ *25 km (15 mi) south of Diakofto.*

The mountain air here is refreshing, breezy, and cool at night, even in the middle of summer, making the town a favorite retreat for people from Patras and Diakofto. The ruins of a **Frankish castle, the Church of the Dormition,** and a **small museum** are worth seeing, but Greeks remember Kalavrita primarily as the site of the Nazis' most heinous war crime on Greek soil. On December 13, 1943, the occupying forces rounded up and executed the town's entire male population over the age of 15 (1,436 people) and then locked women and children into the school and set it on fire. They escaped, but the Nazis later returned and burned the town to the ground. The clock on the church tower is stopped at 2:34 PM, marking the time of the execution. Signs point the way to the **Martyr's Monument** (⊠ Off Vasileos Konstantinou), a white cross on a cypress-covered hill that stands as a poignant commemoration of the 1943 Nazi massacre.

Where to Stay

$$ ⊡ **Filoxenia.** Built in traditional style, this modern hotel caters largely to skiers who enjoy the slopes on nearby Mt. Helmos (accordingly, winter rates are approximately double summer rates). All the rooms have balconies that look either to the gorge or the mountains, and are quite welcoming, with wood floors, contemporary wooden furnishings, and sparkling, well-equipped bathrooms. The friendliness of the staff and the public rooms with their fireplaces add an extra touch of charm as well. ⊠ *Ethnikis Antistasios 10, 25001* ☎ *26920/22290* 🖷 *26920/ 23009* ⊕ *www.hotelfiloxenia.gr* 🖵 *28 rooms* ⭦ *In-room safes, minibars, bar* ▤ *AE, DC, MC, V* ▯◎▯ *BP.*

Sports & the Outdoors

The European path E4 skirts the slopes of Mt. Helmos, and the village of Diaselo Avgou on the mountain has the **B. Leondopoulos Mountain Refuge** for hikers, with a capacity of 12 to 16. Contact the **Kalavrita Alpine Club** (⊠ Top end of Pl. Martiou 25, Kalavrita ☎ 26920/22661), usually open weekdays 7–3. The leading ski facility in the area, the **Kalavrita Ski Center** (⊠ Near Kalavrita ☎ 26920/22661 ⊕ www.kalavrita-ski.gr), is 14 km (9 mi) from town and has 12 ski runs and seven lifts, as well as a restaurant; facilities are open December–April, daily 9–4. **Trekking Hellas** (⊠ Fillelinon 7, 10557 Athens ☎ 210/331–0323 ⊕ www.trekking. gr) runs a six-day "Mountains and Monasteries" hiking tour on Mts. Ziria and Helmos.

Rion

Ρίο

③⑦ *49 km (30 mi) west of Diakofto, 5 km (3 mi) east of Patras.*

Rion was long known as the point from which ferries connected the Peloponnese with Antirion in central Greece; these days, traffic zooms across the Rion–Antirion suspension bridge, providing a much faster route between Rion and the rest of the Peloponnese and other parts of mainland Greece. Rion is distinguished by the **Castle of the Morea,** built by Sultan Bayazid II in 1499. It sits forlorn amid roadways and a field of oil storage tanks. Here the Turks made their last stand in 1828, holding out for three weeks against the Anglo-French forces. Along with the Castle of Roumeli on Antirion's shore opposite, it guarded the narrows leading into the Gulf of Corinth. ⊠ *Waterfront, Rion* ☎ *2610/990691* ⌨ *Free* ☉ *Tues.–Sun. 8:30–7.*

Beach

Ayios Vassilios (⊠ Off E65, near Rion) has received one of the highest cleanliness ratings from Perpa, Greece's ministry of the environment. Even so, crowds from Patras (this is the closest sandy beach to the city); freighter traffic; and the looming presence of the Rion bridge make for a less than idyllic experience.

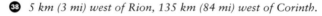

Patras

Πάτρα

38 *5 km (3 mi) west of Rion, 135 km (84 mi) west of Corinth.*

Patras, the third-largest city in Greece and a major harbor, begins almost before Rion is passed. Unless you come to town to catch a ferry to Italy or Corfu, you might want to zoom right by. The municipality has launched an extensive improvement plan, paving the harbor roads and creating pedestrian zones on inner-city shopping streets. Even so, earthquakes and mindless development have laid waste to most of the elegant European-style buildings that earned Patras the nickname "Little Paris of Greece" in the 19th and early 20th centuries.

Like all respectable Greek cities, Patras has an ancient history. Off the harbor in 429 BC, Corinthian and Athenian ships fought inconclusively, and in 279 BC the city helped defeat an invasion of Celtic Galatians. Its acropolis was fortified under Justinian in the 6th century, and Patras withstood an attack by Slavs and Saracens in 805. Silk production, begun in the 7th century, brought renewed prosperity, but control passed successively to the Franks, the Venetians, and the Turks, until the War of Independence. Thomas Palaiologos, the last Byzantine to leave Patras before the Turks took over in 1458, carried an unusual prize with him—the skull of the apostle St. Andrew, which he gave to Pius II in exchange for an annuity. St. Andrew had been crucified in Patras and had been made the city's patron saint. In 1964 Pope Paul VI returned the head to Patras, and it now graces St. Andrew's Cathedral, seat of the Bishop of Patras.

Patras is Greece's major western port and the city has the international, outward-looking feel common to port cities. The waterfront is pleasant enough. You'll find lots of mediocre restaurants, some decent hotels, the bus and train stations, and numerous travel agents (caveat emptor for those near the docks). Back from the waterfront, the town gradually rises along arcaded streets, which provide welcome shade and rain protection. Of the series of large platias, tree-shaded Platia Olga (Queen Olga Square) is the nicest. Patras is built on a grid system, and it is easy to find your way around. For a pleasant stroll, take Ayios Nikolaos street upward through the city until it comes to the long flight of steps leading to the Kastro, the medieval Venetian castle overlooking the harbor. The narrow lanes on the side of Ayios Nikolaos are whitewashed and lined with village-style houses, many of which are being restored.

The **Archaeological Museum's** small rooms are laden with Mycenaean-through Roman-period finds, including sculptures, cups, and jewelry. Many items are from the ancient Roman odeon in town, still in use for a summer festival. It's a pleasant surprise to find these antiquities in a city not known for them. ⊠ *Mezonos 42* ☎ *2610/275070* ⊕ *www.culture. gr* ☜ *Free* ☉ *Tues.–Sun. 8:30–2:30.*

Platia Olga (⊠ 2 blocks uptown from Othonos Amalias, off Kolokotronis) is the most appealing of Patras's many popular squares—locals sip their ouzo and observe their fellow townspeople as they eat, drink, shop, and play in this quintessentially Greek meeting place. Other popular squares include **Platia Martiou 25** and **Platia Ypsila Alonia.**

In the evening the **Kastro** (⊠ End of Ayios Nikolaos, on hill uptown, southeast of train station), a Frankish and Venetian citadel overlooking Patras, draws many Greek couples seeking a spectacular view. The sight of the shimmering ships negotiating the harbor stirs even the most travel-weary.

A **Roman odeon** (⊠ Off Pl. Martiou 25) remains in use in Patras, almost 2,000 years after it was first built. Today the productions of summer arts festivals are staged in the well-preserved theater, which was discovered in 1889 and heavily restored in 1960.

St. Andrew's Cathedral (⊠ At end of Trion Navarhon at western edge of city center) dates from the early 20th century but is built next to a spring that's been used for thousands of years. In antiquity, the waters were thought to have prophetic powers. The church is one of the largest in Greece and an important pilgrimage sight for the faithful—the cavernous interior houses the head of St. Andrew, who spread Christianity throughout Greece and was crucified in Patras in AD 60. The church is open daily 8–8.

Achaia Clauss winery (⊠ 8 km [5 mi] west of Patras, exit 3, Achaia ☎ 2610/ 325051) operates tours and provides tastings. The oldest in Greece, the winery was founded by the Bavarian Gustav Clauss in 1854, and continues to produce a distinctive line of wines. Mavrodaphne, a rich dessert wine, is the house speciality, and oak barrels still store vintages from Gustav's day. The winery, set on a hilltop amid fragrant pines, is open for visits May–October, daily 9–7:30, and November–April, daily 9–5.

Beaches

The nicest beach near Patras is **Kalogria** (⊠ Off E55, about 32 km [20 mi] west of Patras), a long, sandy stretch backed by a pine forest and a grassy plain where cattle graze. Much favored by Greeks, Kalogria is crowded on weekends and in August, and it is often buffeted by bracing winds that can whip up a wild surf. The nearest town is Metohi. A river behind the beach forms estuaries that are great for bird-watching. People swim in them as well, but you may feel like Hercules if you are joined by nonvenomous, yard-long snakes.

Where to Stay & Eat

Avoid most of the indifferent restaurants along much of Patras's waterfront. For lighter fare or after-dinner ice cream, coffee, and pastries, choose one of the cafés along upper Gerokostopoulou street, which is closed to traffic, in Platia Olga, or in Platia Psila Alonia—a favorite watering hole of locals near the Kastro, which, as a bonus, has a panoramic view of the harbor. The streets, including Papadiamatopoulou, leading through the old town up to the south end of the Kastro, have many small *mezedopoleia,* which serve mezedes, Greek-style tapas.

¢–$$ ✕ **To Konaki.** Nouli and Andonis Andrikopoulou take pride in offering local specialties at this homey inn near the train station. *Hortopites* (pies filled with wild greens and feta) and *midhia saganaki* (mussels in a tomato, cheese, and pepper casserole) are among the favorites. On Saturday night a group occasionally plays traditional Greek music. In summer this place closes and the family moves down the coast to a seaside restaurant, set under an arbor on the beach in the idyllic village of Kato Ararchovitika, past Rion, 15 km (9 mi) from Patras. ⊠ *Aratou and Karaiskai 44* ☎ *2610/275096* ☰ *No credit cards* ☽ *Closed May–Aug.*

¢ ✕ **Krini.** The sloping streets heading up to the Kastro are the setting for this *oinopoleia,* or wine shop, which sells wine from barrels to a loyal clientele and serves simple but excellent fare. The rustic taverna room and rear garden are the places to sample delicacies like the spicy meatball sausages known as soutzoukakia or rabbit braised with white wine and rosemary. ⊠ *Pandokratoros 57* ☎ *No phone* ☰ *No credit cards* ☽ *Closed last 2 wks of Aug. No lunch.*

★ $$–$$$ ▦ **Primarolia.** Step through the doors of the most distinctive hotel in town (located in a former distillery), and workday Patras seems far away. Modernist furniture by Greek artists fills the soothing public rooms. Dramatic fabrics and wallpapers add flair to the handsome, well-equipped guest rooms, where the emphasis is on comfort as well as design. Some rooms have balconies with harbor views. ⊠ *Othonos Amalias 33, 26221* ☎ *2610/624900* 🖷 *2610/623559* ⊕ *www.arthotel.gr* 🛏 *11 rooms, 3 suites* ⌂ *Restaurant, in-room safes, minibars, cable TV, in-room data ports, bar, meeting rooms* ☰ *AE, DC, MC, V* ❘⊙❘ *BP.*

$ ▦ **Acropole.** Well-kept, comfortable, and even a bit stylish, the tidy rooms here are filled with light and wonderful views. Sitting on your balcony and watching the sunset might be the highlight of an evening. The port, train and bus stations, and the center of town are all within an easy walk, making this a satisfactory choice if you're stuck in Patras between connections. ⊠ *Zaimi and Kapsali 9, 26221* ☎ *2610/279809* 🖷 *2610/221533* 🛏 *27 rooms* ⌂ *Bar* ☰ *MC, V* ❘⊙❘ *BP.*

¢ ▦ **Rannia.** Just off the harbor and near the train and bus stations, this budget option faces a quiet street and is a nice retreat from the hubbub of Patras. Rooms are simply furnished but spotless and appealing, and all have balconies. ⊠ *Riga Fereou 53, 26500* ☎ *2610/220114* 🖷 *2610/220537* 🛏 *30 rooms* ⌂ *Café* ☰ *MC, V* ❘⊙❘ *BP.*

Nightlife & the Arts

BARS & CAFÉS For nightlife, in general it's best to ask around when you arrive, as the scene changes. On the northern side of Platia Martiou 25 are the steps at the head of Gerokostopoulou street, below the odeon. Closed to traffic along its upper reaches, this street has myriad cafés and music bars, making it a good choice for a relaxing evening. It is the place to be for the young and hip of Patras.

FESTIVALS The Patras tourist office (EOT) can provide information about local festivals and events linked to the EU's designation of Patras as the 2006 Cultural Capital of Europe.

Patras holds a lively **summer arts festival** (⊠ Office: Ayios Georgios 104 ☎ 2610/278730) with concerts and dance performances at the Roman odeon. It usually runs from mid-June to early October.

If you're lucky enough to be in Patras in late January to February, you're in for a treat: the **Carnival** (⊠Office: Ayios Georgios 104 ☎2610/226063), which lasts for several weeks before the start of Lent, is celebrated with masquerade balls, fireworks, and the Sunday Grand Parade competition for the best costume. Room rates can double or even triple during this time; tickets for seats (€10) at the Grand Parade, held in front of the Municipal Theater at Platia Georgiou, are sold at the Carnival office.

NIGHTCLUBS Worth a spin on the dance floor is the music club **Privé** (⊠ Germanou 55 ☎ 2610/274912). Especially in summer, though, the nighttime action centers on the waterfront in Rion.

Shopping

Patras is a major city, and you'll find fashionable clothing, jewelry, and other products here. The best shops are on Riga Fereou, Maizonas, and Korinthou streets, near Platia Olga. An outlet of the venerable London department store **Marks and Spencer** (⊠ Mezonos 68 ☎ 2610/623247) is a good stop if you realize you're missing a vacation essential. Patras also has shops that sell handmade and machine-made Greek icons, which make beautiful decorations. At night in the narrow streets surrounding the Kastro, Greek craftspeople burn the midnight oil in their workshops and stores painting images of saints on wood and stone.

Chlemoutsi Castle

Κάστρο Χλεμουτσίου

39 *56 km (35 mi) west of Patras.*

The little village of Kastro sits at the foot of Chlemoutsi Castle, the best-preserved Frankish monument in the Peloponnese. Geoffrey I de Villehardouin, who built it in a commanding position over the Ionian Sea from 1220 to 1223, named the fortress Clairmont. The Venetians called it Castel Tornese, perhaps on account of the Frankish *tournoi* (coins) minted in nearby Glarentza, stamped with the facade of St. Martin's Church in Tours. The Byzantine despot Constantine Palaiologos captured it in 1427 and used it as a base from which to attack Patras, the last Frankish stronghold. The castle has a huge irregular-hexagon keep, with vaulted galleries around an open court. After 1460 the Turks strengthened the gate and altered the galleries. The Venetians captured the castle in 1687 and shortly thereafter ceded it to the Turks. On the southwest side you can see a breach made by Ibrahim Pasha's cannon during the War of Independence. If the sky is clear, you can get a lovely view of a number of Ionian islands. Basically untended, the castle is open for exploring at all hours. ⊠ *Off E55, Kastro* ⊕ *www.culture.gr* ▨ *Free.*

Beaches

The coast south of Chlemoutsi Castle toward **Loutra Killinis** is a beach resort area and its wide, sandy beach is among the best in Greece. Farther south of Chlemoutsi Castle, near Gastouni, is the fine beach **Katakolo** (⊠ Off Hwy. 9). A bit farther south, near the large commercial town of Pyrgos (and therefore crowded on weekends), is **Spiantza** (⊠ Off Hwy. 9).

Olympia

Ολυμπία

★ ⚐ *65 km (40 mi) southeast of Chlemoutsi Castle, 112 km (69 mi) south of Patras.*

Ancient Olympia, with the Sanctuary of Zeus, was the site of the ancient Olympic Games. Located at the foot of the tree-covered Kronion hill, set in a valley near two rivers, today it is one of the most popular sites in Greece. You'll need at least two hours to see the ruins and the museum, and three or four hours would be better. Modern Olympia, an attractive mountain town surrounded by pleasant hilly countryside, has hotels and tavernas, convenient for visitors to the ancient site.

Although the first Olympiad is thought to have been in 776 BC, bronze votive figures of the Geometric period (10th–8th century BC) reveal that the sanctuary was in use before that date. The festival took place every four years over a five-day period in the late summer during a sacred truce, observed by all Greek cities. Initially only native speakers of Greek (excepting slaves) could compete, but Romans were later admitted. Foreigners could watch, but married women, Greek or not, were barred from the sanctuary during the festival on pain of death. (One woman caught watching was spared, however, since not only all her sons but her husband and father had won Olympic victories.) The events included the footrace, boxing, chariot and horse racing, the pentathlon (combining running, jumping, wrestling, and both javelin and discus throwing), and the *pankration* (a no-holds-barred style of wrestling in which competitors could break their opponent's fingers and other body parts). By and large the Olympic festival was peaceful, though not without problems. The Spartans were banned in 420 BC for breaking the sacred truce; in 364 BC there was fighting in the Altis between the Eleans and the Pisans and Arcadians in front of the crowd who had come to watch the games; the Roman dictator Sulla (138–78 BC) carried off the treasure to finance his army and five years later held the games in Rome. The 211th festival was delayed for two years so that Nero could compete, and despite a fall from his chariot, he was awarded the victory.

The long decline of Olympia began after the reign of Hadrian. In AD 267, under threat of an invasion, many buildings were dismantled to construct a defensive wall; Christian decrees forbade the functioning of pagan sanctuaries and caused the demolition of the Altis. The Roman emperor Theodosius I, a Christian, banned the games, these "pagan rites," in AD 393. Earthquakes settled the fate of Olympia, and the flooding of the Alpheios and the Kladeos, together with landslides off the Kronion hill, buried the abandoned sanctuary.

Olympia's ruins are fairly compact, occupying a flat area at the base of the Kronion hill where the Kladeos and Alpheios rivers join. It's easy to get a quick overview and then investigate specific buildings or head to the museum. The site is very pleasant, with plenty of trees providing shade. It is comprised of the sacred precinct, or **Altis,** a large rectangular enclosure south of the Kronion, with **administrative buildings, baths, and workshops** on the west and south and the **Stadium** and **Hippodrome** on the east. In 1829, a French expedition investigated the Temple of Zeus and brought a few metope fragments to the Louvre. The systematic excavation begun by the German Archaeological Institute in 1875 has continued intermittently to this day.

40 South of the entrance are the remains of a small **Roman bath** and the
41 **Gymnasion,** essentially a large, open practice field surrounded by stoas.
42 The large complex opposite the Gymnasion was the **Prytaneion,** where
the *prytaneis* (magistrates in charge of the games) feted the winners and
where the Olympic flame burned on a sacred hearth. South is the gateway to the Altis, marked by two sets of four columns. Beyond is the
43 **Philippeion,** a circular shrine started by Philip II and completed after
his death by Alexander the Great.

Directly in front of the Philippeion is the large Doric temple of Hera,
44 the **Heraion** (circa 600 BC). It is well preserved, especially considering
that it is constructed from the local coarse, porous shell limestone. At
first it had wooden columns, which were replaced as needed, so although
they are all Doric, the capitals don't exactly match. Three of the
columns, which had fallen, have been set back up. A colossal head of
a goddess, possibly from the statue of Hera, was found at the temple
and is now in the site museum. South of the Heraion are the remains
45 of a 6th-century BC pentagonal wall built to enclose the **Pelopeion**
(Shrine of Pelops), at the time an altar in a sacred grove. According to
Pausanias, the **Altar of Olympian Zeus** was southeast of the temple of
Hera, but no trace of it has been found. Some rocks mark its supposed
location, the most sacred spot in the Altis, where daily blood sacrifices
are said to have been made.

46 There is no doubt about the location of the **Nymphaion,** or Exedra, which
brought water to Olympia from a spring to the east. A colonnade
around the semicircular reservoir had statues of the family of Herodes
47 Atticus and his imperial patrons. The 4th-century **Metroon,** at the bottom of the Nymphaion terrace, was originally dedicated to Cybele,
Mother of the Gods, and was taken over by the Roman imperial cult.
Nearby, at the bottom of the steps leading to the Treasuries and outside
the entrance of the Stadium, were **16 bronze statues of Zeus,** called the
Zanes, bought with money from fines levied against those caught cheat-
ing at the games. Bribery seems to have been the most common offense
(steroids not being available). Olympia also provides the earliest case
of the sports-parent syndrome: in the 192nd Olympiad, Damonikos of
Elis, whose son Polyktor was to wrestle Sosander of Smyrna, bribed the
latter's father in an attempt to buy the victory for his son.

48 On the terrace itself are the city-state **Treasuries,** which look like small
temples and were used to store valuables, such as equipment used in rit-
49 uals. Just off the northeast corner of the Altis is the **Stadium,** which at
first ran along the terrace of the Treasuries and had no embankments
for the spectators to sit on; embankments were added later but were never
given seats, and 40,000–50,000 spectators could be accommodated. The
starting and finishing lines are still in place, 600 Olympic feet (about
630 feet) apart.

50 The **House of Nero,** a 1st-century villa off the southeastern corner of
the Altis, was hurriedly built for his visit. Nearby was found a lead water
pipe marked NER. AUG. Beyond this villa, running parallel to the Sta-

51 dium, was the **Hippodrome,** where horse and chariot races were held. It hasn't been excavated, and much has probably been eroded away by the Alpheios River. Beyond the Altis's large southeastern gate, ap-
52 pended to its southern wall, is the **Bouleuterion** and, south of it, the
53 **South Hall.** The Bouleuterion consisted of two rectangular halls on either side of a square building that housed the Altar of Zeus Horkios, where athletes and trainers swore to compete fairly.

54 In the southwestern corner of the Altis is the **Temple of Zeus.** Only a few column drums are in place, but the huge size of the temple platform is impressive. Designed by Libon, an Elean architect, it was built from about 470 to 456 BC. The magnificent sculptures from the pediments are on view in the site's museum. A gilded bronze statue of Nike (Victory) stood above the east pediment, matching a marble Nike (in the site museum) that stood on a pedestal in front of the temple. Both were the work of the sculptor Paionios. The cult statue inside the temple, made of gold and ivory, showed Zeus seated on a throne, holding a Nike in his open right hand and a scepter in his left. It was created in 430 BC by Pheidias, sculptor of the cult statue of Athena in the Parthenon, and was said to be seven times life size; the statue was one of the Seven Wonders of the Ancient World. It is said that Caligula wanted to move the statue to Rome in the 1st century AD and to replace the head with one of his own, but the statue laughed out loud when his men approached it. It was removed to Constantinople, where it was destroyed by fire in AD 475. Pausanias relates that behind the statue there was "a woolen curtain . . . decorated by Assyrian weavers and dyed with Phoenician crimson, dedicated by Antiochos." It is possible this was the veil of the Temple at Jerusalem (Antiochos IV Epiphanes forcibly converted the Temple to the worship of Zeus Olympias in the 2nd century BC).

Outside the gate at the southwestern corner of the Altis stood the
55 **Leonidaion,** at first a guesthouse for important visitors and later a residence of the Roman governor of the province of Achaea. Immediately
56 north of the Leonidaion was **Pheidias's workshop,** where the cult statue of Zeus was constructed in a large hall of the same size and orientation as the interior of the temple. Tools, clay molds, and Pheidias's own cup (in the site museum) make the identification of this building certain. It
57 was later used as a Byzantine church. North of the workshop is the **Palaestra,** built in the 3rd century BC, for athletic training. The rooms around the square field were used for bathing and cleansing with oil, for teaching, and for socializing. ⊠ *Off Ethnikos Odos 74, ½ km (¼ mi) outside modern Olympia* ☎ *26240/22517* ⊕ *www.culture.gr* ⊠ *€6, combined ticket with Archaeological Museum €9* ⊙ *May–Oct., daily 8–7; Nov.–Apr., daily 8:30–5.*

The **Archaeological Museum at Olympia,** located in a handsome glass and marble pavilion at the edge of the ancient site, has in its magnificent collections the sculptures from the Temple of Zeus and the Hermes of Praxiteles, discovered in the Temple of Hera in the place noted by Pausanias. The central gallery of the museum holds one of the greatest sculptural achievements of classical antiquity: the pedimental sculptures and metopes from the Temple of Zeus, depicting Hercules's Twelve Labors.

The Hermes was buried under the fallen clay of the temple's upper walls and is one of the best-preserved classical statues. Also on display is the famous Nike of Paionios. Other treasures include notable terra-cottas of Zeus and Ganymede; the head of the cult statue of Hera; sculptures of the family and imperial patrons of Herodes Atticus; and bronzes found at the site, including votive figurines, cauldrons, and armor. Of great historic interest are a helmet dedicated by Miltiades, the Athenian general who defeated the Persians at Marathon, and a cup owned by the sculptor Pheidias. ⊠ *Off Ethnikos Odos 74, north of Ancient Olympia site* ☎ *26240/22742* ⊕ *www.culture.gr* ✑ *€6, combined ticket with Ancient Olympia €9* ☉ *May–Oct., Mon. 11–7, Tues.–Sun. 8–7; Nov.–Apr., Mon. 10:30–5, Tues.–Sun. 8:30–3.*

The **Museum of the Olympic Games** is just about the only tourist attraction in modern Olympia. The collection of medals and other memorabilia of the contemporary games is of some, if not great, interest. ⊠ *Spiliopoulou* ☎ *26240/22544* ✑ *€2* ☉ *Weekdays 8–3:30, weekends 9–2:30.*

Where to Stay & Eat

¢–$ ✕ **Aegean.** Don't let the garish signs depicting menu offerings put you off: the far-ranging offerings are excellent. You can eat lightly on a gyro or pizza, but venture into some of the more serious fare, especially such local dishes as fish, oven-baked with onion, garlic, green peppers, and parsley. The house's barrel wine is a nice accompaniment to any meal. ⊠ *Douma, near Hotel New Olympia* ☎ *26240/22540* ▱ *MC, V.*

¢–$ ✕ **Bacchus.** The best restaurants in Greece are often in villages, and Dimitris Zapantis's family-run taverna in the village of Miraka (3 km [2 mi] outside Olympia, along road to Lambia) is one such establishment. Locals start to trickle in around 10:30 PM. Try the delectable chicken with oregano and enjoy an evening in a small village. ⊠ *Miraka* ☎ *0624/22498* ▱ *No credit cards* ☉ *Closed Dec.–Feb.*

¢–$ ✕ **Zeus.** A seat on the attractive terrace gives you a nice view of the comings and going through the center of town. Offerings are straightforward Greek fare, but nicely prepared. ⊠ *Praxitelous Kondili, near Commercial Bank* ☎ *26240/23913* ▱ *MC, V* ☉ *Closed Nov.–Mar.*

$$ ✕⌑ **Europa Best Western.** White stucco, pine, and red tiles offset the somewhat generic resort feel of this hilltop hotel, just above the ancient site. Rooms are large, with queen-size beds, marble bathrooms, and small terraces; most have sunken sitting areas and face the attractive pool, which is set in an olive-shaded garden. The summertime-only outdoor taverna (¢–$$), serves excellent grilled meats and vegetables. It's the best choice in town for an alfresco meal on a warm night. The Greek fare in the handsome, year-round indoor restaurant is commendable, too. ⊠ *Oikismou Drouba, off road to Ancient Olympia, 27065* ☎ *26240/22650 or 26240/22700* ▤ *26240/23166* ⊕ *www.hoteleuropa.gr* ⇗ *78 rooms, 2 suites* ♺ *2 restaurants, refrigerators, cable TV, tennis court, pool, 3 bars, shop* ▱ *AE, DC, MC, V* ⓞ| *BP.*

$$ ⌑ **Olympia Palace.** There's a slick, big-city air at the best hotel in town, with its spacious public rooms, garden café, sleek bar, and shopping mall. The rooms, too, are more sophisticated than those in most other Greek

towns: each has three telephones and most have print bedspreads and wooden furniture. The room rate is often negotiable when the hotel is not full; always ask for the best available price. ⊠ *Praxitelous Kondili 2, 27065* ☎ *26240/23101* ⊠ *26240/22525* ⊕ *www.olympia-palace.gr* ⇨ *58 rooms, 6 suites* ⚐ *2 restaurants, in-room safes, minibars, cable TV, in-room data ports, bar, shops, business services* ☰ *AE, DC, MC, V* ❢❶ *BP.*

★ $ 🔲 **Hotel Pelops.** Suzanna and Theo Spiliopoulou set the gold standard for a small hotel. The stylish and comfortable wood-floor rooms overlook the nearby mountains, and there is a welcoming breakfast room with a large fireplace. Their hospitality extends to dispensing information about Ancient Olympia and other locations in the Peloponnese. They can even provide cooking lessons and other activities; Suzanna is a well-known chef in Greece and will, on request, prepare a Peloponnesian feast for a group. Guests can use the Europa Best Western's pool. ⊠ *Varela 2, 27065* ☎ *26240/22543* ⊠ *26240/22213* ⊕ *www.hotelpelops.gr* ⇨ *26 rooms* ⚐ *Restaurant, bar* ☰ *MC, V* ❢❶ *BP.*

Shopping

★ The shop of the **Archaeological Museum** (⊠ Off Ethnikos Odos 74, north of Ancient Olympia site ☎ 26240/22742) carries an appealing line of figurines, bronzes, votives, and other replicas of objects found in the ruins.

★ At **Atelier Exekias** (⊠ Kondoli ☎ 6936/314054) Sakis Doylas sells exquisite, handmade and hand-painted ceramic bowls and urns, fashioned after finds in Ancient Olympia; the glazes and colors are beautiful.

NORTHERN PELOPONNESE A TO Z

To research prices, get advice from other travelers, and book travel arrangements, visit www.fodors.com.

AIR TRAVEL

There is no commercial plane service to the Northern Peloponnese (the small airport at Patras handles private aviation and limited charters). The closest airports are in Athens and in Kalamata (in the Southern Peloponnese).

BOAT & FERRY TRAVEL

The Nafplion Port Authority and Patras Port Authority can advise you about entry and exit in their ports for yachts. Patras's tourist office (⇨ Visitor Information) is at the port.

HYDROFOILS Hellenic Seaways high-speed car ferries sail four times daily in summer from Piraeus to Porto Heli (two hours; about €23); you can purchase tickets online. In winter the schedule is much reduced.

🛈 **Hellenic Seaways** ⊠ August 25, Heraklion, Crete ☎ 2810/346185 ⊕ www.hellenicseaways.gr. **Nafplion Port Authority** ☎ 27520/27022. **Patras Port Authority** ☎ 2610/341002. **Piraeus Port Authority** ☎ 210/422–6000.

BUS TRAVEL

The association of regional bus companies (KTEL) provides frequent service at reasonable prices from Athens to Patras, Pyrgos (for Olympia),

Corinth, Argos, Epidauros, Nafplion (for Mycenae), and Xylokastro. Buses leave from Terminal A on the outskirts of Athens at Kifissou 100 (take Bus 51 at corner of Zinonos and Menandrou streets, near Omonia Square; from the airport, take Bus E93). Pick up a bus schedule from the Athens EOT (⇨ Visitor Information) or call the number listed below for departure times or seat reservations.

Bargain prices and an extensive network make bus travel a viable alternative to renting a car. Service from Athens to Corinth and Patras, for instance, operates as frequently as every half hour from 6 AM to the late evening, takes only three hours, and spares you a hair-raising drive; the cost is €12.25. In addition to serving major centers such as Nafplion, Argos, Corinth, and Patras, KTEL buses travel to virtually every village in the Northern Peloponnese. Schedules are posted at local KTEL stations, usually on the main square or main street.

🚌 **Terminal A** ✉ Kifissou 100, Athens ☎ 210/512–4910 ⊕ www.ktel.org.

CAR TRAVEL

The roads are fairly good in the Northern Peloponnese, and driving can be the most enjoyable way to see the region, giving you the freedom to visit the sights at leisure. You can take a bus to Patras or Nafplion and rent a car there, or rent a car at the airport in Athens and head south. The toll highway, known simply as Ethnikos Odos, or National Road, runs from Athens to the Isthmus of Corinth (84 km [52 mi], 1¼ hours), and from there continues (toll only in parts) to Nafplion, Patras, and Olympia; the system is well maintained. Have change ready, as a toll of about €2 is collected intermittently. The highway between Corinth and Patras is two lane for the most part and can be dangerous, with impatient drivers using the two lanes as four lanes. Slow-moving traffic is forced onto the shoulder. No speed limit is enforced, and the asphalt becomes very slippery when wet. The accident rate is high.

An alternative route from Athens to Patras is via Delphi and the Rion–Antirion bridge. Many people also enter the region on the car ferry between Italy (Ancona, Bari, or Brindisi) and Patras.

EMERGENCIES The Automobile Touring Club of Greece (ELPA) can assist with repairs and information. During the Epidauros Festival, ELPA road-assistance vehicles patrol the roads around there.

🚗 **Automobile Touring Club of Greece** (ELPA) ✉ Odos Mesoyion 2, Athens ☎ 104 road assistance, 210/606–8800 other information.

EMERGENCIES

Tourist police, who often speak English, can be useful in emergencies; they can also help you find accommodations, restaurants, and sights. Pharmacies, clearly identified by red-cross signs, take turns staying open late. A listing is published in the local newspaper; it is best to check at your hotel to find out not only which pharmacy is open but how to get there.

🚔 Tourist Police **Corinth** ✉ Ermou 51 ☎ 27410/23282. **Nafplion** ✉ Pl. Martiou 25 ☎ 27520/28131. **Olympia** ✉ Douma 13 ☎ 26240/22550. **Patras** ✉ Patreos 53 ☎ 2610/451833 or 2610/451893.

TOURS

CHAT Tours and Key Tours are among the many operators who organize whirlwind one-day tours from Athens to Corinth, Mycenae, Epidauros, and Nafplion; cost is about €75. These no-frills tours, aimed at those who don't expect a lot of hand-holding, can be booked at travel agencies and at larger hotels. CHAT, Key, and other operators also offer a more leisurely two-day tour of Corinth, Mycenae, and Epidauros, with an overnight stay in Nafplion; cost is about €140.

If you are in Nafplion or Patras, many local travel agencies can arrange day tours of the classical sites. Pegasus Cruises and other agencies in Nafplion and Tolo also arrange cruises to Hydra, Poros, and other nearby islands.

🔒 **CHAT Tours** ✉ Xenofontos 9, Athens ☎ 210/323-0827 ⊕ www.chatours.gr. **Key Tours** ✉ Kallirois 4, Athens ☎ 210/923-3166 ⊕ www.keytours.com. **Pegasus Cruises** ✉ Sekeri 10, Tolo ☎ 27520/59430 ⊕ www.pegasus-cruises.gr.

TRAIN TRAVEL

Traveling by train from Athens to some places in the Northern Peloponnese is sometimes convenient and is relatively inexpensive. Trains from Athens depart from the Peloponnissos station; take Bus 057, which leaves every 10 minutes from Panepistimiou, or take Line 2 of the metro to the Larissa station, which is adjacent to the Peloponnissos station.

Trains run from Athens to Corinth, and then the route splits; you can go south to Argos and Nafplion or west along the coast to Patras and then south to Pyrgos and Kalamata. Alternatively you can go directly through the Peloponnese to Kalamata via Tripoli. On the western route the train stops at Kiato, Xylokastro, Diakofto (where a narrow-gauge branch line heads inland to Kalavrita), and Aigion, before arriving in Patras. In summer the trains between Patras and Athens can be crowded with young people arriving from or leaving for Italy on ferries from Patras. Branch lines leave the main line at Kavasila for Loutra Killinis and at Pyrgos for Olympia. If you know you are returning by train, buy a round-trip ticket (good for a month); there is a substantial discount.

There are five departures daily from Athens to Nemea–Mykines–Argos–Nafplion; the trip to Nafplion takes 3 to 5 hours. Thirteen trains run daily from Athens to Corinth, a 2-hour trip; the reliable, more expensive InterCity express takes 1½ hours. Eight trains leave Athens daily for Patras, a trip of 3½ to 4½ hours; the InterCity express is 4 hours. A line running along the west coast connects Kalamata with Patras (6 hours). Going to Olympia by train from Athens isn't worth the trouble; the trip takes almost 8 hours, with a change at Pyrgos.

As of this writing, extensive track work is being done on the Peloponnesian line, with a goal of significantly improving service between Athens and Patras. Check for service interruptions and station changes by contacting one of the offices listed below or in Train Travel in Smart Travel Tips.

🔒 **Greek National Railway (OSE) offices** ✉ Fillelinon 17, Athens ☎ 210/323-6747 ✉ Sina 6, Athens ☎ 210/362-4402. **Patras Railway Station** ✉ Patras ☎ 2610/221311, 2610/

277441, or 2610/273694. **Peloponnissos Station** ✉ Leoforos Theodorou Deligianni, Athens ☎ 210/522-4302.

VISITOR INFORMATION

The Greek National Tourism Organization (GNTO or EOT) has offices in Olympia and Patras. Nafplion has a municipal tourist office across from the OTE (telephone-company) building (✉ Pl. Martiou 25 ☎ 27520/24444). For tourist information and general help in places without tourist offices, it's best to contact the local tourist police, who often speak English and can be extremely helpful. (⇨ Emergencies).

🇬🇷 **Greek National Tourism Organization** ✉ Tsochas 7, Athens ☎ 210/870-7000 ✉ EOT Bldg., 1st fl., Zea Marina, Piraeus ☎ 210/452-2591 or 210/452-2586 ⊕ www.gnto.gr. **Olympia** ✉ Praxitelous Kondili 75 ☎ 26240/23100. **Patras** ✉ Filopimenos 26 ☎ 2610/621992.

Southern Peloponnese

8

BASSAE, METHONI, THE MANI, MYSTRAS & MONEMVASSIA

WORD OF MOUTH

"Monemvassia is called the Gibraltar of Greece. The main street is about 4 feet wide; all materials coming into town must be carried by pack mule. The streets are a maze of twisting alleyways down to the fortress wall. I felt tempted to turn my watch back about five centuries.

. . . The drive around the Mani took us 5 hours but we stopped a lot including at the Pirgos Dirou Caves. The caves are full of water and there is a half hour boat ride through one of the most spectacular caves I have ever seen. Greek mythology places Hades in Mani, and I wonder if this could be the river Styx."

—stanbr

Updated by
Stephen
Brewer

ANCIENT RUINS AND MEDIEVAL MONUMENTS pervade the landscape, along with olive groves, rugged mountains, dizzying gorges, and languorous beaches. Ungainly yet amiable towns like Tripoli, Sparta, and Kalamata are set amid startling natural beauty. Enter the forbidding mountains of the Taygettus range in the center of the Peloponnese to discover not only the forgotten stone towns of Arcadia—Stemnitsa, Dimitsana, and medieval Karitena—but also the remote Temple of Apollo in Bassae. Farther south on the sandy cape of Messinia are such low-key seaside retreats as Methoni, and nearby Ancient Messene, with its mammoth fortifications from the 4th century BC. The Mycenaean ruins of Nestor's Palace, almost a millennium older than Ancient Messene, are surrounded by olive groves on a remote hilltop, and the harbor at Pylos, a whitewashed village that is now a pleasant fishing port and quiet resort, was the scene of a famous 1827 sea battle that paved the way for Greek independence.

Across the Taygettus lies Laconia, where the disciplined armies of the ancient Spartans practiced and where Byzantium's final flourish left the well preserved town of Mystras. Except for the foundations of Artemis's sanctuary and some fragments of Apollo's shrine at Amyklae, nothing remains of ancient Sparta—fitting tribute perhaps to what was the first totalitarian state. As you move on, at the very tip of continental Europe dangles the Mani peninsula, where the colorful port of Gythion faces the Gulf of Laconia and underground rivers flow through the caves of Pirgos Dirou. Throughout the stark landscapes are nearly deserted villages studded with tower houses of up to four stories; these defensive structures survive as vestiges of the Mani's blood feuds and vendettas. Finally, carved into a rock face on Laconia's southeast peninsula sits the inhabited medieval city of Monemvassia, a Byzantine gem.

Despite the waves of invaders over the centuries—Franks, Venetians, and Turks—this land is considered the distillation of all that is Greek, with its indulged idiosyncrasy, intractable autonomy, and appreciation of simple pleasures. The Southern Peloponnese is somewhat isolated from the rest of Greece, especially politically, but its people are great respecters of *filoxenia* (hospitality). Though it may be less accessible than other areas of Greece, this part of the Peloponnese has the advantage of a less-hectic pace and fewer crowds. The best moments come to those who stray beyond the familiar, who take time to have a coffee in the square of a village on Mt. Taygettus, a picnic at the ruins of Bassae, or a sunset swim beneath the brooding towers of a Maniote fishing hamlet.

Exploring the Southern Peloponnese

Politically, the Southern Peloponnese is divided into regions established by the ancients—Messinia in the southwest, Laconia in the southeast, and Arcadia to the north. Massive mountain ranges sweep down the fingers of the peninsula; the beaches are some of the finest and least developed in Greece. For the traveler, the area is best divided into the three regions listed above and the rugged Mani, which is separated from the rest of the Peloponnese by the Taygettus range (part of the Mani is administered by Messinia and the other part by Laconia). Arcadia is the most accessible region from Athens, and Messinia and Laconia are nearby. The Mani is well worth the trip to the southern tip of the region.

About the Restaurants

The Southern Peloponnese is not as popular a travel destination as the Northern Peloponnese and services and resources are proportionally limited. Be prepared to find a reduced selection of restaurants and hotels. Many dining spots in resort areas close from November through March. You won't find many fancy restaurants here, but don't go by looks. A hole-in-the-wall may serve the town's best meals, and what's available is what the butcher, fisherman, and grocer sold that day, despite the printed menu. Even the smallest villages come to life in the evenings, when the tavernas and kafeneia (coffeehouses) buzz with activity. As in the rest of Greece, it's customary to eat around 10 PM or so, though restaurants generally open for dinner around 7 or 7:30 to serve their non-Greek guests.

About the Hotels

Except for a few luxury complexes along the coast, most hotels are standard, with plain rooms. Newer hotels may have more services and a bit more decorative flair—and, fortunately, are more likely to have air-conditioning. Bathrooms usually have showers instead of tubs. Wherever you stay in the warm months, come prepared with mosquito protection since most windows are screenless and the pests are ubiquitous.

Reserve ahead if you plan to travel in the high season (July and August), especially in coastal hotels that cater to groups. It's often cheaper to book larger hotels through a travel agent, and some of these hotels post special offers online. If a hotel is not full, you can usually negotiate a lower-than-official rate, especially in the low season. If the hotels are full, you can always find private rooms, though often without a private bath. Keep in mind that in resort areas, many places close from November through March. Ask the tourist police or a local travel agency for assistance. Most hotels include breakfast in the price, and the offerings range from toast and coffee to lavish buffets.

WHAT IT COSTS In euros					
	$$$$	**$$$**	**$$**	**$**	**¢**
RESTAURANTS	over €20	€16–€20	€12–€15	€8–€11	under €8
HOTELS	over €160	€121–€160	€91–€120	€60–€90	under €60

Restaurant prices are for one main course at dinner or, for restaurants that serve only *mezedes* (small dishes), for two mezedes. Hotel prices are for two people in a standard double room in high season, including taxes.

Timing

Snow renders many of the mountain regions inaccessible in winter, while in summer temperatures can soar to uncomfortable reaches in many regions, especially the Mani. May, September, and October are especially comfortable months here, with pleasant temperatures (it's warm enough to swim) and little rain. As with the rest of Greece, on Monday most state museums and sites are closed. On some Sundays many have free admission.

8

The Southern Peloponnese is a relatively uncrowded region, and you'll appreciate it most if you take time to linger in a village or savor the landscape over a picnic lunch. A short visit forces you to make some difficult choices: any of the four areas covered in this chapter can be explored in a few days, but in that time you may be tempted to explore more than *one* region. The suggested three-day itinerary has several options and takes in highlights of several regions, but you're moving around quickly. An eight-day tour gives you time to appreciate all the different regions.

Numbers in the text correspond to numbers in the margin and on the Southern Peloponnese map.

If you have 3 days

On a three-day trip, you might make a quick visit to **Tripoli** ❶ ☛, from where you can continue to the Arcadian mountain village of ⊡ **Andritsena** ❺ and the **Temple of Apollo at Bassae** ❻. These places and a string of other mountain villages—**Stemnitsa** ❷, **Dimitsana** ❸, and **Karitena** ❹—can be visited in a full day. On the second day, head south through **Sparta** ❷⓪ and the spectacular Byzantine ruins of **Mystras** ❷❶ to the harbor town of ⊡ **Gythion** ❶❾ and the rugged Mani. Continue to the medieval town of ⊡ **Monemvassia** ❷❷ on the third day. As an alternative route, on the second day go southwest from Andritsena through **Kalamata** ❼ to the nearby ruins of **Ancient Messene** ❽ and from there west to ⊡ **Pylos** ❶❶ and the resort town of ⊡ **Methoni** ❶❷. On the third day retrace your steps through **Kalamata** and then drop south into the Mani, with an overnight in ⊡ **Kardamyli** ❶❸ or ⊡ **Areopolis** ❶❻.

If you have 5 days

Pass through **Tripoli** ❶ ☛ and explore the Taygettus mountain villages of **Stemnitsa** ❷, **Dimitsana** ❸, **Karitena** ❹, and ⊡ **Andritsena** ❺ and the **Temple of Apollo at Bassae** ❻. Spend the night in the fresh, cool air of Dimitsana or Andritsena, then descend to ⊡ **Kalamata** ❼ and continue west to the ancient Mycenaean **Nestor's Palace** ❶⓪ and ⊡ **Pylos** ❶❶, with its beautiful bay, for a night in the pleasantly low-key resort of ⊡ **Methoni** ❶❷, dominated by a remarkable Venetian fortress. Then it's on to the Mani, where you can settle for at least two days in ⊡ **Kardamyli** ❶❸, ⊡ **Areopolis** ❶❻, or one of the character-filled hotels around **Vathia** ❶❽. From there, continue to **Sparta** ❷⓪ and the Byzantine city of **Mystras** ❷❶, and spend your final night in medieval ⊡ **Monemvassia** ❷❷, carved out of rock and set high above the crashing surf.

If you have 8 days

Begin by exploring Arcadia, passing through **Tripoli** ❶ ☛ to the surrounding Taygettus mountain villages of **Stemnitsa** ❷, **Dimitsana** ❸, **Karitena** ❹, and ⊡ **Andritsena** ❺ and the **Temple of Apollo at Bassae** ❻. After a day in these pine- and mulberry-scented mountains, make your way west to Messinia's major center, ⊡ **Kalamata** ❼, and from there to the ancient Mycenaean **Nestor's Palace** ❶⓪ and the port town of ⊡ **Pylos** ❶❶, for its archaeological museum, fortresses, and a beautiful bay. Drop farther south to ⊡ **Methoni** ❶❷, where a remarkable Venetian fortress presides over a quiet beach and port.

Next venture into the Mani and base yourself for at least two days in ⊡ **Kardamyli** ❶❸ or ⊡ **Areopolis** ❶❻, the sun-baked gateway to the Inner Mani. You might want to have a boatman row you along the underground rivers of the eerie **Pirgos Dirou Caves** ⑰ and travel all the way down the stark Mani peninsula to **Vathia** ⑱ and Cape Tenaro. For Byzantine ruins, cross the Langada Pass from Kalamata to **Sparta** ⑳, where you can stomp about the Laconian plain, seeing the last jewel in the Byzantine crown, **Mystras** ㉑, followed by a sojourn in the colorful Laconian port of ▧ **Gythion** ⑲. Then move on to ▧ **Monemvassia** ㉒, a medieval town tucked into a rock face.

ARCADIA

ΑΡΚΑΔΙΑ

Arcadia was named after Arcas, whom Zeus fathered with Callisto. According to one version of the legend, Callisto's father chopped Arcas into bite-size pieces and served him to Zeus for dinner. Zeus managed to give his son new life as a bear, but in a fit of ingratitude, Arcas eventually had his wicked way with his mother. That's when Zeus decided to turn both mother and son into the constellations Ursa Major and Minor, the Big and Little Dipper.

Arcadians are believed to be among the oldest inhabitants of the Peloponnese; this group of tribes first united when they entered the Trojan War. They later founded the powerful Arcadian League, but after Corinth fell to Rome in 146 BC, the region slipped into decline. When the Goths invaded in AD 395, Arcadia was almost entirely deserted. Several centuries later the Franks conquered the area and built many castles; they were succeeded by the Byzantines and then the Turks, who ruled until the War of Independence.

No conqueror ever really dominated the Arcadians. Even when Tripoli was the Turks' administrative center, the mountain villagers lived much as they pleased, maintaining secret schools to preserve the rudiments of Greek language and religion and harassing the Turks in roaming bands. Forested mountainsides and valley farms still lend themselves to a decidedly rural way of life, and the very word "arcadia" has come to suggest the sorts of pastoral pleasures you will encounter here. In recent years many locals have abandoned their pastoral life to look for work in Athens; Arcadia now has no more people than Corinthia, a region half its size.

Tripoli

Τρίπολη

➤ ❶ *150 km (93 mi) southwest of Athens, 70 km (43 mi) southwest of Corinth.*

Regardless of the direction from which you approach the southern half of the Peloponnese, history, along with the practicalities of the road network in this part of Greece, suggests you're sure to at least pass through

Tripoli. In the days of the Ottoman Empire, this crossroads was the capital of the Turkish pasha of the Peloponnese, and during the War of Independence it was the first target of Greek revolutionaries. They captured it in 1821 after a six-month siege, but the town went back and forth between the warring sides until 1827, when Ibrahim Pasha's retreating troops burned it to the ground.

Tripoli is a workaday town with few attractions to keep you here, although if you do hang around, you'll get an eyeful of Greek life. Its most attractive feature is the mountain scenery, with attendant hillside villages, that surrounds it; you will soon understand why this region is nicknamed the Switzerland of Greece. Unless you run out of daylight, you'll probably want to move on from Tripoli to one of these villages.

Catch an authentic Greek experience by visiting one of the kafeneia on Platia Agiou Vasiliou. Here Greek men smoke, play cards, and talk politics; women may feel a little uncomfortable but will be treated with great respect if they enter. You can also grab a quick and juicy (and very inexpensive) souvlaki at E Gonia in a corner of the square (*gonia* means "corner" in Greek).

You can observe Greek life in the squares in the center of town, especially **Platia Areos,** one of the largest and most beautiful *platias* (central squares) in Greece—definitely the place to while away the time if marooned in Tripoli.

If you have some extra time, visit Tripoli's small **Panarcadic Archaeological Museum** to see the artifacts from the nearby sites of the classical cities of Mantinea and Tegea and elsewhere. There are some excellent inscriptions dating from the Achaean League as well as some beautiful early Christian funerary stele. ⊠ *Euaggelistrias 8* ☎ *2710/242148* ⊕ *www.culture.gr* ✏ *€2* ⊗ *Tues.–Sun. 8:30–3.*

Where to Stay & Eat

¢–$$ ✕ **Petit Trianon.** The best restaurant in Tripoli, on one side of the huge Platia Areos, serves excellent Greek fare in an ornate room festooned with gold statues and mini-obelisks. Most diners prefer the large front terrace facing the square. Special dishes include *argitiko* (beef with pearl onions slow-cooked in a ceramic dish) and bacon-wrapped filet mignon with mouthwatering potatoes. ⊠ *Pl. Areos 24* ☎ *2710/237413* ⊟ *DC, MC, V.*

¢ ✕ **Café Kallisto.** Sit under the large white umbrellas of this café on Platia Areos and order an exotic fruit tea, raisin crepes soaked in Grand Marnier, baklava, or the chef's special cake. Or savor drinks with a plate of *pikilia* (appetizers) such as meats, smoked trout, shrimp, olives, and cheese. The rosy pink interior with Hollywood prints is cozy, and a large evil-eye charm over the bar will protect you from jealous admirers. ⊠ *Pl. Areos 5* ☎ *2710/237019* ⊟ *No credit cards.*

$$ ▦ **Mainalon Hotel.** The fairly luxurious amenities here include a tasteful mix of traditional and contemporary furnishings, silk fabrics in the guest rooms, and commodious marble bathrooms. Ask for a room in the front of the hotel and enjoy a balcony overlooking Platia Areos. The hotel's café on the square is one of the town's most popular hangouts.

✉ *Pl. Areos, 22100* ☎ *2710/230300* 🖷 *2710/230327* ⊕ *www. mainalonhotel.gr* ⇨ *42 rooms, 3 suites* ↺ *Café, minibars, in-room data ports, bar, meeting rooms* ⊟ *AE, MC, V* ❒ *BP.*

¢ 🏨 **Arcadia**. This six-story green cement box is not fancy, but the saving graces are the high ceilings, pleasantly ornate furnishings, terraces, and a roof garden. ✉ *Pl. Kolokotronis 1, 22100* ☎ *2710/225551 through 2710/225553* 🖷 *2710/222464* ⇨ *45 rooms* ↺ *Restaurant, bar* ⊟ *No credit cards* ❒ *CP.*

Sports

Mt. Menalon ski center (☎ 2710/232243), at Oropedio Ostrakina (4,310 feet) northwest of the city, has five downhill runs and three tows; food and overnight accommodations are available. The center is 30 km (19 mi) from Tripoli.

Stemnitsa

Στεμνίτσα

❷ *43 km (27 mi) northwest of Tripoli.*

This town, also called Ipsous, is wondrously perched 3,444 feet above sea level amid a forest of fir and chestnut trees. For centuries it was one of the Balkans' best-known metalworking centers, and today a minuscule school is still staffed by local artisans. Above the lively village square rises the bell tower of the church of Ayios Giorgios, and at the top of a nearby hill is the monument to fighters in the 1821 War of Independence against the Turks. The views throughout the town are phenomenal, especially at night when the village lies beneath of canopy of bright stars.

From the north side of town, a well-marked path leads through the mountains to the isolated monastery of **Moni Ayiou Ioannitou**, with a little chapel covered in frescoes that is generally open. From the monastery other paths lead through a beautiful, wooded valley to the banks of the River Lousios.

The unusual **folklore museum** devotes one floor to mock workshops for indigenous crafts such as candle making and bell casting; the other two floors house re-created traditional rooms and a haphazard collection of costumes, weapons, icons, and plates. ✉ *Off main Rd.* ☎ *27950/81252* ⊕ *www.culture.gr* 🎫 *Free* ⊙ *Oct.–June, Mon., Wed.–Fri. 11–1; weekends 11–2; July–Sept., Mon. 11–1, Wed., Thurs., and Sat. 11–1 and 6–8, Fri. 6–8.*

Dimitsana

Δημητσάνα

❸ *10 km (6 mi) north of Stemnitsa, 50 km (31 mi) northwest of Tripoli.*

Dimitsana has stunning views of the Arcadian mountains. Leave your car at the entrance to town, stroll the maze of narrow cobbled lanes, and study the town's ancient churches. Archaeologists found ruins of a cyclopean wall (irregular stones without mortar) and classical build-

8

Ancient & Medieval Sites
A journey through the Southern Peloponnese provides a unique opportunity for time travel, since you can explore a rich diversity of classical and medieval sites in the course of a single day. For an almost mind-boggling experience, consider a morning tour of the ruined buildings and colorful frescoes of the Byzantine city of Mystras, followed by stops at Ancient Messene, dating to the 4th century BC, and then Nestor's Palace, even older and mentioned in Homeric legend. In the evening you can dine in the shadows of the 13th-century Venetian citadel that still guards the harbor at Methoni. Don't miss the still-inhabited Byzantine town of Monemvassia, with its evocative buildings and superb coastal views.

Beaches
The best beaches are in the southernmost stretches of the region. You'll find nice sand and clean, warm seas in and around Methoni, in Messinia, and on the little island of Elafonisi. The Mani also has some good sand beaches, especially at the tip of the peninsula, at Porto Kayio and Marmari, near Cape Tenaro. Methoni and Pylos are the best-equipped resorts for windsurfing, sailing, and other water sports.

Folk Dances
Dance performances, accompanied by traditional music, are common in the region. In the *tsakonikos,* the dancers wheel tightly around each other and then swing into bizarre spirals; this dance resembles the sacred dance of Delos, first performed by Theseus to mime how he escaped from the Labyrinth. The popular *kalamatianos* is a circular dance from Kalamata. The *tsamikos,* from Roumeli in central Greece, is an exclusively male dance showcasing agility and derring-do. You will see your fill of dancing at local festivals to celebrate a town or village's patron saint, usually in summer. Dancing is also part of a Greek wedding, and it's not entirely unlikely that you might attend one. The guest list usually includes the entire population of a village or section of town, and if you happen to be staying there at the time of a wedding, you may well be invited.

Great Flavors
Countless local tavernas and simple *estiatoria* (restaurants) serve memorable Greek home cooking and plenty of fresh fish. Villages here were the source of such international favorites as avgolemono soup and lamb fricassee. There are several local specialties to watch for: in the mountain villages near Tripoli, order *stifado* (beef with pearl onions), *arni psito* (lamb on the spit), *kokoretsi* (entrails on the spit), and thick, creamy yogurt. In Sparta, look for *bardouniotiko* (a local dish of chicken stuffed with cheese, olives, and walnuts), and, around Pylos, order fresh ocean fish (priced by the kilo). In the rest of Laconia, try *loukaniko horiatiko* (village sausage), and in the Mani, ask for ham. As for wines, the light white from Mantinea is a favorite, and whenever possible, sample the *hima* (barrel wines), which range from light, dry whites to heavy, sleep-inducing reds.

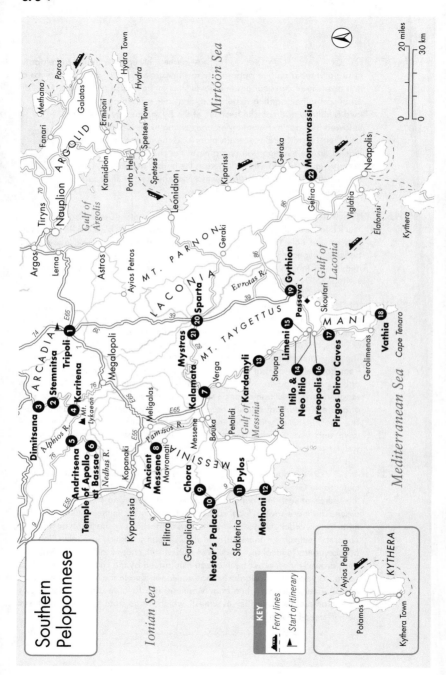

Southern Peloponnese

KEY

Ferry lines

▲ Start of itinerary

Mirtóön Sea

Mediterranean Sea

Ionian Sea

Gulf of Argolis

Gulf of Laconia

Gulf of Kardamyli

ARGOLID

ARCADIA

LACONIA

MESSINIA

MANI

MT. PARNON

MT. TAYGETTUS

Mt. Lykaeon

Alphios R.

Nedhas R.

Pamisos R.

Evrotas R.

Messinia

Poros
Methana
Fanari
Hydra Town
Hydra
Galatas
Ermioni
Spetses Town
Kranidion
Spetses
Porto Heli
Leonidion
Kiparissi
Geraka
Neapolis
Kythera
Elafonisi
Viglafia
Skoutari
Gerolimenas
Cape Tenaro
Koroni
Petalidi
Boúka
Messene
Meligalas
Kopanaki
Kyparissia
Filitra
Gargaliani
Mavromati
Sfakteria
Verga
Stoupa
Tiryns
Argos
Lerna
Astros
Ayios Petros
Geraki
Nauplion
Megalopoli

1 Tripoli
2 Stemnitsa
3 Dimitsana
4 Karitena
5 Andritsena
6 Temple of Apollo at Bassae
7 Kalamata
8 Ancient Messene
9 Chora
10 Nestor's Palace
11 Pylos
12 Methoni
13
14 Itilo & Neo Itilo
15 Liméni
16 Areopolis
17 Pirgos Dirou Caves
18 Vathia
19 Gythion
20 Sparta
21 Mystras
22 Monemvassia

Passava
Gefira

74
E65
72
1
76
E55
9
9
39
82
86
70
39

20 miles
30 km

KYTHERA

Ayios Pelagia
Potamos
Kythera Town

ings near the town; the ruins belonged to the acropolis of Teuthis, an ancient city.

The **Ecclesiastical Museum** houses manuscripts and other artifacts from the former School of Greek Letters, which at one time educated Germanos, a bishop of Patras, and other church leaders. ⊠ *Off main road Sq.* ☎ *27950/31360* 💶 *€1.50* ☉ *Fri.–Tues. 10–1:30 and 5–7.*

On the River Lousios below town is the **Open Air Water Power Museum,** which includes a water mill, tannery, and gunpowder mill. Displays and demonstrations reveal why water power was the force behind the region's economy until the first part of the 20th century. ⊠ *Off main road, south of town* ☎ *27950/31217* 💶 *€1.50* ☉ *Wed.–Mon. 10–4.*

The **town library** displays manuscripts, rare books, and memorabilia from the Greek revolutionary period, when Dimitsana was a center for revolutionary activity against the Turks. ⊠ *Main Sq.* ☎ *27950/31219* 💶 *Free* ☉ *Apr.–Oct., weekdays 8–2, Sat. 8–noon.*

$ 🏨 **Hotel Dimitsana.** The lounges, restaurant, and many rooms hang right over the deep gorge of the River Lousios, providing stunning views. All rooms have balconies (those over the gorge seem to be suspended in midair), while rooms in front of the hotel overlook the surrounding mountains. In summer the hotel can arrange rafting trips and mountain treks; rates jump in winter when skiers use the hotel as a base for the slopes on Mt. Menalon and other nearby ski centers. ⊠ *Main road, south end of town, 22007* ☎ *27950/31518* 🖷 *27950/31040* ✍ *dimitsana@yahoo. gr* 🛏 *20 rooms* ⚒ *Restaurant, shop, Internet room* ▭ *MC, V* ⊖ *BP.*

Sports & the Outdoors

The **E2 hiking path,** part of the European trail system, passes through Dimitsana. You can follow the path south along the gorge of the River Lousios or east into the surrounding mountains. The trek south brings you to several small monasteries tucked into the walls of the gorge and the scanty ruins of the ancient city of Gortys.

Karitena

Καρύταινα

❹ *26 km (16 mi) south of Dimitsana, 54 km (33 mi) west of Tripoli.*

Karitena, a medieval village of stone houses topped by a Frankish castle, is inhabited by fewer than 300 people, though the population was 20,000 during the Middle Ages. The buildings reveal the influence of the Franks, Byzantines, and Turks who occupied the area. For a stunning view of the gorge and the town, walk over to the multiarched Frankish bridge that spans the Alpheios.

When the Franks took over from the Byzantines in 1209, they gave the town to Hugo de la Bruyères, who built the hilltop **Frankish castle** (⊠ Off town Sq.) in 1245 and then bequeathed it to his son Geoffrey, the only well-liked Frankish overlord (he was praised in the *Chronicle of Morea* for his chivalry). The castle was known as the Toledo of Greece because of its strategic position at the mouth of the Alpheios Gorge. Later, during the revolution against the Turks, the hero Theodore Kolokotronis again made use of its location, repairing the fortifications and building a house and a church within the walls as his base, out of reach of Ibrahim Pasha. The castle, now partly in ruin, is not open to the public, though you can climb to the walls.

The 11th-century church of **Ayios Nikolaos** (⊠ Below town Sq.) has vivid and generally well-preserved frescoes, though some of the faces were scratched out during the Ottoman era. Ask in the square for the caretaker, who has the keys.

Andritsena

Ανδρίτσαινα

❺ *29 km (18 mi) southwest of Karitena, 83 km (51 mi) west of Tripoli.*

Andritsena is a pleasant little collection of stone houses. A small **library** houses 15th-century Venetian and Vatican first editions and documents relating to the War of Independence. ⊠ *On main road, 100 yds after Sq.* ☎ *26260/22242* 🎫 *Free* 🕓 *Weekdays 8:30–3.*

Where to Stay

¢ 🏨 **Theoxenia Hotel.** The only hotel for miles is geared to basic comfort, but the rooms are large and pleasantly furnished and offer vistas of mountains and woods. The hotel serves lunch and dinner in summer, but you're better off at one of the eateries surrounding the main square. ⊠ *On main road on edge of village as you enter from Karitena, 27061* ☎ *26260/22219* 🛏 *40 rooms* 🍴 *Restaurant; no a/c, no room phones, no room TVs* ▭ *No credit cards* 🕓 *Closed Jan. and Feb.* ¶◉ *CP.*

Temple of Apollo at Bassae

Ναός του Απόλλωνα στις Βάσσες

★ ⓒ **❻** *14 km (9 mi) south of Andritsena, 97 km (60 mi) southwest of Tripoli.*

Isolated amid craggy, uncompromising scenery, the Temple of Apollo Epikourios at Bassae is elegant and untouched by vandalism or commercialism. Despite its setting, the temple has lost some of its impact—it is veiled by a canopy during ongoing restoration due to weather damage. For many years it was believed that this temple was designed by Iktinos, the Parthenon's architect. Although this theory has recently been disputed, it is one of the best-preserved classical temples in Greece, superseded in its state of preservation only by the Hephaistion in Athens. The residents of nearby Phygalia built it atop an older temple in 420 BC to thank Apollo for delivering them from an epidemic; *epikourious* means "helper." Made of local limestone, the temple has some unusual details: exceptional length compared to its width; a north–south orientation rather than the usual east–west (probably because of the slope of the ground); and Ionic half columns linked to the walls by flying buttresses. Here, too, were the first known Corinthian columns with the characteristic acanthus leaves—only the base remains now—and the earliest example of interior sculptured friezes illustrating the battles between the Greeks and Amazons (now in the British Museum).

Climb to the **summit** northwest of the temple for a view overlooking the Nedhas River, Mt. Lykaeon, and, on a clear day, the Ionian Sea. ⊠ *Off Rte. 76 and then up a 1-lane Rd.* ☎ *26260/22254* ⊕ *www.culture.gr* ⊠ *€2* ⊙ *Daily 8:30–3.*

MESSINIA

ΜΕΣΣΗΝΙΑ

Euripides called this region "a land of fair fruitage and watered by innumerable streams . . . neither very wintry in the blasts of winter, nor yet made too hot by the chariot of Hellos." Long, relatively cool summers and mild winters may be Messinia's blessing, but nature was no ally in 1986 when a major earthquake razed its capital, Kalamata, which has been rebuilt with an eye to efficiency rather than charm. The region remains deeply rural, and Kalamata has given its name to the olives that grow in mile after mile of groves, punctuated by such ancient sites as Ancient Messene and Nestor's Palace.

Kalamata

Καλαμάτα

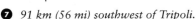 *91 km (56 mi) southwest of Tripoli.*

Though not Greece's most attractive city, Kalamata does have the animated air of a busy market town. The city is built atop ancient Pharai, described by Homer as subject to the kingdom of Agamemnon. In the 8th century BC, Pharai was annexed as a province of Laconia and, like most towns in the area, was not independent again until the Battle of Leuctra ended Spartan domination, prompting the Theban general Epaminondas to erect the great fortifications of Messene.

The effects of the severe earthquake that nearly leveled the city in 1986 are still evident in the remaining rubble and an ongoing rebuilding boom. Kalamata is a crossroads between such places as Pylos and Ancient Messene to the west, Sparta and Mystras to the east, and the Mani to the south.

The small, well-organized **Benakeion Archaeological Museum** exhibits local stone tools, proto-Geometric and Geometric pottery, and a 1st-century AD Roman mosaic floor depicting Dionysos with a panther and a satyr. ⊠ *Benaki and Papazoglou, near Pl. Martiou 25* ☎ *27210/26209* ⊕ *www.culture.gr* ⊠ *Free* ⊙ *Tues.–Sun. 8:30–3.*

In the early 13th century William de Champlitte divided the Peloponnese into 12 baronies, bestowing Kalamata on Frankish knight Geoffrey de Villehardouin, who built a winter **Kastro** (⊠ At the end of Ipapandis). Through the centuries the castle was bitterly fought over by Franks, Slavs, and Byzantines, and today it's difficult to tell what of the remains is original. From Platia Martiou 25, walk up Ipapandis past the church, take the first left at the castle gates (which are always open), and climb the small hill; the views of the town, coast, and the Messinian plain are lovely.

The oldest church here is the 13th-century **Ayii Apostoli** (Holy Apostles; ⊠ Pl. Martiou 25), a small Byzantine church dedicated to the Virgin of Kalamata ("of the good eye"), from whom the town may get its name. Restored after the 1986 earthquake, it is one of Greece's double churches, with two naves—one for the Roman Catholics and one for the Orthodox—that resulted from 13th- and 14th-century ecumenical efforts. The Greek War of Independence was formally declared here on March 23, 1821, when Theodoros Kolokotronis captured Kalamata from the Turks. The church is usually open in the late afternoon (5–7).

Beaches

About 30 km (19 mi) west of Kalamata at **Petalidi** is the beginning of a long chain of sandy beaches that are ideal for children because of the shallow water. **Verga,** about 6 km (4 mi) east of town, and the more crowded **Bouka,** 10 km (6 mi) west of town, both have showers and changing rooms.

Where to Stay & Eat

★ **$–$$** ✕ **Koinakos.** The large, waterfront terrace and handsome dining room are the best places in town to enjoy grilled octopus and fish, mussels steamed in wine, and other seafood dishes, always fresh and deftly prepared. Rather than ordering off the menu, ask to step into the kitchen and see what's fresh that day. ⊠ *Navarinou 12* ☎ *27210/ 22016* 🖃 *MC, V.*

¢–$$ ✕ **Selitsa.** Take in Kalamata and the Gulf of Messinia from the tables at this hillside taverna, set in pine woods next to a stream. It's worth the trip up for the hearty meats such as *katsiki tou fournou* (roasted goat) and roasted lamb. Next door is a small castle, which in summer is a drinks-only bistro. Ask for directions; everyone in Kalamata knows this place well. ⊠ *About 3 km (2 mi) northeast of the center; follow Navarinou south toward Verga; signs indicate turn for Selitsa village, Selitsa* ☎ *27210/41331* 🖃 *No credit cards.*

¢–$ ✕ **Kaloutas.** Watch the men laying out their nets to dry at this waterfront restaurant, while you eat copious helpings of tender beef *kokkinisto* (stew) and *arni lemonato* (lamb cooked in a light lemon sauce). Mr. Kaloutas prides himself on his selection, and if he's not too busy, he takes requests. He also prepares large breakfasts with croissants, eggs, orange juice, and drip coffee instead of the drearily ubiquitous *nes* (boiled Nescafé). ⊠ *Navarinou 98* ☎ *27210/29097* 🖃 *No credit cards.*

★ **$** 🖫 **Hibiscus Hotel.** A chance to spend a night in this neoclassical house, about a five-minute walk from both the main shopping area and the beach, is reason enough to make a stopover in Kalamata. The Koulis family has filled the guest rooms and lounges with appealing antiques and comfortable sofas and lounge chairs, and installed commodious, well-equipped bathrooms. The downstairs sitting room opens to a shady garden. ⊠ *Faron 196, 24100* ☎ *27210/62511* 🖷 *27210/82323* ⊕ *www. traditionalhomes.gr* ⇆ *7 rooms* ⌂ *Cable TV* 🖃 *AE, MC, V* ♚⊙♜ *BP.*

¢ 🖫 **Haikos.** The Haikos brothers run their well-kept seaside hotel meticulously, extend a friendly welcome and readily dispense advice to their guests, and charge very fairly for what they offer. Most of the cool blue bedrooms have balconies and ocean views, and all have showers and comfy chairs and sofas; a pebble-and-sand beach is a few steps away. Breakfast is €6 extra and served in an airy lounge that's a pleasant place to enjoy a coffee or snack any time of the day. ⊠ *Navarinou 115, 24100* ☎ *27210/82886 or 27210/82888* 🖷 *27210/23800* ⊕ *www. haikos.com* ⇆ *65 rooms* ⌂ *Café, room service, in-room data ports* ⊟ *No credit cards* ⏉ *CP.*

Festivals
The annual **Independence Day celebration** is held on or around March 25, the national holiday date. Stick around for the festivities—dancing, local bands, and a spirited parade. Contact the Greek National Tourism Organization (GNTO or EOT) for information. In summer Kalamata holds a **theater festival** (☎ 27210/29909).

Shopping
Kalamata is most famous for its fleshy black olives and olive oil, but is also known for *pasteli* (sesame-seed-and-honey candy) and figs. Nuns from the convent of the Kalograies (⊠ Just below the kastro, off the square of the church of the Virgin Ypapanti) weave beautiful silk scarves and table linens, for sale in a shop just inside the entrance; ask to step into the tranquil cloister while you're there.

Ancient Messene

Αρχαία Μεσσήνη

★ ❽ *31 km (19 mi) north of Kalamata, 75 km (47 mi) southwest of Tripoli.*

The ruins of Ancient Messene, about 20 km (12 mi) north of the modern city of the same name, are set amid olive groves and pine forests on the slopes of majestic Mt. Ithomi (also known as Voulkanos). Epaminondas, the Theban leader, built Ancient Messene, which today incorporates the village of **Mavromati**, in 370–369 BC as a defense against the Spartans, with whom the Messenians had battled during two Messenian Wars, in 743–724 BC and 650–620 BC.

The most striking aspect of the ruins is the city's **circuit wall**, a feat of defensive architecture that rises and dips across the hillsides for an astonishing 9 km (5½ mi). Four gates remain; the best preserved is the north or **Arcadian Gate**, a double set of gates separated by a round courtyard. On the ancient paving stone below the arch, grooves worn by ancient chariot wheels are still visible. The heart of the walled city is now occupied by the village, but excavations have uncovered the most important public buildings, including a **theater,** whose seats have now been restored; the **Synedrion,** a meeting hall for representatives of independent Messene; the **Sebasteion,** dedicated to worship of a Roman emperor; the **sanctuary to the god Asklepios;** and a **temple to Artemis Orthia.** Outside the walls lie a **stadium** and a **cemetery.** The site is a bit confusing, as the ruins are spread over the hillside and approached from different paths; follow the signposts indicating the theater, gates, and other major excavations. Some of the finds are in the village's **small museum.** After exploring the ruins, enjoy a beverage in one of the tavernas that surround the main square of Mavromati. ✉ *From modern town of Messene, turn north at intersection of signposted road to Mavromati* ☎ 27240/51257 ⊕ *www.culture.gr* ▨ *Free* ⊘ *Daily 8–dusk.*

Chora

Χώρα

❾ *48 km (29¾ mi) west of Kalamata, 64 km (39¾ mi) west of Ancient Messene.*

Chora's **Archaeological Museum** (follow the confusing signs from Nestor's Palace; it's at the edge of town) displays golden cups and jewelry from the Mycenaean period; fragments of frescoes from nearby Nestor's Palace, including a warrior in a boar's-tusk helmet described by Homer; and plaster casts of the Linear B tablets—the originals are in the National Archaeological Museum in Athens. ✉ *Marinatou* ☎ 27630/31358 ⊕ *www.culture.gr* ▨ *€2* ⊘ *Tues.–Sun. 8:30–3.*

Nestor's Palace

Ανάκτορο του Νέστορα

❿ *4 km (2½ mi) south of Chora.*

Nestor's Palace belonged to the king of Pylos, commander, according to Homer, of the fleet of "ninety black ships" in the Trojan War. Nestor founded the town around 1300 BC—only Mycenae was larger—but the palace was burned a century later. It was here, the *Iliad* recounts, that Telemachus came to ask for news of his father, Odysseus, from Nestor, who welcomed the young man to a feast at the palace. Most of the palace rooms are clearly marked, but it's a good idea to buy the guidebook (available at the site) prepared by the University of Cincinnati, whose archaeologists excavated the site. The illustrations will help you imagine the palace in its original glory, which is indicated by the sheer size of the foundations and wall fragments. Archaeologists believe the complex, excavated in 1952, was similar to those found in Crete and Mycenae, except that it was unfortified, an indication that surrounding towns had sworn strict allegiance to and depended economically on Pylos. In the **main building**, a simple **entrance gate** is flanked by a **guard chamber** and two **archives**, where 1,250 palm-leaf-shape tablets were discovered on the first day of excavation. The tablets—records of taxes, armament expenses, and debts in Linear B script—were the first such unearthed on the Greek mainland, thus linking the Mycenaean and Minoan (Crete) civilizations, because the writing (like that in Knossos) was definitely Greek.

The entrance gate opens into a spacious **courtyard** with a balcony where spectators could watch the royal ceremonies. To the left are a **storeroom** that yielded thousands of tall-stemmed vases and a **waiting room** with built-in benches. Beyond the courtyard a **porch of the royal apartments** and a **vestibule** open onto a richly decorated **throne room**. In the middle of the room is a ceremonial **hearth** surrounded by four wooden columns (only the stone bases remain) that probably supported a shaft. Now completely destroyed, the throne once stood in the center of the wall to the right. Each **frescoed wall** depicted a different subject, such as a griffin (possibly the royal emblem) or a minstrel strumming his lyre. Even the columns and the wooden ceiling were painted. Along the southern edge of the throne room were seven **storerooms** for oil, which together with the one on the floor immediately above fueled the fire that destroyed the palace.

Off a corridor to the right of the entrance are a **bathroom,** where the oldest known bathtub stands, along with jars used for collecting bathwater. Next to it are the **Queen's apartments.** In the largest room a hearth is adorned with a painted flame, the walls with hunting scenes of lions and panthers. Other rooms in the complex include the **throne room** from an earlier palace, a **shrine, workshops,** and a **conduit** that brought water from a nearby spring. Several **beehive tombs** were also found outside the palace. ☒ *On highway south of Chora* ☏ *27630/31437* 🎫 *€3* ☼ *Tues.–Sat. 8:30–3.*

Pylos

Πύλος

⑪ *22 km (14 mi) south of Chora, 52 km (32 mi) southwest of Kalamata.*

With its bougainvillea-swathed, pristine white houses fanning up Mt. St. Nicholas and the blue waters of its port, Pylos will remind you of an island town. It was built according to a plan drawn by French engineers stationed here from 1828 to 1833 with General Maison's entourage and was the site of a major naval battle in the War of Independence. Ibrahim Pasha chose Sfakteria, the islet that virtually blocks Pylos Bay, from which to launch his attack on the mainland. For two years Greek forces flailed under Turkish firepower until, in 1827, Britain, Russia, and France came in to support the Greek insurgents. They sent a fleet to persuade Turkey to sign a treaty, were accidentally fired upon, and found themselves retaliating. At the end of the battle the allies had sunk 53 of 89 ships of the Turko-Egyptian fleet without a single loss among their 27 war vessels. The sultan was forced to renegotiate, which paved the way for Greek independence. A column rising between a Turkish and a Venetian cannon in the town's main square, Platia Trion Navarchon (Three Admirals Square), commemorates the leaders of the fleets.

For a closer look of the bay, take an hour-long boat tour to the various monuments on **Sfakteria,** sunken Turkish ships, and the neighboring rock of **Tsichli-Baba,** which has a vast, much-photographed natural arch, nicknamed Tripito, a former pirate hideout with 144 steps. The boats can also take you to the weed-infested 13th-century **Paleokastro,** one of the two fortresses guarding the channels on either side of Sfakteria, and make a stop also at **Nestor's cave.** Boat trips cost about €25; walk along the dock and negotiate with the captains, or ask at the waterside kiosk (staffed only occasionally). The trip is less expensive if you go with a group, but these trips are usually prearranged for the tour buses that drop down to Pylos from Olympia. ☒ *West of Pylos Port.*

For views of Pylos, the bay, and the Kamares Roman aqueduct, the **Neokastro,** the newer fortress that dominates the town, is unbeatable. It was built by the Turks in 1573 to control the southern—at that time, the only—entrance to the bay (an artificial embankment had drastically reduced the depth of the northern channel). Neokastro's well-preserved walls enclose the **Church of the Transfiguration,** originally a mosque; cannons; and two anchors from the battle. The highest point of the castle is guarded by a hexagonal fort flanked by towers. A prison in the 18th and 19th centuries, the fort was more secure than most other Greek prisons, because it sometimes housed convicts from the Mani, who continued their blood feuds while behind bars. ⊠ *Access is by trail from south side of town or off road to Methoni* ☎ *27230/22897* ✉ *€2* ⊙ *Daily 8–7.*

The small **Antonopouleion Museum,** dedicated to archaeology, has a collection of Hellenistic pottery, Roman bronze statues, engravings, battle memorabilia, gold pots, jewelry, and other objects of the Mycenaean period. ⊠ *Methonis 8* ☎ *27230/22448* ⊕ *www.culture.gr* ✉ *€2* ⊙ *Tues.–Sun. 8:30–3.*

Where to Stay & Eat

¢–$ ✕ **Ta Pente Aderfia.** Grilled meats, popular Greek *magirefta* (precooked dishes served at room temperature), and fresh seafood are served in a plain but attractive room or on the waterfront terrace. Order the special dish called *navomahia* (a seared fillet of beef) served in wine sauce or the *psari macaronada* (an unusual combination of fish and pasta), which has to be ordered a day ahead. All in all, a meal here is a real treat. ⊠ *Waterfront* ☎ *27230/22564* ⊟ *No credit cards.*

$$ 🏨 **Karalis Beach.** Set on a piney bluff at the end of town and clinging to rocks above the sea, the bright rooms and their balconies hang directly over the water. The setting can also be appreciated from a roof terrace that doubles as a breakfast room in good weather. The same management runs the nearby Karalis ($), on a bluff above the bay. ⊠ *Paralia, 24001* ☎ *27230/23021 or 27230/23022* 🖷 *27230/22970* ⊕ *www. karalis.roomstorent.info* 🛏 *14 rooms* ⌂ *Café, bar* ⊟ *MC, V* ⊙ *Closed Nov.–Mar.* ⊚ *CP.*

Sports & the Outdoors

If you want to putter around the bay on your own, rent a small launch from **Pilos Marine** (⊠ Kalamatis 10 ☎ 27230/22408 ⊕ www.pilosmarine. com). Boats seat four to five people, and the cost is €50 for half a day, €60 for a day. A license is not required.

Methoni

Μεθώνη

⑫ *14 km (9 mi) south of Pylos, 98 km (61 mi) southwest of Kalamata.*

Surrounded by olive groves and vineyards on a cape south of Pylos, Methoni, a small fishing and farming village and quiet resort, is so delightful it was one of the seven towns Agamemnon offered Achilles to appease him after his beloved Briseis was carried off. According to Homer, Pedasos, as it was called, was "rich in vines," and tradition says that the town got its modern name because *onoi* (donkeys) carrying the town's wine became *methoun* (intoxicated) from the aroma. Modern Methoni is two towns—a low-key settlement huddled on the beach beneath the fortress, and, just above, an animated old town on the crest of a rise.

★ ☺ Methoni's principal attraction is its **Kastro,** an imposing, well-kept citadel. After the Second Messenian War in the 7th century BC, the victorious Spartans gave Methoni to the Nafplions, who had been exiled from their homeland for their Spartan alliance. With its natural harbor, the town was an important stop on trade routes between Europe and the East during the Middle Ages. The Venetians took control of Methoni in 1209, building the impressive Kastro along the shoreline. A stone bridge leads over the dry moat to the citadel; various coats of arms mark the walls, including those of Genoa and Venice's Lion of St. Mark. A second bridge joins the Kastro with the **Bourtzi,** an octagonal tower built above the crashing surf on a tiny islet during the Turkish occupation (shortly after 1500). ⊠ *By coast* ☎ *27310/25363* 🖾 *Free* ☉ *Nov.–Mar., daily 8:30–3; Apr.–Oct., daily 8:30 AM–9 PM.*

Where to Stay & Eat

$–$$ ✕ **To Akrogiali.** You might want to take off your shoes to reach this seaside fish taverna, tucked against the walls of the fortress right on the beach. The town's small fishing fleet bobs beyond the dining terrace, ensuring that such simple dishes as grilled octopus and mullet are as fresh as you're ever going to find them. ⊠ *On beach below fortress* ☎ *27230/ 31520* ▭ *No credit cards* ☉ *Closed Nov.–Mar.*

¢–$ ✕ **Alector.** Except in the coldest weather seating here is right in the street—so you get a nice view of village life while enjoying souvlaki and other meats off the wood-fired grill. You can also step into the busy kitchen to choose from the several dishes that are prepared for each meal. ⊠ *Main street of town center* ☎ *27230/31830* ▭ *No credit cards.*

¢–$ ✕ **Nikos's.** "The only time this kitchen closes is if I'm sick," says Nikos Vile, who insists on cooking everything from *mamboulas* (a moussaka made with tomatoes) to *maridakia* (lightly fried whitebait) each day. You can sip an aperitif at the bar or hide out in the vine-covered courtyard. ⊠ *Miali Rd., near fortress* ☎ *27230/31282* ▭ *No credit cards.*

$ 🏠 **Amalia.** Situated on a hilltop and surrounded by lush gardens, this hotel has a flair that puts it many leagues ahead of other hotels in this category. The basic but pleasant rooms have huge verandas that face the sea and the town, with stunning views of the fortress, about a 15-minute walk away. ⊠ *Coastal road to Finikoundas, 24006* ☎ *27230/ 31129 or 27230/31193* 🖨 *27230/31195* 🛏 *34 rooms* ⚒ *Restaurant, refrigerators, bar* ▭ *MC, V* ☉ *Closed Nov.–Apr.* ⦿ *BP.*

★ ¢ 🏠 **Ulysses.** From the shady, well-manicured side garden to the attractive traditional furnishings in the spotless rooms, all aspects of this hotel extend a warm welcome. Balconies have views over the town and sea and each room has an individual heating and cooling unit (important when the mosquitoes are out in force). The breakfast spread is lavish, with fresh orange juice, local yogurt with honey, and freshly baked breads. ⊠ *Paralia, 24006* ☎ *27230/31600* 🖨 *27230/31646* 🛏 *12 rooms* ⚒ *Restaurant, bar* ▭ *MC* ⦿ *BP.*

Festival

On **Kathari Deftera** ("Clean Monday"), before Lent, Methoni holds a mock Koutroulis village wedding at the town platia, a riotous annual performance, in which both the bride and groom are played by men.

MANI

МАΝΗ

Fodor'sChoice ★ On its western side, the Mani stretches from Kardamyli to Cape Tenaro, the mythical entrance to the underworld, and on its eastern side from Cape Tenaro up to Gythion. The western half is the Messinian Mani, while the eastern half is the Laconian Mani. Isolated and invincible, this was the land of bandits and blood feuds. The Dorians never reached this far south, Roman occupation was perfunctory, and Christianity was not established here until the 9th century. Neither the Venetians nor the Turks could quell the constant rebellions.

The Maniotes are thought to be descended from the ancient Spartans and to have been expelled from northern Laconia by invading Slavs in the 7th century. An aristocracy arose—the Nyklians—whose clans began building defensive tower houses (the oldest dates to the 15th century) up to four stories high and fighting for precious land in this barren landscape. The object in battle was to annihilate the enemy's tower house, as well as its entire male population. Feuds could last for years, with the women—who were safe from attack—bringing in supplies. Mani women were famous throughout Greece for their singing of the *moirologhi* (laments), like the ancient choruses in a Greek tragedy.

A truce had to be called in long-lasting feuds during the harvest, but a feud ended only with the complete destruction of a family or its surrender, called *psychiko* (a thing of the soul), in which losers filed out of their tower house one by one, kissing the hand of the enemy clan's parents. The victor then decided under what conditions the humbled family could remain in the village. When King Otho tried to tame this incorrigible bunch in 1833, his soldiers were ambushed, stripped naked, and held for ransom. Today few people live in the Mani. If you have the good luck to share a shot of fiery raki with a Maniote, you may notice a Cretan influence in his dress—older men still wear the baggy breeches, black headbands, and decorated jackets wrapped with heavy belts.

Kardamyli

Καρδαμύλη

★ ⑬ *31 km (19 mi) southeast of Kalamata, 122 km (76 mi) southwest of Tripoli.*

Kardamyli is the gateway to the Mani on the Messinian side. It is considered part of the outer Mani, an area less bleak and stark than the inner Mani that begins at Areopolis. Here the foothills of the Mt.

Taygettus range are still verdant and the sun is more forgiving. The quiet and attractive stone town has become a tourist destination for the more discerning traveler attracted to its remoteness, stark beauty, and the hiking paths that surround it. Kardamyli's most famous resident is Patrick Leigh-Fermor, an Anglo-Irish writer who has written extensively on Greece and on the Mani in particular.

If you're approaching the Kardamyli and the Mani from Kalamata, turn off the main road beyond the eastern outskirts of Kalamata and follow the narrow coastal route through the seaside villages of Mikri Mantinea and Avia before rejoining the main road south of Kambos. Drive slowly, as the route is full of hairpin turns, and consider pulling over to appreciate one of the many stretches of beach or to have a meal at one of the seaside tavernas. The old section of Kardamyli, northwest of the modern town, is on a pine-scented hillside dotted with small clusters of **tower houses,** some of which are being restored; stone-paved paths cut through the enclave. At the edge of the old town is the church of **Ayios Spiridhon** (☒ Northwest of modern town), with some fine wall decorations; it's usually open only during services or when the custodian is around.

Beaches

Kardamyli's **main beach,** at the northern edge of town, is a long stretch of sand and pebbles backed by stands of pines. You can also swim off the dock in the clear, deep waters of the town's small harbor. Other beaches are tucked into coves as you drive south on the main road. **Stoupa,** about 10 km (6 mi) south of Kardamyli, is a low-key collection of seaside tavernas and rooms for rent that stretches along a beautiful sandy beach; it's a good place to come for lunch and a swim.

Where to Stay & Eat

¢ ✕🖾 **Lela's Taverna Pension.** Mrs. Lela is famous for her cooking—the
Fodor'sChoice secret is probably in the fragrant homemade olive oil and the exceed-
★ ingly fresh tomatoes and herbs. Chicken with rosemary, light moussaka, and fish soup are typical dishes that you can sample on the seaside terrace of this oleander-covered stone building. Carefully chosen wines from throughout Greece are excellent accompaniments. The commodious rooms above the taverna have soothing sea views and handsome furnishings that include traditional fabrics and prints of indigenous flowers; two are suites, with small sitting rooms and balconies. ☒ *Seaside, above rocky beach near old soap factory, 24022* 🖾🖾*27210/73541* ✎*notoshotel@kal.forthnet.gr* ✍ *3 rooms, 2 suites* ♙ *Restaurant; no a/c, no room TVs* 🖃 *No credit cards.*

★ $$ 🖾 **Notos Hotel.** These delightful self-catering apartments are scattered across a hillside in handsome stone houses. The bleached-wood furnishings are attractive, kitchens are well equipped, baths are beautifully tiled, and each unit has a large terrace overlooking the sea. ☒ *Above beach, about 1 km (½ mi) north of town center, 24022* 🖾 *27210/73730 or 27210/64130* 🖾*27210/64130* ⊕*www.notoshotel.gr* ✍*13 apartments* ♙*Kitchenettes* 🖃 *No credit cards.*

¢ 🖾 **Hotel Patriarcheas.** The marble-floored rooms in this pleasant stone hotel in the old town are unusually large. There is a delightful garden and terrace, where breakfast is served throughout summer. Rooms in the front face the sea, but also hang above the main road—double-glazed windows and air-conditioning ensure a good night's sleep, but you might want to forego the sea view and choose one of the rear rooms to enjoy the quiet setting from your balcony. ⊠ *Old town, 24022* 🕾 *27210/73366* 🖷 *27210/73660* 🛏 *16 rooms* ⚒ *Refrigerators* 🖃 *No credit cards* ❢❢ *CP.*

---

off the beaten path

VYROS GORGE – North of town, the Vyros Gorge cuts deep into the flanks of Mt. Taygettus. Well-maintained hiking paths follow the gorge to two monasteries at the base of its sheer cliffs, and other paths crisscross the hillsides above the gorge; some lead to the attractive mountain village of Exohori. Shops in Kardamyli sell walking maps of the gorge.

Itilo & Neo Itilo

Οίτυλο & Νέο Οίτυλο

🔟 *37 km (23 mi) south of Kardamyli, 68 km (42 mi) southwest of Kalamata.*

Itilo and Neo Itilo are, respectively, the upper and lower parts of the same town. Neo Itilo is plunk on the curve of an enormous bay with a white-pebble beach ideal for swimming; its uphill counterpart, Itilo, is nestled in a ravine amid slender cypresses. Formerly the capital of the Mani, verdant Itilo looks better from afar, with its red-tile roofs and bright blue window frames; up close, the houses are falling apart, neglected by a dwindling population. From the 16th to the 18th century, the harbor was infamous as a base for piracy and slave trading (Maniotes trading Turks to Venetians and vice versa).

Outraged by the piracy and hoping to control the pass to the north, the Turks built the nearby and deserted **Castle of Kelefa** (⊠ Across gorge from Itilo). You may walk or drive to Kelefa on a road that turns off to the right 4 km (2½ mi) before the Limeni junction.

Beach

Neo Itilo sits on a beautiful large bay with a **white-pebble beach.** Enjoy a swim as you watch the fishermen fixing their nets, checking their ship hulls, and talking among themselves amid the din of their portable radios.

Where to Stay & Eat

$–$$ ✕ **Black Pirate.** You won't find fresher seafood than at this pleasant and friendly taverna. Seating is in a simple room or under a canopy right on the beach. Boats laden with the day's catch pull up out front, you make your choice, and the staff cleans, grills, and serves your fish with a delicious salad and some barrel wine. ⊠ *On waterfront* 🕾 *27330/59363* 🖃 *No credit cards.*

$$ 🏠 **Porto Vitilo.** This stone house set amid olive and cypress trees at the edge of the bay feels like a private villa. There are shady terraces, a large garden, and inviting stone-walled lounges. Guest rooms are attractive and comfortable; many have beamed ceilings and fireplaces, and most

have balconies overlooking the sea or the mountains. ⊠ *South side of village, 23062 Itilo* ☎ *27330/59220* 🖷 *27330/59210* ⊕ *www.portovitilo. gr* ➳ *13 rooms, 1 suite* ♿ *Restaurant, bar* 🚫 *No credit cards* ❦ *BP.*

Limeni

Λιμένι

⑮ *2 km (1 mi) south of Itilo and Neo Itilo, 70 km (43 mi) southwest of Kalamata.*

In Limeni the restored tower of War of Independence hero Petrobey Mavromichaelis now guards little more than a string of cottages with their backs to the sea and a main street crammed with tiny shops. You may be mesmerized by the coastal scenery, but keep an eye out for donkeys, sheep, and flocks of goats that may suddenly trot into the road.

Where to Eat

$–$$ ✕ **To Limeni.** The fish and seafood—priced by the kilo and served at the water's edge—is some of the freshest and best prepared in the region. This is an excellent stop for lunch on the drive south down the Mani peninsula from Kalamata. ⊠ *On waterfront* ☎ *27330/51327* 🚫 *No credit cards.*

Areopolis

Αρεόπολη

⑯ *4 km (2½ mi) south of Limeni, 74 km (46 mi) southwest of Kalamata.*

In Areopolis the typical Maniote tower houses began to appear in earnest, spooky sentinels in the harsh landscape. The town was renamed after the god of war Ares, because of its role in the War of Independence: Petrobey Mavromichaelis, governor of the Mani, initiated the local uprising against the Turks here (his statue stands in the square). Areopolis now enjoys protection as a historical monument by the government, but although the town seems medieval, most of the tower houses were built in the early 1800s. The Taxiarchis (Archangels) church, which looks as if it has 12th-century reliefs over the doors, was actually constructed in 1798. It's easy to slip vicariously into a time warp as you meander down Kapetan Matapan street through the fields to the sea or along the dark cobblestone lanes past the tower houses with their enclosed courtyards and low-arched gateways.

Where to Stay & Eat

★ **¢–$$** ✕ **Taverna Barba Petros.** An appealing, high-ceilinged room and terrace are the pleasant settings for the best meal in Areopolis. The kitchen uses only market-fresh vegetables and locally raised meat, which appear in simple and delicious preparations. Try the baked zucchini, potatoes, and grilled lamb ribs. Dessert—try the honey cake—is on the house. ⊠ *Main St.* ☎ *27330/51026* 🚫 *No credit cards.*

★ **$** 🏨 **Hotel Trapela.** An old stone house just off the main square is a comfortable and stylish base for exploring the Mani. The stone-floored, wood-ceilinged rooms open off communal terraces and overlook a small garden. The suites have three and four beds and are well suited for families. An excellent buffet breakfast is served in the lounge or garden. ✉*Near center of town, 23062* ☎*27330/52690* 🖷*27330/52290* 🌐*www.trapela. gr* 🖘 *8 rooms, 4 suites* ⚷ *Refrigerators, bar* 🖃 *MC, V* ⦿ *BP.*

$ 🏨 **Kapetanakos Tower.** This traditional stone tower, dating from 1826, is a simple but atmospheric hotel. Five of the whitewashed rooms, two with sleeping lofts, are in the tower, reached by ladderlike stairs, and two are in a stone outbuilding. An excellent breakfast is served in a pretty garden in warm weather. ✉ *Near Archangels church at edge of town, 23062* ☎ *27330/51233* 🖷 *27330/51401* 🖘 *7 rooms* ⚷ *Refrigerators* 🖃 *No credit cards* ⦿ *BP.*

Pirgos Dirou Caves

Σπήλαια Πύργου Διρού

🕒 ⑰ *10 km (6 mi) south of Areopolis, 84 km (52 mi) south of Kalamata.*

Carved out of the limestone by the slow-moving underground River Vlychada on its way to the sea, the **Alepotripia** and **Glyfada** caves were places of worship in Paleolithic and Neolithic times and hiding places millennia later for Resistance fighters during World War II. You climb aboard a boat for a 25-minute tour of Glyfada's grottoes—with formations of luminous pink, white, yellow, and red stalagmites and stalactites that resemble surreal "buildings" and mythical beasts. The cave is believed to be at least 70 km (43 mi) long, with more than 2,800 waterways, perhaps extending as far as Sparta. At the end of the tour you walk for several hundred yards (about a fifth of a mile) through Glyfada before emerging on a path above the crashing surf. The close quarters in the passageways are not for the claustrophobic, and even in summer the caves are chilly. During high season you may wait up to two hours for a boat, so plan to arrive early. In low season you may have to wait until enough people arrive to fill up a boat. A small **archaeological museum** (✉ Methonis 8 ☎ 27330/52222 or 27330/52223 🎫 €2 🕒 Tues.–Sun. 8:30–3) houses the few Neolithic finds from the caves. ✉ *Along southern coast, 5 km (3 mi) west of Areopolis–Vathia Rd.* ☎ *27330/52222 or 27330/ 52223* 🎫 *€12* 🕒 *Nov.–Mar., daily 8:30–3; Apr.–Oct., daily 8:30–5:30.*

⎛ en route ⎞ The pleasant village of **Gerolimenas** (about 10 km [6 mi] north of Vathia) recalls an island port. Located at the end of a long natural harbor, around which cluster a few tavernas and shops, Gerolimenas was an important port in the late 19th and early 20th centuries. Sleepy as Gerolimenas now is, it's the most tourist-friendly place in this stark part of the Mani.

Vathia

Βαθειά

★ 🕒 ⑱ *22 km (14 mi) south of Pirgos Dirous Caves, 107 km (66 mi) southeast of Kalamata.*

Vathia, now virtually a ghost town, is worth a visit simply because of the density of the tower houses and the pervasive feeling of emptiness.

Its two- and three-story stone towers have small windows and tiny openings over the doors through which boiling oil was poured on the unwelcome. About 15 km (9 mi) north of Vathia, you can turn off to the hamlet of Stavri and Tsitsiris Castle; from Stavri you can make a memorable one-hour trek to the Castle of Mina, built by the Franks in 1248 into the rock face at the end of a long promontory surrounded by crashing surf.

off the beaten path

CAPE TENARO – The landscape becomes more rugged and even more forbidding south of Vathia, on the way to Cape Tenaro at the tip of the peninsula. The road winds around the mountainsides to Porto Kayio, where a few tavernas face a lovely beach, and then to more beaches at Marmari. A narrow road leads south to barren Cape Tenaro, where the ruins of a small Roman settlement include a mosaic that is perilously open to the elements. An underwater cave here, to which you might be able to convince a boatman to take you, is one of several alleged entrances to the classical underworld. From the cape you can look out over the Mani peninsula and the Gulf of Laconia and Gulf of Messinia.

Where to Stay

$$–$$$$
Fodor'sChoice
★

🏨 **Kyrimai Hotel.** The finest hotel in the Mani is a welcoming assemblage of stone, wood, courtyards, arches, and external staircases at the edge of the sea. The Kyrimis family has carefully restored several 19th-century stone warehouses to create this beautiful retreat. Rooms are furnished with exquisite antiques and a tasteful mix of traditional and contemporary pieces; many have balconies and sleeping lofts. The outdoor dining room, pool, and terraces are so close to the sea that you'll think you're on a yacht. ⊠ Gerolimenas, 23071 ☎ 27330/54288 🖷 27330/59338 ⊕ www.kyrimai.gr ➦ 22 rooms, 3 suites ♿ Restaurant, in-room safes, minibars, cable TV, pool, dock, bar ☰ AE, MC, V ⌾ BP.

$

🏨 **Faros.** The accommodations at this small waterside hotel on a street of mostly deserted and ruined houses are surprisingly delightful. Rooms are large and bright, accented with colorful fabrics and traditional brass and wood pieces, and have modest cooking facilities and terraces. Breakfast is not served, but you can fend for yourself at a taverna in the town, which is 10 km (6 mi) north of Vathia. ⊠ 23071 Gerolimenas ☎ 27330/54271 🖷 27330/54269 ➦ 8 rooms ♿ Kitchenettes ☰ No credit cards.

★ **$**

🏨 **Tsitsiris Castle.** In a tiny hamlet about 15 km (9 mi) north of Vathia, this 200-year-old fortified manor house has lounges and guest rooms with stone floors and wood beams. Many rooms have sleeping lofts and surround a well-tended garden. A roof terrace is a pleasant retreat in which to catch an evening breeze. Basic meals are served in a dining room with a stone-vaulted ceiling or in a tree-shaded courtyard. ⊠ 23062 Stavri ☎ 27330/56297 or 27330/56298 ➦ 20 rooms ♿ Restaurant; no room TVs ☰ No credit cards ⌾ CP.

en route

As you head up the east side of the Mani peninsula, you'll come to the sandy beach of Mavrovouni and the castle of **Passava,** about 10 km (6 mi) south of Gythion. Originally constructed in 1254 by French baron Jean de Neuilly, the castle was rebuilt by the Turks in the 18th century. The walk to the hilltop castle is challenging, especially since there is no regular path, but the view takes in two bays.

Gythion

Γύθειο

⑲ *46 km (29 mi) south of Sparta, 79 km (49 mi) north of Vathia.*

Gythion, at the foot of the Mt. Taygettus range, will seem terribly cosmopolitan if you've been exploring the Mani. Graceful pastel 19th-century houses march up the steep hillside, and along the busy harbor, fruit-laden donkeys sidestep the peanut vendors and gypsies hawking strings of garlic. Laconia's main port, the town is the Laconian gateway to the Mani peninsula. It claims Hercules and Apollo as its founders and survives today by exporting olives, oil, rice, and citrus fruits.

Gythion has a few rather insignificant ruins, including a well-preserved **Roman theater** (⊠ Archaio Theatrou) with stone seats intact. Some remains of the ancient town (Laryssion) are visible on **Mt. Koumaros** (⊠ 2 km [1 mi] north along the road to Monemvassia), a settlement that in Roman times exported the murex shell for dyeing imperial togas purple.

> **need a break?** Take a late-afternoon break for grilled octopus and ouzo; Gythion is the octopus capital of Greece. The best place is **Nautilia** (⊠ Southern end of waterfront, across from pier); look for the octopuses dangling in the doorway.

On the tiny islet of **Marathonissi** (⊠ East of Gythion), once called Kranae, Paris and Helen (wife of Menelaos) consummated their love affair after escaping Sparta, provoking the Trojan War described in the *Iliad*. A causeway now joins Marathonissi to Gythion. The **Pyrgos Tzannetaki Tower** on the island houses a museum of the Mani. ⊠ *Marathonissi* ☎ *27330/ 22676* 🖃 *€2* ⊙ *Daily 9:30–5.*

Beaches

Near Gythion there are beaches on the coast between Mavrovouni and Skoutari and north of town on the road to Monemvassia. About 10 km (6 mi) north of Gythion the Monemvassia road passes a long, sandy beach that, aside from the presence of a rusted freighter that ran aground here, is clean and idyllic.

Where to Stay & Eat

★ ¢–$$ ✕ **Isalos.** Though hardwood floors and tasteful pale walls lend Isalos a sophisticated air, at heart this is a friendly waterfront taverna with seating on the sidewalk and alongside the harbor—and a focus on the freshest fish. The menu lists some pastas and other Italian dishes, alongside traditional Greek fare. All can be accompanied by barrel wine from the family vineyard. ⊠ *Vassileos Pavlou 35* ☎ *27330/24024* 🖃 *No credit cards.*

¢–$ ✕ **Sinantisi.** The freshest seasonal local produce—artichokes in spring, squash and eggplant in summer, wild greens in winter—enhances the *catsarolas* (casserole-style dishes) at this grill. You may also order fresh fish, appetizers such as tzatziki and *taramosalata* (pink fish-roe dip), and homemade sweets such as clove-scented baklava. The restaurant is about 2 km (1 mi) south of Gythion off the main road to Areopolis. ⊠ *Town square, Mavrovouni* ☎ *27330/22256* ▤ *MC, V* ☺ *No lunch.*

$ ⊡ **Aktaion.** All of the rooms in this neoclassical building face the sea, and all have balconies. The style throughout is traditional, with some modern furnishings and old prints of Maniote life, and the overall ambience is that of a comfortable, well-maintained hotel. ⊠ *Vassileos Pavlou 39, 23200* ☎ *27330/23500 or 27330/23501* 🖷 *27330/22294* ⇨ *22 rooms* ▤ *No credit cards* ⏐◌⏐ *CP.*

$ ⊡ **Gythion Hotel.** A former gentleman's club from 1864 is now a waterfront hotel, entered off a flight of steps from the harbor. Rooms are rather narrow but have high ceilings and face the sea, and many have several beds to accommodate families; two apartments have kitchenettes. A hearty breakfast is served in a vaulted lounge. ⊠ *Vassileos Pavlou 33, 23200* ☎ *27330/23452* 🖷 *27330/23523* ⊕ *www.gythionhotel.gr* ⇨ *5 rooms, 2 apartments* ⚲ *Some kitchenettes, minibars* ▤ *No credit cards* ⏐◌⏐ *BP.*

LACONIA

ΛΑΚΩΝΙΑ

The Laconian plain is surrounded on three sides by mountains and on one side by the sea. Perhaps it was the fear that enemies could descend those mountains at any time that drove the Spartans to make Laconia their training ground, where they developed the finest fighting force in ancient Greece. A mighty power that controlled three-fifths of the Peloponnese, Sparta contributed to the Greek victory in the second Persian War (5th century BC). Ultimately, Sparta's aggressiveness and jealousy of Athens brought about the Peloponnesian War, which drained the city's resources but left it victorious. The Greek world found Sparta to be an even harsher master than Athens, and this fact may have led to its losses in the Boeotian and Corinthian wars, at the Battle of Leuctra, and, in 222–221 BC, at the hands of the Achaean League, who liberated all areas Sparta had conquered. A second period of prosperity under the Romans ended with the barbarian invasions in the 3rd century AD, and Sparta declined rapidly.

Laconia can also claim two important medieval sites: Mystras and Monemvassia. Jewels in the Byzantine crown, the former is an intellectual and political center, the latter a sea fortress meant to ward off invaders from the east.

Sparta

Σπάρτη

➋⓪ *60 km (37 mi) south of Tripoli, 60 km (37 mi) east of Kalamata.*

For those who have read about ancient Sparta, the bellicose city-state that once dominated the Greek world, the modern city on the broad Eu-

CloseUp

THE SPARTAN ETHIC

THE SPARTANS' RELENTLESS MILITARISM *set them apart from other Greeks in the ancient world. They were expected to emerge victorious from a battle or not at all, and for most of its existence Sparta was without a wall, because according to Lykourgos, who wrote Sparta's constitution sometime around 600 BC, "chests, not walls, make a city." The government was an oligarchy, with two kings who also served as military leaders. Spartan society had three classes: a privileged elite involved with warfare and government; farmers, traders, and craftspeople, who paid taxes; and the numerous Helots, a serf class with few rights.*

Selected boys in the reigning warrior class were taken from their parents at the age of seven and submitted to a training without parallel in history for ruthlessness. Their diet involved mostly herbs, roots, and the famous black broth, which included pork, the blood of the pig, and vinegar. Rich foods were thought to stunt growth. Forbidden to work, boys and young men trained for combat and practiced stealing, an acceptable skill—it was believed to teach caution and cunning—unless one was caught. One legend describes a Spartan youth who let a concealed fox chew out his bowels rather than reveal his theft. Girls also trained rigorously in the belief they would bear healthier offspring; for the same reason, newlyweds were forbidden to make love frequently.

The kingdom's iron coinage was not accepted outside Sparta's borders, creating a contempt for wealth and luxury (and, in turn, rapacious kings and generals). Sparta's warrior caste subjugated the native Achaean inhabitants of the region. Today all that remains of this realm founded on martial superiority is dust.

rotas River might be a disappointment, since ruins are few and far between. Given the area's earthquakes and the Spartans' no-frills approach—living more like an army camp than a city-state—no elaborate ruins remain, a fact that so disconcerted Otto, Greece's first king, that in 1835 he ordered the modern city built on the ancient site. The modern town is not terribly attractive, but it's pleasant enough, with a pedestrian-only city center.

At the **Temple of Artemis Orthia** (⊠ Tripoli road, down path to Eurotas River), outside town, the young Spartan men underwent *krypteia* (initiations) that entailed severe public floggings. The altar had to be splashed with blood before the goddess was satisfied. Traces of two such altars are among sparse vestiges of the 6th-century BC temple. The larger ruins are the remains of a grandstand built in the 3rd century AD by the Romans, who revived the flogging tradition as a public spectacle.

Ancient Sparta's **acropolis** (⊠ North end of town) is now part archaeological site, part park. Locals can be seen here strolling, along with many young couples stealing a romantic moment amid the fallen limestone and shady trees. The ruins include a **theater**, a **stadium**, and a **sanctuary to Athena**.

Stop a moment and contemplate the stern **Statue of Leonidas** (✉ End of Konstantinou). During the Second Persian War in the 5th century BC, with 30,000 Persians advancing on his army of 8,000, Leonidas, ordered to surrender his weapons, jeered, "Come and get them." For two days he held off the enemy, until a traitor named Efialtes (the word has since come to mean "nightmare" in Greek) showed the Persians a way to attack from the rear. Leonidas ordered all but 300 Spartans and 700 Thespians to withdraw, and when forced to retreat to a wooded knoll, he is said to have commented, "So much the better, we will fight in the shade." His entire troop was slaughtered.

The eclectic collection of the **archaeological museum** reflects Laconia's turbulent history and is worth an hour: Neolithic pottery; jewels and tools excavated from the Alepotripia cave; Mycenaean tomb finds; bright 4th- and 5th-century Roman mosaics; and objects from Sparta. Most characteristic of Spartan art are the bas-reliefs with deities and heroes; note the one depicting a seated couple bearing gifts and framed by a snake (540 BC). ✉ *Ayios Nikonos between Dafnou and Evangelistria* ☎ *27310/28575* ⊕ *www.culture.gr* 🗫 *€2* ☉ *Tues.–Sat. 8:30–3, Sun. 8:30–12:30.*

Olives are thick on the ground in these parts, so it's only fitting that Sparta is home to the **Museum of the Olive and Greek Olive Oil,** a quirky and appealing collection of apparatus and culture related to the staple of Greek economy since ancient times. Ancient oil lamps and storage jars are especially beautiful, and exhibits tracing the botany and cultivation of the olive are fascinating. ✉ *Othonos-Amalias 129* ☎ *27310/89315* ⊕ *www.piop.gr* 🗫 *€2* ☉ *Wed.–Mon. 10–6.*

> **need a break?**
>
> If you find yourself waiting for a bus out of Sparta at dinnertime, cross the street to **Parthenon** (✉ Vrasidou 106 ☎ 27310/23767) for the best gyro you may ever eat. The meat, which has a local reputation for being a cut above the usual, is served in pita with the right amount of chew and generous doses of onion, tomato, and tzatziki sauce.

Where to Stay & Eat

¢–$ ✕ **Diethnes.** Locals claim this is one of Sparta's best restaurants. Classic specialties include a fish dish made with garlic, wine, oil, and rusks; *bardouniotiko* (chicken cooked with cheese and olives) and, occasionally, sheep's heads cooked on a spit. The tree-shaded garden rounds out a perfect meal. ✉ *Paleologou 105* ☎ *27310/28636* 🚫 *No credit cards.*

¢–$ ✕ **Stelakos.** This spot 5 km (3 mi) south of Sparta, on the road to Mystras, is known for excellent chicken dishes. After enjoying its rustic pleasures, take a stroll outside for an unimpeded view of the Taygettus mountain range. You can sip an after-dinner coffee or ouzo in one of the tavernas in the main square, where waterfalls rush down a cliff face. ✉ *Off village square, Parori* ☎ *27310/83346* 🚫 *No credit cards* ☉ *Closed Sun.*

★ $$ ✕🏨 **Maniatis Hotel.** The sleek style here begins in the modern marble lobby and extends through the handsome guest rooms, with their contemporary, light-wood furnishings and soft, soothing colors. All rooms have balconies, wall-to-wall carpeting, and sparkling baths. The restaurant serves such specialties as *arni araxobitiko* (lamb with onions, cheese, red sauce, and walnuts) and *bourekakia* (honey-and-nut pastries). ⊠ *Paleologou 72, 23100* ☎ *27310/22665* ⊟ *27310/29994* ⊕ *www.maniatishotel.gr* ⇨ *80 rooms* △ *Restaurant, bar, lobby lounge* ⊟ *MC, V* ⏐⦶⏐ *BP.*

$$ ⌕ **Menelaion Hotel.** The pool sparkling in the courtyard—a welcome sight after a hot day of exploring the ruins of nearby Mystras—is the best thing about this city-center hotel. Guest rooms are nicely if somewhat blandly furnished and well equipped, with modern bathrooms, most with tubs. ⊠ *Paleologou 91, 23100* ☎ *27310/22161 through 27310/22165* ⊟ *27310/26332* ⊕ *www.menelaion.com* ⇨ *30 rooms* △ *Restaurant, café, cable TV, pool, bar* ⊟ *AE, MC, V* ⏐⦶⏐ *BP.*

Mystras

Μύστρας

🌣 ㉑ *4 km (2½ mi) west of Sparta, 64 km (40 mi) southwest of Tripoli.*

Fodor'sChoice
★

At ethereal Mystras, with its abandoned gold and stone palaces, churches, and monasteries lining serpentine paths, the scent of herbs and wild-flowers permeates the air, goat bells tinkle, and the silvery olive trees glisten with the slightest breeze. An intellectual and cultural center where philosophers like Chrysoloras, "the sage of Byzantium," held forth on the good and the beautiful, Mystras seems an appropriate place for the last hurrah of the Byzantine emperors in the 14th century. Today the splendid ruins are a UNESCO World Heritage Site and one of the most impressive sights in the Peloponnese.

In 1249 William de Villehardouin built the castle in Mystras in an attempt to control Laconia and establish Frankish supremacy over the Peloponnese. He held court here with his Greek wife, Anna Comnena, surrounded by knights of Champagne, Burgundy, and Flanders, but in 1259 he was defeated by the Byzantines. As the Byzantines built a palace and numerous churches (whose frescoes exemplified several periods of painting), the town gradually grew down the slope.

At first the seat of the Byzantine governor, Mystras later became the capital of the Despotate of Morea. It was the despots who made Mystras a cultural phenomenon, and it was the despots—specifically Emperor Constantine's brother Demetrios Palaiologos—who surrendered the city to the Turks in 1460, signaling the beginning of the end. For a while the town survived because of its silk industry, but after repeated pillaging and burning by bands of Albanians, Russians, and Ibrahim Pasha's Egyptian troops, the inhabitants gave up and moved to modern Sparta.

In spring Mystras is resplendent with wildflowers and butterflies, but it can be oppressively hot in summer, so get an early start. It's easy to spend half a day here. Bring water and sturdy shoes for the slippery rocks and the occasional snake.

Among the most important buildings in the lower town (Kato Chora) is **Ayios Demetrios,** the *mitropolis* (cathedral) founded in 1291. Set in its floor is a stone with the two-headed Byzantine eagle marking the spot where Constantine XII, the last emperor of Byzantium, was consecrated. The cathedral's brilliant frescoes include a vivid depiction of the Virgin and the infant Jesus on the central apse and a wall painting in the narthex of the Second Coming, its two red-and-turquoise-winged angels sorrowful as they open the records of Good and Evil. One wing of the church houses a **museum** that holds fragments of Byzantine sculptures, later Byzantine icons, decorative metalwork, and coins.

In the Vrontokion monastery are **Ayios Theodoros** (AD 1295), the oldest church in Mystras, and the 14th-century **Church of Panagia Odegetria,** or **Afendiko,** which is decorated with remarkable murals. These include, in the narthex, scenes of the miracles of Christ: *The Healing of the Blind Man, The Samaritan at the Well,* and *The Marriage of Cana.* The fluidity of the brushstrokes, the subtle but complicated coloring, and the resonant expressions suggest the work of extremely skilled hands.

The **Pantanassa monastery** is a visual feast of intricate tiling, rosette-festooned loops, and myriad arches. It is the only inhabited building in Mystras; the hospitable nuns still produce embroidery that you can purchase. Step out onto the east portico for a view of the Eurotas River valley below.

Every inch of the tiny **Perivleptos monastery,** meaning "attracting attention from all sides," is covered with exceptional 14th-century illustrations from the New Testament, including *The Birth of the Virgin*; in a lush palette of reds, yellows, and oranges; *The Dormition of the Virgin* above the entrance (with Christ holding his mother's soul represented as a baby); and, immediately to the left of the entrance, the famous fresco the *Divine Liturgy.*

In the upper town (Ano Chora), where most aristocrats lived, stands a rare Byzantine civic building, the **Palace of Despots,** home of the last emperor. The older, northeastern wing contains a guardroom, a kitchen, and the residence. The three-story northwest wing contains an immense reception hall on its top floor, lighted by eight Gothic windows and heated by eight huge chimneys; the throne probably stood in the shallow alcove that's in the center of a wall.

In the palace's **Ayia Sofia chapel,** the Italian wives of Emperors Constantine and Theodore Palaiologos are buried. Note the polychromatic marble floor and the frescoes that were preserved for years under whitewash, applied by the Turks when they transformed this into a mosque. Climb to the **castle** and look down into the gullies of Mt. Taygettus, where it's said the Spartans, who hated weakness, hurled their malformed babies. ⊠ *Ano Chora* 🕾 *27310/83377* 🕾 *All Mystras sites €5* ⊕ *www. culture.gr* 🕙 *Nov.–Apr., daily 8:30–3; May and Oct., daily 8–5; Sept., daily 8–6; June–Aug., daily 8–7.*

Sports & the Outdoors
The Athens travel agency **Trekking Hellas** (⊠ Fillelinon 7, 10557 Athens 🕾 210/331–0323 ⊕ www.trekking.gr) arranges weekend hiking trips to Mystras and a six-day walk through the Taygettus foothills, with visits to the Mani and Mystras.

Monemvassia

Μονεμβασία

🕐 ② *96 km (60 mi) southeast of Sparta.*

Fodor'sChoice
★

The Byzantine town of Monemvassia clings to the side of the 1,148-foot rock that rises out of the sea. The rock is part of what was once a headland, but in AD 375 was separated from the mainland by an earthquake. The town was first settled in the 6th century AD, when Laconians sought refuge after Arab and Slav raids. Monemvassia—the name *moni emvasia* (single entrance) refers to the narrow passage to this walled community—once enjoyed enormous prosperity, and for centuries dominated the sea lanes from Western Europe to the Levant. During its golden age in the 1400s, Monemvassia was home to families made wealthy by their inland estates and the export of malmsey wine, a sweet variety of Madeira praised by Shakespeare. When the area fell to the Turks, Monemvassia was controlled first by the pope and then by the Venetians, who built the citadel and most of the fortifications. The newer settlement that has spread out along the water on the mainland is not as romantic as the old town, but it's pleasant and well-equipped with shops and services.

Well-to-do Greeks once again live on the rock in houses they have restored as vacation homes. Summer weekends are crowded, but off-season Monemvassia is nearly deserted. Houses are lined up along steep streets only wide enough for two people abreast, and remnants of another age—escutcheons, marble thrones, Byzantine icons—evoke the sense that time has stopped. It's a delight to wander through the back lanes and along the old walls and to find perches high above the town or the sea.

If you walk or take a taxi from the adjoining town of Gefira, the rock looks uninhabited until you suddenly see castellated walls with an opening wide enough for one person. An overnight stay here allows you to enjoy this strange place when the tour groups have departed.

Christos Elkomenos (Christ in Chains; ✉ Pl. Tzamiou along main St.) is reputedly the largest medieval church in southern Greece. The carved peacocks on its portal are symbolic of the Byzantine era; the detached bell tower—like those of Italian cathedrals—is a sign of Venetian rebuilding in the 17th century.

The 10th-century **Ayios Pavlos** (✉ Across from Pl. Tzamiou), though converted into a mosque, was allowed to function as a church under the Ottoman occupation, an unusual indulgence.

For solitude and a dizzying view, pass through the upper town's wooden entrance gates, complete with the original iron reinforcement. Up the hill is a rare example of a domed octagonal church, **Ayia Sofia** (✉ At top of mountain), founded in the 13th century by Emperor Andronicus II and patterned after Dafni monastery in Athens. Follow the path to the highest point on the rock for a breathtaking view of the coast.

<table>
<tr><td>

off the
beaten
path

</td><td>

ISLAND OF ELAFONISI – Following the Laconic peninsula south from Monemvassia toward Neapolis for 35 km (22 mi) brings you to the village of Viglafia, where car ferries depart about every half hour (€2 for foot passengers, €8 for cars) for the 15-minute crossing to the island of Elafonisi. This is where Greeks retreat for a fish lunch in the delightful little port town and then spend the afternoon on miles-long sandy strands that may well be the best, and least-discovered, beaches in Greece. A number of small hotels on the island may tempt you to linger.

</td></tr>
</table>

Beaches

Some people swim off the rocks at the base of the old town and along the road leading to the main gate, but safer and more appealing is the pebble beach in the new town. For the most rewarding beach experience, head to the sandy strands at Pori, about 5 km (3 mi) northwest of Monemvassia.

Where to Stay & Eat

¢–$$ ✕ **To Kanoni.** After you roll out of bed, wander over to the Kanoni, which serves breakfast on a terrace overlooking the square's *kanoni* (cannon). Choose from omelets, ham and eggs, or thick, creamy yogurt and honey. Among the lunch and dinner offerings are eggplant baked with other fresh vegetables and feta, and *yiouvetsi* (beef baked in a clay pot with orzolike pasta). ⊠ *Old town* ☎ 27320/61387 ⊟ *No credit cards.*

¢–$ ✕ **Marianthi.** You'll feel as if you're dropping into someone's home at dinner here: family photos of stern, mustachioed ancestors hang on the walls along with local memorabilia, and the service, at tables on the street in good weather, is just as homey. Order the wild mountain greens, any of the fish—especially the fresh red mullet—the addictive potato salad (you may have to order two plates), and the marinated octopus sprinkled with oregano. ⊠ *Old town* ☎ 27320/61371 ⊟ *No credit cards.*

★ $$ ▥ **Byzantinon.** These comfortable and unusual accommodations are in buildings throughout the old town. All the rooms are different, embellished with tile work and other distinctive decorations, and some are multilevel. Less-expensive rooms do not have terraces or sea views but are still quite charming. If mobility is a concern, be advised that reaching many of the rooms requires clambering down narrow, unevenly paved lanes and climbing stairs. ⊠ *Old town, 23070* ☎ 27320/61351 or 27320/61254 ⊟ 27320/61436 ✎ byzantino@yahoo.gr ➫ 25 rooms ♿ *Kitchenettes in some rooms; no room TVs* ⊟ *MC, V.*

★ $$ ▥ **Malvasia.** Three restored buildings in the old town (reached on a trek over sometimes steep and uneven pavement) provide atmospheric lodgings. Rooms are tucked into nooks and crannies under cane-and-wood or vaulted brick ceilings. Each is decorated with bright patchwork rugs, embroidered tapestries, antique marble, and antique wood furniture. Many rooms have terraces and sea views, and some have fireplaces. Reserve well ahead in July and August. ⊠ *Old town, 23070* ☎ 27320/61323 or 27320/61113 ⊟ 27320/61722 ➫ 32 rooms ♿ *Kitchenettes, bar; no room TVs* ⊟ *AE, MC, V* ⦿ *CP.*

¢ ▥ **Hotel Pramataris.** When there is no room at the old town's inns, or if you don't like the idea of carting your baggage, this bright and sparkling seaside hotel in the new town is a wonderful alternative and a real bargain. The management is friendly and helpful; the bright, tile-floored rooms have balconies; and the beach is steps away, making this an excellent choice for families. Some units have connecting doors and can be combined. ⊠ *New town, on sea, 23070* ☎ *27320/61833* ✍ *hotelpr@hol.gr* 🛏 *15 rooms, 1 suite* ♿ *Minibars, beach* ▱ *MC, V* ⦿ *CP.*

¢ ▦ **Ta Kellia.** Built in an old monastery (*kellia* means "cells"), this establishment is now run, albeit a little haphazardly, by the Greek National Tourism Office. Though the hotel is not glamorous like the competition, the rough-hewn rooms are a good, comfortable alternative. Only a few rooms on the second floor have ocean views, but all face an airy plaza above the sea. ⊠ *Old town, on lower square opposite Church of Panagia Chrissafitissa, 23070* ☎ *27320/61520* 🛏 *11 rooms* ♿ *No a/c, no room TVs* ▱ *No credit cards.*

Shopping

Ioanna Anghelatou (⊠ Main street, old town ☎ 27320/61163), established by Ms. Anghelatou in the 1980s, has a loyal clientele for her extraordinary collection of antique and contemporary jewelry, much of it crafted by artisans from throughout Greece.

SOUTHERN PELOPONNESE A TO Z

To research prices, get advice from other travelers, and book travel arrangements, visit www.fodors.com.

AIR TRAVEL

CARRIERS Olympic Airlines offers daily one-hour flights from Athens to Kalamata's airport, 10½ km (6½ mi) outside town near Messinia.

🛈 **Olympic Airlines** ☎ 210/926–7555 Athens reservations line ⊠ Giatrakou 3, Kalamata ☎ 27210/86410 ⊕ www.olympic-airways.gr.

AIRPORTS

For the latest flight information in Kalamata, contact the Kalamata Airport.

🛈 **Kalamata Airport** ☎ 27210/69442.

BIKE & MOPED TRAVEL

A number of agencies in the area rent mopeds. For information on cycling in Greece, contact the Greek Cycling Federation.

🛈 **Greek Cycling Federation** ⊠ Bouboulinas 28, Athens ☎ 210/883–1413. **Maniatis** ⊠ Iatropoulou 1, Kalamata ☎ 27210/27694 ⊠ Faron 202, Kalamata ☎ 27210/26025.

BOAT & FERRY TRAVEL

The *Martha* runs five times weekly in winter and daily in summer between Gythion, Neapolis, and Kythera. In the Peloponnese, call the local port authority for the latest information on boat travel.

🛈 **Port Authorities** ☎ 27330/22262 in Gythion, 27210/22218 in Kalamata, 27210/23100 in Pylos, 27320/61266 in Monemvassia.

BUS TRAVEL

The association of regional bus companies (KTEL) provides frequent service at reasonable prices from Athens to the Southern Peloponnese, with buses several times daily for Gythion, Kalamata, and Tripoli and once a day for Andritsena, Monemvassia, and Pylos. Buses leave from Terminal A on the outskirts of Athens at Kifissou 100 (take Bus 051 at corner of Zinonos and Menandrou streets, near Omonia Square; from the airport, take Bus E93). Pick up a bus schedule from the Athens EOT (⇨ Visitor Information in Chapter 1) or call the number listed below for departure times or seat reservations.

In the Peloponnese, you may buy tickets at a local bus station. The network of bus routes lets you move easily, even to more remote sites such as the Pirgos Dirou Caves and Nestor's Palace museum in Chora. There are fewer buses in winter and on weekends. For short distances, you may buy tickets on board; otherwise purchase them in advance at the station.
🗲 **KTEL (Greek Coach Services) Station Office** ☎ 210/513-4574 in Andritsena, 210/512-4913 in Gythion, 210/513-4293 in Kalamata, 210/512-4913 in Monemvassia, 210/513-4293 in Pylos, 201/512-4913 in Sparta, 210/513-2834 in Tripoli. **Local bus stations** ✉ Main square, Andritsena ☎ 26260/22239 ✉ Ebrikleous at north end of harbor, Gythion ☎ 27330/22228 ✉ Artemidos 50, Kalamata ☎ 27210/22851 ✉ Off main square, Monemvassia ☎ 27320/61432 ✉ Pl. Trion Navarchon, Pylos ☎ 27230/22230 ✉ Vrasidou and Paleologou, Sparta ☎ 27310/26441 ✉ Pl. Kolokotronis, Tripoli ☎ 2710/224314. **Terminal A** ✉ Kifissou 100, Athens ☎ 210/512-4910 ⊕ www.ktel.org.

CAR RENTALS
🗲 Local Agencies **Hertz** ✉ Faron 186, Kalamata ☎ 27210/88268 ⊕ www.hertz.com. **Kottaras Rent-A-Car** ✉ Menelaon 54, Sparta ☎ 27310/28966 ⊕ www.kottaras-car-rentals.com. **Stephany's Tours** ✉ Deligianni 23, Tripoli ☎ 2710/239577.

CAR TRAVEL
Especially off-season, when buses don't run regularly, it's most rewarding to explore this region by car. You can rent a car in Athens or in any of the Peloponnese's bigger towns, such as Kalamata, Tripoli, Gythion, and Sparta.

Even if highways have assigned numbers, no Greek knows them by any other than their informal names, usually linked to their destination. For those traveling on the E92 from Athens to Tripoli, the section of the highway (the Corinth–Tripoli road) now cuts travel time in half, to little more than two hours. From Olympia in the northwest Peloponnese, you may take a smaller local road (74, the Pirgos–Tripoli road). Both approaches have mountainous stretches that occasionally close in winter because of snow, but conditions are otherwise good.

EMERGENCIES The Automobile Touring Club of Greece (ELPA) provides assistance for light repairs around the clock. There are also ELPA main offices in Kalamata and Tripoli.
🗲 **Automobile Touring Club of Greece** (ELPA) ☎ 104 road assistance, 210/606-8800 other information.

EMERGENCIES
Emergency information is listed below by region.
🗲 **Medical assistance** ☎ 27330/51259 first aid in Areopolis, 27330/22315 hospital in Areopolis, 27330/22001 through 27330/22003 clinic in Gythion, 27210/25555 first aid in Kalamata, 27210/23561 hospital in Kalamata, 2731/28671 first aid in Sparta, 2731/28672

hospital in Sparta. **Police** ☎ 27330/51209 in Areopolis, 27330/22100 in Gythion, 27210/23187 in Kalamata, 27230/31203 in Methoni, 27320/61210 in Monemvassia, 27230/22316 in Pylos, 27310/28701 in Sparta, 2710/222411 in Tripoli.

SPORTS & THE OUTDOORS

CAMPING There are several camping sites throughout the Southern Peloponnese; contact the **EOT** (⇨ Visitor Information in Chapter 1) for a free camping guide.

HIKING & Throughout the Peloponnese there are many small trails, or *kalderimi* CLIMBING (mule paths), to explore, as well as the international E4 European Rambler Trail, which starts in the Pyrenees, winds through Eastern Europe, and traverses Greece to Gythion. The southern half, from Delphi to Gythion, is considered less difficult than the northern section and can be walked most of the year; the best time is mid-May through early October. Pick up the southern section at Menalon Refuge and continue through Vresthena, Sparta, Taygettus Refuge, and Panagia Yiatris monastery to Gythion.

🎽 **Greek Alpine Club** ✉ Kapnikereas 2, Athens ☎ 210/321–2355. **Hellenic Federation of Mountaineering and Climbing** ✉ Milioni 5, Athens ☎ 210/363–6617 or 210/364–5904 ⊕ www.sportsnet.gr. **Sparta Alpine Club** ☎ 27310/24135. **Tripoli Alpine Club** ☎ 2710/232243.

SAILING Sailing in Greece isn't restricted to the Aegean Islands. Many people prefer to sail to the islands near Methoni, with stops at Sapientsa, Skiza, and Venetiko. When you rent a sailboat or charter a yacht, the agency will usually indicate where to find water and fuel. The local port authority (⇨ Boat & Ferry Travel) can give information on sailing. You can moor at Gythion, which has water and fuel; in Kalamata repair service and moorings are usually available; for sailing around the Messinian cape, the port authority at Pylos can be of help.

TAXIS

If you have trouble reaching a site—for example, there is no public transportation to Ancient Messene—take a taxi from a town's main square, which is always near the bus station. In rural areas drivers may not switch on the meter if the destination has a fixed price, but make sure you agree on the cost before getting in—remember that it's the same price whether you're alone or in a company of four. It's the mileage that counts. When leaving town limits, the driver may switch his meter to the higher rate (Tarifa 2). The price also goes up after midnight. If you think you've been had, don't hesitate to protest or threaten to report the driver to the police.

TOURS

Unlike in the Northern Peloponnese, the choice of English-language tours in the south is extremely limited. If an agency does venture into the region, it's usually a detour through Tripoli and Sparta for a cursory visit to Mystras, as part of a package to the Northern Peloponnese.

TRAIN TRAVEL

Train travel into the area is slower and much more limited than bus travel. Buy tickets before you leave; prices shoot up 50% when purchased on board. If you're traveling during a national holiday, when many Athenians head to the Peloponnese, it's worth paying extra for first class to ensure a seat, especially in no-smoking compartments. Train food is dismal, so stock up for long trips.

Trains run from Athens to Kalamata five times daily with stops in Corinth, Mycenae, and Tripoli, not to be confused with those traveling a second, longer route to Kalamata via Patras. In Athens, the Greek National Railway (OSE) offices are the most convenient if you're staying near Platia Syntagma (Constitution Square); otherwise purchase your ticket before departure at the Peloponnissos station. You can reach the station by Bus 057, which leaves every 10 minutes from Panepistimiou, or take Line 2 of the metro to the Larissa station, which is adjacent to the Peloponnissos station.

As of this writing, extensive track work is being done on the Peloponnesian line, with a goal of significantly improving service between Athens and Patras. Check for service interruptions and station changes by contacting one of the numbers below or in Train Travel in Smart Travel Tips.
🚹**Greek National Railway (OSE) offices** ✉Fillelinon 17, Athens ☎210/323–6747 ✉Sina 6, Athens ☎ 210/362–4402. **Kalamata station** ✉ Sidirodromikou Stathmou ☎ 27210/23904. **Peloponnissos station** ✉ Karilou 1, Athens ☎ 210/522–4302. **Tripoli station** ✉ Grigoris Lambraki at Xeniou Dios ☎ 2710/222402.

VISITOR INFORMATION
Tourist police often speak English and can help you find accommodations, restaurants, and sights. Because of the absence of Greek National Tourism Organization offices in the Southern Peloponnese, you will come to count on these officials for help and information. You can reach them by dialing 171 or local numbers. Beware of good-intentioned locals if you ask for directions to the tourist office—they may lead you to private travel agents (who can indeed be helpful) or to municipal offices that are not geared to helping the public.
🚹 **Tourist police** ☎ 171, 27210/95555 in Kalamata, 27310/20492 in Sparta, 2710/222411 in Tripoli.

The Cyclades

ANDROS, TINOS, MYKONOS, DELOS,
NAXOS, PAROS & SANTORINI

WORD OF MOUTH

"I'd always heard that Naxos has the best beaches in the Cyclades and our visit there last year confirmed it."

—repete

"Just next to Fira [on Santorini] is Firostefani, sometimes not designated as a separate village. This is a much shorter walk from Fira than Imerovigli, so if you can get a hotel there you will have the quiet and caldera view without the crowds."

—brotherleelove2004

"Yes, I would bring the ring [to Santorini] . . . suggest a romantic restaurant with a sunset view of the caldera. Catch her at that moment! If she loves you and has a pulse she can't say no."

—worldinabag

Updated by
Jeffrey and
Elizabeth
Carson

THE MAGICAL WORDS "GREEK ISLANDS" conjure up beguiling images. If for you they suggest sun and sea, blazing bare rock and mountains, olive trees and vineyards, white peasant architecture and ancient ruins, fresh fish and fruity oils, the Cyclades are isles of quintessential plenty, the ultimate Mediterranean archipelago. "The islands with their drinkable blue volcanoes," wrote Odysseus Elytis, winner of the Nobel Prize for poetry, musing on Santorini. That Homer—who loved these islands—is buried here is unverifiable but spiritually true.

The six major stars in this constellation of islands in the central Aegean Sea—Andros, Tinos, Mykonos, Naxos, Paros, and Santorini—are the archetype of the islands of Greece. Here, it always seems—at least in summer—Zeus's sky is faultlessly azure, Poseidon's sea warm, and Dionysus's nightlife swinging (especially in Mykonos's discos). The prevailing wind is the northern *vorias*; called *meltemi* in summer, it cools the always-sunny weather. In a magnificent fusion of sunlight, stone, and sparkling aqua sea, the Cyclades offer both culture and hedonism: ancient sites, Byzantine castles and museums, lively nightlife, shopping, dining, and beaches plain and fancy.

These arid, mountainous islands are the peaks of a deep, submerged plateau, and their composition is rocky, with few trees. They are volcanic in origin, and Santorini (also known as Thera), southernmost of the group, actually sits on the rim of an ancient drowned volcano that exploded about 1600 BC. The dead texture of its rock is a great contrast to the living, warm limestone of most Greek islands. Santorini's geological colors— black, pink, brown, white, or pale green—are never beautiful; as you arrive by boat, little shows above the cliff tops but a string of white villages—like teeth on the vast lower jaw of some giant monster. Still, the island was called Kállisti, "Loveliest," when it was first settled, and today, appreciative visitors find its mixture of vaulted cliff-side architecture, European elegance, and stunning sunsets all but irresistible.

A more idyllic rhythm of life can still be found on many of the other Cyclades (and, of course, in off-season Santorini). Well-to-do Andros, where ship-owning families once lived, retains an air of dignity, and its inhabitants go about their business largely indifferent to visitors. It's a good place for adults in search of history, museums, and quiet evenings. Tinos has stayed authentically Greek, since its heavy tourism is largely owing to its miracle-working icon and not to its beautiful villages. In the town of Mykonos, the whitewashed houses huddle together against the meltemi winds, and backpackers rub elbows with millionaires in the mazelike white-marble streets. The island's sophistication level is high, the beaches fine, and the shopping varied and upscale. It's also the jumping-off place for a mandatory visit to tiny, deserted Delos. That windswept islet, birthplace of Apollo, still watched over by a row of marble lions, was once the religious and commercial center of the eastern Mediterranean.

Naxos, greenest of the Cyclades, makes cheese and wine, raises livestock, and produces potatoes, olives, and fruit. For centuries a Venetian stronghold, it has a shrinking, aristocratic Roman Catholic population,

Venetian houses and fortifications, and Cycladic and Mycenaean sites. Paros, a hub of the ferry system, has reasonable prices and is a good base for trips to other islands. It's also good for lazing on long, white-sand beaches and for visiting fishing villages. Of course, throughout the Cyclades, there are countless classical sites, monasteries, churches, and villages to be explored. The best reason to visit them may be the beauty of the walk, the impressiveness of the location, and the hospitality you will likely find off the beaten track. Despite its depredations, the automobile has brought life back to Cycladic villages. Many shuttered houses are being authentically restored, and much traditional architecture can still be found in Ia on Santorini, Kardiani on Tinos, and Apeiranthos on Naxos—villages that are part of any deep experience of the islands. In the countryside, many of the sites and buildings are often or permanently closed, though the fencing around sites may have fallen, and monks and nuns may let you in if you are polite and nicely dressed—and the gods are still out there.

Exploring the Cyclades

Each island in the Cyclades differs significantly from its neighbors, so how you approach your exploration of the islands will depend on what sort of experience you are seeking. The busiest and most popular islands are Santorini, with its fantastic volcanic scenery and dramatic cliff-side towns of Fira and Ia, and Mykonos, a barren island that insinuates a sexy jet-set lifestyle, flaunts some of Greece's most famous beaches, and has a perfectly preserved main town. Santorini and Mykonos have the fanciest accommodations. Naxos has the best mountain scenery and the longest, least-developed beaches, and Andros, too, is rugged and mountainous, covered with forests and laced with waterfalls. Tinos, the least visited and most scenic of the Cyclades, is the place to explore mountain villages, hundreds of churches, and fanciful dovecotes.

All these islands are well connected by ferries and catamarans, with the most frequent service during the summer season. Schedules change frequently, and it can be difficult to plan island-hopping excursions in advance. So be flexible and the islands are yours.

About the Restaurants

Eating is a lively social activity in the Cyclades, and the friendliness of most taverna owners compensates for the lack of formal service. In fact, you might be surprised to notice simple furnishings and friendly informality even at the most expensive restaurants on Mykonos and Santorini—these restaurant owners have borrowed what's best from the local tradition. At just about any restaurant, from the simplest taverna to the most expensive place, dining is outdoors, on a terrace or sometimes simply at a table in the street.

Unless you order intermittently, at most restaurants the food comes all at once (this is not the case at some of the more expensive, international restaurants in the islands). In many tavernas you will not be given a menu but will be escorted into the kitchen and shown what's being prepared fresh that day. Fish, ironically, is rather expensive in the islands; expect

There is no bad itinerary for the Cyclades. The islands differ remarkably, and are all beautiful. It is possible to "see" any island in a day, for they are small and the "must-see" sights are few—Delos, Santorini's caldera, the Minoan site at Akrotiri, and Paros's Hundred Doors Church. So planning a trip depends on your sense of inclusiveness, your restlessness, your energy, *and* your ability to accommodate changing boat schedules.

Numbers in the text correspond to numbers in the margin and on the Cyclades, Mykonos Town, Delos, Naxos, and Santorini maps.

9

If you have
3 days

In summer, when high-speed ferries and fast interisland boats run frequently, you can easily visit both Mykonos and Santorini in three days. On ⊠ **Mykonos** ❶–❿ ▶ you can spend the first day and evening enjoying appealing Mykonos town, where a maze of beautiful streets are lined with shops, bars, restaurants, and discos; spend time on one of the splendid beaches; and, if you want to indulge in some hedonism, partake of the wild nightlife. The next morning take the local boat to nearby **Delos** ⓫–㉛ for one of the great classical sites in the Aegean; you'll be back in time to board a fast boat to ⊠ **Santorini** ㊺–㊿. Once you've settled in, have a sunset drink on a terrace overlooking the caldera, one of the world's great sights; you'll find many view-providing watering holes in Fira, the capital, or Ia, Greece's most-photographed village. The next day, visit the extensive prehistoric site at Akrotiri and the Museum of Prehistoric Thera; then have a swim one of the black-sand beaches at Kamari or Perissa.

Alternatively, say if off-season boat schedules make it too difficult to visit both Santorini and Mykonos in so short a time, after a day and a morning on Mykonos and Delos go to nearby ⊠ **Tinos.** Here, you can visit Greece's most popular pilgrimage site and also drive through beautiful villages, such as Kardiani.

If you have
5 days

Follow the three-day itinerary for ⊠ **Mykonos** ❶–❿ ▶ (and **Delos** ⓫–㉛) and ⊠ **Santorini** ㊺–㊿ above, but between Mykonos and Santorini pull into ⊠ **Naxos** ㉜–㊹. Plan on arriving from Mykonos in the late afternoon or evening, and begin with a predinner stroll around Naxos town, visiting the Portara (an ancient landmark), the castle, and other sights in the old quarter. The next morning, visit the Archaeological Museum; then drive through the island's mountainous center for spectacular views. Along the way, visit such sights as the Panayia Drosiani, a church near Moni noted for 7th-century frescoes; the marble-paved village of Apeiranthos; and the Temple of Demeter. If you have time, stop for a swim at one of the beaches facing Paros, say Mikri Vigla; then board a fast boat for the sail down to Santorini, arriving in time to see the sun set over the caldera.

If you have
8 days

If you want a good overview of the Cyclades, with time out for some hiking, visits to Byzantine churches, and relaxation, begin with a day and a night in elegant, nontouristy ⊠ **Andros** ▶, where you might want to settle into Andros town for the night or, if you want to be on the beach, Batsi. Spend the morning and early afternoon of the next day driving around the island to explore its small villages and lush mountainsides. The next stop is ⬚ **Tinos,** for an overnight in Tinos town and, the next morning, a visit to Panayia Evangelistria (Church of the Annunciate Virgin), Greece's most popular pilgrimage site, and a few of the island's many beautiful villages, including Pirgos. Then it's on to ⬚ **Mykonos** ❶–❿ for two days and nights, with a visit to **Delos** ⓫–㉛, some downtime on one of the island's splendid beaches, and visits to such sights as the Archaeological Museum ❷ and the Monastery of the Panayia Tourliani in Ano Mera ❿. Continue south for an overnight on ⬚ **Naxos** ㉜–㊹, where you'll want to see Naxos town and to make at least a short drive into the mountainous center. Then head to ⬚ **Paros,** where you should enjoy a meal in the little fishing harbor of Naousa and, on a morning drive around the island, visit the lovely mountain village of Lefkes. Finally, it's time to head to beautiful ⬚ **Santorini** ㊺–㊱ for the final two days of the itinerary. Should you have time and energy, you may well decide to continue exploring the other Cycladic islands, especially Siphnos and Melos—all have their own beauties.

---

to pay about €45 per kilo—that translates to about €15 a serving, at least. You are welcome to eat as simply as you choose and will not be frowned on if you simply order a large Greek salad and another *meze* (small dish) or any other combination that appeals to you.

Reservations are not required unless otherwise noted, and casual dress is the rule. Restaurant schedules on the Cyclades vary; some places close for lunch, most close for siesta, and all are open late. Many, many restaurants close from late October into late March or mid-April or so. Those that remain open, though, are usually the traditional tavernas that serve excellent food to a local clientele.

About the Hotels

Island accommodations range from run-down pensions to bedrooms in private houses to luxury hotels. Overall, the quality of accommodations in the Cyclades is high. The best rooms and service (and noticeably higher prices) are on Mykonos and Santorini, where luxury resort hotels are mushrooming. Wherever you stay in the Cyclades, make a room with a view, and a balcony, a priority.

Unless you're traveling at the very height of the season (July 15–August 30), you're unlikely to need advance reservations; often the easiest—and most recommended—way to find something on the spot is to head for a tourist office and describe your needs and price range. Alternatively, walk around town and ask where you can rent a room, but take a good look first, and check the bathroom before you commit. If there are extra beds in the room, clarify in advance that the amount agreed on is for the entire room—owners occasionally try to put another person in the same room. When approached by one of the touts who meet the ferries, make sure he or she tells you the location of the rooms being pushed, and look before you commit. Avoid places on main roads or near all-night discos. Rates, which are regulated by the Greek National Tourism Organization (EOT), vary tremendously from month to month; in the off-season, rooms may cost half of what they do in August.

In August water pressure may be low, and only expensive hotels provide hot water 24 hours a day; in some hotels you must turn on a thermostat for a half hour to heat water for a shower (don't forget to turn it off). Signs tell you that water is in short supply in the Cyclades, reminding you to conserve it.

WHAT IT COSTS In euros					
	$$$$	**$$$**	**$$**	**$**	**¢**
RESTAURANTS	over €20	€16–€20	€12–€15	€8–€11	under €8
HOTELS	over €160	€121–€160	€91–€120	€60–€90	under €60

Restaurant prices are for one main course at dinner or, for restaurants that serve only *mezedes* (small dishes), for two mezedes. Hotel prices are for two people in a standard double room in high season, including taxes.

Timing

In July and August, the Cyclades are crowded and less personal and more expensive than they are at other times of the year. Walkers, nature lovers, and devotees of classical and Byzantine Greece would do better to come in spring and fall, ideally in late April–June or September–October, when temperatures are lower and the islands are less tourist-riddled. The only problem with off-season travel in the islands is less-frequent boat service; in fact, there is sometimes no service at all between November and mid-March, when stormy weather can make the seas too rough for sailing. In late March the islands begin to burst with thousands of varieties of wildflowers, and sprightly crimson poppies dapple stern marble blocks; the sea begins to warm up for comfortable swimming in late May. Autumn's days are shorter, but the sea remains alluringly swimmable well into October. Autumn travel to the islands also brings rustic pleasures: grapes are pressed in September, and zesty olives are gathered and fields plowed in October.

ANDROS

ΑΝΔΡΟΣ

▶ The northernmost and second largest of the Cycladic islands, rugged, mountainous Andros is about 32 km by 16 km (nearly 20 mi by 10 mi). The highest peak, Mt. Kouvari, reaches 3,260 feet. A network of springs gives birth to streams, which whirl down from the mountaintops, feeding lush valleys; unlike the other Cyclades, Andros is green with pines, sycamores, mulberries, and oaks. In ancient times it was called Hydroussa, or "Well-Watered." The springs, streams, and falls have a cooling effect that, together with summer's northerlies (meltemia), ameliorate the Aegean heat. Spring's southerlies bring heat and many birds.

Foreign tourism is in an early stage on Andros, and most of the islanders are indifferent to it. Perhaps the reason for this snobbishness is that Andros has been a wealthy island since silk production began in the 12th century; today, Andros thrives on Greeks who own villas and bring their own cars on the two-hour ferry journey from Rafina. The well-known Goulandris shipping family from Andros has founded two museums of modern art and the Archaeological Museum in Andros town, all splendid. Though Andros is an island for the cultured, low tourism means low prices for restaurants and hotels (but not cafés), compared to Mykonos or Santorini.

Across the entire landscape of Andros you will notice a striking system of stone walls that marks the boundaries between the fields of different owners. In a building style unique to Andros, the walls are interrupted at regular intervals, and each gap is filled with a large, flat, upright slab. This saves stone and labor and allows herders to move the large slab for the passage of animals. Dovecotes, also seen on Mykonos and especially Tinos, are a common sight on Andros. The Venetians introduced these square towers, whose pigeonholes form decorative geometric design, in the 13th century. Though many fell into disuse, when hard times struck the islands in the 20th century, local farmers started breeding the pigeons and selling them abroad as a delicacy. Today only a few dovecotes are still maintained.

Gavrio

Γαύριο

75 km (46½ mi) east of Rafina Port, 35 km (22 mi) northeast of Andros town.

Gavrio, on the northwest coast, used to be the dull little port town of Andros. But it has developed conscientiously and well, with restaurants, cafés, hotels, and a newly designed quayside. It is now attractive, lively, and the gateway to the beauties of the north. From here roads north and west lead to unspoiled beaches (Felos, Kaminaki, and Pisolomnionas, for example), magnificent agricultural land, and historic landmarks (the ruined Byzantine church at Vitali and the Hellenistic tower at Ayios Petros). The more developed beaches on the main road to the south (Iagios Petros and Kipri, for example) have tavernas with nightlife.

Where to Stay & Eat

$$ ✕ **Sails.** Captain Nikos Tzouanos's quayside fish taverna serves fresh fish that he catches himself. If his large fishing boat, the *Hagios Demetrios,* is not moored out front, then Nikos is out fishing. His mother Vasiliki cooks, and other family members are usually in evidence. There is a good selection of starters, but the catch of the day is the main thing. Price depends on the fish, but you can eat cheaply here. ⊠ *Gavrio (waterfront)* ☎ *22820/71333* ☐ *No credit cards.*

$$ 🔲 **Anastasia Traditional House.** On a winding road up the wooded mountain behind Gavrio is where Nikos and Anastasia Paraskevopoulos decided to build their rural dream house. The large stone house has two cool apartments with wood-beamed ceilings and deep-color, traditional fabrics. The kitchens are fully equipped, and the view of verdant valley and blue sea is sublime. The price includes transfers. ⊠ *Ano Gavrio, 84501* ☎ *22820/72287 or 69379/72014* ⊕ *www.villasinandros. com* 🛏 *2 rooms* ⚲ *Kitchens* ☐ *No credit cards* ☉ *Closed Nov.–Mar.*

$ 🔲 **Aktio Studios.** Five minutes from the beach is this cream-color building draped with bougainvillea. All of the large, airy rooms have terraces

Beaches & Water Sports

The best sport in the islands is swimming, and the islands gleam with beaches, from long blond stretches of sand to tiny pebbly coves. Waterskiing, parasailing, scuba diving, and especially windsurfing have become ever more popular, though venues change from season to season. Anyone who invests in a mask, snorkel, and flippers has entry to intense, serene beauty. The best beaches are probably those on the southwest coast of Naxos, though the ones on Mykonos are trendier. Beaches on Tinos and Andros tend to be less crowded than those on other islands in the Cyclades. The strands on Santorini, though strewn with plenty of bathers, are volcanic; you can bask on sands that are strikingly red and black.

9

Cubism, Cyclades Style

One of the real draws of the Cyclades is the sight of miragelike, white clusters of houses appearing alongside blue waters or tumbling down cliffs and hillsides. Ia and Fira, the two caldera-side towns on Santorini, are the best places to see this typical Cyclades style of architecture, where cubical, whitewashed houses are built one atop another. Mykonos town, a warren of square, white houses arrayed along mazelike streets to confound invaders, is another architectural delight. Distinctive architecture will catch your eye throughout these islands: the stone walls and fanciful dovecotes on Andros; the marble squares in the town of Pirgos, on Tinos; Venetian landmarks in Naxos town.

Great Flavors

Dishes in the Cyclades are often wonderfully redolent of garlic and olive oil. Many of the islands, such as Andros, are still more geared to agriculture than to tourism, so you can expect the freshest tomatoes, peppers, olives, and other vegetables to appear on the table. Grilled seafood is an island favorite, and you should try grilled octopus with ouzo at least once in your travels. Lamb is a staple in the Cyclades, as it is everywhere in Greece, and a simply grilled lamb chop can be a memorable meal; lamb on a skewer and *keftedes* (spicy meatballs) also appear on many menus. Likewise, a light meal of fresh fried calamari with a salad garnished with locally made feta cheese is the Cyclades equivalent of fast food but is invariably excellent. The volcanic soil of Santorini is hospitable to the grape, and Greeks love the Santorini wines. In fact, Santorini and Paros now proudly produce officially recognized "origin" wines, which are sought throughout Greece. Barrel or farmer's wine is common, and except in late summer when it starts to taste a bit off, it's often good.

Hiking

The Cyclades are justly famous for their hiking, with the islands of Andros and Naxos being the largest and least explored. Ancient goat and donkey trails go everywhere—through fields, over mountains, along untrodden coasts. Rarely is the sea out of view, and almost never are you more than an hour's walk from a village. Since tourists tend to visit Greece for classical sites, for nightlife, and for the beach, walking is uncrowded even in July and August. Prime walking months, though, are April and May, when temperatures are reasonable, wildflowers seem to cover every surface, and birds fly over on their migration. October is also excellent for hiking, again because the weather is pleasant and bird-watching is prime—plus, olive groves provide their own sort of spectacle when dozens of "gatherers" descend upon them to place nets beneath the trees and shake the ripe olives off the branches. You can usually pick up maps of trails and guides in tourist offices and in local bookshops, and travel agencies on Andros and Naxos sometimes arrange group hiking trips.

Shopping

Mykonos, with Santorini taking a close second, is the best island in the Cyclades for shopping. You can buy anything from Greek folk items to Italian designer clothes, cowboy boots, and leather jackets from the United States. Although island prices are better than in the expensive shopping districts of Athens, there are many tourist traps in the resort towns, with high-pressure sales tactics and inflated prices for inferior goods. The Greeks have a word for naive American shoppers—*Americanakia*. Among the standard shops there are still craftspeople who make at least some of their own items. Each island has a unique pottery style that reflects its individuality. Santorini potters like the bright shades of the setting sun, though the best pottery islands are Paros and Siphnos. Island specialties are icons hand-painted after Byzantine originals; weavings and embroideries; local wines; and gold worked in ancient and Byzantine designs. Don't be surprised when many stores close between 2 and 5:30 in the afternoon and reopen in the evening; even on the chic islands most everybody takes a siesta.

---

with sea views. The mostly Greek clientele returns year after year. The price includes transfers. ⊠ *On main road south of Gavrio, Paralia, Vardia, 84501* ☏ *22820/71607* 🖷 *22820/71773* ⊕ *www.aktiostudios.gr* 🛏 *10 rooms, 2 suites* ♿ *Refrigerators, fans, bar* 🖃 *No credit cards* ⏐⊘︎ *BP.*

Batsi

Μπατσί

16 km (10 mi) southeast of Gavrio, 27 km (17 mi) northwest of Andros town.

Originally a small fishing village, Batsi has developed over the past 15 years into a simple resort town, where many of the businesses have a friendly, nonhustling quality. On the hillside, a few lovely houses from a century ago look down to the promenade along the sea. Many people stay here because the social life is a bit more lively than it is in Andros town and because there is a beach with windsurfing equipment and paddleboat rentals.

Beaches

Batsi beach is sandy, accessible, and protected from the north wind. Windsurfing equipment and paddleboats can be rented by the hour here. To the south are **Dellavoya** beach and **Ayia Marina** beach, both with tavernas and places to stay. **Xylokaryda,** to the north, is also lovely.

Where to Stay & Eat

★ $–$$$ ✕ **Stamatis.** The best taverna in town is open year-round. Outside, green tables are crammed into the gleaming white alleys. The air-conditioned interior is homey and rustic; the walls display hunting relics. Stamatis's son Yannis will invite you to have a look at the wonderful dishes in the kitchen. If the sea is too rough for a fresh fish haul, try the roasted chicken with Andros cheese stuffing or the phyllo-wrapped lamb with green peppers and onions; on Wednesday, *kleftiko* (the special house lamb) is prepared. The good barrel wine is their own. The light crème caramel is the perfect dessert. ⊠ *One street up from main quay* ☎ 22820/41020 ▤ *MC, V.*

★ ¢–$ ✕ **Balcony of the Aegean.** Ask an Andriot what his favorite restaurant is, and he will name this one. Located in Ano Aprovato (6 km [4 mi] up from Batsi; follow signs), it has a spectacular sunset view and serves lovingly traditional food. Upon your arrival Socrates and Stella Kolitsas usually offer a raki. Sip it with *dra*, a spread made from fresh butter, or with unaged *kopanistí*, a sharp soft cheese. Stella is especially proud of her *fourtalia* (sausage omelet), and Socrates his finely toned meats, since he is a butcher who raises it all himself. With everything homemade or homegrown, this is what Greek food is supposed to taste like. It's open for dinner all year and for lunch in season. ⊠ *Ano Aprovato* ☎ 22820/41020 ▤ *No credit cards.*

$$ ▥ **Mare e Vista–Epaminondas.** Looking something like a cross between
Fodor's Choice a dovecote and a monastery, the exterior of this quiet complex—all terra-
★ cotta and white plaster—climbs Batsi's northern hillside, about 15 minutes by foot from the town center. The cool, spacious interiors of the duplexes and triplexes are tasteful and relaxing, with marble floors and traditionally embroidered curtains. Most rooms have kitchenettes, and all have huge verandas overlooking Batsi Bay. The hotel's deep freshwater pool is lighted all night. ⊠ *On road to lower Batsi, on left, 84503* ☎ *22820/41682 or 22820/41177* 🖷 *22820/41681* ⊕ *www.mare-vista.com* ➪ *23 apartments* ♿ *Some kitchenettes, refrigerators, cable TV, pool, billiards, Ping-Pong* ▤ *MC, V* ⊙ *Closed Nov.–Mar.* ⬚ *BP.*

¢ ▥ **Nora–Norita.** These comfortable, quiet apartments (two to six persons) in a residential area—white cubes on a green hillside—overlook Batsi bay and are 3 minutes from a little beach and 15 minutes by foot from town. All have terraces, sea views, and simple island furnishings; though breakfast is not served, you can make your own in the kitchenettes in each unit. Look for the white houses with red tile roofs as you enter Batsi from Gavrio. ⊠ *84503* ☎ *22820/41252* 🖷 *22820/41608* ⊕ *www.bookandros.com* ➪ *15 apartments* ♿ *Fans, kitchenettes* ▤ *MC, V.*

Nightlife

There are several music bars on the Batsi waterfront where the young congregate: follow your ears. Try **Porto Batsi** (☎ 22820/42026), which is located by Batsi's southern parking lot, right on the sea; there's live music on weekends. On Batsi Square, up the stairs, is the **Capriccio Music Bar** (☎ 22820/41770), which has a view over the harbor; it starts with Greek music and later gets creative.

Shopping

At **Meleti** (⊠ Batsi, one street up from main quay ☎ 22840/42003) potter Sofia Meleti, who studied in Athens, sells distinctive plates, cups, and decorative items and engages her customers in a chat. Each piece is decorated with a bee.

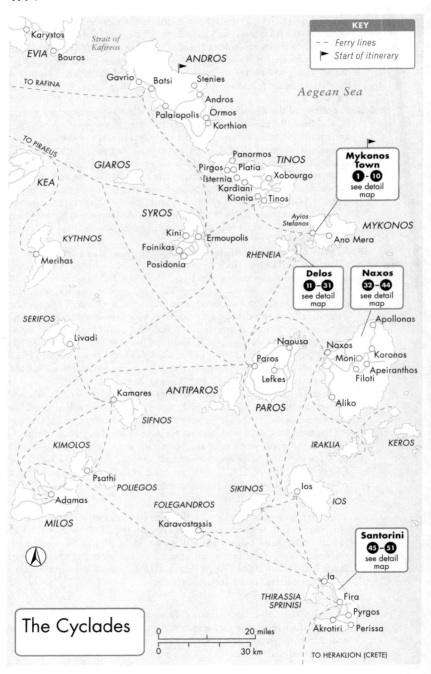

The Cyclades

KEY
-- Ferry lines
► Start of itinerary

Aegean Sea

Karystos
EVIA Bouros
Strait of Kafireos
ANDROS
Gavrio Batsi Stenies
TO RAFINA
Andros
Palaiopolis Ormos
Korthion

TO PIRAEUS
GIAROS
KEA
Panormos TINOS
Pirgos Platia
Isternia Xobourgo
Kardiani
Kionia Tinos

KYTHNOS
SYROS
Kini Ermoupolis
Foinikas
Posidonia
Merihas

Ayios Stefanos
RHENEIA
MYKONOS
Ano Mera

Mykonos Town
1-10
see detail map

Delos
11-31
see detail map

Naxos
32-44
see detail map

SERIFOS
Livadi

Naousa
Paros
Lefkes
ANTIPAROS
PAROS

Apollonas
Naxos
Moni Koronos
Apeiranthos
Filoti
Aliko

Kamares
SIFNOS

IRAKLIA KEROS

KIMOLOS
Psathi POLIEGOS
Adamas
MILOS

SIKINOS
FOLEGANDROS
Karavostassis

Ios
IOS

Santorini
45-51
see detail map

THIRASSIA SPRINISI
Ia
Fira
Pyrgos
Akrotiri Perissa

TO HERAKLION (CRETE)

0 20 miles
0 30 km

Palaiopolis

Παλαιόπολη

9 km (5½ mi) south of Batsi.

Most of Palaiopolis, the ancient capital of Andros, lies beneath the sea, destroyed in the 4th century BC either by an earthquake or a landslide. The town today is a quiet but gorgeous village that stretches down the slope of Mt. Kouvari to the shore. The road cuts through the **upper town,** where you'll find a café and an excellent roadside taverna. From the taverna you can look up to the hill and see the site of an **ancient acropolis,** 984 feet above the sea, now occupied by a small **Orthodox chapel;** some **waterfalls** are a short climb up. In 1832 a farmer turned up the famous **statue of Hermes** in this area, which is now on display in the Archaeological Museum in Andros town. Opposite the café in the upper town, 1,039 steps lead down through the **lower village,** in the shade of flowering vines and trees heavy with lemons. Scattered near the **beach** are marble remnants of early buildings and statues. Though the site has not been systematically excavated, archaeologists did enough digging around here in 1956 to conjecture that the bits and pieces are remains from the ancient agora.

need a break? Stop in Menites to see the sacred springs and have a glass of local wine and a bite to eat at the shaded **Karydes taverna** (⊠ ½ km [¼ mi] off main road, halfway between the fork in the road and Andros town ☎ 22820/51556), where you can order a whole rooster, an Andriot specialty. Mineral spring water tumbles from a series of lion-head spouts along a stone wall, and hidden by greenery in the background is Panayia tis Koumulous, an Orthodox church supposedly built on the site of a temple to Dionysos. According to legend, these are the very springs whose water turned to wine each year on the god's feast day.

Andros Town

Άνδρος (Χώρα)

27 km (17 mi) southeast of Batsi.

Andros town (Chora) has been the capital of the island since the Venetian occupation in the 13th century. The city is built on a long, narrow peninsula, at the end of which is a small island with the remains of a Venetian castle built about 1220.

Take a leisurely stroll down the center's **marble promenade** (⊠ Main St.), past the impressive 13th-century **Palatiani Church** and the interesting **gift shops** that sell the local pottery. Handsome 19th-century stone mansions line the streets, and over their doors are carved galleons, indicating that the original owners were shipowners or sea captains. The town is deliberately kept traditional, and its tidy appearance and the distinction of its neoclassical houses bear witness to its long-standing prosperity.

The main street leads to **Kairis Square** (⊠ At tip of peninsula), where in the center stands a bust of **Theophilos Kairis,** a local hero. Born in Andros town in 1784, Kairis was educated in Paris and returned to Andros in 1821 to become one of the leaders in the War of Independence. A philosopher, scholar, and social reformer, he toured Europe to raise money for an orphanage and school, which he founded in 1835. The school became famous in Greece, and enrollment eventually rose to 600, but the Orthodox church closed it down and tried Kairis as a heretic for his individualistic religious beliefs. He died in a Syros prison in 1852.

★ The pride of Andros's **Archaeological Museum** is the life-size marble statue of Hermes discovered in Palaiopolis and thought to be a copy of a Praxiteles. The collections range from the Mycenaean through Roman eras. Upstairs is an extensive display on Zagora, the earliest known settlement in Andros, a town built during the Geometric period on the southwest coast, on a promontory 529 feet above sea level, surrounded by jagged cliffs. It was the main settlement from 900 BC to 700 BC, before the rise of Palaiopolis. The site is not open, but the museum provides a model. ⊠ *Kairis Sq.* 🖼🖼 *22820/23664* 🎫 *€4* ⊙ *Tues.–Sun. 8:30–2:30.*

★ The **Museum of Modern Art** is the first of the three museums on Andros funded by the Goulandris Foundation. Its summer exhibitions of contemporary international and Greek artists are posted online, as well as conferences and other events. ⊠ *On the stepped street down from Kairis Sq., next to Museum of Sculpture* 🖼 *22820/22444* ⊕ *www. moca-andros.gr* 🎫 *€6, includes admission to Museum of Sculpture* ⊙ *Sat.–Mon. 10–2 and 6–8, Sun. 10–2.*

The **Museum of Sculpture,** displays rotating exhibitions by Greece's best modern artists and a permanent collection of the works of sculptor Michael Tombros (1889–1974), whose parents were born on Andros. ⊠ *On the stepped street down from Kairis Sq., next to Museum of Modern Art* 🖼 *22820/22444* 🎫 *€6, includes admission to Museum of Modern Art* ⊙ *Sat.–Mon. 10–2.*

Beaches
Nimborio Beach (⊠ About 300 ft from Andros town center), on the edge of Andros town, is very developed. About 2 km (1 mi) north of Andros town is **Yialia beach** (⊠ Stenies), with two tavernas.

Where to Stay & Eat
¢–$ ✕ **Parea.** This shaded taverna perched high above a windswept beach is a good place to lunch on cheese croquettes or stuffed eggplant and tomatoes. Veal in lemon sauce is more substantial. ⊠ *Kairis Sq.* 🖼 *22820/23721* 🖃 *MC, V.*

$$ 🖼 **Hotel Pighi Sariza.** This peaceful hotel is in a green mountain village near the Sariza mineral springs (be sure to buy a bottle) and is wonderful for a break from the summer heat. From here you can hike the many mountain trails nearby, view waterfalls, and—sigh—hear nightingales. Half the comfortable rooms have sea views and half have (just as good) mountain views. The spacious restaurant has an international menu. Nature lovers will appreciate the fact that the hotel is open year-round. ⊠ *Apikia road, 5 km (3 mi) north of Andros town, 84500* 🖼 *22820/*

23799 ⊠ 22820/22476 ⊕ *www.andros.gr/pighi-sariza/index_en.htm*
🛏 *42 rooms ♨ Restaurant, minibars, cable TV, pool, sauna, recreation
room* 🖃 *AE, DC, MC, V* ⊗ *Closed Nov.–Mar.* ⊠️ *BP.*

$$ 🏨 **Hotel Stagira.** Andros town's most pleasant hotel is peaceful, welcoming,
attractive, and quiet. The lobby, contrasting Aegean white with dark wood,
leads onto a terrace with an Italianate view of the cypresses of the Li-
vadia valley framing the sea. The suites, similarly designed, have bal-
conies or gardens and full kitchens. Some suites have two baths.
⊠ *Dexameni (turn left after Paradise hotel; after 10 yds turn up hill on
right), 84500* ☎ *22820/23525* ⊠ *22820/24502* ⊕ *androsnetcenter.gr/
Chora/stageira.htm* 🛏 *24 rooms, 8 suites ♨ Kitchenettes, bar* 🖃 *AE,
DC, MC, V.*

$ 🏨 **Niki.** This elegant stately home, right off Kairis Square, fills up when-
ever there is an event at the museums, which is often. The hotel's wood-
paneled cafeteria has marble floors and a ceiling painting of old sailing
ships. Half the rooms, all with balconies and loft beds, face the market
street, while the preferred rooms overlook the sea. The homemade
breakfast costs extra. ⊠ *Andros town, 84500* ☎☎ *22820/29155*
⊕ *www.androsgreece.gr/HOTELS_EN/NIKI_EN.htm* 🛏 *7 rooms ♨ Re-
frigerators, bar* 🖃 *No credit cards.*

The Arts
Check the Museum of Modern Art for lectures, recitals, and opening
nights.

Sports & the Outdoors
The mountainous geography and lush greenery make Andros a pleas-
ant island for hiking, especially Palaiopolis and near Messaria (south),
Apikia (west), and Stenies (north). The 5-km (3-mi) hike from the lit-
tle village of Lamira to Andros town is popular. Andros Travel in Batsi
organizes many hiking trips, their specialty.

Shopping
Nearly unique, Andros's main street hasn't changed much in 50 years.
A number of gift shops sell local pottery, embroidery, ship's models, and
other handmade objects. Through the arch on Kairis Square (notice the
ancient columns in it), Embeirikou street has fixed up its fine neoclas-
sical houses, and some quality shops have opened. They include a gallery
showing Greek and international artists; an art bar; a clothing store with
all Greek fabrics; the local music academy; a natural cosmetics store;
and more.

ART   **Christos Eustathiou** (☎ 22820/22328) is the eponymous shop where
Christos sells his paintings and small sculpted figures.

GIFTS   Katerina Agapaloglou's gift shop, **Detis** (☎ 22820/24855), offers a se-
lection of small items by Greek craftsmen.

SWEETS   Andros is noted for candies and sweetmeats, and several shops in An-
dros town maintain the tradition. Perhaps the best sweetshop is **Kon-
stantinos Laskaris** (⊠ Main St. ☎ 22820/22305), where bitter almond
taffy, rose petals in syrup, and *kaltsounia* (walnut-honey sweetmeat) are
among the once-common, now exotic, items for sale.

TINOS

ΤΗΝΟΣ

Perhaps the least visited of the major Cyclades, Tinos (or, as archaeologists spell it, Tenos) is among the most beautiful and most fascinating. The third largest of the Cyclades after Naxos and Andros, with an area of 195 square km (121 square mi), it is inhabited by nearly 10,000 people, many of whom still live the traditional life of farmers or craftsmen. Its long, mountainous spine, rearing amid Andros, Mykonos, and Syros, makes it seem forbidding, and in a way it is. It is not popular among tourists for several reasons: the main village, Tinos town (Chora), lacks charm; the beaches are undeveloped; there is no airport; and the prevailing north winds are the Aegean's fiercest (passing mariners used to sacrifice a calf to Poseidon—ancient Tinos's chief deity—in hopes of avoiding shipwreck). For Greeks, a visit to Tinos is essential: its great Church of the Evangelistria is the Greek Lourdes, a holy place of pilgrimage and miraculous cures; 799 other churches adorn the countryside. Encroaching development here is to accommodate those in search of their religious elixir and not, as on the other islands, the beach-and-bar crowd.

Tinos is renowned for its 1,300 dovecotes, which, unlike those on Mykonos or Andros, are mostly well maintained; in fact, new ones are being built. Two stories high, with intricate stonework, carved-dove finials, and thin schist slabs arranged in intricate patterns resembling traditional stitchery, the dovecotes have been much written about—and are much visited by doves.

Tinos is dotted with possibly the loveliest villages in the Cyclades, which, for some welcome reason, are not being abandoned. The dark arcades of Arnados, the vine-shaded sea views of Isternia and Kardiani, the Venetian architecture of Loutra, the gleaming marble squares of Pirgos: these, finally, are what make Tinos unique. A map, available at kiosks or rental agencies, will make touring these villages by car or bike somewhat less confusing, as there are nearly 50 of them.

Tinos Town

Τήνος (Χώρα)

55 km (34 mi) southeast of Andros's port.

Civilization on Tinos is a millennium older than Tinos town, or Chora, founded in the 5th century BC. On weekends and during festivals, Chora is thronged with Greeks attending church, and restaurants and hotels cater to them. As the well-known story goes, in 1822, a year after the War of Independence began (Tinos was the first of the islands to join in), the Virgin sent the nun Pelagia a dream about a buried icon of the Annunciation. On January 30, 1823, such an icon was unearthed amid the foundations of a Byzantine church, and it started to heal people immediately.

Fodor'sChoice The Tiniots, hardly unaware of the icon's potential, immediately built
★   the splendid **Panayia Evangelistria,** or Church of the Annunciate Virgin,

TRADITIONAL FESTIVALS

ALL OVER GREECE, villages, towns, and cities have traditional celebrations that vary from joyous to deeply serious, and the Cyclades are no exception. These festivals commemorate significant religious and secular events in all kinds of ways—with special foods, dancing, music, and other activities. Whatever islands you're visiting, check out what's happening and participate if you can. It's a wonderful way to discover the unique spirit of a place and to see the locals. You may even be able to join in some of the dances.

Ano Aprovato, a village south of Batsi on Andros, holds a paneyiri (festival) on August 15, for the Dormition of the Virgin Mary, with feasting and dancing along with the religious rites.

In Tinos town on Tinos, the healing icon from Panayia Evangelistria church is paraded with much pomp on Annunciation Day, March 25, and especially Dormition Day, August 15. As it is carried on poles over the heads of the faithful, cures are effected, and religious emotion runs high. On July 23, in honor of St. Pelagia, the icon is paraded from Kechrovouni Nunnery, and afterward the festivities continue long into the night, with music and fireworks.

If you're on Santorini on July 20, you can partake in the celebration of St. Elias's name-day, when a traditional pea-and-onion soup is served, followed by walnut and honey desserts and folk dancing.

Naxos has its share of festivals to discover and enjoy. Naxos town celebrates the Dionysia festival during the first week of August, with concerts, costumed folk dancers, and free food and wine in the square. During Carnival, preceding Lent, "bell wearers" take to the streets in Apeiranthos and Filoti, running from house to house making as much noise as possible with strings of bells tied around their waists. They're a disconcerting sight in their hooded cloaks, as they escort a man dressed as a woman from house to house to collect eggs. In Apeiranthos, villagers square off in rhyming-verse contests: on the last Sunday of Lent, the paliomaskari, their faces blackened, challenge each other in improvising kotsakia (satirical couplets). At the May Day Festival in Koronos, wildflower garlands are made, and there's lively dancing. On July 14, Ayios Nikodemos Day is celebrated in Chora with a procession of the patron saint's icon through town, but the Dormition of the Virgin on August 15 is, after Easter and Christmas, the festival most widely celebrated, especially in Sangri, Filoti (where festivities take place on August 4), and Apeiranthos.

On Paros each year on August 23, Naousa celebrates the heroic naval battle against the Turks, with children dressed in native costume, great feasts, and traditional dancing. The day ends with 100 boats illuminated by torches converging on the harbor.

on the site, using the most costly marble from Tinos, Paros, and Delos. The church's **marble courtyards** (note the green-veined Tiniot stone) are paved with pebble mosaics and surrounded by offices, chapels, a health station, and **seven museums.** Inside the **upper three-aisle church** dozens of beeswax candles and precious votives—don't miss the golden orange tree near the door donated by a blind man who was granted sight—dazzle the eye. You must often wait in line to see the little icon, which is encrusted with jewels, donated as thanks for cures. To beseech the icon's aid, a sick person sends a young female relative or a mother brings her sick infant. As the pilgrim descends from the boat, she falls to her knees, with traffic indifferently whizzing about her, and crawls painfully up the faded red padded lane on the main street—1 km (½ mi)—to the church. In the church's courtyards, she and her family camp for several days, praying to the magical icon for a cure, which sometimes comes. This procedure is very similar to the ancient one observed in Tinos's temple of Poseidon. The **lower church,** called the Evresis, celebrates the finding of the icon; in one room a baptismal font is filled with silver and gold votives. The chapel to the left commemorates the torpedoing by the Italians, on Dormition Day, 1940, of the Greek ship *Helle*; in the early stages of the war, the roused Greeks amazingly overpowered the Italians. ⊠ *At end of Megalohari* ☎ *22830/22256* 🖼 *Free* ⊘ *Daily 8:30–3.*

On the main street, near the church, is the small **Archaeological Museum;** its collection includes a sundial by Andronicus of Cyrrhus, who in the 1st century BC also designed Athens's Tower of the Winds. Here, too, are Tinos's famous huge, red storage vases, from the 8th century BC. ⊠ *Megalohari* ☎ *22830/22670* 🖼 *€4* ⊘ *Tues.–Fri. 8–2.*

One and a half kilometers (¾ mi) from Chora you'll see a copse of pines shading a small parking lot, from which a path leads down to Stavros (Holy Cross) chapel; right on the water is the unmarked **Markos Velalopoulos's Ouzeri** (⊠ Under church ☎ 22830/23276), which serves *strophia* (raki), ouzo, and traditional snacks such as fried cheese or figs with sesame. This is Tinos's most romantic spot to watch the sunset. It is also good for swimming. Note that the sunken breakwater along the coastal road in front of the *ouzeri* (casual bar) is ancient.

---

off the beaten path

MOUNTAIN VILLAGES ABOVE CHORA – At night the lights of the hill villages surrounding Tinos's highest mountain, Mt. Tsiknias—2,200 feet high and the ancient home of Boreas (the wind god)—glitter over Chora like fireworks. By day they are worth visiting. Take the good road that runs through Dio Horia and Monastiri, ascending and twisting around switchbacks, passing fertile fields and a few of Tinos's most fanciful old dovecotes. After 9 km (5½ mi) you reach **Kechrovouni,** or just Monastiri, which is a veritable city of nuns, founded in the 10th century. One cell contains the head of St. Pelagia in a wooden chest; another is a small icon museum. Though a nunnery, Kechrovouni is a lively place, since many of the church's pilgrims come here by bus. Out front, a nun sells huge garlic heads and braids to be used as charms against misfortune; the Greeks call these "California garlic." One kilometer (½ mi) farther on, Tinos's telecommunications towers spike the sky, marking the entrance to **Arnados,** a strange village 1,600 feet up, overlooking Chora. Most of the streets here are vaulted, and thus cool and shady, if a bit claustrophobic; no medieval pirate ever penetrated this warren. In one alley is the **Ecclesiastical Museum,** which displays icons from local churches. Another 1½ km (¾ mi) farther on are the **Dio Horia**

(Two Villages), with a marble fountain house, unusual in Tinos. The spreading plane tree in front of it, according to the marble plaque, was planted in 1885. Now the road starts winding down again, to reach **Triandaros,** which has a good restaurant. Many of the pretty houses in this misty place are owned by Germans. Yannis Kyparinis, who made the three-story bell tower in Dio Horia, has his workshop and showroom here.

Beaches

There is a series of beaches between Chora and Kionia (and beyond, for walkers). **Stavros** is the most romantic of the area beaches. **Ayios Yannis** (⊠ Near Porto) is long, sandy, and peaceful. **Pachia Ammos** (⊠ Past Porto, reached by a dirt Rd.) is undeveloped and sparkling.

Where to Stay & Eat

¢–$$$ ✕ **Metaxi Mas.** On a trellised lane by the harbor, Euripides Tatsionas's restaurant, the best in Tinos, turns out to be no more expensive than a taverna. The name means "between us," and a friendly air prevails. The decor is traditional—pale yellow walls, wooden furniture, high stone arches—and the staff is welcoming. From starters to desserts, the food is homemade, but with a haute-Athenian flair. For a starter, try deep-fried sun-dried tomatoes or hot eggplant slices wrapped around cheese, mint, and green pepper. Among the main dishes, the spicy lamb cooked in paper is especially succulent; the beef fillet with peppers is also exceptional. With a fireplace in winter and an air conditioner for summer, this place stays open year-round. ⊠ *Kontogiorgi alley* ☎ *22830/25945* ▭ *AE, MC, V.*

¢–$ ✕ **To Koutouki tis Elenis.** On a little alley (first right as you start up Evangelistria street), this place is usually full: Eleni Skoutari's food is well known; even the *skordato* cheese, good with raki, is homemade. For starters, Eleni fries her own sun-dried tomatoes in batter; the "Koutouki" meatballs, made from both beef and pork, are full of herbs. Good main dishes include pork cooked in wine with rosemary and feta, and rabbit stew with thyme. ⊠ *5 Gafou* ☎ *22830/24857* ▭ *AE, MC, V.*

★ $$ ✕▥ **Alonia Hotel.** Ordinary-looking from the road, this is Tinos's most pleasant hotel. Comfortable, family-run, and quietly efficient, it is for you if you dislike snazzy resorts and want to be out of (but still convenient to) hectic Chora. The fairly large rooms all have dazzling views (those overlooking the pool are best) over palms and olive trees to the sea; the bathrooms have bathtubs, a rarity in island hotels. Tinos's largest freshwater pool is surrounded by lawns, trees, and gardens—not baking cement. The price includes transfers. The restaurant (¢) serves home-style meals prepared by the owners: to begin, try marinated raw fish fillets or grilled fresh vegetables. Entrées include chicken breasts stuffed with bacon, cheese, and herbs, or beef stew with wine and onions—the menu changes, so ask what's available that day. The barrel wine is excellent. ⊠ *2 km (1 mi) from Chora toward Porto (Agios Ioannis), 84200* ☎ *22830/23541 through 22830/23543* ▤ *22830/23544* ⊕ *www. aloniahotel.gr* ⇄ *34 rooms, 4 suites* ⌂ *Restaurant, pool, bar* ▭ *AE, MC, V* ⦿| *BP.*

$$$ ⊞ **Porto Tango.** This ambitiously up-to-date resort-hotel strives for the best in decor and service. Greece's late prime minister, Andreas Papandreou, stayed here during his last visit to Tinos. Modular Cycladic architecture lends privacy; the lobby, where an art exhibition is usually on display, has a wooden ceiling, marble floors, and Tiniot furnishings, both modern and antique. Rooms are simple, white, and private, with basic wood furniture. There are extensive spa facilities, for ultimate relaxation. The price includes transfers. ⊠ *Follow signed road up hill, 84200 Porto–Agios Ioannis* ☎ *22830/24411 through 22830/24415* 🖷 *22830/24416* ⊕ *www.tinosportotangohotel.com* ⋙ *55 rooms, 7 suites* ⚒ *Restaurant, cable TV, pool, gym, sauna, spa, bar* ☰ *AE, D, MC, V* ⊘ *Closed Nov.–Mar.* ❙⊘❙ *BP.*

$ ⊞ **Akti Aegeou.** The family that runs this little resort is lucky to own such a valuable piece of property. Akti Aegeou, or "Aegean Coast," is right on the uncrowded beach at Porto. All the airy rooms come with sea-view balconies, marble floors, and traditional rag rugs. The good restaurant specializes in fresh fish. A fishing caïque is set up next to the saltwater pool, which looks out to Delos. ⊠ *Beach of Ayios Ioannis, 84200 Agios Ioannis* ☎ *22830/24248* 🖷 *22830/23523* ⊕ *www.aktiaegeou.gr* ⋙ *5 rooms, 6 apartments* ⚒ *Restaurant, kitchenettes, pool, bar* ☰ *AE, MC, V* ⊘ *Closed Nov.–Mar.* ❙⊘❙ *BP.*

$ ⊞ **Anna's Rooms.** A 10-minute walk from town and 5 minutes from Stavros beach, this small pension is and perfect for families, since each apartment has a full kitchen. The apartments, arranged around a green courtyard, all have balconies with sea views. Except for fresh bread, there is no breakfast. The price includes transfers. ⊠ *Kiona road, about ½ km (¼ mi) outside town, 84200* ☎ *22830/22877* ⊕ *www.tinos.nl* ⋙ *7 rooms* ⚒ *Kitchens, Internet room* ☰ *No credit cards.*

Nightlife

Tinos has fewer bars and discos than the other big islands, but there is plenty of late-night bar action behind the waterfront between the two boat docks. People go back and forth among the popular clubs **Syvilla, Volto,** and **Metropolis,** on the street behind the fish market next to the Archeio Bar.

Sports

Of all the major islands, Tinos is the least developed for sports. The strong winds discourage water sports, and concessions come and go.

Shopping

FARMERS' & FLEA MARKETS   Tinos is a rich farming island, and every day but Sunday, farmers from all the far-flung villages fill the **square** (⊠ Between 2 docks) with vegetables, herbs, and *kritamos* (pickled sea-plant leaves). In a square near town, the local pelican (a rival to Mykonos's Petros) can often be found cadging snacks from the **fish market.**

Tinos produces a lot of milk. A short way up from the harbor, on the right, is the little store of the **Enosis** (Farmers' Cooperative; ⊠ Megalohari, up from harbor ☎ 22830/23289), which sells milk, butter, and cheeses, including sharp *kopanistí*, perfect with ouzo; local jams and honeys are for sale, too.

Evangelistria, the street parallel to the church, is closed to traffic and is a kind of **religious flea market,** lined with shops hawking immense candles, chunks of incense, tacky souvenirs, tin votives, and sweets. There are several good jewelers' shops on the market street, where, as always on Tinos, the religious note is supreme.

JEWELRY At **Artemis d and b** (⊠ Evangelistria 18 ☎ 22830/24312), owned by the Artemis brothers, Christos paints the seascapes; Dimitris, a retired captain, makes ship models; and the classic jewelry is all by Teniots. The selection at **Ostria** (⊠ Evangelistria 20 ☎ 222830/23893 ☏ 22830/24568) is especially good; in addition to delicate silver jewelry, it sells silver icon covers, silver plate, and 22-karat gold.

WEAVINGS The 100-year-old weaving school, or **Biotechniki Scholi** (⊠ Evangelistria, three-quarters of the way up from sea ☎ 22830/22894), sells traditional weavings—aprons, towels, spreads—made by its students, local girls. The largest of its three high-ceiling, wooden-floored rooms is filled with looms and spindles.

Kionia

Κιονία

2½ km (1¼ mi) northwest of Tinos town.

The reason to come to this small community outside Tinos town is to visit the large, untended **Sanctuary of Poseidon** (⊠ Northwest of Tinos town), also dedicated to the bearded sea god's sea-nymph consort, Amphitrite. The present remains are from the 4th century BC and later, though the sanctuary itself is much older. The sanctuary was a kind of hospital, where the ailing came to camp and solicit the god's help. The marble dolphins in the museum were discovered here. According to the Roman historian Pliny, Tinos was once infested with serpents (goddess symbols) and named Serpenttown (Ophiousa), until supermasculine Poseidon sent storks to clean them out. The sanctuary functioned well into Roman times.

Beach

The Kiona road ends at a long, sheltered beach, which is unfortunately being worn away by cars heading for the two pretty coves beyond, including the Gastrion cave, whose entrance bears Byzantine inscriptions.

Where to Stay & Eat

¢–$ ✕ **Tsambia.** Abutting the sanctuary of Poseidon and facing the sea, this multilevel taverna home makes traditional fare. For starters try the indigenous specialties: *louza* (hung pork fillet preserved in wax), local Tiniot cheeses rarely sold in stores (especially fried local goat cheese), and homegrown vegetables. Fresh fish is available, depending on the weather. Tried-and-true are pork in red wine with lemon, or goat casserole with oregano. To get here, follow signs for TRADITIONAL TAVERNA before the Sanctuary of Poseidon. ⊠ *Cement Rd.* ☎ *22830/23142* ▭ *No credit cards.*

$$$ ⊡ **Tinos Beach Hotel.** Part of the government's all-too-successful sponsorship to promote tourism in the '70s, this is Tinos's most varied resort: big, somewhat impersonal, and efficient. The huge, cool lobby

features lots of stone and tile. Most rooms have splendid sea views, and there are suites and bungalows with marble floors that sleep four. ⊠ *Tinos beach, at end (3 km [2 mi]) of Kionia road, past sanctuary to Poseidon, 84200* ☎ *22830/22626* 🖷 *22830/23153* ⊕ *www.tinosbeach. gr* ➩ *110 rooms, 5 suites, 47 bungalows* ⟑ *Restaurant, café, 2 tennis courts, 2 pools, Ping-Pong, volleyball, bar, shops* ▤ *AE, D, MC, V* ⊗ *Closed Nov.–Mar.* ⦿ *BP.*

Isternia

Ιστέρνια

24 km (15 mi) northwest of Tinos town.

The village of Isternia (Cisterns) is verdant with lush gardens. Many of the marble plaques hung here over doorways—a specialty of Tinos—indicate the owner's profession, for example, a sailing ship for a fisherman or sea captain. A long, paved road winds down to a little port, **Ayios Nikitas,** with a **beach** and two **fish tavernas**; a small boat ferries people to Chora in good weather.

Pirgos

Πύργος

★ *32 km (20 mi) northwest of Tinos town, 8 km (5 mi) north of Isternia.*

The village of Pirgos, second in importance to Chora, is inland and up from the little harbor of Panormos. Tinos is famous for its marble carving, and Pirgos, a prosperous town, is noted for its sculpture school (the town's highest building) and marble workshops, where craftsmen make fanlights, fountains, tomb monuments, and small objects for tourists; they also take orders. The village's main square is aptly crafted of all marble; the five cafés, noted for *galaktoboureko* (custard pastry), and one taverna are all shaded by an ancient plane tree. The quarries for the green-veined marble are north of here, reachable by car. The cemetery here is, appropriately, a showplace of marble sculpture.

The marble-working tradition of Tinos survives here from the 19th century and is going strong, as seen in the two adjacent museums **Museum Iannoulis Chalepas and Museum of Tenos Artists,** which house the work of Pirgos's renowned sculptor, and other works. ⊠ *1 block from bus stop* ☎ *22830/31262* 🖳 *€5* ⊗ *Daily 10–2 and 6–8.*

Beaches

The **beaches next to Panormos** are popular in summer.

Shopping

A number of marble carvers are, appropriately, found in Pirgos. You may visit the shop of probably the best master carver, **Lambros Diamantopoulos** (⊠ Near main Sq. ☎ 22830/31365), who accepts commissions for work to be done throughout Greece. He makes and sells traditional designs to other carvers, who may bring a portable slab home to copy, and to visitors.

Panormos Bay

Όρμος Πανόρμου

35 km (22 mi) northwest of Tinos town, 3 km (2 mi) north of Pirgos.

Panormos Bay, an unpretentious port once used for marble export, has ducks and geese, a row of seafood restaurants, and a good beach with a collapsed sea cave. More coves with secluded swimming are beyond, as is the islet of Panormos. There are many rooms to rent.

Where to Eat

$$ ✕ **The Fishbone.** This small taverna, decorated with lots of blue and two Tenian fanlights, is on the quay; boats right out front bring in fresh fish, which owners Belasarius Lais and Nikos Menardos serve with flare. Among the appetizers are small fish pies and mussels in mustard sauce. Fresh fish wrapped in paper to preserve succulence is a specialty; sole with mushrooms is also a top choice. ⊠ *Panormos* ☎ *22830/31362* 🖃 V ⊘ *Closed Nov.–Apr.*

MYKONOS & DELOS

ΜΥΚΟΝΟΣ ΚΑΙ ΔΗΛΟΣ

Put firmly on the map by Jackie O, Mykonos has become one of the most popular of the Aegean islands. Although the dry, rugged island is one of the smallest of the Cyclades—16 km (10 mi) by 11 km (7 mi)—travelers from all over the world are drawn to its many stretches of sandy beach, its thatched windmills, and its picturesque port town of Mykonos. Happily, the islanders seem to have been able to fit cosmopolitan New Yorkers or Londoners gracefully into their way of life. You may see, for example, an old island woman leading a donkey laden with vegetables through the town's narrow streets, greeting the suntanned vacationers walking by. The truth is, Mykoniots regard a good tourist season as a fisherman looks at a good day's catch; for many, the money earned in July and August will support them for the rest of the year. Not long ago Mykoniots had to rely on what they could scratch out of the island's arid land for sustenance, and some remember suffering from starvation under Axis occupation during World War II. In the 1950s a few tourists began trickling into Mykonos on their way to see the ancient marvels on the nearby islet of Delos, the sacred isle.

For almost 1,000 years Delos was the religious and political center of the Aegean and host every four years to the Delian games, the region's greatest festival. The population of Delos actually reached 20,000 at the peak of its commercial period, and throughout antiquity Mykonos, eclipsed by its holy neighbor, depended on this proximity for income, as it partly does today. Anyone interested in antiquity should plan to spend a morning on Delos. Most travel offices in Mykonos town run guided tours that cost about €30, including boat transportation and entry fee. Alternatively, take one of the caïques that visit Delos daily from the port: the round-trip costs about €9, and entry to the site (with no guide) is €6. They leave between 8:30 AM and 1 PM and return noon to 2 PM.

Mykonos Town

Μύκονος (Χώρα)

16 km (10 mi) southeast of Tinos town.

For some, Mykonos town remains the Saint-Tropez of the Greek islands. The scenery is memorable, with its whitewashed streets, Little Venice, the Kato Myli ridge of windmills, and Kastro, the town's medieval quarter. Its cubical two-story houses and churches—with their red or blue doors and domes and wooden balconies—have been long celebrated as some of the best examples of classic Cycladic architecture. Pink oleander, scarlet hibiscus, and trailing green pepper trees form a contrast amid the dazzling whiteness—kept up by frequent renewal of whitewash. Any visitor who has the pleasure of getting lost in its narrow streets (made all the narrower by the many outdoor stone staircases, which maximize housing space in the crowded village) will appreciate how its confusing layout was designed to foil pirates. After Mykonos fell under Turkish rule in 1537, the Ottomans allowed the islanders to arm their vessels against pirates, which had a contradictory effect: many of them found that raiding other islands was more profitable than tilling arid land. At the height of Aegean piracy, Mykonos was the principal headquarters of the corsair fleets—the place where pirates met their fellows, found willing women, and filled out their crews. Eventually the illicit activity evolved into a legitimate and thriving trade network.

❶ A bust of Mando Mavroyennis, the island heroine, stands on a pedestal in the **main square.** In the 1821 War of Independence the Mykoniots, known for their seafaring skills, volunteered an armada of 24 ships, and in 1822, when the Ottomans later landed a force on the island, Mando and her soldiers forced them back to their ships. After independence, a scandalous love affair caused her exile to Paros, where she died.

The best time to visit the **central harbor** is in the cool of the evening, when the islanders promenade along the **esplanade** to meet friends and visit the numerous cafés. By the open-air fish market, Petros the Pelican preens and cadges eats, disdaining a group of ducks. In the 1950s a group of migrating pelicans passed over Mykonos, leaving behind a single exhausted bird; Vassilis the fisherman nursed it back to health, and locals say that the pelican in the harbor is the original Petros, though there are several.

The main shopping street, **Matoyanni** (⊠ Perpendicular to harbor), is lined with jewelry stores, clothing boutiques, chic cafés, and candy shops. The **Public Art Gallery** (⊠ Matoyanni ☎ 22890/27190) is also here, with exhibitions changing often.

❷ The **Archaeological Museum** affords insight into the intriguing history of the Delos shrine. The museum houses Delian funerary sculptures discovered on the neighboring islet of Rhenea, many with scenes of mourning. The most significant work from Mykonos is a 7th-century BC *pithos* (storage jar), showing the Greeks in the Trojan horse and the sack of the city. ⊠ *Ayios Stefanos road, between boat dock and town* ☎ 22890/22325 ▧ €3 ☉ *Wed.–Mon. 8:30–2:30.*

Aegean Maritime
Museum **3**

Ano Mera **10**

Archaeological
Museum **2**

Church of
Paraportiani . . .**7**

Folk
Museum **6**

Greek Orthodox
Cathedral of
Mykonos **8**

Little Venice . . .**4**

Main square . . .**1**

Mykonos
windmills **5**

Roman Catholic
Cathedral **9**

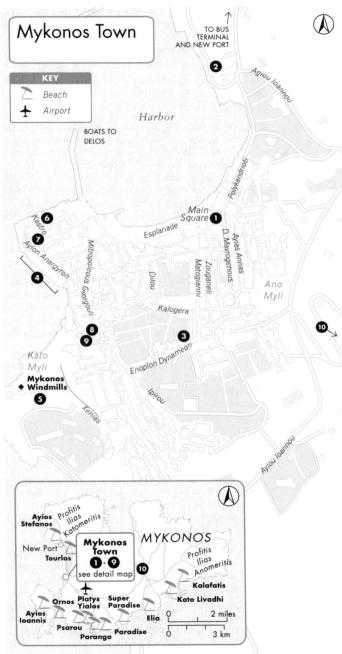

Mykonos Town

KEY

Beach

Airport

TO BUS
TERMINAL
AND NEW PORT

Agiou Ioannou

Harbor

BOATS TO
DELOS

Polykandrioti

*Main
Square* **1**

Esplanade

Kastro

6

7

Ayion Anargyron

4

Mitropoleous Georgouli

Diliou

Kalogera

Ayias Annas

D. Mavrogenous

Zouganeli

Matogianni

*Ano
Myli*

8

9

3

10

*Kato
Myli*

♦ **Mykonos
Windmills**

5

Xenias

Enoplon Dynameon

Ipirou

Ayiou Ioannou

MYKONOS

**Ayios
Stefanos**

*Profitis
Ilias
Katomeritis*

New Port

Tourlos

**Mykonos
Town**
1 - **9**
see detail map

10

*Profitis
Ilias
Anomeritis*

Kalafatis

Kato Livadhi

Ornos

**Platys
Yialos**

**Super
Paradise**

**Ayios
Ioannis**

Psarou

Paranga

Paradise

Elia

0		2 miles
0		3 km

❸ The charming **Aegean Maritime Museum** contains a collection of model ships, navigational instruments, old maps, prints, coins, and nautical memorabilia. The backyard garden displays some old anchors and ship wheels and a reconstructed 1890 lighthouse, once lighted by oil. ⊠ *Enoplon Dynameon* ☎ *22890/22700* 🎟 *€3* ⊙ *Daily 10:30–1 and 6:30–9.*

Take a peek into **Lena's House,** an accurate restoration of a middle-class Mykonos house from the 19th century. ⊠ *Enoplon Dynameon* ☎ *22890/ 22591* 🎟 *Free* ⊙ *Apr.–Oct., daily 7 PM–9 PM.*

Many of the early ship's captains built distinguished houses directly on the sea here, with wooden balconies overlooking the water. Today this
★ **❹** neighborhood, at the southwest end of the port, is called **Little Venice** (⊠ Mitropoleos Georgouli). A few of the old houses have been turned into stylish bars, which are quite romantic at twilight (but disco-loud at night). A block inland are many of Mykonos's famous clubs. Over-
❺ looking them on the high hill are the famous **Mykonos windmills,** echoes of a time when wind power was used to grind the island's grain.

The **Mykonos Agricultural Museum** displays a 16th-century windmill, traditional outdoor oven, waterwheel, dovecote, and more. ⊠ *Petassos, at top of Mykonos town* ☎ *22890/22591* 🎟 *Free* ⊙ *June–Sept., daily 4–6 PM.*

❻ The **Folk Museum,** housed in an 18th-century house, exhibits a bedroom furnished and decorated in the fashion of that period. On display are looms and lace-making devices, Cycladic costumes, old photographs, and Mykoniot musical instruments that are still played at festivals. ⊠ *South of boat dock* ☎ *22890/22591 or 22890/22748* 🎟 *Free* ⊙ *Mon.–Sat. 4–8, Sun. 5:30–8.*

Mykoniots claim that exactly 365 churches and chapels dot their land-
★ **❼** scape, one for each day of the year. The most famous of these is the **Church of Paraportiani** (Our Lady of the Postern Gate; ⊠ Ayion Anargyron, near folk museum). The sloping, whitewashed conglomeration of four chapels, mixing Byzantine and vernacular idioms, has been described as "a confectioner's dream gone mad," and its position on a promontory facing
❽ the sea sets off the unique architecture. The **Greek Orthodox Cathedral of Mykonos** (⊠ On square that meets both Ayion Anargyron and Odos Mitropolis) has a number of old icons of the post-Byzantine period. Next
❾ to the Greek Orthodox Cathedral is the **Roman Catholic Cathedral** (⊠ On square that meets both Ayion Anargyron and Odos Mitropolis) from the Venetian period. The name and coat of arms of the Ghisi family, which took over Mykonos in 1207, are inscribed in the entrance hall.

Beaches

There is a beach for every taste in Mykonos. Beaches near Mykonos town, within walking distance, are **Tourlos** and **Ayios Ioannis. Ayios Stefanos,** about a 45-minute walk from Mykonos town, has a minigolf course, water sports, restaurants, and umbrellas and lounge chairs for rent. The south coast's **Psarou,** protected from wind by hills and surrounded by restaurants, offers a wide selection of water sports and is often called the finest beach. Nearby **Platys Yialos,** popular with families, is also lined with restaurants and dotted with umbrellas for rent. **Ornos** is also perfect for families. **Paranga, Paradise, Super Paradise,** and **Elia** are all on the southern coast of the island, and are famously nude, though getting less so. **Super Paradise** is half gay, half straight, and swings at night. All have tavernas on the beach. At the easternmost end of the south shores is **Kalafatis,** known for package tours, and between Elia and Kalafatis there's a remote beach at **Kato Livadhi,** which can be reached by road.

Where to Stay & Eat

$$–$$$$
Fodor's Choice
★
✕ **La Maison de Catherine.** This hidden restaurant's Greek and French cuisine and hospitality—Katerina is still in charge—are worth the search. The splendid air-conditioned interior mixes Cycladic arches and white-wash with a French feeling and a faded 16th-century tapestry from Constantinople. Candles and classical music set the tone for baby squid stuffed with rice and Greek mountain spices, or soufflé, puffed to perfection and loaded with cheese, mussels, and prawns. For entrées, try leg of lamb with mint sauce or pasta with lobster. The apple tart is divine. ⊠ *Ayios Gerasimos* ☎ *22890/22169* 🖷 *22890/26946* 🕭 *Reservations essential* ▭ *AE, DC, MC, V.*

$$–$$$$
✕ **Mediterraneo.** Haute cuisine in a tasteful room of wood-beam ceilings and quiet colors, overlooking Mykonos Bay on one side and a pool on the other, makes for elegant dining. Chef Simos Avrambos smiles, but he is serious about food. Start with marinated baby herring on fava-bean puree, or slices of lemon-cured bream with vegetable tagliatelle. Follow with dorado fillet and wild greens in a fresh ouzo–herb sauce. The fish is always fresh and delicately prepared. The warm chocolate fondant with ice cream and citrus custard sauce is excellent. ⊠ *Hotel Cavo Tagoo, 15 mins by foot north of Mykonos town on sea Rd.* ☎ *22890/23692 through 22890/23694* 🕭 *Reservations essential* ▭ *AE, DC, MC, V.*

$–$$$$
✕ **Sea Satin Market–Caprice.** On the far tip of land below the windmills, Sea Satin Market, the preferred place for Greek shipowners, sprawls out onto a seaside terrace and even onto the sand. Prices vary according to weight. Shellfish is a specialty, and everything is beautifully presented. If the wind is up, the waves sing. Live music and dancing add to the liveliness in summer. ⊠ *On seaside under windmills* ☎ *22890/24676* ▭ *AE, MC, V.*

$–$$$
✕ **Chez Maria's.** Dine at this 30-year-old garden restaurant for lively atmosphere—sometimes with live music and dancing—for the zest of Greek living in a lovely candlelit garden. Octopus in wine, great cheese pies, and the fillet of beef with cheese and fresh vegetables will keep you in the mood. So will the apple tart with ice cream and walnuts. ⊠ *Kalogera 30* ☎ *22890/27565* ▭ *AE, MC, V.*

$–$$
✕ **Lotus.** For over 30 years, Giorgos and Elsa Cambanis have lovingly run this tiny restaurant. A good starter is the mushroom "Lotos" with cream and cheese. The roast leg of lamb with oregano, lemon, and wine is succulent, and the moussaka is one of Greece's best. For dessert, have *pralina,* which resembles tiramisu. It's open year-round: the porch is covered with bougainvillea in summer, and there's a fireplace in winter. ⊠ *Matoyanni 47* ☎ *22890/22881* ▭ *No credit cards.*

$–$$
✕ **Kounelas.** This long-established fresh-fish taverna is where many fishermen themselves eat, for no frills and solid food. The menu depends

on the weather—low winds means lots of fish. Note: even in simple places such as Kounelas, fresh fish can be expensive. ⊠ *Off port near Delos boats* ☎ *No phone* ▤ *No credit cards.*

$$$$ ✕▥ **Royal Myconian.** You may never leave this light-filled, luxurious hotel, a 20-minute drive from Mykonos town, set high on the bare mountain overlooking quiet Elia beach. The rooms' stone terraces overlook the sea, and suites have private Jacuzzis. The price includes transfers. Chef Yannis Argiriou, one of Greece's very best, is at the helm of the large, elegant restaurant. Start with grilled haloumi cheese wrapped in grape leaves in lime sauce. Sautéed turkey with dried grains in Chios mastic sauce is a fine entrée, as is stuffed sea bass with crab and vegetables in fennel sauce. All the pasta is homemade. For the ultimate chocolate dessert, try the Vesuvius. ⊠ *Elia Beach, 84600* ☎ *22890/72000* 🖷 *22890/ 72027* ⊕ *www.royal-myconian.gr* ⤸ *129 rooms, 20 suites* ⌂ *2 restaurants, minibars, cable TV, pool, spa* ▤ *AC, D, MC, V* ⊙ *Closed Nov.–Mar.* ⦿ *BP.*

$$$$ ▥ **Belvedere.** The clublike atmosphere, convenient location, and view over Mykonos town and harbor ensure this hotel's popularity, though you can cut the "cool" attitude with a knife. The poolside bar is surrounded by greenery and views, and the sushi restaurant is fashionable with yuppies. Some rooms have sea views, and all are dramatically decorated. ⊠ *School of Fine Arts district, 84600* ☎ *22890/25122* 🖷 *22890/ 25126* ⊕ *www.belvederehotel.com* ⤸ *42 rooms, 6 suites* ⌂ *Restaurant, minibars, cable TV, pool, bar, Internet room* ▤ *AE, MC, V* ⊙ *Closed Nov.–Mar.* ⦿ *BP.*

★ **$$$$** ▥ **Cavo Tagoo.** This hotel seems to emerge from its cliff-side backdrop and reach out to the sea 150 feet below. A first-prize winner for its environmentally sensitive architecture in a competition sponsored by the Greek environmental ministry, this medley of white cubical suites has roof-level sunset terraces and an alluring saltwater pool. The reception area, restaurant, and guest rooms all have marble floors, beamed ceilings, and wood furniture. It's a 15-minute walk to town. ⊠ *Follow coast road, north of port, 84600* ☎ *22890/23692 through 22890/23695* 🖷 *22890/24923* ⊕ *www.cavotagoo.gr* ⤸ *68 rooms, 5 suites* ⌂ *Restaurant, cable TV, pool, bar* ▤ *AE, MC, V* ⊙ *Closed Nov.–Mar.* ⦿ *BP.*

★ **$$$$** ▥ **Deliades.** Manager Steve Argiriadis had a hand in the design of this relaxed and well-run hotel, and maybe that's why Deliades (which translates as "Delian nymphs") is so appealing. The capacious, airy rooms all have sea views and big terraces, the marble carvings were made specially for this hotel, and the stark white of the architecture is softened with accents in muted sand and sea shades. Eating dinner at the quiet poolside café-restaurant, overlooking the bay, is especially pleasant. It's a short walk to Ornos beach. The price includes transfers. ⊠ *Far end of Ornos beach, follow road up 30 yards, 84600 Ornos* ☎ *22890/79430 or 22890/79470* 🖷 *22890/26996* ⊕ *www.hoteldeliadesmykonos.com* ⤸ *21 rooms* ⌂ *Restaurant, minibars, cable TV, in-room data ports, pool, bar* ▤ *AE, MC, V* ⊙ *Closed Nov.–Mar.* ⦿ *BP.*

★ **$$$$** ▥ **Kivotos Clubhotel.** Spyros Michopoulos's deluxe hotel is architecturally ambitious, in a richly decorative island style, with statues in niches and stone-mosaic work, and unexpected little courtyards with bright flowers. The rooms, most with sea views, display local crafts. A hotel minibus runs into town, about 3 km (2 mi) away, and to the airport. ✉ *Ornos Bay, 2 km (1 mi) from Mykonos town, 84600* ☎ *22890/25795 or 22890/ 25796* 🖷 *22890/22844* 🌐 *www.kivotosclubhotel.gr* ⇥ *35 rooms, 5 suites* ⟅ *2 restaurants, minibars, cable TV, in-room data ports, 5 pools, hot tub, sauna, 3 bars* ▤ *AE, D, MC, V* ⊘ *Closed Nov.–Mar.* ⦿ *BP.*

★ **$$$$** 🖭 **Semeli.** The carved-marble entrance doorway leads to an old stately home that has been expanded into an elegant hotel in the high Mykoniot style. Each of the large rooms, some with sea views, is differently and traditionally furnished. Though convenient to the town, the pool area, with its terraces and garden view, will tempt you to linger. ✉ *On ring road, 84600* ☎ *22890/27466 or 22890/27471* 🖷 *22890/27467* 🌐 *www.semelihotel.gr* ⇥ *42 rooms, 3 suites* ⟅ *Restaurant, minibars, cable TV, pool, bar, Internet room* ▤ *AE, MC, V* ⦿ *BP.*

$$–$$$$ 🖭 **Petinos.** This casual resort community of four hotels on Platys Yialos beach is comfortable, convenient, and friendly, a favorite among families and visitors planning a long stay on Mykonos. The wind-protected crowded beach, dotted with umbrellas and lounge chairs, is noisy with water sports, snack bars, and restaurants; a boat goes to five other beaches. The four hotels differ in price according to room size, location, and decor. ✉ *Platys Yialos Beach, 2 km (1 mi) from Mykonos town, 84600* ☎ *22890/22913, 22890/24310, or 22890/25925* 🖷 *22890/23680* 🌐 *www.petinosbeach.gr* ⇥ *130 rooms* ⟅ *Restaurant, snack bar, cable TV, 2 pools, gym, hot tub, bar, laundry service* ▤ *AE, MC, V* ⊘ *Closed Nov.–Mar.* ⦿ *BP.*

$$ 🖭 **Villa Konstantin.** This complex of small apartments, studios, and rooms, located on the ring road, is a 700-meter (765-yard) downhill walk to the town. The owners themselves live here all year, and go to lengths to make it attractive and friendly, as their many returning customers attest. The decor is traditional Mykoniot with built-in furniture, and all rooms have terraces or balconies with sea views. ✉ *Box 1030, 84600* ☎ *22890/26204* 🖷 *22890/26205* 🌐 *www.villakonstantin-mykonos. gr* ⇥ *19 units* ⟅ *Kitchenettes, cable TV, in-room data ports,* ▤ *MC, V* ⊘ *Closed Nov.–Mar.*

$ 🖭 **Hotel Philippi.** Of the inexpensive hotels scattered throughout the town, this is the most attractive. The rooms have balconies that overlook the garden—owner Christos Kontizas is a passionate gardener. You can't get there by vehicle, but once there you are in the center of things. ✉ *Kalogera 25, 84600* ☎ *22890/22294* 🖷 *22890/24680* ✎ *chriko@otenet.gr* ⇥ *13 rooms* ⟅ *Cable TV, refrigerators* ▤ *AE, MC, V* ⊘ *Closed Nov.–Mar.*

Nightlife & the Arts

Whether it's bouzouki music, break beat, or techno, Mykonos's nightlife beats to an obsessive rhythm until undetermined hours—little wonder Europe's gilded youth comes here *just* to enjoy the night scene. After midnight, they often head to the techno bars along the Paradise and Super Paradise beaches. Some of Little Venice's nightclubs become gay in more than one sense of the word, while in the Kastro, convivial bars welcome all for tequila-*sambukas* during sunset. What is "the" place of the moment? The scene is ever-changing—so you'll need to track the buzz once you arrive.

BARS & DISCOS   Little Venice is a good place to begin an evening, and Damianos Griparis's **Galleraki** (✉ Little Venice ☎ 22890/27118) is one of the best cocktail bars in town; it's so close to the water you may get wet when a boat passes. Upstairs in the old mansion (Delos's first archaeologists lived here), you'll find an art gallery—a handy sanctum for drinks on windy nights. Kostas Karatzas's long-standing **Kastro Bar** (✉ Behind Paraportiani ☎ 22890/23072), with heavy beamed ceilings and island furnishings, creates an intimate environment for enjoying the evening sunset over the bay; classical music sets the tone. **Montparnasse** (✉ Little Venice ☎ 22890/23719) hangs paintings by local artists; its superb sunset view precedes nights of live cabaret and musicals. At the famous gay **Pierro's** (✉ Matoyanni ☎ 22890/22177), you can find late-night wild dancing to American and European rock. **Remezzo** (✉ North of waterfront) is a high-tech, wild dance club.

Sports & the Outdoors

DIVING   **Mykonos Diving Center** (✉ Psarou ☎ 22890/24808 ⊕ www.dive.gr) has a variety of scuba courses and excursions at 30 locations.

TENNIS   **Aphrodite Beach Hotel** (✉ Kalafati Beach ☎ 22890/71367 🖷 22890/71525) has courts the public can use. The **Kochyli Hotels** (✉ On hill above Mykonos town ☎ 22890/22929) has tennis courts.

WATER SPORTS   The windy northern beaches on Ornos Bay are best for water sports; you can rent surfboards and take lessons. There's windsurfing and waterskiing at Ayios Stefanos, Platys Yialos, and Ornos. **Aphrodite Beach Hotel** (✉ Kalafati Beach ☎ 28890/71367 🖷 22890/71525) has water sports. The program at **Surfing Club Anna** (✉ Agia Anna ☎ 22890/71205) is well organized.

Shopping

FASHION   Yiannis **Galatis** (✉ Platysa Manto, opposite LALAoUNIS ☎ 22890/22255) has outfitted such famous women as Elizabeth Taylor, Ingrid Bergman, and Jackie Onassis. Yiannis will probably greet you personally and show you some of his coats and costumes, hostess gowns, and long dresses. He also has men's clothes. **Jella's** (✉ Nikiou 3 ☎ 22890/24153), a tiny boutique filled with custom-made silk knits that drape with special elegance, and silk slippers from Turkistan, is next to La Maison de Catherine restaurant; nearby, shops are rife. **Loco** (✉ Kalogera 29 N. ☎ 22890/23682) sells cotton and linen summer wear in lovely colors. The Marla knits are from the family factory in Athens.

FINE & DECORATIVE ART   Soula Papadakou's **Venetia** (✉ Ayion Anargyron 16, Little Venice ☎ 22890/24464) carries authentic copies of traditional handmade embroideries in clothing, tablecloths, curtains, and such, all in white; the women who work for her come from all over Greece, including a nunnery in Ioannina. Mykonos used to be a weaver's island, where 500 looms clacked away. Two shops remain. In **Nikoletta** (✉ Little Venice), Nikoletta Xidakis sells her skirts, shawls, and bedspreads made of local wool. **Ioanna Zouganelli** (☎ 22890/22309), whose father used to sell the family's weavings from a trunk on his Delos excursion boat, makes mohair shawls and traditional Mykonian weavings in her tiny shop on the square in front of Paraportiani.

JEWELRY **Ilias LALAoUNIS** (✉ Polykandrioti 14, near taxis ☎ 22890/22444 🖷 22890/24409 ⊕ www.lalaounismykonos.com) is known internationally for jewelry based on classic ancient designs, especially Greek; the shop is as elegant as a museum. The new collections take their designs from DNA and the theme, "The Harmony of Chaos." **Precious Tree** (✉ Dilou 2 ☎☎ 2289024685) is a tiny shop aglitter in gems elegantly set at the workshop in Athens.

SWEETS Since 1950, Efthemios and family have been making traditional almond biscuits and almond milk (mix with five parts ice water) at **Efthemios** (✉ Florou Zouganeli 4 ☎ 22890/22281).

Ano Mera

Άνω Μερά

❿ *8 km (5 mi) east of Mykonos town.*

Monastery buffs should head to Ano Mera, a village in the central part of the island, where the **Monastery of the Panayia Tourliani,** founded in 1580 and dedicated to the protectress of Mykonos, stands in the central square. Its massive baroque iconostasis (altar screen), made in 1775 by Florentine artists, has small icons carefully placed amid the wooden structure's painted green, red, and gold-leaf flowers. At the top are carved figures of the apostles and large icons depicting New Testament scenes. The hanging incense holders with silver molded dragons holding red eggs in their mouths show an Eastern influence. In the hall of the monastery, an interesting **museum** displays embroideries, liturgical vestments, and wood carvings. A good taverna is across the street. ✉ *On central Sq.* ☎ *0289/71249* ⊙ *By appointment only; call in advance.*

Delos

Δήλος

Fodor'sChoice *25-minute caïque ride southwest from Mykonos.*
★

Why did Delos, an islet with virtually no natural resources, become the religious and political center of the Aegean? One answer is that Delos, shielded on three sides by other islands, provided the safest anchorage for vessels sailing between the mainland and the shores of Asia. The saga begins back in the times of myth:

Zeus fell in love with gentle Leto, the Titaness, who became pregnant. When Hera discovered this infidelity, she forbade Mother Earth to give Leto refuge and ordered the Python to pursue her. Finally Poseidon, taking pity on her, anchored the floating island of Delos with four diamond columns to give her a place to rest. She gave birth first to the virgin huntress Artemis on Rhenea and then, clasping a sacred palm on a slope of Delos's Mt. Kynthos, to Apollo, god of music and light.

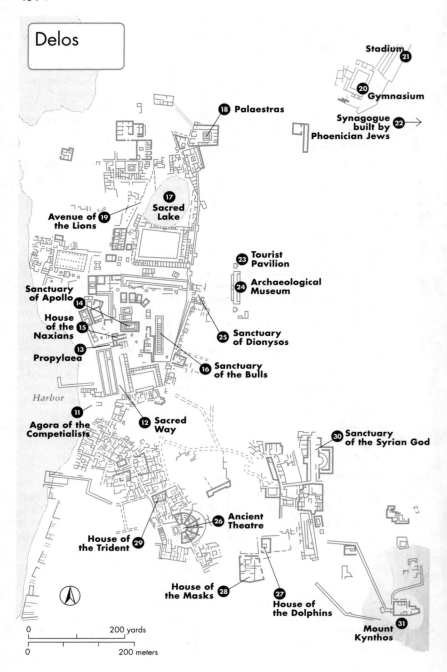

Delos

18 Palaestras

21 Stadium

20 Gymnasium

22 Synagogue built by Phoenician Jews →

17 Sacred Lake

19 Avenue of the Lions

23 Tourist Pavilion

24 Archaeological Museum

14 Sanctuary of Apollo

15 House of the Naxians

13 Propylaea

25 Sanctuary of Dionysos

16 Sanctuary of the Bulls

Harbor

11 Agora of the Competialists

12 Sacred Way

30 Sanctuary of the Syrian God

26 Ancient Theatre

29 House of the Trident

28 House of the Masks

27 House of the Dolphins

31 Mount Kynthos

0 — 200 yards

0 — 200 meters

By 1000 BC the Ionians, who inhabited the Cyclades, had made Delos their religious capital. Homeric Hymn 3 tells of the cult of Apollo in the 7th century BC. A difficult period began for the Delians when Athens rose to power and assumed Ionian leadership. In 543 BC an oracle at Delphi conveniently decreed that the Athenians purify the island by removing all the graves to Rhenea, a dictate designed to alienate the Delians from their past.

After the defeat of the Persians in 478 BC, the Athenians organized the Delian League, with its treasury and headquarters at Delos (in 454 BC the funds were transferred to the Acropolis in Athens). Delos had its most prosperous period in late Hellenistic and Roman times, when it was declared a free port and quickly became the financial center of the Mediterranean, the focal point of trade, where 10,000 slaves were sold daily. Foreigners from as far as Rome, Syria, and Egypt lived in this cosmopolitan port, in complete tolerance of one another's religious beliefs, and each group built its various shrines. But in 88 BC Mithridates, the king of Pontus, in a revolt against Roman rule, ordered an attack on the unfortified island. The entire population of 20,000 was killed or sold into slavery. Delos never fully recovered, and later Roman attempts to revive the island failed because of pirate raids. After a second attack in 69 BC, Delos was gradually abandoned.

In 1872, the French School of Archaeology began excavating on Delos— a massive project, considering that much of the island's 4 square km (1½ square mi) is covered in ruins. The work continues today.

⓫ On the left from the harbor is the **Agora of the Competialists** (circa 150 BC), members of Roman guilds, mostly freedmen and slaves from Sicily who worked for Italian traders. They worshipped the *Lares Competales,* the Roman "crossroads" gods; in Greek they were known as Hermaistai, after the god Hermes, protector of merchants and the crossroads.

⓬ The **Sacred Way**, east of the agora, was the route, during the holy Delian festival, of the procession to the sanctuary of Apollo.

⓭ The **Propylaea**, at the end of the Sacred Way, were once a monumental white marble gateway with three portals framed by four Doric columns.

⓮ Beyond the Propylaea is the **Sanctuary of Apollo**; though little remains today, when the Propylaea were built in the mid-2nd century BC, the sanctuary was crowded with altars, statues, and temples—three of them to

⓯ Apollo. Inside the sanctuary and to the right is the **House of the Naxians**, a 7th- to 6th-century BC structure with a central colonnade. Dedications to Apollo were stored in this shrine. Outside the north wall a massive rectangular **pedestal** once supported a colossal statue of Apollo (one of the hands is in Delos's Archaeological Museum, and a piece of a foot is in the British Museum). Near the pedestal a bronze palm tree was erected in 417 BC by the Athenians to commemorate the palm tree under which Leto gave birth. According to Plutarch, the palm tree toppled in a storm and brought the statue of Apollo down with it.

⓰ Southeast of the Sanctuary of Apollo are the ruins of the **Sanctuary of the Bulls**, an extremely long and narrow structure built, it is thought, to display a trireme, an ancient boat with three banks of oars, dedicated to Apollo by a Hellenistic leader thankful for a naval victory. Maritime symbols were found in the decorative relief of the main halls, and the head and shoulders of a pair of bulls were part of the design of an interior entrance. A short distance north of the Sanctuary of the Bulls is

(17) an oval indentation in the earth where the **Sacred Lake** once sparkled. It is surrounded by a stone wall that reveals the original periphery. According to islanders, the lake was fed by the River Inopos from its source high on Mt. Kynthos until 1925, when the water stopped flow-

(18) ing and the lake dried up. Along the shores are two ancient **palaestras,** buildings for physical exercise and debate.

(19) One of the most evocative sights of Delos is the 164-foot-long **Avenue of the Lions.** These are replicas; the originals are in the museum. The five Naxian marble beasts crouch on their haunches, their forelegs stiffly upright, vigilant guardians of the Sacred Lake. They are the survivors of a line of at least nine lions, erected in the second half of the 7th century BC by the Naxians. One, removed in the 17th century, now guards

(20) the Arsenal of Venice. Northeast of the palaestras is the **gymnasium,** a square courtyard nearly 131 feet long on each side. The long, narrow

(21) structure farther northeast is the **stadium,** the site of the athletic events of the Delian Games. East of the stadium site, by the seashore, are the

(22) remains of a **synagogue built by Phoenician Jews** in the 2nd century BC.

(23) A road south from the gymnasium leads to the **tourist pavilion,** which

(24) has a meager restaurant and bar. The **Archaeological Museum** is also on the road south of the gymnasium; it contains most of the antiquities found in excavations on the island: monumental statues of young men and women, stelae, reliefs, masks, and ancient jewelry.

(25) Immediately to the right of the museum is a small **Sanctuary of Dionysos,** erected about 300 BC; outside it is one of the more boggling sights of ancient Greece: several monuments dedicated to Apollo by the winners of the choral competitions of the Delian festivals, each decorated with a huge phallus, emblematic of the orgiastic rites that took place during the Dionysian festivals. Around the base of one of them is carved a light-hearted representation of a bride being carried to her new husband's home. A marble phallic bird, symbol of the body's immortality, also adorns this corner of the sanctuary.

(26) Beyond the path that leads to the southern part of the island is the **ancient theater,** built in the early 3rd century BC in the elegant residential quarter inhabited by Roman bankers and Egyptian and Phoenician merchants. Their one- and two-story **houses** were typically built around a central courtyard, sometimes with columns on all sides. Floor mosaics of snakes, panthers, birds, dolphins, and Dionysus channeled rainwater into cisterns

(27) below; the best-preserved can be seen in the **House of the Dolphins,** the

(28) (29) **House of the Masks,** and the **House of the Trident.** A dirt path leads east to the base of Mt. Kynthos, where there are remains from many **Middle**

(30) **Eastern shrines,** including the **Sanctuary of the Syrian Gods,** built in 100

(31) BC. A flight of steps goes up 368 feet to the summit of **Mt. Kynthos** (after which all Cynthias are named), on whose slope Apollo was born. ⊠ *Delos island and historic site, take a caïque from Mykonos town* ☎ *22890/22259* ⊕ *www.culture.gr* ⌖ *€5* ⊘ *Apr.–Oct., Tues.–Sun. 8:30–3.*

NAXOS

ΝΑΞΟΣ

"Great sweetness and tranquillity" is how Nikos Kazantzakis, premier novelist of Greece, described Naxos, and indeed a tour of the island leaves you with an impression of abundance, prosperity, and serenity. The greenest, most fertile of the Cyclades, Naxos, with its many potato fields, its livestock and its thriving cheese industry, and its fruit and olive groves framed by the pyramid of Mt. Zas (3,295 feet, the Cyclades' highest), is practically self-sufficient. Inhabited for 6,000 years, the island has memorable landscapes—abrupt ravines, hidden valleys, long and sandy beaches—and towns that vary from a Cretan mountain stronghold to the seaside capital that strongly evokes its Venetian past.

Naxos Town

Νάξος (Χώρα)

32 *Seven hours by ferry from Piraeus; 35 km (22 mi) east of Paros town.*

As your ferry chugs into the harbor, you see before you the white houses of Naxos town (Chora) on a hill crowned by the one remaining tower of the Venetian castle, a reminder that Naxos was once the beautiful capital of the Venetian semi-independent Duchy of the Archipelago. The tiny church of **Our Lady of Myrtle** (⊠ Perched on sea rock off waterfront) watches over the local sailors, who built it for divine protection.

While the capital town is primarily beloved for its Venetian elegance and picturesque blind alleys, Naxos's most famous landmark is ancient: the

★ **Portara** (⊠ At harbor's far edge), a massive doorway that leads to nowhere. The Portara stands on the islet of **Palatia,** which was once a hill (since antiquity the Mediterranean has risen quite a bit) and in the 3rd millennium BC was the acropolis for a nearby Cycladic settlement. The Portara, an entrance to an unfinished Temple of Apollo that faces exactly toward Delos, Apollo's birthplace, was begun about 530 BC by the tyrant Lygdamis, who said he would make Naxos's buildings the highest and most glorious in Greece. He was overthrown in 506 BC, and the temple was never completed; by the 5th and 6th centuries AD it had been converted into a church; and under Venetian and Turkish rule it was slowly dismembered, so the marble could be used to build the castle. The gate, built with four blocks of marble, each 16 feet long and weighing 20 tons, was so large it couldn't be demolished, so it remains today, along with the temple floor. Palatia itself has come to be associated with the tragic myth of Ariadne, princess of Crete.

Ariadne, daughter of Crete's King Minos, helped Theseus thread the labyrinth of Knossos and slay the monstrous Minotaur. In exchange, he promised to marry her. Sailing for Athens, the couple stopped in Naxos, where Theseus abandoned her. Jilted Ariadne's curse made Theseus forget to change the ship's sails from black to white, and so his grieving father Aegeus, believing his son dead, plunged into the Aegean. Seeing Ariadne's tears, smitten Dionysos descended in a leopard-drawn

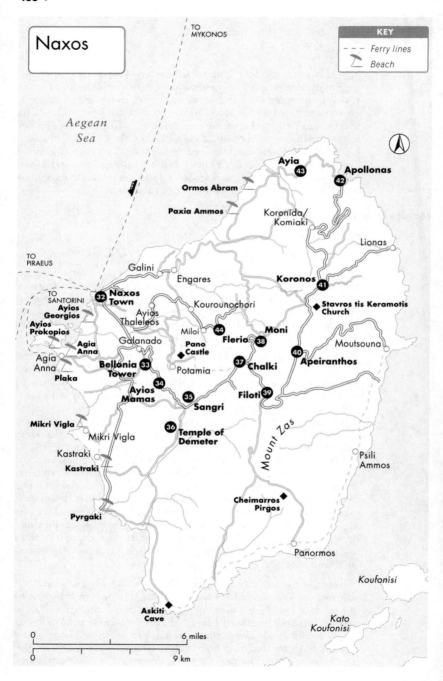

Naxos

TO MYKONOS

Aegean Sea

Ayia 43
Apollonas 42
Ormos Abram
Paxia Ammos
Koronida/ Komiaki
Lionas

TO PIRAEUS

Galini
Engares
Koronos 41
Naxos Town 32
TO SANTORINI
Ayios Georgios
Ayios Prokopios
Kourounochori
Ayios Thaleleos
Stavros tis Keramotis Church
Miloi
Flerio 44
Moni
Agia Anna
Galanado
Pano Castle
38
40
Moutsouna
Apeiranthos
Agia Anna
Bellonia Tower 33
Potamia
37
Chalki
Plaka
34
Ayios Mamas
35
Filoti 39
Mikri Vigla
Sangri
Mikri Vigla
36
Temple of Demeter
Mount Zas
Kastraki
Kastraki
Psili Ammos
Pyrgaki
Cheimarros Pirgos
Panormos
Koufonisi
Askiti Cave
Kato Koufonisi

0   6 miles
0   9 km

chariot to marry her, and set her bridal wreath, the Corona Borealis, in the sky, an eternal token of his love.

The myth inspired one of Titian's best-known paintings, as well as Strauss's opera *Ariadne auf Naxos.*

North of Palatia, **underwater remains of Cycladic buildings** are strewn along an area called **Grotta.** Here are a series of large worked stones, the remains of the mole, and a few steps that locals say go to a tunnel leading to the islet of Palatia; these remains are Cycladic (before 2000 BC).

Old town (⊠ Along quay, left at first big Sq.) possesses a bewildering maze of twisting cobblestone streets, arched porticoes, and towering doorways, where you're plunged into cool darkness and then suddenly into pockets of dazzling sunshine. The old town is divided into the lower section, **Bourgos,** where the Greeks lived during Venetian times, and the upper part, called **Kastro** (castle), still inhabited by the Venetian Catholic nobility.

★ You won't miss the gates of the **castle** (⊠ Kastro). The south gate is called the **Paraporti** (side gate), but it's more interesting to enter through the northern gate, or **Trani** (strong), via Apollonos street. Note the vertical incision in the gate's marble column—it is the Venetian yard against which drapers measured the bolts of cloth they brought to the noblewomen. Step through the Trani into the citadel and enter another age, where sedate Venetian houses still stand around silent courtyards, their exteriors emblazoned with coats of arms and bedecked with flowers. Half are still owned by the original families; romantic Greeks and foreigners have bought up the rest.

The entire citadel was built in 1207 by Marco Sanudo, a Venetian who, three years after the fall of Constantinople, landed on Naxos as part of the Fourth Crusade. For two months he laid siege to the Byzantine castle at t'Apilarou and upon its downfall made Naxos the headquarters of his duchy. He divided the island into estates and distributed them to his officers, who built the *pirgi* (tower houses) that still dot the countryside. When in 1210 Venice refused to grant him independent status, Sanudo switched allegiance to the Latin emperor in Constantinople, becoming Duke of the Archipelago. Under the Byzantines, "archipelago" had meant "chief sea," but after Sanudo and his successors, it came to mean "group of islands," i.e., the Cyclades. For three centuries Naxos was held by Venetian families, who resisted pirate attacks, introduced Roman Catholicism, and later rebuilt the castle in its present form. In 1564 Naxos came under Turkish rule, but even then, the Venetians still ran the island, while the Turks only collected taxes. The rust-color Glezos tower was home to the last dukes; it displays the coat of arms: a pen and sword crossed under a crown.

The **Domus Venetian Museum,** in the 800-year-old Dellarocca-Barozzi house, lets you, at last, into one of the historic Venetian residences. The house's idyllic garden, built into the Kastro wall, provides a regular venue in season for a concert series, from classical to jazz to island music. ⊠ *At Kastro north gate* ☎ *22850/22387* ≊ *€4, tour €5* ☉ *June–Aug., daily 10–3 and 7–10; check ahead for other times.*

The **cathedral** (⊠ At Kastro's center) was built by Sanudo in the 13th century and restored by Catholic families in the 16th and 17th centuries. The marble floor is paved with tombstones bearing the coats of arms of the noble families. Venetian wealth is evident in the many gold and silver icon frames. The icons reflect a mix of Byzantine and Western influences: the one of the Virgin Mary is unusual because it shows a Byzantine Virgin and Child in the presence of a bishop, a cathedral benefactor. Another 17th-century icon shows the Virgin of the Rosary surrounded by members of the Sommaripa family, whose house is nearby.

The **convent and school of the Ursulines** (⊠ A few steps beyond cathedral, in the Kastro) was begun in 1739. In a 1713 document, a general of the Jesuits, Francis Tarillon, mentions that the proposed girls' school should be simple; grandeur would expose it to the Turks' covetousness. Over the years, extensions were added, and the Greek state has now bought the building for use in part as the Archaeological Museum. Wealthier Naxian women still recall the good education the Ursulines provided.

Today the convent and school of the Ursulines houses the **Naxos Archaeological Museum,** best known for its Cycladic and Mycenaean finds. During the early Cycladic period (3200 BC–2000 BC) there were settlements along Naxos's east coast and outside Naxos town at Grotta. The finds are from these settlements and graveyards scattered around the island. Many of the vessels exhibited are from the early Cycladic I period, hand-built of coarse-grain clay, sometimes decorated with a herringbone pattern. Though the museum has too many items in its glass cases to be appreciated in a short visit, you should try not to miss the white marble Cycladic statuettes, which range from the early "violin" shapes to the more detailed female forms with their tilted flat heads, folded arms, and legs slightly bent at the knees. The male forms are simpler and often appear to be seated. The most common theory is that the female statuettes were both fertility and grave goddesses, and the males servant figures. ⊠ *Kastro* ☎ *22850/ 22725* ⊕ *www.culture.gr* 🖾 *€3* ☉ *Tues.–Sun. 8:30–3.*

The **Greek Orthodox cathedral** (⊠ Bourgos) was built in 1789 on the site of a church called Zoodochos Pigis (Life-giving Source). The cathedral was built from the materials of ancient temples: the solid granite pillars are said to be from the ruins of Delos. Amid the gold and the carved wood, there is a vividly colored iconostasis painted by a well-known iconographer of the Cretan school, Dimitrios Valvis, and the Gospel Book is believed to be a gift from Catherine the Great of Russia.

The **Ancient Town of Naxos** was directly on the square in front of the Greek Orthodox cathedral. You'll note that several of the churches set on this square, like the cathedral itself, hint at Naxos's venerable history as they are made of ancient materials. In fact, this square was, in succession, the seat of a flourishing Mycenaean town (1300–1050 BC), a classical agora (when it was a 167-foot by 156-foot square closed on three sides by Doric stoas, so that it looked like the letter "G"; a shorter fourth stoa bordered the east side, leaving room at each end for an entrance), a Roman town, and early Christian church complex. Although much of the site has been refilled, under the square a **mu-**

seum (🖾 Free ☉ Tues.–Sun. 8–2:30) gives you a well-marked sampling of the foundations. City, cemetery, tumulus, hero shrine: no wonder the early Christians built here. For more of ancient Naxos, explore the nearby precinct of Grotta.

Beaches

The southwest coast of Naxos, facing Paros and the sunset, offers the Cyclades' longest stretches of beaches. All these have tavernas and rooms. They are listed, in order, heading south. **Ayios Georgios** is now part of town and very developed. **Ayios Prokopios** has a small leeward harbor and lagoons with waterfowl. **Ayia Anna,** very crowded, has a small harbor with connections to Paros. **Plaka,** ringed by sand dunes and bamboo groves, is about 8 km (5 mi) south of town. Nude **Mikri Vigla** is sandy and edged by cedar trees. Semi-nude **Kastraki** has white marble sand. **Pyrgaki** is the least-developed beach, with idyllic crystalline water.

Where to Stay & Eat

$–$$ ✕ **Gorgona.** Bearded Dimitris and Koula Kapris's beachfront taverna is popular both with sun worshippers on Ayia Anna beach and locals from Chora, who come here winter and summer to get away and sometimes to dance until the late hours, often to live music. The menu is extensive and fresh daily—the fresh fish comes from the caïques that pull up at the dock right in front every morning. Two good appetizers are *kakavia* (fish stew) and shrimp saganaki (with cooked cheese), while spaghetti with crab is a fine entrée. The barrel wine is their own (they also bottle it). The small hotel next door is also theirs. 🖂 *Ayia Anna near dock* ☎ *22850/41007* ▤ *No credit cards.*

¢–$$ ✕ **Meltemi.** Mihalis Mathiassos's restaurant is typically Greek: no frills. But it is by the sea and cool for an outdoor lunch. It's known locally as the place to go for inexpensive Greek staples such as lamb *exohiko* (cooked in paper with vegetables), barbecued fish, and pans of *gigantes* (giant white beans in olive oil) and *tsoutsoukakia* (meat patties made from spicy sausage). *Kaloyero* (eggplant with ham and béchamel) is a bit more unusual. Service is efficient, even when the place is packed. 🖂 *Naxos town waterfront, at other end from dock* ☎ *22850/22654* ▤ *No credit cards.*

★ ♻ ¢–$$ ✕ **Old Inn.** Berlin-trained chef Dieter von Ranizewski's "dream place" is one of the Cyclades' best restaurants. In a courtyard under a chinaberry tree, with rough whitewashed walls and ancient marbles, two of the old church's interior sides open into the wine cellar and gallery; on the fourth side, with beams and wood paneling, is a fireplace. The menu is extensive. For starters you might try sausages with beer sauce, smoked ham, or liver pâté—all homemade. For entrées, have the signature steak with tomatoes, olives, Roquefort, and bacon-flecked roast potatoes. Barbecue spareribs are also especially good. For dessert the mousse beckons voluptuously. There is a children's menu and small playground. 🖂 *Naxos town; take car road off waterfront, turn right into 2nd alley* ☎ *22850/26093* ⊕ *www.theoldinn.gr* ▤ *No credit cards.*

¢–$ ✕ **Apolafsis.** Rightly named "Enjoyment," Lefteris Keramideas's second-floor restaurant offers a balcony with a great view of the harbor and sunset. You'll enjoy live music (always in summer; often in winter), as well as a large assortment of appetizers (try spinach or zucchini tart), local barrel wine, and fresh fish. The sliced pork in wine sauce is good, too. ✉ *Naxos town waterfront* ☎ *22850/22178* 🖃 *AE, MC, V.*

$$$ 🏨 **Galaxy.** All whitewash and marble, this hotel is perfect if you want to be on the beach yet close to town. Its three buildings have wide stone arches and wooden doors in shades of green and blue, and balconies with grillwork depicting swans. Archways also span the large rooms, which have beamed ceilings and orange accessories, plus plants, kitchenettes, and dining areas. Most rooms have ocean views (the beach is a minute away). The carefully tended grounds glow with yellow roses and a fountain. ✉ *Ayios Georgios Beach, 84300* ☎ *22850/22422 or 22850/22423* 🖷 *22850/22889* ⊕ *www.hotel-galaxy.com* 🛏 *43 studios, 11 rooms* ♿ *Snack bar, kitchenettes, cable TV, pool, playground* 🖃 *AE, MC, V* ⊙ *Closed Nov.–Mar.* ¹⊙¹ *BP.*

$$ 🏨 **Lianos Village.** Naxian Yannis Lianos's resort hotel resembles the Cycladic village where he grew up. A 10-minute walk from Ayios Prokopios beach, the hotel has island furnishings, very private rooms with magnificent sea views across the lagoons and straits to Paros, plenty of greenery, and immaculate and unobtrusive service. You can swim and watch the sun set at the same time. If you stay out of town, try to get a room at Lianos. ✉ *Ayios Prokopios Beach, 84300* ☎ *22850/26366 or 22850/26380* 🖷 *22850/26362* ⊕ *www.lianosvillage.com* 🛏 *42 rooms* ♿ *Snack bar, refrigerators, cable TV, pool, Internet room* 🖃 *AE, MC, V* ⊙ *Closed Nov.–Mar.* ¹⊙¹ *BP.*

★ $ 🏨 **Apollon.** In addition to being comfortable, attractive, and quiet (it's a converted marble workshop), this hotel is convenient to everything in town. Even better, it offers parking facilities, a rarity in town. The lobby blends wood, warm marble, deep greens, and many plants. The rooms are simple and have balconies; bathrooms are small. The outside, of ocher plaster and stone, is adorned with a feast of marble decoration. ✉ *Behind Orthodox cathedral, car entrance on road out of town, 84300 Chora* ☎ *22850/22468* 🖷 *22850/25200* ⊕ *www. greekhotel.com/cyclades/naxos/chora/apollonhotel* 🛏 *12 rooms, 1 suite* ♿ *Cable TV,* 🖃 *AE, MC, V.*

★ $ 🏨 **Chateau Zevgoli.** If you stay in Chora, try to settle in here. Each room in Despina Kitini's fairy-tale pension, in a comfortable Venetian house, is distinct. The living room is filled with dark antique furniture, gilded mirrors, old family photographs, and locally woven curtains and tablecloths. One of the nicest bedrooms has a private bougainvillea-covered courtyard and pillows handmade by Despina's great-grandmother; the honeymoon suite has a canopy bed, a spacious balcony, and a view of the Portara. Despina also has roomy studios, in Chora's old town, including several on the kastro—stay a day and you'll stay a month. ✉ *Chora old town (follow signs stenciled on walls), 84300* ☎ *22850/ 22993 or 22850/26143* 🖷 *22850/25200* ⊕ *www.vacation-greece.com/ hotels/cyclades/naxos/chateauzevgoli* 🛏 *8 rooms, 1 suite* ♿ *In-room safes, minibars, refrigerators, cable TV, Internet room* 🖃 *AE, MC, V.*

★ $ 🏨 **Iria Beach.** Maria Refene's hotel is right on the crowded Naxos town beach and echoes Chora's old town with its stucco arches, peaceful nooks and crannies, sunlit courtyard, and bright red and blue shutters. The reception area has huge glass doors, a cool marble floor, and brass details. The owners have eschewed the usual Greek hotel furniture for un-lacquered wood with a gray wash and an interior color scheme of light blue, gray, and white for the spacious one- and two-room apartments, all with balconies. ⊠ *Ag. Anna, 84300 Agia Anna* ☎ *22850/42600* 🖷 *22850/42603* ⊕ *www.iriabeach-naxos.com* ↩ *17 rooms, 7 apartments* ⚊ *Kitchenettes* 🖃 *MC, V* ☾ *Closed Nov.–Mar.* ⦿⎮ *BP.*

¢ 🎦 **Orkos Village Hotel.** When Norwegian doctor Kaare Oftedal first saw Orkos beach years ago, he fell in love with the almost isolated strand ringed by sand dunes and cedars. Every April he returns from Norway to open his small, popular hotel, whose guests seem perfectly content never to leave their idyllic surroundings. The hotel's white bungalows, which stagger down the hillside, are simply furnished and decorated with dried flowers and blue wooden shutters. All have sea views and veran-das; most have an additional sitting area. The stone bar is a nice spot to gather after returning from the idyllic beach (a pool would be pro-fane here). ⊠ *Orkos beach between Plaka and Mikri Vigla, 84300* ☎ *22850/75321* 🖷 *22850/75320* ⊕ *www.orkoshotel.gr* ↩ *28 apartments* ⚊ *Restaurant, kitchenettes, bar* 🖃 *No credit cards.*

Nightlife & the Arts

BARS   Nightlife in Naxos is quieter than it is on Santorini or Mykonos, but there are several popular bars at the south end of Chora. **Ocean Dance** (⊠ Chora ☎ 22850/26766) opens at 11:30, all year round. Head for **Super Island** (⊠ Grotta road, Chora) for a large, soundproof space with a Portara view; it's active till dawn.

ARTS EVENTS   The **Catholic Cultural Center** (⊠ Kastro, near church ☎ 22850/24729), among other things, runs art exhibitions; watch for posters. The **Domus Venetian Museum** (⊠ At Kastro north gate, Chora ☎ 22850/22387), in the 800-year-old Dellarocca-Barozzi house, offers a summer concert se-ries in its lovely garden. The **Town Hall Exhibition Space** (⊠ Chora's south end ☎ 22850/37100) offers an ambitious program of art exhi-bitions, concerts, and other events.

Sports & the Outdoors

HORSEBACK   The three-hour sunset ride at **Naxos Horse Riding** (⊠ Chora ☎ 69488/
RIDING   09142) costs €40. Call Iris Neubauer and she'll come get you.

SAILING &   For windsurfing rental and lessons near Chora, contact **Naxos-Surf Club**
WATER SPORTS   (⊠ Ayios Yorgios beach ☎ 22850/29170). For windsurfing on distant, par-adisal Plaka beach, contact **Plaka Watersports** (⊠ Plaka beach ☎ 22850/41264).

Shopping

ANTIQUE   Vassilis Koutelieris's **Loom** (⊠ Dimitriou Kokkou 8, in Old Market, off
COSTUMES &   main square, 3rd street on right ☎☎ 22850/25531) exhibits museum-
JEWELRY   quality handwoven goods and antique silver jewelry, and sells quality cotton clothes made mostly in Greece (including a new line in earth col-ors). Loom's second store, across the street, sells works by local artists and craftspeople.

ANTIQUES   Eleni Dellarocca's shop, **Antico Veneziano** (⊠ In Kastro, down from mu-seum ☎ 22850/26206 or 22850/22702), is in the basement of her Vene-tian house, built 800 years ago. The columns inside come from Naxos's

ancient acropolis. In addition to antiques, she has handmade embroideries, porcelain and glass, mirrors, old chandeliers, and vintage photographs of Naxos. One room is an art gallery.

BOOKS   At Eleftherios Primikirios's bookstore **Zoom** (⊠ Chora waterfront
☎ 22850/23675 or 22850/23676), there's an excellent selection of English-language books about Naxos and much else. No other island
bookstore is this well stocked.

FOOD, WINE &   A large selection of the famous *kitro* (citron liqueur) and preserves, as
LIQUEUR   well as Naxos wines and thyme honey, packed in attractive gift baskets,
can be found at **Promponas Wines and Liquors** (⊠ Chora waterfront
☎ 22850/22258), which has been around since 1915. Free glasses of
kitro are offered.

JEWELRY   At **Midas** (⊠ Old town, up main street behind Promponas on Chora waterfront ☎ 22850/24852), owner Fotis Margaritis creates talismans in
different settings. All include a "Naxos eye," which is the operculum,
or door, of a seashell with a spiral design that fishermen bring him. The
workshop of **Nassos Papakonstantinou** (⊠ Ayiou Nikodemou street, on
old town's main Sq. ☎☎ 22850/22607) sells one-of-a-kind pieces both
sculptural and delicate. His father was a wood-carver; Nassos has inherited his talent. The shop has no sign—that is Nassos's style.

TRADITIONAL   The embroidery and knitted items made by women in the mountain vil-
CRAFTS, CARPETS   lages are known throughout Greece. They can be bought at **Techni**
& JEWELS   (⊠ Persefonis street, old town ☎ 22850/24767 ⊕ www.techni.gr).
Techi's three shops, almost facing one another, also sell carpets, jewelry
in old designs, linens, and more.

en route   On your way to Bellonia, on the main road from Naxos town you'll
go southeast past Galanado and drive through the reed beds, cacti,
and plains of the **Livadi valley.**

Bellonia Tower

Πύργος του Μπελόνια

③③ *5 km (3 mi) south of Naxos town.*

The graceful Bellonia tower (Pirgos Bellonia) belonged to the area's ruling Venetian family, and like other fortified houses, it was built as a refuge
from pirates and as part of the island's alarm system. The towers were
located strategically throughout the island; if there was an attack, a large
fire would be lighted on the nearest tower's roof, setting off a chain reaction from tower to tower and alerting the islanders. Bellonia's thick
stone walls, its Lion of St. Mark emblem, and flat roofs with zigzag chimneys are typical of these pirgi. The unusual 13th-century **"double church"**
of St. John (⊠ In front of Bellonia tower) exemplifies Venetian tolerance. On the left side is the Catholic chapel, on the right the Orthodox
church, separated only by a double arch. A family lives in the tower,
and the church is often open. From here, take a moment to gaze across

the peaceful fields to Chora and imagine what the islanders must have felt when they saw pirate ships on the horizon.

Ayios Mamas

Άγιος Μάμας

34 *3 km (2 mi) south of Bellonia Tower, 8 km (5 mi) south of Naxos town.*

A kilometer (½ mi) past a valley with unsurpassed views is one of the island's oldest churches (9th century), Ayios Mamas. St. Mamas is the protector of shepherds and is regarded as a patron saint in Naxos, Cyprus, and Asia Minor. Built in the 8th century, the stone church was the island's cathedral under the Byzantines. Though it was converted into a Catholic church in 1207, it was neglected under the Venetians and is now falling apart. You can also get to it from the Potamia villages.

Sangri

Σαγκρί

35 *3 km (2 mi) south of Ayios Mamas, 11 km (7 mi) south of Naxos town.*

Sangri is the center of an area with so many monuments and ruins spanning the Archaic to the Venetian periods, it is sometimes called little Mystras, a reference to the famous abandoned Byzantine city in the Peloponnese. The name Sangri is a corruption of Sainte Croix, which is what the French called the town's 16th-century monastery of **Timios Stavros** (Holy Cross). The town is actually three small villages spread across a plateau. During the Turkish occupation, the monastery served as an illegal school, where children met secretly to learn the Greek language and culture. Above the town, you can make out the **ruins of t'Apilarou** (⊠ On Mt. Profitis Ilias), the castle Sanudo first attacked. It's a hard climb up.

Temple of Demeter

Ναός της Δήμητρας

★ **36** *5 km (3 mi) south of Sangri.*

Take the asphalt road right before the entrance to Sangri to reach the Temple of Demeter, a marble Archaic temple, circa 530 BC, lovingly restored by German archaeologists during the 1990s. Demeter was a grain goddess, and it's not hard to see what she is doing in this beautiful spot. There is also a small museum here (admission is free).

Chalki

Χαλκί

37 *6 km (4 mi) northeast of Sangri, 17 km (10½ mi) southeast of Naxos town.*

You are now entering the heart of the lush Tragaia Valley, where in spring the air is heavily scented with honeysuckle, roses, and lemon blossoms and many tiny Byzantine churches hide in the dense olive groves.

In Chalki is one of the most important of these Byzantine churches: the white, red-roof **Panayia Protothrone** (First Enthroned Virgin Church). Restoration work has uncovered frescoes from the 6th through the 13th centuries, and the church has remained alive and functioning for 14 centuries. The oldest layers, in the apse, depict the Apostles. ⊠ *On main Rd.* ☉ *Mornings.*

Chalki itself is a pretty town, known for its neoclassical houses in shades of pink, yellow, and gray, which are oddly juxtaposed with the plain but stately 17th-century Venetian **Frangopoulos tower.** ⊠ *Main road, next to Panayia Protothrone* 🖾 *Free* ☉ *Sometimes in morning.*

Moni

Μονή

🔵 *6 km (4 mi) north of Chalki, 23 km (14¼ mi) east of Naxos town.*

Owing to a good asphalt road, Moni ("monastery"), high in the mountains overlooking Naxos's greenest valley, has become a popular place for a meal or coffee on a hot afternoon. Local women make embroideries for Chora's shops.

Just below Moni is one of the Balkans' most important churches, **Panayia Drosiani** (☎ 22850/31003), which has faint, rare Byzantine frescoes from the 7th and 8th centuries. Its name means Our Lady of Refreshment, because once during a severe drought, when all the churches took their icons down to the sea to pray for rain, only the icon of this church got results. The fading frescoes are visible in layers: to the right when you enter are the oldest—one shows St. George the Dragon Slayer astride his horse, along with a small boy, an image one usually sees only in Cyprus and Crete. According to legend, the saint saved the child, who had fallen into a well, and there met and slew the giant dragon that had terrorized the town. Opposite him is St. Dimitrios, shown killing barbarians. The church is made up of three chapels—the middle one has a space for the faithful to worship at the altar rather than in the nave, as became common in later centuries. Next to that is a very small opening that housed a secret school during the revolution. It is open mornings and again after siesta; in deserted winter, ring the bell if it is not open.

Filoti

Φιλότι

🔵 *6½ km (4 mi) south of Moni, 20 km (12½ mi) southeast of Naxos town.*

Filoti, a peaceful village on the lower slopes of Mt. Zas, is the interior's largest. A three-day festival celebrating the Dormition starts on August 14. In the center of town is another Venetian tower that belonged to the Barozzi and the Church of Filotissa (Filoti's Virgin Mary) with its marble iconostasis and carved bell tower. There are places to eat and rooms to rent.

Sports & the Outdoors

Filoti is the starting place for several walks in the countryside, including the climb up to **Zas Cave** (⊠ Southeast of town of small dirt track), where obsidian tools and pottery fragments have been found; lots of bats live inside. Mt. Zas, or Zeus, is one of the god's birthplaces; on the path to the summit lies a block of unworked marble that reads *Oros Dios Milosiou,* or "boundary of the temple of Zeus Melosios." (Melosios, it is thought, is a word that has to do with sheep.) The islanders say that under the Turks the cave was used as a chapel, and two stalagmites are called the Priest and the Priest's Wife, who are said to have been petrified by God to save them from arrest.

The **Cheimarros Pirgos** (Tower of the Torrent), a cylindrical Hellenistic tower, can be reached from Filoti by a road that begins from the main road to Apeiranthos, outside town, or by a level, 3½-hour hike with excellent views. The walls, as tall as 45 feet, are intact, with marble blocks perfectly aligned. The tower, which also served as a lookout post for pirates, is often celebrated in the island's poetry: "O, my heart is like a bower/And Cheimarros's lofty tower!"

Apeiranthos

Απείρανθος

★ ⑩ *12 km (7½ mi) northeast of Filoti, 32 km (20 mi) southeast of Naxos town.*

Apeiranthos is very picturesque, with views and marble-paved streets running between the Venetian Bardani and Zevgoli towers. As you walk through the arcades and alleys, notice the unusual chimneys—no two are alike. The elders sit in their doorsteps chatting, while packs of children shout "Hello, hello" at any passerby who looks foreign.

A very small **Archaeological Museum,** established by a local mathematician, Michael Bardanis, displays Cycladic finds from the east coast. The most important of the artifacts are unique gray marble plaques from the 3rd millennium BC with roughly hammered scenes of daily life: hunters and farmers and sailors going about their business. If it's closed, ask in the square for the guard. ⊠ *Off main Sq.* ⊠ *Free* ⊙ *Daily 8:30–3.*

Koronos

Κόρωνος

④ *4 km (2½ mi) north of Apeiranthos, 36 km (23 mi) east of Naxos town.*

The paved road from Apeiranthos to Apollonas, winding and narrow in places, passes through the lovely village of Koronos, which tumbles spectacularly down the green mountainside. On the right you come to the **Stavros tis Keramotis church,** the only point from which you can see both the east and west coasts of Naxos.

Apollonas

Απολλώνας

④ *12 km (7½ mi) north of Koronos via road from Komiaki, 54 km (39½ mi) northeast of Naxos town.*

Apollonas is a small resort town on Naxos's northeast corner. Look for the steps leading to the unfinished 35-foot **kouros of Apollonas,** a statue of a nude bearded man that lies in an ancient quarry. It's thought to represent Dionysos. Initially, the Greeks represented gods with small idols; as their experience widened, so their statues grew. This early-6th-century figure was probably abandoned because cracks developed in the marble while the work was in progress. It lies on its back, eroded by the winds. ⊠ *On main road past Apollonas, on left* 🖾 *Free.*

Beaches

In the far northeast, **Apollonas** is a spread-out beach with small white marble pebbles. Much more rewarding are the **bays of Abram, Ayias Mamas, Xilia Brisi, and Pachia Ammos,** small sand beaches to the west that are seldom crowded. Most of these can be reached by bus.

Where to Eat

¢–$ ✕ **Venetiko.** In Apollonas the pickings are slim, but this is the best of the tavernas encircling the harbor—it's so close to the water you can feed the fish. Between frying potatoes and garnishing Greek salads, Voula and Dimitris can often be found sitting down to chat with customers. Vegetables, cheeses, and most meats are local, and you can see where the fish comes from. Other options include fresh (local) cockerel in wine sauce or fresh rabbit stew with onions, along with some pleasant barrel wine from the mountain village of Komiaki. ⊠ *Apollonas waterfront* 🕾 *22850/67108* 🖃 *No credit cards.*

Ayia

Αγία

🟡 *2½ km (1¼ mi) west of Apollonas.*

The coast road from Apollonas to Naxos town passes, in a lush valley, the **Ayia tower,** once a lookout post for northwestern Naxos. At the nearby church, during the feast of the Dormition (August 15), women who had taken a vow to the Virgin used to attend the service after walking barefoot from Apollonas along the rough paths.

Beaches

The road from Apollonas to Chora runs along steep cliffs, traversing inlets and secluded beaches; the most accessible is **Ormos Abram,** 5 km (3 mi) west of Apollonas, which has a pension and taverna and is pleasant when the north winds aren't blowing.

Flerio

Φλεριό

🟡 *12 km (7½ mi) east of Naxos town.*

★ The island's second famous **kouros** (the first is at Apollonas) is at Flerio, in the Melanes Valley; though smaller (26 feet), it is more detailed and lies in a beautiful private orchard; it has become one of Naxos's more popular sights. The silent kouros, like Ozymandias, is a reminder of a once-glorious age. Archaeologists think the 6th-century statue was abandoned because its leg broke (as you'll see). Also, when the tyrant Lygdamis came to power, he confiscated all the orders of the rich that were still in the quarries. When he couldn't find a way to dispose of some of the kouroi, he tried to sell them back to former owners. ⊠ *On right before small white shack; through small gate* 🖃 *Free* ⊙ *May–Oct., daily 8–sunset.*

need a break?

After seeing the kouros, relax in the **garden** (⊠ On right before small white shack), among bougainvillea and lilac, and order the local family's homemade kitro preserves or a shot of citron liqueur. Once refreshed, ask directions to a second abandoned kouros, up a path from the first.

PAROS

ΠΑΡΟΣ

In the golden age, the great sculptor Praxiteles prized the Parian marble that came from the quarries here; in the 19th century, Paros was beloved by Byron. Today, Paros is favored by people for its lower prices, golden sandy beaches, and charming fishing villages. It may lack the chic of Mykonos and have fewer top-class hotels, but at the height of the season it often gets Mykonos's overflow. The island is large enough to accommodate the traveler in search of peace and quiet, yet the lovely port towns of Paros town (also known as Parikia), the capital, and Naousa also have an active nightlife. Paros is a focal point of the Cyclades ferry network, and many people stay here for a night or two while waiting for a connection. Paros town has a good share of bars and discos, though Naousa has a more chic island atmosphere.

Paros Town

Πάρος (Παροικία)

35 km (22 mi) west of Naxos town, 10 km (6 mi) southwest of Naousa.

Your first impressions of Paros town will not necessarily be positive. The waterfront is crammed with travel agencies dispensing information and a multitude of car and motorbike rental agencies, and the new parking area on landfill is one of the Cyclades' disasters. If you walk east on the harbor road you will see a lineup of bars, fast-food restaurants, and coffee shops—some owned by Athenians who come to Paros to capitalize on tourism in summer. Past them are the bus stop, fishing-boat dock, ancient graveyard, and post office; then the beaches start. Head into town, though, where it is easy to get lost in the maze of narrow, stone-paved lanes that intersect with the streets of the quiet residential areas.

Fodor's Choice
★

The splendid square above the port, to the northwest, was built to celebrate the church's 1,700th anniversary. From there you will see a white gate, the front of the former monastic quarters that surround the magnificent **Panayia Ekatontapyliani** (Hundred Doors Church), the earliest remaining Byzantine church in Greece. According to legend, 99 doors have been found in the church and the 100th will be discovered only after Constantinople is Greek again. Inside, the subdued light mixes with the dun, reddish, and green tufa (porous volcanic rock). The columns are classical and their capitals Byzantine. At the corners of the dome are two fading Byzantine frescoes depicting six-winged seraphim. The 6th-century iconostasis (with ornate later additions) is divided into five frames by marble columns. One panel contains the 14th-century icon of the Virgin, with a silver covering from 1777. The Virgin is carried in procession on the church's crowded feast day, August 15, the Dormition. The adjacent **Baptistery**, nearly unique in Greece, also built from the 4th to the 6th century, has a marble font and bits of mosaic floor.

In 326, St. Helen—the mother of Emperor Constantine the Great—took a ship for the Holy Land to find the True Cross. Stopping on Paros, she had a vision of success and vowed to build a church there. She founded it but died before it was built. Her son built the church in 328 as a wooden-roof basilica. Two centuries later Justinian the Great, who ruled the Byzantine Empire in 527–65, had it splendidly rebuilt with a dome. He appointed Isidorus, one of the two architects of Constantinople's famed Ayia Sophia, to design it; Isidorus decided to send an apprentice, Ignatius, to Paros. Folk legends say that, upon its completion, Isidorus arrived in Paros for an inspection and discovered the dome to be so magnificent that, consumed by jealousy, he pushed the young apprentice off the roof. Ignatius grasped his master's foot as he fell, and the two tumbled to their death together. Two folk sculptures near the toilets at the sanctuary's baroque left portal portray them as two fat men, one pulling his beard with remorse and the other holding his cracked head. The church **museum**, at right, contains post-Byzantine icons. ⊠ *750 ft east of dock* ☎ *22840/21243* ⌚ *€1.50* ☉ *Daily 8 AM–10 PM.*

The **Archaeological Museum** contains a large chunk of the famed Parian chronicle, which recorded cultural events in Greece from about 1500 BC until 260 BC (another chunk is in Oxford's Ashmolean Museum). It interests scholars that the historian inscribed detailed information about artists, poets, and playwrights, completely ignoring wars and shifts in government. Some primitive pieces from the Aegean's oldest settlement, Saliagos (an islet between Paros and Antiparos), are exhibited in the same room, on the left. In the large room to the right rests a marble slab depicting the poet Archilochus in a banquet scene, lying on a couch, his weapons nearby. The ancients ranked Archilochus, who invented iambic meter and wrote the first signed love lyric, second only to Homer. When he died in battle against the Naxians, his conqueror was cursed by the oracle of Apollo for putting to rest one of the faithful servants of the muse. Also there are a monumental Nike and three superb pieces found in the last decade: a waist-down kouros, a gorgon, and a dancing-girl relief. ⊠ *Behind Hundred Doors Church* ☎ *22840/21231* ⊕ *www. culture.gr* ⌚ *€3* ☉ *Tues.–Sun. 8:30–2:30.*

Anthemion Museum. The Kontogiorgos family has lovingly gathered a large, valuable collection of books, manuscripts, prints, coins, jewels, embroideries, weapons, ceramics, and much more mostly pertaining to Paros, and lovingly displays it in this house-turned-museum. ⊠ *Airport road, before Punta split* ☎☎ *22840/91010* ⌚ *€5* ☉ *Tues.–Sun. 8:30–2:30.*

Beaches

From Paros town, boats leave throughout the day for beaches across the bay: to sandy **Krios** and the quieter **Kaminia. Livadia,** a five-minute walk, is very developed but has shade.

Where to Stay & Eat

★ **$–$$** ✕ **Levantis.** Owner George Mavridis does his own cooking—always a good sign. Though this spot looks like a garden taverna and, amazingly, is priced like one, the food is sophisticated and eclectic, as George often returns from winter travels with exotic new recipes. Two intriguing starters are garlic spiced prawns with spinach-rice, and eggplant rolls filled with *myzithra* (like ricotta), sun-dried tomatoes, and basil oil. Such entrées as braised lamb in honey with apples, prunes, and almonds, and sesame-coated marinated pork with wild mushrooms and Chinese noodles keep the interest high. The white-chocolate and amaretto mousse with sour cherries is divine. Unusual in Greece, there is a nonsmoking section. ✉ *Central market St.* ☎ *22840/23613* ▤ *AE, MC, V* ☉ *Closed Nov.–Apr.*

★ **$–$$** ✕ **Porphyra.** Yannis Gouroyannis knows everything about fish; he fishes, dives, prepares, and greets you with a plate of marinated fish. Yannis's wife, Roula, cooks, assisted by their daughter Xanthi—it's a family place, and their sons sometimes help as well. The various croquettes and fish salad are great favorites. The mussels are always superb, and the *kakavia* (fish soup with a whole fish in each plate) and fresh fish (it changes) in an aromatic white sauce remind you that Paros is seagirt. The interior is simple and authentic, while the outdoor tables border a romantic ancient ruin. All ingredients are local and of the highest quality in Paros's best seafood restaurant. ✉ *Along waterfront toward post office* ☎ *22840/23410* ▤ *AE, MC, V.*

¢ ✕ **Gelato Sulla Luna.** Many of the evening strollers on the waterfront of Parikia cannot pass this authentic gelateria; their willpower melts faster than the gelato. Denise Marinucci's father made ice cream in New Jersey, and Denise continues the tradition, but her recipes come from Venice. She makes everything on the premises. ✉ *Paros* ☎ *22840/22868* ⊕ *www. parosweb.com/sullaluna* ▤ *No credit cards* ☉ *Closed Dec.–Mar.*

$$ ⊡ **Pandrossos Hotel.** If you want a good night's sleep away from the pulse of Paros town but you don't want to give up shopping, nightlife, restaurants, and cafés, the Pandrossos—built on a hill with a splendid view overlooking Paros Bay—is the best choice. The lobby, restaurant, and terrace form one great expanse of marble, perfect for sunset watching—unless you're watching it from your room's sea-view balcony. To get to this hotel's hill location, take the seaside road from Paros town. ✉ *On hill at southwest edge of Paros town, 84400* ☎ *22840/22903* ▤ *22840/22904* ⊕ *www.pandrossoshotel.gr* ⌨ *41 rooms, 5 suites* ♢ *Restaurant, cable TV, pool, bar* ▤ *AE, MC, V* ☉ *Closed Nov.–Mar.* ⦿ *BP.*

$ ⊡ **Parian Village.** This shady, quiet hotel at the far edge of Livadia beach has small rooms, all with balconies or terraces, most with spectacular views over Parikia bay. The pool is pretty, but the sea is close. Breakfast costs €5. ✉ *15-min sea walk from center of Paros town, 84400* ☎ *22840/23187* ▤ *22840/23880* ⊕ *www.paros-accommodations.gr/parianvillage* ⌨ *28 rooms* ♢ *Refrigerators, pool* ▤ *MC, V* ☉ *Closed Nov.–Apr.*

¢ ☒ **Pension Evangelistria.** Voula Maounis's rooms, all with balconies, are usually full of returnees—archaeologists, painters, and the like—who enjoy its central location near the Hundred Doors Church, olive trees, and gracious welcome. The house is built over a Roman-period ruin; the hotel is open all year. ☒ *Near dock in Paros town, 84400* ☎ *22840/ 21481* 🖷 *22840/22464* ✉ *parosrealmarket@otenet.gr* ⇗ *9 rooms* ♨ *Kitchenettes* ▤ *No credit cards.*

Nightlife & the Arts

MUSIC & BARS Turn right along the waterfront from the port in Paros town to find the town's famous bars; then follow your ears. At the far end of the Paralia is the laser-light-and-disco section of town, which you may want to avoid. In the younger bars, cheap alcohol, as everywhere in tourist Greece, is often added to the more colorful drinks. For a classier alternative to noisy bars, head for **Pebbles** (☒ On Kastro hill ☎ 22840/ 22283), which often has live jazz (Greece's best jazz guitarist, Vasilis Rakopoulos, who summers on Paros, likes to drop by with local bassist Petros Varthakouris) and overlooks the sunset.

THE ARTS The **Aegean Center for the Fine Arts** (☒ Main cross street to market St. ☎ 22840/23287 ⊕ www.aegeancenter.org), a small American arts college, periodically stages readings, concerts, lectures, and exhibitions in its splendidly restored mansion. It is run by John Pack, an American photographer who lives on the island with his family. Since 1966 the center has offered courses (two three-month semesters) in writing, painting, and photography, among other disciplines.

The **Archilochos Cultural Society** (☒ Near bus stop ☎ 22840/23595 ⊕ www.archilochos.gr) runs a film club in winter and offers concerts, exhibitions, and lectures throughout the year (for instance, in 2005 the International Archilochos Conference was held here). The **Paros Summer Musical Festival** brings musicians from around the world to perform at the Archilochos Hall. Watch for posters.

Sports & the Outdoors

GYM Fotis Skiadas's well-appointed **Gymnasium** (☒ Hotel Zanet, near Livadia beach ☎ 22840/22233), for aerobics and bodybuilding, is air-conditioned and has a sauna.

HORSEBACK For riding along the coast, **Kokou Riding Center** (☒ Livadi ☎ 22840/51818) RIDING has horses; the cost is €30 for two hours.

MOUNTAIN For organized mountain-bike tours (one includes Naxos) and rentals, BIKING there's **Hellas Bike Travel** (☎ 22840/52010 🖷 22840/51720).

WATER SPORTS Many beaches offer water sports, especially windsurfing. **Aegean Diving College** (☒ Golden Beach ☎🖷 22840/43347) offers scuba lessons and takes you to reefs, shipwrecks, and caves. Director Peter Nikolaides, who discovered the oldest shipwreck known, is a marine biologist involved in many of Greece's ecological projects. Every summer the **F2 Windsurfing Center** (☒ New Golden Beach, at Philoxenia Hotel, near Marpissa ☎ 22840/41878) hosts the International Windsurfing World Cup.

Shopping

JEWELRY Vangelis Skaramagas and Yannis Xenos have been making their own delicate, precious jewelry at **Jewelry Workshop** (✉ End of market St. ☎ 22840/21008) for more than 20 years. Local Phaidra Apostolopoulou, who studied jewelry in Athens, now has a tiny shop, **Phaidra** (✉ Near Zoodochos Pyghi church ☎ 22840/23626), where she shows her silver pieces, many lighthearted for summer.

LOCAL FOODS **Enosis** (Agricultural Cooperative's shop; ✉ Manto Mavroyennis Sq., at front of Paros town under police station ☎ 22820/22181) sells home-made pasta, honey, cheeses, and especially Paros's renowned wines. The varietal wine Monemvasia (officially rated "Appellation of High Quality Origin Paros") is made from white monemvasia grapes, indigenous to Paros. You can visit the winery for an evocative slide show, a photography exhibition of Paros's agricultural traditions, and a wine tasting. For an appointment call Alexis Gokas at 22840/22235.

 Halfway from Paros town to Naousa, on the right, the 17th-century **Monastery of Longovarda** (☎ 22840/21202) shines on its mountainside. The monastic community farms the local land and makes honey, wine, and olive oil. Only men, dressed in conservative clothing, are allowed inside, where there are post-Byzantine icons, 17th-century frescoes depicting the Twelve Feasts in the Life of Christ, and a library of rare books; it is usually open mornings.

Naousa

Náουσα

★ *10 km (6 mi) northeast of Paros town.*

Naousa, impossibly pretty, long ago discovered the benefits of tourism. Its outskirts are mushrooming with villas and hotels that exploit it further. Along the harbor, red and navy-blue boats knock gently against one another as fishermen repair their nets and foreigners relax in the ouzeris—Barbarossa being the traditional favorite—by the water's edge. Navies of the ancient Persians, flotillas from medieval Venice, and the imperial Russian fleet have anchored in this harbor. The half-submerged ruins of the Venetian fortifications still remain; they are a pretty sight when lighted up at night.

Beaches

A boat goes regularly to **Lageri** (✉ North of Naousa), a long, sandy beach with dunes. The boat that goes to Lageri also travels to **Santa Maria** (✉ Northeastern shore of Paros), the windsurfers' beach. A boat crosses the bay to **Kolimbithres** (✉ Directly across bay from Naousa), noted for its anfractuous rock formations, water sports, a choice of tavernas, and two luxury hotels. **Ayios Ioannis** (✉ Across from Naousa), served by the boat that goes to Kolimbithres, is quieter.

Where to Stay & Eat

★ **$$$–$$$$**   ✕ **Mario.** Good food is enhanced here by the pretty location, a few feet from the fishing boats on Naousa's harbor. The taverna specializes in fresh fish and also such dishes as eggplant confit, or pastry rolls stuffed with shrimp and soft cheese. For a main dish, have fresh fish wrapped in bacon, or a fillet of beef on potato puree in wine sauce. The fresh strawberry liquor will keep you sitting longer. ✉ *On fishing-boat harbor* ☎ *22840/51047* ⚖ *Reservations essential* ▤ *AE, MC, V.*

$$$–$$$$ ✕ **Poseidon.** Eat here for elegant dining away from the fray, on a spacious terrace with two pools, dozens of palm trees, and the bay of Naousa in front of you. All the vegetables are from their own garden, the fish is fresh, and the kitchen (where everything is made) is immaculate. To start, try beef carpaccio, or vegetables tossed with smoked salmon, prawns, and caviar in citrus sauce. Two excellent main courses would be veal with pasta, and *carrée d'agneau,* lamb with an herb dressing and merlot wine sauce on a bed of sautéed arugula. If you can still manage dessert (you will want to sit here a long time), try the "Pandesi," a dark chocolate cake with amaretto and berry sauce. ✉ *Astir hotel, Kolymbithres, Paros* ☎ *22840/51976* ⊕ *www.astirofparos.gr* ▤ *AE, MC, V* ☯ *Closed Nov.–Apr.*

★ **$$$–$$$$**   ✕ **Taverna Christos.** For more than 25 years Christos has been Naousa's best restaurant; it still is. Its cool, white, spacious garden—the walls are an art gallery—has an easy elegance; the service is both efficient and gracious. Excellent first courses include *myzethra* (a local, soft goat cheese similar to ricotta) quiche, and mussels steamed in wine. Among entrées, try fresh guilthead bream wrapped in vine leaves, or veal escalope cooked in sweet Cypriot wine and cardamom. The white-chocolate tart in fruit-of-the-season sauce is sinful. Christos always has local specialties, so ask. ✉ *Up hill from central Sq.* ☎ *22840/51442* ⊕ *www. christos-restaurant.gr* ▤ *AE, MC, V* ☯ *Closed Oct.–May.*

$$$$ ▦ **Astir of Paros.** Across the bay from Naousa twinkle the lights of this deluxe resort hotel, an elegant and expensive retreat, with green lawns, tall palm trees, lush gardens, and an art gallery. Rooms are pretty and spacious—perfect for romantic couples of taste—with antiques, artwork, and views of the sparkling Naousa Bay. Its bars are popular and its two restaurants are excellent. ✉ *Take Kolymbithres road from Naousa, 84401* ☎ *22840/51976 or 22840/51984* ⊟ *22840/51985* ⊕ *www. astirofparos.gr* ⤴ *11 rooms, 46 suites* ⚭ *2 restaurants, refrigerators, cable TV, tennis court, pool, gym, sauna, 2 bars* ▤ *AE, DC, MC, V* ☯ *Closed Nov.–Mar.* ⊠ *BP.*

$ ▦ **Svoronos Bungalows.** These bungalow apartments always seem to be fully occupied. The friendly Sovronos family tends the lush garden, and the comfortable apartments and Cycladic whitewashed courtyards are decorated with antiques and objects from the family's extensive travels. Though quiet, the hotel is within easy reach of Naousa's lively shopping and nightlife. There is no air-conditioning, but it is cool. ✉ *Behind big church, 1 block in from Santa Maria road, 84401* ☎ *22849/51211 or 22840/51409* ⊟ *22840/52281* ⊕ *www.parosweb. gr/svoronos* ⤴ *19 apartments* ⚭ *Kitchenettes, bar; no a/c, no room TVs* ▤ *MC, V* ☯ *Closed Nov.–Apr.*

Nightlife & the Arts

BARS **Linardo's** (⊠ At fishing harbor) is lively and is open into the wee hours. **Agosta** (⊠ At fishing harbor) is a pretty spot.

DANCE The group **Music–Dance "Naousa Paros"** (☎ 22840/52284), formed in 1988 to preserve the traditional dances and music of Paros, performs all summer long in Naousa in the costumes of the 16th century and has participated in dance competitions and festivals throughout Europe. Keep an eye out for posters.

Sports & the Outdoors

If you're traveling with children, **Aqua Paros Waterpark** (⊠ Kolymbithres, next to Porto Paros Hotel ☎ 22840/53271), with its 13 waterslides big and small, will cool a hot afternoon. Admission is €12. **Santa Maria Surf Club** (⊠ Santa Maria beach, about 4 km [2½ mi] north of Naousa) is popular, with windsurfing, jet-skiing, waterskiing, and diving.

Shopping

ART & JEWELRY Paros is an art colony and exhibits are everywhere in summer. Petros Metaxas's **Metaxas Gallery** (⊠ On 2nd street from harbor toward main church ☎ 22840/52667) is especially devoted to the jewelry of Aristotelis and Lilly Bessis, who run it, too. There are also exhibits by local artists.

FASHION Kostas Moyzedakis's **Tango** (⊠ On 2nd street from harbor toward main church ☎ 22840/51014) has been selling classic sportswear for two decades; its most popular line is its own Tangowear.

Marathi

Μαράθι

10 km (6 mi) east of Paros town.

During the classical period the island of Paros had an estimated 150,000 residents, many of them slaves who worked the ancient marble quarries in Marathi. The island grew rich from the export of this white, granular marble known among ancient architects and sculptors for its ability to absorb light. They called it *lychnites* ("won by lamplight").

Marked by a sign, **three caverns** (⊠ Short walk from main Rd.) are bored into the hillside, the largest of them 300 feet deep. The most recent quarrying done in these mines was in 1844, when a French company cut marble here for Napoléon's tomb.

Shopping

At **Studio Yria** (⊠ 1½ km [1 mi] east of Marathi, above road to Kostos village ☎ 22840/29007 ⊕ www.studioyria.com) master potters Stelios and Monique Ghikas and other craftspeople can be seen at work. Marble carvers, metalsmiths, painters, and more all make for a true Renaissance workshop. Both the ceramic tableware and the works of art make use of Byzantine and Cycladic motifs in their designs; they have even made ceramic designs for the Prince of Wales. Easily accessible by bus, taxi, and rental car, the studio is usually open daily 8–8; call ahead in the off-season.

Lefkes

Λεύκες

6 km (4 mi) south of Marathi, 10 km (6 mi) southeast of Paros town.

Rampant piracy in the 17th century forced thousands of people to move inland from the coastal regions; thus for many years the scenic village of Lefkes, built on a hillside in the protective mountains, was the island's capital. It remains the largest village in the interior and has maintained a peaceful, island feeling, with narrow streets fragrant of jasmine and honeysuckle. Farming is the major source of income, as you can tell from the well-kept stone walls and olive groves.

Two **17th-century churches** of interest are **Ayia Varvara** (St. Barbara) and **Ayios Sotiris** (Holy Savior). The big 1830 neo-Renaissance **Ayia Triada** (Holy Trinity) is the pride of the village.

Beaches

Piso Livadi (⊠ On road past Lefkes) was the ancient port for the marble quarries and today is a small resort town convenient to many beaches; the harbor, from where boats go to Naxos and Delos, is being expanded.

Where to Stay & Eat

¢–$ ✕ **Taverna Klarinos.** You go to Nikos and Anna Ragousis's place for the real thing. Nikos grows the vegetables, raises the meat, makes the cheese (even the feta) from his own goats, and makes the wine from his own vineyards; Anna cooks. Traditional dishes such as fried zucchini or beets with garlic sauce are the best you'll taste, and the grilled meats make the gods envious. ⊠ *Main entrance street, opposite square, on 2nd fl.* ☎ 22840/41608 ▭ *No credit cards* ♥ *Closed Oct.–May.*

★ $$$ ▦ **Lefkes Village.** All the rooms in this elegant hotel are white, and the wooden furniture and fabrics are reproductions of traditional styles; all have balconies with magnificent views down the olive-tree valley and over the sea to Naxos. The restaurant is noted for its traditional Greek food; the folk museum here is chockablock with interesting objects. ⊠ *East of Lefkes on main road, 84400* ☎ *22840/41827 or 22840/42398* ⊕ *www.lefkesvillage.gr* ➷ *20 rooms* ♿ *Restaurant, refrigerators, pool, bar* ▭ *AE, DC, MC, V* ♥ *Closed Nov.–Mar.* ⅼ◑ *BP.*

Shopping

POTTERY & CRAFTS One street above the lower café square, **Yria Interiors** (☎ 22840/28198) has a shop and exhibition rooms in three old Lefkes houses. The shop, in addition to pottery from Studio Yria, sells weavings by Eleni Kouvara (you'll see her loom), dried herbs, and imported European home furnishings.

WEAVINGS On the main street above the lower café square, Nikoletta Haniotis's shop, **Anemi** (☎ 22840/41182), sells handwoven weavings colored with natural dyes and local designs. Also for sale are iron pieces made by her father, Lefkes' blacksmith.

Petaloudes Park

Πεταλούδες

4 km (2½ mi) south of Paros town.

A species of moth returns year after year to mate in Petaloudes (the Valley of the Butterflies), a lush oasis of greenery in the middle of this dry island. In May, June, and perhaps July, you can watch them as they lie dormant during the day, their chocolate-brown wings with yellow stripes still against the ivy leaves. In the evening they flutter upward to the cooler air, flashing the coral-red undersides of their wings as they rise. A notice at the entrance asks visitors not to disturb them by taking photographs or shaking the leaves. ⊠ *Petaloudes* 🖾 €3 🕙 *Mid-May–mid-Sept., daily 9–8.*

need a break? Even when the butterflies are not there, it is pleasant to have coffee in the small ***kafeneio*** (coffeehouse; ⊠ Inside entrance to park) and enjoy the shade of the cypress, olive, chestnut, mulberry, and lemon trees.

On the summit of a hill beyond the garden reigns a lopped **Venetian tower.** Its founder's name, Iakovos Alisafis, and the date, 1626, are inscribed on it.

Sports & the Outdoors

You can rent tennis courts at the **Holiday Sun Hotel** (⊠ Pounda ☎ 22840/91284 or 22840/91285), which also has an exercise room and sauna.

en route A 15-minute walk or 2-minute drive back toward Paros town from the Valley of the Butterflies leads to the convent known as **Christos sto Dasos** (Christ in the Wood), from where there's a marvelous view of the Aegean. The convent contains the tomb of St. Arsenios (1800–77), who was a schoolteacher, an abbot, and a prophet. He was also a rainmaker whose prayers were believed to have ended a long drought, saving Paros from starvation. The nuns are a bit leery of tourists. If you want to go in, be sure to wear long pants or skirt and a shirt that covers your shoulders, or the sisters will turn you away.

SANTORINI (THERA)

ΣΑΝΤΟΡΙΝΗ (ΘΗΡΑ)

Undoubtedly the most extraordinary island in the Aegean, crescent-shape Santorini remains a mandatory stop on the Cycladic tourist route—even if it's necessary to enjoy the sensational sunsets from Ia, the fascinating excavations, and the dazzling white towns with a million other travelers. Arriving by boat, you are met by one of the world's truly breathtaking sights, the caldera: a crescent of cliffs, striated in black, pink, brown, white, and pale green, rising 1,100 feet, with the white clusters of the towns of Fira and Ia perched along the top. The encircling cliffs are the ancient rim of a still-active volcano, and you are sailing east across its flooded caldera.

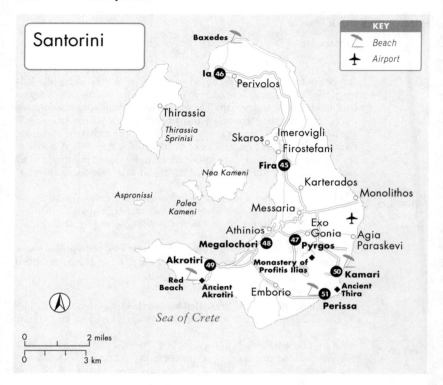

Santorini and its four neighboring islets are the fragmentary remains of a larger landmass that exploded about 1600 BC: the volcano's core blew sky high, and the sea rushed into the abyss to create the great bay, which measures 10 km by 7 km (6 mi by 4½ mi) and is 1,292 feet deep. The other pieces of the rim, which broke off in later eruptions, are Thirassia, where a few hundred people live, and deserted little Aspronissi ("White Isle"). In the center of the bay, black and uninhabited, two cones, the "Burnt Isles" of Palea Kameni and Nea Kameni, appeared between 1573 and 1925. The ancients called Santorini's island group Strongyle ("Round") and Kalliste ("Loveliest"); the island was named Thera, and it still officially is. Its medieval name of Santorini (a corruption of Sant' Irene) is more common.

There has been too much speculation about the identification of Santorini with the mythical Atlantis, mentioned in Egyptian papyri and by Plato (who says it's in the Atlantic), but myths are hard to pin down. This is not true of old arguments about whether or not tidal waves from Santorini's cataclysmic explosion destroyed Minoan civilization on Crete, 113 km (70 mi) away. The latest carbon-dating evidence, which points to 1645 as the probable year of eruption, clearly indicates that the Minoans outlasted the eruption by a couple of hundred years.

Since antiquity, Santorini has depended on rain collected in cisterns for drinking and irrigating—the well water is often brackish—and the serious shortage is alleviated by the importation of water. The volcanic soil produces small, intense tomatoes with tough skins used for tomato paste (good restaurants here serve them); the famous Santorini fava beans, which have a light, fresh taste; barley; wheat; and white-skin eggplants. The locals say that in Santorini there is more wine than water, and it may be true; Santorini produces more wine than any two other Cyclades. The volcanic soil, high daytime temperatures, and humidity at night produce 36 varieties of grape, and these unique growing conditions are ideal for the production of distinctive white wine now gaining international recognition. Farmers twist the vines into a basketlike shape, in which the grapes grow, protected from the wind.

Sadly, unrestrained tourism has taken a heavy toll on Santorini. Fira and Ia could almost be described as "a street with 40 jewelry shops"; many of the natives are completely burned out by the end of the peak season (the best times to come here are shoulder periods); and, increasingly, business and the loud ringing of cash registers have disrupted the normal flow of Greek life here. For example, if a cruise ship comes in during afternoon siesta, all shops immediately open. And you will have a pushy time walking down Fira's main street in August, so crowded is it. Still and all, if you look beneath the layers of gimcrack tourism, you'll find that Santorini is a beautiful place.

Fira

Φηρά

45 *10 km (6 mi) west of the airport, 14 km (8½ mi) southeast of Ia.*

Tourism, the island's major industry, adds more than 1 million visitors per year to a population of 7,000. As a result, Fira, the capital, midway along the west coast of the east rim, is no longer only a picturesque village but a major tourist center, overflowing with discos, shops, and restaurants. Many of its employees, East Europeans or young travelers extending their summer vacations, hardly speak Greek.

It soon becomes clear what brings the tourist here: with its white, cubical white houses clinging to the cliff hundreds of feet above the caldera, Fira is a beautiful place.

To experience life here as it was until only a couple of decades ago, walk down the much-photographed, winding **staircase** that descends from town to the water's edge—walk or take the cable car back up, avoiding the drivers who will try to plant you on the sagging back of one of their bedraggled-looking donkeys.

The modern Greek Orthodox cathedral of **Panayia Ypapantis** (⊠ Southern part of town) is a major landmark; the local priests, with somber faces, long beards, and black robes, look strangely out of place in summertime Fira. Along **Eikostis Pemptis Martiou** (25th of March street; ⊠ East of Panayia Ypapantis), you'll find inexpensive restaurants and accommodations. The blocked-off Ypapantis street (west of

Panayia Ypapantis) leads to **Kato Fira** (Lower Fira), built into the cliff side overlooking the caldera, where prices are higher and the vista wonderful. For centuries the people of the island have been digging themselves rooms-with-a-view right in the cliff face—many bars and hotel rooms now occupy the caves.

★ The **Museum of Prehistoric Thera** displays pots and frescoes from the famed excavations at Akrotiri. Note the fresco fragments with the painted swallows (who flocked here because they loved the cliffs) and the women in Minoan dresses. The fossilized olive leaves from 60,000 BC prove the olive to be indigenous. ⊠ *Mitropoleos, behind big church* ☎ *22860/23217* ⊕ *www.culture.gr* ☒ *€5 including Archaeological Museum, €8 including Archeological Museum and Akrotiri* ⊙ *Tues.–Sun. 8:30–3.*

The **Archaeological Museum** displays pottery, statues, and grave artifacts found at excavations mostly from ancient Thira and Akrotiri, from the Minoan through the Byzantine periods. ⊠ *Stavrou and Nomikos, Mitropoleos, behind big church* ☎ *22860/22217* ☒ *€5 including Museum of Prehistoric Thera* ⊙ *Tues.–Sun. 8:30–3.*

off the beaten path

NEA KAMENI – To peer into a live, sometimes smoldering volcano, join one of the popular excursions to Nea Kameni, the larger of the two Burnt Isles. After disembarking, you hike 430 feet to the top and walk around the edge of the crater, wondering if the volcano is ready for its fifth eruption during the last hundred years—after all, the last was in 1956. Some tours continue on to Therasia, where there is a village. Tours (about €15) are scheduled regularly by **Bellonias Tours** (☎ 22860/22469, 22860/23604 Fira, 22860/31117 Kamari) and **Nomikos Travel** (☎ 22860/23660 ☒ 22860/23666 ⊕ www. nomikosvillas.gr).

Where to Stay & Eat

$$$$ ✕ **Sphinx.** When Fira locals want more than a taverna, they come to this vaulted room, which opens onto several terraces with caldera views. Owner George Psichas is his own chef, and every dish is evidence of his loving care (even the bread and pasta are homemade); his brother Dimitris manages graciously. Starters include seafood carpaccio with arugula and capers, and delicately stuffed mussels au gratin. Fresh fish is always available—try the fresh grouper steak with grape and grappa sauce. Among the meat dishes, the fillet steak with mushrooms and truffle oil is especially good. Desserts change day by day, but they are noted for their crème brûlée. The wine list is long. ⊠ *Cliff-side walkway in front of Panayia Ypapantis* ☎ *22860/23823* ⊕ *www.sphinx-santorini.com* ✍ *Reservations essential* ⊟ *AE, MC, V.*

$$–$$$$ ✕ **Selene.** The terrace at Fira's best place for elegant dining has a splendid caldera view, and the interior is an old cliff house with a vaulted ceiling and dark-wood furniture; the banquettes are the built-in benches intrinsic to traditional island houses. The menu is full of interesting starters, such as a salad of pulses and pomegranate seeds with *apokti* (local cured pork); and sardines with pine nuts and black raisins in lemon-orange aspic. The entrées include baked mackerel with caper leaves and tomato wrapped in a fava crepe, and rabbit casserole in egg-cheese sauce. For dessert try eggplant confit with chocolate mousse and almonds. In summer, owners Evelyn and George give daylong cooking classes. ⊠ *Cliff-side walkway, 310 ft to left of Hotel Atlantis* ☎ *22860/22449* ⊕ *www. selene.gr* ⚓ *Reservations essential* ▭ *AE, DC, MC, V* ⊘ *Closed Nov.–Mar.*

$–$$$ ✕ **Camille Stéfani.** Ares has moved his popular restaurant from Kamari back to Fira, where he started 20 years ago. Perched on top of the small Fabrica shopping plaza off the cliff-side walkway, its enclosed terrace with wooden decor is open to the breezes from the bay and the southern sea. The menu is large; the meats—steak with green peppers is a specialty—are especially good. ☎ *22860/28938* ▭ *AE, MC, V.*

¢–$ ✕ **Nicholas.** This is Santorini's oldest taverna, where you'll find locals in winter. Island dishes are prepared well and served in a simple, attractive room. Try the local yellow lentils and the lamb fricassee with an egg-lemon sauce. ⊠ *2 streets in from cliff side on Erythrou Stavrou* ☎ *No phone* ▭ *No credit cards.*

$$$$ 🏨 **Aigialos.** Aigialos ("seashore") occupies a cluster of buildings from the 18th and 19th centuries and provides the most comfortable and discreetly luxurious—as well as the most poetic—place to stay in Fira. The one- and two-bedroom villas, with marble floors and beautiful furniture, have terraces or balconies overlooking the caldera—no need to venture out at sunset. There's maid service twice daily, impeccable 24-hour service, and fresh flowers. The restaurant serves its Mediterranean cuisine only to residents, and you can eat on your private terrace. It is always serenely quiet. ⊠ *South end of cliff-side walkway, 84700* ☎ *22860/ 25191 through 22860/25195* 🖷 *22860/22856* ⊕ *www.aigialos.gr* ⤶ *16 villas* ⚒ *Dining room, refrigerators, cable TV, pool, spa, bar* ▭ *AE, DC, MC, V* ⊘ *Closed Nov.–Mar.* ⫶❶ *BP.*

Fodor'sChoice
★

$$$$ 🏨 **Hotel Anteliz.** This little hotel, a family's cliff-side house rigorously redone according to tradition, is quiet, sparkling, and isolated, and a mere 10-minute walk along the caldera from either Fira or Firostefani. Guests find it hard to leave the little gated courtyard with its caldera view. The spacious apartments have handsome traditional furnishings and two bathrooms. ⊠ *Next to Nomikos Conference Centre, 84700* ☎ *22860/28842* 🖷 *22860/28843* ⊕ *www.anteliz.gr* ⤶ *8 apartments* ⚒ *Kitchenettes, cable TV, pool, bar* ▭ *MC, V* ⊘ *Closed Nov.–Mar.* ⫶❶*BP.*

$$$$ 🏨 **Hotel Aressana.** Though the Aressana lacks a view of the caldera, its own slant of sea view is effulgent. The large freshwater pool, spacious lobby with traditional furnishings and wood-paneled bar, excellent service, famous breakfast, and location in central Fira make it first-rate. The Aressana specializes in traditional wedding receptions and provides charming bridal suites—so don't be surprised at how many Americans honeymoon here. ⊠ *South end of cliff-side walkway, 84700* ☎ *22860/ 23900 or 22860/23901* 🖷 *22860/23902* ⊕ *www.aressana.gr* ⤶ *42 rooms, 8 suites* ⚒ *Cable TV, in-room data ports, pool, bar, Internet room* ▭ *AE, DC, MC, V* ⊘ *Closed Nov.–Mar.* ⫶❶ *BP.*

$$$$ 🏨 **Theoxenia Hotel.** Nestled among the jewelry stores on the main street is the narrow door leading up marble steps to this hotel. Upstairs, the hotel is an oasis of simplicity, taste, and cleanliness, a tribute to the Mendrinos family, who owns it, and to manager Andrzej Weglarz, who runs it. All rooms have attractive traditional furnishings; those on the top floor have caldera views. Stays here include use of Aressana's pool. ⊠ *Via D'Oro, 84700* ☎ *22860/22740 or 22860/22545* 🖷 *22860/22950* ⊕ *www.theoxenia.net* ⤳ *9 rooms* ⚭ *Refrigerators, cable TV, in-room data ports, hot tub* ⊟ *AE, DC, MC, V* ⏁◎⏁ *BP.*

$ 🖾 **Loizos Apartments.** Lefteris Anapliotis's pension, located in a quiet and convenient section of Fira, is the perfect budget choice. The rooms, some with sea views, are spacious and the garden is pretty. The price includes transfers. The excellent breakfast costs €5. Anapliotis also runs the even cheaper Loizos Hotel 3 km (2 mi) outside town. ⊠ *On cobbled road up from main traffic street, near Town Hall, 84700* ☎ *22860/24046* 🖷 *22860/25118* ⊕ *www.loizos.gr* ⤳ *10 rooms* ⚭ *Snack bar, refrigerators, cable TV, in-room data ports* ⊟ *AE, MC, V.*

$ 🖾 **Pension Delphini I.** Vassilis Rouuseas's pension, on the busy main traffic street, is well run, inexpensive, friendly, and open all year. His mother tends the lovely little garden. ⊠ *Main traffic street, opposite Piraeus Bank, 84700* ☎ *22860/22780* 🖷 *22860/22371* ⊕ *www.delfinisantorini.gr* ⤳ *10 rooms* ⚭ *Refrigerators, cable TV, in-room data ports* ⊟ *No credit cards.*

Nightlife & the Arts

DANCING   The **Koo Club** (⊠ North end of cliff-side walkway ☎ 22860/22025) is Fira's most popular outdoor disco by far. **Santorinia** (⊠ Next to Nomikos Conference Center ☎ 22860/23777) is the place for live Greek music and dancing. Nothing happens before midnight. **Casablanca Soul** (⊠ Fira ☎ 697/757–5191) is in the maze to the north; there is often live music.

FESTIVAL   Thank pianist Athena Capodistria for September's **Santorini Music Festival** (⊠ Nomikos Conference Center ☎ 22860/22220), which always includes internationally known musicians.

MUSIC   The popular **Franco's Bar** (⊠ Below cliff-side walkway ☎ 22860/24428) plays classical music and serves champagne cocktails. It has a caldera view.

Sports & the Outdoors

SAILING   The **Santorini Sailing Center** (⊠ Merovigli ☎ 22860/23058 or 22860/23059), near Fira, arranges charters and runs weekly two- to three-day sailing trips around the Cyclades for groups of up to 10.

TENNIS   The **Santorini Tennis Club** (⊠ Santorini Tennis Club Hotel, Kartaradoes ☎ 22860/22122) has two concrete courts where two people can play in high season for €7 per hour; it's open April–October.

Shopping

ART GALLERY   **Phenomenon.** Christoforos Asimis studied painting at Athens University, and has had many exhibitions there and abroad. The nearby cathedral's murals are his. His paintings specialize in the light and landscape of his home island. His wife, Eleni, who also studied in Athens, shows sculptures, ceramics, and jewelry. ⊠ *Ypapantis Walkway, Palia Fabrika* ☎ 22860/23041 ⊕ *www.santorini.info/paliafabrika/index.html.*

EMBROIDERY   **Costas Dimitrokalis** and Matthew Dimitrokalis sell locally made embroideries of Greek linen and Egyptian cotton, rugs, pillowcases in hand-crocheted wool with local designs, and more. Purchases can be mailed any-where. ⊠ *1 block from cable car* ☎☎ *22860/22957* ☰ *AE, D, MC, V.*

JEWELRY **Kostas Antoniou Jewelry** is well known, and many of Kostas's original pieces were many inspired by ancient Thera; some solid gold necklaces are magnificent enough to earn their own names, such as Earth's En-gravings, Ritual, and Motionless Yielding. The work is both classic and creative. ⊠ *Opposite cable car* ☎☎ *22860/22633* ☰ *AE, MC, V.*

Firostefani

Φηροσζεφάνι

Firostefani used to be a separate village, but now it is an elegant sub-urb north of Fira. The 10-minute walk between them, along the caldera, is one of Santorini's highlights. From Firostefani's single white cliff-side street, walkways descend to traditional vaulted cave houses, which are fast becoming pensions. Though close to the action, Firostefani feels calm and quiet.

Where to Stay & Eat

★ **$$–$$$** ✕ **Vanilia.** Set in a windmill—built in 1872 and preserved by the gov-ernment after the 1956 earthquake—Vanilia also encompasses pretty ter-races, providing a lovely place to enjoy excellent food. You might start with roasted eggplant with smoked Metzova cheese or a salad of mar-inated oranges with chilies and feta. An intriguing entrée is homemade pasta with ouzo, shrimp, mussels, and garlic. The Vanilia cheesecake, with *anthotiro* cheese, will make you want to linger at this friendly place. ⊠ *Main Sq.* ☎ *22860/25631* 🖷 *22860/71800* ☰ *AE, D, MC, V.*

★ **$–$$** ✕ **Aktaion.** In his tiny taverna, Vangelis Roussos uses mostly his grand-father's recipes. The paintings on the walls are Vangelis's own. Salad Santorini, his mother's recipe, has raw cod flakes, caper leaves, and sea-sonal ingredients. The moussaka, made with white eggplant, is incom-parable. ⊠ *Main Sq.* ☎ *22860/22336* ☰ *MC, V.*

★ **$$$$** ▦ **Tsitouras.** There's no sign; guests are met (at the airport or harbor) and brought to these extraordinary apartments—sparkling white cubes with volcanic stone trimmings built around an 18th-century mansion. The cavelike rooms are long, cool, and elaborately furnished. Dimitris Tsitouras is a well-known art collector, and each room displays a different aspect of his collection—porcelain, sketches of Nureyev, portraits (including a fetch-ing beauty beloved by Lord Byron); even the hotel's wreath-insignia is de-signed by Greece's most famous artist, Ghika. The elegant terrace overlooks the caldera. ⊠ *Firostefani cliff face, next to St. Mark's, 84700* ☎ *22860/ 23747* 🖷 *22860/23918* ⊕ *www.tsitouras.gr* ↵ *5 apartments* ⟳ *Restau-rant, minibars, cable TV, Internet room* ☰ *AE, D, MC, V* ¶⊙¶ *BP.*

★ **$–$$$$** ▦ **Reverie Traditional Apartments.** Georgios Fytros has converted his family home into an inexpensive and attractive hotel, all cream-color with marble insets. Each of the large rooms, white with dark-toned wood furniture, has a winding staircase to a balcony with a metal frame bed. ⊠ *Between Firostefani walkway and main traffic road, 84700* ☎ *22860/ 23322* 🖷 *22860/23044* ⊕ *www.reverie.gr* ↵ *13 rooms, 2 suites* ⟳ *Re-frigerators, cable TV, pool, Internet room* ☰ *AE, D, MC, V.*

Imerovigli

Ημεροβίγλι

Imerovigli, on the highest point of the caldera's rim, is what Firostefani was like a decade and a half ago. It is now being developed, and for good reasons: it is quiet, traditional, and less expensive. The 25-minute walk from Fira, with incredible views, should be on everyone's itinerary. The lodgments, some of them traditional cave houses, are mostly down stairways from the cliff-side walkway. The big rock backing the village was once crowned by Skaros castle, where Venetial the conqueror raised his flat in 1207; it housed the island's administrative offices. It collapsed in an earthquake, leaving only the rock.

Where to Stay & Eat

$ ✗ **Skaros Fish Taverna.** This rustic open-air taverna, one of three restaurants in Imerovigli, has spectacular caldera views. It serves fresh fish and Santorini specialties, such as octopus in onion sauce, and mussels with rice and raisins. ⊠ *On cliff-side walkway* ☎ *22860/23616* ⊟ *AE, MC, V* ☯ *Closed Nov.–Mar.*

$$$$ ☷ **Phenix Studios and Apartments.** White and cool blue-gray are the dominant hues at this cliff-side complex. Rooms vary greatly but all are handsomely equipped and have caldera views; the superior rooms have in-room Jacuzzis. The pool terrace overlooks the caldera and the bar is popular in the evening. ⊠ *Box 47 Fira, but in Imerovigli on cliff-side walkway, 84700* ☎ *22860/22116* 🖷 *22860/23809* ⊕ *www.phenix.gr* ⇱ *14 rooms, 6 studios* ♧ *Snack bar, some kitchenettes, cable TV, pool, Internet room* ⊟ *MC, V* ☯ *Closed Nov.–Mar.*

$–$$ ☷ **Annio.** The rooms in this cliff-side lodgment are attractive and simple, with local furnishings both new and old. All have terraces and caldera views. Christos Nomikos built it himself on his family property, and his daughter Katerina runs it. They don't provide transfers, but rather lots of beauty, peace, comfort, and quiet. ⊠ *Imerovigli, 84700* ☎ *22860/ 24714* 🖷 *22860/23550* ⊕ *www.annioflats.gr* ⇱ *11 rooms* ♧ *Refrigerators, cable TV, in-room data ports* ⊟ *MC, V* ☯ *Closed Nov.–Apr.*

$–$$ ☷ **Heliades Apartments.** Owner Olympia Sarri knows she has something special. Her father mostly built the apartments, consisting of four cave houses, white with blue-green accents, with verandas and caldera views. The couches and loft beds are traditional, and the arches are outlined in Santorini tufa; the living room areas are especially spacious. ⊠ *On cliff-side walkway, behind the church of the Panaghia Maltesa, near parking and bus stop, 84700* ☎ *22860/24102* 🖷 *22860/25587* ⊕ *www.heliades-apts.gr* ⇱ *4 houses* ♧ *Kitchens, cable TV* ⊟ *No credit cards* ☯ *Closed Nov.–Mar.*

Ia

Οία

● **46** *80 km (50 mi) southeast of Paros town, 14 km (8½ mi) northwest of*
FodorśChoice *Fira.*
★

At the tip of the northern horn of the island sits Ia (or Oia), Santorini's second-largest town and the Aegean's most-photographed village. Ia is more tasteful than Fira (for one thing, no establishment here is allowed to play music that can be heard on the street), and the town's cubical white houses stand out against the green, brown, and rust-color layers of rock, earth, and solid volcanic ash that rise from the sea. Every summer evening, travelers from all over the world congregate at the caldera's rim—sitting on whitewashed fences, staircases, beneath the town's windmill, on the old castle—each looking out to sea in anticipation of the performance: the Ia sunset. The three-hour rim-edge walk from Ia to Fira at this hour is unforgettable.

In the middle of the quiet caldera, the volcano smolders away eerily, adding an air of suspense to an already awe-inspiring scene. The 1956 eruption caused tremendous earthquakes (7.8 on the Richter scale) that left 48 people dead (thankfully, most residents were working outdoors at the time), hundreds injured, and 2,000 houses toppled. The island's west side—especially Ia, until then the largest town—was hard hit, and many residents decided to emigrate to Athens, Australia, and America. And although Fira, also damaged, rebuilt rapidly, Ia proceeded slowly, sticking to the traditional architectural style. The perfect example of that style is the restaurant 1800, a renovated ship-captain's villa.

Ia is set up like the other three towns—Fira, Firostefani, and Imerovigli—that adorn the caldera's sinuous rim. There is a car road, which is new, and a cliff-side walkway, which is old. Shops and restaurants are all on the walkway, and hotel entrances mostly descend from it—something to check carefully if you cannot negotiate stairs easily. In Ia there is a lower cliff-side walkway writhing with stone steps, and a long stairway to the tiny blue bay with its dock below. Short streets leading from the car road to the walkway have cheaper eateries and shops. There is a parking lot at either end, and the northern one marks the end of the road and the rim. Nothing is very far from anything else.

The **Naval Museum of Thera** is in an old mansion. It displays ships' figureheads, seamen's chests, maritime equipment, models, and more. ⊠ *Near telephone office* ☎ *22860/71156* ⊡ *€4* ☉ *Tues.–Sun. 8:30–3.*

Beach
There are no beautiful beaches close to Ia, but you can hike down Ia's cliff side or catch a bus to the small sand beach of **Baxedes** (⊠ Port of Armoudhi).

Where to Stay & Eat
$$$–$$$$ ✕ **1800.** Owner, architect, and restaurateur John Zagelidis has lovingly
Fodor'sChoice restored a magnificent old captain's house (the name refers to its date)
★ with original furnishings and colors (white, olive green, and gray). For starters try grilled summer vegetables wrapped in Spanish ham, or smoked eel with watercress and arugula. Entrées include fresh fillet of sea bream with cherry tomatoes, olives, and fennel; and baked shank of lamb on couscous with celery and tomato comfit. For dessert try a pear cooked in muscat filled with marzipan, date puree, and amaretto. The wine list is extensive. Clearly, this captain lived graciously. ⊠ *Main St.* ☎ *22860/ 71485* ⊟ *22860/72317* ⊕ *www.oia-1800.com* ⊟ *AE, DC, MC, V.*

$–$$$ ✕ **Red Bicycle.** This sophisticated café, wine bar, and art gallery is located at the north end of the main walkway, just down the steps; its balcony overlooks the bay. It has a large wine list and serves delicious sandwiches, salads, canapés, and desserts. The menu changes daily, but you might find baked cheese in pastry with olive paste and caper leaves. The Greek cheese cake with rose preserves is both traditional and unusual. ⊠ *Ia* ☎ *22860/71856* ▭ *No credit cards.*

★ **$–$$$**   ✕ **Kastro.** Spyros Dimitroulis's restaurant is primarily patronized for its view of the famous Ia sunset, and at the magical hour it is always filled. Happily, the food makes a fitting accompaniment. The menu changes frequently, but he almost always has grilled fruit with honey sauce. The lamb fillet with fava is especially good. Lunch is popular. ⊠ *Near Venetian castle* ☎ *22860/71045* ▭ *AE, MC, V.*

$$$$ ▥ **Katikies.** This sumptuously appointed, immaculately white cliff-side complex layered on terraces has sleek modern design, including Andy Warhol wall prints, stunning fabrics, and handsome furniture. Chic as the surroundings are, the barrel-vaulted ceilings and other architectural details lend a traditional air to the place. Suites and villas are small and private; all overlook the caldera and and are luxuriously appointed. ⊠ *Ia cliff face, edge of main town, 84702* ☎ *22860/71401* 🖷 *22860/71129* ⊕ *www.katikies.com* 🛏 *7 rooms, 33 suites, 7 villas* ♿ *3 restaurants, kitchenettes, cable TV, 2 pools, 2 bars, laundry service, Internet room* ▭ *AE, MC, V* ⊘ *Closed Nov.–Mar.* ⦿ *BP.*

$$$$ ▥ **Lampetia Villas.** This EOT Traditional Settlement, 800 feet up the cliff from the sea, offers charm, comfort, and friendliness. The owner, Tom Alafragis, has a charm all his own. Each of the accommodations—all have private balconies with a view—is different in size and furnishings. ⊠ *Nomikou, Ia cliff face, down from main street, 84702* 🖷🖷 *22860/* ⊕ *www.lampetia.gr* 🛏 *8 houses* ♿ *Kitchenettes, pool* ▭ *No credit cards* ⊘ *Closed Nov.–Mar.* ⦿ *BP.*

$$$$ ▥ **Perivolas.** Some photographs of the pool here may make it seem that a swimmer could float off the edge into the caldera's blue bay 1,000 feet below. This effect is nearly accurate. The vaulted apartments, converted from old wineries, are sculpted into the red cliffs and simply but stunningly furnished with handmade wooden pieces and weavings. Each house has its own terrace. ⊠ *Nomikou, Ia cliff face, 15 mins by foot from cliff-side street, 84702* ☎ *22860/71308* 🖷 *22860/71309* ⊕ *www. perivolas.gr* 🛏 *17 houses* ♿ *Restaurant, kitchenettes, pool, bar* ▭ *AE, MC, V* ⊘ *Closed Nov.–Mar.* ⦿ *BP.*

$ ▥ **Delfini Villas.** If you think a comfortable, convenient room in Ia with caldera view and terrace has to be expensive, think again: Rena Halari's place is affordable and warmly charming. ⊠ *Lower main traffic street, opposite Piraeus Bank, 84702* ☎ *22860/71600* 🖷 *22860/71601* ⊕ *www. delfinivillas.com* 🛏 *6 rooms, 4 apartments* ♿ *Kitchenettes, refrigerators, cable TV* ▭ *No credit cards* ⊘ *Closed Nov.–Mar.*

Nightlife

A peaceful note: establishments here are forbidden to play loud music. In Ia, sophistication and architectural splendor are the selling points of the **1800** (⊠ Main St. ☎ 22860/71485) bar and restaurant. Those in search of a happy-hour beer go to **Zorba's** (⊠ On cliff side).

Shopping

Ia is the right place for finding locally crafted items. The inhabitants are sophisticated, and here you will find art galleries, "objets" shops, crafts shops, and icon stores.

ANTIQUES & COLLECTIBLES — Chara Kourti's **Loulaki** (⊠ Main shopping St. ☎ 22860/71856) sells antiques, odd pieces, jewelry, and art; exploring the shop is a pleasure. Alexandra Solomos's painted plates are a favorite.

ART — **Art Gallery** (⊠ Main shopping St. ☎☎ 22860/71448) sells large, three-dimensional representations of Santorini architecture by Bella Kokeenatou and Stavros Galanopoulos. Their lifelike depth invites the viewer to walk through a door or up a flight of stairs. **Caldera** (⊠ Main shopping St. ☎☎ 22860/71363), in a vaulted cliff-side room, shows paintings and sculptures by artists on Santorini, and also objets and rugs.

BOOKS — **Atlantis Books** (⊠ North end of main shopping St. ☎ 22869/72346 ⊕ www.atlantisbooks.org) is a tiny English bookshop that would be at home in New York's Greenwich Village or London's Bloomsbury; its presence here is a miracle. Only good literature makes it onto the shelves. Writers stop by to chat and give readings.

Pyrgos

Πύργος

47 *5½ km (3½ mi) south of Fira.*

Though today Pyrgos has only 500 inhabitants, until the early 1800s it was the capital of the island. Stop there to see its medieval houses, stacked on top of one another and back to back for protection against pirates. The beautiful neoclassic building on the way up is a luxury hotel. The view from the ruined Venetian Castle is panoramic. And reward yourself for the climb up the picturesque streets, which follow the shape of the hill, with a stop at panoramic terrace of the Café Kastelli, for Greek coffee and homemade sweets. In Pyrgos you are really in old Santorini—hardly anything has changed.

The **Monastery of Profitis Ilias** is at the highest point on Santorini, which spans to 1,856 feet at the summit. From here you can see the surrounding islands and, on a clear day, the mountains of Crete, more than 100 km (66 mi) away. You may also be able to spot ancient Thira on the peak below Profitis Ilias. Unfortunately, radio towers and a NATO radar installation provide an ugly backdrop for the monastery's wonderful bell tower.

Founded in 1711 by two monks from Pyrgos, Profitis Ilias is cherished by islanders because here, in a secret school, the Greek language and culture were taught during the dark centuries of the Turkish occupation. A **museum** in the monastery contains a model of the secret school in a monk's cell, another model of a traditional carpentry and blacksmith shop, and a display of ecclesiastical items. The monastery's future is in doubt because there are so few monks left. ⊠ *At highest point on Santorini* 🎫 *Free* ☉ *No visiting hrs; caretaker is sometimes around.*

Megalochori

Μεγαλοχώρι

48 *4 km (2½ mi) east of Pyrgos, 9 km (5½ mi) southwest of Fira.*

Megalochori is a picturesque, half-abandoned town set. Many of the village's buildings were actually *canavas,* wine-making facilities. The tiny main square is still lively in the evening.

On your way south from Megalochori to Akrotiri, stop at **Antoniou Winery** (✉ Megalochori ☎🖷 22860/23557) and take a tour of the multilevel old facility. It's so beautiful, local couples get married here. An enologist leads a wine tasting with snacks, and a slide show describes local wine production; it costs €5. Many think Antoniou's white wines are Santorini's best—and that's saying a lot.

Where to Stay

★ $$$$ 🖵 **Vedema.** One of Santorini's most deluxe hotels is a world unto itself. Vedema's buildings are designed around a beautiful 15th-century winery, and in this authentic setting every luxury is provided and the service is impeccable. The old vaulted dining room is the prettiest on Santorini; the wine cellar, with its many valuable wines, is worth exploration (there are wine tastings nightly). The spacious suites, in pastel-hue town houses, all have marble bathrooms, island-style furnishings, and terraces. Vedema is not cheap, but you'll get what you're paying for, in spades. A shuttle service ferries you to other parts of the island. ✉ *84700 Megalochori* ☎ *22860/81796 or 22860/81797* 🖷 *22860/81798* ⊕ *www.vedema.gr* 🖵 *35 rooms, 7 suites* ⟡ *2 restaurants, some kitchenettes, cable TV, pool, exercise equipment, laundry service* ▤ *AE, D, MC, V* ⊗ *Closed Nov.–Mar.* ⭐ *BP.*

Akrotiri

Ακρωτήρι

49 *13 km (8 mi) south of Fira, 7 km (4½ mi) west of Pyrgos.*

★ If you visit only one archaeological site during your stay on Santorini, it should be **ancient Akrotiri,** near the tip of the southern horn of the island. At this writing, the site was closed temporarily for structural repairs, so check ahead before you plan your visit.

In the 1860s, in the course of quarrying volcanic ash for use in the Suez Canal, workmen discovered the remains of an ancient town. The town was frozen in time by ash from an eruption 3,600 years ago, long before Pompeii's disaster. In 1967 Spyridon Marinatos of the University of Athens began excavations, which occasionally continue. It is thought that the 40 buildings that have been uncovered are only one-thirtieth of the huge site and that excavating the rest will probably take a century. You enter from the south, pass the ticket booth, and walk 100 yards or so up a stone-paved street to a vast metal shed that protects 2 acres of the site from wind and sun. A path punctuated by explanatory signs in English leads through the ancient town.

Marinatos's team discovered great numbers of extremely well-preserved frescoes depicting many aspects of Akrotiri life, most now displayed in the National Archaeological Museum in Athens; Santorini wants them back. Meanwhile, postcard-size pictures of them are posted outside the houses where they were found. The antelopes, monkeys, and wildcats they portray suggest trade with Egypt. One notable example, apparently representing a festival, shows two ports: the left village has ordinary people in skins and tunics, and a symbolic lion runs overhead; and the other, probably Akrotiri, more aristocratic, has in its center a fleet of sailing ships at sea, with playful dolphins swimming alongside.

Culturally an outpost of Minoan Crete, Akrotiri was settled as early as 3000 BC and reached its peak after 2000 BC, when it developed trade and agriculture and settled the present town. The inhabitants cultivated olive trees and grain, and their advanced architecture—three-story frescoed houses faced with masonry (some with balconies) and public buildings of sophisticated construction—is evidence of an elaborate lifestyle. Unlike at Pompeii, no human remains, gold, silver, or weapons were found here—probably tremors preceding the eruption warned the inhabitants to pack their valuables and flee. After the eruptions Santorini was uninhabited for about two centuries while the land cooled and plant and animal life regenerated. The site is accessible by public bus or guided tour. ⊠ *South of modern Akrotiri, near tip of southern horn* ☎ *22860/81366* ⊕ *www.culture.gr* ⊠ *€5* ⊘ *Tues.–Sun. 8:30–3.*

Beach
Red Beach (⊠ On southwest shore below Akrotiri) is quiet and has a taverna.

Kamari

Καμάρι

⑳ *6 km (4 mi) south of Fira, 6½ km (4¼ mi) east of Akrotiri.*

★ Archaeology buffs will want to visit the site of **ancient Thira**. There are relics of a Dorian city, with 9th-century BC tombs, an engraved phallus, Hellenistic houses, and traces of Byzantine fortifications and churches. At the sanctuary of Apollo, graffiti dating to the 8th century BC record the names of some of the boys who danced naked at the god's festival (Satie's famed musical compositions, *Gymnopedies,* reimagine these). To get there, hike up from Perissa or Kamari or take a taxi up **Mesa Vouna**. On the summit are the scattered ruins, excavated by a German archaeology school around the turn of the 20th century; there's a fine view. ⊠ *On a switchback up mountain right before Kamari, 2,110 ft high* ☎ *22860/31366* ⊕ *www.culture.gr* ⊠ *€5* ⊘ *Tues.–Sun. 8:30–3.*

Beaches
The black-sand beaches of **Kamari** (and of Perissa) are a natural treasure of Santorini and are consequently overdeveloped. Deck chairs and umbrellas can be rented, and tavernas and refreshment stands abound.

Where to Stay & Eat

¢–$$ ✕ **Galini.** This taverna is halfway between Kamari and Monolithos—about a 10-minute drive, and a worthwhile one. Some of the tables are on the quiet sandy beach. Manolis Prekas and his sister Anna cook good traditional Santorini food, including fresh fish, tomato croquets, and fava. For something heavier, try rabbit in red sauce. If you have had trouble finding Santorini's famous *chloro* cheese, eat it here. ⊠ *Ayia Paraskevi beach* ☎ *22860/32924* ▭ *No credit cards.*

$ 🏠**Hotel Astro.** Makarios Sigalas owns and manages the Astro, and his friendly nature permeates the place. Redone in marble, the hotel is looking spiffier than ever. It is a short walk to the black-sand beach and minutes away from the local nightlife. Rooms on the lower level have verandas; those on the second floor have balconies facing the mountains or the Aegean. After spending the day at the sea, it's great to take a dip in the freshwater pool in the evening. ⊠ *84700 Central Kamari* ☎ *22860/31366* 🖷 *22860/31732* ⊕*www.astro-hotel.com* ➥*35 rooms, 6 apartments, 2 studios* ♺*Coffee shop, refrigerators, cable TV, pool, Internet room* ▭ *MC, V* ⧖*BP.*

Nightlife

In Kamari the younger set heads for the disco **Dom Club** (⊠ Off promenade, behind Mango Bar ☎ 22860/33420) and the other bars along the beach promenade.

Perissa

Περίσσα

51 *5½ km (3½ mi) south of Fira.*

In the southern corner of the island, on the other side of the mountain from Kamari, Perissa, a 7-km-long (4½-mi-long) black sandy beach, is rapidly being developed, with hotels, restaurants, taverns, beach chairs, and bars. Because the beach is so long, however, sections of it remain fairly pristine. On August 29 and September 14, Perissa's Byzantine church of Aghia Irini (St. Irene) holds festivals in honor of Santorini's patron saint, who died on the island while in exile in AD 304. Ancient Thira is a picturesque hike up Mesa Vouna mountain. One kilometer (½ mi) from Perissa, the beautiful village of Emporio is filled with traditional Cycladic architecture, peasant and neoclassical.

Beach

The shadowy-hued grains covering the beach in **Perissa** are actually volcanic sands, not rocks. As at Kamari, deck chairs and umbrellas are available, and there is no shortage of food options in the surrounding area.

Where to Stay & Eat

¢ ✕ **Lava Taverna.** Located in Limnes, the undeveloped southern edge of Perissa, Yannis Rigos's beach tavern is fittingly unpretentious, and so is the fresh homemade food. Good appetizers, the specialty here, include peppers *florina* (stuffed with wheat, raisins, pine nuts, and pistachios), and baked eggplant stuffed with feta; the baked stuffed onions are also excellent. The main dishes emphasize fresh fish and grilled meats. ⊠ *Limnes* ☎ *22860/81776* ▭ *No credit cards.*

$ ⌨ **Chrissi Ammos Hotel.** This simple, comfortable hotel is a two-minute walk from a quiet section of Perissa's black beach. Owner Vangelis Denaxas and family keep the atmosphere friendly and the garden green. The rooms all have balconies, most with sea view. ⊠ *Perissa, 84703* ☎ *22860/81065* 🖨 *22860/81109* 📶 *18 rooms* ♨ *Snack bar, refrigerator; no room TVs* ▤ *No credit cards* ⊙ *Closed Nov.–Apr.*

THE CYCLADES A TO Z

To research prices, get advice from other travelers, and book travel arrangements, visit www.fodors.com.

AIR TRAVEL
Schedules change seasonally and are often revised; reservations are always a good idea. There are no airports on Andros or Tinos.

CARRIERS Olympic Airways has seven flights daily to Mykonos (10 daily during peak tourist season). There are also summer flights between Mykonos and Heraklion (on Crete), and between Mykonos and Rhodes. The Olympic Airways offices in Mykonos are at the port and at the airport. Olympic Airways has four flights daily between Athens and Naxos airport. Olympic also offers five daily flights to the Paros Airport from Athens (up to seven a day in high season) and six daily flights to Santorini Airport from Athens in peak season. In summer there are flights to Mykonos and Salonica about three times per week.

Aegean Airlines has two daily flights to Mykonos and three to Santorini. Some European countries now have charter flights to Mykonos.
🚩 **Aegean Airlines** ☎ 210/626-1000 ⊕ www.aegeanair.com. **Olympic Airways** ⊠ Port, Mykonos town ☎ 22890/22490 or 22890/22495 ⊠ Ayia Athanassiou, Santorini, Fira ☎ 22860/22493 or 22860/22793.

AIRPORTS
🚩 **Mykonos Airport** ⊠ 4 km [2½ mi] southeast of Mykonos town ☎ 22890/22327. **Naxos Airport** ⊠ 1 km [½ mi] south of Naxos town ☎ 22850/23969. **Paros Airport** ⊠ Near Alyki village, 9 km [5½ mi] south of Paros town ☎ 22840/91257. **Santorini Airport** ⊠ On east coast, 8 km [5 mi] from Fira, Monolithos ☎ 22860/31525.

BIKE TRAVEL
All the major islands have car- and bike-rental agencies at the ports and in the business districts. Motorbikes and scooters start at about €10 a day, including third-party liability coverage. Don't wear shorts or sandals, and get a phone number, in case of breakdown.

BOAT & FERRY TRAVEL
Most visitors use the island's extensive ferry network, which is constantly being upgraded. Ferries sail from Piraeus (Port Authority) and from Rafina, 35 km (22 mi) northeast of Athens (Port Authority). Leaving from Rafina cuts traveling time by an hour; buses leave for the one-hour trip from Rafina to Athens every 20 minutes 6 AM–10 PM. Traveling time from Piraeus varies with the speed (and price) of the boat. Interisland catamarans are fast, but they cannot operate when seas are rough.

Third-class boat tickets cost roughly one-quarter the airfare, and passengers are restricted to seats in the deck areas and often-crowded indoor seating areas. For Blue Star Ferries, get a seat number. A first-class ticket, which sometimes buys a private cabin and better lounge, costs about half an airplane ticket. For information on interisland connections, contact the port authorities on the various islands. High season is June through September; boats are less frequent in the off-season. All schedules must be checked soon before departure, as they change with the season, for major holidays, for weather, and for reasons not ascertainable.

🚢 **Piraeus Port Authority** ☎ 210/451-1311 or 210/415-1321. **Rafina Port Authority** ☎ 22940/22300.

ANDROS For Andros, you must take a ferry from Rafina (not Piraeus); they leave two or three times a day in summer, and the trip takes about two hours. From Andros (contact the Port Authority for more details) boats leave twice daily for Tinos and Mykonos. Boats leave five times weekly for Paros, Naxos, Ios, and Crete. An excursion boat goes daily to Mykonos and Delos, returning in the late afternoon.

🚢 **Andros Port Authority** ☎ 22820/22250.

MYKONOS In summer, there are two to three ferries daily to Mykonos from Piraeus and Rafina. From the Mykonos Port Authority, there are daily departures to Paros, Syros, Tinos, and Andros, and five to seven departures per week for Santorini, Naxos, Ios, and Crete. Possible destinations change monthly. Check which dock they leave from.

🚢 **Mykonos Port Authority** ✉ Harbor, above National Bank ☎ 22940/22218.

NAXOS In summer, ferries leave Piraeus for Naxos at least three times a day. (The trip takes about four to seven hours.) Boats go daily from Naxos (Port Authority) to Mykonos, Ios, Paros, Syros, Tinos, and Santorini; check for other places served. Boats from Naxos serve the Little Cyclades, Iraklia, Schinousa, Koufonisi, and Donousa.

🚢 **Naxos Port Authority** ☎ 22850/22300.

PAROS About three ferries leave Piraeus for Paros every day in summer. Paros has daily ferry service to Santorini, Ios, Mykonos, Tinos, Andros, Syros, and Naxos; check for other places served. Boats to Antiparos leave from Parikia and car ferries leave from Pounda. Cruise boats leave daily from Paros town and Naousa for excursions to Delos and Mykonos.

🚢 **Paros Port Authority** ☎ 22840/21240.

SANTORINI Santorini is served at least twice daily from Piraeus; from Santorini, ferries make frequent connections to the other islands—daily to Paros, Naxos, Ios, Anaphi, and Crete. All ferries dock at Athinios port, where taxis and buses take passengers to Fira, Kamari, and Perissa Beach. Travelers bound for Ia take a bus to Fira and change there. The port below Fira is used only by small steamers and cruise ships. Passengers disembarking here face a half-hour hike, or they can take the cable car (or ride up on the traditional donkeys; but please spare the poor things). The port police can give information on ferry schedules.

🚢 **Port Police** ☎ 22860/22239.

TINOS Tinos is served in summer by four boats a day from Rafina. There are daily connections with Andros, Syros, Paros, Naxos, and Mykonos and regular boats to Santorini, and sometimes other islands. An excursion boat goes daily to nearby Delos, returning in the afternoon. The Port Authority in Chora gives information, but it's not more reliable than that given at the agencies clustered near the old harbor.

🗎 **Port Authority in Chora** ☎ 22830/22348.

BUS TRAVEL

ANDROS About six buses a day from Andros town (to right of marble walkway) go to and from the harbor, in conjunction with the ferry schedule; all buses stop in Batsi. Daily buses also go to and return from Stenies, Apikia, Strapouries, Pitrofos, and Korthi.

MYKONOS In Mykonos town the Ayios Loukas station near the Olympic Airways office is for buses to Ornos, Ayios Ioannis, Platys Yialos, Psarou, the airport, and Kalamopodi. Another station near the Archaeological Museum is for Ayios Stefanos, Tourlos, Ano Mera, Elia, Kalafatis, and Kalo Livadi.

NAXOS On Naxos, the bus system is reliable and fairly extensive. Daily buses go from Chora (at the waterfront) to Engares, Melanes, Sangri, Filoti, Apeiranthos, Koronida, and Apollonas. In summer there is added daily service to the beaches, including Ayia Anna, Pyrgaki, Ayiassos, Pachy Ammos, Ayios Mamas, and Abram. The bus office is near the dock.

PAROS From the Paros town bus station (three minutes away from the town, east of the dock), there is service every hour to Naousa and less-frequent service to Alyki, Pounda, and the beaches at Piso Livadi, Chrissi Akti, and Drios. Schedules are posted.

SANTORINI On Santorini buses leave from the main station in central Fira (Deorgala) for Perissa and Kamari beaches, Ia, Pyrgos, and other villages. Schedules are posted.

TINOS On Tinos, buses run several times daily from the quay of Chora to nearly all the many villages in Tinos, and in summer buses are added for beaches.

🗎 **Bus Information** ☎ 22820/22316 in Andros, 22890/23360 in Mykonos, 22850/22440 in Naxos, 22840/21133 in Paros, 22890/25404 in Santorini, 22830/22440 in Tinos.

CAR RENTALS

All the major islands have car- and bike-rental agencies at the ports and in the business districts. Car rentals cost about €45 per day, with unlimited mileage and third-party liability insurance. Full insurance costs about €6 a day more. Four-wheeled semi-bikes (jeeps and dune buggies), that look—but are not—safer than bikes, are also available in Santorini, Mykonos, Paros, Tinos, and Naxos. Choose a dealer that offers 24-hour service and a change of vehicle in case of a breakdown. Beware: all too many travelers end up in Athenian hospitals owing to poor roads, slipshod maintenance, careless drivers, and excessive partying.

ANDROS   Cars can be rented in Gavrio at Rent a Car Tasos, which has good cars and friendly service. Helena Prodromou of Andros Travel can also arrange for your needs.

🚗 Local Agencies **Andros Travel** ✉ Opposite Batsi beach, Batsi ☎ 22820/41252 🖨 22820/41608. **Rent a Car Tasos** ✉ Near ferryboat quay, opposite beach, Gavrio ☎ 22820/71040.

MYKONOS   No cars are permitted in town. Many car rentals line the street above the bus terminal, and in the Maouna area near the windmills. Beware of sharp dealing. For friendly, trustworthy service go to Apollon Rent a Car, run by the Andronikos family. They'll meet you at the boat with a car, or bring one to your hotel; they also have offices at Mykonos Airport and at Ornos. Their in-town parking is a boon.

🚗 Local Agency **Apollon Rent a Car** ✉ Maouna, Mykonos ☎ 22890/24136 🖨 22890/23447 ⊕ www.apolloncars.com.

NAXOS   Car-rental outfits are concentrated in the Chora new town: try Naxos Vision. Or let Despina Kitini, of the Tourist Information Centre(⇨ Tours), make arrangements for you.

🚗 Local Agency **Naxos Vision** ✉ Chora, near post office ☎ 22850/26200 🖨 22850/26201 ⊕ www.naxosvision.com.

PAROS   It is a good idea to rent a vehicle here, because the island is large; there are many beaches to choose from, and taxis are in demand. There are many reputable agencies near the port. Kostas Soukantos's Motor Plan is reliable and friendly.

🚗 Major Agency **Sixt** ✉ Car-rental desk in Polos Travel, by OTE office, Paros town ☎ 22840/21309 ⊕ www.polostours.gr/english/rentacar ✉ Naousa ☎ 22840/51544. 🚗 Local Agency **Motor Plan** ✉ On waterfront, past post office, before Asteria Hotel, Parikia ☎ 22840/24678.

SANTORINI   Europcar has offices in Fira and at Santorini Airport. Ia's Drossos delivers anywhere.

🚗 Major Agency **Europcar** ☎ 22860/24610 in Fira, 22860/33290 airport ⊕ www.europcar.com.gr. 🚗 Local Agency **Drossos** ☎ 22860/71492, 22860/71668 at port ⊕ www.drossos.gr.

TINOS   Vidalis Rent-a-Car and Dimitris Rental, almost next door to each other, are reliable.

🚗 Local Agencies **Dimitris Rental** ✉ Alavanou, Tinos town ☎ 22830/23585 🖨 22830/22744. **Vidalis Rent-a-Car** ✉ Alavanou 16, Tinos town ☎ 22830/24300 🖨 22830/25995 ⊕ www.vidalis-rentacar.gr.

CAR TRAVEL

To take cars on ferries you must make reservations. Though there is bus service on the large and mountainous islands of Andros and Naxos, it is much more convenient to travel by car.

Although islanders tend to acknowledge rules, many roads on the islands are poorly maintained, and tourists sometimes lapse into vacation inattentiveness. Drive with caution, especially at night, when you may well be sharing the roads with motorists returning from an evening of drinking.

EMERGENCIES

ANDROS **🚹 Health center** ☎ 22820/22222 in Andros town. **Medical Assistance** ☎ 22820/41326 in Batsi, 22820/71210 in Gavrio. **Police** ☎ 22820/71220 in Gavrio, 22820/41204 in Batsi, 22820/22300 in Andros town.

MYKONOS The hospital in Mykonos has 24-hour emergency service with pathologists, surgeons, pediatricians, dentists, and X-ray technicians.
🚹 First Aid ✉ Ano Mera ☎ 22890/71395. **Hospital** ✉ Mykonos town ☎ 22890/23998 or 22890/23994. **Police** ☎ 2289/22235.

NAXOS The Health Center outside Chora is open 24 hours a day.
🚹 Health Center ☎ 22850/23333 or 2285/23676. **Medical Center of Naxos** ✉ Quay, Chora ☎ 22850/23234 🖷 22850/23576. **Police** ☎ 22850/22100 in Chora, 22850/31244 in Filoti.

PAROS **🚹 Medical Center** ☎ 22840/22500 in Paros town, 22840/51216 in Naousa, 22840/61219 in Antiparos. **Police** ☎ 22840/23333 in Paros town, 22840/51202 in Naousa.

SANTORINI **🚹 Medical assistance** ☎ 22860/22237 in Fira, 22860/71227 in Ia. **Police** ☎ 22860/22649 in Fira.

TINOS **🚹 Medical assistance** ✉ East end of town, Chora ☎ 22830/22210 ✉ Isternia ☎ 22830/31206. **Police** ☎ 22830/22255 in Chora, 22830/31371 in Pirgos.

TAXIS

On Andros, there are taxi stands off the main street, near the bus station in Andros town, and in Batsi, at the small quayside square beneath the Dolphins restaurant. Call the number listed for Andros to reach either location.

Meters are not used on Mykonos; instead standard fares for each destination are posted on a notice bulletin board. There is a taxi stand on Naxos near the harbor, and in Paros, there is one across from the windmill on the harbor. Note that in high season taxis are often busy.

The main taxi station on Santorini is near Fira's central square (25th of March street). In Tinos, taxis wait near the central boat dock, on the quay.
🚹 Taxis ☎ 22820/22171 in Andros, 22890/22400, 22890/23700 in Mykonos, 22850/22444 in Naxos, 22840/21500 in Paros, 22860/22555 in Santorini, 22830/22470 in Tinos.

TOURS

ANDROS Helena Prodromou's Andros Travel arranges coach tours and especially walking tours, from strolling to climbing. Helena, a British Cypriot, is friendly and very knowledgeable.
🚹 Andros Travel ✉ Opposite beach, Batsi ☎ 22820/41252 🖷 22820/41608 ⊕ www.bookandros.com.

MYKONOS Sunspots Travel takes a group every morning for a day tour of Delos (€30). The company also has half-day guided tours of the Mykonos beach towns, with a stop in Ano Mera for the Panagia Tourliani Monastery (€20). Windmills Travel runs excursions to nearby Tinos (€35–€50); arranges private tours of Delos and Mykonos and off-road jeep trips

(€50); charters yachts; and, in fact, handles all tourist services. John van Lerberghe's office is small, but he can tailor your trip from soup to nuts.

📑 **John van Lerberghe Travel Services** ✉ In picturesque old building, up the steep staircase Enoplon Dynameon 10, Mykonos town ☎ 22890/23160 🖷 22890/24137 ⊕ mykonos-accommodation.com. **Sunspots Travel** ✉ Near airport bus stop, into town, on left, 2nd fl., Mykonos town ☎ 22890/24196 🖷 22890/23790. **Windmills Travel** ✉ Fabrica ☎ 22890/26555 or 22890/23877 🖷 22890/22066 ⊕ www.windmillstravel.com.

NAXOS   The Tourist Information Centre, run by Despina Kitini of the Chateau Zevgoli, offers round-the-island tours (€18). Despina can usually tell exactly what you want after a short discussion and then swiftly arrange it. Zas Travel runs two good one-day tours of the island sights with different itineraries, each costing about €18, and one-day trips to Delos (about €35) and Mykonos (about €35).

📑 **Tourist Information Centre** ✉ Waterfront, Chora ☎ 22850/22993 🖷 22850/25200. **Zas Travel** ✉ Chora ☎ 22850/23330 or 22850/23331 🖷 22850/23419 ✉ Ayios Prokopios ☎ 22850/24780.

PAROS   Trips by land and sea, such as a tour around Antiparos, are arranged by Kostas Akalestos's Paroikia Tours. Erkyna Travel runs many excursions by boat, bus, and foot.

📑 **Erkyna Travel** ✉ On main square, Naousa ☎ 22840/22654, 22840/22655, or 22840/53180 ⊕ www.erkynatravel.com/islands/paros.htm ✉ Paros town ☎ 22840/22654 or 22840/22655 🖷 22840/22656. **Paroikia Tours** ✉ Market street, Paros town ☎ 22840/22470 or 22840/22471 🖷 22840/22450.

SANTORINI   Bellonias Tours runs coach tours that include Akrotiri, ancient Thira, Ia, wine tastings, and churches; it also has daily boat trips to the volcano and Thirassia (half day €12, full day €25) and arranges private tours. Nomikos Travel has tours to the same sights and to the island's wineries and the Monastery of Profitis Elias. This is the place to sign up for a caldera submarine trip (€50).

📑 **Bellonias Tours** ✉ Fira ☎ 22860/22469 or 22860/23604 ✉ Kamari ☎ 22860/31117. **Nomikos Travel** ✉ Fira ☎ 22860/23660 🖷 22860/23666 ⊕ www.nomikosvillas.gr.

TINOS   Windmills Travel runs daily guided bus tours of the island for €10, specialty tours by jeep, and unguided Delos–Mykonos trips (€20).

📑 **Windmills Travel** ✉ Above outer dock, behind playground, Chora ☎🖷 22830/23398 ⊕ www.windmillstravel.com.

TRANSPORTATION AROUND THE CYCLADES

On all islands, caïques leave from the main port for popular beaches and interisland trips. For popular routes, captains have posted signs showing their destinations and departure times.

VISITOR INFORMATION

ANDROS   The police station in Gavrio lists available accommodations. Your best bet is to ask Andros Travel for additional help in planning your stay.

📑 **Andros Travel** ✉ Batsi waterfront, opposite beach ☎ 22820/41252 🖷 22820/41608 ⊕ www.bookandros.com. **Police Station** ✉ Across from ferry dock, Gavrio ☎ 22820/71220.

MYKONOS George Ghikas's Sunspots Travel is superefficient, with a multitude of services. Very personal service can be found at John van Lerberghe Travel Services.

📩 **John van Lerberghe Travel Services** ✉ In picturesque old building, up the steep staircase Enoplon Dynameon 10, Mykonos town ☎ 22890/23160 🖨 22890/24137 ⊕ mykonos-accommodation.com. **Sunspots Travel** ✉ Near airport bus stop, into town, on left, Mykonos town ☎ 22890/24196 🖨 22890/23790 ⊕ www.sunspotstravel. com. **Tourist police** ✉ Mykonos town harbor, near departure point for Delos ☎ 22890/22716.

NAXOS Despina Kitini's Tourist Information Centre has free booking service, bus and ferry schedules, international dialing, luggage storage, laundry service, and foreign exchange at bank rates. You can also book airline tickets and rent Kastro houses.

📩 **Tourist Information Centre** ✉ Waterfront, Chora ☎ 22850/24525, 22285/24358, or 22850/22993 🖨 222850/25200.

PAROS For efficient and friendly service—tickets, villa rentals for families, apartments, and quality hotel reservations—try Kostas Akalestos's Paroikia Tours. Kostas, efficient and full of the Greek spirit, has many repeat customers. Polos Tours is big, inclusive, and efficient and will deliver tickets to your Athens hotel. Erkyna Travel has extensive services. There is also a Paros town office.

📩 **Erkyna Travel** ✉ On main square, Naousa ☎ 22840/22654, 22840/22655, 22840/53180 Paros town 🖨 22840/22656. **Paroikia Tours** ✉ Market street, Paros town ☎ 22840/22470 or 22840/22471 🖨 22840/22450. **Polos Tours** ✉ Next to dockside OTE office, Paros town ☎ 22840/22333 🖨 222840/21983.

SANTORINI Nomikos Travel, which has offices in Fira and Perissa, can handle most needs.

📩 **Nomikos Travel** ☎ 22860/23660 🖨 22860/23666 ⊕ www.nomikosvillas.gr.

TINOS For all tourist services (schedules, room bookings, tours, happenings), see friendly Sharon Turner, manager of Windmills Travel; she's a gold mine of information—there's nothing she doesn't know about her adopted island.

📩 **Windmills Travel** ✉ Above outer dock, behind playground, Chora ☎🖨 22830/23398 ⊕ www.windmillstravel.com.

Crete

WORD OF MOUTH

"Under most circumstances, I would consider it a no-brainer to stay in Hania rather than Heraklion. But if all you want to do is visit the [Archaeological] Museum and [the Palace of] Knossos, you should definitely stay in Heraklion . . . you will want to allow yourself a few hours at the museum in Heraklion. It contains all the best artifacts, wall frescoes, etc. that were removed from Knossos for better preservation and safety in the museum, including quite a few pieces of world reknown."

—Marilyn

"I would consider Crete number one for the exceptional scenery, snowcapped mountains, the great beaches, and of course the city of Hania, my screen name."

—Hania

Updated by
Stephen
Brewer

MOUNTAINS, SPLIT WITH DEEP GORGES and honeycombed with caves, rise in sheer walls from the sea. Snowcapped peaks loom behind sandy shoreline, vineyards, and olive groves. Miles of beaches, some with a wealth of amenities and others isolated and unspoiled, fringe the coast. But spectacular scenery is just the start of Crete's appeal: vestiges of Minoan civilization, one of the most brilliant and amazing cultures the world has ever known, abound at Knossos, Phaistos, and many other archaeological sites around the island. Hania, Rethymnon, and other towns and villages are attractive and have rich histories.

Around 1500 BC, while the rest of Europe was still in the grip of primitive barbarity, prehistoric Cretan civilization approached its finest, and final, hours. In fact, the Minoans had founded Europe's first urban culture as far back as the 3rd millennium BC. The sophisticated elegance of King Minos's court on the island of Crete was an appropriate manifestation of imperial power patiently built up over centuries, and the island's rich legacy of art and architecture strongly influenced both mainland Greece and the Aegean islands in the Bronze Age. From around 1900 BC the Minoan palaces at Knossos (near present-day Heraklion), Mallia, Phaistos, and elsewhere were centers of political power, religious authority, and economic activity—all concentrated in one sprawling complex of buildings. Their administration seems to have had much in common with contemporary cultures in Egypt and Mesopotamia. Another thing that set the Minoans apart from the rest of the Bronze Age world was their art. It was lively and naturalistic, and they excelled in working in miniature. From the scenes illustrated on their frescoes, stone vases, seal stones, and signet rings, it is possible to build a picture of a productive, well-regulated society.

Yet research suggests that prehistoric Crete was not a peaceful place; there may have been years of warfare before Knossos became the island's dominant power, around 1600 BC. It may well be that political upheaval, rather than the devastating volcanic eruption on the island of Santorini, triggered the violent downfall of the palace civilization around 1450 BC. Nor did peace come easily in the modern era: rebellion was endemic for centuries—against Arab invaders, Venetian colonists, Ottoman pashas, and German occupiers in World War II. Today, though, the island welcomes outsiders. Openly inviting to guests who want to experience the real Greece, Cretans remain family oriented and rooted in tradition. One of the greatest pleasures on Crete is immersing yourself in the island's lifestyle.

Exploring Crete

You can take in a lot of Crete simply by driving around the island, where in the course of a relatively few miles you might see the setting change from coastal plain to high mountains and from city center to rural village. English is spoken widely. Since Crete is long and narrow, approximately 257 km (159 mi) long and 60 km (37 mi) at its widest, the island is often approached in halves. Western Crete is especially rugged, with inland mountains and the equally craggy southern shoreline; some of the best beaches on the island are on the western coast, especially those at Elafonisi and surrounding the town of Falasarna. Hania and Rethymnon, both lovely, mysterious old cities that trace their roots to the Arab and Venetian worlds, are here in the west. The east begins at Crete's largest town, Heraklion, and its most important archaeological site, Knossos, and includes many of its most developed resorts. In both the east and the west of Crete, the greatest development is on the north shore; for the most part the southern coast remains blessedly unspoiled.

About the Restaurants

Dinner is an event here, as it is elsewhere in Greece, and is usually served late; in fact, when non-Greeks are finishing up around 10:30 or so, locals usually begin arriving. You will almost certainly eat better in a taverna or restaurant than at a hotel, where, unless you are staying at a first-class resort, the menu is usually of the bland "international" variety. From April through October, most restaurants serve outdoors, and enjoying a dinner beneath a Cretan sky is one of the island's most memorable pleasures. In restaurants, *magirefta* (dishes cooked ahead in the oven and often served at room temperature) are prepared in the morning and are best eaten at lunch. As a rule, it is hard to go hungry in Crete; in a village *kafeneio* (traditional Greek coffeehouse), you can almost always order salad and an omelet, or eggs fried with cheese.

Hotel desk clerks willingly recommend a choice of tavernas. Dress is invariably casual, though except in the most casual places shorts are not worn in the evening. Reservations are unnecessary unless noted. Credit cards are usually accepted only in more expensive restaurants.

About the Hotels

For an authentic experience on Crete, opt for simple, whitewashed, tile-floor rooms with rustic pine furniture in mountain and seaside villages. You'll find these in simple hotels or in the ubiquitous "room to rent" establishments, which are basically simple hotels, often occupying purpose-built structures or converted barns. Another common term is "studio," which implies the presence of a kitchen or at least basic cooking facilities; many of these are quite simple, while others can be very nicely appointed. In the west especially, old houses, Venetian palaces, and 19th-century mansions are being sensitively restored as small hotels. Hania has several such hotels, and they are excellent. Luxury resort properties have sports and entertainment facilities that compare with those anywhere in the Mediterranean. Some of Greece's finest resorts line the shores of Elounda peninsula, outside the town of Ayios Nikolaos. Many rooms, especially those in more expensive hotels, are decorated with traditional Cretan furnishings, which can be quite elegant: highly polished, carved hardwood divans, seats upholstered in the striped weavings typical of the island; dark, polished-wood armchairs with curvaceous arms and cane seats, often complemented by colorful pillows; floors covered with wool rugs woven locally. Unfortunately, there are also many undistinguished, concrete-block hotels, mostly along the north coast around Mallia and Limin Hersonissos.

Prices rise in July and come down again in mid-September, but even in high season you can often negotiate a discount at medium-price hotels if you are staying more than a night or two. Resort hotels sometimes

Although Crete is a large island, you can see the greatest of the island's Minoan sights even on a one-day stopover: in the north, at least, the island is crossed by a good highway and serviced by a good bus system. A three-day tour allows you to taste the pleasures of Heraklion and the cities of western Crete, and seven days allows time to see most of the major towns and sights.

Numbers in the text correspond to numbers in the margin and on the Eastern Crete, Heraklion, and Western Crete maps.

10

**If you have
1 day**

Often cruise-ship passengers stop in Crete for a day en route from Santorini to Rhodes. This stopover doesn't allow much time to get to know the island, and it makes for an intense day of sightseeing. Start with a visit to ▦ **Heraklion** ❶–❿ ▶, and the **Archaeological Museum** ❻, with its stunning displays of Minoan culture. Move on to the island's largest and most well-preserved Minoan sight, the **Palace of Knossos** ⓫. In the afternoon, make the hour-long trip to the **Palace of Phaistos** ㉑, another great Minoan site overlooking the south coast, and before returning to Heraklion dip your toes into the sea at the nearby, low-key resort of **Matala** ㉓.

**If you have
3 days**

▦ **Heraklion** ❶–❿ ▶ is the best starting point for any visit to the island. Spend one day visiting that city, the **Archaeological Museum** ❻, and the nearby **Palace of Knossos** ⓫. The next day, follow the north coast west to the city of **Rethymnon** ㉖, with its Venetian and Arab heritage, and later in the afternoon travel on to ▦ **Hania** ㉘, one of the most beautiful cities in Greece and, with its gorgeous harbor and fascinating old town, a delightful place to spend two nights. Sip coffee by the old harbor, walk through the narrow lanes, and explore the archaeological, folk, and naval museums. For a day trip, you might slip west from Hania to the glorious beach at Falasarna, or drive south through the dramatically high and craggy white mountains to the tiny seaside villages of Souyia or Paleochora, on the Libyan Sea. One of the island's most memorable experiences is a hike through the nearby Samaria Gorge. En route back to Heraklion, detour south from Rethymnon and stop at the Minoan **Palace of Phaistos** ㉑.

**If you have
7 days**

A week allows time to see all of Crete, if not exactly at leisure, at least at an enjoyable pace. Begin in ▦ **Heraklion** ❶–❿ ▶, where a stay of two nights allows enough time to see the city, the museums, and the **Palace of Knossos** ⓫. The third day, head east from Heraklion; your first stop is the **Lasithi plateau** ⓬, where you can experience one of the most scenic corners of rural Crete. After lunch there, return to the north shore and stop to see the Minoan ruins at the **Palace of Mallia** ⓭ and then the pleasant town of **Ayios Nikolaos** ⓮. The nearby ▦ **Elounda** ⓯, with its hotels and wonderful views of the Gulf of Mirabello, is an excellent place to stay. On Day 4 continue along the north coast to the Minoan city of Gournia, and then dip south to **Ierapetra** ⓱. After lunch and maybe a swim, it's back up to the north coast to ▦ **Siteia** ⓲—where you can find accommodation in a simple pension or room in a private home—and the beautiful beach at **Vai** ⓳. The next morning begins with a swim and is devoted to driving, all the way to ▣ **Rethymnon** ㉖ on the western side of the island. The distance is a little more than 200 km (120 mi), and the highway along the north coast is wide and well paved. After an evening in Rethymnon, preferably staying in the charming old town, make the short trip on to ▣ **Hania** ㉘. Spend two nights here, allowing time to see the city and to explore the area. You might, for instance, want to take a day trip to the Samaria Gorge, to the beaches in the far west, or to the rugged southern coast around Paleochora or Souyia. On your last day take the long route from Hania back to Heraklion, making a loop south at Rethymnon to visit the Minoan **Palace of Phaistos** ㉑, then turning back to the north coast.

---

require half-board (MAP); many give substantial discounts at the beginning and end of the season. Travel agencies, the local Greek National Tourism Organization (GNTO or EOT) offices, and the tourist police can all help you find accommodation at short notice. In villages, ask at the kafeneio about rooms for rent; these are common throughout Crete and usually cost €30 or less. Standards of cleanliness are high in Crete, and service is almost always friendly.

WHAT IT COSTS In euros					
	$$$$	$$$	$$	$	¢
RESTAURANTS	over €20	€16–€20	€12–€15	€8–€11	under €8
HOTELS	over €160	€121–€160	€91–€120	€60–€90	under €60

Restaurant prices are for one main course at dinner or, for two *mezedes* (small dishes) at restaurants that serve only mezedes. Hotel prices are for two people in a standard double room in high season, including taxes.

Timing

The best times for visiting Crete are April and May, when every outcrop of rock is ablaze with brilliant wildflowers, or September and October, when the sea is still warm and the light golden but piercingly clear. In July and August the main Minoan sites and the coastal towns, especially those on the north coast, come close to overflowing. Such places as Mallia and Limin Hersonissos, hideously developed towns where bars and pizzerias fill up with heavy-drinking northern Europeans, should be avoided in any other season as well. Driving can be hazardous in July and August amid the profusion of buses, rented jeeps, and motorbikes.

EASTERN CRETE

ΑΝΑΤΟΛΙΚΗ ΚΡΗΤΗ

Eastern Crete includes the towns and cities of Heraklion, Ayios Nikolaos, Siteia, and Ierapetra, as well as the archaeological sites of Knossos and Gournia. Natural wonders lie amid these man-made places, including the palm-fringed beach at Vai and the stunning Elounda peninsula.

Heraklion

Ηράκλειο

> *175 km (109 mi) south of Piraeus, 69 km (43 mi) west of Ayios Niko-laos, 78 km (49 mi) east of Rethymnon.*

The narrow, crowded alleys and thick stone ramparts of Heraklion, Crete's largest city and the fourth-largest city in Greece, recall the days when soldiers and merchants clung to the safety of a fortified port. In Minoan times, this was a harbor for Knossos, the largest palace and effective power center of prehistoric Crete. But the Bronze Age remains were built over long ago, and now Heraklion, with more than 120,000 inhabitants, stretches far beyond even the Venetian walls. Today's city is busy, and much of the new town is haphazardly constructed and rather unattractive. Even so, a walk down Dedalou and the other pedestri-ans-only streets around it provides plenty of amusements, and the city has more than its share of outdoor cafés where you can sit and watch life unfold. Oddly, Heraklion has turned away from the sea and the waterfront is rather derelict, though the seaside promenades are slowly coming back to life, thanks to ongoing restoration. In any event, the nearby Palace of Knossos and the city's renowned Archaeological Mu-seum make Heraklion a mandatory stop for anyone even remotely in-terested in ancient civilizations.

a good walk

You can nicely explore the compact old town in a walk of an hour or two, beginning at **Ta Leontaria** ➊ ☞ with its famous fountain and cathe-dral of **Ayios Markos** ➋. Proceed northeast across the busy intersection, and you come to a remnant of Venetian occupation, the **Loggia** ➌, then the church of **Ayios Titos** ➍, named for the patron saint of Crete. From here you can follow 25 Avgoustou, or a warren of little lanes, north to the seaside Venetian fortifications known as the **Koules** ➎ and the inner harbor to watch the fishing boats or ogle at the yachts. By following the old city walls inland from the waterfront, you arrive at the famed **Archaeological Museum** ➏, filled with Minoan treasures, and the busy **Pla-tia Eleftherias** ➐. Day and evening, residents come here to stroll and to sit on café terraces. Continue west to Odos 1866; you are in the heart of Heraklion's market. The market ends in **Platia Kornarou** ➑, dominated by a Venetian fountain and a Turkish pavilion (now the site of a café). Follow Kyrillou east and you pass many of Heraklion's most famous churches: the cathedral of **Ayios Minas** ➒, dedicated to Heraklion's pa-tron saint, and the medieval church of the same name, then the church of **Ayia Aikaterina** ➓, where El Greco is said to have studied. A right turn onto Leoforos Kalokorinou, another major shopping thoroughfare, brings you back to Ta Leontaria.

TIMING   If you have just a day in Heraklion, your time will be tight. Get an early start and spend a couple of hours in the morning doing this walk, step-ping into the churches if they're open and poking around the lively mar-ket. Save your energy for the Archaeological Museum and nearby Knossos, which will occupy most of the rest of the day. If you're stay-ing overnight in or near Heraklion, take an evening stroll in the busy area around Ta Leontaria and Platia Kornarou; half the population seems to converge here.

What to See

⑥ Archaeological Museum. Housed here are many of the treasures brought to light by the legendary excavations at the Palace of Knossos and other great monuments of Cretan culture. The Minoan civilization of 3,000 years ago is superbly illustrated by the unique collection, which compares favorably to similar exhibits in the great museums of western Europe. Among the holdings are the famous seal stones with Linear B script, which first attracted British archaeologist Sir Arthur Evans's attention. The best seal stone is the so-called "Phaistos Disk," found at Phaistos Palace in the south. Yet it is the sophisticated frescoes upstairs, restored fragments found in Knossos, that most catch the eye. They depict broad-shouldered, slim-waisted youths, their large eyes fixed with an enigmatic expression on the Prince of the Lilies; ritual processions and scenes from the bull ring, young men and women somersaulting over the back of a charging bull; and groups of court ladies, whose flounced skirts led a French archaeologist to exclaim in surprise, "*Des Parisiennes!,*" a name still applied to this striking fresco.

Even before great palaces with frescoes were being built around 1900 BC, the prehistoric Cretans excelled at metalworking and carving stone vases, such as those seen in Gallery I. They were also skilled at producing pottery, such as the eggshell-thin Kamaresware decorated in delicate abstract designs (in Gallery III). Other specialties were miniature work such as the superbly crafted jewelry (in Galleries VI and VII), and the colored seal stones (in Gallery III) that are carved with lively scenes of people and animals. Though naturalism and an air of informality distinguish much Minoan art from that of contemporary Bronze Age cultures elsewhere in the eastern Mediterranean, you can also see a number of heavy, rococo set pieces, such as the fruit stand with a toothed rim and the punch bowl with appliquéd flowers (both in Gallery III). The Linear B script, inscribed on clay tablets (Gallery V), is now recognized as an early form of Greek, but the earlier Linear A script (Gallery V) and that of the Phaistos Disk (Gallery III) have yet to be deciphered.

The Minoans' talents at modeling in stone, ivory, and a kind of glass paste known as faience peaked in the later palace period (1700 BC–1450 BC). A famous rhyton, a vase for pouring libations, carved from dark serpentine in the shape of a bull's head, has eyes made of red jasper and clear rock crystal with horns of gilded wood (Gallery IV). An ivory acrobat—perhaps a bull-leaper—and two bare-breasted faience goddesses in flounced skirts holding wriggling snakes (both Gallery IV) were among a group of treasures hidden beneath the floor of a storeroom at Knossos. (Bull-leaping, whether a religious rite or a favorite sport, inspired some memorable Minoan art.) Three vases, probably originally covered in gold leaf, from Ayia Triada (Gallery VII) are carved with scenes of Minoan life thought to be rendered by artists from Knossos: boxing matches, a harvest-home ceremony, and a Minoan official taking delivery of a consignment of hides. The most stunning rhyton of all, from Zakro, is made of rock crystal (Gallery VIII). Commodities were stored in the palaces: an ele-

Great Flavors Crete isn't a center of gastronomy, but ingredients here are always fresh, and the family-run tavernas take pride in their cooking. The island produces top-quality fruit and vegetables—cherries from the Amari Valley in June, oranges from the groves around Hania in winter, tomatoes and cucumbers all year round, and, increasingly, avocados and bananas. The Cretans enjoy grilled meat, generally lamb and pork, but there is also plenty of fresh fish. Cretan *graviera*, a hard, smooth cheese, is a blend of pasteurized sheep's and goat's milk that resembles Emmanthal in flavor and texture—not too sharp, but with a strong, distinctive flavor. *Mizythra* (a creamy white cheese) is also prized. Cretan olive oil is famous throughout Greece; it's heavier and richer than other varieties. The island's wines are improving fast: look for Boutari Kritikos, a crisp white, and Minos Palace, a smooth red. Make sure you try the *tsikouthia* (also known as raki), the Cretan firewater made from fermented grape skins, which is drunk at any hour, often accompanied by a dish of raisins, or walnuts drenched in honey. Many restaurants offer raki free of charge at the end of a meal. Retsina is not part of Cretan tradition, but it can be found in town restaurants.

10

Museums & Minoan Ruins It's not classical ruins that draw archaeologically inclined visitors to Crete, but the remains of the ancient Minoan civilization. You'll find the extensive ruins of Minoan palace complexes at Knossos, Phaistos, and Mallia, but there are many other Minoan sites around the island as well. Crete also has many excellent museums; take some time off from the beach and other outdoor activities to enjoy them. In addition to the outstanding Archaeological Museum in Heraklion, many towns and villages have folklife museums that pay homage to the island's traditional past. One of the finest collections is in Vori, southwest of Heraklion; there are also excellent folk collections at the Historical and Folk Art Museum in Rethymnon and the Historical Museum of Crete in Heraklion. October through April, museum hours are often reduced.

Nightlife & Festivals An evening out in Crete can pleasantly be spent in a *kentron* (a taverna that hosts traditional Cretan music and dancing). The star performer is the *lyra* player, who can extract a surprisingly subtle sound from the small pear-shape instrument, held upright on the thigh and played with a bow. Cretan dances range from monotonous circling to astonishing displays of athletic agility, but much depends on the *kefi* (enthusiasm) of participants. In cold weather, the kentron moves indoors and becomes a more typical bouzouki joint. Ask at your hotel where the best-known lyra players are performing.

Almost every town and village has a *panigyri*, a celebration of its patron saint with food, drink, traditional music, and dancing usually lasting until dawn. If you are lucky, you may be invited to a *glendi* (local party), or even a traditional Cretan wedding, where the celebrations can last 24 hours.

Crete has few serious arts activities and events. Though the island attracts painters from all over Europe, they rarely exhibit locally. In Heraklion, Rethymnon, and Hania, however, local authorities sometimes organize concerts, theater, and folk-dancing events from June to August. Athenian and even some foreign musical groups stage open-air performances in the Koules fort at Heraklion and the Fortessa at Rethymnon. Ask at the EOT offices for up-to-date information.

Shopping

Crete is a serendipitous place for the shopper: by poking around the backstreets of Heraklion, Rethymnon, and Hania, you can find things both useful and exotic—and sometimes even beautiful. Crete was famous even in Minoan times for its weaving. You still occasionally come across the heavy scarlet-embroidered blankets and bedspreads that formed the basis of a traditional dowry chest. Woven wool rugs in plain geometric designs from the village of Axos on the slopes of Mt. Ida are attractive, as are heavy sweaters in natural oily wool. All the villages on the Lasithi plateau have shops selling embroidered linens, made in front of the stove during the cold months. All over the island, local craftspeople produce attractive copies of Minoan jewelry in gold and silver, as well as some with original modern designs. A shepherd's kit (a striped woven haversack) and a staff are useful for the hiker. A Cretan knife, whether plain steel or with a decorated blade and handle, makes a handy kitchen or camping implement (remember to pack it in your checked luggage when you fly home). Boot makers in Heraklion and Hania can make you a pair of heavy Cretan leather knee boots to order. In the village of Thrapsano, 20 km (12½ mi) southeast of Heraklion, potters make terra-cotta vases, candlesticks, and other objects, including *pithoi*, tall earthenware jars used by the Minoans for storing wine and oil. They are still popular today, often as a flowerpot (*pithos*, singular). You can have yours air-freighted home.

---

phant tusk and bronze ingots (Gallery VIII) were found at Zakro and Ayia Triada. It's best to visit the museum first thing in the morning, before the tour buses arrive. ⊠ *Pl. Eleftherias* ☎ *2810/224630* ⊕ *www.culture.gr* ⊠ *€6; combined ticket for museum and Palace of Knossos, €10* ☉ *Apr.–mid-Oct., daily 8–7:30; mid-Oct.–Mar., daily 8–5.*

❿ Ayia Aikaterina. Nestled in the shadow of the Ayios Minas cathedral is one of Crete's most attractive small churches, Ayia Aikaterina, built in 1555. The church now contains a museum of icons by Cretan artists, who traveled to Venice to study with Italian Renaissance painters. Look for six icons (Nos. 2, 5, 8, 9, 12, and 15) by Michael Damaskinos, who worked in both Byzantine and Renaissance styles during the 16th century. ⊠ *Kyrillou Loukareos* ☎ *No phone* ⊠ *€2* ☉ *Mon. and Wed. 9:30–1, Thurs. and Sat. 9–1 and 5–7, Fri. 9–1.*

❷ Ayios Markos. This 13th-century church (now an exhibition space) is named for Venice's patron saint, but, with its modern portico and narrow interior, it bears little resemblance to its grand namesake in Venice. Hours are irregular; the church is open only for exhibitions. ⊠ *Pl. Eleftheriou Venizelou* ☎ *No phone.*

❾ Ayios Minas. This is a huge, lofty, but ultimately unprepossessing 1895 cathedral that can hold up to 8,000 worshippers. ⊠ *Kyrillou Loukareos.*

❹ Ayios Titos. A chapel to the left of the entrance contains St. Tito's skull, set in a silver-and-gilt reliquary. He is credited with converting the islanders to Christianity in the 1st century AD on the instructions of St. Paul. ☒ *Set back from 25 Avgoustou.*

Historical Museum of Crete. An imposing mansion houses a varied collection of early Christian and Byzantine sculptures, Venetian and Ottoman stonework, artifacts of war, and rustic folklife items. Look out for the *Lion of St. Mark* sculpture, with an inscription that says in Latin I PROTECT THE KINGDOM OF CRETE. Left of the entrance is a room stuffed with memorabilia from Crete's bloody revolutionary past: weapons, portraits of mustachioed warrior chieftains, and the flag of the short-lived independent Cretan state set up in 1898. The 19th-century banner in front of the staircase sums up the spirit of Cretan rebellion against the Turks: ELEFTHERIA O THANATOS (Freedom or Death). Upstairs, look in on a room arranged as the study of Crete's most famous writer, Nikos Kazantzakis (1883–1957), the author of *Zorba the Greek* and an epic poem, *The Odyssey, a Modern Sequel*. The top floor contains a stunning collection of Cretan textiles, including the brilliant scarlet weavings typical of the island's traditional handwork, and another room arranged as a domestic interior of the early 1900s. ☒ *Kalokorinou, in a warren of little lanes near the seafront* ☏ 2810/283219 ☑ €3 ◷ Weekdays 9–5, Sat. 9–2.

❺ Koules. Heraklion's inner harbor, where fishing boats land their catch and yachts are moored, is dominated by the Turkish-named fortress. Koules was built by the Venetians and decorated with three stone lions of St. Mark, symbol of Venetian imperialism. On the east side of the fortress are the vaulted arsenal; here Venetian galleys were repaired and refitted, and timber, cheeses, and sweet malmsey wine were loaded for the three-week voyage to Venice. The view from the battlements takes in the inner as well as the outer harbor, where freighters and passenger ferries drop anchor, and the sprawling labyrinth of concrete apartment blocks that is modern Heraklion. To the south rises Mt. Iuktas and, to the west, the pointed peak of Mt. Stromboli. ☒ *North end of 25 Avgoustou* ☏ 2810/288484 ☑ €2 ◷ Tues.–Sun. 8:30–3.

❸ Loggia. A gathering place for the island's Venetian nobility, this loggia was built in the early 17th century by Francesco Basilicata, an Italian architect. Now restored to its original Palladian elegance, it adjoins the old Venetian Armory, now the City Hall. ☒ *25 Avgoustou.*

> **need a break?**
>
> Stop in at Kir-Kor, a venerable old ***bougatsa shop*** (☒ Pl. Eleftheriou Venizelou), for this envelope of flaky pastry that's either filled with a sweet, creamy filling and dusted with cinnamon and sugar, or stuffed with soft white cheese. A double portion served warm with Greek coffee is a nice treat. Thick Cretan yogurt and ice cream are other indulgences on offer.

Martinengo Bastion. Six bastions shaped like arrowheads jut out from the well-preserved Venetian walls. Martinengo is the largest, designed by Micheli Sanmicheli in the 16th century to keep out Barbary pirates

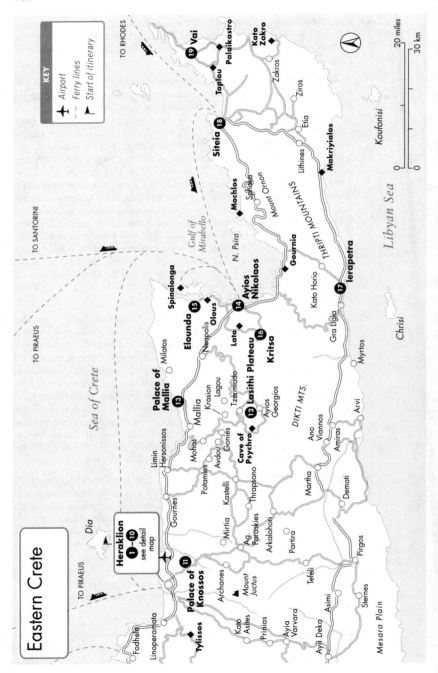

Eastern Crete

KEY
- ✈ Airport
- --- Ferry lines
- ▲ Start of itinerary

TO PIRAEUS

TO SANTORINI

TO RHODES

Heraklion
①–⑩ see detail map

⑪ Palace of Knossos

Tylissos

Fodhele

Linoperamata

Dia

Sea of Crete

Gournes

Limin Hersonissos

Mohos

Avdou

Gonies

Potamies

Kastelli

Mirtia

Ag. Paraskies

Arkalohori

Partira

Asimi

Ayii Deka

Ayia Varvara

Prinias

Kato Ashes

Archanes

Mount Juctus ▲

Tefeli

Pirgos

Sternes

Mesara Plain

⑬ Palace of Mallia

Mallia

Krasion

Lagou

Tzermiado

⑫ Lasithi Plateau

Cave of Psychro

Ayios Georgios

Ano Viannos

Martha

Demati

Amiras

Arvi

Myrtos

DIKTI MTS.

Milatos

Neapolis

⑮ Elounda

Olous

⑭ Ayios Nikolaos

⑯ Lato **Kritsa**

Spinalonga

Gulf of Mirabello

N. Psira

Gournia

Kato Horio

Gra Ligia

⑰ Ierapetra

THRIPTI MOUNTAINS

Chrisi

Libyan Sea

Mochlos

Sfaka

Mount Ornon

⑱ Siteia

Lithines

Etia

Ziros

Makriyialos

Koufonisi

Toplou

⑲ Vai

Palaikastro

Kato Zakro

Zakros

0   20 miles
0   30 km

N

and Turkish invaders. When the Turks overran Crete in 1648, the garrison at Heraklion held out for another 21 years in one of the longest sieges in European history. General Francesco Morosini finally surrendered the city to the Turkish Grand Vizier in September 1669. He was allowed to sail home to Venice with the city's archives and such precious relics as the skull of Ayios Titos—which was not returned until 1966. Literary pilgrims come to the Martinengo to visit the **burial place of writer Nikos Kazantzakis.** The grave is a plain stone slab marked by a weathered wooden cross. The inscription, from his writings, says: I FEAR NOTHING, I HOPE FOR NOTHING, I AM FREE. ⊠ *South of Kyrillou Loukareos on N. G. Mousourou.*

❼ Platia Eleftherias. The city's biggest square is paved in marble and dotted with fountains. The Archaeological Museum is off the north end of the square; at the west side is the beginning of Daidalou, the city's main street, which follows the line of an early fortification wall and is now a pedestrian walkway lined with tavernas, boutiques, jewelers, and souvenir shops. ⊠ *Southeast end of Daidalou.*

❽ Platia Kornarou. This square is graced with a Venetian fountain and an elegant Turkish stone kiosk. Odos 1866, which runs north from the square, houses Heraklion's lively open-air market, where fruit and vegetable stalls alternate with butchers' displays of whole lambs and pigs' feet. ⊠ *At Odos 1866, south of Ta Leontaria.*

St. Peter's. Only a shell remains of this medieval church, which was heavily damaged during World War II in the bombing before the German invasion in 1941. ⊠ *West of harbor along seashore Rd.*

▶ **❶ Ta Leontaria.** "The Lions," a stately marble Renaissance fountain, remains a beloved town landmark. It's the heart of Heraklion's town center— Platia Eleftheriou Venizelou, a triangular pedestrian zone filled with cafés and named after the Cretan statesman who united the island with Greece in 1913. This was the center of the colony founded in the 13th century, when Venice bought Crete, and Heraklion became an important port of call on the trade routes to the Middle East. The city, and often the whole island (known then as Candia), was ruled by the Duke of Crete, a Venetian administrator. ⊠ *Pl. Eleftheriou Venizelou.*

Where to Stay & Eat

¢–$$ ✕ **Prassein Aloga.** Although the center of Heraklion is chockablock with places to eat, few are as pleasant as the Green Horse. Dine in the simply decorated little room or, when weather permits, at tables outside on a quiet side street near Ta Leontaria. Grilled meats, fish, and traditional Greek dishes are the mainstays, though the menu also includes a nice selection of Mediterranean-inspired salads and pasta dishes. ⊠ *Kindonias 21, off Handakos* ☎ *2810/283429* ☒ *MC, V.*

¢–$$ ✕ **Terzakis.** Choose half a dozen or more dishes from a long list of fish, dips, and salads at Heraklion's most popular *mezedopoleio* (a restaurant serving small, appetizer-size dishes, or mezedes). Traditionally, mezes are accompanied by ouzo, but beer or wine is equally acceptable. The place is always busy, so you might have to wait for a table. The

bustling establishment spills into a narrow lane off 25 Avgoustou. ⊠ *Loh. Marineli 17, behind Ayios Dimitrios church* ☎ *2810/221444* ▭ *MC, V* ☉ *No dinner Sun.*

¢–$ ✕ **Pantheon.** The liveliest restaurant in Heraklion's covered meat market has grilled and spit-roasted meats, as well as deftly prepared versions of moussaka and other traditional dishes. The surroundings are simple, but that doesn't stop locals from pouring in at all hours for a meal, which is nicely accompanied by salads made from the freshest Cretan produce. ⊠ *Market off Pl. Kornarou* ☎ *2810/241652* ▭ *No credit cards.*

$$$$ ▦ **Astoria Capsis.** This sleek hotel opposite the Archaeological Museum in the most animated part of the city is attractive and welcoming, though it's become a bit overpriced compared with other lodging options in Heraklion. Contemporary rooms are decorated in cool shades and furnished with blond wood; others are done in an extremely tasteful traditional, darker-wood style. All have balconies and all of the modern baths are equipped with bathtubs. Retreat to the rooftop swimming pool from June to August, when bar service is provided, or have coffee at the ground-floor bar, open 24 hours. Rates include a buffet breakfast that is nothing short of lavish. ⊠ *Pl. Eleftherias, 71201* ☎ *2810/343080* ⎙ *2810/229078* ⊕ *www.astoriacapsis.gr* ⇥ *117*

rooms, 14 suites ⚐ Restaurant, coffee shop, room service, minibars, cable TV, in-room data ports, pool, bar, dry cleaning, laundry service, business services, meeting rooms, car rental, travel services ⊟ AE, DC, MC, V ⍾ BP.

$$$$ ▦ **Megaron.** A 1930s office building that for decades stood derelict
Fodor'sChoice above the harbor now houses an unusually luxurious and restful hotel,
★ by far the best in town. Handsome public spaces include a welcoming library/lounge, a rooftop restaurant with stunning views of the city and sea, and a top-floor terrace where a swimming pool is perched dramatically at the edge of the roof. The large and sumptuous guest rooms bring together a tasteful combination of rich fabrics, marble, and woods, and the teak-floored baths are lavish. Special Internet rates are often lower than those at other hotels in this class, making the Megaron a relatively affordable indulgence. ⊠ *Doukos Bofor 12, 71202* ☏ *2810/305300* ☏ *2810/305400* ⊕ *www.gdmmegaron.gr* ⤚ *38 rooms, 8 suites ⚐ Restaurant, café, room service, cable TV, Wi-Fi, pool, gym, bar, meeting rooms, no smoking rooms ⊟ MC, V ⍾ CP.*

$ ▦ **El Greco.** Ask for a garden-facing room for a quieter night, or request a street-side balcony to watch the action steps from Ta Leontaria fountain. The carpeted rooms are simply but pleasantly furnished with wood beds and a desk. Rates include a full breakfast, but air-conditioning costs €7 a day extra. Even so, the word is out about what a bargain this is, so it's best to reserve far in advance. ⊠ *Odos 1821 4, 71202* ☏ *2810/281071* ☏ *2810/281072* ⊕ *www.elgrecohotel.gr* ⤚ *90 rooms ⚐ Snack bar, recreation room; no a/c in some rooms ⊟ DC, MC, V ⍾ BP.*

$ ▦ **Marin Hotel.** A quiet oasis like this is welcome in busy Heraklion. Sleek, contemporary decor and furnishings in the public spaces and guest rooms alike make this small inn on a narrow street just above the harbor especially soothing and restful. The handsome rooms have stylish wood floors and balconies, some with views of the sea; all of the city sights are just a short walk away. ⊠ *Doukos Bofor 12, 71202* ☏ *2810/300018* ☏ *2810/300019* ⊕ *www.marinhotel.gr* ⤚ *44 rooms ⚐ Restaurant, in-room safes, minibars, cable TV, in-room data ports, bar ⊟ AE, MC, V ⍾ CP.*

¢ ▦ **Dedalos.** You'd have to look hard to find a more fairly priced accommodation in the city center. On pedestrian-only Daidalou, this place is an easy walk to the Archaeological Museum and other sights. Rooms are modest and not a lot of care goes into the decor, but they're comfortable and all have balconies. Be sure to ask for one that faces the sea and not the street, which is loud with merrymakers into the wee hours. Breakfast is available for €6. ⊠ *Daidalou 15, 71202* ☏ *2810/244812* ☏ *2810/244391* ⤚ *58 rooms ⚐ Dining room; no a/c ⊟ MC, V.*

Palace of Knossos

Ανάκτορο Κνωσού

⑪ *5 km (3 mi) south of Heraklion.*

Fodor'sChoice
★ The palace of Knossos belonged to King Minos, who kept the Minotaur, a hybrid monster of man and bull, in an underground labyrinth.

Palace of Knossos

This most amazing of archaeological sites once lay hidden beneath a huge mound hemmed in by low hills. Heinrich Schliemann, father of archaeology and discoverer of Troy, knew it was here, but Turkish obstruction prevented him from exploring his last discovery. Cretan independence from the Ottoman Turks made it possible for Sir Arthur Evans, a British archaeologist, to start excavations in 1899. A forgotten and sublime civilization thus came again to light with the uncovering of the great Palace of Knossos. The site was occupied from Neolithic times, and the population spread to the surrounding land. Around 1900 BC, the hilltop was leveled and the first palace constructed; around 1700 BC, after an earthquake destroyed the original structure, the later palace was built, surrounded by houses and other buildings. Around 1450 BC, another widespread disaster occurred, perhaps an invasion: palaces and country villas were razed by fire and abandoned, but Knossos remained inhabited even though the palace suffered some damage. But around 1380 BC the palace and its outlying buildings were destroyed by fire, and at the end of the Bronze Age the site was abandoned. Still later, Knossos became a Greek city-state.

You enter the palace from the west, passing a bust of Sir Arthur Evans, who excavated at Knossos on and off for more than 20 years. A path leads you around to the monumental **south gateway.** The **west wing** encases lines of long, narrow storerooms where the true wealth of Knossos was kept in tall clay jars: oil, wine, grains, and honey. The **central court** is about 164 feet by 82 feet long. The cool, dark **throne-room complex** has a griffin fresco and tall, wavy-back gypsum throne, the oldest in Europe. The most spectacular piece of palace architecture is the **grand staircase,** on the east side of the court, leading to the domestic apartments. Four flights of shallow gypsum stairs survive, lighted by a deep light well. Here you get a sense of how noble Minoans lived; rooms were divided by sets of double doors, giving privacy and warmth when closed, coolness and communication when open. The **queen's megaron** (apartment or hall) is decorated with a colorful dolphin fresco and furnished with stone benches. Beside it is a bathroom, complete with a clay tub, and next door a toilet, whose drainage system permitted flushing into a channel flowing into the Kairatos stream far below. The east side of the palace also contained **workshops.** Beside the staircase leading down to the **east bastion** is a stone water channel made up of parabolic curves and settling basins: a Minoan storm drain. Northwest of the east bastion is the **north entrance,** guarded by a relief fresco of a charging bull. Beyond is the **theatrical area,** shaded by pines and overlooking a shallow flight of steps, which lead down to the **royal road.** This, perhaps, was the ceremonial entrance to the palace.

Although excavations have revealed houses with mosaic floors, statuary, and a wealth of information about the Minoan civilization, colorful—and controversial—concrete reconstructions form much of the site. Opinions vary, but these restorations and fresco copies do impart a sense of what Knossos must have once looked like. Without the recreation it would be impossible to experience a full Minoan palace—long, pillared halls; narrow corridors; deep stairways and light wells; and curious reverse-tapering columns. For a complete education, consider touring Knossos, then traveling south to the Palace of Phaistos, another great Minoan site, which has not been reconstructed. To reach Knossos by bus, take No. 2 (departing every 15 minutes) from Odos Evans, close to the market, in Heraklion. ☎ *2810/231940* ⊕ *www. culture.gr* ✉ *€6; combined ticket for Knossos and Archaeological Museum in Heraklion, €10* ⊗ *Apr.–mid-Oct., daily 8–7:30; mid-Oct.–Mar., daily 8–5.*

off the beaten path

ARCHANES – If you continue inland from Knossos, after about 3 km (2 mi) you'll come to a well-marked road to Archanes, about 5 km (3 mi) beyond the turnoff. After the town received EU funds to do a makeover, streets were repaved with cobblestones, houses were restored and painted in bold shades of ocher and pastels, many fine neoclassical stone structures were spruced up, and new trees and flowers planted everywhere in town. Archanes now looks a bit like a stage set, but it's lovely, and the handsome *platia* and surrounding streets are well equipped with places for a snack or a meal—accompany either with a glass of wine from the vineyards that cover the slopes around town.

Lasithi Plateau

Ομοπέδιο Λασιθίς

★ ⑫ *47 km (29 mi) southeast of the Palace of Knossos, 52 km (32 mi) southeast of Heraklion.*

The Lasithi plateau, 2,800 feet high and the biggest of the upland plains of Crete, lies behind a wall of barren mountains. Windmills still pump water for fields of potatoes and the apple and almond orchards that are a pale haze of blossom in early spring. The plateau is remote and breathtakingly beautiful, and ringed by small villages where shops sell local weaving and embroidery.

The **Cave of Psychro** is an impressive, stalactite-rich cavern that was once a Minoan sanctuary and has long since been a popular tourist attraction on the plateau. It's where Zeus, the king of the gods, was supposedly born. Approach it from the large parking lot on foot or by donkey. ⊠ *Near village of Psychro* ☎ *No phone* 🎫 *€4* ☼ *July and Aug., daily 8–7; Sept.–June, daily 8:30–3.*

An old village house in Ayios Georgios contains the delightful **Cretan Folklore Museum.** The house stands as it was when generations of farmers lived here, and the simple furnishings, embroidery, tools, and combination of living quarters and stables provide a chance to see domestic life as it was, and indeed still is, for many residents. ⊠ *Ayios Georgios* ☎ *No phone* 🎫 *€2.50* ☼ *Mid-Apr.–late Oct., daily 10–4.*

Where to Eat

★ $ ✕ **Kronio.** The promise of a meal in this cozy, family-run establishment is alone worth the trip up to the plateau. Delicious meat and vegetable pies as well as homemade casseroles and lamb dishes emerge from the kitchen, to be accompanied by fresh-baked bread and the house wine and followed up with homemade desserts. The charming proprietors, Vassilis and Christine, encourage you to linger over your wine or raki, and point you to what to see on the plateau. ⊠ *Tzermiado* ☎ *28440/22375* ▭ *No credit cards* ☼ *Closed Nov.–Mar.*

Shopping

Shops selling distinctive embroidered goods and other handiwork can be found across the Lasithi plateau. **Katerina** stocks tablecloths, napkins, clothing, cloth bags, and other items, and the owner will most likely offer you a refreshment as you shop. ⊠ *Tzermiado* ☎ *28440/22622.*

Palace of Mallia

Ανάκτορο Μαλίων

★ ⑬ *50 km (31 mi) north of Lasithi plateau, 37 km (23 mi) east of Heraklion.*

In its effort to serve mass tourism, the town of Mallia has submerged whatever character it might once have had. The sandy beach, overlooked by the brooding Lasithi mountains, is backed by a solid line of hotels and vacation apartments. The town itself may not be worth a visit, but the Minoan Palace of Mallia on its outskirts definitely is. Like the palaces of Knossos and Phaistos, it was built around 1900 BC, but it was less sophisticated both in architecture and decoration. The layout, however, is similar. Across the west court, along one of the paved raised walkways, is a double row of **round granaries** sunk into the ground, which were almost certainly roofed. East of the granaries is the **south doorway,** beyond which is the large, circular limestone table, or *kernos* (on which were placed offerings to a Minoan deity), with a large hollow at its center and 34 smaller ones around the edge. The **central court** has a shallow pit at its center, perhaps the location of an altar. To the west of the central court are the remains of an imposing staircase leading up to a second floor, and a terrace, most likely used for religious ceremonies; behind is a long corridor with **storerooms** to the side. In the north wing is a large **pillared hall,** part of a set of public rooms. The **domestic apartments** appear to have been in the northwest corner of the palace, entered through a narrow dogleg passage. They are connected by a smaller **northern court,** through which you can leave the palace by the **north entrance,** passing two giant old *pithoi* (large earthenware jars for storage of wine or oil). Much excavation has been done nearby, but only a few of the building sites are open. ⊠ *3 km (2 mi) northeast of Mallia town* ☎ *28970/31597* ⊕ *www.culture.gr* ⌨ *€4* ☉ *Nov.–May, daily 8:30–3; June–Oct., daily 8:30–7.*

Ayios Nikolaos

Άγιος Νικόλαος

★ ⑭ *32 km (20 mi) southeast of Mallia, 69 km (43 mi) east of Heraklion.*

Ayios Nikolaos, built over a century ago by Cretans from the southwest of the island, is clustered on a peninsula alongside the Gulf of Mirabello, a dramatic composition of bare mountains, islets, and deep blue sea. Behind the crowded harbor lies a natural curiosity, tiny Lake Voulismeni, linked to the sea by a narrow channel. Hilly, with narrow, steep streets that provide sea views, the town is a welcoming place: you can stroll miles of waterside promenades, cafés line the lakeshore, and many streets are open only to pedestrians.

The **archaeological museum** at Ayios Nikolaos displays some interesting artifacts, such as the *Goddess of Myrtos,* a statue of a woman cradling a large jug in her spindly arms. The early Minoan rhyton comes from a site on the southeast coast. There are also examples of late Minoan pottery in the naturalist marine style, with lively octopus and shell designs. ⊠ *Odos Palaiologou 74* ☎ *28410/24943* ⌨ *€3* ☉ *Tues.–Sun. 8:30–3.*

The excellent **folk museum** showcases exquisite weavings, along with walking sticks, tools, and other artifacts from everyday rural life. ⊠ *Odos Palaiologou 2* ☎ *28410/24943* ⌨ *€3* ☉ *Sun.–Fri. 11–3.*

need a break? A walk around town should include a stop at **Chez Georges** (⊠ Kornarou 2 ☎ 28410/26130), an airy café high above the lake. Sit down before stunning views and enjoy ice cream, coffee, and cocktails, served throughout the day late into the night.

Beaches

You can dip into the clean waters that surround Ayios Nikolaos from several good beaches right in town. **Kitroplatia** and **Ammos** are both only about a 5- to 10-minute walk from the center. You can rent lounges and umbrellas at both.

Where to Stay & Eat

¢-$$$ ✕ **Migomis.** Dress well (no shorts), try to nab a seat by the windows, and partake of an excellent meal accompanied by stunning views of the town and the sea. At one of the best restaurants in town, the menu embraces both Greece and Italy, with some excellent pastas and Tuscan steaks as well as the freshest fish and other seafood. ✉ *Plasira near 28th October* ☎ *28410/24353* ⌂ *Reservations essential in summer* ⊟ *AE, MC, V.*

¢-$ ✕ **Itanos Restaurant.** This old-fashioned taverna is a much better value than the seafront establishments and offers a very palatable house wine from a row of barrels in the kitchen. The *tzoutzoukakia* (oven-cooked meatballs) are tender and spicy, and vegetable dishes, such as braised artichokes or green beans with tomato, are full of flavor. ✉ *Pl. Iroon* ☎ *28410/25340* ⊟ *No credit cards.*

¢   ✕ **Sarris.** Irini Sarris shows off her deft culinary skill best in traditional dishes, such as *stifado* (a rich stew made with lamb and sometimes with hare), and in the many *mezedes* (small dishes). The delightful, shady arbor set with tables overlooks an old church. ✉ *Kyprou 15* ☎ *28410/28059* ⊟ *No credit cards* ⊙ *Closed Nov.–Feb.*

¢   ✕▥ **Hotel Du Lac.** The handsomely appointed dining room with lakeside terrace ($–$$$) is one of the best places in town for a meal. Attentive and polished servers present house specialties such as steaks, other grilled meats, and seafood that's always fresh. The rooms upstairs are airy, spacious, and nicely done with simple, contemporary furnishings; studios, with kitchens and large baths, are enormous and an especially good value. Outlooks from all rooms and their balconies are pleasant, but ask for a room overlooking the lake. ✉ *28th October 17, 72100* ☎ *28410/22711* ⊟ *28410/27211* ⊕ *www.dulachotel.gr* ⇥ *18 rooms, 6 studios* ⌂ *Some kitchens, refrigerators* ⊟ *AE, MC, V.*

¢   ▥ **Hotel Kastro.** At the end of a quiet street, on top of a hill just above the city center, watch the goings-on at the port from your private balcony. In the pleasant and plain rooms, which cling to the hillside below the main entrance, arches form the doorways and beds are tucked into alcoves. Although rooms have cooking facilities, a homemade breakfast is served in the morning. ✉ *Lathenous 23, 72100* ☎ *28410/24918* ⊟ *28410/25827* ⌀ *www.meraki.gr* ⇥ *12 rooms* ⌂ *Kitchenettes; no room TVs* ⊟ *MC, V* ⏍ *BP.*

Shopping

An appealing array of beads, quartz and silver jewelry, woven tablecloths and scarves, and carved bowls and other handicrafts fills **Chez Sonia** (✉ 28th October ☎ 28410/28475). You can get a very nice taste of the island at **Elixir** (✉ Koundourou 15 ☎ 28410/82593), well stocked with Cretan olive oils and wines and locally harvested honey and spices, as well as handmade olive oil soaps.

Elounda

Εχούντα

⑮ *11 km (7 mi) north of Ayios Nikolaos, 80 km (50 mi) east of Heraklion.*

Traversing a steep hillside, a narrow road with spectacular sea views runs north from Ayios Nikolaos around the Gulf of Mirabello to Elounda. The beaches tend to be narrow and pebbly, but the water is crystal clear and sheltered from the *meltemi* (the fierce north wind that blows in July and August). Elounda village is becoming a full-scale resort destination: dozens of villas and hotels dot the surrounding hillsides, and the shore of the gulf south of Elounda is crowded with some of the most luxurious hotels in Crete. Don't come here in search of the authentic Greece; expect to meet fellow international travelers.

Olous (⊠ 3 km [2 mi] east of Elounda) is an ancient city, the sunken remains of which are visible beneath the sea; snorkelers can easily see them.

off the
beaten
path

SPINALONGA – A small, narrow island in the center of the Gulf of Mirabello, Spinalonga is a fascinating, if somewhat macabre, place to visit. The Venetians built a huge, forbidding fortress here in the 17th century, and in the early 1900s the island became a leper colony. To reach it you must take a boat trip. Travel agents in Ayios Nikolaos and Elounda can arrange excursions, some complete with a midday beach barbecue and a swim on a deserted islet. As you cruise past the islet of Ayioi Pantes, a goat reserve, look for the *agrimi* (Cretan wild goat), with its impressive curling horns.

Where to Stay & Eat

\$–\$\$\$ ✕ **Marilena.** In good weather, meals are served in the large rear garden, or you can choose a table on a sidewalk terrace facing the harbor. The kitchen prepares an excellent fresh, grilled fish and a rich fish soup; any meal here should begin with a platter of assorted appetizers. ⊠ *Harborside, main Sq.* 🕾🕾 *28410/41322* 🖃 *MC, V* ☉ *Closed late Oct.–early Mar.*

¢–\$ ✕ **Pefko.** Despite the presence of a hideous resort at the edge of town, Plaka remains a delightful fishing village and Pefko (the Pine Tree) a pleasant place to take in village life and sea views. The menu offers a nice assortment of appetizers, salads, and such basics as moussaka and lamb, to be enjoyed on a shady terrace or in a cozy dining room where music is played some evenings. ⊠ *Near the beach in center of town, Plaka* 🕾 *28410/42510* 🖃 *No credits cards.*

\$\$\$\$ 🏨 **Elounda Beach.** One of Greece's most renowned resort hotels, on 40 acres of gardens next to the Gulf of Mirabello, Elounda Beach has inspired dozens of imitators. The architecture reflects Cretan tradition: whitewashed walls, shady porches, and cool flagstone floors. You can have a room in the central block or a bungalow at the edge of the sea; 25 of the suites have their own swimming pools. Two sandy beaches are the jumping-off point for numerous water sports, including scuba diving. ⊠ *3 km (2 mi) south of village, 72053* 🕾 *28410/41412* 🖃 *28410/41373* ⊕ *www.eloundabeach.gr* 🛏 *215 rooms, 28 suites* 🕭 *6 restaurants, cable TV with movies, miniature golf, 5 tennis courts, pool,* *health club, sauna, steam room, beach, windsurfing, boating, parasailing, waterskiing, 3 bars, cinema, shops* ▭ *AE, DC, MC, V* ⊘ *Closed Nov.–Mar.* ⦿ *BP.*

$$$$ ▦ **Elounda Mare.** If you plan to stay at one luxurious resort in Crete,
FodorśChoice make it this extraordinary Relais & Châteaux property on the Gulf of
★ Mirabello, one of the finest hotels in Greece. More than half of the rooms, all bathed in cool marble and stunningly decorated in a soothing and comfortable blend of traditional and contemporary furnishings, are in villas set in their own gardens with private pools. Verdant gardens line the shore above a sandy beach and terraced waterside lounging areas, a stone's throw from the large pool. ⊠ *3 km (2 mi) south of village, 72053* ☎ *28410/41102 or 28410/41103* 🖷 *28410/41307* ⊕ *www. eloundamare.gr* ⇝ *38 rooms, 44 bungalows* ⟡ *3 restaurants, minibars, cable TV, in-room data ports, 9-hole golf course, 2 tennis courts, pool, gym, sauna, steam room, beach, windsurfing, boating, waterskiing* ▭ *AE, DC, MC, V* ⊘ *Closed Nov.–mid-Apr.* ⦿ *BP.*

$ ▦ **Akti Olous.** This friendly, unassuming hotel on the edge of the Gulf of Mirabello is a step away from a strip of sandy beach and provides sweeping views of the sea and peninsula. The rooftop pool and terrace are especially pleasant at sunset, and there is a waterside taverna and bar. The bright rooms, decorated in a handsome, modern neoclassical style, all have balconies overlooking the sea. ⊠ *Waterfront road, 72053* ☎ *28410/41270* 🖷 *28410/41425* ⊕ *www.greekhotels.net/aktiolous* ⇝ *70 rooms* ⟡ *Restaurant, refrigerators, pool, beach, bar* ▭ *MC, V* ⊘ *Closed Nov.–mid-Apr.* ⦿ *BP.*

Kritsa

Κριτσά

⑯ *20 km (12½ mi) south of Elounda, 80 km (50 mi) southeast of Heraklion.*

The village of Kritsa, 9 km (5½ mi) west of Ayios Nikolaos, is renowned for its weaving tradition and surrounds a large, shady town square filled with café tables. The lovely Byzantine church here, the whitewashed **Panayia Kera,** has an unusual shape, with three naves supported by heavy triangular buttresses. Built in the early years of Venetian occupation, it contains some of the liveliest and best-preserved medieval frescoes on the island, painted in the 13th century. ⊠ *On main road before town* 🎫 *€1* ⊘ *Sat.–Thurs. 9–3.*

One of the best views in Crete can be had at **Lato,** an ancient city built in a dip between two rocky peaks. Make your way over the ancient masonry to the far end of the site: on a clear day you can see the island of Santorini, about 135 km (84 mi) across the Cretan Sea. ⊠ *1 km (½ mi) northeast of Panayia Kera; follow the dirt track.*

The Minoan site of **Gournia** was excavated in 1904 by Harriet Boyd Hawes, the first woman archaeologist to work here, along with her team of Cretan workmen and a chaperon. Most of what you see dates from the later palace period, though Gournia had only a small mansion set among dozens of small houses. Excavations indicated that this fishing and weaving community was destroyed around 1400 BC and never re-settled. ⊠ *8 km (5mi) east of Kritsa, to right of main highway, on low hillside* ☎ *No phone* ⊕ *www.culture.gr* ⊠ *€2* ⊙ *Daily 8:30–3.*

Ierapetra

Ιεράπετρα

⓱ *23 km (14 mi) southeast of Kritsa, 114 (70 mi) southeast of Heraklion.*

Cross the narrowest part of Crete to Ierapetra, the only major town on the south coast. The prosperity of the flourishing agricultural center is based in the plastic-covered greenhouses where early tomatoes and cucumbers are grown and exported all over Europe. The climate in this part of Crete is North African; you are nearer to Libya than to mainland Greece.

Beaches

Ierapetra's greatest attraction is the turquoise sea that washes onto a white beach stretching the length of the town. Markopoulou, a mostly pedestrian avenue that runs along the beach, is lined with restaurants and cafés that offer nice views from their terraces. Tourism is fast developing to the east of Ierapetra, where there are some sandy beaches. At the village of **Makriyialos** (⊠ 28 km [17 mi] east of Ierapetra), you can take your pick of sandy spots; even in July and August you might

★ have most of a cove to yourself. The best beaches are those on **Krissi island,** (⊠ In middle of the Libyan Sea due south of Ierapetra); the island is essentially a sandbar with only a few tavernas. Boats make the trip from Ierapetra twice in the morning, at about 8 and 10, with two afternoon returns, usually at about 3 and 5. Among the many agencies in town that sell boat tickets is **South Crete Tours** (⊠ Lesthenous 36 ☎ 28420/22892); the round-trip fare is about €20.

Where to Stay & Eat

¢ ✕☷ **El Greco.** The small, tidy rooms are plain, but all have balconies and many hang over the beach. The terrace of the beachfront restaurant (¢–$$) is one of the most popular places in town for a meal; the menu includes everything from pizzas to simply prepared fish dishes. ⊠ *Kothri 42, 72200* ☎ *28420/28471* 🖷 *28420/24515* ➙ *30 rooms* 🍴 *Restaurant* 🖃 *AE, MC, V* ⦿ *CP.*

Siteia

Σητεία

⓲ *23 km (14 mi) northeast of Ierapetra, 143 km (87 mi) east of Heraklion.*

Like Ierapetra, Siteia is an unpretentious town where agriculture is more important than tourism: raisins and, increasingly, bananas are the main crops. Siteia's waterfront, lined with cafés and tavernas, is lively from June through August. A long, sandy beach stretches to the east of the waterfront. From Siteia you can fly to Rhodes or take a ferry there via the small islands of Kassos and Karpathos. In July and August, there are usually weekly ferries between Siteia and Piraeus.

An old Venetian fort, the **Kazarma,** overlooks Siteia from a height in the west. The view across the bay is spectacular. ⊠ *Follow road up hill from waterfront.*

Siteia's **archaeological museum,** in addition to other artifacts, contains a rare treasure: a Minoan ivory and gold statuette of a young man, found on the east coast at Palaikastro. The figure dates from around 1500 BC and, though incomplete, is a masterpiece of Minoan carving. ⊠ *Siteia–Ierapetra road, outskirts of town* ☎ *28430/23917* ⊕ *www.culture.gr* 🎫 *€2* ⊗ *Tues.–Sun. 8:30–3.*

The fierce north wind that sweeps this region has twisted the few trees on hillsides surrounding the fortified monastery at **Toplou** into strange shapes. Only a few monks live here now, and the monastery is slowly being renovated. Inside the tall loggia gate, built in the 16th century, the cells are arranged around a cobbled courtyard with a 14th-century church at its center. Each of 61 scenes in its famous icon was inspired by a phrase from the Orthodox liturgy. ⊠ *13 km (8 mi) east of Siteia, off road to Palaikastro* ☎ *No phone* 🎫 *€3* ⊗ *Daily 9–1 and 2–6.*

Where to Stay

¢   🏨 **Hotel El Greco.** This friendly establishment on a narrow street several blocks above the waterfront is perfectly comfortable and not without charm. Many of the simple rooms have balconies overlooking the old town and the sea. Don't count on the sea breeze to keep you cool—opt for a room with air-conditioning, which is €5 extra. Breakfast is available for a small additional fee. ⊠ *G. Arkadiou, 72300* ☎ *28430/23133* 🖷 *28430/26391* 🛏 *15 rooms* ⚐ *Lobby lounge; no a/c in some rooms* 🖃 *MC, V* ⊗ *Closed Nov.–Apr.*

Vai

Βάι

🔟 *27 km (17 mi) east of Siteia, 170 km (104 mi) east of Heraklion.*

Unique in Europe, the palm grove of the renowned beach at Vai existed in classical Greek times. The sandy stretch with nearby islets set in clear turquoise water is one of the most attractive in Crete, but in July and August it gets very crowded.

Follow a narrow track through olive groves to the sandy beach at **Palaikastro.** It's rarely crowded, and service is welcoming at the waterside tavernas. The sprawling Minoan town, currently being excavated by British and American archaeologists, lies off to the right. ⊠ *9 km (5½ mi) south of Vai, follow sign for Marina Village.*

The ruins of the **Palace of Kato Zakro** are smaller than those of the other Minoan palaces on the island. You can drive down to the town and site by a circuitous but spectacular route, or stop at Ano Zakro (Upper Zakro), 20 km (12½ mi) south of Palaikastro village; a path leads down through a deep ravine past caves used for early Minoan burials to the Minoan palace. The walk down and back up is steep but not overly arduous, and takes about two hours. The site is surrounded by a terraced village, Zakro, with narrow cobbled streets. On the fine beach is a cluster of tavernas with a few rooms to rent. ⊠ *38 km (25 mi) south of Vai, ascend paved Minoan road from Kato Zakro harbor through gateway to northeast court down stepped ramp* ☎ *28410/22462* 🖃 *€3* ⊙ *Tues.–Sun. 8–3.*

WESTERN CRETE

Much of Western Crete's landscape—soaring mountains, deep gorges, and rolling green lowlands—remains largely untouched by mass tourism; in fact, only the north coast is developed. There is a wealth of interesting byways to be explored. This region is abundant in Minoan sites—including the palace at Phaistos—as well as Byzantine churches and Venetian monasteries. Two of Greece's more appealing cities are here: Hania and Rethymnon, both crammed with the houses, narrow lanes, and minarets that hark back to Venetian and Turkish occupation. Friendly villages dot the uplands, and there are some outstanding beaches on the west and south coasts. Immediately southwest of Heraklion lies the traditional agricultural heartland of Crete: long, narrow valleys where olive groves alternate with vineyards of sultana grapes for export.

Ayii Deka

Άγιοι Δέκα

 45 km (28 mi) south of Heraklion.

After climbing through a vine- and olive-clad valley, the narrow road southwest from Heraklion swings toward Ayii Deka and on to the Mesara plain. The village contains the church where St. Tito is reputed to be buried, the 6th-century Christian basilica **Ayios Titos.** The plain, filled with silver-gray olive trees interspersed with plastic greenhouses for growing early tomatoes and cucumbers, rises again to the craggy Asterousia Mountains; beyond them is the Libyan Sea. In summer especially, the temperature rises sharply as you descend.

The main road divides a huge expanse of scattered archaeological ruins at the ancient Greco-Roman city of **Gortyna** (also known as Gortys or Gortyn). Look for the **odeion,** a small amphitheater where musical recitals were staged in the 1st century AD. In a brick building behind it, the **Gortyna Law Code** is displayed. Inscribed on a set of stone blocks, it dates from the first half of the 5th century BC (the earliest code discovered in Europe). The 600 lines detail the laws concerning marriage, divorce, inheritance, adoption, assault and rape, and the status of slaves. A path climbs a few hundred feet uphill to the **Acropolis of Gortyna,** which has a view across the plain. Italian archaeologists, who have dug here since the 1880s, compiled a map—posted at several points around the site—to help you to find your way through the olive trees to several temples, a small theater, and the public baths. Made a Roman capital in AD 67, Gortyna was destroyed by Arab raiders in the 7th century and never rebuilt. The ruins provided most of the building material for the town of Ayii Deka. Fragments of ancient sculpture and inscriptions can

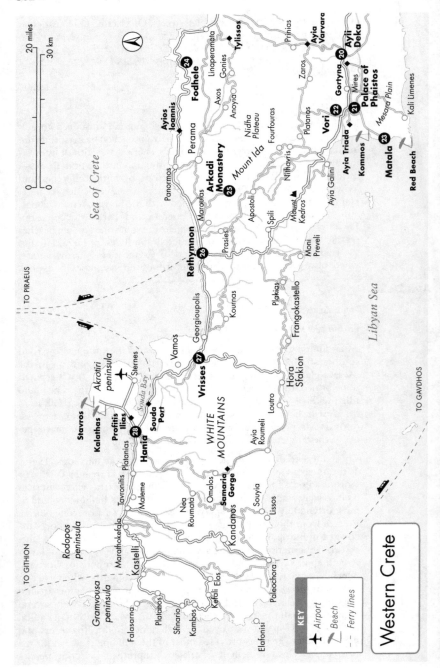

Western Crete

KEY

✈ Airport

⌇ Beach

-- Ferry lines

Sea of Crete

Libyan Sea

TO PIRAEUS

TO GITHION

TO GAVDHOS

20 miles

30 km

Rodopos peninsula

Gramvousa peninsula

Akrotiri peninsula

Souda Bay

WHITE MOUNTAINS

Nidha Plateau

Mount Ida

Mount Kedros

Mesara Plain

Falasarna
Platanos
Sfinaria
Kambos
Elafonisi
Kefali Elos
Kastelli
Marathokefala
Tavronitis
Maleme
Nea Roumata
Platanias
28 **Hania**
Stavros
Kalathas
Profitis Ilias
Sternes
Souda Port
Vamos
Georgioupolis
27 **Vrisses**
Omalos
Samaria Gorge
Kandanos
Souyia
Lissos
Ayia Roumeli
Loutro
Hora Sfakion
Paleochora
Frangokastello
Plakias
Moni Preveli
Ayia Galini
Kournas
Panormos
26 **Rethymnon**
Prasies
Maroulas
25 **Arkadi Monastery**
Apostoli
Spili
Nifhavris
Fourfouras
Platanos
Zaros
Axos
Anoyia
Gonies
Linaperamata
24 **Fodhele**
Ayios Ioannis
Perama
Tylissos
Prinias
Ayia Varvara
20 **Ayii Deka**
Gortyna
Mires
22 **Vori**
21 **Palace of Phaistos**
Ayia Triada
Kommos
23 **Matala**
Red Beach
Kali Limenes

still be seen in the 13th-century village church there. ⊠ *Next to Ayios Titos* ☎ *28920/31144* ⊕ *www.culture.gr* ☑ *€2* ⊙ *June–Oct., daily 8:30–7; Nov.–May, daily 8:30–5.*

Palace of Phaistos

Ανάκτορο Φαιστού

㉑ *11 km (7 mi) west of Ayii Deka, 50 km (31 mi) southwest of Heraklion.*

Fodor'sChoice
★

On a steep hill overlooking olive groves and the sea on one side, and high mountain peaks on the other, Phaistos is the site of one of the greatest Minoan palaces. Unlike Knossos, Phaistos has not been reconstructed, though the copious ruins are richly evocative. The palace was built around 1900 BC and rebuilt after a disastrous earthquake around 1650 BC. It was burned and abandoned in the wave of destruction that swept across the island around 1450 BC.

You enter down a flight of steps leading into the west court, then climb a grand staircase. From here you pass through the **Propylon porch** into a light well and descend a narrow staircase into the **central court.** Much of the southern and eastern sections of the palace have eroded away. But there are large pithoi still in place in the old **storerooms.** On the north side of the court the recesses of an elaborate doorway bear a rare trace: red paint in a diamond pattern on a white ground. A passage from the doorway leads to the **north court** and the **northern domestic apartments,** now roofed and fenced off. The **Phaistos Disk** was found in 1903 in a chest made of mud brick at the northeast edge of the site. East of the central court are the **palace workshops,** with a metalworking furnace fenced off. South of the workshops lie the **southern domestic apartments,** including a clay bath. From there you have a memorable view across the Mesara plain. ⊠ *Cross Geropotamos River and ascend hill* ☎ *28920/42315* ⊕ *www.culture.gr* ☑ *€3; combined ticket with Ayia Triada, €6* ⊙ *Daily 8–7:30.*

Vori

Βώροι

㉒ *5 km (3 mi) north of Palace of Phaistos, 65 km (40½ mi) southwest of Heraklion.*

Vori is a pleasant farming town of whitewashed houses on narrow lanes; locals congregate at the cafés on the lively main square.

★ The **Foundation Museum of Cretan Ethnology** has a rich collection of Cretan folk items, including exquisite weavings and pottery, all displayed in a well-designed museum building. ⊠ *Edge of village center* ☎ *28920/91112* ☑ *€3* ⊙ *Daily 10–6.*

Ayia Triada dates from the later palace period and was destroyed at the same time as Phaistos, which is only a few miles away. It was once thought to have been a summer palace for the rulers of Phaistos but now is believed to have been a group of villas and warehouse areas. From the archaeological site there's a magnificent view toward the Paximadia islets in the Mesara Gulf. Rooms in the L-shape complex of buildings were once paneled with gypsum slabs and decorated with frescoes: the two now hanging in the Archaeological Museum in Heraklion show a woman in a garden and a cat hunting a pheasant. ⊠ *Follow signs from main road, 3 km (2 mi) southwest of Vori* ☎*28920/91360* ⊕*www.culture. gr* ⊡ *€3; combined ticket with Phaistos €6* ☉ *Tues.–Sun. 10–4:30.*

Where to Stay

★ ¢ 🏠 **Portakali Studios.** "My little piece of paradise" is how Gudrun Krasagaki describes the small inn she has created at the edge of Vori. The extremely attractive beamed-ceiling apartments are decorated with tasteful furnishings and local art and photographs, and have well-equipped kitchens. All open onto a large, shady, well-tended garden that is the perfect place to spend a hot afternoon or to catch an evening breeze. Mrs. Krasagaki gladly dispenses advice on exploring the region. ⊠ *Vori, 70200* ☎☎ *28920/91188* ⊕ *www.messara.gr* ⤴ *4 apartments* ⌂ *Kitchens, room TVs, bicycles; no room phones* ☱ *No credit cards.*

Matala

Μάταλα

❷ *10 km (6 mi) southwest of Vori, 70 km (42 mi) southwest of Heraklion.*

Renowned in the 1960s as a stopover on the hippie trail across the eastern Mediterranean, Matala today is a small, low-key beach resort and a stop on the Phaistos–Ayia Triada tourist circuit. The 2nd-century AD Roman tombs cut in the cliff side (where the hippies lived) are now fenced off but continue to attract day-trippers on coach tours from Heraklion. Once the crowds leave (usually by the early afternoon), the town beach is pleasant though rather bland. The excellent **Red Beach** is accessible only by a 20-minute walk across a rocky promontory reached from the steep path on the south side of town. ⊠ *1 km (½ mi) south of town.*

One of the best, and least crowded, beaches on the south coast, **Kommos** lies below the Minoan harbor site where excavations are ongoing. ⊠ *2 km (1 mi) off Mires–Matala road, near village of Pitsidia.*

Where to Stay & Eat

★ ¢ ✕🏠 **Taverna and Studios Sigelakis.** Residents from villages for miles around come to Sivas to enjoy a meal (¢–$) of *briam* (baked vegetables) *pastitsio* (the traditional casserole of pasta, ground lamb or beef, cheese, and a creamy béchamel sauce), and other specialties, along with friendly service and a free glass of raki and a sweet. Sit out on the front terrace in warm seasons or in the stone-walled, hearth-warmed dining room when the weather's cold. The Sigelakis family also rents out extremely comfortable and tastefully furnished apartments in a hillside house around the corner. All have separate bedrooms or sleeping areas as well as such nice touches as stone walls and archways and terraces that overlook the surrounding hills and olive groves; some have fireplaces. ⊠ *6 km (4 mi) northeast of Matala, 70200 Sivas* ☎ *69748/10905* ⊕ *www.sigelakis-studios.gr* ⤴ *8 apartments* ⌂ *Kitchens, room TVs; no room phones* ☱ *MC, V.*

Fodhele

Φόδελε

㉔ *80 km (43 mi) northeast of Matala, 13 km (8 mi) west of Heraklion, 10 km (6 mi) northwest of Tylissos.*

The straggling village of Fodhele is said to be the birthplace of Domenico Theotokopoulos, the 16th-century Cretan painter known as El Greco.

The road to the Minoan site at **Tylissos** gradually winds uphill through vineyards. The pine-shaded complex reveals three later palace-period buildings: workshops, living quarters, and storerooms. ✉ *10 km (6 mi) southeast of Fodhele, off Heraklion–Hania road at Gazi* ☎ *2810/ 831372* 🎟 *€3* ⊗ *Daily 8:30–3.*

The monastery of **Ayios Ioannis** is dedicated to John the Baptist. Inside is a historic small chapel, but there is rarely anyone around to let you in. It's above the highway, with a spectacular view from its terrace across the Cretan Sea. ✉ *23 km (14 mi) west of Fodhele, Heraklion–Hania Rd.*

Arkadi Monastery

Μονή Αρκαδίου

★ **㉕** *18 km (11 mi) south of Fodhele, 30 km (19 mi) west of Heraklion.*

Follow a gorge inland before emerging into the flat pastureland that is part of the Arkadi Monastery's holdings. The monastery is a place of pilgrimage for Cretans and one of the most stunning pieces of Renaissance architecture on the island. The ornate facade, decorated with Corinthian columns and an elegant belfry above, was built in the 16th century of a local, honey-color stone. In 1866 the monastery came under siege during a major rebellion against the Turks, and Abbot Gabriel and several hundred rebels, together with their wives and children, refused to surrender. When the Turkish forces broke through the gate, the defenders set the gunpowder store afire, killing themselves together with hundreds of Turks. ✉ *South of town of Perama, off old Heraklion–Hania Rd.* 🎟 *€1* ⊗ *Daily 8–5.*

Rethymnon

Ρέθυμνο

★ **㉖** *54 km (33½ mi) west of Arkadi Monastery, 78 km (48½ mi) west of Heraklion.*

Rethymnon is Crete's third-largest town, after Heraklion and Hania. As the population (about 30,000) steadily increases, villagers move into new houses on the outskirts of town. Much of Rethymnon's charm perseveres in the old Venetian quarter, which is being restored: this is where you'll want to spend your time. Wandering through the narrow alleyways, you come across handsome carved-stone Renaissance doorways belonging to vanished mansions, fountains, archways, and wooden

Turkish houses. A long strip of beach to the east of the old town has been tastelessly developed with large hotels and other resort facilities catering to tourists on package vacations. Ferries run between Rethymnon's port and Piraeus.

One of the few surviving minarets in Greece is on the **Neratze,** a mosque–turned–concert hall. You can climb its 120 steps for a panoramic view; access is possible only when a performance takes place. ⊠ *Odos Verna and Odos Ethnikis Adistaseos.*

Don't miss the carefully restored **Venetian loggia:** the colonnade was once the clubhouse of the local nobility. ⊠ *Arkadiou, near town center.*

Rethymnon's small **Venetian harbor,** with its restored 13th-century lighthouse, comes to life in warm weather, when restaurant tables clutter the quayside. ⊠ *Waterfront.*

Rethymnon is dominated by the huge, fortified Venetian castle known as the **Fortessa.** High, well-preserved walls enclose a large empty space occupied by a few scattered buildings—and filled with wildflowers in spring. Forced laborers from the town and surrounding villages built the fortress from 1573 to 1583. It didn't fulfill its purpose of keeping out the Turks: Rethymnon surrendered after a three-week siege in 1646. ⊠ *West end of town* 🖼 *€3* 🕘 *Sat.–Thurs. 8:30–7.*

At the local **archaeological museum,** look for the collection of bone tools from a Neolithic site at Yerani (west of Rethymnon). An unfinished statue of Aphrodite, the goddess of love, is interesting: the ancient chisel marks show clearly. The museum building used to be a Turkish prison. ⊠ *West end of town, next to entrance of Fortessa* 🕾 *28310/54668* 🖼 *€3* 🕘 *Tues.–Sun. 8:30–3.*

One of the town's most delightful attractions is the **Historical and Folk Art Museum,** in a restored Venetian palazzo near the mosque. Rustic furnishings, tools, and costumes provide a charming and vivid picture of what life on Crete was like until well into the 20th century. ⊠ *Vernadou 28* 🕾 *28310/29975* 🖼 *€3* 🕘 *Daily 9:30–2.*

Where to Stay & Eat

★ **$$-$$$$** ✕ **Avli.** A stone, barrel-vaulted dining room and a multitiered garden are the attractive settings for creative interpretations of Cretan cuisine, made only from grass-fed lamb, fresh-caught fish, and garden vegetables, and other organic and natural ingredients. Even a simple *horiatiki* (Greek salad) and grilled lamb chop can be transporting here, as is the excellent selection of the island's finest wines. Reservations are a good idea in summer. ⊠ *Paleologou 22* 🕾 *28310/26213* 🖃 *MC, V.*

¢-$$ ✕ **Cavo D'Oro.** This is the most stylish of the handful of fish restaurants around the tiny Venetian harbor, and one of the finest restaurants in Crete. Lobster and fish dishes are always served fresh. The high-ceilinged, wood-paneled dining room was once a medieval storeroom; diners also sit on the old cobbled waterfront. ⊠ *Nearchou 42–43* 🕾 *28310/24446* 🖃 *DC, MC, V.*

¢-$ ✕ **Kyria Maria.** At this simple, family-run taverna in the center of the old town, good home cooking is served from a small menu of traditional

Greek specialties. Neighborhood life buzzes around the tables set beneath an arbor in a narrow lane. The place is so popular that the family has opened two nearby outposts, one around the corner near the port on Fotaki street and another one, with a nice garden, beneath the castle on Himarras street. All are open for breakfast, lunch, and dinner. ⊠ *Moschovitou* ☎ *28310/29078* ➟ *MC, V.*

★ **$$$$** 🏠 **Palazzino di Corina.** Rethymnon has several hotels occupying old palaces; Corina is the most luxurious and provides stylish surroundings that include a courtyard with wood chaises, topiary planters, and statuary surrounding a small pool. Guest rooms, with exposed-stone walls and wooden beams, are furnished with a mix of antiques and contemporary pieces. ⊠ *Damvergi and Diakou, 74100* ☎ *28310/21205* 📠 *28310/21204* ⊕ *www.corina.gr* ➟ *21 suites* ⚹ *Restaurant, room service, minibars, cable TV with movies, pool* ➟ *MC, V* ⍾⊙⍾ *BP.*

$ 🏠 **Hotel Fortezza.** Only steps from the fortress, the old town, and the beach, you can enjoy many of the advantages of the larger hotels on Rethymnon's charmless beach strip. The tile-floor rooms, with handsome traditional wood furnishings, are built around a marble atrium and sunny courtyard; many have balconies. Breakfast is served as a buffet. ⊠ *Melisinou 16, 74100* ☎ *28310/55551* 📠 *28310/54073* ⊕ *www.fortezza.gr* ➟ *54 rooms* ⚹ *Restaurant, snack bar, pool, recreation room* ➟ *AE, DC, MC, V* ⍾⊙⍾ *BP.*

The Outdoors
The **Happy Walker** (⊠ Tombazi 56 ☎ 28310/52920) arranges easy hiking tours in the surrounding mountains; €28 a walk.

Shopping
★ The **Archaeological Museum Shop** (⊠ Paleologou ☎ 28310/54668) has an excellent selection of books, as well as reproductions of artifacts from its collections and from other sites in Crete and throughout Greece. For a souvenir that will be light to carry, stop in at **Kalymnos** (⊠ Arabatzoglou 18), filled to the rafters with sponges harvested off the eponymous island.

Vrisses

Βρύσες

㉗ *26 km (14 mi) west of Rethymnon, 105 km (65 mi) west of Heraklion.*

This appealing old village, a welcome retreat from the untidy beachfront developments that have sprung up around nearby Georgioupolis, is famous throughout Crete for its thick, creamy yogurt. Served in the cafés beneath the plane trees at the center of the village, it's best eaten with a large spoonful of honey on top.

en route The road from Vrisses to Hania climbs across the Vamos peninsula and past **Souda Bay** (5 km [3 mi] east of Hania). This deep inlet, considered the best harbor in the eastern Mediterranean, can shelter the entire U.S. Sixth Fleet; indeed, the U.S. Navy maintains a naval support base here. Taking photos in the area is forbidden, a regulation to be taken seriously: if you are caught doing so you may be charged with spying. At the top of the bay is the port where passenger ferries arrive from Piraeus.

Hania

Χανιά

28 *52 km (33 mi) west of Vrisses, 78 km (48 mi) west of Rethymnon.*

Fodor's Choice
★

A long avenue lined with eucalyptus trees leads to the outskirts of Hania, where signs guide you around the one-way system to the large, cross-shape covered market in the town center. Some of the outskirts are a bit scrappy; the town's beauty resides in well-preserved Venetian and Turkish quarters, around the harbor and its centuries-old waterside warehouses, and in leafy residential neighborhoods of small villas. It was here that the Greek flag was raised in 1913 to mark Crete's unification with Greece, and until 1971 Hania was the island's capital.

From Hania's market, work your way through a maze of narrow streets to the waterfront, which is a pedestrian zone in July and August. Walk around the inner harbor, where the fishing boats moor, and east past the Venetian arsenals. Both Theotokopoulou and Zambeliou streets access narrow alleyways with predominantly Venetian and Turkish houses. If you head around to the old lighthouse, you get a magnificent view of the town with the imposing White Mountains looming beyond.

Kastelli hill, where the Venetians first settled, became the quarter of the local nobility, but it had been occupied much earlier: parts of what may be a Minoan palace have been excavated at its base. ⊠ *Above harbor.*

On Sunday, Hania's time-honored flag-raising ceremony is repeated at the **Firka,** the old Turkish prison, which is now the naval museum. Exhibits, more riveting than might be expected, trace the island's seafaring history from the time of the Venetians. Look for the photos and mementos from the World War II Battle of Crete, when Allied forces moved across the island and, with the help of Cretans, ousted the German occupiers. ⊠ *Waterfront at far west end of port* ☎ *28210/91875* 🖂 *€2* ☉ *Daily 9–4.*

The **Janissaries Mosque** was built when the Turks captured the town in 1645 after a two-month siege and now holds temporary exhibits. Hours vary from show to show; the place is most often closed. ⊠ *East side of inner harbor.*

The **Etz Hayyim Synagogue,** restored in 1999 after being stripped of all religious objects by the Nazis in 1944, testifies to the long presence of Jews on Crete. The building was formerly the Venetian church of St. Catherine; it became a synagogue in the 17th century. It contains Venetian Gothic arches, a *mikveh* (ritual bath), and the tombs of three rabbis. ⊠ *Parodos Kondylaki, outer harbor* ☎ *28210/86286* ⊕ *www.etz-hayyim-hania. org* 🖂 *Free* ☉ *May–mid-Oct., Mon.–Wed. 9–8, Thurs. and Fri. 9–5:30; mid-Oct.–Apr., Mon. 9:30–8, Tues. 9:30–5:30, Wed.–Fri. 9:30–2.*

Artifacts on display at the **archaeological museum** come from all over western Crete: the painted Minoan clay coffins and elegant late Minoan pottery indicate that the region was as wealthy as the center of the island in the Bronze Age, though no palace has yet been located. The museum occupies the former Venetian church of St. Francis. ⊠ *Chalidron* ☎ *28210/90334* ▨ *€2* ☉ *Tues.–Sun. 8:30–3.*

A folklife museum, the **Cretan House** is bursting at the seams with farm equipment, tools, household items, wedding garb, and a wealth of other material reflecting the island's traditional heritage. ⊠ *Off courtyard at Chalidron 46, near archaeological museum* ☎ *28210/90816* ▨ *€1.50* ☉ *Mon.–Sat. 9–3 and 6–9.*

The **Profitis Ilias** neighborhood is lined with neoclassical mansions dating to the turn of the 20th century, when Britain, France, Russia, and Italy were active in Cretan politics. A panoramic view from here takes in Hania and its surrounding villages, along with much of the northwest coast. ⊠ *5 km (3 mi) east of center, Halepa.*

North of Hania lie two worthy sand **beaches:** Kalathas and Stavros, both about 15 km (9 mi) north of Hania, near the Akrotiri peninsula's monasteries.

Lands at the northeast corner of the Akrotiri peninsula are the holdings of several monasteries. The olive groves that surround and finance these institutions are said to yield some of the island's finest oil, which is available for sale in a shop at **Ayia Triada.** ⊠ *16 km (10 mi) north of Hania, follow road from Chordaki* ☎ *No phone* ☉ *Daily 9–3.*

★ From the monastery at **Goubermetou,** on the Akrotiri peninsula, a path leads down the flanks of a seaside ravine past several caves used as hermitages and churches. A 20-minute walk brings you to the remote monastery of St. John the Hermit; follow the path along a riverbank for another 20 minutes or so to a delightful cove that is the perfect place for a refreshing dip. The return walk requires a steep uphill climb. ⊠ *19 km (12 mi) north of Hania, follow road north from Chordaki* ☎ *No phone* ▨ *Free* ☉ *Daily 9–3.*

off the beaten path

Fodor'sChoice ★

SAMARIA GORGE – Drive south of Hania to the deep, verdant crevice that extends 10 km (6 mi) from near the village of Xyloskalo to the Libyan Sea. The gorge's landscape—of forest, sheer rock faces, and running streams—is magnificent. Buses depart the central bus station in Hania at 7:30 and 8:30 AM for Xyloskalo. Boats leave in the afternoon from the mouth of the gorge (most people don't hike back up) at Ayia Roumeli for Hora Sfakion, from where buses return to Hania. Travel agents also arrange day trips to the gorge. ⊠ *25 km (15 mi) south of Hania, Omalos.*

Where to Stay & Eat

$–$$ ✕**Apostolis.** What is reputed to be the freshest and best-prepared fish in town is served on a lively terrace toward the east end of the old harbor, near the Venetian arsenals. Choose your fish from the bed of ice and decide how you would like it prepared, or opt for the rich fish soup. ⊠ *Akti Enoseos* 📞 28210/41767 ▭ *MC, V.*

¢–$ ✕ **Faka.** Much to the delight of the many neighborhood residents who dine here regularly, Faka concentrates on traditional Cretan cooking. House specialties include *boureki,* a delicious casserole of zucchini, potato, and cheese, and *papoutsakia,* a baked dish with ground lamb, eggplant, and béchamel sauce. The generous meze platter is a meal in itself. ⊠ *Off Archoleon, behind Venetian arsenals* 📞 28210/42341 ▭ *MC, V.*

¢–$ ✕ **Tamam.** An ancient Turkish bath has been converted to one of the most atmospheric restaurants in Hania's old town. Specialties served up in the tiled dining room, and on the narrow lane outside, include peppers with grilled feta cheese and eggplant stuffed with chicken. ⊠ *Zambeliou 49* 📞 28210/96080 ▭ *No credit cards.*

¢–$ ✕ **Well of the Turk.** It's an adventure just finding this restaurant: ask your way, because everyone in the neighborhood knows the place. Behind the Venetian warehouses on the harbor, it stands in a narrow alley near the minaret in the old Arab quarter. The food ranges from simple Greek fare (a prerequisite is the wonderful, large appetizer platter) to some Continental dishes, such as sautéed chicken in a wine sauce. ⊠ *Kalinikou Sarpaki 1–3, Splantiza* 📞 28210/54547 ▭ *No credit cards.*

★ $$$$ ▦ **Casa Delfino.** In the 1880s this Venetian Renaissance palace was the home of Pedro Delfino, an Italian merchant; today it belongs to two of his descendants. The dramatically decorated guest rooms, four of which are housed in an adjoining building of the same era, are entered through graceful stone archways surrounding a courtyard paved in pebble mosaic. Most have upscale, contemporary wood furniture and rich fabrics, and distinctive architectural details—some occupy two levels, some have enormous marble baths, some have private terraces. ⊠ *Theofanous 9, Palio Limani, 73100* 📞 28210/87400 🖷 28210/96500 ⊕ *www.casadelfino.com* ⇝ *21 suites* ⇱ *Minibars, cable TV, some in-room data ports, bar, laundry service* ▭ *AE, DC, MC, V* ⑩ *BP.*

$$$$ ▦ **Villa Andromeda.** The German high command occupied this seaside villa during World War II (Rommel supposedly enjoyed the old swimming pool that is still next to a larger one in the garden). The yellow, neoclassical mansion contains large suites, some on two levels with sleeping areas upstairs, that overlook the garden or face the sea. Ornate painted ceilings, marble floors, and tapestry rugs add to the elegance of the communal spaces. ⊠ *Pl. Eleftheriou Venizelou 150, 73100* 📞 28210/28300 or 28210/28301 🖷 28210/28303 ⊕ *www.villandromeda.gr* ⇝ *8 suites* ⇱ *Minibars, pool, bar* ▭ *DC, MC, V* ⑩ *CP.*

★ $$ ▦ **Doma.** Feel at home for a night in a 19th-century seaside mansion on the eastern edge of town; it stands about a 20-minute walk along the water from the Venetian harbor. With their elegant, Cretan-style dark-wood furnishings, the simple guest rooms face either the luxuriant garden or the sea. Carved-wood sofas and local and family photos fill the sitting room, and an exquisite collection of headdresses from around the world is displayed off the wicker-filled garden room. Breakfast, a lavish spread, includes fresh breads, homemade jams, and yogurt with a Turkish topping: a delicious mix of spices, quince preserves, and honey. On request the owners will prepare a traditional Cretan dinner for guests or nonguests and serve it in an airy upstairs dining room. ⊠ *Pl. Eleftheriou Venizelou 124, 73100* ☎ *28210/51772 or 28210/51773* 📠 *28210/41578* ⊕ *www.hotel-doma.gr* 🛏 *22 rooms, 3 suites* ⚐ *Dining room, minibars; no TVs in some rooms* ▤ *DC, MC, V* ⊙ *Closed Nov.–Mar.* ⦿ *BP.*

$$ ⊞ **Hotel Amphora.** Relax on the rooftop terrace and gaze out at views of the harbor, town, and mountains. This comfortable, well-run, and character-filled hotel is in a 14th-century Venetian mansion on a lane above the inner harbor. Rooms are large and many have sea views, as well as such extras as beamed ceilings, fireplaces, private balconies, and kitchenettes. The hotel serves a lavish buffet breakfast for €10, and the dining room, which is on the harbor-front promenade, serves excellent, basic Greek fare and good wines at a discount to you as a hotel patron. ⊠ *Parodos Theotokopoulou, 73100* ☎ *28210/93224* 📠 *28210/93226* 🛏 *18 rooms* ⚐ *Restaurant, some kitchenettes* ▤ *AE, MC, V.*

$ ⊞ **Casa Leone.** A Venetian courtyard with a fountain, and a salon and balcony that hang over the harbor are among the dramatic flourishes at this 600-year-old mansion in the old town. The large and comfortable bedrooms are enhanced with modern baths and such details as curved walls, paneled ceilings, sleeping lofts, and private terraces. ⊠ *Theotokopoulou 18, 73100* ☎📠 *28210/76762* 🛏 *5 rooms* ⚐ *Minibars, bar* ▤ *MC, V* ⦿ *CP.*

$ ⊞ **Porto del Colombo.** This renovated Venetian town house is full of architectural surprises: wood ceilings and floors; small, deep-set windows; two-story rooms with lofts. The wood furnishings throughout are traditional Cretan. Weather permitting, breakfast is served on the narrow, old-town street out front. ⊠ *Theofanous and Moshon, 73100* ☎📠 *28210/70945* 🛏 *10 rooms* ⚐ *Minibars, bar* ▤ *MC, V* ⦿ *CP.*

Shopping

One or two souvenir stores on the waterfront sell English-language books and newspapers. The most exotic shopping experience in town is a stroll through Hania's covered market to see local merchants selling rounds of Cretan cheese, jars of golden honey, lengths of salami, salt fish, lentils, and herbs.

★ The silver jewelry and ceramics at **Carmela** (⊠ Odos Anghelou 7 ☎ 28210/90487) are striking. The store represents contemporary jewelers and other craftspeople from Crete and throughout Greece, as well as the work of owner Carmela Iatropoulou.

★ **Top Hanas** (⊠ Odos Anghelou 3 ☎ 28210/98571) sells a good selection of antique blankets and rugs, most of them made for dowries from homespun wool and natural dyes.

off the beaten path

WESTERN BEACHES – Drive west from Hania to the magnificent beaches on the far coast, such as **Falasarna,** near Crete's northwestern tip, and, on the southwestern tip of Crete, **Elafonisi.** These are rarely crowded even in summer. Elafonisi islet has white-sand beaches and black rocks in a turquoise sea (to get there you wade across a narrow channel). You can also head south from Hania across the craggy White Mountains to explore the isolated Libyan Sea villages of Paleochora, the area's main resort, and Souyia. In summer, boat service operates along the southwest coast, connecting such towns as Paleochora, Ayia Roumeli, and Hora Sfakion.

CRETE A TO Z

To research prices, get advice from other travelers, and book travel arrangements, visit www.fodors.com.

AIR TRAVEL

Olympic Airways connects Athens, and other islands, with Heraklion and Hania. Aegean Airlines flies between Athens and Heraklion and Hania.

⏴ Carriers Aegean Airlines ☎ 210/998-8300 in Athens ⊕ www.aegeanairlines.gr. **Olympic Airways** ☎ 28210/57702 in Hania, 210/966-6666 in Athens ⊕ www.olympic-airways.gr.

AIRPORTS

The principal arrival point on Crete is Heraklion Airport, where up to 16 flights daily arrive from Athens, daily flights arrive from Rhodes and Thessaloniki, and two weekly flights arrive from Mykonos. Heraklion is also serviced directly by charter flights from other European cities. There are several daily flights from Athens to Hania Airport.

⏴ Hania Airport ⊠ 15 km [9 mi] northeast of Hania, off road to Sterne, Souda Bay ☎ 28210/63264. **Heraklion Airport** ⊠ 5 km [3 mi] east of town, off road to Gournes, Heraklion ☎ 2810/245644.

AIRPORT TRANSFERS A municipal bus (⇨ Bus Travel, *below*) just outside Heraklion Airport can take you to Platia Eleftherias in the Heraklion town center. Tickets are sold from a kiosk next to the bus stop; the fare is €0.80. From Hania Airport, Olympic Airlines buses take you to the airline office in the center for €2. Cabs line up outside Heraklion and Hania airports; the fare into the respective towns is about €5 for Heraklion and €7 for Hania.

BIKE & MOPED TRAVEL

Motorbikes are available for rent in almost every town and village. The law, and common sense, mandates that you wear a helmet. Be cautious—motorbike accidents account for numerous fractures and other injuries among tourists every year. Reliable rentals can be arranged through Crete Travel in Heraklion and at the Grecotel Rithymna Beach hotel in Rethymnon.

⏴ Crete Travel ⊠ Epimenidou 20-22, Heraklion ☎ 2810/227002 ⊕ www.cretetravel.com. **Grecotel Rithymna Beach Hotel** ⊠ Beachfront, Rethymnon ☎ 28310/71002.

BOAT & FERRY TRAVEL

Heraklion and Souda Bay (5 km [3 mi] east of Hania) are the island's main ports, and there is regular service as well to Rethymnon. Two Cretan shipping companies, Anek and Minoan Lines, have daily ferry service from Piraeus, near Athens, to these Cretan ports year-round. The overnight crossing takes eight hours on Anek and about six hours on

Minoan. Hellenic Seaways runs high-speed, four-hour service between Piraeus and Heraklion and Hania; Minoan Lines catamarans also operate between Santorini and Heraklion, cutting travel time to just less than two hours.

On the overnight runs, you can book a berth or an aircraft-style seat, and there are usually cafeterias, dining rooms, shops, and other services on board. A one-way fare from Piraeus to Heraklion, Rethymnon, or Hania without accommodation costs about €22, from about €44 with accommodation, with a small discount for round-trips. Car fares are about €70 each way, depending on vehicle size.

In July and August, a boat service around the Samaria Gorge operates along the southwest coast from Hora Sfakion to Loutro, Ayia Roumeli, Souyia, Lissos, and Paleochora, the main resort on the southwest coast. Ferries also sail from Paleochora to Ghavdos, an island south of Crete, and from Ierapetra to Krissi, an island also to the south. A ferry links Siteia with the Dodecanese islands of Kassos, Karpathos, and Rhodes. There are weekly sailings from Heraklion to Limassol, in Cyprus, to Haifa, Israel, and to Venice. A weekly trip connects Kastelli, west of Hania, with Gythion, in the Peloponnese.

Most travel agencies sell tickets for all ferries and hydrofoils; make reservations several days in advance during the July to August high season.
🔏 **Anek** ✉ Karamanlis Ave., Hania ☎ 28210/24163 ⊕ www.anek.gr. **Hellenic Seaways** ✉ 25 August, Heraklion ☎ 2810/346185 ⊕ www.hellenicseaways.gr. **Minoan Lines** ✉ 25 August, Heraklion ☎ 2810/346185 ⊕ www.ferries.gr/minoan.

BUS TRAVEL
The public bus company (KTEL) has regular, inexpensive service among the main towns. You can book seats in advance at bus stations. Unfortunately, finding the right bus in Heraklion is a difficult task. The bus station for western Crete is opposite the port; the station for the south is outside the Hania Gate to the right of the archaeological museum; and the station for the east is at the traffic circle at the end of Leoforos D. Bofor, close to the old harbor. Ask someone at the tourist information office to tell you exactly where to find your bus and to show you the spot on a map.

KTEL's efficient village bus network operates from the bus station in each *komopolis,* or market town.
🔏 **KTEL** ☎ 28410/22234 in Ayios Nikolaos, 28210/93052 in Hania, 2810/245020 in Heraklion, 28310/22785 in Rethymnon ⊕ www.ktel.org.

CAR RENTALS
You can rent cars and jeeps in any of the island's main towns, or you can arrange beforehand with a major agency in the United States or in Athens to pick up a car on arrival in Crete. Many local car-rental agencies have offices in the airports and in the cities, as well as in some resort villages. For example, Sixt has offices in Ayios Nikolaos, Hania, and Heraklion. For the most part, these local agencies are extremely reliable and charge very low rates. Even without advance reservations, ex-

pect to pay about €40 or less a day in high season for a medium-size car with unlimited mileage. Weekly prices are negotiable, but with unlimited mileage rentals start at about €200 in summer. Rates are less and usually negotiable out of season. Cars are often not available from the outlets at the Heraklion Airport unless you've booked in advance, but even at the height of season you can usually find a car at one of the agencies in town—there are many around Platia Eleftherias.

Avis ⊠ Akti Koundourou 12, Ayios Nikolaos ☎ 28410/28497 ⊕ www.avis.com ⊠ Hania Airport ☎ 28210/63080 ⊠ Heraklion Airport ☎ 2810/229402. **Hertz** ⊠ Akti Koundourou 17, Ayios Nikolaos ☎ 28410/28311 ⊕ www.hertz.com ⊠ Hania Airport ☎ 28210/63385 ⊠ Heraklion Airport ☎ 2810/330452. **Sixt** ⊠ Akti Konudourou 28, Ayios Nikolaos ☎ 28410/82055 ⊕ www.sixt.com ⊠ Hania Airport ☎ 28210/20905 ⊠ Heraklion Airport ☎ 2810/280915.

CAR TRAVEL

Roads on Crete are not too congested, but driving in the main towns can be nerve-racking, especially during the lunchtime rush hour. Apart from the north-coast highway, outlying roads tend to be winding and narrow. Most are now asphalt, but dirt tracks between villages are still found in mountainous regions. Most road signs are in Greek and English. Gas stations are not plentiful outside the big towns, and road maps are not always reliable, especially in the south. Sheep and goats frequently stray onto the roads, with or without their shepherd or sheepdog.

Drive defensively wherever you are, as Cretan drivers are aggressive and liable to ignore the rules of the road. In July and August, tourists on motor scooters can be a hazard. Night driving is not advisable.

EMERGENCIES

Your hotel can help you call an English-speaking doctor. Pharmacies stay open late by turns, and a list of those open late is displayed in their windows.

Emergency Services Hospitals ☎ 28410/66000 in Ayios Nikolaos, 28210/22000 in Hania, 2810/368000 in Heraklion, 28310/87100 in Rethymnon. **Tourist Police** ☎ 28410/26900 in Ayios Nikolaos, 28210/5332 in Hania, 2810/289614 in Heraklion, 28310/28156 in Rethymnon.

ENGLISH-LANGUAGE MEDIA

English-language books, magazines, and newspapers are available in the major towns and resorts, but difficult to find once you get off the well-beaten tourist path. In some of the larger hotels you may find CNN, Star News, or other English-language television broadcasts from the United States and the United Kingdom.

English-Language Bookstores Astrakianakis ⊠ Pl. Eleftheriou Venizelou, Heraklion ☎ 2810/284248. **International Press Bookshop** ⊠ Pl. Eleftheriou Venizelou 26, Rethymnon. **Kouvidis-Manouras** ⊠ Daidalou 6, Heraklion ☎ 2810/220135.

MAIL & SHIPPING

Post offices are open weekdays 8–3. You can sometimes buy stamps at magazine kiosks.

Post offices ⊠ Tzanakaki 3, Hania ⊠ Pl. Daskaloyianni, Heraklion ⊠ Koundourioti, Rethymnon.

SPORTS & THE OUTDOORS

The Greek National Tourism Organization (GNTO or EOT) can provide information about hiking on Crete. Alpine Travel offers many hiking tours throughout western Crete. The Greek Federation of Mountaineering Associations operates overnight refuges in the White Mountains and on Mt. Ida.

🖪 **Alpine Travel** ✉ Bonaili 11, Hania ☎ 28210/50939 ⊕ www.alpine.gr. **Greek Federation of Mountaineering Associations** ☎ 28210/44647 in the White Mountains, 2810/289440 on Mt. Ida, 2810/227609 in Heraklion.

TELEPHONES

You can often make metered calls overseas from kiosks and kafeneia, even in small villages. To avoid heavy surcharges imposed by hotels on long-distance calls, you can make them from offices of the Greek phone company, known as OTE.

🖪 **OTE** ✉ Tzanakaki 5, Hania ✉ El Greco Park, Heraklion ✉ Koundourioti, Rethymnon.

TOURS

Resort hotels and large agents, such as Canea Travel, organize guided tours in air-conditioned buses to the main Minoan sites; excursions to spectacular beaches such as Vai in the northeast and Elafonisi in the southwest; and trips to Santorini and to closer islands such as Spinalonga, a former leper colony off Ayios Nikolaos. El Greco Tours organizes hikes through the Samaria Gorge and other local excursions. The Crete Travel Web site is an excellent one-stop source for tour information, with insights on many of the island's more worthwhile sights, as well as car rental and distinctive accommodation.

A tour of Knossos and the Archaeological Museum in Heraklion costs about €40; a tour of Phaistos and Gortyna plus a swim at Matala costs about €20; a trip to the Samaria Gorge costs about €25. Travel agents can also arrange for personal guides, whose fees are negotiable.

🖪 **Canea Travel** ✉ Bonaili 12–13, Hania ☎ 28210/52301 ⊕ www.helsun.gr. **Crete Travel** ✉ Monaho, Armenoi Chanion ☎ 28250/32690 ⊕ www.cretetravel.com. **El Greco Tours** ✉ Kydonias 76, Hania ☎ 28210/86018 ⊕ www.elgrecotours.com.

VISITOR INFORMATION

The Greek National Tourism Organization (GNTO or EOT) is open daily 8–2 and 3–8:30. The municipality of Ayios Nikolaos operates its own tourist office and provides a wealth of information on the town and island as well as help with accommodation and local tours; it's open daily 8:30–9:30

🖪 **Ayios Nikolaos** ✉ Koundourou 21 A ☎ 28410/22357. **Greek National Tourism Organization** ✉ Xanthoudidou 1, Heraklion ☎ 2810/246106 ⊕ www.gnto.gr ✉ Odos Kriari 40, Hania ☎ 28210/92624 ✉ Sofokli Venizelou, Rethymnon ☎ 28310/56350.

Rhodes & the Dodecanese

KOS, SYMI & PATMOS

WORD OF MOUTH

"Water parks, discos, night clubs, crowded resorts? Yes, they exist but we didn't go looking for them. We spent a perfectly pleasant week [on Rhodes with plenty to explore, good beaches to relax on, and good food, too—it is still possible to find all the things that attracted people to the island in the first place . . . . Kos town was well worth a visit—we spent 2 half days and an evening there. For anyone who enjoys wandering round ruins, there were plenty, from 2,000-year-old Greek and Roman remains, to a huge Crusader castle. There was a good pedestrian area with shops, restaurants and bars, and a little market hall where I bought loads of cheap herbs and spices."

—Maria_H

By Stephen Brewer

Updated by Angelike Contis

LYING AT THE EASTERN EDGE OF THE AEGEAN SEA, wrapped enticingly around the shores of Turkey and Asia Minor, is the southernmost group of Greek islands, the Dodecanese (Twelve Islands), sometimes known as the Southern Sporades. The archipelago has long shared a common history: Romans, Crusaders, Turks, and Venetians left their mark with temples, castles, and fortresses in exotic towns of shady lanes and tall houses. Of the 12 islands, 4 are highlighted here: strategically located Rhodes has played by far the most important role in history and was for many years one of the most popular vacation spots in the Mediterranean. Kos comes in second in popularity and has vestiges of antiquity; the Sanctuary of Asklepeios, a center of healing, drew people from all over the ancient world. Symi is a virtual museum of 19th-century neoclassical architecture almost untouched by modern development, and Patmos, where St. John wrote his *Revelation,* became a renowned monastic center during the Byzantine period and continues as a significant focal point of the Greek Orthodox faith. Symi and Patmos both have a peace and quiet that in large part has been lost on overdeveloped Rhodes and Kos. But despite the invasion of sunseekers, there are still delightful pockets of local color in the Dodecanese.

Exploring Rhodes & the Dodecanese

Rhodes and Kos unfold in fertile splendor, creased with streams and dotted with large stretches of green; their major towns sit next to the sea on almost flat land, embracing exceptionally large and well-protected harbors facing the mainland of Asia Minor. Both islands are worth visiting for a couple of days each. Patmos and Symi, however, resemble in some ways more the Cycladic islands: rugged hills and mountains are almost devoid of vegetation, with villages and towns clinging in lovely disarray to craggy landscapes. Symi is the closest island to Rhodes, an easy 50-minute hydrofoil ride away.

About the Restaurants

Throughout the Dodecanese, especially on Rhodes, you can find sophisticated restaurants, as well as simple tavernas serving excellent food. Because Rhodes and Kos produce most of their own foodstuffs, you can count on fresh fruit and vegetables. Fish, of course, is readily available on all islands. Tiny, tender Symi shrimp, found only in the waters around this island, have such soft shells they can be easily popped in the mouth whole. They are used in dozens of local dishes. Wherever you dine, ask about the specialty of the day, and check the food on display in the kitchen of tavernas. With the exception of one or two very high-end spots on Rhodes, dress on all the islands is casual; reservations are not necessary unless specified.

About the Hotels

Except for Athens, Rhodes probably has more hotels per capita than anywhere else in Greece. Most of them are resort or tourist hotels, with sea views and easy access to beaches, that cater to package tours from northern Europe. High season is extremely crowded and you may have difficulty finding a room in Rhodes if you don't book well in advance. Mass tourist accommodations are also plentiful on Kos but, as in

Rhodes, most lodging isn't especially Greek in style. Symi has more small hotels with charm, since the island never encouraged the development of mammoth caravansaries. Similarly, Patmos has attractive, high-quality lodgings that tend to be both more elegant and traditional than its resort-magnet neighbors. Many hotels throughout the Dodecanese are closed from November through April. Lodgings in water-poor Symi and Patmos remind you to limit water use. Resorts rates usually include morning refreshments that resemble expanded Continental breakfast, with yogurt, fresh fruit, baked goods, and sometimes eggs.

WHAT IT COSTS In euros				
$$$$	**$$$**	**$$**	**$**	**¢**
RESTAURANTS over €20	€16–€20	€12–€15	€8–€11	under €8
HOTELS over €160	€121–€160	€91–€120	€60–€90	under €60

Restaurant prices are for one main course at dinner or, for restaurants that serve only *mezedes* (small dishes), for two mezedes. Hotel prices are for two people in a standard double room in high season, including taxes.

Timing

High season is from about March or April through October, when all establishments are open and the weather is most agreeable. Be warned that in August tourists pack the islands and prices shoot up.

RHODES

Ρόδος

The island of Rhodes (1,400 square km [540 square mi]) is the fourth-largest Greek island and, along with Sicily and Cyprus, one of the great islands of the Mediterranean. It lies almost exactly halfway between Piraeus and Cyprus, 18 km (11 mi) off the coast of Asia Minor, and it was long considered a bridge between Europe and the East. Geologically similar to the Turkish mainland, it was probably once a part of it, separated by one of the frequent volcanic upheavals this volatile region has experienced.

Rhodes saw successive waves of settlement, including the arrival of the Dorian Greeks from Argos and Laconia sometime early in the first millennium BC. From the 8th to the 6th century BC Rhodian cities established settlements in Italy, France, Spain, and Egypt and actively traded with mainland Greece, exporting pottery, oil, wine, and figs. Independence and expansion came to a halt when the Persians took over the island at the end of the 6th century BC and forced Rhodians to provide ships and men for King Xerxes's failed attack on the mainland (480 BC). A league of city-states rose under Athenian leadership. In 408 BC the united city of Rhodes was created on the site of the modern town, much of the populace moved there, and the history of the island and the town became synonymous. As the new city grew and flourished, its political organization became the model for the city of Alexandria in Egypt.

11

If you have at least two weeks, exploring the Dodecanese by boat makes for a marvelous holiday. Even on a short visit, you can partake of the diverse pleasures of the Dodecanese by combining a visit to one of the busier islands with a retreat to a quieter place.

Numbers in the text correspond to numbers in the margin and on the Rhodes and the Dodecanese map.

If you have 3 days

Start your visit to Rhodes in ▦ **Rhodes town** ❶ ▶, where you can spend a day walking through the fascinating old town and visiting the Palace of the Grand Masters and other sights. Definitely make a day trip to the old city of **Lindos** ❸, where you can also enjoy a beach, and stop in **Petaloudes** ❽, the Valley of the Butterflies, en route back to Rhodes town. Alternatively, consider taking the night boat from Athens directly to ▦ **Patmos** island to spend three days. It's a magical place where the hilly landscape is as mystical as its famous monastery.

If you have 5 days

The island of ▦ **Rhodes** ❶ ▶ –❾ is a good place to base yourself for a short tour of the Dodecanese. Follow the three-day itinerary above, perhaps overnighting in **Lindos** ❹. On Day 4, take a hydrofoil trip to spend the next two days on ▦ **Symi,** a quiet, beautiful island with neoclassical architecture and striking, arid landscape.

If you have 7 days

After exploring ▦ **Rhodes** ❶ ▶ –❾ and ▦ **Symi** for four days, take a hydrofoil or catamaran to ▦ **Kos** on Day 5 for two days. After touring the mosque and museums of ▦ **Kos town**, make the trip out of town to the archaeological site of Asklepieion; then venture farther afield to other archaeological sites and the island's excellent beaches. From Kos, travel by boat to stunning ▦ **Patmos** for a night. Visit the Monastery of the Apocalypse, where the prophet John wrote the *Revelation*. Spend the night on the island, perhaps in ▦ **Skala,** absorbing the otherworldly scene before taking a ferry to Athens or Rhodes, from where you can fly on.

In 42 BC, Rhodes came under the hegemony of Rome, and through the years of the empire it was fabled as a beautiful city where straight roads were lined with porticoes, houses, and gardens. According to Pliny, who described the city in the 1st century AD, the town possessed some 2,000 statues, at least 100 of them of colossal scale. One of the most famous examples of the island's sculptural school is the *Laocöon*—probably executed in the 1st century BC—which showed the priest who warned the Trojans to beware of Greeks bearing gifts (it stands in the Vatican today). The ancient glory of Rhodes has few visible remnants. The city was ravaged by Arab invaders in AD 654 and 807, and only with the expulsion of the Arabs, and the reconquest of Crete by the Byzantine emperors, did the city begin to revive. Rhodes was a crucial stop on the road to the Holy Land during the Crusades. It came briefly under Venetian influence, then Byzantine, then Genoese, but in 1309, when the Knights of St. John took the city from its Genoese masters, its most glorious modern era began.

The Knights of St. John, an order of Hospitalers, organized to protect and care for Christian pilgrims. By the beginning of the 12th century the order had become military in nature, and after the fall of Acre in 1291, the Knights fled from Palestine, withdrawing first to Cyprus and then to Rhodes. In 1312, the Knights inherited the immense wealth of the Templars (another religious military order, which had just been outlawed by the pope) and used it to fortify Rhodes. But for all their power and the strength of their walls, moats, and artillery, the Knights could not hold back the Turks. In 1522 the Ottomans, with 300 ships and 100,000 men under Süleyman the Magnificent, began what was to be the final siege, taking the city after six months.

During the Turkish occupation, Rhodes became a possession of the Grand Admiral, who collected taxes but left the Rhodians to pursue a generally peaceful and prosperous existence. They continued to build ships and to trade with Greece, Constantinople (later Istanbul), Syria, and Egypt. The Greek mainland was liberated by the War of 1821, but Rhodes and the Dodecanese remained part of the Ottoman Empire until 1912, when the Italians took over. After World War II, the Dodecanese were formally united with Greece in 1947. In the years post–World War II, tourism became king, Rhodes town expanded, and the island's farming activities shrank.

Today Rhodes retains its role as the center of Dodecanese trade, politics, and culture. Sprawling resort hotels line much of the coast, but the island is large and diverse enough to have grand archaeological sites, and even a taste of rural life, in addition to beach entertainment and water sports.

Rhodes Town

Ρόδος (Πόλη)

▶ ❶ *463 km (287 mi) east of Piraeus.*

Fodor'sChoice
★
Early travelers described Rhodes as a town of two parts: a castle or high town (Collachium) and a lower city. Today Rhodes town is still a city of two parts: the old town, a UNESCO World Heritage site that incorporates the high town and lower city, contains Orthodox and Catholic churches, Turkish structures, and houses, some of which follow the ancient orthogonal plan. Public buildings are all similar in style: staircases are on the outside, either on the facade or in the court; the facades are elegantly constructed of well-cut limestone from Lindos; windows and doors are often outlined with strongly profiled moldings and surmounted by arched casements. Careful reconstruction in recent years has enhanced the harmonious effect. Spreading away from the walls that encircle the old town is the modern metropolis, or new town. You can purchase a multisight ticket (€10) which gets you admission to the Palace of the Grand Masters, Archaeological Museum, Museum of Decorative Arts, and Byzantine Museum.

Ancient Splendors

The ruins of the ancient world still litter these islands, and though these antiquities are not necessarily as well known as those elsewhere in Greece, coming upon them can be a transporting experience. The famed Colossus of Rhodes stands no more, but the Acropolis of Lindos remains as a mighty testament to the island's importance in antiquity. Other ruins litter the island, including those of the ancient cities of Kameiros and Ialyssos. Ancient Greeks and Romans also left their mark on Kos, the location of one of the great healing centers of antiquity, the Asklepieion. Meanwhile, contemporary Kos town wraps enticingly around the evocative ruins of the Roman agora and harbor and other ancient remnants.

11

Beaches

In the Dodecanese it's never hard to find a beautiful beach, or at least a rock from which to swim. Although many beaches on Rhodes and Kos have been developed to the last grain of sand, on Rhodes the sheltered southeastern coast has long, exquisite, and undeveloped stretches of fine sand. The Gulf of Kefalos on Kos is a haven for those wishing to escape the tourist fray— broad, sandy, scenically magnificent, and for much of its length devoid of development, curving around an enchanting bay. One of the pleasures of being on Patmos is to seek out yet another perfect beach every day: in the morning, caïques make regular runs from Skala to several of the beaches; some can be reached by car or bus, and many delightfully empty strands are the reward for a short trek on foot. The rocky shores of Symi provide many a cove for superb swimming.

Medieval Might

As much as sand, sun, and nightlife, the monuments the Knights of St. John built some 700 years ago are what draw duly impressed visitors to the island of Rhodes. Here, on cobbled lanes within perfectly preserved walls, are the palaces and halls where the knights lived and gathered after this order of knighthood, returning from the Crusades, took the island from the Genoese. In few other places in the world are there as many monuments from the Middle Ages concentrated in one place. To walk through the medieval city of Rhodes town, especially in the relative quiet of the early morning or evening, is to be transported to a different time.

Majestic Monasteries

Two of Greece's most famous and most visited monasteries, the Monastery of St. John the Theologian and the Monastery of the Apocalypse, are on Patmos. They pay homage to St. John, who was banished to this island in AD 95 and wrote his *Revelation* here. Today these hallowed shrines attract thousands of pilgrims. Another particularly appealing monastery is that of Taxiarchis Michael Panormitis, the protector of sailors, in a remote part of the small island of Symi. Here, mosaics, frescoes, and the scent of pine and incense create a quiet sense of great spirituality.

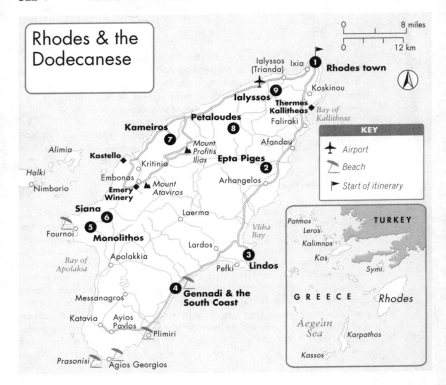

In the castle area, a city within a city, the Knights of St. John built most of their monuments. The **Palace of the Grand Masters**, at the highest spot of the medieval city, is the best place to begin a tour of Rhodes; here you can get oriented before wandering through the labyrinthine old town. Of great help is the permanent exhibition downstairs, with extensive displays, maps, and plans showing the layout of the city. The palace building withstood unscathed the Turkish siege, but in 1856, an explosion of ammunition stored nearby in the cellars of the Church of St. John devastated it; the present structures are 20th-century Italian reconstructions. Note the Hellenistic and Roman mosaic floors throughout, which came from the Italian excavations in Kos. ⊠ *Ippoton, old town* ☎ *22410/23359* ⊕ *www.culture.gr* 🎫 *€6* ⊙ *May–Oct., Mon. 12:30–7, Tues.–Sun. 8:30–7; Nov.–Apr., Tues.–Sun. 8–3.*

In front of court of Palace of the Grand Masters is the **Loggia of St. John,** on the site where the Knights of St. John were buried in an early church. From the Loggia, the **Street of the Knights** descends toward the **Commercial Port,** bordered on both sides by the **Inns of the Tongues,** where the Knights supped and held their meetings.

The **Inn of France** was the largest of the Knights' gathering spots and is now the French Consulate. The facade is carved with flowers and heraldic patterns and bears an inscription that dates the building between 1492 and 1509. ⊠ *About halfway down Str. of the Knights from Loggia of St. John.*

The hospital was the largest of the Knights' public buildings, completed in 1489. The imposing facade opens into a courtyard, where cannonballs remain from the siege of 1522. Today it contains the **Archaeological Museum.** On the main floor there's a collection of ancient pottery and sculpture, including two well-known representations of Aphrodite: the *Aphrodite of Rhodes,* who, while bathing, pushes aside her hair as if she's listening; and a standing figure, known as *Aphrodite Thalassia,* or "of the sea," as she was discovered in the water off the northern city beach. Other important works include a 6th-century BC *kouros* (a statue of an idealized male youth, usually nude) that was found in Kameiros, and the beautiful 5th-century BC funerary stele of Timarista bidding farewell to her mother, Crito. ⊠ *Pl. Mouseou* ☎ *22410/25500* ⊕ *www. culture.gr* ☞ *€3* ☉ *Tues.–Sun. 8:30–2:30.*

The **Byzantine Museum** collection of icons is displayed within the 11th-century Lady of the Castle church. ⊠ *Off Pl. Mouseou* ☎ *22410/ 23359* ☞ *€2* ☉ *Tues.–Sun. 8:30–2:30.*

The **Museum of Decorative Arts** exhibits finely made ceramics, crafts, and artifacts from around the Dodecanese. ⊠ *Pl. Argyrokastrou* ☎ *22410/ 23359* ☞ *€2* ☉ *Tues.–Sun. 8:30–2:30.*

The **Mosque of Süleyman,** at the top of Sokratous street, was built circa 1522 and rebuilt in 1808. At this writing, the site was closed indefinitely for restoration work. The **Turkish Library** dates to the late 18th century. Striking reminders of the Ottoman presence, the library and the mosque are still used by those members of Rhodes's Turkish community who stayed behind after the population exchange of 1922. ⊠ *Sokratous opposite the Mosque of Süleyman* ☎ *22410/74090* ☞ *Free* ☉ *Mon.–Sat. 9:30–4.*

The **walls** of Rhodes in themselves are one of the great medieval monuments in the Mediterranean. Wonderfully restored, they illustrate the engineering capabilities as well as the financial and human resources available to the Knights. (The 20th-century Italian rulers erased much of the Ottoman influence, preferring to emphasize the Knights' past when restoring architecture.) For 200 years the Knights strengthened the walls by thickening them, up to 40 feet in places, and curving them so as to deflect cannonballs. The moat between the inner and outer walls never contained water; it was a device to prevent invaders from constructing siege towers. Part of the road that runs along the top for the entire 4 km (2½ mi) is accessible through municipal guided tours. ⊠ *Old town, tours depart from Palace of the Grand Masters entrance* ☎ *22410/23359* ☞ *Tour €6* ☉ *Tours Tues. and Sat. at 2:45 (arrive at least 15 mins early).*

The soaring vaults of the ruins of **Our Lady of the Bourg,** once a magnificent Gothic church, are a startling reminder of Rhodes's Frankish past. ⊠ *Inside remains of walls, access through Panagias Gate.*

The **Commercial Harbor,** at the "mouth" of the old town, is Rhodes's largest. The port authority and customs offices are here. ⊠ *Near St. Catherine's Gate.*

CloseUp

THE GREAT COLOSSUS

AT THE END OF THE 4TH CENTURY BC *the Rhodians commissioned the sculptor Chares, from Lindos, to create the famous Colossus, a huge bronze statue of the sun god, Helios, one of the Seven Wonders of the Ancient World. Two bronze deer statues mark the spot where legend says the Colossus statue once straddled the Mandraki Harbor entrance. The 110 foot-high statue only stood for half a century. In 227 BC, when an earthquake razed the city and toppled the Colossus, help poured in from all quarters of the eastern Mediterranean. After the calamity the Delphic oracle advised the Rhodians to let the great Colossus remain where it had fallen. So there it rested for some eight centuries, until AD 654 when it was sold as scrap metal and carted off to Syria allegedly by a caravan of 900 camels. After that, nothing is known of its fate.*

The medieval old town of Rhodes is now completely surrounded by the **new town.** The city first spread outside town walls during Ottoman domination. Today, there are many circa 1950s–1970s buildings that resemble those in Athens, though they have fewer stories overall. ⊠ *North of old town walls, bordering Mandraki Harbor.*

The city's municipal buildings, an open-air bazaar, and the main shopping areas are along **Mandraki Harbor.** The town's cathedral, Evagelismos Church, which is modeled after the destroyed Church of St. John in the Collachium, dominates the waterfront. The Governor's Palace is constructed in an arcaded Venetian Gothic style. ⊠ *New town.*

Mt. Smith rises about 2 km (1 mi) to the west of Rhodes center. Villas and gardens dot its slopes, but many more of them have been torn down to make way for modern apartment buildings. For a dramatic view, walk to the westernmost edge of Mt. Smith, which drops via a sharp and almost inaccessible cliff to the shore below, now lined with enormous hotels. Atop Mt. Smith are the freely accessible ruins of the **acropolis.** These include a heavily restored **theater,** a **stadium,** the three restored columns of the **Temple of Apollo Pythios,** and the scrappy remains of the **Temple of Athena Polias.** ⊠ *Mt. Smith* ☎ *No phone.*

As you leave Rhodes town and travel south along the east coast, a strange sight meets you: the buildings of the **Thermes Kallitheas** (⊠ 10 km [6 mi] south of Rhodes town) look as if they have been transplanted from Morocco. In fact, this mosaic-tile bath complex was built in 1929 by the Italians. As far back as the early 2nd century BC, area mineral springs were prized; the great physician Hippocrates of Kos extolled the springs for alleviating liver, kidney, and rheumatic ailments. Though the baths are no longer in use, you can wander through the ruins of the buildings' ornate arches and swim on the nearby beach.

Beaches

The beach at **Elli** (⊠ North of old town, near Rhodes Yacht Club) has fine sand; an easy slope; chairs, umbrellas, and pedal boats for rent; showers; and plenty of sunbathing tourists. All of the coast around Rhodes town is developed, so you can reach some of the best beaches only through the hotels that occupy them.

Where to Stay & Eat

★ **$$$$** ✕ **Ta Kioupia.** In a group of humble farm buildings, Ta Kioupia is anything but modest. The white-stucco rooms with exposed ceiling beams exude rustic elegance: antique farm tools are on display, and linen tablecloths, fine china, and crystal set the tables. In summer you dine in an enclosed garden. Food is presented on large platters and you select what you fancy: pine-nut salad, *tiropita* (four-cheese pie), an eggplant dip that regulars say can't be beat, cheese-and-nut *bourekakia* (stuffed phyllo pastries), *kokorosouvlaki* (rooster kebab) . . . the list goes on; the food is extraordinary in its variety and quality. ⊠ *7 km (4½ mi) west of Rhodes town, Tris* ☎ *22410/91824* ⊕ *www.kioupia.com* ✍ *Reservations essential* ▤ *AE, DC, MC, V* ☉ *Closed Sun. No lunch.*

★ **$$$–$$$$** ✕ **Dinoris.** The great hall that holds Dinoris was built in AD 310 as a hospital and then converted into a stable for the Knights in 1530. The fish specialties and fine service lure appreciative and demanding clients, from the mayor to hotel owners and visiting VIPs. For appetizers, try the variety platter, which includes *psarokeftedakia* (fish balls made from a secret recipe) as well as mussels, shrimp, and lobster. Other special dishes are grilled prawns, and sea-urchin salad. An outdoor terrace is in the planning stages. ⊠ *Pl. Mouseou 14a* ☎ *22410/25824* ✍ *Reservations essential* ▤ *AE, MC, V* ☉ *Closed Jan.*

★ **$–$$$$** ✕ **Alexis.** Continuing the tradition begun by his father in 1957, Yiannis Katsimprakis serves the very best seafood and speaks passionately of eating fish as though it were a lost art. Don't bother with the menu; just ask for suggestions and then savor every bite, whether you choose caviar, mussels in wine, smoked eel, or sea urchins. He even cooks up *porphyra*, the mollusk yielding the famous purple dye of the Byzantine emperors. A side dish might be sautéed squash with wild *glistrida* (purslane). ⊠ *Sokratous 18* ☎ *22410/29347* ▤ *AE, MC, V* ☉ *Closed Nov.–Apr. No lunch Sun. June–Aug.*

$–$$$$ ✕ **Palia Istoria.** Chef Mihalis Boukouris creates culinary delights ensconced in an old house with high ceilings and genteel murals. Tantalizing entrées include shrimp ouzo with orange juice, pork tenderloin in garlic and wine sauce, and spearmint-spice *keftedes* (meatballs). Cleopatra's Salad, with arugula and dried fig, reigns over the extensive salad choices. Choose from among 100 Greek wines. The flambéed banana dessert wrapped in phyllo and topped with a portlike Komantaria liqueur could complete the meal. Palia Istoria is a bit out of the way, in the new town— about €3 by taxi from the old town. ⊠ *Odos Mitropoleos 108, Ayios Dimitrios* ☎ *22410/32421* ▤ *MC, V* ☉ *Closed Dec.–Apr. No lunch.*

¢ ✕ **People & People.** On principle, the owners of this Mandraki Harbor café insist on keeping the price of all coffee at €1.50. They also serve feather-light doughnut drops with fresh strawberry centers, homemade ice cream, pastries (packed to-go in artistic gift boxes), and sandwiches. Hang out under the umbrellas outside or the dinerlike interior of this 1972 landmark, open Monday–Saturday 7 AM–11 PM. ⊠ *Ethnarhou Makariou 4, new town* ☎ *22410/36025* 🖃 *No credit cards* ⊙ *Closed Sun.*

$$$$ 🏨 **Rodos Park.** Nestled in a green corner of the new town, Rhodes's most luxurious hotel is also one of its most quiet retreats, with more staff than guests. The hotel's welcoming common spaces include a warm lounge with a cigar-cognac bar, a tranquil landscaped pool area, and a wood-and-stone spa. The less-impressive guest rooms are either simple carpeted doubles or large, marble-floor suites with whirlpool tubs. Stunning views look over the old town, which is a few minutes' walk away. ⊠ *Odos Riga Fereous 12, 85100* ☎ *22410/24612* 🖶 *22410/24613* ⊕ *www.rodospark.gr* 🛏 *30 rooms, 30 suites* ♨ *Restaurant, room service, some in-room hot tubs, minibars, cable TV, pool, gym, sauna, spa, steam room, bar, lounge, business center* 🖃 *AE, DC, MC, V* ⑩ *BP.*

★ **$$–$$$$** 🏨 **Marco Polo Mansion.** Entering this renovated 15th-century Ottoman mansion is like stepping into another world. The trip begins in the maze of the old town's colorful Turkish section, which gives a flavor of what's to come inside. Individually styled rooms are painted in deep, warm colors, with Oriental rugs adorning the pitch-pine floors and soft embroidered cushions beckoning from low sofas. Most of the Eastern furnishings are unusual antiques, including the large beds draped with translucent canopies. It's no wonder this truly beautiful hotel has been featured in dozens of glossy magazines. Homemade marmalades and cakes are served at breakfast. ⊠ *Aghiou Fanouriou 40–42, 85100* ☎ *22410/25562* ⊕ *www.marcopolomansion.web.com* 🛏 *10 rooms* ♨ *Café; no a/c, no room phones, no room TVs* 🖃 *AE, MC, V* ⑩ *CP.*

$–$$$$ 🏨 **S. Nikolis Hotel.** A charming old-town accommodation occupies a restored house on the site of an ancient agora. The small but tidy rooms are enlivened by arches and other architectural details, and many have balconies overlooking a lovely garden. Excellent service, including laundry, is administered by Sotiris and Marianne Nikolis with care. Breakfast is served on the roof terrace. ⊠ *Odos Ippodamou 61, 85100* ☎ *22410/34561* 🖶 *22410/32034* ⊕ *www.s-nikolis.gr* 🛏 *10 rooms, 4 suites* ♨ *Some in-room hot tubs, some kitchens, refrigerators, laundry service* 🖃 *AE, MC, V* ⑩ *CP.*

$$$ 🏨 **Grand Hotel.** A cut above other resort hotels in the new town, the Grand is near the beach and the nightclub scene, and not far from the old town. Though the hotel is not exceptional from the outside, once you enter, the name makes sense: the atrium lobby is spacious, with giant plants and views onto the portico-covered pool and garden. The best rooms are in the newer wing, with pink marble floors and pretty paintings of nymphs and goddesses. They have subdued blue and rose furnishings, trompe l'oeil touches, and bathtub alcoves. ⊠ *Akti Miaouli 1, 85100* ☎ *22410/54700, 210/291–7027 in Athens* 🖶 *22410/35589* ⊕ *www.mitsishotels.com* 🛏 *401 rooms, 5 suites* ♨ *Restaurant, cable TV, tennis court, 3 pools (1 indoor), gym, sauna, bar, nightclub, shops* 🖃 *DC, MC, V* ⑩ *BP.*

$ 🏨 **Hotel Andreas.** The owners of this old-town pension, set in a rather ramshackle 15th-century house, say it once belonged to a Turkish vizier and that most of the rooms were bedrooms for his wives. You can guess what the status was of each occupant—some rooms are lovely and have sea views, others are tiny with bathrooms outside the room (though still private). All are decorated individually with soft washes of color on stucco walls, romantic bed canopies, international folk art, and tapestry bedspreads. Continental breakfast is €5, a full breakfast is €6. You eat on the huge, plant-filled terrace with a magical view of the old town. ⊠ *Omirou 28D, 85100* ☎ *22240/34156* 🖷 *22410/74285* ⊕ *www.hotelandreas.com* ⤴ *11 rooms* ⚓ *No a/c in some rooms, no TV in some rooms* ▤ *AE, MC, V.*

¢ 🖷 **Pension Sofia.** The old town is full of rooms to rent, but budget-priced Sofia's is bright, pleasant, and framed by trailing jasmine; each room has a little bath. ⊠ *Aristofanous 27, 85100* ☎ *22410/36181 or 22410/75166* ⤴ *10 rooms* ⚓ *Fans; no a/c in some rooms, no room phones* ▤ *No credit cards.*

Nightlife & the Arts

BARS & DISCOS Sophisticated Greeks have created a stylish nightlife using the medieval buildings and flower-filled courtyards of the old town. Some bars and cafés here are open all day for drinks, and many—often those with beautiful medieval interiors—stay open most of the year. Nighttime-only spots in the old town open up around 10 PM and close around 3 or 4 AM. The action centers around narrow, pebble-paved Miltiadou street, where seats spill out from trendy bars set in stone buildings. Another hot spot is Platia Arionos.

Those wanting to venture to the new town's throbbing discos should head to Orfanidou street, where bronzed, scantily clad tourists gyrate 'til dawn at massive clubs. New town clubs rock well through sunrise. As always in Greece, nightspots come and go, so check with your concierge or the free *Rodos News,* available at the Greek National Tourism Organization (GNTO or EOT) office.

Baduz (⊠ Pl. Arionos ☎ 69366/74466) plays progressive international music and is decorated with old marble basins. *Rembetika* (acoustic music, with blueslike lyrics, played on the bouzouki) fans head to tiny **Cafe Chantant** (⊠ Aristotelous 42 ☎ 22410/32277) for live music. The biggest area disco is the three-stage complex **Colorado** (⊠ Orfanidou and Akti Miaouli, new town ☎ 22410/75120) with live rock, as well as dance hits and R&B.

Hammam (⊠ Aischylou 26 ☎ 22410/33242), in an Ottoman bathhouse, hosts live Greek bands. Mellow **Selini** (⊠ Evripidou 4B ☎ No phone) has frescoes of the moon, art exhibits, cushioned outdoor benches, and jazz. The candlelit **Theatro** (⊠ Miltiadou 2 ☎ 22410/76973) plays funk and electronic music and even hosts live theater events.

CASINO You must show your passport to get into Rhodes's **casino** (⊠ Hotel Grande Albergo Delle Rose, Papanikolaou 4, new town ☎ 22410/97500 ⊕ www.casinorodos.gr). The entry fee is €15, and tables are open Monday–Thursday 6 PM–6 AM. On Friday, tables open at 2 PM and stay open continuously through 6 AM Monday. Slot machines are open 24 hours, and drinks are free. You have to be at least 23 years old to play.

PERFORMANCES   The **Nelly Dimoglou Folk Dance Theatre** (✉ Andronikou 7, behind Turkish baths, old town ☎ 22410/20157) has kept alive the tradition of Greek dance since 1971, with strict adherence to authentic detail in costume and performance. From June until October performances (€12) are held Monday, Wednesday, and Friday at 9:20 PM. The theater also gives dance lessons.

From May through October the **Sound-and-Light Show** (✉ Grounds of Palace of the Grand Masters ☎ 22410/21922 ⊕ www.hellenicfestival. gr) tells the story of the Turkish siege. English-language performances are Monday, Wednesday, and Friday at 9:15 PM; Tuesday, Thursday, and Saturday at 11:15 PM. In September and October, performances start one hour earlier; the cost is €6; free for children up to 10 years old.

Sports

For €50 **Dive Med College** (✉ Lissavonas 33, Rodini ☎ 22410/61115 ⊕ www.divemedcollege.com) takes you by boat to Thermes Kallitheas and after a 45-minute theory lesson and practice in shallow water, you descend for a 20-minute dive. Out of fear of theft of underwater antiquities, diving is forbidden everywhere in Rhodes except off Thermes Kallitheas.

Shopping

In Rhodes town you can buy good copies of Lindos ware, a delicate pottery decorated with green and red floral motifs. The old town's shopping area, on Sokratous, is lined with boutiques selling furs, jewelry, and other high-ticket items. The owner of **Astero Antiques** (✉ Ayiou Fanouriou 4, at Sokratous ☎ 22410/34753) travels throughout Greece each winter to fill his shop.

AROUND THE ISLAND

The island's east coast is blessed with white-sand beaches and dotted with copses of trees, interspersed with fertile valleys full of figs and olives. This beauty has meant that long stretches of country are now given over to vast resort hotels and holiday villages. Even so, there are still some wonderfully un-trammeled sections of beach to be found all around the island, and the town of Lindos alone warrants an excursion from Rhodes town.

Epta Piges

Επτά Πηγές

❷ *30 km (19 mi) south of Rhodes town.*

Seven Springs, or Epta Piges, is a deeply shaded glen watered by mountain springs. In the woods around the springs, imported peacocks flaunt their plumage. The waters are channeled through a 164-yard-long tunnel, which you can walk through, emerging at the edge of a cascading dam and a small man-made lake where you can swim. Here an enterprising local shepherd began serving simple fare in 1945, and his sideline turned into the busy taverna and tourist site of today. Despite its many visitors, Seven Springs' beauty remains unspoiled. To get here, turn right on inland road near Kolymbia and follow signs.

Where to Eat

¢–$$$ ✕ **Epta Piges.** The family-run taverna spreads out below the plane and pine trees, directly overlooking the springs. There's always charcoal-grill lamb or fish on the menu and starters include dishes like *pitaroudia* (fried potato balls) or thin fried zucchini and eggplant. ☎ *22410/56259* ⊕ *www.eptapiges.com* ▭ *MC, V* ⊙ *Closed Nov.–Mar.*

Lindos

Λίνδος

❸ *19 km (12 mi) southwest of Epta Piges, 48 km (30 mi) southwest of Rhodes town.*

Lindos, cradled between two harbors, had a particular importance in antiquity. Before the existence of Rhodes town, it was the island's principal maritime center. Lindos possessed a revered sanctuary, consecrated to Athena, whose cult probably succeeded that of a pre-Hellenic divinity named Lindia, and the sanctuary was dedicated to Athena Lindia. By the 6th century BC, an impressive temple dominated the settlement, and after the foundation of Rhodes, the Lindians set up a *propylaia* (monumental entrance gate) on the model of that in Athens. In the mid-4th century BC, the temple was destroyed by fire and almost immediately rebuilt, with a new wooden statue of the goddess covered by gold leaf, and with arms, head, and legs of marble or ivory. In the Hellenistic period, the acropolis was further adorned with a great portico at the foot of the steps to the propylaia. Lindos prospered into Roman times, during the Middle Ages, and under the Knights of St. John. Only at the beginning of the 19th century did the age-old shipping activity cease. The population decreased radically, reviving only with the 20th-century influx of foreigners.

Lindos is remarkably well preserved, and many 15th-century houses are still in use. Everywhere are examples of the Crusader architecture you saw in Rhodes town: substantial houses of finely cut Lindos limestone, with windows crowned by elaborate arches. Many floors are paved with black-and-white pebble mosaics. Intermixed with these Crusader buildings are whitewashed, geometric, Cycladic-style houses with square, blue-shuttered windows. Most of Lindos's mazelike streets don't have conventional names or addresses; instead, buildings are numbered, from 1 through about 500. Lower numbers are on the north side of town, higher numbers on the south.

Like Rhodes town, Lindos is enchanting off-season, but can get unbearably crowded otherwise, since pilgrims make the trek from Rhodes town daily. The main street is lined with shops selling clothes and trinkets, and since the streets are medieval in their narrowness and twisting course, the passage slows to a snail's pace. Spend a night in Lindos to enjoy its beauties after the day-trippers leave. Only pedestrians and donkeys are allowed in Lindos because the town's narrow alleys are not wide enough for vehicles. If you're arriving by car, park in the lot above town and walk the 10 minutes down (about 1200 feet) to Lindos.

The **Church of the Panayia** (✉ Off main Sq.) is a graceful building with a beautiful bell tower. The body of the church probably antedates the Knights, although the bell tower bears their arms with the dates 1484–90. The interior has frescoes painted in 1779 by Gregory of Symi.

Fodor'sChoice
★

For about €5, you can hire a donkey for the 15-minute climb from the modern town up to the **Acropolis of Lindos.** The winding path leads past a gauntlet of Lindian women who spread out their lace and embroidery over the rocks like fresh laundry. The final approach ascends a steep flight of stairs, past a marvelous 2nd-century BC **relief** of the prow of a Lindian ship, carved into the rock, and through the main gate.

The entrance to the Acropolis takes you through the **medieval castle,** with the Byzantine **Chapel of St. John** on the next level above. On the **upper terraces** are the remains of the elaborate **porticoes** and **stoas.** As is the case with Sounion, on the mainland southeast of Athens, the site and temple command an immense sweep of sea, making a powerful statement on behalf of the deity and city to which they belonged; the lofty white columns on the summit must have presented a magnificent picture. The main portico had 42 Doric columns, at the center of which an opening led to the staircase up to the **propylaia.** The temple at the very top is surprisingly modest, given the drama of the approach. As was common in the 4th century BC, both the front and the rear are flanked by four Doric columns, like the Temple of Athena Nike on the Acropolis of Athens. Numerous inscribed statue bases were found all over the summit, attesting in many cases to the work of Lindian sculptors, who were clearly second to none. The effects of major restoration work, started in 1993 and scheduled to finish in 2008, are visible. Much of the iron and cement used to prop up the Temple of Athena and the Hellenistic Stoa in the 1930s—as well as wooden supports added later—have been removed. ✉ *Above new town* ☎ *22440/31258* ⊕ *www.culture.gr* 💶 *€6* ⊙ *May–Oct., daily 8:30–6:45; Nov.–Apr., Tues.–Sun. 8:30–2:40.*

Escape the crowds by trekking to the **Tomb of Kleoboulos,** which archaeologists say is incorrectly named after Lindos's early tyrant Kleoboulos. After about 3 km (2 mi), a 30-minute scenic walk, you encounter the small, rounded stone tomb of a wealthy family of the 1st–2nd century BC. You can peer inside and see the candle marks, which testify to its later use as the church of St. Emilianos. ✛ *Look for sign at the parking lot above the main square. Follow dirt path along the hill that is on the opposite side of bay from the Acropolis* ☎ *No phone* ⊕ *www.culture.gr.*

Where to Stay & Eat

In Lindos it's possible through travel agents to rent **rooms** in many of the traditional homes that have mosaic courtyards, gardens, and sea views; an entire house may even be for rent. *Savaidis Travel* ☎ *22440/31347* ⊕ *www.savaidis-travel.gr. Lindos Sun Tours* ☎ *22440/31333* ⊕ *www. lindosuntours.gr.*

$–$$$$ ✕ **Mavrikos.** The secret of this longtime favorite is an elegant, perfect simplicity. Seemingly straightforward dishes, such as sea-urchin salad, fried *manouri* cheese with basil and pine nuts, swordfish in caper sauce, and lobster risotto, become transcendent with the magic touch of third-generation chef Dimitris Mavrikos. He combines the freshest ingredients with classical training and an abiding love for the best of Greek village cuisine. ⊠ *Main square, Lindos* ☎ *22440/31232* ⊟ *MC, V* ☉ *Closed Nov.–Mar.*

★ **$$$$** ▥ **Melenos Hotel.** Michalis Melenos worked for years to make this 12-room stone villa overlooking Lindos bay into a truly special boutique hotel. Each room has a built-in, traditional Lindian village bed with hand-carved woodwork and antique furnishings brought from throughout Greece and Turkey. Colorful Turkish fountains splash throughout the grounds. A tranquil terrace, bathed by lamplight in the evenings, is the stage for the restaurant's inspired Mediterranean cuisine. If you didn't bring your own computer, the staff will let you check e-mail at the reception desk. ⊠ *At edge of Lindos, on path to Acropolis, 85107* ☎ *22440/32222* ⎙ *22440/31720* ⊕ *www.melenoslindos.com* ⤶ *12 suites* ⚙ *Restaurant, room service, minibars, cable TV, in-room broadband* ⊟ *MC, V* ⎰ *BP.*

¢ ▥ **Pension Electra.** Linger on the spacious terrace or down in the blossoming garden of the pension owned by multilingual Sophy Agouros. The old-style house has high ceilings and several levels. Many rooms have sea views and air-conditioning. You can whip up your own breakfasts in one of two large kitchens. ⊠ *No. 66, 85107* ☎ *22440/31266, 210/2028326 in Athens* ⤶ *11 rooms* ⚙ *Some kitchens; no a/c in some rooms, no room phones, no room TVs* ⊟ *No credit cards.*

Nightlife

Most of Lindos's bars cater to a young, hard-drinking crowd; few are without a television showing soccer. Many are open year-round to serve the locals. The **Captain's House** (⊠ Akropoleos 243 ☎ 22440/31235), set, naturally, in an old captain's house with a courtyard, plays lounge, ethnic, and Greek music. **Gelo Blu** (⊠ Near Theotokou Church ☎ 22440/31761), run by the owners of Mavrikos, serves homemade ice cream by day and drinks day and night in its cool, blue-cushioned interior and pebbled courtyard. Relaxed **Rainbird** (⊠ On road to Pallas beach ☎ 22440/32169) is open for coffee and drinks all day and has a romantic sea-view terrace.

Gennadi & the South Coast

Γεννάδι & νότια παράλια

❹ *20 km (12½ mi) south of Lindos, 68 km (42 mi) south of Rhodes town.*

The area south of Lindos is less traveled than the rest of the island. The sandy beaches are fewer and the soil is less fertile, so there is much less development. The pretty and inexpensive coastal village of Gennadi has pensions, rooms for rent, tavernas, and a handful of nightclubs and DJ-hosted beach parties.

Beaches

The long **Lachania** beach begins a mile before Gennadi and stretches south, uninterrupted for several miles; drive alongside until you come to a secluded spot. Past Lachania is a quiet beach, **Plimiri** (✉ 10 km [6 mi] south of Gennadi), which is reached by following a sign for Taverna Plimiri from the main road. If you're on a quest for the perfect strand and are armed with four-wheel-drive and a good map, aim for the pristine, cedar-lined beach at **Ayios Georgios**—though it will take some doing. (Rental car companies discourage you from taking regular cars on the poor road.) About 4 km (2½ mi) past Plimiri, you can see the abandoned monastery of Agios Pavlos. Just before the monastery, if you dare, turn left down the cypress-lined dirt road. Follow the route about 8 km (5 mi) to a church, where the road forks. Keep going straight to reach the beach at Ayios Georgios, one of Rhodes's loveliest secret spots. Head to the southern island tip of **Prasonisi** (✉ 17 km [10½ mi] south of Plimiri), for some of Greece's best windsurfing. You can rent boards and wet suits at the beach.

Monolithos

Μονόλιθος

❺ *28 km (17 mi) northwest of Gennadi, 74 km (46 mi) southwest of Rhodes town.*

The medieval fortress of Monolithos—so named for the jutting, 750-foot monolith on which it is built—rises above a fairy-tale landscape of deep green forests and sharp cliffs plunging into the sea. Inside the fortress there is a chapel, and the ramparts provide magnificent views of Rhodes's emerald inland and the island of Halki. Take the western road from the middle of the village of Monolithos; near the hairpin turn there's a short path up to the fortress.

Beach

Keep heading down the narrow, twisting road past the Monolithos fortress to reach the tiny beach at **Fournoi**. This secluded spot is beautiful, but the water can be choppy.

Siana

Σιάνα

❻ *5 km (3 mi) north of Monolithos, 69 km (43 mi) southwest of Rhodes town.*

The town perches above a vast, fertile valley and sits in the shadow of a rock outcropping crowned with the ruin of a castle. Siana is known for *souma* (a local grape liquor, resembling flavored schnapps); look for roadside stands selling the intoxicant. The village's renowned honey and walnuts can be obtained at **Manos** (✉ Past town church, on main Rd. ☎ 22460/61209).

The **Kastello** (✉ 13 km [8 mi] northeast of Siana), a fortress built by the Knights in the late 15th century, is an impressive ruin, situated high above the sea with good views in every direction.

en route   Beyond Siana, the road continues on a high ridge through thick pine forests, which carpet the precipitous slopes dropping toward the sea. To the east looms the bare, stony massif of Mt. Ataviros, Rhodes's highest peak, at 3,986 feet. If you follow the road inland rather than continue north along the coast toward Kritinia, you climb the flanks of the mountains to the traditional, arbor-filled village of Embonas, in Rhodes's richest wine country. The well-respected **Emery Winery** makes many good wines, and occasionally, a few outstanding ones. Tastings are free. ⊠ *Embonas* ☎ *22460/41208* ⊕ *www.emery.gr* ⊗ *Weekdays 8–4:30.*

As you continue east you come into the landscape that, in medieval times, earned Rhodes the moniker "emerald of the Mediterranean." The exquisite drive up Mt. Profitis Ilias, overlooking dark green trees carpeting mountains that plunge into the sea, is one of the loveliest passages of scenery in Greece. Near the 2,200-foot-high summit is the small Church of Profitis Ilias. From the church, you can follow the well-trodden path down to the village of Salakos. It's about a 45-minute walk through the woods.

Kameiros

Κάμειρος

❼ *23 km (14 mi) northeast of Siana, 34 km (21 mi) south of Rhodes town.*

The site of classical Kameiros is one of the three ancient cities of Rhodes. The apparently unfortified ruins, excavated by the Italians in 1929, lie on a slope above the sea. Most of what is visible today dates to the classical period and later, including impressive remains of the early Hellenistic period. ⊠ *Off main Rhodes road, turn at sign for Ancient Kameiros* ☎ *22410/40037* ⊕ *www.culture.gr* 💶 *€4* ⊗ *Tues.–Sun. 8:30–2:40.*

Petaloudes

Πεταλούδες

★ ❽ *22 km (14 mi) east of Kameiros.*

The Valley of the Butterflies, Petaloudes, lives up to its name, especially in July and August. In summer the *callimorpha quadripunctaria*, actually a moth species, cluster by the thousands around the low bushes of the pungent storax plant, which grows all over the area. Through the years their number has diminished, partly owing to busloads of tourists clapping hands to see them fly up in dense clouds. Don't agitate the butterflies. Access to the valley is through a main road and admission booth. ⊠ *25 km (16 mi) southwest of Rhodes town* 💶 *€5* ⊗ *Late Apr.–Oct., daily 8–sunset.*

Ialyssos

Ιαλυσός

❾ *18 km (11 mi) northeast of Petaloudes, 14 km (9 mi) southwest of Rhodes town.*

Mt. Filerimos is capped by the site of Ialyssos, an ancient Rhodian community. There are some remains of an early Hellenistic Temple of

Athena, as well as those of a Byzantine church. Because of its strategic position, Filerimos also was used by the Knights for a fortress, which stands above a monastery of Our Lady of Filerimos. ⊠ *Take turnoff, going on coast road west from Petaloudes, at Trianda and head south for 5 km (3 mi)* ☎ *22410/92202* ⊕ *www.culture.gr* ⊠ *€3* ⊘ *May–Oct., Mon.–Sun. 8:30–2:40; Nov.–Apr., Tues.–Sun. 8:30–2:40.*

The **Rhodes Windsurfing Academy** (⊠ Odos Ferenikis ☎ 22410/91666 ⊕ www.rwa.gr) in coastal Ialyssos (Trianda) has windsurfing, sailing, canoe, and other sea-sport lessons, and equipment rental and repair.

SYMI

ΣΥΜΗ

The island of Symi, 45 km (27 mi) north of Rhodes, is an enchanting place, with its star attraction being Chorio, a 19th-century town of neoclassical mansions. The island has few beaches and almost no flat land, so it is not attractive to developers. As a result, quiet Symi provides a peaceful retreat for travelers, who tend to fall in love with the island on their first visit and return year after year.

Nireus, the ancient king of Symi, who sailed with three vessels to assist the Greeks at Troy, is mentioned in Homer. Symi was later part of the Dorian Hexapolis dominated by Rhodes, and it remained under Rhodian dominance throughout the Roman and Byzantine periods. The island has good natural harbors, and the nearby coast of Asia Minor provided plentiful timber for the Symiotes, who were shipbuilders, fearless seafarers and sponge divers, and rich and successful merchants. Under the Ottomans their harbor was proclaimed a free port and attracted the trade of the entire region. Witness to their prosperity are the neoclassical mansions that line the harbor and towns. The Symiotes' continuous travel and trade and their frequent contact with Europe led them to incorporate foreign elements in their furnishings, clothes, and cultural life. At first they lived in Chorio, high on the hillside above the port, and in the second half of the 19th century spread down to the seaside at Yialos. There were some 20,000 inhabitants at this acme, but under the Italian occupation at the end of the Italo-Turkish war in 1912, the island declined; the Symiotes lost their holdings in Asia Minor and were unable to convert their fleets to steam. Many emigrated to work elsewhere, and now there are just a few thousand inhabitants in Chorio and Yialos. Symi is an hour ride by hydrofoil from Rhodes town.

Yialos

Γιαλός

45 km (27 mi) north of Rhodes.

As the boat from Rhodes to Symi rounds the last of many rocky barren spurs, the port of Yialos, at the back of a deep, narrow harbor, comes into view. The shore is lined with mansions with ground floors that have been converted to cafés that have waterside terraces perfect for whiling away lazy hours.

The **Church of Ayhios Ioannis** (⊠ Near center of Yialos village), built in 1838, incorporates in its walls fragments of ancient blocks from a temple that apparently stood on this site and is surrounded by a plaza paved in an intricate mosaic, fashioned from inlaid pebbles.

Sponge-diving tools, model ships, 19th-century navigation tools, and anchors fill the teeny **Symi Naval Museum.** It's hard to miss the ornamental blue-and-yellow building. The sea memorabilia within gives a good taste of life in Symi in the 19th and early 20th centuries. ⊠ *Yialos waterfront* ☜ *€2* ⊗ *Tues.–Sun. 11–2:30.*

Where to Stay & Eat

★ **$$$–$$$$** ✕**Mylopetra.** Dine in an old flour mill, where decorations include an ancient tomb embedded in glass beneath the floor, or out on the candlelit terrace. This extraordinary restaurant is the creation of a German couple, Hans and Eva Sworoski, who painstakingly oversaw the delightful conversion and tend to the excellent cooking and gracious service. The menu changes daily, though perpetual favorites include a wonderful lasagna with prawns and sea bream in a light mustard sauce. ⊠ *Behind church on the back St.* ☎ *22460/72333* ⚓ *Reservations essential* ▤ *MC, V* ⊗ *Closed mid-Oct.–Apr.*

¢–$ ✕**Trawlers.** Anna Kanli's home cooking is behind one of Yialos's most successful, inexpensive tavernas. She prepares traditional meat and fish dishes, not to mention vegetarian moussaka. Weather permitting, you can also dine in a pretty square a few steps from the port. ⊠ *Pl. Economou, harbor front* ☎ *22460/71411* ▤ *No credit cards* ⊗ *Closed Nov.–Apr.*

★ **$$$–$$$$** ⌸ **Aliki Hotel.** A three-story, 1895 mansion on the waterfront houses this attractive hotel. Each of the rooms is different, but all are furnished with a tasteful mix of antiques and newer pieces. The best rooms, of course, are those that face the water—two rooftop rooms share a tiled terrace. Breakfast is included and in good weather is served on a waterside terrace that doubles as a bar in the evening. ⊠ *Yialos waterfront, 85600* ☎ *22460/71665* ⌨ *22460/71655* ⊕ *www.hotelaliki.gr* ⇗ *13 rooms, 2 suites* ⚐ *Café, bar, lobby lounge; no room TVs* ▤ *MC, V* ⦿ *CP.*

Beaches

One reason Symi's beaches are so pristine is that almost none are reachable by car. From the main harbor at Yialos, boats leave every half hour between 10:30 and 12:30 to the beautiful beaches of **Aghia Marina, Aghios Nikolas, Aghios Giorgos,** and **Nanou Bay.** Return trips run 4–6 PM. The round-trips cost €5–€10.

For a swim near Yialos, you can go to the little strip of beach beyond the Yialos harbor—follow the road past the bell tower and the Aliki Hotel and you come to a seaside taverna that rents umbrellas and beach chairs. If you continue walking on the same road for about 3 km (2 mi), you come to the pine-shaded beach at **Niborios Bay,** where there is another taverna.

Festival

The **Symi Festival** brings free dance, music, theater performances, and cinema screenings to the island every year from July through September. Most events take place in the main harbor square in Yialos, but some are scheduled in other places around the island. A schedule of events is posted at the square, and programs can be found at local shops, travel agents, and the town hall.

Chorio

Χωριό

1 km (½ mi) east of Yialos.

It's a 10-minute walk from the main harbor of Yialos up to the hilltop town of Chorio, along a staircase of some 400 steps, known as Kali Strata. There is also a road that can be traveled in one of the island's few taxis or by bus, which makes a circuit with stops at the harbor in Yialos, Chorio, and the seaside community of Pedi. The Kali Strata is flanked by elegant neoclassical houses with elaborate stonework; lavish pediments; and intricate wrought-iron balconies. Just before the top of the stairs (and the welcome little Kali Strata bar), a line of windmills crowns the hill of **Noulia.** Most of Chorio's many churches date to the 18th and 19th centuries, and many are ornamented with richly decorated iconostases and ornate bell towers. Donkeys are often used to carry materials through the narrow streets for the town's steady construction and renovation work.

The collection at the **archaeological museum** displays Hellenistic and Roman sculptures and inscriptions as well as more recent carvings, icons, costumes, and handicrafts. ⊠ *Follow signs from central square to Lieni neighborhood* ☎ *22460/71114* 🗐 *€2* ☉ *Tues.–Sun. 8–2:30.*

The **kastro** (Castle; ⊠ At top of town, in ancient acropolis) incorporates fragments of Symi's history in its walls. A church and several teeny chapels dominate the area with only a few remnants of the castle walls. The view from here takes in the village of Pedi as well as both Chorio and Yialos.

Where to Stay & Eat

$–$$$$ ✕ **Georgio and Maria's Taverna.** Meals at this simple Chorio taverna, which is as popular with locals as it is with tourists, are served in a high-ceilinged, whitewashed dining room or on a terrace that is partially shaded by a grape arbor and affords wonderful views over the sea and surrounding hills. Fish is a specialty, and simply prepared *mezedes* (small dishes), such as roasted peppers topped with feta cheese and fried zucchini, can constitute a delicious meal in themselves. If you're lucky, one of the neighbors will stroll in with instrument in hand to provide an impromptu serenade. ⊠ *Off main Sq.* ☎ *22460/71984* ⊟ *AE, MC, V.*

$–$$ ✕ **The Windmill.** An old mill at the top of the Kali Strata has been converted into a multifloor restaurant serving breakfast and takeout by day and casual dining by night. British proprietor Amanda Wall aims for light, summery food, from creative salads and bruschetta to pasta shells with seafood. The desserts served in the eatery's elevated courtyard are more decadent, including chocolate-coated cheesecake. ⊠ *Off main Sq., 85600* ☎ *22460/71871* ⊟ *No credit cards* ☉ *Closed Oct.–Apr.*

$ 🏠 **Village Hotel.** On a small lane, this hotel occupies a traditional neo-classical mansion. It has good views in all directions . . . and a steep climb home after you've had a morning coffee in the port. All the rooms open onto a balcony or terrace and surround an attractive garden. ⊠ *Off main square, 85600* 🖷 *22460/71800* 🖶 *22460/71802* 🖫 *17 rooms* 🍴 *Dining room, refrigerators, bar; no room TVs* 🖃 *No credit cards* 🕙 *Closed Nov.–Apr.* ¶⊙¶ *CP.*

★ ¢–$ 🏠 **Hotel Fiona.** This bright, cheerful hotel is perched on the hillside in Chorio, with splendid views. Just about all of the large rooms, with spotless white-tile floors and attractive blue-painted furnishings and pastel fabrics, have a sea-facing balcony. Breakfast, with yogurt, homemade cakes, and marmalade, is served in the breezy, attractive lobby lounge. ⊠ *Near main square, 85600* 🖷🖶 *22460/72088* 🖫 *14 rooms* 🍴 *Lobby lounge; no room TVs* 🖃 *No credit cards* 🕙 *Closed Nov.–Apr.* ¶⊙¶ *CP.*

Monastery of Taxiarchis Michael Panormitis

Μονή Ταξιάρχη Μιχαήλ Πανορμίτη

7 km (4½ mi) south of Chorio.

The main reason to venture to the atypically green, pine-covered hills surrounding the little gulf of Panormitis is to visit the Monastery of Taxiarchis Michael Panormitis, dedicated to Symi's patron saint, and also the protector of sailors. The entrance to the site is surmounted by an elaborate **bell tower,** of the multilevel wedding-cake variety already seen in Yialos and Chorio. In the **courtyard,** which is surrounded by a vaulted stoa, a black-and-white pebble mosaic adorns the floor. The interior of the **church,** entirely frescoed in the 18th century, contains a marvelously ornate wooden iconostasis, flanked by a heroic-size 18th-century representation of Michael, completely covered with silver. Note also the collection of votives, including ship models, gifts brought from all over, and bottles with money in them, which, according to local lore, traveled to Symi on their own after having been thrown into the sea. Any trip to the monastery should be accompanied by a refreshing swim in the deep-blue harbor. The monastery allows you to stay overnight free of charge in simple rooms for up to a week; rooms with kitchens are available for €18–€28 a night. ⊠ *Symi's south side, at harbor* 🖷 *22460/72414* 🖃 *Free* 🕙 *Daily 7 AM–8 PM.*

KOS

ΚΩΣ

The island of Kos, the third largest in the Dodecanese, is certainly one of the most beautiful, with verdant fields and tree-clad mountains, surrounded by miles of sandy beach. Its highest peak, part of a small mountain range in the northeast, is less than 2,800 feet. All this beauty has not gone unnoticed, of course, and Kos undeniably suffers from the effects of mass tourism: its beaches are often crowded, most of its seaside towns have been recklessly overdeveloped, and the main town is noisy and busy between June and September.

In Mycenaean times and during the Archaic period, the island prospered. In the 6th century BC it was conquered by the Persians but later joined the Delian League, supporting Athens against Sparta in the Peloponnesian War. Kos was invaded and destroyed by the Spartan fleet, ruled by Alexander and various of his successors, and has twice been devastated by earthquakes. Nevertheless, the city and the economy flourished, as did the arts and sciences. The painter Apelles, the Michelangelo of his time, came from Kos, as did Hippocrates, father of modern medicine. Under the Roman Empire, the island's Asklepieion and its renowned healing center drew emperors and ordinary citizens alike. The Knights of St. John arrived in 1315 and ruled for the next two centuries, until they were replaced by the Ottomans. In 1912 the Italians took over, and in 1947 the island was united with Greece.

Kos Town

Κως (Πόλη)

92 km (57 mi) north of Rhodes.

The modern town lies on a flat plain encircling a spacious harbor called Mandraki and is a pleasant assemblage of low-lying buildings and shady lanes. The fortress, which crowns its west side, where Hippocrates is supposed to have taught in the shade of a large plane tree, is a good place to begin your exploration of Kos town. On one side of Platia Platanou, the little square named after the tree, stands the graceful Loggia, actually a mosque, built in 1786.

The **Castle of the Knights,** built mostly in the 15th century and full of ancient blocks from its Greek and Roman predecessors, is a repository of fragments of ancient inscriptions, funerary monuments, and other sculptural material. A walk around the walls affords good views over the town, whose flat skyline is pierced by a few remaining minarets and many palm trees. ⊠ *Over bridge from Pl. Platanou* ☎ *22420/27927* 🎫 *€3* ☉ *Tues.–Sun. 8:30–2:30.*

Excavations by Italian and Greek archaeologists have revealed ancient **agora and harbor ruins** (⊠ Over bridge from Pl. Platanou, behind Castle of the Knights) that date from the 4th century BC through Roman times. Remnants include parts of the walls of the old city, of a Hellenistic stoa, and of temples dedicated to Aphrodite and Hercules. The ruins, which are not fenced, blend charmingly into the fabric of the modern city; they are a shortcut for people on their way to work, a place to sit and chat, an outdoor playroom for children. In spring the site is covered with brightly colored flowers, which nicely frame the ancient gray-and-white marble blocks tumbled in every direction.

★ The **Archaeological Museum** contains extremely important examples of Hellenistic and Roman sculpture by Koan artists. Among the treasures are a renowned statue of Hippocrates; a group of sculptures from various Roman phases, all discovered in the House of the Europa Mosaic; and a remarkable series of Hellenistic draped female statues mainly from the Sanctuary of Demeter at Kyparissi and the Odeion. ⊠ *Pl. Elefthe-*

rias west of agora through gate leading to Pl. Platanou ☎ 22420/28326
📠 €3 ☉ *Tues.–Sun. 8–2:30.*

The **west excavations** (✉ Southwest of the agora and harbor ruins) have
uncovered a portion of one of the main Roman streets with many
houses, including the **House of the Europa Mosaic.** Part of the **Roman
baths** (near main Roman street), it has been converted into a basilica.
The **gymnasium,** distinguished by its partly reconstructed colonnade, and
the so-called **Nymphaion,** a lavish public latrine that has been restored,
are also of interest. These excavations are always open with free access.

Beaches

If you must get wet but can't leave Kos town, try the narrow pebble
strip of beach, immediately south of the main harbor. The pebble
beach at **Empros Thermes** (✉ 8 km [5 mi] southeast of Kos town) has
the added attraction of a bubbling, seaside hot springs. **Tingaki** (✉ On
north coast, 13 km [8 mi] west of Kos town) has pretty, sandy, but
heavily developed resort beaches. At **Mastichari** (✉ On north coast, 32
km [20 mi] west of Kos town) there's a wide sand beach, tavernas,
rooms for rent, and a pier where boats sail on day trips to the uncrowded
islet of Pserimos.

Where to Stay & Eat

$–$$$ ✕ **Petrino.** Greek-Canadian brothers Mike and George Gerovasilis have
created a calm oasis a few streets in from the hustle and bustle of Kos
harbor. A 150-year-old stone house provides cozy dining in cool months,
and tables fill a garden full of private nooks, fountains, and gentle
music in summer. The enormous menu lists Greek recipes, like zucchini
pancakes and liver with oregano, side-by-side with European classics
like chateaubriand. Actor Tom Hanks has been among the VIP guests.
✉ *Pl. Ioannou Theologou* ☎ *2220/27251* ⊕ *petrino.kosweb.com*
▤ *AE, DC, MC, V.*

$–$$$ ✕ **To Limanaki.** Buttery Symi shrimp, tender calamari, and lightly fried
atherines (tiny smelt fish) stand out among the many seafood choices.
If fish isn't your thing, the menu also has all the Greek basics. The family-run taverna is even open for bacon and eggs in the morning. On one
side of the restaurant is a buzzing street, on the other, silent ruins and
the chapel of St. Ann. ✉ *Odos Megalou Alexandrou 11* ☎ *22420/
21153* ▤ *MC, V.*

★ $$$$ ⌂ **Grecotel Kos Imperial.** On a hillside over the Aegean, this spa resort
has a private beach as well as seawater and freshwater pools and artificial rivers and lagoons. Indoors, there are glimmering glass-tile hy-
drotherapy pools, dozens of spa treatments, and many guest rooms with
private hot tubs and pools. Grecotel's signature style of simple but
beautifully designed luxury is everywhere in evidence, as in the airy rooms
with bamboo furniture, sheer white linen, and sweeping blue sea views.
✉ *4 km (2½ mi) east of Kos town, 85300 Psalidi* ☎ *22420/58000*
📠 *22420/25192* ⊕ *www.grecotel.gr* ➥ *122 rooms, 207 bungalows, 55
suites* ⚒ *3 restaurants, some in-room hot tubs, in-room safes, cable TV,
indoor pool, 3 saltwater pools, wading pool, spa, beach, shops, laundry service* ▤ *AE, DC, MC, V* ⍩ *BP.*

¢ ⊞ **Hotel Afendoulis.** Simple and friendly, the plain, whitewashed rooms with dark-wood furniture are spotless and of far better quality than most in this price range; they're also far enough off the main road, so it stays quiet at night. You can walk to most places in Kos town from here. Enjoy breakfast, which is extra, in the open marble lobby. ⊠ *Evripilou 1, 85300* ☎ *22420/25321* 🖷 *22420/25797* 20 rooms ♨ Lobby lounge, laundry facilities; no room TVs 🗃 MC, V.

Nightlife

Things start cooking before 7 PM and roar on in many cases past 7 AM on Akti Koundourioti and in the nearby Exarhia area, which includes rowdy Nafklirou and Plessa streets. Competing bars try to lure in bar-hoppers with ads for cheap beer and neon-color drinks.

Fashion (⊠ Odos Kanari 2 ☎ 22420/22592), a massive club off of Akti Koundourioti, has an outdoors bar, happy hour, and a throbbing indoor dance floor. Guest DJs seek to provide young, international tourists the kind of club music they'd hear back home.

A quiet spot for live Greek music is **Cafe Bar 4** (⊠ Riga Fereou 13 ☎ 22420/24743). The loungey, seaside club **H20** (⊠ Aktis Art Hotel, beachfront, Vasileos Georgiou 7 ☎ 22420/47207) has a small, sleek interior as well as outdoor seating.

Festival

Every summer from July through mid-September Kos hosts the **Hippocrates Festival** (☎ 22420/28665). Music, dance, movie screenings, and theater performances enliven the Castle of the Knights. The festival also includes daytime activities for children.

Sports & the Outdoors

The island of Kos, particularly the area around the town, is good for bicycle riding. Ride to the Asklepieion for a picnic, or visit the Castle of Antimacheia. Note: be aware of hazards such as cistern openings; very few have security fences around them. You can rent bicycles everywhere—in Kos town and at the more popular resorts. Try the many shops along Eleftheriou Venizelou street in town. Renting a bike costs about €6 per day.

Asklepieion

Ασκληπιείον

4 km (2½ mi) west of Kos town.

One of the great healing centers of antiquity, the Asklepieion is framed by a thick grove of cypress trees and laid out on several **broad terraces** connected by a monumental staircase. The lower terrace probably held the Asklepieion Festivals. On the middle terrace is an **Ionic temple,** once decorated with paintings by Apelles, including the renowned depiction of Aphrodite often written about in antiquity and eventually removed to Rome by the emperor Augustus. On the uppermost terrace is the **Doric Temple of Asklepieios,** once surrounded by colonnaded porticoes. ⊠ *Asklepieion* ☎ *22420/28763* 🎫 *€4* ☉ *Tues.–Sun. 8:30–2:30.*

| off the beaten path |

MOUNTAIN VILLAGES – Leaving the main road southwest of the Asklepieion (turnoff is at Zipari, 9 km [5½ mi] southwest of Kos town), you can explore an enchanting landscape of cypress and pine trees on a route that climbs to a handful of lovely, whitewashed rural villages that cling to the craggy slopes of the island's central mountains, including Asfendiou, Zia, and Lagoudi. The busiest of them is Zia, with an appealing smattering of churches; crafts shops selling local honey, weavings, and handmade soaps; and open-air tavernas where you can enjoy the views over the surrounding forests and fields toward the sea.

Where to Eat

¢ ✕ **Asklipios.** The town is noted for its Muslim minority, and you can have

Fodor's Choice a memorable Turkish-inspired meal at the little restaurant called "Ali."

★ Sit in the shade of an ancient laurel tree and try the selection of exquisite mezedes: *imam bayaldi* (baked eggplant), bourekakia, and home-prepared *dolmadakia* (small dolmades). An array of kebabs includes excellent *soutzoukakia* (elongated meatballs); even the boiled cauliflower is perfect. ⊠ *3 km (2 mi) west of Kos town, on main square, Platani* ☎ *22420/25264* ▤ *MC, V.*

★ ¢ ✕ **Taverna Ampavris.** The surroundings and the food are both delightful at this charming, rustic taverna, outside Kos town on a lane leading to the village of Platani. Meals are served in the courtyard of an old farmhouse, and the kitchen's emphasis is on local country food—including wonderful stews and grilled meats, accompanied by vegetables from nearby gardens. ⊠ *Ampavris, Platani* ☎ *22420/25696* ▤ *No credit cards.*

Castle of Antimacheia

Κάστρο Αντιμάχειας

21 km (13 mi) southwest of Asklepieion, 25 km (15 mi) southwest of Kos town.

The thick, well-preserved walls of this medieval fortress look out over the sweeping Aegean and Kos's green interior. Around the fortress, which has a coat of arms from the Knights of the Order of St. John of Rhodes, are the remains of a ruined settlement. ⊠ *On main road from Kos, turn left 3 km (2 mi) before village of Antimacheia, following signs to castle.*

Kefalos Bay

Κόλπος Κέφαλου

10 km (6 mi) south of the Castle of Antimacheia, 35 km (22 mi) southwest of Kos town.

On Kefalos Bay, the little beach community of Kamari is pleasant and less frantic than the island's other seaside resorts. On a summit above is the lovely old town of Kefalos, a pleasant place to wander for its views and quintessential Greekness. Close offshore here is a little rock formation holding a chapel to St. Nicholas. Opposite are the ruins of a magnificent 5th-century Christian basilica.

Beaches

A chunk of the **Ayios Stefanos** beach, just north of Kamari, is now occupied by a Club Med; the rest belongs to beach clubs renting umbrellas and chairs and offering activities that include waterskiing and jet-skiing. Nearby **Paradise Beach** (⊠ 3 km [2mi] north of Kalmari) has plenty of parking, and thus crowds, but the broad, sandy beach is magnificent and gives its name to a long stretch of sand that curves around the enchanting Gulf of Kefalos and, at its northern end, is undeveloped, almost deserted (and popular with nude bathers).

Where to Stay & Eat

¢–$$ ✕ **Faros.** It's not surprising that fish rules the menu at this seaside taverna at the very end of the beach in Kamari. In fact, some patrons arrive by dinghies from their yachts anchored offshore. The friendly staff will take you into the kitchen and show you the fresh catch of the day; then they'll grill or bake it to your liking. ⊠ *Beachfront, Kamari* ☎ *22420/71240* ▭ *MC, V.*

¢ ▦ **Studio Eleni.** Rows of sunflowers and giant basil plants decorate this family-run group of studio apartments located along the waterfront of the relatively quiet community of Kamari. The rooms are large and better equipped than most in this price range; all have kitchens and outdoor terraces. ⊠ *Waterfront, 85300 Kamari* ☎ *22420/71267, 22420/71048 winter* ➶ *6 studios* ⌂ *Kitchenettes; no a/c, no room TVs* ▭ *No credit cards.*

PATMOS

ΠΑΤΜΟΣ

Rocky and barren, the small, 34-square-km (21-square-mi) island of Patmos lies beyond the islands of Kalymnos and Leros, northwest of Kos. Here on a hillside is the Monastery of the Apocalypse, which enshrines the cave where St. John received the Revelation in AD 95. Scattered evidence of Mycenaean presence remains on Patmos, and walls of the classical period indicate the existence of a town near Skala. Most of the island's approximately 2,500 people live in three villages: Skala, medieval Chora, and the small rural settlement of Kambos. The island is popular among the faithful making pilgrimages to the monastery as well as with vacationing Athenians and a wealthy international set who have bought homes in Chora. Administrators have carefully contained development, and as a result, Patmos retains its charm and natural beauty—even in the busy month of August.

Skala

Σκάλα

161 km (100 mi) north of Kos.

Skala, the island's small but sophisticated main town, is where almost all the hotels and restaurants are located. It's a popular port of call for cruise ships, and in summer, the huge liners often loom over the chic shops and restaurants. There's not much to see in the town, but it is lively and very attractive, and, since strict building codes have been enforced, even new buildings have traditional architectural detail. The medieval town of Chora, only 5 km (3 mi) above Skala, and the island's legendary monasteries are nearby.

Beaches

Although most of Patmos's beaches, which tend to be coarse shingle, are accessible by land, many sun worshippers choose to sail to them on the caïques that make regular runs from Skala, leaving in the morning; prices vary with the number of people making the trip (or with the boat). Ask for several "bids" to find out the going rate and the time of return, and don't be shy about negotiating. Transport to and from a beach for a family for a day may cost around €35.The beach at **Melloi,** a 20-minute walk north of Skala or a quick caïque ride, is a sand-and-pebble strip with cafés and tavernas nearby. The beach at **Kambos Bay,** a 15- to 20-minute caïque ride or 10 minutes by car or bus from Skala, is the most popular on the island. It has mostly fine pebble and sand, nearby tavernas, windsurfing, waterskiing, and pedal boats for rent. **Psili Amos** on the south shore, has sand, but requires a 45-minute caïque ride (€10) or a 20-minute walk from the taverna near the end of the road to the south end of the island.

off the beaten path	**LIVADI KALOGIRON** – Beyond Kambos, on the northern end of the island, Livadi Kalogiron beach—a combination of sand and pebbles backed by pine trees—is accessible by road, 8 km (5 mi) north of Skala. The **Livadi Beach Restaurant** (✛ Take turnoff along narrow road that follows coast from Kambos toward Livadi Kalogiron beach ☎ No phone) sits above the beach and from June to August serves simple food, including delicious zucchini pancakes. It's an excellent place to retreat from the heat of the day and enjoy a beverage.

Where to Stay & Eat

★ **$–$$** ✕ **Benetos.** A native Patmian, Benetos Matthaiou, and his American wife, Susan, operate this lovely restaurant where you dine on a flowery terrace. Here you are surrounded by a seaside garden that supplies the kitchen with fresh herbs and vegetables. Homegrown ingredients, including aromatic cherry tomatoes, find their way into a selection of Mediterranean-style dishes that include phyllo parcels stuffed with spinach and cheese, the island's freshest Greek salad, and seafood pastas. Accompany your meal with a selection from the eclectic Greek wine list. Service is gracious and friendly. ⊠ *On harborside road between Skala and Grikos, Sapsila* ☎ *22470/33089* ⊕ *www.benetosrestaurant.com* ☐ *MC, V* ☉ *Closed Mon. and mid-Oct.–May.*

¢–$$ ✕ **Ostria.** After a long day of swimming or boating, locals gravitate to this frill-free fish taverna on the harbor. Basic wooden furniture, plastic tablecloths, and bare lightbulbs are the only decor in the tented summer eating area. But this is the perfect place for watching Skala's human traffic pass by while sipping an ouzo and tackling an overflowing fried seafood *pikilia* (appetizer sampler). ⊠ *Waterfront* ☎ *No phone* ☐ *No credit cards* ☉ *Closed mid-Oct–May.*

★ $$$–$$$$ ▦ **Porto Scoutari.** It seems only fitting that Patmos should have a hotel that reflects the architectural beauty of the island while providing luxurious accommodations. Guest rooms are enormous and have sitting and sleeping areas, in addition to large terraces that face the sea and a verdant garden with a swimming pool. Furnishings differ from room to room and include brass beds and reproduction Greek antiques; the lobby and breakfast rooms are also exquisitely decorated with traditional pieces. Owner Elina Scoutari, who lived in Washington, D.C., for many years, is on hand to see to your needs. ⊠ *1 km (½ mi) northeast of Skala center, 85500* ☎ *22470/33123* 📠 *22470/33175* ⊕ *www.portoscoutari. com* 🛏 *30 rooms* ⚹ *Café, kitchenettes, minibars, cable TV, in-room data ports, pool, bar, travel services* ▭ *MC, V* ⊗ *Closed Nov.–Mar.* ⦿ *BP.*

$ ▦ **Blue Bay Hotel.** A Greek-Australian family has returned to open this hotel, which is outside Skala and within a 10-minute walk of everything. Its location, with a view over the open sea (shared by all but two of the rooms), is one of its great charms, as are the neatly decorated, immaculate rooms, all with stone slab floors and terraces or balconies. ⊠ *South edge of Skala Harbor, 85500* ☎ *22470/31165* 📠 *2247032303* ⊕ *www. bluebay.50g.com* 🛏 *27 rooms* ⚹ *Refrigerators, lobby lounge, Internet room; no TVs in some rooms* ▭ *MC, V* ⊗ *Closed Nov.–Mar.* ⦿ *CP.*

★ $ ▦ **Captain's House.** One of the very special places to stay in Patmos, largely because the owners are so pleasant, this small pink hotel with green shutters faces the sea at the edge of Skala. The feel of old Patmos has been re-created with stone arches accenting the multilevel lobby. The white-painted rooms with their simple wood furniture are spotless and breezy; all have balconies that face either the harbor or the pool area. The TV in the lounge gets satellite stations. ⊠ *Inland, south of main street, 85500* ☎ *22470/31793* 📠 *22470/34077* ⊕ *www.captainshouse.net* 🛏 *19 rooms* ⚹ *Café, pool, lobby lounge, car rental* ▭ *MC, V* ⊗ *Closed mid-Oct.–Mar.* ⦿ *CP.*

Shopping

Patmos has some elegant boutiques selling jewelry and crafts, including antiques, mainly from the island. **Katoi** (⊠ Skala–Chora Rd. ☎ 22470/ 31487 or 22470/34107) has a wide selection of ceramics, icons, and silver jewelry of traditional design. **Parousia** (⊠ Past square at beginning of road to Chora ☎ 22470/32549) is a good place to purchase Byzantine-style icons, wooden children's toys, and small religious items.

Chora

Χώρα

5 km (3 mi) south above Skala.

Atop a hill due south of Skala, the village of Chora, clustered around the walls of the Monastery of St. John the Theologian, has become a preserve of international wealth. Though the short distance from Skala may make walking seem attractive, a steep incline can make this challenging. A taxi ride is not expensive, about €6, and there is frequent bus service from Skala and other points on the island (€1).

In AD 95, during the emperor Domitian's persecution of Christians, St. John the Theologian was banished to Patmos, where he lived until his reprieve two years later. He writes that it was on Patmos that he "heard . . . a great voice, as of a trumpet," commanding him to write a book and "send it unto the seven churches." According to tradition, St. John wrote the text of *Revelation* in the little cave, the Sacred Grotto,
★ now built into the **Monastery of the Apocalypse.** The voice of God spoke through a threefold crack in the rock, and the saint dictated to his follower Prochorus. A slope in the wall is pointed to as the desk where Prochorus wrote, and silver haloes are set on the stone that was the apostle's pillow. The grotto is decorated with wall paintings of the 12th century and icons from the 16th. The monastery was constructed in the 17th century from architectural fragments of earlier buildings, and further embellished in later years; it also contains chapels to St. Artemios and St. Nicholas. In early September, the monastery hosts the **Festival of Sacred Music of Patmos,** with world-class Byzantine and ecclesiastical music performances in an outdoor performance space. ⊠ *2 km (1 mi) south on Skala–Chora Rd.* ☎ *22470/31234 monastery, 22470/29363 festival* 🖅 *Free* ⊘ *Mon., Wed., Fri., and Sat. 8–1:30; Tues., Thurs., and Sun. 8–1:30 and 4–6.*

Fodor'sChoice ★ The **Monastery of St. John the Theologian,** on its high perch, is one of the finest extant examples of a fortified medieval monastic complex. Hosios Christodoulos, a man of education, energy, devotion, and vision who built the Theotokos Monastery in Kos, came to Patmos in 1088 to set up the island's now-famous monastery. From its inception, it attracted monks of education and social standing, who made sure that it was ornamented with the best sculpture, carvings, and paintings. It was an intellectual center, with a rich library and a tradition of teaching, and by the end of the 12th century it owned land on Leros, Limnos, Crete, and Asia Minor, as well as ships, which carried on trade exempt from taxes. A broad staircase leads to the entrance, which was fortified by towers and buttresses. The complex consists of buildings from a number of periods: in front of the entrance is the 17th-century **Chapel of the Holy Apostles;** the **main church** dates from the time of Christodoulos; the **Chapel of the Virgin** (not open to the public) is 12th century.

The **treasury** contains relics, icons, silver, and vestments, most dating from 1600 to 1800. Many of the objects are votives dedicated by the clerics, nobles, and wealthy individuals; one of the most beautiful is an 11th-century icon of St. Nicholas, executed in the finest mosaic work, in an exquisitely chased silver frame. Another treasure is an El Greco icon. On display too are some of the library's oldest codices, dating to the late 5th and the 8th centuries, such as pages from the Gospel of St. Mark and the Book of Job. The more than 600 vestments are of luxurious fabrics, elaborately embroidered with gold, silver, and multicolor silks. A new wing, opened in 2005, contains folk art and Patmos antiquities.Though not open to the public, the **library** contains extensive treasures: illuminated manuscripts, approximately 1,000 codices, and more than 3,000 printed volumes. The collection was first cataloged in 1200; of the 267 works of that time, the library still has 111. The archives preserve a near-continuous record, down to the present, of the history of the monastery as well as the political and economic history of the region. ✉ *3 km (2 mi) south of Monastery of Apocalypse* ☎ *22470/31398* 🖼 *Church and chapel free, treasury €6* ⊘ *Daily 8–1:30, Sun., Tues., and Thurs. 8–1:30 and 4–6.*

Where to Eat

¢–$ ✕ **Vangelis.** At this pleasant taverna on the main square, you can choose between a table there or in the back garden, where a raised terrace has stunning views of the sea. Fresh grilled fish and lamb are the specialties, and simple dishes such as fried eggplant and *tzatziki* (yogurt and cucumber dip) are excellent. The management is happy to help find rooms in private homes in Chora. ✉ *Main Sq.* ☎ *22470/31967* 🖃 *No credit cards.*

RHODES & THE DODECANESE A TO Z

AIR TRAVEL

There are more than eight flights per day to Rhodes from Athens on Olympic Airlines or Aegean Airlines, and extra flights are added during high season. The 45-minute flight costs about €100 one-way. Olympic flies flights to Rhodes from Heraklion (one hour, €87) and several times a week from Thessaloniki (75 minutes, €117). It is possible to fly directly to Rhodes from a number of European capitals, especially on charters.

To Kos, Olympic Airlines runs three to four daily flights from Athens, and three flights a week from Rhodes. Schedules are reduced in winter. Neither Patmos nor Symi have airports.

🛂 Carriers **Aegean Airlines** ✉ Rhodes Airport, Rhodes town, Rhodes ☎ 22410/98345, 210/998-8300 in Athens ⊕ www.aegeanair.gr. **Olympic Airlines** ✉ Ierou Lochou 9, Rhodes town, Rhodes ☎ 22410/24555, 22420/24571, 210/966-6666 in Athens 🖷 210/966-6111 ✉ Vasileos Pavlou 22, Kos town, Kos ☎ 22420/28331 or 22420/28332 ⊕ www.olympicairlines.com.

AIRPORTS

Rhodes Airport is about 20 minutes from Rhodes town, and it's best to take a taxi (about €14). Though private vehicles must have permits to enter the old town, a taxi may enter if carrying luggage, no matter what a reluctant driver tells you. A bus runs between the Olympic Airways office in Kos and the Kos airport about 30 minutes away.

🛂 **Kos Airport** ☎ 22420/51229. **Rhodes Airport** ☎ 22410/88700.

BIKE & MOPED TRAVEL

You can rent bicycles, including mountain bikes, as well as motor scooters, in Rhodes town from Margaritis Rent a Moto. Bicycle shops are plentiful in Kos.

🛂 Rentals **Margaritis Rent a Moto** ✉ Kazouli 23, Rhodes town, Rhodes ☎ 22410/37420.

BOAT & FERRY TRAVEL

When traveling from Piraeus to Rhodes by ferry (12–18 hours, €35–€90), you first make several stops, including at Patmos (6–10 hours, €25–€81) and Kos (10–16 hours, €30–€80). Bringing a car aboard can quadruple costs. Of the several ferry lines serving the Dodecanese, Blue Star Ferries and G&A Ferries have the largest boats and the most frequent service, both sailing several times a week out of Piraeus. The Athens–Dodecanese ferry schedule changes seasonally, so contact ferry lines, the Piraeus Port Authority, any Athens EOT, or a travel agency for details.

The easiest way to get among the Dodecanese islands is by hydrofoil or catamaran, which takes almost half the time of a ferry (and costs more). Dodekanisos Shipping Co. catamarans travel between Rhodes and Symi (50 minutes, €14), Kos (2 hours and 15 minutes, €28), Patmos (5 hours, €43), and other islands daily. ANES also has hydrofoils and catamarans running between Symi and Rhodes and other islands.

ANES ⊠ Harbor front, Yialos, Symi ☎ 22460/71444 ⊕ www.anes.gr. **Blue Star Ferries** ⊠ Akti Poseidonas 26, Piraeus ☎ 210/891–9800 ⊕ www.bluestarferries.com. **Dodekanisos Shipping Co.** ⊠ Australia 3, Rhodes town, Rhodes ☎ 22410/70590 ⊕ www.12ne.gr. **G&A Ferries** ⊠ Kantharou 2, at Akti Miaouli, Piraeus ☎ 210/458–2640. **Piraeus Port Authority** ☎ 210/422–6000. **Rhodes Port Authority** ☎ 22410/22220.

BUS TRAVEL

There is a good bus network on all the islands. Buses from Rhodes town leave from the bus stop for points on the east side of the island and from Averoff street for the west side.

Averoff ⊠ Next to new market, Rhodes town, Rhodes ☎ 22410/26300. **Rhodes bus stop** ⊠ Alexander Papagou, near Pl. Rimini, Rhodes town, Rhodes ☎ 22410/27706.

CAR RENTALS

Agencies **Budget Drive Rent-a-Car** ⊠ 1-km mark on Tsairi–airport road, Rhodes town 22440/32177, Rhodes ☎ 22410/68243 ⊠ Airport, Rhodes ☎ 22410/81011. **Holiday Autos** ⊠ Karaiskaki 9, Kos town, Kos ☎ 22420/22997 ⊟ 22420/27608.

Local Agencies **Helen's** ⊠ Ramira Beach Hotel, Psalidi, Kos ☎ 22420/28882 ⊟ 22420/21013. **Roderent** ⊠ Al. Diakou 64, Rhodes town, Rhodes ☎ 22410/31831. **Tassos** ⊠ Skala, Patmos ☎ 22470/31753 ⊟ 22470/32210.

CAR TRAVEL

You may take a car to the Dodecanese on one of the large ferries that sail daily from Piraeus to Rhodes and less frequently to the smaller islands. On Rhodes, the roads are good, there are not many of them, and good maps are available. It is possible to tour the island in one day if you rent a car. Traffic is likely to be heavy only from Rhodes town to Lindos and again as you near Kameiros.

In Kos, a car is advisable only if you are very pressed for time; most of what you want to see in Kos can by reached by bicycle or public transportation. In Patmos, a car or motorbike makes it easy to tour the island, though most other sights and outlying restaurants are easily reached by bus or taxi, and beaches can be reached either by bus or boat. Symi, which has only one road suitable for cars, is best explored on foot or by boat.

EMERGENCIES

As elsewhere in Greece, pharmacies in the Dodecanese post in their windows a list showing which locations are open 24 hours and on which days.

Hospital ☎ 22410/22222 in Rhodes, 22420/22300 in Kos, 22470/31211 in Patmos. **Emergency** ☎ 166 in Rhodes and Kos. **Police** ⊠ Ethelondon Dodekanissou 45, Rhodes town,

Rhodes ☎ 100 in Rhodes and Kos, 22470/31303 in Patmos, 22460/71111 in Symi. **Tourist police** ✉ Odos Karpathou 1, Rhodes town, Rhodes ☎ 22410/27423, ✉ Akti Miaouli 2, Kos town, Kos ☎ 22420/22444.

ENGLISH-LANGUAGE MEDIA

The free *Rodos News,* an English-language paper with insiders' evaluations of the sites and events, is available at tourist spots. On Symi, the useful English-language newspaper *Symi Visitor,* available at tourist spots, has information on events and activities around the island, along with bus and ferry schedules. The Web site also has weather updates and information on finding accommodations on Symi.

🔹 *Symi Visitor* ⊕ www.symivisitor.com.

TAXIS

Taxis are available throughout the island of Rhodes, including at most resorts. All taxi stands in Rhodes have a sign listing set fares to destinations around the island. Expect a delay when calling radio taxis in high season.

🔹 **Taxis** ✉ Off Pl. Rimini, Rhodes town, Rhodes ☎ 22410/64712 or 22410/64756.

TOURS

From April to October, local island boat tours take you to area sights and may include a picnic on a remote beach or even a visit to the shores of Turkey. For example, Triton Holidays of Rhodes organizes a visit to Lindos by boat; a caïque leaves Mandraki Harbor in Rhodes town in the morning, deposits you in Lindos for a day of sightseeing and beachgoing, and returns you in the evening for €20. You can also take their boat trip to Marmaris, Turkey (€35, plus €14 Turkish port tax), which includes a free guided tour of the city. On Symi, Symi Tours and Kalodoukas Tours run boat trips to the Monastery of Panormitis, as well as to secluded beaches and islets, which include swimming and a barbecue lunch. Aeolos Travel in Kos organizes one-day cruises to other islands. A1 Yacht Trade Consortium organizes sailing tours around the Greek islands near the Turkish coast.

If you're not renting a car on Rhodes, it can be worth it to take a bus tour to its southern points and interior. Triton Holidays has, among other trips, a guided bus tour to Thermes Kallitheas, Epta Piges, and Lindos (€30); a bus tour to Kameiros, Filerimos, and Petaloudes (€30); and a full-day trip through several points in the interior and south (€ 35). Astoria Travel provides day bus trips to Patmos's St. John the Theologian Monastery and the Monastery of the Apocalypse (€20).

On Symi, George Kalodoukas of Kalodoukas Tours leads wonderful guided hiking tours around the island. They also sell a short book by Frances Noble that outlines 25 walks around the island. On Rhodes, you can pick up a book with 18 walks from the Rhodes town GNTO or EOT office (⇨ Visitor Information).

🔹 **Aeolos Travel** ✉ Annetas Laoumzi 8, Kos ☎ 22420/26203 🖶 22420/25948. **Astoria Travel** ✉ Skala Harbor, Patmos ☎ 22470/31205 or 22470/31208 🖶 22470/31975. **Kalodoukas Tours** ✉ Behind Trawler's taverna, Yialos, Symi ☎ 22460/71077 🖶 22460/71491 ⊕ www.symi-greece.com. **Symi Tours** ✉ Symi Harbor, Symi ☎ 22460/71307

🖨 22460/70011 ⊕ www.symitours.com. **Triton Holidays** ✉ Plastira 9, Rhodes, Rhodes ☎ 22410/21690 🖨 22410/31625 ⊕ www.tritondmc.gr. **A1 Yacht Trade Consortium** ✉ Vyronas 1, at Canada, Rhodes town, Rhodes ☎ 22410/22927 ⊕ www.a1yachting.com.

TRAVEL AGENCIES
Triton Holidays on Rhodes, Aeolos Travel on Kos, and Kalodoukas Tours on Symi (⇨ Tours) are helpful in organizing transport, lodging, activities, and other travel arrangements around the Dodecanese.

VISITOR INFORMATION
In Rhodes, the Greek National Tourism Organization (GNTO or EOT), close to the medieval walls in the new town, has brochures and bus schedules. It's open June–September, weekdays 9–9 (8–3 the rest of the year). The central Rhodes Municipal Tourism Office, near the bus station, is open May–October, Saturday–Monday 8–7 and Sunday 8–2:30. The city of Rhodes maintains a helpful English Web site.

🚩 **City of Rhodes** ⊕ www.rhodes.gr. **Greek National Tourism Organization (GNTO or EOT)** ✉ Archbishop Makarios and Papagou, Rhodes town, Rhodes ☎ 22410/44335 or 22410/44336 ⊕ www.gnto.gr ✉ Vasileos Georgiou 1, Kos town, Kos ☎ 22420/24460 ✉ Near ferry dock, Skala, Patmos ☎ 22470/31666. **Rhodes Municipal Tourism Office** ✉ East side of Pl. Rimini, Rhodes town, Rhodes ☎ 22410/35945.

The Northern Islands

12

LESBOS, CHIOS & SAMOS

WORD OF MOUTH

"[Samos] is not the 'green' haven . . . but it has great history, amazing archaeological sites and museums, and a fun nightlife if that's something you'd be into. It's also only a few kilometers from Turkey, so there are day trips one can take."
—tessiegrace

"[Molyvos] is a beautiful little town scattered down a mountainside, with lovely little rooms everywhere, nice restaurants, and a main street that's covered in wisteria. You can walk to a nearby hot springs (we picnicked on the way). I can honestly say I've never smelled anywhere like Lesbos— the air is full of scents of herbs and flowers. And there are birds everywhere. It's a must to visit."
—Collette

www.fodors.com/forums

Updated by
Shane
Christensen

QUIRKY, SEDUCTIVE, FERTILE, sensual, faded, sunny, worldly, ravishing, long-suffering, hedonistic, luscious, mysterious, legendary—these adjectives only begin to describe the islands of the northeastern Aegean. This startling and rather arbitrary archipelago includes a number of islands, such as Ikaria, Samothraki, and Thassos; in this book we focus on the three largest—Lesbos, Chios, and Samos. Closer to Turkey's coast than to Greece's, and quite separate from one another, these islands are hilly, sometimes mountainous, with dramatic coastlines and uncrowded beaches, brilliant architecture, and unforgettable historic sites. Lesbos, Greece's third-largest island and birthplace of legendary artists and writers, is dense with gnarled olive groves and dappled with mineral springs. Chios, though ravaged by fire, retains an eerie beauty and has fortified villages, old mansions, Byzantine monasteries, and stenciled-wall houses. Samos, the lush, mountainous land of wine and honey, whispers of the classical wonders of antiquity.

Despite the Northern Islands' proximity to Asia Minor, they are the essence of Greece, the result of 4,000 years of Hellenic influence. Lesbos, Chios, and Samos prospered gloriously in the ancient world as important commercial and religious centers, though their significance waned under the Ottoman Empire. They also were cultural hothouses, producing such geniuses as Pythagoras, Sappho, and probably Homer.

Tourism has not obscured the magnificent history, rich enduring culture, and spectacular scenery of the Northern Islands. Indeed, the region's pace seems to progress as it must have for ages, and the growing number of summertime visitors has not dimmed the islanders' warmth and openness. Signs of traditional ways of life abound, which you can see as much in the people's interactions with each other as in their longtime activities making ouzo, olive oil, mastic, and wine. The University of the Aegean, with schools in Lesbos, Chios, and Samos, signals the continued importance of arts and letters for the inhabitants of these islands, and year-round festivals demonstrate the prevalence of their cultures.

These are not strictly sun-and-fun islands with the extent of tourist infrastructure of, say, the Cyclades. Many young backpackers and party seekers seem to bypass the northern Aegean. To be sure, you can still carve out plenty of beach time by day and wander into lively restaurants and bars at night. But these islands reveal a deeper character, tracing histories that date back to ancient, Byzantine, and post-Byzantine times, and offering landscapes that are both serene and unspoiled. Visitors to the Northern Islands should expect to find history, culture, beauty, and hospitality. These islands offer commodities that are valued ever more highly by travelers—a sense of discovery and the chance to interact with rich, enduring cultures.

Exploring the Northern Islands

The island of Lesbos is carved by two large, sandy bays, the gulfs of Yera and Kalloni. Undulating hills and cultivated valleys, pine-clad mountains, beaches, springs, desert, and even a petrified forest are also part of the Lesbos terrain. Deep green valleys and rolling hills punctuated by mastic villages characterize Chios. Samos, bathed in green, is filled with pine forests, olive groves, citrus trees, and grapevines, as well as soft hills that fall into the breathtaking Aegean sea.

About the Restaurants

Although waterfront restaurants in the touristed areas can be mediocre, you can most often find delightful meals, especially in the villages. Unless noted, reservations are unnecessary, and casual dress is always acceptable. Go to the kitchen and point to what you want (the Greek names for fish can be tricky to decipher), or be adventurous and let the waiter choose for you (although you may wind up with enough food to feed a village). Fresh fish is very expensive across the islands, €50 and up per kilo, with a typical individual portion measured at about half a kilo. The price for fish is not factored into the price categories below. Lobster is even more expensive. Many restaurants close from October to May.

About the Hotels

Restored mansions, village houses, sophisticated hotels, and budget accommodations are all options. Reserve early in high season for better-category hotels, especially in Pythagorio on Samos and Molyvos on Lesbos. Off-season you can usually bargain down the official prices and you may be able to avoid paying for a compulsory breakfast. Lodging in general remains less costly here than elsewhere in Greece. Most hotel rooms are basic, with simple pine furniture and sparse furnishings often created by local craftspeople. Islanders are extremely friendly hosts, and although they may become more standoffish when the multitudes descend in August, they treat you as a guest rather than a billfold.

WHAT IT COSTS In euros				
	$$$$	**$$$**	**$$**	**$**	**¢**
RESTAURANTS	over €20	€16–€20	€12–€15	€8–€11	under €8
HOTELS	over €160	€121–€160	€91–€120	€60–€90	under €60

Restaurant prices are for one main course at dinner or, for restaurants that serve only *mezedes* (small dishes), for two mezedes. Hotel prices are for two people in a standard double room in high season, including taxes.

Timing

Ask locals and they'll usually say May is the best time to visit these islands. But April, June, September, and October are also especially lovely periods—the weather is ideal, wildflowers and shrubs are in bloom, and the crowds have thinned. Since these three islands are not yet overrun with tourists even in summer, you can find isolated nooks where you can enjoy the therapeutic sounds of the wind, the birds, and the lapping water.

When booking, keep in mind the enlightening cultural events and religious festivals called *paniyiri,* which usually take place on a saint's day or patriotic holiday. Easter is a movable feast. On Lesbos a cultural week of drama, dance, and music exhibitions occurs each May. On Chios festivities take place during Lent and in summer. For more information, *see* the Island Celebrations box, *below.*

Seeing all three islands is a planning challenge: boats sail between Lesbos and Chios almost daily, but sometimes only one ferry runs per week to Samos from those islands. Frequent ferries run to all three islands from Piraeus.

Numbers in the text correspond to numbers in the margin and on the Lesbos and Chios & Samos maps.

If you have 5 days In five days you can manage an overview of Lesbos and Chios. On Day 1 explore the capital of Lesbos, and your lodging base, 🚹 **Mytilini ❶** ⛵. The next two days take excursions out into the countryside: to northern villages such as dreamy **Molyvos ❸**; to Sappho's birthplace in **Skala Eressou ❹**; and to the hill village of **Agiassos ❺**. Take the ferry to Chios for two nights in 🚹 **Chios town ❻**; don't miss the old quarter. Vist nearby **Nea Moni ❼**, a monastery with fine mosaics and tragic history. Then travel via Lithi and Vessa to the southern mastic villages of stenciled **Pirgi ❽** and labyrinthine 🚹 **Mesta ❾**. An alternative would be to take the ferry from Piraeus directly to 🚹 **Samos town ❿**, the capital of Samos. Spend the five days circling the island, with stops at 🚹 **Pythagorio ⓫** and the ancient temple at **Heraion ⓬**, one of the Seven Wonders of the Ancient World. Then travel through mountain villages and to the fishing village of **Kokkari ⓮**.

If you have 7 days Follow the five-day itinerary for Lesbos and Chios above and plan your timing carefully to catch a ferry from Chios to 🚹 **Samos ❿–⓮** for the last two days. You can go on from Samos to other Greek islands, to the Turkish coast, or back to Athens or Piraeus.

If you have 10 days Stick to the seven-day schedule, plugging in three extra days, wherever they fit best, on the islands of your choice, for relaxing and recreation—hiking, enjoying water sports, shopping, or just lazing on an Aegean beach. You might bird-watch on 🚹 **Lesbos ❶–❺** or study ancient ruins on 🚹 **Samos ❿–⓮**. You could visit the other nearby north-Aegean islands and islets, or take a ferry to **Turkey** from Chios, Lesbos, or Samos.

LESBOS

ΛΕΣΒΟΣ

The Turks called Lesbos the "garden of the empire" for its fertility: in the east and center of the island, about 12 million olive trees line the hills in seemingly endless undulating groves. The western landscape is filled with oak trees, sheep pastures, rocky outcrops, and mountains. Wildflowers and grain cover the valleys, and the higher peaks are wreathed in dark green pines. This third-largest island in Greece is filled with beauty, but its real treasures are the creative artists and thinkers it has produced and inspired though the ages.

Lesbos was once a major cultural center, known for its Philosophical Academy, where Epicurus and Aristotle taught. It was also the birthplace of the philosopher Theophrastus, who presided over the Academy in Athens; of the great lyric poet Sappho; of Terpander, the "father of Greek music"; and of Arion, who influenced the later playwrights Sophocles and Alcaeus, inventors of the dithyramb (a short poem with an erratic strain). Even in modernity, artists have emerged from Lesbos: Theophilos, a poor villager who earned his ouzo by painting some of the finest naive modern art Greece has produced; novelists Stratis Myrivilis and Argyris Eftaliotis; and the 1979 Nobel prize–winning poet Odysseus Elytis.

The island's history stretches back to the 6th century BC, when its two mightiest cities, Mytilini and Mythimna (now Molyvos), settled their squabbles under the tyrant Pittacus, considered one of Greece's Seven Sages. Thus began the creative era, but later times brought forth the same pillaging and conquest that overturned other Greek islands. In 527 BC the Persians conquered Lesbos, and the Athenians, Romans, Byzantines, Venetians, Genoese, and Turks took their turns adding their influences. After the Turkish conquest, from 1462 to 1912, much of the population was sent to Turkey, and traces of past civilizations that weren't already destroyed by earthquakes were wiped out by the conquerors. Greece gained sovereignty over the island in 1923. This led to the breaking of trade ties with Asia Minor, diminishing the island's wealth and limiting the economy to agriculture. Lesbos was occupied by the Germans in World War II, and only after that period did they begin a slow, steady transformation to a more modern society.

Lesbos has more inhabitants than either Corfu or Rhodes, with only a fraction of the tourists, so here you can get a good idea of real island life in Greece. Many Byzantine and post-Byzantine sites dot the island's landscape, including castles and archaeological monuments, churches, and monasteries. The traditional architecture of stone and wood, inspired by Asia Minor, adorns the mansions, tower houses, and other homes of the villages. Beach composition varies throughout the island from pebble to sand. Some of the most spectacular sandy beaches and coves are in the southwest.

Mytilini

Μυτιλήνη

▶ ❶ *350 km (217 mi) northeast of Piraeus.*

Set on the ruins of an ancient city, Mytilini (so important through history that many call Lesbos by the port's name alone), sprawls across two bays like an amphitheater. This busy main town and port, with stretches of grand waterfront mansions and a busy old bazaar area, were once the scene of a dramatic moment in Greek history. Early in the Peloponnesian War, Mytilini revolted against Athens but surrendered in 428 BC. As punishment, the Athens assembly decided to kill all men in Lesbos and enslave all women and children, and a boat was dispatched to carry out the order. The next day a less-vengeful mood prevailed; the

Village Treasures

Many wonderful villages dot the islands, and they are a pleasure to discover and explore; especially magical are the fortified, labyrinthine mastic villages in the interior of Chios. On Lesbos you come upon picturesque places like the port of Skala Sikaminias and the cobbled and tiled town of Molyvos. Appealing spots on Samos include seaside Kokkari and mountainside Manolates. Some of Greece's best-preserved Byzantine monasteries are near small villages scattered throughout these islands—among them are Nea Moni, with its mosaics, on Chios, and hilltop Timiou Stavrou on Samos. The bearded, ponytailed monks in their long black robes are often friendly and informative, happy to enlighten you on Greek Orthodox rituals and history. Be sure to dress modestly, and show respect for the sanctity of the premises.

12

Great Flavors

Hospitality and good, fresh food abound on the Northern Islands. Fish is relatively expensive; lobster (crayfish to Americans) is popular, and pricey, and sweet fresh shrimp comes from Lesbos's Kalloni gulf. *Kakavia* is a fisherman's soup made with small fish, tomatoes, and onions. Besides being recognized for its mastic products, Chios is known for tangerines; preserved in syrup, they are served as a *gliko koutaliou*, or spoon sweet, meaning you spoon them into water or another beverage, or eat them with a spoon. Lesbos, especially, is known for its good food: try the *keskek* (a special meat mixed with wheat served most often at festivals) and Kalloni bay sardines, the fleshiest in the Mediterranean, which are salted for a few hours and eaten raw. Octopus, simmered in wine or grilled, goes perfectly with the famous island ouzo, of which there are several dozen brands. Fresh figs, almonds, and raisins are delicious; a local Lesbos dessert is *baleze* (almond pudding). Samos is known for its thyme-scented honey, *yiorti* (the local version of keskek), and *revithokeftedes* (chickpea patties).

Shopping

Unique products, not hard to find in Athens—and on other Greek islands—make interesting and original gifts. Snatch up the Samian wine, honey, and ceramics. The wine comes in several varieties: Samena Gold is a dry white with a light note of pear; Fokianos is a rosé; Nectar and Dux are two familiar names for the sweet dessert wines favored by locals. *Moschato* is a sweet white. On Lesbos, olive oil, chestnuts, ouzo, wood products, and pottery are popular. On Chios look for the unique mastic resin products, preserved fruits, handwoven fabrics, and wine.

Beaches

From golden sand to black and red pebbles, from isolated turquoise coves to long sweeps of sunny coastline, beaches here are varied and often excellent. After the busy strands of the Cyclades, they seem empty. Most sunbathers are Greek families wearing suits, but nudity and toplessness are allowed on many beaches away from towns. The islands' ragged coastlines, calm and uncrowded waters, strong winds, and deserted beaches make sailing a particular pleasure. There's a taverna or two near the beaches, with some of them renting sun beds and umbrellas in summer.

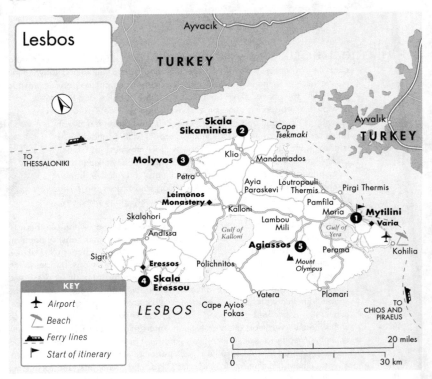

assembly repealed its decision and sent a second ship after the first. The second ship pulled into the harbor just as the commander of the first finished reading the death sentence. Just in time, Mytilini was saved.

The bustling waterfront just south of the headland between the town's two bays is where most of the town's sights are clustered. Stroll the main bazaar street **Ermou,** which goes from port to port. Walk past the fish market on the southern end, where men haul in their sardines, mullet, and octopuses. Narrow lanes are filled with antiques shops and grand old mansions.

The elegant seaside suburb of Varia was home to the modern "naïve" artist Theophilos; Tériade, the publisher of the modern art journals; and 20th-century poet Odysseus Elytis.

The pine-covered headland between the bays—a nice spot for a picnic—supports a **kastro,** a stone fortress with intact walls that seem to protect the town even today. Built by the Byzantines on a 600 BC temple of Apollo, it was repaired with available material (note the ancient pillars crammed between the stones) by Francesco Gateluzzi of the famous Genoese family. Look above the gates for the two-headed eagle of the Palaiologos emperors, the horseshoe arms of the Gateluzzi family, and inscriptions made by Turks, who enlarged it; today it is a **military bastion.** Inside the castle there's only a crumbling **prison** and a **Roman cistern,** but you should make the visit for the fine view. ⊠ *On pine-covered hill* ☎ *22510/27297* 🖭 *€2* ⊗ *Tues.–Sun. 8:30–3.*

The only vestige of ancient Mytilini is the freely accessible ruin of an **ancient theater,** one of the largest in ancient Greece, from the Hellenistic period. Pompey admired it so much that he copied it for his theater in Rome. Though the marbles are gone, the shape, carved out of the mountain, remains beautifully intact. ⊠ *In pine forest northeast of town.*

The enormous post-baroque church of **Ayios Therapon,** built in the 19th century, is reminiscent of some styles in Italy. It has an ornate interior, a frescoed dome, and, in its courtyard, a **Vizantino Mouseio,** or Byzantine Museum, filled with icons. ⊠ *Southern waterfront* ☎ *22510/28916* 🖭 *Church and museum €2* ⊗ *Mon.–Sat. 9–1.*

In front of the cathedral of Ayios Athanasios there is a **traditional Lesbos house,** restored and furnished in 19th-century style. Call owner Marika Vlachou to arrange a visit. ⊠ *Mitropoleos 6* ☎ *22510/28550* 🖭 *Free* ⊗ *By appointment only.*

The **Archaeological Museum of Mytilene,** in a 1912 neoclassical mansion, displays finds from the Neolithic through the Roman eras, a period of 5,000 years. A garden in the back displays the famous 6th-century Aeolian capitals from Klopedi's temples. The museum's modern wing, at the corner of Noemvriou and Melinas Merkouri, contains finds from prehistoric Thermi, mosaics from Hellenistic houses, reliefs of comic scenes from the 3rd-century Roman house of Menander, and temporary exhibits. ⊠ *Mansion: Argiri Eftaliotis 7, behind ferry dock; modern wing: Noemvriou and Melinas Merkouri* ☎ *22510/28032* ⊕ *www.culture.gr* 🖭 *€3 for both* ⊗ *Mansion Tues.–Sun. 8:30–3, modern wing Tues.–Sun. 8–7:30.*

Crammed to the ceiling in the **Museum of Theophilos** are 86 of the eponymous artist's naive, precise works detailing the everyday life of local folk such as fishermen and farmers, and fantasies of another age. Theophilos lived in poverty but painted airplanes and cities he had never seen. He painted in bakeries for bread, and in cafés for ouzo, and walked around in ancient dress. ⊠ *4 km (2½ mi) southeast of Mytilini, Varia* ☎ *22510/41644* 🖭 *€3* ⊗ *Tues.–Sun. 10–1 and 4:30–8.*

The **Musée–Bibliothèque Tériade** was the home of Stratis Eleftheriadis, better known by his French name, Tériade. His Paris publications *Minotaure* and *Verve* helped promote modern art. Among the works on display are lithographs done for him by Picasso, Matisse, Chagall, Roualt, Giacometti, and Miró. The museum is set among the olive trees of Varia, near the Museum of Theophilos. ⊠ *4 km (2½ mi) southeast of Mytilini, Varia* ☎ *22510/23372* 🖭 *€3* ⊗ *Tues.–Sun. 9–2 and 3–5.*

off the beaten path

LOUTROPOULI THERMIS – This village, 11 km (7 mi) northwest of Mytilini, is aptly named for its *loutra* (hot springs). These sulfur baths are dramatically enclosed with vaulted arches. A settlement existed here, centered on the spa's curative properties, from before

3000 BC until Mycenaean times. In all, remnants of five cities have been excavated at this site. The nearby beach of Mystegna, with its tiny white pebbles and crystal-clear waters, is beautiful. *Therapeutic center:* ⊠ *on road to Thermi, at junction of road from Mytilini to Mantamados* ☎ *22510/71242* ☉ *May–Oct., weekdays 7–1 and 5–7, weekends 7–1.*

Where to Stay & Eat

¢–$$ ✕ **Kostaras.** One in a lineup of fish taverns on the picturesque little fishing port of Panayiouda, Kostaras is widely considered by locals to be the best restaurant in the area. Fresh fish, sold by weight, is the specialty, accompanied by cold ouzo. Crab salad makes for an appealing appetizer, followed by fresh squid in wine sauce. ⊠ *5 km (3 mi) north of Mytilini, Panayiouda* ☎ *22510/31275* ☒ *No credit cards.*

¢–$$ ✕ **Polytechnos.** Locals and visiting Athenians pack the outdoor tables— a solid indication this restaurant has earned its reputation. Some folks choose from the impressive fish selection, others order simple, traditional Greek dishes like souvlaki or succulent pork medallions, and get a small salad of tomatoes and cucumbers to go with it. This casual restaurant lies across from the municipal building on the waterfront, and is the first along the quay. ⊠ *Fanari quay* ☎ *22510/44128* ☒ *No credit cards.*

¢–$ ✕ **O Stratos.** This no-nonsense, no-decoration restaurant serves the best fish in town. No surprise, then, that waterfront tables are hard to come by, so plan to come early if you want to sit outside. Ask for the catch of the day, or go into the kitchen to take a look at the *sargoi* (sea bream), *tsipoures* (dorado), or *barbounia* (red mullet) before making your pick. If fish is not what you're in the mood for, the barbecue chicken is a worthy substitute. Consider an accompanying wine from the island of Limnos. ⊠ *Fanari quay* ☎ *22510/21739* ☒ *V.*

¢ ✕ **Hermes.** Founded in 1790 in a building 100 years older, this *ouzeri* (ouzo bar, though the sign calls it a *kafeneio,* or coffeehouse) is where local and visiting artists, poets, and politicians prefer to sip their ouzo on a vine-shaded terrace, with marble-topped tables. You might try octopus in wine sauce, long-cooked chickpeas, or homemade sausages. The interior, a popular gathering spot in winter, provides a glimpse of traditional Lesbos design with old wood and mirrors. ⊠ *Kornarou 2, near end of Ermou* ☎ *22510/26232* ☒ *No credit cards.*

★ $$$$ ⊞ **Loriet Hotel.** The area's top hotel has two distinct characters. One is the 1880 stone mansion, where high frescoed ceilings, friezes, and antique furniture set the mood—and where visiting dignitaries often stay. The rooms here are called "suites" and start at €550 in high season. These are considerably more enticing than the utilitarian character of rooms and studios in the hotel's modern section, which is separated from the mansion by a beautiful pool and a grove of tall pines. An on-site restaurant is open July and August. The hotel lies across from the beach and is a five-minute drive from town and the airport. ⊠ *2 km (1 mi) south of Mytilini, 81100 Varia* ☎ *22510/43111* ☒ *22510/41629* ⊕ *www.loriet-hotel.com* ⇎ *26 modern rooms, 7 mansion rooms* ☖ *Restaurant, some kitchenettes, minibars, pool, bar, meeting rooms* ☒ *AE, MC, V.*

$$$ 🏨 **Pyrgos of Mytilene.** A carefully restored 1916 mansion in the ornate Second Empire style provides modern-day amenities and 19th-century nostalgia. The guest rooms are lavish, with period furniture, chandeliers, and stucco moldings, and each has its own style and color scheme, ranging from pistachio green to Venetian red. Particularly charming are the round rooms in the towers. The reception rooms are inviting, elegant, and spacious. Included in the price is a breakfast of local breads, fruits, preserves, and other products. ✉ *Eleftherios Venizelou 49, 81100* ☎ *22510/27977 or 22510/25069* 🖷 *22510/47319* ⊕ *www.pyrgoshotel. gr* 🖙 *12 rooms* ♨ *Room service, minibars, cable TV, bar* 🚭 *AE, V* ⓧ *CP.*

$$ 🏨 **Porto Lesvos.** If you want to stay in the center of Mytilini, this tall, narrow hotel is a solid moderately priced choice. In the furnishings and service, you can feel the Papadakis family touch throughout the old, carefully renovated building a block back from the harbor. The rooms all have exposed stonework and some have sea views, and the breakfast room is nicely done in wood and stone. ✉ *Koniaki 21, 81100* ☎ *22510/ 41771* 🖷 *22510/28034* ⊕ *www.portolesvos.gr* 🖙 *12 rooms* ♨ *Refrigerators, bar* 🚭 *MC* ⓧ *CP.*

Nightlife

The cafés along the harbor turn into bars after midnight, generally closing at 3 AM. To start the evening off with a cocktail in a relaxed Caribbean-like way, stop by **Hacienda** (✉ East end of port ☎ 22510/ 46850). You need transportation to reach **Kohilia** (✉ 7 km [4½ mi] south of Mytilini, on beach opposite the airport ☎ No phone), an outdoor beach bar with an upscale, artistic beat.

Shopping

Much of the best shopping is along the Ermou street bazaar; here you can buy a little of everything, from food (especially olive oil and ouzo) to pottery, wood carvings, and embroidery. Lesbos produces 50 brands of ouzo, and George Spentzas's shop, **Veto** (✉ J. Arisarchi 1 ☎ 22510/ 24660), right on the main harbor, makes its own varieties on the premises and has since 1948. Other local foods are also for sale.

Skala Sikaminias

Σκάλα Συκαμινιάς

★ ❷ *35 km (22 mi) northwest of Mytilini.*

At the northernmost point of Lesbos, past Pelopi (the ancestral village of 1988 presidential candidate Michael Dukakis), is the exceptionally lovely fishing port of Skala Sikaminias, a miniature gem—serene and real, with several good fish tavernas on the edge of the dock. The novelist Stratis Myrivilis used the village as the setting for his *The Mermaid Madonna.* Those who have read the book will recognize the tiny chapel at the base of the jetty. The author's birthplace and childhood home are in Sikaminia, overlooking the Turkish coast from high above the sea.

en route | To get to Molyvos, most people take the main road a bit inland from Sikaminia. But there is a little-trafficked unpaved coastal route rimming the water from Skala Sikaminias. To drive on this narrow path takes about half an hour; to walk, about three hours. You are amply rewarded along the way with close-up views of passing fishing boats and fresh sea breezes. In summer you can also take a caïque from Skala Sikaminias to Molyvos.

Where to Eat

¢–$ ✕ **Skamnia.** Sit at a table of Skala Sikaminias's oldest taverna, under the same spreading mulberry tree where Myrivilis wrote, to sip a glass of ouzo and watch the fishing boats bob. Eat a plate of stuffed zucchini blossoms or cucumbers and tomatoes tossed with local olive oil. Or you might go for some fresh shrimp with garlic and parsley, or chicken in grape leaves—the menu is creative. ✉ *On waterfront* ☏ *22530/55319* 🖶 *AE, MC, V.*

Molyvos

Μόλυβος

❸ *17 km (10½ mi) southwest of Skala Sikaminias, 61 km (38 mi) west of*
Fodor's Choice *Mytilini.*
★

Molyvos, also known by its ancient name, Mythimna, is a place that has attracted people since antiquity. Legend says that Achilles besieged the town until the king's daughter fell for him and opened the gates; then Achilles killed her. Before 1923 the Turks made up about a third of the population, living in many of the best stone houses. Today these balconied buildings with center staircases are weighed down by roses and geraniums; the red-tile roofs and cobblestone streets are required by law. Attracted by the town's charms, many artists live here. Don't miss a walk down to the picture-perfect harbor front.

Come before high season and walk or drive up to the **kastro,** a Byzantine-Genoese fortified castle, for a hypnotic view down the tiers of red-tile roofs to the glittering sea. At dawn the sky begins to light up from behind the mountains of Asia Minor, casting silver streaks through the placid water as weary night fishermen come in. Purple wisteria vines shelter the lanes that descend from the castle and pass numerous Turkish fountains, some still in use. ✉ *Above town* ☏ *22530/71803* 🎫 *€2* 🕓 *Tues.–Sat. 8–2:30.*

★ The stunning 16th-century **Leimonos Monastery** houses 40 chapels and an impressive collection of precious objects. Founded by St. Ignatios Agalianos on the ruins of an older Byzantine monastery, it earned its name from the "flowering meadow of souls" surrounding it. The intimate St. Ignatios church is filled with colorful frescoes and is patrolled by peacocks. A **folk-art museum** with historic and religious works is accompanied by a **treasury** of 450 Byzantine manuscripts. Women are not allowed inside the main church. ✉ *Up a marked road 5 km (3 mi) northwest of Kalloni, 15 km (9 mi) southwest of Molyvos* 🎫 *Museum and treasury €1.50* 🕓 *Daily 9–1 and 5–7:30.*

Where to Stay & Eat

★ $$ ✕ **Captain's Table.** At the end of a quay, this wonderful taverna serves seafood caught on its own trawler, moored opposite. The best way to go is to mix

ISLAND CELEBRATIONS

FESTIVALS PROVIDE A WONDERFUL *view into age-old traditions—and lots of fun.* Greek Carnival is celebrated to varying degrees throughout the islands, mixing folk traditions with myth and legend. Chios has some notable pre-Lenten events. Greek Carnival reaches a climax in Thimiana, south of Chios town, where islanders reenact the expulsion of the Berber pirates in the Festival of Mostras. There on the last Friday of Carnival, youths masquerade and wear old men's and women's clothes. In villages across the island Clean Monday is celebrated with the custom of Agas, when an "Aga" is chosen to judge and sentence the people who are present in a humorous, recreational affair. On the evening before Easter the effigy of Judas is burned in Mesta. In Pirgi on August 15 and August 23, villagers perform the local dance, the pyrgoussikos, to commemorate the death of the Virgin Mary.

On Lesbos, Clean Monday brings Carnival to a close in late February–early March with lavish costume parades and theater performances at Agiassos. On August 15 the islanders of Lesbos flock to Agiassos to celebrate the Feast of the Dormition of the Virgin with dancing, drinking, and eating.

Samos has many celebrations: a wine festival in late summer to early fall pleases with Panhellenic dances in Samos town. In high summer, a fisherman's festival centers on the harbor at Pythagorio. Swimming races in Pythagorio commemorate the battle of Cavo Fonias on August 6, a day of celebration for the entire island. On September 14, the Timiou Stavrou monastery celebrates its feast day with a service followed by a paniyiri (feast), with music, firecrackers, coconut candy, and loukoumades (honey-soaked dumplings).

and match a series of small dishes, or *mezedes*: maybe try *aujuka* (spicy eggplant slices), smoked mackerel with olives, vegetarian souvlaki, or grilled veggies and rice. Fresh fish may include red snapper, sea bream, lobster, and gilt. Owners Melinda and Theo, who are wonderful resources for visitors, also rent rooms in a house that's a 10-minute walk from the restaurant. ⊠ *Molyvos Harbor across from Ayios Nikolaos chapel* ☎ 22530/ 71241 ⊟ *MC, V* ⊙ *Closed mid-Oct.–mid-Apr.*

$ ✕ **Gatos.** Gaze at the island and the harbor from the veranda, or sit inside and watch the cooks chop and grind in the open kitchen: Gatos is known for its grilled meats. The beef fillet is tender, the lamb chops nicely spiced, and the salads fresh. You might also consider ordering the *kokkinisto* (beef in tomato sauce) with garlic and savory onion. ⊠ *One street up from main pedestrian St.* ☎ 22530/71661 ⊟ *V.*

¢–$ ✕ **Panorama.** High over the town, this terraced restaurant cooks terrific Greek food and has a spectacular view. It is worth coming here just for a sunset drink, to see the sun illumine the red roofs of Molyvos and the sea beyond. Good appetizers include spicy cheese salad, and fried stuffed peppers; among the main courses are meat on the grill and fresh fish. It is also open for breakfast. ⊠ *Under kastro* ☎ 22530/71848 ⊟ *No credit cards.*

$ ⌂ **Aeolis.** Relax by the swimming pool (preferable to the mediocre beach down below) or kick back in the lounge's deep-seated sofas near the fireplace and potted plants. These beachside rooms have two or three low-to-the-ground beds, bathrooms with showers or baths, and French doors opening onto a veranda. The view from the veranda takes in the sea and Molyvos castle. A hotel shuttle service runs up to town, as does the local bus. ☒ *On road to Eftalou, 81108* ☎ *22530/71772* ☒ *22530/71773* ⊕ *www.aeolishotel.gr* ⟿ *71 rooms* ♿ *Restaurant, some kitchenettes, pool, 2 bars* ☰ *MC, V* ☉ *Closed Nov.–Mar.* ⍟| *BP.*

★ **$** ⌂ **Sea Horse Hotel.** This delightful stone-front hotel on Molyvos Harbor overlooks the restaurants and cafés of the picture-perfect quay; the lobby even extends into a waterfront café. Twelve of the rooms—simply decorated but perfectly charming with painted wood furniture—have full sea views, an additional three have partial sea views, and one room has a village view. ☒ *Molyvos quay, 81108* ☎ *22530/71320 or 22530/71630* ☒ *22530/71374* ⊕ *www.seahorse-hotel.com* ⟿ *16 rooms* ♿ *Restaurant, refrigerators, cable TV, bar* ☰ *MC, V* ☉ *Closed mid-Oct.–mid-Apr.* ⍟| *CP.*

Nightlife & the Arts

The best-known celebration on the islands is the **Molyvos Theater Festival** (☎ 22530/71323 tickets) in July and August. With the castle as backdrop, artists from Greece and elsewhere in Europe stage entertainments that range from a Dario Fo play to contemporary music concerts.

Molly's Bar (☒ One street above harbor ☎ 22530/71209) has relaxed music in an environment that's ideal for quiet conversations. **Music Cafe Del Mar** (☒ Harbor front ☎ 22530/71588) hosts live acoustic bouzouki music and has a cocktail terrace with a sea view.

Shopping

The **Earth Collection** (☒ Molyvos quay ☎ 22530/72094) sells organic clothes using only natural products. **Evelyn** (☒ Pl. Kyriakou ☎ 22530/72197) sells a wide variety of local products, including ceramics, pastas, olive oil, wines, ouzo, sauces, and marmalades.

Skala Eressou

Σκάλα Ερεσού

★ ❹ *40 km (25 mi) southwest of Molyvos, 89 km (55 mi) west of Mytilini.*

The poet Sappho, according to unreliable late biographies, was born here circa 612 BC. Dubbed the Tenth Muse by Plato because of her skill and sensitivity, she perhaps presided over a finishing school for marriageable young women. She was married herself and had a daughter. Some of her songs erotically praise these girls and celebrate their marriages. Sappho's works, proper and popular in their time, were burned by Christians, so that mostly fragments survive; one is "and I yearn, and I desire." Sapphic meter was in great favor in Roman and medieval times; both Catullus and Gregory the Great used it, and in the 19th century, Tennyson did, too. Today, many gay women come to Skala Erresou to celebrate Sappho (the word "lesbian" derives from Lesbos), although the welcoming town is also filled with heterosexual couples.

On the **acropolis** (⊠ 1 km [½ mi] north of Skala Eressou) of ancient Eressos overlooking the coastal area and beach are **remains of pre-Hellenic walls, castle ruins,** and the 5th-century church, **Ayios Andreas.** The church has a mosaic floor and a tiny adjacent **museum** housing local finds from tombs in the ancient cemetery.

The old village of **Eressos** (⊠ 11 km [7 mi] inland, north of Skala Eressou), separated from the coast by a large plain, developed to protect its inhabitants from pirate raids. Along the mulberry tree–lined road leading from the beach you might encounter a villager wearing a traditional head scarf (*mandila*), plodding by on her donkey. This village of two-story, 19th-century stone and shingle houses is filled with superb architectural details. Note the huge wooden doors decorated with nails and elaborate door knockers, loop-hole windows in thick stone walls, elegant pediments topping imposing mansions, and fountains spilling under Gothic arches.

Beaches

Some of the island's best beaches are in this area, which has been built up very rapidly—and not always tastefully. Especially popular is the 4-km long (2½-mi long) town beach at **Skala Eressou,** where the wide stretch of dark sand is lined with tamarisk trees. A small island is within swimming distance, and northerly winds lure windsurfers as well as swimmers and sunbathers. There are many rooms to rent within walking distance of the beach.

Where to Eat

$–$$ ✕ **Soulatso.** The enormous anchor outside is a sign that you're in for some seriously good seafood here. On a wooden deck, tables are set just a stone's throw from the break of the waves. Owner Sarandos Tzinieris serves, and his mother cooks. Fresh grilled squid is sweet, and the fish are carefully chosen every morning. ⊠ *At beach center* ☎ *22530/52078* ▭ *DC, MC, V.*

¢–$ ✕ **Parasol.** Totem poles, colored coconut lamps, and other knickknacks from exotic travels make this beach bar endearing. The owner and his wife serve omelets, fruits, yogurt, and sweet Greek coffee for breakfast, and simple dishes like pizzas, veggie spring rolls, and cheese platters the rest of the day. But the most obvious reason to come here is to relax after sundown with one of the bar's creative drinks, such as the signature green cocktail, the Wooloomooloo Wonder made with vodka and fresh melon. The music might be characterized as sophisticated lounge; the owner calls it "intellectual." ⊠ *Beachfront* ☎ *No phone* ▭ *No credit cards* ☉ *Closed Nov.–Apr.*

Agiassos

Αγιάσος

★ ❺ *87 km (53 mi) northwest of Skala Eressou, 28 km (17½ mi) southwest of Mytilini.*

Agiassos village, the prettiest hill town on Lesbos, sits in an isolated valley amid thousands of olive trees, near the foot of Mt. Olympus, the highest peak. (In case you're confused, 19 mountains in the Mediterranean are named Olympus, almost all of them peaks sacred to the local sky god, who eventually became associated with Zeus.) Exempted from taxes by the Turks, the town thrived. The age-old charm of Agiassos can be seen in its gray stone houses, cobblestone lanes, medieval castle, and local handicrafts, particularly pottery and woodwork. The church of **Panayia Vrefokratousa** (Madonna Holding the Infant) was founded in the 12th century to house an icon of the Virgin Mary, believed to be the work of St. Luke, and remains a popular place of pilgrimage. Built into its foundation are shops whose revenues support the church, as they have through the ages. The **Church Museum** has a little Bible from AD 500, with legible, elegant calligraphy. ✉ *€0.50* ☉ *Daily 8–1 and 5:30–8:30.*

need a break?   Stop at one of several cafés in the winding streets of the old bazaar area past the church of Panayia Vrefokratousa. On weekend afternoons sip an ouzo and listen to a *santoúri* band (hammered dulcimer, accompanied by clarinet, drum, and violin). As the locals dance, rather haphazardly, on the cobblestones, you might be tempted to join in the merriment.

Where to Eat

¢ ✕ **Dagielles.** If nothing else, you must stop here for a coffee made by owner Stavritsa and served by her no-nonsense staff. You might also try the *kolokitholouloudo* (stuffed squash blossoms) and the dishes that entice throughout winter: *kritharaki* (orzo pasta) and *varkoules* ("little boats" of eggplant slices with minced meat). For a few short weeks in spring the air is laden with the scent of overhanging wisteria. ✉ *Near bus stop* ☎ 22520/22241 ▤ *No credit cards.*

Shopping

Local crafts are a specialty of Agiassos. For handmade, hand-painted pottery, have a look in **Ceramic Workshop Antonia Gavve** (✉ On main St. ☎ 22520/93350), where you can watch the artist paint. For woodwork inspired by Byzantine art and Hellenism, stop by the functioning workshop of **D. Kamaros & Son** (✉ Next to church ☎ 22213/22520); the store is opposite the shop. Dimitris Kamaros exports his woodwork throughout the Orthodox world. Although specializing in walnut furniture (the trees are local), the store also sells small pieces such as chessboards, backgammon tables, carved religious pieces, and jewelry boxes.

CHIOS

ΧΙΟΣ

"Craggy Chios" is what local boy Homer, its first publicist, so to speak, called this starkly beautiful island, which almost touches Turkey's coast and shares its topography. The island may not appear overly charming when you first see its principal city and capital, Chios Town, but consider its misfortunes: the bloody Turkish massacre of 1822 during the fight for Greek independence; major earthquakes, including one in 1881 that killed almost 6,000 Chiotes; severe fires, which in the 1980s burned

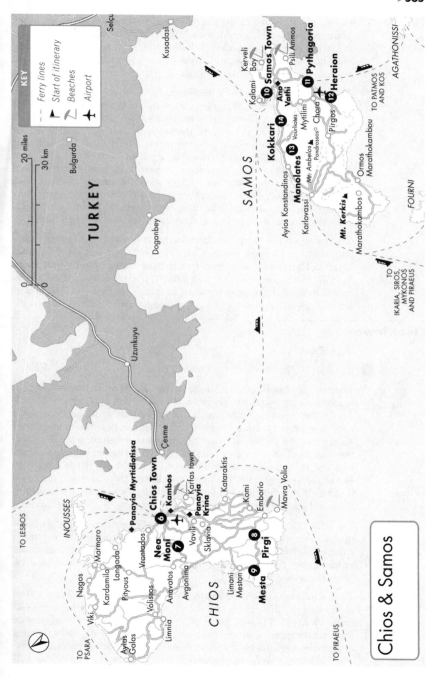

KEY

- - - Ferry lines
▲ Start of itinerary
≥ Beaches
✈ Airport

TURKEY

Selçu
Kusadasi
Bulgurda
Doganbey
Çesme
Uzunkuyu

20 miles
30 km

TO LESBOS
INOUSSES
TO PSARA

Vki
Ayias
Galas
Limmia
Volissos
Pityous
Kardamila
Langada
Nagos
Marmaro
Vrontados
Panayia Myrtidiotissa
Chios Town
Kambos
Karfas town
Panayia Krina
Kataraklis
Komi
Emborio
Mavra Volia
6
Nea Moni
7
Vavili
Sklavia
Avgonima
Anavatos
Limani
Meston
Mesta
9
Pirgi
8

CHIOS

TO PIRAEUS

Chios & Samos

SAMOS

Kerveli
Samos Town
10
Kalami
Kalami Bay
Psili Ammos
Ano Vathi
Pythagoria
11
12 Heraion
Mytilini
Chora
Pirgos
Pondrossos
Ayios Konstandinos
Manolates
Vourliotes
13
Kokkari
14
Karlovassi
Mt. Ambelos
Mt. Kerkis
Marathokambos
Ormos
Marathokambou

TO PATMOS
AND KOS

AGATHONISSI

FOURNI

IKARIA, SIROS,
TO MYKONOS
AND PIRAEUS

two-thirds of its pine trees; and, through the ages, the steady stripping of forests to ax-wielding boatbuilders. Yet despite these disadvantages, the island remains a wonderful destination, with friendly inhabitants, and villages so rare and captivating that even having just one of them on this island would make it a gem.

The name Chios comes from the Phoenician word for "mastic," the resin of the *Pistacia lentisca,* evergreen shrubs that with few exceptions thrive only here, in the southern part of the island. Every August, incisions are made in the bark of the shrubs; the sap leaks out, permeating the air with a sweet fragrance, and in September it is harvested. This aromatic resin, which brought huge revenues until the introduction of petroleum products, is still used in cosmetics and chewing gum sold on the island today. Pirgi, Mesta, and other villages where the mastic is grown and processed are quite enchanting. In these towns you can wind your way through narrow, labyrinth-like Byzantine streets protected by medieval gates and peered over by homes that date back half a millennium.

Chios is also home to the elite families that control Greece's private shipping empires: Livanos, Karas, Chandris; even Onassis came here from Smyrna. The island has never seemed to need tourists, nor to draw them. Yet Chios intrigues, with its deep valleys, uncrowded sand and black-pebble beaches, fields of wild tulips, Byzantine monasteries, and haunting villages—all remnants of a poignant history.

Chios Town

Χίος (Πόλη)

❻ *285 km (177 mi) northeast of Piraeus, 24 km (15 mi) northeast of Pirgi.*

The main port and capital, Chios town, or Chora (which means "town"), is a busy commercial settlement on the east coast, across from Turkey. This is the best base from which to explore the island, and you don't need to venture far from the port to discover the beautiful mansions of Kambos or the captivating orange groves just south of town. The daytime charm of the port area is limited, in part because no buildings predate the 1881 earthquake, and in part because it just needs a face-lift. But in the evening when the lights twinkle on the water and the scene is softened by a mingling of blues, the many cafés begin to overflow with ouzo and good cheer, and locals proudly promenade along the bayside.

The capital is crowded with half the island's population, but its fascinating heart is the sprawling **bazaar district.** Merchants hawk everything from local mastic gum and fresh dark bread to kitchen utensils in the morning, but typically close in the afternoon. ⊠ *South and east of Pl. Vounakiou, the main Sq.*

The **old quarter** is inside the **kastro** (castle) fortifications, built in the 10th century by the Byzantines and enlarged in the 14th century by the Genoese Giustiniani family. Under Turkish rule, the Greeks lived outside the wall; the gate was closed daily at sundown. A deep dry moat remains on the western side. Note the old wood-and-plaster houses on the narrow backstreets, typically decorated with latticework and jutting balconies. An air of mystery pervades this old Muslim and Jewish neighborhood, full of decaying monuments, fountains, baths, and mosques. ✉ *On northern highlands.*

The **Giustiniani Museum,** inside a 15th-century building that may have acted as the headquarters of the Genoese, exhibits Byzantine murals and sculptures, post-Byzantine icons, and other small Genoese and Byzantine works of art. ✉ *Just inside old quarter* ☎ *22710/22819* ⊕ *www. culture.gr* 🎫 *€3* ☉ *Tues.–Sun. 9–2:30.*

In **Platia Frouriou** (✉ In fort's small square, old quarter), look for the **Turkish cemetery** and the large **marble tomb** (with the fringed hat) of Kara Ali, chief of the Turkish flagship in 1822. Along the **main street** are the elegant **Ayios Georgios** church (closed most of the time), which has icons from Asia Minor; houses from the Genoese period; and the **remains of Turkish baths** (north corner of fort).

In 1822, in the tiny **prison,** 75 leading Chiotes were jailed as hostages before they were hanged by the Turks, part of the worst massacre committed during the War of Independence. The Turks drove out the Genoese in 1566, and Chios, spurred by Samians who had fled to the island, joined the rest of Greece in rebellion in the early 19th century. The revolt failed, and the Sultan retaliated: the Turks killed 30,000 Chiotes and enslaved 45,000, an event written about by Victor Hugo and depicted by Eugène Delacroix in *The Massacre of Chios.* The painting, now in the Louvre, shocked Western Europe and increased support for Greek independence. Copies of *The Massacre of Chios* hang in many places on Chios. ✉ *Inside main gate of castle, near Giustiniani Museum.*

The only intact mosque in this part of the Aegean, complete with a slender minaret, houses the **Byzantine Museum,** which at this writing is closed indefinitely for renovation. It holds a *tugra* (the swirling monogram of the sultan that indicated royal possession), rarely seen outside Istanbul; its presence indicated the favor Chios enjoyed under the sultan. Housed inside are the Jewish, Turkish, and Armenian gravestones leaning with age in the courtyard, a silent reminder of past suffering. ✉ *Pl. Vounakiou* ☎ *22710/26866.*

The **Chios Maritime Museum** celebrates the sea-based heritage of the island with exquisite ship models and portraits of vessels that have belonged to Chios owners over time. One exhibit highlights the Liberty ships and others constructed during World War II that contributed to the beginning of Greece's postwar shipping industry. ✉ *Stefanou Tsouri 20* ☎ *22710/44139* 🎫 *Free* ☉ *Mon.–Sat. 10–1.*

The **Chios Archaeological Museum** has a collection that ranges from proto-Helladic pottery dug up in Emborio to a letter, on stone, from Alexander the Great addressed to the Chiotes and dated 332 BC. It also displays beautiful Ionian sculptures crafted by Chiotes. ✉ *Michalon 5* ☎ *22710/44239* ⊕ *www.culture.gr* 🎫 *€2* ☉ *Tues.–Sun. 8:30–1.*

The **Philip Argenti Museum** houses a historic and folkloric collection, and sits on the second floor above the **Korais Library,** Greece's third largest. The museum displays meticulously designed costumes, embroidery, pastoral wood carvings, and furniture of a village home. ⊠ *Korais 2, near cathedral* ☎ *22710/23462* ✉ *€1* ⊙ *Mon.–Thurs. 8–2, Fri. 8–2 and 4–7:30, Sat. 8–12:30.*

Mastodon bones were found in the **Kambos district,** a fertile plain of tangerine, lemon, and orange groves just south of Chios town. In medieval times and later, wealthy Genoese and Greek merchants built ornate, earth-color, three-story mansions here. Behind forbidding stone walls adorned with coats of arms, each is a world of its own, with multicolor sandstone patterns, arched doorways, and pebble-mosaic courtyards. Some houses have crumbled and some still stand, reminders of the wealth, power, and eventual downfall of an earlier time. These suburbs of Chios town are exceptional, but the unmarked lanes can be confusing, so leave time to get lost and to peek behind the walls into another world. ⊠ *4 km (2½ mi) south of Chios town.*

Daskalopetra (Teacher's Rock) where Homer is said to have taught his pupils, stands just above the port of Vrontados, 4 km (2½ mi) north of Chios town. Archaeologists think this rocky outcrop above the sea is part of an ancient altar to Cybele; you can sit on it and muse about how the blind storyteller might have spoken here of the fall of Troy in the *Iliad.*

Beaches

Karfas beach (⊠ 8 km [5 mi] south of Chios town) fronts a shallow sandy bay. Tavernas are in the area, and in summer there is transportation to town. Farther south, Komi has a fine, sandy beach.

Where to Stay & Eat

¢–$$$ ✕ **Bella Vista.** On the coastal road toward the airport, just outside the port, Bella Vista serves the island's best Italian food. Selections include salads with fresh mozzarella, thick crisp pizzas, and numerous pastas, such as spaghetti with fresh, juicy lobster—accompanied by fresh-baked bread. The delicious shrimp "terminator" are large shrimp smothered with mushrooms, peppers, and cream. The dining room has a mesmerizing tropical aquarium; street noise can disturb the tranquillity of the outdoor veranda. ⊠ *South of center, Livanou 2* ☎ *22710/41022* ▭ *MC, V.*

¢–$$$ ✕ **Pyrgos.** Attentive service, fine food, and pretty surroundings characterize a meal at the poolside garden restaurant of the Grecian Castle hotel. Beef carpaccio and spinach salad are excellent starters, followed by beef *pagiar,* a fillet stuffed with *mastello* (the local goat cheese), sun-dried tomatoes, and pesto-olive sauce. Or try the pork with prunes, mushrooms, and *vin santo* (a sweet wine) sauce. The extensive menu also includes crepes, pastas, and seafood. Mastic ice cream with rose syrup closes a meal on a richly local note. ⊠ *Chios Harbor* ☎ *22710/44740* ▭ *AE, D, MC, V.*

★ ℭ ¢–$ ✕ **Tavern of Tassos.** Dependably delicious traditional food is why so many locals eat here in a garden courtyard beneath a canopy of trees. Fresh fish and seafood, lamb chops and other meats, stuffed peppers and cooked greens—you can't go wrong. Expect Greek owner Dimitrius Doulos and his son, the chef, to warmly welcome you. The tavern lies at the south edge of town toward the airport, and there's a playground for kids. ⊠ *Livanou 8, south toward airport* ☎ *22710/27542* ▭ *DC, MC, V.*

$$$ 🏨 **Chios Chandris.** Only a few minutes' walk from the village center, Chios Chandris has the best location of any hotel in Chios Town: it looks out at both the sea and the harbor, and has an inviting pool with panoramic views of both. Balconies have views of the mountains or of the ferries and fishing boats plying the harbor. Although the outside looks a bit worn, comfortable rooms are brightly decorated in shades of Aegean blue and yellow. ⊠ *Between port and beach, 82100 Prokymea* 🕾 *22710/ 44401 through 22710/44410* 🖷 *22710/25768* ⊕ *www.chandris.gr* 📠 *123 rooms, 16 suites* ⚑ *Restaurant, some kitchenettes, cable TV, pool, hair salon, bar, meeting rooms* ☰ *AE, MC, V* ⊗ *BP.*

★ $–$$$ 🏨 **Grecian Castle.** The Grecian Castle hotel sets a high standard for Chios. A stone exterior of the main building, originally a pasta factory, was influenced by Chios's medieval castle; it's complemented by the elegant wood furnishings of the lobby and breakfast room. Spacious rooms are housed in a series of additional stone buildings and furnished in warm, neutral tones. The sophisticated hotel has a pretty pool and carefully landscaped grounds. It lies near the sea, toward the airport. ⊠ *Leoforos Enosseos, 1 km (½ mi) south toward airport, 82100* 🕾 *22710/44740* 🖷 *22710/44052* ⊕ *www.greciancastle.gr* 📠 *51 rooms, 4 suites* ⚑ *Restaurant, room service, minibars, cable TV, pool, 2 bars, meeting rooms* ☰ *AE, D, MC, V.*

$–$$ 🏨 **Perleas Mansion.** More than a thousand trees, mostly citrus, grow on the beautiful grounds of this stunning estate, which includes the main stone house from 1640. Owners Vangelis and Claire Xydas have painstakingly restored the house and two smaller buildings. Guest rooms, which look out to the orchards, are filled with antique furnishings and the fragrance of jasmine. Common rooms have books and board games, and there are wonderful spots for walking, reading, and relaxing. The service here makes you feel like an aristocrat from a previous era. The staff prepares an elegant dinner (extra charge) served under the stars three nights per week. ⊠ *Vitiadou, Kambos district, 4 km (2½ mi) south of center, 82100* 🕾 *22710/32217 or 22710/32962* 🖷 *22710/32364* ⊕ *www.perleas.gr* 📠 *7 rooms* ⚑ *Dining room, minibars; no room TVs* ☰ *MC, V* ⊗ *BP.*

Fodor'sChoice ★

★ $ 🏨 **Kyma.** Begun in 1917 for a shipping magnate, this neoclassical villa on the waterfront was completed in 1922, when it served as Colonel Plastiras's headquarters after the Greek defeat in Asia Minor (Plastiras went on to become a general and Prime Minister of Greece). Now the villa is the prettiest hotel in town, run by the friendliest staff under Theo Spordilis. Many of Kyma's rooms have balconies with sea views, and some are equipped with hot tubs. A large breakfast, including fruits, juices, eggs, jams, yogurt, and honey, is served under frescoed ceilings in the breakfast room. ⊠ *Chandris 1, 82100* 🕾 *22710/44500* 🖷 *22710/ 44600* ✎ *kyma@chi.forthnet.gr* 📠 *59 rooms* ⚑ *Some in-room hot tubs, some refrigerators* ☰ *No credit cards* ⊗ *CP.*

$ 🏨 **Pension Perivoli.** Behind an ornate pediment-top gate and across from the Villa Argentiko, this grand yet informal two-story 18th-century mansion is in an orange orchard (think fresh-squeezed juice at breakfast in the large garden). Fireplaces, a massive outdoor staircase of native stone, a waterwheel, and local furnishings and antiques evoke another time. The rooms are spare, but the grounds are beautiful and loud with birdsong. ⊠ *Argenti 9–11, Kambos district, 4 km (2½ mi)* *south of center, 82100* ☎ *22710/31513* 🖨 *22710/32042* 🛏 *15 rooms* ♨ *Restaurant, minibars; no room TVs* 🝙 *MC, V.*

¢ ⌨ **Fedra.** This neoclassical mansion, built in 1879, is run as a pension by a playwright, painted ocher, and planted with jubilant flowers. Rooms have twin beds. The summer outdoor café generates some noise, so ask for a back room. Off-season, local and visiting musicians perform in the bar. ✉ *Livanou 13, 82100* ☎ *22710/41129 or 22710/41130* 🖨 *22710/41128* 🛏 *9 rooms* ♨ *Café, bar* 🝙 *No credit cards.*

Nightlife & the Arts

Stylish nightspots along the harbor are more sophisticated than those on most of the other northern Aegean islands, and many of the clubs are filled with well-off young tourists and locals. You can just walk along, listen to the music, and size up the crowd; most clubs are open to the harbor and dramatically lighted. **Cosmo** (✉ Aigeou 100 ☎ 22710/81695) stands out as an inviting cocktail lounge playing international and Greek music.

Shopping

The resinous gum made from the sap of the mastic tree is a best buy in Chios; the brand is Elma, which makes a fun souvenir and conversation piece. You can also find mastic liquor called *mastíha,* and *gliko koutaliou,* sugar-preserved fruit added to water. Stores are typically closed on Sunday, and open mornings only on Monday through Wednesday.

At the elegant shop of **Mastic Spa** (✉ Aigaiou 12, on waterfront a block from dock ☎ 22710/40223), all the beauty and health products contain the local balm. **Moitafiz** (✉ Venizelou 7 ☎ 22710/25330) sells mastíha, fruit preserves, and other sweets and spirits. **Yiogos Varias** (✉ Venizelou 2 ☎ 22710/22368) has a passion for pickles. His tiny store is crammed with 36 varieties, including melon, chestnut, and fig. **Zaharoplasteion Avgoustakis** (✉ Psychari 4 ☎ 22710/44480) is a traditional candy store where you can buy *masourakia* (crispy rolled pastries dripping in syrup and nuts) and *rodinia* (melt-in-your-mouth cookies stuffed with almond cream).

Nea Moni

Νέα Μονή

❼ *17 km (10½ mi) west of Chios town.*

FodorsChoice
★

Almost hidden among the olive groves, the island's most important monastery—with one of the finest examples of mosaic art anywhere—is the 11th-century Nea Moni. Emperor Constantine VIII Monomachos (Dueler) ordered the monastery built where three monks found an icon of the Virgin in a myrtle bush. The octagonal *katholikon* (medieval church) is the only surviving example of 11th-century court art—none survives in Constantinople. The church has been renovated a number of times: the dome was completely rebuilt following an earthquake in 1881, and a great deal of effort has gone into the restoration and preservation of the mosaics over the years. The distinctive three-part vaulted sanctuary has a double narthex, with no buttresses supporting the dome. This design, a single square space covered by a dome, is rarely seen in Greece. Blazing with color, the church's interior gleams with marble slabs and mosaics of Christ's life, austere yet sumptuous, with azure blue, ruby red, velvet green, and skillful applications of gold. The saints' expressiveness comes from their vigorous poses and severe gazes, with heavy shadows under the eyes. On the iconostasis hangs the icon—a small Virgin and Child facing left. Also inside the grounds are an **ancient refectory, a vaulted cistern, a chapel** filled with victims' bones from the massacre at Chios, and a large **clock** still keeping Byzantine time, with the sunrise reckoned as 12 o'clock. ✉ *In mountains west of Chios town* ☎ *22710/79391* 💰 *Donations accepted* ☉ *Tues.–Sun. 8–1 and 4–7.*

Pirgi

Πυργί

★ ⑧ *20 km (12½ mi) south of Chios town.*

Beginning in the 14th century, the Genoese founded 20 or so inland, fortified villages in southern Chios. These villages shared a defensive design with double thick walls, a maze of narrow streets, and a square tower, or *pyrgos,* in the middle—a last resort to hold the residents in case of pirate attack. The villages prospered on the sales of mastic gum and were spared by the Turks because of the industry. Today they depend on citrus, apricots, olives—and tourists.

Pirgi is the largest of these mastic villages, and in many ways the most wondrous. It could be a graphic designer's model or a set from a mad moviemaker or a town from another planet. Many of the buildings along the tiny arched streets are adorned with *xysta* (like Italian sgraffito). They are coated with a mix of cement and volcanic sand from nearby beaches, then whitewashed and stenciled, often top to bottom, in traditional patterns of animals, flowers, and geometric designs. The effect is both delicate and dazzling. This exuberant village has more than 50 churches (people afraid of attack tend to pray for a continuation of life).

About 50 people named Kolomvos live in Pirgi, claiming kinship with Christopher Columbus, known to have been from Genoa, the power that built the town (some renegade historians claim Columbus, like Homer, was really born on Chios).

Look for especially lavish xysta on buildings near the main square, including the **Kimisis tis Theotokou church** (Dormition of the Virgin church), built in 1694. ✉ *Off main Sq.* ☉ *Daily 9–1 and 4–8.*

Check out the fresco-embellished 12th-century church **Ayioi Apostoli** (Holy Apostles), a very small replica of the katholikon at the Nea Moni Monastery. The 17th-century frescoes that completely cover the interior, the work of a Cretan artist, have a distinct folk-art leaning. ✉ *Northwest of main Sq.* ☉ *Tues.–Sun. 8:30–3.*

In the small mastic village of **Armolia**, 5 km (3 mi) north of Pirgi, pottery is a specialty. In fact, the Greek word *armolousis* ("man from Armola") is synonymous with potter. **Earthal Art** sells hand-painted pottery and handicrafts, as well as quality, inexpensive oil paintings of the Greek islands. ⊠ *Pirgi–Armolia Rd.* ☎ *22710/72693.*

Beaches

From Pirgi it's 8 km (5 mi) southeast to the glittering black volcanic beach near Emborio, known by locals as **Mavra Volia** (Black Pebbles). The cove is backed by jutting volcanic cliffs, the calm water's dark-blue color created by the deeply tinted seabed. Here perhaps was an inspiration for the "wine-dark sea" that Homer wrote about.

Mesta

Μεστά

❾ *11 km (7 mi) west of Pirgi, 30 km (18½ mi) southwest of Chios town.*

Fodor's Choice
★

Pirgi may be the most unusual of the mastic villages, but Mesta is the island's best preserved: a labyrinth of twisting vaulted streets link two-story stone-and-mortar houses that are supported by buttresses against earthquakes. The enchanted village sits inside a system of 3-foot-thick walls, and the outer row of houses also doubles as protection. In fact, the village homes were built next to each other to form a castle, reinforced with towers. Most of the narrow streets, free of cars and motorbikes, lead to blind alleys; the rest lead to the six gates. The one in the northeast retains an iron grate.

One of the largest and wealthiest churches in Greece, the 18th-century church of **Megas Taxiarchis** (Great Archangel) commands the main square; its vernacular baroque is combined with the late-folk-art style of Chios. The church was built on the ruins of the central refuge tower. Ask at the main square for Elias, the gentle old man in the village who is the keeper of the keys.

Beaches

Escape to the string of secluded coves, between Elatas and Trahiliou bays, for good swimming. The **nudist beach** (⊠ 2 km [1 mi] north of Lithi) has fine white pebbles.

Where to Stay & Eat

★ ¢–$ ✕ **Restaurant Café Mesconas.** A traditional Greek kitchen turns out the delicious food served on outdoor tables in the small village square, adjacent to the central tower which is now a church. You dine surrounded by medieval homes and magical lights at night, but the setting is lovely even just for coffee and relaxed conversation. The best dishes include rabbit *stifado* (stew), made with shallots, tomatoes, and olive oil, and *pastitsio*, a meat pie with macaroni and béchamel sauce. All of the recipes use local ingredients and natural herbs and spices. *Soyma* is the local equivalent of ouzo. ⊠ *Main Sq.* ☎ *22710/76050* ⊟ *MC, V.*

¢ ✕ **Limani Meston.** The fishing boats bobbing in the water only a few feet away supply Limani Meston with a rich daily fish selection. The friendly, gracious owner may well persuade you to munch on some of his smaller catches, such as sardines served with onions and pita, accompanied by calamari and cheese balls. Meats served at the simple taverna include homemade sausage and lamb or beef on the spit. You can sit outside among the ivy and blossoms, where Mesta's working harbor unfolds before you; on colder days, enjoy the fireplace with the locals. The owner rents studio apartments within walking distance. ⊠ *Mesta Harbor, 3 km (2 mi) north of Mesta village* ☎ *22710/76367 or 22710/76265* 🚫 *No credit cards.*

★ ¢ 🏠 **Anna Floradi.** The charming Floradi family has remodeled a medieval home into a guesthouse with four studio rooms and a two-bedroom apartment. All have rustic furnishings and cooking facilities—not bad for Byzantine accommodations smack in the center of a mastic village. Ask for one of the rooms upstairs; they open out onto an alfresco den built around an old wood oven, and one has a balcony. Anna Floradi leaves breakfast items (bread, honey, yogurt, or cheese pie) for guests to prepare on their own. ⊠ *Village center, 82102* ☎ *22710/28891* 🖨 *22710/76455* 📧 *floradis@internet.gr* 🛏 *4 rooms, 1 apartment* △ *Kitchens* 🚫 *MC, V* �| *CP.*

Nightlife

Karnayio (⊠ Leoforos Stenoseos, outside town on road to airport ☎ No phone) is a popular spot for dancing.

Shopping

Artists and craftspeople are attracted to this ancient area. **Agnitha** (⊠ Delfon 34 ☎ 22710/76031) is a magical shop selling handwoven textiles, silver jewelry, and local art. **Ilias Likourinas** (⊠ Workshop, Delfon) is an icon artist who will paint to order. The shop of **Sergias Patentas** (⊠ Mesta–Limenas Harbor road, 3 km [2 mi] north of Mesta) sells sculptural fantasies he creates based on mythology and history.

> **en route**
>
> As you head out of town, on the way to Chios town, near Vavili, is the 12th-century **Panayia Krina** (Our Lady of the Source; ⊠ On road to left marked TO SKLAVIA), where three layers of frescoes span six periods. The earliest period is represented by portraits of the saints facing the entrance; most of the restored frescoes hang in the Giustiniani palace, now a museum, in Chios town. The church is rarely open, but the finely worked exterior makes the trip worthwhile.

SAMOS

ΣΑΜΟΣ

The southernmost of this group of three north Aegean islands, Samos lies the closest to Turkey of any Greek island, separated by only 3 km (2 mi). It was, in fact, a part of Asia Minor until it split off during the Ice Age. Samos means "high" in Phoenician, and its abrupt volcanic mountains soaring dramatically like huge hunched shoulders from the rock surface of the island are among the tallest in the Aegean, geologically part of the great spur that runs across western Turkey. As you approach from the west, Mt. Kerkis seems to spin out of the sea, and in the distance Mt. Ambelos guards the terraced vineyards that produce the famous Samian wine. The felicitous landscape has surprising twists, with lacy coasts and mountain villages perched on ravines carpeted in pink oleander, red poppy, and purple sage.

When Athens was young, in the 7th century BC, Samos was already a political, economic, and naval power. In the next century during Polycrates's reign, it was noted for its arts and sciences and was the expanded site of the vast Temple of Hera, one of the Seven Wonders of the Ancient World. The Persian Wars led to the decline of Samos, however, which fell first under Persian rule, and then became subordinate to the expanding power of Athens. Samos was defeated by Pericles in 439 BC and forced to pay tribute to Athens.

Pirates controlled this deserted island after the fall of the Byzantine empire, but in 1562 an Ottoman admiral repopulated Samos with expatriates and Orthodox believers. It languished under the sun for hundreds of years until tobacco and shipping revived the economy in the 19th century.

Small though it may be, Samos has a formidable list of great Samians stretching through the ages. The fabled Aesop, the philosopher Epicurus, and Aristarchos (first in history to place the sun at the center of the solar system) all lived on Samos. The mathematician Pythagoras was born in Samos's ancient capital in 580 BC; in his honor, it was renamed Pythagorio in AD 1955 (it only took a couple of millennia). Plutarch wrote that in Roman times Anthony and Cleopatra took a long holiday on Samos, "giving themselves over to the feasting," and that artists came from afar to entertain them.

In the last decade Samos has become packed with other holiday travelers—European charter tourists—in July and August. Thankfully the curving terrain allows you to escape the crowds easily and feel as if you are still in an undiscovered Eden.

Samos Town

Σάμος (Πόλη)

❿ *278 km (174 mi) east of Piraeus.*

On the northeast coast at the head of a sharply deep bay is the capital, Samos town, also known as Vathi (which actually refers to the old settlement just above the port). Red-tile roofs sweep around the arc of the bay and reach toward the top of red-earth hills. In the morning at the sheltered port, fishermen still grapple with their nets, spreading them to dry in the sun, and in the early afternoon everything shuts down. Slow summer sunsets over the sparkling harbor match the relaxed pace of locals. Tourism has not altered this centuries-old schedule.

★ The stepped streets ascend from the shopping thoroughfare, which meanders from the port to the city park next to the **Archaeological Museum,** the town's most important sight. The newest wing holds the impressive **kouros from Heraion,** a statue of a nude male youth, built as an offering to the goddess Hera and the largest freestanding sculpture surviving from ancient Greece, dating from 580 BC. This colossal statue, the work of a Samian artist, is made of the typical Samian gray-and-white-band marble. Pieces of the kouros were discovered in various peculiar locations: its thigh was being used as part of a Hellenistic house wall, and its left forearm was being used as a step for a Roman cistern; it's so large (16½ feet tall) that the wing had to be rebuilt specifically to house it. The museum's older section has a collection of pottery and cast-bronze griffin heads (the symbol of Samos). Samian sculptures from past millennia were considered among the best in Greece, and examples here show why. An exceptional collection of tributary gifts from ancient cities far and wide, including bronzes and ivory miniatures, affirms the importance of the shrine to Hera. ☒ *Pl. Dimarhiou* ☎ *22730/27469* ⊕ *www.culture.gr* ▱ *€3* ☾ *Tues.–Sun. 8:30–7:30.*

In the quaint 17th-century enclave of **Ano Vathi** (☒ Southern edge of Samos town, beyond museum, to the right), wood-and-plaster houses with pastel facades and red-tile roofs are jammed together, their balconies protruding into cobbled paths so narrow that the water channel takes up most of the space. From here you have a view of the gulf.

> ### off the beaten path
>
> **TURKEY –** From Samos town (and Pythagorio), you can easily ferry to Turkey. Once you're there, it's a 13 km (8 mi) drive from the Kuşadası Kud on the Turkish coast, where the boats dock, to Ephesus, one of the great archaeological sites and a major city of the ancient world. (Note that the Temple of Artemis in Ephesus is a copy of the Temple of Hera in Heraion, which is now in ruins.) Many travel agencies have guided round-trip full-day tours to the site (€100), although you can take an unguided ferry ticket for under €30. You leave your passport with the agency, and it is returned when you come back from Turkey.

Beaches

One of the island's best beaches is **Psili Ammos** (☒ Southeast of Samos town, near Mesokambos), a pristine, sandy beach protected from the wind by cliffs. There are two tavernas here. The beach at **Kerveli Bay** (☒ On the coast east of Samos town) has an enticing pebbly beach with calm, turquoise waters.

Where to Stay & Eat

$–$$ ✕ **The Steps.** Climb the steps and enter a softly lighted, airy terrace draped with ivy and overlooking the harbor. One of the chef's specialties is the mixed plate, which gives you a chance to try the lamb, chicken, beef fillet, and beef steak. He also serves *exohiko*, swordfish grilled with lemon-oil sauce. ☒ *Off Samos waterfront, behind Catholic church* ☎ *22730/28649* ☖ *Reservations essential* ▭ *MC, V* ☾ *Closed Nov.–Apr. No lunch.*

¢–$ ✕ **Artemis.** Tucked in a bend on the road out of town, this unassuming local haunt does standard Greek cuisine the right way, with fresh ingredients, perfected traditional recipes, and warm service. Sit in the glass enclosed terrace, or on the outside patio, to enjoy a view of the Aegean across the street, as well as the excellent moussaka, *giouvetsi Samos* (meat, pasta, vegetables, and cheese baked in a clay dish), or octopus in wine sauce. To find Artemis, go past the port police station on the main road out of town toward the hospital. ⊠ *Kefalopoulou* ☎ *22730/23639* 🍽 *No credit cards.*

★ ¢–$ ✕ **Karavi.** From the shape of one of Samos town's oldest port-side tavernas it's easy to see that *karavi* in Greek means boat. To your benefit—and to the frustration of neighboring restaurants—the owner here has arranged for most local fish to be delivered to him. Fish soup, made the local way with vegetables and Aegean fish, tastes like a first-rate bouillabaisse. Other outstanding choices include the fresh grilled calamari, scampi, crawfish spaghetti, and lobster. When you're finished, stop for a cocktail at the stylish adjacent beach bar. ⊠ *Kefalopoulou 3–5* ☎ *22730/24293* ⌕ *Reservations essential* 🍽 *AE, DC, MC, V.*

♺ ¢–$ ✕ **Ostrako.** Greeks come here, amid colored lights, seashell-covered walls, and flowering trees, to devour octopus snacks, steaming hot mussels, shrimp *saganaki* (baked in a red sauce with cheese), crawfish pasta, stuffed calamari, and sea bream fish. As with other local favorites, Ostrako is a place to order and share mezedes (small dishes, like appetizers). Meat lovers can choose from among 20 dishes, including lamb chops and grilled tenderloin. Follow dinner by fruit and Samoan doughnuts topped with honey and cinnamon. All the action takes place on the restaurant's back garden patio, which has a small kids' playground next to it. ⊠ *Them. Soufouli 141, east side of the port* ☎ *22730/27070* 🍽 *No credit cards.*

$ 🏨 **Hotel Samos.** Sleek modern rooms come equipped with soundproof windows, wireless Internet, minifridges, and hair dryers—uncommon amenities in this price range. A small marble lobby connects to a chic, street-level café along the town's waterfront, a perfect place for people-watching. There's also a rooftop pool and hot tub. ⊠ *Them. Soufouli 11, 83100* ☎ *22730/28377* 🖷 *22730/23771* ⊕ *www.samoshotel.gr* ⟿ *98 rooms, 2 suites* ⌕ *Café, room service, refrigerators, cable TV, Wi-Fi, pool, hot tub, bar* 🍽 *AE, DC, MC, V.*

$ 🏨 **Ino Village Hotel.** North of the port on a sloping hill in residential Kalami is a tranquil alternative to the bustle of Samos town: sand-color stucco buildings draped with fuchsia bougainvillea surround a luminous pool at the Ino Village Hotel. All rooms have balconies, dark-wood furnishings, and some black-and-white etchings of ancient Samos. Superior rooms include TVs, small refrigerators, and air-conditioning. Ask for those in the 800 block for a spectacular view of Samos Bay and the mountains beyond. The 15-minute walk to Samos town is downhill (you can call the hotel to arrange for transport back up). ⊠ *1 km (½ mi) north of Samos town center, 83100 Kalami* ☎ *22730/23241* 🖷 *22730/23245* ⊕ *www.inovillagehotel.com* ⟿ *65 rooms* ⌕ *Restaurant, snack bar, some refrigerators, pool, bar, travel services; no a/c in some rooms, no TVs in some rooms* 🍽 *AE, D, DC, MC, V.*

Nightlife

Bars generally are open May to September starting between 8 and 10 PM and closing at 3 AM. Begin your evening at **Escape** (⊠ Past port police station, on main road out of town, near hospital ☎ 22730/28095), a popular gathering place, with a sunset cocktail on the spacious seaside patio (drinks are half price from 8 to 10 PM daily). The music picks up later and so does the dancing. Friday is theme night (rock, reggae, or funk, for example) and there are full-moon parties.

Next to Karavi restaurant, **Selini** (✉ Kefalopoulou 3–5 ☎ 22730/24293) is a stylish beachfront cocktail bar designed in Cycladic white. A fashionable Greek and international crowd mixes outside, as blue lights reflect off the sea below. Lounge and dance music is played.

Pythagorio

Πυθαγόρειο

⑪ *14 km (8½ mi) southwest of Samos town.*

Samos was a democratic state until 535 BC, when the town now called Pythagorio (formerly Tigani, or "frying pan") fell to the tyrant Polycrates (540–22 BC). Polycrates used his fleet of 100 ships to make profitable raids around the Aegean, until he was caught by the Persians and crucified in 522 BC. His rule produced what Herodotus described as "three of the greatest building and engineering feats in the Greek world." One is the Heraion, west of Pythagorio, the largest temple ever built in Greece and one of the Seven Wonders of the Ancient World. Another is the ancient mole protecting the harbor on the southeast coast, on which the present 1,400-foot jetty rests. The third is the Efpalinio tunnel, built to guarantee that water flowing from mountain streams would be available even to besieged Samians. Pythagorio remains a picturesque little port, with red-tile-roof houses and a curving harbor filled with fishing boats, but it is popular with tourists. There are more trendy restaurants and cafés here than elsewhere on the island.

The underground aqueduct, the **To Efpalinio Hydragogeio**, or Efpalinio tunnel, was finished in 524 BC with primitive tools and without measuring instruments. Polycrates, not a man who liked to leave himself vulnerable, ordered the construction of the tunnel to ensure that Samos's water supply could never be cut off during an attack. Efpalinos of Megara, a hydraulics engineer, set perhaps 1,000 slaves into two teams, one digging on each side of Mt. Kastri. Fifteen years later, they met in the middle with just a tiny difference in the elevation between the two halves. The tunnel is about 3,340 feet long, and it remained in use as an aqueduct for almost 1,000 years. More than a mile of (long-gone) ceramic water pipe once filled the space, which was also used as a hiding place during pirate raids in the 7th century. Today the tunnel is exclusively a tourist site, and though some spaces are tight and slippery, you can walk the first 1,000 feet. ✉ *Just north of town* ☎ *22730/ 61400* ⚊ *€4* ⊙ *Tues.–Sun. 8:45–7:30.*

Among acres of excavations, little remains from the **archaia polis** (ancient city; ✉ Bordering small harbor and hill) except a few pieces of the **Polycrates wall** and the **ancient theater** a few hundred yards above the tunnel.

Pythagorio's quiet cobblestone streets are lined with mansions and filled with fragrant orange blossoms. At the east corner sits the crumbling ruins of the **kastro** (castle, or fortress), probably built on top of the ruins of the acropolis. Revolutionary hero Lykourgou Logotheti built this 19th-century edifice; his statue is next door, in the **courtyard** of the church built to honor the victory. He held back the Turks on Transfiguration Day, and a sign on the church announces in Greek: CHRIST SAVED SAMOS 6 AUGUST, 1824. On some nights the villagers light votive candles in the church cemetery, a moving sight with the ghostly silhouette of the fortress and the moonlit sea in the background.

The tiny but impressive **Samos Archaeological Museum** contains local finds, including headless statues, grave markers with epigrams to the dead, human and animal figurines, and beautiful portraits of the Roman emperors Claudius, Caesar, and Augustus. Hours are approximate. ⊠ *Pl. Pythagora, in municipal bldg.* ☎ *22730/61400* ⊕ *www.culture.gr* ⊠ *Free* ⊙ *Tues.–Sun. 9–2:30.*

At the ruins of the **Romaika Loutra** (Roman Baths), the doorways still stand intact. A bit west of the baths are the remains of the ancient Aegean harbor, long ago bustling with the mighty naval fleets of *samains*, ships with five tiers of oarsmen. That harbor is now a silted-in lake and the ships a mere memory. ⊠ *West side* ☎ *22730/61400* ⊠ *Free* ⊙ *Tues.–Sat. 8:30–2:45.*

Where to Stay & Eat

¢–$ ✕ **Maritsa.** A regular Pythagorio clientele frequents Maritsa, a simple fish taverna in a garden courtyard on a quiet, tree-lined side street. You might try shrimp souvlaki, red mullet, octopus, or squid garnished with garlicky *skordalia* (a thick lemony sauce with pureed potatoes, vinegar, and parsley). The usual appetizers include a sharp *tzatziki* (tangy lemon-yogurt dip) and a large salad of *horiatiki* (wild greens), piled high with tomatoes, olives, and feta cheese. Additional recommendations include lamb on the spit, the mixed grill, and stuffed tomatoes. ⊠ *Off Lykourgou Logotheti, 1 block from waterfront* ☎ *22730/61957* ⊟ *MC, V.*

$$$$ 🏨 **Doryssa Bay Hotel-Village.** Guests here choose between accommodations in the plush main hotel building with a view of Pythagorio beach and the sea or in the painstakingly created "village," with its winding cobblestone streets, colorful town-house facades, and rustic main square, complete with shops. Either choice provides elegant contemporary furnishings and gives you access to a well-trained professional staff and a wealth of resort facilities, including an on-site folklore museum. The hotel is popular with Greek and international travelers and receives many tour groups in summer. ⊠ *On road to airport, 83103* ☎ *22730/88300 or 22730/88400* 🖶 *22730/61463* ⊕ *www.doryssa-bay.gr* 🛏 *172 rooms, 125 bungalows, 5 suites* 🍴 *2 restaurants, snack bar, in-room safes, minibars, cable TV, miniature golf, tennis court, pool, gym, hair salon, spa, sauna, beach, boating, waterskiing, billiards, Ping-Pong, volleyball, 2 bars, shops, playground, Internet room, convention center, some pets allowed* ⊟ *AE, DC, MC, V* ⊙ *Closed Nov.–Mar.*

★ $$$$ 🏨 **Proteas Bay.** Standing on the sweeping terrace of the hotel restaurant, or on the balcony of one of the luxurious bungalows that cascade down the steep hillside, is like being on the bridge of a ship. All you see are the blue sea and sky and the mountains of Turkey rising up from the water. The hotel is notably quiet. It's designed in a clean, contemporary style with large, airy spaces, gardens planted with local flowers, an

Olympic-size pool, and a beautiful secluded-cove beach. ⊠ *Samos town–Pythagorio road, 83103* ☎ *22730/62144 or 22730/62146* 🖷 *22730/62620* ⊕ *www.proteasbay.gr* ⇥ *20 rooms, 72 suites* ⚹ *2 restaurants, refrigerators, cable TV, in-room data ports, tennis courts, 2 pools (1 indoor), wading pool, gym, sauna, spa, beach, Ping-Pong, volleyball, 3 bars, shop, babysitting, playground, laundry service, Internet room, business services, convention center, travel services* ▭ *AE, DC, MC, V* ⊙ *Closed Oct.–May.*

$ 🏨 **Fito Bay Bungalows.** Individual white bungalows with terra-cotta roofs neatly wrap around a sparkling long pool just steps from Pythagorio beach. The grounds are beautifully kept, and paths wind between beds of roses and lavender. The rooms themselves are spare, but this is not a place to linger indoors: take breakfast on the vine-covered terrace, relax in a lounge chair on the beach, or have a meal in the excellent taverna. The knowledgeable and warm staff make you feel at home, and this is a relaxed, economical option for families. ⊠ *Pythagorio beach, on road to airport, 83103* ☎ *22730/61314* 🖷 *22730/62045* ⊕ *www. fitobay.gr* ⇥ *87 rooms, 1 suite* ⚹ *Restaurant, snack bar, pool, wading pool, beach, bar, recreation room, babysitting, Internet room, ; no room TVs* ▭ *AE, MC, V* ⊙ *Closed Oct.–Apr.*

Sports

Sun Yachting (⊠ Poseidonos 21, Kalamaki, Athens ☎ 210/983–7312 ⊕ www.sunyachting.gr) in Athens specializes in charter rentals to Samos; you can pick up the boat in Piraeus or Pythagorio for one- and two-week rentals.

Heraion

Ηραίον

★ ⑫ *6 km (4 mi) southwest of Pythagorio, 8 km (5 mi) southwest of Samos town.*

The early Samians worshipped the goddess Hera, believing she was born here beneath a bush near the stream Imbrassos and that there she also lay with Zeus. Several temples were subsequently built on the site in her honor, the earliest dating back to the 8th century BC. Polycrates rebuilt the To Hraio, or Temple of Hera, around 540 BC, making it four times larger than the Parthenon and the largest Greek temple ever conceived, with two rows of columns (155 in all). The temple was damaged by fire in 525 BC and never completed, owing to Polycrates's untimely death. In the intervening years, masons recycled the stones to create other buildings, including a basilica (foundations remain at the site) to the Virgin Mary. Today you can only imagine the To Hraio's massive glory; of its forest of columns only one remains standing, slightly askew and only half its original height, amid acres of marble remnants in marshy ground thick with poppies.

At the ancient celebrations to honor Hera, the faithful approached from the sea along the **Sacred Road,** which is still visible at the site's northeast corner. Nearby are replicas of a 6th-century BC sculpture depicting an aristocratic family, whose chiseled signature reads "Genelaos made me." The kouros from Heraion was found here, and now is in the Archaeological Museum in Samos town. Hours may be shortened in winter. ⊠ *Near Imvisos River* ☎ *22730/95277* ⊕ *www.culture.gr* ✉ *€3* ☉ *Apr.–Oct. daily 8–7:30.*

off the beaten path

MONI TIMIOU STAVROU – The hilltop monastery 20 km (13 mi) north of Heraion, near the village of Mavratzeoi, was built in 1592 and is considered Samos's most important monastery. It is worth a stop to enjoy the icons, carved-walnut iconostasis, and the bishop's throne. The surrounding region produces distinctive honey with a hint of the herbs that the Samian bees buzz around.

Manolates

Μανωλάτες

⓭ *13 km (8 mi) southwest of Samos town.*

Driving up the steep, winding mountain road to Manolates from Karlovassi is an adventure in itself. The hushed village of 120 inhabitants lies amid impenetrable verdant forest in the foothills of Mt. Ambelos. Narrow streets whitewashed with floral designs wind through squares lined with balconied stone houses with tile roofs. At night the town is so silent it almost seems deserted. Unscathed by tourism, Manolates provides a glimpse of Samos as it was a century ago and is definitely worth the trip. The village has a small central plaza with cafés and traditional tavernas, as well as a number of working ceramics shops and stores. Hikers set out from here to admire coastal panoramas or watch for birds. Steep vineyards on these lower slopes of Mt. Ambelos produce white and rosé wines and have wide-ranging views; the best time to visit is in September when the grapes are harvested. Most restaurants on the island sell the local wine.

Where to Eat

¢ ✕ **Pigi.** In Greek, *pigi* means "spring water," and this casual Greek eatery stands high on a hilltop just above a natural spring. Claim one of the eight outdoor tables with a panoramic view of the sea, and settle in for a fine Greek meal. Traditional plates like rabbit stifado, souvlaki, and meatballs are recommended. End with the incredibly delicious baklava or the wonderful apple pie (yes, it seems strange for this location). The owner grew up in this tiny town and has operated the restaurant for more than 15 years. ⊠ *First restaurant on right as you enter Manolates* ☎ *69749/84364* ☰ *No credit cards* ☉ *Closed Nov.–Mar.*

Kokkari

Κοκκάρι

★ **⓮** *8 km (5 mi) northeast of Manolates, 5 km (3 mi) southwest of Samos town.*

Beyond the popular beaches of Tsabou, Tsamadou, and Lemonakia, the spectacular stretch of coast road lined with olive groves and vineyards ends in the fishing village of Kokkari, one of the most appealing spots on the island. Until 1980, not much was here except for a few dozen houses between two headlands, and tracts of onion fields, which gave the town its name. Though now there are a score of hotels, and many European tourists, you can still traipse along the rocky, windswept beach and spy fishermen mending trawling nets on the paved quay. Cross the spit to the eastern side of the headland and watch the moon rise over the lights of Vathi (Samos town) in the next bay. East of Kokkari you pass by Malagari, the winery where farmers hawk their harvested grapes every September.

Beaches

Acclaimed coves of the north coast with small pebbly beaches and gorgeous blue-green waters include **Lemonakia, Tsamadou,** and **Tsabou;** all are just a few minutes from one another, and they're to be avoided when the *meltemi* (northern winds) blow, unless you're a professional windsurfer.

Where to Stay & Eat

¢–$ ✕**Akrogiali Tavern.** Although this small beach shack is not nearly as stylish as some other restaurants up the beach, Akrogiali Tavern serves the town's tastiest fish. Sold by the kilo, the daily selections vary but are always extensive. Among the possible catches are red mullet, swordfish, mackerel, salmon, squid, and a host of other fish caught in the Aegean. The menu clearly indicates what's fresh and what's frozen, and Samos olive oil is used in the cooking. Try the local white wine, made from muscat grapes, with your meal. ⊠ *Kokkari promenade* ☎ *22730/92423* ▤ *No credit cards* ⊘ *Closed Nov.–Mar.*

¢–$ ✕**Ammos Plaz.** Smack on the beach, you stare out from the restaurant to the turquoise water. Ammos Plaz serves what many locals consider the best traditional Greek food in Kokkari. Expect the dishes to change daily, but you may find choices like lamb fricassee and rabbit stifado. The owner's father is a fisherman, and he brings his fresh catch to the restaurant daily. Octopus in a sweet white wine sauce and grilled lobster are two favorites, but considerably more expensive than many selections on the menu. ⊠ *Kokkari promenade* ☎ *22730/92463* ▤ *AE, MC, V* ⊘ *Closed Nov.–Mar.*

$ 🏨**Olympia Beach/Olympia Village.** Flowery Samian ceramics decorate the spare, immaculate rooms with balconies overlooking the sea at the bright-white Olympic Beach hotel. The Olympic Village has apartments with a bedroom, a living room, two baths, and a kitchen. From here you can walk to Tsamadou cove, favored for its shallow water, pine trees, and seclusion. ⊠ *Northwest beach road, 83100* ☎ *22730/92324 or 02730/92353* 🖷 *22730/92457* ⊕ *www.olympiabeach.gr* ⇥ *12 rooms, 22 apartments* ⧄ *Restaurant, some kitchens, refrigerators, cable TV, beach, bar* ▤ *MC, V* ⊘ *Closed Nov.–Apr.* ⑩| *CP.*

¢ 🏨**Galini.** "Galini" means "tranquillity," and this quiet hotel deserves the name. Markela Moshous is a wonderfully hospitable host; she serves breakfast in either the garden or the charming breakfast room. Rooms have simple wood furnishings and impressive marble floors, and they come with balconies or terraces facing the town or sea (and access to a refrigerator). ⊠ *Panayotis Moshous, 83100* ☎ *22730/92331, 22730/*

92365, or 22730/28039 🛏 *9 rooms* ⚐ *Fans, lobby lounge; no a/c, no room TVs* 🖃 *No credit cards* ⊘ *Closed Nov.–Apr.* ⏋◎⏌ *CP.*

Sports & the Outdoors

In summer **Kokkari Surf and Bike Center** (✉ On road to Lemonakia ☎ 22730/92102 ⊕ www.samoscenter.gr) rents windsurfing equipment, motorboats, sea kayaks, and mountain bikes. They also provide windsurfing instruction and run treks for hikers and mountain bikers.

THE NORTHERN ISLANDS A TO Z

To research prices, get advice from other travelers, and book travel arrangements, visit www.fodors.com.

AIR TRAVEL

Even if they have the time, many people avoid the 10- to 12-hour ferry ride from Athens and start their island-hopping trip by taking air flights to all three islands; they take less than an hour. Olympic Airlines has at least a dozen flights a week from Athens to Lesbos and Chios in summer; fewer to Samos. Aegean Airlines flies daily from Athens to Chios. There are several Olympic Airlines flights a week from Chios to Lesbos, Limnos, Rhodes, and Thessaloniki; and several a week from Lesbos to Chios, Limnos, and Thessaloniki. From Samos there are several weekly Olympic flights to Limnos, Rhodes, and Thessaloniki; there are few flights (usually only one per week) between Samos and the other Northern Islands.

Be aware that overbooking happens; if you have a reservation, you should be entitled to a free flight if you get bumped.

🛈 Carriers **Aegean Airlines** ✉ Koundouriotou 87, Mytilini, Lesbos ☎ 22510/37355 ⊕ www.aegeanair.gr. **Olympic Airlines** ☎ 801/120000 or 210/626–1000 Athens ⊕ www. olympicairlines.com ✉ Egeou, Chios town, Chios ☎ 22710/44727 ✉ Kavetsou 44, Mytilini, Lesbos ☎ 22510/28660 ✉ Kanari 5, Samos town, Samos ☎ 22730/27237.

AIRPORTS

Lesbos Airport is 7 km (4½ mi) south of Mytilini. Chios Airport is 4½ km (3 mi) south of Chios town. The busiest airport in the region is on Samos, 17 km (10½ mi) southwest of Samos town. More than 40 international charters arrive every week in midsummer.

🛈 **Chios Airport** ☎ 22710/81400. **Lesbos Airport** ☎ 22510/38700. **Samos Airport** ☎ 22730/61219.

BOAT & FERRY TRAVEL

Expect ferries from any of the Northern Islands to/from Piraeus, Athens port, to take 10 to 12 hours. There are at least four boats per week from Piraeus and three per week from Thessaloniki to Lesbos. Boats arrive daily to Chios from Piraeus. Ferries arrive on Samos at ports in Samos town and Karlovassi four to nine times per week from Piraeus, stopping at Paros and Naxos; and most of the year two or three ferries weekly serve Pythagorio from Kos and Patmos. There is daily service between Lesbos and Chios. The regular ferry takes 3½ hours; the fast ferry 1½ hours. There can be as few as one ferry per week between Lesbos or Chios and Samos (both 3-hour trips). The only other way to reach Samos from Lesbos or Chios is to fly via Athens (an expensive alternative), on Olympic Airlines. Ferries and hydrofoils to Kuşadası, the Turkish coast, leave from Samos town. Owing to sudden changes, no advance ferry schedule can be trusted. Port authority offices have the most recent ferry schedule information and the Greek Travel Pages Web site is helpful.

🚢 **Chios Port Authority** ☎ 22710/44433, 22710/44434 in Chios town. **Greek Travel Pages** ⊕ www.gtp.gr. **Lesbos Port Authority** ☎ 22510/47888 in Mytilini. **Piraeus Port Authority** ☎ 210/422-6000. **Samos Port Authority** ☎ 22730/27318 in Samos town, 22730/30888 in Karlovassi, 22730/61225 in Pythagorio.

BUS TRAVEL

Buses leave the town of Chios several times per day for Mesta and Pirgi. Lesbos's bus system is infrequent, though there are several buses a day from Mytilini to Molyvos via Kalloni. Samos has excellent bus service, with frequent trips between Pythagorio, Samos town, and Kokkari.

🚌 **Chios Blue and Green Bus System** ✉ Vlatarias 13, Chios town, Chios ☎ 22710/23086 or 22710/24257. **Lesbos Bus Station** ✉ Pl. Konstantinopoleos, Mytilini, Lesbos ☎ 22510/28873 ✉ Ioannou Lekati and Kanari, Samos town, Samos ☎ 22730/27262.

CAR TRAVEL

Lesbos and Chios are large, so a car is useful. You might also want to rent a car on Samos, where mountain roads are steep; motorbikes are a popular mode of transport along the coast. Expect to spend about €35–€40 per day for a compact car with insurance and unlimited mileage. Note that you must have an international driver's license to rent a car on Chios. American driver's licenses are accepted on the other islands.

Budget, at Lesbos Airport, has newer cars and is cheaper than other agencies. Vassilakis on Chios has reliable, well-priced vehicles. Aramis Rent-a-Car, part of Sixt, has fair rates and reliable service on Samos.

🚗 Agencies **Aramis Rent-A-Car** ✉ Directly across from port, Samos town, Samos ☎ 22730/23253 🖶 22730/23620 ✉ On main street near National Bank, Pythagorio, Samos ☎ 22730/62267 ✉ Town center, opposite Commercial Bank, Kokkari, Samos ☎ 22730/92385. **Budget** ✉ Airport, Mytilini, Lesbos ☎ 22510/61665 ⊕ www.budget.com. **Vassilakis** ✉ Chandris 3, Chios town, Chios ☎ 22710/29300 🖶 22710/23205 ⊕ www.rentacar-chios.com.

EMERGENCIES

🚑 **Ambulance** ☎ 166. **Fire** ☎ 199. **Police** ☎ 100.

TOURS

Aeolic Cruises on Lesbos runs several island tours. In Molyvos, Panatella Holidays has two tours that take in villages, monasteries, and other sights. Chios Tours organizes land excursions to the south, central, and northern regions of that island, as well as day trips to Izmir in Turkey. Samina Tours, on Samos, runs an island tour, a one-day boat trip to Patmos island, and a picnic cruise.

🚢 **Aeolic Cruises** ✉ Prokymea, Mytilini, Lesbos ☎ 22510/23960 or 22510/23266 🖶 22510/43694. **Chios Tours** ✉ Aigeou, waterfront, Chios town, Chios ☎ 22710/29444 or 22710/29555 🖶 22710/21333 ⊕ www.chiostours.gr. **Panatella Holidays** ✉ Possidonion, at town entrance, Molyvos, Lesbos ☎ 22530/71520, 22530/71643, or 22530/71644

🖨 22530/71680 ⊕ www.panatella-holidays.com. **Samina Tours** ✉ Them. Sofouli 67, Samos town, Samos ☎ 22730/22425 ⊕ www.samina.gr.

VISITOR INFORMATION
🚩 **Chios Municipal Tourist Office** ✉ Kanari 18, Chios town, Chios ☎ 22710/44389 or 22710/44344 ⊕ www.chios.gr. **Greek National Tourism Organization** (GNTO or EOT) ⊕ www.gnto.gr. **Mesta's Tourist Information Office** ✉ Main square, Chios town, Chios ☎ 22710/76319. **Lesbos Municipal Tourist Office** ✉ Harbor front, Mytilini, Lesbos ☎ 22510/44165 ⊕ www.lesvos.gr. **Samos Municipal Tourist Office** ✉ Ikostipemptis Martiou 4, Samos town, Samos ☎ 22730/81031 ⊕ www.samos.gr. **Tourist police** ✉ Harbor front, Mytilini, Lesbos ☎ 22510/22776 ✉ Neoriou 37, Chios town, Chios ☎ 22710/81539 ✉ Harbor front, Samos town, Samos ☎ 22730/87344.

UNDERSTANDING GREECE

GREEK ARCHITECTURE

The Megaron
Showing the development from the "House of the People" to the "House of the God"

A. TROY II

B. TIRYNS

C. OLYMPIA —
Temple of Zeus

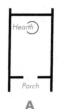

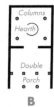

The Orders of Greek Architecture

Doric

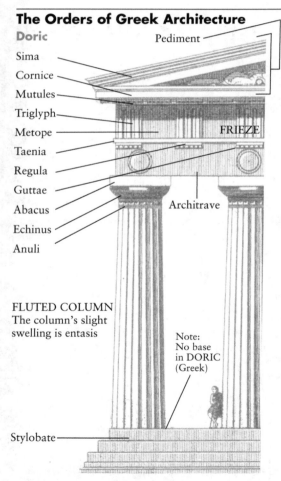

- Pediment
- Sima
- Cornice
- Mutules
- Triglyph
- Metope
- Taenia
- Regula
- Guttae
- Abacus
- Echinus
- Anuli

FRIEZE

Architrave

FLUTED COLUMN
The column's slight swelling is entasis

Note:
No base in DORIC (Greek)

Stylobate

Corinthian

Ionic

Composite

BOOKS & MOVIES

Books

A. R. Burn's *The Penguin History of Greece* takes the reader from the Neolithic pioneers to the splendors of Athens to the last dark days when the philosophic schools were closed, capturing the culture of an amazing people. Extremely fluid, it is written for those who are not experts in classical literature. Just as erudite and enthusiastic is the *Oxford History of Greece and the Hellenistic World,* edited by John Boardman, Jasper Griffin, and Oswyn Murray, a comprehensive but never boring view of the ancient Greek world and its achievements. A late convert to classical Greece, Peter France will engage even the laziest reader in his *Greek as a Treat* (Penguin); theme by theme, with a sharp wit, he introduces readers to the greats—Homer, Pythagoras, Aeschylus, Socrates, and Plato—demonstrating how they still can enrich our 20th-century lives.

In *Sailing the Wine-Dark Sea: Why the Greeks Matter* (Nan A. Talese/Doubleday), Thomas Cahill engagingly explores the contributions of the ancient Greeks and examines six key figures (warriors, philosophers, and artists) who exemplify these achievements. Mary Beard's *The Parthenon* (Harvard University Press) is an elegant cultural guide to one of the world's most influential buildings.

C. M. Woodhouse's *Modern Greece: A Short History* (Faber and Faber) succinctly covers the ensuing development of Greece, from the fall of the Byzantine empire to the War of Independence and the monarchy to the ongoing struggle between the socialist PASOK party and the conservative New Democracy party. *The Greeks: The Land and People Since the War* (Penguin; out of print), by James Pettifer, takes readers behind the postcard imagery of lazy beaches and sun-kissed villages to modern Greece's contradictions as the author examines the far-reaching effects of the country's recent troubled past, including civil war and dictatorship. Richard Clogg's *Concise History of Greece* (Cambridge University Press) focuses on the period from the late 1700s to the present. *Eleni* (Ballantine) is journalist Nicholas Gage's account of his mother's struggle for the freedom of her children and her execution in the late 1940s.

John Julius Norwich's three-volume *Byzantium* (Knopf), or his condensed one-volume *A Short History of Byzantium* (Vintage), is a good introduction to the medieval Byzantine empire. Timothy Ware's *The Orthodox Church* (Penguin) provides an introduction to the religion of the Greek people, while Paul Hetherington's *Byzantine and Medieval Greece, Churches, Castles, and Art* (DIANE Publishing) offers a useful introduction to Byzantine and Frankish mainland Greece.

Unearthing Atlantis (Avon), by Charles Pellegrino, is a fascinating book linking Atlantis to Santorini. The idyllic youth of naturalist Gerald Durrell on the island of Corfu is recalled in many of his books, such as *My Family and Other Animals* (Penguin), which are written with an unpretentious, precise style in a slightly humorous vein and are underrated as works of literature. Lawrence Durrell's 1945 memoir *Prospero's Cell* describes an earlier era on Corfu. Henry Miller's *The Colossus of Maroussi* (New Directions), an enjoyable seize-the-day-as-the-Greeks-do paean that veers from the profound to the superficial—sometimes verging on hysteria—is the product of a trip Miller took to Greece, during which he experienced an epiphany. *Roumeli: Travels in Northern Greece* and *Mani: Travels in Southern Peloponnese,* written by Patrick Leigh Fermor in the mid-20th century, are out of print but worth seeking out for the writer's exquisite evocations of these areas of Greece.

An American poet's account of a year (1992–93) spent in Athens, *Dinner with Persephone* (Vintage), by Patricia Storace, is an unsentimental portrait of modern

Greek life and values. Fodor's *Athens: The Collected Traveler,* edited by Barrie Kerper, brings together articles about the city and surrounding areas and extensive bibliographies. *The Most Beautiful Villages of Greece* (Thames & Hudson), by Mark Ottaway and with luscious color photographs by Hugh Palmer, could inspire anyone's travel itinerary.

Greece's premier writer, Nikos Kazantzakis (1883–1957), captured the strengths and weaknesses and the color of traditional Greek culture in his wonderful novel *Zorba the Greek*; he also wrote the classics *Christ Recrucified* and *The Odyssey*. Other modern Greek fiction will immerse readers in the joys and woes of Greece today: Kedros Books has an excellent series, *Modern Greek Writers,* distributed in the United Kingdom by Forest Books, which includes *Farewell Anatolia,* by Dido Sotiriou, chronicling the traumatic end of Greek life in Asia Minor, and *Fool's Gold,* by Maro Douka, about an aristocratic young woman who becomes enamored of and then disillusioned with the resistance movement to the junta. Noted for his translations of Kazantzakis, the late Kimon Friar demonstrated exquisite taste in his superb translations of modern Greek verse, including works by C. P. Cavafy, and the Nobel Laureates George Seferis and Odysseus Elytis. Friar's *Modern Greek Poetry* is published by the Efstathiadis Group in Athens but is available elsewhere. Readers may have less difficulty finding Edmund Keeley and Philip Sherrard's *Voices of Modern Greek Poetry* (Princeton University Press); both Keeley and Sherrard have written about modern Greek literature.

Some people like to go back to the classics while in Greece. Try either Robert Fitzgerald's or Richmond Lattimore's translations of the *Iliad* and *Odyssey* of Homer, done in verse, unlike the clumsy prose translations you probably read in school. Take the *Iliad* as a pacifist work exposing the uselessness of warfare; read the *Odyssey* keeping in mind the relationships between men and women as illustrated by Odysseus and Penelope, Circe, and Calypso. Lattimore also translated Greece's early lyric poets, Sappho and her lesser-known contemporaries, in a collection titled *Greek Lyric Poetry.* Aristophanes's play *The Wasps* is one of the funniest pieces of literature ever written; the dramas of Aeschylus, Sophocles, and Euripides are important texts in Western culture. Although it isn't light reading, Thucydides's *Peloponnesian War* details the long struggle of Athens and Sparta, fought openly and through third parties, for and against democracy and autocracy. Pausanias's *Guide to Greece* (Penguin, two volumes) was written to guide Roman travelers to Greece in the 2nd century AD.

Movies

A determination to live for the moment coupled with lingering fatalism still pervades Greek society. No film better captures this than Michael Cacoyannis's *Zorba the Greek* (1964; in English), starring the inimitable Anthony Quinn, Alan Bates, and Irene Pappas. Graced with the music of Mikis Theodorakis (the score won an Oscar even though Theodorakis's music was banned at the time in Greece), the film juxtaposes this zest for life with the harsh realities of traditional village society.

In perhaps the second-best-known film about Greece, Hellenic joie de vivre meets American pragmatism in *Never on Sunday* (1960; in English), directed by Jules Dassin. The late Melina Mercouri, a national icon (she also served as the minister of culture in the 1980s), plays a Greek hooker, who in her simple but wise ways takes on the American who has come to reform her and teaches him that life isn't always about getting ahead.

The epic musical drama *Rembetiko* (1983; English subtitles), directed by Costas Ferris and awarded the Silver Bear in 1984, follows 40 years in the life of a rembetika

(Greek blues) singer, played by smoldering, throaty-voiced Sotiria Leonardou. The film, notable for its authenticity and the music's raw energy, spans the turbulent political history of Greece and the development of rembetika blues, which flourished from the 1920s until the '40s as 1.5 million Greeks were displaced from Asia Minor. They brought with them their haunting minor-key laments, as well as the Anatolian custom of smoking hashish; today rembetika is enjoying a resurgence with young Greeks.

Mediterraneo (1991; English subtitles) is a nostalgic, humorous depiction of life on a tiny, distant Greek island, occupied by Italian soldiers during World War II. The soldiers become inextricably involved with the island's vivid personalities—to the point that some refuse to leave when finally informed that the war has long been over. The movie, which won an Oscar for Best Foreign Film, features Vanna Barba, a popular Greek actress whose lusty yet stern gaze captivates the lead role.

One of Greece's leading directors, Theodoros Angelopoulos, has made several internationally acclaimed films, including *Journey to Kythera* (1984; English subtitles), which won for Best Screenplay in the 1984 Cannes festival. Considerably shorter than most of his films, it blends the mythical with the contemporary, detailing the life of a Greek civil-war fighter who returns from the Soviet Union to reunite with his son in an adventure that leaves him and his wife on a raft bound for Kythera island. Manos Katrakis, considered one of Greece's finest stage actors, performs superbly (he died soon after), and the music and striking cinematography evoke Cavafy's famous poem, "Journey to Ithaki," familiar to all Greeks: "But do not hurry the voyage at all. It is better to let it last for long years; and even to anchor at the isle when you are old, rich with all that you have gained on the way."

A recent film that portrays life in Greece since tourism hit in the late '60s is *Shirley Valentine* (1989; in English). Set amid marvelous island scenes, the story is a cautionary tale about a bored British housewife who leaves her stultifying life to vacation in Greece. Here, she regains her identity through a liberating romance with the local flirt (Tom Conti, speaking abominable Greek). Although a bit dated, since the "kamaki" (men who prey on foreign women) is no longer in full force given the increased independence of Greek women, the movie is full of humor, sharp dialogue, and dazzling shots of the Aegean.

Captain Corelli's Mandolin (2001; in English) adapted Louis de Bernières's novel of the same name about an Italian captain on the fascist-occupied island of Cephalonia during World War II. Political complexities are simplified into a love story between the captain and a young Greek woman—portrayed by Nicolas Cage and Penelope Cruz—but the Greek scenery is magnificent.

CHRONOLOGY

Neolithic Period to the Establishment of Democracy

ca. 6000 BC   Beginning of Neolithic period in Greece, with introduction of domesticated plants and animals from Anatolia

ca. 3000 BC   Development of early Bronze Age cultures: on Crete called "Minoan" after the legendary monarch, Minos, and on the mainland known as "Helladic"

ca. 1900 BC   Rise of important settlement at Mycenae

1900 BC–1400 BC   Height of Minoan culture. On Crete the Palace of Minos at Knossos is built, which includes indoor plumbing. Its mazelike complexity gives rise to the legend of the labyrinth

1400 BC–1200 BC   Height of Mycenaean power: Crete is taken, and the city of Troy in Asia Minor is sacked. At Mycenae and Pylos impressive tombs mark this warrior culture

1200 BC–1100 BC   Mycenaean civilization falls as Bronze Age civilizations of the Eastern Mediterranean collapse

1100 BC–750 BC   The "dark ages": writing disappears. The legendary poet Homer narrates a history of the Trojan War and describes an aristocratic society; this oral tradition is later written down as the *Iliad* and the *Odyssey*

ca. 750 BC   Establishment of the *polis,* or city-state, as the characteristic form of political and civic organization in Greece

ca. 725 BC   The poet Hesiod describes rural life in *Works and Days* and establishes the pantheon of Greek gods in *Theogony*. The Olympic Games are established as a Panhellenic event, during which peace prevails

700 BC–500 BC   Colonization builds Greek city-states throughout the Mediterranean. Meanwhile, social pressures at home lead to the rule of tyrants

621 BC   Dracon publishes a notoriously severe legal code in Athens

ca. 600 BC   The legendary ruler Lykourgos establishes the Spartan system of a highly controlled, militaristic society. Thales of Miletus, the first Greek philosopher, starts wondering about the world

594 BC   Solon is given extraordinary powers to reform the Athenian government and constitution

ca. 550 BC   Establishment of the Peloponnesian League, a military alliance of city-states dominated by Sparta. The philosopher Pythagoras propounds a famous theorem and sets up a monastic colony in southern Italy; the poet Sappho of Lesbos describes a particular kind of love

508 BC–501 BC   Cleisthenes establishes Athenian democracy

The Classical Era

499 BC–479 BC Persian wars: Athens leads Greek states against Kings Darius and Xerxes. 490 BC: Battle of Marathon is a critical victory for Athens. 480 BC: Xerxes invades Greece; the Greek League, which includes Athens and Sparta, defeats him in a series of battles at Thermopylae, Salamis, and Plataea

478 BC–477 BC Founding of Delian League of city-states under Athenian hegemony; it will evolve into an empire

ca. 475 BC– 400 BC Golden age of classical Greek culture, centered at Athens. Aeschylus (525 BC–456 BC), Sophocles (circa 496 BC–406 BC), and Euripides (circa 485 BC–402 BC) form the great triumvirate of classical drama; the comedies of Aristophanes (circa 450 BC–385 BC) satirize contemporary mores. Socrates (469 BC–399 BC) and his disciple Plato (circa 429 BC–347 BC) debate the fundamental questions of knowledge and meaning. Herodotus (circa 484 BC–420 BC) and Thucydides (471 BC–402 BC) invent historical writing. The Acropolis epitomizes the harmony and precision of classical architecture and sculpture

462 BC Pericles (circa 495 BC–429 BC) rises to the leadership of Athens and leads the city to its cultural height

460 BC–445 BC First Peloponnesian War between Athens and Sparta ends with the "Thirty Years' Peace" and recognition of the Athenian Empire. At the height of his power, Pericles rebuilds Athens

432 BC The Second, or Great, Peloponnesian War begins when Sparta declares war on Athens

429 BC A disastrous plague kills more than one-third of the Athenian population, including Pericles

415 BC–413 BC Athens's disastrous invasion of Sicily reopens the war and sets the stage for its downfall

404 BC Athens falls to Sparta and its walls are dismantled, ending an era

398 BC–360 BC Rule of Agesilaus at Sparta, whose aggressive policies lead to its ruin

394 BC Spartan fleet destroyed by Persians

386 BC Plato founds the Academy in Athens, a school of philosophy that trains statesmen

384 BC Birth of Aristotle, the greatest ancient philosopher and scientist (died 322 BC)

378 BC Second Athenian Confederation marks the resurgence of Athens

362 BC Death of Epaminondas at the battle of Mantinea ends Theban dominance, documented by Xenophon (circa 434 BC–355 BC)

355 BC Second Athenian Confederation collapses, leaving Greece in chaos

The Hellenistic Era

351 BC   Demosthenes (384 BC–332 BC) delivers the First Philippic, warning Athens of the dangers of Macedonian power

342 BC   Aristotle becomes tutor to a young Macedonian prince named Alexander (356 BC–323 BC)

338 BC   Alexander's father, Philip of Macedon (382 BC–336 BC) defeats the Greek forces at Chaeronea and establishes Macedonian hegemony

336 BC   Philip is assassinated, leaving his empire to his son Alexander, soon to be known as "the Great." Aristotle founds his school, the Lyceum, at Athens

323 BC   Having conquered the known world and opened it to Greek culture, Alexander dies of a fever in Babylon

ca. 330 BC–   Hellenistic culture blends Greek and other influences in a
200 BC   cosmopolitan style. Epicureanism, Stoicism, and Cynicism enter philosophy; Hellenistic sculpture blends emotion and realism. At the new city of Alexandria in Egypt, Greek science and mathematics flourish with Euclid (300 BC) and Archimedes (circa 287 BC–212 BC); Aristarchus (circa 310 BC–230 BC) asserts that Earth revolves around the sun

The Roman Era

215 BC   The outbreak of the First Macedonian War signals Rome's rise in the Mediterranean

146 BC   Rome annexes Greece and Macedonia as provinces. Roman culture becomes increasingly Hellenized

49 BC–31 BC   Greece is a battleground for control of Rome's empire. In 48 BC Julius Caesar defeats Pompey at Pharsalus; in 42 BC Caesar's heir, Octavian, defeats Brutus at Philippi; in 31 BC Octavian defeats Mark Antony at Actium and becomes, as Augustus, the first Roman emperor

AD 125   The guidebook of Pausanias makes Greece a favored tourist stop; the emperor Hadrian undertakes the renovation of ancient monuments

394   The emperor Theodosius declares Christianity the official religion of the Roman Empire and bans pagan cults, suppressing the Olympic Games and closing the oracle at Delphi

The Medieval Era

476   The fall of Rome leaves Greece open to waves of invaders, though it remains nominally under the hegemony of the Byzantine emperors at Constantinople

529   The Byzantine emperor Justinian closes Plato's Academy in Athens

1054   The Great Schism divides the Christian Church into Greek and Roman orthodoxies

1204–1261	Greece briefly reenters the sphere of Western influence with the Latin capture of Constantinople in the Fourth Crusade
1453	The fall of Constantinople to the Ottoman Turks leads to nearly four centuries of Turkish rule in Greece

The Modern Era

1770	The Russian prince Orloff attempts but fails to establish a Greek principality
1814	The *Philike Hetairia,* a "friendly society" established by Greek merchants at Odessa (Russia), is instrumental in the growth of Greek nationalism
1821–1829	The Greek War of Independence. 1821: the Greek Patriarch, Archbishop Germanos, declares Greek independence, and war with the Turks breaks out. Among those aiding Greece in her struggle is the English poet Lord Byron. 1826: a Greek defeat at Missolonghi stirs European sympathy. 1827: the Triple Alliance of Great Britain, France, and Russia intervene against the Turks and their Egyptian allies. 1829: the Turks are defeated and Greece is declared an independent state, guaranteed by the Triple Alliance
1832	Prince Otho of Bavaria is offered the Greek throne by the Triple Alliance
1834	King Otho chooses Athens as his capital
1844	Greece adopts a constitution that establishes a constitutional monarchy
1863	As a result of Otho's pro-Russian policies during the Crimean War, he is forced to abdicate and is replaced on the throne by Prince George of Denmark
1896	Birth of the modern Olympic Games, which are held in Athens
1909–1910	The Military League, a group of young army officers, leads a peaceful revolt and installs as prime minister Eleftherios Venizelos, who enacts a series of reforms
1912–1913	Greece gains Macedonia, Epirus, and Crete as a result of the Balkan Wars
1917–1918	Greece fights on the Allied side in World War I
1924	Greece is declared a republic
1935	Monarchy is restored; in the next year, King George II allows General Joannes Metaxas to establish a military dictatorship
1940	Italy invades Greece, leading to four years of Axis occupation
1946	Greece becomes a charter member of the United Nations
1946–1949	Communist rebellion is defeated with U.S. help
1952	Women are given the right to vote

1963 George Seferis wins the Nobel Prize for Literature

1967 A military coup ousts King Constantine II

1974 In the wake of the Cyprus crisis (Turkey invades northern Cyprus), the military government of Greece collapses and the first elections in 10 years are held. Constantine Karamanlis is named prime minister. The republic is confirmed by popular vote

1980 Odysseus Elytis becomes the second Greek to win the Nobel Prize for Literature

1981 Greece joins the European Economic Community

1993 Andreas Papandreou returns to power

1994 Minister of Culture Melina Mercouri dies

1996 Former prime minister Andreas Papandreou dies; Costas Simitis becomes leader and wins a vote of confidence shortly after Papandreou's death, when he was elected to the position of PASOK party president, a position that Papandreou never relinquished

2002 Euro bills and coins enter circulation in 12 countries of the European Union, including Greece. The drachma is withdrawn from circulation. The Greek police arrest presumed members of the elusive November 17 terrorist group, responsible for various bombings and 22 killings since 1975

2004 Athens hosts the XXVII Summer Olympic Games

GREEK VOCABULARY

The Greek ABC's

The proper names in this book are transliterated versions of the Greek name, so when you come upon signs written in the Greek alphabet, use this list to decipher them.

Greek	Roman	Greek	Roman
A, α	a	N, υ	n
B, β	v	Ξ, ξ	x or ks
Γ, γ	g or y	O, o	o
Δ, δ	th, dh, or d	Π, π	p
E, ε	e	P, ρ	r
Z, ζ	z	Σ, σ, ς	s
H, η	i	T, τ	t
Θ, θ	th	Y, υ	i
I, ι	i	Φ, φ	f
K, κ	k	X, χ	h or ch
Λ, λ	l	Ψ, ψ	ps
M, μ	m	Ω, ω	o

Basics

The phonetic spelling used in English differs somewhat from the internationalized form of Greek place names. There are no long and short vowels in Greek; the pronunciation never changes. Note, also, that the accent is a stress mark, showing where the stress is placed in pronunciation.

Do you speak English?	Miláte angliká?
Yes, no	Málista *or* Né, óchi
Impossible	Adínato
Good morning, Good day	Kaliméra
Good evening, Good night	Kalispéra, Kaliníchta
Goodbye	Yá sas
Mister, Madam, Miss	Kírie, kiría, despiní
Please	Parakaló
Excuse me	Me sinchórite *or* signómi
How are you?	Ti kánete *or* pós íste
How do you do (Pleased to meet you)	Chéro polí
I don't understand.	Dén katalavéno.
To your health!	Giá sas!
Thank you	Efcharistó

Numbers

one	éna
two	dío
three	tría
four	téssera
five	pénde
six	éxi
seven	eptá
eight	októ
nine	enéa
ten	déka
twenty	íkossi
thirty	triánda
forty	saránda
fifty	penínda
sixty	exínda
seventy	evdomínda
eighty	ogdónda
ninety	enenínda
one hundred	ekató
two hundred	diakóssia
three hundred	triakóssia
one thousand	hília
two thousand	dió hiliádes
three thousand	trís hiliádes

Days of the Week

Monday	Deftéra
Tuesday	Tríti
Wednesday	Tetárti
Thursday	Pémpti
Friday	Paraskeví
Saturday	Sávato
Sunday	Kyriakí

Months

January	Ianouários
February	Fevrouários
March	Mártios
April	Aprílios
May	Maíos

June	Ióunios
July	Ióulios
August	Ávgoustos
September	Septémvrios
October	Októvrios
November	Noémvrios
December	Dekémvrios

Traveling

I am traveling by car . . . train . . . plane . . . boat.	Taxidévo mé aftokínito . . . me tréno . . . me aeropláno . . . me vapóri.
Taxi, to the station . . . harbor . . . airport	Taxí, stó stathmó . . . limáni . . . aerodrómio
Porter, take the luggage.	Akthofóre, pare aftá tá prámata.
Where is the filling station?	Pou íne tó vensinádiko?
When does the train leave for . . . ?	Tí óra thá fíyi to tréno ya . . . ?
Which is the train for . . . ?	Pío íne to tréno gía . . . ?
Which is the road to . . . ?	Piós íne o drómos giá . . . ?
A first-class ticket	Éna isitírio prótis táxis
Smoking is forbidden.	Apagorévete to kápnisma.
Where is the toilet?	Póu íne í toaléta?
Ladies, men	Ginekón, andrón
Where? When?	Póu? Póte?
Sleeping car, dining car	Wagonlí, wagonrestorán
Compartment	Vagóni
Entrance, exit	Íssodos, éxodos
Nothing to declare	Den écho típota na dilósso
I am coming for my vacation.	Érchome giá tis diakopés mou.
Nothing	Típota
Personal use	Prossopikí chríssi
How much?	Pósso?
I want to eat, to drink, to sleep.	Thélo na fáo, na pió, na kimithó.
Sunrise, sunset	Anatolí, díssi
Sun, moon	Ílios, fengári
Day, night	Méra, níchta
Morning, afternoon	Proí, mesiméri, *or* apóyevma
The weather is good, bad.	Ó kerós íne kalós, kakós.

On the Road

Straight ahead	Kat efthían
To the right, to the left	Dexiá, aristerá
Show me the way to . . . please.	Díxte mou to drómo . . . parakaló.
Where is . . . ?	Pou íne . . . ?
Crossroad	Diastávrosi
Danger	Kíndinos

In Town

Will you lead me? take me?	Thélete na me odigíste? Me pérnete mazí sas?
Street, square	Drómos, platía
Where is the bank?	Pou íne i trápeza?
Far	Makriá
Police station	Astinomikó tmíma
Consulate (American, British)	Proxenío (Amerikániko, Anglikó)
Theater, cinema	Théatro, cinemá
At what time does the film start?	Tí óra archízi ee tenía?
Where is the travel office?	Pou íne to touristikó grafío?
Where are the tourist police?	Pou íne i touristikí astinomía?

Shopping

I would like to buy	Tha íthela na agorásso
Show me, please.	Díxte mou, parakaló.
May I look around?	Boró na ríxo miá matyá?
How much is it?	Pósso káni? (*or* kostízi)
It is too expensive.	Íne polí akrivó.
Have you any sandals?	Échete pédila?
Have you foreign newspapers?	Échete xénes efimerídes?
Show me that blouse, please.	Díxte mou aftí tí blouza.
Show me that suitcase.	Díxte mou aftí tí valítza.
Envelopes, writing paper	Fakélous, hartí íli
Roll of film	Film
Map of the city	Hárti tis póleos
Something handmade	Hiropíito
Wrap it up, please.	Tilixteto, parakaló.
Cigarettes, matches, please.	Tsigára, spírta, parakaló.
Ham	Zambón
Sausage, salami	Loukániko, salámi
Sugar, salt, pepper	Záchari, aláti, pipéri
Grapes, cherries	Stafília, kerássia

Apple, pear, orange	Mílo, achládi, portokáli
Bread, butter	Psomí, voútiro
Peach, figs	Rodákino, síka

At the Hotel

A good hotel	Éna kaló xenodochío
Have you a room?	Échete domátio?
Where can I find a furnished room?	Pou boró na vró epiploméno domátio?
A single room, double room	Éna monóklino, éna díklino
With bathroom	Me bánio
How much is it per day?	Pósso kostízi tin iméra?
A room overlooking the sea	Éna domátio prós ti thálassa
For one day, for two days	Giá miá méra, giá dió méres
For a week	Giá miá evdomáda
My name is. . . .	Onomázome. . . .
My passport	Tó diavatirió mou
What is the number of my room?	Piós íne o arithmós tou domatíou mou?
The key, please.	To klidí, parakaló.
Breakfast, lunch, supper	Proinó, messimergianó, vradinó
The bill, please.	To logariasmó, parakaló.
I am leaving tomorrow.	Févgo ávrio.

At the Restaurant

Waiter	Garsón
Where is the restaurant?	Pou íne to estiatório?
I would like to eat.	Tha íthela na fáo.
The menu, please.	To katálogo, parakaló.
Fixed-price menu	Menú
Soup	Soúpa
Bread	Psomí
Hors d'oeuvre	Mezédes, orektiká
Ham omelet	Omelétta zambón
Chicken	Kotópoulo
Roast pork	Psitó hirinó
Beef	Moschári
Potatoes (fried)	Patátes (tiganités)
Tomato salad	Domatosaláta
Vegetables	Lachaniká
Watermelon, melon	Karpoúzi, pepóni

Desserts, pastry	Gliká *or* pástes
Fruit, cheese, ice cream	Fróuta, tirí, pagotó
Fish, eggs	Psári, avgá
Serve me on the terrace.	Na mou servírete sti tarátza.
Where can I wash my hands?	Pou boró na plíno ta héria mou?
Red wine, white wine	Kokivó krasí, áspro krasí
Unresinated wine	Krasí aretsínato
Beer, soda water, water, milk	Bíra, sóda, neró, gála
Greek (formerly Turkish) coffee	Ellenikó kafé
Coffee with milk, without sugar, medium, sweet	Kafé gallikó me, gála skéto, métrio, glikó

At the Bank, at the Post Office

Where is the bank? . . . post office?	Pou íne i trápeza? . . . to tachidromío?
I would like to cash a check.	Thélo ná xargiróso mía epitagí.
Stamps	Grammatóssima
By airmail	Aëroporikós
Postcard, letter	Kárta, grámma
Letterbox	Tachidromikó koutí
I would like to telephone.	Thélo na tilephonísso.

At the Garage

Garage, gas (petrol)	Garáz, venzíni
Oil	Ládi
Change the oil.	Aláksete to ládi.
Look at the tires.	Rixte mia matiá sta lástika.
Wash the car.	Plínete to aftokínito.
Breakdown	Vlávi
Tow the car.	Rimúlkiste tó aftokínito.
Spark plugs	Buzí
Brakes	Fréna
Gearbox	Kivótio tachitíton
Carburetor	Karbiratér
Headlight	Provoléfs
Starter	Míza
Axle	Áksonas
Shock absorber	Amortisér
Spare part	Antalaktikó

INDEX

PHOTO CREDITS

ABOUT OUR WRITERS

Stephen Brewer is a New York–based writer and editor who travels to Crete and other Mediterranean shores for various national magazines and guidebooks. He has climbed many a terrifying hairpin-bend on the roads between Knossos and Phaestos. His Fodor's assignment was Crete and the Northern and Southern Peloponnese.

Jeffrey and Elizabeth Carson, native New Yorkers, have lived on Paros for nearly 35 years; they teach at the Aegean Center for the Fine Arts. Jeffrey, a poet, translator, and critic, has published many articles and books. Elizabeth is a photographer who has had numerous solo exhibitions, and has been published widely, including the book *The Church of 100 Doors*. Their assignment was the Cyclades.

Shane Christensen, who covered the Sporades and Northern Islands, has written for Fodor's around the world and has found no destination more enchanting than the Greek islands. A California native, Shane has also worked as a U.S. diplomat and contributes regularly to *Fodor's Washington, D.C.* He is currently finishing a Master's in Public Administration at Harvard.

Angelike Contis was raised in Vermont, but took her first baby steps while visiting her grandparents in Arcadia. She has lived in Greece for eight years, working at the *Athens News* and *Odyssey* magazine. In revisiting Rhodes & the Dodecanese for her assignment, she was happy to discover that it is still possible to eat well and escape the crowds on these very popular and photogenic islands.

Wendy Holborow, who updated the Corfu chapter, fell in love with the island on numerous trips from the U.K. before permanently relocating nine years ago. She now lives on Corfu year-round as a writer and English teacher.

Tania Kollias is a writer and editor based in her father's hometown of Athens. She travels extensively, and formerly was a columnist at the *Athens News* and editor of *Now in Athens* magazine. Tania also edited Greece's first comprehensive English-language listings book (the *OTE Blue Pages*), and now regularly writes for the foreign press. She updated the Northern Greece chapter.

Silvi Rigopoulou, a native Athenian, is an editor, translator, and writer. She provided the Greek translations throughout this edition of *Fodor's Greece*.

Diane Shugart was lured back to her mother's homeland eleven years ago by the laid-back lifestyle and the stark, yet stunning, landscape. A journalist and translator, she makes her home in Athens—a city's whose cultural and history she has explored in the book *Athens by Neighborhood*. Diane updated Smart Travel Tips and the Athens and Attica chapters for this edition.

Adrian Vrettos first traveled to Greece from London over a decade ago to work as a field archaeologist on prehistoric and classical excavations. All he managed to uncover, however, was the ancient inscription, "The laptop is mightier than the trowel" (loosely translated from Linear B). Thus he set to work decoding modern Greek life instead, and is now a freelance journalist and editor based in Athens. Adrian updated the Epirus & Thessaly chapter.